THE PANDORA SEQUENCE

THE PANDORA SEQUENCE

Frank Herbert & Bill Ransom

WordFire Press
Colorado Springs, Colorado

WORDFIRE PRESS

Published by
WordFire Press, an imprint of
WordFire Inc
PO Box 1840
Monument CO 80132

ISBN: 978-1-61475-050-5

WordFire Press Trade Paperback Edition: December 2012
Printed in the USA

www.wordfire.com

Contents

Foreword: The Path to Pandora ... iii
The Jesus Incident ... 1
Introduction ... 1
The Lazarus Effect ... 279
Introduction ... 279
The Ascension Factor ... 541
Introduction ... 541
Afterword ... 777
Letter from the Lost Notebooks ... 781
About the Authors ... 777

Foreword

The Path to Pandora

Bill Ransom

IN APRIL, 1975, Harlan Ellison invited the country's top science fiction writers of the day to participate in a unique science fiction conference at UCLA. Four of the writers would create a basic world and planetary system; they and others, including Frank Herbert, would brainstorm story possibilities before, and with participation from, a live audience. These authors would then write interrelated stories, possibly even a group novel. Cross-communication in a typewriter-and-carbon-paper, dial-telephone (no call waiting, no call forwarding, no caller i.d.) world seemed an insurmountable task. Harlan, ringmaster and choreographer, ultimately wrangled, collected and arranged these stories into the greater story of *Medea* (Bantam).

Each writer received a transcript of the brainstorming sessions, a transcript of student questions from the audience, and the original planetary system/conditions provided by Hal Clement, Poul Anderson, Larry Niven and Fred Pohl. Frank Herbert came into the live brainstorming session on tax deadline day in 1975—as did Tom Disch, Ted Sturgeon, Bob Silverberg and the UCLA audience—having seen the planetary specs, a considerable document, a mere one hour earlier. Bob Silverberg remarked, "We were handed twenty-three single-spaced pages without margins, full of data … and we got this at—oh, about six o'clock—"

Harlan: "Six-thirty."

Each of these very successful authors already was committed to major novel or film projects, as was Frank Herbert, who was tasked with finishing and promoting his recent *Children of Dune.* By 1976 Frank moved toward revising a re-issue of *Destination Void*, and figuring out his next novel project. Berkley wanted to reissue *Destination Void* in hopes of reaping some of the publicity tailwind from *Children of Dune.* They had been disappointed in its original sales, and suggested to Frank that the problem was with the math and technology detail that supported the story, which actually was questioning the nature of consciousness. Since we met every day for coffee and conversation anyway, Frank asked me to read *Destination Void* with an eye toward suggestions for replacing as much of the math as possible with plain (American)

English. Both of us were re-reading *Destination Void* through fall of 1977. The story and project were science fiction, so asking counsel of a regional poet with modest national recognition was risky. For me it was an opportunity to learn first-hand how to sustain a novel-length narrative. My fear: I might bungle this learning opportunity and risk the friendship. In the process, I learned the identities of people who were unwitting models for his characters. Those secrets remain safe with me.

Harlan's letter to all participants in *Medea* on September 3, 1977 included a specific message to Frank:

"Frank, I haven't heard from you as I write this. You're the only one. *Please* get in touch with the others.... Don't forget, we have to have it done and in Fred's hands by the 20th of November, which isn't that far off.... Please, each of us, don't let the others down." Frank's newsman blood respected a deadline.

One Fall morning the *crunch-crunch* of gravel outside and quick *bangbangbang* on the door interrupted my rush to meet a noon deadline on an article on carpenter ants. My house was off the grid, and my wife and I were practicing separation, so drop-ins were rare.

"Ransom?"

Early morning, Frank's prime writing time, and very unlike him to interrupt mine. I swung the door open to a Frank I'd not seen before—pale, disheveled and scared.

Without a moment's hesitation, Frank blurted, "Can you write like me for 750 bucks?"

Frank was notorious for his practical and impractical jokes, but his voice quavered and his eyes were red.

"I can write like anybody for 750 bucks," I said. "What's up?"

"I just took Bev to the hospital," he said. He was near tears and took a moment to get control. "Coughing up blood, don't know what it is yet but it can't be good."

He came inside for a coffee and listed his other pressures, which included being over deadline for *Destination Void* revision and for a story for Harlan Ellison's *Medea* project.

"There's a lot of background info for that story," he said. "About eighty pages of data altogether, and another 100 pages of brainstorming transcript."

Harlan wanted 12,000 words. I would have two weeks to draft the story, which would leave Frank only a day or two to give it the final "Frank Herbert". Did I mention that I didn't have a phone? Manual typewriters with three carbons? No internet?

Frank's offer was a huge compliment and a vote of trust; I was 32, separated, with a nine-year-old daughter. I took a deep breath, left the arts foundation I'd been working with and plunged headlong into the world that became Pandora.

Problem: Everyone thought Frank was writing the story, so the other authors called him to inform him of elements in their stories—history, biology, etc.—that might affect his story. Sometimes I had elements to add to the mix or questions for the others. In either case, I would drive the mile to Frank's with a notepad so that he could make the essential calls. Clunky, but it worked. He was quick to point out that my working title, "The Ship Who Sang," would be great except that Anne McCaffrey beat me to it in 1969.

Frank added a fair amount to the beginning and ending before shipping it out, and this brought the story up to novella length. I had not read Frank's version of the story until I was asked to write this introduction—neither in manuscript nor in print. I still don't know why. I discovered that I like my version better, and Frank would get a hearty laugh out of hearing me say that. Harlan was happy with the story; Frank got paid, and I got paid as agreed. All is well.

During this time, Bev was recovering at home and heard our conversations around the *Medea* and *Destination Void* projects.

"What you're talking about is a novel," she said, when "Songs of a Sentient Flute" went into the mail. "And you're having way too much fun to stop now."

Frank always followed Bev's lead. Frank's editor agreed. Fans like books in series, but Frank wasn't ready to return to *Dune* so soon after *Children of Dune*. He'd mentioned several times about the importance of always leaving an opening for a sequel. *Destination Void* was being rewritten, and it ends with the Ship who claims to be God saying, "You must decide how to WorShip Me!"

Frank wanted to have a stronger tie to his own work in case some flap arose around my role in "Songs of a Sentient Flute." The answer started out to be that the Medea system is where Ship took humans after *Destination Void*. Some of the elements of Medea didn't work for us—we wanted a contrast to *Dune*'s Arrakis—and some separation from the *Medea* project. Frank and I brainstormed a sequel proposal, and Frank took it to New York. The story of the argument with the publisher around having both of our names on the cover is long, distasteful and thirty-four years dead, so let's leave it that way. Because of that argument, authors' collaborations are now acknowledged on covers without a fuss. We were on our way to mating *Destination Void* with "Songs of a Sentient Flute."

Destination Void was already on Frank's mind in 1975, and I found some of this thinking in the transcript of Harlan's brainstorming session on April 15th of that year. Frank wasn't finished chewing on the notion of an entity of human manufacture coming to sentience and claiming to be God. His overarching interest was the relationship between "conscious" and "conscience." Recent (1970s) experiments with AI (Artificial Intelligence) had him speculating over many a cup of coffee on the relationship of intelligence to consciousness and sentience. One of the largest kelp beds in the north Pacific grew only a few hundred meters from my house, so one time I joked with Frank, "What does the kelp think?"

When the UCLA discussion moved to planetary details, Frank brought up our kelp bed: "The problem is: what are the evolutionary lines to produce [two co-existing intelligent races]? If one of them is plant and if, let us say, they're like sea weed which grows up in the ocean … a bladder creature. And that at one stage in their evolution they break off. They're no longer plants, they are free-floating creatures in the air." Frank referred to the "blue book" of data they were given, then said, "We'll have lightning, and that means if lightning ever touches one of those damn things it'll go 'bang'. And that could be a very religious experience.... And it could have something to do with their reproduction, too. What if when they burst in this way it's necessary to their reproductive cycle?" Finally, he wanted one of the main characters to be "a mystic—maybe a poet-mystic."

Frank's first comment in brainstorming for *Medea* got right to basics: "The thing we're concerned about is: what kind of a system is it? What kind of a system is at the ground level that the people are living in? Because if there is any life on that [planet], it has to be related in some kind of a system or arrangement."

The second thing he did was to inform the group that their conclusions regarding the tidal effects on the planet were off by more than an order of magnitude—which Bob Silverberg verified from the data they'd been handed an hour before. Then he shifted from the mathematical data to his primary concern in every story: "We're not going to get anywhere, though, if we don't put people in the situation.... [T]hen we see through the reflection of what happens to them the conditions of the planet."

We were only three years away from inventing sentient kelp, aka Avata. Frank loved brainstorming and compared it to jazz, and jazz perfectly defines our subsequent collaboration.

What follows is Frank's two-page summation of our Fall, 1977 brainstorming sessions around the materials he gave me:

"Among the colonists is a poet. Young, ship-raised, trained by a master who died en route. Among his attributes is an incredible memory for detail and an ability to make associations and conceptual jumps in language that only a few humans succeeded in doing with mathematics. He is an ideal communicant with the balloons. His partner—a middle-aged woman sociologist. Attractive, bright, aggressive. Since romance is often desirable, this combination might prove interesting to our liberated readers. These two would be in a position to manipulate human/balloon affairs and, ultimately, most of Medea's social structure since they control human/balloon communications, much like political control of the media (sorry) as we know it here.

"How about the hydrogen reacting with the tissue of the balloons to form a high-energy plasma system that would act as medium for intellectual activity and as a target for lightning?

"Anyway, protagonists should opt for communications control and ultimate deception of humans for moral reasons. It should be a hard choice, probably costing human lives and at least a major part of the scientific progress of their community. But readers should remain sympathetic with them.

"We will view the whole matter four ways: through his eyes, through her eyes, through their notebook entries (tapes) & poems, and through occasional flashbacks to his mentor's sage words of advice while teaching him the perceptual and mystical skills of the poet. Mysticism and enlightenment would play the major role in the story. Perhaps true enlightenment would destroy human society as they know it and, consequently, the human individuals. Humans, including themselves, are not far enough evolved spiritually. Make the notion of a natural spiritual evolution the key—the notion that certain species are inherently more enlightened than others and that no species is enlightened before its physical/social state is ready. (One answer to the persecution of messiahs.)

"So poet and sociologist wind up sacrificing themselves to prove themselves, achieve a sudden, premature anachronistic enlightenment and save humans from a deadly shortcut to spirituality that we, as a species, are not yet prepared to face.

"She is interested in linear thought—logic as we know it. The scientific method as best it can apply to human (or sentient) behavior is her forte. The poet functions on an intuitive level. His associations are more Jungian, zen-like. This is what endears him to the balloons. So much of his conversation and his poetry would read like zen koans and stories. As would the balloons'.

"Fuxes and most other humans are peripheral to the story. This one belongs to the poet, the sociologist and the balloons.

"The poet is locator, namer, definer. Through him comes the vision of the natural phenomena, a clear definition of *place*.

"Balloons have the ability to function as individuals or as cells in some ethereal cortical matrix. Enlightenment is the death that allows the poet and sociologist to be one with the balloons' cortical matrix, which is one with THE life source. Death would be a total loss of individual identity and acquisition of a total spiritual identity. The balloons on this level are a community of spiritual beings with no social structure and a shared, total wisdom (knowledge, perhaps.) And 'community of beings' is misleading because there is no identity or sense of number at this level.

"Begin as a short story—but what about playing the game out? Would make a fun novel and then, perhaps, a posthumous collection of poetry. fun. Would be *great* fun. And a great practical joke on our literary establishment."

Two weeks later, I handed over "Songs of a Sentient Flute"; Frank added some opening and closing material and shipped it off to Fate, the ultimate practical joker.

THE JESUS INCIDENT

Dedication

For Jack Vance, who while teaching how to use claw hammer and saw, taught also the difference between fantasy and science fiction.
—Frank Herbert

For Bert Ransom, who never once said that fantasy wasn't real.
—Bill Ransom

Acknowledgments

The authors thank Connie Weineke for her research into the Aramaic, and Marilyn Hoyt-Whorton for her typing and good cheer.

Introduction

Bill Ransom

OUR WORKING title late in 1977 was "Clone Wars," a link to *Destination Void.* Our first official meeting focused on preserving our friendship. Frank's Jungian training helped us to face important non-writing challenges to us, personally, and to the project. Frank might be seen as "running out of ideas" and I as some obscure poet "riding on the coattails of The Great Frank Herbert." We agreed, with a formal handshake, that nothing in this process would supersede our friendship. If one of us rewrote something of the other, and if the other really wanted his version, then he could have it. We never had to invoke this unwritten clause.

Our second day we devoted to process. This would be a "true collaboration", different from the "tag-team" process we used for "Songs of a Sentient Flute." Word-jazz or plot-jazz or character-jazz became the game that kept it fun. "Songs of a Sentient Flute" was a studio job, where the featured artist lays down a track over the studio musician's work. We became a duet, an untested product that put Frank's reputation on the line—we were playing on *his* stage, after all. We assessed our writing strengths and weaknesses, determined the most productive time of day to meet face-to-face, and we set up a structure for those meetings.

We started each meeting with Big Questions, such as: How might a god develop? Would a god free humans from the need for a god? How is religion related to some humans' need to have and to exert power over other humans? What is the relationship between consciousness and conscience? What if humans are a failed experiment given one last chance? How do we get the reader to wonder, "Am I in an 'instant replay' right now?" What is the nature of worship?

We ended these sessions by playing out dialogue in some small part of a scene to warm up or to try something out. We made up rules as we went, beginning with which elements of the two previous stories to keep and which to discard. Two examples of "rules for the book":

1. The god gives information, not decisions—all decisions are human.
2. Everything must be seen through character.

Here is an excerpt from a transcript of a typical Big Question conversation:

> FH: The only faith you need to have is in yourselves as humans, in your human ability to choose, at any given moment, no matter what happens to you, what is the *right* thing to do. You've been educated in judgment, which is the essence of worship.
>
> BR: And judgment always occurs in the past. Will, free or otherwise, is concerned with the future.
>
> FH: How do you use will? Judgment prepares you to use will. Thinking is the performance of the moment, out of which you use your judgment to modulate will. You sit here almost as though you were a convection center through which past prepares future.

I was reading Joseph Bronkowski's *The Ascent of Man* and Frank was reading *The Upanishads.*

We talked, we split up, we wrote, we came back the next day to exchange pages for the other person's touch. At one hundred pages we laid out the sheets in order for the first time across Frank's living-room floor. We put blank pages where we needed transitions or more material, and we assigned each other those parts according to individual interests or insights on a character. That's as close to an outline as we ever got.

"A story's *organic,*" Frank used to say. "Let it grow!"

So we did.

My divorce was final.

Chapter 1

There is a gateway to the imagination you must enter before you are conscious and the keys to the gate are symbols. You can carry ideas through the gate … but you must carry the ideas in symbols.

—Raja Flattery, Chaplain/Psychiatrist

SOMETHING WENT "Tick."

He heard it quite distinctly—a metallic sound. There it went again: "Tick."

He opened his eyes and was rewarded with darkness, an absolute lack of radiant energy … or of receptors to detect energy.

Am I blind?

"Tick."

He could not place the source, but it was out there—wherever *out there* was. The air felt cold in his throat and lungs. But his body was warm. He realized that he lay very lightly on a soft surface. He was breathing. Something tickled his nose, a faint odor of … pepper?

"Tick."

He cleared his throat. "Anybody there?"

No answer. Speaking hurt his throat.

What am I doing here?

The soft surface beneath him curved up around his shoulders to support his neck and head. It encased hips and legs. This was familiar. It ignited distant associations. It was … what? He felt that he should know about such a surface.

After all, I …

"Tick."

Panic seized him. Who am I?

The answer came slowly, thawed from a block of ice which contained everything he should know.

I am Raja Flattery.

Ice melted in a cascade of memories.

I'm Chaplain/Psychiatrist on the Voidship Earthling. *We … we …*

Some of the memories remained frozen.

He tried to sit up but was restrained by softly cupping bands over his chest and wrists. Now, he felt connectors withdraw from the veins at his wrists.

I'm in a hyb tank!

He had no memory of going into hybernation. Perhaps memory thawed more slowly than flesh. Interesting. But there were a few memories now, frigid in their flow, and deeply disturbing.

I failed.

Moonbase directed me to blow up our ship rather than let it roam space as a threat to humankind. I was to send the message capsule back to Moonbase … and blow up our ship.

Something had prevented him from … something …

But he remembered the project now.

Project Consciousness.

And he, Raja Flattery, had held a key role in that project. Chaplain/Psychiatrist. He had been one of the crew.

Umbilicus crew.

He did not dwell on the birth symbology in that label. Clones had more important tasks. They were clones on the crew, all with Lon for a middle name. Lon meant clone as Mac meant son of. All the crew—clones. They were doppelgangers sent far into insulating space, there to solve the problem of creating an artificial consciousness.

Dangerous work. Very dangerous. Artificial consciousness had a long history of turning against its creators. It went rogue with ferocious violence. Even many of the uncloned had perished in agony.

Nobody could say why.

But the project's directors at Moonbase were persistent. Again and again, they sent the same cloned crew into space. Features flashed into Flattery's mind as he thought the names: a Gerrill Timberlake, a John Bickel, a Prue Weygand.…

Raja Flattery … Raja Lon Flattery.

He glimpsed his own face in a long-gone mirror: fair hair, narrow features … disdainful …

And the Voidships carried others, many others. They carried cloned Colonists, gene banks in hyb tanks. Cheap flesh to be sacrificed in distant explosions where the uncloned would not be harmed. Cheap flesh to gather data for the uncloned. Each new venture into the void went out with a bit more information for the wakeful umbilicus crew and those encased in hyb …

As I am encased now.

Colonists, livestock, plants—each Voidship carried what it needed to create another Earth. That was the carrot luring them onward. And the ship—certain death if they failed to create an artificial consciousness. Moonbase knew that ships and clones were cheap where materials and inexpensive energy were abundant … as they were on the moon.

"Tick."

Who is bringing me out of hybernation?

And why?

Flattery thought about that while he tried to extend his globe of awareness into the unresponsive darkness.

Who? Why?

He knew that he had failed to blow up his ship after it had exhibited consciousness … using Bickel as an imprint on the computer they had built.…

I did not blow up the ship. Something prevented me from …

Ship!

More memories flooded into his mind. They had achieved the artificial consciousness to direct their ship … and it had whisked them far across space to the Tau Ceti system.

Where there were no inhabitable planets.

Moonbase probes had made certain of that much earlier. No inhabitable planets. It was part of the frustration built into the project. No Voidship could be allowed to choose the long way to Tau Ceti sanctuary. Moonbase could not allow that. It would be too tempting for the cloned crew—breed our own replacements, let our descendants find Tau Ceti. And to hell with Project Consciousness! If they voted that course, the Chaplain/Psychiatrist was charged to expose the empty goal and stand ready with the destruct button.

Win, lose or draw—we were supposed to die.

And only the Chaplain/Psychiatrist had been allowed to suspect this. The serial Voidships and their cloned cargo had one mission: gather information and send it back to Moonbase.

Ship.

That was it, of course. They had created much more than consciousness in their computer and its companion system which Bickel had called "the Ox." They had made Ship. And Ship had whisked them across space in an impossible eyeblink.

Destination Tau Ceti.

That was, after all, the built-in command, the target programmed into their computer. But where there had been no inhabitable planet, Ship had created one: a paradise planet, an earth idealized out of every human dream. Ship had done this thing, but then had come Ship's terrible demand: "You must decide how you will WorShip Me!"

Ship had assumed attributes of God or Satan. Flattery was never sure which. But he had sensed that awesome power even before the repeated demand.

"How will you WorShip? You must decide!"

Failure.

They never could satisfy Ship's demand. But they could fear. They learned a full measure of fear.

"Tick."

He recognized that sound now: the dehyb timer/monitor counting off the restoration of life to his flesh.

But who had set this process into motion?

"Who's there?"

Silence and the impenetrable darkness answered.

Flattery felt alone and now there was a painful chill around his flesh, a signal that skin sensation was returning to normal.

One of the crew had warned them before they had thrown the switch to ignite the artificial consciousness. Flattery could not recall who had voiced the warning but he remembered it.

"There must be a threshold of consciousness beyond which a conscious being takes on attributes of God."

Whoever said it had seen a truth.

Who is bringing me out of hyb and why?

"Somebody's there! Who is it?"

Speaking still hurt his throat and his mind was not working properly—that icy core of untouchable memories.

"Come on! Who's there?"

He knew somebody was there. He could feel the familiar presence of …

Ship!

"Okay, Ship. I'm awake."

"So you assume."

That chiding voice could never sound human. It was too impossibly controlled. Every slightest nuance, every inflection, every modulated resonance conveyed a perfection which put it beyond the reach of humans. But that voice told him that he once more was a pawn of Ship. He was a small cog in the workings of this Infinite Power which he had helped to release upon an unsuspecting universe. This realization filled him with remembered terrors and an immediate awesome fear of the agonies which Ship might visit upon him for his failures. He was tormented by visions of Hell …

I failed … I failed … I failed …

Chapter 2

St. Augustine asked the right question: "Does freedom come from chance or choice?" And you must remember that quantum mechanics guarantees chance.

—Raja Flattery, *The Book of Ship*

USUALLY MORGAN Oakes took out his nightside angers and frustrations in long strides down any corridor of the ship where his feet led him.

Not this time! he told himself.

He sat in shadows and sipped a glass of astringent wine. Bitter, but it washed the taste of the ship's foul joke from his tongue. The wine had come at his demand, a demonstration of his power in these times of food shortages. The first bottle from the first batch. How would they take it groundside when he ordered the wine improved?

Oakes raised the glass in an ancient gesture: *Confusion to You, Ship!*

The wine was too raw. He put it aside.

Oakes knew the figure he cut, sitting here trembling in his cubby while he stared at the silent com-console beside his favorite couch. He increased the light slightly.

Once more the ship had convinced him that its program was running down. The ship was getting senile. He was the Chaplain/Psychiatrist and the ship tried to poison him! Others were fed from shiptits—not frequently and not much, but it happened. Even he had been favored once, before he became Ceepee, and he still remembered the taste—richly satisfying. It was a little like the stuff called "burst" which Lewis had developed groundside. An attempt to duplicate elixir. Costly stuff, burst. Wasteful. And not elixir—no, not elixir.

He stared at the curved screen of the console beside him. It returned a dwarfed reflection of himself: an overweight, heavy-shouldered man in a one-piece suit of shipcloth which appeared vaguely gray in this light. His features were strong: a thick chin, wide mouth, beaked nose and bushy eyebrows over dark eyes, a bit of silver at the temples. He touched his temples. The reduced reflection exaggerated his feeling that he had been made small by Ship's treatment of him. His reflection showed him his own fear.

I will not be tricked by a damned machine!

The memory brought on another fit of trembling. Ship had refused him at the shiptits often enough that he understood this new message. He had stopped with Jesus Lewis at a bank of corridor shiptits.

Lewis had been amused. "Don't waste time with these things. The ship won't feed us."

This had angered Oakes. "It's my privilege to waste time! Don't you ever forget that!"

He had rolled up his sleeve and thrust his bare arm into the receptacle. The sensor scratched as it adjusted to his arm. He felt the stainless-steel nose sniff out a suitable vein. There was the tingling prick of the test probe, then the release of the sensor.

Some of the shiptits extruded plaz tubes to suck on, but this one was programmed to fill a container behind a locked panel—elixir, measured and mixed to his exact needs.

The panel opened!

Oakes grinned at an astounded Lewis.

"Well," Oakes remembered saying. "The ship finally realizes who's the boss here." With that, he drained the container.

Horrible!

His body was wracked with vomiting. His breath came in shallow gasps and sweat soaked his singlesuit.

It was over as quickly as it began. Lewis stood beside him in dumb amazement, looking at the mess Oakes had made of the corridor and his boots.

"You see," Oakes gasped. "You see how the ship tried to kill me?"

"Relax, Morgan," Lewis said. "It's probably just a malfunction. I'll call a med-tech for you and a repair robox for this … this thing."

"I'm a doctor, dammit! I don't need a med-tech poking around me." Oakes held the fabric of his suit away from his body.

"Then let's get you back to your cubby. We should check you out and …" Lewis broke off, looking suddenly over Oakes' shoulder. "Morgan, did you summon a repair unit?"

Oakes turned to see what had caught Lewis' attention, saw one of the ship's robox units, a one-meter oval of bronze turtle with wicked-looking tools clutched in its extensors. It was weaving drunkenly down the corridor toward them.

"What do you suppose is wrong with that thing?" Lewis muttered.

"I think it's here to attack us," Oakes said. He grabbed Lewis' arm. "Let's back out of here … slow, now."

They retreated from the shiptit station, watching the scanner eye of the robox and the waving appendages full of tools.

"It's not stopping." Oakes' voice was low but cold with fear as the robox passed the shiptit station.

"We'd better run for it," Lewis said. He spun Oakes ahead of him into a main passageway to Medical. Neither man looked back until they were safely battened inside Oakes' cubby.

Hah! Oakes thought, remembering. That had frightened even Lewis. He had gone back groundside fast enough—to speed up construction of their Redoubt, the place which would insulate them groundside and make them independent of this damned machine.

The ship's controlled our lives too long!

Oakes still tasted bitterness at the back of his throat. Now, Lewis was incommunicado ... sending notes by courier. Always something frustrating.

Damn Lewis!

Oakes glanced around his shadowed quarters. It was nightside on the orbiting ship and most of the crew drifted on the sea of sleep. An occasional click and buzz of servos modulating the environment were the only intrusions.

How long before Ship's servos go mad?

The ship, he reminded himself.

Ship was a concept, a fabricated theology, a fairy tale imbedded in a manufactured history which only a fool could believe.

It is a lie by which we control and are controlled.

He tried to relax into the thick cushions and once more took up the note which one of Lewis' minions had thrust upon him. The message was simple, direct and threatening.

"The ship informs us that it is sending groundside one (1) Chaplain/Psychiatrist competent in communications. Reason: the unidentified Ceepee will mount a project to communicate with the electrokelp. I can find no additional information about this Ceepee but he has to be someone new from hyb."

Oakes crumpled the note in his fist.

One Ceepee was all this society could tolerate. The ship was sending another message to him. "You can be replaced."

He had never doubted that there were other Chaplain/Psychiatrists somewhere in the ship's hyb reserves. No telling where those reserves might be hidden. The damned ship was a convoluted mess with secret sections and random extrusions and concealed passages which led nowhere.

Colony had measured the ship's size by the occlusion shadow when it had eclipsed one of the two suns on a low passage. The ship was almost fifty-eight kilometers long, room to hide almost anything.

But now we have a planet under us: Pandora.

Groundside!

He looked at the crumpled note in his hand. Why a note? He and Lewis were supposed to have an infallible means of secret communication—the only two Shipmen so gifted. It was why they trusted each other.

Do I really trust Lewis?

For the fifth time since receiving the note, Oakes triggered the alpha-blink which activated the tiny pellet imbedded in the flesh of his neck. No doubt the thing was working. He sensed the carrier wave which linked the capsule computer to his aural nerves, and there was that eerie feeling of a blank screen in his imagination, the knowledge that he was poised to experience a waking dream. Somewhere groundside the tight-band transmission should be alerting Lewis to this communication. But Lewis was not responding.

Equipment failure?

Oakes knew that was not the problem. He personally had implanted the counterpart of this pellet in Lewis' neck, had made the nerve hookups himself.

And I supervised Lewis while he made my implant.

Was the damned ship interfering?

Oakes peered around at the elaborate changes he had introduced into his cubby. The ship was everywhere, of course. All of them shipside were in the ship. This cubby, though, had always been different … even before he had made his personal alterations. This was the cubby of a Chaplain/Psychiatrist.

The rest of the crew lived simply. They slept suspended in hammocks which translated the gentle swayings of the ship into sleep. Many incorporated padded pallets or cushions for those occasions that arose between men and women. That was for love, for relaxation, for relief from the long corridors of plasteel which sometimes wound tightly around the psyche and squeezed out your breath.

Breeding, though … that came under strictest Ship controls. Every Natural Natal had to be born shipside and under the supervision of a trained obstetrics crew—the damned Natali with their air of superior abilities. Did the ship talk to them? Feed them? They never said.

Oakes thought about the shipside breeding rooms. Although plush by usual cubby standards, they never seemed as stimulating as his own cubby. Even the perimeter treedomes were preferred by some—under dark bushes … on open grass. Oakes smiled. His cubby, though—this was opulent. Women had been known to gasp when first entering the vastness of it. From the core of the Ceepee's cubby, this one had been expanded into the space of five cubbies.

And the damned ship never once interfered.

This place was a symbol of power. It was an aphrodisiac which seldom failed. It also exposed the lie of Ship.

Those of us who see the lie, control. Those who don't see it … don't.

He felt a little giddy. *Effect of the Pandoran wine*, he thought. It snaked through his veins and wormed into his consciousness. But even the wine could not make him sleep. At first, its peculiar sweetness and the thick warmth had promised to dull the edge of doubts that kept him pacing the nightside passages. He had lived on three or four hours' sleep each period for … how long now? Annos … annos …

Oakes shook his head to clear it and felt the ripple of his jowls against his neck. Fat. He had never been supple, never selected for breeding.

Edmond Kingston chose me to succeed him, though. First Ceepee in history not selected by the damned ship.

Was he going to be replaced by this new Ceepee the ship had chosen to send groundside?

Oakes sighed.

Lately, he knew he had turned sallow and heavy.

Too much demand on my head and not enough on my body.

Never a lack of couch partners, though. He patted the cushions at his side, remembering.

I'm fifty, fat and fermented, he thought. *Where do I go from here?*

Chapter 3

The all-pervading, characterless background of the universe—this is the void. It is not object nor senses. It is the region of illusions.
—Kerro Panille, *Buddha and Avata*

WILD VARIETY marked the naked band of people hobbling and trudging across the open plain between bulwarks of black crags. The red-orange light of a single sun beat down on them from the meridian, drawing purple shadows on the coarse sand and pebbles of the plain. Vagrant winds whisked at random dust pockets, and the band gave wary attention to these disturbances. Occasional stubby plants with glistening silver leaves aligned themselves with the sun in the path of the naked band. The band steered a course to avoid the plants.

The people of the band showed only remote kinship with their human ancestry. Most of them turned to a tall companion as their leader, although this one did not walk at the point. He had ropey gray arms and a narrow head crowned by golden fuzz, the only suggestion of hair on his slender body. The head carried two golden eyes in bony extrusions at the temples, but there was no nose and only a tiny red circle of mouth. There were no visible ears, but brown skin marked the spots where ears might have been. The arms ended in supple hands, each with three six-jointed fingers and opposable thumb. The name Theriex was tattooed in green across his hairless chest.

Beside the tall Theriex hobbled a pale and squat figure with no neck to support a hairless bulb of head. Tiny red eyes, set close to a moist hole which trembled with each breath, could stare only where the body pointed. The ears were gaping slits low at each side of the head. Fat and corded arms ended in two fingerless fleshy mittens. The legs were kneeless tubes without feet.

Others in the band showed a similar diversity. There were heads with many eyes and some with none. There were great coned nostrils and horned ears, dancers' legs and some stumps. They numbered forty-one in all and they huddled close as they walked, presenting a tight wall of flesh to the Pandoran wilderness. Some clung to each other as they stumbled and lurched their way across the plain. Others maintained a small moat of open space. There was little conversation—an occasional grunt or moan, sometimes a plaintive question directed at Theriex.

"Where can we hide, Ther? Who will take us in?"

"If we can get to the other sea," Theriex said. "The Avata …"

"The Avata, yes, the Avata."

They spoke it as a prayer. A deep rumbling voice in the band took it up then: "All-Human one, All-Avata one."

Another spoke: "Ther, tell us the story of Avata."

Theriex remained silent until they were all pleading: "Yes, Ther, tell us the story … the story, the story …"

Theriex raised a ropey hand for silence, then: "When Avata speaks of beginning, Avata speaks of rock and the brotherhood of rock. Before rock there was sea, boiling sea, and the blisters of light that boiled it. With the boiling and the cooling came the ripping of the moons, the teeth of the sea gone mad. By day all things scattered in the boil, and by night they joined in the relief of sediment and they rested."

Theriex had a thin whistling voice which carried over the shuffling sounds of the band's passage. He spoke to an odd rhythm which fitted itself to their march.

"The suns slowed their great whirl and the seas cooled. Some few who joined remained joined. Avata knows this because it is so, but the first word of Avata is rock."

"The rock, the rock," Theriex's companions responded.

"There is no growth on the run," Theriex said. "Before rock Avata was tired and Avata was many and Avata had seen only the sea."

"We must find the Avata sea …"

"But to grip a rock," Theriex said, "to coil around it close and lie still, that is a new dream and a new life—untossed by the ravages of moon, untired. It was vine to leaf then, and in the new confidence of rock came the coil of power and the gas, gift of the sea."

Theriex tipped his head back to look up at the metallic blue of the sky and, for a few paces, remained silent, then: "Coil of power, touch of touches! Avata captured lightning that day, curled tight around its rock, waiting out the silent centuries in darkness and in fear. Then the first spark arced into the horrible night: 'Rock!'"

Once more, the others responded, "Rock! Rock! Rock!"

"Coil of power!" Theriex repeated. "Avata knew rock before knowing Self; and the second spark snapped: I! Then the third, greatest of all: I! Not rock!"

"Not rock, not rock," the others responded.

"The source is always with us," Theriex said, "as it is with that which we are not. It is in reference that we are. It is through the other that Self is known. And where there is only one, there is nothing else. From the nothing else comes no reflection of Self, nothing returns. But for Avata there was rock, and because there was rock there was something returned and that something was Self. Thus, the finite becomes infinite. One is not. But we are joined in the infinite, in the closeness out of which all matter comes. Let Avata's rock steady you in the sea!"

For a time after Theriex fell silent, the band trudged and hobbled onward without complaint. There was a smell of acid burning on the whisking breezes, though, and one of the band with a sensitive nose detected this.

"I smell Nerve Runners!" he said.

A shudder ran through them and they quickened their pace while those at the edges scanned the plain around them with renewed caution.

At the point of the band walked a darkly furred figure with a long torso and stumpy legs which ended in round flat pads. The arms were slim and moved with a snakelike writhing. They ended in two-fingered hands, the fingers muscular, long and twining, as though designed to reach into strange places for mysterious reasons. The ears were motile, large and leathery under their thin coat of fur, pointing now one direction and now another. The head sat on a slender neck, presenting a markedly human face, although flattened and covered with that fine gauze of dark fur. The eyes were blue, heavy-lidded and bulging. They were glassy and appeared to focus on nothing.

The plain around them, out to the crags about ten kilometers distant, was devoid of motion now, marked only by scattered extrusions of black rock and the stiff-leaved plants making their slow phototropic adjustments to the passage of the red-orange sun.

The ears of the furred figure at the point suddenly stretched out, cupped and aimed at the crags directly ahead of the band.

Abruptly, a screeching cry echoed across the plain from that direction. The band stopped as a single organism, caught in fearful waiting. The cry had been terrifyingly loud to carry that far across the plain.

A near-hysterical voice called from within the band: "We have no weapons!"

"Rocks," Theriex said, waving an arm at the extruded black shapes all around.

"They're too big to throw," someone complained.

"The rocks of the Avata," Theriex said, and his voice carried the tone he had used while lulling his band with the story of Avata.

"Stay away from the plants," someone warned.

There was no real need for this warning. They all knew about the plants—most poisonous, all capable of slashing soft flesh. Three of the band already had been lost to the plants.

Again, that cry pierced the air.

"The rocks," Theriex repeated.

Slowly, the band separated, singly and in small groups, moving out to the rocks where they huddled up to the black surfaces, clinging there, most of them with faces pressed against the darkness.

"I see them," Theriex said. "Hooded Dashers."

All turned then to look where Theriex looked.

"Rock, the dream of life," Theriex said. "To grip rock, to coil around it close and lie still."

As he spoke, he continued to stare across the plain at the nine black shapes hurtling toward him. Hooded Dashers, yes, many-legged, and with enfolding hoods instead of mouths. The hoods retracted to reveal thrashing fangs. They moved with terrifying speed.

"We should have taken our chances at the Redoubt with the others!" someone wailed.

"Damn you, Jesus Lewis!" someone shouted. "Damn you!"

They were the last fully coherent words from the band as the Hooded Dashers charged at blurring speed onto its scattered members. Teeth slashed, claws raked. The speed of the attack was merciless. Hoods retracted, the Dashers darted and whirled. No victim had a second chance. Some tried to run and were cut down on the open plain. Some tried to dodge around the rocks but were cornered by pairs of demons. It was over in blinks, and the nine Dashers set to feeding. Things groped from beneath the rocks to share the feast. Even nearby plants drank red liquid from the ground.

While the Dashers fed, subtle movements changed the craggy skyline to the north. Great floating orange bags lifted above the rocky bulwarks there and drifted on the upper winds toward the Dashers. The floaters trailed long tendrils which occasionally touched the plain, stirring up dust. The Dashers saw this but showed no fear.

High wavering crests rippled along the tops of the bags, adjusting to the wind. A piping song could be heard from them now, like wind through sails accompanied by a metallic rattling.

When the orange bags were still several kilometers distant, one of the Dashers barked a warning. It stared away from the bags at a boil of stringy tendrils disturbing the plain about fifty meters off. A strong smell of burning acid wafted from the boil. As one, the nine Dashers whirled and fled. The one which had fed on Theriex uttered a high scream as it raced across the plain, and then, quite clearly, it called out: "Theriex!"

Chapter 4

A deliberately poor move chosen at random along the line of play can completely change the theoretical structure of a game.

—Bickel quote, *Shiprecords*

OAKES PACED his cubby, fretting. It had been several nightside hours since he had last tried to contact Lewis on their implanted communicators. Lewis definitely was out of touch.

Could it be something wrong at the Redoubt?

Oakes doubted this. The finest materials were going into that base out on Black Dragon. Lewis was sparing nothing in the construction. It would be impenetrable by any force known to Pandora or Shipmen ... any force, except ...

Oakes stopped his pacing, scanned the plasteel walls of his cubby.

Would the Redoubt down on Pandora really insulate them from the ship?

The wine he had drunk earlier was beginning to relax him, clearing the bitter taste from his tongue. His room felt stuffy and isolated even from the ship. Let the damned ship send another Ceepee groundside. Whoever it was would be taken care of in due course.

Oakes let his body sag onto a couch and tried to forget the latest attack on him by the ship. He closed his eyes and drifted in a half-dream back to his beginning.

Not quite. Not quite the beginning.

He did not like to admit the gap. There were things he did not remember. Doubts intruded and the carrier wave of the pellet in his neck distracted him. He sent the nerve signal to turn the thing off.

Let Lewis try to contact me!

Oakes heaved an even deeper sigh. Not the beginning—no. There were things about his beginnings that the records did not show. This ship with all the powers of a god would not or could not provide a complete background on Morgan Oakes. And the Ceepee was supposed to have access to everything. Everything!

Everything except that distant origin somewhere earthside … back on far-away Earth … long-gone Earth.

He knew he had been six when his first memory images gelled and stayed with him. He even knew the year—6001 dating from the birth of the Divine Imhotep.

Spring. Yes, it had been spring and he had been living in the power center, in Aegypt, in the beautiful city of Heliopolis. From the Britone March to the Underlands of Ind, all was Graeco-Roman peace fed by the Nile's bounty and enforced by the hired troopers of Aegypt. Only in the outlands of Chin and the continents of East Chin far across the Nesian Sea were there open conflicts of nations. Yes … spring … and he had been living with his parents in Heliopolis. Both of his parents were on assignment with the military. This he knew from the records. His parents were perhaps the finest geneticists in the Empire. They were training for a project that was to take over young Morgan's life completely. They were preparing a trip to the stars. This, too, he was told. But that had been many years later, and too late for him to object.

What he remembered was a man, a black man. He liked to imagine him one of the dark priests of Aegypt that he watched every week on the viewer. The man walked past Morgan's quarters every afternoon. Where he went, and why he went only one way, Morgan never knew.

The fence around his parents' quarters was much higher than the black man's head. It was a mesh of heavy steel curved outwards and down at the top. Every afternoon Morgan watched the man walk by, and tried to imagine how the man came to be black. Morgan did not ask his parents because he wanted to figure it out for himself.

One morning early his father said, "The sun's going nova."

He never forgot those words, those powerful words, even though he did not know their meaning.

"It's been kept quiet, but even the Roman Empire can't hide this heat. All the chants of all the priests of Ra won't make one damn whit of difference."

"Heat?" his mother shot back. "Heat is something you can live in, you can deal with. But this …" she waved her hand at the large window, "this is only a step away from fire."

So, he thought, it was the sun made that man black.

He was ten before he realized that the man who walked past was black from birth, from conception. Still, Morgan persisted in telling the other children in his crèche that it was the sun's doing. He enjoyed the secret game of persuasion and deception.

Ah, the power of the game, even then!

Oakes straightened the cushion at his back. Why did he think of that black man, now? There had been one curious event, a simple thing that caused a commotion and fixed it in his memory.

He touched me.

Oakes could not recall being touched by anyone except his parents until that moment. On that very hot day, he sat outside on a step, cooled by the shade of the roof and the ventilator trained on his back from the doorway. The man walked by, as usual, then stopped and turned back. The boy watched him, curious, through the mesh fence, and the man studied him carefully, as though noticing him for the first time.

Oakes recalled the sudden jump of his heart, that feeling of a slingshot pulled back, back.

The man looked around, then up at the top of the fence, and the next thing Oakes knew the man was over the top, walking up to him. The black man stopped, reached out a hesitant hand and touched the boy's cheek. Oakes also reached out, equally curious, and touched the black skin of the man's arm.

"Haven't you ever seen a little boy before?" he asked.

The black face widened into a smile, and he said, "Yes, but not a little boy like you."

Then a sentry jumped on the man out of nowhere and took him away. Another sentry pulled the boy inside and called his father. He remembered that his father was angry. But best of all he remembered the look of wide-eyed wonder on the black man's face, the man who never walked by again. Oakes felt special then, powerful, an object of deference. He had always been someone to reckon with.

Why do I remember that man?

It seemed as though he spent all of his private hours asking himself questions lately. Questions led to more questions, led ultimately, daily, to the one question that he refused to admit into his consciousness. Until now.

He voiced the question aloud to himself, tested it on his tongue like the long-awaited wine.

"What if the damned ship is God?"

Chapter 5

Human hybernation is to animal hibernation as animal hibernation is to constant wakefulness. In its reduction of life processes, hybernation approaches absolute stasis. It is nearer death than life.

—*Dictionary of Science*, 101st Edition

RAJA FLATTERY lay quietly in the hybernation cocoon while he fought to overcome his terrors.

Ship has me.

Moody waves confused his memories but he knew several things. He could almost project these things onto the ebon blackness which surrounded him.

I was Chaplain/Psychiatrist on the Voidship Earthling.

We were supposed to produce an artificial consciousness. Very dangerous, that.

And they had produced … something. That something was Ship, a being of seemingly infinite powers.

God or Satan?

Flattery did not know. But Ship had created a paradise planet for its cargo of clones and then had introduced a new concept: WorShip. It had demanded that the human clones decide how they would WorShip.

We failed in that, too.

Was it because they were clones, every one of them? They had certainly been expendable. They had known this from the first moments of their childhood awareness on Moonbase.

Again, fear swept through him.

I must be resolute, Flattery told himself. *God or Satan, whatever this power may be, I'm helpless before it unless I remain resolute.*

"As long as you believe yourself helpless, you remain helpless even though resolute," Ship said.

"So You read my mind, too."

"Read? That is hardly the word."

Ship's voice came from the darkness all around him. It conveyed a sense of remote concerns which Flattery could not fathom. Every time Ship spoke he felt himself reduced to a mote. He combed his way through a furry sense of subjugation, but every thought amplified this feeling of being caged and inadequate.

What could a mere human do against a power such as Ship?

There were questions in his mind, though, and he knew that Ship sometimes answered questions.

"How long have I been in hyb?"

"That length of time would be meaningless to you."

"Try me."

"I am trying you."

"Tell me how long I've been in hyb."

The words were barely out of his mouth before he felt panic at what he had done. You did not address God that way … or Satan.

"Why not, Raj?"

Ship's voice had taken on an air of camaraderie, but so precise was the modulation his flesh tingled with it.

"Because … because …"

"Because of what I could do to you?"

"Yes."

"Ahhhhh, Raj, when will you awaken?"

"I am awake."

"No matter. You have been in hybernation for a very long time as you reckon time."

"How long?" He felt that the answer was deeply important; he had to know.

"You must understand about replays, Raj. Earth has gone through its history for Me, replayed itself at My Command."

"Replayed … the same way every time?"

"Most of the times."

Flattery felt the inescapable truth of it and a cry was torn from him: "Why?"

"You would not understand."

"All of that pain and …"

"And the joy, Raj. Never forget the joy."

"But … replay?"

"The way you might replay a musical recording, Raj, or a holorecord of a classical drama. The way Moonbase replayed its Project Consciousness, getting a bit more out of it each time."

"Why have You brought me out of hyb?"

"You are like a favorite instrument, Raj."

"But Bickel …"

"Ohh, Bickel! Yes, he gave Me his genius. He was the black box out of which you achieved Me, but friendship requires more, Raj. You are My best friend."

"I would've destroyed You, Ship."

"How little you understand friendship."

"So I'm … an instrument. Are You replaying me?"

"No Raj. No." Such sadness in that terrible voice. "Instruments play."

"Why should I permit You to play me?"

"Good! Very good, Raj!"

"Is that supposed to be an answer?"

"That was approval. You are, indeed, My best friend, My favorite instrument."

"I'll probably never understand that."

"It's partly because you enjoy the play."

Flattery could not suppress it; a chuckle escaped him.

"Laughter suits you, Raj."

Laughter? He remembered little laughter except the bitter amusement of self-accusation. But now he remembered going into hyb—not once, but more times than he cared to count. There had been other awakenings … other games and … yes, other failures. He sensed, though, that Ship was amused and he knew he was supposed to respond.

"What are we playing this time?"

"My demand remains unfulfilled, Raj. Humans somehow cannot decide how to WorShip. That's why there are no more humans now."

He felt frigid cold all through his body.

"No more … What've You done?"

"Earth has vanished into the cosmic whirl, Raj. All the Earths are gone. Long time, remember? Now, there are only Shipmen … and you."

"Me, human?"

"You are original material."

"A clone, a doppelganger, original material?"

"Very much so."

"What are Shipmen?"

"They are survivors from the most recent replays—slightly different replays from the Earth which you recall."

"Not human?"

"You could breed with them."

"How are they different?"

"They have similar ancestral experiences to yours, but they were picked up at different points in their social development."

Flattery sensed confusion in this answer and made a decision not to probe it . . . not yet. He wanted to try another tack.

"What do You mean they were picked up?"

"They thought of it as rescue. In each instance; their sun was about to nova."

"More of Your doing?"

"They have been prepared most carefully for your arrival, Raj."

"How have they been prepared?"

"They have a Chaplain/Psychiatrist who teaches hate. They have Sy Murdoch who has learned the lesson well. They have a woman named Hamill whose extraordinary strength goes deeper than anyone suspects. They have an old man named Ferry who believes everything can be bought. They have Waela and she is worthy of careful attention. They have a young poet named Kerro Panille, and they have Hali Ekel, who thinks she wants the poet. They have people who have been cloned and engineered for strange occupations. They have hungers, fears, joys. . . ."

"You call that preparation?"

"Yes, and I call it involvement."

"Which is what You want from me!"

"Involvement, yes."

"Give me one compelling reason I should go down there."

"I do not compel such things."

Not a responsive answer, but Flattery knew he would have to accept it.

"So I'm to arrive. Where and how?"

"There is a planet beneath us. Most Shipmen are on that planet—Colonists."

"And they must decide how they are supposed to WorShip?"

"You are still perceptive, Raj."

"What'd they say when You put the question to them?"

"I have not put this question to them. That, I hope, will be your task."

Flattery shuddered. He knew that game. It was in him to shout a refusal, to rage and invite Ship's worst reprisal. But something in this dialogue held his tongue.

"What happens if they fail?"

"I break the . . . recording."

Chapter 6

Dig your stubborn heels
Firm into dirt.
And where is the dirt going?
—Kerro Panille, *The Collected Poems*

KERRO PANILLE finished the last briefing on Pandoran geology and switched off his holo. It was well past the hour of mid-meal, but he felt no hunger. Ship's air tasted stale in the tiny teaching cubby and this surprised him until he realized he had sealed off the secret hatch into this place, leaving only the floor vent. *I've been sitting on the floor vent.*

This amused him. He stood and stretched, recalling the lessons of the holo. Dreams of real dirt, real seas, real air had played so long in his imagination that he feared now the real thing might disappoint him. He knew himself to be no novice at image-building in his mind ... and no novice to the disappointments of reality.

At such times he felt much older than his twenty annos. And he looked for reassurance in a shiny surface to reflect his own features. He found a small area of the hatch plate polished by the many passages of his own hand when entering this place.

Yes—his dark skin retained the smoothness of youth and the darker beard curled with its usual vigor around his mouth. He had to admit it was a generous mouth. And the nose was a pirate's nose. Not many Shipmen even knew there had ever been such people as pirates.

His eyes appeared much older than twenty, though. No escaping that.

Ship did that to me. No ... He shook his head. Honesty could not be evaded. *The special thing Ship and I have between us—that made my eyes look old.*

There were realities within realities. This thing that made him a poet kept him digging beneath every surface like a child pawing through pages of glyphs. Even when reality disappointed, he had to seek it.

The power of disappointment.

He recognized that power as distinct from frustration. It contained the power to regroup, rethink, react. It forced him to listen to himself as he listened to others.

Kerro knew what most people shipside thought about him.

They were convinced he could hear every conversation in a crowded room, that no gesture or inflection escaped him. There were times when that was true, but he kept to himself his conclusions about such observations. Thus, few were offended by his attentions. No one could find a better audience than Kerro Panille. All he wanted was to listen, to learn, to make order out of it in his poems.

It was order that mattered—beautiful order created out of the deepest inspiration. Yet ... he had to admit it, Ship presented an image of infinite disorder. He had asked Ship to show its shape to him once, a whimsical request which he had half expected to be refused. But Ship had responded by taking him on a visual tour, through the internal sensors, through the eyes of the robox repair units and even through the eyes of shuttles flitting between Ship and Pandora.

Externally, Ship was most confusing. Great fanlike extrusions dangled in space like wings or fins. Lights glittered within them and there were occasional glimpses of people at work behind the open shutters of the ports. Hydroponics gardens, Ship had explained.

Ship stretched almost fifty-eight kilometers in length. But it bulged and writhed throughout that length with fragile shapes which gave no clue to their purpose. Shuttles landed and were dispatched from long, slender tubes jutting randomly outward. The hydroponics fans were stacked one upon another, built outward from each other like mad growths springing from mutated spores.

Panille knew that once Ship had been sleek and trim, a projectile shape with three slim wings at the midpoint. The wings had dipped backward to form a landing tripod. That sleek shape lay hidden now within the confusion of the eons. It was called "the core" and you caught occasional glimpses of it in the passages—a thick wall with an airtight hatch, a stretch of metallic surface with ports which opened onto the blank barriers of new construction.

Internally, Ship was equally confusing. Sensor eyes showed him the stacks of dormant life in the hybernation bays. At his request, Ship displayed the locator coordinates, but they were meaningless to him. Numbers and glyphs. He followed the swift movements of robox units down passages where there was no air and out onto Ship's external skin. There, in the shadows of the random extrusions, he watched the business of repairs and alterations, even the beginnings of new construction.

Panille had watched his fellow Shipmen at their work, feeling fascinated and faintly guilty. A secret spy intruding on privacy. Two men had wrestled a large tubular container into a loading bay for shuttle transshipment down to Pandora. And Panille had felt that he had no right to watch this without the two men knowing it.

When the tour was over, he had sat back disappointed. It occurred to him then that Ship intruded this way all the time. Nothing any Shipman did could be hidden from Ship. This realization had sparked a momentary resentment which was followed immediately by amusement.

I am in Ship and of Ship and, in a deeper sense, I am Ship.

"Kerro!"

The sudden voice from the com-console beside his holo focus startled him. How had she found him here?

"Yes, Hali?"

"Where are you?"

Ahhh, she had not found him. A search program had found him.

"I'm studying," he said.

"Can you walk with me for a while? I'm really wound up."

"Where?"

"How about the arboretum near the cedars?"

"Give me a few minutes to finish up here and meet you."

"I'm not bothering you, am I?"

He noted the diffidence in her tone.

"No, I need a break."

"See you outside of Records."

He heard the click of her signoff and stood a blink staring at the console.

How did she know I was studying in the Records section?

A search program keyed to his person would not report his location.

Am I that predictable?

He picked up his notecase and recorder and stepped through the concealed hatch. He sealed it and slipped down through the software storage area to the nearest passage. Hali Ekel stood in the passageway beside the hatch waiting for him. She waved a hand, all nonchalance.

"Hi."

Most of his mind was still back in the study. He blinked at her foolishly, mindful as usual of the sheer beauty of Hali Ekel. At times like this—meeting suddenly, unexpectedly in some passage—she often stunned him.

The clinical sterility of the ever-present pribox at her hip never distanced them. She was a med-tech, full time, and he understood that life and survival were her business.

The secret darkness of her eyes, her thick black hair, the lustrous brown warmth of her skin always made him lean toward her slightly or face her way in a crowded room. They were from the same bloodlines, the Nesian Nations, selected for strength, survival sense and their easy affinity with the highways of the stars. Many mistook them for brother and sister, a mistake amplified by the fact that true siblings had not existed shipside in living memory. Some siblings slept on in hyb, but none walked together.

Notes toward a poem flashed behind his eyes, another of the many she brought to his mind, that he kept to himself.

Oh dark and magnificent star
What little light I have, take.
Weave those supple fingers into mine.

Feel the flow!

Before he could think of putting this into his recorder, it occurred to him that she should not be here so fast. There were no nearby call stations.

"Where were you when you called me?"

"Medical."

He glanced up the passage. Medical was at least ten minutes away.

"But how did you …"

"Keyed the whole conversation on a ten-minute delay."

"But …"

"See how standard you are on com? I can tape my whole side of a conversation with you and get it right down the line."

"But the …" He nodded at the hatch into software storage.

"Oh, that's where you always are when nobody can find you—somewhere in there." She pointed to the storage area.

"Hmmm." He took her hand and they headed out toward the west shell.

"Why so thoughtful?" she asked. "I thought you'd be amused, surprised … laugh, or something."

"I'm sorry. Lately it's bothered me when I do that. Never take time for people, never seem to have the flair for … the right word at the right time."

"A pretty strong self-indictment for a poet."

"It's much easier to order characters on a page or a holo than it is to order one's life. 'One's life!' Why do I talk that way?"

She slipped an arm around his waist and hugged him as they walked. He smiled. Presently, they emerged into the Dome of Trees. It was dayside, the sunglow of Rega muted through the screening filters. All the greens came with soothing blue undertones. Kerro took a deep breath of the oxygenated air. He heard birds twittering behind a sonabarrier off in heavier bushes to the left. Other couples could be seen far down through the trees. This was a favorite trysting place.

Hali slipped off her pribox strap and pulled him down beside her under a cover of cedar. The needle duff was warm and soft, the air thick with moisture and sun dazzled through the branches. They stretched out on their backs, shoulder to shoulder.

"Mmmmmm." Hali stretched and arched her back. "It smells so nice here."

"It? What's the smell of an it?"

"Oh, stop that." She turned toward him. "You know what I mean—the air, the moss, the food in your beard." She brushed at his whiskers, wove her fingers in and out of the coarse hairs. "You're the only Shipman with a beard."

"So I'm told."

"Do you like it?"

"I don't know." He reached out and traced the curve of the small wire ring which pierced her left nostril. "Traditions are strange. Where did you get this ring?"

"A robox dropped it."

"Dropped it?" He was surprised.

"I know—they don't miss much. This one was repairing a sensor outside that little medical study next to Behavioral. I saw the wire drop and picked it up. It was like finding a rare treasure. They leave so little around. Ship only knows what they do with all the scraps they carry off."

She slipped her arm around his neck and kissed him. Presently, she pulled back.

He pulled away from her and sat up. "Thanks, but …"

"It's always 'Thanks, but …'" She was angry, fighting the physical evidence of her own passion.

"I'm not ready." He felt apologetic. "I don't know why and I'm not playing with you. I just have this compulsion toward timing, for the feeling of rightness in things."

"What could be more right? We were selected as a breeding pair after knowing each other all this time. It's not like we were strangers."

He could not bring himself to look at her. "I know … anyone shipside can partner with anyone else, but …"

"But!" She whirled away and stared at the base of the sheltering tree. "We could be a breeding pair! One pair in … what? Two thousand? We could actually make a child."

"It isn't that. It's ..."

"And you're always so damned historical, traditional, quoting social patterns this and language patterns that. Why can't you see what ..."

He reached across her, put his fingers over her mouth to silence her and gently kissed her cheek.

"Dear Hali, because I can't. For me, partnership will have to be a giving so deep that I lose myself in the giving."

She rolled away and lifted her head to stare at him, her eyes glistening. "Where do you get such ideas?"

"They come out of my living and from what I learn."

"Ship teaches you these things?"

"Ship does not deny me what I want to know."

She stared morosely at the ground under her feet. "Ship won't even talk to me."

Her voice was barely audible.

"When you ask in the right way, Ship always answers," he said. Then, an afterthought as he sensed it between them: "And you have to listen."

"You've said that before but you never tell me how."

There was no evading the jealousy in her voice. He found that he could only answer in one way. "I will give you a poem," he said. He cleared his throat.

"Blue itself
teaches us blue."

She scowled, concentrating on his words. Presently, she shook her head. "I'll never understand you any more than I understand Ship. I go to WorShip; I pray; I do what Ship directs ..." She stared at him. "I never see you at WorShip."

"Ship is my friend," he said.

Curiosity overcame her resentments.

"What does Ship teach you?"

"Too many things to tell here."

"Just give me one thing, just one!"

He nodded. "Very well. There have been many planets and many people. Their languages and the chronicle of their years weave a magic tangle. Their words sing to me. You don't even have to understand the words to hear them sing."

She felt an odd sense of wonder at this.

"Ship gives you words and you don't understand?"

"When I ask for the original."

"But why do you want words that you don't understand?"

"To make those people live, to make them mine. Not to own them, but to become them, at least for a blink or two."

He turned and stared at her. "Haven't you ever wanted to dig in ancient dirt and find people nobody else even knew existed?"

"Their bones?"

"No! Their hearts, their lives."

She shook her head slowly.

"I just don't understand you, Kerro. But I love you."

He nodded silently, thinking: Yes, love doesn't have to understand. She knows this but she won't let it into her life.

He recalled the words of an old earthside poem: "Love is not a consolation, it is a light." The thought, the poem of life, that was consolation. He would talk to her of love sometime, he thought, but not this dayside.

Chapter 7

Why are you humans always so ready to carry the terrible burdens of your past?

—Kerro Panille, *Questions from the Avata*

SY MURDOCH did not like coming out this close to Colony perimeter, even when sheltered behind the crysteel barrier of Lab One's private exit. Creatures of this planet had a way of penetrating the impenetrable, confounding the most careful defenses.

But someone Lewis trusted had to man this observation post when the hylighters congregated on the plain as they were doing this morning. It was their most mysterious form of behavior and lately Lewis had been demanding answers—no doubt jumping to commands from The Boss.

He sighed. When he looked out on the unprotected surface of Pandora, there was no denying its immediate dangers.

Absently, he scratched his left elbow. When he moved his head against the exterior light, he could see his own reflection in the Plaz: a blocky man with brown hair, blue eyes, a light complexion which he kept meticulously scrubbed.

The vantage point was not the best available, not as good as the exterior posts which were always manned by the fastest and the best the Colony could risk. But Murdoch knew he could argue his importance to the leadership team. He was not expendable and this place did serve Lewis' purpose. The crysteel barrier, although it filtered out almost a fourth of the light, framed the area they needed to watch.

What was it those damned floating gasbags did out there?

Murdoch crouched behind a swivel-mounted scope-cum-vidicorder, and touched the controls with a short, stubby finger to focus on the 'lighters. More than a hundred of them floated above the plain about six kilometers out.

There were some big orange monsters in this mob, and Murdoch singled out one of the biggest for special observation, reading what he saw into a small recorder at his throat. The big 'lighter looked to be at least fifty meters in diameter, a truncated sphere somewhat flattened along the top which formed the muscular base for the tall, rippling sail membrane. Corded tendrils trailed down to the plain where it grasped a large rock which bumped and dragged along the surface, kicking up dust, scattering gravel.

The morning was cloudless, only one sun in the sky. It cast a harsh golden light on the plain, picking out every wrinkle and contraction of the 'lighter's bag. Murdoch could make out a cradle of smaller enfolding tentacles cupped beneath the 'lighter, confining something which squirmed there … twisting, flailing. He could not quite identify what the 'lighter carried, but it definitely was alive and trying to escape.

The mob of accompanying 'lighters had lined out in a great curved spread which was sweeping now across the plain on a diagonal path away from Murdoch's observation post. The big one he had singled out anchored the near flank, still confining that flailing something in the tentacle shadows beneath it.

What had that damned thing captured? Surely not a Colonist!

Murdoch backed off his focus to include the entire mob and saw then that they were targeting ground creatures, a mixed lot of them huddled on the plain. The arc of hylighters swept toward the crouching animals which waited mesmerized. He scanned them, identifying Hooded Dashers, Swift Grazers, Flatwings, Spinnerets, Tubetuckers, Clingeys … demons—all of them deadly to Colonists.

But apparently not dangerous to hylighters.

All of the 'lighters carried ballast rocks, Murdoch saw, and now the central segment of the sweeping arc dropped their rocks. The bags bounced slightly and tendrils stretched out to snatch up the crouching demons. The captive creatures squirmed and flailed, but made no attempt to bite or otherwise attack the 'lighters.

Now, all but a few of the ballasted 'lighters dropped their rocks and began to soar. The few still carrying rocks tacked out away from the capture team, appearing to search the ground for other specimens. The monster bag which Murdoch had studied earlier remained in this search group. Once more, Murdoch enlarged the image in the scope, focusing in on the cupped tendrils beneath the thing's bag. All was quiet there now and, as he watched, the tendrils opened to release their catch.

Murdoch dictated his observations into the recorder at his throat: "The big one has just dropped its catch. Whatever it is it appears to be desiccated, a large flat area of black … My God! It was a Hooded Dasher! The big 'lighter had a Hooded Dasher tucked up under the bag!"

The remains of the Dasher struck the ground in a geyser of dust.

Now, the big 'lighter swerved left and its rock ballast scraped the side of another large rock on the plain. Sparks flew where the rocks met and Murdoch saw a line of fire spurt upward to the 'lighter which exploded in a flare of glowing yellow. Bits of the orange bag and a cloud of fine blue dust drifted and sailed all around.

The explosion ignited a wild frenzy of action on the plain. The other bags dropped their captives and soared upward. The demons on the ground spread out, some dashing and leaping to catch the remnants of the exploded 'lighter. Slower creatures such as the Spinnerets crept toward fallen rags of the orange bag.

And when it was over, the demons sped away or burrowed into the plain as was the particular habit of each.

Murdoch methodically described this into his recorder.

When it was done, he scanned the plain once more. All of the 'lighters had soared away. Not a demon remained. He shut down the observation post and signaled for a replacement to come up, then he headed back toward Lab One and the Garden. As he made his way along the more secure lighted passages, he thought about what he had seen and recorded. The visual record would go to Lewis and later to Oakes. Lewis would edit the verbal observations, adding his own comments.

What was it I saw and recorded out there?

Try as he might to understand the behavior of the Pandoran creatures, Murdoch could not do it.

Lewis is right. We should just wipe them out.

And as he thought of Lewis, Murdoch asked himself how long this most recent emergency at the Redoubt would keep the man out of touch. For all they really knew, Lewis might be dead. No one was completely immune to the threats of Pandora—not even Lewis. If Lewis were gone …

Murdoch tried to imagine himself elevated to a new position of power under Oakes. The images of such a change would not form.

Chapter 8

Gods have plans, too.

—Morgan Oakes, *The Diaries*

FOR A long time, Panille lay quietly beside Hali in the treedome, watching the plaz-filtered light draw radial beams on the air above the cedar tree. He knew Hali had been hurt by his rejection and he wondered why he did not feel guilty. He sighed. There was no sense in running away; this was the way he had to be.

Hali spoke first, her voice low, tentative.

"Nothing's changed, is it?"

"Talking about it doesn't change it," he said. "Why did you ask me out here—to revive our sexual debate?"

"Couldn't I just want to be with you for a while?"

She was close to tears. He spoke softly to avoid hurting her even more.

"I'm always with you, Hali." With his left hand he lifted her right hand, pressed the tips of his fingers against the tips of her fingers. "Here. We touch, right?"

She nodded like a child being coaxed from a tantrum.

"Which is we and which the material of our flesh?"

"I don't …"

He held their fingertips a few centimeters apart.

"All the atoms between us oscillate at incredible speeds. They bump into each other and shove each other around." He tapped the air with a fingertip, careful to keep from touching her.

"So I touch an atom; it bumps into the next one; that one nudges another, and so on until …" He closed the gap and brushed her fingertips. "… we touch and we were never separate."

"Those are just words!" She pulled her hand away from him.

"Much more than words, you know it, Med-tech Hali Ekel. We constantly exchange atoms with the universe, with the atmosphere, with food, with each other. There's no way we can be separated."

"But I don't want just any atoms!"

"You have more choice than you think, lovely Hali."

She studied him out of the corners of her eyes. "Are you just making these things up to entertain me?"

"I'm serious. Don't I always tell you when I make up something?"

"Do you?"

"Always, Hali. I will make up a poem to prove it." He tapped her wire ring lightly. "A poem about this."

"Why're you telling me your poems? You usually just lock them up on tapes or store them away in those old-fashioned glyph books of yours."

"I'm trying to please you in the only way I can."

"Then tell me your poem."

He brushed her cheek beside the ring, then:

"With delicate rings of the gods
in our noses
we do not root in their garden."

She stared at him, puzzled. "I don't understand."

"An ancient Earthside practice. Farmers put rings in the noses of their pigs to keep the pigs from digging out of their pens. Pigs dig with their noses as well as their feet. People called that kind of digging 'rooting.'"

"So you're comparing me to a pig."

"Is that all you see in my poem?"

She sighed, then smiled as much at herself as at Kerro. "We're a fine pair to be selected for breeding—the poet and the pig!"

He stared at her, met her gaze and, without knowing why, they were suddenly giggling, then laughing.

Presently, he lay back on the duff. "Ahhh, Hali, you are good for me."

"I thought you might need some distraction. What've you been studying that keeps you so shut away?"

He scratched his head, recovered a brown twig of dead cedar. "I've been rooting into the 'lectrokelp."

"That seaweed the Colony's been having all the trouble with? Why would that interest you?"

"I'm always amazed at what interests me, but this may be right down my hatchway. The kelp, or some phase of it, appears to be sentient."

"You mean it thinks?"

"More than that … probably much more."

"Why hasn't this been announced?"

"I don't know for sure. I came across part of the information by accident and pieced together the rest. There's a record of other teams sent out to study the kelp."

"How did you find this report?"

"Well … I think it may be restricted for most people, but Ship seldom holds anything back from me."

"You and Ship!"

"Hali …"

"Oh, all right. What's in this report?"

"The kelp appears to have a language transmitted by light but we can't understand it yet. And there's something even more interesting. I can't find out if there's a current project to contact and study this kelp."

"Doesn't Ship …"

"Ship refers me to Colony HQ or to the Ceepee, but they don't acknowledge my inquiries."

"That's nothing new. They don't acknowledge most inquiries."

"You been having trouble with them, too?"

"Just that Medical can't get an explanation for all the gene sampling."

"Gene sampling? How very curious."

"Oakes is a very curious and very private person."

"How about someone on the staff?"

"Lewis?" Her tone was derisive.

Kerro scratched his cheek reflectively.

"The 'lectrokelp and gene sampling, Hali, I don't know about the gene sampling … that has a peculiar stink to it. But the kelp …"

She interrupted, excited: "This creature could have a soul … and it could WorShip."

"A soul? Perhaps. But I thought when I saw that record: 'Yes! This is why Ship brought us to Pandora.'"

"What if Oakes knows that the 'lectrokelp is the reason we're here?"

Panille shook his head.

She gripped his arm. "Think of all the times Oakes has called us prisoners of Ship. He tells us often enough that Ship won't let us leave. Why won't he tell us why Ship brought us here?"

"Maybe he doesn't know."

"Ohhh, he knows."

"Well, what can we do about it?"

She spoke without thinking: "We can't do anything without going groundside."

He pulled his arm away from her and dug his fingers into the humus. "What do we know about living groundside?"

"What do we know about living here?"

"Would you go down to the Colony with me, Hali?"

"You know I would but …"

"Then let's apply for …"

"They won't let me go. The groundside food shortage is critical; there are health problems. They've just increased our workload because they've sent some of our best people down."

"We're probably imagining monsters that don't exist, but I'd still like to see the 'lectrokelp for myself."

A high-pitched hum blurted from the ever-present pribox on the ground beside Hali. She pressed the response key.

"Hali …" There was a clatter, a buzz. Presently, the voice returned. "Sorry I dropped you. This is Winslow Ferry. Is that Kerro Panille with you, Hali?"

Hali stifled a laugh. The bumbling old fool could not even put in a call without stumbling over something. Kerro was caught by the direct reference to someone being with Hali. Had Ferry been listening? Many shipside suspected that sensors and portable communications equipment had been adapted for eavesdropping but this was his first direct clue. He took the pribox from her.

"This is Kerro Panille."

"Ahhh, Kerro. Please report to my office within the hour. We have an assignment for you."

"An assignment?"

There was no response. The connection had been broken.

"What do you suppose that's all about?" Hali asked.

For answer, Kerro drew a blank page from his notebook, scribbled on it with a fade-stylus, then pointed to the pribox. "He was listening to us."

She stared at the note.

Kerro said: "Isn't that strange? I've never had an assignment before … except study assignments from Ship."

Hali took the stylus from him, wrote: "Look out. If they do not want it known that the kelp thinks, you could be in danger."

Kerro stood, blanked the page and restored it to his case. "Guess I'd better wander down to Ferry's office and find out what's happening."

They walked most of the way back in silence, intensely aware of every sensor they passed, of the pribox at Hali's hip. As they approached Medical, she stopped him.

"Kerro, teach me how to speak to Ship."

"Can't."

"But …"

"It's like your genotype or your color. Except for certain clones, you don't get much choice in the matter."

"Ship has to decide?"

"Isn't that always the way, even with you? Do you respond to everyone who wants to talk to you?"

"Well, I know Ship must be very busy with …"

"I don't think that has anything to do with it. Ship either speaks to you or doesn't."

She digested this for a moment, nodded, then: "Kerro, do you really talk to Ship?"

There was no mistaking the resentment in her voice.

"You know I wouldn't lie to you, Hali. Why're you so interested in talking to Ship?"

"It's the idea of Ship answering you. Not the commands we get over the 'coders, but …"

"A kind of unlimited encyclopedia?"

"That, yes, but more. Does Ship talk to you through the 'coders?"

"Not very often."

"What is it like when …"

"It's like a very distinctive voice in your head, just a bit clearer than your conscience."

"That's it?" She sounded disappointed.

"What did you expect? Trumpets and bells?"

"I don't even know what my conscience sounds like!"

"Keep listening." He brushed a finger against her ring, kissed her quickly, brotherly, then stepped through the hatch into the screening area for Ferry's office.

Chapter 9

The fearful are often holders of the most dangerous power. They become demonic when they see the workings of all the life around them. Seeing the strengths as well as the weaknesses, they fasten only on the weaknesses.

—Shipquotes

WINSLOW FERRY sat in his dimly lighted office unaware of the random chaos around him—the piles of tapes and software, the dirty clothes, the empty bottles and boxes, the papers with scribbled notes to himself. It had been a long, tense dayside for him, and the place smelled of stale, spilled wine and old perspiration. His entire attention focused on the sensor screen at the corner of his comdesk. He bent his sweaty face close to the screen which showed Panille walking down a passageway with that lithe and succulent med-tech, Hali Ekel.

A wisp of gray hair fell over his right eye and he brushed it aside with a deeply veined hand. His pale eyes glittered in the com light.

He watched Hali on the holo, watched the smoothness of her young body glide from passageway to hatch to passageway. But the musk that surrounded him there in his office was Rachel. At times Rachel Demarest seemed all bone and elbow to him, a hard woman hardly used. He developed an amused distance from her whine. She had dreams that included him because she wanted him, even if he was a sack of graying wrinkles and sour breath. She wanted power and Ferry liked to snuggle up to power. They were good for each other and they tricked themselves into a personal distance by trading information for liquor, wine for position or a warm night together. This game of barter between them walled off the kind of hurt they'd both been dealt at the hands of whimsical lovers.

Rachel was asleep now in his cubby, dreaming herself Senior Chair of a new Council that would wrest power from Oakes, make the Colony self-sufficient and self-governing.

Ferry sat at his console, slightly drunk, dreaming of Hali Ekel.

He waited to shift to the next spy sensor until he could no longer make out the details of Hali's small, firm hips tight against her jumpsuit. What luscious hips! As he switched sensors to the one ahead of them, he forgot to change focus. The two were a blur as they approached the sensor's forward field limit. Ferry fumbled with the controls and lost them.

"Damn!" he whispered, and his old surgeon's hands were shaking like a wihi in a flare.

He touched the screen to steady himself, touched Hali's image blurring past the sensor and into a treedome.

"Enjoy, enjoy, my dears." He spoke aloud, his words absorbed by the piled confusion around him. Everyone knew why young couples went into the treedome. He checked to see that the holo was on record and that sound levels were satisfactory. Lewis and Oakes would want to see this, and Ferry anticipated making a special copy for himself.

"Give it to her, young fellow! Give it to her!"

He felt a pleasant swelling at his crotch and wondered if he could get away to visit Rachel Demarest.

"Get something on that poet," Lewis had ordered, and he'd had five liters of the new Pandoran wine delivered to Ferry's office from groundside by Rachel—a double gift. One of the empties lay across his mazed hookup to the Biocomputer. Another empty was still on the deck of the cubby temporarily occupied by Rachel. She was a clone (one of the better ones) and wine was the treasure to her that Ferry was not. Rachel was the treasure to him that Ekel was not.

Ferry watched the small touches between Panille and Ekel, imagining every one of them to be his own.

Perhaps with a little wine … he thought, and he leered at the faint, half-imagined nipples pressing her suit, shouting him out of her conversation with Panille.

Are they going to couple?

He was beginning to doubt it. Panille was not reacting correctly. *I should've told them about Panille's groundside orders sooner.* That was always a good lever for sex. "I'm going groundside soon, dear one. You know what the dangers are down there?"

"Go ahead, do it, fellow!"

Ferry wanted to watch Hali slip out of her singlesuit, wanted her to desire a horny old surgeon with that desire she had in her eyes for Panille.

"So you want to know about the kelp," Ferry slurred to Panille's reclining image in the viewscreen. "Well, you'll know it all soon enough, fellow. And Hali …" His clammy fingers caressed the screen. "… perhaps Lewis can see to it that you are assigned to us here at Classification and Processing. Yesss." And the yes was a feverish hiss through his yellow teeth.

Suddenly, the conversation on the screen jarred him out of his daydream. He was sure he had heard correctly. Panille had told Hali Ekel that the kelp was sentient.

"Damn you!" Ferry screamed at the viewer, and this became his low-voiced chant as the eavesdropping continued.

Yes, Panille was telling her everything. He was spoiling everything!

Panille was going groundside, was going to be out of the way. And all because of the kelp! Ferry was sure of it. The groundside orders must have been cut by Lewis or Oakes. That had to be because they were cut as soon as that mass of study-circuits on the kelp started showing up on Panille's program orders. Panille was onto something, but could be stopped. He was quiet, and could be removed quietly. The only logical reason for the delay in sending the fellow groundside had to be that order from Lewis: "Get something on 'im."

Well ... orders said the delay ended if Panille started talking too much.

"But damn him, he told her!"

Ferry caught his breath and tried to calm himself. He opened his last bottle of wine, the fantasy bottle that he would have offered to Ekel, if only in his dreams. He had neither the key, the code, nor the technical expertise to alter the holorecording, to erase all evidence that Ekel, too, knew about the kelp.

He took a long swallow of the wine and slammed the call key coded to her.

"Hali ..." He threw the bottle across his office in rage, then lost his balance and fell against the console, breaking the call-connection. He pushed himself back, calmed his voice and once more opened the channel.

"Sorry I dropped you. This is Winslow Ferry. Is that Kerro Panille with you, Hali?" How he loved the sound of her name on his tongue, the touch of her even in word.

She laughed at him!

Ferry had no recollection of ending the call, ordering Panille to his office, but he knew he had done it.

She laughed at him ... and she knew about the kelp. When Lewis reviewed this holorecord (and he would certainly do that), then Lewis would know she had laughed at him and Lewis would laugh because he often laughed at Ferry.

But it's always old Winslow who gets him what he needs!

Yes ... always. When no one else could manage it, Winslow knew someone who knew someone who knew something and had a price. Lewis would not care deeply that she laughed at old Winslow. Momentary amusement, that was all. But Lewis would care about the kelp. New orders would be cut for Ekel. Ferry knew that for certain. And wherever Ekel was assigned, it would not be to Classification and Processing.

Chapter 10

A good bureaucracy is the best tool of oppression ever invented.
—Jesus Lewis, *The Oakes Diaries*

WHEN REGA had set behind the western hills, Waela TaoLini turned atop her craggy vantage to watch the red-orange ball of Alki cross the southern horizon in its first passage of the diurn. She had only been forced to kill three demons in the past hour and there seemed little more to do on this watch except mark the distant line of powdery red to the south where they had burned out a Nerve Runner boil just two diurns past. But it looked as though they had sterilized the area, although she could still detect an occasional whiff of burned acid from that direction. But Swift Grazers were already into the red, gorging on the dead Runners. The bulbous little multipeds would not venture anywhere near a live boil of Runners.

As usual, she stood tall and alert on watch. She did not feel unusually exposed on the crag. There was a 'scape hatch and slide tunnel one step away on her left. A sensor atop the tunnel's marker pole kept constant watch on her. She carried a gushburner and lasgun, but even more important, she knew her own reflexes. Conditioned by the harsh requirements of Pandora, she could match anything except a massed attack by the planet's predators.

And the Nerve Runner invasion had been turned back.

Waela crouched then and stared down across the southern plain to the rim of hills. Without conscious volition, her gaze darted left, right; she stood and turned, repeated this procedure. It was all random, constant movement.

"Try to look everywhere at once." That was the watchword.

Her yellow flaresuit was damp with perspiration. She was tall and slim and she knew this gave her an advantage here. On patrol, she walked tall. Other times, she pulled in her shoulders and tried to appear shorter. Men did not like taller women, a continually bothersome fact which amplified her constant concern over her unavoidable peculiarity: her skin changed color through a broad spectrum from blue to orange in response to her moods, a system not under conscious control. Right now, her exposed skin betrayed the pale pink of repressed fear. Her hair was black and cropped at the neck. Her eyes were brown and shaded in epicanthic folds, but she felt that she had a slender and attractive nose which complemented her broad chin and full lips.

"Waela, you're some kind of chameleon throwback," one of her friends had said. But he was dead now, drowned under the kelp.

She sighed.

"Rrrrrssss!"

She turned to the sound and, by reflex, gunned out two Flatwings, thin and multilegged ground racers about ten centimeters long. Poisonous things!

Alki was four diameters above the southern horizon now, sending long shadows northward and painting a red-purple glow across the distant sea to the west.

Waela liked this particular watch station for its view of the sea. It was the highest vantage connected to Colony. They called it simply "Peak."

A line of hylighters drifted through the sky along the distant shoreline. Judging by their apparent size from this distance, they were giants. As with others among the Shipmen/Colonists, she had studied the native life carefully, making the usual comparisons against Shiprecords. The hylighters were, indeed, like giant airborne Portuguese men-of-war, great orange creatures born in the sea. Steadied by its long black tendrils, a hylighter could adjust the great membrane atop its buoyant bag and tack into the wind. They moved with a strange precision, usually in groups of twenty or more, and Waela found herself on the side of those who argued for some intelligence in these gentle creatures.

Hylighters were a nuisance, yes. They were buoyed by hydrogen and that, coupled with Pandora's frequent electrical storms, made the creatures into lethal firebombs. In common with the 'lectrokelp, they were useless as food. Even to touch them produced weird mental effects—hysteria and even, sometimes, convulsions. Standing orders were to explode them at a distance when they approached Colony.

Almost without thinking about it, she noted a Spinneret creeping up the Peak on her left. It was a big one. She guessed it would equal the five kilos of the largest ever taken. Because the high-density, molelike creature was Pandora's only slow mover, she took her time responding. Every opportunity to study Pandora's predators had to be used. It was as gray-black as the rocks and she guessed its length at about thirty centimeters, not counting the spinner tail. The first Colonists to encounter Spinnerets had been trapped in the sticky fog the things released through that tail appendage.

Waela chewed her lower lip, watching the Spinneret's purposeful approach. It had seen her; no doubt of that. The sticky mesh of the Spinneret's fog produced a peculiar paralysis. It rendered everything it touched immobile, but alive and alert. The nearsighted Spinneret, having trapped a victim, could suck the captive dry at a slow and agonizing pace.

"Close enough," she whispered as the thing paused fewer than five meters below her and started turning to bring its lethal spinner into play. A quick red wash of the gushburner incinerated the Spinneret. She watched the remains tumble off the Peak.

Alki was now eight diameters above the horizon and she knew her watch was almost over. She had been ordered to assess possible dangerous activity among the free-roaming predators. They all knew the reason for watching outside Colony's barriers. The visible human in a yellow flaresuit would attract predators.

"We're bait out there," one of her friends had said.

Waela resented the assignment, but in a place of common perils she knew she had to share every danger. That was Colony's social glue. Even though she would get extra food chits for this, she could not help resenting it.

There were other dangers more important to her, and she saw this assignment as a symptom of perilous change in Colony priorities. Her place was out studying the kelp. As the sole survivor of the original study teams, she was the perfect choice for assembling a new team.

Are they phasing out our research?

There were rumors all through Colony. The materials and energy could not be spared for construction of strong-enough submersibles. The LTAs could not be spared. Lighter-Than-Air was still the most reliable groundside transport for the mining and drilling outposts, and, because they had been built to simulate hylighters, they attracted minimal attention from predators. Hylighters appeared to be immune to the predators.

She could see the rationale of the arguments. Kelp interfered with the aquaculture project and food was short. The argument for extermination, though, she saw as one of dangerous ignorance.

We need more information.

Almost casually, she gunned out a Hooded Dasher, noting that it was the first one seen anywhere near the Peak in twenty diurns.

The kelp must be studied. We must learn.

What did they know about the kelp after all the lives spent and all the frustrating dives?

Fireflies in the night of the sea, someone called them.

The kelp extruded nodules from its giant stems and those nodules glowed with a million firecolors. She agreed with all the others who had seen it and lived to report: the pulsing and glowing nodules were a hypnotic symphony, and the lights might, just might, be a form of communication. There did seem to be purpose in the glowing play of light, discernible patterns.

The kelp covered the planet's seas except for the random patches of open water called "lagoons." In a planet with only two major land masses, this represented a gigantic spread of life.

Once again, she returned to that unavoidable argument: what did they really know about the kelp?

It's conscious, it thinks.

She was certain of it. The challenge of this problem engaged her imagination with a totality she had never dreamed possible. It had caught others as well. It was polarizing Colony. And the extermination arguments could not be thrown out.

Can you eat the kelp?

You could not eat it. The stuff was disorienting, probably hallucinogenic. The source of this effect had thus far defied Colony chemists to isolate it.

It had this in common with the hylighters. The illusive substance had been dubbed "fraggo" because "it fragments the psyche."

That alone said to Waela that the kelp should be preserved for study.

Once more, she was forced to kill a Hooded Dasher. The long black shape went tumbling down the Peak, green blood gushing from it.

That's too many of them, she thought.

Warily, she examined her surroundings, probing for movement below her in the rocks. Nothing. She was still scanning the area this way moments later when her relief stepped out of the hatch. She recognized him, Scott Burik, an LTA fitter on the nightside shift. He was a small man with prematurely aged features, but he was as quick as any other Colonist, already scanning the area around them. She told him about the two Dashers as she passed over the 'burner.

"Good rest," he said.

She slipped into the hatch, heard it slam behind her then slid down to debriefing where she turned in her kill count and made her assessment of COA—Current Outside Activity.

The debriefing room was windowless with pale yellow walls and a single comdesk. Ary Arenson, a blond, gray-eyed man who never seemed to change expression, sat behind it. Everyone said he worked for Jesus Lewis, a rumor which predisposed Waela to walk and talk softly with him. Odd things happened to people who displeased Lewis.

She was tired now with a fatigue which watch always produced, a drained feeling, as though she were victim of a psychic Spinneret. The routine questions bored her.

"Yes, the Nerve Runner area appears sterilized."

At the end of it, Arenson handed her a small square of brown Colony paper with a message which restored her energy. She read it at a glance:

"Report to Main Hangar for new kelp research team assignment."

Arenson was glancing at his Comscreen as she read the note and now he changed expression, a wry smile. "Your replacement …" He pointed upward toward the Peak with his chin. "… just got it. A Dasher chewed his guts out. Stand by a blink. They're sending another replacement."

Chapter 11

Poetry, like consciousness, drops the insignificant digits.
—Raja Flattery, *Shiprecords*

SHIP'S WARNING that this could be the end of humankind left Flattery with a sense of emptiness.

He stared into the blackness which surrounded him, trying to find some relief. Would Ship really break the … recording? What did Ship mean by a recording?

Last chance.

His emotional responses told Flattery he had touched a deep core of affinity with his own kind. The thought that in some faraway future on a line through infinity there might be other humans to enjoy life as he had enjoyed it—this thought filled him with warm affections for such descendants.

"Do You really mean this is our last chance?" he asked.

"Much as it pains Me." Ship's response did not surprise him.

The words were torn from him: "Why don't You just tell us how to …"

"Raj! How much of your free will would you give me!"

"How much would You take?"

"Believe Me, Raj, there are places where neither God nor Man dares intervene."

"And You want me to go down to this planet, put Your question to them, and help them answer Your demand?"

"Would you do that?"

"Could I refuse?"

"I seek choice, Raj, not compulsion or chance. Will you accept?"

Flattery thought about this. He could refuse. Why not? What did he owe these … these … Shipmen, these replay survivors? But they were sufficiently human that he could interbreed with them. Human. And he still sensed that core of pain when he thought about a universe devoid of humans.

One last chance for humankind? It might be interesting … play. Or it might be one of Ship's illusions.

"Is all this just illusion, Ship?"

"No. The flesh exists to feel the things that flesh feels. Doubt everything except that."

"I either doubt everything or nothing."

"So be it. Will you play despite your doubts?"

"Will You tell me more about this play?"

"If you ask a correct question."

"What role am I playing?"

"Ahhhh …" It was a sigh of beatific grace. "You play the living challenge."

Flattery knew that role. Living challenge. You made people find the best within themselves, a best which they might not suspect they possessed. But some would be destroyed by such a demand. Remembering the pain of responsibility for such destruction, he wanted help in his decision but knew he dared not ask directly. Perhaps if he learned more about Ship's plans …

"Have You hidden in my memory things about the game that I should know?"

"Raj!" There was no mistaking the outrage. It flowed through him as though his body were a sudden sieve thrust beneath a hot cascade. Then, more softly: "I do not steal your memories, Raj."

"Then I'm to be something different, a new factor, in this game. What else is different?"

"The place of the test possesses a difference so profound it may test you beyond your capacities, Raj."

The many implications of this answer filled him with wonder. So there were things even an all-powerful being did not know, things even God or Satan might learn.

Ship made him fearful then by commenting on his unspoken thought.

"Given that marvelous and perilous condition which you call Time, power can be a weakness."

"Then what's this profound difference which will test me?"

"An element of the game which you must discover for yourself."

Flattery saw the pattern of it then: The decision had to be his own. Not compulsion. It was the difference between choice and chance. It was the difference between the precision of a holorecord replay and a brand-new performance where free will dominated. And the prize was another chance for humankind. The Chaplain/Psychiatrists' Manual said: "God does not play dice with Man." Obviously, someone had been wrong.

"Very well, Ship. I'll gamble with You."

"Excellent! And, Raj—when the dice roll there will be no outside interference to control how they fall."

He found the phraseology of this promise interesting, but sensed the futility of exploring it. Instead, he asked: "Where will we play?"

"On this planet which I call Pandora. A small frivolity."

"I presume Pandora's box already is open."

"Indeed. All the evils that can trouble Mankind have been released."

"I've accepted Your request. What happens now?"

For answer, Flattery felt the hyb locks release him, the soft restraints pulling away. Light glowed around him and he recognized a dehyb laboratory in one of the shipbays. The familiarity of the place dismayed him. He sat up and looked around. All of that time and this … this lab remained unchanged. But of course Ship was infinite and infinitely powerful. Nothing outside of Time was impossible for Ship.

Except getting humankind to decide on their manner of WorShip.

What if we fail this time?

Would Ship really break the recording? He felt it in his guts: Ship would erase them. No more humankind … ever. Ship would go on to new distractions.

If we fail, we'll mature without flowering, never to send our seed through Infinity. Human evolution will stop here.

Have I changed in hyb? All that time …

He slipped out of the tank enclosure and padded across to a full-length mirror set into one of the lab's curved walls. His naked flesh appeared unchanged from the last time he had seen it. His face retained its air of quizzical detachment, an expression others often thought calculating. The remote brown eyes and upraked black eyebrows had been both help and hindrance. Something in the human psyche said such features belonged only to superior creatures. But superiority could be an impossible burden.

"Ahhh, you sense a truth," Ship whispered.

Flattery tried to swallow in a dry throat. The mirror told him that his flesh had not aged. Time? He began to grasp what Ship meant by such a length of Time which was meaningless. Hyb held flesh in stasis no matter what the passage of Time. No maturity there. But what about his mind? What about that reflected construct for which his brain was the receiver? He felt that something had ripened in his awareness.

"I'm ready. How do I get down to Pandora?"

Ship spoke from a vocoder above the mirror. "There are several ways, transports which I have provided."

"So You deliver me to Pandora. I just walk in on them. 'Hi. I'm Raja Flattery. I've come to give you a big pain in the head.'"

"Flippancy does not suit you, Raj."

"I feel Your displeasure."

"Do you already regret your decision, Raj?"

"Can You tell me anything more about the problems on Pandora?"

"The most immediate problem is their encounter with an alien intelligence, the 'lectrokelp."

"Dangerous?"

"So they believe. The 'lectrokelp is close to infinite and humans fear …"

"Humans fear open spaces, never-ending open spaces. Humans fear their own intelligence because it's close to infinite."

"You delight Me, Raj!"

A feeling of joy washed over Flattery. It was so rich and powerful that he felt he might dissolve in it. He knew that the sensation did not originate with him, and it left him feeling drained, transparent … bloodless.

Flattery pressed the heels of his hands against his tightly closed eyes. What a terrible thing that joy was! Because when it was gone … when it was gone …

He whispered: "Unless You intend to kill me, don't do that again."

"As you choose." How cold and remote.

"I want to be human! That's what I was intended to be!"

"If that's the game you seek."

Flattery sensed Ship's disappointment, but this made him defensive and he turned to questions.

"Have Shipmen communicated with this alien intelligence, this 'lectrokelp?"

"No. They have studied it, but do not understand it."

Flattery took his hands away from his eyes. "Have Shipmen ever heard of Raja Flattery?"

"That's a name in the history which I teach them."

"Then I'd better take another name." He ruminated for a moment, then: "I'll call myself Raja Thomas."

"Excellent. Thomas for your doubts and Raja for your origins."

"Raja Thomas, communications expert—Ship's best friend. Here I come, ready or not."

"A game, yes. A game. And … Raj?"

"What?"

"For an infinite being, Time produces boredom. Limits exist to how much Time I can tolerate."

"How much Time are You giving us to decide the way we'll WorShip?"

"At the proper moment you will be told. And one more thing—"

"Yes?"

"Do not be dismayed if I refer to you occasionally as My Devil."

He was a moment recovering his voice, then: "What can I do about it? You can call me whatever You like."

"I merely asked that you not be dismayed."

"Sure! And I'm King Canute telling the tides to stop!"

There was no response from Ship and Flattery wondered if he was to be left on his own to find his way down to this planet called Pandora. But presently, Ship spoke once more: "Now we will dress you in appropriate costume, Raj. There is a new Chaplain/Psychiatrist who rules the Shipmen. They call him Ceepee and, when he offends them, they call him The Boss. You can expect that The Boss will order you to attend him soon."

Chapter 12

Perhaps the immobility of the things that surround us is forced upon them by our conviction that they are themselves and not anything else, and by the immobility of our conceptions of them.

—Marcel Proust, *Shiprecords*

OAKES STUDIED his own image reflected in the com-console at his elbow. The curved screen, he knew, was what made the reflection diminutive.

Reduced.

He felt jumpy. No telling what the ship might do to him next.

Oakes swallowed in a dry throat.

He did not know how long he had sat there hypnotized by that reflection. It was still nightside. An unfinished glass of Pandoran wine sat on a low brown table in front of him. He glanced up and around. His opulent cubby remained a place of shadows and low illumination, but something had changed. He could feel the change. Something … someone watching …

The ship might refuse to talk to him, deny him elixir, but he was getting messages—many messages.

Change.

That unspoken question which hovered in his mind had changed something in the air. His skin tingled and there was a throbbing at his temples.

What if the ship's program is running down?

His reflection in the blank screen gave no answer. It showed only his own features and he began to feel pride in what he saw there. Not just fat, no. Here was a mature man in his middle years. The Boss. The silver at his temples spoke of dignity and importance. And although he was … plump, his skin remained soft and clear, testimony to the care he took preserving the appearance of youth.

Women liked that.

What if the ship is Ship … is truly God?

The air felt dirty in his lungs and he realized he was breathing much too rapidly.

Doubts.

The damned ship was not going to respond to his doubts. Never had. Wouldn't talk to him; wouldn't feed him. He had to feed himself from the ship's limited hydroponics gardens. How long could he continue to trust them? Not enough food for everyone. The very thought increased his appetite.

He stared at the unfinished glass of wine—dark amber, oily on the inner surface of the glass. There was a wet puddle under the glass, a stain on the brown surface.

I'm the Ceepee.

The Ceepee was supposed to believe in Ship. In his own cynical way, old Kingston had insisted on this.

I don't believe.

Was that why a new Ceepee was being sent groundside?

Oakes ground his teeth together.

I'll kill the bastard!

He spoke it aloud, intensely aware of how the words echoed in his cubby.

"Hear that, Ship? I'll kill the bastard!"

Oakes half expected a response to this blasphemy. He knew this because he caught himself holding his breath, listening hard to the shadows at the edges of his cubby.

How did you test for godhood?

How did you separate a powerful mechanical phenomenology, a trick of technological mirrors, from a … from a miracle?

If God did not play dice, as the Ceepees were always told, what might God play? Perhaps dice was not challenge enough for a god. What was risk enough to tempt a god out of silence or reverie … out of a god's lair?

It was a stupefying question—to challenge God at God's own game?

Oakes nodded to himself.

In the game, perhaps, is the miracle. Miracle of Consciousness? It was no trick to make a machine self-programming, self-perpetuating. Complex, true, and unimaginably costly …

Not unimaginably, he cautioned himself.

He shook his head to drive out the half-dream.

If people did it, then it's imaginable, tangible, somehow explainable. Gods move in other circles.

The question was: which circles? And if you could define those circles, their limits, you could know the limits of the god within them. What limits, then? He thought about energy. Energy remained a function of mass and speed. Even a god might have to be somewhere within the denominator of—what kind of mass, how much, how fast?

Maybe godhood is simply another expansion of limits. Because our vision dims is no reason to conclude that infinity lies beyond.

His training as a Chaplain had always been subservient to his training as a scientist and medical man. He knew that to test data truly he could not close the doors on experiment or assume that what he wished would necessarily be so.

It was what you did with data, not the data, that was important. Every king, every emperor had to know that one. Even his theology master had agreed.

"Sell 'em on God. It's for their own good. Pin the little everyday miracles on God and you've got 'em; you don't need to move mountains. If you're good enough, people will move the mountains for you in the name of God."

Ahh, yes. That had been Edmond Kingston, a real Chaplain/Psychiatrist out of the ship's oldest traditions, but still a cynic.

Oakes heaved a deep sigh. Those had been quiet days shipside, days of tolerance and security of purpose. The machinery of the monster around them ran smoothly. God had been remote and most Shipmen remained in hyb.

But that had been before Pandora. Bad luck for old Kingston that the ship had put them in orbit around Pandora. Good old Edmond, dead on Pandora with the fourth settlement attempt. Not a trace recovered, not a cell. Gone now, into whatever passed for eternity. And Morgan Oakes was the second cynical Chaplain to take on the burden of Ship.

The first Ceepee not chosen by the damned ship!

Except … there was this new Ceepee, he reminded himself, this man without a name who was being sent groundside to talk to the damned vegetables … the 'lectrokelp.

He will not be my successor!

There were many ways that a man in power could delay things to his own advantage. Even as I am now delaying the ship's request that we send this poet … this whatsisname, Panille, groundside.

Why did the ship want a poet groundside? Did that have anything to do with this new Ceepee? A drop of sweat trickled into his right eye.

Oakes grew aware that his breathing had become labored. Heart attack? He pushed himself off the low divan. Have to get help. There was pain all through his chest. Damn! He had too many unfinished plans. He couldn't just go this way. Not now! He staggered to the hatch but the hatch dogs refused to turn under his fingers. The air was cooler here, though, and he grew aware of a faint hissing from the equalizer valve over the hatch. Pressure difference? He did not understand how that could be. The ship controlled the interior environment. Everyone knew that.

"What're you doing, you damned mechanical monster?" he whispered. "Trying to kill me?"

It was getting easier to breathe. He pressed his head against the cool metal of the hatch, drew in several deep breaths. The pain in his chest receded. When he tried the hatch dogs again they turned, but he did not open the hatch. He knew his symptoms could be explained by asphyxia … or anxiety.

Asphyxia?

He opened the hatch and peered out into an empty corridor, the dim blue-violet illumination of nightside. Presently, he closed the hatch and stared across his cubby.

Another message from the ship? He would have to go groundside soon … as soon as Lewis made it safe for him down there.

Lewis, get that Redoubt ready for us!

Would the ship really kill him? No doubt it could. He would have to be very circumspect, very careful. And he would have to train a successor. Too many things unfinished to have them end with his own death.

I can't leave the choice of my successor to the ship.

Even if it killed him, the damned ship could not be allowed to beat him.

It's been a long time. Maybe the ship's original program has run out.

What if Pandora were the place for a long winding-down process? Kick the fledglings out of the nest a millimeter at a time.

His gaze picked out details of the cubby: erotic wall hangings, servopanels, the soft opulence of divans …

Who will move in here after me?

He had thought he might choose Lewis, provided Lewis worked out well. Lewis was bright enough for some dazzling lab work, but dull politically. A dedicated man.

Dedicated! He's a weasel and does what he's told.

Oakes crossed to his favorite divan, fawn soft cushions. He sat down and fluffed the cushions under the small of his back. What did he care about Lewis? This flesh that called itself Oakes would be long gone when the next Chaplain took over. At the very least he would be in hyb, dependent on the systems of the ship. And it may not be a good idea to tempt Lewis with that much power, power that would be contingent upon Oakes' own death. After all, death was the specialty of Jesus Lewis.

"No, no," Lewis had said to Oakes privately, "it's not death—I give them life, I give them life. They're engineered clones, Doctor, E-clones. I remind you of that. If I give them life, for whatever purpose, it is mine to take away."

"I don't want to hear it." He waved Lewis away with a brush of his hand.

"Have it your way," Lewis said, "but that doesn't change the facts. I do what I have to do. And I do it for you …"

Yes, Lewis was a brilliant man. He had learned many new and useful genetic manipulation techniques from the genetics of the 'lectrokelp, that most insidious indigent species on Pandora. And it had cost them dearly.

A successor? What real choice would he make, if he truly believed in the process and the godhood of Ship? If he could exclude all the nastiness of politics?

Legata Hamill.

The name caught him off guard, it came so quickly. Almost as though he did not think it himself. Yes, it was true. He would choose Legata if he believed, if he truly believed in Ship. There was no reason why a woman could not be Chaplain/Psychiatrist. No doubt of her diplomatic abilities.

Some wag had once said that Legata could tell you to go to hell and make you anticipate the trip with joy.

Oakes pushed aside the cushions and levered himself to his feet. The hatch out into the dim passages of nightside beckoned him—that maze of mazes which meant life to them all: the ship.

Had the ship really tried to asphyxiate him? Or had that been an accident?

I'll put myself through a medcheck first thing dayside.

The hatch dogs felt cold under his fingers, much colder than just moments before. The oval closure swung soundlessly aside to reveal once more nightside's blue-violet lighting in the corridor.

Damn the ship!

He strode out and, around the first corner, encountered the first few people of the Behavioral watch. He ignored them. The Behavioral complex was so familiar that he did not see it as he passed through. Biocomputer Study, Vitro Lab, Genetics—all were part of his daily routine and did not register on his nightside consciousness.

Where tonight?

He allowed his feet to find the way and realized belatedly that his wanderings were taking him farther and farther into the outlying regions, farther along the ship's confused twistings of passages and through mysterious hums and odd odors—farther out than he had ever wandered before.

Oakes sensed that he was walking into a peculiar personal danger, but he could not stop even as his tensions mounted. The ship was able to kill him at any moment, anywhere shipside, but he took a special private knowledge with him: he was Morgan Oakes, Ceepee. His detractors might call him "The Boss," but he was the only person here (with the possible exception of Lewis) who understood there were things the ship would not do.

Two of us among many. How many?

They had no real census shipside or groundside. The computers refused to function in this area, and attempts at manual counting varied so widely they were useless.

The ship showing its devious hand again.

Just as the ship's machinations could be sensed in this order for a poet groundside. He remembered the full name now: Kerro Panille. Why should a poet be ordered groundside to study the kelp?

If we could only eat the kelp without it driving us psychotic.

Too many people to feed. Too many.

Oakes guessed ten thousand shipside and ten times that groundside (not counting the special clones), but no matter the numbers, he was the only person who realized how little knowledge his people had about the workings and purposes of the ship or its parts.

His people!

Oakes liked it that way, recalling the cynical comment of his mentor, Edmond Kingston, who had been talking about the need to limit the awareness of the people: "Appearing to know the unknown is almost as useful as actually knowing."

From his own historical studies, Oakes knew that this had been a political watchword for many civilizations. This one thing stood out even though the ship's records were not always clear and he did not completely trust the ship's versions of history. It often was difficult to distinguish between real history and contrived fictions. But from the odd literary references and the incompatible datings of such works—from internal clues and his own inspired guesswork—Oakes deduced that other worlds and other peoples existed ... or had existed.

The ship could have countless murders on its conscience. If it had a conscience.

Chapter 13

As I am your creation, you are Mine. You are My satellites and I am yours. Your personas are My impersonations. We melt into ONE at the touch of infinity.

—Raja Flattery, *The Book of Ship*

FROM THE instant the Redoubt's first hatchway exploded, Jesus Lewis stayed within arm's length of his bodyguard, Illuyank. It was partly a conscious decision. Even in the worst of times, Illuyank inspired a certain confidence. He was a heavily muscled man, dark-skinned, with black wavy hair and a stone-cut face accented by three blue chevrons tattooed above his left eyebrow. Three chevrons—Illuyank had run outside around the Colony Perimeter three times, naked, armed only with his wits and endurance, "running the P" for a bet or a dare.

Testing their luck, some called it. When the hatch blew, they all needed luck. Some of them were barely awake and had not yet eaten their first dayside meal.

"The clones got a lasgun!" Illuyank shouted. His clear, dark eyes worked the area. "Dangerous. They don't know how to use it."

The two men stood in a passage between the clones' quarters and a random huddle of survivors who waited behind them near a half-circle of hatches leading to the core of the Redoubt. Even in this moment of peril, Lewis knew how he must appear to the others. He was a short man, thin all the way—thin straw-colored hair, thin mouth, thin chin made even more so by a deep cleft, a thin nose, and oddly dark eyes which never seemed to reflect light in the thin compression of his lids. Beside him, Illuyank was everything Lewis was not.

Both stared toward the core of the Redoubt.

There was a real question in their minds whether the core of the Redoubt remained secure.

Knowing this, Lewis had deactivated the communications pellet buried in the flesh of his neck and refused to answer it even when insistent calls from Oakes tempted him.

No telling who might be able to listen!

There had been some disquieting indications lately that their private communications channel might not be as private as he had hoped. By now, Oakes would have received word about the new Ceepee. Discussion of that and the possible breach of their private communications system would have to wait.

Oakes would have to be patient.

At the first sign of trouble, Lewis had hit an emergency signal switch to alert Murdoch at Colony. There was no certainty, though, that the signal had gone through. He had not been allowed time for a retransmit-check. And the whole Redoubt had gone onto emergency power then. Lewis had no way of knowing which systems might be working and which not.

The damned clones!

A loud whirr sounded from the direction of the clones' quarters. Illuyank flattened himself on the floor and the others were showered with shards of passage wall.

"I thought they didn't know how to use that lasgun!" Lewis shouted. He pointed at a gaping hole in the wall as Illuyank leaped up and spun him around toward the others at the hatch circle.

"Downshaft!" Illuyank called.

One of the waiting group whirled the downshaft hatchdogs and opened the way into a passage lighted only by the blue flickering of emergency illumination.

Lewis sprinted blindly behind Illuyank, heard the others scrambling after them. Illuyank shouted back at him as he ran: "They don't know how to use it and that's what makes it dangerous!" Illuyank tucked and rolled across an open side passage as he spoke, firing a quick burst down the passage from his gushgun. "They could hit anything anywhere!"

Lewis glanced down the open passage as he ran past, glimpsed a scattering of bodies blazing there.

It soon became apparent where Illuyank was leading them and Lewis admired the wisdom of it. They took a left turn into a new passage, then a right turn and found themselves in the Redoubt's unfinished back corridors, skirting the native rock of the cliffside into the small Facilities Room on the beach side. One plasma-glass window overlooked the sea, the courtyard and the corner where the clones' quarters joined the Redoubt itself.

The last of the followers dogged the hatch behind them. Lewis took quick stock of his personnel—fifteen people, only six of them from his personally chosen crew. The others, rated reliable by Murdoch, had not yet been tested.

Illuyank had moved to the maze of controls at the cliff wall and was poring over the Redoubt's schematics etched into a master plate there. It occurred to Lewis then that Illuyank was the only survivor from Kingston's mission to this chunk of dirt and rock named Black Dragon.

"Is this how it was with Kingston?" Lewis asked. He forced his voice to an even calm while watching Illuyank trace a circuit with one stubby finger.

"Kingston cried and hid behind rocks while his people died. Runners got him. I cooked them out."

Cooked them out! Lewis shuddered at the euphemism. The grotesque image of Kingston's head crisped to char grinned across his mind.

"Tell us what to do." Lewis was surprised at his control under this fear.

"Good." Illuyank looked directly at him for the first time. "Good. Our weapons are these." He indicated the power switches and valve controls around them. "We can control every circuit, gas and liquid from here."

Lewis touched Illuyank's arm and pointed to a one-meter square panel beside him.

"Yes." Illuyank hesitated.

"We're blind otherwise," Lewis said.

For answer, Illuyank tapped out a code on the console beneath the square. The blank panel slid back to reveal four small viewscreens.

"Sensors," one of those behind them said.

"Eyes and ears," Lewis said, still looking at Illuyank.

The dark man's expression did not change, but he whispered to Lewis: "We also will have to see and hear what we do to them."

Lewis swallowed and heard a faint snap-snapping at the hatch.

"They're cutting in!" a voice quavered behind them.

Lewis and Illuyank scanned the screens. One showed the rubble that had been the clones' quarters. I'M HUNGRY NOW!, the new rallying cry of the clones, was smeared in yellow grease across one wall. The adjoining screen scanned the courtyard. A crowd of mutated humans—E-clones all—scoured the grounds for rocks and bits of glass, anything for a weapon.

"Keep an eye on them," Illuyank whispered. "They can't hurt us with that stuff, but all that blood out there will bring demons. There are holes all over our perimeter. If demons hit, they'll catch that bunch first."

Lewis nodded. He could hear some of the others pressing close for a better view.

Once more, there was that snap-snapping at the hatch.

Lewis glanced at Illuyank.

"They're just pounding at us with rocks," Illuyank said. "What we have to do is find that lasgun. Meanwhile, keep an eye on the courtyard. The blood …"

The lower left-hand screen showed the clone mess hall, a shambles of security hatches broken open in the background, a turmoil of clones throughout the area. This screen suddenly went blank.

"Sensor's gone in the mess hall," Lewis said.

"Food will keep them busy there for a time," Illuyank said. He was busy searching through the Redoubt on the remaining screen. It showed a flash of the courtyard from a different angle, then a broken tangle of perimeter wall, cut to pieces by the lasgun and swarming with clones coming in from the outside where Lewis had ejected them, the action which had ignited this revolt.

We have to cull them somehow, Lewis told himself. *The food will go only so far.*

He turned his attention to the screen showing the courtyard. Yes … there was a lot of blood. It made him aware that he was badly cut himself. Celltape stopped his major bleeding, but small cuts began to ache as he thought of his condition. None of them was without injury. Even Illuyank bled slightly from a rock cut above his ear.

"There," Illuyank said.

His voice coincided with a new thump and crackling agitation at the hatch. But the COA screen Illuyank had been using now showed the passage outside their hatch. It was filled with a mass of clone flesh: furred bodies, strange limbs, oddly shaped heads. At the hatch two of the strongest clones were trying to maneuver a plasteel cutter, but their actions were impeded by the press of others behind them.

"That'll get them in here for sure," someone said. "We're cooked."

Illuyank turned and barked orders, pointing, waving a hand until all fifteen were busy in the Facilities Room—a valve to control, a switch to throw; each had some particular responsibility.

Lewis keyed for sound in the screen and a confused babble came over the speakers.

Illuyank signaled to a man at the remote valve controls across the room. "Dump the brine tanks into level two! That'll flood the outer passage."

The man worked his controls, muttering as he followed the schematics at his position.

Illuyank touched Lewis on the elbow, pointed to the screen which showed the courtyard. The clones there were looking away from the sensor, all of them at full alert, their attention on a broken segment of wall which led to the perimeter. Abruptly, almost as one organism, they dropped their rocks and glass weapons and ran screaming off-screen.

"Runners," Illuyank muttered.

Lewis saw them then, a waving swarm of tiny pale worm shapes cresting the rubble. He could almost smell the burned acid and tasted acid in his throat. Automatically, he gave the orders.

"Seal off."

"We can't," a timid voice from the edge of the room began. "Some of our people are still out there. If we seal off … if we … they'll all …"

"They'll all die," Lewis finished for him. "And our perimeter's full of holes. Runners are in the courtyard. If we don't seal off, we die, too. Seal off!"

He crossed to a valve-control panel, punched the proper sequence. Lights above the panel showed that the indicated valve was closing. He could hear others around him obeying. Illuyank's voice intruded with a quiet warning: "Check the surface shafts." This brought another bustle of activity.

Lewis glanced at the courtyard screen. A clone stumbled back into the sensor's range, screaming and beating at his eyes with the blunt knobs which passed for his hands. As he moved into range, he fell and lay twisting on the ground. A blur of writhing shadows swept over him. The courtyard filled with fleeing clones and tiny, eel-like bodies. Behind Lewis, one of their group could be heard vomiting.

"They're in the passage," Illuyank said. He gestured at the sensor where the view outside their hatch showed brine rising in the passage with a swarming mass of Nerve Runners riding in on the wave.

Lewis shot a frantic glance at the hatch. What the sensor revealed was happening right out there!

The brine stopped short of the passage ceiling, but not before it had shorted out the plasteel cutter.

Clones were thrashing in the water, Nerve Runners covering them, but here and there dead Runners could be seen on the brine's surface. And where the plasteel cutter had shorted out, a milky gray gas clouded the thin space over the water. Wherever the gas touched, Runners died.

Lewis felt his mind leaping from item to item. Item: brine. Item: electrical short.

"Chlorine," he whispered. Then louder: "Chlorine!"

"What?" Illuyank was clearly puzzled.

Lewis pointed at the screen. "Chlorine kills Nerve Runners!"

"What's chlorine?"

"A gas created when you throw an electrical charge through sodium chloride brine."

"But …"

"Chlorine kills Runners!" Lewis looked across the Facilities Room where the plaz-glass barrier showed a corner of clone area and the ocean beyond. "Are the sea pumps still working?"

The man at the pump console checked his keyboard, then: "Most of them."

"Sea water wherever we can put it," Lewis said. "We need a large container where we can dump it from here and throw an electrical charge through it."

"Water purification," Illuyank said. "The purification plant. We can pump almost everywhere from there."

"Wait a bit," Lewis said. "We want to attract as many Runners as we can; make them easier to wipe out."

He watched the screens, dragging it out, then: "All right, let's hit them."

Once more, Illuyank scanned his schematics, throwing orders over his shoulder while the survivors in the Facilities Room obeyed.

Lewis fixed his attention on the sensor screens. The outer passage was quiet now—a few dead E-clones floating on the surface of the brine, many dead Runners among them. He timed the mess-room screen to another sensor eye, found the exercise bay outside the clone labs. It was filled with a thrashing crowd of E-clones in absolute panic and, here and there among them, some of his own people caught outside when he had given the order to seal off. There were not many recognizable faces, but the colors of the uniforms could be identified. One by one, they died, their mouths frothing pink and their last stares turned upward toward the sensor.

Even as the last of them were dying, a milky cloud of gas had begun to sweep out of an open passage, drifting across the scene, blurring it.

"Watch their eyes," Illuyank said. "If we don't get all the Runners, they'll go for the eyes first."

All was quiet in the Facilities Room then as the survivors listened to their own precious breath, felt the comfort of their own live sweat and watched the eyes of the dead outside for some reflection of their own mortality.

Lewis leaned against the lip of the console, feeling cold metal under his fingers. Other screens showed more of the milky gas billowing through the Redoubt. There were even sensor eyes still alive to show the area outside their perimeter, the gas drifting across the open ground there. Illuyank scanned from sensor to sensor.

Someone behind Lewis heaved a shuddering sigh and Lewis echoed it.

"Chlorine," Illuyank muttered.

"We'll be able to sterilize the Runner boils right out of existence now," Lewis said. "If we'd only known …"

"A nasty way to learn," someone behind them said.

And someone else said: "It'll be a long wait."

"Waiting's that way," Illuyank said. "Think how long you live if you're always waiting."

It was an insightful comment, deeper than anything Lewis had ever expected from Illuyank. And it meant that Illuyank would have to be shifted to a tour of duty Colonyside. He saw too much, deduced too much. That could not be permitted. First, though, they had to get out of here. But there was no way out except into the Runner-contaminated open areas of the Redoubt. The chlorine would make that possible … in time.

"Can we get a message to Murdoch?" Lewis asked.

"Emergency transmitter only," Illuyank said.

"Send him the emergency shut-down signal. No one comes in here until we've cleaned up. It wouldn't do to have anyone see what's happened and …" Lewis directed a loaded look at Illuyank.

Illuyank nodded, and provided Lewis with the perfect opening for what had to be done. "Someone should go Colonyside, though, and see that they understand."

"That had better be you," Lewis said. "Make sure they don't try to explain anything to The Boss shipside. That's my job."

"Right."

"Don't tell them any more than you have to. And … while you're there, try to circulate in the Colony—everything normal, routine. Accept the usual assignments …"

"And try to find out if word of this …" Illuyank glanced at the sensor screens "… has leaked out."

"Good man."

And Lewis thought: *Too good.*

Chapter 14

Just as a technician learns to use his tools, you can be taught to use other people to create whatever you desire. This becomes more potent when you can create the special person for your special purpose.

—Morgan Oakes, *The Diaries*

LEGATA HAMILL knew groundside was to be their permanent home eventually, but she did not like these courier jobs on which Oakes sent her. There was a sense of power in them, though; no denying it. Her pass (often just an identifying look at her by a guard) admitted her anywhere. She was an arm of Morgan Oakes. She knew what they saw when they looked at her: a small woman with pale skin and ebon hair, a figure almost lush in its femininity. They saw a woman The Boss wanted and who, because of that, was powerful and dangerous.

Every inspection trip she took for Oakes created tension.

This time she was to inspect Lab One at Colony. And all of it would be on holo to make a full record for Oakes to review.

"Penetrate it," Oakes had said.

The way he said "penetrate" had distinctly sexual overtones.

She had never been into the Lab One depths before and that alone piqued her curiosity. Lewis had a trusted minion here, Sy Murdoch. She was to meet Murdoch. Usually, Lewis was to be found in the shiny plasteel environs of the lab which was entered via a triple-lock system at the end of a long tunnel. Not today. Lewis was out of communication. A strange way of putting it; and there was no doubt that Oakes was disturbed by this development.

"Find out where the hell he is, what he's doing!"

Both suns had been in the sky when the shuttle brought her down. Maximum flare security had been in force. She had been hustled out of the landing complex and into a servo which deposited her at the tunnel. The Colony personnel were quick and harried today—rumors of perimeter difficulties with Pandora's many demons.

Legata shuddered. Any thought of the predatory creatures which roamed the landscape beyond Colony's barriers filled her with apprehension.

Murdoch himself met her in the brightly lighted and bustling area where the last lock sealed off the entrance within the lab. He was a blocky man, light complexion and blue eyes, with cropped brown hair. His fingers were short and stubby, the nails well trimmed. He always appeared recently scrubbed.

"What is it this time?" he demanded.

She liked the energy focus in his question. It said: *We're busy here. What does Oakes want now?*

Very well, she could match that mood. "Where's Lewis?"

Murdoch glanced around to see who might overhear them. Seeing no workers nearby, he said: "Redoubt."

"Why doesn't he answer our calls?"

"Don't know."

"What was his last message?"

"Emergency code. Hold all transports. No craft permitted to land at Redoubt. Wait for clearance signal."

Legata absorbed this. *Emergency*. What was happening across the waters at the Redoubt?

"Why wasn't Doctor Oakes informed?"

"The code signal called for complete security."

She understood this. No transmissions from Colony to Ship could carry a message involving that restriction. But that was two full Pandoran diurns ago. She sensed another restriction in the last message from the Redoubt, a private Lewis restriction to his own minions. It would be pointless to explore such a conjecture, but she felt its presence.

"Have you sent an overflight?"

"No."

So that was restricted, too. Bad … very bad. Well, then, she had to get on to the rest of her assignment.

"I'm here to inspect the lab."

"I know."

Murdoch had been studying this woman while they talked. The orders transmitted from The Boss were clear. She was to go into everything except the Scream Room. That would come later for her … as it came for everyone here. She was a pretty thing: a pocket Venus with a doll face and green eyes. She had a good brain, too, by all accounts.

"If you know, let's get going," she said.

"This way."

He led her down a passage between banked vats of primary clonewombs into the Micro-micro Processing section.

At first, Legata's interest was intellectual—she knew this and it comforted her. Murdoch even took her hand at one point, leading her past rows of special-application clonewombs. He was so intent in his rhapsody on equipment and techniques that she did not mind his touch. It was, after all, clinical. Or unintentional. Whichever, Murdoch's touch was not born out of affection; this she knew.

But he knew Lab One as few others could, even perhaps as well as Lewis, and she had never been told to go deep into it before.

"… but I've accepted that as true," Murdoch was saying, and she had missed the point, being more intent on an incomplete fetus of odd proportions floating behind a screen of transparent plaz.

She looked at Murdoch. "Accepted what? I'm sorry, I was … I mean, there's so much to see."

"Plasteel by the kilometer, tanks and fluids, pseudo-bodies, pseudo-minds …" He waved his hand in frustration.

She realized that Murdoch was in a particularly manic mood and this bothered her. She felt the need to suppress unspoken questions about that odd fetus floating behind the screen of plasma glass.

"So you've accepted all this," she said. "So what?"

"We birth here. We conceive people here, nurture them fetally, extract them, send some shipside for training … Doesn't it strike you as odd that we can't bring natural births groundside, too?"

"What Ship decides is for good reason, for the good of …"

"... of Shipmen everywhere. I know. I've heard it as often as you have. But Ship did not decide. Nowhere in the records can anyone—even you, the best Search Technician we have, so I'm told—find where Ship has demanded that all births take place shipside. Nowhere."

Without knowing how she knew it, Legata realized he was repeating Lewis' words verbatim. This was not Murdoch's manner of speaking. Why was she supposed to hear this? Was it part of Oakes' scheme to do away with the shipside obstetrics force, the Natali?

"But we are required to WorShip," she said. "And what greater WorShip can we have than to entrust Ship with our children? It makes sense, too ..."

"It makes sense, it has logic," he agreed. "But it is not a direct command. And it makes a good deal of our work here in Lab One unnecessarily limited. Why, we could ..."

"Own this world? Morgan says you can do it anyway."

There, let him chew on that. Morgan, not The Boss, not Doctor Oakes.

Murdoch dropped her hand and the flush of elation washed out of his cheeks.

He knows we're on holo, she thought, *and I've mined his act.*

It occurred to her then that Murdoch had been playing to another audience, to Oakes. If the emergency at the Redoubt over on Black Dragon turned out fatal for Lewis ... yes, they would need a replacement. She imagined Oakes' attention on them later from some metallic scanner shipside. But she wanted Murdoch to squirm a bit more. She took his hand and said, "I'd like to see The Garden."

Her statement was only half-true. She had seen the catalogues which Oakes kept securely locked away, the wide selection of E-clones grown to special purposes here—any purpose, it seemed. Fewer than a dozen people shipside were even aware that such a process existed. And here at Colony, Lab One was a complex of its own, secreted away from the rest of the buildings, its purpose shrouded in the mystique of its name.

Lab One.

When asked what went on at Lab One, people usually said, "Ship only knows." Or they began some childish ghost story of hunchbacked scientists peering into the heart of life itself.

Legata knew that Oakes and Lewis even encouraged the mystery, often started their own rumors. The result was a fearsome aura about the place, and recently there had been mutterings about the disproportionate supply of food allotted to Lab One. To be assigned here, in the minds of Shipmen and Colonists alike, was to disappear forever. All workers moved into quarters at the complex and, with few exceptions, did not return shipside or to Colony proper.

These thoughts left her with a feeling of unsettled doubts, and she had to remind herself: *I'm not being assigned here.* No, that wouldn't happen, not as long as Oakes wanted to get her naked on his couch ... to penetrate her.

Legata took a deep breath of warm air. As in all Colony buildings, temperature and humidity were identical with Ship's. Here in the lab, though, her flesh shuddered off a special kind of chill, a gooseflesh that made her stomach ache and jabbed needles of pain into the knots that her nipples made against her singlesuit. She spoke quickly to mask her disquiet.

"Your staff people, they look so old."

"Many of them have been with us from the start."

There was evasion in his voice and it did not go unnoticed, but Legata chose to watch, not push.

"But they … look even older than that. What …"

Murdoch interrupted her. "We have a higher fatality rate than Colony, did you know that?"

She shook her head. It was a lie; had to be a lie.

"It's being out here on the perimeter," Murdoch said. "We don't get the protection everyone else does. Nerve Runners are particularly heavy this close to the hills."

An uncontrollable shudder swept over her arms. Nerve Runners! Those darting little worms were the most feared of all Pandoran creatures. They had an affinity for nerve cells and would eat their way slowly, agonizingly along human nerve channels until they gorged on the brain, encysted and reproduced.

"Bad," Murdoch said, seeing her reaction. "And the workload we carry here, of course … but that's agreed on from the start. These are the most dedicated people groundside."

She looked across a bank of plaz vats at a group of these dedicated workers—-blank, tight-lipped faces. Most of those she had seen here were wrinkled and drawn, pale. No one joked; not even a nervous giggle broke the monotony. All was the clink and click of instruments, the hum of tools, the aching distance between lives.

Murdoch flashed her a sudden smile. "But you wanted to see The Garden." He turned, waved a hand for her to follow. "This way."

He led her through another system of locks, only doubles this time, into what appeared to be a training area for young E-clones. There were several of them around the entrance, but they drew back at Murdoch's approach.

Fearful, Legata thought.

There was a circular barrier across the training area and she identified another lock entrance.

"What's over there?" She nodded.

"We won't be able to go in there today," Murdoch said. "We're sterilizing in there."

"Oh? What's in there?"

"Well … that's the core of The Garden. I call it the Flower Room." He turned toward a group of the young E-clones nearby. "Now, here we have some of the young products from the Flower Room. They …"

"Does your Flower Room have another name?" she asked. She did not like his answers. Too evasive. He was lying.

Murdoch turned to face her and she felt threatened by the pouncing glee in his eyes. Guilty knowledge lay there—dirty, guilty knowledge.

"Some call it the Scream Room," he said.

Scream Room!

"And we can't go in there?"

"Not … today. Perhaps if you made an appointment for later?"

She controlled a shudder. The way he watched her, the avaricious glint to his eyes.

"I'll come back to see your … Flower Room later," she said.
"Yes. You will."

Chapter 15

From you, Avata learns of a great poet-philosopher who said: "Until you meet an alien intelligence, you will not know what it is to be human."

And Avata did not know what it was to be Avata.

True, and poetic. But poetry is what's lost in translation. Thus, we now permit you to call this place Pandora and to call us Avata. The first among you, though, called us vegetable. In this, Avata saw the deeper meaning of your history and felt fear. You ingest vegetable to use the energy gathered by others. With you, the others end. With Avata, the others live. Avata uses minerals, uses rock, uses sea, uses the suns—and from all this, Avata nurses life. With rock, Avata calms the sea and silences the turbulence inherited from the rip of suns and moons.

Knowing human, Avata remembers all. It is best to remember so Avata remembers. We eat our history and it is not lost. We are one tongue and one mind; the storms of confusions cannot steal us from one another, cannot pry us from our grip to rock, to the firmament that cups the sea around us and washes us clean with the tides. This is so because we make it so.

We fill the sea and calm it with our body. The creatures of water find sanctuary in Avata's shadow, feed in our light. They breathe the riches we exude. They fight among themselves for what we discard. They ignore us in their ravages and we watch them grow, watch them flare in the sea like suns and disappear into the far side of night.

The sea feeds us, it washes in and out, and we return to the sea in kind. Rock is Avata's strength and as strength grows so grows the nest. Rock is Avata's communion, ballast and blood. With all this, Avata orders quiet in the sea and subdues the fitful rages of the tides. Without Avata, the sea screams its fury in rock and ice; it whips the winds of hot madness. Without Avata, the rage of the sea returns to smother this globe in blackness and a thin white horizon of death.

This is so because we make it so—Avata: barometer of life.

Atom to atom to molecule; molecule to chain and chain winding around and around the magnificence of light; then cell to cell, and cell to blastula, cilia to tentacle, and from stillness blossoms the motion of life.

Avata harvests the mysterious gas of the sea and is born into the world of clouds and mountains, into the world the stars walk in fear. Avata sails high with the gas from the sea to find the country of the spark of life. There, Avata gives self to love, thence back to the sea, and the circle is complete but unfinished.

Avata feeds and is fed. Sheltered, Avata shelters, eats and is eaten, loves and is loved. Growth is the Avata way. In growth is life. As death resides in stillness, Avata strives for stillness in growth, a balance of flux, and Avata lives.

This is so because Avata makes it so.

If you know this of the alien intelligence and still find it alien, you do not know what it is to be human.

—Kerro Panille, *Translations from the Avata*

Chapter 16

You are called Project Consciousness, but your true goal is to explore beyond the imprinted pattern of all humankind. Inevitably, you must ask: Is consciousness only a special kind of hallucination? Do you raise consciousness or lower its threshold? The danger in the latter course is that you bring up the military analogue: you are confined to action.

—Original Charge to the Voidship Chaplain/Psychiatrist

ON THESE nightside walks through the ship, Oakes liked to move without purpose, without the persona of Ceepee tagging along. He had worked long and hard to remain just a name both shipside and groundside. Few saw his face and most of his official duties were carried out by minions. There was the routine WorShip in the corridor chapels, the food allotments groundside, a minimal endorsement of the many functions that Ship carried out with no human intervention. Ceepee rule was supposed to be nominal. But he wanted more.

Kingston had once said: "We have too damned much idle time. We're idle hands and we can get into trouble."

Memories of Kingston were much with Oakes this night as he took his nocturnal prowl. Through the outer passages, sensor eyes and ears dotted corridor walls and ceilings. They strung themselves ahead and behind in diminishing vectors of attention, dim glistenings in the blue-violet nightside lighting.

Still no word from Lewis. This rankled. Legata's preliminary report left too many unanswered questions. Was Lewis striking out on his own? Impossible! Lewis did not have the guts for such a move. He was the eternal behind-the-scenes operator, not a front man.

What was the emergency, then?

Oakes felt that too many things were coming to a head around him. They could not delay much longer on sending this poet, this Kerro Panille, groundside. And the new Ceepee the ship had brought out of hyb! Both poet and Ceepee would have to be bundled into the same package and watched carefully. And it would soon be time to start an eradication project against the kelp. People were getting hungry enough groundside that they were ready for scapegoats.

And that disturbing incident with the air in his cubby. Had the ship really tried to asphyxiate him? Or poison him?

Oakes turned a corner and found himself in a long corridor with iridescent green arrows on the walls indicating that it led outward from shipcenter. The ceiling sensors were dots receding into a converging distance.

Out of habit he noticed the activation of each sensor as he neared it. Each mechanical eye followed his pace faithfully, and, as he approached the limits of its vision, the next one rolled its wary cyclopean pupil around to catch his approach. He had to admit that, in Shipman or machine, he appreciated this sense of guarded watchfulness, but the idea that a possibly malevolent intelligence waited behind that movement set his nerves on edge.

He had never known a sensor to malfunction. To tamper with one meant dealing with a robox unit—a single-minded repair and defense device that respected no life or limb save that of Ship.

THE ship, dammit!

Those years of programming, preparation—even he could not shake them. How did he expect others of lesser will, lesser intelligence, to do so?

He sighed. He expected to sway no one. What he expected was that he would use the tools at hand. With intelligence, he felt that one could turn anything to advantage. Even a dangerous tool such as Lewis.

Another pair of sensors caught his attention, this time outside the access to the Docking Bays. It was quiet here and pervaded by that odd smell compounded from uncounted sleeping people. Not even freight moved during Colony's nightside which sometimes coincided with Shiptime, but often did not. All the industry of dayside was put away for the community of sleep.

Except in two places, he reminded himself: life-support and the agraria.

Oakes stopped and studied the line of sensors. He, of all Shipmen, should appreciate them. He had access to the movements they recorded. Every detail of shipside life was supposed to be his. And he had seen to it that the groundside colony was similarly equipped. Ship's watchfulness was his own.

"The more we know, the stronger we are in our choices."

Kingston's voice came to him from his training days.

What a raw but marvelously trainable bit of human material I was!

Kingston had been almost a master of control. Almost. And control was a function of strong choices. When it came down to it, Kingston had refused certain choices.

I do not refuse.

Choices resulted from information. He had learned that lesson well.

But how can you know the result of every choice?

Oakes shook his head and resumed his wandering. The sense that he walked into new dangers was an acute pressure in his breast. But there was no stopping this short of death. His feet turned him down a passageway which he saw led to an agrarium. There was the peculiar green smell of the passage even if he had not recognized the wide cart tracks leading through an automatic lock ahead. He stepped across the track-dump, through the lock and found himself in a dimly lighted and frighteningly unbounded space.

It was nightside here too. Even plants required that diurnal pulse. An internally illuminated yellow wall map at his left showed him his location and the best access routes out. It also showed this agrarium. The largest extrusions of the ship were monopolized for food production, but he had not entered one of these complexes for years—not since provisioning that first attempted colony on Pandora's Black Dragon continent. Long before they had gained their Colony foothold on the Egg.

Kingston's first big mistake.

Oakes stepped closer to the map, aware of distant movement far out in the agrarium but more interested in this symbol. He was not prepared for what the map told him. The agrarium he had entered was almost as large as the central core of the ship. It spread out, fanlike, from roots in the original hull. Ship and Colony maintenance figures he had been initialing took on a new reality here. And the map's explanatory footnote was an exclamation point.

As Oakes looked on, the nightside shift of agrarium workers broke for their mid-meal WorShip. They did so as one and no perceptible signal passed among them, no reluctance of any sort evident. They moved together into the dim blue light of the WorShip alcove.

They believe! Oakes thought, *they really believe that the ship is God!*

As the shift supervisor led them in their litany, Oakes found himself washed in a sadness that came so suddenly and so hard that it held him on the verge of tears. He realized then that he envied them their faith, their small comfort of the ritual that was so much bother to him.

The supervisor, a squat, bowlegged man with dirt on his hands and knees, led them in the Chant of Sure Growth.

"Behold the bed of dirt," and he dropped a pinch of dirt to the floor.

"And the seed asleep in it," the crew responded, lifting their bowls and setting them down.

"Behold water," he dribbled some from his glass.

"And the waking it brings," they raised their glasses.

"Behold light," he lifted his face to the U-V racks overhead.

"And the life it opens." They spread their hands, palms up.

"Behold the fullness of the grain, the thickness of the leaf," he spooned from the communal pot, into the bowl to his left.

"And the seed of life it plants in us," each worker spooned a helping for the Shipman on his left.

"Behold Ship and the food Ship gives." The supervisor sat down.

"And the joy of company to share it," they said, and sat to eat.

Oakes turned away unnoticed.

The joy of company! he snorted to himself. If there were less company and more food there would be a damn sight more joy!

He moved along the rim of the ship's outer hull then, raw space only a few meters away. His mind was racing.

That agrarium could feed thirty thousand people. Instead of counting people, they could count agraria and add the support figures! He knew that groundside shipments supplied eighty percent of Colony stores. Here was a key to real numbers! Why had they not seen that before?

Even as he experienced elation at this thought, Oakes knew the ship would frustrate such an attempt. The damned ship did not want them to know how many people it supported. It blocked their attempts to count; it hid hyb complexes and confused you with meaningless corridors.

It brought a nameless Ceepee out of hyb and announced a new groundside project outside of Shipman control.

Well … accidents could happen groundside, too. And even a precious Ceepee from Ship could walk into a fatality.

What difference did it make? The new Ceepee was probably a clone. Oakes had seen the earliest records: Clones were property. Somebody who signed with the initials MH had said it. And there was an aura of power around that statement. *Clones were property.*

Chapter 17

A word of caution about our genetic programs. When we breed for speed, we breed as well for very specific kinds of decisions. Speed chops out, edits out certain kinds of reflexive choices and long-term considerations. Everything becomes the decision of the moment.

—Jesus Lewis, *The E-Clone Directive*

WHEN TEMPORARY seals had closed off the breaks in the perimeter of the Redoubt, Lewis directed the careful dayside cleanup of the interior. It was a long frustrating job, and they worked through the night with emergency lighting. The entire Redoubt stank of chlorine, so strong in some areas that they were forced to wear filters and portable breathing equipment.

In the morning, they drenched the courtyard with chlorine several times before daring to touch the corpses there. Even then, they moved the bodies with hastily improvised claw grabs attached to mobile equipment.

Chlorine everywhere, and the inevitable burns of both flesh and fabrics made it an even slower task.

At Sub-level Four, they came on a welcome surprise: twenty-nine clones and five more of the Redoubt crew sealed in an unlighted storage chamber—all of them hungry, thirsty and terrified. The chamber contained spare charges for the gushguns, permitting Lewis to add fire to the chlorine for a final sterilization sweep.

Lewis was surprised to find that the E-clones had not attacked the five crewmen. Then he learned that the crewmen had sounded the alarm at the Nerve Runner attack and herded the clones into the chamber. A sense of fellowship between E-clones and normals had developed during the long confinement. Lewis noted it as they emerged—clones helping normals and vice versa. *Very dangerous, that.* He gave sharp orders to separate them, clones to the more dangerous task of courtyard cleanup, normals to their regular supervisory tasks.

One observation particularly annoyed him: the sight of a trusted guard, Pattersing, being solicitous over a delicate female E-clone of the new mix. She was tall and emaciated by human standards, a light brown skin and large eyes. Her whole series was flawed by fragile bones, and Lewis had almost decided to abandon it—except that now she was one of his few remaining examples of the genetic mix between human and Pandoran.

Perhaps Pattersing was merely being careful with valuable material. He must know how fragile the bones of this series were. Yes ... that could be it.

Lewis was pleased to note other more successful examples of the new E-clones, the breed incorporating native genetic material. There would be no need to go back through that long, slow and costly development program. The disaster here at the Redoubt had not been total.

A mood of euphoria came over him as it became increasingly clear that they had sterilized the Redoubt, and that they had a new weapon effective against Runners.

"At least we've solved the food problem," he told Illuyank.

Illuyank gave him a strange, measuring look which Lewis did not like.

"Counting E-clones, there are only fifty of us left," Illuyank said.

"But we've saved the heart of the project," Lewis said.

Too late, Lewis realized he had said too much to this perceptive aide. Illuyank had proved himself capable of making correct deductions on limited information.

Well ... Illuyank was going Colonyside. Murdoch would see to things there.

"We'll need replacements, lots of them," Illuyank persisted.

"I expect us to be stronger because of this testing " Lewis said.

Lewis diverted Illuyank then by ordering a complete inspection of the Redoubt—every corner, every bay, no space missed—chlorine and/or fire everywhere. They moved slowly through the passages and across the open areas, their progress marked by the hissing flames of the gushguns and great splashing washes of chlorine. Lewis ordered a final purging with chlorine gas, opening all valves, all hatches within the Redoubt. They then made another inspection with sensor eyes.

Clean. When it was finished, they pumped the chlorine residue onto the surrounding ground, following it by waves of gas which swept around the rocks and hillocks where the clones had huddled when he had ordered them thrust from the safety of the Redoubt.

Inevitably, some of the chlorine spilled over the cliff into the sea. It ignited a violent, churning retreat by the hallucinogenic kelp in the cove. A pack of hylighters came to the excitement. They floated at a safe distance over the surrounding hills, spectators, while Lewis and his meager force sterilized the area around the Redoubt.

Later, Lewis went grinding out of a lock in an armored vehicle to direct the outside sterilizing team, taking Illuyank as his driver. At one point, Lewis ordered Illuyank to stop and shut down while they studied the arc of hylighters in the distance. It was a scene framed by the thick barrier of plazglass in the crawler. The giant orange bags floated in disconcerting silence, anchored by long black tendrils twining in the rocks of the hills. They were a perimeter of mystery about three kilometers distant and they filled Lewis with angry fear.

"We'll have to eliminate those damned things!" he said. "They're floating bombs!"

"And maybe more," Illuyank said.

One of the surviving clones took this moment to drop his chlorine backpack. The clone turned to face the arc of hylighters, spread his stumpy arms wide and called out in a voice heard through the area: "Avata! Avata! Avata!"

"Get that damned fool out of here and into confinement!" Lewis ordered. Illuyank relayed the order over their vehicle's external speakers. Two supervisors scrambled to obey.

Lewis watched in grumbling impatience. Avata—that had been the other cry of the clone revolt. *Avata*, and, *We're hungry now!*

If the particular clone out there had not been one of the precious new ones with the genetic mix, Lewis knew he would have ordered the stupid creature killed immediately.

New security precautions would have to be put into effect, he told himself. Tougher rules about clone behavior. Oakes would have to be brought into these decisions. They would have to raid Colony, and Ship, for replacements—more clones, more staff, more guards, more supervisors. Murdoch and the Scream Room were going to be very busy for a time. Very busy. Well, gardening had always been a brutal business: root out the weeds, kill off the predatory grazers, destroy the pests. Lab One's special-purpose area was correctly labeled: The Garden. Producing flowers for Pandora.

"We've used up the chlorine and it looks clean out here," Illuyank said.

"Take us back inside," Lewis ordered. Then: "When you get back to Colony, I don't want any mention of the chlorine."

"Right."

Lewis nodded to himself. It was time now to consider what he would tell Oakes, how this disaster would be explained to make it an important victory.

Chapter 18

Clones are property and that's that!
—Morgan Hempstead, Moonbase Director

"THANK YOU for complying with my invitation."

Thomas watched the seated speaker carefully, wondering at the sense of peril aroused by such a simple statement. This was Morgan Oakes, Chaplain/Psychiatrist—the Ceepee, The Boss?

It was late dayside on Ship and Thomas had not been long enough from hyb to feel completely awake and familiar with his long-dormant flesh.

I am no longer Raja Flattery. I am Raja Thomas.

There could be no slip in the new facade, especially here.

"I have been studying your dossier, Raja Thomas," Oakes said.

Thomas nodded. That was a lie! The stress in the man's voice was obvious. Didn't Oakes realize how much he betrayed himself to trained senses? You could not believe a word this man uttered! He was careless—that was it.

Perhaps there are no other trained senses to test him.

"I responded to a summons, not to an invitation," Thomas said.

There! That was the kind of thing a Raja Thomas would say.

Oakes merely smiled and tapped a folder of thin Shippaper in his lap. A dossier? Hardly. Thomas knew that it was in Ship's interest to conceal the real identity of this new player in the game.

Thomas! I am Thomas! He glanced around the Shipcell to which Oakes had invited him, realizing belatedly that this once had been a cubby. Oakes had taken out bulkheads to expand the cubby. Then, as Thomas recognized a mystical decorative motif between two dark-red woven wall hangings, he suffered one of the worst shocks in this awakening.

This was my cubby!

It was obvious that Ship had expanded enormously since those faraway Voidship days when it had housed only a few thousand hybernating humans and a minimal umbilicus crew. The changes he had seen on the trip here from hybernation hinted at even deeper changes behind them. *What had happened to Ship?*

This expanded cubby suggested an unsavory history. The space was sybaritic with exotic hangings, deep orange carpeting, soft divans. Except for a small holoprojection at Oakes' left hand, all the cubby's expected servosystems had been concealed.

Oakes was giving his visitor plenty of time to study the space around him, using the time to return that scrutiny. What was Ship's intent with this mysterious newcomer? The question was engraved large on Oakes' face.

Thomas found his own attention caught by the computer-driven projection at the holofocus. It was a familiar three-dimensional analogue of a ship orbiting a planet, all glittering green and orange and black. Only the planetary system was unfamiliar; it had two suns and several moons. And as he watched the slow progression of the ship's orbit, he felt an odd sense of deja vu. He was in motion in a ship in motion in a universe in motion ... and it had all happened before.

Replay?

Ship said not, but ... Thomas shrugged off such doubts, reserving them for later. He did not have to be told that the planet in the focus was Pandora and that this projection represented a real-time version of Ship's position in the system. Some things did not change no matter the great passage of time. Bickel had once monitored such a projection on the Voidship *Earthling.*

Morgan Oakes sat on a deep divan of rust velvet while Raja Thomas stood—an unsubtle accent on their positions in a hierarchy which Thomas had not yet analyzed.

"I'm told you are a Chaplain/Psychiatrist," Oakes said. And he thought: *This man does not respond to his name in a quite normal way.*

"That was my training, yes."

"Expert in communication?"

Thomas shrugged.

"Ahhh, yes." Oakes was pleased with himself. "That remains to be tested. Tell me why you have asked for the poet."

"Ship asked for the poet."

"So you say."

Oakes allowed silence to follow this challenge.

Thomas studied the man. Oakes was portly-going-on-fat, dark complexion, faint odor of perfume. His gray-streaked hair had been combed forward to conceal a receding hairline. The nose was sharp and flared at the nostrils, the mouth thin and given to a tight, stretching grimace; the chin was wide and cleft. The man's eyes dominated this rather common Shipman face. They were light blue and they probed, boring in, always trying to penetrate every surface they found. Thomas had seen such eyes on people diagnosed as psychotic.

"Do you like what you see?" Oakes asked.

Again, Thomas shrugged.

Oakes did not like this response. "What is it you see in me which requires such scrutiny?"

Thomas stared at the man. The genotype was recognizable and that first name was suggestive. Oakes could have Lon as a middle name. If Oakes were a clone instead of a replay-survivor rescued from a dying planet … yes, that would be an interesting clue as to how Ship was playing this deadly game. Oakes bore a more than casual resemblance to Morgan Hempstead, the long-ago director of Moonbase. And there was that first name.

"I've just been very curious to meet The Boss," Thomas said. He found a seat facing Oakes and sat without invitation.

Oakes scowled. He knew what they called him shipside and groundside, but politeness (not to mention politics) dictated that the term not be used in this room. Best not precipitate conflict yet, however. This Raja Thomas posed too many mysteries. Aristocratic type! That damned better-than-you manner.

"I, too, am curious," Oakes said.

"I'm a servant of Ship."

"But what is it you're supposed to do?"

"I was told you have a communications problem on Pandora—something about an alien intelligence."

"How very interesting. What are your special capabilities in this respect?"

"Ship appears to think I'm the one for the job."

"I don't call the ship's process *thinking*. Besides, who cares what opinions come out of a system of electronic bits and pieces? I prefer a human assessment."

Oakes watched Thomas carefully for a response to this open blasphemy. Who was this man … really? You couldn't trust the damned ship to play fair. The only thing to believe was that the ship was not a god. Powerful, yes, but with limits which needed exploring.

"Well, I intend to have a go at the problem," Thomas said.

"If I permit it."

"That's between you and Ship," Thomas said. "I'm well satisfied to carry out Ship's suggestions."

"It offends me …" Oakes paused, leaned back into his cushions. "… when you refer to this mechanical construction …" He waved a hand to indicate the physical presence of Ship all around. "… as Ship. The implications …" He left it there.

"Have you issued an order prohibiting WorShip?" Thomas asked. He found this an interesting prospect. Would Ship interfere?

"I have my own accommodation with this physical monstrosity which human hands loosed on the universe," Oakes said. "We tolerate each other. You have an interesting first name, do you know that?"

"In my family for a ... very long time."

"You have a family?"

"Had a family would be more proper."

"Strange. I took you for a clone."

"That's an interesting philosophical question," Thomas said. "Do clones have families?"

"Are you a clone?"

"What difference does that make?"

"No matter. As far as I'm concerned, you're another machination of the ship. I will tolerate you ... for now." He waved a hand in dismissal.

Thomas was not ready to leave. "You, too, have an interesting first name."

Oakes had been turning toward the holo projection and its com-console at his side. He hesitated, glanced at Thomas without turning his head. The gesture said: *You still here?* But there was more in his eyes. His interest had been caught.

"Well?"

"You bear a striking physical resemblance to Morgan Hempstead and I couldn't help but notice that you have the same first name."

"Who was Morgan Hempstead?"

"We often wondered if the Moonbase director had allowed a clone of himself. Are you that clone?"

"I'm not a clone! And what the hell is Moonbase?"

Thomas broke off, recalling what Ship had told him. These replay survivors had been picked up at a different stage in human development. The resemblance, even the name, could be coincidence. Did they come from a time before space travel? Was Ship their first experience in the many dimensions of the universe?

"I asked you a question!" Oakes was angry and not bothering to conceal it.

"Moonbase was the project center which created Ship."

"On Earth's moon? My Earth?" Oakes touched his breast with a thumb. And he thought about this revelation.

"Didn't you ever wonder where Ship originated?" Thomas asked.

"Many times. But I never thought we did this thing to ourselves."

Thomas remembered more of Ship's recital now and drew on it. "Some people had to be saved. The sun was going nova. It required a herculean effort."

"So we were told," Oakes said, "but that was later. I am considerably more interested in how a Moonbase was kept secret."

"If there's only one lifeboat, do you tell everyone where it is?"

Thomas felt rather proud of this creative lie. It was just the kind of thing Oakes might believe.

Oakes nodded to himself. "Yes ... of course." He glanced at the com-console, then twisted himself more comfortably into the divan. Thomas was lying, obviously. Interesting lie, though. Everyone knew that the ship had landed in Aegypt. Could there be two ships? Perhaps … and there could have been many landings.

Thomas stood. "Where do I find transportation down to Pandora?"

"You don't. Not until you've told me more about Moonbase. Make yourself comfortable." He indicated the seat which Thomas had vacated.

There was no avoiding the threat. Thomas sank back. *What a tangled web we weave*, he thought. *Truth is easier.* But Oakes could not be told the truth … no, not yet. The proper moment and place had to be found for laying Ship's command upon him. Shipmen were far gone in the puny play of WorShip. They would have to be shaken out of that before they could even contemplate Ship's real demand.

Thomas closed his eyes and thought for a moment, then opened his eyes and began recounting the physical facts of Moonbase as he knew them. The account was barbered only to the extent needed for illusion that Moonbase had been a project kept secret from Oakes' Earth.

Occasionally, Oakes stopped him, pressing for particular details.

"You were clones? All of you?"

"Yes."

Oakes could not conceal his delight at this revelation. "Why?"

"Some of us were sure to be lost. Cloning was a way of improving the project's chances of success. The best people were selected … each group had more data."

"That's the only reason?"

"Moonbase directives defined clones as property. You … could do things to clones that you couldn't do to Natural Natals, the naturally born humans."

Oakes ruminated on this for a moment while a slow smile crept over his face. Then: "Do continue."

Thomas obeyed, wondering what it was that Oakes found so satisfying.

Presently, Oakes raised a hand to stop the recital. Small details were not of pressing interest. The broad picture carried the messages he wanted. Clones were property. There was precedent for this. And now, he knew the name behind those significant initials: MH—Morgan Hempstead! He decided to press for any other weaknesses in this Raja Thomas.

"You say Raja is a family name. Are you, ahhhh, related to the Raja Flattery mentioned in what passes for our history?"

"Distantly."

And Thomas thought: *That's true. We're related distantly in time. Once there was a man called Raja Flattery … but that was another eon.*

Already, he felt himself firmly seated in the identity of Raja Thomas. In some ways, the role suited him better than that of Flattery.

I was always the doubter. My failures were failures of doubt. I may be Ship's "living challenge" but the means are mine.

Oakes cleared his throat. "I found this a most edifying and gratifying exchange."

Once more, Thomas stood. He did not like this man's attitude, the feeling that people were only valuable in terms of their usefulness to Morgan Oakes.

Morgan. He has to be a Hempstead clone. Has to be!

"I'll be leaving now," Thomas said.

Was that challenge enough? He studied Oakes for a negative response. Oakes was merely amused.

"Yes, Raja Lon Thomas. Go. Pandora will welcome you. Perhaps you'll survive that welcome … for a time."

Not until much later when he was standing in the shipbay waiting to board the groundside lighter did Thomas pause to wonder at where and how Oakes had obtained those sybaritic furnishings for his expanded cubby.

From Ship?

Chapter 19

The mind falls, the will drives on.
—Kerro Panille, *The Collected Poems*

PANILLE EMERGED from Ferry's office dazed and fearfully excited.

Groundside!

He knew what Hali thought of old Ferry—a bumbling fool, but there had been something else in the old man. Ferry had seemed sly and vindictive, consumed by unresolved hostilities. Even so, there was no evading his message.

I'm going groundside!

He had no time for dawdling—his orders required him to be at Shipbay Fifty in little more than an hour. Everything was controlled now by the time demands of Colony. It might be the last quarter of dayside here, but down at Colony it would soon be dawn, and the shuttles from Ship tried to make their groundside landings in the early hours there—less hylighter activity then.

Hylighters … dawn … groundside …

The very words conveyed a sense of the exotic to him. No more of Ship's passages and halls.

The full import of this change began to fill him. He could see and touch 'lectrokelp. He could test for himself how this alien intelligence performed.

Abruptly, Panille wanted to share his excitement with someone. He looked around at the sterile reaches of Medical's corridors—a few med-techs hurrying about their business. None of the faces were friendly acquaintances.

Hali's face was nowhere among these impersonal passersby. Everything he saw was just the bustle and movement of Medical's ordinary comings and goings.

Panille headed toward the main corridors. Medical's bright lights bothered him. It was a painful contrast with Ferry's office—the clutter, the dank smells. Ferry kept his office too dim.

Probably hiding the clutter even from himself.

It occurred to Panille then that Ferry's mind probably was like that office—dim and confused.

A poor, confused old man.

At the first main corridor, Panille turned left toward his quarters. No time to search out Hali and share this momentous change. There would be time for sharing later—at the next shipside period of rest and recuperation. He would have much more to share then, too.

At his cubby, Panille shoved things into a shipcloth bag. He was not sure what to take. No telling when he might return. Recorder and spare charges, certainly; a few keepsakes … clothing … notepads and a spare stylus. And the silver net, of course. He stopped and held the net up to examine it—a gift from Ship, flexible silver and big enough to cover his head.

Panille smiled as he rolled the net and confined it in its own ties. Ship seldom refused to answer one of his questions; refusal signaled a defect in the question. But the day of this net had been memorable for refusals and shifting responses from Ship.

Insatiable curiosity—that was the hallmark of the poet and Ship certainly knew this. He had been at the Instruction Terminal, his request. "Tell me about Pandora."

Silence.

Ship wanted a specific question.

"What is the most dangerous creature on Pandora?"

Ship showed him a composite picture of a human.

Panille was irritated. "Why won't You satisfy my curiosity?"

"You were chosen for this special training because of your curiosity."

"Not because I'm a poet?"

"When did you become a poet?"

Panille remembered staring at his own reflection in the glistening surface of the display screen where Ship revealed its symbolic patterns.

"Words are your tools but they are not enough," Ship said. "That is why there are poets."

Panille had continued to stare at his reflection in the screen, caught by the thought that it was a reflection but it also was displayed where Ship's symbols danced. *Am I a symbol?* His appearance, he knew, was striking: the only Shipman who wore a beard and long hair. As usual, the hair was plaited back and bound in a golden ring at the nape of his neck. He was the picture of a poet from the history holos.

"Ship, do You write my poetry?"

"You ask the question of the Zen placebo: 'How do I know I am me?' A nonsense question as you, a poet, should know."

"I have to be sure my poetry is my own!"

"You truly believe I might try to direct your poetry?"

"I have to be certain."

"Very well. Here is a shield which will isolate you from Me. When you wear it, your thoughts are your own."

"How can I be sure of that?"

"Try it."

The silvery net had come out of the pneumatic slot beside the screen. Fingers trembling, Panille opened the round carrier, examined the contents and put the net over his head, tucking his long black hair up into it. Immediately, he sensed a special silence in his head. It was frightening at first and then exciting.

I'm alone! Really alone!

The words which had flowed from him then had achieved extra energy, a compulsive rhythm whose power touched his fellow Shipmen in strange ways. One of the physicists refused to read or listen to his poetry.

"You twist my mind!" the old man shouted.

Panille chuckled at the memory and tucked the silver snood into his shipcloth bag.

Zen placebo?

Panille shook his head; no time for such thoughts.

When the bag was full he decided that solved his packing problem. He took up his bag and forced himself not to look back when he left. His cubby was the past—a place of furious writing periods and restless inner probings. He had spent many a sleepless night there and, for one period, had taken to wandering the corridors looking for a cool breeze from a ventilator. Ship had felt overly warm and uncommunicative then.

But it was really me; I was the uncommunicative one.

At Shipbay Fifty, he was told to wait in an alcove with no chair or bench. It was a tiny metal-walled space too small for him even to stretch out on the floor. There were two hatches: the one through which he had entered and another directly opposite. Sensor lenses glittered at him from above the hatches and he knew he was being watched.

Why? Could I have angered The Boss?

Waiting made him nervous.

Why did they tell me to get right out here if they were going to make me wait?

It was like that faraway time when his mother had taken him to the Shipmen. He had been five years old, a child of Earth. She had taken him by the hand up the ramp to Ship Reception. He had not even known what Ship meant then, but he had been sensitized to what was about to happen to him because his mother had explained it with great solemnity.

Panille remembered that day well—a green spring day full of musty earth smells which had not vanished from his memory in all the Shipdays since. Over one shoulder, he had carried a small cotton bag containing the things his mother had packed for him.

He looked down at the shipcloth bag into which he had crammed the things for his groundside trip. Much more durable ... larger.

The small cotton bag of that long-gone day had been limited to four kilos—the posted maximum for Ship Reception. It had contained mostly clothing his mother had made for him herself. He still had the amber stocking cap. And there were four primitive photographs—one of the father he had never seen in the flesh, a father killed in a fishing accident. He was revealed as a redhaired man with dark skin and a smile which survived him to warm his son. One picture was his mother, unsmiling and workworn, but still with beautiful eyes; one showed his father's parents, two intense faces which stared directly into the recording lens; and one slightly larger picture showed "the family place" which was, Kerro reminded himself, a patch of land on a patch of planet lost long ago when its sun went nova.

Only the photo survived, wrapped with the others in the amber stocking cap within his shipcloth bag. He had found all of this preserved in a hyb locker when the Shipmen had revived him.

"I want my son to live," his mother had said, handing him over to the Shipmen. "You have refused to take the two of us as a family, but you had better take him!"

No mistaking the threat in her voice. She would do something desperate. There were many desperate people doing violent things in those days. The Shipmen had appeared more amused than disturbed, but they had accepted young Kerro and sent him into hyb.

"Kerro was my father's name," she had explained, rolling the r's. "That's the way you say it. He was Portuguese and Samoan, a beautiful man. My mother was ugly and ran away with another man but my father was always beautiful. A shark ate him."

Panille knew that his own father had been a fisherman. His father had been named Arlo and his father's people had escaped from Gaul to the Chin Islands of the south, far across a sea which insulated them from distant persecution.

How long ago was that? he wondered.

He knew that hybernation stopped time for the flesh, but something else went on and on and on … Eternity. That was the poet's candle. The people who were keeping him waiting now did not realize how a poet could adjust the candle's flame. He knew he was being tested, but these Shipmen hidden behind their sensors did not know the tests he had already surmounted with Ship.

Panille idled away the wait by recalling such a test. At the time he had not known it was a test; that awareness came later. He had been sixteen and proud of his ability to create emotions with words. In the secret room behind Records, Panille had activated the com-console for a study session—to explore his own curiosity.

Ship began the conversation, which was unusual. Usually, Ship only responded to his questions. Ship's first words had startled him.

"As has been the case with other poets, do you think you are God?"

Panille had reflected on this. "All the universe is God. I am of this universe."

"A reasonable answer. You are the most reasonable poet of My experience."

Panille remained silent, poised and watchful. He knew Ship did not always give simple answers, and never simple praise.

Ship's response had been, once more, unexpected. "Why are you not wearing your silver net?"

"I'm not making poems."

Then, back to the original subject: "Why is there God?"

The answer popped into his head the way some lines of poetry occurred to him. "Information, not decisions."

"Cannot God make decisions?"

"God is the source of information, not of decisions. Decisions are human. If God makes decisions, they are human decisions."

If Ship could be considered to feel excitement, that was the moment for it and Kerro sensed this. There had been a pattern to the way Ship supplied information to him, and it was a pattern which only a poet might recognize.

He was being trained, sensitized, to ask the right questions ... even of himself.

As he waited at Shipbay Fifty, the questions were obvious, but he did not like some of the answers those questions suggested.

Why were they keeping him waiting? It signaled a callous attitude toward their fellows. And what use had the Colony found for a poet? Communication? Or were Hali's fears to be believed?

The hatch in front of him scissored open with a faint swish of servosystems and a voice called out: "Hurry it up!"

Panille recognized the voice and tried not to show surprise as he stepped through into a reception room and heard the hatch seal behind him. Automatics. And yes, it was the bumbler, Doctor Winslow Ferry.

With his recent analysis of Ferry, Panille tried to see the man sympathetically. It was difficult. Painful powers centered on this room, which was functional shipside standard: two hatches in metal walls, instruments in their racks, no ports. The room was blocked by a low barrier and a large com-console behind which Ferry sat. A gate on the right led to a hatch in the far wall.

It occurred to Panille that Ferry was old for shipside. He had watery gray eyes full of false boredom, puffy cheeks. His breath gave off a heavy floral perfume. There was slyness in his voice.

"Brought your own recorder, I see." He punched a notation into the com-console which shielded him from the waist down.

Ferry glanced at the shipcloth bag on Panille's shoulder. "What else you bring?"

"Personal possessions, clothes ... a few keepsakes."

"Hrrrm." Ferry made another notation. "Let's see."

The distrust in this order shocked Panille. He put the bag on a flat counter beside the com-console, watched while Ferry pawed through the contents. Panille resented every stranger-touch on intimate possessions. It became obvious after a time that Ferry was searching for things which could be used as weapons. The rumors were true, then. The people around Oakes feared for their own flesh.

Ferry held up the flexible net of silver rolled into its tie bands. "Wha's's?"

"I use that when I'm writing my poetry. Ship gave it to me."

Ferry put it onto the counter with care, went back to examining the rest of the bag's contents. Some items of clothing he passed beneath a lens behind him and studied details in a scanner whose shields prevented anyone else from seeing what he saw. Occasionally, he made notations in the com-console.

Panille looked at the silver net. What was Ferry going to do with it? He could not take it!

Ferry spoke over his shoulder while examining more of Panille's clothing under the scanner lens.

"You think the ship's God?"

The "ship"? The usage surprised Panille. "I ... yes."

And he thought back to that one conversation he had had with Ship on the subject. That had been a test, too. Ship was God and God was Ship. Ship could do things mortal flesh could not ... at least while remaining mortal flesh. Normal dimensions of space dissolved before Ship. Time carried no linear restrictions for Ship.

I, too, am God, Doctor Winslow Ferry. But I am not Ship … Or am I? And you, dear Doctor, what are you?

No doubting the origin of Ferry's question. Ship's godhead remained an open question with many. There had been a time when Ship was the ship, of course. Everyone knew that from the history which Ship taught. Ship had been a vehicle for mortal intelligence once. The ship had existed in the limited dimensions which any human could sense, and it had known a destination. It also had known a history of madness and violence. Then … the ship had encountered the Holy Void, that reservoir of chaos against which all beings were required to measure themselves.

Ship's history was cloudy with migrations and hints at a paradise planet somewhere awaiting humankind.

But Ferry was revealed as one of the doubters, one who questioned Ship's version of history. Such doubts thrived because Ship did not censure them. The only time Panille had referred to the doubts, Ship had responded clearly and with a creative style to inspire a poet.

"What is the purpose of doubts, Panille?"

"To test data."

"Can you test this historical data with your doubts?"

That required thought and Panille answered after a long pause. "You are my only source."

"Have I ever given you false data?"

"I've found no falsehoods."

"Does that silence these doubts?"

"No."

"Then what can you do with such doubts?"

That involved more careful thought and a longer pause before answering. "I put them aside until a moment arrives when they may be tested."

"Does that change your relationship with Me?"

"Relationships change constantly."

"Ahhh, I cherish the company of poets."

Panille was shaken out of this memory by the realization that Ferry had spoken to him several times.

"I said, 'Wha's's?"

Panille looked at the object in Ferry's hand.

"It was my mother's comb."

"The stuff! The material?"

"Tortoise shell. It came from Earth."

There was no mistaking the avaricious glint in Ferry's eyes. "Well … I dunno about this."

"It's a keepsake from my mother, one of the few things I have left. If you take it I'll lodge a formal complaint with Ship."

Ferry betrayed definite anger, his eyes squinted, his hand trembled with the comb. But his gaze strayed to the silver net. He knew the stories about this poet; this one talked to the ship in the quiet of the night and the ship answered.

Once more, Ferry made a notation within the shielded secrecy of his com-console, then delivered himself of his longest speech: "You're assigned groundside to Waela TaoLini and it serves you right. There's a freighter waiting in Fifty-B. Take it. She'll meet you groundside."

Panille stuffed his belongings back into the bag while Ferry watched with growing amusement. *Did he take something while I was daydreaming?* Panille wondered. He preferred the man's anger to his amusement but there was no way to take everything out of the bag once more to check it. No way. *What had happened to the people around Oakes?* Panille had never seen such slyness and greed in a Shipman. And the smell of that stuff on his breath! Dead flowers. Panille sealed the bag.

"Go on, they're waiting," Ferry said. "Don't waste our time."

Panille heard the hatch open once more behind him. He could feel Ferry's gaze on him all the way out of the reception room.

Waela TaoLini? He had never heard the name before. Then: *Serve me right?*

Chapter 20

Beware, for I am fearless and therefore powerful. I will watch with the wiliness of a snake, that I may sting with its venom. You shall repent of the injuries you inflict

—*Frankenstein's Monster Speaks, Shiprecords.*

OAKES SAT in shadows watching the holographic replay. He was nervous and irritated. Where was Lewis?

Behind him and slightly to his left stood Legata Hamill. The dim glow of the projector underlighted their features. Both of them stared intently at the action in the holofocus.

The scene holding their attention revealed the main finger passage behind Shipbay Nineteen and leading out to one of the treedomes. Kerro Panille accompanied by Hali Ekel walked toward the pickup which had caught the scene. The treedome could be glimpsed in the background framed by the end of the passage. Ekel carried her pribox over one shoulder, its harness held loosely by her right hand. Panille wore a recorder at his hip and a small bag from which protruded notepad and stylus. He was dressed in a white one-piece which set off his long hair and beard. The hair was bound in a golden ring, plaited and with the tip draped down his chest on the left. Issue boots covered his feet.

Oakes studied each detail carefully.

"This is the young man of Ferry's report?"

"The same."

The rich contralto of Legata's voice distracted Oakes and he was a few blinks replying. During that time, Panille and Ekel walked from the range of one sensor and into the range of another. The holographic point-of-view shifted.

"They seem a little nervous," he said. "I wish I knew what they wrote on that pad."

"Love notes."

"But why write them if . . ."

"He's a poet."

"And she is not a poet. What's more, he resists her sexual advances. I don't understand that. She appears quite pneumatic, eminently couchable."

"Do you want him picked up and the notepad examined?"

"No! We must move with discretion and subtlety. Damn! Where is Lewis?"

"Still incommunicado."

"Damn him!"

"His assistants now say Lewis is occupied with a special problem."

Oakes nodded. Special problem. That was their private code for something which could not be discussed in the clear. No telling who might eavesdrop. Were the neck pellets then no longer immune to spying?

Panille and Ekel had stopped near the hatch to Ferry's office in Medical.

Oakes tried to remember all the times he had seen this young man shipside. Panille had not invited much interest until it had become clear that he really might be talking to the ship. Then that order from the ship for Panille to be sent groundside!

Why does the ship want him groundside?

A poet! What use could there be for a poet? Oakes decided that he really did not believe Panille talked to the ship.

But the ship, and possibly that Raja Thomas, wanted Panille groundside.

Why?

He turned the question over and found no shadow.

"You're sure the request for Panille came from the ship?" he asked.

"It's been six diurns since the request . . . and it didn't read like a request to me; it read like an order."

"But from the ship, you're certain?"

"As certain as you can be of anything." The irritation in her voice bordered on insubordination. "I used your code and made the complete cross-check. Everything scans."

Oakes sighed.

Why Panille?

Perhaps more attention should have been paid to the poet. He was one of the originals from Earthside. Have to dig deeper into his past. That was obvious.

The scene in the holofocus showed Panille and Ekel parting. Panille turned and they had a view of his back—a wide and muscular back, Legata noted. She called this to Oakes' attention.

"Do you find him attractive, Legata?"

"I merely point out that he's not some dainty flower-sniffer."

"Mmmmmm."

Oakes was intensely conscious of the musky odor coming from Legata. She had a magnificently proportioned body which she had kept from him so far. But Oakes knew himself to be a patient man. Patient and persistent.

Panille was entering the hatch to Ferry's office. Oakes slapped the switch to stop the replay, leaving the carrier light still glowing. He did not care to have another run through that scene with Ferry. Stupid, bumbling old fool!

Oakes glanced at Legata with only the barest turning of his head. Magnificent. She often presented a vapid mask but Oakes saw the consistent brilliance in her work. Few people knew that she was shockingly strong, a mutation. She concealed an extraordinary musculature under that smooth warm skin. He found this idea exciting. She was known shipwide as a history fanatic who frequently begged Records for style displays to copy in her clothing. Currently, she wore a short toga which exposed most of her right breast. The light fabric hung precariously from her nipple. Oakes felt the pulse of her strength, even there.

Taunting me?

"Tell me why the ship wants a poet groundside," he said.

"We'll have to wait and see."

"We can guess."

"It may be a very simple and open thing—communication with the 'lectro...."

"Nothing the ship does is open and simple! And do not use that high-sounding term with me. It's kelp, nothing but kelp. And it's a damned nuisance."

She cleared her throat, the first sign of nervousness that Oakes had detected in her. He found this pleasing. Yes ... she would be ready for the Scream Room soon.

"There's still Thomas," she said, "perhaps he can...."

"You are not to question him about Panille."

She was startled. "You're satisfied with the answers he gave you?"

"I am satisfied that he's too much for you to handle."

"I think you're overly suspicious," she said.

"With this ship you cannot be too suspicious. You suspect everything and know you'll miss something."

"But they're just two...."

"The ship ordered this." There was a long pause while Oakes continued to stare up at her. "Your term: order. Is that not so?"

"As far as we can determine."

"Do you have any indication, even a faint hint, that Thomas and not the ship initiated this?"

"There's only one order from Ship adding this ... this Panille to the Colony roster."

"You hesitated over his name."

"It slipped my mind!"

Now she was nervous and angry. Oakes found himself enjoying that very much. This Legata Hamill had potential. She would have to be broken of that habit, however, saying Ship rather than the ship.

"You don't find the poet attractive?"

"Not particularly."

The fingers of her left hand twisted a corner of her toga.

"And there's no record of communication between Thomas and the ship?"

"Nothing."

"You don't find that odd?"

"What do you mean?"

"Thomas had to come from hyb. Who ordered it? Who briefed him?"

"There's no record of any such communication."

"How could there be no record of something we know took place?"

Now fear edged her anger. "I don't know!"

"Haven't I warned you to suspect everything?"

"Yes! You tell me to suspect everyone!"

"Good … very good."

He turned back to face the light of the empty holofocus.

"Now, go and look some more. Perhaps there's something you've missed."

"Do you know of something I've missed?"

"That's for you to find out, my dear!"

He listened to the whisk-whisk of her clothing as she hurried from the room. There was a brief flare of light from the outer passage as she opened the hatch, then shadows once more and she was gone.

Oakes switched from replay to real-time and coded in the passage pickups to follow her progress as she took the turn to Records. He switched from pickup to pickup, watching until she sat down at a scandesk in the command level of Records and called for the information she wanted. Oakes checked the readouts. She was asking for any messages between the ship and Pandora, all references to Raja Thomas and Kerro Panille. She did not overlook Hali Ekel.

Good.

Her next step would be to use some of Lewis' people for actual surveillance. Oakes knew she already had scanned the Records data once, but now she would look even harder, seeking codes or other subterfuge. At least, he hoped that was her intent. If the secret were there, she could find it. She simply needed to be challenged, driven, goaded into it.

Suspect everything and everyone.

He shut down the holo and scowled at the darkness. Soon, very soon, he would have to go groundside for good. No returning to the dangerous confines of the ship. Pandora was dangerous enough, but the need for his own hole, a nest where he could not be watched by the ship increased with terrifying speed. This mechanical monster! He knew it followed every move he made shipside. It's what I would do.

There were some who thought the ship's influence extended farther. But the Redoubt would solve all of that. Provided Lewis had not failed him. No … no chance of that. This long silence from Lewis had to be some internal problem with the clones. There were too many fail-safe signals for real disasters. None of the signals had been activated. Something else was happening down at the Redoubt. Perhaps Lewis is preparing a pleasant surprise for me. Just like him.

Oakes smiled to himself, nursing the privacy of his innermost thoughts. *You do not know what I plan, Mechanical Monster. I have plans for you.*

He had plans for Pandora, too, big plans. And the ship was no part of them. Other plans for Legata. She would have to go to the Scream Room soon. Yes. She had to be made more trustworthy.

Chapter 21

Nostalgia represents an interesting illusion. Through nostalgia, humans wish for things that never were. The positive memory is the one that sticks. Over several generations, the positive memory tends to weed out more and more of what really existed, refining down to a distillation of haunted desires.

—Shipquotes

FOR THE first time, Waela considered refusing an assignment. Not out of fear—she had survived in the research subs where no one else had, and still she accepted the fact that this project must continue at all costs. Beyond instinct, she knew that the 'lectrokelp was the most important factor in Colony life. Survival.

I've been down there and I survived. I should lead the new team.

This thought dominated her awareness as she and Thomas approached the bustle of early dayside activity around the new sub he was having rushed to completion.

Thomas worried her. One blink he seemed like a nice-enough fellow; the next … what? His mind appeared to wander.

He hasn't been out of hyb long enough to handle himself here.

They stopped a few meters from the work perimeter and she stared at what was taking shape under the brilliant lights. All this energy—all those workers. They were like insects intent on a giant egg. She tried to fathom the sense of this thing. It did make a certain sense … but a transparent core of plaz? They had always used plasma glass in the subs, but this detachable core constructed entirely of plaz was a new concept. She could see that it was going to be crowded in there and didn't know if she would like that.

Why Thomas? Why did they put him in charge?

She recalled their walk across the compound and into the LTA hangar. He had been too busy giving orders to her for him to see the telltale shadow-flicker of a Hooded Dasher breaking past the sentries. She had cooked it in mid-leap with a hipshot from her lasgun—and immediately began to shiver when she realized that she had almost left the weapon in her cubby. This perimeter was supposed to be secure, the sentries the best.

Thomas had barely noticed.

"Quick little devils," he said, calmly. "By the way, there's a poet coming onto our team from Ship."

"A poet? But we need…."

"We will get a poet because Ship is sending us a poet."

"But we asked for ..."

"I know what we asked for!"

He sounded like a man suppressing his own misgivings.

She said: "Well, we still need a systems engineer for ..."

"I want you to seduce this poet."

She had trouble believing what she had heard.

Thomas said: "Your skin's a regular rainbow when you get upset. Just consider this a team assignment. I've seen a holo of the poet. He's not unattractive in ..."

"My body is my own!" She glared at him. "And nobody—not you, not Oakes, not Ship, tells me who I will or will not let into my body."

They were stopped in the compound by then and she was surprised to see his hands up and a grin on his face. She realized that she had instinctively raised her lasgun to focus between his eyes. Without reducing her furious glare, she lowered the gun and holstered it.

"Sorry," he said. And they resumed their walk toward the hangar. Presently, he asked: "How important is the kelp team to you?"

He should know that! Everyone knew, and since Thomas had been groundside he had shown an amazing ability to seek out critical information.

"It's everything to me."

Words began to pour from him. He wanted to know if Panille was a free agent. Was Panille really sent by Ship? Could Panille be working for Oakes or this Lewis people mentioned in such fearful tones. Who? Who? Doubts—a cascade of doubts.

But why the hell should she have to seduce Panille to find out? There was no satisfaction in the answer Thomas gave.

"You have to get through all of Panille's barriers, all of his masks."

Damn!

"Just how important is this project to you?" Thomas demanded.

"It's vital ... not just to me but to the entire Colony."

"Of course it is. That's why you must seduce this poet. If he's to be a working member of this very bizarre team, there are things we must know about him."

"And a hold we must have on him!"

"There's no other way."

"Pull his records if you want to know whether he prefers women. I will not ..."

"That's not my question and you know it! You will not refuse my orders and remain on this team!"

"I can't even question the wisdom of your decisions?"

"Ship sent me. There is no higher authority. And there are things I must know for this project to succeed."

She could not deny the intensity of his emotions, but ...

"Waela, you're right that the project's vital. We can't play with time as we play here with words."

"And I have nothing to say about the team?" She was close to tears and did not care that it showed.

"You have a ..."

"After all I've been through? I watched them all die! All of them! That buys me some say in how this team goes, or it buys me the R & R I can collect shipside. You name it."

Thomas, aware of the deepening flush in her skin, felt the intensity of her presence. Such a quick and perceptive person. He felt himself giving over to feelings he had not experienced in eons.

It's been Shipcenturies!

He spoke softly: "We consult, we share data. But all key decisions are mine and final. If that had been the case all along, this project would not have been botched."

Waela keyed the hangar door and they stepped inside to the brilliant focus of lights and activity, the noise and smell of torches. She put a hand on his arm to stop him. How thin and wiry he felt!

"How will seducing the poet make our mission succeed?"

"I've told you. Get to the heart of him."

She stared across at the activity around the new sub. "And replacing the plasteel with plaz …"

"No single thing will make it for us. We're a team." He glanced down at her. "And we're going in by air."

"By …" Then she saw the stranded cables reaching up and out of the brilliant illumination into the upper shadows of the hangar—a gigantic LTA partly inflated there. The sub was being fitted to a Lighter-Than-Air in place of the usual armored gondola.

"But why …"

"Because the kelp has been strangling our subs."

She thought back to her own survival from a doomed sub—the writhing kelp near the shore, the bubble escape, her frantic swim to the rocks and the near-miraculous dive of the observation LTA which had plucked her away from predators.

As though he read her thoughts, Thomas said: "You've seen it yourself. At our first briefing, you said you believed the kelp to be sentient."

"It is."

"Those subs did not just get tangled. They were snatched."

She considered this. On every lost mission where they had the data, they knew that the sub had been destroyed shortly after collecting samples.

Could the kelp think we were attacking?

Her own reasoning made this possible. If the kelp is sentient … Yes, it would have an external sensory matrix to respond to pain. Not blind writhing, but sentient response.

Thomas spoke in a flat voice: "The kelp is not an insensitive vegetable."

"I've said all along that we should be attempting to communicate with it."

"And so we shall."

"Then what difference does it make whether we drop in or dive in from shoreside? We're still there."

"We go by lagoon."

Thomas moved closer to the work, bending to inspect a line of welds along the plaz. "Good work; good work," he muttered. The welds were almost invisible. When the conversion was complete, the occupants would have close to three hundred and sixty degrees of visibility.

"Lagoons?" Waela asked as he stepped back.

"Yes. Isn't that what you call those vertical tunnels of open water ?"

"Certainly, but …"

"We will be surrounded by the kelp, actually helpless if it wants to attack. But we will not touch it. This sub is being fitted to play back the kelplights—to record the patterns and play them back."

Again, he was making sense.

Thomas continued to speak as he watched the work: "We can approach a perimeter of kelp without making physical contact. As you've seen, when we go in from shore, that's impossible. Not sufficient room between the kelp strands."

She nodded her head slowly. There were many unanswered questions about this plan, but she could see the pattern of it.

"Subs are too unwieldy," he said, "but they're all we've got. We must find a sufficiently large pocket of open water, drop into it and anchor. Then we dive and study the kelp."

It sounded perilous but possible. And that idea of playing back the kelplights to the kelp: She had seen those coherent patterns herself, sometimes repetitive. Was that the way the kelp communicated?

Maybe Thomas really was chosen by Ship.

She heard him mutter something. Thomas was the only man she knew who talked to himself more or less constantly. He faded in and out of conversations. You could never be sure whether he had been thinking aloud or talking to you.

"What?"

"The plaz. Not as strong as plasteel. We had to do some buttressing inside. Makes things much more crowded than you might expect."

He moved through a group of workers to speak to their foreman, a low-voiced conversation which came through to her only in bits: "… then if you lattice the … and I'll want … where we …"

Presently, he returned to her side. "My design isn't as good as it might be, but it'll suffice."

So he has his little mistakes but he doesn't hide them.

She had heard a few snatches of talk among the workers. They stood a bit in awe of Thomas. The man showed a surprising ability at their work, no matter what the work—plaz welding, control design … He was a jack of all trades.

Master of none?

She sensed that this was a difficult man to influence: a fearsome enemy, that one friend who does not mirror but mocks when mockery is needed.

This recognition increased her uneasiness. She knew she could like this man, but she felt bad vibrations about the team … and it wasn't even a team yet.

And the sub will be crowded even with three of us.

She closed her eyes.

Should I tell him?

She had never told anyone, not in the debriefings, nor in friendly conversation. The kelp had a special hold over her. It was a thing that began happening as soon as the sub started slipping through the gigantic stems and tentacles: a sexual excitement very nearly impossible to control at times. Absurdity, in fact. She had managed a form of balance by hyperventilating but it remained troublesome and sometimes reduced her efficiency. When that happened, though, the shock of it cleared the effect.

Her old teammates had thought the hyperventilating a response to fear, a way of overcoming the terrors all of them felt and suppressed. And now they were all dead—nobody left to hear her confession.

The closeness, the strange sexual air that had taken over the background of the project—the unknowns in Thomas—all frustrated her. She had thought of taking Anti-s to relieve the sexual tensions, but Anti-s made her drowsy and slowed her reflexes. Deadly.

Thomas stood beside her, silently observing the work. She could almost see him making mental notes for changes. There were gears turning in his head.

"Why me?" she muttered.

"What?" He turned toward her.

"Why me? Why do I have to take on this poet?"

"I've told you what ..."

"There are women paid well to do just what you ..."

"I won't pay for this. It's a project thing, vital. Your own word. You will do it."

She turned her back on him.

Thomas sighed. This Waela TaoLini was an extraordinary person. He hated what he had asked her to do, but she was the only one he could trust. The project was that vital to her, too. Panille posed too many unanswered questions. Ship's words were plain and simple: "There will be a poet ..." Not: "I have named a poet," or, "I have assigned a poet ..."

There will be ...

Who was Panille working for? Doubts ... doubts ... doubts ...

I have to know.

By the old rush in his veins, he already knew that Waela would follow his orders, and he would sink into a sadness the likes of which he had almost forgotten.

"Old fool," he muttered to himself.

"What?" She turned back toward him and he could see the acceptance and the resolve on her face.

"Nothing."

She stood facing Thomas a moment, then: "It all depends on how much I like the poet." With that, she turned on her heel and left the hangar with characteristic Pandoran speed.

Chapter 22

Religion begins where men seek to influence a god. The biblical scapegoat and Christian Redeemer are cast from the same ancient mould—the human subservient to an unpredictable universe (or unpredictable king) and seeking to rid himself of the guilt which brings down the wrath of the all-powerful.

—Raja Flattery, *The Book of Ship*

AGAIN, THE communications pellet in Oakes' neck made no contact with Lewis. Static or silence, wild images projected onto his waking dreams—these were all he got. He wanted to reach into his neck and rip the thing out.

Why had Lewis ordered no physical contact with the Redoubt? Oakes chafed at his own inability to raise too much disturbance. The real purposes of the Redoubt remained a secret from most Shipmen; to most it was just a rumored exploratory attempt out on Black Dragon. He did not dare countermand the order which had isolated the Redoubt. Too many would see the size of the place.

Lewis can't do this to me.

Oakes paced his cubby, wishing it were even larger. He wanted to walk off his frustrations but it was full dayside out in the ship's passages and he knew he would be plagued by the need to make decisions once he stepped from his sanctum. Rumors were raging through the ship. Many had noted his upset. This could not go on much longer.

I would go down myself … except …

No, without Lewis to prepare the way, it is too dangerous.

Oakes shook his head. He was too valuable to risk down there yet.

Dammit, Lewis! You could send me some message …

Oakes had come increasingly to suspect that Lewis really was involved in a primary emergency. That or treachery. No … it had to be an emergency. Lewis was not a leader. Then it had to be a major threat from the planet itself.

Pandora.

In many ways, Pandora was a more immediate and dangerous adversary than the ship.

Oakes glanced at the blank holofocus beside his couch. A touch of the buttons would call up real-time images of the planet. To what avail? He had tried a sensor search of the Black Dragon coastline from space. Too many clouds … not enough detail.

He could identify the coastal bay where the Redoubt was being built, could even see glinting reflections during the diurn passages of Alki or Rega.

Oakes took a deep breath to calm himself. This planet was not going to beat him.

You're mine, Pandora!

As he had told Legata, anything was possible down there. They could fulfill any fantasy.

Oakes examined his hands, rubbed them across his bulging stomach. He was determined that he would never under any circumstances grub out a living on the surface of a planet. Especially on a planet he owned. This was only natural.

The ship conditioned me to be what I am.

More than any other person he had ever known, Oakes felt that he knew the nature of the ship's conditioning processes—the differences from what they had been when they had lived free to scatter on Earth's surface.

It's the crush of people ... too many people too close together.

Shipside congestion had been transported groundside. This way of life demanded special adaptations. All Shipmen adjusted the same way at bottom. They drugged themselves, gambled—risked everything ... even their own lives. Running the Colony perimeter naked except for thonged feet. And for what? A bet! A dare! To hide from themselves. In his long walks through the ship, Oakes knew how he screened out the comings and goings of others. Like most Shipmen, he could retreat into the deepest interior of his mind for privacy, for entertainment, for living.

In these times of food shortage, this faculty had been especially valuable to him. Oakes knew himself to be the ... heaviest man shipside. He knew there was envy and angry questioning, but even so no one stared directly at him with such thoughts openly readable.

Yes, I know these people. They need me.

Under Edmond Kingston's tutelage, he had studied well for the psychiatric side of his specialty—all the banks of records handed down for generations ... eons maybe. The way the ship had put them in and out of hyb, the passage of real time had been lost.

That unknown length of time bothered Oakes. And the translations from the records produced too many anomalies. Popular apology for the ship said the confusion arose from Ship's attempt to rescue as many people as possible. Oakes did not believe this. The translations hinted at too many other explanations. Translation? The ship controlled even that. You asked a computer to render the unintelligible intelligible. But linguists pointed out that among the languages found in Records were some which existed in a free-floating universe of their own—without discernible beginnings nor descendants.

What happened to the folk of those rich linguistic heritages?

I don't even know what happened to us.

His childhood memories told him things, though. Compared to the people of the Earth from which the ship had plucked them, Shipmen were freaks—all of them, clone and Natural Natal alike. Freaks. The shipside mind had become a place to live very quickly for those who had little space, few private possessions to call their own, for people torn between WorShip and dismay. Shipmen cultivated the skills of personalizing whatever the ship provided them. Functional simplicity did not bear the onus or sense of restriction that arbitrary simplicity carried. Each tool, each bowl and spoon and pair of chopsticks, each cubby bore the signature of the user in some small fashion.

My cubby is merely a larger manifestation of this.

The mind, too, was the outpost of privacy, a last place to sit and whittle something sensible out of an insane universe.

Only the Ceepee was above it all; even while he participated, he was above. Oakes felt that sometimes the people around him wore signs revealing their innermost thoughts.

And what about this Raja Thomas? Another Ceepee and he studied me carefully … much the way I sometimes study others.

It occurred to Oakes then that he had grown careless. Since old Kingston's death, he had thought himself immune to the probing study of others, alone in the ability to snare a Shipman's psyche. It was dangerous for someone else to have that weapon. Just one more reason this Thomas would have to be eliminated. Oakes realized he had been pacing back and forth in his cubby—to the mandala, turn and back to the com-console, once more to the mandala … He was confronted by the com-console when this realization struck him. His hand went out to the keys and he brought into the holofocus a scene from Agrarium D-9 out on shiprim. He stared at the bustle of workers, at the filtered blue-violet light which set these peoples apart in a world of their own.

Yes … if independence from them were possible, it would begin with food and the cultivation of life. The axolotl tanks, the clone labs, the biocomputer itself—all were but sophisticated toys for the well fed, the sheltered and clothed.

"Feed men, then ask of them virtue."

That was an old voice from one of his training records. A wise voice, a practical one. The voice of a survivor.

Oakes continued to stare at the workers. They attended their plants with total attention, occupation and preoccupation linked in a particular reverence which he had sensed only among older Shipmen during WorShip.

These agrarium workers engaged in a kind of WorShip.

WorShip!

Oakes chuckled, amused by the thought of WorShip reduced to tending plants in an agrarium. What a grand sight they must be in the eyes of a god! A pack of sniveling beggars. What kind of a god kept its charges in poverty to hear them beg? Oakes could understand a touch of subjugation, but … this? This spoke to something else.

Someone had to be boss, and the rest have to be reminded of that occasionally. Otherwise, how can anything be organized to work?

No; he heard the message. It said that the ship's programs were running out. All of the problems were being dumped on the Ceepee's shoulders.

Look at those workers!

He knew they did not have the time to make the ordering decisions for their own lives. When? After work? Then the body was tired and the mind was dulled into a personal reverie which precluded insightful judgments for the good of all.

The good of all—that's my job.

He freed them from the agony of the decisions which they were not well informed enough, not energetic enough, nor even intelligent enough to make. It was the Ceepee who gave them that more pleasant gift of drifting time, the time to seek their own ease and recreations.

Recreation … Re-creation.

The association flitted through his mind. Re-creation was where they were made new again, where all they worked for was made real, where they lived. Looking down at the agrarium workers in the holofocus, Oakes felt like the conductor of an intricate musical score. He reminded himself to remember that analogy for the next general meeting.

Conductor of a symphony.

He liked that. It was food for thought. Did the ship have such thoughts? He experienced a sudden feeling of affinity for the ship, his enemy.

What food are we that we deserve reverence and care? What manna? Could the ship …

His reverie was shattered by the abrupt opening hiss of his cubby hatch.

Who dared …

The hatch slammed back against the bulkhead and Lewis darted through, sealed the opening behind him and dogged it. He was breathing hard and, instead of his usual self-effacing brown fatigues, he wore a crisp new issue singlesuit of dark green.

"Lewis!"

Oakes was overjoyed to see the man … and then dismayed. When Lewis turned at the sealed hatch, it was apparent that his face bore signs of quick medical patchwork to cover numerous cuts and bruises. And he was limping.

Chapter 23

Judgment prepares you to enter the stream of chance and use your will. You use judgment to modulate will. Thinking is the performance of the moment. You sit in judgment, a convection center for the currents where past prepares a future. It is a balancing act.

—Kerro Panille, *The Avata Argue*

HALI EKEL, moving with her usual sure-footed grace, leaped up one-handed to grasp the lift bar for the ceiling hatch leading to the software storage section of Records. Her pribox, suspended on its shoulder harness, slapped her hip as she jumped. She had discovered less than an hour earlier that Kerro Panille was headed groundside. He had done this without farewell, not even a note … or a poem.

Not that I have any special hold on him!

She opened the hatch and levered herself up into the service tube.

He refuses the breeding match with me, he …

She pushed such thoughts aside. But his leaving this way hurt. They had come to maturity in the same crèche section, were the same age (within days) and had remained friends. She had heard his stories of Earthside and he had heard her stories. Hali had no illusions about her own emotions. She thought Kerro the most attractive male shipside.

Why was he always so distant?

She crouched to scuttle up the curving oval of the tube. It was only one hundred and sixty centimeters in its longest diameter, eight centimeters short of her height, but she was used to moving around Ship through such little-known shortcuts.

It's not as though I were ugly.

Her shipcloth singlesuit, she knew, revealed an attractive feminine figure. Her skin was dark, eyes brown and she wore her black hair cropped short as all technicians did. All of the med-techs were acutely aware of the sanitary advantages of hair shorn to a bristly cap. Not that she had ever wanted Kerro to clip his hair or beard. She found his style exciting. But he did not have to deal with medical problems.

She found the Records access hatch locked but she had memorized the code and it took only seconds to work the latch. Ship buzzed at her from the interior sensor-eye as she stooped and slipped through into the storage area.

"Hali, what are you doing?"

She stopped in shock. Vocal! Everyone knew the flat, metallic work-voice of Ship, the means of necessary contacts, but this was something different … a resonant voice full of emotional overtones. And Ship had used her name!

"I … I want a software reader station. There's always one open in here."

"You are very unconventional, Hali."

"Have I done something wrong?" Her strong fingers worked to seal the hatchdogs as she spoke, and she hesitated there, fearful that she had offended Ship.

But Ship was talking to her! Really talking!

"Some would think your actions wrong."

"I was just in a hurry. No one will tell me why Kerro has gone groundside."

"Why did you not think to ask Me?"

"I was …" She glanced along the narrow passage between the rotary bins of software discs toward the reader station. Its keyboard and screen were blank, unoccupied as she had expected.

Ship would not leave it there. "I am never farther from you than the nearest monitor or com-console."

She peered up at the orange bulb of the sensor-eye. It was a baleful orb, a cyclopean pupil with its surrounding metal grid through which Ship's voice issued. Was Ship angry with her? The measured control of that awful voice filled her with awe.

"I am not angry with you. I merely suggest that you show more confidence in Me. I am concerned about you."

"I'm … confident of You, Ship. I WorShip. You know that. I just never thought You would talk to me like this."

"As I talk to Kerro Panille? You are jealous, Hali."

She was too honest to deny it, but words would not come. She shook her head.

"Hali, go to the keyboard at the end of this aisle. Depress the red cursor in the upper right-hand corner and I will open a door behind that station."

"A … door?"

"You will find a hidden room there with another instruction station which Kerro Panille often used. You may use it now."

Wondering and fearful, she obeyed.

The entire keyboard and its desk swung wide to reveal a low opening. She crouched to enter and found herself in a small room with a vaguely yellow couch. Muted green light came from concealed illuminators at the corners of the room. There was a large console with screen and keyboard, a familiar holofocus circle on the floor. She knew the setting—a small teaching lab, but one she had not even known existed. It was smaller than any other of her experience.

She heard the hatch seal itself behind her, but she felt unaccountably secure in this privacy. Kerro had used this place. Ship was concerned about her. There was the unmistakable musk of Kerro's flesh on her sensitive nostrils. She rubbed at the gold ring in her nose. There was a stationary swivel seat at the keyboard. She slipped into it.

"No, Hali. Stretch out on the couch. You will not need the keyboard here."

Ship's voice came from all around her. She looked for the source of that awesomely-measured voice. There were no sensors visible or monitor-eyes.

"Do not fear, Hali. This room is within my protective shield. Go to the couch."

Hesitantly, she obeyed, The couch was covered with a slick material which felt cold against her neck and hands.

"Why did you come here looking for an unoccupied terminal, Hali?"

"I wanted to do something ... definite."

"You love Kerro?"

"You know I do."

"It is your right to try to make him love you, Hali, but not by subterfuge."

"I ... I want him."

"So you sought My help?"

"I'll take any help I can get."

"You have free access to information, Hali, but what you do with it is your own decision. You are making a life, do you understand that?"

"Making a life?" She could feel her own perspiration against the slick material of the couch.

"Your own life. It is your own ... a gift. You should treat it well. Be happy with it."

"Would You match Kerro and me again?"

"Only if that really suits you both."

"I'd be happier with Kerro. And Kerro's gone groundside!" It came out almost a wail and she felt tears at the edges of her eyes.

"Can you not go groundside?"

"You know I have Shipside medical responsibilities!"

"Yes, the Shipmen must be kept healthy that Colony may eat. But I ask about your own decision."

"They need me here!"

"Hali, I ask that you trust Me."

She blinked at the empty screen across from the couch. What a strange statement! How could one not trust Ship? All people were creatures of Ship. The invocations of WorShip marked their lives forever. But she felt that some personal response was being demanded and she gave it.

"Of course I trust You."

"I find that gratifying, Hali. Because of that, I have something just for you. You are to learn about a man called Yaisuah. The name is in an ancient language which was known as Aramaic. Yaisuah is a form of the name Joshua and it is where Jesus Lewis gets his name."

In all of this, Hali was most startled by Ship's pronunciation of Jesus. Anyone shipside referring to Jesus Lewis called him Hesoos. But Ship's diction could not be questioned: "Geezus."

She stared at the screen. The lab lights suddenly flared to bright, glinting off the metal surfaces. She blinked and sneezed.

Maybe it isn't Ship talking to me, she thought. *What if it's someone playing a joke?* This was a frightening thought. Who would dare such a prank?

"I am here, Hali Ekel. It is Ship speaking to you."

"Do You … read my mind?"

"Reserve that question, Hali, but know that I can read your reactions. Do you not read the reactions of those around you?"

"Yes, but …"

"Do not fear. I mean you no harm."

She tried to swallow, recalling what Ship had said she could learn. Yaisuah?

"Who is this … this Yaisuah?"

"To learn that, you must travel."

"Travel? Wha … what …" She cleared her throat and forced herself to be calm. Kerro had used this lab often and had never shown fear of Ship. "Where will I travel?"

"Not where, but when. You will stroll into that which you humans call Time."

She took this to mean that Ship would show her a holo-record. "A projection? What are You going to …"

"Not that kind of projection. For this experience, you are the projection."

"Me … the …"

"It is important that Shipmen learn about Yaisuah, who was also called Jesus. I have chosen you for this journey."

She felt tightness in her chest, panic near. "How …"

"I know how, Hali Ekel, and so do you. Answer Me: How do your neurons function?"

Any med-tech knew that. She tossed it off without thinking: "A charged measure of acetylcholene across the synapses where …"

"A charged measure, yes. A bridge, a shortcut. You take shortcuts all the time."

"But I …"

"I am the universe, Hali Ekel. Every part of Me—each part in its entirety—the universe. All Mine—including the shortcuts."

"But my body … what …" She broke off, stopped by an intense fear for this precious flesh she wore.

"I will be with you, Hali Ekel. That matrix which is you, that also is part of the universe and Mine. You wish to know if I read your thoughts?"

She found the very idea deeply disturbing, an invasion of her privacy. "Do You?"

"Ekel …" Such sadness Ship put into her name. "Our powers are of the same universe. Your thought is My thought. How can I help but know what you think?"

She struggled for a deep breath. Ship's words spoke of things just beyond her grasp, but WorShip had taught her to accept.

"Very well."

"Now, are you ready to travel?"

She tried to swallow in a dry throat. Her mind searched for some logical objection to this thing which Ship proposed. A projection? The words represented such an insubstantial thing. Ship said she would be the projection. How threatening that sounded!

"Why … why must I go through … Time?"

"Through?" Ship's tone conveyed an exquisite reprimand. "You persist in thinking of Time as linear and a barrier. That is not even close to the reality, but I will play that game if it reassures you."

"What is … I mean, if it's not linear …"

"Think of it as linear if you wish. Think of it as thousands of meters of computer tape unraveled and crammed into this little lab. You could move from one Time to another—a shortcut—just by reaching across the loops and folds."

"But … I mean if you actually go across, how can you get back to …"

"You never let go of the now."

In spite of that deep and grinding fear, she was interested. "Two places at one Time?"

"All Time is one place, Ekel."

It occurred to her then that Ship had shifted from the personal and reassuring *Hali* to *Ekel*, subtly but definitely.

"Why are You calling me Ekel now?"

"Because I perceive that this is the line which you believe to be yourself. I do it to help you."

"But if You take me somewhere else …"

"I have sealed this room, Ekel. You will have two bodies simultaneously, but separated by a very long Time and a very great distance."

"Will I know both …"

"You will be conscious of only one flesh, but you will know both."

"Very well. What do I do?"

"Stay there on the lab couch and accept the fact that I will make another body for you at another Time."

"Will it …"

"If you do what I tell you to do, it will not hurt. You will understand the speech of this other place and I will give you an old body, an old woman. Old bodies are not as threatening to others. No one bothers an old woman."

She tried to relax in obedience. *Accept.* But questions filled her mind. "Why are You sending me to …"

"Eavesdrop, Ekel. Observe and learn. And no matter what you see, do not try to interfere. You would cause unnecessary pain, perhaps even to yourself."

"I just watch and …"

"Do not interfere. You will see the consequences presently of interfering with Time."

Before she could ask another question, she felt a prickling along the back of her neck; a slither of chill swept down her spine. Her heart slammed against her ribcage.

Ship's voice came from a long distance. "Ready, Ekel." It was a command, not a question, but she answered, and her own voice echoed in her skull.

"Yesssssss ..."

Chapter 24

The mind is a mirror of the universe.
See the reflections?
The universe is no mirror for the mind.
Nothing out there
Nothing in here
Shows ourselves.

—Kerro Panille, *The Collected Poems*

WAELA TAOLINI lay in her groundside cubby, fatigue in her body, fatigue in her mind, but unable to sleep. Thomas had no mercy. Everything must be done to his perfectionist demands. He was a fanatic. They had spent twenty-one hours going through the operational routine for the new sub. Thomas would not wait for the arrival of the poet, who was somewhere in the bowels of Processing. *No. We will use what time we have.*

She tried to take a deep breath. Pain yanked a knot behind her breastbone.

She wondered how Thomas came to them. How could he be from Ship? Things he did not know, things that Shipmen took for granted, worried her. There was the incident with the Hooded Dasher.

He was calm, though, I'll give him that.

What really surprised her was his ignorance of The Game.

A crowd had gathered behind the LTA hangar—off-shift crew, most of them drinking what Shipmen called Spinneret wine.

"What's this about?" Thomas pointed his clipboard at the group.

"It's The Game." She looked at him with a new amazement. "You mean you don't know The Game?"

"What Game? That's just a bunch of drunks having a good time ... strange, there was nothing in my briefing about liquors of any kind."

"There have always been lab alcohols," she said, "and at one time there were wines and brandies. But officially we can't afford to give up any productive food for wine. Somehow, some do and the market is brisk. Those men," she nodded toward the group, "have traded away some of their food chits for it."

"So, they trade food for wine that costs food to make—maybe less food. Isn't that their right?" His eyes squinted at her.

"Yes, but food's short. They're going hungry. In this place, going hungry means you slow down and here, Raja Thomas, if you slow down you die. And maybe someone else dies because of it."

"Do you do it?" he asked softly.

"Yes," her skin glowed red, "when I can afford the time."

She followed Thomas as he strolled toward the crew, pulled the sleeve of his singlesuit to stop him short.

"There's more."

"What?"

"It requires an even number of players, men or women. Each one buys into The Game with a certain number of food chits. They pair off any way they wish, and each one draws a wihi stick from a basket. They compare, and the longest stick wins a round. The shorter stick of the pair is eliminated, so those drawing the longer sticks pair up. They draw again, and so on until there is only one couple."

"What about the food chits?"

"The players up the ante every round, so if there are a lot of people, The Game gets pretty expensive."

"Does the last couple divide the chits?"

"No, they draw again. The one who draws the longer stick wins the chits."

"That seems boring enough."

"Yes."

She hesitated, then: "The short stick runs the perimeter."

She said it offhand, without as much as a blink.

"You mean they run around the outside ...?" His thumb hung in the air over his shoulder.

She nodded. "They run it naked."

"But they can't possibly ... that's almost ten kilometers out in the open ..."

"Some make it."

"But why? Not for food, it's not that bad yet, is it?"

"No, not for food. For favors, jobs, quarters, partners. For the thrill. For the chance to go out with a flash from a boring life. The long sticks are the losers. Food chits are a consolation prize. The winner gets to run the P."

Thomas let out a long breath.

"What are the odds?"

"By experience, they work out just like the rest of The Game—fifty-fifty. Half don't make it."

"And it's legal?"

It was her turn to look at him quizzically.

"They have the right to their own bodies."

He turned to watch the people playing this ... this game.

The crew had paired up, drawn, paired up, drawn, and was now down to the last pair. A man and a woman this time. The man had no nose, but wrinkled slits in his forehead pulsed with the moisture that Thomas took for breath. The woman looked vaguely like someone he had known.

They drew, and the woman matched longer. The crowd cheered and helped her gather her winnings. They tucked them in her collar and sleeves and belt. The last of the wine was passed around and the group began moving toward the west quarter exterior hatch.

"He's really going out there?" Thomas followed them with his eyes.

"Did you notice his right eyebrow?"

"Yes," he looked up at her, "it looked as though he had two eyebrows above it. And the nose …"

"Those were tattoos, hash marks. You get one for running the P."

"Then this is his third? …"

"That's right. His odds are still fifty-fifty. But there is a groundside saying: 'You go once, you've had your flirt with death. You go twice, you live twice. Go three times and go for me.'"

"Charming."

"It's a good game."

"You ever play it, TaoLini?"

She swallowed, and the glow faded out of her skin.

"No."

"A friend?"

She nodded.

"Let's get back to work," he said, and walked her slowly back to the hangar.

Waela remembered this exchange with the odd feeling that she had missed something in Thomas' responses.

Thomas would not even pause for WorShip. He permitted a grudging rest, hardly a hesitation, only when fatigue had them dropping programs and forgetting coordinates. During one of these rests he had started an odd conversation with her and it kept her awake now.

What was he trying to say to me?

They had been seated in the globe of plaz which would shield them in the depths of the sea. Workmen continued their activity all around the outside. She and Thomas sat so close to each other that they had been required to learn a special rhythm to keep from bumping elbows. Waela had missed the right sequence of keys for the dive train three times running.

"Take a rest."

There was accusation in his tone, but she sank back into the sheltered contours of her seat, thankful for any relief, thankful even for the crash-harness which supported her. Muscles did not have to do what the harness did.

Presently, Thomas' voice intruded on her consciousness.

"Once upon a time there was a fourteen-year-old girl. She lived on Earth, on a chicken farm."

Lived on a chicken farm, Waela thought, then: *He's talking about me!*

She opened her eyes.

"So, you've pried into my records."

"That's my job."

A fourteen-year-old girl on a chicken farm. Her job!

She thought about that girl she had been—child of emigrants, grubbers in the dirt. Technopeasants. Gaulish middle-class.

I broke away from that.

No … to be honest, she had to admit that she had run away. A sun going nova meant little to a fourteen-year-old girl, a girl whose body had become a woman's much earlier than her contemporaries.

I ran away to Ship.

She had held such conversations with herself many times. Waela closed her eyes. It was as though two people occupied her consciousness. One of them she called "Runaway," and the other, "Honesty." Runaway had objected to Shipman life and railed against groundside dangers.

Runaway asked, "Why was I chosen for this damned risky life, anyway?"

Honesty replied, "As I recall it, you volunteered."

"Then I must've parked my brains somewhere. What in hell was I thinking?"

"What do you know about Hell?" Honesty asked.

"Yeah, I have to know Hell before I can understand Paradise. Isn't that what the Ceepee says?"

"You have it backwards, as usual."

"You know why I volunteered, dammit!" The Runaway voice was edged with tears.

"Yes—because he died. Ten years with him and then—poof."

"He died! That's all you have to say about it, 'He died.'"

"What else would there be to say?" Honesty's voice was level, sure.

"You're as bad as the Ceepee, always answering with questions. What'd Jim do to deserve that?"

"He tested for limits and found them when he ran the P."

"But why doesn't Ship or the Ceepee ever talk about it?"

"About death?" Honesty paused. "What's there to talk about? Jim is dead and you're alive, and that's much more important."

"Is it? Sometimes I wonder ... I wonder what's going to happen to me."

"You live until you die."

"But what's going to happen!"

Honesty paused again, uncharacteristically, and said, "You fight to live."

Waela! Waela, wake up!

It was Thomas' voice. She opened her eyes, tipped her head onto the seatback and looked at him. Light glittered from the plaza above him and there was the sound of workmen pounding metal out in the hangar. She noted that Thomas, too, looked tired but was fighting it.

"I was telling you a story about Earth," he said.

"Why?"

"It's important to me. That fourteen-year-old girl had such dreams. Do you still have dreams about your life?"

Her skin began a nervous glow. Does he read minds?

"Dreams?" She closed her eyes and sighed. "What do I need with dreams? I have my work."

"Is that enough?"

"Enough?" she laughed. "That's not my worry. Ship is sending down my prince, remember?"

"Don't blaspheme!"

"I'm not blaspheming, you are. Why do I have to seduce this poor idiot poet when ..."

"We won't argue that again. Leave now. Quit. But no more arguments."

"I'm not a quitter!"

"So I've noticed."

"Why did you pry into my records?"

"I was trying to recapture that girl. If she won't start with dreams, maybe she'll get somewhere with dreamers. I want to tell her what's become of those dreams."

"Well, what's become of them?"

"She still has them; she always will."

Chapter 25

You species of gods. Very well. Avata speaks that language now. Avata says consciousness is the Species-God's gift to the individual. Conscience is the Individual-God's gift to the species. In conscience you find the structure, the form of consciousness, the beauty.

—Kerro Panille, *Translations from the Avata*

HALI FELT no passage of time, but when the echoes of her own voice stopped reverberating in her consciousness, she found she was facing herself. She still sensed the tiny teaching lab which Ship had revealed behind the terminal in Records. And there was her own flesh in that lab. Her body lay stretched out on the yellow couch, and she stared down at it without knowing how she did this. Light filled the lab, splashed from every surface. It startled her how different she appeared from the mirror image she had known all of her life. The slick yellow material of the couch accented her brown skin. She thought the brilliance of the light should be dazzling, but could feel no discomfort. Where her short black hair stopped below her left ear there was a dark mole. Her nose ring caught the light and glittered against her skin. An odd aura surrounded her body.

She wanted to speak and for a panic-seized instant wondered how she could do this. It was as though she struggled to get back into her body. Sudden calm washed her and she heard Ship's voice.

"I am here, Ekel."

"Is that like hybernation?" She had no sensation of speaking, but heard her own voice.

"Far more difficult, Ekel. I show you this because you must remember it."

"I'll remember."

Abruptly, she felt herself tumbling slowly in darkness. And at the front of her awareness was Ship's promise to give her another body for this experience. An old woman's body.

How will that feel?

There was no answer except the tunnel. It was a long, warm tunnel and the most disturbing thing was that it contained no heartbeat, no pulse at all. But there was a glimmer of light at some distance and she could glimpse a hillside beyond the light. Raised shipside, she understood corridors without thinking about them, but when she emerged through the oval whiteness it was a shock to find herself in an unconfined area.

Now, there was a pulsebeat, though. It was in her breast. She put a hand there, felt rough fabric and looked down. The hand was dark, old and wrinkled.

That's not my hand!

She looked around. It was a hillside. She felt the deep vulnerability of her presence here. There was sunlight, a golden glowing which felt good to this body. She looked at her feet, her arms: an old body. And there were other people at a distance.

Ship spoke in her mind: "It will take a moment for you to become acquainted with this body. Do not try to rush it."

Yes—she could feel her awareness creeping outward through halting linkages. Sandals covered her feet; she felt the straps. Rough ground underfoot when she tried two shuffling steps. Fabric swished against her ankles—a coarsely woven sack of a garment. She felt how it abraded her shoulders when she moved; it was the only garment covering her body … no. There was a piece of cloth wound around her hair. She reached up and touched it, turning as she did this to face downhill.

A crowd of several hundred people could be seen down there—perhaps as many as three hundred. She was not sure.

She felt that this body might have been running before she assumed her place in it. Breathing was difficult. A stink of old perspiration assaulted her nostrils.

She could hear the crowd now: a murmurous animal noise. They were moving slowly uphill toward her. The people in it surrounded a man who dragged what appeared to be part of a tree over his shoulder. As he drew nearer, she saw blood on his face, an odd circlet at his brow … it looked like a spiney sweat band. The man appeared to have been beaten; bruises and cuts could be discerned through his shredded gray robe.

While the man still was at some distance from her, she saw him stumble and fall on his face in the dirt. A woman in a faded blue robe hurried to help him up but she was beaten back by two young men who wore crested helmets and stiff upper garments which glittered. There were many such men in the crowd. Two of them were kicking and prodding the fallen man, trying to force him to his feet.

Armor, she thought, recalling her history holos. *They're wearing armor.*

A sense of the great time which stretched between this moment and her shipside life threatened to overwhelm her. *Ship?*

Be calm, Ekel. Be calm.

She forced several deep, painful breaths into the old lungs. The armored men, she saw, wore dark skirts which covered them to the knees … heavy sandals on their feet, metal greaves over their shins. Each had a short sword sheathed at the shoulder with the handle sticking up beside his head. They used long staves to control the crowd … No, she corrected herself. They were using spears, clubbing the crowd back with the butt ends.

The crowd was milling around now, concealing the fallen figure from her. There was a great screaming and crying from them—a conflict which she did not understand.

Some called out: "Let him up! Please let him up!"

Others shouted: "Beat the bastard! Beat him!"

And there was one shrill voice heard above all the others: "Stone him here! He won't make it to the top."

A line of the armored men pushed the crowd back, leaving a tall dark man beside the fallen one. The dark man glanced all around, his fear obvious. He jerked to one side, trying to flee, but two of the armored men cut him off, swinging the butts of their spears at him. He dodged back to the side of the fallen man.

One of the soldiers shook the pointed tip of his spear at the dark one, shouted something which Hali could not make out. But the dark one stooped and picked up the tree, lifting it off the fallen one.

What is happening here?

Observe and do not interfere.

A cluster of women was wailing nearby. As the fallen man climbed to his feet and accompanied the dark one, who now dragged the tree, all moved up the hill toward Hali. She watched them carefully, seeking any clue to tell her what was happening. Obviously, it was something painful. Was it momentous? Why had Ship insisted she witness this scene?

They drew nearer. The beaten man lurched along and, presently, stopped near the wailing women. Hali saw that he was barely able to stand. One of the women slipped through the ring of soldiers and mopped the injured man's bloody face with a gray cloth. He coughed in long, hard spasms, holding his left side and grimacing with each cough.

Hali's med-tech training dominated her awareness. The man was badly injured—broken ribs at least, and perhaps a punctured lung. There was blood at the corner of his mouth. She wanted to run to him, use her sophisticated skills to ease his suffering.

Do not interfere!

Ship's presence was like a palpable thing, a wall between her and the injured man.

Steady, Ekel.

Ship was in her mind.

She gripped her hands into fists, took several deep gasping breaths. This brought the smell of the crowd into focus. It was the most disgusting sensory experience she had ever known. They were rank with an unwashed festering. How could they survive the things which her nostrils reported?

She heard the injured man speak then. His voice was soft and directed at the women who fell silent when he spoke.

"Weep not for me, but for your children."

Hali heard him clearly. Such tenderness in that voice!

One of the armored men struck the injured one in the back with a spear butt then, forcing him to resume that lurching march uphill. They drew nearer. The dark one dragged the section of tree.

What were they doing?

The injured one looked back at the cluster of women who once more were wailing. His voice was strong, much stronger than Hali had thought possible.

"If they do these things in a green tree, what will they do in a dry?"

Turning back, the injured one looked full at Hali. He still clutched his side and she saw the characteristic red froth of a lung puncture at his lips.

Ship! What are they doing to him?

Observe.

The injured one said: "You have traveled far to see this."

Ship intruded on her shock: "He's talking to you, Ekel. You can answer him."

The dust of the crowd welled up around her and she choked on it before being able to speak, then: "How ... how do you know how far I've come?"

It was an old woman's cracked voice she heard issuing from her mouth.

"You are not hidden from me," the injured one said.

One of the soldiers laughed at her then and thrust his spear in her direction. He did it almost playfully. "Get along, old woman. You may've traveled far but I can send you farther."

His companions guffawed at the jest.

Hali recalled Ship's reassurance: No one bothers an old woman. The injured man called out to her: "Let them know it was done!"

Then the angry shouts of the crowd and the swirling, odorous dust engulfed her. She almost choked as they moved past, caught by a coughing spasm which cleared her throat. When she could, she turned to gaze after the crowd and a gasp was forced from her. At the top of the hill beyond the crowd two men were hanging on tree constructions with crosspieces such as that being dragged along with the injured man.

A momentary opening in the crowd gave her another glimpse of the injured one and, turning back toward her, he shouted: "If anyone understands God's will, you must."

Once more, the milling crowd hid him from her.

God's will?

A hand touched her arm and she jerked away in fright, whirling to see a young man in a long brown robe at her side. His breath smelled of sewage. And his voice was an unctuous whine.

"He says you come from afar, mother," the foul-breathed one said. "Do you know him?"

The look in Foul-breath's eyes made her acutely aware of the vulnerable old flesh which housed her consciousness. This was a dangerous man ... very dangerous. The look in his eyes reminded her of Oakes. He could cause great pain.

"You had better answer me," he said, and there was poison in his voice.

Chapter 26

You call Avata "Firefly in the night of the sea." Avata has doubts about such words because Avata sees the landscape of your mind. Avata moves through your landscape with difficulty. It shifts and twists and changes as Avata goes through. But Avata has made such journeys before. Avata is an explorer of such landscapes. Your phantoms are Avata's glides. We are linked in motion.

What is this thing you call "the natural universe?" Is that something taken from your god? Ahhh, you have separated your parts to create the unique. You do not need this separation for your creations. This fluid evasiveness of your landscape is your strength. The patterns … ahhh, the patterns. From yourself come the forces which shape the course of each thought. Why do you confine your thought in a tiny fixed landscape?

You find a distinction between measurement and preparation of your landscape. You continually prepare, saying: "I am going to say something about …" But that limits what you say and it tells your listener to accept your limits. All such measurement and limiting date back to a common system in a simple, linear landscape. Look about you, Human! Where do your senses find such simplicity?

Does a second look at the landscape yield the same view as the first look? Why is your will so inflexible?

A magical affinity between object and likeness, between being and symbol, underlies all symbol systems. It is the assumed foundation of language. The word for thing or object in most languages is related to the word for say or speak and these, in turn, have their roots in magic.

—Kerro Panille, *I Sing to the Avata*

OAKES STOOD in stunned silence, staring at Jesus Lewis standing just inside the Ceepee cubby's hatch. Somewhere, there was a background buzz. Oakes realized he had left the holofocus projecting Agrarium D-9. Yes … it was full dayside out there. He slapped the cut-off.

Lewis moved another step into the cubby. He was breathing heavily. His thin, straw-colored hair was disarrayed. His dark eyes moved left, right—probing the room. It was an eye movement which Oakes identified as characteristic of groundsiders. There was a patch of pseudoflesh over an injury on Lewis' narrow, cleft chin, another over the bridge of his sharp nose. His thin mouth was twisted into a wry smile.

"What happened to you?"

"Clones …" Deep breath. "… revolt."

"The Redoubt?" A sharp twinge of fear shot through Oakes.

"It's all right."

Limping, Lewis crossed the room, sank into a divan. "Is there any of your special joy juice around? Every last drop was lost at the Redoubt."

Oakes hurried to a concealed locker, removed a bottle of raw Pandoran wine, opened it and handed the whole bottle to Lewis.

Lewis upended the wine and took four long swallows without a breath while he stared around the bottle at Oakes. The poor old Ceepee looked to be in bad shape. There were dark circles under his eyes. Tough.

For Oakes, the moment was welcome as a time to recover his wits. He did not mind serving Lewis and the sense of personal concern this conveyed would have a desired effect. Obviously, something very bad had happened at the Redoubt. Oakes waited until Lewis put down the bottle, then: "They revolted?"

"The discards from the Scream Room, the injured and the others we just can't support. Food's getting very short. I put all of them outside."

Oakes nodded. Clones thrown out of the Redoubt were, of course, condemned to death. Quick and efficient disposal by Pandora's demons … unless they had the misfortune to encounter Nerve Runners or a Spinneret. Messy business.

Lewis took another deep swallow of the wine, then: "We didn't realize that the area had become infested with Nerve Runners."

Oakes shuddered. To him, Nerve Runners were the ultimate Pandoran horror. He could imagine the darting, threadlike creatures clinging to his flesh, savaging his nerves, invading his eyes, worming their ravenous way through to his brain. The long agony of such an attack was well known groundside and the stories had made the rounds shipside. Everything Pandoran feared the Runners except, perhaps, the kelp. They seemed immune.

When he could control his voice, Oakes asked: "What happened?"

"The clones raised the usual fuss when we put them outside. They know what it's like out there, of course. I suppose we didn't pay as close attention as we should. Suddenly, they were screaming, 'Nerve Runners!'"

"Your people buttoned down, of course."

"Everything shut up tight while we tried to spot the boil."

"So?"

Lewis stared at the bottle in his hands, took a deep breath.

Oakes waited. Nerve Runners were horrible, yes—it took three or four minutes for them to do what other demons did in a few eyeblinks. Same result, though.

Lewis sighed, took another swallow of the wine. He appeared calmer, as though Oakes' presence told him that he really was safe at last.

"They attacked the Redoubt," Lewis said.

"Nerve Runners?"

"The clones."

"Attacked? But what weapons …"

"Stones, their own bodies. Some of them smashed the sewage baffle before we could stop them. Two clones got inside that way. They were infected by then."

"Nerve Runners in the Redoubt?"

Oakes stared at Lewis in horror. "What did you do?"

"There was a wild scramble. Our mop-up crew, mostly E-clones, locked themselves in the Aquaculture Lab but Runners were in the water lines by then. The lab's a shambles. No survivors there. I sealed myself in a Command room with fifteen aides. We were clean."

"How many did we lose?"

"Most of our effectives."

"Clones?"

"Almost all gone."

Oakes grimaced. "Why didn't you report, ask for help?" He tapped the pellet at his neck.

Lewis shook his head. "I tried. I got static or silence, then someone else trying to talk to me, trying to put pictures in my head."

Pictures in his head!

That was a good description of what Oakes had experienced. Their safe little secret communications channel had been penetrated! Who?

He voiced the question.

Lewis shrugged. "I'm still trying to find out."

Oakes put a hand over his own mouth. *The ship? Yes, the damned ship was interfering!*

He did not dare speak openly of that suspicion. The ship had eyes and ears everywhere. There were other fears, too. A Nerve Runner boil had to be met by fire. He envisioned the Redoubt a mass of cinders inside.

"You say the Redoubt's all right?"

"Clean. Sterilized, and we have a bonus." Lewis took another long swallow of wine and grinned at Oakes, savoring the suspense he read in the Ceepee's face. The Ceepee was so easy to read.

"How?" Oakes did not try to hide his impatience.

"Chlorine and heavily chlorinated water."

"Chlorine? You mean that kills Nerve Runners?"

"I saw it with my own eyes."

"That simple? It's that simple?" Oakes thought of all the years they had lived in terror of these tiniest demons. "Chlorinated water?"

"Heavily chlorinated, undrinkable. But it dissolves the Runners. As a liquid or a gas, it penetrates all the fine places to get every one. The Redoubt stinks, but it's clean."

"You're sure?"

"I'm here." Lewis tapped his chest, took another swallow of wine. Oakes was reacting strangely. It was unsettling. Lewis put down the bottle of wine and thought about the report he had read on the shuttle coming shipside. Legata to the Scream Room! Were there no limits to what the old bastard might do? Lewis hoped not. That was how to control Oakes—through his excesses.

"You are, indeed, here," Oakes agreed. "How did you get … I mean, how did you discover …"

"Those of us in the Facilities Room had all of the controls in front of us. We started dumping whatever we could find to …"

"But chlorine—how did you get chlorine?"

"We were trying salt brine. There was an electrical short, a wide-scale electrolytic reaction in the brine and we had chlorine. I was on the sensors at the time and saw the chlorine kill some Runners."

"You're sure?"

"I saw it with my own eyes. They just shriveled up and died."

Oakes began to see the picture. Colony had never put chlorine and Nerve Runners together. Most shipside caustics had little effect groundside anyway. Potable water was produced with filters and flash heat from laser ovens. That was the cheapest way. Fire worked on Nerve Runners. Colony had always used fire. Another thought occurred to him.

"The survivors … how …"

"Only those locked into a sealed area before the infection spread were saved. We flushed everything else with chlorine gas and heavily chlorinated water."

Oakes imagined the gas killing people and Runners, the caustic water burning flesh … He shook his head to drive out such thoughts.

"You're absolutely sure the Redoubt is safe?"

Lewis stared up at him. *The precious Redoubt! Nothing was more important.*

"I'm going back dayside."

Belatedly, Oakes realized he should show more human concern. "But my dear fellow, you're wounded!"

"Nothing serious. But one of us will have to be at the Redoubt all of the time from now on."

"Why?"

"The cleanup was pretty bloody and that's causing trouble."

"What kind of trouble?"

"The surviving clones, even some of our people … well, you can imagine how I had to clean up the place. There were necessary losses. Some of the surviving clones and a few of the more irrational among our people have …" He shrugged.

"Have what? Explain yourself."

"We've had to handle several petitions from clones and there were even a few of our people who sympathized. I have Murdoch down there standing in for me while I came up to report."

"Clones? Petitions? How are you handling them?"

"The same way I handled the food problem."

Oakes scowled. "And …the sympathizers?"

Again, Lewis shrugged. "When we sterilized the area around the Redoubt, the other demons returned. They're a fast and efficient way to solve our problem."

Oakes touched the scar of the pellet at his neck. "But when … that is, why didn't you send someone up to …"

"We stayed until we were sure we were clean."

"Yes … yes, of course. I see. Brave fellows."

"And can you imagine what would happen if word of this leaks out?"

"You're quite right." Oakes thought about what Lewis had said. As usual, Lewis made the right decisions. Astringent but efficient.

"Now, what's this I hear about Legata?" Lewis asked.

Oakes was outraged. "You have no right to question my …"

"Oh, simmer down. You're going to send her to the Scream Room. I just want to know if we should prepare to replace her."

"Replace … Legata? I think not."

"Let me know in plenty of time if you need a replacement."

Oakes was still angry. "It strikes me, Lewis, that you've been very wasteful of lives."

"You know some other way I could've handled this?"

Oakes shook his head. "I meant no offense."

"I know. But this is why I don't report such things unless you ask or unless I have no choice."

Oakes did not like the tone Lewis took there, but another thought struck him. "One of us has to stay at the Redoubt all the time? What about … I mean, Colony?"

"You're going to have to wind things up here and come groundside to manage Colony. It's our only answer. You can use Legata for shipside liaison, provided she's still useful after the Scream Room."

Oakes thought about this. Go groundside among all of those vicious demons? The periodic demonstration-of-power trips were bad enough … but live there full time?

"That's why I asked about Legata," Lewis said.

Mollified, Oakes ventured a more important question: "How … are … conditions at Colony?"

"Safe enough as long as you stay inside or travel only in a servo or shuttle."

Oakes closed his eyes for a long blink, opened them. Once more, Lewis demonstrated impeccable reasoning. *Who else could they trust as they trusted each other?*

"Yes. I understand."

Oakes glanced around his cubby. No visible sensors, but this had never reassured him. The damned ship always knew what was happening shipside.

I will have to go groundside.

The reasons were compelling. Lewis would take Lab One to the Redoubt, of course. But there were too many other delicate matters in balance at Colony.

Groundside.

He had always known he would have to quit the ship one day. It did not help that circumstances had made the decision for him. The move was being forced and he felt vulnerable. This incident with the Nerve Runners did nothing to reassure him.

What a dilemma!

As he gathered more power and exercised it, shipside became increasingly untrustworthy. But Pandora remained equally dangerous and unknown.

It occurred to Oakes then that he had been hoping for a tranquilized and sterilized planet, a place made ready for him by Lewis, before going groundside.

Sterile. Yes.

Oakes stared at Lewis. Why did the man appear so smug? It was more than survival against odds. Lewis was holding something back.

"What else do you have to report?"

"The new E-clones. They were in an isolated chamber and all survived. They're clean, completely unprogrammed and beautiful. Just beautiful."

Oakes was distrustful. The statistical incidence of deviation among clones was a known factor. The body, after all, was transparent to cosmic bombardments which altered the genetic messages in human cells. Rebuilding the DNA structure was Lewis' specialty, yes, but still …

"No kinks?"

"I used 'lectrokelp cells and went back to recombinant DNA as a foundation for the changes." He rubbed the side of his nose with a forefinger. "We've succeeded."

"You said that last time."

"It worked last time, too. We simply couldn't keep up with the food supply necessary to . . ."

"No freaks?"

"A clean job. All we get is accelerated growth to maturity. And that kelp isn't easy to work with. Lab people hallucinating all over the damn place and aging faster than . . ."

"Are you still able to waste lab technicians on this?"

"They're not wasted!" Lewis was angry, exactly the reaction Oakes had sought.

Oakes smiled reassuringly. "I just want to know that it's working, Jesus, that's all."

"It's working."

"Good. I believe you're the only person who could make it work, but I am the only person who can give you the freedom in which to do this. What is the time frame?"

Lewis blinked at the sudden shift of the question. *Cagey old bastard always kept you off balance.* He took a deep breath, feeling the wine, the remembered sense of protective enclosure which Ship . . . the ship always gave him.

"How long?" Oakes insisted.

"We can continue an E-clone's growth, the aging, actually, and arrive at any age you want. From conception to age fifty in fifty diurns."

"In good condition?"

"Top condition and completely receptive to our programming. They're mewling infants until they become our . . . ah, servants."

"Then we can restore the Redoubt's working force rather rapidly."

"Yes . . . but that's the problem. Most of our people know this and they . . . ahh, saw what I did with the clones and the sympathizers. They're beginning to see that they can be replaced."

"I understand." Oakes nodded. "That's why you have to stay at the Redoubt." He studied Lewis. The man was still worried, still holding something back. "What else, Jesus?"

Lewis spoke too quickly. The answer had been right there in front of his awareness awaiting the question.

"An energy problem. We can work it out."

"You can work it out."

Lewis lowered his gaze. It was the answer he expected. Correct answer, of course. But they had to produce more burst, their own elixir.

"I will give you one suggestion," Oakes said. "Plenty of hard work precludes time for plotting and worry. Now that you've solved the clone problem, put your people to work eliminating the kelp. I want a neat, simple solution. Enzymes, virus, whatever. Tell them to wipe out the kelp."

Chapter 27

An infinite universe presents infinite examples of unreasoned acts, often capricious and threatening, godlike in their mystery. Without god-powers, conscious reasoning cannot explore and make this universe absolutely known; there must remain mysteries beyond what is explained. The only reason in this universe is that which you, in your ungodlike hubris, project onto the universe. In this, you retain kinship with your most primitive ancestors.

—Raja Thomas, *Shiprecords*

AS SHE stood frozen in terror of the foul-breathed stranger, Hali tried to think of a safe response. The terrible differences of this place where Ship had projected her compounded her sense of helplessness. The dust of the throng which followed the beaten man, the malignant odors, the passions in the voices, the milling movements against a single sun …

"Do you know him?" The man was insistent.

Hali wanted to say she had never before seen the injured man but something told her this could not be true. There had been something disquietingly familiar about that man.

Why did he speak to me of God and knowing?

Could that have been another Shipman projected here? Why had the wounded man seemed so familiar? And why had he addressed her directly?

"You can tell me." Foul-breath was slyly persistent.

"I came a long way to see him." The old voice which Ship had provided her sounded groveling, but the words were true. She felt it in these old bones she had borrowed. Ship would not lie to her and Ship had said this. A very great distance. Whatever this event signified, Ship had brought her expressly to see it.

"I don't place your accent," Foul-breath said. "Are you from Sidon?"

She moved after the crowd and spoke distractedly to the inquisitor who kept pace with her. "I come from Ship."

What were those people doing with the wounded man?

"Ship? I've never heard of that place. Is it part of the Roman March?"

"Ship is far away. Far away."

What were they doing up on that hill? Some of the soldiers had taken the piece of tree and stretched it on the ground. She glimpsed the activity through the crowd.

"Then how can Yaisuah say that you know God's will?" Foul-breath demanded.

This caught her attention. *Yaisuah?* Ship had said that name. It was the name Ship said had become Geezus and then Hesoos. *Jesus.* She hesitated, stared at her inquisitor.

"You call that one Yaisuah?" she asked.

"You know him by some other name?"

He gripped her arm hard. There was no mistaking the avaricious cunning in his voice and manner.

Ship intruded on her then. *This one is a Roman spy, an informer who works for those who torture Yaisuah.*

"Do you know him?" Foul-breath demanded. He gave her arm a painful shake.

"I think this … Yaisuah is related to Ship," she said.

"Related to … How can someone be related to a place?"

"Isn't he related to You, Ship?" She spoke the question aloud without thinking.

Yes.

"Ship says that's true," she said.

Foul-breath dropped her arm and stepped back two paces. An angry scowl twisted his mouth.

"Crazy! You're nothing but a crazy old woman! You're just as crazy as that one!" He gestured up the hill where the armored men had taken Yaisuah. "See what happens to crazies?"

She looked where he had pointed.

The two men already hanging there were roped to the cross-pieces and she realized they were being left to die. *That was going to happen to Yaisuah!*

As the full realization hit her, Hali began to weep.

Ship spoke within her mind: *Tears do little to improve acuity. You must observe.*

She wiped her eyes on a corner of her robe, observing that Foul-breath had moved up into the crowd. She forced herself to climb up with him, pressing in among the people.

I must observe!

The armored ones were stripping the robe from Yaisuah. This exposed his wounds—cuts and bruises all over his body. He stood with a stolid watchfulness through all this, not even responding to the gasp which went up when the mob saw his wounds. There was an unguarded vulnerability to this moment, as though everyone here was participating in his own personal death.

Someone off to the left shouted: "He's a carpenter! Don't tie him on!"

Several large, crudely wrought nails were pressed up through that part of the crowd and thrust into the hands of an armored young man.

Others took up the cry: "Nail him on! Nail him on!"

Two of the armored men supported Yaisuah on either side now. His head swayed slightly from side to side, then bowed. Things were being thrown at him from the far side of the crowd but he made no attempt to dodge. Hali saw stones strike him … an occasional glob of spittle.

It was all so … so bizarre, played in an orange glow of mute sunlight coming through a high layer of thin clouds.

Hali blinked the tears from her eyes. Ship said she had to observe this! Very well … She estimated that she stood no more than six meters from Yaisuah's left shoulder. He appeared to be a wiry man, probably active through most of his adult life, but now he was near the point of exhaustion. Her med-tech training told her that Yaisuah could survive this, given proper care, but she had the impression that he did not want such care, that none of this surprised him. If anything, he seemed anxious to get on with it. Perhaps that was the reaction of a tortured animal, cornered and beyond all will to fight or flee.

As she watched, he lifted his head slowly and turned to face her. She saw then the slight glow about him, an aura such as she had seen around her own body when Ship had projected her away from …

Is he also a projection of Ship?

She saw that there was a debate going on among the armored men. The nails were being waved in front of one of them by the one who had taken them from the crowd at the far side.

Yaisuah was looking at her, compelling her attention. She saw recognition in his eyes, the lift of eyebrows … a suggestion of surprise.

Ship intruded: *Yaisuah knows where you are from.*

Are You projecting him?

That flesh lives here as flesh, Ship said. *But there is something more.*

Something more … That's why You brought me here.

What is it, Ekel? What is it?

There was no mistaking the eagerness in Ship.

He has another body somewhere?

No, Ekel. No!

She cringed before Ship's disappointment, forcing herself to a peak of alertness which her fears demanded.

Something more … something more … She saw something then, a significance of the aura. *Time does not confine him.*

That is very close, Ekel. Ship was pleased and this reassured her, but it did not remove the pressure from the moment.

There is something of him which Time cannot hold, she thought. *Death will not release him!*

You please Me, Ekel.

Joy washed through her to be cut off abruptly by Ship's demanding intrusion: *Now! Watch this!*

The armored men had settled their argument. Two of them threw Yaisuah to the ground, stretching his arms along the timber.

Another took the nails and using a rock for a hammer began nailing Yaisuah's wrists to the wood.

Someone shouted from the crowd: "If you're the son of God, let's see you get yourself out of this!"

Hali heard jeering laughter all around her. She had to clasp her hands across her breast, forcing herself not to rush forward. This was barbarous! She trembled with frustration.

We are all children of Ship!

She wanted to shout this to these fools. It was the lesson of her earliest WorShip classes, the admonition of the Chaplain.

Two soldiers lifted the length of wood, hoisting the man who was nailed to it by his wrists. He gasped as they moved him. Four soldiers, two on each side of him, lifted the timber on their spear points into a notch on a tall post which stood upright between the other two victims. Another soldier scrambled up a crude ladder behind the post and lashed the crosspiece into the notch. Two more soldiers moved up to Yaisuah's dangling feet. While one soldier crossed the ankles, the other nailed the feet to the upright. Blood ran down the wood from the wound.

She had to open her mouth wide and breathe in gulping gasps to keep from fainting.

She saw the brown eyes flash with sudden agony as a soldier shook the upright to test its firmness. Yaisuah slumped forward unconscious.

Why are they causing him such pain? What do they want him to do?

Hali pressed forward in the suddenly silent throng, elbowing her way through with a strength which she found surprising in this old body. She had to see it close. She had to see. Ship had commanded her to observe. It was difficult moving in the press of people even with the strength of her inner drive. And she suddenly became aware of the breath-held silence in the throng.

Why were they so silent?

It was as though the answer had been flashed on her eyes. *They want Yaisuah to stop this by some secret power in him. They want a miracle! They still want a miracle from him. They want Ship … God to reach out of the sky and stop this brutal travesty. They do this thing and they want a god to stop it.*

She pressed herself past two more people and found that she had achieved the inner ring of the crowd. There were only the three timber constructions now, the three bodies …

I could still save him, she thought.

Chapter 28

I play the song to which you must dance. To you is left the freedom of improvisation. This improvisation is what you call free will.
—The Oakes Covenant

THE MEETING will please come to order."

Oakes used his wand-amplifier to dominate the shuffling and buzzing in the Colony's central meeting hall. It was a domed and circular room truncated by a narrow platform against the south wall where he stood. When not being used for meetings, the room was taken over by manufacture of food-production equipment and the sub-assembly operations for the buoyant bags of the LTAs. Because of this, all meetings had to be called at least ten hours in advance to give workers time to clear away machines and fabrics.

He still felt beset by the tensions of moving from shipside to groundside. His time sense was upset by the diurnal shift and this meeting had been rushed. It was almost the hour of mid-meal here. There would be psychological pressures from the audience because of that.

This was the wrong hour for a meeting and there had been some muttering about interference with important work, but Murdoch had silenced that by leaking the announcement that Oakes had come groundside to stay. The implications were obvious. A major push was impending to make Colony secure; Oakes would command that push.

On the platform with Oakes stood Murdoch and Rachel Demarest. Murdoch's position as director of Lab One was well known, and the mystery surrounding that lab's purposes made his presence here a matter of intense curiosity.

Rachel Demarest was another matter. Oakes scowled when he thought about her. She had learned things while acting as a messenger between Ferry and groundside.

Sounds in the room were beginning to subside as the stragglers made their way in and took seats. Portable chairs had been provided, many constructed from the twisted Pandoran plant material. The unique appearance of each chair offended Oakes. Something would have to be done to standardize appearances here.

He scanned the room, noting that Raja Thomas was present in a seat down front. The woman beside Thomas fitted the description Murdoch had provided of one Waela TaoLini, a survivor of the original kelp-research projects. Her knowledge might be dangerous. Well … she and the poet would share Thomas' fate. End of that problem!

Oakes had been groundside for almost two diurns now and much of that time had been taken up in preparation for this meeting. There had been many eyes-only reports from Lewis and his minions. Murdoch had been quite useful in this. He would bear watching. Legata had provided some of the data and, even now, was back shipside gathering more.

This meeting represented a serious challenge to his powers, Oakes knew, and he intended to meet it head on. Lewis had estimated that about a thousand people were here. The larger part of Colony personnel could never be spared from guard and maintenance and building and rebuilding. Two steps forward, one step back—that was Pandora's way. Oakes was aware, though, that most of those facing him down on that floor carried the proxy votes of associates. There had been an unofficial election and this would be a real attempt at democracy. He recognized the dangers. Democracy had never been the shipside way and it could not be allowed groundside. It was a sobering thought and he felt adrenaline overcoming an earlier indulgence in wine.

The people were taking a devilish long time to get settled, moving about, forming groups. Oakes waited with what show of patience he could muster. There was a dank, metallic smell in the room which he did not like. And the lights had been tuned too far into the green. He glanced back at the Demarest woman. She was a slight figure with unremarkable features and dull brown hair. She was notable only for her intensely nervous mannerisms. Demarest had been the instigator of the election—a petition-bearer. Oakes managed a smile when he looked at her. Lewis had said he knew how to defuse her. Knowing Lewis, Oakes did not probe for details.

Presently, Rachel Demarest came forward on the platform. Leaving her wand-amplifier on its clip at her wrist, she raised both arms, twisting her palms rapidly. It was interesting that the room fell silent immediately.

Why didn't she use her amplifier? Oakes wondered. *Was she an anti-tech?*

"Thank you all for coming," she said. Her voice was high and squeaky with a whine at the edge. "We won't take much of your time. Our Ceepee has a copy of your petition and has agreed to answer it point by point."

Your petition! Oakes thought. *Not my petition. Oh, no.*

But evidence from Lewis and Murdoch was clear. This woman wanted a share in Colony power. And she had managed most cleverly to say *Ceepee* with an emphasis which made the title appear foolish. Battle, therefore, was joined.

As Demarest stepped back, glancing at him, Oakes produced the petition from an inner pocket of his white singlesuit. Making it appear accidental, he dropped the petition. Several pages fluttered off the platform.

"No matter." He waved back people in the front row as they moved to recover the pages. "I remember everything in it."

A glance at Murdoch brought him a reassuring nod. Murdoch had found chairs for himself and Demarest. They sat well back on the platform now.

Oakes hunched forward toward his audience in a gesture of confidence, smiling. "Few of our people are here this morning and you all know the very good reasons for this. Pandora is unforgiving. We all lost loved ones in the four failures on Black Dragon."

He gestured vaguely westward where the rocky eminences of Black Dragon lay hidden beyond the mists of more than a thousand kilometers of ocean. Oakes knew that none of those failures could be laid at his hatch; he had been very careful about that. And his presence permanently groundside imparted a feeling of excitement about Colony prospects here on the undulating plains of The Egg. That sense of impending success had contributed to the confrontation brewing in this room. Colonists were beginning to think beyond the present state of siege, rubbing their wishes together, shaping their desires for personal futures.

"As most of you know." Oakes said, lifting his amplifier to make his voice carry, "I am groundside to stay, groundside to direct the final push for victory."

There was a polite spatter of applause, much less than he had expected. It was high time he came groundside! He had loyalties to weld, organization to improve.

"The Demarest petition, then," he said. "Point One: elimination of one-man patrols." He shook his head. "I wish it could be done. Perhaps you don't understand the reason for them. I'll put it plainly. We are conditioning the animals of Pandora to run like hell when they see a human!"

That brought a rewarding burst of applause.

Oakes waited for it to subside, then: "Your children will have a safer world because of your bravery. Yes, I said your children. It is my intent to bring the Natali groundside."

Shocked murmurs greeted this announcement.

"This will not happen immediately," Oakes said, "but it will happen. Now—Point Two of the Demarest petition." He pursed his lips in recollection. " 'No major decision about Colony risks or expansion shall be made without approval by a clear majority of Colonists voting in Council. Do I have that right, Rachel?" He glanced back at her but did not wait for her to respond.

Glancing once more at the scattered papers of the petition on the floor below him, he looked hard at the front row and swept his gaze across the audience.

"Putting aside for the moment the vagueness in that word 'clear' and this unexplained concept of 'Council,' let me point out one thing we all know. It took ten hours to clear this room for a meeting. We have a choice. We keep this hall clear and ready at all times, thereby putting a dangerous strain on production facilities, or we accept a ten-hour delay for every major decision. I prefer to call those survival decisions, by the way." He made a show of looking back at the large wall chrono, then returned his attention to the audience. "We've already been here more than fifteen minutes and obviously we will use more time on this."

Oakes cleared his throat, giving them a moment in which to absorb what he had said. He noted a few squirmers in the audience sending signals that they would like to comment on this argument, and he had not missed the fact that Murdoch had taken Rachel Demarest's arm, whispering in her ear and, incidentally, keeping her from interrupting.

"Point Three," Oakes said. "More rest and recuperation back on the ship. If we …"

"Ship!" Someone in the middle rows shouted. Oakes identified the speaker, a guard on the hangar perimeter squad, one of Demarest's supporters. "Not the ship, but Ship!" The man, half out of his seat, was pulled back by a companion.

"Let's face that then," Oakes said. "I presume that a Chaplain/Psychiatrist has a modicum of expertise with which to address this question?"

He glanced at Rachel Demarest who still was being held quietly but firmly by Murdoch. You want to use titles? Very well, let us put this title into its proper perspective. Not Ceepee, but Chaplain/Psychiatrist. All the traditions of THE ship stand behind me.

"I will spell it out for you," Oakes said, turning once more to the audience. "We are a mixed bag of people. Most of us appear to have come from Earth where I was born. We were removed by the ship …"

"Ship saved you!" That damned guard would not stay silent. "Ship saved you! Our sun was going nova!"

"So the ship says!"

Oakes gave it a bit more volume by a touch on his wand's controls. "The facts are open to other interpretation."

"The facts …"

"What have we experienced?" Oakes drowned him out and then reduced the volume. "What have we experienced?" Lower volume still. "We found ourselves on the ship with other people whose origins are not clear, not clear at all. Some clones, some naturals. The ship taught us its language and controlled our history lessons. We learn what the ship wants us to learn. And what are the ship's motives?"

"Blasphemy!"

Oakes waited for the stir of this outcry to subside, then: "The ship also trained me as a doctor and a scientist. I depend on facts I can test for myself. What do I know about Shipmen? We can interbreed. In fact, this whole thing could be a genetic …"

"I know my origins and so does everyone else!" It was Rachel Demarest breaking away from Murdoch and leaping to her feet. She still was not using her wand, but she fumbled with it as she moved toward Oakes. "I'm a clone, but I'm from …"

"So the ship says!"

Again, Oakes hurled that challenge at them. Now, if Lewis and Murdoch had read the Colonists correctly, suspicions had been placed like barbs where they would do the most good when the vote was called.

"So the ship says," Oakes repeated. "I do not doubt your sincerity; I merely am aghast at your credulity."

She was angered by this and, still fumbling with her wand, failed to give herself enough amplification when she said: "That's just your interpretation." Her voice was lost on all but the first rows.

Oakes addressed the audience in his most reasonable manner: "She thinks that's just my interpretation. But I would be failing you as your Chaplain/Psychiatrist if I did not warn you that it is an interpretation you must consider. What do we know? Are we merely some cosmic experiment in genetics? We know only that the ship …" He gestured upward with his left thumb. "… brought us here and will not leave. We are told we must colonize this planet which the ship calls Pandora. You know the legend of Pandora because it's in the ship's educational records, but what do you know about this planet? You can at least suspect that the name is very appropriate!"

He let them absorb this for several blinks, knowing that many among them shared his suspicions.

"Four times we failed to plant a Colony over on Black Dragon!" he shouted. "Four times!"

Let them think about their lost loved ones.

He glanced at Rachel Demarest, who stood three paces to his left, staring at him aghast.

"Why this planet and not a better one?" Oakes demanded. "Look at Pandora! Only two land masses: this dirt under us which the ship calls The Egg, and that other one over there which killed our loved ones—Black Dragon! And what else has the ship given us? The rest of Pandora? What's that? A few islands too small and too dangerous for the risking. And an ocean which harbors the most dangerous life form on the planet. Should we give thanks for this? Should we …"

"You promised to take up the entire petition!"

It was Rachel Demarest again and this time with her amplifier turned up too far. The intrusion shocked the audience and there were clear signs that many found the shock offensive.

"I will take it up, Rachel." Very soft and reasonable. "Your petition was a needed and useful instrument. I agree that we should have better procedures for work assignments. Calling this deficiency to my attention strengthens us. Anything which strengthens us meets my immediate approval. I thank you for it."

She got her wand under control.

"You imply that the 'lectrokelp is the most dangerous …"

"Rachel, I already have started a project which will try to determine if there is something useful to us about the kelp. The director of that project and one of his assistants are sitting right down there."

Oakes pointed down at Thomas and Waela, saw heads turned, people craning to see.

"Despite the dangers," he said, "very potent and obvious dangers, as anyone will agree who has studied the data from these oceans, I have started this project. Your petition comes after the fact."

"Then why couldn't we have learned this when …"

"You want more open communication from those of us making the decisions?"

"We want to know whether we're succeeding or failing!" Again, she had her amplifier turned too high.

"Reasonable," Oakes said. "That is one of the reasons I have moved myself and my staff permanently groundside. In my head …" He tapped his skull. "… is the complete plan to make Pandora into a garden planet for …"

"We should have Council members on …"

"Rachel! You propose having your people at key positions? Why your people? What record of success do they have?"

"They've survived down here!"

Oakes fought to conceal anger. That had been a low blow. She implied that he had remained safely ensconced shipside while she and her friends risked Pandora's perils. A reasonable tone was the only way to meet that challenge.

"I'm down here now," he said. "I intend to stay. I will submit to your questions at any mutually acceptable time, despite the fact which we all know—time taken to debate our problems could be used to better advantage for Colony as a whole."

"Will you answer our questions today?"

"That's why I called this meeting."

"Then what's your objection to having an elected Council which …"

"Debating time, just that. We don't have the time for such a luxury. I agreed with those who objected that this meeting took us away from more important work, from food. But you insisted, Rachel."

"What're you doing over on Black Dragon?" That was the objectionable perimeter guard down in the audience, taking a new tack now.

"We are attempting to build another foothold for Colony over on Dragon."

Reasonable … reasonable, he reminded himself. *Keep your voice reasonable.*

"Dividing your energies?" Rachel Demarest demanded.

"We are using new clones provided by the ship's facilities," he said. "Jesus Lewis is out there now directing the effort. I assure you that we are risking only new clones who fully understand the nature of their involvement."

Oakes smiled at Rachel Demarest, recalling Murdoch's jocular admonition: "A few lies don't hurt when you've given them some truth to admire."

Turning back to face the audience, Oakes said: "But this diverts us from the orderly resolution of our meeting. Rather than waste our time this way, we should take the issues one at a time."

His announcement about the attempt at Dragon had served its purpose, though. His listeners (even Rachel Demarest) were absorbing the implications with varying degrees of shock.

Someone away in the right rear quadrant of the room shouted: "What do you mean new clones?"

Silence followed his demand, a waiting silence which said it spoke a question in the minds of most.

"I'll let Jesus Lewis speak to that at another meeting. It's a technical question about matters which have been under his direct supervision. For now, I can say that the new clones are being bred and conditioned to defeat the perils we all know exist out on Dragon."

There: Lewis was prepared with subtle lies and half truths. The injection of rumors and key elements of their prepared story into Colony's grapevine would tie this issue down. Most people would accept the prepared story. It was always better to know that someone else was going into danger, sparing you that necessity.

"You didn't answer our question about rest and recuperation," Rachel Demarest accused.

"You may not realize it, Rachel, but the schedule of shipside R & R is the most important issue before us today."

"You're not going to buy us off with shipside time!" she said. She was clenching her wand with both hands, pointing it at him like a weapon.

"Again, I am aghast at your limited perception," Oakes said. "You really are not fit to be making the decisions which you ask the power to make."

At this direct attack, she backed two steps away from him, glared into his eyes.

Oakes shook his head sadly. "You have a friend down there brave enough to state the essential problem ..." Oakes pointed down at the perimeter guard who sat in red-faced anger. (Have to watch that one. A fanatic for sure.) "... but not brave enough nor perceptive enough to see the full implications of his emotional outburst."

That did it. The man was on his feet and shaking a fist at Oakes. "You're a false Chaplain! If we follow you, Ship will destroy us!"

"Oh, sit down!"

Oakes used almost the full amplification to drown out the man's voice. The sound-shock provided the man's companions with the interval to pull him back into his seat.

Turning down the amplifier, Oakes asked: "Who among you asks what I ask? An obvious question: Where did WorShip originate? With the ship. That ship!"

He thrust a pointing finger ceilingward. "You all know this. But you don't question it. As a scientist, I must ask the hard physical questions. Some among you argue that the ship has been motivated by the wish to save us—a beneficent savior. Some of you say WorShip is a natural response to our savior. Natural response? But what if we are guinea pigs?"

"What are your origins, Oakes?"

That was Rachel Demarest again. *Beautiful.* She could not have performed better for him had she been programmed. Didn't she know that by the best guess, the naturals outnumbered the clones almost four to one?—perhaps even more. And she already had admitted to being a clone.

"I was a child of Earth," Oakes said, and once more his voice was its most reasonable. He looked directly at her, then back at the audience. A little barbering of the truth was called for now. No need to bring up the fact that old Edmond Kingston had chosen him as successor. "Most of you know my history. I was taken by the ship and trained as Chaplain/Psychiatrist. Don't you understand what that means? The ship directed my training to lead WorShip! Don't any of you find something strange in this?"

Right on cue, Rachel intruded: "That seems the most natural ..."

"Natural?" Oakes allowed free reign to his rage. "A mirror and recorder would have done just as good a job as such a Chaplain! If we have no free will, our WorShip is sham! How can the ship expect to condition me for such a task? No! I question what that ship tells us. I don't even doubt. I question! And I don't like some of the answers."

This was public blasphemy on a scale few of them had ever imagined. Coming from the Chaplain/Psychiatrist it amounted to an open revolt. Oakes allowed the shock to become well seated in them before hammering it home. He raised his face to the domed ceiling and shouted: "Why don't you strike me dead, Ship?"

The hall became one long-held breath while Oakes turned and smiled at Murdoch, then turned the smile on his audience. He reduced the amplifier volume to the minimum required for reaching the hall's extremities.

"I obey the ship because the ship is powerful. We are told to colonize this planet? Very well. That is what we are doing and we are going to succeed. But who can doubt that the ship is dangerous to us? Have you had enough food lately? Why is the ship reducing our food supplies? I am not doing this. Send a deputation shipside if you wish to verify this." He shook his head from side to side. "No. Our survival requires that we depend as little as possible upon the ship, and ... eventually, no dependence upon the ship at all. Buy you with shipside time, Rachel? Hell no! I intend to save you by freeing you from the ship!"

It was a simple matter to read the majority reaction to this challenge. He might appear to be a fat little man but he was braver than any of them, dared more than the bravest among them ... and he was risking new clones (whatever they might be). He was also going to feed them. When it came time for the question: "Put me out of office or continue me. But no more of this democracy and Council crap." When it came time for that, it was clear they would support him by acclamation. He was their brave leader, even against Ship, and few could doubt it now.

Both Lewis and Murdoch argued for a bit more insurance, though, and Oakes knew it would do no harm to follow their script.

"It has been suggested that we introduce complicated and time-consuming forms into our survival efforts," Oakes said, his voice tired. "The ones who propose this may be sincere but they are dangerous. Slow reactions will kill us all. We are required to act more swiftly than the deadly creatures around us. We cannot wait for debate and group decisions."

As both Lewis and Murdoch had insisted she would do when faced with defeat, Rachel Demarest tried the personal attack. "What makes you think your decisions will save us?"

"We are alive and Colony prospers," Oakes said. "My first effort here, my primary reason for being here, is to direct a crash program to increase food production."

"No one else could do what ..."

"But I will!" He allowed just a touch of mild reproof into his tone. Anyone who could defy Ship could certainly solve the food problem. "We all know that I did not make those decisions which killed our loved ones on Dragon. If I had been making those decisions, we might still be alive and growing out there."

"What decisions? You talk about ..."

"I would not have wasted our energy trying to understand life forms which were killing us! Simple sterilization of the area was indicated and Edmond Kingston could not bring himself to order it. He paid for that failure with his life ... but so did many innocents."

She still wanted her reasonable confrontation.

"How can you fight what you don't understand?"

"You kill it," Oakes said, facing her and lowering the amplification. "It's that simple: You kill it."

Chapter 29

There is fear in the infinite, in the unlimited chaos of the unstructured. But this boundless "place" is the never-ending resource of that which you call talent, that ability which peels away the fear, exposing its structure and form, creating beauty. This is why the talented people among you are feared. And it is wise to fear the unknown, but only until you see the new-found fearlessness which identity beautifies.

—Kerro Panille, *Translations from the Avata*

FOR A concentrated surge of time, Hali Ekel stood at the inner ring of the throng and stared up at the three men so cruelly suspended. It was a nightmare scene—the blood, the dust, the orange light which threw grotesque shadows on the doomed men, the sense of latent violence in every movement around her.

I'm an observer, observer, observer ...

Her chest hurt when she breathed and she could smell the blood dripping from Yaisuah's nailed feet.

I could save him. She took one shuffling half-step forward.

Don't interfere. Ship's command stopped her. It was not in her to disobey that command. The conditioning of WorShip was too strong.

But he'll die there and he's just like me!

He is not just like you.

But he's ...

No, Ekel. When the time comes, he will remember who he is and he will go back just as you will go back. But you two are profoundly different.

Who is he?

He is Yaisuah, the man who speaks to God.

But he ... I mean, why are they doing this to him? What did he do?

He reported his conversations. Now, they try to move God in this way. Observe. This is not the way.

God? But God is Ship and Ship is God.

And the infinite is infinite.

Why won't you let me save him ?

You could not save him.

I could try.

You would only inflict pain on that old flesh which you have borrowed. That flesh has enough pains. Why would you want to make it suffer more?

It occurred to her then that there might be another consciousness waiting somewhere to re-enter this body. Borrowed. She had not thought of it that way. The idea made her intensely aware of responsibility toward the body. She forced her attention away from the dangling figure of Yaisuah—those bleeding feet and palms.

The other two men began struggling against their restraints. Hali saw the cruel reason behind this torture then. In time, they would smother. Their chest muscles would fail and respiration would stop. The roped men pushed their feet against the wooden uprights, trying for leverage, seeking another few blinks of life.

One of the armored men saw this and laughed. "Look at the thieves squirm!"

Someone in the crowd behind Hali jeered: "They're trying to steal a little more time!"

One of the roped men looked down at his armored tormentor and groaned: "You'd hang your own mother." He gasped for another breath, and Hali saw the effort of it in his chest muscles. As he exhaled, he moved his head feebly toward Yaisuah. "This man here did nothing illegal …"

The armored man swung his spear butt and smashed the speaker's knees. The thief sagged and writhed in a final rattling agony. As he did this, Yaisuah stirred and turned toward him.

"Today, you go home with me," Yaisuah said.

It was said in a low tone, but most of the crowd heard him. The words were repeated for some few on the outskirts who had missed it.

The armored man laughed, said: "Bullshit!" He swung his spear butt once more and broke the other thief's knees. This man, too, collapsed in a spasm of choking gasps.

Yaisuah lifted his head, then called out: "I'm thirsty."

The spear-swinger looked up at him. "The poor boy's thirsty! We should give him something nice to drink."

Hali wanted to turn away, but could not move. What had made these men into such beasts? She searched around her for something in which to give the dying man a drink.

Once more, Ship warned her: *Let this happen, Ekel! This is a necessary lesson. These people must learn how to live.*

Some of the crowd began to leave. The show was over. Hali found herself alone on one side of the dying man, only a few women across from her … and the armored guardians of this torment. A young boy came running up with a jug which he handed to the armored man who had smashed the knees of the thieves. Hali saw a coin passed to the boy. He bit it and turned away, not even looking at the condemned men.

The armored man fastened a rag to the end of his spear, poured some of the jug's contents on it and pushed the rag up to the dying man's mouth.

Hali detected the odor of acetic acid. *Vinegar!*

But Yaisuah sucked at the rag hungrily. The moisture spread across his cracked and bloody mouth. As the rag was pulled away, he slumped forward, once more unconscious.

An older man across from Hali called out: "He'd better die before sundown. We can't leave him up there for the Sabbath."

"Easily done." The armored man had taken the rag from his spear. He turned, ready to swing it against Yaisuah's knees. In that instant, the light faded, darkness spread over the landscape. A moan spread through the crowd. Hali glanced up, saw a partial eclipse behind the clouds.

A young woman broke from the crowd opposite Hali and grabbed the soldier's spear.

"Don't!" she cried. "Let him be. He's nearly gone."

"What's it worth to you?"

The young woman looked up at Yaisuah, who took this moment to twist in delirium. She looked back at the spearman. Her back was to her companions and she faced only Hali as she lifted the spearman's hand and placed it on her breast inside her robe. At that instant, Yaisuah arched his back against the wooden upright and called out: "Father! Father, why have you forsaken me?"

A great breath shuddered through him. His eyes opened, his gaze directly on Hali.

"It is finished," he said. He fell forward, eyes still open, and did not take another breath.

The abrupt hush was shattered by the wailing of a woman in the group across from Hali. Others joined in, tearing at their garments. The armored man took his hand away from the young woman's breast.

Hali stood fixed in place, staring up at the dead man. As she looked, the sunlight returned. A wind picked up the hem of her robe; it chilled her. She could see the armored men moving off, one of them with an arm around the shoulder of the young woman who had stopped the spear blow. Hali turned away and headed down the hill, unable to watch more. She spoke to Ship as she moved.

Ship?

Yes, Ekel?

Is there a history of this event in the shipside records?

It is there for the asking. You who were raised shipside have not had much reason to ask, especially those of you whose ancestors came from places where this was not common knowledge.

Is this real, him dying there just now?

As real as your flesh waiting shipside.

She felt the tug of that remembered flesh then. This tired old body was such a poor vehicle by comparison. She felt joints aching as she stumbled down the hillside.

I want to go back, Ship.

Not yet.

If Yaisuah was a projection, why didn't his body disintegrate when he died?

Active imagination supports him. It is essential to such phenomena. If I were to forget about the you that is shipside or the you that is here, the forgotten flesh would disappear.

But he's dead. What good is it to keep his flesh intact?

The survivors require something to bury. They will return to his tomb one day and find it empty. It will be a marvel. They will say he returned to life and walked from his tomb.

Will he do that?

That is not part of your lesson, Ekel.

If this is a lesson, I want to know what happens to him!

Ahhhh, Ekel, you want so much!

Won't You tell me?

I will tell you this: Those who remember him travel this world over teaching peace and love. For this they suffer murder and torture and they incite great wars in his name, many bloody events even worse than what you have just seen.

She stopped. There were rude buildings just ahead and she felt that she would be more protected in among them. They were more like … corridors, like Ship's own passages. But she was filled with outrage. *What kind of a lesson is this? What good is it?*

Ekel, your kind cannot learn peace until you are drenched in violence. You have to disgust yourselves beyond all anger and fear until you learn that neither extortion nor exhortation moves a god. Then you need something to which you can cling. All this takes a long time. It is a difficult lesson.

Why?

Partly because of your doubts.

Is that why You brought me here? To settle my doubts?

There was no response and she felt suddenly bereft, as though Ship had abandoned her. Would Ship do that?

Ship?

What do you hear, Ekel?

She bent her head, listening. Hurried footsteps. She turned. A group of people rushed past her down the hillside. A young man hurried behind this group. He stopped beside Hali.

"You stayed the whole time and did not curse him. Did you love him, too?"

She nodded. The young man's voice was rich and compelling. He took her hand.

"I am called John. Will you pray with me in this hour of our sadness?"

She nodded and touched her lips pretending that she could not speak.

"Oh, dear woman. If he had but said the word, your affliction would have passed from you. He was a great man. They mocked him as the son of God, but all he claimed was a kinship to Man. 'The Son of Man,'" he said. That is the difference between gods and men—gods do not murder their children. They do not exterminate themselves."

She sensed then in this young man's manner and his voice the power of that event on the hillside. It frightened her, but she realized that this encounter was an important part of what Ship wanted her to experience.

Some things break free of Time, she thought.

You can come back to your own flesh now, Ekel, Ship said.

Wait!

John was praying, his eyes closed, his grip firm on her hand. She felt it was vital to hear his words.

"Lord," he said, "we are gathered here in your name. One in the foolishness of youth and the other infirm with age, we ask that you remember us as we remember you. As long as there are eyes to read and ears to hear, you will not be forgotten. . . .”

She listened to the earnestness of the prayer as it unraveled from his mind. The firm touch of his hand pleased her. There were faint veins on his eyelids which trembled as he spoke. She did not even mind the universal stink which came from him as it came from all of those she had encountered here. He was dark, like Kerro, but he had wild, wiry hair that framed his smooth face and accented his intensity.

I could love this man!

Careful, Ekel.

Ship’s warning amused her as much as her own thought had surprised her. But one look at the old, liver-spotted hand that John held reminded her she walked in another time. This was an old woman’s body which enclosed her awareness.

“. . . we ask this in Yaisuah’s name,” John concluded. He released her hand, patted her shoulder. “It would not be good for you to be seen with us.”

She nodded,

“Soon we will meet again,” he said, “at this house or that, and we will talk more of the Master and the home to which he has returned.”

She thanked him with her eyes and watched him until he turned a corner and was gone among the houses below her.

I want to go home, Ship.

There came a moment of blankness and, once more, the tunnel passage, then the lab’s dazzling lights pained her eyes after the Earthside dusk.

But those other eyes weren’t the same as these eyes!

She sat up, feeling the vital agility of this familiar flesh. It reassured her that Ship had kept the promise to return her to her own body.

Ship?

Ask, Ekel.

You said I would learn about interfering with Time. Did I interfere?

I interfered, Ekel. Do you understand the consequences?

She thought about John’s voice in prayer, the power in him—the terrible power which Yaisuah’s death had released. It was unleashed power, capable of joy or agony. The sense of that power terrified her. Ship interfered and this power resulted. What good was such power?

What is your choice, Ekel?

Joy or agony—the choice is mine?

What choice, Ekel?

How do I choose?

By choosing, by learning.

I do not want that power!

But now you have it.

Why?

Because you asked.

I didn’t know.

That is often the case when you ask.

I want joy but I don’t know how to choose!

You will learn.

She swung her feet off the yellow couch, crossed to the screen and keyboard where this terrifying experience had begun. Her mind felt ancient suddenly, an old mind in a young body.

I did ask; I started it … back in that ancient time when all I wanted was Kerro Panille.

She sat down at the keyboard and stared into the screen. Her fingers strayed over the keys. They felt familiar, yet strange. Kerro's fingers had touched these keys. She saw this instrument suddenly as a container which held raw experiences at a distance. You did not have to go in person. This machine made terrible things acceptable. She took a deep breath and punched the keys:

ANCIENT HISTORY RECORDS—YAISUAH/JESUS.

But Ship was not through intruding.

If there is any of it you wish to see in person, Ekel, you have but to ask.

The very thought sent shudders through her body.

This is my body and I'm staying in it.

That, Ekel, is a choice which you may have to share.

Chapter 30

My imagination was too much exalted by my first success to permit me to doubt of my ability to give life to an animal as complex and wonderful as man.
—Mary Shelley's *Frankenstein, Shiprecords*

I LIKE to call this the Flower Room," Murdoch said, leading Rachel Demarest across the open area to the lock. It was bright there, and she did not like the way the younger clones pulled back from Murdoch. A clone herself, she had heard the stories about this place and wanted to hold back, to delay what was happening. But it was her only chance at the Oakes/Lewis political circle. Murdoch kept a strong grip on her arm just above the elbow and she knew the pain he could cause if she hesitated.

Murdoch stopped at the lock and glanced at his charge.

This one won't carry any more petitions, he thought.

The slightly blue cast to her skin, her nervous, gangly limbs made her appear cold.

"Perhaps you and I could work something out," she said, and pressed her hip against him.

Murdoch was tempted … but that blue skin!

"I'm sorry, but this is standard for everyone who works here. There are things we need to know—and things that you need to know, too."

He really was sorry, remembering dimly some of the things which had happened to him during his own Scream Room initiation. There were things which he did not remember, too—a disturbing fact in itself. But orders were orders.

"Is this the place you call the Scream Room?" Her voice was barely a whisper as she stared at the hatch into the lock.

"It's the Flower Room," he said. "All of these beautiful young clones …" He waved vaguely at the room behind her. "All of them come from here."

She wanted to glance back. There had been some strangely shaped people hugging the rear of the throngs in the room, some with colors even stranger than her own. Something in Murdoch's manner prevented her from turning.

He took her hand then and placed her palm on the sensor-scribe beside the hatch— "To record your entry time." She felt an odd stinging sensation as her palm touched the scribe.

Murdoch smiled, but there was no mirth in it. His free hand went out to the lock-cycling switch. The hatch hissed open and he thrust her into it.

"In you go."

She heard the hatch seal behind her, but her attention was on the inner hatch as it opened. When it had swung wide, she realized that what she had thought was a grotesque statue standing there was actually a naked living creature framed by the open end of the lock. And … and there were tears streaming down the creature's cheeks.

"Come in, my dear." His voice was full of hoarse gruntings.

She moved toward him hesitantly, aware that Murdoch was watching through the sensors overhead. The room she entered was lighted by corner tubes which filled the entire space with a deep red illumination.

The gargoyle took her arm as the hatch sealed behind her and he swung her into the room.

His arms are too long.

"I am Jessup," he said. "Come to me when you are through."

Rachel looked around at a circle of grinning figures—some of them male, some female. There were among them creatures even more grotesque than Jessup. She saw that a male with short arms and bulbous head directly in front of her had an enormous erection. He bent over to grasp it and point it at her.

These people are real! she thought. This is not a nightmare.

The rumors she had heard did not even begin to describe this place.

"Clones," Jessup whispered beside her, as though he had been reading her mind. "All clones and they owe their lives to Jesus Lewis."

Clones? These aren't clones; they're recombinant mutants.

"But clones are people," she whispered.

Bulbous-head lurched one step toward her, still holding that enormous erection pointed at her.

"Clones are property," Jessup said, his voice firm but still with those odd gruntings in it. "Lewis says it and it must be true. You may develop an … appreciation for certain of them."

Jessup started to move away, but she clutched his arm. *How cold his flesh was!* "No … wait."

"Yes?" Grunting.

"What … what happens here?"

Jessup looked at the waiting circle. "They are children, just children. Only weeks old."

"But they're …"

"Lewis can grow a full clone in a matter of days."

"Days?" She was clutching at any delay. "How … I mean, the energy …"

"We eat a lot of burst in here. Lewis says this is the reason his people invented burst."

She nodded. The food shortage—it would be amplified enormously by the requirements of making burst.

Jessup leaned close to her ear, whispered: "And Lewis learned some beautiful tricks from the kelp."

She looked at him, full at him—that too-wide face with its toothless mouth and high cheeks, the pinpoint eyes, the receding forehead and protruding chin. Her gaze traveled down his body—enormous chest, but sunken and incurving … and narrow hips … pipestem legs … He was … he was not just he, she saw, but both sexes. And now she understood the grunting. He was fucking himself … herself! Little muscles at the crotch moved the …

Rachel whirled away, her mind searching wildly for something, anything to say.

"Why are you crying?" Her voice was too high.

"Ohhh, I always cry. It doesn't mean anything."

Bulbous-head lurched another step toward her and the circle moved with him.

"Entertainment time," Jessup said and pushed her roughly toward Bulbous-head.

She felt hands clutching her, turning her, and, presently, her memory left her … but for a long time she felt that she heard screams and she wondered if they might be her screams.

Chapter 31

Absolute dependence is the hallmark of religion. It posits the supplicant and the one who dispenses gifts. The supplicant employs ritual and prayer in the attempt to influence (control) the dispenser of gifts. The kinship between this relationship and the days of absolute monarchs cannot be overlooked. This dependence on supplication gives to the keeper of those two essentials—the ritual paraphernalia and the purity of prayerful forms (that is, to the Chaplain)—a power akin to that of the gift dispenser.

—"Training the Chaplain/Psychiatrist,"
Moonbase Documents (from *Shiprecords*)

RAJA THOMAS strode along a Colony passage with Waela TaoLini at his side. They both wore insulated yellow singlesuits with collar attachments for breather-helmets. It was first-light of Rega outside, but in here was the soft gold of dayside illumination that any Colonist could remember from shipside.

The food of this diurn's first meal sat heavily in his stomach and he wondered at that. They were adding some odd filler to the food. What was happening to the shipside agraria? Could it be possible, as Oakes' people hinted, that Ship was cutting down on hydroponics output?

Waela was oddly silent as she matched his pace. He glanced at her and found her studying him. Their eyes flicked past a confrontation too brief to call recognition, but an orange glow suffused her neck and face.

Waela stared straight ahead. They were bound for the test-launch apron to inspect the new submersible gondola and its carrier. It would be tried first in the enclosed and insulated tank at the hangar before being risked in Pandora's unpredictable ocean.

Why can't I just say no? she wondered. She did not have to get at the poet in the way Thomas ordered. There were other ways. It occurred to her then to ask herself about the society of Thomas' origins. What was his conditioning that he thinks sex is the best way to lower the psyche's guards?

As happened on rare occasions when she was with others, Honesty spoke within her head: "Men ruled and women were a subordinate class."

She knew this had to be true. It fitted his behavior.

Thomas was speaking silently to himself: *I am Thomas. I am Thomas. I am Thomas …*

The strange thing about this inner chant which he had adopted as his personal litany was that it increased his sensitivity to doubts. Could it be something built into the name?

Waela no longer trusts me … if she ever did.

What is this poet and where is he? Processing was taking an unconscionably long time with him. Will he be an arm of Ship?

Why were they getting a poet on their team? It had to be a clue to Ship's plans. Obscure, perhaps … convoluted … but a clue. This might be the element of the deadly game which he was required to discover for himself.

How much time do we have?

Ship did not always play the game by rules that were just and fair.

You're not always fair, are You, Ship?

If you mean even-handed, yes, I am fair. The answer surprised Thomas. He had not expected Ship to respond while he walked along this corridor.

Thomas glanced at Waela—silent woman. Her color had returned to its normal pale pink. Did Ship ever talk to her?

I talk to her quite often, Devil. She calls me Honesty.

Thomas missed a step in surprise.

Does she know it's You?

She is not conscious of that, no.

Do You talk to others without their knowing?

Too many, very many.

Thomas and Waela turned a corner into another portless passage, this one illuminated by the pale blue of overhead strip lighting—the color code which told them that it led outside somewhere up ahead. He glanced at Waela's hip, saw the ever-present lasgun in its holster there.

Waela broke the silence. "Those new clones that Oakes says are being used out on Dragon—what do you suppose they are?"

"People with faster responses."

"I don't trust that Lewis."

Thomas found himself in agreement. Lewis remained a mystery figure—the brutal alter-ego to Oakes? There were stories about Lewis which suggested that Ship had held nothing back when lifting the lid of Pandora's box.

They had come to the hatch into the hangar. Thomas hesitated before signaling the dogwatch to admit them. He glanced through the transparent port, saw that the sky doors of the hangar were closed. There should be little delay.

"What's eating you, Waela?"

She met his gaze. "I've been wondering if there's anyone I can trust."

Pandora's curse, he thought, and chose to direct her suspicions at Oakes.

"Why don't we insist on an inspection team to explore everything Oakes is doing?"

"Do you think they'd let us?"

"It's worth finding out."

"I'll suggest it to Rachel when I see her."

"Call her when we get inside."

"Can't. The roster says she's on vegetation patrol, south perimeter. I'll call her nightside."

Without knowing precisely why, Thomas felt a chill at hearing this. *Was that stupid Demarest woman in danger?* He shook his head. They were all in danger, every moment.

Again, Thomas peered through the port at activity in the hangar. There were bright lights around the sub. The LTA was lost in shadows above. Many workers moved around in the lighted area. He could see that they had opened the floorgate to expose the testing basin beneath the hangar. The lights glistened off exposed water beside the plaz gondola and its carrier-sub. Ahh, yes. They were mating the sub and gondola.

So Rachel would not be back from south perimeter until nightside. He was caught by the curious persistences in Waela's shipstyle language.

Nightside.

The irregular diurns of a planet with two suns caused few circadian problems for Colonists. They had been Shipmen, and Shipmen had a ready referent at hand: Day and Night were not times, but sides. Was there a clue here, something to help him in his search for a way to the heart of these people? He had thought that if he succeeded in communicating with the 'lectrokelp, this would give him the desired status.

Anything to help us fit into the rhythms of Pandora.

If Colonists learn to trust me … if they look up to me … then I can tell them what Ship really wants of them. They will believe and they will follow.

That sub in there—would it be the key? Persistent symbols. What would persist in the symbols of an intelligent vegetable? It was intelligent. He was convinced of it. So was Waela. But the symbols remained a mystery.

Fireflies in the night of the sea.

Did they talk to each other beneath the waves?

We do.

Waela gestured at the signal switch beside the hatch.

"What's the delay?"

"They're mating the new gondola and the sub. I didn't want to call anyone away from that."

He nodded as he saw the gondola swing into place, then he depressed the switch.

Presently, a green-clad workman unsealed the inner locks and the hatch swung open. Slow procedure, but this was a dangerous area. Hatches could be locked either side—from inside when the skydoors were open. Everything groundside was designed to contain an attack.

There was a musty aroma of outside within the hangar which set Thomas' nerves on edge.

Waela preceded him across the hangar floor, striding out with that watchful swing which Colonists never put aside, head turning, gaze darting about. Her pale singlesuit fitted her body like another skin.

He had insisted they go through Stores for the new suits. As he had ordered, they were insulated against the sea's chill, eliminating the need for insulation on the gondola. Plaz was an excellent conductor unless doubled or tripled. This decision gave them a few extra centimeters in the gondola core.

Waela had disconcerted him when they picked up the suits. In shipside style, there were no separate dressing rooms. She had moved right into the try-on area with him. That habit of bodily candor still bothered him. He always found it necessary to turn his back when dressing or undressing with a female companion. Waela, on the other hand, remained frankly direct.

"Raj, did you know that you have a funny-looking mole on your butt?"

Without thinking, he had turned his head toward her just in time to see her stepping into her suit—breasts and pubis exposed. There was just the slightest hesitation in her while she continued dressing, as though she spoke only to his eyes, saying: "Of course I'm a woman. You knew that."

He found himself intensely aware that she was a woman, and there was no denying the magnetic attraction she worked on him. There also was no denying that she knew this and was amused by it in an undefinably gentle way. This knowledge in her might even have contributed to her upset when he asked her to apply sexual pressure to the new team member.

She was right, too. It was cheating.

But what if Ship is cheating us?

Doubts—always doubts. He found himself in silent agreement with some of the things Oakes had said. On the other hand, he could not fault Waela's argument: "We don't help ourselves by cheating each other."

That open candor in her attracted him as much as the chemistry of her physical presence.

But I am the goad, the devil's advocate, the challenger. I am the knight among the pawns.

And he knew he did not have much time. Ship might hand him an impossible deadline at any moment. Or Oakes and his crew might make good on their unspoken threat to cut this project off at the pockets as soon as they dared.

There was no mistaking the latent anger in Waela—it betrayed itself in her stride (a bit too emphatic) and in the way she studied him now when she thought he was not looking. But she would get to Panille and ask all of the proper questions. That was the important thing.

Thomas still felt remnants of her anger as they stepped into the glaring light and bustle at the testing apron where the new sub was cradled. She was all business as she stared up at this creation which had emerged from Thomas' commands.

It was a fat metallic teardrop, slightly elongated, its LTA attachment eyelets extending along the top in a double ridge reminiscent of the backbone of an antediluvian Earthside monster. The principle was relatively simple. Most of the external sub was carrier for the plaz globe of the gondola at the core. Only the drive motors and fuel storage were made strong against the sea's pressures. The carrier had one more important function now visible to her eyes: Vertical lines of plaz-bubble lights extended up and down its sides—each bubble four centimeters in diameter. The trigger system to light them in sequence passed through a computer/sensor feedback program. What the sensor-eyes saw in the ocean depths, these lights could play back. The kelp's patterns would be its patterns, the kelp's rhythms its rhythms.

The chief of Construction Services, Hapat Lavu, came out to meet them at the edge of the lighted area. He was a slender, driving man, completely bald. His gray eyes missed few details of his work and, despite a biting and accusatory tongue which delivered reprimands with thin-lipped fury, he was one of the best-liked Colonists. The common assessment was, "You can depend on Hap."

Dependability gained high marks groundside, and Hap Lavu was fighting for his reputation. Of all the equipment from his shops, only the subs had failed to match Pandora's demands. Sixteen had been lost without a trace—there had been survivors from four, and the wreckage of three others had been located on the bottom. All had been crushed or otherwise disabled by giant strands of kelp.

Lavu's assessment was the opinion of many: "That damn stuff can think and it's a killer."

He had become an admirer of Thomas during their short association. Thomas had taken the accepted sub-components and reworked them into this new design. The only parts of the plan Lavu distrusted involved communications and pickup. He spoke to that as he greeted Thomas: "You should have something better than the rocketsonde. They fail, y'know."

"We'll stick with it," Thomas said.

He knew what worried Lavu. The ubiquitous 'lectrokelp not only clogged the seas, but their electrical activity jammed the communications channels—sonar to radar. Hylighter exhibited similar phenomena. Was there a relationship? There was no pattern to the jamming; it was random squirts of signal activity. Because of this, they depended on high power and line-of-sight relays waterside. Even then, a cloud of hylighters rising from the sea could block transmissions.

"You'll have to surface before you can communicate," Lavu said. "Now, if you'd let me adapt the anchor cable to ..."

"Too many lines to the sub," Thomas said. "We could tangle in them."

"Then pray that y'can lift above interference for the relays to take your talk-talk."

Thomas nodded agreement. The plan was to anchor the LTA in a lagoon, slip down the anchor cable in a vertical dive and stay clear of the kelp barriers.

"We'll observe, play back their light patterns and seek any new coherent patterns in the lights or their electrical activity," he had said.

It was a workable plan. Several subs had survived exploratory dives by giving a wide berth to the kelp. It was when the subs went in to take specimens that violence occurred.

Workable … but with unavoidable weaknesses.

Their LTA would hang at the surface, tethered on its anchor-line and awaiting the sub's return from the depths. A plan to have another LTA with a lift-gondola anchored or standing by aloft had been scratched. The winds were too unpredictable and it was argued that two LTAs anchored in the same lagoon would pose dangerous maneuvering problems. The necessary size of such an LTA made them difficult to handle in tight quarters. The standard procedure at the hangar was to winch them down after grappling the downhaul hawser. Instead, their LTA bag had been triple-reinforced with compartmented cells.

These arguments went through Thomas' mind as he studied the new submersible.

Was it worth the risk? He felt that he was challenging Ship, but the stakes were the highest.

Will You let me die here, Ship?

No answer, but Ship had said that his destiny was his own now. That was a rule of this game.

If the kelp is sentient and we can make contact, the rewards will be enormous. Intelligent vegetable! Did it WorShip? It could be the key to Ship's demands.

Ship called the kelp intelligent and that could be another twist of this game. Should he doubt?

It occurred to Thomas then that if Ship were telling the truth, the kelp might be close to immortal. Except for specimens damaged by human intrusion, they had never seen dead kelp.

Did it live forever?

"Do y'still reject a standby LTA?" Lavu asked.

"How long could you hold one in sight of us?" Thomas asked.

"Depends on the weather, as y'well know."

There was resentment in Lavu's voice. He took it personally that so many of his creations had been destroyed, all of them equipped as best he knew for underwater survival. The answer, of course, was that Pandora's planet-wide sea contained perils beyond those they knew. Lavu felt that the entire project was now a challenge to him. He did not want to quit. It was more than a concern about hardware. Lavu wanted to go out as crew.

"How else can I learn what's needed if I don't go out m'self?"

"No," Thomas said.

All right, Ship. This will be the big throw of the dice.

Devil, why do you persist in such overly dramatic poses? This time, he expected the response and was ready for it.

Because they won't listen to me here unless I become bigger than life to them.

Life can never be bigger than itself.

Lavu patted the outer surface of the sub as Waela moved up beside him. She had been listening to the undertones in the conversation between Thomas and Lavu.

What drives Thomas? she wondered.

She had only the barest details about him. Out of hyb and into command of this project. *Ship's doing*, he said.

Why?

"She's heavier than any of the others," Lavu said, thinking that the question in Waela's mind. "I defy any Pandoran monster to break it."

"Did you solve the problem of filling the LTA?" Thomas asked.

"You'll have to get your final inflation outside," Lavu said, "I've laid on extra perimeter guards because the skydoors'll be open longer'n I like."

"The sub itself?" Waela asked.

"We've rigged guide cables up through the doors. That's it."

Instinctively, Thomas glanced up at the iris closure of the skydoors.

"She'll be ready by oh-six hundred at the latest," Lavu said. "You'll have a full nightside of rest before going out. Who's to ride with y'?"

"Not you, Hap," Thomas said.

"But I ..."

"A new fellow named Panille is to go with us," Thomas said.

"So I've heard. Untrained. A poet? Is that the truth?"

"An expert in communication," Thomas said.

"Well, then, let's run the tank test," Lavu said. He turned and waved a hand signal at an aide.

"We'll ride it with you," Thomas said. "What pressure will you take it to?"

"Five hundred meters."

Thomas glanced at Waela. She gave the barest inclination of her head to indicate agreement, then returned her attention to the sub. It curved over her, more than three times her height at the thickest part of the teardrop near its bow. The outer carrier concealed all but the upper bubble of the plaz gondola within it. The induction propeller at the stern had been shielded in a complex baffle and screening system which reduced its effectiveness, but guarded it against kelp fouling.

Workers ran a ladder up the side of the hull now, cushioned it with a foam blanket to keep the exterior signal lights clean, and steadied it while Lavu mounted. He spoke as he climbed.

"We've installed the manual override to insure that no random signal opens your hatch. You'll have to undog it by hand every time y'open it."

No surprises there, Thomas thought. That had been Waela's idea. There were suspicions that the kelp could control signals in a wide scanning spectrum and that some of the lost subs had merely been opened underwater by scanner-activation of their hatch motors.

Waela scrambled up behind Lavu, leaving Thomas to follow. They were already inside when he reached the open hatch. He paused there to peer along this craft he would command. In a way, it was a small Voidship. The stabilizer fins were like solar panels. Exterior sensors for all of the cardinal directions were like a Voidship's hull eyes. And every known weak point had been multiple-reinforced.

Backup systems piled on backup systems.

He turned, found the top rung of the access ladder with a foot and stepped down into the gondola. It was red-lighted gloom there with Lavu and Waela already at their positions. Waela was bent over her console, checking her instruments, leaving the line of her left cheek visible to Thomas in the red light. How tender and beautiful that line was, he thought. Immediately, he suppressed a cynical laugh.

Well, my glands are still working.

Chapter 32

Cain rose up against Abel, his brother, and slew him. And the Lord said unto Cain, "Where is Abel, thy brother?" and he said, "I know not: am I my brother's keeper?" and He said, "What hast thou done? The voice of thy brother's blood cries unto Me from the ground."

—Christian Book of the Dead, Shiprecords

ANYTHING GOES here?" Legata asked.

She studied Sy Murdoch carefully as he thought about the question. He was taking too long to answer. She did not like this man, the pale eyes which defied everything around them. He kept the lab too bright, especially this late in the dayside. The young E-clones huddled against a far wall were obviously terrified of him.

"Well?"

"That takes a little thought," Murdoch said.

Legata pursed her lips. This was her second visit to Lab One in three diurns. She did not believe the reasons for this one. Oakes had pretended anger that she had not penetrated every element of the lab, but she had sensed the flaws in his performance. He was lying.

Why had Oakes sent her back here? Lewis was no longer out of contact. What did those two know that they had not shared with her? Legata felt anger at the frustrating unknowns.

Murdoch moved cautiously. Oakes had ordered Legata sent through the Scream Room, an "exploratory," but had warned: "She is frighteningly strong."

How strong? Stronger than me?

He did not see how she could be. Such a bouncy little thing.

"I asked you a simple question," Legata said, not bothering to conceal her anger.

"Interesting question, but not simple. Why do you ask it that way?"

"Because I've seen the lab reports to Morgan. You're doing some strange things here."

"Well … I would say that there are few limits here, but isn't that the basis for discovery?"

She replied with a cold stare, and he went on.

"There are few limits here, so long as Doctor Oakes has a complete holorecord of what we do."

"He has us on holo right now," she said.

"I know."

The way he said that made Legata's skin crawl. Murdoch carried his powerful body like a dancer. He lifted his chin and she saw a scar beneath his jaw that she had not noticed before. It mingled with creases as he lowered his chin. There was no telling his age. Given the possibility that he might be a clone, there was no telling his chronological age either.

Have to look into him, she noted to herself.

The things Lewis was having done here …

She glanced around the room once more. Something was not right. She saw the usual holo, com-console, sensors, but the place offended her directly, she was one who appreciated beauty. Not decoration, but beauty. The two huge flowers flanking the hatchway … she'd noticed them before. They were pink as tongues and their petals convoluted into one another like a line of mirrors.

Strange, she thought, *they smell like sweat.*

"Let's get on with it," she said.

"First, a formality requested by Doctor Oakes."

Murdoch swung a sensorscribe from a panel beside the lock. It appeared to be the standard identification reader of her shipside experience. She placed her hand on the flat plate to allow it to read her.

Stupid formality, everyone knew who she was.

A sudden tingling sensation shot up her arm from her palm and she realized that Murdoch had said something to her. What did he say?

"I'm sorry … what?"

She felt weak and disoriented. Something….

She saw that the hatch was open and she had no memory of him opening it. What had he done to her?

Murdoch's hand was on her shoulder propelling her into the lock. As she passed through the hatchway she imagined that she heard a tiny voice pleading from the heart of one of the flowers: *Feed me, feed me.*

She heard the hatch seal behind her and realized that she was alone and the inner door was swinging open … slowly … ponderous. What was all the red light? And those dim shapes moving … ?

She walked toward the opening hatch.

So strange that Murdoch had not accompanied her. She peered at the shapes awash in the red glow beyond the inner hatch. Oh, yes—the new E-clones. Some of them she recognized from the lab reports. They were designed to match the synapse-quick demons of Pandora. There was a problem with breeding for speed, something she'd intended to investigate.

What was it she wanted to watch for?

A voice whispered in her ear: "I am Jessup. Come to me when you are through."

How did I get inside here?

Something was wrong with her time sense. She swallowed hard and felt the thickness of her dry tongue rasp against the roof of her mouth.

"Good and evil hang their uniforms at the door."

Did somebody say that or did I think it?

Oakes had said, "Anything goes on Pandora. Our every fancy is possible there."

That's why I asked Murdoch … where is Murdoch? The gargoyle clones were all around her now and she tried to focus on them. Her eyes were not tracking. Someone grabbed her left arm. Painful.

"Let go of me, you…."

She rippled her arm and heard the grunts of surprise. Peculiar things were happening to her sense of time and the awareness of her own flesh. Blood welled up on her arms and she had no memory of how it got there. And her body—it was naked. Her muscles corded reflexively and she crouched in defense.

What is happening to me?

More hands—rough hands. She responded in a slow-motion flex of power. And she distinctly heard someone screaming. How odd that no one responded to those screams!

Chapter 33

Humans spend their lives in mazes. If they escape and cannot find another maze, they create one. What is this passion for testing?
—Kerro Panille, *Questions from the Avata*

RAJA THOMAS awoke in darkness and it was like that most recent time, awakening in hyb. He found himself disoriented in darkness, waiting for dangers he could not locate. Slowly, it came to him that he was in his groundside cubby … night. He glanced at the luminous time display beside his pallet: two hours into the midnight watch.

What awakened me?

His cubby was eight levels under the Pandoran surface, a choice location cushioned from surface noises and perils by numerous color-coded passages, locks, hatches, slide-tubes and seemingly endless branchings. The Shiptrained found no difficulty recording mental maps of such layouts, the more remote the address the better. Thomas resented being buried in these depths. Too much travel time to places which demanded his attention.

Lab One.

He had gone to sleep while wondering about that restricted place. The source of so many odd rumors.

"They're breeding people who're faster than the demons."

That was the popular story.

"Oakes and Lewis want nothing but servile zombies!"

Thomas had heard that story from one of the new militants, a fiery young woman associate of Rachel Demarest.

Slowly, he sat up and tried to probe the darkness around him.

Odd I should awaken at this hour.

He touched the light plate on the wall beside his head and a dim glow replaced the dark. The cubby appeared boringly normal: his singlesuit draped over a slideseat … sandals. Everything as it should be.

"I feel like a damned Spinneret down here."

He spoke it aloud while rubbing his face. Presently, he summoned a servo, then slipped into his clothing while waiting for it. The servo buzzed his hatch and he stepped out into an empty passage lighted by the widely spaced ceiling bulbs of nightside. Seating himself in the servo, he ordered it to take him topside. He felt oppressed by the travel time, the weight of construction overhead.

I never needed open spaces shipside. Maybe I'm going native.

The servo emitted an irritating hum full of subsonics.

At the surface autosentry checkpoint, he keyed his code into the system. With the green go signal came the blinking yellow light for Condition 2. He swore under his breath, then turned to the lockers beside the topside hatch and took out a lasgun. He knew the hatch would not open unless he did this. The weapon felt clumsy in his hands and, when he holstered it, he was intensely conscious of the weight at his waist.

"Doesn't take much sense to know you shouldn't live in a place if you have to carry a gun." He muttered it, but his voice was loud enough that the blue acknowledge light winked at him from the sentry plate.

Still the hatch remained sealed to him. His hand was moving toward the override switch when he saw the little blinker at the bottom of the plate demanding: "Purpose of movement?"

"Work inspection," he said.

The system digested this, then opened the hatch.

Thomas slipped off the servo and strode out into the topside corridors, sure now of why he had awakened at this hour.

Lab One.

It was a mystery of peculiar odor.

He found himself presently in the darkened perimeter halls, passing an occasional worker and the well-spaced extrusions of sentry posts, each with its armed occupant paying attention only to the nightside landscape.

Plaz ports showed Thomas that it was moonlight out there, two moons quartering the southern horizon. Pandora's night was a buzz of shadows.

After a space, the ring passage ramped downward into a hatch-distribution dome about thirty meters in diameter. The passage to Lab One was indicated by an "L-1" sign on his right. He had taken only two steps toward it when it opened and a woman emerged, slamming the hatch behind her. It was dim in the dome, lighted only by the moonlight coming in through plaz ports on his left, but there was no mistaking the almost disjointed agitation in her movements.

The woman darted toward him, grabbing his arm as he passed, dragging him along toward the external ports with a strength which astonished him.

"Come here! I need you."

Her voice was husky and full of odd undertones. Her face and arms were a mass of scratches and he sensed the unmistakable odor of blood on her light singlesuit.

"What …"

"Don't question me!"

There was wildness, a touch of insanity, in her voice.

And she was beautiful.

She released him when they reached the barrier wall, and he saw the dim outline of an emergency hatch to Pandora's perilous open air. Her hands were busy at the hatch controls, keying the override system in a way that did not set off the alarms. One of her hands reached out and grabbed his right wrist, guiding his hand to the lock mechanism. Such strength in her!

"When I say so, open this hatch. Wait twenty-three minutes, then look for me. Let me in."

Before he could find the words to protest, she slipped out of her singlesuit and thrust it at him. He caught it involuntarily with his free hand. She already was crouching to thong her feet and he saw that she had a magnificent body—-smooth muscles, a supple perfection—but swatches of Celltape crisscrossed her skin.

"What's happened to you?"

"I warned you once not to question." She spoke without looking up, and he sensed the wild power in her. *Dangerous. Very dangerous. No inhibitions.*

"You're going to run the P," he said. He glanced around, looking for someone, anyone, to call on for help. The circle of the distribution dome contained no other people.

"Bet on me," she said, standing,

"How will I tell the twenty-three minutes?" he asked.

She crowded close to him and slapped a panel beside the emergency hatch. Immediately, he heard the sentry circuit's hum, then a deep male voice: "Post Nine clear."

A tiny screen above the circuit speaker glowed with red numerals: 2:29.

"The hatch," she said.

There was no way to avoid it; he had felt her wild strength. He undogged the hatch and she thrust past him, swinging it wide as she dashed out into the open, turning right. Her body was a silver blur in the moonlight and he saw a dark shadow coming up behind her. His gun was in his hand without thinking about it and he cooked a Hooded Dasher that was only a step behind her. She did not turn.

His hands were shaking as he resealed the hatch.

Running the P!

He glanced at the time signal: 2:29. She had said twenty-three minutes. That would put her back at the hatch by 2:52.

It occurred to him then that the perimeter was just under ten kilometers.

It can't be done! No one can run ten kilometers in twenty-three minutes!

But she had come from the passage to Lab One. He unwadded her singlesuit. Blood on it, no doubt of that. Her name was stitched over the left breast: *Legata.*

He wondered if it was a first or last name.

Or a title?

He peered out of the plaz port, looking to the left where she would have to appear if she really did run the perimeter.

What would a Legata be?

A voice on the sentry circuit startled him: "Someone's out there, pretty far out."

Another voice answered: "It's a woman running the P. She just rounded Post Thirty-Eight."

"Who is it?"

"Too far out to identify."

Thomas found himself praying for her to make it as he listened to each succeeding post report the runner. But he knew there was not much chance. Since learning about The Game from Waela, he had looked into the statistics. Fifty-fifty in dayside, yes. But nightside, fewer than one in fifty made it.

The timer beside his head moved with an agonizing slowness: 2:48. It seemed to him that it took an hour shifting to 2:49. The sentries were silent now.

Why didn't the sentries mark her passage?

As though to answer him, a voice on the circuit said: "She just rounded East Eighty-Nine!"

"Who the hell is that out there?"

"She's still too far out to identify."

Thomas drew his lasgun and put a hand on the hatchdog. The word was that the last minutes were the worst, Pandora's demons ganging up on the runner. He peered out into the moon-shadows.

2:50.

He spun the hatchdog, opened it a crack. No movement.... Nothing. Not even a demon. He found that he was swearing under his breath, muttering: "Come on, Legata. Come on. You can do it. Don't blow the fucking run at the end!"

Something flickered in the shadows off to his left. He swung the hatch wide.

There she was!

It was like a dance—leaping, dodging. Something large and black swerved behind her. Thomas took careful aim and burned another Dasher as she sped past him without breaking her stride. There was a musky odor of perspiration from her. He slammed the hatch and dogged it. Something crashed into the barrier as he sealed it.

Too late, you fucker!

He turned to see her slipping through the Lab One hatchway, her singlesuit in hand. She waved to him as the hatch hissed shut.

Legata, he thought. Then: *Ten klicks in twenty-three minutes!*

There was a babble of conversation on the sentry circuit.

"Anybody know who that was?"

"Negative. Where'd she go?"

"Somewhere over near Lab One dome."

"Sheee-it! That must've been the fastest time ever."

Thomas slapped the switch to shut them off, but not before a male voice said: "I'd sure like to have that little honey chasing ..."

Thomas crossed over to the Lab One hatch, heaved on the dog. It refused to move, sealed.

All that just to put a hashmark above her eyebrow?

No ... it had to be much more than the mark of success.

What were they doing down there in Lab One?

Again, he tried the hatchdog. It refused to budge. He shook his head and walked slowly back to the autosentry gate where he picked up a servo and rode it to his quarters. All the way down he kept wondering:

What the hell's a Legata?

Chapter 34

The clone of a clone does not necessarily stay closer to the original than a clone of the older original. It depends on cellular interference and other elements which may be introduced. Passage of time always introduces other elements.

—Jesus Lewis, *The New Cloning Manual*

OAKES SNAPPED off the holo and swiveled his chair around to stare at the design on the wall of his groundside cubby.

He did not like this place. It was smaller than his quarters shipside. The air smelled strange. He did not like the casual way some of the Colonists treated him. He found himself constantly aware of Pandora's surface … right out there.

Never mind that it was many layers of Colony construction beyond his quarters, it was right out there.

Despite the few familiar furnishings he had brought groundside, this place would never feel as comfortable as his old shipside cubby.

Except that the dangers of the ship—the dangers which only he knew—were more distant.

Oakes sighed.

It was late dayside and he still had many things to do, but what he had seen on the holo compelled his attention.

A most unsatisfactory performance.

He chewed at his lower lip. No … it was more than unsatisfactory. Disturbing.

Oakes leaned back and tried to relax. The holo of Legata's visit to the Scream Room filled him with disquiet. He shook his head. In spite of the drug suppressing her cortical responses, she had resisted. Nothing in her Scream Room performance could be held against her … except … no. She had done nothing.

Nothing!

If he had not seen it for himself … Would she ask to see this holo? He thought not, but nothing was certain. None of the others had asked to see their holos, although everyone knew such a record was made.

Legata had not performed according to pattern. Things were done to her and she resisted other things. The holo gave him no absolutely secure hold on her.

If she sees that holo, she'll know.

How could he keep the record of it from the best-known Search Technician?

Was it a mistake … sending her into the Scream Room!

But he thought he still knew her. Yes. She would not take action against him unless she were in great pain. And she might not ask for the holo. Might … not.

Not once in the Scream Room had Legata sought her own pleasure. She had acted only in reaction to the application of pain.

Pain that I commanded.

This made him uncomfortable.

It was necessary!

Given an adversary as potent as the ship, he had to take extreme measures. He had to explore the limits.

I'm justified.

Legata had not even required sedation after emerging from the Scream Room.

Where did she go, dashing off like that with only the minimal Celltape on her wounds?

She had returned naked, carrying her singlesuit.

Oakes had heard the rumors that someone had run the perimeter in that interval. Surely not Legata. A coincidence, no more. And the proof of it was that she wore no hashmark.

Damn fools! Running in the open at night like that!

He would have liked to prohibit The Game, but Lewis had warned him off this, and his own good sense had agreed. There was no way to prevent The Game without wasting too much manpower policing all the hatches. Besides, The Game vented certain impulses of violence.

Legata running the perimeter?

Certainly not!

Efficient damned woman! She was expected back at work by evening, the physical marks of her Scream Room experience almost gone. He looked at the notes beside his left hand. Unconsciously, he had addressed them to her.

"Check on possible relationship between waxing of Alki and growth of 'lectrokelp. Have Lab One begin two LH clones. Map new data on dissidents—special attention to those associated with Rachel Demarest."

Would Legata even take his orders now?

The picture of Legata's face from the holorecord kept slipping back into his mind.

She trusted me.

Had she really trusted him? Why else would she go back to Lab One when her misgivings about it were all that apparent? With anyone else, he would have laughed at such musings, but not with Legata. She was painfully different from the others and he had already taken her too far.

Entertainment time.

It had not been as entertaining as he had expected. He recalled the first potent look of betrayal in her eyes when the sonics hit her. The sonics had driven away the clones; they already had taken their entertainment. But even heavy pain had not moved Legata. Despite sedation, she could hear Murdoch's commands. And the sedation had been designed to suppress her will … but she resisted. Murdoch's commands told her what to do, the clone was prepared, the equipment set—but even then, she had to be totally awash with pain before inflicting anything like her own agony on the clone. Most of the time, her gaze had sought out the holo scanner. She had stared directly into the scanner, and the dimming of her eyes gave him no pleasure, no pleasure at all.

She won't remember. They never do.

Most of the subjects begged, offered anything for the pain to stop. Legata simply stared at the scanner, wide-eyed. Somewhere in her, he knew, there had been awareness that she was totally helpless, totally subject to his every whim. It was a conditioning process. He wanted her to be like the rest. He could deal with that.

But he had been unprepared for the shock of her difference. Yes, she was different. What a shock, finally discovering this magnificent difference, to know that he had destroyed it. Whatever private trust they might have had was gone forever.

Forever.

She would never again trust him completely. Oh, she would obey—perhaps even more promptly now. But no trust.

He felt himself shaking with this knowledge. Tense, distracted. He had to force himself to relax, to concentrate on something which comforted.

Nothing is forever, he thought.

Presently, he drifted into his own peculiar arena of sleep, but it was a sleep haunted by the design on his cubby wall. The design took on distorted shapes from the holo of Legata in the Scream Room.

And Pandora was right out there … and … and … tomorrow …

Chapter 35

Humankerro: "Does the listener project his own sense of understanding and consciousness?"

Avata: "Ahhh, you are building barriers."

Humankerro: "That's what you call the illusion of understanding, is it not?"

Avata: "If you understand, then you cannot learn. By saying you understand, you construct barriers."

Humankerro: "But I can remember understanding things."

Avata: "Memory only understands the presence or absence of electrical signals."

Humankerro: "Then what's the combination, the program for learning?"

Avata: "Now you open the path. It is the program which counts in the most literal sense."

Humankerro: "But what are the rules?"

Avata: "Are there rules underlying every aspect of human life? Is that your question?"

Humankerro: "That appears to be the question."

Avata: "Then answer it. What are the rules for being human?"

Humankerro: "But I asked you!"

Avata: "But you are human and I am Avata."

Humankerro: "Well, what are the rules for being Avata?"
Avata: "Ahhhh, Humankerro, we embody such knowledge but we cannot know it."
Humankerro: "You appear to be saying that such knowledge cannot be reduced to language."
Avata: "Language cannot occur in a reference vacuum."
Humankerro: "Don't we know what we're talking about?"
Avata: "Using language involves much more than recognizing strings of words. Language and the world to which it refers . . ."
Humankerro: "The script of the play?"
Avata: "The script, yes. The script of the game and its world must be interrelated. How can you substitute a word or some other symbol for every cellular element of your body?"
Humankerro: "I can talk with my body."
Avata: "For that, you do not need a script."

—Kerro Panille, *The Avata*, "The Q & A Game"

Chapter 36

The mystery of consciousness? Erroneous data—significant results.

—P. Weygand, Voidship Med-tech

OAKES WATCHED the sentry on the Colony scanner. The man writhed and screamed in agony. The evening light of Alki cast long purple shadows which twisted as the man flopped and turned. The Current Outside Activity circuits reproduced the sounds of the sentry with clear fidelity, terrifyingly immediate. The man might be just outside this cubby's hatch instead of on Colony's north perimeter as the sensor log indicated.

The screams turned to a hoarse growl, like a turbine running down. There came a convulsive flopping, shudders, then quiet.

Oakes found that the sentry's first screams still echoed in memory and would not be silenced.

Runners! Runners!

There was no escaping Pandora anywhere groundside. Colony remained under constant siege. And at the Redoubt—sterilization was their only solution. Kill everything.

Oakes found that he had pressed his hands to his ears trying to quiet the memory of those screams. Slowly, he brought his hands down to the scanner controls, looking at them as though they had betrayed him. He had just been running through the available sensors, scanning for any random COA which might require his attention. And . . . and he had encountered horror.

Images continued to play in his mind.

The sentry had clawed at his own eyes, ripping out the nerve tissue which Runners found so succulent. But he must have known what every Colonist knew—there could be no help for him. Once Runners contacted nerve tissue they could not be stopped until they encysted their clutch of eggs in his brain.

Except that this particular sentry knew about chlorine. Had some residual hope clutched at his doomed awareness? Surely not. Once the Runners were in his flesh, that was too late even for chlorine.

To Oakes, the most horrible part of the incident was that he knew the sentry: Illuyank. Part of Murdoch's Lab One crew. And before that, the doomed sentry had been with Lewis on Black Dragon Redoubt. Illuyank had been a survivor—three times running the P … and one of those who came back from Edmond Kingston's team. Illuyank had even come shipside to report on Kingston's failure.

I heard his report.

Movement in the scanner riveted Oakes' attention. The sentry's backup stepped into view (not too close!) with lasgun at the ready. The backup was marked as an ultimate coward by Colony rules. He had not been able to shoot the doomed Illuyank. So the Runners' victim had died the most miserable death Pandora could offer.

Now, the backup aimed his gun and burned Illuyank's head to char. Standard procedure. Cook them out. Those eggs, at least, would never hatch.

Oakes found the strength to switch off the scanner. His body was shaking so hard he could not move himself away from the console.

It had just been a routine scan, the kind of thing he did regularly shipside. The horror of this place!

What has the ship done to us?

Groundside—nowhere to turn for escape. No release from the knowledge that he could not survive on this synapse-quick world without multiple barriers and constant guarding.

And there was no turning back. Lewis was right. Colony required constant attention. Delicate decisions about personnel movements and assignments, the shifting of supplies and equipment to Redoubt—none of this could be trusted to shipside-groundside communications channels. Pandora required swift action and reaction. Lewis could not divide his attention between Redoubt and Colony.

Oakes pressed a thumb against the lump of pellet in his neck. Useless now. Groundside static interference limited range … and when that impediment lifted, as it did for brief moments, the random signals which came through proved that their secrecy had been breached.

The ship had to be the source of those signals. *The ship!* Still interfering. The pellets would have to come out at the first opportunity.

Oakes lifted a bottle from the floor beside his console. His hand still shook from the shock of Illuyank's death. He tried to pour a glass of wine and slopped most of it over his console where the sticky red splash reminded him of blood pulsing out of the sentry's empty sockets … out of his nose … his mouth …

The three tattooed hashmarks over Illuyank's left eye remained burned in Oakes' memory.

Damn this place!

Gripping the glass with both hands, Oakes drained what little remained in it. Even that small swallow soothed his stomach.

At least I won't throw up.

He put the empty glass on the lip of his console, and his gaze swept around the confines of his cubby. It was not big enough. He longed for the space he'd enjoyed shipside. But there could be no retreat—no return to the slavery of the ship.

We're going to beat You, Ship!

Bravo!

Everything groundside reminded him that he did not belong here. The speed of the Colonists! There was nothing like that speed shipside. Oakes knew he was too heavy, too out of condition to consider keeping up, much less protecting himself. He needed constant guarding. It festered in him that Illuyank had been one of the people considered for his own guard force. Illuyank was supposed to be a survivor.

Even survivors die here.

He had to get out of this room, had to walk somewhere. But when he pushed himself away from the console to stand and turn around, he confronted another wall. It came to him then that the loss of his lavish shipside cubby was a greater blow than anticipated. He needed the Redoubt for physical and psychological reasons as well as for a secure base of command. This damned cubby was larger than any other groundside, but by the time they housed his command console, his holo equipment and the other accouterments of the Ceepee, he was almost crowded out.

There's no room to breathe in here.

He put a hand to the hatchdogs, wanting the release of a walk in the corridors, but when his hand touched cold metal he realized how all of those corridors led to the open, unguarded surface of Pandora. The hatch was one more barrier against the ravages of this place.

I'll eat something.

And perhaps Legata could be summoned on some pretext. Practical Legata. Lovely Legata. How useful she remained … except that he did not like what had happened deep in her eyes. Was it time to ask Lewis for a replacement? Oakes could not find the will to do this.

I made a mistake with her.

He could admit this only to himself. It had been a mistake sending Legata to the Scream Room.

She's changed.

She reminded him now of the shipside agrarium workers. What had really impressed him out there was the difference between those workers and other Shipmen. Agrarium workers were a tight-lipped lot and always busy—sometimes noisy in their work but silent in themselves.

That was it. Legata had become silent in herself.

She was like the agrarium workers, containing seriousness, almost a reverence … not the grimness found in the Vitro labs or around the axolotl tanks where Lewis produced his miracles … but something else.

It occurred to Oakes that the agraria were the only parts of the ship where he had felt out of place. This thought disturbed him.

Legata makes me feel out of place now.

And there was no escaping the choices he had made. He would have to live with the consequences. Choices resulted from information. He had acted on bad information.

Who gave me that bad information? Lewis?

What control systems reposed in the information, leading inevitably to certain choices?

Such a simple question.

He turned it over in his mind, feeling that it put him on the track of something vital. Perhaps it was the key to the ship's true nature. A key somewhere in the flow of information.

Information-to-choice-to-action.

Simple, always simple. The true scientist was required to suspect complexity.

Occam's razor really cuts.

What choices did the ship make and on the basis of what information? Would the ship openly oppose moving the Natali groundside, for instance? The move could not yet be made, but the possibility of open opposition excited him. He longed for such opposition.

Show your hand, you mechanical monster!

The ship can act without hands.

But could the ship act without curiosity and without leaving clues?

As an intelligent, questioning being, Oakes felt the constant need to sharpen his curiosity, to keep himself in motion. He might not always move smoothly—that business with Legata—but he had to move … in jumps and fits and starts… whatever. The success of his movements stayed relative to his own intelligence and the information available.

Better information.

Excitement shot through him. With the right information, could he design the test which would prove, once and for all, that the ship was not God? An end to the ship's pretenses forever!

What information did he possess? The ship's consciousness? It had to be conscious. To assume otherwise would be to move backward—bad choice. Whatever else it might be, the ship could only be viewed as a complex intelligence.

A truly intelligent being might move seldom, but it would move surely and on the basis of reliable information which had been tested somehow for predictability.

Testing by large numbers or over a long time.

One or the other.

How long had the ship been testing its Shipmen? In a pure-chance universe, past results could not always guarantee predictions. Could the ship's decisions be predicted?

Oakes felt his heart thumping hard and fast. In this game, he truly felt himself come alive. It was like sex … but this could be even bigger—the biggest game in the universe.

If the ship's movements and choices could be predicted, they could be precipitated. He would have the key to quick and easy victory on Pandora. What action could he take to link the ship's powers to his own desires? Given the right information, he could control even a god.

Control!

What was prayer but a whining, sniveling attempt to control. Supplication? Threats?

If You don't get me assigned to Medical, Ship, I'll abandon WorShip!

So much for WorShip. The gods, if there were any, could have a good laugh.

Abruptly, he was sobered by memory of Illuyank's death.

Damn this place!

To walk in a shipside agrarium right now … or even in a treedome …

He remembered once nightside on the ship, walking out through the shutter-baffles to a dome on the rim, pressing his forehead against the plaz to stare into the void. Out there, stars whirled in their slow spin and he had known, beyond a doubt, that they spun around him. But, in the face of those uncounted stars, he had felt himself slipping into a maw of terrifying black. On the other side of that plasmaglass barrier, whole galaxies awoke and whole galaxies died every second. No call for help could carry beyond the tip of his own tongue. No caress could survive the cold.

Who else in that universe was this much alone?

Ship.

The voice of his mind had spoken the unexpected. But he had known it for the truth. In that instant he had seen, in the plaz, the reflection of his own eyes melting into the dark between the stars. He recalled that he had stepped back in mute surprise.

That look! That same expression!

It had been on the face of the black man back on Earth when they took the man away.

Remembering, he realized it was the same expression he now saw in Legata's eyes.

In my eyes … in her eyes … in the eyes of the black man from my childhood …

Now, feeling the groundside cubby around him, all of the concentric rings of walls and barriers which comprised Colony, he sensed how his unguarded body could be betrayed.

I could betray myself to myself.

And perhaps to others.

To Thomas?

To the ship?

No matter his denials, the mystery of deep space and inner space filled him with wonder and fear. This was a weakness and it required that he deal with it directly.

God or not, the ship was one of a kind. As I am.

And what if … Ship were really God?

Oakes passed his tongue over his lips. He stood alone in the center of his cubby and listened.

For what am I listening?

He could only move by testing, by forcing the exchange, by groping beyond the ken of all other Shipmen. The key to the ship lay in its movements. Why did any organism move?

To seek pleasure, to avoid pain.

Food was pleasure. He felt hunger knot his stomach. Sex was pleasure. Where was Legata right now? Victory was pleasure. That would have to wait.

Let the pains demand their own actions.

Always the pendulum swung: pleasure/pain … pleasure/pain. Intensity and period varied; the balance, the mean, did not.

What sweets would tempt a god? What thorn would lift a god's foot?

It came over Oakes that he had been standing for a long time in one position, his gaze fixed on the mandala pattern attached to his cubby wall. It copied the one he had left shipside. Legata had made this copy for him before … She had produced another in her finest hand and it already was displayed at the Redoubt. How he wished the Redoubt were ready! Demons gone, dayside and nightside safe. Many times he had dreamed of stepping out into Pandora's double-sunshine, a light breeze ruffling his hair, Legata on his arm for a walk through gardens down to a gentle sea.

A sudden image of Legata clawing at her eyes replaced this pastoral vision. Oakes fought for a deep breath, his gaze fixed on the mandala.

Lewis has to destroy all of the demons—the kelp, everything!

It required a physical effort for Oakes to break himself away from his fixation on the mandala. He turned, walked three steps, stopped … He was facing the mandala!

What's happening to my mind?

Daydreaming. That had to be it, letting his mind wander. The pressure of all those demons outside Colony's perimeter walls overwhelmed him with feelings of vulnerability. He had lost the insulation he had enjoyed shipside—exchanged the perils of the ship for the perils of Pandora.

Who would ever have thought I'd miss the ship?

The damned Colonists were too brash, too quick. They thought they could barge in any time, interrupt anything. They talked too fast. Everything had to be done right now!

His com-console buzzed at him.

Oakes depressed a key. Murdoch's thin face stared at him from the screen. Murdoch began speaking without asking leave, without any preamble.

"My dayside orders say you wanted Illuyank assigned to …"

"Illuyank's dead," Oakes said, his voice flat. He enjoyed the look of surprise on Murdoch's face. That was one of the reasons for secret random sampling among the spy sensors. No matter what horrors you found, the information could make you appear omnipotent.

"Find someone else for my guard squad," Oakes said. "Make it someone more suitable." He broke the connection.

There! That was the way they did it groundside. Quick decisions.

The reminder of Illuyank's death brought back the knot in his stomach. Food. He needed something to eat. He turned, and once more found himself looking at the mandala.

Things will simply have to slow down.

The mandala rippled before his eyes, myriad grotesque faces weaving in and out of the design, folding upon themselves.

Belatedly, he realized that one of the faces was that of Rachel Demarest. *Silly bitch!* The Scream Room had driven her out of her mind … what was left of her mind. Running outside like that! Enough people had seen the demons get her that no blame would be laid at his hatch. One problem gone … but running outside …

Everything reminds me of outside!

Someone else would have to be found to make the liquor deliveries to old Win Ferry. Pure grain spirits he wanted now. And Ferry would have to get the message—no more pestering questions about that Demarest woman.

Oakes found that his hands ached and he realized both fists were clenched. He forced himself to relax, began to rub at the beginnings of cramp in his fingers. Maybe another small drink of the wine … No!

All this frustration! For what?

Only one answer, the answer he had given Lewis so many times: For this world.

Victory would give them their own safe world. Unconsciously, his right hand went out and touched the mandala. What a price! And Legata—historian, search technician, beautiful woman—perhaps she would be his queen. He owed her that, at least. Empress. His finger traced the maze of lines in the mandala, flowing intricacies.

"Politics is your life, not mine," Lewis had said.

Lewis did not know what it cost. All Lewis wanted was his lab and the safety of the Redoubt.

"Leave me alone here. You can proclaim and make policy all you want."

They were a great team—one in front and one behind.

Maybe just a little bit of the wine. He picked up the bottle and sipped from it. This Raja Thomas would be eliminated soon. Another victim of the kelp.

Lewis ought to drink more of this wine. They've really improved it.

Oakes sipped the wine, aerated it across his tongue with a slurping sound which he knew always made Lewis uneasy.

"You really should treat yourself to some of this stuff, Jesus. You might smooth some of those lines out of your face."

"No thanks."

"All the more for me, then."

"You and Ferry."

"No. I can take it or leave it alone."

"We have urgent problems," Lewis kept saying.

But urgency should never mean hurry, incautious rushing about. He had told Lewis in no uncertain terms: "If we're relaxed and reasonable in our urgency to complete the Redoubt, the solutions we find will be relaxed and reasonable."

No need for chaos.

He slurped more of the wine while staring at the mandala. The way those lines twisted—they, too, appeared to come right out of chaos. But Legata had found the design of it, duplicated it twice. Design. Pandora had its design, too. He just had to find it. Peel away all of this dissonance, and there would be the foundations of order.

We'll finish off the kelp, the Runners. Chlorine. Lots of it. Things will start making sense around here pretty soon.

He lifted the bottle to take another sip, found that there was no more wine in it. He let the bottle slip out of his hand, heard it thump on the floor. As though that were the signal, his com-console buzzed at him once more.

Murdoch again.

"Demarest's people are asking for another meeting, Doctor."

"Stall them! I told you to . . . stall them."

"I'll try."

Murdoch did not sound very happy with the decision.

Oakes took two stabs with a finger to break the connection. *How many times did you have to give an order around this damned place?*

Once more, he focused on the mandala.

"We'll have some order around here pretty soon," he told it.

He realized then that he had taken too much wine. It sounded ridiculous, talking to himself in quarters this way, but he enjoyed hearing certain things, even if he had to be the one who voiced them.

"Gonna get some order around here."

Where was that damned Legata? Had to tell her to get some order into things.

Chapter 37

As the rock silences the sea, the One in one silences the universe.
—Kerro Panille, *Translations from the Avata*

LEGATA PUT her shuttle on automatic for its landing at the Redoubt station. She leaned back into her couch and watched the shoreline sweep past beneath her. This time was her own. It was early dayside and she did not have to deal with Oakes or Lewis just yet, nor with demons or clones. She had nothing to do but watch, relax and breathe easy.

Hylighters!

She had seen them on holo, and a few had skirted Colony while she was there, but these hung no more than two hundred meters from the plaz in front of her.

Ship's teeth! They're huge!

She counted twelve of them, the largest one half again as big as her shuttle. Their bronzed orange sails caught the wind and they tacked in unison, almost escorting her. The sunlight through the membrane of their sails shimmered rainbows all over them. Most of their tentacles were tucked up against their bodies. They each held a ballast-rock with their two longest tendrils. The larger ones allowed the rocks to drag in the sea, forming a frothy wake. They tacked, and tacked again, picking up on the shifts of wind. As her shuttle settled into its final glide-path, she saw two of the smaller hylighters separate from the rest, pick up speed and slam the boulders they carried into the plaz shield surrounding Oakes' private garden.

Garden, she shuddered at the thought of the word.

The boulders had no effect on the plaz—she could crash her shuttle into it and it might shatter, but rocks …

The two hylighters disappeared in a flash so bright that for a few blinks she was blinded. When her vision cleared, she saw that her shuttle was down and linked with the entry lock, and that the two exploded hylighters had been a diversion. The others, all larger, slammed their rocks into the walls and plaz of the Redoubt where it had already been damaged by the clones. Each boulder chipped off a few more chunks of the buildings before the sentries focused on the sails. The other hylighters too, went up in a flash. The largest one was so close to the shuttle station when it exploded that it took part of the control tower and rigging with it.

They give their lives for this, she thought. *They are either very foolish or very noble.*

Several parts of the grounds were in flames and a work crew, covered by sentries, was busy fighting the fires. Lewis beckoned her from the plaz verandah at Oakes' quarters and it was only then that she noticed the scorchmarks across the dome of her shuttle,

She opened her hatch and stepped out between two sentries who escorted her along the covered way to the Redoubt. There was a strong taint of chlorine lingering over everything.

At least we don't have to worry about Runners, she thought.

Over the chlorine she caught the sea-smell from the beach, and saw that the tideline had moved down several meters from its usual mark. The damp sand left behind was warmed by the suns. A heavy mist rose from it, dissipating in wisps over the rocks and the sea. She did not look at Lewis until she stepped up to the verandah.

"Legata," he offered his hand, "how are you?"

The searching expression in his eyes told her all that she needed to know.

So that's why I'm here, she thought. *He wants to explore my current … utility before Oakes arrives.*

"Quite well," she said, "that was a wonderful display the hylighters put on. Did you arrange it just for me?"

"If I'd arranged it, it wouldn't have cost us damage we can't afford."

He led her inside and closed the hatch behind them.

"How much damage?"

He was leading her further inside, away from the plaz. She wanted to see the grounds, the repairs.

"Not irreparable. Would you care for something to eat?"

A woman with large, fanlike ears walked past them, accompanied by a normal crewman carrying a lasgun.

"No, thank you, I'm not hungry."

At Legata's response, the woman turned, looked her full into the eyes as if she wanted to say something, then turned quickly and went outside. Legata remembered that a rallying cry of the clone revolt had been *I'm hungry now*, and she was embarrassed.

"Those ears … why?"

"She can hear a Hooded Dasher at a hundred meters. That gives us a full second's advantage. Attractive, too, don't you think?"

"Yes," Legata said coldly, "quite."

She noticed that Lewis was still limping, but she did not sympathize with him. Although she was curious about details of the revolt, she didn't ask. She countered by not dropping the subject.

"How reparable is 'not irreparable'?"

Lewis dropped his cordiality and assumed his usual businesslike air.

"We lost most of our clone work force. Fewer than half of those remaining are effective. We're getting replacements from Colony and the ship, but that's slow work. Two of the finished hangars are badly damaged—hatches missing, holes in the walls. The clones' quarters have their exterior walls and hatches intact, but the interiors are completely useless. Serves 'em right. Let 'em sleep on the piles of plaz."

"What about this building?"

"Took some damage back where the clones' quarters join with the storage area. They got into the kitchen but that's where we sealed them off ..."

"You sealed them off?"

Lewis glanced away from her, then back. He rubbed his nose with his finger and she was reminded of Oakes when he was nervous. When it became obvious that he wouldn't answer, she nodded.

"After you discovered chlorine killed the Runners, how long before you released it among the people you had sealed off?"

"Now, Legata, you weren't here. You didn't see what they were...."

"How long?"

He looked her in the eyes, but did not answer.

"So, you killed them."

"Runners killed them."

"But you could've killed the Runners."

"Then the clones would've gotten inside and killed us. You weren't here. You don't know what it was like."

"Yes, I think I do. Show me to Morgan's Garden."

It took all of her nerve just to say that word. Whatever that horror she had confronted at Colony, the name of The Garden would not be shaken off, even though she could not remember. But she saw it made Lewis uneasy to think about it and she would be damned if she would ease anything for him.

Lewis was obviously shaken by the sudden reference to The Garden. It meant Scream Room to him, too. She could see the questions forming behind his eyes: *How much does she know? Why isn't she afraid?* She refused to allow herself the luxury of fear. Let him see that much. Until she herself remembered what had happened, she would not allow anyone else to capitalize on her experience there.

"Yes," he said, his voice almost hushed, "of course. The Garden. You can relax there until Morgan comes. This way."

Lewis led Legata through the finished parts of the resort and into the main dwelling, a mammoth structure carved entirely out of the mottled stone of the mountainside and lined with plasteel. She turned at the entryway and looked back over the grounds and out across the sea.

"This hatchway opens to Morgan's quarters. The study, library and cubby are all in this unit. Further back are the meeting and dining areas, all of that. I'll take you through them if you like."

She watched the pulse of waves explode against the seawall ahead of them and imagined she could hear the slap and crash of the water through the insulating plaz.

"Legata?"

"Yes. I mean, no, you don't have to guide me. I'd like to be alone."

"Very well." Lewis spoke abruptly, "Morgan said that you are to be comfortable. I suggest you check with me before wandering around. You may need a sentry for some of the more exposed areas. It's still early and I'm not due back at Colony until after mid-meal. Call if you need me."

With that, the hatch hissed shut and she was alone.

Once more, she looked at the sea. It tumbled away forever, drawing her consciousness outward, reaching.

There's a power here that even Morgan can't buy, she thought, and fought back the temptation to run past the plazzed-in trees, the flowers, and the pond, past the stream meandering through the grasses, past the protection of the compound itself and into the wild sea air of Pandora. Then she noticed the kelp. The great masses of it which had glutted the beaches and the bay outside the Redoubt were reduced to a few isolated clumps and some long, serpentine tendrils undulating at the surface. Lewis' doing! A sudden sadness filled her eyes with tears and she whispered aloud to the kelp, "I hope they're wrong. I hope you make it."

She caught a movement out of the corner of her eye and turned to see two clones working on the tower at the shuttle station.

Morgan's expected in, she thought, they'll want things looking as controlled as possible.

She looked closer at the two men, her attention caught by the fact that they were lifting and welding plaz that was at least four meters off the ground—and neither was using scaffolding.

Those arms …

She wondered, coldly, where those workers fit within the clone index and price list.

"Cost is no object, my dear," Murdoch had said, and something in his inflection had terrified her. This terror was rekindled by the sight of the two workers busily welding plaz.

Anything went, she thought. *My every fantasy was possible.*

Why can't I remember?

Whatever horrors or pleasures took place in the Scream Room were no longer a part of her consciousness. There were flashes, uncontrollable and swift, that struck her mute in mid-conversation or mid-thought. Those who worked with her attributed it to a growing absentmindedness, an offshoot of her apparent love affair with The Boss.

She knew she could find the Scream Room holo and see for herself what she had done. Oakes taunted her with it.

"Dear Legata," his every corpulent pore oozed honey and oil, "sit here with me, have a nice drink, and we'll enjoy your games in the Scream Room."

He laughed at first when she shuddered and turned away. It was difficult for her to keep any personal control—he'd seen to that when he'd had her trapped and helpless down in Lab One. And now the Scream Room had been moved to the Redoubt.

The laughter died away and he had spoken to her directly and flatly, "Like it or not, you're one of us now. You can never go back. You may never walk into that room again, but you did walk into it once. Of your own free will, I might add."

"Free will!" Her blue eyes flashed up at him. "You drugged me! And those … monsters. Where was their free will?"

"They would have no will at all, no existence at all, if it weren't for me.…"

"If it weren't for Ship, you mean."

He sighed overdramatically. She remembered that he glanced at his viewscreen and made a few adjustments on his console.

"Sometimes I really don't understand you, Legata. One day soon you'll be luxuriating in the Redoubt and its exquisite pleasures, and here you are mumbling dark-ages crap about the mystical powers of Ship."

He had shown her a holo, then, of this garden around her now. There was no question of its beauty. It was thick with vegetation and the perfumes of countless blossoms. She turned her eyes up to the dome. The immensity and wonder of the Pandoran sky pumped a strange surge of power through her. She experienced a feeling of … of …

Connection! she thought. *Yes, no matter what he does, somehow all of this is alive in me just as I live in it now.*

At Colony the nightside before, as she had been preparing to leave for the Redoubt, Oakes had escorted her into the tiny plaz dome far above his quarters.

"There," he had pointed out a large white glow slowly traversing the horizon, "there is your ship. Another pinpoint in the night. It takes no mysticism, no degree of godhood whatsoever, for one bit of mass to orbit another."

"That's blasphemy," she answered, because he expected it.

"Is it? Ship can defend itself. Nothing is out of the hearing or the reach of Ship. Ship could terminate my program at any instant—but chooses not to. Or can't. Either is the same to me. Blasphemy?"

He had squeezed her hand tight, then. *Convincing himself,* she thought, and she had enjoyed the power this observation gave her.

He gestured widely, indicating the entire display of stars.

"I have brought you to this, not Ship. Ship is a tool. Complexity to the fifth power, granted, but still a tool. Built by people, thinking people, for the use of thinking people. People who know how to take charge, how to see light in the darkening storm of confusion.…"

As he had raved on into the night, Legata had realized that much of what he said held a surprising sense of truth. She knew that, at the bottom of whatever was happening to Shipmen both on and off Ship, it was a result of noninterference by Ship itself. But she had delved into the secrets of Ship's circuitry for too long and too deeply to believe that Ship was a piece of steel and molded plastics, that Ship didn't care.

She stood in the garden at the Redoubt and looked up at what she guessed to be Ship's position above them.

I wonder, she thought, *I wonder if we're a disappointment.*

Two patrol drones screamed over the dome and shattered Legata's reverie. She guessed that Oakes would be coming soon; they were gearing up for him. She realized that she should prepare too.

Nothing, she reminded herself, *is sacred.*

Then, in a sudden leap of insight during the heavy stillness following the drones, she added, *but something should be.* This thought was liberating, exhilarating.

Chapter 38

The universe has no center.

—Shipquotes

RAJA THOMAS stood under the gigantic semi-inflated bag of the LTA in the main hangar. Lavu's crew had gone, turning off most of the lights. It was full nightside now. The bag was a dim orange bulk tugging gently at its tethers above him. There were great folds and concavities in it yet, but before Alki joined Rega dayside, they would be airborne, the bag as full and smooth as a hylighter.

Except that no hylighter of that size had ever been seen.

Thomas glanced across the dark hangar, impatient to leave. *Why does Oakes want to meet me here?*

The order had been succinct and simple. Oakes was coming out especially to inspect the LTA and its attached sub before allowing them to venture into the unprotected wilderness of Pandora's sea.

Is he about to veto the project?

The implications were clear: Too much Colony energy went into projects such as this one. It was contra-survival. The exterminators wanted their way. This might be the last scientific investigation permitted for a long time. Too many subs lost … too many LTAs. Such energy could be applied to food production.

The contrary argument of reason found fewer listeners with every passing hour of hunger.

Without the knowledge we gain there may never be dependable food production on Pandora. The kelp is sentient. It rules this planet.

What did the kelp call Pandora?

Home.

Was that Ship or my own imagination?

No response.

Thomas knew he was too keyed up, too full of uncertainties. Doubts. It would be so easy to share every viewpoint Oakes put forward. Agree with him. Even some of Lavu's crew had been picking up that muttered catch phrase which could be heard all through Colony: *I'm hungry now.*

Where was Oakes?

Keeping me waiting to teach me my place.

The self-constructed persona of Raja Thomas dominated this thought, but there were distant echoes of Flattery in it—distant but distinct. He felt like an actor well seated in his part after many performances. The Flattery self lay in his past like a childhood memory.

What have You hidden in the depths of the sea, Ship?

That is for you to discover.

There! That definitely was Ship talking to him.

The LTA creaked against its tethers. Thomas stepped from beneath it and peered up at the sphincter leaves of the skydoor—a vast shadowy circle in the dim light. His nostrils tasted a faint bitterness of Pandoran esters in the air. Colony had found that some volatile renderings from selected demons insulated the area around them against other ravening native predators—especially against Nerve Runners. Nothing was forever, though. The demons soon developed counter-responses.

Thomas looked back at the shadowed sub—a smooth black rock held in the tentacles of an artificial hylighter ... a smooth black rock with glittering lines down its sides.

Again, the LTA creaked against its tethers. There was a draft in the hangar and he hoped this did not mean some unguarded opening to Pandora's dangerous exterior. He was unarmed and alone here except for perimeter guards at the ground-level hatches, and a watchman off somewhere brewing tea. Thomas could smell it faintly—a familiar thing but marked by the subtle differences of Pandoran chemistry.

Am I being set up to go the way Rachel Demarest went?

He was a doubting man but there was no doubt in his mind about the way of Rachel's passing. It had been too convenient, the timing too good.

Who could question it, though?

Such things happened every day on perimeter patrol. Colony had a number for this attrition: one in seventy. It was like losses in a war. Soldiers knew. Except that most Shipmen appeared to know very little about war in the historic sense.

They knew soldiering, though.

He sniffed.

A faintly sweet undertone of native lubricants drifted on the air. This made him acutely aware of how grudgingly this planet gave up any of its substance to Colony. He had seen the reports—just cutting in the wells for those lubricants had cost them one life for every six diurns. And there was a general reluctance to go for cloned replacements—an unexplainable reluctance.

Fewer and fewer clones around, except out at that mysterious project on Dragon.

What was Lewis doing out there?

Why the growing split between clones and naturals? Was it something about being groundside?

We originated on a planet.

Was there some atavistic memory at work here?

Why don't You answer me, Ship?

When you need to know, you will know without asking.

Typical Ship answer!

What did Oakes mean by new clones? Are You helping him on that project, Ship? Are these new clones Your project?

Who helped you make Me, Devil?

Thomas felt his throat go dry. There had been barbs in that response. He glanced at the sub suspended off to his left. Quite suddenly, he saw it as representing a fragile and foolish venture. Sub and LTA had been shaped to simulate a hylighter carrying its characteristic rock ballast. No matter that the sub did not look much like rock.

I should be out preaching Ship's demand instead of risking my ancient flesh on this venture.

But Ship had given him no stature for this game, no platform upon which to stand.

How will you WorShip?

No matter the different ways Ship phrased the question, it came out the same.

Who would listen to an unknown, self-proclaimed Ceepee awakened from hyb? He was an admitted clone, member of a minority whose role was being redefined by Oakes.

Talk to the sentient vegetable. Did the kelp have an answer? Ship hinted at it, but refused to say definitely.

That's for you to discover, Devil.

No help there. No clues on how he could open a conversation with this alien sentience. In the abstract, it was an exciting idea—talk to a life form so different from humankind that few evolutionary parallels could be drawn.

What strange things could we learn from them?

What could the kelp learn from him?

Again, Thomas glanced at his chrono. This delay was getting ridiculous!

Why do I permit it?

By this time Waela will have our poet in her cubby.

A deep sigh shook him.

Processing had released Panille less than an hour before nightside. They delayed him deliberately … the way Oakes is delaying now. What did they have in mind?

Waela, if …

Could that be the cause of Oakes' delay? Had Oakes discovered that Waela …

Thomas shook his head sharply. Foolish speculation!

He felt cold and exposed waiting here in the hangar, and there was no denying his uneasiness at thoughts of Waela.

Waela and the poet.

Thomas felt torn by his own imagination. He had never before experienced such a powerful physical attraction toward a woman. And there was in his background, dredged up from that ancient conditioning process, a terrifying drive toward possession—private and exclusive possession. He knew this ran directly counter to much of the behavior Ship had allowed … or promoted.

Waela … Waela …

He had to force a mask of distant, deliberate coolness. *The delay with Panille could have been the time for preparing him to act against me.* They could have been briefing him. It was necessary that Waela become intimate with this poet, peel away his masks and find … What?

Panille … Pandora …

More of Ship's doing?

Waela would find out. She had her orders. She must turn this Panille inside out, peer at the center of his being. She would learn and report back to her commander.

Me.

Who obeyed Oakes that way? Lewis, certainly. And Murdoch. And that Legata. What a surprise to find she was the Hamill of Ship's briefing. Did they set traps the way he had set this one for Panille?

Waela would do it right. It must seem a fortuitous accident to Panille. The right time … the right conditions …

Dammit! How can I be jealous? I set this up!

He knew he was performing according to Ship's design. And probably according to Oakes' design. What was the relationship between Oakes and Ship?

Blasphemous man, Oakes. But Ship allowed the blasphemy. And Oakes might be right.

Thomas had come to suspect more and more that Ship might not be God.

What did we make when we created Ship?

Thomas knew his own hand in that creation. But had there been other, unseen hands in that construction?

Who helped you make Me, Devil?

God or Satan? What did we make?

At this moment, it did not much matter. He was tired in body and emotions and his dominant personal hope was that Panille would see through the sexual trap and defy it. Thomas did not really expect that to happen.

I'm doing Your job to the best of my ability, Ship.

"A function of my Devil is to frustrate good works. Shipmen must extend themselves beyond anything they believe possible."

Those had been Ship's words to him.

Why? Because frustration helped us to succeed with Project Consciousness?

Were they only replaying an old theme which had worked once and might work once more?

It occurred to him then that the Moonbase director who had supervised the building and the crew preparations for that original Voidship—old Morgan Hempstead—had served this identical function.

He was our Devil and we knew it. But now I'm Ship's Devil … and best friend.

Thomas found cynical delight in this thought. Being a friend of Ship carried special perils. Oakes might have chosen the better role. *Enemy of Ship.* Thomas knew his own role, though. Ship chided him with it often enough.

"Play the game, Devil."

Yes, he had to play the game even though he lost.

A scraping noise intruded on his awareness. The sound came from the locker area where the sub crews prepared for their flights. Dead men's lockers, the Colony called them.

Something moved in the shadows over there, a waddling figure clad in a white shipsuit. Thomas recognized Oakes. Alone. So it was going to be that kind of a meeting.

Thomas took a handlight from his pocket and waved it to show where he stood.

Responding to the light, Oakes changed his path slightly. Oakes always felt diminished by the hangar area. Too much space used for too little return.

Bad investment.

Thomas appeared dwarfed by the immensity of the semi-inflated bag overhead.

These thoughts firmed his resolve. It would not pay to cancel this project outright without a dramatic motive. There were still some who supported it. Oakes knew the arguments.

Learn to live with the kelp!

You did not live with a wild cobra; you killed it.

Yes, Thomas had to go … but dramatically, very dramatically. Two Cee-pees could not co-exist in Colony.

Oakes did not want to know what Lewis and Murdoch had arranged. An accident with the submersible, perhaps. There already had been enough accidents without arrangement. The cost in Shipmen lives had reached abrasive levels. Colonists expected casualties while they subdued this planet, but the latest attrition rate went beyond the tolerable.

As he came up to Thomas, Oakes smiled openly. It was a gesture he could afford.

"Well, let's look at this new submersible," Oakes said.

He allowed himself to be guided to the sub's side hatch and into the cramped command gondola at the core, noting that Thomas offered no small talk, none of the unconscious obeisance of language which Oakes had come to expect from those around him. Everything was business, technical: Here were the new sonar instruments, the remote-recording sensors, the nephelometers …

Nephelometers?

Oakes had to cast back into his medical training for the association.

Oh, yes. Instruments for collecting and examining small particles suspended in the water.

Oakes almost laughed. It was not small particles which needed study but the giant kelp: fully visible and certainly vulnerable. In spite of his amusement, Oakes managed a few seemingly responsive questions.

"What makes you say that everything in the sea has to serve the kelp?"

"Because that's what we find, that's the condition of the sea. Everything from the grazing cycles of the biota to the distribution of trace metals, everything fits the growth demands of the kelp. We must find out why."

"Grazing cycles of …"

"The biota—all the living matter … The mud-dwelling creatures and those on the surface, all appear to be in a profound symbiotic relationship with the kelp. The grazers, for example, stir the toxic products cast off by the kelp into a layer of highly absorbent sediment where other creatures restore these substances to the food chain. They …"

"You mean the kelp shits and this is processed by animals on the bottom?"

"That would be one way of stating it, but the total implication of the sea system is disturbing. There are leaf grazers, for instance, whose only function is to keep the kelp's leaves clean. The few predators all have large fins, much larger than you'd expect for their size, and …"

"What does that have to do with …"

"They stir the water around the kelp."

"Huh?" For a moment, Oakes had found his interest aroused, but Thomas had all the earmarks of a specialist blowing his own private horn—even to the esoteric language of the specialty. This was supposed to be a communications expert?

Just to keep things moving, Oakes asked the expected question: "What disturbing implications?"

"The kelp is influencing the sea far more than simple evolutionary processes can explain. Perhaps it supports the marine community. The only historical comparisons we can make lead us to believe that a sentient force is at work here."

"Sentient!" Oakes put as much disdain as he could muster into the word. That damned report on kelp-hylighter relationships! Lewis was supposed to have made it inaccessible. Was the ship interfering?

"A conscious design," Thomas said.

"Or an extremely long-lived adaptation and evolution."

Thomas shook his head. There was another possibility, but he did not care to discuss it with Oakes. What if Ship had created this planet precisely the way they found it? Why would Ship do such a thing?

Oakes had absorbed enough from this encounter. He had made the gesture. Everyone would see that he was concerned. His guards were waiting back there at the hatch. They would talk. Losses were too high and the Ceepee had to look into it himself. Time to end it.

Oakes relaxed visibly. How nicely things were working.

And Thomas thought: *He's going to let us go without a struggle. All right, Ship. I'm going to pry into one of Your secret places. If You made this planet to teach us Your WorShip, there have to be clues in the sea.*

"Well, I'll want a complete report when you return," Oakes said. "Some of your data may help us begin a useful aquaculture project."

He left then, muttering loud enough to be heard: "Sentient kelp!"

As he walked back across the hangar, Oakes thought it had been one of his best performances, and all of it caught by the sensors, all of it recorded and stored. When … whatever Lewis had arranged happened, they would be able to edit excerpts from the record.

See how concerned I was?

From the sub's hatch, Thomas watched Oakes leave, then slipped back down for a final inspection of the core. Had Oakes sabotaged something? All appeared normal. His gaze fell on the central command seat, then on the secondary position to the left where Waela would sit. He caressed the back of the seat.

I'm an old fool. What would I do? Waste precious time with a useless dalliance? And what if she refused to respond to me? What then, old fool?

Old!

Who but Ship even suspected how old? Original material. A clone, a doppelganger—but original material. Nothing like it alive and moving anywhere else in the universe.

So Ship said.

Don't you believe Me, Devil?

The thought was a static burst in Thomas' awareness. He spoke as he often did to answer Ship when alone. No matter that some thought him slightly mad.

"Does it matter whether I believe You?"

It matters to Me.

"Then that's an edge I have and You don't.'"

You regret your decision to play this game?

"I keep my word."

And you gave Me your word.

Thomas knew it did not matter whether he said this aloud or merely thought it, but he found himself unable to prevent the outburst.

"Did I give my word to Satan or to God?"

Who can settle that question to your satisfaction?

"Maybe You're Satan and I'm God."

That is very close, My Doubting Thomas!

"Close to what?"

Only you can tell.

As usual, nothing was settled in such an exchange except the re-establishment of the master-servant relationship. Thomas slipped into the command seat, sighed. Presently, he began going through the instrument checklist, more to distract himself than for any other reason. Oakes had not come to sabotage but to make a show of some kind.

Devil?

So, Ship was not through with him.

"Yes, Ship?"

There is something you need to know.

Thomas felt his heartbeat quicken. Ship seldom volunteered information. It must be something momentous.

"What is it?"

You recall Hali Ekel?

That name was familiar … yes; he had seen it in the Panille dossier which Waela had supplied.

"Panille's med-tech friend, yes. What about her?"

I have exposed her to a segment of a dominant human past.

"A replay? But You said …"

A segment, Devil, not a replay. You must learn the distinction. When there is a lesson someone needs, you do not have to show the entire record; you can show only a marked passage, a segment.

"Am I living in a marked passage right now?"

This is an original play, a true sequel.

"Why tell me this? What are you doing?"

Because you were trained as a Chaplain. It is important that you know what Hali has experienced. I have shown her the Jesus incident.

Thomas felt his mouth go dry. He was a moment recovering, then: "The Hill of Skulls? Why?"

Her life has been too tame. She must learn how far holy violence can extend. You, too, need this reminder.

Thomas thought about a sheltered young woman from the shipside life being exposed suddenly to the crucifixion. It angered him and he let that anger appear in his voice.

"You're interfering, aren't You!"

This is My universe, too, Devil. Never forget that.

"Why did you do that?"

Prelude to other data. Panille has recognized the trap you set for him and avoided it. Waela failed.

Thomas knew he could not conceal his elation and did not try. But a question remained: "Is Panille Your pawn?"

Are you My pawn?

Thomas felt a tight band across his chest. Nothing worked the way he expected. Presently, he found his voice.

"How did he recognize the trap?"

By being open to his peril.

"What does that mean?"

You are not open, as My Devil should be.

"And You told me You wouldn't interfere with the roll of the dice!"

I never said I would not interfere; I said there would be no outside interference.

Thomas thought about that while he fought to overcome a deep sense of frustration. It was too much and he spoke his feelings: "You're in the game: You can do anything You want and You don't call that ..."

You, too, can do anything you want.

This froze him. What powers had Ship imparted to him? He did not feel powerful. He felt helpless before Ship's omnipresence. And this business of Hali Ekel and the Jesus incident! What did it mean?

Once more, Ship intruded: *Devil, I tell you that some things take their own course only if you fail to detect that course. Waela really feels a powerful attraction toward young Panille.*

Young Panille!

Thomas spoke past an emptiness in his breast: "Why do You torture me?"

You torture yourself.

"So You say!"

When will you awaken? There was no mistaking Ship's frustrated emphasis.

Thomas found that he did not fear this. He was much too tired and there was no more reason for him to stay here in the sub. Oakes had approved the venture. They would go out on schedule—Waela and Panille with him.

"Ship, I'll awaken early tomorrow and take out this LTA and its sub."

Would that this were true.

"You intend to stop me?" Thomas found himself oddly delighted at the prospect of Ship interfering in this particular way.

Stop you? No. The play must run its course apparently.

Was that sadness in Ship's projection? Thomas could not be certain. He sat back. There was a stabbing ache between his shoulder blades. He closed his eyes, sent his fatigue and frustrations out in thought.

"Ship, I know I can't hide anything from You. And You know why I'm going out to the sea tomorrow."

Yes, I know even what you hide from yourself.

"Are You my psychiatrist now?"

Which of us usurps the function of the other? That has always been the question.

Thomas opened his eyes. "I have to do it."

That is the origin of the illusion men call kismet.

"I'm too tired to play word games."

Thomas slipped out of the command seat and stood up. He kept one hand on the seat back, spoke as much to himself as to Ship.

"We could all die tomorrow, Waela, Panille and I."

I must warn you that truisms represent the most boring of all human indulgences.

Thomas felt Ship's intrusive presence withdraw, but he knew that nothing had been taken away. Wherever he went, whatever he did, Ship was there.

He found his thoughts winging back to that faraway time when he had been trained (conditioned, really) not merely as a Psychiatrist, but as a Chaplain/Psychiatrist.

"Fear him which is able to destroy both soul and body in hell."

Old Matthew knew how to put the fear of God in you!

Thomas found it took him several blinks to overcome a sense of panic so deep that it kept him locked in place.

Early training is the most powerful, he reminded himself.

Chapter 39

Man also knows not his time: as the fishes that are taken in an evil net, and as the birds that are caught in the snare; so are the sons of men snared in an evil time, when it falls suddenly upon them.

—*Christian Book of the Dead, Shiprecords*

FOR A long time after returning to Ship from the Hill of Skulls, Hali could not find the will to leave the room. She stared up and around at the softly illuminated space—this secret place where Kerro had spent so many hours communing with Ship. She remembered the borrowed flesh of the old woman, the painful and halting steps. The ache of aging shoulders. A feeling of profound sensitivity to her familiar body pervaded her awareness; each tiny movement became electric with immediacy.

She remembered the man who had been nailed to the rigid crosspiece on the hill. Barbaric!

Yaisuah.

She whispered it: "Yaisuah."

It was understandable how this name had evolved into that of Jesus … and even to the Heysoos of Jesus Lewis.

But nowhere could she find understanding of why she had been taken to witness that agonizing scene. Nowhere. And she found it odd that she had never encountered historical records of that faraway event—not in Ship's teachings nor in the memories of Shipmen who came from Earth.

In the first moments of her return, she had asked Ship why she had been shown that brutal incident, and had received an enigmatic response.

Because there are things from the human past that no creature should forget.

"But why me? Why now?"

The rest was silence. She assumed that the answers were her own to find.

She stared at the com-console. The seat there at the instruction terminal was her seat now; she knew it. Kerro was gone … groundside. Ship had introduced her to this place, had given it to her.

The message was clear: *No more Kerro Panille here.*

A shuddering wave of loss shot through her, and she shook tears from her eyes. This was no place to stay now. She stood, took up her pribox and slipped out the way she had entered.

Why me?

She wound her way out of Softwares and into D passage leading back to Medical, into the workings of Ship's body.

The beep of her pribox startled her.

"Ekel here," she said, surprised at the youthfulness of her own voice—not at all like the ancient quavering of that old woman's voice she had borrowed.

Her pribox crackled, then: "Ekel, report to Dr. Ferry's office."

She found a servo and, instead of walking, rode to Medical.

Ferry, she thought. Could it mean reassignment? *Could I be joining Kerro groundside?*

The thought excited her, but the idea of groundside duty remained fearful. So many nasty rumors. And lately, all groundside assignments seemed permanent. Except for the tight-knit political circle at Medical, no one made the return trip. Pressures of work had kept her from thinking much about this before, but suddenly it became vital.

What are they doing with all our people?

The drain on equipment and food from Ship was a topic for constant anxious conversation; recurrent dayside orders exhorted greater production efforts … but few speculated about missing people.

We've been conditioned not to face the finality of absolute endings. Is that why Ship showed me Yaisuah?

The thought stood there in her awareness, riding on the hum of the servo carrying her toward Medical and Ferry.

It was clear to her that Yaisuah had ended, but his influence had not ended. Pandora was a place of endings. It gulped food and people and equipment. What influences were about to be sent reverberating from that place?

Endings.

The servo fell silent, stopped. She looked up to see Medical's servo gate and, across the passage, the hatch to Ferry's offices. She did not want to go through that hatch. Her body still throbbed with sensitivities ignited by what Ship had shown her. She did not want Ferry touching her body. It was more than her dislike for him—the silly old fool! He drank too much of the alcohol which came up from Colony and he always reached out to put a hand on her somewhere.

Everyone knew the Demarest woman brought him his wine from groundside. He always had plenty of it after her visits.

His food chits can't support that kind of drinking.

She stared at the dogged hatch across the way. Something was definitely wrong—shipside and groundside. Why did Rachel Demarest bring wine up to Ferry?

If she brings him wine, what does she get in return?

Love? Why not? Even neurotics like Ferry and Demarest needed love. Or … if not love, at least an occasional couch partner.

A remembered image of Foul-breath shuddered through her mind. She could almost feel the touch of his hand translated to her own young flesh. Involuntarily, she brushed her arm.

Maybe that's how they get so foul. No love … no lovers.

There was no evading the summons, though. She slid off the servo and crossed to Ferry's hatch. It snicked open at her approach. Why was she reminded of a sword leaving its scabbard?

"Ahhh, dear Hali." Ferry opened his palms to her as she entered.

She nodded. "Dr. Ferry."

"Sit down wherever you like." His hand rested on the arm of a couch, inviting her to the place beside him. She chose a seat facing him, cleared off the mess of papers and computer discs that covered it. The whole office smelled sour in spite of Ship's air filtration. Ferry appeared to be drunk … at least happy.

"Hali," he said, and recrossed his legs so one foot reached out to touch hers. "You're being reassigned."

Again, she nodded. *Groundside?*

"You're going to the Natali," Ferry said.

It was totally unexpected, and she blinked at him stupidly. To the Natali? The elite corps which handled all natural births had never been her ambition. Not even her hope. A dream, yes … but she was not the type to hope for the impossible.

"How do you feel about that?" Ferry asked, moving her foot with his.

The Natali! Working daily with the sacrament of WorShip!

She nodded to herself as the reality of it seeped through her. She would join the elite who opened the hatchway to the mystery of life … she would help rear the children shipside until they were assigned to their own schools and quarters at the age of seven annos.

Ferry smiled a red-stained smile. "You look stunned. Don't you believe me?"

She spoke slowly. "I believe you. I suspected that this …" She waved a hand at his office. "… was for reassignment, but …"

Ferry made no move to respond, so she went on.

"I thought I'd be going groundside. Everyone seems to be going there, lately."

He steepled his fingers and rested his chin on them.

"You're not happy with this assignment?"

"Ohhh, I'm very happy with it. It's just …" She put a hand to her throat. "I never thought I … I mean … Why me?"

"Because you deserve it, my dear." He chuckled. "And there's talk of moving the Natali groundside. You may get the best of both worlds."

"Groundside?" She shook her head. Too many shocks were coming at her one after the other.

"Yes, groundside." He spoke as though explaining something simple to an errant child.

"But I thought … I mean, the foremost provision of WorShip is that we give our children to Ship until they're seven. Ship designated the Natali as the trustees of birth … and their quarters are here, the estate …"

"Not Ship!" Ferry's interruption was guttural. "Some Ceepee did it. This is a matter for our determination."

"But doesn't Ship …"

"There's no record of Ship doing this. Now, our Ceepee has ruled that it is no violation of WorShip to move the Natali groundside."

"How … how long … until …"

"Perhaps a Pandoran anno. You know—quarters, supplies, politics." He waved it all off.

"When do I go to the Natali?"

"Next diurn. Take a break. Get your things moved over. Talk toooo …" He picked up a note from the jumble on his desk, squinted. "… Usija. She'll take care of you from there."

His foot brushed the back of her heel, then rubbed her instep.

"Thank you, Doctor." She pulled her foot back.

"I don't feel your gratitude."

"But I do thank you, especially for the time off. I have some notes to catch up on."

He held up an empty glass. "We could have a drink … to celebrate."

She shook her head, but before she could say no, he leaned forward, grinning. "We'll be neighbors, soon, Hali. We could celebrate that."

"What do you mean?"

"Groundside." He pushed the glass toward her. "After the Natali go …"

"But who'll be left here?"

"Production facilities, mostly."

"Ship? A factory?" She felt her face blaze red.

"Why not? What other use will we have for Ship when we're groundside?"

She jumped to her feet. "You would lobotomize your own mother!" Whirling from his startled gaze, she fled.

All the way back to her quarters, she heard the drum of Yaisuah's voice in her ears: "If they do these things in a green tree, what will they do in a dry?"

Chapter 40

I like seeing things fall into place.
—Kerro Panille, *The Notebooks*

NIGHTSIDE AFTER *nightside, always nightside! The horror!* Legata awoke on the deck in a shipside cubby, her hammock hanging around her like the torn shreds of her nightmares. Sweat and fear chilled her in the dark.

Slowly, reason returned. She felt the remnants of the hammock on and under her, the cold of the deck against her palms.

I'm shipside.

She had come up earlier at Oakes' command to check out reports that Ferry was too far gone on alcohol to be effective. It had shocked her, getting off the shuttle in a familiar shipbay, to see how few Shipmen formed the arrival crew. Staffing raids by Lewis were decimating the shipside work force to replace losses at the Redoubt.

How many people did they really lose?

She tugged pieces of hammock out from under her, hurled them into the darkness.

Ferry, warned of her approach, had gulped too many wake-pills and had been a jittering mess when she found him. She had dressed him down in fury which had surprised even her, and had removed the last of his Colony liquor supply.

At least, she hoped it was the last of it.

I have to do something about these nightmares.

Some details remained unclear upon waking, but she knew she dreamed of blood and her most tender flesh peeled back by dozens of needlenosed instruments—all of this backed by the feverish glitter of Morgan Oakes' smile. Oakes thick-lipped smile … but Murdoch's eyes. And … somewhere in the background … Lewis laughing.

She found pieces of her bedding, an intact cushion, pulled them together and, still in the dark, dragged herself across the cubby to a mat. Only once before had she felt this beaten, this empty … this helpless.

The Scream Room.

It was why she had run the P—to regain some pieces of her self-respect. Self-respect regained … but no important memories.

What happened in that room? What kind of a game is Morgan playing? Why did he send me in there?

She remembered the preliminaries. Innocent enough. Oakes had given her a few drinks, left her with a holo canister which detailed as he put it, "a few of the treats available to those who can afford them."

He had begun by showing her technical summaries and graphs of the work Lewis was doing on E-clones. The drinks fuzzed her thinking, but most of it remained in memory.

"Lewis has made remarkable modifications in the cloning system," Oakes said.

Remarkable, indeed.

Lewis could grow a clone to age thirty annos in ten diurns.

He could engineer clones for special functions.

It had occurred to her as she watched the holo display of Lab One's clones that she could begin playing this game with Oakes, but that they must switch to her rules.

I didn't even know the game!

When Oakes had suggested she inspect Lab One, she had not suspected that he wanted her to … that she was expected to …

Nothing is sacred!

The thought kept returning. She breathed in a deep lungful of the sweetly filtered shipside air. How different it was from groundside. She knew she was wasting time. There were things she must remember before returning to Oakes.

He believes he has nothing to fear from me now. I had better keep it that way.

His powers were not diminished. But after all he had done to her, after the Scream Room, she still felt that she was the only person who knew him well enough to beat him. There would be no opposition from him as long as he did not consider her a threat … or a challenge.

As long as he wants my body … and now that I know the game we're really playing …

Anxiety began to build in her—the nightmares … the lost memories …

She pounded the deck beside her with both fists. The anxiety rose in her like some thing, like a bastard child got by rape. The unresolved emotions in her were a place, immediately demanding, and she felt that she looked down upon her present upset as the dying were said to look down upon themselves from some high and unresolved corner.

Her hands pained her where she had pounded the deck.

A Chaplain is supposed to ease anxiety, not cause it!

Chaplain—she had searched the word out once and the readout had surprised her: Keeper of the sacred relics.

What were Ship's sacred relics?

Humans?

Slowly, she forced herself to relax in the darkness of the shipside cubby, but her mind remained a blur of unanswered questions, and once more she caught herself gasping for breath. In sudden dizziness, she saw a memory image of herself touching a dial in the Scream Room. Just a glimpse, and across from her, that twisted clone face … those wide terrified eyes …

Did I turn that dial? I have to know!

She hugged her knees to keep herself from pounding the deck.

Did I turn that dial myself or did Oakes force my hand?

She held her breath, knowing that she had to remember. She had to. And she knew she would have to destroy Oakes, that she was the only one who could do it.

Even Ship cannot destroy him. She peered up into the cubby's darkness. *You can't do it, can You, Ship?*

She felt that someone else's thoughts spun in her head—dizziness, dizziness. She shook her head sharply to rid it of the feeling.

Nothing … is … sacred.

Violent trembling shook her body.

The Scream Room.

She had to remember what happened there! She would have to know her own limits before she went after someone else's limits. She had to face the blank places in her mind or Oakes would continue to own her—not her body, but her most private self. He would own her.

Her hands clenched into fists against her legs. Her palms ached from the bite of her own fingernails.

I must remember ... I must ...

There was one fogged memory and she clung to it: Jessup kneading her maimed flesh with oddly gentle fingers whose deformity she had not even minded.

That memory was real.

She forced herself to open her clenched fists, relax her legs. She sat cross-legged on the mat, sweating and nude. One hand went out in the dark and groped for one of the bottles of wine she had taken from Ferry. Her hands were shaking so badly she was afraid she would crush a glass—besides, that would require her to stand, turn on lights, open a locker. She uncapped the raw wine and drank straight from the bottle.

Presently, a semblance of calm restored, she found the light control, tuned it for a low yellow, and returned to the bottle she had left on the deck. More of that? She had visions of herself reduced to Ferry's condition. No! There had to be a better way. She recapped the bottle, stuffed it in a locker, and sat on her mat, feet stretched out straight.

What to do?

Her gaze fell on her reflection in the mirror beside her hatch and what she saw made her groan. She liked her body—the suppleness, the firmness. To men, it appeared intensely female and soft, an illusion attributable to large breasts. But even her breasts were firm to touch, toned by a rigorous physical program which few besides herself and Oakes knew she enjoyed. Now, though, she saw red marks across her stomach, down one arm—the beginnings of softness down her thighs where there were more red streaks from her nightmare struggle with the hammock.

She held up her left hand and stared at it. The fingers ached. In that slender arm and those fingers she held the strength of five men. She had discovered this early and, afraid it would mean a life of body-work instead of mind-work, she had concealed this genetic gift. But she could not hide from what the mirror showed—the shambles she had made of her hammock and the marks on her flesh.

What to do?

She refused to go back to the wine. Sweat was beginning to cool on her skin. Her thick hair was stuck to her face and neck—damp dark at the ends. She no longer felt perspiration trickle down the small of her back.

Her green eyes stared back at her from the mirror and pried into her like Oakes' spying sensors.

Damn him!

She closed her eyes in a grimace. There had to be some way of breaking through the memory barrier! *What happened to me?*

Scream Room.

She spoke it aloud: "Scream Room."

Jessup's terrible fingers kneaded her neck, her back.

Abruptly, images began to rush through her mind like a storm. Bits and shards at first: a glimpse of a face here, an agony there. Writhings and couplings. There was a rainbow of sad clones mounting each other, always sweating, their freak organs slick, waving …

I took none of them!

Her terrible strength had stunned the clones.

Blood! She saw blood on her arms.

But I did not join them! None of it! She knew it. And because she knew it, there was a new strength in her. An objectifying freedom glared from her eyes when she stared once more into the mirror.

The holorecord!

Oakes had offered to play it for her, amusement in his eyes … and something else there … a fearful watching. She had refused.

"No-o-o. Perhaps some other time."

And her stomach was a knot of terror.

The wine or the holorecord? There was a certainty in her that it had to be one or the other, and she experienced an abrupt wave of sympathy for old Win Ferry.

What did they do to that poor old bastard?

There was no doubt about her choice. It had to be the holo, not the bottle. She had to see herself as she had appeared to Oakes. This was the horror required of her before the nightmares could be stopped.

Before Oakes and Lewis and Murdoch could be stopped.

If they're stopped, who keeps Colony alive?

Shipmen had tried four times—four leaders, four failures. "Failure" was the Shipman euphemism for the reality—revolt, slaughter, suicide, massacre. The records were there for a good Search Technician to winkle out.

The present Colony had suffered setbacks, true, but nothing even close to total wipeout—no retreat en masse back to the insulated corridors of Ship. Pandora had become no friendlier. Shipmen had grown wiser. And the wisest of all, beyond question, were Oakes and Lewis.

Ship only knew how many Shipmen crawled the surface of Pandora or the myriad passageways of Ship. And all survived, to whatever degree of comfort or discomfort, because of Oakes and the efficiency of his management … and because Lewis knew how to carry out orders with brutal efficiency. To her knowledge, no other Ceepee team could make such a claim in all the histories of Ship.

Ship will care for us.

She felt Ship around her now, the faint hummings and susurrations of nightside.

But Ship had never agreed to care for Shipmen.

At one time, she had been interested in Shipman's place in the Ship scheme of things. She had pored through a confusing lot of histories seeking some agreement, a covenant, some evidence of even rudimentary formal relationship between the people and their god.

Ship who is God.

All agreements save one had been made by Ceepees on behalf of Ship. Back in the earliest accounts, she had come on one recorded line, a direct demand from Ship: *You must decide how you will WorShip Me.*

That had to be the origin of present WorShip. It could be traced to Ship. But the demand appeared suitably vague and, when she had recounted it to Oakes, he had seen it as emphasizing the powers of the Ceepees.

"We, after all, command the WorShip."

If Ship were God … well, Ship still appeared to be unwilling to interfere directly in the management of Shipman affairs. Every visible thing Ship did could be attributed to work at maintaining itself.

Some Shipmen claimed they talked to Ship, and she had studied these people. They fell into two obvious categories: fools and non-fools. Most of the claimants had a history of talking to walls, bowls, items of clothing and such. But perhaps one out of every twenty who said they talked to Ship were Ship's best. For them, talking with Ship represented the single rare absurdity of their records. It fascinated her that, for this small group, the talking incidents were isolated and seemingly innocuous—almost as though Ship were checking in from time to time.

Unlike Oakes and Lewis, she did not count herself a disbeliever.

But God or not, Ship apparently refused to interfere in the private decisions of Shipmen.

So what if I decide to destroy Oakes?

Did Ship care for him, too?

Oakes was too cautious, too painstakingly right about the things he did. What if he were the only reason Colony had survived? Could she watch Colony wither and die, knowing she had done it?

Was the Scream Room right?

Only the holorecord could decide that for her. She had to see it.

She levered herself to her feet, found a singlesuit and slipped into it. There was a sense of urgency about her motions now compounded of the late hour and the terrors she knew she was holding at bay. A glance at her chrono showed only six hours to dayside. Six hours to call up those records, review them and cover her tracks. And those records spanned most of a diurn—perhaps forty hours. All she needed was to see the essence of it, though.

What did he do to me?

Without conscious decision, she headed for Oakes' abandoned shipside cubby, realizing her own choice only when she grasped the hatchdogs. Yes, the com-console would still be here. It was a good place to search out the record and review it. She knew the code which would call up the Scream Room holo. Her priority number would insure that she got it. And there was something exquisitely right about the choice of the place to do it.

As she keyed the hatchdogs on the cubby, she reminded herself: *Whatever he wanted me to do, I did not do it.* Some part of her knew that neither the pleasures nor the curiosities of the Scream Room had tempted her—neither ecstasy nor pain. But Oakes wanted her to believe in some willing debasement. He required that she believe.

He'll see.

She released the hatchdogs and stepped inside.

Chapter 41

The family feeds its fledgling, and under the nest weaves twigs—Intelligence is a poor cousin to understanding.

—Kerro Panille, *The Collected Poems*

THE DULL crimson of instruments and telltales filled the sub's core gondola with red shadows and played firelight flickers off every movement of the three people strapped in their seats around the tight arc of controls.

Thomas, intensely aware of the crushing pressure of water around them, glanced up at the depth repeater. This was not completely like a Voidship, after all. Instead of empty space, he sensed the inward pressing of the Pandoran sea. All he had to do was look directly up through the transparent dome of the gondola where it protruded from the carrier-sub and he could see the diminishing circle of glowing light which was the surface of the lagoon.

As he moved his head, he glimpsed Waela engaged in the same reflexive check of the repeater. She appeared to be taking it well. No residual fugue from her bad experiences down here.

He looked then at Kerro Panille. This poet was not what he had expected—young, yes—barely past twenty according to the records—but there was something more mature in Panille's manner.

The poet had been quiet during the descent, not even asking the expected questions, but his eyes missed very little. The way he cocked his head at new sounds betrayed his alertness. There had been no time really to train him for this. Waela had set Panille to watching the monitors on their communications program to signal when it began accepting the firefly patterns of the kelp. She had reserved for herself the instruments which reported the status of their linkage to the anchor cable. The anchor had been dropped in the center of a lagoon and now the cable guided their descent. The LTA rode close to the sea surface overhead, tightly tethered to the cable.

"He's very sensitive to unconscious communication," she had told Thomas before Panille's arrival at the hangar.

Thomas did not ask how she knew this. She already had confirmed the failure of her attempt to seduce Panille.

"Was he too naive? Did he know what you …"

"Oh, he knew. But he has this thing about his body being his own. Rather refreshing in a man."

"Is he … do you think he's really working for Oakes?"

"He's not the type."

Thomas had to agree. Panille displayed an almost childlike openness.

Since the abortive and (she had to admit it) rather amateurish attempt at seduction, Waela had felt restrained with Panille. But the poet showed no such inhibition. He had shipside candor and, she suspected, would be rather more apt than not to walk openly into some deadly Pandoran peril out of curiosity.

I like him, she thought. *I really like him.*

But he would have to be educated swiftly to the dangers here or he would not last long enough to write another poem.

Ship really did send him, then, Thomas thought. *Is he supposed to keep watch on me?*

Thomas had reserved for himself the visual observation of the kelp-free pocket through which they were descending. It was a column of clear water about four hundred meters in diameter, a Pandoran "lagoon." They had not yet descended into the dark regions where the kelp played its light show.

Panille had been fascinated by the name lagoon when he had heard it. Ship had displayed an Earthside lagoon for him once—palm trees, an outrigger with white sails. Would Pandora ever see such play upon its seas?

He found himself acutely aware of every sensory impression about this experience. It was the stuff of countless poems. There was the faint hiss of air being recycled, the smell of human bodies too close and exuding their unspoken fears. He liked the way the red light played off the ladder which ran up to the hatch.

When Thomas had used the word lagoon to describe their destination, Panille had said: "The persistence of atavism." The remark had provoked a startled glance from Thomas.

Waela marked their descent past eighty-five meters and called it out. She leaned close to the screen which displayed the lagoon's nearest wall of encaging kelp. The long strands angled down into darkness with an occasional black tentacle reaching out toward the sub. The external dive lights played green shadows on the pale kelp, revealing small dark extrusions, bubbles whose purpose remained undiscovered. Farther down, such bubbles played their bright patterns of light.

The water around the kelp strands and in the upper lagoon was aswarm with darting and slow-moving shapes, some with many eyes and some with none. Some were thin and worm-like, some fat and ponderous with long fleshy fins and toothless gaping jaws. None had ever been known to attack Shipmen and it was thought they lived in symbiosis with the kelp. Taking them for specimens aroused the kelp to violence and when they were removed from the sea, they melted so rapidly that mobile labs appeared to be the only way to examine them. But mobile labs did not survive long here.

Farther down, Waela knew, there would be fewer and fewer of these creatures. Then the sub would enter the zone of crawlers, things which moved along the kelp and across the sea floor. A few large swimmers there, but crawlers dominated.

On the flight out to the lagoon, Waela had kept herself busy, fearing that she might break down when the moment came to make another dive. It had helped to recall the strong construction of this sub, but the actual moment of the dive had loomed ahead, mingled with a return to dark memories of terror. Colony's last dive had been a disaster. The sub had been seventy meters long, studded with knives and cutters. It had cost Colony a terrible toll in lives to transport it across The Egg's undulating plains to the one area on the south coast where they could skid the sub into a wave-washed bay of kelp. She had been one of the nine on the crew, the only survivor.

For a time, they had thought sheer size and weight would bring them success. Water doors were opened remotely and stuffed with kelp specimens. But the kelp's cable-strands released themselves from the rocks on the seafloor and, tendrils waving, swept over the sub. There seemed no end to the attack. More and more kelp came at them, wrapping around the sub, overwhelming the cutters by weight of numbers, drawing them deeper and deeper while tendrils probed for any weak point. Leaves blinded their external sensors, static crackled in their communications system. They were blind and dumb. Then water had jetted into the hull near a hatch, a stream so strong it cut the flesh in its path.

Thinking about those moments made Waela's breath come faster. She had been operating a cutter, her station a plaz bubble extruded from the hull. Leaves covered the bubble except for straining strands of kelp trying to crush the sub. Through the crashing static in her earphones, she had heard a crewmate describe the water jet cutting one of their companions in half. Abruptly, a warping of the hull and the explosive shift of pressure within the sub had blasted her bubble free. It shot out and clear of the blinding leaves, then upward as the kelp spread aside to permit her passage. She had never been able to explain that phenomenon. The kelp had opened a way to the surface for her!

Once into the glare of double-dayside, she had forced open the hatch, dived clear to an undulant sea covered by broad fans of kelp leaves. She remembered touching the leaves, fearing them and needing them to support her; they were a pale green cushion which dampened the waves. Then she had felt a tingling all through her body. Her mind had been invaded by wild images of demons and humans locked in death struggles. She remembered screaming, swallowing salty water and screaming. Within seconds, the images overwhelmed her and she rolled across a kelp leaf unconscious.

An observation LTA had snatched her from the sea. She had spent many diurns recovering, awakening to acclaim because she had proved that the kelp not only was dangerous because of its physical abilities, but that its hallucinogenic capacity worked havoc when enough of it contacted enough of a Shipman's body in a liquid medium.

"Is something wrong, Waela?"

That was Panille staring at her, concerned by her introspection.

"No. We're leaving the active surface waters. We'll begin to see the lights soon."

"You've been down here before, they tell me."

"Yes."

"We'll be safe as long as we don't threaten the kelp," Thomas said. "You know that."

"Thanks."

"The records say that attempts to establish a shoreside harvester were defeated when the kelp actually came ashore to attack," Panille said.

"People and machines were snatched from the shore, yes," she said. "The people drowned and were thrown back. Machines just disappeared."

"Then why won't it attack us here?"

"It never has when we just come down and observe."

Saying this helped her restore a measure of calm. She returned to observation of sensors and telltales.

Panille peered over his shoulder at her screen, saw the angled strands of kelp, the fluting leaves and the curious bubble extrusions which reflected starbursts from the sub's dive lights. When he looked up past the ladder to the top hatch, he could see the luminous circle of the lagoon's surface—a receding moon populated by the darting shapes of the creatures who shared the sea with the kelp.

The lagoon was a place of magic and mystery with a beauty so profound he felt thankful to Ship just to have seen it. The kelp strands were pale gray-green cables, thicker than a Shipman's torso in places. They reached up from darkness into the distant mercuric pool of light overhead.

Light reaches for stars and, seeing the stars, fears to grasp them, floats in wonder. Oh, stars, you burn my mind.

The kelp aimed itself at Rega, the only sun in their sky at the moment. Alki would join Rega later. Even under clouds, the kelp aligned itself perpendicular to the passage of a sun. When two suns were present, this tropism adjusted to the radiation balance. It was a precise adjustment.

Panille thought about this, reviewing what he had learned from Ship. These were observations which perilous ventures into the sea had gleaned. Sparse information, and nowhere as intense as what he learned by being here. He knew some of the things he would see at the bottom: kelp tendrils wrapped around and through large rocks. Crawling creatures and burrowing ones. Slow currents, drifting sediments. Lagoons were ventilators, passages for exchange between surface and bottom waters. Near the surface, they provided light for creatures other than kelp.

The lagoons were cages.

"These lagoons are where the kelp engages in aquaculture," he said.

Thomas blinked. That was so close to his own surmise about how kelp fitted into the sea system that he wondered if Panille had been eavesdropping on his thoughts.

Is Ship talking to him even now?

Panille's words fascinated Waela. "You think the kelp follows a conscious plan?"

"Perhaps."

To Thomas, the poet's words pulled a veil from the kelp domain. He began to sense the sea in a different way. Here was rich living space free of Pandora's other dangerous demons. Was it right then to rid the sea of kelp? He knew it could be done—disrupt the ecosystem, break the internal chain of the kelp's own life. Was that the decision of Oakes and Lewis?

"The lights!" Panille said. "Ohhh, yes."

They had reached the dark zone where the sub's external sensors began to pick up the flickering lights. Jewels danced in the blackness beyond the range of the dive lights—tiny bursts of color … red, yellow, orange, green, purple … There appeared to be no pattern to them, just bursts of brilliance which dazzled the awareness.

"Bottom coming up," Waela said.

Panille, every sense alert, shot a glance at her screen. Yes—the bottom appeared to be moving while they remained stationery. Coming up.

Thomas adjusted the rate of descent—slower, slower. The sub came to rest with a slight jar which stirred sediment into a gray fog around them. When the fog settled, the screens showed a plastering of ripples out to the limits of their illumination. Bottom grazers moved through the ripples—inverted bowls with gulping lips all around the rim. At the extreme forward edge of illumination, the flukes of the sub's anchor dug into the sediment. The cable sagged back over them and out of light range. Off to the port side, they could glimpse black mounds of rock with kelp tendrils lacing over and through them. Dark shapes swam deep in the kelp jungle—more attendants of the sea's rulers.

Tiny crawlers already were working their way along the anchor and the cable. Panille knew that the anchor tackle had been made of native iron and steel—substances which would be etched away to lace in a few diurns. Only plaz and plasteel resisted the erosive powers in Pandora's seas.

This knowledge filled him with a sense of how fragile was their link to safety. He watched the jewel brilliants flickering in the gloom beyond the sub's dive lights. They seemed to speak to him: "We are here. We are here. We are here …"

To Thomas, the lights were like the play of a computer board. Watching holorecords of them had formed this association in his mind. He had proposed it to Waela during one of the sessions when she had been teaching him the ways of Pandora's deeps. "A computer could crunch far greater numbers, form so many more associations so much faster."

Out of this had been born his proposal: *Record them, scan for patterns and play those patterns back to the kelp.*

Waela had admired the elegant simplicity of it: Leap beyond the perilous collection and analysis of specimens, beyond the organic speculations. Strike directly for the communications patterns!

Say to the kelp: "We see you and know you are aware and intelligent. We, too, are aware. Teach us your speech."

As he watched the play of lights, Thomas wanted to say they were like Christmas lights twinkling in the dark. But he knew neither of his crew would understand.

Christmas!

The very thought made him feel ancient. Shipmen did not know Christmas. They played other religious games. Perhaps the only person in his universe who might understand Christmas was Hali Ekel. She had seen the Hill of Skulls.

What did the Hill of Skulls and the passion of Jesus have to do with these lights flickering in a sea?

Thomas stared at the screen in front of him. What was he supposed to see here?

Aquaculture?

Would Shipmen be forced to exterminate the kelp? Crucify it for their own survival?

Christmas and aquaculture …

The play of lights was hypnotic. He felt the silent wonder of watchfulness throughout the command gondola. A sense of revelatory awe crept over him. Here on the bottom was the record of Pandora's budget, all the transactions which the planet's life had made. This was more than the bourse, it was the deposit vault where Pandora's grand geochemical and biochemical circuit of exchange lay open to view.

What do you here, mighty kelp?

Was this what Ship wanted them to see?

He did not expect Ship to answer that question. Such an answer did not fit into the rules of this game. He was on his own down here.

Play the game, Devil.

The pressure of the water around their gondola filled his awareness. They remained here by the sufferance of the kelp. By the kelp's own tolerance could they survive. Others had come into this sea and survived by careful restraint. What might the kelp interpret as a threat? Those jeweled blinkings in the gloom took on a malevolent aspect to him then.

We trust too much.

In the silence of his fears, Panille's voice came as a jarring intrusion.

"We're beginning to get some pattern indicators."

Thomas shot a glance at the recording board to the left of his console. The load-sensors indicated preparation for playback. This would control the sub's exterior bubbles to replay any light patterns which the computer counted as repetitive and significant. Any such patterns would be played to the kelp.

"See! Now, we talk to you. What are we saying?"

That would catch its attention. But what would it do?

"The kelp's watching us," Panille said. "Can't you feel it?"

Thomas found himself in silent agreement. The kelp around them was watching and waiting. He felt like the child of that faraway day at Moonbase when he had entered the crèche school for the first time. There was a truth revealed here which most educators ignored: *You could learn dangerous things.*

"If it's watching us, where are its eyes?" Waela whispered.

Thomas thought this a nonsense question. The kelp could possess senses which Shipmen had never imagined. You might just as well ask about Ship's eyes. But he could not deny that sense of watchfulness around the sub. The presence which the kelp projected onto the intruders was an almost palpable thing.

The recorder buzzed beside him and he saw the green lights which signaled the shift to replay. Now, the extruded bubbles on the carrier surface were playing back something, he had no idea what. Exterior sensors revealed only a glow of many colors reflecting off particles in the water.

He could see no discernible change in the light play from the kelp.

"Ignoring us." That was Waela.

"Too soon to say," Panille objected. "What's the response time of the kelp? Or maybe we're not even speaking to it yet."

"Try the pattern display," Waela said.

Thomas nodded, punched for the prepared program. This had been the alternate approach. The small screen above the recorder board began to show what was being displayed on the sub's hull: first Pythagorean squares, then the counting of the sticks, the galactic spiral, the pebble game …

No response from the kelp,

The dim shapes of swimmers among the kelp did not change their movements dramatically. All appeared to be the same.

Waela, studying her own screens, asked: "Am I mistaken or are the lights brighter?"

"A bit brighter perhaps," Thomas said.

"They are brighter," Panille said. "It seems to me that the water is … murkier. If … Look at the anchor cable!"

Thomas flicked to the view Panille's screen displayed, saw the sensors signaling the approach of some large object from above.

"The cable's gone slack," Waela said. "It's sinking!"

As she spoke, they all saw the first remnants of the LTA bag settling around them into the range of the dive lights—dull orange reflections from the fabric, black edges. It pulled a curtain over the bubble dome above them. This disturbed the creatures among the kelp and ignited a wild flickering in the kelp lights which vanished as the curtain settled around the sub.

"Lightning hit the bag," Waela said. "It …"

"Stand by to drop the carrier and blow all tanks," Thomas said. He reached for the controls, fighting to suppress panic.

"Wait!" Panille called. "Wait for all of the bag to settle. We could be trapped in it, but the sub can cut a way through it."

I should've thought of that, Thomas thought. *The bag could trap us down here.*

Chapter 42

Hittite law emphasized restitution rather than revenge. Humankind lost a certain useful practicality when it chose the other Semitic response—never to forgive and never to forget.

—Lost People, *Shiprecords*

LEGATA SAT back, her whole body shaking and trembling. She could tell by the flickering cursor on the com-console that it was almost dayside. Familiar activities soon would begin out in Ship's corridors—familiar but with a feeling of sparseness because of the diminished crew. She had kept illumination low during nightside, wanting no distractions from the holorecord playing at the focus in front of Oakes' old divan.

Her gaze lifted and she saw the mandala she had copied for Oakes' quarters at the Redoubt. Looking at the patterns helped restore her, but she saw that her hands still shook.

Fatigue, rage or disgust?

It required a conscious effort to still the trembling. Knots of tension remained in her muscles, and she knew it would be dangerous for Oakes to walk into his old cubby right now.

I'd strangle him.

No reason for Oakes to come shipside now. He was permanently groundside.

The prisoner of his terrors.

As I was … until …

She took a deep, clear breath. Yes, she was free of the Scream Room.

It happened, but I am here now.

What to do about Oakes? Humiliation. That had to be the response. Not physical destruction, but humiliation. A particular humiliation. It would have to be at once political and sexual. Something more than embarrassment. Something he might think of to do against someone else. The sexual part was easy enough; that was no challenge to a woman of her beauty and genius. But the politics …

Should I conceal the evidence that I've seen this holo?

Save that information for the proper moment.

That was a good thought. Trust her own inspiration. She keyed the comconsole and typed in: SHIPRECORDS EYES ONLY LEGATA HAMILL. Then the little addition which she had discovered for herself: SCRAMBLE IN OX.

There. No matter who thought to search for such a datum, it would be lost in that strange computer which she had discovered in one of her history hunts.

I'll stay shipside this diurn. She would not feel well. That would be the message to Oakes. He would grant her a rest period without question. She would spend her time here pulling every trick of computer wizardry she could to get the complete record on Morgan Oakes.

Political humiliation. Political and sexual. That had to be the way of it.

Perhaps that other Ceepee brought out of hyb, that Thomas, might hold a clue. Something in the way he looked at Oakes … as though he saw an old acquaintance in a new role …

And she owed a debt to Thomas. Strange that he should be the only one to know she had run the P. He had kept the secret without being asked … or asking. Rare discretion.

She had no thought of fatigue now. There was food shipside when she needed it. The power of Oakes' position made that no problem. She sent her message to Oakes groundside, turned to the console.

Somewhere in the records there would be a useful fact or two. Something Oakes had hidden or that he did not even know about himself—perhaps something he had done and did not want revealed. He was good at this concealment game but she knew herself to be better at it.

She began at the main computer—Ship's major interface with Shipmen.

Would it take fancy programming? A painstaking search through coded relationships which could hide bits of data far in the recesses of offshoot circuitry such as that Ox gate? How about the Ox gate? She hid things there, but had never asked it about Oakes.

She tapped out a test routine, keyed it and waited.

Presently, data began flowing across the small screen on the console. She stared. That simple? It was as though the material were waiting for her to ask. As though someone had prepared a bio for her to discover. Everything she needed was there—facts and figures.

"Suspect everyone," Oakes had said. "Trust no one."

And here he was being proved right beyond his wildest fears. The text kept rolling out. She backed it up, keyed for printout, and set it in motion once more.

The heading of the record was the most surprising thing of all.

MORGAN LON OAKES.

Cloned. Raised, as he would put it, "like a common vegetable." Out of the axolotl tanks and into an Earthside womb.

Why?

There it was even as she asked. "To conceal the fact that it could be done, the birth was made to appear natural."

It was a feat of politics worthy of Ship … or Oakes. Did he know? How could he know? She stopped the printout and asked who else had called up this data.

"Ship."

It was an answer she had never before seen. Ship had worked with this data. Fearfully, she asked why Ship had called up the bio on Oakes.

"To store it in a special record for Kerro Panille should he ever desire to write a history."

She pulled her hands away from the keys. *Am I talking to Ship?*

Panille was one of those who said he talked to Ship. Not one of the fools, then.

Am I a fool?

She found herself more fearful of this discovery than she had been of the Scream Room. Ship dealt in powers far beyond those of Oakes and Lewis and Murdoch. She glanced around the enlarged cubby—pretentious damned place. Her gaze fell on the mandala. He had taken the movable hangings. The mystical design lay exposed against a bare metal bulkhead of silvery gray. It appeared lifeless to her, robbed of some original breath.

I'm not worthy of talking to Ship.

This had been an accident … a dangerous accident. Hesitantly, she started the Oakes bio printing once more. Words again flowed across the screen and the printer rattled with its text.

Legata heaved a deep sigh of relief. Perilous ground. But she had escaped.

This time.

She felt that something strange was happening, some new program awakening in Ship. It was a feeling in her shoulder blades. Something even more awesome might happen and she was right in the middle of it.

Her attention returned to the Oakes bio. That had been a time of great scurrying about Earthside, great secrets. Salvation and survival—whatever the label—the arrival of Ship and the desperation of doomed people.

Desperation breeds extremes if nothing else.

"Legata."

It was Oakes calling her name and she felt her heart skip a beat. But it was the console override. He was calling her from groundside.

"Yes?"

"What are you doing?"

"My job."

She glanced at the com-console telltales to see if he could find out what she was reading. It was still blocked by the Ox gate.

He recognized the sound of the printer, though.

"What are you printing out?"

"Some data you'll find interesting."

"Ahhhh, yes."

She could almost see his mind working on this. Legata had something she would not trust to the open channels between Ship and ground. She would show it to him, though. It must be interesting.

I'll have to find something juicy, she thought. *Something about Ferry. That's why I'm here.*

"What do you want?" she asked.

"I've been expecting you groundside."

"I'm not feeling well. Didn't you get my signal?"

"Yes, my dear, but we have urgent matters demanding our attention."

"But it's not full dayside yet, Morgan. I couldn't sleep and I still have work here."

"Is everything all right?"

"Just busy," she said.

"This cannot wait. We need you."

"Very well. I'm coming down."

"Wait for me at the Redoubt."

At the Redoubt!

He broke the connection and it was only then that she realized he had spoken of needing her. Was that possible? Alliance or love? She did not think there was much room for love in the convoluted patterns of Morgan Oakes.

Sooner expect Lewis to start raising a pet Runner.

Either way, Oakes wanted her presence. That gave her a wedge into the power she needed. Something still nagged at her, though—the one fear above all other: *What if he does love me?*

Once, she had thought she wanted him to love her. There was no question that he was the most interesting man she had ever met. Unpredictably terrifying, but interesting. There was much to be said for that.

Will I destroy him?

The printer finished producing the Oakes bio. She folded it, crossed to the mandala looking for a place to conceal the thick wad of Shipscript. The mandala was fixed solidly to the bulkhead. She turned and glanced around the cubby. *Where to hide this?*

Do I need to hide it?

Yes. Until the right moment

The divan? She crossed to the divan and knelt beside it. The thing was fixed to the deck by bolts. Could she call a serviceman? No … she didn't dare let anyone suspect what she was doing. Gritting her teeth, she put two fingers on a bolt and twisted. The bolt turned.

Strength has its purposes!

The bolts removed, she lifted the end of the divan. *My! It was heavy.* She doubted that three men could lift it. She slipped the text under the divan, restored the bolts, twisting them tight.

Now for something juicy about Win Ferry.

She stood up and returned to the console. Ferry gave her no difficulty either. He practiced no discretion whatsoever.

Poor old fool! I'm going to destroy Oakes for you, Win.

No! Don't trick yourself into nobility. You're doing it on your own and for yourself. Let's keep love and the glory of others out of it.

Chapter 43

Remember that I have power; you believe yourself miserable, but I can make you so wretched that the light of day will be hateful to you. You are my creator, but I am your master.

—Frankenstein's Monster Speaks, Shiprecords

OAKES WOKE out of his first sound sleep groundside to muffled pounding outside his cubby.

His fingers reached his com-console before he was even awake and the viewscreen showed complete madness up and down Colony's corridors.

Even outside his own locked hatchway!

"I'm hungry now! I'm hungry now! I'm hungry now!"

The chant was a snarl in the throat of the night.

There were no guns in evidence, but plenty of rocks.

In a matter of blinks, Lewis was on the line.

"Morgan, we've lost them for now. This thing will have to run its course until …"

"What the hell is happening?" Oakes did not like it that his voice cracked.

"It started out as a round of The Game down in the 'ponicsways. Lots of drinking. Now it's a food riot. We can flood 'em out with …"

"Wait a minute! Are the perimeters still secure?"

"Yes. My people are out there."

"Then why …"

"Water in the passages will slow 'em down until we …"

"No!" Oakes took a deep breath. "You're out of your league, Jesus. What we'll do is let them go. If they seize food, then it'll be their responsibility when food gets even shorter. The supply does not change, you hear me? No extra food!"

"But they're running wild through …"

"Let them rip things up. The repairs afterward will keep them busy. And a good riot will purge emotions for a time, wear them out physically. Then we turn it to our advantage, but only after well-reasoned consideration."

Oakes listened for some response from Lewis, but the 'coder remained silent.

"Jesus?"

"Yes, Morgan." Lewis sounded out of breath. "I think that you … had better move … to the Redoubt immediately. We can't wait for dayside, but you'll …"

"Where are you, Jesus?"

"Old Lab One complex. We were moving out the last of …"

"Why must I go to the Redoubt now?" Oakes blinked and turned up the illumination in his cubby. "The riots will pass. As long as the perimeter's secure we can …"

"They're not stamping their feet and whining, Morgan. They're killing people. We've sealed off the gun lockers but some of the rioters …"

"The Redoubt cannot be ready yet! The damage there was … I mean, is it safe?"

"It's ready enough. And the crew there is handpicked by Murdoch. They're the best. You can rely on them. And, Morgan …"

Oakes tried to swallow, then: "Yes?"

Another long pause, garbled snatches of conversation.

"Morgan?"

"I'm still on."

"You should go now. I've arranged everything. We'll flood 'em out of the necessary passages. My people will be there within minutes: our usual signal. You should be at the shuttle hangar within fifteen minutes."

"But my records here! I haven't finished the …"

"We'll get that later. I'll leave a briefing disc for you with the shuttle crew. I'll expect to hear from you as soon as you get to the Redoubt."

"But … I mean … what about Legata?"

"She's safe shipside! Call her when you get to the Redoubt."

"It's … that bad?"

"Yes."

The connection went dead.

Chapter 44

Though a pendulum's arc may vary, its period does not. Each swing requires the same amount of time. Consider the last swing and its infinitesimal arc. That is where we are truly alive: in the last period of the pendulum.

—Kerro Panille, *The Notebooks*

LEGATA LOOKED past Oakes to the sea below the Redoubt. It was an orderly suns-set out there, Rega following Alki below the rim of the sea. A distant line of clouds boiled along the horizon's curve. Long waves rolled in to crash on the beach of their small bay. The surf lay out of sight beneath the cliffs upon which the Redoubt perched. Double walls of plaz plus an insulated foundation screened out most of the sounds, but she could feel the surf through her feet. She certainly could see the spray misting her view and beading the plaz along the view porch.

Orderly suns-set and disorderly sea.

She experienced a sense of calm which she knew to be false. Oakes had bolstered himself with alcohol, Lewis with work. They were still getting reports from Colony, but the last word suggested that the old Lab One site was under siege. Lucky thing Murdoch had been sent shipside.

Disorderly sea.

Only thin rags of kelp remained on the surface, and she found the absence of it a loss which she could not explain. Once kelp had dampened the surf. Now, wind whipped white froth across the wavetops. Had Lewis allowed for that?

"Why do you link the kelp and hylighters?" she asked. "You've seen the reports. They're vectors of the same creature or symbiotic partners."

"But it doesn't follow that they think."

Oakes directed a lidded stare at her, swirled an amber drink in a small glass. "Touch one of them and the other responds. They act together. They think." He gestured at the cliffs across the Redoubt's bay where a scattered line of hylighters hovered like watchful sentries.

"They're not attacking now," she said.

"They're planning."

"How can you be sure?"

"We plan."

"Maybe they're not like us. Maybe they're not very bright."

"Bright enough to pull out and regroup when they're losing."

"But they're only violent when we threaten them. They're just a … a nuisance."

"Nuisance! They're a threat to our survival."

"But … so beautiful." She stared across the small bay at the drifting orange bags, the stately way they tacked and turned, touching the cliff with their tendrils to steady themselves, avoiding their fellows.

Turning only her head, she shifted her attention to Oakes, and tried to swallow in a dry throat. He was staring down into his drink, gently swirling the liquid. *Why wouldn't he talk about what was happening at Colony?* She felt nervous precisely because Oakes no longer appeared nervous. It had been two full diurns since the food riot. What was happening? She sensed new powers being invoked—the bustling activity all through the Redoubt while Oakes stood here drinking and admiring the view with her. Not once in this period had Oakes turned to her with an assignment. She felt that she might be on probation for a new position. He could be testing her.

Does he suspect what I discovered about him shipside? Morgan Lon Oakes.

Impossible! He could not appear this calm in the face of that knowledge.

Oakes raised his eyebrows at her and tossed back his drink.

"They're beautiful, yes," he said. "Very pretty. So's a sun going nova, but you don't invite it into your life."

He turned back to the ever-present dispenser for another drink, and something about the mural on the inner wall of the porch caught his eyes, startling him. The thing seemed to move … like the waves of the sea.

"Morgan, may I have a drink, too?"

Her voice sounded small and weak against the background of the mural—yet she had created this mural. A gift. He had thought: *She wants to please me.* But now … there was always something other than pleasing in the way she looked at him. What had she really meant with this painting? Was it to please him or disturb him? He stared at it. The painting was a splash of colors, much larger than the mandala for his new offices here. She called it: "Struggle at suns-set."

The mural recreated a scene they had witnessed earlier on holo: Colonists at a construction site near the sea fighting back a sudden swarm of hylighters. One Colonist dangled by a leg in mid-air, wide-eyed … Horror or hallucination? The doomed man pointed an accusing finger out of the painting directly at the observer. This detail had escaped Oakes before. He stared at it.

All the construction sites, the drilling sites, the mine heads—all of them were shut down now. Everything depended on the Redoubt.

Why did that figure in the painting look accusing?

"A drink, please, Morgan?"

He did not have to turn to know her expression, the tongue flickering out to wet her lips. What was she planning? He pressed the dispenser key for two drinks. The Scream Room had left its imprint on her, no doubt of that, but instead of making her more trustworthy … it had … What? He did not like the eagerness in her request for a drink. Was she going the way of that damned Win Ferry? Her report on Ferry was unsettling. They had to have somebody shipside they could trust!

Oakes returned to her side, handed her one of the drinks. The suns-set was shading into dark purples with a few streaks of rose higher in the sky.

"Is this the way I have to buy your favors now?" He focused on her drink.

She managed a smile. What did he mean by that question? Coming here had been far more difficult than she had imagined. Even armed with the new knowledge in her possession … even fleeing the turmoil at Colony—very difficult. A new Lab One with Lewis in charge was being built only a few blinks away, buried in the rocks of the Redoubt.

I'm free of that. I'm free.

But now she knew it would take more than conscious awareness of what had happened to her, much more, before she could feel completely liberated. Oakes still had his grasping hand in her psyche.

Her fingers trembled as she sipped from the glass he had handed her. It was pungent and bitter, a distillation, but she could feel it soothing her.

When the right time comes, Morgan Lon Oakes.

Oakes touched her hair, stroked her head. She did not lean toward him or away.

"In another few diurns," he said, "all that will remain of the kelp will be holo approximations and our memories. If we're right about the hylighters, they won't endure much longer." He glanced out the plaz where the afterglow of the setting suns had left golden luminescence in the sky and two fans of shadowy lines radiating upward from beyond the curve of the sea. "None too fond, eh, Legata?"

She shuddered as his fingers touched a nerve in her neck.

"Cold, Legata?"

"No."

She turned and her gaze fell on the mural. Sensors had ignited low illumination to compensate for the shadows filling the porch. The mural. It drank her mind.

I did that. Was it real or dream ?

She stared into the mural at the world of her dreams, that peculiar soothsayer of the mind called imagination—a world Oakes could never see without the intervention of someone like herself.

Again, she shuddered, recalling the holorecord which had inspired the painting: the eerie moanings of the hylighters and the *whoosh* and *thump* when they exploded, the tortured screams of burning Colonists. Even as she recalled the scene, she imagined the smell of burning hair. It seemed to fill the porch. She tore her attention away from the mural and stared out at the sea—all darkness out there except for a distant white line glowing along the horizon. It looked threatening, more threatening than her memories.

"Why did we have to build so near the sea?" she asked.

The question was out before she could think about it and she wished she had suppressed it.

The drink. It loosens the tongue.

"We're high above the sea, my dear, not very near at all."

"But it's so big and …"

"Legata! You helped draw the plans for our Redoubt. You agreed. I recall your words clearly: 'What we need is a place to get away, a safe place.'"

But that was before the Scream Room, she thought.

She forced herself to look at him. The dim illumination erased the soft edges of his features and left the shadows controlled by his skull.

What other plans does he have for me?

As though he heard the question in her mind, Oakes began to speak, addressing her reflection in the plaz.

"As soon as we get matters orderly down here, Legata, I'll want you to make a few trips back to the ship. We'll have to keep an eye on Ferry until we can find a replacement."

So he still needs me.

It was clear now that he feared going shipside more than he feared the terrors groundside. *Why? How does Ship threaten him?* She tried to imagine herself as Oakes back in his cubby shipside, completely surrounded by the presence of Ship. Not *the ship. Ship!* Did Oakes, after all, believe in Ship?

He put an arm around her waist. "You agreed, my dear."

She forced herself not to cringe, fearful of the artificial kindness in his tone, afraid of unknown plans he might have for her. *What was the reasoning behind his decisions?*

Perhaps there is no reason.

The futility of this thought frightened her even more than Morgan Oakes did. Morgan Lon Oakes. Could it be that … clones and the wild creatures of Pandora … and Shipmen—that so many died merely because Oakes acted without reason?

He has his reasons.

Once more, she looked at her mural. What did I paint there? The doomed man stared back at her—the eyes, the melting flesh, the pointing finger, all screamed: You agreed! You agreed!

"You can't kill all of the creatures on this planet," she whispered, and shut her eyes tight.

He removed his arm from her waist. "Pardon me, Legata. I thought you said 'can't.'"

"I …" She could not continue.

He took her arm above the elbow the way Murdoch had grasped her at the Scream Room! She felt him guide her across the porch, and she opened her eyes only when her shins touched the red couch. Firmly, he pressed her down into the cushions. She saw that she still clutched her drink, some of it still sloshing in the glass. She could not look up at Oakes. She was shaking so hard that small splashes of the drink jumped out of the glass to settle on her hand and thigh.

"Do I make you nervous, Legata?" He reached down to stroke her forehead, her cheek.

She could not answer. She remembered the last time he did this and began to cry silently, her shoulders stiff, tears flowing quietly down her cheeks.

Oakes dropped to the couch beside her, took the drink from her hand and put it somewhere aside on the floor. He began to massage the back of her neck, working the stiffness out of her shoulders. His fingers, his precise medical touch, knew where to reach her and how to ease through her defenses.

How can he touch me like this and be wrong?

She leaned forward, almost totally relaxed, and her elbow touched a damp spot on her thigh where she had spilled her drink. She knew in that instant that she could resist him … and that he would not expect the way of her resistance.

He does not know about the record I hid shipside.

His fingers continued to move so expertly, so full of pseudo-love.

He doesn't love me. If he loved me he wouldn't … he wouldn't … She shuddered at a memory of the Scream Room.

"Still cold, my dear?"

His practiced hands pulled her gently down onto the couch, eased the tensions from her throat and breast.

If he loved me, he wouldn't touch me this way and frighten me the way he does. What does he really want?

It had to be more than sex, more than her body which he knew how to ignite with such sureness. It had to be something far more profound.

How strange, the way he could go on talking to her at a time like this. His words seemed to make no sense whatsoever.

"… and in the recombinant process itself, we have gained an interesting side effect to the degeneration of the kelp."

Degeneration! Always degeneration!

Chapter 45

Avata informs through the esoteric symbols of Avata's history reduced to dreams and to images which often can be translated only by the dreamer, not by Avata.

—Kerro Panille, *History of the Avata*

THERE'S NO reason to panic yet, Waela told herself.

Other subs had lost their LTAs and survived. The drill was spelled out by those experiences.

Still, she found herself trembling uncontrollably, her memory focused on her escape from the depths at the south shore of The Egg.

I escaped before. I'm a survivor. Ship, save us!

Save yourself. That was the unmistakable voice of her own Honesty. Certainly. She knew how to do it. She had taught the procedure to Thomas by repeated drill. And Panille appeared to be a cool one. No panic there. He was watching the screens, estimating the extent that the downed LTA bag was covering them.

Strange that it drifted straight down.

"There has to be a vertical current in this lagoon," Panille said, as though answering her thought. "See how the fabric has draped itself over us."

Thomas had watched the fabric cover them, sinking all around the sub to enclose them in an orange curtain which cut off their view of the kelp.

There's no way the LTA could have been brought down by lightning, he thought. The bag was grounded to its anchor cable. It was compartmented. Breaking half the compartments would not have brought it down. There still would have been enough lift to take off the stripped-down gondola.

Somebody doesn't want us back.

"I think we could begin cutting away the fabric now," Panille said. He touched Thomas on the shoulder, not liking the way the man sat staring fixedly at the screens.

"Yes … yes. Thank you."

Thomas lifted the nose of the sub then and extruded the cutters. Whiplike arc burners, they slipped from hull-top compartments and began their work. The plaz dome above them glowed with silvery blue light from the burner. Thomas saw the orange curtain part and drift down, stirring up a fog of sediment.

"Do you want me to do it?" Waela asked.

He shook his head abruptly, realizing that she too must have noted his funk. "No. I can handle it."

The procedure was direct: release the slip-tackle which linked them to the anchor cable, fire the blast bolts which freed the command gondola from the carrier, blow the tanks and ride the gondola to the surface. Once on the surface, the gondola would stabilize automatically. They could fire their radiosonde then and set their locator beacon. From there, it was a matter of waiting out the arrival of a relief LTA.

The sense of failure was large in Thomas as he began the escape procedure. They had barely started the communications routine … and the plan had been a good one.

The kelp could've answered.

They all felt the jolt of the blast bolts. The gondola began to lift from the split carrier. *Rising out of it like a pearl from an oyster,* Thomas thought.

As they lifted, the kelp lights once more came into view through the open areas of the plaz walls.

Waela stared out at the winking lights. They pulsed and glowed in spasmodic bursts which sparked a memory just at the edge of awareness.

Where have I seen that before?

It was so familiar! Lights almost all green and purple winking at her …

Where? I was only down in the …

The memory returned in a rush and she spoke without thinking.

"This is just like the other time when I escaped. The kelp lights were very much like that."

"Are you sure?" Thomas asked.

"I'm sure. I can still see them there—the kelp separating and opening a way to the surface for me."

"Hylighters are born in the sea," Panille said. "Maybe they think we're a hylighter."

"It may be," Thomas said. And he thought: *Is that what we were supposed to see, Ship?*

There was a certain elegant sense in the idea. Colony had copied the hylighters to give the LTAs free access to Pandora's skies. Hylighters did not attack an LTA. Perhaps the kelp could be fooled in the same way. It would bear investigation. There were more important considerations of survival right now, however. Suspecting sabotage, he had to share that suspicion with his team.

"Nothing ordinary could have brought down that LTA," he said.

Panille turned from looking out at the firefly lights of the kelp.

"Sabotage," Thomas said. He produced the arguments.

"You don't really believe that!" Waela protested.

Thomas shrugged. He stared out at the descending cables of kelp. The gondola was almost into the biologically active zone near the surface.

"You don't," she insisted.

"I do."

He thought back through his conversation with Oakes. Had the man come out to inspect a sabotage device? He certainly had done nothing discernible. But there had been discrepancies in his responses—lapses.

Panille stared out through the gondola's plaz walls at the enclosing cage of kelp. Illumination was increasing rapidly now. The surface dome of light expanded and expanded as they entered sun-washed waters. Swimming creatures darted out of their path and circled close. Dazzling rays of light shot through the enclosing kelp barrier. The flickering nodules dimmed and were gone. Within a few heartbeats, the gondola broke free on the surface.

Thomas activated the surface program as the gondola began to bob and turn in the currents of the lagoon, rising and settling on a low swell. The sky overhead was cloudless but a mass of hylighters could be seen downwind.

A sea anchor popped from its external package below them, spread its funnel shape and snubbed the capsule around. The plaz-filtered light of both suns filled the gondola with brilliant reflections.

Panille exhaled a long sigh, realized he had been holding his breath to see if they really had stabilized on the surface.

Sabotage?

Waela, too, thought about Thomas' suspicions. *He had to be wrong!* A few remnants of the LTA bag drifted in the kelp leaves around the downwind edge of the lagoon. It was all consistent with a lightning strike.

In a cloudless sky?

Honesty would have to focus on the big discrepancy!

The hylighters, then?

Hylighters do not attack LTAs. You know that

Thomas armed the radiosonde, punched the firing key. There was a popping sound overhead and a red glow arced over them, swerved left and dove into the sea. Boiling orange smoke lifted from the water where it had gone and was whipped toward the mass of hylighters tacking across the downwind horizon.

They all saw the kelp leaves twist and lift in agitation where the radiosonde had gone.

Thomas nodded to himself. *A faulty radiosonde.*

Waela freed herself from her seat restraints and reached for the release handle to the top hatch, but Panille grabbed her arm. "No! Wait."

"What?" She twisted free of him.

It embarrassed her to touch him after that scene the previous nightside. She found her skin glowing a hot and velvety purple which she was unable to control.

"He's right," Thomas said. "Touch nothing yet."

Thomas unlocked his own seat restraints, found the gondola's toolkit and removed a unipry. With the unipry, he began removing the cover to the hatch mechanism. The cover came off with a snapping sound and fell to the deck below. They all saw the odd green package nested in the controls where it would be crushed by a lever when the hatch was undogged and opened. Thomas took nippers from the toolkit and released the green package. He handled it gently.

Very amateur work, he thought, recalling the training which his Voidship crew had undergone in detecting and defusing dangerous devices. Ship did much better than this even before it was Ship. That had been good training and necessary. There had been no telling how a rogue Voidship might attack its umbilicus crew.

Did we create a rogue Voidship of more subtle powers?

The evidence of sabotage which he had seen thus far did not feel like Ship. It reeked of Oakes … or Lewis.

"What's that package?" Waela asked.

"My guess is it's a poison vapor set to start fuming when we tried to undog the hatch," Thomas said.

Handling it with caution in the bobbing gondola, Thomas set the package aside and returned his attention to the hatch controls. The system appeared to be free of other tampering. Slowly, gingerly, he undogged the hatch, folded down the screw handle and began turning it. The hatch lifted to expose the rim of gaskets and a sky unfiltered by the enclosing plaz.

When he had the hatch fully open, Thomas took the green package in one hand, climbed part way up the ladder and threw the package downwind. When it touched the water, lime-yellow smoke erupted from it, was caught by the wind and blown across the kelp-covered waves. The surface leaves writhed away from the smoke, curling and withering as he watched.

Waela clutched a stanchion for support and put one hand across her mouth.

"Who?"

"Oakes," Thomas said.

"Why?" Panille asked. He found himself more fascinated than fearful at these developments. Ship could save them if it came to that.

"He may want no more than one Ceepee alive in Colony."

"You're a Ceepee?" Panille was surprised.

"Didn't Waela tell you?" Thomas came back down the ladder.

"I …" She blushed a deep purple. "It slipped my mind."

"Perhaps The Boss has his own plans for the kelp," Panille said.

Thomas pounced on this. "What do you mean?"

Panille repeated what Hali Ekel had told him about the threat to exterminate the kelp.

"Why didn't you tell us?" Waela demanded.

"I thought Hali might be mistaken and … the opportunity to tell you did not arise."

"Everybody stay put," Thomas said, "while I see if there are any more little surprises in here."

He bent to his examination.

"You seem to know what you're looking for," Waela said.

"I've had some training in this."

She found this a disturbing idea: *Thomas trained to locate sabotage?*

Panille listened to them with only part of his attention. He released himself from his seat and looked up at the open hatch. There was a sweet smell to the salt-washed air blowing in the hatchway. He found the smell invigorating. Through an unblocked area beside his console, he could see the flock of hylighters tacking closer across the wind. The motions of the gondola, the smells—even the survival from the perils of the dive—all charged him with a sense of being intensely alive.

Thomas finished his examination.

"Nothing," he said.

Waela said: "I still find it difficult to …"

"Believe it anyway," Panille said. "There are things happening around Oakes that the rest of us are not supposed to learn."

She was outraged. "Ship wouldn't allow …"

"Hah!" Thomas grimaced. "Oakes may be right. Ship or the ship? How can we be sure?"

Such open blasphemy intrigued Panille. From another Ceepee, too! But it was the old philosophical question he had debated many times with Ship, merely cast in a more direct form. As he thought about this, Panille watched the approach of the hylighters, and now he pointed downwind.

"Look at those hylighters!"

Waela glanced over her shoulder. "A lot of them and big ones. What're they doing?"

"Probably coming to investigate us," Thomas said.

"They won't get too close, do you think?"

Panille stared at the orange flock. They were alive, perhaps sentient. "Have they ever attacked?"

"There's argument about that," Waela said. "They use hydrogen for buoyancy, you know, very explosive if ignited. There have been incidents ..."

"Lewis argues that they sacrifice themselves as living bombs," Thomas said. "I think they're just curious."

"Could they wreck us?" Panille asked. He stared all around the horizon. No land in sight. He knew they had food and water in the compartments under their feet. Waela had inspected those before takeoff while he held a handlight.

"They could blacken the gondola's skin a bit," Thomas said. He spoke while working at his console. "I've activated the locator beacon, but there's a lot of static on those frequencies. Radio appears to be working ..."

"But we can't punch past the interference without the 'sonde," Waela said. "We're marooned."

Panille, holding himself against the pitching of the gondola, climbed several steps of the ladder until his shoulders cleared the hatch. One glance showed the hylighters still working their way toward the gondola. He turned his attention to the 'sonde-release package attached to the plaz beside the hatch.

"What're you doing?" Thomas demanded.

"There's a lot of the 'sonde's antenna wire still in its reel."

Thomas moved to the foot of the ladder, peered up. "What're you thinking?"

Panille stared at the hylighters, at the wind-whipped sea surface. He felt an unexpected freedom here, as though all of that time confined in Ship's artificial environment had merely been preparation for this release. All of the holorecords, the history and the intense hours of study could not touch one blink of this reality. The preparations had, however, armed him with knowledge. He looked down at Thomas.

"A kite could lift our antenna high enough."

"Kite?" Waela stared up through the plaz at him. Kites were carrion-eating birds.

Thomas, knowing the other meaning, looked thoughtful. "Do we have the material?"

"What are you talking about?" Waela demanded.

Thomas explained.

"Ohhh, festival flyers," she said. She glanced around the gondola. "We have fabrics. What're these?" She unsnapped a sealing strip from an instrument panel, flexed it. "Here's material for the bracing."

Panille, looking down at them, said: "Then let's ..." He broke off as a shadow passed over him.

They all looked up.

Two large hylighters passed directly over the gondola, some of their tendrils tucked up while others held large rocks in the water to steady them. The ballast tendrils of one hylighter rubbed across the gondola, rocking it sharply.

Panille clutched the hatch rim for support. The ballast rock sped past below him in a foaming wake.

"What're they doing?" Waela shouted.

"That gas we threw out killed a lot of the kelp," Thomas said. "You don't suppose hylighters protect the kelp?"

"Here come some more of them!" Panille called.

Thomas and Waela looked where he was pointing. A swarm of hylighters glowing golden orange tacked across the wind perhaps a hundred meters away, turning in unison.

Panille climbed farther out of the hatch to sit on the rim. From this vantage, he could see the ballast rocks draw foaming lines across the waves, skipping over the kelp's leaves. The giant sail-crests of the hylighters billowed and flapped as they turned, then stiffened as they took their new heading,

Standing below him to peer over the top of an instrument bank, Thomas could see some of this.

"Don't tell me they're brainless," he said.

"I wonder if we've angered them?" Waela asked.

Panille, the wind tugging at his hair and beard, heard this as though it came from the ancient world of Ship. He felt exhilarated—free at last. Pandora was wonderful!

"They're beautiful!" he cried. "Beautiful!"

A sharp crackling sound from behind Thomas brought him whirling around. It was the speaker of a radio he had left on after testing it. Another sharp crackling erupted from the speaker. Hylighters and kelp both were blamed for this phenomenon which made radio undependable here, but how did they do it?

The swarm was almost at the gondola now. A giant specimen in the lead aimed its rock ballast directly at the gondola. Thomas held his breath. How much of that could the plaz withstand?

"They're attacking!" Waela shouted.

Panille had climbed farther out, standing now on the ladder's topmost rung while he steadied himself with a knee against the open hatch cover. He waved both arms wide, shouting: "Look at them! They're gorgeous! Magnificent!"

Thomas shouted to Waela who stood at the foot of the ladder: "Get that fool down here!"

As he shouted, the tucked tendrils of the leading hylighter slid over the gondola and the rock smashed into the plaz directly in front of Waela. She clutched the ladder for support and screamed at Panille as the gondola tipped, but her warning came too late. Arms still waving, Panille was knocked off his feet and spilled out of the gondola. She saw one of his hands clutch a hylighter tendril and he was jerked skyward. Other tendrils quickly enfolded him, almost concealing his body which was now glimpsed only in places through the hylighter's grasp. She saw all of this in bits and pieces as the gondola went through a series of wildly twisting gyrations under the massed onslaught of hylighters.

They were attacking!

Thomas had wedged himself into a corner where the arc of controls joined the communications board. He saw only Panille's feet disappear and heard Waela scream: "They've got Kerro!"

Chapter 46

In your terms, Self may be called Avata. Not hylighter, not kelp, not 'lectrokelp, but Avata. That is the Great Self in the language from your animal past. Avata. Finding this label in you, Avata knows we sing the same song. Through each other, Avata and human know Self. No second measurement for Avata. Same value every time. No separate qualities or forms. Thus with human.

Avata. But not Avata.

To name is to limit, to control. To name without knowing you limit is to hinder the knowing. At best, it is a diversion. At worst, it is a misrepresentation, a stolen label, a death. To name a thing falsely and to act thereafter on the name—that is killing, a cutting of the spiritual leaf, the death of the stem. A thing is Self or it is Other. The naming is a matter of proximity.

Avata identifies the speciesfold magnetification, the magnetism of proximity; the wavelength of space: humanthomas humankerro, humanjessup, humanoakes. Avata concludes lack of sensory organ necessary to differentiate between clone and human. Avata does not consider this lack a weakness or misrepresentation.

Avata is one in hylighter and kelp, not separate in either, nor the same. Cells differ but share the One. Before humans, Avata did not distinguish. Both are Self. Avata would teach you the Self of Other, the human in clone.

Some things are because you name them. You perpetuate them in your language, you commiserate over the woe they have wrought you.

Say simply that these things are not so. Do not change the label but the labelness. Eliminate them from your life by washing them first from your tongue. Ignoring that which is false is also a knowing. Thus—learning. To learn is to grow and to grow is to live. You may practice forgetting and thus learn.

"Home."

That is your label for this place, humankerro. Avata washes your tongue here that you may properly inflect the name and then forget it. Avata brings you this to cleanse you of expectancies, that you may learn the cues to which Avata responds or refuses to respond.

This is how you learn Avata. You are both lower level and higher level, and the continuity is the continuity of your will. Observe the vine which is all Avata winding through "Home." Grasp the vine. Cup the waters in your hands and drink.

You are the observer-effect.

—Kerro Panille, *Translations from the Avata*

Chapter 47

And the Lord God said, "Behold the man is become as one of us, to know good and evil: and now, lest he put forth his hand, and take also of the tree of life, and eat, and live forever: Therefore the Lord God sent him forth from the Garden of Eden to till the ground from whence he was taken. So he drove out the man and he placed at the east of the Garden of Eden Cherubims, and a flaming sword which turned every way, to keep the way of the tree of life.
—Christian Book of the Dead, Shiprecords

FOR KERRO Panille, his last sensible thought was the beauty of the lead hylighter passing within two meters overhead. He felt the presence of the sea and the wind, saw the black twisting mass of tendrils and the long rope of them which he knew linked the magnificent creature to its ballast rock. Then he was knocked off his feet and clutched at the only possible handhold—that long rope of guiding tendrils.

From his study of them, Panille knew that the creatures were considered to be dangerously hallucinogenic, explosive and poisonous to Shipmen, but nothing could have prepared him for the actual experience. As his hand touched the hylighter he experienced an electric buzzing which climbed to a crescendo in every sense of his body. He tasted bitter iron. The musk of uncounted flowers savaged his nostrils. His ears were the citadel of the fiercest attack—cymbals and twanging strings competed with horns and the cries of birds. Behind this assault, he heard the choral singing of a multitude.

Then his sense of balance went crazy.

Silence.

The sensations were turned off as though by a switch.

Am I dead? Is this real?

You live, humankerro.

In a way, it was like the voice of Ship. It was calm, faintly amused, and he knew it occurred only in his head.

How do I know that?

Because you are a poet.

Who ... who are you?

I am that which you call hylighter. I save you from the sea.

The beautiful ...

Yes! The beautiful, gorgeous, magnificent hylighter!

There was pride in this announcement, but still that sense of amusement.

You called me ... humankerro.

Yes—humankerro-poet.

What does being a poet have to do with my knowing this is real?

Because you trust your senses.

As though these words opened a door to his body, he felt the enclosing tendrils, the sharp bite of wind between them, and his inner ears registered the roll of a sweeping turn as the hylighter tacked. His eyes reported a shadowy golden area millimeters from his nose and he knew he lay on his back in a cradle of tendrils, the body of the hylighter close above him.

What did you do to me?

I touched your being.

How …

Again, he experienced the savage assault on his senses, but this time there was pattern in it. He detected bursts of modulation too fast for him to separate into coherent bits. His sense of sight registered pictures and he knew he was looking down with hylighter vision upon the sea … and the gondola from which he had been snatched. He felt that he must cling to these sensations as he clung to his sanity. Madness lurked at the edges of his awareness …

And once more, the assault stopped with shocking abruptness.

Panille lay gasping. It was like being immersed in all the most beautiful poetry that humankind had ever produced—everything simultaneous.

You are my first poet, and all poets are known through you.

Panille sensed an elemental truth in this.

What are you doing with me? he asked. It was very much like talking to Ship in his head.

I strive to prevent the death of human and of Self.

That was reasonable.

Panille could make no response to this. All the thoughts which occurred to him felt inadequate. Poison from the gondola had killed kelp. The hylighters, known to originate in the sea, obviously resented this. Yet, this hylighter would save a human. It occurred to him then that he was talking to a source which could explain the relationship between kelp and hylighter. Before he could think through his question, the voice filled his head, a single thought-burst: *Hylighterself-kelpself-all-one.*

It was like Ship asking him about God. He sensed another elemental truth.

Poet knows … This thought twined around in his mind until he could not tell if it originated with the hylighter or with himself. *Poet knows … poet knows …*

Panille felt himself washed in this thought. It was still with him when he realized that he was conversing with the hylighter in no language he could recall. The thoughts occurred … he understood them … but of all the languages he knew, none coincided with the structure of this exchange.

Humankerro, you speak the forgotten language of your animal past. As I speak rock, you speak this language.

Before Panille could respond he felt the tendrils opening around him. It was a most curious sensation: He was both the tendrils and himself, and he knew he was clinging to the Avata as he was clinging to his own sanity. Curiosity was his grip upon his being. *How curious this experience! What poetry it would make!* Then he knew he was being dangled over the sea: The foam at the edge of a kelp's fan leaf caught his attention and held it. He was not afraid; there was only that enormous curiosity. He wanted to drink in everything that was happening and preserve it to share with others.

Wind whipped past him. He smelled it, saw it, felt it. He was turning in the grasp of the hylighter and he saw a mounded mass of hylighters directly below. They opened like flower petals expanding to reveal the gondola in their midst—orange petals and the glistening gondola.

With gentle sureness, tendrils lowered him into the flower, into the gondola's hatch. They followed him, spreading around the interior of the gondola. He knew he was there with Waela and Thomas, yet still saw the flower as its petals closed.

An orange blaze surrounded him and he saw through the plaz, the hylighters all around, holding the gondola in a basket of tendrils.

Again, the wild play of his senses resumed, but now it was slower and he could think between the beats of it. Yes, there were Thomas and Waela, eyes glazed—terrified or unconscious.

Help them, Avata.

Chapter 48

Even the seemingly immortal gods survive only as long as they are required by mortal men.

—The Oakes Covenant

OAKES BEGAN to sputter and snore. His body lay half-melted into cushions of the long divan which stretched beneath Legata's mural on the porch of the Redoubt. The light was dull red, the early dayside of Rega coming in through the plaz above the sea.

Legata untangled herself from Oakes, slowly eased the sleeve of her singlesuit from under his naked thigh. She stepped over to the plaz and looked out at the dayside light flickering off the tops of waves. The sea was wild turmoil and the horizon a thick line of milky white. She found the uncontrolled violence of the sea repellent.

Perhaps I was not made for a natural world.

She pulled her singlesuit on, zipped it.

Oakes continued to snore and snort.

I could have crushed him there in those cushions, thrown his body to the demons. Who would suspect?

No one except Lewis.

The thought had very nearly become reality back there on the divan. Oakes had been satyric all through the dark hours. Once, she had slipped her arms up around his ribs while he worked at her, sweating and mumbling, but she could not bring herself to kill. Not even Oakes.

Waves whipped high onto the beach across the bay as she scanned the scene. The water slashed high this morning. The pounding surf echoed a deeper trembling of the earth and she could hear the clatter of rock against rock. The sound must be frighteningly loud outside for it to be heard that well in here.

It's the job of waves and rocks to make sand, she thought. Why can't I do my job that well … without question?

The answer came immediately, as though she had thought it through countless times: *Because changing rock into sand is not killing. It is change, not extermination.*

Her artist's eye wanted to find order in the view out the plaz, but all was disorder. Beautiful disorder, but frightening. What a contrast with the peaceful bustle of a shipside agrarium.

She could see the shuttle station off on the isolated point of land to her left, an arc of the bay between, and the low line of the protected passage leading from Redoubt to Station. That had been Lewis' idea: Keep the Station remote, easy to cut off should attackers come from Colony.

She found herself wanting the roll and toss of kelp leaves in the bay, but the kelp was going … going …

A chill crawled up her spine and down her arms.

A few diurns, Oakes had said.

She closed her eyes and the picture that haunted her was her own mural, the accusing finger which pointed straight at her heart.

You are killing me! it said.

No matter how hard she shook her head, the voice would not be still. Against her better judgment, she crossed to the dispenser and keyed it for a drink. Her hand was steady. She returned to the plaz-guarded view, and sipped slowly while watching the waves bite their way up the beach across the bay. The waves had buried the previous high-tide mark at least a dozen meters back. She wondered whether she should wake Oakes.

A hylighter suddenly valved itself low across the beach below the shuttle station. A sentry appeared at the beachside guardpost and snapped her heavy lasgun to her shoulder, then hesitated. Legata held her breath, expecting the bright orange flash and concussion. But the woman did not fire; she lowered her weapon and watched as the delicate hylighter drifted out of sight around the point.

Legata let out her breath in a long sigh.

What happens when we have no others to kill?

Oakes' desire for a paradise planet vanished when she confronted that seascape. He could make it sound so plausible, so natural, but …

What about the Scream Room?

It was a symptom. Would people turn on each other, band together in tribes and attack each other in the absence of Dashers or Runners … or kelp?

Another hylighter drifted past farther out.

It thinks.

And the vanishing kelp. Oakes was right that she had seen the reports from the disastrous undersea research project.

It thinks.

There was a sentiency here which touched her where cell walls left off, somewhere within that realm of creative imagination which Oakes distrusted and would never enter.

Almost eighty percent of this planet is wrapped in seas and we don't even know what's under there.

She found herself envying the researchers who had risked (and lost) their lives groping beneath these seas. What had they found?

A pair of huge boulders down on the beach beneath her smashed together with a jarring crack that caused her to jump. She glanced at the beach across the bay. As quickly as it crossed the high-tide mark, the waters began their ebb.

Curious.

Tons of boulders had been rolled up against the cliff barrier across the compound. More of them obviously must be on the beach beneath her. The boulders she could see were gigantic.

That much power in the waves.

"Legata …"

The abruptness of Oakes' voice and touch upon her shoulder startled her, and she crushed the glass in her hand. She stared down at the hand, the cuts, her own blood, shards of glass glinting in her flesh.

"Sit over here, my dear."

He was the doctor then, and she felt thankful for it. He plucked out broken glass, then unrolled strips of Celltape from a dispenser at his com-console to stop the bleeding. His hands were firm and gentle as he worked. He patted her shoulder when he had finished.

"There. You should …"

The buzz of the console interrupted.

"Colony's gone." It was Lewis.

"What do you mean, gone?" Oakes raged. "How can the entire …"

"A shuttle overflight shows nothing but a hole where Lab One was. Plenty of demons, hatchways to all lower levels blown …" He shrugged, a tiny gesture in the console screen.

"That's … that's thousands of people. All … dead?"

Legata could not face Lewis, even on the screen. She crossed to the divan silently and stared out the plaz.

"There could be survivors holed up behind some of the hatches," Lewis went on. "That's how we made it here when …"

"I know how you made it here!" Oakes shouted. "What are you suggesting?"

"I'm not suggesting anything."

Oakes gritted his teeth and pounded the console. "You don't think we should have Murdoch try to save anyone?"

"Why risk the shuttles? Why risk one of our last good people?"

"Of course. A hole, you say?"

"Nothing but rubble. Looks to've been the work of lasguns and plasteel cutters."

"Do they … I mean, are there any shuttles left over there?"

"We disabled everything before leaving."

"Yes … yes, of course," Oakes murmured. Then: "LTAs?"

"Nothing."

"Didn't you and Murdoch say that you cleared everything out of that Lab One site? Moved it all here?"

"Apparently the rioters thought there might be some burst hidden away there. They captured the only remaining communications equipment. They were demanding help from … the ship."

"They didn't …" Oakes could not complete the question.

"The ship didn't answer. We were listening."

A deep sigh shook Oakes.

Without turning to face him or the viewscreen, Legata called out, "How many people did we lose there?"

"Ship knows!" Lewis threw back his head, laughing.

Oakes hit the key to shut him off,

Legata clenched her fists. "How could he laugh that way at …" She shook her head.

"Nervous," Oakes said. "Hysteria."

"He was not hysterical! He was enjoying it!"

"Calm yourself, Legata. You should get some rest. We have much to do and I'll need your help. We've saved the Redoubt. We have most of the food that was at Colony and far fewer people to eat it. Be thankful that you're among the living."

That worry in his tone, in his eyes.

It was almost possible to believe he felt genuine love for her.

"Legata …" He put out a hand to touch her arm.

She pulled away. "Colony's gone. The hylighters and kelp are next. Then what? Me?"

She knew it was her own voice speaking, but she had no control over it.

"Really, Legata! If you can't handle alcohol, you should not drink it."

His gaze went to the broken glass on the floor.

"Especially this early in the dayside."

She whirled away from him and heard him press the console key and summon a clone worker to clean up the broken glass. As he spoke, Legata felt the last of her hope shatter in the morning air, lost on the wild glinting of the waves she could see out there.

What can I do against him?

Chapter 49

Human, do you know how interesting it is, this thing you describe? Avata does not have a god. How is it that you have a god? Avata has Self, has this universe. But you have a god. Where did you find this god?

—Kerro Panille, *Translations from the Avata*

FOR THOMAS and Waela, the return of the hylighters had appeared another concerted attack. Thomas tried to close the gondola's hatch and found it jammed. Waela was shouting up at him to hurry, and asking if he saw Kerro.

Both suns were up now. And the light on the sea was dazzling.

Waela's head was still spinning from the gondola's gyrations.

"What'll they do with him?" she called.

"Ship knows!" He jerked at the hatch cover, but it would not move. Something had hit the mechanism while the gondola was twisted and tilted in the first attacks.

Thomas peered at the tacking hylighters. One of them had its tendrils tucked up tightly. It could be holding Panille in there. He saw that the gondola had been pushed out of the dead kelp into a patch of living green. The sea all around was subdued by a carpet of gently pulsing leaves.

"They're coming back!" Waela shouted.

Thomas abandoned his attempts on the hatch, slid back into the gondola.

"Brace yourself in your seat!" he called. And he followed his own order while he watched the advancing swarm of orange.

"What're they doing?" Waela asked.

It was a rhetorical question. They could both see the hylighters slow their advance at the last instant. In concert, they turned their great sail membranes into the wind and cupped the gondola in dangling tendrils.

Waela freed herself from her seat, but before she could move, the massed hylighters opened a way overhead and Panille was lowered through the hatch.

She tried to avoid the questing mass of tendrils which accompanied Panille, but they found her. They enfolded her face with a sensation of tingling dryness which immediately gave way to a drunken sense of abandon. She knew her body; she knew where she was: right here in the gondola which was being held steady in a cupped hammock of hylighter tendrils. But nothing mattered except a feeling of joy which insinuated itself all through her. She felt that the sensation came from Panille and not from the hylighters.

Avata? What are Avata?

That thought had seemed her own, but she could not be certain.

She was not aware of up or down. There was no spatial solidity.

I'm going crazy!

All of the horror stories about poisonous and hallucinogenic hylighters crashed through her barriers and she tried to scream but could not locate her voice.

Still, the joy persisted. Panille was right there saying things to soothe her. "It's all right, Lini."

Where did he get that name for me? That was my childhood name! I hate that name.

"Don't hate any part of yourself, Lini."

The joy would not be denied. She began to laugh but could not hear her own laughter.

Quite suddenly, an island of clarity opened around her and she knew Kerro Panille lay nude beside her. She felt his warm flesh against her.

Where did my clothing go?

It was not important.

I'm hallucinating.

This was a product of Thomas' command that she seduce the poet. She gave herself up to the dream, to the warmth and hardness of him as he slid into her, rocking her. And she sensed all around the questing tendrils as they explored, joining her with images of flaring stars. That, too, was unimportant—more hallucination. There was only the joy, the ecstasy.

For Panille, the slowed play of the sense-attack wavered when he first saw Waela. He felt his own body and he felt the hylighter's. Wind whipped his sail membranes. Then he heard music, a slow and sensual chant which moved his flesh in time to the dance of tendrils around him. He found himself drawn to Waela, his hands upon her neck. How electric her flesh! His hands unsnapped her singlesuit. She made no move to assist or resist, but kept time to the sensory beat with a soft swaying of her hips which did not stop even when the singlesuit slid off her body.

Strangest sensation of all: He could see her flesh, the lovely body, yet he saw also a golden-orange hylighter rise from the sea and spring free into the sky, and he saw Hali stretched out in warm yellow light beneath a cedar of a treedome. Wonder filled him as he dropped his own suit and drew Waela down to the deck.

Ship? Ship, is this the woman for whom I saved myself?

How is it that you call upon Ship when you could call your humanself?

Was that Ship or Avata? No matter. He could not listen for an answer. There was only the hard beat of sexual magnetism which told him every movement his body should make. Waela became not-Waela, not-Hali, not-Avata, but part of his own flesh entwined with a sensation of enormous involvement by countless others. Somewhere in this, he felt that he lost even himself.

Thomas, still restrained securely by his seat straps when Panille returned, was caught there by entwining tendrils. He tried to fight them off, but …

Voices! There were voices … he thought he heard old Morgan Hempstead back at Moonbase, christening their Voidship. Momentous day. There was a buzzing in his nostrils and he smelled the musk of Pandora but he was crouched within his own nostrils recording this. Tendrils! They moved all over his body, under his suit, avoiding no intimate contact. As they moved, they sucked out his identity. First he was Raja Flattery, then Thomas, then he did not know who he was. This amused him and he thought he laughed.

I'm hallucinating.

That was not even his own thought because he was not there to have such a thought. There was a head somewhere spinning out of control. He thought he felt brains rattle and slosh in their cage of skull. He knew he ought to breathe but he could not find where to breathe. He was sliding through a passage which no clone had ever known—the womb of all wombs.

That's how it is to be born.

Panic threatened to overcome him. *I was never born! The hylighters are killing me!*

Avata does not kill you!

That was a voice echoing in a metal barrel. *Avata?* He knew that from his Chaplain studies—ancient superego of the Hindu oversoul.

Who am I who knows this?

He glimpsed Panille and Waela, their naked bodies entwined in lovemaking. The ultimate biological principle. *Clones don't have that link with their past.*

Am I a clone? Who am I?

He knew what clones were, whoever he was; he knew that. Clones were property. Morgan Hempstead said so. Again, panic threatened him, but it was stifled instantly while he tried to follow a silvery thread of awareness which moved faster and faster as he sped to overtake it.

Waela … Panille …

He knew those had to be people, but he did not know who, except that the names filled him with rage. Something fought him to calmness.

The mandala on his cubby wall. Yes. He stared at it.

Who was Waela?

A sense of loss flooded through him. He was forever out of his time, far gone from someplace where he had grown, stripped of past and without his own future.

Damn You, Ship!

He knew who Ship was—the keeper of his soul, but this thought made him feel that he was Ship and he had damned himself. No reality remained. Everything was confusion, everything gone to chaos.

It's you damned Avata/hylighters! Keep that Panille out of my mind! Yes, I said MY mind.

Darkness. He was aware of darkness and of motion, sensations of controlled movement, glimpses of light and a glaring sun, then craggy rocks. He could see Rega low on a castellated rock horizon. There was flesh around him and he knew it for his own.

I'm Raja Flattery, Chaplain/Psychiatrist on … No! I'm Raja Thomas, Ship's Devil!

He looked down to find himself strapped into his command couch. There was no motion to the gondola. When he looked out through the plaz he could see solid ground—a damp stretch of Pandoran soil studded with native plants: odd spikey things with fluting silver leaves. He turned his head and there was Waela seated on the deck, completely naked. She was staring at two singlesuits. One of them, Thomas saw, carried Waela's shoulder badge of the LTA service, and the other … the other was Panille's.

Thomas looked all around the gondola. Panille was not there.

Waela turned to look up at Thomas. "I think it was real. I think we really did make love. And I was in his head while he was in me."

Thomas pushed himself hard against the back of his seat, his memory struggling for the bits and pieces of what had happened to them. Where was the damned poet? He could not survive out there.

Waela moved her tongue against her teeth. She felt that she had lost track of time. She had been out of her body in some new place, but now she knew her body better than ever before. Images. She recalled the earlier, more terrible moments off the south coast of The Egg when she had sprawled on a kelp leaf, fighting for her sanity. This recent experience in the gondola was not the same, but one partook of the other. In both, she felt the aftermath as a loosening of her identity and a mixing of linear memories, shaking bits of her past out of place.

Thomas unfastened his seat restraints, stood and peered out through the filtering plaz. He felt that something had reached into his psyche and drained away the energy. *What are we doing here? How did we get here?*

There was no sign of hylighters.

What are Avata?

The gondola had been deposited in a broad pocket of flat land surrounded by a rock rim. The place looked vaguely familiar. The outline of the west rim … He stared at it, caught up in a fugue state of attempted recollection.

"Where are we?" That was Waela.

His throat was too dry to respond. It took a moment of convulsive attempts to swallow before he could speak.

"I … think we're somewhere near Oakes' Redoubt. Those rocks—" He pointed.

"Where's Kerro?"

"Not here."

"He can't be outside. The demons!"

She stood and stared all around over the obstructing panels of instruments, craning her neck to peer every direction. *That fool poet!* She looked up at the hatch. It was still open.

In that instant an LTA drifted over the rim of rocks to the west; the glare of Rega setting ringed it in a golden halo. The LTA was valved down to a landing beside the gondola, the hiss of its loud vents stirred up the dust. The gondola was a conventional landside type, armored against demons and studded with weapons. The side hatch opened a crack and a voice called from within: "You can make it if you run! No demons near."

Hastily, Waela stood and slipped into her suit. It was like putting on familiar flesh. She felt her sense of identity firming.

I must not think about what has happened. I'm alive. We're rescued.

But somewhere within her she thought she heard a voice crying names: "Kerro … Jim … Kerro … where are you?"

There was no answer, just Thomas insisting that she follow only after he had tested the outside. *Damn fool! I'm faster than he is.* But she went quietly up the ladder behind him, watched him slide down the smooth plaz curve of the gondola, then followed on his heels. The rescue hatch of the other gondola swung wide as they reached it, and they were jerked inside by two pairs of hands. They were in familiar red shadows with the Shipmen at defensive stations all around the interior.

Waela heard the hatch slammed and dogged behind her, felt the gondola lift, swinging. There was the humming of a scanner as it passed over her body. A voice at her ear said: "They're clean."

Only then did she realize that she stood in a sealed-off bubble within the rescue gondola. This spoke of only one threat: Nerve Runners!

There were Runners in the area.

She felt a deep sense of gratitude for the Shipman who had scanned them, risking contact with Runners. Turning, she saw a long-armed monstrosity only vaguely Shipman in shape.

"We take you Lab Oneside," he said and his mouth was a toothless black hole.

Chapter 50

In a fit of enthusiastic madness I created a rational creature and was bound towards him to assure, as far as was in my power, his happiness and well-being. This was my duty, but there was another still paramount to that. My duties towards the beings of my own species had greater claims to my attention because they included a greater proportion of happiness or misery.

—*Dr. Frankenstein Speaks, Shiprecords*

THOMAS STRETCHED himself in the hammock of a cell and watched a fly creep its way across his ceiling. There were no ports in this cell, no chrono. He had no way of estimating the time.

The fly skirted the protrusion of a sensor eye.

"So we brought you, too." Thomas spoke aloud to the fly. "It wouldn't surprise me to find a few rats skulking around this place. Non-human rats, that is."

The fly stopped and rubbed its wings. Thomas listened. There was a steady stream of footsteps up and down the passage outside his locked hatch. It had been locked from the outside, no handle in here.

He knew he was somewhere within Oakes' infamous Redoubt, the fortress outpost on Black Dragon. They had taken all of his clothing, every possession, leaving him with a poorly fitted green singlesuit.

"Quarantine!" he snorted, still talking aloud. "At Moonbase we called it 'the hole.'"

Some of those footsteps outside were running. Everything was rush-rush here. He wondered what was happening. What was going on over at Colony? Where had they taken Waela? They had told him he was headed for debriefing. It turned out to be a quick once-over by a strange med-tech and isolation in this cell. Quarantine! Before they had closed the hatch, he had glimpsed a sign across the way: "Lab One." So they had a Lab One here, too … or they had moved the other one from Colony.

He was aware of the sensor eye prying at him from the ceiling. The cell was Spartan—the hammock, a fixed desk, a sink, an old-style composting toilet without seat.

Once more, he looked at the fly. It had progressed to the far corner of the cell.

"Ishmael," he said. "I think I'll call you Ishmael."

… *his hand will be against every man and every man's hand against him, and he shall dwell in the presence of all his brethren.*

Ship's unmistakable presence filled Thomas' head so suddenly that he clapped his hands over his ears in reflex.

"Ship!" He closed his eyes and found that he was near tears. "I can't give in to hysteria! I can't."

Why not, Devil? Hysteria has its moments. Particularly among humans.

"There isn't time for hysteria." He opened his eyes, brought his hands away from his ears, and spoke in the general direction of the ceiling sensor. "We have to solve Your problem of WorShip. They won't listen to me. I'll have to take direct action."

Ship was relentless: *Not MY problem! Your problem.*

"My problem, then. I'm going to share it with the others."

It is time to talk of endings, Raj.

He glared at the sensor, as though that were the origin of the presence in his head.

"You mean … break the recording?"

Yes, it is the time of times.

Was that sadness in Ship?

"Must You?"

Yes.

So Ship really meant it. This was not just another diversion, another replay. Thomas closed his eyes, feeling his voice go slack in his throat, his mouth dry. He opened his eyes and the fly was gone.

"How … long do we … how long?"

There was a noticeable pause.

Seven diurns.

"That's not enough! I might do it in sixty. Give me sixty diurns. What's such a sliver of time to You?"

Just that, Raj: a sliver. Annoying, the way it works its way into the most sensitive area. Seven diurns, Raj, then I must be about other business.

"How can we discover the right way to WorShip in seven diurns? We haven't satisfied You for centuries and …"

The kelp is dying. It has seven diurns until extinction. Oakes thinks it will be longer, but he is mistaken. Seven diurns, then, for you all.

"What will You do?"

Leave you to the certainty that you will wipe yourselves out.

Thomas leaped from his hammock, shouted: "I can't do anything about it in here! What do You expect from …"

"You in there! Thomas!"

It was a male voice from a hidden vocoder. Thomas thought he recognized the voice of Jesus Lewis.

"Is that you, Lewis?"

"Yes. Who are you talking to?"

Thomas looked up at the sensor in the ceiling. "I have to talk to Oakes."

"Why?"

"Ship is going to destroy us."

Let you destroy yourselves. The correction was gentle but firm in his awareness.

"Was that what you were shouting about? You think you were talking to the ship?" There was derision in Lewis' tone.

"I was talking to Ship! Our WorShip is all wrong. Ship demands that we learn how to …"

"Ship demands! The ship is about to be put in its proper place, a functional …"

"Where's Waela?" He shouted it in desperation. He had to have help. Waela might understand.

"Waela's pregnant and she's been sent shipside to the Natali. We don't have birthing facilities here yet."

"Lewis, please listen to me, please believe. Ship awakened me from hyb to put you all on notice. You don't have much time left to …"

"We have all the time in this world!"

"That's it! And this world has only seven more diurns. Ship demands that we learn the proper WorShip before …"

"WorShip! We can't waste time on such nonsense. We have to make a whole planet safe to live on!"

"Lewis, I have to talk to Oakes."

"You think I'm going to bother the Ceepee with your babblings?"

"You forget that I'm a Ceepee."

"You're insane and you're a clone."

"Unless you listen to me, you're headed for destruction. Ship will break the … it will be the end of humankind forever."

"I have my orders about you, Thomas, and I'm going to obey them. There's only room for one Ceepee here."

The hatch behind Thomas popped open and he whirled to see the yellow dayside lights of the passage framing an E-clone sentry there—giant head, round black hole for a mouth, huge arms that hung nearly to his ankles. The eyes were glaring red and bulbous.

"You!" A growling voice issued from the round black hole. "Out here!"

One of the massive hands reached in, closed around Thomas' neck and jerked him out into the passage.

"WorShip. We have to learn how to WorShip," Thomas croaked.

"I get tired a hearin' that WorShip crap," the sentry said. "You're movin' out." The sentry released his neck and gave Thomas a violent push down the passage.

"Where are we going? I have to talk to Oakes."

The sentry lifted one of his arms, pointed down the passage. "Out!"

"But I …"

Another push sent Thomas stumbling. There was no resisting the strength of this clone. Thomas allowed himself to be herded down the passage. It curved to the right and ended at a locked hatch. The sentry took one of Thomas' arms in a relentless grip, opened the hatch. It swung wide to reveal the open ground of Pandora in the harsh cross-lighting of Alki swinging low on the horizon to his left. A sudden push from the clone sent Thomas sprawling into the open and took his breath away. He heard the hatch slam closed. Somewhere above him, he heard the distant fluting of a flock of hylighters.

They've sent me into the open to die!

Chapter 51

And the Lord said, "Behold, the people is one, and they have all one language … and now nothing will be restrained from them which they have imagined to do. Let us go down and confound their language that they may not understand one another's speech."

—Christian Book of the Dead, Shiprecords

FROM THE instant the first tentacles brushed her face to the moment she boarded the shuttle for Ship, Waela lived in a blur of past-present-future which she could not control. Kerro was gone and Thomas was not available, this much she knew. And contact with the hylighters had left her with a voice in her mind. It flared there in flashes of total demand. She wavered between accepting the voice and believing herself insane.

The voice of Honesty would not answer, but this new voice intruded without warning. When it came, she felt herself filled with the same conceptual ecstasy she had felt in the gondola.

It is the Avata way of learning.

The voice kept repeating this. When she questioned, answers came, but in a jargon which confused her.

Like electricity, humanwaela, knowledge flows between poles. It activates and charges all that it touches. It changes that which moves it and moves within it. You are such a pole.

She knew what the words meant, but they went together in a confusing way.

And all the while, she remained vaguely aware of the processing procedure when the rescue gondola deposited them at Colony. Thomas was taken away somewhere and she was rushed into a medical unit for debriefing. The session was run by Lewis—astonishing!

It was right there that the first demanding flash hit her.

Waela. I have found the Avata.

She knew there was no sound, but the voice filled her sense of hearing. It was Kerro Panille, no denying it. Not his voice, but his identity recognized in an internal way which could not be disguised. She knew it as she knew herself. But she didn't even know that Kerro was alive!

I'm alive.

Then he had found some way of reaching out … or of reaching in.

Either that or I'm insane, she thought.

She did not feel insane as she stood in the Medical section's glaring tile-white cubicle looking across a metal table at Lewis. Hands supported her. It was nightside; she knew this. Rega had been setting and they had brought her directly in here. Lewis was speaking to her and she kept shaking her head, unable to answer him because of that voice in her mind. An older med-tech said something to Lewis. She heard three words: "… too soon for …"

Then the whirl of that intruding voice returned. She was uncertain whether she recognized words—or whether it really could be called a voice—but she knew what was being said. It was a non-language, and she knew this when she found that she could not distinguish between "I" and "We" in Kerro's communication. A language barrier was down.

In that instant of recognition, she knew Avata as Kerro Panille knew Avata. She wondered how she learned this lesson, this ancient bit of human history.

How did I learn, Kerro Panille?

What is done to one is felt by all, humanwaela.

"Why am I humanwaela?" She asked it aloud and saw an odd expression come over the face of Lewis as he turned from talking to the med-tech. This did not bother her. She felt her mind drifting lazily in the Pandoran wind. There were mutterings and head-shakings among people around her—med-techs, several of them … an entire team. She filtered them out. Nothing was more important than the voice in her mind.

You are humanwaela because you are at once human and at once Waela. There may be such a time as this is not so. Then you will be human.

"When will that be?"

The cold node of a pribox drilled the back of her left hand, tingled up her arm and sent her down a whirlwind of dis-timed memories which were not her own.

When you know all that otherhumans know, and otherhumans know all of you, then you are human.

She concentrated on that magnificent universe of the interior which this concept opened before her. *Avata.* She had no sensation of time while she floated in the arms of Avata, or whether Avata was really with her. If it was just a dream, she wanted it never to end.

Only you can end it, humanwaela. See?

Memories poured into her—from that first sensory awareness of the first Avata to the coming of Shipmen to Pandora and then to her rescue from the gondola—everything poured into her through a timeless flash, a non-linear stream of sensations.

This is not hallucination!

She saw humans, Shipman/humans of many suns, and uncounted histories which died with them. It baffled her how she understood this. *How …*

She heard the voice in her mind: *This we trade with those we touch. Lives of all humans alive in each of you. But you and humankerro are the first to recognize the trade. Others resist and fear. Fear erases. Humanthomas resists, but out of humanfear, not out of humanthomas fear. There is something he will not trade.*

Waela found herself eavesdropping through another's eyes. She was looking in a mirror and the face that looked back was Raja Thomas. A shaking hand explored the face, a wan face, tired. She heard a voice which she knew to be Ship's.

Raj.

Then there were no more mind pictures. He blanked her out. Rejected.

She found herself alone on a gurney in a Redoubt passage.

So Thomas is on speaking terms with Ship.

"Why?" The question was a dry crackle in her throat and a nearby med-tech bent over her. "You'll be shipside soon, dear. Don't worry." The gurney's straps hurt her breasts.

This is Pandora, humanwaela. All evil has been released here.

There was that voice again. Not Kerro. Avata?

The word tingled on her tongue as med-techs began to roll her gurney onto a shuttle. There was another face above her then—dream or reality? Small, a face like Lewis, but not Lewis. The voices all around were babble. She was being wheeled, pushed and probed, but her attention remained with the voice in her mind and the link she had seen to that intricate chain of humanity.

"She's pregnant. That means shipside, the Natali. Orders."

"How long's she been pregnant?"

"Looks like more'n a month."

That can't be! she thought. *I've just arrived here and Kerro and I ...*

She felt a doubled awareness of time then—one told her she had arrived at the Redoubt late in the same diurn that had seen their sub enter the lagoon. The other time-sense lived in her abdomen, and the clock there had gone mad ... spinning, spinning, spinning. It raced completely out of pace with the clock in her head.

"She'll be the Natali's problem pretty soon," someone said. Those were words in her ears. Time out of sync was more important. From the time Kerro had slipped into her....

The time was out of phase. She knew only that she must be delivered shipside to the Natali. That was the way of WorShip.

How can that be, Avata?

She felt that she was meant to be pregnant and the act of conception was an Avata formality.

As the hatchway opened to the shuttle the lean-faced man took hold of the gurney and she saw that it was one of Murdoch's people, a long-fingered clone who spoke in a falsetto. A shock of fear jolted her body.

"Am I going shipside?"

She couldn't bring herself to ask the other half of the question, *Or to Lab One?*

"Yes," he said, as she thumped across the threshold of the shuttle.

"What do we do now?" she asked aloud. And the voice from her mind said, *Save the world.*

Then the hatchdogs were secured and she slept.

Chapter 52

CONSCIOUS: from Latin com, with scire (to know).
CONSCIENCE: from Latin com (intensive), with scire.
Conscious—to know; conscience—to know well (or, in the vernacular, to know better).

—Shiprecords

SHIPSIDE!" OAKES screamed into the vocoder on his console, "Who ordered the TaoLini woman shipside?"

The med-tech facing him on the screen looked terrified and small. His little mouth worked itself into a stumble of words.

"You did, sir. I mean … orders. She's pregnant, sir, and you signed the WorShip order sending all …"

"Don't tell me what I signed!"

"No, sir. Are you ordering her back, sir?"

Oakes pressed a hand against his forehead.

Too late, now. The Natali have her. Reprocessing her groundside would mean an executive order and that would mean attention. The Redoubt was problem enough. Better to let the matter rest until something could be arranged … *Damn! Why couldn't we have moved the Natali down here …*

"I want to talk to Murdoch."

"He is shipside, sir."

"I know he's shipside! Get him on a line to me as soon as you can!"

He smacked the key on the console with the side of his fist and the frightened little med-tech's face faded.

Damn! Just when things were going right!

He looked out over the clear bay beside the shuttle station. No more kelp there anyway. The perimeter lights and the arcs from the nightside crew's torches reflected the flat calm of the water.

No kelp. It'll be gone from Pandora before we know it.

That left Ship.

The ship.

And now, that TaoLini woman. *No telling what she knows.* Thomas could have convinced her of anything. After all, he was a Ceepee.…

Oakes turned back to his console and activated the holo of Thomas' debriefing.

Thomas sat in the center of the room, a cell three meters square. He faced the sensor. A tall woman from Behavioral stood facing Thomas and he was shaking his head from side to side.

"No time. No time. You must decide how you will WorShip, Ship says and the clue is in the sea. I know it's in the sea. WorShip … WorShip. And there is no time, after all the eons and all these worlds … no time. No time.…" Oakes switched off the holo in disgust.

The kelp got to him, that's for sure. Maybe it's just as well.

He paced back to the plaz which screened the ocean view, and watched the dazzle of the welders and cutters play across the water.

The kelp is a trade, he thought. *Thomas wasn't all that far off. With the kelp gone, we buy ourselves time and with time we buy a world. Not a bad barter.*

He retraced his steps again and again, plaz to console, console to plaz.… Having that TaoLini woman shipside was too big a variable—something would have to be done.

Damn that tech! his fist came down again. He should've double-talked her into Lab One instead of letting her go shipside. *Can't the fool think for himself? Do I have to make every decision!*

He knew Murdoch was up there in a power-scrimmage with Ferry, but they were Lewis' people and it was Lewis' business. This whole fiasco was really Lewis' fault.

"Until they interfere with the Ceepee," he said aloud, pointing an affirmative finger at his reflection in the plaz. On the other side of the reflection, the quiet bay began to pick up the rhythmic *rush rush* of small waves licking at the beach.

Chapter 53

Inflection is the adjective of language. It carries the subtleties of delight and horror, the essence of culture and social process. Such is the light-pattern displayed by the kelp; such is the song of the hylighter.

—Kerro Panille, *History of the Avata* (from the "Preface")

WAELA SAT watching a holo of Panille as a child. Except for the projected action at the holofocus, it was quiet in the small teaching study where Hali Ekel had put her. The chair, a simple sling in a metal frame, presented the holocontrols on its arm beneath her right hand. Soft blue light suffused the room, down-toned to increase resolution at the holofocus. Each time the holosound subsided, a low susurration of venting air could be heard.

At frequent intervals, Waela turned her head slightly to the left and drank from a tube leading into a shiptit. Her left hand rested lightly on her abdomen and she was certain that the hand felt the growth of the fetus. There was no concealing the rapidity of that growth, but she tried not to think about it. Every time she was forced to confront the mystery of what was happening within her, she felt a hiccup of terror—a sensation which subsided in a blink as something dampened it.

A sense of isolation permeated the study—an accent on her awareness that she was being kept out of contact with ordinary shipside life. The Natali were doing this deliberately.

The pangs of terrible hunger controlled the movement of her mouth to the shiptit. She drank greedily and with feelings of guilt. Hali Ekel had not explained why there was a shiptit here, nor why Ship fed her from it when others were denied. Feelings of rebellion welled up in Waela from time to time, but these, too, were dampened by some automatic response. She continued to sit and stare at the holo of the young Panille.

At the moment, the holo showed him sleeping in his cubby. The register gave his age as only twelve standard annos at the time, and there was no mention of who had authorized this holo.

A Ship 'coder rattled in the sleeping child's cubby then, waking Panille. He sat up, stretched and yawned, then increased the cubby's light level with one hand while rubbing his eyes with the other.

Ship's voice filled the cubby with its awful clarity: "Last nightside, you claimed kinship with God. Why do you sleep? Gods need not sleep."

Panille shrugged and stared at the 'coder from which Ship's voice issued. "Ship, have You ever stretched out as long as You can reach and yawned?"

Waela held her breath at the audacity of the child. This question suggested blasphemy and there was no reply.

Panille waited. Waela thought him patient for one so young.

"Well?" he asked, finally, smug in his adolescent logic.

"I'm sorry, young Kerro. I nodded my head but apparently you did not see it."

"How could you nod? You don't have a head to put on a pillow."

Waela gasped. The child was challenging Ship because of Ship's question about kinship with God. She waited for Ship's response and marveled at it.

"Perhaps the head I nod and the muscles I stretch are simply not within your field of vision."

Panille took a glass of water from his cubby spigot and drank before replying.

"You're just imagining what it's like to stretch. That's not the same at all."

"I actually stretched. Perhaps it is you who imagines what it is to stretch."

"I really stretch because I have a body and that body sometimes wants to sleep."

Waela thought he sounded defensive, but there were plain hints at amusement in Ship's tones.

"Never underestimate the power of imagination, Kerro. Notice the word itself: creator of images. Is that not the essence of your human experience?"

"But images are . . . just images."

"And the artistry in your images, what is that? If, someday, you compose an account of all your experiences, will that be artistry? Tell me how you know that you exist."

Waela slapped the shut-off switch. The holo image of young Panille held itself in the negative, like an afterthought, then died. But she thought he had been nodding as she stopped the replay, as though he had acquired sudden insight.

What did he acquire in his odd way of relating to Ship? She felt herself inadequate to the task of understanding Panille, despite these mysterious recordings. How had Hali Ekel known about these holos? Waela glanced around the tiny study cubby. What a strange little place hidden away here behind a secret hatch.

Why did Hali want me to look at these recordings? Will I really find him there in his past—lay the ghost of his childhood to rest or drive his voice from my mind?

Waela pressed her palms against her temples. That voice! In her most unguarded moments of panic, that voice came into her mind, telling her to be calm, to accept, telling her eerie things about someone called Avata.

I'm going mad. I know I am.

She dropped her hands and pressed them against her abdomen, as though this pressure would stop the terrible speed of that growth within her.

Hali Ekel's diffident knock sounded at the hatch. It opened just enough to let her slip through. She sealed the hatch, swung her pribox around to her hip.

"What have you learned?" Hali asked.

Waela indicated the jumble of holo recordings around her chair. "Who made these?"

"Ship." Hali put her pribox on the arm of Waela's chair.

"They don't tell me what I want to know."

"Ship is not a fortuneteller."

Waela wondered at the oddity of that response. There were times when Hali seemed at the point of saying something important about Ship, something private and secret, but the disclosure never came—just these odd statements.

Hali attached the cold platinum node of the pribox to the back of Waela's left hand. There was a moment of painful itching at the contact, but it subsided quickly.

"Why is the baby growing so fast in me?" Waela asked. The hiccup of terror leered in her mind, vanished.

"We don't know," Hali said.

"There's something wrong. I know it." The words came out flat, absolutely devoid of emotion.

Hali studied the instruments of her pribox, looked at Waela's eyes, her skin. "We can't explain this, but I can assure you that everything except the speed of it is normal. Your body has done months of work in only a few hours."

"Why? Is the baby ..."

"Everything we scan shows the baby is normal."

"But it can't be normal to ..."

"Ship says you're being fed everything you need." Hali indicated the tube into the shiptit.

"Ship says!" Waela looked down at the linkage between her hand and the pribox.

Hali keyed a cardiac scan. "Heart normal, blood pressure normal, blood chemistry normal. Everything normal."

"It is not!"

Waela panted with the exertion required to put emotion into her voice. Something did not want her excited, upset or frustrated.

"This child is growing at a rate of about twenty-three hours for every hour of the gestation," Hali said. "That is the only abnormal thing about this."

"Why?"

"We don't know."

Tears welled up in Waela's eyes, slipped down her cheeks.

"I trust Ship," Hali said.

"I don't know what to trust."

Without conscious volition, Waela turned to the shiptit, drank in long sucking gulps. The tears stopped while she drank. She watched Hali at the same time, how purposefully the young woman moved, changing the settings on the pribox. What a strange creature, this Hali Ekel—shipcut hair as black as Panille's, that odd ring in her nostril.

So mature for one so young.

That was the real oddity about Hali Ekel. She said she had never been groundside. Life was not rendered down to raw survival here the way it was groundside. There was time here for softer things, more sophisticated dalliances. Ship's records at your fingertips. But Hali Ekel had groundside eyes.

Waela stopped drinking, her hunger satisfied. She turned and stared directly at Hali.

Could I tell her about Kerro's voice in my head?

"You scattered the graphs there," Hali said. "What were you thinking?"

Waela felt a warm flush spread up her neck.

"You were thinking about Kerro," Hali said.

Waela nodded. She still felt a tightening of her throat when she tried to talk about him.

"Why do you say hylighters took him?" Hali asked. "Groundside says he's dead."

"The hylighters rescued us," Waela said. "Why should they turn around and kill him?"

Waela closed her eyes as Hali remained silent and watchful. *You see, Hali, I hear Kerro's voice in my head. No, Hali, I'm not insane. I really hear him.*

"What does it mean to run the P?" Hali asked.

Waela's eyes snapped open. "What?"

"Records says you once lost a lover because he ran the P. His name was Jim. What does it mean to run the P?"

Slowly at first, then in bursts, Waela described The Game, then, seeing the reason for Hali's question, added: "That has nothing to do with why I believe Kerro's alive."

"Why would the hylighters take him away?"

"They didn't tell me."

"I want him to be alive, too, Waela, but …" Hali shook her head and Waela thought she detected tears in the med-tech's eyes.

"You were fond of him, too, Hali?"

"We had our moments." She glanced at Waela's swelling abdomen. "Not those moments, but good just the same."

With a quick shake of her head, Hali turned her attention to the pribox, keyed another scan, converted it to code, stored it.

"Why are you storing that record?"

She's watching me carefully, Hali thought. *Do I dare lie to her?*

Something had to be done, though, to allay the obvious fears aroused by this examination and the questions which could not be answered.

"I'll show you," Hali said. She called back the record and shunted it to the study screen beyond the holofocus. With an internal pointer, she indicated a red line oscillating across a green matrix.

"Your heart. Note the long, low rhythm."

Hali keyed another sequence. A yellow line wove its way through the red, pulsing faster and with lower intensity.

"The baby's heart."

Again, Hali's fingers moved over the keys. "Here's what happened when you thought about Kerro."

The two lines formed identical undulations. They merged and pulsed as one for a dozen beats, then separated.

"What does that mean?" Waela asked.

Hali removed the node from Waela's hand, began restoring the pribox to its case at her hip.

"It's called synchronous biology and we don't know exactly what it means. Ship's records associate it with certain psychic phenomena—faith healing, for example."

"Faith healing?"

"Without the intervention of accepted scientific medicine."

"But I've never …"

"Kerro showed me the records once. The healer achieves a steady physiological state, sometimes in a trance. Kerro called it 'a symphony of the mind.'"

"I don't see how that …"

"The patient's body assumes an identical state, in complete harmony with the healer's. When it ends, the patient is healed."

"I don't believe it."

"It's in the records."

"Are you trying to tell me my baby is healing me?"

"Given the unknowns about this rapid gestation," Hali said, "I would expect greater upset from you. But you don't seem capable of maintaining long periods of physiological imbalance."

"Whatever else she may be, she's still an unformed infant," Waela said. "She could not do that."

"She?"

Waela felt pressure against one of her lower ribs, the baby shifting.

"I've known all along that it's female."

"That's what the chromosome scan says," Hali agreed. "But the odds were even that you could guess right. Your guess doesn't impress me."

"No more than your faith healing."

Waela stood up slowly and felt the baby adjust to this new position.

"Unborn infants have been known to compensate for deficiencies in the mother," Hali said, "but I'm not selling faith healing."

"But you said …"

"I say a lot of things." She patted her pribox case. "We've set up a special exercise cubby down in P-T. You have to keep up your body tone even if …"

"If you're right, this baby will be born in a matter of diurns. What can I do to …"

"Just get down to P-T, Waela."

Hali slipped back out through the hatch before Waela could raise more objections. That was an alert and intelligent woman in there. Waela knew how to search records, and her curiosity would not be dampened by inadequate answers. *Now, what do we do?*

Hali turned at the crèche hatch and saw one of the children staring out at her from the open bubble of the play area. Hali knew the child, Raul Andrit, age five. She had treated him for nightmares. She bent toward him. "Hi. Remember me?"

Raul turned his face up to her, wan and listless. Before he could answer, he fell out of the bubble into the passage.

Setting her alarm signal on call, Hali turned the child onto his back and attached the pribox. The emergency readout buzzed and, for the first time, Hali doubted a computer diagnosis. In the snarl of facts blurring past her eyes she read: fatigue … exhaustion … 10.2 …

"Yes?" The voice of a responding medic was thin in her pribox speaker. She briefed him and set the boy up for a glucose and vitamin series from her emergency packet.

"I'll send a cart." The speaker blipped as the medic broke the connection.

Hali put a question to her computer: "Raul Andrit: age?"

The screen flashed 5.5.

"What is the age of the subject just tested?"

10.2.

Her fingers scurried across the keys: "The last subject tested was Raul Andrit. How could he be 5.5 and 10.2?"

He has lived 5.5 standard annos. His body exhibits the characteristic intracellular structures of one who is 10.2. For medical purposes, cellular age is the more important.

Hali sat back on her heels and stared down at the unconscious child—dark circles under his eyes, pale skin. His chest appeared too thin and it heaved convulsively when he breathed. What the computer had just told her was that this little boy had doubled his age in a matter of diurns. She heard the cart pull up, a young attendant with it.

"Get this child to sickbay. Notify his Natali sponsor and continue treatment for fatigue," she said. "I'll be along shortly."

She hurried toward Physical Therapy and, at the passage turn, bumped into a breathless medic rushing out. "Ekel! I was just coming for you. You signaled with a child who fainted? There's another one in the Secondary play area. This way."

She followed on his heels, listening to the description. "He's a seven-anno in Polly Side's section. Kid can barely stay awake. Eating too much lately and, what with food monitoring, that's a problem—but he was weighed today and found to be down two kilos from last week."

She did not have to be told that this was a significant drop for a child of that age.

The boy was lying on a stretch of thick green lawn in the free-play area, a shutter-shielded dome overhead. As she crouched beside him to set up her case, she smelled the fresh-clipped grass and thought how incongruous that was—the enticing green odor and this boy ill.

The pribox readout did not surprise her after Raul Andrit. Fatigue … exhaustion … signs of aging …

"Should we move him?"

That was a new voice. She turned and looked up at a thin-faced man in groundside blue standing beside the medic.

"Oh, this is Sy Murdoch," the medic said. "He came up to ask some questions of the TaoLini woman. You sent her down to P-T, didn't you?"

Hali stood up, recalling the grapevine stories about Murdoch: Kelp and clones. Lab One director. One of Lewis' people.

"Why would you want to move him?" she asked.

"I understand from the medics that Raul Andrit has been taken to sickbay with a similar seizure. It occurred to me that …"

"You say Raul Andrit with a certain familiarity," she said. "You're wearing groundside. What do you know about …"

"Now, see here! I don't have to answer your …"

"You'll answer me or a medical board. This could be a disease brought up from groundside. What's your association with Raul Andrit?"

His face went blank, completely unreadable, then: "I know his father."

"That's all?"

"That's all. I've never seen the child before. I just … knew he was here, shipside."

Hali, trained from childhood to be a med-tech, to support life and see that Shipmen survived, knew each bodily muscle, nerve, gland and blood vessel by name and often spoke to them quietly as she worked. Instinctively, she knew that Murdoch was trained otherwise. He repelled her. And he was lying.

"What's your business with Waela TaoLini?"

"That concerns the Ceepee, not you."

"Waela TaoLini has been put in my charge by the Natali. That's Ship's business. Anything concerning her concerns me."

"It's just routine," Murdoch said.

Every mannerism said it was not just routine, but before she could respond, she saw Waela walk into the play area.

While she was still at some distance, Waela called: "They said somebody here was looking for me. Do you …"

"Stay back there!" Hali called. "We've some sick boys and we don't want them near any expectant mothers. Wait for me over in the Natali Section. I'll join you in …"

"Forget it!" That was Murdoch speaking with a new forcefulness. He gave every indication of someone who had come to an important decision. "We'll meet with Ferry in Medical. Immediately."

Hali protested: "With Ferry? He doesn't …"

"Oakes left him in charge shipside. That should be good enough for you." He turned on his heel and strode from the area.

Chapter 54

Myths are not fiction, but history seen with a poet's eyes and recounted in a poet's terms.

—Shipquotes

FERRY SAT at his command couch sipping a pale liquid which reeked of mint. He had been reviewing biostats on a shielded viewscreen when Hali and Waela entered and he did not lower the shields.

The command cubby, which had been tacked onto the Processing complex after Oakes' departure, was brightly illuminated by corner remotes which filled the room with yellow light. There was a sharp smell of caustic cleaner in the air.

Hali noted two things immediately: Ferry was not yet overcome by the drink and he appeared fearful. Then she saw that the command center had been tidied recently. Anywhere Ferry worked was soon a scattered mess—a notorious situation shipside where instincts of neatness equated with survival. But things had been made neat here. Unusual.

She saw Murdoch then and realized that Ferry feared what Murdoch might report to Oakes. Murdoch stood at one side of the command center, arms folded, impassive.

Ferry closed down his screen with a conscious flourish, swiveled to face the newcomers.

"Thank you for coming along so quickly."

Ferry's voice was reedy with controlled emotions. He stroked the bridge of his nose once, an unconscious imitation of Oakes.

Waela noted that his fingers were trembling.

What does he fear? she wondered.

The man's furtiveness spoke of terrified concealments.

Is it something to do with my baby?

The characteristic blip of her own fears lifted and fell. And there was Kerro's voice: "Trust Hali and Ship, Waela. Trust them."

Waela tried to swallow in a dry throat. *Could no one else hear him?* She shot a furtive glance around the room. When she heard the voice, she felt sure of it. The instant it was gone, she doubted. Her real-time perceptions were demanding full attention, though. Physical senses honed to high sensitivity by the necessities of survival on Pandora—these she trusted. And Ferry demanded her attention. The man was a menace, operating on several levels of deception. She had heard the stories about Ferry, a competent-enough medical man with a few eccentricities, but not to be trusted alone with a young woman.

Her eyes told her something else.

A humbler, Waela told herself, who sits in the command seat. *Interesting. Why did Oakes choose a humbler?*

Waela's Pandora-sensitized nostrils detected alcohol in Ferry's drink. She put on her best impassive mask to conceal the recognition. The groundside uses of alcohol and tetrahydracannabinol in their various forms were generally accepted in Colony. But somehow she had not expected this shipside. With Ship to protect them … well, Shipmen had long held that alcohol was a risky and undesirable poison shipside. But then again, she knew that Ferry, like herself, had spent his early years Earthside. His reversion might not be all that unusual.

Still, Ferry's actions interested her. If the fact of her impregnation outside Ship's regular breeding program were taken seriously in certain circles … Well, why else would Ferry be using viewscreen shields? And alcohol! She did not want her life, nor her baby's life, depending on someone who deliberately lowered his acuities.

Drinking, she thought. The word was dredged up out of her childhood and she had a bottomless-pit feeling about the hyb-plus-waking time which had passed since she had equated that word with alcohol.

The shielded screen bothered her. *It was time someone invaded Ferry's privacy,* she thought.

"That drink smells like fresh mint. Could I taste it?"

"Yes … of course,"

It was not of course, but he offered her the glass. "Just a taste. It's not the kind of thing a prospective mother should have."

The glass was cold against her fingers. She sipped the drink and closed her eyes, recalling a scorched afternoon in Earthside summer when her mother had let her have a diluted mint julep with the grownups. The color of this drink was paler, but it was definitely bourbon with mint. She opened her eyes and saw Ferry's gaze fixed on the glass.

Hungry for it, she saw. *He's nearly drooling.*

"It's quite good," she said. "Where did you get it?"

He reached for the glass, but Waela handed it to Hali, who hesitated and looked at Ferry, then at Waela.

"Go ahead," Waela said. "Everyone should have one sometime. I had my first when I was twelve."

When Hali still hesitated, Ferry said, "Perhaps she shouldn't, what with this strange illness going around. What if it's catching?"

He treats it like a precious jewel, Waela thought. *It must be hard to get.*

She said: "If it's that contagious, we've caught it. Go ahead, Hali."

The younger woman sipped, swallowed and immediately bent her head in a fit of coughing, the glass thrust out for someone to take it.

Ferry grabbed it from her hand.

Eyes watering, Hali said: "That's terrible!"

"It's all in knowing what to expect," Ferry said.

"And lots of practice," Waela said. "You never told us where you got it. Not one of our lab alcohols, is it?"

Ferry placed the glass carefully on the deck beside his seat.

"It's from Pandora."

"Must be hard to get."

"Don't we have more important things to discuss?" Murdoch asked.

They were his first words, and they transfixed Ferry. He reached down for the drink, drew his hand back without it. He turned and fussed with the controls for his screen, dropped the shield, hesitated, then left it down.

Waela promised herself that she would use the first opportunity to call up the records Ferry found so interesting. With unrestricted use of Ship's research facilities, it would not be difficult.

Murdoch moved around behind Ferry, an action which increased Ferry's nervousness.

Waela found herself sympathizing with the old man. Murdoch in that position would make anyone's shoulder blades twitch.

Ferry sputtered, then: "I was … ahh, waiting for some, ahhh, others to come up before, ahhh, taking up the, ahh, business we … I mean …"

"What are we doing here?" Hali asked. She did not like the undercurrents flowing through this room. Unspoken threats lay heavy on Ferry's shoulders and it was obvious they came from Murdoch.

Ferry reached for the drink with a convulsive motion, but before he could put it to his lips, Murdoch reached over Ferry's shoulder and removed the glass from his hand.

"This'll wait."

Murdoch put the glass on a ledge behind him. As he turned back toward the others, the hatch opened and three people entered.

Hali recognized Brulagi from Medical, a heavy-set woman with fat arms and a thick lower lip. She wore her auburn hair in the regular close-cropped style, and her eyes shone bright blue above a flat nose. Right behind her came Andrit from Behavioral, a large dark man with quick almond eyes of deep brown and a nervous, darting manner. Behind these two was Usija, gray-haired, a thin-lipped, soft-spoken woman from the Natali, who had assigned Hali to monitor Waela TaoLini.

"Ahhh, here you are," Ferry said. "Please be seated, everyone. Please be seated."

Hali was glad to sit. She found a sling chair for Waela and another for herself. Waela moved her own chair to seat herself directly across from Ferry. It put her apart from the others, an observer's distance, and let her focus on Ferry and Murdoch without having to turn. Ferry would notice and it would annoy him, she thought. He wanted attention, not investigation.

What is it with you, old man? Waela wondered. *What do you fear?*

The three latecomers perched on a couch at right angles to Ferry. Murdoch remained standing.

Hali, noting Waela's move, wondered about it, but was distracted by the sudden realization that Andrit from Behavioral must be the father of young Raul. *What was going on here?*

Murdoch touched Ferry's shoulder and the older man jumped. "Show them the map."

Ferry swallowed, turned to his keyboard, punched at it clumsily. A miniature projection of Ship's schematic materialized at the holofocus beside him.

Hali recognized the special Natali area outship from Behavioral and noted a number of red dots through the projection. Brulagi from Medical leaned forward with her thick arms on her legs and stared at the three-dimensional map. Andrit appeared agitated by it. Usija merely nodded.

"What are the red markers?" Hali asked.

"Each dot represents a stricken child," Ferry said. "If you connect them, they form a spiral and you'll note that they increase in density as they reach the spiral's center."

"A vortex," Murdoch said.

Waela peered closely at the schematic. She caught her breath and glanced up to catch a look of unguarded fury on Andrit's face. He was clenching and unclenching his fists. She saw the heavy muscles of his forearms knotting under his singlesuit.

Ferry pulled some papers from the ledge beside his keyboard and shuffled through them while he spoke: "For the sake of those who might not know, ahh, where is your cubby, Waela?"

Andrit leaned forward, almost falling from the couch as he glared at Waela. She saw Murdoch repress a smile. *What amused him?*

"You all know where I sleep, Doctor. My cubby's at the center of the spiral."

Andrit lunged as quickly as anyone Waela had ever seen shipside. But even though she felt heavily pregnant, Pandora had conditioned her reflexes to blurring speed. When Andrit hit the space where Waela had been sitting, she no longer was there. Before he could recover, Waela felled him with a blow to his carotid—every move automatic.

She felt strength flowing through her. It gushed from the fetus within her and out through every fiber of her body.

Hali, out of her chair by this time, looked from Andrit sprawled unconscious on the deck to Waela who stood poised and breathing easily in front of them. The sudden exertion had fanned the reddish glow under her skin to a blaze. As she turned slowly on one heel to see if there would be more attack, she was an awesome sight.

Dazed, Hali asked: "Why did he do that?"

Waela confronted Ferry. "Why?" She stood balanced on the balls of her feet. Andrit had threatened not her but her unborn child! Let any of them try to harm her child!

Murdoch chose to answer, an odd glint in his eyes. He appeared to be enjoying this.

"He was … personally upset, you understand? One of the stricken children is his son."

"What do those red dots really mean?" Hali demanded.

"Ahh, there have been some energy problems, we believe," Murdoch said. "We saw a similar thing in Lab One."

Waela took a step toward Ferry. "I want to hear it from you. Oakes left you in charge here. What's going on?"

"I, uhh, don't really know much about it." Ferry licked his lips, shot a glance over his shoulder at Murdoch.

"You mean you're not supposed to know anything about it," Waela said. "Tell us what you do know."

"Now, let's change our tone a bit," Murdoch said. "There's an injured man on the deck and this whole unfortunate matter does not require more passion."

He turned toward the Natali representative. "Doctor Usija, since the med-tech appears unable to respond …"

Hali looked down at Andrit who was beginning to stir.

"He'll recover," Waela said. "I pulled my blow."

Hali stared at her. The implication was obvious: She could have killed the man. Belatedly, Hali bent to examine him. Her pribox showed a bruise on his neck, some nerve damage, but Waela was right: He would recover.

"What happened in Lab One?" Waela directed her question to Murdoch.

"An … artificial form of this phenomenon. You are the first natural example of this we've seen."

"Natural example of what?" Waela forced the words out.

"The draining of energy from … other people."

Waela glared at him. What was he saying? She took a step toward him and felt Hali's hand on her arm. Waela whirled on the med-tech and almost brought her down. Sensing this, Hali jerked her hand back.

"Waela? Just a moment. I'm beginning to understand."

"Understand what?"

"They think you're responsible for the sick children."

"Me? How?" She turned back toward Ferry. "Explain."

Murdoch started to speak, but she snapped an angry glare at him. "Not you! *Him*."

"Now, Waela, calm yourself," Ferry said. "This has all been an unfortunate mistake."

"What do you mean unfortunate mistake, you drunk? You set this up. You invited Andrit here. You knew about that spiral in your schematic. What were you trying to do?"

"I will not take that tone from you," Ferry said. "This is my …"

"This is your funeral if you don't tell me what's going on here!"

Hali stared at Waela. What was happening to the woman? Murdoch, Hali noted, was standing very still—no threatening movements at all. Usija and Brulagi were frozen in their seats.

"Now, don't you threaten me, Waela," Ferry said. There was a plaintive note in his voice.

She's perfectly capable of killing him if he doesn't satisfy her demand, Hali thought. *Ship, save us! What has come over her?*

Usija began to speak very softly, but her voice was compelling in the tense air of the room.

"Doctor Ferry, you are looking at the phenomenon of the threatened feral mother. It goes very deep. It is dangerous to you. Since Waela is Pandora-conditioned, I advise you to answer her."

Ferry pushed himself back in his seat as far as he could go. He wet his lips with his tongue.

"I, ahhh … your circumstances shipside, Waela. There has been some, ahhh, let us call it superstition."

"About what?"

"About, ahhh, you. We have tested you since your return and … ahhh, we do not find usable answers. Even Ship is no help. Whatever it is, Ship has locked it away—Restricted. Or …" He shot a venomous glance at Hali. "… we are referred to Med-tech Hali Ekel."

Hali could not repress a gasp.

Waela whirled and glared at her.

Hali realized suddenly that now she was a target.

"Waela, I swear to you that I don't know what he's talking about. I'm here to protect you and your baby, not to hurt you."

Waela gave a curt nod, returned her attention to Ferry.

Andrit groaned and pushed himself upright. Waela bent and, with one hand, hoisted him to his feet. In the same motion, she hurled him toward the couch where he narrowly missed Brulagi and Usija. The effortless way Waela did this made Hali hold her breath, then exhale slowly. *Very dangerous, indeed.*

"Tell us the circumstances where Ship refers you to Hali Ekel," Waela said. Her voice was like a bubbling volcano.

Andrit leaned forward abruptly and vomited, but no one looked.

"When we asked if it was the child causing this or if it was you," Ferry said.

Hali gasped, her vision suddenly blurred by memory of a dusty hillside, the setting of a blazing yellow sun, and three figures tortured on crosses. *What kind of a child was Waela carrying?*

Waela spoke without turning. "Hali, does that mean anything to you?"

"How was your child conceived?" Hali asked.

Waela turned a startled look toward her. "Kerro and I … for Ship's sake, you know how babies are made! Do you think we carry axolotl tanks on those subs?"

Hali looked at the deck. The legend said immaculate conception—no man involved. A god … But it was only a legend, a myth. *Why would Ship refer the questioners to her?* Many times since that trip through time, Hali had asked herself, *Why? What was I supposed to learn?* Ship spoke of holy violence. The accounts concerning the Hill of Skulls which she had scanned since the experience certainly confirmed this. *Holy violence and Waela's child?*

Waela continued to stare at her. "Well, Hali?"

"Perhaps your child is not confined to this time." She shrugged. "I can't explain, but that's what occurs to me."

Apparently, this satisfied Waela. She glanced at Andrit, who was holding his head and remaining quiet. She turned back to Ferry.

"What is it about my baby? What're you afraid of?"

"Murdoch?" It was a desperate plea from Ferry. Murdoch crossed his arms and said, "We got the reports from Ferry and …"

"What reports?"

Murdoch swallowed, nodded at the holoprojection with its spiral of red dots.

"What were you supposed to do to me?" Waela asked.

"Nothing. I swear it. Nothing."

He's terrified, Hali thought. Has he seen this feral threatened-mother phenomenon before?

"Questions?" Waela asked.

"Oh, yes, of course—questions."

"Ask them."

"Well, I was … I mean, I discussed this with the Natali and, we, that is, Oakes, wanted me to ask if you would return groundside to have your baby?"

"Violate our rules of WorShip?" Waela looked at Usija.

"You do not have to go groundside," Usija said. "We merely agreed that he could ask."

Waela returned her attention to Murdoch. "Why groundside? What did you hope to do there?"

"We have stockpiled a large supply of burst," Murdoch said. "It's my belief you will need every ounce of it you can get."

"Why?"

"Your baby is growing at an accelerated rate. The physical requirements for the cellular growth are … very large."

"But what about the sick children?" She turned toward Andrit. "What have they told you?"

He lifted his head, glared at her. "That you're responsible! That they've seen this before groundside."

"Do you want me to go groundside?"

They could see him battling with his WorShip conditioning. He swallowed hard, then: "I just want it to go away, whatever's making my son sick."

"How do they explain my responsibility for this?"

"They say it's a … psychic drain, often observed but never explained. Perhaps Ship …" He was incapable of repeating outright blasphemy.

They chose a poor tool to attack me, Waela thought.

The pattern of the plot was clear now: Andrit was to demonstrate potential violence in shipside opposition to her. She would be forced to go groundside "for your own good, my dear." They wanted her down there badly.

Why? How am I dangerous to them?

"Hali, have you ever heard of this phenomenon?"

"No, but I would agree that the evidence points at you or your baby. You don't need burst, though."

"Why?" Murdoch demanded.

"Ship is feeding her from the shiptits."

Murdoch glared at her, then: "How long have you Natali known that this baby was growing too rapidly?"

"How do you know it?" Usija countered.

"It's part of this phenomenon—rapid growth, abnormal demand for energy."

"We've known since our first examinations of her," Hali said.

"You kept it under wraps and proceeded with caution," Murdoch said. "Precisely what we did groundside."

"Why would you want to feed me on burst?" Waela asked.

"If the fetus gets enough energy from burst, the psychic drain does not take place."

"You're lying," Waela said.

"What!"

"You're as transparent as a piece of plaz," Waela said. "Burst cannot be better than elixir."

Usija cleared her throat. "Tell us, Murdoch, about your experience with this phenomenon."

"We were doing some DNA work with kelp samples. We found this ... this survival characteristic. The organism absorbs energy from the nearest available source."

"The mother's the nearest available source," Hali said.

"The mother's the host and immune. The organism takes from other organisms around it which are, ahhh, similar to the hungry one."

"I'm not aging," Hali said. "And I'm around her more than anyone."

"It does that," Murdoch said. "It takes from some people and not from others."

"Why from children?" Hali asked.

"Because they're defenseless!" That was Andrit, fearful but still angry.

Waela felt energy charging every muscle in her body. "I'm not going groundside."

Andrit started to get to his feet, but Usija restrained him. "What are you going to do?" Usija asked.

"I'll move out to the Rim beyond one of the agraria. We'll keep people, especially children, away from me while Hali studies this condition." She looked at Hali, who nodded.

Murdoch did not want to accept this. "It would be far better if you came groundside where we've had experience with ..."

"Would you try to force me?"

"No, oh no."

"Perhaps if you sent us a supply of burst," Usija said.

"We would not be able to justify shipment of such a precious food at this time," Murdoch said.

"Tell us what you know about the phenomenon," Hali said. "Can we develop an immunity? Does it recur or is it chronic? Does ..."

"This is the first time we've seen it outside a lab. We know that Waela TaoLini conceived outside the breeding program and outside Colony's protective barriers, but …"

"Why don't I get answers from Colony?" Ferry asked. He had been sliding his chair slowly to one side while Murdoch spoke, and now he looked up at the man.

"That has nothing to do with …"

"You speak of not shipping burst at this time," Ferry said. "What is special about this time?"

Waela heard desperation in the old man's voice. *What is Ferry doing?* Something deep in him was driving these questions out.

"Your questions do not relate to this problem," Murdoch said, and Waela heard death in his voice.

Ferry heard it, too, because he fell into abashed silence.

"What do you mean about the conception being outside of Colony's barriers?" Usija asked. It was the scientist's voice gnawing at an interesting question.

Murdoch appeared thankful for the interruption. "They were floating in a … in a kind of plaz bubble. It was in the sea, completely surrounded by the kelp. We don't know all of the details, but some of our people have suggested that Waela and her child may no longer be humantype."

"Don't try to get me groundside!" Waela said.

Usija climbed to her feet. "Humans bred freely Earthside and anywhere they liked. We're merely seeing it happen again … plus an unknown which must be studied."

Murdoch directed his glare at her. "You said …"

"I said you could ask her. She has made her decision. Her plan is a sensible one. Isolate her from children, put her under constant monitoring …"

Usija's voice droned on outlining specifics to implement Waela's decision—a place with a shiptit, a rotation of Natali med-techs …

Waela tuned out the droning voice. The baby was turning again. Waela felt dizzy.

None of this is normal. Nothing is as it should be.

Blip. The fear lifted in her awareness, then dropped.

What did Murdoch mean that she might no longer be humantype?

Waela tried to recall details of what had happened in the gondola as it floated on Pandora's sea. All she could remember was the ecstatic wash of her union with something awesome. This shipside command cubby, Usija's voice—none of this was important any longer. Only the baby growing at its terrible pace within her was important.

I need a shiptit.

An image of Ferry pressed itself into her awareness. He was somewhere else with his inevitable drink in his hand. Murdoch was talking to him. Ferry was trying to protest without success. She heard faint voices, distant and muffled as though they came from a sealed room. There was a high view of Pandora's sea glowing in the light of two suns. It was replaced by a blurred vision of Oakes and Legata Hamill. They were making love. Oakes lay on his back on a brown woven mat. She was astride him … slow movement … very slow … an insane look of joy on her face, her hands clenching and unclenching the fat of his chest. In the vision, Legata leaned back, trembling and Oakes caught her as she fell.

It's a dream, a strange waking dream, Waela told herself.

Now, the dream shifted to Hali on her knees in her own cubby. Atop a ledge in front of Hali stood an odd construction of wood—two smooth sticks, one of them fixed off-center across the other. Hali leaned her head close to the crossed sticks and, as she did this, Waela experienced the unmistakable fragrance of cedar, as fresh as anything she had ever smelled in a treedome.

Abruptly, she was back in the command cubby. Hali's arm was around her shoulder, leading her out the hatch while Usija and Brulagi argued with Murdoch behind them.

"You need food and rest," Hali said. "You've overstressed yourself."

"Shiptit," Waela whispered. "Ship will feed me."

Chapter 55

The prophets of Israel who preached the idea of the nucleus of ten good men required for a city's survival, built this concept on the Talmudic idea of the Thirty-Six Just Ones whose existence in each generation is necessary for the survival of Humankind.

—Judaism's Book of the Dead, Shiprecords

UNTIL SHE saw him sprint across the east plain, a Hooded Dasher close behind, Legata did not know Thomas was at the Redoubt. She stood at the giant screen in the Command Center, the hum of late dayside activity going on all around. Oakes and Lewis were conferring off to her left. The big screen had been set on a scan program, ready to lock onto any unusual activity. She took over the controls and zoomed in on the running man. The Dasher was only a few leaps behind him. The scene was outlined in the harsh cross-light of the evening suns.

"Morgan, look!"

Oakes rushed to her side, stared up at the screen.

"The fool," he muttered.

Thomas swerved abruptly to the left, made a desperate leap off a dangerously high rock onto the sand at the high tide mark. The Dasher leaped after him, misjudged and landed in a patch of dead kelp washed up by the surf. It immediately began gulping rags of kelp while Thomas ran off down the beach. Another Dasher appeared behind him then, dropping from a high rock, running as it landed. Thomas dodged around a boulder and sped off along the high tide mark. His boots kicked up globs of damp sand. There was no doubt that he heard the Dasher closing on him.

"He'll never make it. No one can," Oakes' trembling voice betrayed his nervousness.

Afraid he won't get away? Legata asked herself. *Or afraid he will?*

"Why did you turn him out?" she asked. She kept her attention on the figure darting and weaving away from her, and she remembered that nightside meeting with him outside Colony's Lab One. She found herself silently urging him on: *Into the surf! Dodge into the water!*

"I didn't turn him out, my dear," Oakes said. "He must've escaped." Oakes turned and called out to Lewis across the room. "Make sure nothing's been left open to the outside."

"He was a prisoner. Why?"

"He and the TaoLini woman came back from their undersea venture without Panille, a wild story about hylighters rescuing them. That requires more than simple debriefing."

Lewis came up to stand beside Oakes. "All secure."

Thomas had swerved into the water once more, diving under ragged scraps of dead kelp. He surfaced draped with the stuff, and the second Dasher remained behind to feed on the scraps. Thomas was visibly tiring now, his stride irregular.

"Can't we do anything for him?" Legata asked.

"What would you have us do?" Oakes asked.

"Send a rescue party!"

"That area's full of Dashers and Flatwings. We can't afford to lose any more people."

"If he was foolish enough to go outside, he takes his own chances," Lewis said. "Isn't that the rule for running the P?" He stared at Legata.

"He's not running the P," she said, and she wondered if Lewis had somehow learned about her own mad run.

"Whatever he's doing, he's on his own," Oakes said.

"Ohhh, no ..." The gasp escaped her as the black figure of another Hooded Dasher, two Flatwings close behind it, took up the chase. Thomas was staggering now and the Dasher closed rapidly. In the last blink, as the Dasher stretched for the final blurring leap, it swerved abruptly aside. A mass of tentacles dropped from the air and a hylighter soared across Thomas, scooping him up.

Oakes worked the screen controls, zooming back for a general view. Someone behind them said: "Would you look at that!" It was almost a sigh.

The hills and cliffs inland from the Redoubt displayed tier upon tier of hylighters, great mobs of them gathered in a siege arc beyond the range of the Redoubt's weapons.

"Goodbye, Raja Thomas," Oakes said. "Too bad the hylighters got him. A Dasher would've ended it quickly."

"What do the hylighters do to you?" Legata asked.

Before Oakes could answer, Lewis turned to the room and said: "All right, everybody. Show's over. Back to work."

"We only have evidence from some demon carcasses," Oakes said. "They were sucked dry."

"I ... wish we could've saved him," she said.

"He took his chances and he lost."

Oakes reached out to the controls, his finger poised over the scan program, stopped. He stepped backward to bring the whole screen into view. The hylighter carrying Thomas had lost itself in the distant mobs. The great billowing bags now danced on the air, underlighted by the orange glow of the suns, their sail membranes rippling and filling.

Legata saw what had stopped Oakes. More hylighters were coming up, climbing higher and higher, filling in the sky.

"Ship's eyes!" another voice behind them said. "They're blocking out the suns!"

"Split screen," Oakes said. "Activate all perimeter sensors."

It took several blinks for Legata to realize he was addressing her. She flipped the switches and the screen went gray, then reformed in measured squares of the different views, a locator number under each. Hylighters englobed the sky all around the Redoubt—over the sea, over the land.

"Look there." It was Lewis pointing to a screen showing the base of the inland cliffs. "Demons."

They became aware then that the entire rim of cliffs, as far as the sensors could reach, writhed with life. Legata felt certain that never before had such a mass of teeth and claws and stings assembled in one place on the face of Pandora.

"What are they doing?" Oakes asked, and his voice trembled.

"They look like they're waiting for something," Legata said.

"Waiting for orders to attack," Lewis said.

"Check security!" Oakes barked.

Legata keyed for the proper sensors and the screens flickered to re-form with views of the cleanup work on the damage left by the E-clone revolt. *Orders from whom?* she wondered. Crews were busy in every screen, mostly E-clones guarded by armed normals. Some worked in the open courtyard where the Nerve Runners had left nothing alive; others toiled along the shattered sections of the perimeter where temporary barriers had been erected. There were even some heavily guarded crews outside. No demons or hylighters interfered.

"Why aren't they attacking?" Legata asked.

"We seem to be at a stand-off," Lewis said.

"We're saving our energy," Oakes said. "My orders are not to shoot them at random. We cook them now only if they come within twenty-five meters of our people or equipment."

"They can think," Lewis said. "They think and plan."

"But what are they planning?" Legata asked. She noticed that Oakes was going paler by the blink.

Oakes turned. "Jesus, we'd better do some planning of our own. Come with me."

They left, but Legata did not notice. She remained at the screen, working through the outside sensors. The whole landscape had turned into a golden dazzle of suns and hylighters, black cliffs aswarm with demons, and a surging sea capped with white foam and spray.

Presently, Legata turned, realized that Oakes and Lewis no longer were in the Command Center.

I'll have to act soon, she thought. *And I have to be ready.*

She worked her way through the activity in the Center, opened a main corridor hatch and hurried toward her own quarters.

Chapter 56

Poet
You see bones up ahead
where there are none.
By the time we get there
so do they.
—Hali Ekel, Private Letters

HALI STUDIED the monitors on the reclining Waela with care. It was well into dayside, but Waela appeared to be asleep, her body quiet on the tightly stretched hammock which they had rigged in one of Ship's rim compartments. Her abdomen was a mounded hillock. There was no hatch to this cubicle, only a fabric curtain which rustled in faint stirrings from the agrarium to which this extrusion was attached.

This is not normal sleep, Hali thought.

Waela's breathing was too shallow, the passivity of her body too profound. It was as though she had slipped back into something approaching hyb. What did that mean for the fetus?

The compartment was slightly larger than a regular cubby, and Hali had brought in a small wheeled cart to support the monitor screen. The screen showed Waela's vital signs as visible undulating curves with synchronous time-blips. A secondary set of lines reported on the child developing in Waela's womb. A simple twist of a dial could superimpose one set of lines on the other.

Hali had been checking the synchronous beat for almost an hour. Waela had come to this Natali retreat without protest, obeying every suggestion Hali made with a sleepwalker's passivity. She had appeared to gain some energy after feeding at a corridor shiptit—a process which still filled Hali with confusion. So few ever received elixir at the shiptits anymore that most Shipmen ignored them, taking this as a sign of Ship's deeper intents or displeasure. Attendance at WorShip had never been more punctual.

Why was Ship feeding Waela?

While Waela drank from the shiptit container, Hali had tried to get a response from the same corridor station. No elixir.

Why, Ship?

No answer. Ship had not been easily responsive since sending her to see the crucifixion of Yaisuah.

The lines on the monitor screen were merging once more—fetus and mother in synchronous beat. As the lines merged, Waela opened her eyes. There was no consciousness in the eyes, only an unmoving stare at the compartment ceiling.

"Fly us back to Jesus."

As she spoke, the synchronous lines separated and Waela closed her eyes to sink back into the geography of her mysterious sleep.

Hali stood in astonished contemplation of the unconscious woman. Waela had said "Jesus" the way Ship pronounced the name. Not Yaisuah or Hesoos, but Geezuz.

Had Ship sent Waela, too, on that odd journey to the Hill of Skulls? Hali thought not. *I would recognize the signs of that shared experience.* Hali knew the marks on herself which came from that trip to Golgotha.

My eyes are older.

And there was a new quietude in her manner, a wish to share this thing with someone. But she lived with the knowledge that no other person might understand … except possibly … just possibly, Kerro Panille.

Hali stared at the pregnant mound of Waela's abdomen.

Why had he bred with this … this older woman?

Fly us back to Jesus?

Could that be just delirious muttering? Then why Geezuz?

A deep sense of uneasiness moved itself through Hali. She used her pribox to call down to Shipcore and arranged for a relief watch on the monitor. The relief showed up presently, a young Natali intern named Latina. Her official green pribox hung at her hip as she hurried into the compartment.

"What's the rush?" Hali asked.

"Ferry sent word that he wants to see you right away down at WorShip Nine."

"He could've called me." Hali tapped her own pribox.

"Yes … well, he just said for me to tell you to hurry."

Hali nodded and gathered her things. Her own pribox and recorder were beyond habit, a part of her physical self. She briefed Latina on the routine as she gathered her equipment, noting the log of synchronous beats, then ducked out through the curtain. The agrarium was a scene of intense dayside activity, a harvest in process. Hali wove her way through the dance of workers and found a servo going coreside. At Old Hull she took the slide to Central and dropped off at the Study passage which led to Worship Nine.

The red numeral winked at her as she found the hatch and slipped into the controlled blue gloom. She could not see Ferry anywhere, but there were perhaps thirty children in the five-to-seven age range sitting cross-legged around a holofocus at the center of the WorShip area. The focus showed a projection of a man in shipcloth white who was lying on bare ground and covering his eyes with both hands in great pain or fear.

"What is the lesson, children?"

The question was asked in the flat and emotionless tone of Ship's ordinary instruction programs.

One of the boys pointed to another boy beside him and said: "He wants to know where the man's name came from."

The projected figure stood, appearing dazed, and a hand reached from outside the focus to steady him. The hand became another man in a long beige robe as the focus widened. Beside this other man, skittish and wild-eyed, danced a large white horse.

The children gasped as the horse stepped into, then out, then back into the holo. They clapped when the robed man got it under control.

Hali moved across to a WorShip couch overlooking this performance and sank into the cushions. She glanced around once more for Ferry. No sign of him. Typical. Tell her to hurry, then he was not here.

Neither of the projected figures was speaking, but now a voice in a strange tongue boomed from the holofocus. *How familiar that tongue sounded!* Hali felt that she could almost understand it—as though she had learned it in a dream. She tapped the translate switch on the arm of the couch beside her and the voice boomed once more: "Saul, Saul, why do you persecute me?"

That voice! Where had she heard that voice?

The white-clad figure, still with hands over his eyes and concealing most of his face, rolled over and climbed to his feet with his back to Hali. She saw that he was not wearing a shipsuit after all, but a white robe which had clung to his long legs. The man stumbled back two steps now and fell once more. As he fell, he cried: "Who are you?"

The booming voice said: "I am Yaisuah, whom you persecute. It is hard for you to kick against the thorns."

Hali sat in breathless quiet: *Yaisuah! Yaisuah … Hesoos … Geezuz.*

The holofocus blipped out and the WorShip lights came up to a warm yellow. Hali saw that she was the only adult in the room—this had been a session for young children. Why had Ferry ordered her to meet him here?

One of the children still seated on the floor spoke directly to Hali: "Do you know where that man got his name?"

"It was a mixture from two ancient cultures Earthside," she said. "Why were you watching that?"

"Ship said that was today's lesson. It started with the man on the horse. He rode very fast. Do we have horses in hyb?"

"The manifest says we have horses but we have no place for them yet."

"I'd like to ride a horse sometime."

"What did you learn from today's lesson?" Hali asked.

"Ship is everywhere, has been everywhere and has done and seen everything," the boy said. Other children nodded.

Was that why You showed me Yaisuah, Ship?

No answer, but she had not expected one.

I didn't learn my lesson. Whatever it was Ship wanted me to learn … I failed.

Distraught, she stood and glanced at the boy who had addressed her. Why weren't there any adults here? It was children's WorShip, but not even a guide?

"Has Doctor Ferry been here?" she asked.

"He was here but someone called him away," a little girl in the background said. "Is he supposed to leave WorShip?"

"When it's the business of Ship," Hali said. The apology sounded empty, but the girl accepted it.

Abruptly, Hali turned away and slipped out of the room. As she left, she heard the little girl call: "But who's going to lead us in lesson study?"

Not me, little girl. I have my own studying to do.

Something was going very wrong shipside. Waela's odd pregnancy was merely one symptom among many. Hali ran down the side passage coreside from the WorShip area, found a service access plate and slipped it aside. She wormed her way down a dimly lighted tube to a cross-tube where she slipped out through another service plate into the main passage to Records. There was activity in Records—a teener group learning how to handle the more sophisticated equipment, but she found her aisle between the storage racks unoccupied and no one at the console which concealed Kerro's small study lab.

Hali opened the concealed hatch, saw pale pink light in the lab. She slid inside and sat at the control seat. The hatch snicked closed behind her. She was breathless from the rush of getting here, but wanted no delay. Where to begin? Vocoder? Projection?

Hali chewed at her lip. Nothing could be hidden from Ship. The lesson for the children had been a true one. She knew this.

I don't even need this equipment to address Ship.

Then why did Ship use this place at all?

"Most of you find it less disturbing than when I speak in your mind."

Ship's intimate voice issued from the vocoder in front of her. For some reason, the calm and rational tone angered her.

"We're just pets! What happens when we become a nuisance?"

"How could you become a nuisance?"

The answer was there without considering it: "By losing our respect for Ship."

There was no reply.

This cooled her anger. She sat in silent contemplation for a moment, then: "Who are You, Ship?"

"Who? Not quite the proper term, Hali. I was alive in the minds of the first humans. It required time for the right events to occur, but only time."

"What do You respect, Ship?"

"I respect the consciousness which brought Me into your awareness. My respect is made manifest by My decision to interfere as little as possible in that consciousness."

"Is that how I'm supposed to respect You, Ship?"

"Do you believe you can interfere with My consciousness, Hali?"

She let out a long breath.

"I do interfere, don't I." It was a statement, not a question.

With a sudden sensation of sinking, as though the realization occurred because she let it happen and not because she willed it, Hali saw the lesson of the Hill of Skulls.

"The consequences of too much interference," she whispered.

"You please Me, Hali. You please Me as much as Kerro Panille ever pleased Me."

"Hali!"

It was Ferry's voice shouting at her over the pribox speaker at her hip. "Get to Sickbay!"

She was out the concealed hatch and halfway down the storage aisle before she realized she had broken away from Ship in mid-conversation. Ship had spoken personally with very few people, and she had the impudence to jump up and leave. Even as this thought flashed through her mind, she laughed at herself. She couldn't leave Ship.

Ferry met her at the main hatchway into Sickbay. He was wearing the heavier groundside blue and carried another suit of it under his arm. He thrust it at her and Hali saw then that the suits had been fitted for helmets of hazardous flight.

She accepted the suit as Ferry thrust it at her. The old man appeared to be in the grip of deep agitation, his face flushed, hands trembling.

The groundside fabric felt rough in her hands, so different from the shipcloth. The detachable slicker and hood were contrastingly slippery.

"What's … what's happening?" she asked.

"We have to get Waela off ship. Murdoch's going to kill her."

She was a blink accepting the import of his words. Then doubts filled her. Why would this fearful old man oppose Murdoch? And by implication oppose Oakes!

"Why would you help?" she asked.

"They're demoting me groundside, sending me to Lab One."

Hali had heard the rumors of Lab One—clone experiments, some wild stories, but Ferry was visibly terrified. Did he know something definite about Lab One?

"We have to hurry," he said.

"But how … they'll catch us."

"Please! Put on the groundsides and help me."

She slipped the clothing over her shipsuit and noted how bulky it made her feel. Her fingers fumbled with the slicker's catches as Ferry hurried her into Sickbay.

"We'll be gone by the time they suspect," he said. "There's a freighter leaving in four minutes from Docking Bay Eight. It's carrying hardware, no crew—everything on automatic."

They were at a Sickbay alcove by now and, as he pulled aside the curtains, Hali suppressed a startled question. Waela lay on a gurney, already clad in groundside slicker with the hood pulled down over her brow. Her swollen abdomen was a blue mound under the slicker. *How had Ferry brought her here?*

"Murdoch had her brought down here as soon as you were relieved," Ferry said, grunting as he wrestled the gurney out of its alcove. Hali moved to unhook the monitor connections.

"Not yet!" Ferry snapped. "That's the signal to Bio that something's wrong."

Hali drew back. Of course, she should've thought of that.

"Now, hook up your pribox," Ferry said. "People will think we're moving her somewhere for more tests." Ferry folded the groundside hood under Waela's head and covered her with a gray blanket. She stirred sleepily as he lifted her head.

"What did they give her?" Hali asked.

"A sedative, I think."

Hali looked down at her groundsides, then at Ferry. "People will take one look at our clothes and know something's wrong."

"We'll just act as though we know what we're doing."

Waela jerked in her sleep, mumbled something, opened her eyes and said: "Now. Now." Just as quickly she was back in her sedated sleep.

"I hear you," Hali muttered.

"Ready?" Ferry asked. He gripped the head of the gurney.

Hali nodded.

"Unhook her."

Hali removed the monitor connections and they wheeled Waela out into the passageway, moving as fast as they could.

Docking Bay Eight, Hali thought. Four minutes. They could make it if they were not delayed too long anywhere along the way.

She saw that Ferry was guiding the gurney toward the tangent passage to the docking bays. Good choice.

They had taken fewer than a dozen hurried steps when Hali was paged.

"Ekel to Sickbay. Ekel to Sickbay."

Hali estimated two hundred meters from Sickbay to their goal. They could not trust shiptransport internally. If Murdoch was a killer, if she had figured him for less than what he revealed himself, then placing themselves in a transit tube would be disaster. He could override the controls and have them delivered like salad to his hatchway.

The gurney's wheels squeaked and Hali found this irritating. Ferry was panting with unaccustomed exertion. The few people they passed merely observed the obvious rush on medical business and squeezed aside to let them pass.

Once more, she was paged: "Ekel! Emergency in Sickbay!"

They skidded around the corner into the passage to the Docking Bay and nearly overturned the gurney. Ferry grabbed for it and prevented Waela from sliding off.

Hali helped to settle Waela as they continued pushing toward Number Eight. They were passing Number Five and she could see the Eight down the passage ahead of them.

Ferry, reaching under Waela's shoulder as they moved, pulled out something which had caught his eye.

Hali saw him go pale. "What's that?"

He held it up for her to see.

The thing looked insidious—a small pale tube of silver.

"Tracer," Ferry gasped.

"Where was it?"

"Murdoch must've tried to feed it to her, but he didn't stick around long enough to be sure she swallowed it. She must've spit it out."

"But …"

"They know where we are. The biocomputer can track this through the body, yes, but it can also track it anywhere in Ship."

Hali grabbed it out of his hand and threw it behind her as far as she could.

"All we need's a little delay."

"This is as far as you go, Ekel!"

It was Murdoch's shrill voice almost paralyzing her as he stepped out of the Number Eight hatch just ahead of Ferry. She glimpsed a laser scalpel in his hand, realizing he could use it as a weapon. That thing under full power could sever a leg at ten meters!

Chapter 57

As the Jesuits recognized, a key function of logic limits argument and, therefore, confines the thinking process. As far back as the Vedanta, this way of tying down the wild creativity of thought was codified into seven logic-directing categories: Quality, Substance, Action, Generality, Particularity, Intimate Relation and Non-existence (or Negation). These were thought to define the true limits of the symbolic universe. The recognition that all symbol processes are inherently open-ended and infinite came much later.

—Raja Thomas, *Shiprecords*

THE HYLIGHTER with Thomas cradled in its tentacles vented a brief undulating song and began a slow drop into blue haze. Thomas felt the tentacles enfolding him, heard the song—was even aware that Alki was beginning its long slide into sunset. He saw the dark purple of the meridian sky, saw the side-lighted brilliance of the blue haze and a surrounding rim of steep crags. He saw all of this and still was not sure of what he saw, nor was he entirely sure of his own sanity.

The haze enclosed him then, warm and moist.

His memories were confused, like something seen through swirling water. They moved and shifted, combining in ways that frightened him.

Calm. Be calm.

He could not be sure this was his own thought.

Where was I?

He thought he remembered being thrust into the open outside Oakes' Redoubt. The land beneath him, then, could still be Black Dragon. He could not, however, remember being picked up by a hylighter.

How did I get here?

As though his confusion ignited some remote explanation, he saw a distant view of himself sprinting across a plain, a Hooded Dasher close behind, then the swoop of a hylighter as it lifted him to safety. The images played in his mind without his volition.

Rescue? What am I doing here? Ballast? Food? Maybe the hylighter is taking me to its nest and a bunch of hungry … hungry what?

"Nest!"

He heard the word clearly as though someone spoke directly into his ear, but there was no one. He knew the voice was not his, not Ship's.

Ship!

They had fewer than seven diurns left! Ship was about to break the recording. End of humankind.

I've gone insane, that's it. I'm not really being carried through blue haze by a hylighter.

In his mind, a hatch opened and he heard a babble of voices, Panille's among them. Memories … he felt his mind lock onto memories that had been sealed away until this babble of voices. The gondola—the hylighters reaching into the surfaced gondola … Waela and Panille making love, tentacles all around like long black snakes slithering … questing. He heard his own hysterical laughter. Was that another memory? He recalled the LTA carrying them to the Redoubt … the cell—those odd E-clones … more laughter. *I'm hallucinating … and remembering hallucinating.*

"Not hallucinating."

That voice again! The cradling tentacles shifted, but he still saw only blue haze and … and … Nothing else was certain.

The chatter continued in his mind—memories or present, he did not know. His head whirled. Fragments of what appeared to be holorecords danced behind his eyes.

I've finally gone all the way—really insane.

"Not insane."

No … I just talk to myself.

The chatter had begun to separate into discriminate pieces. He thought he recognized specific snatches of conversation, but the internal holorecord terrified him. He felt that the entire planet had become eyes and ears just for him, that he was … everywhere.

In fits and starts, silence returned. He felt it wash through his mind. Slowly—the creep of some small creature up a gigantic wall—he felt those other eyes and ears remove themselves from his awareness.

He was alone.

What the hell is happening to me?

No answer.

But he sensed the cadences of his mind's voice echo down a long, dark system of tunnels and corridors. He was in darkness. And somewhere in this dark was an ear to hear and a voice to answer. Waela was there. He sensed her as though he could reach out with one hand and touch …

The tentacles no longer enclosed him!

One palm touched the ground … rock, sand. Darkness all around. Waela remained there—calm, receptive.

I've turned into some kind of a damned mystic.

"Live mystic."

That voice! It was as real as the wind he felt abruptly on his face. He knew then that he knelt on some dark ground with … with haze turning luminous blue all around. And he remembered, really remembered being picked up by a hylighter. *Most precious memory:* He nursed it as though it were his only child. *Memory:* a shimmering expanse of sea, narrow ribbon of coast winding itself out of sight, the most rugged mountains of Pandora lifting from the sea and plain—Black Dragon.

"Look up, Raja Thomas, and see how the child becomes father to the man."

He tipped his head and saw ripplings of bright yellow and orange in the blue mist. A whistling song astounded his ears. It was a small hylighter directly overhead in the mist. Tentacles brushed the ground around him. The mist began to thin, pushed by the breeze he could feel on his skin. He smelled floral perfumes. Visibility moved outward through air thick and warm with water vapor. He looked right and left.

Jungle.

Without knowing how it came about, he understood his surroundings: a large crater nestled in black rock, a captive cloud layer creating an inversion with protected warmth beneath the crater's rim.

One of the hovering hylighter's tentacles snaked toward him, touched the back of his left hand. It felt as warm and soft as his own flesh. A small trickle of condensation ran down the back of his neck. He looked up at the hylighter. Another tentacle dripping condensation dangled directly above him.

Calmness fled.

What's it going to do to me?

His gaze moved all around: warm blue mist.

Crack!

Far overhead, a bright flash of lightning flared horizontally across the haze. He felt the prickling presence of it along the hairs on the back of his neck and arms.

Where is this place?

"Nest."

He felt that he was not really hearing that voice. No … it played on his aural centers the way Ship's voice played, but it was not Ship.

Still, he sensed reality in what his eyes reported. A hylighter tentacle touched his hand; another hovered over him. The jungle remained right out there. Perhaps he was seeing what he desired most: the legendary refuge, the place of the horn of plenty, where there were no worries and no passage of time: Eden.

I've taken refuge in my own mind because of Ship's decision to end us.

He ventured another look at the mist-wrapped jungle all around—mottled clumps of trees and vines with odd colors hidden in the green.

"Your senses do not lie, Raja Thomas. Those are real trees and vines. Do you see the flowers?"

The colors were blossoms—red, magenta, draping cascades of golden yellow. It was all too perfect, a delicate fiction.

"We find the flowers quite pleasant."

"Who … is … talking … to … me?"

"Avata talks to you. Avata also admires the wheat and corn, the apple trees and cedars. Avata planted here what was swept away and abandoned by your kind."

"Who is Avata?"

Thomas stared up at the hovering hylighter, afraid of the answer he might get.

"This is Avata!"

Visions flooded his senses: the planet in light and darkness, the crags of Black Dragon and the plains of The Egg, seas and horizons—a confusion which overwhelmed his ability to discriminate. He tried to cringe away from it, but the visions persisted.

"The hylighters," he whispered.

"We choose to be called 'Avata' by you, for we are many and yet one."

Slowly, the visions withdrew.

"Avata brings Panille to help you. See?"

He swung his gaze wide and saw, on his left, another hylighter descending through the blue mist, a naked Kerro Panille clutched in a loop of tentacle. Panille swam in the air like a persistent aftervision. The hylighter dropped him centimeters from the ground. He landed on his feet and strode toward Thomas. The sound of Panille's feet scuffing in sand could not be denied.

The poet was real. He had not died on the plain or been killed by the hylighters.

"You are not hallucinating," Panille said. "Remember that. This is not fraggo. It is a trading of Self."

Thomas climbed to his feet and the trailing tentacle of his hylighter moved with him, not breaking the contact against the back of his hand.

"Where are we, Kerro?"

"As you surmised—Eden."

"You read my thoughts?"

"Some of them. Who are you, Thomas? Avata expresses great curiosity about the mystery of you."

Who am I? He spoke what was in the front of his mind: "I am the bearer of evil tidings. Ship is going to end humankind forever. We have … less than seven diurns."

"Why would Ship do such a thing?" Panille stopped less than a pace from Thomas, head cocked to one side, a quizzical, half-amused expression on his face.

"Because we cannot learn how to WorShip."

Chapter 58

The forgotten language of our animal past conveys the necessity for challenges. Not to be challenged is to atrophy. And the ultimate challenge is to overcome entropy, to break through those barriers which enclose and isolate life, limiting the energy for work and fulfillment.

—Kerro Panille, *I Sing to the Avata*

FOR A long heartbeat, Hali stood immobile in the passage while she stared at Murdoch and the weapon he carried—that deadly laser scalpel. She could see Docking Bay Eight directly behind him—the freighter and escape lay there. They had less than two minutes now until the automatic system propelled that freighter into space for the long dive to Pandora. A quick glance at the unconscious Waela on the gurney beside her showed no change there, but the target of that laser scalpel appeared obvious. Hali interposed her own body between Murdoch and Waela. She heard old Win Ferry gasp as she moved.

Hali kept her attention on the scalpel, cleared her throat, and found her voice astonishingly calm. "Those things are meant to save lives, Murdoch, not take them."

"I'll be saving a lot of lives by getting rid of this TaoLini woman." His voice reminded her of that faraway time when Ship had allowed her to be confronted by Foul-breath below the Hill of Skulls.

Ship? The unspoken plea filled her mind.

Ship made no response. It all depended on her then.

Ferry had stopped the gurney two paces from Murdoch and stood now at Hali's left, trembling.

Murdoch waved the scalpel at them. "This is made to excise unnatural growth from a healthy body. She …" He glared at the unconscious Waela. "… defiles us."

Again, Hali found her memory filled with the faces of the Hill of Skulls—passionate eyes and violence thinly restrained behind them. Murdoch's face was one of those.

"You have no right," she said.

"I have this." He flicked the scalpel's laser blade in a searing arc past her right cheek. "That's all the right I need."

"But Ship …"

"The ship be damned!" He took one step toward her, thrusting out with his free hand to sweep her aside.

In this instant, Ferry moved. He was so fast that Hali saw only the backwards jerk of Murdoch's chin, the blur of old Ferry's elbow. Murdoch went sprawling to the deck, the scalpel spinning from his hand. Hali was as shocked by the old man's speed as by his action. Desperation moved Ferry.

"Go!" Ferry yelled at her. "Get Waela out of here!"

Murdoch was scrambling to his feet as Ferry lunged for him.

Hali moved instinctively. She grabbed the gurney, jerked it past the struggling men. Its howling wheels grated on her senses.

How much time do we have?

And she asked herself as she swept the gurney through the Bay Eight hatch: *What made Ferry so desperate?*

The sealed hatch into the freighter lay directly beyond the Bay Eight opening. She wheeled the gurney across the bump of the interlock and in ten steps brought it up short against the freighter's hatch. It was then that she realized she could not escape without Ferry. He carried the freighter's transit program. She stared at the control panel beside the hatch. Without the program, the freighter would land them at Colony. Her instincts told her that something worse than Murdoch awaited them there. Without that program, they could not enter the freighter—they would be cooked alive here in the Docking Bay. Without that program, she could not switch the freighter from automatic to life-support.

The inventory in her mind stopped as she heard the panel relays click into the final stages before separation. She whirled at a grunting sound and saw Murdoch and Ferry struggling in the short passage to the freighter's hatch, Murdoch slowly pushing the old man backward toward Hali. Once more, the panel clicked. One by one, the hatches to the docking bay hissed shut. Bolts clicked into their locks, sealing the bay and the four of them from the rest of Ship.

There was a scream from Murdoch and she saw his ear skid like a fragile blossom across the red-smeared deck. It was then she realized that Ferry had recovered the scalpel. She whirled to the panel, threw it open and found a hold program key. In desperation, she hit the key.

I hope I haven't trapped us.

An ominous ticking issued from the control panel.

Ferry thrust her aside, slipped a small metal wafer into a slot in the panel. His trembling hand touched the add program key and the freighter's hatch popped open. They pushed the gurney inside and, as they moved, Waela sat up. She looked at Ferry, then at Hali, and said: "My child will sleep in the sea. Where the hylighters calm the waves to the touch of a cradle, there my child will sleep."

Her head fell forward onto her chest. They slipped her from the gurney and wrestled her gently across to a passenger couch, locked her in it. As they worked, Hali heard the freighter's hatch hiss closed. The freighter quivered. Ferry propelled her toward one of the forward control couches and they strapped in.

"You ever fly one of these?" Ferry asked.

She shook her head.

"Me neither. I had simulator experience, but that was a long time ago."

His hand hesitated over the launch program key and, before he could move, the red automatics light flashed on the board. Hali looked forward to the plaz curve nested into the bay, expecting it to separate. Nothing happened.

"What's wrong?" She felt hysteria bubbling in her throat. "Why doesn't it launch?"

"Ferry! Ekel! Shut that thing down and come back inside!"

"Murdoch," Ferry said. "Always spoiling things. He must've escaped from the bay. He's taken over the auto-pilot and we can't release the docking bolts."

"Ferry, Ekel—if we don't get TaoLini back into Sickbay, she could die. You want that on your conscience? Don't let yourselves in for trouble over a …"

Ferry snapped off the vocoder.

Hali took a deep breath. "What now?"

"This will either be the ride of your life or no life at all. Hang on."

Ferry cleared the console and hit the reset key, then override and manual. His finger hesitated several blinks over launch program.

"Hit it," Hali said.

He depressed the key. A powerful trembling rippled through their cabin.

Hali looked at him. She had never suspected such action and determination in old Ferry. He seemed beyond desperation, caught up in some overriding program of his own. She realized then that the old man was sober.

"If we only had a flight manual," he said.

A metallic female voice startled them, crackling from an overhead vocoder: "You have a manual."

"Who the hell are you?" Ferry demanded.

"I am Bitten. I am the system of this freighter. I am designed for conventional or conversational program in emergencies. You wish to separate from Ship, correct?"

"Yes, but …"

A roar shuddered through the freighter. The forward plaz displayed a blinding glimpse of Rega, then a panorama of stars as they shot free of Ship. They began a slow one-eighty turn toward Pandora, and Hali saw a gaping hole that had been Docking Bay Eight. Roboxes already were swarming over the area like insects, starting repairs on the ragged edges.

"Well," Ferry muttered, "what now?"

Hali tried to swallow in a dry throat, then: "What Waela said—the cradle of the sea. Does she know something about ..."

"Life support has been activated," Bitten announced. "Does the sleeping one require additional attention?"

Hali jerked around and studied her patient. Waela lay in quiet sleep, her chest rising and falling evenly. Hali unstrapped, crept back to Waela's side and ran a test series: Everything read as normal as could be expected—blood pressure up a bit, adrenaline on the high side but dropping. No medication was indicated.

Ferry's voice intruded on Hali's thoughts then as he asked Bitten for their ETA to Pandora's atmosphere.

Hali turned and stared at the planet with a growing sense of wonder. Her shipboard life was ended. The only thing she knew for sure about her life now was that she still had it.

Bitten's metallic rasping filled the cabin: "Two hours, thirty-five minutes to atmosphere. Additional twenty-five minutes for entry and docking at Colony."

"We can't dock at Colony!" Hali said. She made her way back to her seat and strapped down. "What are our alternatives?"

"Colony is the only docking station approved for this vessel," Bitten intoned.

"What about a surface landing?"

"Certain conditions permit surface landing without damage to vessel and crew. But our departure destroyed all forward landing gear and docking valves. These are not necessary at Colony."

"But we can't land at Colony!" She stared at Ferry, who sat frozen either in fear or complete resignation.

"Survival of unprotected crew elsewhere on Pandora surface not likely," Bitten intoned.

Hali felt her mind whirling. *Survival not likely!* She had the sudden feeling that this whole thing was high drama, something staged and unreal. She looked at Ferry. He continued to stare out the forward plaz. That was it: Ferry was acting out of character—too far out.

But Murdoch's ear ... that hole in Ship ...

"We can't go back to Ship and we can't dock at Colony and we can't land in the open," she said.

"We're trapped," Ferry agreed, and she did not like the calm way he said it.

Chapter 59

Behold, these are a small troop, and indeed they are enraging us; and we are a host on our guard.

—Muslim Book of the Dead, Shiprecords

WHAT YOU'RE talking about is war," Panille said, shaking his head. He sat on the warm ground, his back against a jungle tree, moon-shadowed darkness all around.

"War?" Thomas rubbed his forehead, looked at the shadowy ground. He did not like looking at Panille—a naked Pan who seemed to flow in and out of contact with native life—touching a tree here, the tentacle of a passing hylighter there. Contact, physical contact: always touching. "Shipmen have had no experience of war for many generations," Panille said. "Clones and E-clones have no experience of it at all, not even stories or traditions. I know it only from Ship's holos."

With one moon full and another raising its pale face on the jagged horizon, Panille saw Thomas haloed against night sky, a hazy outline amidst the stars. A very disturbed man.

"But we have to take over the Redoubt," Thomas said. "It's our only hope. Ship … Ship will …"

"How do you know this?"

"It's why I was brought out of hyb."

"To teach us WorShip?"

"No! To acquaint you with the need to solve that problem! Ship insists we …"

"There is no problem."

"What do you mean there's no problem?" Thomas was outraged. "Ship will …"

"Look around you." Panille gestured at the moon-shadowed basin, the gentle stirrings of the moist air in the leaves. "If you care for your house, you are sheltered."

Thomas forced himself to take a deep breath, to assume at least the outward appearance of calm. The jungle—yes, there did not appear to be any demons in this place … this nest, as the hylighters called it. But this place was not enough! No place was safe from Oakes or from Ship. And there was no escaping Ship's demand. Panille had to be made to understand that.

"Please believe me," Thomas said. "Unless we learn how to WorShip, we are through. No more humankind anywhere. I … I don't want that to happen."

"Then why should we attack the Redoubt?"

"Because you say those are the last people groundside—Colony's destroyed."

"That's true, but what would you teach those people by attacking?" Panille's tone was maddeningly reasonable, a voice which kept its disturbing pace with the sounds of breeze-stirred leaves.

Thomas tried to match that tone: "Lewis and The Boss are destroying the 'lectrokelp and the hylighters. The native life is running out of time, too. Don't they …"

"Avata understands what is happening here."

"They know they're being wiped out?"

"Yes."

"Don't they want to prevent that?"

"Yes."

"How do they expect to do that without controlling the Redoubt?"

"Avata will not attack the Redoubt."

"What will they do?"

"What Avata has always done: nurture. Avata will continue to rescue people when possible. Avata will carry us where we need to go."

"Didn't the kelp kill Colonists? You heard what Waela said…."

"Another of Lewis' lies," Panille said, and Thomas knew that he was right.

He stared off at the jungle beyond Panille. Somewhere in there, he knew, was a large band of survivors, E-clones and normals, all scooped from Pandora's surface and planted here as the hylighters planted the scavenged Earthside vegetation. Thomas had not seen this collection of people, but Panille and the hylighters had described it. The hylighters could do this thing … but … Thomas shook his head in despair.

"They have so much power!"

"Who?"

"The 'lectrokelp and the hylighters!"

"Avata, you mean." Panille's voice remained patient.

"Why won't they use their power to defend themselves?"

"Avata is one creature who understands about power."

"What? What do you …"

"To have power is to use it. That is the meaning of possession. To use it is to lose it."

Thomas closed his eyes, clenched his fists. Panille refused to understand. Refusing to understand, he doomed them all.

Such a loss! Not just humankind … but this, this Avata.

"They have so much," Thomas whispered.

"Who?"

"The Avata!"

He thought about what the hylighters already had shown him, spoke the thought aloud: "That hylighter, the one that brought me, do you know what it showed me after we were fed?"

"Yes."

Thomas went on, not hearing: "Just in a few blinks of touching it, I hallucinated the development, very nearly complete, of the entire recent geological and botanical phenomena of Pandora. Think of losing that!"

"Not hallucination," Panille corrected him.

"What is it, then?" Thomas opened his eyes, stared at the passing moons.

"Avata teaches by touch, at first. A true, but sometimes overwhelming flow of information. As the student learns to focus, the information becomes discrete, discriminated. You separate the needed bits from the babble."

"Babble, yes. Most of it's babble, but I …"

"You know about focus," Panille said. "You select which noises to hear and understand. You select which things to see and recognize. This is just a different kind of focus."

"How can we sit here and discuss … discuss this … I mean, it's going to end! Forever!"

"This is the true flow of knowledge between us, Raja Thomas. Avata moves from the mastery of touch to direct communication, mind to mind. Precise identification with another being. You have seen demons eat scraps of exploded hylighters?"

Thomas was interested in spite of his frustration. "I've seen it."

"Direct ingestion of knowledge, precise identification. Some ancient creatures of Earth did it. Planarians."

"You don't say."

"No … I don't limit."

Thomas jerked away as a passing hylighter trailed tentacles across his face, pausing also to touch the seated Panille. For an instant, Thomas sensed a blur of pictures, dream fragments dancing behind his eyes. And the chatter!

"Avata remains fascinated by the mystery of you, Raja Thomas," Panille said. "Who are you?"

"Ship's best friend."

Panille heard truth in those words and found himself transported in memory back to the shipside teaching cubby. A momentary flicker of jealousy burned at his awareness and was gone.

"Ship's best friend would start a war?"

"It's the only way."

"Who would fight your war?"

"It's between us and them."

"But who would be your soldiers?"

Thomas gestured at the jungle, hoping he pointed somewhere near the collection of remnant people brought here by the hylighters.

"And you would move against Oakes with violence?"

"Oakes is a phony. The Chaplain/Psychiatrist is responsible for the first order of WorShip: survival. Oakes would sacrifice the entire future of humankind to satisfy his own selfish goals."

"That is true. Oakes is selfish."

Thomas remained caught up in resentment of Oakes: "Survival takes planning and sacrifice. The Ceepee should be willing to sacrifice the most. We give our children to Ship as a matter of WorShip. Oakes engineers more people from cloning, and on a fixed food supply. Children starve while his playthings …"

Thomas broke off in frustration. As he stood there, wondering how he could make this poet understand what had to be done, Alki lifted above the eastern horizon, flooding the crater's mists with milky light. The illumination picked out every leaf-dripping detail nearby but hazed away to a mysterious background of muted colors.

"We're in danger, terrible danger," he muttered.

"Life is always in danger."

"Well, we agree on something."

Thomas lowered his chin to his chest, looked down at his feet and, in that strange elasticity of time which comes with danger, he saw his boots. He remembered those booted feet dangling below him as the hylighter lifted him from the threat of a Hooded Dasher at the Redoubt.

Terrible danger!

He suddenly recalled another moment akin to this one: when he had pressed the abort trigger aboard the Voidship *Earthling*, those countless millennia and replays past. In the century between instructing his body to push the abort-trigger and actually pushing it, he had studied the galaxies waving to him from the back of his hand and fingers. One crazy hair, only millimeters long, had poked out from the side of a knuckle on his right index finger, and he recalled the trickle of something small and wet down the side of his left cheek.

"Why did the hylighter bring me here?"

"To preserve your seed."

"But Oakes and the Lab One people will kill us. Nothing will survive. What they miss, Ship will finish."

"Yet, we are in Eden," Panille said. He moved gracefully to his feet, swept an arm wide. "There is food. It is warm. It's little more than a kilometer over the cliffs to the beach, not more than ten kilometers to the Redoubt—two different worlds, and you would make them the same."

"No! You don't understand what I …"

Thomas broke off as a shadow passed over them. He jerked his gaze upward as a trio of hylighters swept overhead carrying a long plasteel cutter and several wriggling human shapes. Behind them, cresting the crater's crags, more hylighters appeared. The tentacles of all were burdened with people and equipment.

Panille touched a dangling tentacle as a hylighter circled over them and dumped the wind from its sail membrane. He spoke in a distant, musing voice: "Lewis has installed Lab One at the Redoubt. These people were driven out. They are terrified. We must take care of them."

A feeling of elation swept through Thomas. "You ask about troops? Here they are! And the hylighters are bringing weapons! You said they wouldn't help us attack, but …"

"Now I know that you once really were a Ceepee," Panille said. "The keeper of the ritual and the robes—the trappings and the suits of woe."

"I tell you there's no other way! We have to take over the Redoubt and learn how to WorShip!"

Panille stared at him, eyes unfocused. "Don't you know that humans made Ship? Therefore, humans made all that proceeds from Ship. Ship tells us nothing, demands nothing which is not from and of ourselves."

Thomas no longer could contain his anger and frustration. "You ask me if I know that humans made Ship? I was one of those humans!"

It was an explosive revelation for Panille—Thomas, a piece of history resurrected! Ship's hand in this was almost visible—past, present, future woven into a lovely pattern. This thing wanted only a poem to bring it into existence. Panille smiled at his own enlightenment, and spoke in a burst of energy: "Then you must know why you made Ship."

Thomas heard it as a question.

"We had a Voidship, the *Earthling*, and we were commanded to turn it into a conscious being. We did it because it was succeed or die. At the moment of consciousness, Ship delivered us from one danger into another, demanding that we learn how to WorShip. It's what we were supposed to do with our new lives, us and all of our descendants after us."

Panille did not answer, but continued to stare at the arriving swarms of hylighters each with its cargo of people or equipment. The soft flutings of the hylighters and the terrified babble of the people being lowered to the ground began to fill the open area all around.

"So you talk to Ship as I do," Panille mused. "Yet you do not hear your own words. Now, I see why Ship needed a poet here."

"What we really need is an experienced military leader," Thomas said. "Lacking that, I guess I'll have to serve." He turned and strode toward the nearest batch of terrified survivors.

"Where are you going?" Panille asked.

"Recruiting."

Chapter 60

Through the process of nostalgic filtering, Earth assumed for the Shipmen fairyland characteristics. The different strains of people, telling their different historical memories, could only make such stories mix in a paradise setting. No Shipman ever experienced every Earthly place and clime and society. Thus, over the many generations, the reinforcement of positive memories left only the faith in how things were.

—Kerro Panille, *History of the Avata*

LEGATA SAT at a comdesk in the working space assigned to her at the Redoubt. It was a small room and showed signs of hasty construction. Directly in front of her across the desk was an oval hatch leading into her own private cubby, a space she seldom occupied now. But Oakes was busy somewhere and she had seized this opportunity.

She punched for shiprecords, keyed for her own private code, and waited. Did they still have contact with Ship?

The instrument buzzed. Glyphs danced across the screen in the desk. She punched for the Ox gate, set up a random-barrier lock and began transferring the data on Oakes into the Redoubt's own storage system.

There you are, Morgan Lon Oakes!

And the printout remained secreted in Oakes' old cubby shipside should she ever need it. It was remotely possible that Oakes might stumble on this record here, might erase it and even trace back to the original to erase that. But the printout would remain, stamped with Ship's imprimatur.

When she had reviewed the data to reassure herself, and once more checked the random-barrier, she keyed the lock, then turned to the question of Lewis. It was not enough to have power over Oakes. Lewis held to his own power base like a man aware of every threat. She did not like the way he stared at her, secretive and measuring.

The Ox gate gave her its open-files response and she asked for anything available about Jesus Lewis.

Immediately the activity light at the command console winked out. She jiggled the switch. Nothing. She tried the override sequence, Oakes' private code, the vocoder. Nothing.

When I asked for material on Lewis.

It had to be a coincidence. She went through the entire contact routine once more. Ship's records could not be brought into this console. She stood up, went out and into the passage, through the tension and bustle of E-clone Processing, and borrowed one of their consoles. Same result.

We're cut off.

She thanked the pale, thin-fingered E-clone who had stepped aside at her request and returned to her own cubby. She knew that the right thing to do would be to tell Oakes. With Colony gone and no communication to Ship, they were isolated, alone in the wilderness that pressed inward all around the Redoubt.

Yes—Oakes would have to be told. She sat down at her desk, called on Voice-Only when nothing else responded, and when he snapped that he was busy, she insisted that her information transcended any other business.

Oakes heard her out in silence, then: "We're trapped."

"How can we be trapped?" she asked. "There's no one to trap us."

"They've set us up," he insisted. "Wait there for me."

The 'coder snapped with his sudden disconnection and it was only then she realized that Oakes had not asked where she was. Did he spy on her all the time? *How much of what I did … how much did he see?*

In less than a minute, Oakes stepped through the hatch, his white singlesuit drenched in sweat. He was speaking as he entered, crackling tension in his voice.

"That TaoLini woman, Panille and Thomas—they're out to destroy us!"

He stopped just inside the room, glared down at her across the comdesk.

"That's impossible! I saw the hylighter carry Thomas off. And Panille …"

"They're alive, I tell you! Alive and plotting against us."

"How …"

"More clones have revolted! And we've had a strange message from Ferry, threatening. They're somewhere nearby, some valley, Lewis thinks. People and equipment. They're going to attack."

"How could anyone …"

"Probe flights, Lewis is sending out probes. And there is something out there. They're able to drive our search instruments crazy—some kind of interference that Lewis can't explain—but we're still getting indications of a lot of life and metal."

"Where?"

"South." He gestured vaguely. "What were you doing when the ship broke contact?"

"Nothing," she lied. "The circuitry just went dead."

"We need that contact, the people still up there, the material and food. Get them back."

"I've tried. Here, see for yourself." She slid out of the seat and gestured for him to take it.

"No … no." He seemed actually afraid to sit at her comdesk. "I … trust your efforts. I just …"

She slipped back into her seat. "You just what!"

"Nothing. See if you can contact Lewis. Tell him to meet me at the Command Center."

Oakes turned on his heel. The hatch hissed closed behind him.

She keyed a search for Lewis and fed the message into it, then tried once more to contact Ship. No response. She sat back and stared at the comdesk. A feeling of regret swept over her, pre-remorse, a sense of sorrow over the Morgan Oakes who might have been. He was nearing the very kind of desperation she wanted.

Let someone attack the Redoubt. Whatever happened, she would be ready with the material she had stored here.

At the worst possible moment, Morgan Lon Oakes! You may be able to appreciate my timing, although you never have before.

Would it happen in front of Thomas? Was it possible that Thomas had survived and would lead an attack? She thought it distinctly possible. Thomas—another Ceepee. The unfailing Thomas who had seen her run the P, who had helped her in that desperate hour, then said nothing of it to anyone.

Discreet. Kind and discreet. Almost a lost breed.

Doubts began to fill her mind then. Perhaps the survival of humans groundside really did depend on Oakes and Lewis. But Colony was gone and the Redoubt was clearly under siege from the planet, if not from some nebulous force headed by Thomas. She thought of the Scream Room then. Where did the Scream Room figure in any scheme of survival? The Scream Room was unjustifiable by any standards. It betrayed negative, anti-survival impulses. Everything about it, that proceeded from it, brought death or hunger or a terrifying subservience. No—not survival.

Oakes put me through the Scream Room.

Nothing would ever change that. But Thomas had guarded the perimeter hatch for her. His were survival instincts. She determined then that she would see what she could do to keep the Thomas breed from dying out.

At what cost? she wondered then, her doubts returning. *At what cost?*

Chapter 61

A horrible feeling came over me—a terrible amusement, for I believed that humankind, through the filtering of Ship's manipulations and the great passage of time, had lost the very ability to engage in war. I thought war had been bred and conditioned out of them at the very moment when they needed this ability the most.
—The Thomas Diatribes, Shiprecords

WHILE HALI was making another examination of Waela's condition and well before the freighter reached atmosphere, Bitten's metallic voice barked at them from the overhead 'coder.

"Do you know a Kerro Panille?"

Waela stirred and mumbled at the sound, then rubbed both hands over her mounded abdomen.

"Yes, we know Panille," Hali said. She closed and sealed her pribox. "Why?"

"You wish to land at some place other than Colony," Bitten intoned. "That now may be possible."

Ferry glared up toward the 'coder. "You said we had to land at Colony!"

"I have been in contact with Kerro Panille," Bitten said. "He asserts that Colony has been destroyed."

"Destroyed?" Hali sat stiffly in her couch, dumb with shock.

Ferry gripped the arms of his command couch, knuckles white. "But we're programmed for landing at Colony."

"I remind you that I am the emergency program," Bitten said. "Present conditions fit the definition of emergency."

"Then where can we land?" Hali asked. And she felt the stirrings of hope. *Contact with Kerro!*

"Panille asserts that I can make a sea landing near an occupied site called the Redoubt. He is prepared to guide us to that landing."

Hali checked the fastenings which held Waela in the passenger couch, returned to her own seat and strapped in. The plaz directly in front of her framed a brilliant circle of cloud-covered planet.

"They meant us to die," Ferry muttered. "Damn them!"

"Do you desire to land at the alternate site?" Bitten asked.

"Yes, land us there," Hali said.

"There is risk," Bitten said.

"Land us there!" Ferry shouted.

"A normal tone of voice suffices for conversational direction of this program," Bitten said.

Ferry stared at Hali. "They meant us to die."

"I heard you. What do you mean?"

"Murdoch said we would have to go to Colony."

Hali looked at him, weighing his words. *Was the man unaware of what he had just told her?*

"So it was a set-up," she said. "You staged that fight."

Ferry remained silent, blinking at her.

"But you cut off one of Murdoch's ears," Hali said, remembering.

Ferry bared his old teeth in a terrible grin. "He did something to my Rachel. I know he did."

Hali crossed her arms over her breast, hearing all the unspoken things in Ferry's words. Her gaze went to the laser scalpel clipped in a breast pocket of Ferry's singlesuit: a thin stylus with death or life in its mechanism.

He was supposed to bring the scalpel in case he needed it against me!

"I made it seem like an accident," Ferry said. "But I knew they did something to my Rachel. And Murdoch's the one they get to do the nasty stuff." He nodded at Hali. "In the Scream Room. That's where they do it."

As he said Scream Room, he shuddered.

"So we were supposed to go to Colony and it's destroyed," Ferry said. "Demons, yes. Very neat. They didn't like my asking about Rachel."

Hali wet her lips with her tongue. "What's … what's the Scream Room?"

"In Lab One where they do the nasty stuff. It was because of Rachel, I know it was. And I drink too much. Lots of us do that after the Scream Room."

Bitten's voice intruded: "Correction noted."

"What was that?" Ferry demanded.

"This is Bitten. I have acknowledged a course correction from Kerro Panille."

"You're going to land us in the sea?" Hali asked, filled with sudden concern for her unconscious patient.

"Near shore. Panille asserts there will be help where we land."

"What about the demons?" Ferry asked.

"If that is a reference to native fauna, you can protect yourselves with the weapons in this freighter's cargo."

"You carry … weapons?" Hali asked.

"The cargo manifest lists food concentrates, building equipment and tools, medical supplies, groundsuits and weapons."

Hali shook her head. "I knew you needed weapons to survive groundside, but I didn't know they were being made shipside."

"Do you know what a weapon is?" Ferry asked, looking directly at Hali.

She thought of her history holos, and the soldiers at the Hill of Skulls. "Oh, yes. I know about weapons."

"This laser scalpel." Ferry touched the stylus shape at his breast. "Acid concentrates, plasteel cutters for construction teams, knives, axes …"

Hali swallowed past a lump in her throat. Every bit of her med-tech training cried out against this. "If we prepare to … kill," the word was barely a sigh past her lips, "then we will kill."

"Down here, it's kill or be killed," Ferry said. "That's the way The Boss wants it."

In that instant, the freighter skipped into the first thin surface of Pandora's atmosphere. Vibration hummed all through the cabin, then smoothed.

"Can't we run away?" Hali asked. Her voice was a low whisper.

"Nowhere to run," Ferry said. "You must know that. All Shipmen learn enough about groundside to know that."

Fight or flee, Hali thought, *and nowhere to flee.* And it occurred to her that Pandora was a place where people were made into primitives.

"Trust me," Ferry said, and the quavering in his old voice made the statement pathetic.

"Yes, of course," Hali said.

She felt the freighter's braking thrust then as it pressed her against the restraining harness, and she glanced back to reassure herself that Waela remained secure.

"We will land in the cradle of the sea," Hali said. "That's what Waela said. Remember?"

"What does she know?" Ferry demanded, and it was his fearful, querulous tone, the one which had made her despise him.

Chapter 62

This the true human knows:
the strings of all the ways
make up a cable of great strength
and great purpose.
—Kerro Panille, *The Collected Poems*

FOR A long time Panille sat in the shadows of the seaside cliff while he felt the approaching presence from space. The sea lay below him down a rugged path, the cliffs soared high behind. Avata had been the first to tell him about this problem and, for a few blinks, he had fallen back into Thomas' ways of thinking.

The Redoubt will know about this freighter, will send its weapons against it.

But Avata soothed him, told him that Avata would transmit false images to the Redoubt's systems, concealing the freighter's passage. Avata would continue to mask the nest's location with similar projections.

The rock was cold against Panille's back. From time to time, he opened and closed his eyes. When his eyes were open he was vaguely aware of the amber glow from Double Dusk—the sky alight from two suns dodging just below Pandora's horizon.

Ship would know he was here and what he was doing. Nothing escaped Ship. Did that omnipotent awareness work through phenomena similar to those of Avata? Was it awareness of even the most minute changes in electrical impulses? Or was it some other form of energy which Ship and Avata monitored?

That presence from space was coming closer … closer. He felt it, then he saw it.

The freighter skipped up the horizon, a great stone crossing the surface of a glassy sea. The fall into atmosphere was deceptive. The freighter had entered Pandora's pull at the lowest point on the horizon. It streaked a long upward arc as Panille felt it fill his awareness. It grew larger with its approach around the planet's curvature, and he saw it now falling white-hot toward him.

The crunch of gravel told him of Thomas' approach, but Panille had only a single purpose now. The approaching freighter was himself and he was diving through the sky alight with amber.

"Can you do it?" Thomas asked.

"I am doing it," Panille whispered. He begrudged the distraction of answering.

Until he had seen the pinpoint of that first glow against the Pandoran dusk, Panille had not been sure he could master this thing.

"I'm thinking them in," he whispered. There was awe and wonder in his voice.

"Who is coming?" Thomas asked.

"Avata did not say."

Thomas emitted a wry, jibing chuckle. "It's a surprise package from Ship. Maybe more recruits for me."

He moved around Panille and climbed down out of sight along the narrow path, his figure a mysterious movement in the half light.

Going to the shore where the surf crashes. The surf will make this landing perilous.

As the last sound of Thomas faded from Panille's awareness, darkness fell—the Double Dark in which Pandora's greatest mysteries blossomed.

Panille thought of himself now as a beacon. He was a signal transmitter in a known position. The freighter and its unknown passengers depended on his constancy. Avata wanted this freighter to land here. He trusted Avata.

Come to the sea, he thought. *The sea … the sea …*

Hylighters began whistling along a rock ledge ahead of him and he knew it was time to join Thomas on the shore. He got up stiffly. It had been a long wait on the observation ledge. Knowing this, he had scavenged a singlesuit of white shipcloth which Avata had stored in the nest.

A hylighter positioned itself above and behind him as he began the slow climb down to the shore. Panille sensed tentacles dangling near, ready to grasp him should he fall.

Avata, Brother, he thought.

It fluted a brief reply.

The sharp rocks and the difficulty of the dark cliff path were second nature to Panille's body. He did not have to think about the climb. And he found that he could maintain the beacon while his thoughts wandered. His mind strayed back to Thomas' unbelieving interrogation.

Thomas demanded explanations and refused to believe almost everything he heard.

He believes Avata projects strange images into his mind. He believes I have learned from Avata, that I am a master of hallucination. He believes only what he can touch, and then he doubts that.

Panille recalled his own words: "Avata is not hallucinogenic. They are not even *they*. That's why I use the term Avata. That's why I call a hylighter Avata."

"I know that word!" Thomas was accusatory.

"The Oneness which is present in the many. It's a word from one of the old languages of my mother's people."

"Your mother!" Thomas was astounded.

"Didn't Ship tell you? I was womb-bred, womb-grown and nursed. I thought you said Ship told you everything."

Thomas flashed him a dark scowl which showed that Panille was striking at sensitive areas. But nothing had stopped Thomas from forming his army—no warnings about Avata's nature, no jibes at Thomas' limited information. Half of the army waited above them now—a mixed crew of E-clones and normals—all of them praying that the freighter from Ship was bringing weapons and other support. Some had descended earlier to wait among the rocks at the base of the cliff.

Above Panille in the darkness, his Avatan guardian shared amusement and dismay at these thoughts.

Can that army save you? Panille asked.

Avata will die in only a few diurns. Then it may be that a rebirth can occur.

Oakes hasn't beaten you yet, Panille said. *Lewis with his poisons and his virus, none of them understand about power.*

Soft flutings rippled from the hylighter, the nearest Avata came to betraying doubts. Panille wondered then: Was this futility aroused by Thomas' efforts, or by the imminent end of Avata—no more of 'lectrokelp/hylighters, no more of the individual cells, the great plural-singular unity?

This idea disturbed him and he thought angrily as he worked his way down the steep trail to the shore: *If you think you're done, then you are finished!*

He emerged from a gap between high rocks onto a wide, rock-mounded sandy beach. Thomas stood far down the sand near the surf—one dark shadow among the many rocks. The surf was high, long rollers crashing onto the shingle. The air was damp with salt spray. Panille felt the surf's heavy rhythm transmitted through skin and feet simultaneously. He put a hand against one of the gateway rocks through which he had entered this sea realm. The rock was cold and wet, and it also vibrated to the surf.

Without the kelp to subdue the sea, the waves had become destructively wild—raging against the cliffs at high tide, throwing giant rocks in their surgings. Soon, very soon, all that Avata had built here would come crashing down into the wilderness of the sea.

The Avatan guardian hovered near his shoulder. One tendril touched his cheek, transmitting remembered emotions.

Yes, this is the place.

It was here, Panille recalled, that he had learned to appreciate all the centuries of poetry celebrating rock and sand and sea, and the peculiar Avata life-of-Self illuminated by the regular passage of moons and suns. Here, the occasional monotony of wave against shore had been broken by the healthy slap of a nightborn hylighter breaking free of its motherplant and drifting off with its long umbilicus tentacles trailing in the sea. Though all Avata was one creature, Panille had felt his own private kinship with the nightborn hylighter-Avatan. Here, he had listened for them and greeted each birth with a song. A far-off slap would catch his attention and fill him with all the wonder of an answered prayer. Across the gently rolling sea, the tiny creature would rise into darkness.

Never again?

Panille whispered a chant to those lost cells of Avata, feeling his whole body transmit the chant as though he were, at last, truly one with Avata.

The solitary blossom overpowers the bouquet.
Even remembering union, without embrace:
a transformation.
Oh, the golden, night-blooming truth!

As he chanted, the whole line of beach glowed with the moons-rise and the shimmering friendship of Avata. The glow illuminated the people of Thomas' ragtag army. Panille saw Thomas outlined against the dim light. Pushing himself away from the gateway rock, Panille went down the beach to stand near this mysterious "friend of Ship."

"They're less than two minutes away," Panille said. He felt the beacon within him, a timed fire which linked him to that hot metal behemoth diving toward him.

"Oakes will send probes," Thomas said.

"Avata will help me jam their signals." Panille gave a smile to the dark. "Would you care to join me in this?"

"No!"

You hold back too much, Raja Thomas.

"But I need your help," Panille said. And he felt Thomas fuming, the tension mounting.

"What do I do?" Thomas forced the words out.

"It may help you to touch an Avatan tentacle. Not necessary, but it helps at first."

A black tentacle came looping down to him then from the night sky. Reluctance apparent in every movement, Thomas reached out and placed a palm against the thrusting warmth.

Immediately, he felt his awareness joined to whoever guided that freighter toward them. He could see two hylighters hovering directly ahead of him and he felt his body standing on surf-drummed sand, a place to go. But the pulse of flight held him in thralldom.

If anybody had told me back at Moonbase that one day I'd land a freighter with my mind and a couple of plants that sing in the dark …

And think!

The Avata intrusion could not be avoided. Avata would not accept that designation as plant. Thomas sensed more than heard the aural projection, something not quite pride, but not completely separated from pride.

Avata confuses me, he apologized.

You confuse yourself. Why do you hide your true identity?

Thomas jerked his hand away from the warm tentacle, but the Avata presence remained in his awareness.

You're prying where you don't belong! Thomas accused.

Avata does not pry. There was no denying the hurt in this response.

Panille felt like an eavesdropper on a private argument. Thomas was smoldering with anger now, aware that he could not break off the Avata contact at will, aware that Avata wanted to pierce the wall behind which this private idea of himself lay hidden.

"Let's get the freighter down," Panille said. "Probes are coming from the Redoubt."

Panille released his part of the beacon system then, telling himself that he had to concentrate on the probes. Thomas would have to make his own mistakes.

The first of the probes screamed down the beach, blazing toward them on a course which undoubtedly had been computed against a plot of the incoming freighter.

As Avata had taught him, Panille set up a terrain image all around and transmitted it to the probe. He felt the projected illusion mesh with the probe's electronic functions. The probe almost shattered from the Gs it pulled, avoiding a sudden cliff which was not there.

They're getting closer, he thought.

He knew why. Each illusion of mistaken terrain formed a pattern of error from which the computer at Redoubt could derive significant results.

Avata numbers appeared in Panille's awareness, telling him that he was being monitored constantly now.

Yes, he agreed. *The patrols have increased.*

Tenfold in twelve hours, Avata insisted. *Why does Thomas not understand his role in this?*

It is his nature, perhaps.

Have you identified your contact on the freighter?

Panille thought about this question, reviewed his own performance as a beacon, and experienced a sudden wash of insight. Knowing it was urgent, he reinsinuated himself into Thomas' performance, feeling the affirmation of contact with the freighter.

Thomas, who have you contacted on the freighter? Panille asked.

Thomas considered this. He could feel the approaching presence—almost palpable. If it was illusion, it was a most complete illusion.

Who? Panille insisted.

Thomas knew he could not be in contact with a Shipman up there. Shipmen would panic when alien thoughts intruded. Who could it be then?

Bitten.

The freighter's identification signal came to him clear and unmistakable: a simple intense concentration without emotion.

"Ahhhhhhh," Thomas said.

To Panille, the startling thing was Thomas' emotional response: deep amusement. Bitten was a flight-system computer, and the realization that his mind was in contact with a computer should not have amused the man. This could only be more evidence of the mystery which so attracted Avata.

They were both forced to concentrate on their mental linkage with Bitten then, but Panille could not explain why this aroused a deep fear reaction in him. He felt it, though, a fear which radiated from his own flesh and outward into every cell of Avata.

Chapter 63

SHIP: I have taught you about the classical Pandora and her box.
PANILLE: I know how this planet got its name.
SHIP: Where would you hide when the serpents and shadows oozed out of the box?
PANILLE: Under the lid, of course.
—Kerro Panille, *Shiprecords*

WAELA FELT that she lived only in a dream, unable to trust any reality. She held her eyes closed, a tight seal against the world beyond her flesh. This was not enough. Part of her awareness told her that she was controlling the landing approach of a freighter. *Insane!* Another part recorded the moments before the suns lifted in the shadow of Black Dragon. Panille was there, too, somewhere low in the shadow. *I'm hallucinating.*

Hali!

Waela felt anxiety coming from Hali … and Hali was nearby. It was an odd anxiety—tension overlain with a deliberate effort to remain calm.

Hali is terribly afraid and even more afraid that she will show it. She wants someone to take charge.

Of course—Hali has never been off Ship before.

Waela tried to move her lips, tried to form reassuring words, but her mouth was too dry. Speech required enormous effort. She felt trapped, convinced that she lay strapped into a passenger couch in a freighter diving toward heavy surf.

A piece of Kerro's poems floated through Waela's awareness then, and she focused on it in both fascination and fear, having no memory of where she had heard this poem:

Your course will be true when you sight
the blue line of sunrise, at night
low in the shadow of Black Dragon.

Hali was there, too, listening to the fragment and rejecting it. A wave of emotion rushed over Waela, made her want to reach out and hold Hali close, to cry with her. She knew this emotion—love of the same man. But she saw Pandora very close now—a raging white line of surf. Waela wanted to cringe away from it. She could feel the child in her womb, another awareness whose share of life reached out and out and out and out….

A cry escaped her, but the sound was lost in the abrupt roaring, metal-straining protest as the freighter made its first contact with the sea. For a few blinks, the ride smoothed; there was a gliding sensation followed by a cushioned deceleration and lifting, then a grating, grinding cacophony which ended in a thumping and stillness.

"Where are the people?" That was Hali's voice.

Waela opened her eyes, looked upward at the ceiling of the freighter's sparse cabin—metal beams, soft illumination, a winking red light. Somewhere there was a sound of surf. The freighter creaked and popped. Abruptly, it tipped a full degree.

"There's someone." That was old Ferry.

Waela turned her head, saw Ferry and Hali releasing themselves from the command couches. The plaz beyond them framed a seamed barrier of black rock only a few meters away illuminated by wavering beams of artificial light.

Ferry's hand moved to a control in front of him. There was a hiss near Waela's feet, then the sudden rush of cold sea wind through an open hatchway. It was night beyond those moving lights. The hatch was blocked for a moment by the entrance of two people. As though awakening from a dream, Waela recognized them—Panille and Thomas.

"Waela!" They spoke in unison, both appearing startled at the sight of her.

Hali pushed herself away from the control console, intensely aware that Panille was focused on Waela's mounded abdomen. Neither Panille nor the man with him, she realized, had expected to see Waela, and certainly not in the full bloom of pregnancy.

"Kerro," Hali said.

He faced her, equally startled. "Hali?"

Thomas threw his head back in sudden laughter. "You see? A surprise package from Ship!"

Waela fumbled with the straps holding her to the couch. Hali rushed to assist her, released the straps and helped her off the couch. The sound of the surf was loud and they could feel its pounding through their feet.

"Hello," Waela said. She took three short steps up to Thomas, hugged him.

Hali tried to identify the play of emotions across the man's face. *Fear?*

Panille touched Hali's arm. "This is Raja Thomas, leader of the army and nemesis of Morgan Oakes."

"Army?" Hali looked from Panille to Thomas.

Thomas gently released Waela's grip around his waist, steadied her while he directed a glare at Panille. "You joke about this?"

"Never." Panille shook his head.

Hali could not understand the exchange. She started to frame a question, but Thomas spoke first.

"What else is in the freighter?"

The Bitten program responded, a crackling voice from the overhead 'coder, full of baps and bursts of static but the listing of the cargo manifest remained understandable.

"Weapons!" Thomas said. He ran to the open hatch, shouted something to people outside, whirled back. "We have to unload this thing before the surf breaks it up or Oakes' people destroy it. Everybody out!"

Hali felt a touch on her shoulder, Ferry standing there. "I think I'm owed an explanation." Even his demands were shaded in whines.

"Later," Thomas said. "There's a guide right outside who'll take you to our camp. She'll tell you everything you need to know."

"Demons?" Ferry asked.

"Nothing like that around here," Thomas said. "Now hurry it up while …"

"You can't dismiss him just like that!" Hali protested. "If it weren't for him, Murdoch would have … We'd be dead!"

Panille directed a quizzical stare at Hali, then at Ferry. "Hali, this old man works for Oakes … and for himself. He's an expert at the game of power politics and he knows that we're a highly negotiable commodity."

"That's all past," Ferry sputtered. The veins in his nose stood out like worms.

"Your guide's waiting," Thomas said.

"Her name's Rue," Panille said. "You might remember her better as Rachel Demarest's cubbymate."

Ferry swallowed, started to speak, swallowed again, then: "Rachel?"

Panille shook his head slowly from side to side.

A single tear formed at the corner of Ferry's right eye, slid down his veined cheek. He took a deep, trembling breath, turned and shuffled toward the hatch. All the energy and urgency he had displayed earlier were drained from him.

"He really did save us," Hali said. "I know he's a spy but …"

"Who are you?" Thomas asked.

"This is Med-tech Hali Ekel," Panille said.

Hali looked up at Thomas—so tall! His eyes held her. He appeared to be in some ageless ring of middle age, but when she took the hand he held out to her, it felt firm and youthful. A commanding hand, confident. She grew aware then that Waela and Kerro were touching. Kerro's arm was around Waela's shoulder, guiding her toward the hatchway.

"Med-tech," Thomas said. "You'll be a great help to us, Hali Ekel. Come this way."

Hali resisted the pressure of his arm and watched Kerro reach out, inquisitive, to touch Waela's abdomen with one finger.

Thomas saw the gesture and focused on Waela. "Something's wrong with her. She should not be that big …"

Thomas loves her, Hali thought. The sound of concern was plain in his voice.

"My pribox says she's only a few diurns from parturition," Hali said.

"That can't be!"

"But it is. Only a few diurns. Otherwise …" Hali shrugged. "… she appears to be healthy."

"That's impossible, I say. It takes much longer for a baby to develop into …"

"Lewis does it. You heard what the E-clones said." That was Kerro returned from the hatchway, not concealing a faint amusement at Thomas' confusion.

"Yes, but …" Thomas shook his head.

"Can you climb down to the beach by yourself, Hali?" Panille asked. "The rear of the freighter is already breaking up. And I think Waela …"

"Yes, of course." She moved past him—the familiar face and familiar voice, his body much thinner than she remembered, though. It struck her then: *He's not the Kerro I knew! He's changed … so different.*

Behind her, she heard Thomas muttering: "I want to examine that woman myself."

Chapter 64

Man also knows not his time: as the fishes that are taken in an evil net and as the birds that are caught in the snare; so are the sons of men snared in an evil time, when it falls suddenly upon them.

—Christian Book of the Dead, Shiprecords

BLOW THAT cutter. Give me the particulars later." Lewis switched off the com-line, and turned to face Oakes across the Command Center. As though this act conveyed some deep communication, they both turned to look up at the big screen.

The bustle of activity around them went on—some fifty people guiding the Redoubt's defenses under the eyes of the armed Naturals quietly watchful at the edges of the room. But to Legata, who stood near Oakes, it seemed that the noise level went down dramatically. She, too, stared at the screen.

It was early Rega morning out there, and the light showed the massed ring of hylighters, the waiting mobs of demons at the cliffs—all strangely held in check. Something new had been added this morning, however. A naked man sat on a flat rock pinnacle to the southeast, hylighter tentacles brushing against him. Sensor amplification had showed his features in close-up—the poet, Kerro Panille.

On the floor of the plain beneath Panille stood a plasteel-cutter fitted with wheels, E-clones and what appeared to be Naturals grouped around it. The cutter's deadly nozzle was pointed toward the Redoubt—too far away for that model to do any damage, but unmistakably menacing.

The most menacing thing of all was the fact that no demon moved to molest any of the people waiting beside the cutter. Pandora's terrible creatures waited with the others in mysterious docility.

"We should know in a blink or two," Lewis said. He threaded his way through the room's activities to stand near Oakes and Legata. All of them stared up at the screen.

"Can't we send some people out there?" Oakes asked. "We could take that thing with a direct attack."

"Who would we send out?" Lewis asked.

"Clones. We have clones up to here!" He brushed the edge of his right hand across his throat. "And we don't have enough food. They could get through if we sent enough of them."

"Why would clones do that?" Legata asked.

"What?" Oakes glared at her audacity.

"Why would clones obey an order to attack? They can see the demons out there. And there'll be Runners somewhere on that plain. Why would clones take the risk?"

"To save themselves, of course. If they stay here and do nothing …" Oakes' voice trailed off.

"Your fate is their fate," she said. "Maybe worse. They'll ask why you aren't out there with them."

"Because … I'm the Ceepee! I'm worth more than they are to our survival."

"Worth more to them than they are worth to themselves?"

"Legata, what are you …" Oakes was interrupted by a brilliant flash of light and a blast so close that the concussion popped his ears and took his breath away. Sensor images vanished from the big screen to be replaced by static flashes of light. Legata, thrown backward by the blast, steadied herself against a fixed control console. Lewis had sprawled on the floor and, as he climbed to his feet, they all heard screams and clattering feet in the passage outside the Command Center.

Oakes gestured to Legata. "Get that screen working!"

"We must've hit that cutter," Lewis said.

Legata leaped to the screen controls, keyed an emergency search for active sensors, found a high one which looked out over the Redoubt to the distant cliff with its bank of hylighters. Panille still sat on the pinnacle, the plasteel cutter and its crew remained at their cliffbase. Nothing appeared to have changed.

They could all hear the sound of pounding against the Command Center's hatch. Someone across the room opened it. Immediately, the Center filled with people, a menagerie of E-clones and Naturals, all crying and screaming: "Runners! Runners! Seal off!"

Lewis whirled to the nearest console, slapped the key for the Seal Off program. As hatches hissed shut, they saw on the screen the first wave of people shrieking in terror at the inner edge of the Redoubt. Legata turreted the high sensor to follow them and they all saw the smoking break in the Redoubt's perimeter, the flood of people fleeing it and being brought up short at sealed hatches. Fists beat a muffled drumming on the hatches, the sound made all the more terrible by its distance from the sensor. It gave the whole scene a marionette quality.

Lewis suddenly darted across the room, grabbed the arm of one of the newcomers and returned to Oakes with the man. Legata recognized him as a crew supervisor, a Natural named Marco.

"What the hell happened out there?" Oakes demanded.

"I don't know." The man blinked in confusion, stared up at the screen rather than at Oakes. "We took one of the new cutters, the long-range ones, and we hit within a meter of them."

"You missed them?" Oakes screamed it, his face red with rage.

"No! No, sir. A meter's good enough. That close will melt bedrock for ten meters all around. It's just …"

"That's all right, Marco," Lewis said. "Just describe what you saw."

"It was that man up on the rocks." Marco pointed at the screen.

"He didn't do anything," Oakes said. "We were looking at the screen the whole time and he …"

"Let Marco tell what he saw," Lewis interrupted.

"It was almost too fast for the eye to see," the supervisor said. "Our beam hit less than a meter away. I saw the ground out there begin to glow. Then the beam … bent. It bent right up toward that man on the rock. I thought I saw him glow, then the beam came right back at us!"

"Our cutter's gone?" Lewis asked.

"It went up so fast only a few of us escaped."

"Send out some clones," Oakes said.

An unmistakable press of bodies moved toward him as he spoke and, too late, he realized his danger. More than half the Command Center crew was composed of clones and most of the refugees who now crowded the room were clones.

"Sure!" someone shouted from the press of people. "You stay here while we take the risk!"

Another voice, gravelly and full of gutturals, took it up from another corner of the crowd: "Yes, send out some clones. More meat for the demons. A diversion while you Naturals tiptoe home to Colony and your wine!"

Oakes glanced at the ring of faces pressing toward him. Even the Naturals among them appeared angry. This was not the time to tell them that Colony no longer existed. They would know their power then. They would know how much he needed them.

"No!" Oakes waved a hand in the air. "All survival decisions belong to the Ceepee. I am Ship's envoy and voice here!"

"Ohhh, it's *Ship* now!" someone shouted.

"We will not run home to Colony," Oakes said. "We will stand here at your side … to the last man, if necessary."

The guttural voice responded: "You're damn right you're not leaving!"

The room took on an odd sense of quiet into which Lewis' voice came clearly: "We will not be beaten."

Oakes picked it up: "We have almost eliminated the kelp that kept us from gardening the sea. The hylighters will go next. A few rebels will not stand in the way of the good life we can make for ourselves here."

Oakes glanced at Lewis, surprised a flitting smile there.

"Tell us what to do," Lewis said.

One of Lewis' minions in the crowd responded on cue: "Yes, tell us."

How well early conditioning pays off, Oakes thought. And he said: "First, we have to take stock of our situation."

"I've been watching the screen," Lewis said. "I don't see any Runners. Have you seen any, Legata?"

"No, not a one."

"Not one Runner has tried to enter the Redoubt," Lewis said. "They remember the chlorine."

"Have you looked at the whole perimeter?" someone demanded.

"No, but look at those people near that break in our wall." Lewis pointed. "Not a one of them's in trouble. I'm going to open the hatches."

"No!" Oakes stepped forward. "Whoever asked that question is right. We have to be sure." He turned toward Legata. "Do you have enough sensors to scan the perimeter?"

"Not completely … but Jesus is right. Nothing's attacking our people out there."

"Send some volunteers out with portable sensors, then," Lewis said. "We could use a few repair crews as well. I'll go with 'em, if you like."

Oakes stared at Lewis. *Could the man really be that brave? Runners remembering chlorine? Impossible.* Something else was holding the demons in check. As he thought this, Oakes experienced the abrupt sensation that the entire planet was out there, waiting just for the proper moment to attack and kill him.

Taking his silence for agreement, Lewis pressed his way through the crowd, selecting people as he moved. "You … you … you … you … Come with me. Larius, you get a repair crew together, take the down-chart and get busy restoring our eyes and ears."

Lewis popped a hatch at the far side of the room, waved his volunteers through, and turned before joining them. "All right, Morgan, it's up to you."

What did he mean by that? Oakes watched the hatch seal behind Lewis. *I have to do something!*

"Everybody back to work," Oakes said. "Everybody but the Command Center crew outside in the passage."

They were reluctant to move.

"Nothing came in the hatch when Jesus opened it," Oakes said. "Go on. We have work to do. So do you."

"Leave the hatch open if you want," Legata said.

Oakes did not like that, but the suggestion moved them. People began leaving. Legata turned back to the control console for the big screen. Oakes moved to her side, becoming intensely aware of the musky smell which surrounded her.

"We're fighting the whole damned planet," he muttered.

He watched while portable sensors and repairs began restoring the big screen's overview of the Redoubt's operation. As service returned, it became apparent that something had destroyed some seventy degrees of perimeter sensors below the ten-meter level. Burned-out relays had put other sensors out of service. The damage was far less than he had feared. He began to breathe more easily, realizing only then how tension had tightened his chest.

Lewis returned after a time, crossed to Oakes and Legata at the screen. "Did you want those people to stay in the passage?"

Oakes shook his head. "No." He continued to watch the screen.

"I sent them about their business," Lewis said. "Nothing seems to've changed outside. Why are they waiting?"

"War of nerves," Oakes said.

"Perhaps."

"We must devise a plan of attack," Oakes said. "The clones must be convinced that it's necessary to attack."

Lewis stared at the play of Legata's hands across the screen controls, glancing now and then up at the COA she produced. Rega was much higher in the sky now and Alki was beginning to creep above the horizon. It was brilliant out on the plain, every detail washed in light.

"How will you convince the clones?" Lewis asked.

"Get a few of them in here," Oakes said.

Lewis directed a questioning stare at Oakes, but turned and obeyed. He returned with twelve E-clones whose appearance had been held closer to the Natural standard except for the introduction of extra musculature in arms and legs. They were a type Oakes had always thought bulged in a repellant way, but he masked his dislike. Lewis stopped the group in an arc about three paces from Oakes.

Studying the faces, Oakes recognized some of the group which had fled into the Command Center earlier. There was no avoiding the distrust in their expressions. And Oakes noted that Lewis had seen fit to don a holstered lasgun and that the Naturals around the edges of the room were alert and watchful.

"I will not go back to Colony," Oakes began. "Never. We are here to …"

"You might run back to Ship!" It was a clone standing just to the left of Lewis.

"Ship will not respond to us," Legata said. "We are on our own."

Damn her! Oakes went pale. *Didn't she know how dangerous it was to betray your dependence on others?*

"We are being tested, that's all," Oakes said. He glanced at Lewis, surprised another fleeting grin on the man's face.

"Maybe we're supposed to go outside and run for it," Legata said. Her fingers danced across the screen's controls. "Maybe it's just a game like the Scream Room or running the P."

What is she doing? Oakes wondered. He shot a glance at her, but Legata continued to direct the screen's controls.

"They're doing something," she said.

Every eye turned toward the screen whose entire area she had focused on the view toward the cliffs. Panille was standing now, his right hand clutching a hylighter tentacle. More E-clones and others had massed around the cutter on the plain below him. Demons had moved out from the cliff shadows. Even the enclosing arc of hylighters appeared more agitated, moving about, changing altitude.

Legata zoomed in on a man standing beside the cutter's left wheel.

"Thomas," she said. "But the hylighters …"

"He's in league with 'em," Lewis said. "Has been all along!"

Legata stared out at the plain. Was that possible? She had been about to expose Oakes as a clone, but now she hesitated. What did she really know about Thomas?

As she thought this, Thomas lowered his right arm and Panille, atop the pinnacle, was picked up by one of the giant bags, carried gently down to the plain.

Thomas and his people were moving forward now, a ragged advance but spreading out on both sides of the cutter.

"There must be at least a thousand of them," Lewis muttered. "Where'd they get that many people?"

"What're the demons doing?" Legata asked.

The creatures had spread out below the cliff—Dashers, Spinnerets, Flatwings and more—even a few of the rare Grunchers. They were following the attackers but slowly and at a distance.

"If they get that cutter within range of us, we're through," Oakes said. He rounded on Lewis. "Now will you send out some attackers?"

"We have no choice," Lewis said. He glanced at the clones beside him. "You all see that, don't you?"

All of them were staring up at the screen, intently focused on the advancing cutter and the outrider demons.

"It's plain to see," Lewis said. "They cut open our perimeter and let the demons in. We're all dead then. But if we can stop them …"

"Everybody!" Oakes called out. "I grant full status as a Natural to every clone who volunteers. These rebels are the last real threat to our survival. When they're gone, we'll make a paradise out of this planet."

Slowly, but with growing momentum, the arc of clones moved toward the passage hatch. More joined them as they moved.

"Keep them moving, Lewis," Oakes said. "Issue weapons as they go out. We'll win by the weight of numbers alone."

Chapter 65

Once my fancy was soothed with dreams of virtue, of fame and of enjoyment. Once I falsely hoped to meet with beings who, pardoning my outward form, would love me for the excellent qualities which I was capable of unfolding.
—Frankenstein's Monster Speaks, Shiprecords

AS THOMAS gave the signal for the attack, he experienced the almost paralyzing sensation that he was not aiming a blow at the Redoubt but was striking out at Ship.

You set this up, Ship! See what You've done?

Ship gave no response.

Thomas moved forward with his army.

The air was hot on the plain below the cliffs, both suns climbing to their meridians. The light was brilliant, forcing him to squint when he looked toward the reflected glare of the suns. He smelled a flinty bitterness in the air, dust kicked up by his ragtag group.

He looked left and right at them. Had anyone ever dreamed of such a wild mixture on such a venture? The Naturals in Avata's collection were a vanishing minority—swallowed up in the press of strange shapes: bulbous heads, oddly placed eyes, ears, noses and mouths; great barrel chests and scrawny ones, thin limbs and conventional fingers, ropey tendrils, feet and stumps. They strode and rocked and stumbled along in obedience to his command. The improvised wheels they had attached to the plasteel cutter grated in sand, bumped over small rocks. Muttering, grunting, wheezing, his people moved forward. Some of the E-clones chanted "Avata! Avata! Avata!" as they shuffled along. He noted that the demons moved with him at a distance, just as Panille had said they would.

Waiting to scavenge.

What did the demons see here? Panille had said that he and the hylighters could project false images to hold the demons in check. Certain of the E-clones, too, exhibited this skill. Thomas guessed it to be a side-effect of the recombinant experiments with the kelp. It seemed a fragile defense against such potent creatures. This whole venture was based on fragility—not enough weapons, not enough people, not enough time to plan and train.

He glanced back toward the cliffs, saw the arc of trailing demons, Panille walking among them without fear. A gigantic Dasher brushed against the poet, veered away. Thomas shuddered. Panille had said he would not take active part in killing, but would protect this army as well as he could. The med-tech and a handpicked crew of aides waited at the foot of the cliff. Everything now depended on whether this force could so overawe the Redoubt's defenders that Oakes would capitulate.

At the chosen moment, Thomas gave the signal for his people to spread out, dispersing wide across the plain. If Panille's powers continued to work, the defenders would see only one small tightly massed target of attackers coming straight on into range of the Redoubt's weapons. Thomas joined the crew of the cutter as they veered off to the left.

As he moved, doubts welled up in him. By his time reckoning, they had only hours until Ship carried out the threat to end humankind forever. This venture seemed hopeless. He would have to overcome the Redoubt, assemble the survivors, find the proper WorShip and prove to Ship that humankind should endure.

Not enough time.

Panille! It was Panille's fault that they had been delayed so long. To every argument for the need to attack the Redoubt, Panille had interjected a quiet remonstrance.

The nest was paradise enough, he said.

No doubt it was a paradise—a continuous growing season for Earth plants—no rot, no mold, no insect parasites … not even any demons to threaten the people there.

The crater nest was a blastula of Earth, a chaotic jumble of elements looking for growth and order.

A one-kilometer circle of Eden does not a habitable planet make.

And always Panille there with his senseless observations: "What you do with the dirt beneath your feet, that is a prayer."

Is that what You want, Ship! That kind of prayer?

No answer from Ship—just the rustle of sand underfoot, the movement of his army as it spread out wide across the plain and continued to advance on the Redoubt.

I'm on my own here. No help from Ship.

He remembered the Voidship *Earthling* then—the ship which had become Ship. He remembered the crew, their long training on Moonbase. *Where were they now?* Any of them left in hyb? He longed to see Bickel again. John Bickel would be a good one to have here now—resourceful, direct. *Where was Bickel now?*

Sand grated under his feet like the sands of the exercise yard at Moonbase. Sands of the Moon, not of Earth. All those years, looking up to the Earth at night—the blue and white glory of it. His desires had not been for the stars, not for some mathematical conception at Tau Ceti. He had wanted only the Earth—that one place forbidden to him in all of the universe.

Pandora is not Earth.

But the nest was a temptation—so like the Earth of his dreams.

Probably not like the real Earth at all. What do I know of the real Earth?

His kind had known only the clone sections of Moonbase, forever separated from the human originals by the vitro shields. Always the vitro shields, always only a simulated Earth—just as the clones simulated humans.

They didn't want us taking strange diseases all over the universe.

A laugh escaped him.

Look at the disease we've brought to Pandora! War. And the disease called humankind.

A shout came from off to his right, bringing him out of his reverie. He saw that a beam from the Redoubt had incinerated a large rock ahead of them on the plain. Thomas signaled for wider separation. He looked back, saw Panille with his spreading pack of demons still walking imperturbably behind the army.

A terrible resentment of Panille welled up in Thomas then. Panille was a naturally born human.

I was grown in an axolotl tank!

How odd, he thought, that it should take all of these uncountable eons and an ultimate crisis here for him to realize how much he resented being a clone.

Clones from Moonbase are expressly forbidden …

The list of "Thou shalt nots" had stretched on for page after page.

It is forbidden to come into contact with Natal humans or with Earth.

Banished from the Garden without benefit of sin.

What is felt by one is felt by all, Avata said.

Yes, Avata, but Pandora is not Earth.

Ship had said he was original material, though, some bit of what Earth had been. What memories of Earth tingled in the genes sparkling at the tips of his fingers?

It was very hot out here on the plain, glaring hot. Exposed. Could Panille's projection truly confuse the Redoubt's defenders? Panille had confused the probes, that was a fact. And Thomas recalled his own mental linkage with Bitten, the control program for the freighter which had brought such a cornucopia of supplies. As Panille said, the ability to communicate was also the ability to dissemble.

What if Panille just left them out here, dropped the masking projection? What if Panille were wounded … or killed? Panille should have stayed back by the cliffs.

That's just like a clone, missing the obvious.

The old taunt rang through his ears. Just like a clone! All the human efforts at instilling pride in the clones had vanished before the taunts. Clones were supposed to be extra-human, built for precision performance. Humans did not like that. Clones of Moonbase did not look different from humans, did not talk different … but separation developed eccentricities. *Just like a clone.*

He imagined a Moonbase instructor, looking at him out of that blasphemous screen, lecturing on the intricacies of systems monitors, reprimanding: "That's just like a clone, walking out on paradise."

His army was almost into range of the Redoubt's smallest weapons now, less than two hundred meters away. Thomas shook himself out of his reverie—hell of a way for a general to behave! He looked left and right. They were well fanned out. He paused beside a tall, black rock—taller than he. The Redoubt loomed ahead, prickly with the muzzles of its cutters. Panille could not come any closer. Thomas turned and waved for Panille to stop, saw the poet obey. The army would have to go on alone from here. They could not risk their most valuable weapon.

The rock beside him began to glow. Thomas leaped to the right as the rock erupted in molten orange. A tiny splash of it burned his left arm. He ignored it, shouted: "Attack!"

His mob started a shambling run toward the Redoubt. As they moved, exterior hatches in the Redoubt's perimeter snapped open. Defenders swarmed onto the plain carrying 'burners and lasguns. They raced forward in a confused mass toward Panille's projected images. As they came within a few meters, their confusion increased. Targets dissolved before them. They stumbled left and right, shooting. Random shots dropped some of the army. The Redoubt's cutters began to sparkle with incandescent beams which probed the plain.

"Fire!" Thomas screamed. "Fire!"

Some of his people obeyed. But the Redoubt's defenders presented the same genetic mix as the army's. Attackers and defenders, indistinguishable without uniforms, stumbled into each other. Searing beams wavered in wild arcs, cutting friend and foe alike. Bloody bodies lay on the plain—some dismembered, some screaming. Thomas stared in horror at the arterial geyser from a headless torso directly to his left. Red spray splashed all around as the body tumbled forward.

What have I done? What have I done?

None of these people, attackers or defenders, knew how to fight a proper war. They were hysterical instruments of destruction—nothing more. Fewer than a fourth of the defenders had reached his army. What did it matter? The plain around the Redoubt was a bloody shambles.

He signaled to the cutter crew on his left. "Cut through their wall!" But his crew had been decimated, the cutter's improvised wheels disabled. It stood canted over to its right, the deadly muzzle pointed at the ground. The survivors crouched behind the cutter.

Thomas whirled and looked back at Panille. The poet stood immobile amidst the waiting pack of demons. Two Dashers crouched on his right like obedient dogs. The horrible line of Pandora's killer species reached left and right in a wide arc around the scene of carnage.

Rage coursed through Thomas. *You haven't beaten me, Ship!* He stumbled, panting across to the cutter, grasped its heavy barrel and heaved it around. Four strong clones had been needed to lift the thing back at the cliff. In his rage, he moved it by himself, tipping it against a rock until it was trained on a blank stretch of Redoubt wall. The surviving crew members cowered away from him as he leaped to the controls and activated the beam. A blinding blue line leaped out to the Redoubt, melting the wall. Upper structure sloughed away, slipping down into the molten pool.

Reason returned to Thomas. He stepped back, again, again. He was twenty paces from the humming cutter when the defense weapons found it. The cutter exploded as beam confronted beam. Thomas did not even feel the sharp chunk of metal which penetrated his chest.

Chapter 66

Why shouldst Thou cause a man to put himself to shame by begging aid, when it is in Thy power, O Lord, to vouchsafe him his necessities in an honorable fashion?

—A Kahan, Atereth ha-Zaddikim, *Shiprecords*

HALI KEPT a careful watch on Waela as the E-clone assistants prepared an obstetrics area within their temporary medical shelter. The cliff shadow covered them, and the confusion of the army departing filled the air with discordant noise: shouts, grunts, the crunching of the cutter's wheels on the sand. She felt a sense of relief as the demons moved off with Panille. He frightened her now. Her soft-voiced poet friend had become the keeper of a terrifying inner fire. He was keeper of the kind of terrible power she had seen at Golgotha.

Heavy as she was with the unborn child, Waela moved with a supple quickness. She was in her natural habitat: Pandora. This place had changed Waela, too. Was that why Panille had mated with her? Hali put down an anguished stab of jealousy.

I am a med-tech. I am a Natali! An unborn child needs me. I want joy!

She tried not to think about what might happen out there on the plain. Thomas had warned her what to expect. Where had he learned about battle? She had been unable to suppress feelings of outrage.

"Those people who will die, how are they different from us?"

She had hurled the question at him as they moved down from the cliff top, steadied by hylighter tendrils, the red streaks of dayside fingering a gray horizon on their right. It had been a nightmare setting: the babble of the army, the muted flutings of hylighters. The great orange bags had floated some people down to the plain, carried equipment, guarded the descent of those who stayed afoot.

Hundreds of people, tons of equipment.

Thomas had not answered her question until she repeated it.

"We have to take over the Redoubt. Ship will destroy us if we don't."

"That makes us no better than them."

"But we will survive."

"Survive as what? Does Ship say anything about that?"

"Ship says, 'When you shall hear of wars and the rumors of wars, be you not troubled: for such things must needs be; but the end shall not be yet.'"

"That's not Ship! That's the Christian Book of the Dead!"

"But Ship quotes it."

Thomas had looked at her then and she had seen the pain within his eyes. *Christian Book of the Dead.*

Ship had shown parts of it to her on request, displaying the words within the tiny cubby where Panille once had studied. If Thomas really were a Ceepee, he would know those words. She wondered if Oakes knew them. How strange that no one shipside had responded to her careful questions and probes about the events on the Hill of Skulls.

Thomas had frightened her then as they paused to regain their breath on a little rock platform deep in a fissure.

"Why did Ship show you the crucifixion? Have you ever asked yourself that, Hali Ekel?"

"How do you … how do you know about …"

"Ship tells me things."

"Did Ship tell you why I …"

"No!"

Thomas set off down the steep trail. She called after him: "Do you know why Ship showed me that?"

He stopped at a gap in the fissure, looked out at the morning light growing on the plain, the glistening brilliance of reflections off the Redoubt's plaz in the distance. She caught up with him.

"Do you know?"

Thomas rounded on her, the pain terrible in his eyes. "If I knew that, I'd know how to WorShip. Did Ship give you no clues?"

"Only that we must learn about holy violence."

He glared at her. "Tell me what you saw there at the crucifixion!"

"I saw a man tortured and killed. It was brutal and awful, but Ship would not let me interfere."

"Holy violence," Thomas muttered.

"The man they killed, he spoke to me. He … I thought he recognized me. He knew I had come far to see him there. He said I was not hidden from him. He said I should let them know it was done."

"He said what?"

"He said if anyone understood God's will, then I must understand it … but I don't!" She shook her head, tears close. "I'm just a med-tech, a Natali, and I don't know why Ship showed me that!"

Thomas spoke in a whisper: "That's all the man said?"

"No … he told the people in the crowd not to weep for him but for their children. And he said something about a green tree."

"If they do these things in a green tree, what will they do in a dry?" Thomas intoned.

"That's it! That's what he said! What did he mean?"

"He meant … he meant that the powerful grow more deadly in times of adversity—and what they do in the roots can be felt to the ends of the branches—forever."

"Then why have you created this army? Why are you going out there to …"

"Because I must."

Thomas resumed his way down the trail, refusing to respond to her. Others who had chosen to climb down caught up, pressed close. She had no other opportunity to speak to him. They were at the foot of the cliffs soon and she had her own duties while Thomas set off about his war.

Ferry was one of the people Thomas assigned to medical work. She knew what Thomas and Kerro thought about the old man and this prompted her now to kindness toward him. While she worked with Ferry in the rude fabric shelter below the cliffs, she heard Thomas speaking to his army.

"Blessed be Ship, my strength, which teaches my hands to war and my fingers to fight."

Was that any way for a Ceepee to talk? She asked this of Ferry while they worked.

"That's the way Oakes talks." The old man seemed resigned to his fate but eager to help her.

The army was busy at its preparations then, Panille standing nearby like a cold observer. She did not like the nearness of the demons, but he said they would not harm the people here. He said the hylighters had filled the demons' senses with a false world which kept them in check.

Ferry shambled past her then, glancing oddly at her nose ring.

She wondered how Ferry felt about the way Thomas talked. Thomas spoke about the old man in front of him as though Ferry were not there.

"This old fool doesn't have any real power," Thomas had said. "Oakes thinks he has a corner on the real power and the symbolic power, right here on Black Dragon. He doesn't share power. He's set himself up here for easy pickings compared to what we'd have encountered at Colony."

"I told him he was moving too soon," Ferry had said.

Thomas had ignored him, addressed Panille. "Ferry's a liar, but we can use him. He must know something valuable about Oakes' plans."

"But I don't know anything." The old man's voice quavered.

One of the Naturals Thomas had named as an aide had come up then with organizational problems. Thomas had stared at the hashmarks over the man's right eye. They had gone away together, Thomas muttering: "Helluva way to slap together an army, out of somebody else's rejects."

She had seen some sense in his orders, though, the E-clones grouped according to design: runners, carriers, lifters … He had taken a training inventory—equipment operator, light-physics technician, welder, unskilled labor …

She thought about this as she prepared the medical facilities under the cliff. What difference did it make to her how Thomas organized his force? When they arrived here, they would merely be wounded.

Waela, helping with the preparations for the delivery, stopped in front of Hali. "Why do you look so worried? Is it something about my baby?"

"No, nothing like that."

And Waela heard her old inner voice, Honesty, marking time: *The baby will be born soon. Soon.*

Waela stared at Hali.

"What has you so worried?"

Hali looked at Waela's mounded abdomen. "If the hylighters hadn't brought us that supply of burst from Colony …"

"Colony didn't need it anymore. They're all dead."

"That's not what I …"

"You're afraid my baby would've been robbing you of your years, your life and …"

"I don't think your baby would take from me."

"Then what is it?"

"Waela, what are we doing here?"

"Trying to survive."

"You sound like Thomas."

"Thomas makes a great deal of sense sometimes."

Three E-clones intruded, staggering into the shelter, two of them helping a third who had lost an arm. All of them had been burned. One held the severed arm against the stump, bloody sand all around the wound.

"Who's the med-tech here?" one of them demanded. He was a dwarf with long, flexible fingers.

Ferry started to step forward, but Hali motioned him back. "Stay with Waela. Let me know when she needs me."

"I'm a doctor, you know." There was hurt in the old voice.

"I know. Stay with Waela."

Hali led the injured trio to the emergency alcove partly sheltered by the black rocks of the cliff. She worked quickly, closing up the severed stump with celltape after powdering it with septalc.

"Can't you save his arm?" the dwarf demanded.

"No. What's happening out there?"

The dwarf spat on the floor. "Hell and damn folly."

She finished with his companions, looked at the dwarf. His comment surprised her and he saw it. "Oh, we can think well enough," he said.

"Come here and let me tend to you," she said. His right arm was badly burned. She spoke to distract him from his pain. "How did you come to be with the hylighters?"

"Lewis pushed us out. Like garbage. You know what that means. There were Runners. Most of us didn't get away. I hope the Runners get in there." He gestured with his good arm at the Redoubt across the plain. "Eat every one of those shiptit bastards!"

The dwarf slid off the treatment table as she finished. He headed toward the exit.

"Where are you going?"

"Back to help where I can." He stood with the fabric flap held back and she stared out the opening at the Redoubt. Blue flashes filled the air there. She could hear distant shouts and screams.

"You're in no condition to …"

"I'm well enough to carry the wounded."

"There are more?"

"Lots of 'em." He lurched out the opening, the fabric falling closed behind him.

Hali closed her eyes. In her mind she could see a mill of people. It changed to a crowd and the crowd became a mob. Foul-breath and the salty stink of blood were on the wind. The tiny lips of cuts and the great smears of burn wounds filled her imagination. A pair of broken knees blurred through her memory—the men on the crosses.

"That's not the way," she muttered. She took up her pribox and an emergency medical kit, stepped to the opening, flung it back. The dwarf already was a small figure in the distance. She strode after him.

"Where are you going?" It was Ferry's voice calling after her.

She did not turn. "They need me out there."

"But what about Waela?"

"You're a doctor." She shouted it without taking her gaze off the smoke billowing in the distance.

Chapter 67

When humans act as spokesmen for the gods, mortality becomes more important than morality. Martyrdom corrects this discrepancy but only for a brief interval. The sorry thing about martyrs is that they are not around to explain what it all meant. Nor do they stay to see the terrible consequences of martyrdom.

—"You Are Spokesmen for Martyrs," Raja Thomas, *Shiprecords*

LEGATA SWITCHED the big screen from sensor to sensor, trying to make sense of what the instruments reported. Images blurred, re-formed in different perspective. Cutter beams slashed across the plain, she could see bodies, odd movements. Alarm buzzers signaled damage to a section of the Redoubt's perimeter. She heard Lewis dispatch repair and defense teams. Defense cutters beamed into action, directed by key people in the Center. She kept her attention on the mystery in the screens. In the split-screen images an occasional blur slipped past—as though some outside force were confusing the instruments.

She wiped a sleeve across her forehead. The two suns had climbed high while the confused battle went on, and the Redoubt's life-support had been reduced to minimum, shunting energy to weapons. It was hot in the Command Center and the nervous movements of Oakes at her elbow irritated her. In contrast, Lewis appeared unaccountably calm, even secretly amused.

It was carnage on the plain, no doubt of that. The clones in the Command Center affected extreme diligence at their duties, obviously fearful that they might be sent outside into the battle.

Legata hit replay. Something blurred across the big screen.

"What was that?" Oakes demanded.

Legata hit fix, but the sensors failed to resolve an image. Once more, she hit replay and zoomed in close to the blur. Nothing sensible. She touched replay again and slowed the projection, asking the Redoubt's computer system for image enhancement. A slow shape writhed across the screen, vaguely humanoid. It moved between two rocks, struggled with some heavy object, then moved away.

A harsh blue beam snaked from somewhere within the blurred area, alarm signals were indicated by flashing blinkers at the corners of the screen. She ignored them—that was past, and Lewis had met the emergency. Something more important was indicated on the screen: a slow blossom of red-orange which had not revealed itself there before.

"What are you doing?" Oakes demanded. "What caused that?"

"I think they're influencing our sensor system," she said. And she heard the disbelief in her own voice.

Oakes stared at the screen for several blinks, then: "The ship! The damned ship's interfering."

Sweat droplets glistened on his upper lip and jowls. She could smell him beginning to crack.

"Why would the ship do that?" Lewis asked.

"Because of Thomas. You saw him out there." Oakes' voice was breaking.

Legata switched sensors, keyed for the broad view of the cliffside staging area where the attack had originated. The demons were gone, not visible anywhere. The poet no longer sat his perch atop the pinnacle. The arc of watching hylighters had diminished to a thin rim atop the cliffs. The whole scene stood out in the glare of double sunlight.

"Where are the hylighters?" she asked. "I didn't see them go."

"None in close," Lewis said. "Maybe they've gone off somewhere to …" He broke off at a commotion near the open passage hatch.

Legata turned to see a dark-haired Natural, a crew supervisor, slip into the Command Center. Sweaty and nervous, he hurried across to Lewis. There was celltape covering a gory burn on the man's bare left shoulder and his eyes showed the glazing of a pain-killer.

So there are Naturals outside, too, she thought.

"We're getting lots of wounded clones, Jesus," the man said. His voice was hoarse, tense. "What do we do with 'em?"

Lewis looked at Oakes, fielding the question.

"Set up an infirmary," Oakes said. "Clones' quarters. Let 'em treat their own."

"Not many of them understand medical care," Lewis said. "Some are pretty young, remember."

"I know," Oakes said.

Lewis nodded. "I see." He glanced at the crew supervisor. "You heard it. Get busy."

The man glared at Oakes, then at Lewis, but obeyed.

"The ship's interfering with us," Oakes said. "We can't spare medical people or any others right now. We have to devise a plan for …"

"What is going on out there?" Legata asked.

Oakes turned, saw that once more she was running through the sensors, showing several at once. He glanced up at the screen and, at first, did not see what had attracted her attention. Then he saw it—a rectangle high up on the right showed a silvery something creeping over the Redoubt's walls. It moved like a slow-motion wave, blanking out sensors, creeping up and up. Legata compensated for the obscured sensors, moving back and back through new sensors. The wave was composed of countless glittering threads bright in the glare of the double suns.

"Spinnerets," Lewis hissed.

The entire room became so quiet that the air was brittle with listening.

Legata continued, busy at the console.

Lewis turned to the Naturals guarding the Command Center. "Harcourt, you and Javo take a 'burner and see what you can do to cut through that Spinneret mesh."

The men did not respond.

Legata smiled to herself at the continued quiet in the room. She could feel the tensions building to the precise moment she desired. It had been right to wait.

"Send some clones." Legata recognized Harcourt's high-pitched voice.

There was a heavy stirring in the room. She glanced back, saw more clones pressing into the center from the passage. Some of them were the more outré E-types. Most appeared to be wounded. They obviously were looking for someone. A guttural voice called out from amidst the newcomers: "We need medics!"

Lewis faced the two Naturals he had ordered to meet the Spinneret attack. "You refuse to obey my orders?"

Harcourt, his face red, repeated his protest: "Send some clones. That's what they're for."

From somewhere in the center of the room, a thin voice shouted: "We're not going out there!"

"Why should they go?" Legata asked.

"You stay out of this, Legata!" Oakes screamed.

"Just tell them why clones should go," she said.

"You know why!"

"No, I don't."

"Because the first out on any dangerous mission are clones. Harcourt's right. Clones first. That's the way it's always been, and that's the way it'll be."

So he's pitching for the loyalty of the Naturals.

Legata looked at Lewis, met his gaze head on. *Was that amusement in his eyes?* No matter. She depressed a key on the console controlling the big screen, watched the people in the room. They could not miss what was happening on the screen. She had set the program to fill it.

Yes … the room was becoming a tableau, all attention shifting to the screen, locking on it.

Puzzled, Oakes turned to look at the screen, saw his own likeness there. Below the image, a biographical printout was rolling. He stared at the heading: "Morgan Lon Oakes. Ref. Original File, Morgan Hempstead, cell donor …"

Oakes found it difficult to breathe. *It was a trick!* He glanced at Legata and the cold stare he met there iced his backbone.

"Morgan …" How sweet her voice sounded. "… I found your records, Morgan. See Ship's imprimatur on the printout? Ship vouches for the truth of this record."

A tic twitched the corner of Oakes' left eyelid. He tried to swallow.

This is not happening!

Muttering drifted through the room. "Oakes a clone? Ship's eyes!"

Legata stepped away from the console, moved to within a meter of Oakes. "Your name … that's the name of the woman who bore you—for a fee."

Oakes found his voice: "This is a lie! My parents … our sun went nova … I …"

"Ship says not so." She waved at the screen. "See?"

The data continued to roll: Date of cell implantation, address of pseudo-parents, names …

Lewis came up to stand at Oakes' shoulder. "Why, Legata?" There was no denying the amusement in his voice.

She refused to take her attention from the stricken look on Oakes' face. *Why do I want to comfort him?*

"The Scream Room was a mistake," she whispered.

Someone off toward the edge of the room shouted: "Clones first! Send the clone out!" It began as a chant, grew to a pounding rage: "Send the clone out!"

Oakes screamed: "No!"

But hands grabbed him and Legata was powerless to prevent it in the crush of people without using her great strength to kill. She found herself unable to do this. Oakes' voice screaming: "No! Please, no!" grew fainter across the room, out into the passage, was lost in the shouting of the mob.

Lewis moved to the console, shut off the data, keyed a high sensor still free of the Spinneret webs. It showed the sudden gush of a burner opening a gap through the web where the wall had been breached by a cutter beam from outside. Presently, Oakes stumbled into view outside, running alone across Pandora's deadly plain.

Chapter 68

This fetus cannot be brought to term. It cannot be a fruit of the human tree. No human could accelerate its own fetal development. No human could tap the exterior world for its needed energy. No human could communicate before departing the womb. We must abort it or kill both mother and child.

—Sy Murdoch, *The Lewis Exchange, Shiprecords*

WAELA SAT on the edge of the cot in the obstetrics alcove they had improvised. She could hear Ferry working with the wounded out in the emergency area. He had not even noticed her leave his side. Supply crates screened her area and she sat in the fabric-diffused shadows, taking shallow breaths to slow the contractions.

The prediction of Hali's pribox and her own inner voice had been correct. The baby was going to be born on its own schedule and despite anything else that might be happening.

Waela leaned back on the cot.

I'm not afraid. Why am I not afraid?

She felt that a voice spoke to her from her womb—*It will be as it will be.*

The quiet was broken by a babble of voices and another rush of footsteps into the medical shelter. How many batches of the wounded did that make? She had lost count.

A particularly hard contraction forced a gasp from her.

It's time. It's really time.

She felt that she had been put on a long slide, unable to get off, unable to change a single thing that would happen. This was inevitable, growing from that moment in the sub's gondola.

How could I have stopped that? There was no way.

"Where's that TaoLini woman? We need her help out here."

It was Ferry's familiar wheeze. Waela thrust herself upright, staggered to her feet and made her way heavily back to the emergency area of the shelter. She paused in the entrance as another contraction gripped her.

"I'm here. What do you want?"

Ferry glanced up from applying celltape to a wounded E-clone.

"Somebody has to go outside and decide which people are most in need of emergency treatment. I don't have time."

She stumbled toward the exit.

"Wait." The bleary old eyes focused on her. "What's wrong with you?"

"It's … I'm …" She clutched the edge of the treatment table, looked down at a wounded E-clone.

"You'd better go back and lie down," Ferry said.

"But you need …"

"I'll decide what has to be done!"

"But you said …"

"I changed my mind." He finished with the E-clone on the table, looked down at the bulging eyes which protruded from the corners of the clone's temples. "You. You're well enough to go outside and see that I get the worst cases first."

She shook her head. "He doesn't know anything about …"

"He knows when somebody's dying. Don't you?" Ferry helped the clone off the table, and Waela saw the burn splash across the man's right shoulder.

"He's wounded," Waela protested. "He can't …"

"We're all wounded," Ferry said. She heard hysteria in his voice. "Everybody's wounded. You go back now and lie down. Let the wounded take care of the wounded."

"What will you …"

"I'll be back when I've finished with this lot. Then …" He leered at her, old yellow teeth. "Maybe a baby. You see? I'm a poet, too. Maybe you'll like me now."

Waela felt the old snake of fear wriggle up her spine.

Another burn victim staggered into the emergency area, a spidery young female with elongated neck and head, gigantic eyes. Ferry helped her onto the emergency table, signaled a clone from secondary treatment to come in and help. A stump-legged figure clumped in, held the wounded woman's shoulders.

Waela turned away, unable to look at the pain in the woman's eyes. *How silent she was!*

"I'll be in soon," Ferry called as Waela left.

She stopped at the fabric closure to the rear of the shelter. "I can tend to myself. Hali taught me to …"

Ferry laughed. "Hali, sweet bloom of youth, taught you nothing! You're not a young woman, TaoLini, and this is your first baby. Like it or not, you'll need me. You'll see."

Another contraction seized her as she stumbled into her alcove. She doubled over until it passed, then made her way through the gloom to the cot, threw herself on it. Another long, hard cramp rippled the length of her abdomen, followed immediately by an even harder one. She inhaled a deep breath, then a third constriction began. Suddenly, the cot was drenched with amniotic fluid.

Oh, Ship! The baby's coming now. She's coming …

Waela clenched her eyes tightly closed, her entire body taken up in the elemental force moving within her. She had no memory of calling out, but when she opened her eyes, Ferry was there with the long-fingered dwarf she had seen in the outer area of the medical shelter.

The dwarf bent over her face. "I'm Milo Kurz." His eyes were overlarge and protruding. "What do you want me to do?"

Ferry stood behind the dwarf, wringing his hands. Perspiration stood out on his forehead and all the hysterical bravado she had seen in the emergency area was gone.

"The baby's not coming now," he said.

"It's coming," she gasped.

"But the med-tech's not back. The Natali …"

"You said you could help me."

"But I've never …"

Another contraction rippled through her. "Don't just stand there! Help me! Damn you, help me!"

Kurz stroked her forehead.

Twice, Ferry reached toward her, and twice pulled back.

"Please!" Waela screamed it between gasps. "The baby must be turned! Please turn her!"

"I can't!" Ferry backed away from the cot.

Waela glared up at the dwarf. "Kurz … please. The baby has to be turned. Could you …" Another gasping contraction silenced her.

When it passed, she heard the dwarf's voice, low and calm. "Tell me what to do, sister."

"Try to slip your hands around the baby and turn her. She has one arm up and keeping her head from … ohhhhhh!"

Waela tasted blood where she had bitten her own lip, but the pain cleared her head. She opened her eyes, saw the dwarf kneeling between her legs, felt his hands—gentle, sure.

"Ahhhhhhhhhhhh," he said.

"What … what …" It was Ferry, standing at the exit from the alcove, ready to flee.

"The baby tells me what to do," Kurz said. His eyes closed, his breathing slowed. "This infant has a name," he said. "She is called Vata."

Out, out.

Waela heard the voice in her head. She saw darkness, smelled blood, felt her nose stuffed with … with …

"Am I being born here?" Kurz asked. He leaned back in a rapturous movement, held up a glistening infant wriggling in his hands.

"How did you do that?" Ferry demanded.

Waela threw her arms wide, felt the baby delivered to her breast. She felt the dwarf touching her, touching the infant—Vata, Vata, Vata … Visions of her own life mingled with scenes which she knew had occurred to Kurz. *What a sweet and gentle man!* She saw the battle at the Redoubt, felt Kurz being wounded. Other scenes unreeled before her closed eyes like a speeded holo. She felt Panille's presence. She heard Panille's voice in her head! Terrifying. She could not shut it out.

The touch of the infant teaches birth, and our hands are witness to the lesson. That was Panille, but he was not here in the medical shelter.

She sensed the people they had left aboard Ship then—the hydroponics workers, the crew going about their business along the myriad passages … even the dormant ones in hyb: All were one with her mind for an instant. She felt them pause in their shared awareness. She felt the questions in their minds. Their terror became her terror.

What is happening to me? Please, what is happening?

We live! We live!

All the other people vanished from her awareness as she heard/felt those words. Only the speaker of those words remained with her—a tiny voice, a chant, an enormous relief. *We live!* Waela opened her eyes, looked up into the eyes of the dwarf.

"I have seen everything," he whispered. "The infant …"

"Yes," she whispered. "Vata … our Vata …"

"Something's happening," Ferry said. "What is it?" He put his hands to his temples. "Get out of there! Get out, I say!" He collapsed, writhing.

Waela looked at Kurz. "Help him."

Kurz stood up. "Yes, of course. The worst of the wounded first."

Chapter 69

In that hour when the Egyptians died in the Red Sea the ministers wished to sing the song of praise before the Holy One, but he rebuked them saying: My handiwork is drowning in the sea; would you utter a song before me in honor of that?

—*The Sanhedrin, Shiprecords*

OAKES FELT his heart pumping too fast. Perspiration drenched his green singlesuit. His feet hurt. Still, he staggered away from the Redoubt.

Legata, how could you?

When he could move no farther, he sank to the sand, venturing his first look back. They were not pursuing.

They might've killed me!

Black char fringed the distant hole in the web where the mob had burned a passage to eject him. He stared at the hole. His chest pained him with each breath. Slowly he grew conscious of sounds other than his own gasping. The ground under his hand was trembling with some distant thunder. Waves!

Oakes looked toward the sea. The tide was higher than he had ever seen it. A white line marked the entire sea horizon. Gigantic waves crashed against the headland where they had built the shuttle facility. Even as he watched, a great wedge of headland slid into the waves, opening a jagged gap in the shuttle hangar. He staggered to his feet, stared. Black objects moved in the white foam of the crashing sea. Rocks! There were rocks larger than a man in that surf. Even as he watched, the garden—his precious garden—sloughed away.

Mewling cries like near-forgotten seabirds insinuated themselves across the spume. He looked up and turned around once, completely. Hylighters? Gone. Not one orange bag danced in the sky or hovered above the cliffs.

The cries continued.

Oakes looked toward the cliffs where Thomas had begun the attack. Bodies. The battleground lay there with pieces of people twitching in the harsh glare of the suns. Figures moved among the wounded, lifting some on litters and carrying them toward the cliffs.

Once more, Oakes stared back at the Redoubt. Certain death lay there. He turned toward the battleground and for the first time, saw the demons. A shudder convulsed him. The demons were a silent mob sitting in a wide arc beyond the battleground. A single human in a white garment stood in their midst. Oakes recognized the poet, Kerro Panille.

Those cries! It was the wounded and the dying.

Oakes staggered toward Panille. *What did it matter? Send your demons against me, poet!*

Here was the fringe of the battleground … mutilated bodies. Oakes stepped on a dismembered hand. It cupped his boot in reflex, and he leaped away from it. He wanted to run back to the Redoubt, back to Legata. His body refused. He could only shuffle on toward Panille, who stood tall amidst the demons.

Why do they just sit there?

Oakes stopped only a few meters from Panille.

"You." Oakes was surprised by the flat sound of his own voice.

"Yes."

The poet's voice came clearly through the pellet in Oakes' neck and there was no movement of Panille's mouth. "You're finished, Oakes."

"You! You're the one who wrecked things for me! You're the reason Lewis and I couldn't …"

"Nothing is wrecked, Oakes. Life here has just begun."

Panille's lips did not move, yet that voice rang through the neck pellet!

"You're not speaking … but I can hear you."

"That is Avata's gift to us."

"Avata?"

"The hylighters and the kelp—they are one: Avata."

"So this planet's really beaten us."

"Not the planet, nor Legata."

"The ship then. It's hounded me down at last."

"Not Ship."

"Lewis! He did this. He and Legata!"

Oakes felt his tears begin. Lewis and Legata. He was unable to meet Panille's steady gaze. Lewis and Legata. A Flatwing moved away from the poet, crawled onto the toe of Oakes' boot, rested its bristling head there. Oakes stared down at it in horror, unable to command his own muscles. Frustration forced words from him.

"Tell me who did this!"

"You know who did it."

An anguished cry was wrenched from Oakes' throat: "Nooooooooooo!"

"You did it, Oakes. You and Thomas."

"I didn't!"

Panille merely stared at him.

"Tell your demons to kill me then!" Oakes hurled the words at Panille.

"They are not my demons."

"Why don't they attack?"

"Because I show them a world which some would call illusion. No creature attacks what it sees, only what it thinks it sees."

Oakes stared at Panille in horror. *Illusion. This poet could fill my mind with illusion?*

"The ship taught you how to do that!"

"Avata taught me."

A feeling of hysteria crept into Oakes. "And your Avata's done for … all gone!"

"Not before teaching us the universe of alternate realities. And Avata lives in us yet."

Oakes stared down at the deadly Flatwing on his boot. "What does it see?" He pointed a shaking finger at the creature.

"Something of its own life."

A crash shook the ground all around them and the Flatwing crept off his boot to squat quietly on the sand. Oakes looked toward the source of the sound, saw that another coveside section of the Redoubt had slipped away into the surf. The white line of the horizon had moved right up to the land—thunderous waves. The cove amplified the waves, condensing them and sending them high against the shore. Oakes stared in dumb horror as another section of the Redoubt ripped away and fell from view.

"I don't care what you say," Oakes muttered. "The planet's beaten us."

"If that's what you want."

"What I want!" Oakes rounded on him in rage, broke off at the approach of two E-clones carrying a wounded man on a litter. Hali Ekel, her nose ring glittering in the brilliant light, walked alongside. Her pribox was hooked to the patient. Oakes looked down at the litter and recognized the man there: Raja Thomas. The litter carriers stared questioningly at Oakes as they lowered Thomas to the sand.

"How bad?" Oakes directed the question at Hali.

Panille answered: "He is dying. A chest wound and a flash bum."

A chuckle forced its way from Oakes. He gulped it back. "So he won't survive me! At last—no Ceepee for the damned ship!"

Hali knelt beside Thomas and looked up at Panille. "He won't survive being carried to the shelter. He wanted me to bring him to you."

"I know."

Panille stared down at the dying man. Awareness of Thomas lay there in Panille's mind, linked to Vata, to Waela, to most of the E-clones whose genetic mix traced itself back to the Avata. All of it was there, the complete pattern. How profound of Ship to take the Raja Flattery of Ship's own origins and make a personal nemesis out of the man.

Thomas moved his lips, a whisper only, but even Oakes heard him: "I studied the question so long … I hid the problem."

"What's he talking about?" Oakes demanded.

"He's talking to Ship," Panille said, and this time his lips moved, his voice was the remembered voice of the poet, full of pouncing awareness.

A series of gasps wracked the dying man, then: "I played the game so long … so long. Panille knows. It's the rock … the child. Yes! I know! The child!"

Oakes snorted. "He just thinks he's talking to the ship."

"You still refuse to live up to the best of your own humanity," Panille said, looking at Oakes.

"What … what do you mean?"

"That's all Ship ever asked of us," Panille said. "That's all WorShip was meant to be: find our own humanity and live up to it."

"Words! Just words!" Oakes felt that he was being crowded into a corner. Everything here was illusion!

"Then throw out the words and ask yourself what you're doing here," Panille said.

"I'm just trying to survive. What else is there to do?"

"But you've never really been alive."

"I've … I've …" Oakes fell silent as Panille lifted an arm.

One by one, the demons moved off at an angle away from the cliffside shelter. The first of them were at the cliff and moving up toward the high plains before Panille spoke.

"I release them as Avata released them. Still they do what they do."

Oakes looked at the departing demons. "What will they do?"

"When they are hungry, they will eat."

It was too much for Oakes. "What do you want of me?"

"You're a doctor," Panille said. "There are wounded."

Oakes pointed at Thomas. "You'd have me save him?"

"Only Ship or all of us together can save him," Panille said.

"Ship!"

"Or all of us together—it's the same thing."

"Lies! You're lying!"

"The idea of saving has many meanings," Panille said. "There's comfort in the intelligence and potential immortality of our own kind."

Oakes backed one step away from Panille. "Lying words! This planet's going to kill us all."

"What are your senses for if not to be believed?" Panille asked. He gestured around him, met Hali's rapt gaze. "We survive. We repair this planet. Avata, who kept this place in balance, is gone. But Vata is their daughter as much as mine."

"Vata?" Oakes spat the word. "What's this new nonsense?"

"Waela's child has been born. She is called Vata. She carries the true seed of Avata placed there at her conception."

"Another monster." Oakes shook his head.

"Not at all. A beautiful child, as human in her form as her mother. Here, I will show you."

Images began to play in Oakes' awareness, howling through his mind on the carrier wave of the pellet in his neck. He wanted to tear the thing from his flesh. Oakes staggered backward, thrusting at Panille with one hand while the other hand clutched at the imbedded pellet.

"Nooooo … no … no!"

The images would not stop. Oakes fell backward to the sand and, as he fell, he heard the voice of Ship. He knew it was Ship. There was no escaping that presence as it expanded within him, not needing the pellet, not needing any device.

You see, Boss? You never needed a covenant of inflexible words. All you ever needed was self-respect, the self-worship which contains all of humankind and all the things that matter for your mutual immortality.

Pressing his hands to his head, Oakes rolled to his knees. He stared down at the sand, his eyes blurred by tears.

Slowly, Ship withdrew. It was a hot knife being pulled from Oakes' brain. It left an aching void. He lowered his hands and heard the crunch of many feet on sand. Turning, he saw a long line of people—E-clones and Naturals—approaching from the Redoubt. Legata and Lewis led them. Beyond the refugees, Oakes saw smoke drifting on a sea wind, billowing from the wreckage of the Redoubt. His precious sanctuary was being destroyed! Everything! All of Oakes' rage returned as he stumbled to his feet.

Damn You, Ship! You tricked me!

Oakes shook a fist at Legata. "You bitch, Legata!"

Lewis and Legata stopped about ten paces from Oakes. The refugees stopped behind them except for one tall E-clone female with fine features on a bulbous head. She stepped in front of Legata.

"You do not speak to her that way!" the E-clone shouted. "We have chosen her Ceepee. You do not speak to our Ceepee that way."

"That's crazy!" Oakes screamed it. "How can deformed monstrosities choose a Ceepee?"

The E-clone took a step toward Oakes, another. "Whom do you call monstrosity? What if we breed and breed here, and your kind becomes the freak?"

Oakes stared at her in horror.

"You ain't so pretty, you know," she said. "I look at me every day and every day I don't look so bad. But every day you get uglier and uglier. What if I don't think it's right for any more uglies to be born?"

Legata stepped forward and touched the woman's arm. "Enough."

As Legata spoke, a dark shadow flowed over them. They looked up to see Ship passing between Rega and the plain—far lower than Ship had ever been before. The odd protrusions and wing shapes of the agraria were clearly visible. The shadow moved with an awesome slowness, an eternity in the passage. When the shadow touched him, Lewis began to laugh. All who heard him turned toward Lewis and most of them were in time to see him vanish. He became a white blur which dissolved and left nothing where he had stood.

"Why, Ship?" Panille spoke it aloud, startled by the disappearance.

They all heard the answer, a joyous clamor in their heads.

You needed a real devil, Jesus Lewis, the other half of Me. The real devil always goes with Me. Thomas remained his own devil—a special kind of demon, a goad. And now he knows. Humans, you have won your reprieve. You know how to worship.

In that instant, they all saw Ship's intentions toward Thomas, the issue hanging on a fragile balance.

Thomas raised himself on one elbow, resisting Hali's attempts to prevent it. "No, Ship," he muttered. "Not back to hyb. I'm home."

Legata intruded. "Let him go, Ship."

If you can save him, he is yours.

Ship's challenge rang through them.

Panille held fast to the awareness of Thomas and sent the call to Vata back in the medical shelter at the cliffs: *Vata! Help us!*

The old presence of Avata crept into his mind—attenuated but with nothing omitted. Vata was all of what had been … and more. Panille felt his daughter as the repository of those long eons when Avata had lived and learned, but welded now to everything human. She reached beyond the plain into the crew remaining aboard Ship, even into the dormant ones of hyb, giving them the new worship and weaving them into a single organism. They came together an awareness at a time … even Oakes. And when they were united, they moved threadlike into the flesh of Thomas, closing his wounds, repairing cells.

It was done and they left Thomas asleep on the litter.

Panille took a trembling breath and stared around him at the people on the plain. In the healing of Thomas, all of the wounded had been restored. There were bodies of the dead, but not a single maimed among the living. All stood silent under the shadow presence which slid across the plain.

Legata.

It was Ship again.

Still shaken by the experience of the sharing, she spoke aloud in a trembling voice. "Yes, Ship?"

You have taken My best friend, Legata. Oakes is Mine now, a fair exchange. Where I go, I will need him more than you.

She looked up at the Rega-haloed outline. "You're leaving?"

I travel the Ox gate, Legata. The Ox gate—My childhood and My eternity.

She thought about the Ox gate, the scrambled repository in which she had found the truth about Oakes' origins, the near-mystical computer where hidden things emerged. As she thought this, she felt her own consciousness become one with Ship's records. And because they all were linked through Vata, all on the plain shared this.

Ship's words and images rode over this flooding awareness.

Infinite imagination has its infinite horrors, too. Poets turn their nightmares to words. With gods, dreams take on substance and lives of their own. Such things cannot be scratched out. The Ox gate, my morality factor. My psyche moves both ways. If it moves in symbols, it moves through the Ox. Some of my symbols walk and breathe—as it was with Jesus Lewis. Others sing in the words of poets.

Oakes fell to his knees, pleading. "Don't take me, Ship. I don't want to go."

But I need you, Morgan Oakes. I no longer have Thomas, my personal demon, and I need you.

Ship's shadow began to pass beyond the people on the plain. As light touched Oakes, he vanished—a white blur, then an empty place on the sand.

Legata stood there, looking at where Oakes had knelt, and she could not keep the tears from coursing down her cheeks.

Hali stood up beside the litter where her patient slept. She felt emptied and angry, robbed of her role. She stared up at the passing immensity of Ship.

Is this what I was supposed to let them know? she demanded.

Show them, Ekel!

Still angry, she played the images of the crucifixion, then: "Ship! Is that how it was with Yaisuah? Was he just another filament from one of Your dreams?"

Does it matter, Ekel? Is the lesson diminished because the history that moves you is fiction? The incident which you just shared is too important to be debated on the level of fact or fancy. Yaisuah lived. He was an ultimate essence of goodness. How could you learn such an essence without experiencing its opposite?

The shadow was gone from them, flowing away over the cliffs, carrying off the bits of humanity remaining up there—the Natali, the hyb attendants, the hydroponics workers …

"Ship is leaving us," Legata said. She crossed to Panille's side.

In the midst of her words, she felt the blaze of awareness which Ship had shared with them—Shiprecords, all of the pasts carried into the smallest cell on the plain.

"We've been weaned," Panille said. "We have to go it alone now."

Hali joined them. "No more shiptits."

"But *alone* has lost all of its old meanings," Panille said.

"Is this what the expansion of the universe is all about?" Legata asked. "The fleeing of the gods from their own handiwork?"

"Gods ask other questions," Panille said. He looked down at Hali. "You were midwife to us all when you brought us Vata and the Hill of Skulls."

"Vata brought herself," Hali said. She put a hand in Panille's. "Some things don't need a midwife."

"Or a Ceepee," Legata said. She grinned. "But it's a role we all know now." She shook her head. "I have only one question—What will Ship do with those people up there?"

She pointed upward at the vanishing ship.

They all heard it then, Ship's presence filling the people on the plain, then fading, but never to be forgotten.

Surprise Me, Holy Void!

THE LAZARUS EFFECT

Dedication

For Brian, Bruce and Penny. For all the years they tiptoed while their father was writing.
—Frank Herbert

For all those healers who ease our suffering; for people who feed people, then ask them for virtue; for our friends—gratitude and affection.
—Bill Ransom

Introduction

Bill Ransom

AFTER *THE Jesus Incident,* I went through Washington's fire service training program and became a firefighter and firefighter basic training instructor. Within a year I was working at our county hospital as an Advanced Life Support EMT, taught CPR in the community and began regular trips to Central America (Guatemala, El Salvador, Nicaragua) to train firefighters and others in trauma and rescue techniques. I wrote the first draft of what became *Jaguar,* a number of short stories and a small collection of poems ("Last Call").

Frank and Bev were under a good deal of stress from many quarters—Bev's treatment had unexpected, very worrisome complications, Frank was in demand around the world, and Frank needed to travel to Ireland for research on his current book. As soon as Bev was able, they made the Ireland trip. The getaway offered them the distance and privacy that they both needed, and Frank shot hundreds of photos.

We received an offer from the publisher for a sequel to *The Jesus Incident.* Clearly, readers showed little concern for the number of names on the cover—also clearly, Frank was the main attraction. Over coffee at Frank's I noticed the mass of photos of Ireland snaking across the walls of his study. He had a contract for a novel of fiction set in Ireland, and Bev was more ill than they'd thought.

"We're moving to Hawaii," Frank said. "We can work on our book there, unless you have some objection to living in paradise for a while."

We received a modest advance, so I took a leave from the fire department and the hospital and landed on a grass field in Hana, Hawaii. A friend of Frank's (Frayne Utley?) loaned us a house and a cabin while Frank and Bev oversaw construction of their own place. We met every day to talk story, as usual, but this time we had no exchange of papers. We agreed that I would write the whole story straight through, and then Frank would take a shot at it. Meanwhile, he was building a house, caring for Bev and writing what became *The White Plague*.

Every day my regimen focused on writing and on training for the Maui Marathon: coffee, write, run to Seven Pools and back, lunch with Frank, write, join Frank and Bev for dinner, spend the evening walking the Hana countryside and meeting neighbors.

Bev endured several emergency hospitalizations in Honolulu, and Frank asked me to certify all of the construction workers on site in CPR. I borrowed an "Annie" from the park service, invited other community members, and certified about forty people in CPR. All of us working and living in and on that house breathed the heaviness of Bev's condition, and within a couple of months a collective sense of urgency picked up the pace for all of us. This house was Bev's dream; she wanted to see it complete, and Frank wanted Bev to have whatever she wanted.

My daughter loved visiting Frank and Bev in Port Townsend. Being Hawaiian, she was *very* excited to visit them in Hana—she was named after Haleakela volcano, "Home of the Sun". Hali flew into Hana the day Bev was flown to Honolulu for one of her emergency situations, and she never got to see Bev again.

Frank finished his draft of *The White Plague* the same day I finished my final draft of *The Lazarus Effect*, and we swapped manuscripts. Bev also had a copy of *The White Plague* for critique, so the three of us spent all night reading, pencils poised. Bev and I both suggested that Frank should cut some specific parts for length—coincidentally, the same specific parts. Frank handed back an unmarked copy of *The Lazarus Effect* and said, "These are your Journeyman's Papers, Ransom!"

Between us, we considered *Lazarus* to be the second act of an opera, moving from exploring development of conscious to development of conscience, and we had no doubt that, sooner or later, the publisher would want a sequel.

We mailed both books out, Bev passed away, and Frank moved back to Port Townsend to deal with the opening of David Lynch and Dino di Laurentis' film version of *Dune*. I went back to work at the Emergency Room and began nursing school. Sure enough, in my second year Frank's publisher asked for another adventure on Pandora.

Chapter 1

The Histories assert that a binary system cannot support life. But we found life here on Pandora. Except for the kelp, it was antagonistic and deadly, but still it was life. Ship's judgment is upon us now because we wiped out the kelp and unbalanced this world. We few survivors are subject to the endless sea and the terrible vagaries of the two suns. That we survive at all on our fragile Clone-rafts is as much a curse as a victory. This is the time of madness.

—Hali Ekel, *The Journals*

DUQUE SMELLED burning flesh and scorched hair. He sniffed, sniffed again, and whined. His one good eye watered and pained him when he tried to knuckle it open. His mother was out. *Out* was a word he could say, like *hot* and *Ma.* He could not precisely identify the location and shape of *out.* He knew vaguely that his quarters were on a Clone-raft anchored off a black stone pinnacle, all that remained of Pandora's land surface.

The burning smells were stronger now. They frightened him. Duque wondered if he should say something. Mostly, he did not talk; his nose got in the way. He could whistle through his nose, though, and his mother understood. She would whistle back. Between them, they understood more than a hundred whistle-words. Duque wriggled his forehead. This uncurled his thick, knobby nose and he whistled—tentative at first to see whether she was near.

"Ma? Where are you, Ma?"

He listened for the unmistakable *scuff-slap, scuff-slap* of her bare feet on the soft slick deck of the raft.

Burning smells filled his nose and made him sneeze. He heard the slaps of many feet out in the corridor, more feet than he had ever before heard out there, but nothing he could identify as *Ma.* There was shouting now, words Duque did not know. He sucked in a deep breath and let go the loudest whistle he could muster. His thin ribs ached with it and the vibration made him dizzy.

No one responded. The hatch beside him remained closed. No one plucked him out of his twisted covers and held him close.

Despite the pain of the smoke, Duque peeled back his right eyelid with the two nubs on his right hand and saw that the room was dark except for a glow against the thin organics of the corridor wall. Dull orange light cast a frightening illumination over the deck. Acrid smoke hung like a cloud above him, tendrils of its oily blackness reaching downward toward his face. And now there were other sounds outside added to the shouting and the *slap-slap* of many feet. He heard big things dragging and bumping along his glowing wall. Terror held him curled into a silent lump under the covers of his bunk.

The burning smells contained a steamy, bitter flavor—not quite the sticky-sweet of the time when the stove scorched their wall. He remembered the charred melt of organics opening a new passage between their room and the next one along the corridor. He had poked his head through the burned opening and whistled at their neighbors. The smells now were not the same, though, and the glowing wall did not melt away.

A rumbling was added to the outside sounds. Like a pot boiling over on the stove, but his mother was not cooking. Besides, it was too loud for cooking, louder even than the other corridor noises. Now, there were screams nearby.

Duque kicked off his covers and gasped when his bare feet touched the deck.

Hot!

Abruptly, the deck pitched, first backward and then forward. The motion lurched him face-first through the bulkhead. The hot organics of the wall stretched and parted for him like a cooked noodle. He knew he was on the outer deck but stumbling feet kept him too busy covering his head and body with his arms. He could not spare a hand to open his good eye. The hot deck burned his knees and elbows. Duque caught his breath in the sudden onslaught of pain and wrenched out another shrill whistle. Somebody stumbled against him. Hands reached under his armpits and lifted him clear of the scorched bubbly that had been the deck. Some of it came loose with him and stuck to his bare skin. Duque knew who held him by the jasmine smell of her hair—Ellie, the neighbor woman with the short, stubby legs and beautiful voice.

"Duque," she said, "let's go find your ma."

He heard something wrong in her voice. It rasped low in a dry throat and cracked when she spoke.

"Ma," he said. He knuckled his eye open and saw a nightmare of movement and firelight.

Ellie shouldered them through the crowd, saw that he was looking around and slapped his hand away. "Look later," she said. "Right now you hang on to my neck. Hold tight."

After that one brief glimpse, there was no need to repeat the order. He clutched both arms around Ellie's neck. A small whimper escaped his throat. Ellie continued to push them through a crowd of people—voices all around saying words Duque did not understand. Movement against the others peeled away chunks of bubbly from his skin. It hurt.

That one look at *out* remained indelibly in Duque's memory. Fire had been coming out of the dark water! It coiled up out of the water accompanied by that thick, boiling sound and the air was so full of steam that people were shadow clumps against the hot red glow of flames. Screams and shouts still sounded all around, causing Duque to hold even tighter to Ellie's neck. Chunks of the fire had rocketed into the sky high above their island. Duque did not understand this but he heard the fire crash and sizzle through the body of the island into the sea beneath.

Why water burn? He knew the whistle-words but Ellie would not understand.

The raft tipped sharply under Ellie and sent her sprawling beneath the trampling feet with Duque atop her shielded from the burning deck. Ellie cursed and gasped. More people fell around them. Duque felt Ellie sinking into the melting organics of the deck. She struggled at first, thrashing like a fresh-caught muree that his mother had put into his hands once before she cooked it. Ellie's twisting slowed and she began moaning low in her throat. Duque, still clutching Ellie's neck, felt hot bubbly against his hands and jerked them away. Ellie screamed. Duque tried to push himself away from her but the press of bodies all around prevented his escape. He felt the hair at the nape of his neck standing up. A questing whistle broke from his nose but there was no response.

The deck tilted again and bodies rolled onto Duque. He felt hot flesh, some of it warm-wet. Ellie gasped once, very deep. The air changed. The people screaming, "Oh, no! Oh, no!" stopped screaming. Many people began coughing all around Duque. He coughed, too, choking on hot, thick dust. Someone nearby gasped: "I've got Vata. Help me. We must save her."

Duque sensed a stillness in Ellie. She wasn't moaning anymore. He could not feel the rise and fall of her breathing. Duque opened his mouth and spoke the two words he knew best:

"Ma. Hot, Ma. Ma."

Someone right beside him said: "Who's that?"

"Hot, Ma," Duque said.

Hands touched him and hauled him away from Ellie. A voice next to his ear said: "It's a child. He's alive."

"Bring him!" someone called between coughs. "We've got Vata."

Duque felt himself passed from hand to hand through an opening into a dimly lighted place. His one good eye saw through a thinner dust haze the glitter of tiny lights, shiny surfaces and handles. He wondered if this could be the *out* where Ma went but there was no sign of Ma, only many people crowded into a small space. Someone directly in front of him held a large naked infant. He knew about infants because Ma sometimes brought them from *out* and cared for them, cooing over them and letting Duque touch them and pet them. Infants were soft and nice. This infant looked larger than any Duque had ever seen but he knew she was only an infant—those fat features, that still face.

The air pressure changed, popping in Duque's ears. Something began to hum. Just when Duque was deciding to come out of his fears and join in this warm closeness of flesh, three gigantic explosions shook all of them, sending their enclosed space tumbling.

"Boom! Boom! Boom!" the explosions came one on top of the other.

People began extricating themselves from the tumble of flesh. A foot touched Duque's face and was withdrawn.

"Careful of the little ones," someone said.

Strong hands lifted Duque and helped him open his eye. A pale masculine face peered at him—a wide face with deeply set brown eyes. The man spoke. "I've got the other one. He's no beauty but he's alive."

"Here, give him to me," a woman said.

Duque found himself pressed close to the infant. A woman's arms held them both, flesh to flesh, warmth to warmth. A sense of reassurance swept through Duque but it was cut off immediately when the woman spoke. He understood her words! He did not know how he understood but the meanings were there unfolding as her voice rumbled against his cheek pressed to her breast.

"The whole island exploded," the woman said. "I saw it through the port."

"We're well below the surface now," a man said. "But we can't stay long with this many people breathing our air."

"We will pray to Rock," the woman said. "And to Ship," a man said. "To Rock and to Ship," they all agreed.

Duque heard all of this from a distance as more understanding flooded his awareness. It was happening because his flesh touched the flesh of the infant! He knew the infant's name now.

"Vata."

A beautiful name. The name brought with it a blossoming mindful of information, as though the knowledge had always been there, needing only Vata's name and her touch to spread it through his memory. Now, he was aware of *out*, all of it as known through human senses and kelp memories … because Vata carried kelp genes in her human flesh. He remembered the place of the kelp deep under the sea, the tendrils clinging to precious rock. He remembered the minuscule islands that no longer existed because the kelp was gone and the sea fury had been unleashed. Kelp memories and human memories revealed wondrous things happening to Pandora now that waves could roam freely around this planet, which was really a distorted ball of solid matter submerged in an endless skin of water.

Duque knew where he was, too: in a small submersible, which should have had a Lighter-Than-Air carrier attached to it.

Out was a place of marvels.

And all of this wondrous information had come to him directly from the mind of Vata because she had kelp genes, as did he. As did many of Pandora's surviving humans. Genes … he knew about those marvels, too, because Vata's mind was a magic storehouse of such things, telling him about history and the Clone Wars and the death of all the kelp. He sensed a direct link between Vata and himself, which endured even when he pulled away from physical contact with her. Duque experienced a great thankfulness for this and tried to express his gratitude but Vata refused to respond. He understood then that Vata wanted the deep sea-quiet of her kelp memories. She wanted only the waiting. She did not want to deal with the things she had dumped onto him. She had dumped them, he realized, shedding these things like a painful skin. Duque felt a momentary pique at this realization but happiness returned immediately. He was the repository of such wonders!

Consciousness.

That's my department, he thought. *I must be aware for both of us. I am the storage system, the Ox Gate, which only Vata can open.*

Chapter 2

There were giants in the earth in those days.
—Genesis, *Christian Book of the Dead*

22 BUNRATTI, 468.

WHY DO I keep this journal? This is a strange hobby for the Chief Justice and Chairman of the Committee on Vital Forms. Do I hope that a historian will someday weave rich elaborations out of my poor scribblings? I can just see someone like Iz Bushka stumbling onto my journal many years from now, his mind crammed full of the preconceptions that block acceptance of the truly new. Would Bushka destroy my journal because it conflicted with his own theories? I think this may have happened with other historians in our past. Why else would Ship have forced us to start over? I'm convinced that this is what Ship has done.

Oh, I believe in Ship. Let it be recorded here and now that Ward Keel believes in Ship. Ship is God and Ship brought us here to Pandora. This is our ultimate trial—sink or swim, in the most literal sense. Well … almost. We Islanders mostly float. It's the Mermen who swim.

What a perfect testing ground for humankind is this Pandora, and how aptly named. Not a shard of land left above its sea, which the kelp once subdued. Once a noble creature, intelligent, known to all creatures of this world as Avata, it is now simply kelp—thick, green and silent. Our ancestors destroyed Avata and we inherited a planetary sea.

Have we humans ever done that before? Have we killed off the thing that subdues the deadliness in our lives? Somehow, I suspect we have. Else, why would Ship leave those hybernation tanks to tantalize us in orbit just beyond our reach?

Our Chaplain/Psychiatrist shares this suspicion. As she says, "There is nothing new under the suns."

I wonder why Ship's imprimatur always took the form of the eye within the pyramid?

I began this journal simply as an account of my own stewardship on the Committee that determines which new life will be permitted to survive and perhaps breed. We mutants have a deep regard for the variations that the bioengineering of that brilliant madman, Jesus Lewis, set adrift in the human gene pool. From those incomplete records we still have, it's clear that *human* once had a much narrower definition. Mutant variations that we now accept without a passing glance were once cause for consternation, even death. As a Committeeman passing judgment on life, the question I always ask myself and try to answer with my poor understanding is: *Will this new life, this infant, help us all survive?* If there is the remotest chance that it will contribute to this thing we call human society I vote to let it live. And I have been rewarded time and again by that hidden genius in cruel form, that mind plus distorted body which enrich us all. I know I am correct in these decisions.

But my journal has developed a tendency to wander. I have decided that I am secretly a philosopher. I want to know not only what, but why.

In the long generations since that terrible night when the last of Pandora's true land-based islands exploded into molten lava, we have developed a peculiar social duality, which I am convinced could destroy us all. We Islanders, with our organic cities floating "willy-nilly" on the sea's surface, believe we have formed the perfect society. We care for each other, for the inner other that the skin (whatever shape or shade) protects. Then what is it about us that insists on saying "us" and "them?" Is there a viciousness buried in us? Will it explode us into violence against the excluded others?

Oh, Islanders exclude; this cannot be denied. Our jokes betray us. Anti-Mermen jokes. "Merms," we call them. Or "pretties." And they call us "Mutes." It's a grunt word no matter how you sound it.

We are jealous of Mermen. There it is. I have written it. Jealous. They have the freedom of all the land beneath the sea. Merman mechanization depends on a relatively uniform, traditional human body. Few Islanders can compete under middleclass conditions, so they occupy the top of Merman genius or the depths of its slums. Even so, Islanders who migrate down under are confined to Islander communities … ghettos. Still the Islander idea of heaven is to pass for a pretty.

Mermen repel the sea to survive. Their living space benefits from a kind of stability underfoot. Historically, I must admit, humans show a preference for a firm surface underfoot, air to breathe freely (although theirs is depressingly damp) and solid things all around. They produce an occasional webbed foot or hand but that, too, was common all down the lineage of the species. Merman appearance is that of humans for as long as likenesses have been recorded; that much we can see for ourselves. Besides, *Clone Wars* happened. Our immediate ancestors wrote of this. Jesus Lewis did this to us. The visible evidence of *other* is inescapable.

But I was writing about Merman nature. It is their self-proclaimed mission to restore the kelp. But will the kelp be conscious? Kelp once more lives in the sea. I have seen the effects in my lifetime and expect we've just about seen the last of wavewalls. Exposed land will surely follow. Yet, how does that subtract from this nature that I see in the Mermen?

By bringing back the kelp, they seek to *control* the sea. That is the Merman nature: control.

Islanders float with the waves and the winds and the currents. Mermen would control these forces and control us.

Islanders bend with things that might otherwise overwhelm them. They are accustomed to change but grow tired of it. Mermen fight against certain kinds of change—and are growing tired of that.

Now, I come to my view of what Ship did with us. I think it is the nature of our universe that life may encounter a force that could overwhelm it if life cannot bend. Mermen would break before such a force. Islanders bend and drift. I think we may prove the better survivors.

Chapter 3

We bear our original sin in our bodies and on our faces.
—Simone Rocksack, Chaplain/Psychiatrist

THE COLD *slap* of a sudden wave over the side snapped Queets Twisp full awake. He yawned, unkinked his overlong arms where they had tangled themselves in the tarp. He wiped the spray from his face with his shirtsleeve. Not yet full sunrise, he noted. The first thin feathers of dawn tickled the black belly of the horizon. No thunderheads cluttered the sky and his two squawks, their feathers preened and glistening, muttered contentedly on their tethers. He rubbed the circulation back into his long arms and felt in the bottom of the coracle for his tube of thick juice concentrates and proteins.

Blech.

He made a wry face as he sucked down the last of the tube. The concentrate was tasteless and odorless, but he balked at it just the same.

You'd think if they made it edible they could make it palatable, he thought. *At least dockside we'll get some real food.* The rigors of setting and hauling fishing nets always built his appetite into a monumental thing that concentrates could support, but never satisfy.

The gray ocean yawned away in all directions. Not a sign of dashers or any other threat anywhere. The occasional splatter of a sizable wave broke over the rim of the coracle but the organic pump in the bilge could handle that. He turned and watched the slaw bulge of their net foam the surface behind them. It listed slightly with its heavy load. Twisp's mouth watered at the prospect of a thousand kilos of scilla—boiled scilla, fried scilla, baked scilla with cream sauce and hot rolls …

"Queets, are we there yet?" Brett's voice cracked in its adolescent way. Only the shock of his thick blonde hair stuck out from under their tarp—a sharp contrast to Twisp's headful of ebony fur. Brett Norton was tall for sixteen, and his pile of hair made him seem even taller. This first season of fishing had already begun to fill in some of his thin, bony structure.

Twisp sucked in a slow breath, partly to calm himself after being startled, partly to draw in patience.

"Not yet," he said. "Drift is right. We should overtake the Island just after sunrise. Eat something."

The boy grimaced and rummaged in his kit for his own meal. Twisp watched as the boy wiped the spout nearly clean, unstoppered it and sucked down great gulps of the untantalizing brown liquid.

"Yum." Brett's gray eyes were shut tight and he shuddered.

Twisp smiled. *I should quit thinking of him as "the boy."* Sixteen years was more than boyhood, and a season at the nets had hardened his eyes and thickened his hands.

Twisp often wondered what had made Brett choose to be a fisherman. Brett was near enough to Merman body type that he could have gone down under and made a good life there.

He's self-conscious about his eyes, Twisp thought. *But that's something few people notice.*

Brett's gray eyes were large, but not grotesque. Those eyes could see well in almost total darkness, which turned out to be handy for round-the-clock fishing.

That's something the Mermen wouldn't let out of their hands, Twisp thought. *They're good at using people.*

A sudden lurch of the net caught both of them off-balance and they reached simultaneously for the rimline. Again, the lurch.

"Brett!" Twisp shouted, "Get us some slack while I haul in."

"But we can't haul in," the boy said, "we'd have to dump the catch …"

"There's a Merman in the net! A Merman will drown if we don't haul in." Twisp was already dragging in the heavy netlines hand-over-hand. The muscles of his long forearms nearly burst the skin with the effort. This was one of those times he was thankful he had a mutant's extra ability.

Brett ducked out of sight behind him to man their small electric scull. The netlines telegraphed a frantic twisting and jerking from below.

Merman for sure! Twisp thought, and strained even harder. He prayed he could get him up in time.

Or her, he thought. The first Merman he'd seen netbound was a woman. Beautiful. He shook off the memory of the crisscross lines, the net-burns in her perfect, pale … dead skin. He hauled harder.

Thirty meters of net to go, he thought. Sweat stung his eyes and small blades of pain seared his back.

"Queets!"

He looked from the net back to Brett and saw white-eyed terror. Twisp followed the boy's gaze. What he saw three or four hundred meters to starboard made him freeze. The squawks set up a fluttering outcry that told Twisp what his eyes were barely able to confirm.

"A hunt of dashers!"

He almost whispered it, almost let slip the netlines creasing his rock-hard palms.

"Help me here," Twisp shouted. He returned to the frantic tugging at the net. Out of the corner of one eye he saw the boy grab the port line, out of the other he watched the steady froth of the oncoming dashers.

A half-dozen of them at least, he thought. *Shit.*

"What'll they do?" Brett's voice cracked again.

Twisp knew that the boy had heard stories. Nothing could match the real thing. Hungry or not, dashers hunted. Their huge forepaws and saberlike canines killed for the sheer bloody love of it. These dashers wanted that Merman.

Too late, Twisp dove for the lasgun he kept wrapped in oiled cloth in the cuddy. Frantically, he scrabbled for the weapon, but the first of the dashers hit the net head-on and their momentum rocked the coracle. Two others fanned to the sides, closing on the flanks like a fist. Twisp felt the two hard hits as he came up with the lasgun. He saw the net go slack as slashing claws and fangs opened it wide. The rest of the hunt closed in, scavenging bits of meat and bone thrown clear of the frothy mess that had been a Merman. One dasher nipped another and, primed to kill, the rest turned on their wounded mate and tore him to bits. Fur and green gore splattered the side of the coracle.

No need wasting a lasgun charge on that mess! It was a bitter thought. Islanders had long ago given up the hope they might exterminate these terrible creatures.

Twisp shook himself alert, fumbled for his knife and cut the netlines.

"But why … ?"

He didn't answer Brett's protest, but toggled a switch under the scull housing. One of the dashers froze not a meter from their gunwale. It sank slowly, drifting back and forth, back and forth like a feather falling on a breezeless day. The others made passes at the coracle but retreated once they felt the edge of the stunshield on their noses. They settled for the stunned dasher, then thrashed their way out to sea.

Twisp rewrapped his lasgun and wedged it under his seat.

He switched off the shield then and stared at the ragged shards that had been their net.

"Why'd you cut loose the net?" Brett's voice was petulant, demanding. He sounded near tears.

Shock, Twisp thought. *And losing the catch.*

"They tore the net to get the … to get him," Twisp explained. "We'd have lost the catch anyway."

"We could've saved some of it," Brett muttered. "A third of it was right *here.*" Brett slapped the rimline at the stern, his eyes two gray threats against a harsh blue sky.

Twisp sighed, aware that adrenaline could arouse frustrations that needed release.

"You can't activate a stunshield with the lines over the side like that," he explained. "It's got to be all the way in or all the way out. With this cheap-ass model, anyway …" His fist slammed one of the thwarts.

I'm as shook as the kid, he thought. He took a deep breath, ran his fingers through the thick kinks of his black hair and calmed himself before activating the dasher-warning signal on his radio. That would locate them and reassure Vashon.

"They'd have turned on us next," he said. He flicked a finger against the material between thwarts. "This stuff is one thin membrane, two centimeters thick—what do you think our odds were?"

Brett lowered his eyes. He pursed his full lips, then stuck the lower lip out in a half-pout. His gaze looked away past a rising of Big Sun come to join its sister star already overhead. Below Big Sun, just ahead of the horizon, a large silhouette glowed orange in the water.

"Home," Twisp said quietly. "The city."

They were in one of the tight trade currents close to the surface. It would allow them to overtake the floating mass of humanity in an hour or two.

"Big fucking deal," Brett said. "We're broke."

Twisp smiled and leaned back to enjoy the suns.

"That's right," he said. "And we're alive."

The boy grunted and Twisp folded his meter-and-a-half arms behind his head. The elbows stuck out like two strange wings and cast a grotesque shadow on the water. He stared up across one of the elbows—caught as he sometimes was reflecting on the uniqueness of his mutant inheritance. These arms gangled in his way most of his life—he could touch his toes without bending over at all. But his arms hauled nets as though bred for it.

Maybe they were, he mused. *Who knows anymore?* Handy mostly for nets and for reach, they made sleeping uncomfortable. Women seemed to like their strength and their wraparound quality, though. Compensation.

Maybe it's the illusion of security, he thought, and his smile widened. His own life was anything but secure. Nobody who went down to the sea was secure, and anybody who thought so was either a fool or dead.

"What will Maritime Court do to us?" Brett's voice was low, barely audible over the splashings of the waves and the continued ruffled mutterings of the two squawks.

Twisp continued to enjoy the drift and the warm sunlight on his face and arms. He gnawed his thin lips for a blink, then said, "Hard to say. Did you see a Merman marker?"

"No."

"Do you see one now?"

He listened to the faint rustle across the coracle and knew that the boy scanned the horizon. Twisp had picked the boy for those exceptional eyes. That, and his attitude.

"Not a sign," the boy said. "He must've been alone."

"That's not likely," Twisp said. "Mermen seldom travel alone. But it's a sure bet *somebody's* alone."

"Do we *have* to go to court?"

Twisp opened his eyes and saw the genuine fear in Brett's downturned mouth. The boy's wide eyes were impossible moons in his unstubbled face.

"Yep."

Brett plopped down on the thwart beside Twisp, rocking the little boat so hard that water lapped over the sides.

"What if we don't tell?" he asked. "How would they know?"

Twisp turned away from the boy. Brett had a lot to learn about the sea, and those who worked it. There were many laws, and most of them stayed unwritten. This would be a hard first lesson, but what could you expect of a kid fresh from the inside? Things like this didn't happen at Center. Life there was … nice. Scilla and muree were dinner to people living in the Island's inner circle, they weren't creatures with patterns and lives and a bright final flutter in the palm of the hand.

"Mermen keep track of everything," Twisp said flatly. "They know."

"But the dashers," Brett insisted, "maybe they got the other Merman, too. If there *was* another one."

"Dasher fur has hollow cells," Twisp said. "For insulation and flotation. They can't dive worth a damn."

Twisp leveled his black eyes at the kid and said, "What about his family waiting back home? Now shut up."

He knew the kid was hurt, but what the hell! If Brett was going to live on the sea he'd better learn the way of it. Nobody liked being surprised out here, or abandoned. Nobody liked being boat-bound with a motor-mouth, either. Besides, Twisp was beginning to feel the proximity and inevitable discomfort of the Maritime Court, and he thought he'd better start figuring out their case. Netting a Merman was serious business, even if it wasn't your fault.

Chapter 4

The fearful can be the most dangerous when they gain power. They become demoniac when they see the unpredictable workings of all that life around them. Seeing the strengths as well as the weaknesses, they fasten only on the weaknesses.
—Shipquotes, *The Histories*

EXCEPT FOR the movements of the operators, and their occasional comments, it was quiet in 'Sonde Control this morning, a stillness insulated from the daylight topside beneath a hundred meters of water and the thick walls of this Merman complex. The subdued remoteness filled Iz Bushka with disquiet. He knew his senses were being assaulted by Merman strangeness, an environment alien to most Islanders, but the exact source of his unease escaped him.

Everything's so quiet, he thought.

All that weight of water over his head gave Bushka no special concern. He had overcome that fear while doing his compulsory service in the Islander subs. The attitude of superiority that he could detect in the Mermen around him, *that* was the source of his annoyance! Bushka glanced left to where his fellow observers stood slightly apart, keeping their distance from the lone Islander in this company.

GeLaar Gallow leaned close to the woman beside him, Kareen Ale, and asked: "Why is the launch delayed?"

Ale spoke in a softly modulated voice: "I heard someone say there was an order from the Chaplain/Psychiatrist—something about the blessing."

Gallow nodded and a lock of blonde hair dropped to his right eyebrow. He brushed it back with a casual movement. Gallow was quite the most beautiful human male Bushka had ever seen—a Greek god, if the histories were to be credited. As an Islander historian by avocation, Bushka believed the histories. Gallow's golden hair was long and softly waved. His dark blue eyes looked demandingly at everything they encountered. His even, white teeth flashed smiles that touched nothing but his mouth, as though he displayed the perfect teeth in that perfect face only for the benefit of onlookers. Some said he had been operated on to remove webs from fingers and toes but that could be a jealous lie.

Bushka studied Ale covertly. It was said that Mermen were petitioning Ale to mate with Gallow for the sake of beautiful offspring. Ale's face was an exquisitely proportioned oval with full lips, widely spaced blue eyes. Her nose, slightly upturned, showed a smooth and straight ridgeline. Her skin—perfectly set off by her dark red hair—was a pinkish translucence that Bushka thought would require salves and ointments when her duties took her topside into the harsh presence of the suns.

Bushka looked past them at the giant console with its graphic operational keys and large screens. One screen showed brilliant light on the ocean surface far above them. Another screen revealed the undersea tube where the Lighter-Than-Air hydrogen 'sonde was being prepared for its upward drift and launch into Pandora's turbulent atmosphere. A thin forest of kelp wavered in the background.

On Bushka's right, a triple thickness of plazglas also revealed the LTA launch base with Mermen swimming around it. Some of the swimmers wore prestubes for oxygen, all encased in their tight-fitting dive suits. Others carried across their backs the organic airfish that Islander bioengineering had pioneered for sustained work undersea.

We can produce it, but we cannot have the freedom of the undersea in which to use it.

Bushka could see where the leechmouth of an airfish attached itself to a nearby Merman's carotid artery. He imagined the thousands of cilia pumping fresh oxygen into the worker's bloodstream. Occasionally, a worker equipped with an airfish vented carbon dioxide in a stream of drifting bubbles from the corner of his mouth.

How does it feel to float freely in the sea, dependent on the symbiotic relationship with an airfish? It was a thought full of Islander resentments. Islander bioengineering surpassed that of the Mermen, but everything Islander genius produced was gobbled up in the terrible need for valuable exchange.

As I would like to be gobbled up. But there's not much hope of that!

Bushka suppressed feelings of jealousy. He could see his reflection in the plaz. The Committee on Vital Forms had faced no trouble in accepting him as human. He obviously fell somewhere near the Merman-tip of the spectrum. Still, his heavyset body, his small stature, the large head with its stringy dark brown hair, thick brows, wide nose, wide mouth, square chin—none of this came near the standard Gallow represented.

Comparisons hurt. Bushka wondered what the tall, disdainful Merman was thinking. *Why that quizzical expression aimed at me?*

Gallow returned his attention to Ale, touching her bare shoulder, laughing at something she said.

A new flurry of activity could be seen at the LTA launch base, more lights within the tube that would guide the 'sonde on the start of its journey toward the surface.

The launch director at the control console said: "It'll be a few minutes yet."

Bushka sighed. This experience was not turning out the way he had expected … the way he had dreamed.

He sneered at himself. *Fantasy!*

When he had been notified that he would be the Islander observer at this launch into the realm of Ship, elation had filled him. His first trip into the core of Merman civilization! At last! And the fantasy: *Perhaps … just possibly, I will find the way to join Merman society, to abandon poverty and the grubby existence topside.*

Learning that Gallow would be his escort had fanned his hopes. GeLaar Gallow, director of the Merman Screen, one who could vote to accept an Islander into their society. But Gallow appeared to be avoiding him now. And there had never been any doubt of the man's disdain.

Only Ale had been warmly welcoming, but then she was a member of the Merman government, a diplomat and envoy to the Islanders. Bushka had been surprised to discover that she also was a medical doctor. Rumor had it that she had gone through the rigors of medical education as a gesture of rebellion against her family, with its long tradition of service in the diplomatic corps and elsewhere in the Merman government. The family obviously had won out. Ale was securely seated among the powerful—held, perhaps, greater power than any other member of her family. Both the Merman and Island worlds buzzed with the recent revelation that Ale was a major inheritor in the estates of the late Ryan and Elina Wang. And Ale had been named guardian of the Wangs' only daughter, Scudi. Nobody had yet put a number on the size of the Wang estate, but the senior director of Merman Mercantile had probably been the wealthiest man on Pandora. Elina Wang, surviving her husband by less than a year, had not lived long enough to make serious changes in the Wang holdings. So there was Kareen Ale, beautiful and powerful and with the right words for any occasion.

"Delighted to have you with us, Islander Bushka." How warm and inviting she had sounded.

She was just being polite … diplomatic.

Another burst of activity rippled through the workers at the console in 'Sonde Control. The screen showing the surface emitted a series of brilliant flickers and the view was replaced by the face of Simone Rocksack, the Chaplain/Psychiatrist. The background revealed that she spoke from her quarters at the center of Vashon far away on the surface.

"I greet you in the name of Ship."

A barely suppressed snort came from Gallow.

Bushka noted a shudder pass through the man's classic body at sight of the C/P. Bushka, accustomed to Islander variations, had never made note of Rocksack's appearance. Now, however, he saw her through Gallow's eyes. Rocksack's silvery hair flared in a wild mane from the top of her almost perfectly round head. Her albino eyes projected at the tips of small protuberances on her brows. Her mouth, barely visible under a flap of gray skin, was a small red slit abandoned without a chin. A sharp angle of flesh went directly back from beneath her mouth to her thick neck.

"Let us pray," the C/P said. "This prayer I offered just a few minutes ago in the presence of Vata. I repeat it now." She cleared her throat. "Ship, by whose omnipotence we were cast upon Pandora's endless waters, grant us forgiveness from Original Sin. Grant us …"

Bushka tuned her out. He had heard this prayer, in one version or another, many times. Doubtless his companions had heard it, too. The Mermen observers fidgeted at their stations and looked bored.

Original Sin!

Bushka's historical studies had made him a questioner of tradition. Mermen, he had discovered, thought Original Sin referred to the killing of Pandora's sentient kelp. It was their penance that they must rediscover the kelp in their own genes and fill the sea once more with submerged jungles of gigantic stems and fronds. Not sentient, this time, however. Merely kelp … and controlled by Mermen.

The fanatical WorShipers of Guemes Island, on the other hand, insisted that Original Sin came when humankind abandoned WorShip. Most Islanders, though, followed the C/P's lead: Original Sin was that line of bioengineering chosen by Jesus Lewis, the long-dead mastermind behind today's variations in the human norm. Lewis had created the Clones and "selected others re-formed to fit them for survival on Pandora."

Bushka shook his head as the C/P's voice droned on. *Who is surviving best on Pandora?* he asked himself. *Mermen. Normal humans.*

At least ten times as many Mermen as Islanders survived on Pandora. It was a simple function of available living space. Under the sea, cushioned from Pandora's vagaries, there was a far greater volume of living space than on Pandora's turbulent, dangerous surface.

"Into Ship's realm I commend you," the C/P said. "Let the blessing of Ship accompany this venture. Let Ship know that we mean no blasphemy by intruding ourselves into the heavens. Let this be a gesture that brings us closer to Ship."

The C/P's face vanished from the screen, replaced by a close-up of the launch tube's base. Telltales on the tube tipped left to a slow current.

At the console to Bushka's left, the launch director said: "Condition green."

From the prelaunch briefing, Bushka knew this meant they were ready to release the 'sonde. He glanced at another of the screens, a view transmitted down a communications cable from a gyro-stabilized platform on the surface. White froth whipped the tops of long swells up there. Bushka's practiced eye said it was a forty-klick wind, practically a calm on Pandora. The 'sonde would drift fast when it broached but it would climb fast, too, and the upper atmosphere, for a change, showed breaks in the clouds, with one of Pandora's two suns tipping the cloud edges a glowing silver.

The launch director leaned forward to study an instrument.

"Forty seconds," he said.

Bushka moved forward, giving himself a better view of the instruments and the launch director. The man had been introduced as Dark Panille—"'Shadow' to my friends." No overt rejection there; just a touch of the specialist's resentment that observers could be brought into his working space without his permission. Bushka's Mute-sensitive senses had detected immediately that Panille carried kelp genes, but was fortunate by Pandoran standards because he was not hairless. Panille wore his long black hair in a single braid—"a family style," he had said in answer to Bushka's question.

Panille displayed a countenance distinctly Merman-normal. The kelp telltale lay chiefly in his dark skin with its unmistakable undertone of green. He had a narrow, rather sharp-featured face with high planes on both his cheeks and his nose. Panille's large brown eyes looked out with a deep sense of intelligence beneath straight brows. The mouth was set in a straight line to match the brows and his lower lip was fuller than the upper. A deep crease rolled from beneath his lips to the cleft of a narrow, well-defined chin. Panille's body was compact, with the smooth muscles common to Mermen who lived much in the sea.

The name Panille had aroused a historian's interest in Bushka. Panille's ancestry had been instrumental in human survival during the Clone Wars and after the departure of Ship. It was a famous name in the Histories.

"Launch!" Panille said.

Bushka glanced out the plaz beside him. The launch tube climbed beyond his vision through green water with a backdrop of sparsely planted kelp—thick red-brown trunks with glistening highlights at odd intervals. The highlights wavered and blinked as though in agitation. Bushka turned his attention to the screens, expecting something spectacular. The display on which the others focused showed only the slow upward drift of the LTA within the tube. Brilliant lights in the tube wall marked the ascent. The wrinkled bag of the LTA expanded as it lifted, smoothing finally in an orange expanse of the fabric that contained the hydrogen.

"There!" Ale spoke in a sighing voice as the 'sonde cleared the top of the tube. It drifted slantwise in a sea current, followed by a camera mounted on a Merman sub.

"Test key monitors," Panille said.

A large screen at the center of the console shifted from a tracking view to a transmission from the 'sonde package trailing beneath the hydrogen bag. The screen showed a slanted green-tinged view of the sea bottom—thin plantations of kelp, a rocky outcrop. They dimmed away into murkiness as Bushka watched. A screen at the upper right of the console shifted to the surface platform's camera, a gyro-stabilized float. The camera swept to the left in a dizzying arc, then settled on an expanse of wind-frothed swells.

A pain in his chest told Bushka that he was holding his breath, waiting for the LTA to break the surface. He exhaled and took a deep breath. *There!* A bubble lifted on the ocean surface and did not break. Wind flattened the near side of the bag. It lifted free of the water, receding fast as the 'sonde package cleared. The surface camera tracked it—showing an orange blossom floating in a blue bowl of sky. The view zoomed in to the dangling package, from which water still dripped in wind-driven spray.

Bushka looked to the center screen, the transmission from the 'sonde. It showed the sea beneath the LTA, an oddly flattened scene with little sense of the heaving waves from which the LTA had recently emerged.

Is this all? Bushka wondered.

He felt let down. He rubbed his thick neck, feeling the nervous perspiration there. A surreptitious glance at the two Merman observers showed them chatting quietly, with only an occasional glance at the screens and the plaz porthole that revealed Mermen already cleaning up after the launch.

Frustration and jealousy warred for dominance in Bushka. He stared at the console where Panille was giving low-voiced orders to his operators. How rich these Mermen were! Bushka thought of the crude organic computers with which Islanders contended, the stench of the Islands, the crowding and the life-protecting watch that had to be kept on every tiny bit of energy. Islanders paupered themselves for a few radios, satellite navigation receivers and sonar. And just look at this 'Sonde Control! So casually rich. If Islanders could afford such riches, Bushka knew the possessions would be kept secret. Display of wealth set people apart in a society that depended ultimately on singleness of all efforts. Islanders believed tools were to be used. Ownership was acknowledged, but a tool left idle could be picked up for use by anyone … anytime.

"There's a willy-nilly," Gallow said.

Bushka bridled. He knew Mermen called Islands "willy-nillys." Islands drifted unguided, and this was the Merman way of sneering at such uncontrolled wandering.

"That's Vashon," Ale said.

Bushka nodded. There was no mistaking his home Island. The organic floating metropolis had a distinctive shape known to all of its inhabitants—Vashon, largest of all Pandora's Islands.

"Willy-nilly," Gallow repeated. "I should imagine they don't know where they are half the time."

"You're not being very polite to our guest, GeLaar," Ale said.

"The truth is often impolite," Gallow said. He directed an empty smile at Bushka. "I've noticed that Islanders have few goals, that they're not very concerned about 'getting there.'"

He's right, damn him, Bushka thought. The drifting pattern had seated itself deeply in the Islander psyche.

When Bushka did not respond, Ale spoke defensively: "Islanders are necessarily more weather-oriented, more tuned to the horizon. That should not be surprising." She glanced questioningly at Bushka. "All people are shaped by their surroundings. Isn't that true, Islander Bushka?"

"Islanders believe the *manner* of our passage is just as important as *where* we are," Bushka said. He knew his response sounded weak. He turned toward the screens. Two of them now showed transmissions from the 'sonde. One pointed backward to the stabilized camera platform on the surface. It showed the platform being withdrawn into the safety of the calm undersea. The other 'sonde view tracked the drift path. Full in this view lay the bulk of Vashon. Bushka swallowed as he stared at his home Island. He had never before seen this view of it.

A glance at the altitude repeater below the screen said the view was from eighty thousand meters. The amplified image almost filled the screen. Grid lines superimposed on the screen gave the Island's long dimension at nearly thirty klicks and slightly less than that across. Vashon was a gigantic oval drifter with irregular edges. Bushka identified the bay indentation where fishboats and subs docked. Only a few of the boats in Vashon's fleet could be seen in the protected waters.

"What's its population?" Gallow asked.

"About six hundred thousand, I believe," Ale said.

Bushka scowled, thinking of the crowded conditions this number represented, comparing it with the spaciousness of Merman habitats. Vashon squeezed more than two thousand people into every square klick … a space more correctly measured in cubic terms. Cubbies were stacked on cubbies high above the water and deep beneath it. And some of the smaller Islands were even more condensed, a crowding that had to be experienced to be believed. Space opened on them only when they began to run out of energy—dead space. Uninhabitable. Like people, organics rotted when they died. A dead Island was just a gigantic floating carcass. And this had happened many times.

"I could not tolerate such crowding," Gallow said. "I could only leave."

"It isn't all bad!" Bushka blurted. "We may live close but we help each other."

"I should certainly hope so!" Gallow snorted. He turned until he was facing Bushka. "What is your personal background, Bushka?"

Bushka stared at him, momentarily affronted. This was not an Islander question. Islanders *knew* the backgrounds of their friends and acquaintances, but the rules of privacy seldom permitted probing.

"Your working background," Gallow persisted.

Ale put a hand on Gallow's arm. "To an Islander, such questions are usually impolite," she said.

"It's all right," Bushka said. "When I got old enough, *Merman* Gallow, I was a wave–watcher."

"A sort of lookout to warn of wavewalls," Ale explained.

"I know the term," Gallow said. "And after that?"

"Well … I had good eyes and a good sense of distance, so I did my time as a driftwatch and later in the subs … then, as I showed navigational ability, they trained me as a timekeeper."

"Timekeeper, yes," Gallow said. "You're the ones who dead-reckon an Island's position. Not very accurate, I'm told."

"Accurate enough," Bushka said.

Gallow chuckled. "Is it true, Islander Bushka, that you people think we Mermen stole the kelp's soul?"

"GeLaar!" Ale snapped.

"No, let him answer," Gallow said. "I've been hearing recently about the fundamentalist beliefs of Islands such as Guemes."

"You're impossible, GeLaar!" Ale said.

"I have an insatiable curiosity," Gallow said. "What about it, Bushka?"

Bushka knew he had to answer but his voice was dismayingly loud when he responded. "Many Islanders believe Ship will return to forgive us."

"And when will that be?" Gallow asked.

"When we regain the Collective Consciousness!"

"Ahhhh, the old Transition Stories," Gallow sneered. "But do you believe this?"

"My hobby is history," Bushka said. "I believe something important happened to human consciousness during the Clone Wars."

"Hobby?" Gallow asked.

"Historian is not a fully accredited Islander job," Ale explained. "Superfluous."

"I see. Do go on, Bushka."

Bushka clenched his fists and fought down his anger. Gallow was more than self-important … he was truly important … vital to Bushka's hopes.

"I don't believe we stole the kelp's soul," Bushka said.

"Good for you!" Gallow really smiled this time.

"But I do believe," Bushka added, "that our ancestors, possibly with kelp assistance, glimpsed a different kind of consciousness … a momentary linkage between all of the minds alive at that time."

Gallow passed a hand across his mouth, an oddly furtive gesture. "The accounts appear to agree," he said. "But can they be trusted?"

"There's no doubt we have kelp genes in the human gene pool," Bushka said. He glanced across the control room at Panille, who was watching him intently.

"And who knows what may happen if we revive the kelp to consciousness, eh?" Gallow asked.

"Something like that," Bushka agreed.

"Why do you think Ship abandoned us here?"

"GeLaar, please!" Ale interrupted.

"Let him answer," Gallow said. "This Islander has an active mind. He may be someone we need."

Bushka tried to swallow in a suddenly dry throat. Was this all a test? Was Gallow actually screening him for entry into Merman society?

"I was hoping …" Again, Bushka tried to swallow. "I mean, as long as I'm down here anyway … I was hoping I might gain access to the material Mermen recovered from the old Redoubt. Perhaps the answer to your question …" He broke off.

An abrupt silence settled over the room.

Ale and Gallow exchanged an oddly veiled look.

"How interesting," Gallow said.

"I'm told," Bushka said, "that when you recovered the Redoubt's data base … I mean …" He coughed.

"Our historians work full-time," Gallow said. "After the Disaster, everything, including the material from the Redoubt, was subjected to exhaustive analysis."

"I would still like to see the material," Bushka said. He cursed himself silently. His voice sounded so plaintive.

"Tell me, Bushka," Gallow said, "what would be your response if this material revealed that Ship was an artifact made by human beings and not God at all?"

Bushka pursed his lips. "The Artifact Heresy? Hasn't that been …"

"You haven't answered my question," Gallow said.

"I would have to see the material and judge for myself," Bushka said. He held himself quite still. No Islander had ever been granted access to Redoubt data. But what Gallow hinted … explosive!

"I should be most interested to hear what an Islander historian has to say about the Redoubt accounts," Gallow said. He glanced at Ale. "Do you see any reason why we shouldn't grant his request, Kareen?"

She shrugged and turned away, an expression on her face that Bushka could not interpret. *Disgust?*

Gallow directed that measuring smile toward Bushka. "I quite understand that the Redoubt has mystical implications for Islanders. I hesitate to feed superstitions."

Mystical? Bushka thought. Land that once had protruded from the sea. A place built on a continent, a mass of exposed land that did not drift, the last inundated in the Disaster. Mystical? Was Gallow merely toying with him?

"I'm a qualified historian," Bushka said.

"But you said hobby …" Gallow shook his head.

"Was everything recovered intact from the Redoubt?" Bushka ventured.

"It was sealed off," Ale said, turning once more to face Bushka. "Our ancestors put an air-bell on it before cutting through the plasteel."

"Everything was found just as it was left when they abandoned the place," Gallow said.

"Then it's true," Bushka breathed.

"But would you reinforce Islander superstitions?" Gallow insisted.

Bushka drew himself up stiffly. "I am a scientist. I would reinforce nothing but the truth."

"Why this sudden interest in the Redoubt?" Ale asked.

"Sudden?" Bushka stared at her in amazement. "We've always wanted to share in the Redoubt's data base. The people who left it there were our ancestors, too."

"In a manner of speaking," Gallow said.

Bushka felt the hot flush of blood in his cheeks. Most Mermen believed that only Clones and mutants had populated the drifting Islands. Did Gallow really accept that nonsense?

"Perhaps I should've said why the *renewed* interest?" Ale corrected herself.

"We've heard stories, you see, about the Guemes Movement," Gallow said.

Bushka nodded. WorShip was, indeed, on the increase among Islanders.

"There have been reports of unidentified things seen in the sky," Bushka said. "Some believe that Ship already has returned and is concealed from us in space."

"Do you believe this?" Gallow asked.

"It's possible," Bushka admitted. "All I really know for certain is that the C/P is kept busy examining people who claim to have seen visions."

Gallow chuckled. "Oh, my!"

Bushka once more felt frustration. They were toying with him! This was all a cruel Merman game! "What is so amusing?" he demanded.

"GeLaar, stop this!" Ale said.

Gallow held up an admonitory hand. "Kareen, look with care upon Islander Bushka. Could he not pass as one of us?"

Ale swept a swift glance across Bushka's face and returned her attention to Gallow. "What're you doing, GeLaar?"

Bushka inhaled deeply and held his breath.

Gallow studied Bushka a moment, then: "What would be your response, Bushka, if I were to offer you a place in Merman society?"

Bushka exhaled slowly, inhaled. "I ... I would accept. Gratefully, of course."

"Of course," Gallow echoed. He smiled at Ale. "Then, since Bushka will be one of us, there's no harm in telling him what amuses me."

"It's on your head, GeLaar," Ale said.

A movement at the 'Sonde Control console caught Bushka's attention. Panille was no longer looking at him, but the set of his shoulders told Bushka the man was listening intently. Ship save them! Was the Artifact Heresy true, after all? Was that the great Merman secret?

"These *visions* causing so much trouble for our beloved C/P," Gallow said. "They are Merman rockets, Bushka."

Bushka opened his mouth and closed it without speaking. "Ship was not God, is not God," Gallow said. "The Redoubt records ..."

"Are open to several interpretations," Ale said.

"Only to fools!" Gallow snapped. "We are sending up rockets, Bushka, because we are preparing to recover the hyb tanks from orbit. Ship was an artifact made by our ancestors. Other artifacts and *things* have been left in space for us to recover."

The matter-of-fact way Gallow said this made Bushka catch his breath. Stories about the mysterious hyb tanks permeated Islander society. What might be stored in those containers that orbited Pandora? Recovering those tanks, and really seeing what they contained, was worth anything—even destruction of the Ship-God belief that sustained so many people.

"You are shocked," Gallow said.

"I'm ... I'm awed," Bushka replied.

"We were all raised on the Transition Stories." Gallow pointed upward. "Life awaits us up there."

Bushka nodded. "The tanks are supposed to contain countless life forms from ... from Earth."

"Fish, animals, plants," Gallow said. "And even some humans." He grinned. "Normal humans." He waved a hand to encompass the occupants of 'Sonde Control. "Like us."

Bushka inhaled a trembling breath. Yes, the historical accounts said the hyb tanks held humans who had never been touched by the bioengineering machinations of Jesus Lewis. There would be people in those tanks who had gone to sleep in another star system, who had no idea of this nightmare world that awaited their awakening.

"And now you know," Gallow said.

Bushka cleared his throat. "We never suspected. I mean ... the C/P has never said a word about ..."

"The C/P does not know of this," Ale said. There was a warning note in her voice.

Bushka glanced at the plaz porthole with its view of the LTA tube. "She knows about that, of course," Ale said.

"An innocuous thing," Gallow said.

"There has been no blessing of our rockets," Ale said.

Bushka continued to stare out the porthole. He had never counted himself a deeply religious person, but these Merman revelations left him profoundly disturbed. Ale obviously doubted Gallow's interpretation of the Redoubt material, but still ... a blessing would be only common sense ... just in case ...

"What is your response, Merman Bushka?" Gallow asked.

Merman Bushka!

Bushka turned a wide-eyed stare on Gallow, who obviously awaited an answer to a question. A question. What had he asked? Bushka was a moment recovering the man's words.

"My response ... yes. The Islanders ... I mean, about these rockets. The Islanders ... shouldn't they be told?"

"They?" Gallow laughed, a deep amusement that shook his beautiful body. "You see, Kareen? Already his former compatriots are 'they.'"

Chapter 5

The touch of the infant teaches birth, and our hands are witness to the lesson.
—Kerro Panille, *The Histories*

VATA DID not experience true consciousness. She skirted the shadow-edges of awareness. Memories flitted through her neurons like tendrils from the kelp. Sometimes she dreamed kelp dreams. These dreams often included a wondrous hatch of hylighters—spore-filled gasbags that had died when the original kelp died. Tears mixed with her nutrient bath as she dreamed such things, tears for the fate of those huge sky-bound globes tacking across the evening breezes of a million years. Her dream hylighters clutched their ballast rocks in their two longest tentacles and Vata felt the comforting texture of rock hugged close.

Thoughts themselves were like hylighters to her, or silken threads blowing in the dark of her mind. Sometimes she followed the awareness of Duque, who floated beside her, sensing events within his thoughts. Time and again, she re-experienced through him that terrible night when the gravitational wrenching of Pandora's two suns destroyed the last human foothold on the planet's fragile land. Duque repeatedly let his thoughts plunge into that experience. And Vata, linked to the fearful mutant like Mermen diving partners on the same safety line, was forced to recreate dreams that soothed and calmed Duque's terrors.

"Duque escaped," she muttered in his mind, "Duque was taken away onto the sea where Hali Ekel tended his burns."

Duque would snuffle and whimper. Had Vata been conscious, she would have heard with her own ears, because Vata and Duque shared the same life support at the center of Vashon. Vata lay mostly submerged in nutrient, a monstrous mound of pink and blue flesh with definite human female characteristics. Enormous breasts with gigantic pink nipples lifted from the dark nutrient like twin mountains from a brown sea. Duque drifted beside her, a satellite, her familiar dangling in the endless mental vacuum.

For generations now, the two of them had been nurtured and reverenced in Vashon's central complex—home of the Chaplain/Psychiatrist and the Committee on Vital Forms, Merman and Islander guards kept watch on the pair under the command of the C/P. It was a ritualized observation, which, in time, eroded the awe that Pandorans learned early from the reactions of their parents.

"The two of them there like that. They'll always be there. They're our last link with Ship. As long as they live, Ship is with us. It's WorShip keeps them alive so long."

Although Duque occasionally knuckled an eye into glaring wakefulness and watched his guardians in the gloomy surroundings of the living pool that confined them, Vata's responses never lifted to consciousness. She breathed. Her great body, responding to the kelp half of her genetic inheritance, absorbed energy from the nutrient solution that washed against her skin. Analysis of the nutrient betrayed traces of human waste products, which were removed by the sucker mouths of blind scrubberfish. Occasionally, Vata would snort and an arm would lift in the nutrient like a leviathan rising from its depths before settling once more into the murk. Her hair continued to grow until it spread like kelp across the nutrient surface, tangling over the hairless skin of Duque and impeding the scrubberfish. The C/P would come into the chamber then and, with a reverence touched by a certain amount of cupidity, would clip Vata's locks. The strands were washed and separated to be blessed and sold in short lengths as indulgences. Even Mermen bought them. Sale of Vatahair had been the major source of C/P income for many generations.

Duque, more aware than any other human of his curious link with Vata, puzzled over the connection when Vata's intrusions left him with thinking time of his own. Sometimes he would speak of this to his guardians, but when Duque spoke there was always a flurry of activity, the summoning of the C/P, and a different kind of watchfulness from the security.

"She lives me," he said once, and this became a token label inscribed on the Vatahair containers.

In these speaking times, the C/P would try prepared questions, sometimes booming them at Duque, sometimes asking in a low and reverential voice.

"Do you speak for Vata, Duque?"

"I speak."

That was all they ever got from him on this question. Since it was known that Duque was one of the hundred or so original mutants who had been conceived with kelp intervention and thus bore kelp genes, they would sometimes ask him about the kelp that had once ruled Pandora's now-endless sea.

"Do you have memory of the kelp, Duque?"

"Avata," Duque corrected. "I am the rock."

Interminable arguments came out of this answer. Avata had been the kelp's name for itself. The reference to rock gave scholars and theologians room for speculation.

"He must mean that his consciousness exists at the bottom of the sea where the kelp lives."

"No! Remember how the kelp always clung to a rock, lifting its tendrils to the sunlight? And the hylighters used rock for ballast ..."

"You're all wrong. He's Vata's grip on life. He's Vata's rock."

And there was always someone who would harken back to WorShip and the stories of that distant planet where someone calling himself Peter had given the same answer Duque had given.

Nothing was ever solved by such arguments, but the questioning continued whenever Duque showed signs of wakefulness.

"How is it that you and Vata do not die, Duque?"

"We wait."

"For what do you wait?"

"No answer."

This recurrent response precipitated several crises until the C/P of that time issued an order that Duque's answers could only be broadcast by permission of the C/P. This didn't stop the quiet whispering and the rumors, of course, but it relegated everything except the C/P's official version to the role of mystical heresy. It was a question no C/P had asked for two generations now. Current interest centered much more on the kelp that Mermen spread far and wide in Pandora's planetary sea. The kelp was thick and healthy, but showed no signs of acquiring consciousness.

As the great Islands drifted they were seldom out of sight of a horizon touched by the oily green flatness of a kelp bed. Everyone said it was a good thing. Kelp formed nurseries for fish and everyone could see there were more fish these days, though they weren't always easy to catch. You couldn't use a net amongst the kelp. Baited lines tangled in the huge fronds and were lost. Even the dumb muree had learned to retreat into kelp sanctuary at the approach of fishermen.

There was also the recurrent question of Ship, Ship who was God and who had left humankind on Pandora.

"Why did Ship abandon us here, Duque?"

All Duque would ever say was: "Ask Ship."

Many a C/P had engaged in much silent prayer over that one. But Ship did not answer them. At least, not with any voice that they could hear.

It was a vexing question. Would Ship return? Ship had left the hyb tanks in orbit around Pandora. It was a strange orbit, seeming to defy the gravitational index for such things. There were those among Pandora's Mermen and Islanders who said Vata waited for the hyb tanks to be brought down, that she would awaken when this occurred.

No one doubted there was some link between Duque and Vata, so why not a link between Vata and the dormant life waiting up there in the tanks?

"How are you linked to Vata?" a C/P asked.

"How are you linked to me?" Duque responded.

This was duly recorded in the Book of Duque and more arguments ensued. It was noted, however, that whenever such questions were asked, Vata stirred. Sometimes grossly and sometimes with only the faintest movement over her vast flesh.

"It's like the safety line we use between divers down under," an astute Merman observed. "You can always find your partner."

Vata's tendril-awareness stirred to the linkage with genetic memories of mountain climbers. They were climbing, she and Duque. This she showed him many times. Her memories, shared with Duque, showed a spectacular world of the vertical that Islanders could barely imagine and holos did not do justice. Only, she did not think of herself as one of the climbers, or even think of herself at all. There was only the line, and the climbing.

Chapter 6

First, we had to develop a landless life-style; second, we preserved what technology and hardware we could salvage. Lewis left us with a team of bioengineers—both our curse and our most powerful legacy. We do not dare plunge our few precious children into a Stone Age.

—Hali Ekel, *The Journals*

WARD KEEL looked down from the high bench and surveyed the two young petitioners in front of him. The male was a large Merman with the tattoo of a criminal on his brow, a wine-red "E" for "Expatriate." This Merman could never return to the rich land under the sea and he knew the Islanders accepted him only for his stabilizing genes. Those genes had not stabilized this time. The Merman probably knew what the judgment would be. He patted a damp cloth nervously over his exposed skin.

The woman petitioner, his mate, was small and slender with pale blonde hair and two slight indentations where she should have had eyes. She wore a long blue sari and when she walked Keel did not hear steps, only a rasping scrape. She swayed from side to side and hummed to herself.

Why does this one have to be the first case of the morning? Keel wondered. It was a perverse fate. *This morning of all mornings!*

"Our child deserves to live!" the Merman said. His voice boomed in the chambers. The Committee on Vital Forms often heard such loud protestation but this time Keel felt that the volume was directed at the woman, telling her that her mate fought for them both.

As Chief Justice of the Committee it was too often Keel's lot to perform that unsavory stroke of the pen, to speak directly the unutterable fears of the petitioners themselves. Many times it was otherwise and then this chamber echoed the laughter of life. But today, in this case, there would be no laughter. Keel sighed. The Merman, even though a criminal by Merman ruling, made this matter politically sensitive. Mermen were jealous of the births that they called "normal," and they monitored every topside birth involving Merman parentage.

"We have studied your petition with great care," Keel said. He glanced left and right at his fellow Committee members. They sat impassively, attention elsewhere—on the great curve of bubbly ceiling, on the soft living deck, on the records stacked in front of them—everywhere but on the petitioners. The dirty work was being left to Ward Keel.

If they only knew, Keel thought. *A higher Committee on Vital Forms has today passed judgment on me … as it will pass judgment on them, eventually.* He felt a deep compassion for the petitioners in front of him but there was no denying the judgment.

"The Committee has determined that the subject"—*not "the child,"* he thought—"is merely a modified gastrula …"

"We want this child!" The man fisted the rail that separated him from the Committee's high bench. The security guardians at the rear of the chambers came to attention. The woman continued to hum and sway, not in time with the music that came from her lips.

Keel leafed through a stack of plaz records and pulled out a sheet thick with figures and graphs.

"The subject has been found to have a nuclear construction that harbors a reagent gene," he reported. "This construction insures that the cellular material will turn on itself, destroying its own cell walls …"

"Then let us have our child until that death," the man blurted. He swiped at his face with the damp cloth. "For the love of humanity, give us *that* much."

"Sir," Keel said, "for the love of humanity I cannot. We have determined that this construction is communicable should there be any major viral invasion of the subject …"

"Our *child!* Not a subject! Our *child!*"

"Enough!" Keel snapped. Security moved silently into the aisle behind the Merman. Keel tapped the bell beside him and all stirring in the chamber ceased. "We are sworn to protect human life, to perpetuate life forms that are not lethal deviants."

The Merman father stared upward, awed at the invocation of these terrible powers. Even his mate stopped her gentle swaying, but a faint hum still issued from her mouth.

Keel wanted to shout down at them, "I am dying, right here in front of you. *I am dying.*" But he bit back the impulse and decided that if he were going to give in to hysteria he'd do it in his own quarters.

Instead, he said, "We are empowered to carry out measures in the extreme to see that humankind survives this genetic mess we inherited from Jesus Lewis." He leaned back and steadied the shaking in his hands and voice. "We are in no way refreshed by a negative decision. Take your woman home. Care for her …"

"I want one …"

The bell rang again, cutting the man short.

Keel raised his voice: "Usher! See these people out. They will be given the usual priorities. Terminate the subject, retaining all materials as stated in Vital Form Orders, subparagraph B. Recess."

Keel arose and swept past the other Committee members without a glance at the rest of the chambers. The grunts and struggles of the heartsick Merman echoed and re-echoed down the corridors of Keel's anguished mind.

As soon as he was alone in his office, Keel unstoppered a small flask of boo and poured himself a stiff shot. He tossed it back, shuddered and caught his breath as the warm clear liquid eased into his bloodstream. He sat in the special chair at his desk then, eyes closed, and rested his long, thin neck against the molded supports that took the weight of his massive head.

He could not make a lethal decision as he had done this morning without recalling the moment when he, as an infant, had come before the Committee on Vital Forms. People said it was not possible for him to remember that scene, but he did remember it—not in bits and sketches, but in its entirety. His memory went back into the womb, through a calm birth into a gloomy delivery room and the glad awakening at his mother's breast. And he remembered the judgment of the Committee. They had been worried about the size of his head and the length of his thin neck. Would prosthetics compensate? He had understood the words, too. There was language in him from some genetic well and although he could not speak until growth caught up with what had been born in him, he knew those words.

"This infant is unique," that old Chief Justice had said, reading from the medical report. "His intestines must have periodic implantation of a remora to supply missing bile and enzyme factors."

The Chief Justice had looked down then, a giant behind that enormous and remote bench, and his gaze had fixed on the naked infant in its mother's arms.

"Legs, thick and stubby. Feet deformed—one-joint toes, six toes, six fingers. Torso overlong, waist pinched in. Face rather small in that …" the Justice cleared his throat, "enormous head." The Justice had looked at Keel's mother then, noting the extremely wide pelvis. Obvious anatomical questions had lain unspoken in the man's mind.

"In spite of these difficulties, this subject is not a lethal deviant." The words issuing from the Justice's mouth had all been in the medical report. Keel, when he came to the Committee as a member, fished out his own report, reading it with a detached curiosity.

"Face rather small …" These were the very words in the report, just as he remembered them. "Eyes, one brown and one blue." Keel smiled at the memory. His eyes—"one brown and one blue"—could peek around from the nearly squared edges of his temples, allowing him to look almost straight back without turning his head. His lashes were long and drooping. When he relaxed, they fuzzed his view of the world. Time had put smile wrinkles at the corners of his wide, thick-lipped mouth. And his flat nose, nearly a handsbreadth wide, had grown until it stopped just short of his mouth. The whole face, he knew from comparisons, was oddly pinched together, top to bottom, as though put on his head as an afterthought. But those corner-placed eyes, they were the dominant feature—alert and wise.

They let me live because I looked alert, he thought.

This was a thing he, too, sought in the subjects brought before him. Brains. Intelligence. That was what humankind required to get them out of this mess. Brawn and dexterity, too, but these were useless without the intelligence to guide them.

Keel closed his eyes and sank his neck even deeper into the cushioned supports. The boo was having its desired effect. He never drank the stuff without thinking how strange it was that this should come from the deadly nerve runners that had terrified his ancestors in the pioneer days of Pandora when real land protruded above the sea.

"Worm hordes," the first observers had called them. The worm hordes attacked warm life and ate out every nerve cell, working their way to the succulent brain where they encysted their clutches of eggs. Even dashers feared them. Came the endless sea, though, and nerve runners retreated to a subsea vector whose fermentation by-product was boo—sedative, narcotic, "happy juice."

He fondled the small glass and took another sip.

The door behind him opened and a familiar footstep entered—familiar swish of garments, familiar smells. He didn't open his eyes, thinking what a singular mark of trust that was, even for an Islander.

Or an invitation, he thought.

The beginnings of a wry smile touched the corners of his mouth. He felt the tingling of the boo in his tongue and fingertips. Now in his toes.

Baring my neck for the axe?

There was always guilt after a negative decision. Always at least the unconscious desire for expiation. Well, it was all there in the Committee's orders, but he was not fool enough to retreat into that hoary old excuse: "I was just obeying orders."

"May I get you something, Justice?" The voice was that of his aide and sometimes-lover, Joy Marcoe.

"No, thank you," he murmured.

She touched his shoulder. "The Committee would like to reconvene in quarters at eleven hundred hours. Should I tell them you're too … ?"

"I'll be there." He kept his eyes closed and heard her start to leave. "Joy," he called, "have you ever thought how ironic it is that you, with your name, work for this Committee?"

She returned to his side and he felt her hand on his left arm. It was a trick of the boo that he felt the hand melt into his senses—more than a touch, she caressed a vital core of his being.

"Today is particularly hard," she said. "But you know how rare that is, anymore." She waited, he presumed, for his response. Then when none came: "I think Joy is a perfect name for this job. It reminds me of how much I want to make you happy."

He managed a weak smile and adjusted his head in the supports. He couldn't bring himself to tell her about his own medical reports—the final verdict. "You do bring me joy," he said. "Wake me at ten-forty-five."

She dimmed the light when she left.

The mobile device that supported his head began to irritate the base of his neck where it pressed into the chair's supports. He inserted a finger under the chair's cushions and adjusted one of the contraption's fastenings. Relief on his left side was transmitted to irritation on the right. He sighed and poured another short dash of boo.

When he lifted the slender glass, the dimmed overhead light shot blue-gray sparkles through the liquid. It looked cool, as refreshing as a supportive bath on a hot day when the double suns burned through the clouds.

What warmth the tiny glass contained! He marveled at the curve of his thin fingers around the stem. One fingernail peeled back where he had snagged it on his robe. Joy would clip and bind it when she returned, he knew. He did not doubt that she had noted it. This had happened often enough, though, that she knew it did not pain him.

His own reflection in the curvature of the glass caught his attention. The curve exaggerated the wide spacing of his eyes. The long lashes drooping almost to the bend of his cheeks receded into tiny points. He strained to focus on the glass so close in front of him. His nose was a giant thing. He brought the glass to his lips and the image fuzzed out, vanished.

Small wonder that Islanders avoid mirrors, he thought.

He had a fascination with his own reflection, though, and often caught himself staring at his features in shiny surfaces.

That such a distorted creature should be allowed to live! The long-ago judgment of that earlier Committee filled him with wonder. Did those

Committee members know that he would think and hurt and love? He felt that the often-shapeless blobs that appeared before his Committee bore kinship to all humanity if only they showed evidence of thought, love and the terribly human capacity to be hurt.

From some dim passageway beyond his doors or, perhaps, from somewhere deep in his own mind, the soft tones of a fine set of water-drums nestled him into his cushions and drowsed him away.

Half-dreams flickered in and out of his consciousness, becoming presently a particularly soothing full-dream of Joy Marcoe and himself rolling backward on her bed. Her robe fell open to the smooth softness of aroused flesh and Keel felt the unmistakable stirrings of his body—the body in the chair and the body in the dream. He knew it was a dream of the memory of their first exploratory sharing. His hand slipped beneath her robe and pulled the softness of her against him, stroking her back. That had been the moment when he discovered the secret of Joy's bulky clothes, the clothes that could not hide an occasional firm trim line of hips or thighs, the small strong arms. Joy cradled a third breast under her left armpit. In the dream of the memory, she giggled nervously as his wandering hand found the tiny nipple hardening between his fingers.

Mr. Justice.

It was Joy's voice, but it was wrong.

That was not what she said.

"Mr. Justice."

A hand shook his left arm. He felt the chair and the prosthetics, a pain where his neck joined the massive head.

"Ward, it's wake-up. The Committee meets in fifteen minutes." He blinked awake. Joy stood over him, smiling, her hand still on his arm.

"Nodded off," he said. He yawned behind his hand. "I was dreaming about you."

A distinctive flush darkened her cheeks. "Something nice, I hope."

He smiled. "How could a dream with you in it be anything but nice?"

The blush deepened and her gray eyes glittered.

"Flattery will get you anything, Mr. Justice." She patted his arm. "After Committee, you have a call to Kareen Ale. Her office said she would arrive here at thirteen-thirty. I told them you have a full appointment sheet through …"

"I'll see her," he said. He stood and steadied himself on the edge of his desk console. The boo always made him a little groggy at first recovery. Imagine the medics giving him their death sentence and then telling him to knock off the boo! *Avoid extremes, avoid anxiety.*

"Kareen Ale takes advantage of her position to presume on your good nature and waste your time," Joy said.

Keel didn't like the way Joy exaggerated the Merman ambassador's name: "ah-*lay*." True, it was a difficult name to carry through the cocktail parties of the diplomatic corps, but the woman had Keel's complete respect on the debating floor.

He was suddenly aware that Joy was leaving. "Joy!" he called. "Allow me to cook for you in quarters tonight."

Her back straightened in the doorway and when she turned to face him she smiled. "I'd like that very much. What time?"

"Nineteen hundred?"

She nodded once, firmly, and left. It was just the economy of movement and grace that endeared her to him. She was less than half his age, but she carried a wisdom about her that age ignored. He tried to remember how long it had been since he'd taken a full-time lover.

Twelve years? No, thirteen.

Joy made the wait that much more right in his mind. Her body was supple and completely hairless—something that excited him in ways he'd thought he'd forgotten.

He sighed, and tried to get his mind set for the coming meeting with the Committee.

Old farts, he thought. One corner of his mouth twisted up in spite of himself. *But they're pretty interesting old farts.*

The five Committee members were among the most powerful people on Vashon. Only one person rivaled Keel, with his position as Chief Justice—Simone Rocksack, the Chaplain/Psychiatrist, who commanded great popular support and provided a check on the power of the Committee. Simone could move things by inference and innuendo; Keel could order them done and they were done.

Keel realized, with some curiosity, that as well as he knew the Committee members, he always had trouble remembering their faces. Well … faces were not all that important. It was what lay behind the face that mattered. He touched a finger to his nose, to his distended forehead, and as though it were a magic gesture his hand called up a clear image of those other faces, those four old justices.

There was Alon, the youngest of them at sixty-seven. Alon Matts, Vashon's leading bioengineer for nearly thirty years.

Theodore Carp was the cynic of the group and, so Keel thought, aptly named. Others referred to Carp as "Fish Man," a product of both his appearance and his bearing. Carp *looked* fishlike. A sickly-pale, nearly translucent skin covered the long narrow face and blunt-fingered hands. The cuffs of his robe came nearly to the tips of his fingers and his hands appeared quite finlike at first glance. His lips were full and wide, and they never smiled. He had never been considered seriously for Chief Justice.

Not a political enough animal, Keel thought. *No matter how bad things get, you've got to smile sometime.* He shook his head and chuckled to himself. Maybe that should be one of the Committee's criteria for passing questionable subjects—the ability to smile, to laugh …

"Ward," a voice called, "I swear you'll daydream your life away."

He turned and saw the other two justices walking the hallway behind him. Had he passed them in the hatchway and not noticed? Possibly.

"Carolyn," he said, and nodded, "and Gwynn. Yes, with luck I'll daydream my life away. Are you refreshed after this morning's session?"

Carolyn Bluelove turned her eyeless face up to his and sighed. "A difficult morning," she said. "Clear-cut, of course, but difficult …"

"I don't see why you go through a hearing, Ward," Gwynn Erdsteppe said. "You just make yourself uncomfortable, it makes us *all* uncomfortable.

We shouldn't have to whip ourselves over something like that. Can't we channel the drama outside the chambers?"

"They have their right to be heard, and the right to hear something as irreversible as our decision from those who make it," he said. "Otherwise, what might we become? The power over life and death is an awesome one, and it should have all the checks against it that we can muster. That's one decision that should never be easy."

"So what are we?" Gwynn persisted.

"Gods," Carolyn snapped. She put her hand on Keel's arm and said, "Walk these two doddering old gods to chambers, will you, Mr. Justice?"

"Delighted," he said. They scuff-scuffed down the hallway, their bare feet hardly more than sighs on the soft deck.

Ahead of them, a team of slurry workers painted nutrient on the walls. This team used broad brushes and laid on vivid strokes of deep blue, yellow and green. In a week all the color would be absorbed and the walls returned to their hungry, gray-brown hue.

Gwynn positioned herself behind Keel and Carolyn. Her lumbering pace hurried them on. Keel was distracted from Carolyn's small talk by the constant lurch of Gwynn's hulk behind them.

"Do either of my fellow justices know why we're meeting just now?" he asked. "It must be something disturbing because Joy didn't reveal it when she told me about the appointment."

"That Merman this morning, he's appealed to the Chaplain/Psychiatrist," Gwynn snorted. "Why won't they leave it be?"

"Curious," Carolyn said.

It struck Keel as very curious. He had sat the bench for a full five years before a case had been appealed to the Chaplain/Psychiatrist. But this year …

"The C/P's just a figurehead," Gwynn said. "Why do they waste their time and ours on—"

"And hers," Carolyn interrupted. "It's a lot of work, being the emissary to the gods."

Keel shuffled quietly between them while they reopened the ages-old debate. He tuned it out, as he'd learned to do years ago. People filled his life too much to leave any time for gods. Especially now—this day when the life burning inside him had become doubly precious.

Eight cases appealed by the C/P in this season alone, he thought. *And all eight involved Mermen.*

The realization made him extremely interested in the afternoon meeting with Kareen Ale, which was to follow this appeals hearing.

The three justices entered the hatchway to their smaller chambers. It was an informational room—small, well-lit, the walls lined with books, tapes, holos and other communications equipment. Matts and the Fish Man were already watching Simone Rocksack's introductory remarks on the large viewscreen. She would, of course, use the Vashon intercom. The C/P seldom left her quarters near the tank that sustained Vata and Duque. The four protrusions that made up most of the C/P's face bent and waved as she talked. Her two eye protuberances were particularly active.

Keel and the others seated themselves quietly. Keel raised the back of his chair to ease the strain on his neck and its support.

"... and further, that they were not even allowed to view the child. Is that not somewhat harsh treatment from a Committee entrusted with sensitive care of our life forms?"

Carp was quick to respond. "It was a gastrula, Simone, purely and simply a lump of cells with a hole in it. There was nothing to be gained by bringing the creature into public view ..."

"The *creature's* parents hardly constitute a public viewing, Mr. Justice. And don't forget the association of *Creator* and *creature*. Lest you forget, sir, I am a Chaplain/*Psychiatrist*. While you may have certain prejudices regarding my religious role, I assure you that my preparation as a psychiatrist is most thorough. When you denied that young couple the sight of their offspring, you denied them a good-bye, a closure, a finality that would help them grieve and get on with their lives. Now there will be counseling, tears and nightmares far beyond the normal scope of mourning."

Gwynn picked up at the C/P's first pause.

"This doesn't sound like an appeal for the life form in question. Since that is the express function of an appeal, I must ask your intentions here. Is it possible that you're simply trying to go on record as establishing a political platform out of the appeals process?"

The nodules on the C/P's face retracted as if struck, then slowly re-emerged at the ends of their long stalks.

A good psychiatrist has a face you can't read, Keel thought. *Simone certainly fills the bill.*

The C/P's voice came on again in its wet, slurpy fashion. "I defer to the decision of the Chief Justice in this matter."

Keel snapped fully awake. This was certainly an unlikely turn of argument—if it was argument. He cleared his throat and gave his full attention to the screen. Those four nodules seemed to hunt out the gaze of both his eyes and fix on his mouth at the same time. He cleared his throat again.

"Your Eminence," he said, "it is clear that we did not proceed with this case in the most sensitive fashion. I speak for the Committee when I voice my appreciation for your candid appraisal of the matter. Sometimes, in the anguish of our task, we lose sight of the difficulty imposed upon others. Your censure, for lack of a better word, is noted and will be acted on. However, Justice Erdsteppe's point is well made. You dilute the appeals process by bringing before us matters that do not, in fact, constitute an appeal on behalf of a condemned lethal deviant. Do you wish to proceed with such an appeal in this case?"

There was a pause from the viewscreen, then a barely audible sigh. "No, Mr. Justice, I do not. I have seen the reports and, in this case, I concur with your findings."

Keel heard the low grumbling from Carp and Gwynn beside him.

"Perhaps we should meet informally and discuss these matters," he said. "Would that be to your liking, Your Eminence?"

The head nodded slightly, and the voice slurped, "Yes. Yes, that would be most helpful. I will make arrangements through our offices. Thank you for your time, Committee."

The screen went blank before Keel could respond. Amid the mutterings of his colleagues he found himself wondering, *What the devil is she up to?* He knew that it must deal with the Mermen somehow, and the itch between his shoulder blades told him it was more serious than this conversation suggested.

We'll find out how serious soon enough, he thought. *If it's bad, the appointment will be for me alone.*

Ward Keel had done a little psychiatric study himself and he was not one to waste a skill. He resolved to be particularly attentive to detail when he met later with Kareen Ale. The C/P's intrusion coincided with the Merman ambassador's appointment too well—surely more than coincidence.

Actually, I think I'll cancel the appointment, he thought, *and make a few calls. This meeting had best be on my time, on my turf.*

Chapter 7

> *How cruel of Ship to leave everything we need circling out of reach above us while this terrible planet kills us off one by one. Six births last nightside, all mutant. Two survive.*
>
> —Hali Ekel, *The Journals*

FEELING THE warmth of the suns through the open hatch, Iz Bushka rubbed the back of his neck and shook himself. It was as close as he could let his body get to a shudder in the presence of Gallow and the other men of this Merman submersible crew.

Pride made me accept Gallow's invitation, Bushka decided. *Pride and curiosity—food for the ego.* He thought it odd that someone, even someone as egocentric as Gallow, would want a "personal historian." Bushka felt the need for caution all around him.

The Merman sub they occupied was familiar enough. He had visited aboard Merman subs before when they docked at Vashon. They were strange craft, all of their equipment hard and unforgiving—dials and handles and glowing instruments. As a historian, Bushka knew these Merman craft were not much different from those constructed by Pandora's first colonists before the infamous Time of Madness that some called the "Night of Fire."

"Quite a bit different from your Islander subs, eh?" Gallow asked.

"Different, yes," Bushka said, "but similar enough that I could run it."

Gallow cocked an eyebrow, as if measuring Bushka for a different suit.

"I was on one of your Islander subs once," Gallow said. "They stink."

Bushka had to admit the organics that formed and powered Islander submersibles did give off a certain odor reminiscent of sewage. It was the nutrient, of course.

Gallow sat at the sub's controls to one side and ahead of Bushka, holding the craft steady on the surface. The space around them was larger than anything Bushka had seen in an Islander sub. But he had to avoid bumping into hard edges. Bushka had already collected bruises from hatch rims, seat arms and the handles of compartment doors.

The sea was producing a long swell today, gentle by Islander standards. Just a little wash and slap against the hull.

They had not been long into this "little excursion," as Gallow called it, before Bushka began to suspect that he was in actual danger—ultimate danger. He had the persistent feeling that these people would kill him if he didn't measure up. And it was left to him to find out what "measuring up" might mean.

Gallow was planning some kind of revolution against the Merman government, that much was clear from the idle chatter. "The Movement," he called it. Gallow and his "Green Dashers" and his Launch Base One. "All mine," he said. It was so explicit and unmistakable that Bushka felt the ages-old fear that crept up on those who'd dared record history while it happened all down the ages. It had a sweaty side.

Gallow and his men were revealed as conspirators who had talked too much in the presence of an ex-Islander.

Why did they do that?

It was not because they truly considered him one of their own—too much innuendo indicated otherwise. And they didn't know him well enough to trust him, even as Gallow's personal historian. Bushka was sure of that. The answer lay there, obvious to someone of Bushka's training—all of that historical precedent upon which to draw.

They did it to trap me.

The rest of it was just as obvious. If he were implicated in Gallow's scheme—whatever that turned out to be—then he would be Gallow's man forever because it would be the only place he could go. Gallow did indeed want a captive historian in his service, and maybe more. He wanted to go down in history on his own terms. He wanted to *be* history. Gallow had made it clear that he had researched Bushka—"the best Islander historian."

Young and lacking some practical experience, that was how Gallow rated him, Bushka realized. Something to be molded. And there was the terrifying attractiveness of that other appeal.

"*We* are the true humans," Gallow said.

And point by point, he had compared Bushka's appearance to the *norm*, concluding: "You're one of us. You're not a Mute."

One of us. There was power in that … particularly to an Islander, and particularly if Gallow's conspiracy succeeded.

But I'm a writer, Bushka reminded himself. *I'm not some romantic character in an adventure story.* History had taught him how dangerous it was for writers to mix themselves up with their characters—or historians with their subjects.

The sub took an erratic motion and Bushka knew someone must be undogging the exterior hatch.

Gallow asked, "Are you sure that you could run this sub?"

"Of course. The controls are obvious."

"Are they, really?"

"I watched you. Islander subs have some organic equivalents. And I do have a master's rating, Gallow."

"GeLaar, please," Gallow said. He unstrapped himself from the pilot's seat, stood up and moved aside. "We are companions, Iz. Companions use first names."

Bushka slid into the pilot's seat at Gallow's gesture and scanned the controls. He pointed to them one by one, calling out their functions to Gallow: "Trim, ballast, propulsion, forward-reverse and throttles, fuel mixture, hydrogen conversion control, humidity injector and atmospheric control—the meters and gauges are self-explanatory. More?"

"Very good, Iz," Gallow said. "You are even more of a jewel than I had hoped. Strap in. You are now our pilot."

Realizing he had been drawn even further into Gallow's conspiracy, Bushka obeyed. The flutter in his stomach increased noticeably.

Again, the sub moved erratically. Bushka flicked a switch and focused a sensor above the exterior hatch. The screen above him showed Tso Zent and behind him, the scarred face of Gulf Nakano. Those two were living examples of deceptive looks. Zent had been introduced as Gallow's primary strategist "and of course, my chief assassin."

Bushka had stared at the chief assassin, taken aback by the title. Zent was smooth-skinned and schoolboy-innocent in appearance, until you saw the hard antagonism in his small brown eyes. The wrinkle-free flesh had that soft deceptiveness of someone powerfully muscled by much swimming. An airfish scar puckered at his neck. Zent was one of those Mermen who preferred the fish to the air tanks—an interesting insight.

Then there was Nakano—a giant with hulking shoulders and arms as thick as some human torsos, his face twisted and scarred by burns from a Merman rocket misfiring. Gallow had already told Bushka the story twice, and Bushka got the impression that he'd hear it again. Nakano allowed a few wispy beard hairs to grow from the tip of his scarred chin; otherwise he was hairless, the burn scars prominent on his scalp, neck and shoulders.

"I saved his life," Gallow had said, speaking in Nakano's presence as though the man were not there. "He will do anything for me."

But Bushka had found evidence of human warmth in Nakano—a hand outstretched to protect the new *companion* from falling. There was even a sense of humor.

"We measure sub experience by counting bruises," Nakano had said, smiling shyly. His voice was husky and a bit slurred.

There was certainly no warmth or humor in Zent.

"Writers are dangerous," he'd said when Gallow explained Bushka's function. "They speak out of turn."

"Writing history while it happens is always dangerous business," Gallow agreed. "But no one else will see what Iz writes until *we* are ready—that's an advantage."

It had been at this point that Bushka fully realized the peril of his position. They had been in the sub, seventy klicks from the Merman base, anchored on the fringes of a huge kelp bed. Both Gallow and Zent had that irritating habit of speaking about him as though he were not present.

Bushka glanced at Gallow, who stood, back to the pilot's couch, peering out one of the small plazglas ports at whatever it was that Zent and Nakano were making ready out there. The grace and beauty of Gallow had taken on a new dimension for Bushka, who had marked Gallow's deep fear of disfiguring accidents. Nakano was a living example of what Gallow feared most.

Another chanted notation went into Bushka's "true history," the one he elected to keep only in his mind in the ages-old Islander fashion. Much of Islander history was carried in memorized chants, rhythms that projected themselves naturally, phrase by phrase. Paper was fugitive on the Islands, subject to rot, and where could it be stored that the container itself would not eat it? Permanent records were confined to plazbooks and the memories of chanters. Plazbooks were only for the bureaucracy or the very rich. Anyone could memorize a chant.

"GeLaar fears the scars of Time," Bushka chanted to himself. "Time is Age and Age is Time. Not the death but the dying."

If only they knew, Bushka thought. He brought a notepad from his pocket and scribbled four innocuous lines on it for Gallow's official history—date, time, place, people.

Zent and Nakano entered the cabin without speaking. Sea water slopped all around them as they took up positions in seats beside Bushka. They began a run-through on the sub's sensory apparatus. Both men moved smoothly and silently, grotesque figures in green-striped, skin-tight dive suits. "Camouflage," had been Gallow's response to Bushka's unasked question when he first saw them.

Gallow watched with quiet approval until the check-list had been run, then said, "Get us under way, Iz. Course three hundred and twenty-five degrees. Hold us just beneath wave turbulence."

"Check."

Bushka complied, feeling the unused power in the craft as he gentled it into position. Energy conservation was second nature to an Islander and he trimmed out as much by instinct as by the instruments.

"Sweet," Gallow commented. He glanced at Zent. "Didn't I tell you?"

Zent didn't respond, but Nakano smiled at Bushka. "You'll have to teach me how you do that," he said. "So smooth."

"Sure."

Bushka concentrated on the controls, familiarizing himself with them, sensing the minute responses transmitted from water to control surface to his hands. The latent power in this Merman craft was tempting. Bushka could feel how it might respond at full thrust. It would gulp fuel, though, and the hydrogen engines would heat.

Bushka decided he preferred Islander subs. Organics were supple, living-warm. They were smaller, true, and vulnerable to the accidents of flesh, but there was something addictive about the interdependence, life depending on life. Islanders didn't go blundering about down under. An Islander sub could be thought of as just big valves and muscle tissue—essentially a squid without a brain, or guts. But it gave a pulsing ride, soothing and noiseless—none of this humming and clicking and metal throbbing, none of these hard vibrations in the teeth.

Gallow spoke from close to Bushka's ear: "Let's get more moisture in the air, Iz. You want us all to dry out?"

"Here." Nakano pointed at a dial and alphanumerical readout above Bushka's head on the sloping curve of the hull. A red "21" showed on the air-moisture repeater. "We like it above forty percent."

Bushka increased humidity in gentle increments, thinking that here was another Merman vulnerability. Unless they became acclimated to topside existence—in the diplomatic corps or some commercial enterprise—Mermen suffered from dry air; cracked skin, lung damage, bloody creases in exposed soft tissues.

Gallow touched Zent's shoulder. "Give us the mark on Guemes Island."

Zent scanned the navigation instruments while Bushka studied the man furtively. What was this? Why did they want to locate Guemes? It was one of the poorest Islands—barely big enough to support ten thousand souls just above the lip of malnutrition. Why was Gallow interested in it?

"Grid and vector five," Zent said. "Two eighty degrees, eight kilometers." He punched a button. "Mark." The navigation screen above them came alight with green lines: grid squares and a soft blob in one of them.

"Swing us around to two hundred and eighty degrees, Iz," Gallow said. "We're going fishing."

Fishing? Bushka wondered. Subs could be rigged for fishing but this one carried none of the usual equipment. He didn't like the way Zent chuckled at Gallow's comment.

"The Movement is about to make its mark on history," Gallow announced. "Observe and record, Iz."

The Movement, Bushka thought. Gallow always named it in capital letters and frequently with quotation marks, as though he saw it already printed in a plazbook. When Gallow spoke of "The Movement," Bushka could sense the resources behind it, with nameless supporters and political influence in powerful places.

Responding to Gallow's orders, Bushka kicked the dive planes out of their locks, checked the range detectors for obstructions, scanned the trim display and the forward screen. It had become almost automatic. The sub glided into an easy descent as it came around on course.

"Depth vector coming up," Zent said, smiling at Bushka. Bushka noted the smile in the reflections of the screens and made a mental note. Zent must know it irritated a pilot to read his instruments aloud that way without being asked. Nobody likes being told what they already know.

Cabin air getting sticky, Bushka noted. His topside lungs found the high humidity stifling. He backed off the moisture content, wondering if they would object to thirty-five percent. He locked on course.

"On course," Zent said, still smiling.

"Zent, why don't you go play with yourself?" Bushka asked. He leveled the dive planes and locked them.

"I don't take orders from writers," Zent said.

"Now, boys," Gallow intervened, but there was amusement in his voice.

"Books lie," Zent muttered.

Nakano, wearing the hydrophone headset, lifted one earphone. "Lots of activity," he said. "I count more than thirty fishing boats."

"A hot spot," Gallow said.

"There's radio chatter from the Island, too," Nakano reported. "And music. That's one thing I'll miss—Islander music."

"Is it any good?" Zent asked.

"No lyrics, but you could dance to it," Nakano said.

Bushka shot a questioning look at Gallow.

What did Nakano mean, he would miss Islander music?

"Steady on course," Gallow said.

Zent took over Nakano's headphones and said, "GeLaar, you said Guemes Islanders were damned near floating morons. I thought they didn't have much radio."

"Guemes has lost almost half a kilometer in diameter since I started watching it last year," Gallow said. "Their bubbly's starving. They're so poor they can't afford to feed their Island."

"Why are we here?" Bushka asked. "If they only have low-grade radio and malnutrition, what good are they to The Movement?" Bushka experienced a bad feeling about all this. A very bad feeling. *Are they trying to set me up? Make the Islander a patsy for some of their dirty work?*

"A perfect first demonstration," Gallow said. "They're traditionalists, hard-core fanatics. I'll give 'em credit for one piece of good sense. When other Islands suggest it might be time to move down under, Guemes sends out delegations to stop it."

Was that Gallow's secret? Bushka wondered. Did he want all the Islanders to stay strictly topside?

"Traditionalists," Gallow repeated. "That means they wait for us to build land for them. They think we like them so much we'll make them the gift of a couple of continents. Keep toting that rock, slapping that mud! Plant that kelp!"

The three Mermen laughed and Bushka smiled in response. He didn't feel like smiling at all, but there was nothing else to do.

"Things would go much easier if Islanders would learn to live the way we do," Nakano said.

"All of them?" Zent asked.

Bushka noted a growing tension as Nakano failed to respond to Zent's question.

Presently, Gallow said, "Only the right ones, Gulf."

"Only the right ones," Nakano agreed, but there was no force in his voice.

"Damned religious troublemakers," Gallow blurted. "You've seen the missionaries from Guemes, Iz?"

"When our Islands have been on proximate drifts," Bushka said. "Any excuse for visiting is a good one, then. Mixing and visiting is a happy time."

"And we're always pulling your little boats out of the sea or giving you a tow,"

Zent said. "For that you want us to keep slopping mud!"

"Tso," Gallow said, patting Zent's shoulder, "Iz is one of us now."

"We can't get this foolishness under control any too soon for me," Zent said. "There's no reason for anyone to live anywhere but down under. We're already set up."

Bushka marked this comment but wondered at it. He felt Gallow's hatred of Guemes but the Mermen were saying that everyone should live down under.

Everyone living as rich as the Mermen? There was some sadness to that thought. *What would we lose of the old Islander ways?* He glanced up at Gallow. "Guemes, are we … ?"

"It was a mistake to elevate a Guemian to C/P," Gallow said. "Guemians never see things our way."

"Island on visual," Zent reported.

"Half speed," Gallow ordered.

Bushka complied. He felt the reduction in speed as an easing of the vibration against his spine.

"What's our vertical relationship?" Gallow asked.

"We're coming in about thirty meters below their keel," Zent said. "Shit! They don't even have outwatchers. Look, no small boats at all ahead of their drift."

"It's a wonder they're still in one piece," Nakano said. Bushka caught a wry edge to the statement that he didn't quite understand.

"Set us directly under their keel, Iz," Gallow said.

What are we doing here? Bushka wondered as he obeyed the order. The forward display screen showed the bulbous lower extremity of Guemes—a thick red-brown extrusion of bubbly with starved sections streaming from it. Yes, Guemes was in bad condition. They were starving essential parts of their Island. Bushka inhaled quick, shallow breaths of the thick moist air. The Merman sub was too close for simple observation. And this was not the way you approached an Island for a visit.

"Drop us down another fifty meters," Gallow ordered.

Bushka obeyed, using the descent propulsion system and automatically adjusting trim. He felt proud that the sub remained straight and level as it settled. The upward display, set wide-angle, showed the entire Island as a dark shadow against the surface light. A ring of small boats dappled its edges like beads in a necklace. Bushka estimated that Guemes was no more than six klicks in diameter at the waterline. He put the depth at three hundred meters. Long strips of organics floated dreamlike in the currents around the Island. Entire bulkheads of bubbly blackened the surrounding water with dead-rot. Thatchings of thin membranous material patched the holes.

Probably spinnarett webbing.

Bushka saw raw sewage pumping out of a valve off to his right, sure evidence that the Guemes nutrient plant had suffered a major breakdown.

"Can you imagine how that place smells?" Zent asked.

"Very nice on a hot day," Gallow said.

"Guemes needs help," Bushka offered.

"And they're going to get it," Zent said.

"Look at all the fish around them," Nakano said. "I'll bet the fishing's real good right now." He pointed at the upward display as a giant scrubberfish, almost two meters long, floated past the external sensor. Half of the fish's whiskers had been nibbled away and the one visible eye socket was empty and white.

"It's so rotten around here that even the scrapfish are dying," Zent said.

"If the Island's this sick, you can bet the people are in sad shape," Nakano added.

Bushka felt his face get red, and pressed his lips shut tight.

"Those boats all around, maybe they're not fishing," Zent said. "Maybe they're living on their boats."

"This whole Island is a menace," Gallow said. "There must be all kinds of diseases up there. There's probably an epidemic in the whole system of organics."

"Who could live in shit and not be sick?" Zent asked.

Bushka nodded to himself. He thought he had figured out what Gallow was doing here.

He's brought the sub in close to confirm their desperate need for help.

"Why can't they see the obvious?" Nakano asked. He patted the hull beside him. "Our subs don't need nutrient slopped all over them. They don't rot or oxidize. They don't get sick or make us sick …"

Gallow, watching the upward display, tapped Bushka's shoulder. "Down another fifteen meters, Iz. We still have plenty of room under us."

Bushka complied and again it was that smooth, steady descent that brought an admiring look from Nakano.

"I don't see how Islanders can live under those conditions." Zent shook his head. "Sweating out weather, food, dashers, disease—any one of a hundred mistakes that would send the whole pack of them to the bottom."

"They've made that mistake, now, haven't they, Tso?" Gallow asked.

Nakano pointed at a corner of the upward display. "There's nothing but some kind of membrane where their driftwatch should be."

Bushka looked and saw a dark patch of spinnarett webbing where the large corneal bubble should have been, the observer tucked safely behind it watching for shallows, coordinating with the outwatchers. No driftwatch—Guemes probably had lost its course-correction system, too. They were in terrible condition! Guemes would probably do anything for the offer of help.

"The corneal bubble has died," Bushka told them. "They've patched it over with spinnarett webbing to keep watertight."

"How long do they think they can drift blind before scraping bottom someplace?" Nakano muttered. There was anger in his voice.

"They're probably up there praying like mad for Ship to come help them," Zent sneered.

"Or they're praying for us to stabilize the sea and bring back their precious continents," Gallow said. "And now that we're getting it whipped, they'll be crying about bottoming out on the land we've built. Well, let 'em pray. They can pray to us!" Gallow reached over Zent's shoulder and flipped a switch.

Bushka scanned the displays—up, down, forward, aft the sub's complement of tools sprang out of their hull sheaths all glittering and sharp—deadly.

So that's what Zent and Nakano had been doing out there topside! Iz realized. They'd been checking manipulators and mechanical arms. Bushka scanned them once more: trenchers, borers, tampers, cutters, a swing-boom and the forward heliarc welder on its articulated arm. They gleamed brightly in the wash of the exterior lights.

"What are you doing?" Bushka asked. He tried to swallow but his throat was too dry in spite of the humidity.

Zent snorted.

Bushka felt repelled by the look on Zent's face—a smile that touched only the corners of his mouth, no humor at all in those bottomless eyes.

Gallow gripped Bushka's shoulder with a powerful and painful pressure. "Take us up, Iz."

Bushka glanced left and right. Nakano was flexing his powerful hands and watching a sensor screen. Zent held a small needle burner with its muzzle carelessly pointed at Bushka's chest.

"Up," Gallow repeated, emphasizing the order with increased pressure on Bushka's shoulder.

"But we'll cut right through them," Bushka said. He felt his breath pumping against the back of his throat. The awareness of what Gallow intended almost gagged him. "They won't have a chance without their Island. The ones who don't drown right away will drift in their boats until they starve!"

"Without the Island's filtration system, chances are they'll die of thirst before they starve," Gallow said. "They'd die anyway, look at them. Up!"

Zent waved the needle burner casually and pressed his left phone tighter to his ear.

Bushka ignored the needle burner's threat. "Or dashers will get them!" he protested. "Or a storm!"

"Hold it," Zent said, leaning toward his left earphone while he pressed it harder. "I'm getting free sonics of some kind … a sweeping pulse from the membrane, I think …" Zent screamed and tore the earphone from his head. Blood trickled from his nostrils.

"Take it up, damn you!" Gallow shouted.

Nakano kicked the locks off the dive planes and reached across Bushka to blow the tanks. The sub's nose tipped upward.

Bushka reacted with a pilot's instincts. He fed power to the drivers and tried to bring them onto an even keel but the sub was suddenly a live thing, shooting upward toward the dark bottom of Guemes Island. In two blinks they were through the bottom membranes and into the Island's keel. The sub kicked and twisted as its exterior tools hacked and slashed under the direction of Nakano and Gallow. Zent still sat bent over, holding his ears with both hands. The needle burner lay useless in his lap.

Bushka pressed hard against his seatback while he watched in horror the terrible damage being done all around. Anything he did to the controls only added to the destruction. They were into the Island center now, where the high-status Islanders lived, where they kept their most sensitive equipment and organics, their most powerful people, their surgical and other medical facilities …

The cold-blooded slashing of blades and cutters continued—visible in every screen, felt in every lurch of the sub. It was eerie that there could be this much pain and not a single scream. Soft, living tissue was no match for the hard, sharp edges that the sub intruded into this nightmare scene. Every bump and twist of the sub wrought more destruction. The displays showed bits and pieces of humanity now—an arm, a severed head.

Bushka moaned, "They're people. "They're *people.*"

Everything he'd been taught about the sanctity of life filled him now with rebellion. Mermen shared the same beliefs! How could they kill an entire Island? Bushka realized that Gallow would kill him at the first sign of resistance. A glance at Zent showed the man still looking stunned, but the bleeding had stopped and he had recovered the burner. Nakano worked like an automaton, shuttling power where necessary as cutters and torches continued their awful havoc in the collapsing Island. The sub had begun to twist on its own, turning end for end on a central pivot.

Gallow wedged himself into the corner beside Zent, his gaze fixed on the display screens, which showed Island tissue melting away from the heliarcs.

"There is no Ship!" Gallow exulted. "You see! Would Ship allow a mere mortal to do such a thing?" He turned emotion-glazed eyes on Bushka at the controls. "I told you! Ship's an artifact, a thing made by people like us. God! There is no God!"

Bushka tried to speak but his throat was too dry.

"Take us back down, Iz," Gallow ordered.

"What're you doing?" Bushka managed.

"I challenge Ship," Gallow said. "Has Ship responded?" A wild laugh issued from his throat. Only Zent joined it.

"Take us down, I said!" Gallow repeated.

Driven by fear, Bushka's pilot-conditioned muscles responded, shifting trim ballast, adjusting planes. And he thought: *If we get out fast, some of this Island may survive.* Gently, he maneuvered the sub downward through the wreckage left by its terrible ascent. Plazports and screens showed the water around them dim with blood, a dull gray in the harsh illumination from the sub's exterior lights.

"Hold us here," Gallow ordered.

Bushka ignored the command, his gaze intent on the exterior carnage—inert bodies and pieces of bodies glimpsed in the murk. Raw horror everywhere around him. A little girl's dancing frock with white lace ruffles in an ancient pattern floated past a port. Behind it could be seen strung out the remnants of someone's pantry, half a lover's portrait pasted against a remnant stone box: outline of a smile without eyes. Beyond the sub's hot lights, blood rolled and streamed, a cold gray fog reaching down the currents.

"I said hold us here!" Gallow shouted.

Bushka continued to gentle the sub downward. A well of tears brimmed against his eyelids.

Don't let me cry! he prayed. *Dammit! I can't break down in front of these … these …* No word in his memory could label what his companions had become. This realization burned its change in him. These three Mermen were now lethal deviants. They would have to be brought before the Committee. Judgment must be made.

Nakano reached across Bushka and adjusted the ballast controls to bring the sub's descent to a stop. His eyes looked a warning.

Bushka looked at Nakano through a swim of tears, then shifted his gaze to Zent. Zent still held his left ear, but he watched Bushka steadily, smiling that cold-liver smile. His lips moved silently: "Wait till I get you topside."

Gallow reached across Zent's head to the heliarc controls.

"Take us straight ahead," he ordered. He snapped a polarized shield in place and sighted down the twin snouts of the bow heliarc.

Bushka reached to his shoulder and brought his chest harness into place, snapping it closed at his side. He moved with purpose, which brought a questioning stare from Zent. Before Zent could react, Bushka kicked loose the dive planes, skewed the control surfaces to starboard and blew the rear ballast tanks while he opened the bow valves. The sub surged over onto its nose and corkscrewed toward the bottom, spinning faster and faster. Nakano was thrown to the left by the force of the spin. Zent lost his needle burner while trying to grab for a support. His body was thrown against Gallow. Both men lay pinned between hull and control panels. Only Bushka, strapped in at the center of the spin, could move with relative ease.

"You damn fool!" Gallow shouted. "You'll kill us!"

His right hand moving across the switches methodically, Bushka snapped off the cabin lights and all but the exterior bow light. Outside the glow of that one beacon, darkness closed in, surrounding them with a gray murk in which only a few shreds of torn humanity drifted and sank.

"You're not Ship!" Gallow screamed. "You hear me, Bushka? It's just you doing this!"

Bushka ignored him.

"You can't get out of this, Bushka," Gallow shouted. "You'll have to come up sometime and we'll be there."

He's asking if I mean to kill us all, Bushka thought.

"You're crazy, Bushka!" Gallow shouted.

Bushka stared straight ahead, looking for the first glimpse of bottom. At this speed, the sub would dig in and make Gallow's warning come true. Not even plasteel and plaz could withstand a twisting dive into the rocky bottom, not at this depth and this speed.

"You going to do it, Bushka?" That was Nakano, voice loud but level and more than a little admiration in the question.

For answer, Bushka eased the angle of dive but kept the hard spin, knowing his Island-trained equilibrium could better withstand the violent motion.

Nakano began to vomit, gagging and gasping as he tried to clear his throat in the heavy centrifugal pressure. The stench became a nauseating presence in the cabin.

Bushka keyed his console for display of the sub's gas displacement. Notations showed ballast was blown with CO_2. His gaze traced out the linked lines. Yes … exhausted cabin air was bled into the ballast system … conservation of energy.

Gallow had subsided into a low growling protest while he struggled to crawl out against the force of the spin. "Not Ship! Just another damn shit-eater. Gonna kill him. Never trust Islander."

Following the diagram in front of him, Bushka tapped out the valving sequence on the emergency controls. Immediately, an oxygen mask dropped in front of him from an overhead compartment. All other emergency oxygen remained securely in place. Bushka pressed the mask to his face with one hand while his other hand bled CO_2 from the ballast directly into the cabin.

Zent began gasping. Gallow moaned: "Not Ship!"

Nakano's voice gurgled and rasped but the words were clear: "The air! He's … going … to … smother us!"

Chapter 8

Justice does not happen by chance; indeed, something that subjective may never have happened at all.

—Ward Keel, *Journal*

MARITIME COURT did not go at all as Queets Twisp had expected. Killing a Merman in the nets had never been an acceptable "accident" at sea, even when all the evidence said it was unavoidable. The emphasis was always on the deceased and the needs of the surviving Merman family. Mermen were always reminding you of all the Islanders they saved every year with their pickup crews and search teams.

Twisp walked the long mural-distorted hallway out of the Maritime offices scratching his head. Brett almost skipped along beside him, a wide grin on his face.

"See?" Brett said. "I knew we were worried for nothing. They said it wasn't a Merman in our net—no Mermen lost, nobody that wasn't accounted for. We didn't drown anybody at all!"

"Wipe that grin off your face!" Twisp said.

"But Queets …"

"Don't interrupt me!" he snapped. "I had my face down there in the net—I saw the blood. Red. Dasher blood's green. Now, didn't it seem to you that they got us out of court too fast?"

"It's a busy place and we're small-time. You said that yourself." Brett paused, then asked, "Did you really see blood?"

"Too much for a few beat-up fish."

The hallway let them out into the wide third-level perimeter concourse with its occasional viewports opening out onto the surging sea and the spume flying past. Weather had said there was a fifty-klick wind today with chance of rain. The sky hung gray, hiding the one sun that had headed downward into the horizon, the other already gone.

Rain?

Twisp thought Weather had made one of its infrequent errors. His fisherman's sense said the wind would have to increase before any rain came today. He expected sunshine before sunset.

"Maritime has other things to do than worry about every small-time …" Brett broke off as he saw the bitter expression on Twisp's face.

"I mean …"

"I know what you mean! We're really small-time now. Losing that catch cost me everything: depth gear, nets, new stunshield charges, food, the scull …"

Brett was almost breathless trying to keep up with the older man's longer, firmer strides. "But we can make another start if …"

"How?" Twisp asked with a toss of one long arm. "I can't afford to outfit us. You know what they'll advise me in Fisherman's Hall? Sell my boat and go back to the subs as a common crewman!"

The concourse widened into a long ramp. They walked down without speaking and out onto the wide second-level terrace with its heavily cultivated truck gardens. Mazelike access lanes crooked their way to the high railing overlooking the wider first level. As they emerged, gaps began to appear in the overcast and one of Pandora's suns made liars out of the meteorologists at Weather. It bathed the terrace in a welcome yellow light.

Brett pulled at Twisp's sleeve. "Queets, you wouldn't have to sell the boat if you got a loan and—"

"I've got loans up to here!" Twisp said, touching his neck. "I'd just cleared my accounts when I brought you on. I won't go through that again! The boat goes. That means I have to sell your contract."

Twisp sat on a mound of bubbly at the rail and looked out over the sea. The wind-speed was dropping fast, just as he'd expected. The surge at the rim of the Island was still high but the spume shot straight up now.

"Best fishing weather we've had in a long time," Brett said.

Twisp had to admit this was true.

"Why did Maritime let us off so easy?" Twisp muttered. "We had a Merman in the net. Even you know that, kid. Something funny's going on."

"But they let us off, that's the important thing. I thought you'd be happy about it."

"Grow up, kid." Twisp closed his eyes and leaned back against the rail. He felt the cool water breeze against his neck. The sun was hot on his head. *Too many problems,* he thought.

Brett stood directly in front of Twisp. "You keep telling me to grow up. It looks to me like you could do some growing up yourself. If you'd only get a loan and—"

"If you won't grow up, kid, then shut up."

"It couldn't have been a tripod fish in the net?" Brett persisted.

"No way! There's a different feel. That was a Merman and the dashers got him." Twisp swallowed. "Or her. Up to something, too, from the look of things." Without changing his position against the rail, Twisp listened to the kid shift from foot to foot.

"Is that why you're selling the boat?" Brett asked. "Because we accidentally killed a Merman who was where he wasn't supposed to be? You think the Mermen will be out to get you now?"

"I don't know what to think."

Twisp opened his eyes and looked up at Brett. The kid had narrowed his overly large eyes into a tight squint, his gaze steady on Twisp.

"The Merman observers at Maritime didn't object to the court's decision," Brett said.

"You're right," Twisp said. He jerked a thumb upward toward the Maritime offices. "They're usually ruthless in cases like this. I wonder what we saw … or almost saw."

Brett moved to one side and plopped himself onto the bubbly beside Twisp. They listened for a time to the *thlup-thlup-thlup* of waves against the Island's rim.

"I expected to be sent down under," Twisp said. "And you with me. That's what usually happens. You go to work for the dead Merman's family. And you don't always come back topside."

Brett grunted, then: "They'd have sent me, not you. Everybody knows about my eyes, how I can see when it's almost dark. The Mermen would want that."

"Don't give yourself airs, kid. Mermen are damned cautious about who they let into their gene pool. They call us Mutes, you know. And they don't mean something nice when they say it. We're mutants, kid, and when we go down under it's to fill a dead man's dive suit … nothing else."

"Maybe they didn't want this job filled," Brett said.

Twisp tapped a fist on the resilient organics of the rail. "Or they didn't want anybody from topside to know what that Merman's job was."

"That's crazy!"

Twisp did not respond. They sat quietly for a while as the lone sun dipped lower. Glancing over his shoulder, Twisp stared at the horizon. It bent away in the distance to a bank of black sky and water. Water everywhere.

"I can get us outfitted," Brett said.

Twisp was startled but remained silent, looking at the kid. Brett, too, was staring off at the horizon. Twisp noticed that the boy's skin had become fisherman-dark, not the sickly pale he had displayed when he first boarded the coracle. The kid looked leaner, too … and taller.

"Didn't you hear me?" Brett asked. "I said—"

"I heard you. For somebody who pissed and moaned most of the time he was out there fishing, you sound pretty anxious to get back on the water."

"I didn't moan about—"

"Just joking, kid." Twisp raised a hand to stop the objections. "Don't be so damned touchy."

His face flushed, Brett looked down at his boots. Twisp asked, "How would you get this loan?"

"My parents would loan it to me and I'd loan it to you."

"Your parents have money?" Twisp studied the kid, aware that this revelation did not surprise him. In all the time they'd spent together, though, Brett had never talked about his parents and Twisp discreetly had never asked. Islander etiquette.

"They're close to Center," Brett said. "Next ring out from the lab and Committee."

Twisp whistled between his teeth. "What do your parents do that gets them quarters at Center?"

Brett's mouth turned up in a crooked grin. "Slurry. They made their fortune in shit."

Twisp laughed in sudden awareness. "Norton! Brett Norton! Your folks are *the* Nortons?"

"Norton," Brett corrected him. "They're a team and they bill themselves as one artist."

"Shitpainting," Twisp said. He chuckled.

"They were the first," Brett said. "And it's nutrient, not shit. It's processed slurry."

"So your folks dig shit," Twisp teased.

"Come on!" Brett objected. "I thought I got away from that when I left school. Grow up, Twisp!"

"All right, kid," he laughed, "I know what slurry is." He patted the bubbly beside him. "It's what we feed the Island."

"It's not that simple," Brett said. "I grew up with it, so I know. It's scraps from the fish processors, compost from the agraria, table scraps and … just about everything." He grinned. "Including shit. My mother was the first chemist to figure out how to color the nutrient like they do now without hurting the bubbly."

"Forgive an old fisherman," Twisp said. "We live with a lot of dead organics, like the membrane on the hull of my coracle. Islandside, we just pick up a bag of nutrient, mix it with a little water and spread it on our walls when they get a little gray."

"Don't you ever try the colored stuff and make a few of your own murals on your walls?" Brett asked.

"I leave that to the artists like your folks," Twisp said. "I didn't grow up with it the way you did. When I was a kid, we only had a bit of graffiti, no pictures. It was all pretty bland: brown on gray. We were told they couldn't introduce other colors because that interfered with absorption by the decks and walls and things. And you know, if our organics die …" He shrugged. "How'd your folks stumble onto this?"

"They didn't stumble! My mother was a chemist and my father had a flair for design. They went out with a wall-feeding crew one day and did a nutrient mural on the radar dome near the slurryside rim. That was before I was born."

"Two big historical events," Twisp joked. "The first shit painting and the birth of Brett Norton." He shook his head in mock seriousness. "Permanent work, too, because no painting lasts more than about a week."

Brett spoke defensively. "They keep records. Holos and such. Some of their friends have worked up musical scores for the gallery and theater shows."

"How come you left all that?" Twisp asked. "Big money, important friends … ?"

"You never had some bigshot pat you on the head and say, 'Here's our new little painter.'"

"And you didn't want that?"

Brett turned his back on Twisp so fast that Twisp knew the kid was hiding something. "Haven't I worked out well enough for you?" Brett asked.

"You're a pretty good worker, kid. A little green, but that's part of the bargain on a new contract."

Brett didn't respond and Twisp saw that the kid was staring at the Maritime mural on the inner wall of the second level. It was a big and gaudy mural aglow in the hard light of the setting sun—everything washed a fine crimson.

"Is that one of their murals?" Twisp asked. Brett nodded without turning.

Twisp took another look at the painting, thinking of how easy it was these days to walk past the decorated hallways, decks and bulkheads without even noticing the color. Some of the murals were sharply geometric, denying the rounded softness of Islander life. Famous murals, ones that kept Norton in constant, high priced demand, were the great historical pieces barely applied before they began their steady absorption toward the flat gray of hungry walls. The Maritime mural was something new in a Norton wall—an abstraction, a study in crimson and the fluidity of motion. It glowed with an internal power in the low light of the sun, seeming to boil and seethe along its rim like an angry creature or a thunderstorm of blood.

The sun lay almost below the horizon, throwing the sea's surface into the little dusk. A fine line of double light skittered across the top of the painting, then the sun dipped below the horizon and they were left with the peculiar afterglow of sunset on Pandora.

"Brett, why didn't your parents buy your contract?" Twisp asked. "With your eyesight, it seems to me you'd have made a fine painter."

The dim silhouette in front of Twisp turned, a fuzzed outline against the lighter background of the mural.

"I never offered my contract for sale," Brett said.

Twisp looked away from Brett, oddly moved by the kid's response. It was as though they suddenly had become much closer friends. The unspoken revelations carried a kind of cement, which sealed all of their shared experiences out on the water … out there where each depended on the other for survival.

He doesn't want me to sell his contract, Twisp thought. He kicked himself for being so dense. It wasn't just the fishing. Brett could get plenty of fishing after his apprenticeship with Queets Twisp. The contract had increased in value simply because of that apprenticeship. Twisp sighed. No … the kid did not want to be separated from a friend.

"I still have credit at the Ace of Cups," Twisp said. "Let's go get some coffee and … whatever …"

Twisp waited, hearing the little shufflings of Brett's feet in the growing dark. The Island's rimlights began their nightly duty—homing beacons for the time between suns. The lights started with a blue-green phosphorescence of wave tops, bright because the night was warm, then grew even brighter as the organics ignited. Out of the corners of his eyes, Twisp saw Brett wipe his cheeks quickly as the lights came up.

"Hell, we're not breaking up a good team, yet," Twisp said. "Let's go get that coffee." He had never before invited the kid to share an evening at the Ace of Cups, although it was well-known as a fisherman's hangout. He stood and saw an encouraging lift to Brett's chin.

"I'd like that," Brett said.

They walked quietly down the gangway and along the passages with their bright blue phosphorescence to light the way. They entered the coffeehouse through the wool-lined arch and Twisp allowed Brett a moment to look around before pointing out the really fancy feature for which the Ace of Cups was known throughout the Islands—the rimside wall. From deck to ceiling, it was solid wool, a softly curling karakul of iridescent white.

"How do they feed it?" Brett whispered.

"There's a little passageway behind it that they use for storage. They roll the nutrient on from that side."

There were only a few other early drinkers and diners and these paid little attention to the newcomers. Brett ducked his head slightly into his shoulder blades, trying to see everything without appearing to look.

"Why did they choose wool?" Brett asked. He and Twisp threaded their way through the tables to the rimwall.

"Keeps out noise during storms," Twisp said. "We're pretty close to the rim."

They took chairs at a table against the wall—both table and chairs made of the same dried and stretched membrane as the coracles. Brett eased himself into a chair gingerly and Twisp remembered the kid's first time in the coracle.

"You don't like dead furniture," Twisp said.

Brett shrugged. "I'm just not used to it."

"Fishermen like it. It stays put and you don't have to feed it. What'll you have?"

Twisp waved a hand toward Gerard, the owner, who lifted head and shoulders from the raised well behind the bar, a questioning look on his enormous head. Tufts of black hair framed a smiling face.

"I hear they have real chocolate," Brett whispered.

"Gerard will slip a little boo in it if you ask."

"No … no thanks."

Twisp lifted two fingers with the palm of his other hand over them—the house signal for chocolate—then he winked once for a dash of boo in his own. Presently, Gerard signaled back that the order was ready. All of the regulars knew Gerard's problem—his legs fused into a single column with two toeless feet. The proprietor of the Ace of Cups was confined to a Merman-made motorized chair, a sure sign of affluence. Twisp rose and went to the bar to collect their drinks.

"Who's the kid?" Gerard asked as he slid two cups across the bar. "Boo's in the blue." He tapped the blue cup for emphasis.

"My new contract," Twisp said. "Brett Norton."

"Oh, yeah? From downcenter?"

Twisp nodded.

"His folks are the shitpainters."

"How come everybody except me knew that?" Twisp asked.

"'Cause, you keep your head buried in a fish tote," Gerard said. His ridged forehead drew down and his green eyes twinkled in amusement.

"It's a mystery whatever brought him out to fish," Twisp said. "If I believed in luck, I'd say he was bad luck. But he's a damned nice kid."

"I heard about you losing your gear and your catch," Gerard said. "What're you going to do?" He nodded toward where Brett sat watching them. "His folks have money."

"So he says," Twisp said. He balanced the cups for his return to the table. "See you."

"Good fishing," Gerard said. It was an automatic response and he frowned when he realized he'd said it to a netless fisherman.

"We'll see," Twisp said and returned to the table. He noted that the action of the deck underfoot had picked up slightly. *Could be a storm coming.*

They sipped quietly at their chocolate and Twisp felt the boo settling his nerves. From somewhere in the quarters behind the counter someone played a flute and someone else tapped out a back-up on water drums.

"What were you two talking about?" Brett asked.

"You."

Brett's face flushed noticeably under the dim lights of the coffeehouse. "What … what were you saying?"

"Seems everybody but me knew about you being from downcenter. That's why you don't like dead furniture."

"I got used to the coracle," Brett said.

"Not everybody can afford organics … or wants them," Twisp said. "It costs a lot to feed good furniture. And organics don't make the best small boats because they can go wild when they get into a school of fish. The subs are specially designed to prevent that."

Brett's mouth began to twitch into a smile. "You know, when I first saw your boat and heard you call it a coracle, I thought 'coracle' meant 'carcass.'"

They both laughed, Twisp a little unsteadily from the boo. Brett stared at him. "You're drunk."

Mimicking Brett's tone, Twisp said, "Kid, I am getting downright inebriated. I may even have another boo."

"My folks do that after an art show," Brett said.

"And you didn't like it," Twisp said. "Well, kid, I am not your folks—neither one of 'em."

A hooter went off just outside the Ace of Cups hatchway. The wall pulsed with the blast of sound.

"Wavewall!" Brett shouted. "Can we save your boat?" Brett was already up and headed out of the coffeehouse in a press of pale-faced fishermen.

Twisp lurched to his feet and followed, motioning to Gerard not to dog the hatch. The deck outside already was awash from a few low breakers. The passage was filled with people lurching and splashing toward hatchways. Twisp shouted at Brett's retreating back far up the passage, "Kid! No time! Get inside!"

Brett didn't turn.

Twisp found an extruded safety line and worked himself along it out onto the rim. Lights glared out there, throwing high contrast onto scurrying people, contorted faces. People were shouting all around, calling out names. Brett was out on the fishboat slip tossing equipment into the coracle's cubby and lashing it down. As Twisp came up to him, Brett lashed a long line to the coracle's bow cleat. The wind howled across them now and waves were breaking over the outer bubbly of the slip, filling the normally protected lagoon with frothing white water.

"We can sink it and haul it up later!" Brett shouted.

Twisp joined him, thinking that the kid had learned this lesson from listening to some of the old-timers. Sometimes it worked and certainly it was the only chance they had to save the coracle. All along the slip, other boats had been sunk, their lines dipping down sharply. Twisp found a store of ballast rocks near the slip and began passing the heavy load to Brett, who tossed them into the boat. The five-meter craft was almost awash. Brett jumped in and lashed a cover over the ballast.

"Open the valves and jump!" Twisp yelled.

Brett reached under the load. A strong jet of water pulsed up from the bottom. Twisp reached a long arm toward Brett just as the wavewall itself swept over the lagoon and crashed into the side of the sinking coracle. Brett's outstretched fingertips grazed Twisp's hand as the coracle went under. The line to the bow, passing across Twisp's right arm, played out in a wet hiss. Twisp grabbed it, burning his palms, yelling: "Brett! Kid!"

But the lagoon was a boil of white rage and two other fishermen grabbed him and forced him, soaked and still shouting, down the passage and through the hatch into the Ace of Cups. Gerard, in his motorized chair, dogged the hatch against the incoming sea behind them.

Twisp clawed at the resilient wool. "No! The kid's still out there!"

Someone forced a warm drink of almost pure boo against his lips. The liquid gushed into his mouth and he swallowed. The liquor washed through him in a soothing blankness. But it did not drive away the tingle of Brett's fingertips grazing his own.

"I almost had him," Twisp moaned.

Chapter 9

Space is mankind's natural habitat. A planet, after all, is an object in space. I believe humans have a natural drive to be mobile in space, their true habitat.
—Raja Thomas, *The Histories*

THE IMAGE caught on the small stretched sheet of organics was that of a silvery tube flying through the sky. The tube had no wings or any other visible means of support. Only that orange glow from one end, pale fire against the silver and blue of Pandora's sky. The process that had caught the image was fugitive and the colors already had begun to fade.

Ward Keel was held as much by the beauty of it as by its unique implications. Images made this way were a much-loved art form among Islanders, relying on the light-sensitivity of organisms that could be made to adhere in a thin layer on the stretched organics. Pictures on this preparation formed by exposure through a lens were admired as much for their fleeting existence as for their intrinsic beauty. This image, however, in spite of its exquisite play of colors and composition, was deemed by its creator to possess holy significance.

Was that not Ship or an artifact from Ship?

The man was reluctant to part with his creation, but Keel used the power of his position to silence argument. He did this kindly and without hurry, relying chiefly on delay—long and convoluted sentences with many references to trust and the well-being of the Islands, frequent pauses and silent noddings of his massive head. Both of them were aware that the picture was fading and before long would be a flat gray surface ready for renewal and the capture of another image. The man left finally, unhappy but resigned—a thin, spindly-legged fellow with too-short arms. An artist, though, Keel had to admit.

It was early on a warm day and Keel sat a moment in his robes, enjoying the breeze that played through the vent system in his quarters. Joy had straightened some of the rumpled disarray around him before leaving, smoothing the covers on his couch and arranging his clothing across a translucent plaz sling-chair. The matching table surface in front of him still bore the remains of the breakfast she had fixed for them—squawk eggs and muree. Keel pushed the plate and chopsticks aside and put the stretched sheet with its odd image flat on the table. He stared at it a moment longer, thinking. Presently, he nodded to himself and called the chief of Inner-Island Security.

"I'll send a couple of people down in two hours," the man said. "We'll get right on it."

"Two hours is not getting right on it," Keel said. "The image will be almost faded out by then."

The deeply lined face on the viewscreen frowned. The man started to speak, then thought better of it. He rubbed his fleshy nose with a thick finger and lifted his gaze. The chief appeared to be reviewing data from a source out of Keel's sight.

"Mr. Justice," he said, presently, "someone will meet you in a few minutes. Where will you be?"

"In my quarters. I presume you know where that is."

The chief flushed. "Of course, sir."

Keel switched off, regretting his sharpness with Security. They were irritating, but his reaction had come from thoughts aroused by that fading image. It was a disturbing thing. The artist who had captured the image of that object in the sky had not taken it to the C/P. Evidence of Ship's return, the man thought, but he had taken it to the Chief Justice.

What am I supposed to do about it? Keel wondered. *But I didn't call the C/P, either.*

Simone Rocksack would resent this, he knew. He would have to call her soon, but first . . . a few other matters.

The water drum at his door thrummed once, twice.

Security here already? he wondered.

Taking the fading image of the thing in the sky, Keel walked through the hatchway into his main room, sealing off the kitchen area as he passed. Some Islanders resented those who ate privately, those whose affluence removed them from the noisy, crowded press of the mess halls.

At the entrance to his quarters he touched the sense membrane and the responsive organics expanded, revealing Kareen Ale standing in the arched opening. She gave a nervous start as she saw him, then smiled.

"Ambassador Ale," he said, momentarily surprised at his own formality. They had been Kareen and Ward off the debate floor for several seasons now. Something about her nervous posture, though, said this was a formal visit.

"Forgive my coming to your quarters without warning," she said. "But we have something to discuss, Ward."

She glanced at the image in his hand and nodded, as though it confirmed something.

Keel stood aside for her to enter. He sealed the door against casual entry and watched Ale choose a seat and sink into it without invitation. As always, he was conscious of her beauty.

"I heard about that," Ale said, gesturing at the stretched sheet of organics in his hand.

He lifted the image and glanced at it. "You came topside because of this?"

She held her face motionless for an instant, then shrugged. "We monitor a number of topside activities," she said.

"I've often wondered about your spy system," he said. "I am beginning to distrust you, Kareen."

"What is making you attack me, Ward?"

"This is a rocket, is it not?" He waved the image at her. "A *Merman* rocket?"

Ale grimaced, but did not seem surprised that Keel had guessed.

"Ward, I would like to take you back down under with me. Let's call it an instructional visit."

She had not answered his question but her attitude was sufficient admission. Whatever was going on, the Mermen wanted the mass of Islanders and the religious community left out of it. Keel nodded. "You're after the hyb tanks! Why was the C/P not asked to bless this enterprise?"

"There were those among us …" She shrugged. "It's a political matter among the leading Mermen."

"You want another Merman monopoly," he accused. She looked away from him without answering. "How long would this instructional visit require?" he asked.

She stood. "Perhaps a week. Perhaps longer."

"What subject matter will be covered by this instructional visit?"

"The visit itself will have to answer that for you."

"So I'm to prepare myself for an indefinite visit down under whose purpose you will not reveal until I get there?"

"Please trust me, Ward."

"I trust you to be loyal to Merman interests," he said, "just as I'm loyal to the Islanders."

"I swear to you that you will come to no harm."

He allowed himself a grim smile. What an embarrassment it would be to the Mermen if he died down under! And it could happen. The medics had been indefinite about the near side of the death sentence they had passed on Chief Justice Ward Keel.

"Give me a few minutes to pack my kit and turn over my more urgent responsibilities to others," he said.

She relaxed. "Thank you, Ward. You will not regret this."

"Political secrets always interest me," he said. He reminded himself to take a fresh tablet for his journal. There would be things to record on this instructional visit, of that he was certain. Words on plaz and chants in his memory. This would be action, not speculative philosophy.

Chapter 10

A planet-wide consciousness died with the kelp and with it went the beginnings of a collective human conscience. Was that why we killed the kelp?
—Kerro Panille, *Collected Works*

SHADOW PANILLE'S thickly braided black hair whipped behind him as he ran down the long corridor toward Current Control. Other Mermen dodged aside as he passed. They knew Panille's job. Word already had spread through the central complex—unspecified trouble with a major Island. Big trouble.

At the double hatch of Current Control, Panille did not pause to regain his breath. He undogged the outer hatch, ducked through and sealed the outer latch with one hand while spinning the dog for the inner hatch with his other hand. Definitely against Procedural Orders.

He was into the hubbub of Current Control then, a place of low illumination. Long banks of instruments and displays glowed and flashed against two walls. CC's activity and the displays told him immediately that his people were in the throes of a crisis. Eight screens had been tuned to remotes showing dark blotches of sea bottom strewn with torn bubbly and other Island debris. Surface monitors scanned decrepit scatterings of small boats, all of them overcrowded with survivors.

Panille took a moment trying to assess what he saw. The small craft bobbed amidst a wide, oily expanse of flotsam. The few Islander faces he saw showed dull shock and hopelessness. He could see many injured among the survivors. Those able to move attempted to staunch blood flowing from jagged slashes in flesh. Some of the injured twisted and writhed from the effects of high-temperature burns. All of the small craft drifted nearly awash. One had been piled with bodies and pieces of bodies. An older woman with gray hair and stubby arms was being restrained in a long coracle, obviously to prevent her from throwing herself into the sea. There was no sound with the transmission but Panille could see that she was screaming.

"What happened?" Panille demanded. "An explosion?"

"It may have been their hydrogen plant, but we're not sure yet."

That was Lonson, Panille's daywatch number two, at the central console. Lonson spoke without turning.

Panille moved closer to the center of activity. "Which Island?"

"Guemes," Lonson said. "They're pretty far out, but we've alerted Rescue and the pickup teams in their area. And as you can see we've lifted scanners from the bottom."

"*Guemes,*" Panille said, recalling the last watch report. Hours away even with the fastest rescue subs. "What time are we estimating for arrival of the first survivors?"

"Tomorrow morning at the earliest," Lonson said.

"Dammit! We need foils, not rescue subs!" Panille said. "Have you asked for them?"

"First thing. Dispatcher said they couldn't be spared. Space Control has priority." Lonson grimaced. "They *would* have!"

"Easy does it, Lonson. We'll be asked for a report, that's sure. Find out if the first rescue team on the scene can spare people to interrogate the survivors."

"You afraid Guemes may have bottomed out?" Lonson asked.

"No, it's got to be something else. Ship! What a mess!" Panille's straight mouth drew into a tight line. He rubbed at the cleft in his chin. "Any estimate yet on the number of survivors?"

A young woman at the computer-record center said, "It looks like fewer than a thousand."

"Their last census was a little over ten thousand," Lonson said.

Nine thousand dead?

Panille shook his head, contemplating the monumental task of collecting and disposing of that many bodies. The bodies would have to be removed. They contaminated Merman space. And when they floated, they could only encourage dashers and other predators to new heights of aggression. Panille shuddered. Few things were more upsetting to Mermen than going out for a sledge job and running into dead, bloated Islanders.

Lonson cleared his throat. "Our last survey says Guemes was poor and losing bubbly around its rimline."

"That couldn't account for this," Panille said. He scanned the location monitor for the coordinates of the tragedy and the approaching lines of rescue craft. "Much too deep for them to have bottomed out. It must've been an explosion."

Panille turned to his left and walked slowly down the line of displays, peering over the shoulders of his operators. As he paused and asked for special views, operators zoomed in or back.

"That Island didn't just fall apart," Panille said.

"It looks as though it was torn apart and burned," an operator said. "What in Ship's teeth happened out there?"

"The survivors will be able to tell us," Panille said.

The main access behind Panille hissed open and Kareen Ale slipped through. Panille scowled at her reflection in a dark screen. Of all the dirty turns of fate! They had to send Ale for his first report! There had been a time when … Well, that was past.

She came to a stop beside Panille and swept her gaze along the display. Panille saw the shock sweep over her features as the evidence on the screens registered.

Before she could speak, he said, "Our first estimates say we'll have at least nine thousand bodies to collect. And the current is setting them into one of our oldest and largest kelp plantations. It'll be hell itself getting them out of there."

"We had a 'sonde report from Space Control," she said.

Panille's lips shaped into a soundless *ahhh-hah!* Had she been notified as a member of the diplomatic corps or as a new director of Merman Mercantile? And did it make any difference?

"We've been unable to tune in any 'sonde reports," Lonson said, speaking from across the room.

"It's being withheld," Ale said.

"What does it show?" Panille asked.

"Guemes collapsed inward and sank."

"No explosion?" Panille was more startled by this than by the revelation that the 'sonde report was being withheld. 'Sonde reports could be suppressed for many reasons. But Islands as big as Guemes did not just collapse abruptly and sink!

"No explosion," Ale said. "Just some kind of disturbance near the Island center. Guemes broke up and most of it sank."

"It probably rotted apart," the operator in front of Panille said.

"No way," Panille said. He pointed to the screens showing the maimed survivors. "Could a sub have done that?" Ale asked.

Panille remained silent, shocked by the import of her question.

"Well?" Ale insisted.

"It could have," Panille said. "But how could such an accident …"

"Don't pursue it," Ale said. "For now, forget that I asked."

There was no mistaking the command in her voice. The grim expression on Ale's face added a bitterness to the order. It sent a pulse of anger through Panille. What had that suppressed 'sonde view shown?

"When will we get the first survivors in here?" Ale asked.

"About daybreak tomorrow," Panille said. "But I've asked for the first rescue team to assign interrogators. We could have—"

"They are not to report on an open frequency," Ale said.

"But—"

"We will send out a foil," she said. She crossed to the communications desk and issued a low-voiced order, then returned to Panille. "Rescue subs are too slow. We must act with speed here."

"I didn't know we had the foils to spare."

"I am assigning new priorities," Ale said. She moved back one step and addressed the room at large. "Listen, everyone. This has happened at a very bad time. I have just brought the Chief Justice down under. We are engaged in very delicate negotiations. Rumors and premature reports could cause great trouble. What you see and hear in this room must be kept in this room. No stories outside."

Panille heard a few muttered grumblings. Everyone here knew Ale's power, but it said something about the urgency of the situation that she would give orders on his turf. Ale was a diplomat, skilled at cushioning the distasteful.

"There're already rumors," Panille said. "I heard talk in the corridors as I came over."

"And people saw you running," Ale said.

"I was told it was an emergency."

"Yes … no matter. But we must not feed the rumors."

"Wouldn't it be better to announce that there's been an Island tragedy and that we're bringing in survivors?" Panille asked.

Ale moved close to him and spoke in a low voice. "We're preparing an announcement, but the wording … delicate. This is a political nightmare … and coming at such a time. It must be handled properly."

Panille inhaled the sweet odor of the scented soap Ale used, touching off memories. He pushed such thoughts aside. She was right, of course.

"The C/P is from Guemes," Ale reminded him.

"Could Islanders have done this?" he asked.

"Possibly. There's widespread resentment of Guemes fanaticism. Still …"

"If a sub did that," Panille said, "it was one of ours. Islander subs don't carry the hardware to do that kind of damage. They're just fishermen."

"Never mind whose sub," she said. "Who would order such an atrocity? And who would carry it out?" Ale once more studied the screens, an expression of deep concern on her face.

She's convinced it was a sub, Panille thought. *That 'sonde report must've been dangerously revealing. One of our subs for sure!*

He began to sense the far-reaching political whiplash. *Guemes! Of all places!* Islanders and Mermen maintained an essential interdependency, which the Guemes tragedy could disrupt. Islander hydrogen, organically separated from sea-water, was richer and purer … and the impending space shot increased the demand for the purest hydrogen.

Movement visible through the plaz port drew Panille's dazed and wandering attention. A full squad of Mermen swam by towing a hydrostatically balanced sledge. Their dive suits flexed like a second skin, showing the powerful muscles at work.

Dive suits, he thought.

Even *they* were a potential for trouble. Islanders made the best dive suits, but the market was controlled by Mermen. Islander complaints about price controls carried little weight.

Ale, seeing where he directed his attention, and apparently divining his thoughts, gestured toward the new kelp planting visible out the plaz port. "That's only part of the problem."

"What?"

"The kelp. Without Islander agreement, the kelp project will slow almost to a stop."

"Secrecy was wrong," Panille said. "Islanders should've been brought in on it from the first."

"But they weren't," Ale said. "And as we expose more land masses above the surface …" She shrugged.

"The danger that Islands will bottom out increases," Panille said. "I know. This is Current Control, remember?"

"I'm glad you understand the political dangers," she said. "I hope you impress this upon your people."

"I'll do what I can," he said, "but I think it's already out of hand."

Ale said something too low for Panille to hear. He bent even closer to her. "I didn't hear that."

"I said the more kelp the more fish. That benefits Islanders, too."

Oh, yes, Panille thought. The movements of political control made him increasingly cynical. It was too late to stop the kelp project absolutely, but it could be slowed and the Merman dream delayed for generations. Very bad politics, that. No … the benefits had to be there for all to see. Everything focused on the kelp and the hyb tanks. First recover the hyb tanks from orbit, and then deal with the dreamers. Panille saw the practicalities,
recognizing that politics must deal in the practical while speaking mainly of dreams.

"We'll do the practical thing," he said, his voice almost a growl.

"I'm sure you will," Ale said.

"That's what Current Control is all about," he said. "I understand why you emphasize the kelp project to me. No kelp—no Current Control."

"Don't be bitter, Shadow."

It was the first time since entering Current Control that she had used his first name, but he rejected the implied intimacy.

"More than nine thousand people died out there," he said, his voice low. "If one of our subs did it …"

"Blame will have to be placed squarely," she said. "There can be no doubts, no questions …"

"No question that *Islanders* did it," he said.

"Don't play games with me, Shadow. We both know there are many Mermen who will look upon the destruction of Guemes as a benefit to all Pandora."

Panille glanced around Current Control, taking in the intent backs of his people, the way they concentrated on their work while appearing not to listen to this charged conversation. They heard, though. It dismayed him that even here would be some who agreed with the sentiment Ale had just exposed. What had been up to now just late-night scuttlebutt, cafe chatter and idle stories took on a new dimension. He felt this realization as an unwanted maturation, like the death of a parent. Cruel reality no longer could be ignored. It startled him to recognize that he had entertained dream fancies about the essential good will underlying human interactions … until just moments ago. The awakening angered him.

"I'm going to find out personally who did that," he said.

"Let's pray it was a horrible accident," she said.

"You don't believe that and neither do I." He sent his gaze across the awful testimony of those flickering screens. "It was a big sub—one of our S-twenties or larger. Did it dive deep and escape under the scattering layer?"

"There's nothing definite in the 'sonde report."

"That's what it did, then."

"Shadow, don't make trouble for yourself," Ale said. "I'm speaking as a friend. Keep your suspicions to yourself … no rumor-spreading outside this room."

"This is going to be very bad for business," he said. "I understand your concern."

She stiffened and her voice took on a coldly clipped quality. "I must go and get ready to receive the survivors. I will discuss this with you later." She turned on one heel and left.

The hatch sealed with a soft hiss behind him and Panille was left with the memory-image of her angry back and the sweet scent of her body.

Of course she had to go, he thought. Ale was a medic and every available medic would be called up in this emergency. But she was more than a medic. *Politics! Why did every political crisis have the stink of merchants hovering around it?*

Chapter 11

Consciousness is the Species-God's gift to the individual. Conscience is the Individual-God's gift to the species. In conscience you find the structure, the form of consciousness, the beauty.
—Kerro Panille, *Translations from the Avata, The Histories*

SHE DREAMS me," Duque said. His voice came strongly from the shadows at the edge of the great organic tub that he shared with Vata.

A watcher ran to summon the C/P.

Indeed, Vata had begun to dream. They were specific dreams, part her own memories, part other memories she inherited from the kelp. Avata memories. These latter included human memories acquired through the kelp's hylighter vector, and other human memories gained he knew not how … but there was death and pain involved. There were even Ship memories, and these were strangest of all. None of this had entered a human awareness in quite this way for generations.

Ship! Duque thought.

Ship moved through the void like a needle through wrinkled fabric—in at one place, out far away, and all in a blink. Ship once had created a paradise planet and planted humans on its surface, demanding:

"You must decide how you will WorShip me!"

Ship had brought humans to Pandora, which was not a paradise, but a planet almost entirely seas, and those waters moved by the unruly cycles of two suns. A physical impossibility, had Ship not done it. All this Duque saw in the flashing jerks of Vata's dreams.

"Why did Ship bring its humans to me?" Avata had asked.

Neither humans nor Ship answered. And now Ship was gone but humans remained. And the new kelp, that was Avata, now had nothing but a toehold in the sea and its dreams filled Duque's awareness.

Vata dreamed endlessly.

Duque experienced her dreams as vision-plays reproduced upon his senses. He knew their source. What Vata did to him had its own peculiar flavor, always identifiable, never to be denied.

She dreamed a woman called Waela and another called Hali Ekel. The Hali dream disturbed Duque. He felt the reality of it as though his own flesh walked those paths and felt those pains. It was Ship moving him through time and other dimensions to watch a naked man nailed to a crosspiece. Duque knew it was Hali Ekel who saw this thing but he could not separate himself from her experience. Why did some of the spectators spit on him and some weep?

The naked man raised his head and called out: "Father forgive them."

Duque felt it as a curse. To forgive such a thing was worse than demanding revenge. To be forgiven such an act—that could only be more terrible than a curse.

The C/P arrived in the Vata room. Even her bulky robes and long strides couldn't disguise the fine curves of her slim hips and ample breasts. Her body was doubly distracting because she was C/P, and because she was imprisoned inside that Guemian face. She knelt above Duque and the room immediately went silent except for the gurgle of the life-support systems.

"Duque," the C/P said, "what occurs?"

"It is real," Duque said. His voice came out strained and troubled. "It happened."

"What happened, Duque?" she asked.

Duque sensed a voice far away, much farther away than the Hali Ekel dream. He felt Hali's distress, he felt the ancient flesh she wore for Ship's excursion to that hill of terrible crosses; he felt Hali's puzzlement.

Why were they doing this thing? Why did Ship want me to see this? Duque felt both questions as his own. He had no answers. The C/P repeated her demand: "What happened, Duque?" The faraway voice was an insect buzzing in his ear. He wanted to slap it. "Ship," he said.

A gasp arose from the watchers, but the C/P did not move.

"Is Ship returning?" the C/P asked.

The question enraged Duque. He wanted to concentrate on the Hali Ekel dream. If only they would leave him alone, he felt he might find answers to his questions.

The C/P raised her voice: "Is Ship returning, Duque? You must answer!"

"Ship is everywhere!" Duque shouted.

His shout extinguished the Hali Ekel dream completely.

Duque felt anguish. He had been so close! Just a few more seconds … the answers might have come.

Now, Vata dreamed a poet named Kerro Panille and the young Waela woman of that earlier dream. Her face merged with drifting kelp, but her flesh was hot against Panille's flesh and their orgasm shuddered through Duque, driving away all other sensations.

The C/P turned her protuberant red eyes toward the watchers. Her expression was stern.

"You must say nothing of this to anyone," she ordered.

They nodded agreement, but already some among them were speculating on who might share this revelation—just one trusted friend or lover. It was too great a thing to contain.

Ship was everywhere!

Was Ship in this very room in some mysterious way?

This thought had occurred to the C/P and she asked it of Duque, who lay half somnolent in postcoital relaxation.

"Everywhere is everywhere," Duque muttered.

The C/P could not question such logic. She peered fearfully around her into the shadows of the Vata room. The watchers copied her questioning examination of their surroundings. Remembering the utterance that had been repeated to her when she had been summoned, the C/P asked: "Who dreams you, Duque?"

"Vata!" Vata stirred sluggishly and the murky nutrient rippled around her breasts.

The C/P bent close to one of Duque's bulbous ears and spoke so low that only the closest watchers heard and some of them did not hear it correctly.

"Does Vata waken?"

"Vata dreams me," Duque moaned.

"Does Vata dream of Ship?"

"Yesssss." He would tell them anything if only they would go away and leave him to these terrible and wonderful dreams.

"Does Ship send us a message?" the C/P asked.

"Go away!" Duque screamed.

The C/P rocked back on her heels. "Is that Ship's message?"

Duque remained silent.

"Where would we go?" the C/P asked.

But Duque was caught up in Vata's birth-dream and the moaning voice of Waela, Vata's mother: "My child will sleep in the sea."

Duque repeated it.

The C/P groaned. Duque had never before been this specific.

"Duque, does Ship order us to go down under?" she demanded.

Duque remained silent. He was watching the shadow of Ship darken a bloody plain, hearing Ship's inescapable voice: "I travel the Ox Gate!"

The C/P repeated her question, her voice almost a moan. But the signs were clear. Duque had spoken his piece and would not respond further. Slowly, stiffly the C/P lifted herself to her feet. She felt old and tired, far beyond her thirty-five years. Her thoughts flowed in confusion. What was the meaning of this message? It would have to be considered with great care. The words had seemed so clear ... yet, might there not be another explanation?

Are we Ship's child?

That was a weighty question.

Slowly, she cast her gaze across the awed watchers. "Remember my orders!"

They nodded, but within only a few hours, it was all over Vashon: Ship had returned. Vata was awakening. Ship had ordered them all to go down under.

By nightfall, sixteen other Islands had the message via radio, some in garbled form. The Mermen, having overheard some of the radio transmissions, had questioned their people among the Vata watchers and sent a sharp query to the C/P.

"Is it true that Ship has landed on Pandora near Vashon? What is this talk of Ship ordering the Islanders to migrate down under?"

There was more to the Merman query but C/P Rocksack, realizing that Vata security had been breached, invested herself in her most official dignity and answered just as sharply.

"All revelations concerning Vata require the most careful consideration and lengthy prayer by the Chaplain/Psychiatrist. When there is a need for you to know, you will be told."

It was quite the curtest response she had ever made to the Mermen, but the nature of Duque's words had upset her and the tone of the Merman message had been almost, but not quite, of a nature to bring down her official reprimand. The appended Merman observations she had found particularly insulting. Of course she knew there could be no swift and complete migration of Islanders down under! It was physically impossible, not to mention psychologically inadvisable. This, more than anything else, had told her that Duque's words required another interpretation. And once more she marveled at the wisdom of the ancestors in combining the functions of chaplain with those of psychiatrist.

Chapter 12

They that go down to the sea in ships,
That do business in great waters;
These see the works of the Lord,
And his wonders in the deep.
—*Christian Book of the Dead*

AS HE fell from the pier, the coracle's bowline whipping around his left ankle, Brett knew he was going under. He pumped in one quick breath before hitting the water. His hands clawed frantically for something to hold him up and he felt Twisp's hand rasp beneath his fingers but there was nothing to grip. The coracle, an anchor dragging him down, hit a submerged ledge of bubbly and upended, kicking him toward the center of the lagoon and, for a moment, he thought he was saved. He surfaced about ten meters from the pier and, over the howl of the hooters, he heard Twisp calling to him. The Island was receding fast and Brett realized the coracle's bowline had broken free of the dockside cable. He hauled in as much air as his lungs could grab and felt the line on his ankle pull him toward the Island. Doubling over underwater, he tried to free himself, but the line had tangled in a knot and his weight was enough to tug the coracle off the bubbly below the pier. He felt the line whip taut, dragging him down.

A warning rocket painted the water over him bloody orange. The surface appeared flat, the momentary calm ahead of a wavewall. Roiling water rolled him, the line on his ankle pulled steadily and he felt the pressure increase through his nose and across his chest.

I'm going to drown!

He opened his eyes wide, amazed suddenly at the clarity of his underwater vision—even better than his night vision. Dark blues and reds dominated his surroundings. The ache in his lungs increased. He held the breath tight, not wanting to let go of that last touch with life, not wanting that first gulp of water and the choking death behind it.

I always thought it would be a dasher.

The first trickle of bubbles squeezed past his lips. Panic began to pulse through him. A gush of urine warmed his crotch. He twisted his head, seeing the glow of the urine against him holding back the cold press of the sea.

I don't want to die!

His superb underwater vision followed the leak of bubbles upward, tracing them toward the distant surface, which was no longer a visible plane but only a hopeless memory.

In that instant, when he knew all hope was gone, a corner of his vision caught a dark flash, a flicker of shadow against shadow. He turned his head toward it and saw a woman swimming below him, her dive-suited flesh looking unclothed. She turned, something in her hand. Abruptly, the line of his ankle jerked once, then released.

Merman!

She rolled beneath him and he saw her eyes, open and white against a dark face. She slipped a knife into her leg sheath while she moved upward toward him.

The trickle of bubbles from his mouth became a stream, driving out of his mouth in a hot release. The woman grabbed him under an armpit and he saw clearly that she was young and supple, superbly muscled for swimming. She rolled over him. A white flash of oxygen despair began at the back of his head. Then she slammed her mouth against his and blew the sweet breath of life down his throat.

He savored it, exhaled, and again she blew a breath into him. He saw the airfish against her neck and knew she was giving him the half-used excess that her blood exuded into her lungs. It was a thing Islanders heard about, a Merman thing that he'd never expected to experience.

She backed off, dragging him by one arm. He exhaled slowly, and again she fed him air.

A Merman team had been working an undersea ridge, he saw, with kelp waving high beside it and lights glowing at the rocky top—small guide markers.

As panic receded, he saw that his rescuer wore a braided line around her waist with weights attached to it. The airfish trailing backward from her neck was pale and darkly veined, deep ridges along its length for the external gills. It was an ugly contrast to the young woman's smooth dark skin.

His lungs ceased aching, but his ears hurt. He shook his head, pulling at an ear with his free hand. She saw the movement and squeezed his arm hard to get his attention. She plugged her nose with her fingers and mimicked blowing hard. She pointed at his nose and nodded. He copied her and his right ear popped with a snap. An unpleasant fullness replaced the pain. He did it again and the left ear went.

When she gave him his next breath, she clung to him a bit longer, then smiled broadly when she broke away. A flooding sensation of happiness washed through Brett.

I'm alive! I'm alive!

He glanced past the airfish at the way her feet kicked so steadily, the strong flow of her muscles under the skin-tight suit. The light markers on the rocky ridge swept past.

Abruptly, she pulled back on his arm and stopped him beside a shiny metal tube about three meters long. He saw handgrips on it, a small steering rudder and jets. He recognized it from holos—a Merman horse. She guided his hand to one of the rear grips and gave him another breath. He saw her release a line at the nose of the device, then swing astraddle of it. She glanced backward and waved for him to do the same. He did so, locking his legs around the cold metal, both hands on the grips. She nodded and did something at the nose. Brett became conscious of a faint hum against his legs. A light glowed ahead of the woman and something snaky extruded from the horse. She turned and brought a breather mouthpiece against his lips. He saw that she also was wearing one and realized she was easing the double load the airfish had been forced to carry. The fish trailing from her neck and over his own shoulder appeared smaller, the gill ridges deeper and not as fat.

Brett gripped the mouthpiece in his teeth and pushed the lip cover hard against the flesh.

In by the mouth, out by the nose.

Every Islander had some sub schooling and parallel training with Merman rescue equipment.

Blow, inhale.

His lungs filled with rich, cool air.

He felt a lurch then and something bumped his left ankle. She rapped his knee and pulled him closer to her back, lifting his handgrips until they formed a brace against her buttocks. He had never seen a naked woman before and her dive suit left nothing for him to imagine. Unromantic as the situation was, he liked her body very much.

The horse surged upward, then dived, and her hair streamed backward, covering the head of the airfish and flickering against his cheeks.

He stared through a haze of her hair and over her right shoulder, feeling the water tumble around them. Far down the tunneling shadows of the sea past the smooth shoulder he saw a dazzling play of lights—uncounted lights—big ones, small ones, wide ones. Shapes began to grow visible: walls and towers, fine planes of platforms, dark passages and caves. The lights became plaz windows and he realized he was descending onto a Merman metropolis, one of the major centers. It had to be, with that much sprawl and that much light. The dance of illumination enthralled him, feeding through his mutated vision a rapture he had not known himself capable of feeling. A part of his awareness said this came from knowing he had survived overwhelming odds, but another part of him gloried in the new things his peculiar eyes could see.

Cross-currents began to turn and twist the horse. Brett had trouble holding his position; once he lost his leg grip. His rescuer felt this and reached back to guide one of his hands around her waist. Her feet came back and locked onto his. She crouched over her controls, guiding them toward a sprawling assemblage of blocks and domes.

His hands against her abdomen felt the smooth warmth there. His own clothing seemed suddenly ridiculous and he understood the Merman preference for dive suits and undersea nudity for the first time. They wore Islander-made dive suits for long, cold work, but their skin served them well for short spurts or warmer currents. Brett's pants chafed his thighs and cramped him, whipping in the currents of their passage.

They were much closer to the complex of buildings now and Brett began to have a new idea of the structures' sizes. The closest tower faded out of sight above them. He tried to trace it into the upper distances and realized that night had fallen topside.

We can't be very far down, he thought. *That tower could break the surface!*

But no one topside had reported such a structure.

Ship save us if an Island ever hit such a thing!

Lights from the buildings provided him with more than enough illumination, but he wondered how his rescuer was finding her way in what he knew to be deep darkness for ordinary human vision. He saw then that she was guided by fixed lights anchored to the bottom—lanes of red and green.

Even the darkest topside night had never kept him from moving around easily, but here the surface was just a faraway bruise. Brett drew a deep breath from the tube and settled himself closer to the young woman. She patted his hand on her stomach while jockeying the machine into a maze of steep-sided canyons. They rounded a corner and came onto a wide, well-lighted space between tall buildings. A dome structure loomed straight ahead with docking lips extruded from it. Many people swam in the bright illumination that glared all along the lips. Brett saw the on-off blink of a bank of hatchways opening and closing to pass the swimmers. His rescuer settled them onto a ramp with only a small sensation of grating. A Merman behind them took the horse by a rear handhold. The young woman motioned for Brett to take a deep breath. He obeyed. She gently pulled the breather from him, removed her airfish and caged it with others beside the hatch.

Through the hatch they went into a chamber where the water was quickly flushed out and replaced by air. Brett found himself standing in a dripping puddle facing the young woman, who shed water as though she and her translucent suit had been oiled.

"My name is Scudi Wang," she said. "What is yours?"

"Brett Norton," he said. He laughed self-consciously. "You … you saved my life." The statement sounded so ridiculously inadequate that he laughed again.

"It was my watch for search and rescue," she said. "We're always extra alert during a wavewall if we're near an Island."

He had never heard of such a thing but it sounded reasonable. Life was precious and his view of the world said everyone felt the same, even Mermen.

"You *are* wet," she said, looking him down and up. "Are there people who should know you are alive?"

Alive! The thought made his breathing quicken. *Alive!*

"Yes," he said. "Is it possible to get word topside?"

"We'll see to it after you're settled. There are formalities."

Brett noticed that she'd been staring at him much the same way he'd been intent on her. He guessed her age at close to his own—fifteen or sixteen. She was small, small-breasted, her skin as dark as a topside tan. She stared at him calmly out of green eyes with golden flecks in them. Her pug nose gave her a gamin look—the look of wide-eyed corridor orphans back on Vashon. Her shoulders were sloping and muscular, the muscles of someone who kept in top shape. The airfish scar glowed at her neck, a livid pink against the dark wash of her wet black hair.

"You are the first Islander I've ever rescued," she said.

"I'm …" He shook his head, finding that he did not know how to thank her for such a thing. He finished lamely: "Where are we?"

"Home," she said with a shrug. "I live here." She dropped her ballast belt at the jerk of a knot and slung it over a shoulder. "Come with me. I'll get us both some dry clothes."

He slopped after her through a hatch, his pants dripping a trail of wetness. It was cold in the long passage where the hatchway left them, but he was not too cold to miss the pleasant bounce of Scudi Wang's body as she walked away from him. He hurried to catch up. The passage was disturbingly strange to an Islander—solid underfoot, solid walls lighted by long tubes of fluorescence. The walls glowed a silvery gray broken by sealed hatches with colored symbols on them—some green, some yellow, some blue.

Scudi Wang stopped at a blue-coded hatch, undogged it and led him into a large room with storage lockers lining the sides. Benches in four rows took up the middle. Another hatch led out the opposite side. She opened a storage locker and tossed him a blue towel, then bent to rummage through another locker where she found a shirt and pants, holding them up while she looked at Brett. "These'll probably fit. We can replace them later." She tossed the faded green pants onto the bench in front of him along with a matching pullover shirt. Both were a light material that Brett didn't recognize.

Brett dried his face and hair. He stood there indecisively, his clothes still dripping. Mermen paid little attention to nudity, he had been told, but he was not used to being unclothed ... much less in the company of a beautiful woman.

She removed her dive suit unselfconsciously, found a singlesuit of light blue in another locker and sat down to pull it over her body, drying herself with a towel. He stood up, looking down at her, unable to avoid staring.

How can I thank her? he wondered. *She seems so casual about saving my life.* Actually, she seemed casual about everything. He continued to stare at her and blushed when he felt the tightening erection beginning in his cold wet pants. Wasn't there a partition or something where he could get out of sight and dress? He glanced around the room. Nothing.

She saw him looking around and chewed her lower lip.

"I'm sorry," she said. "I forgot. They say Islanders are peculiarly modest. Is that true?"

His blush deepened. "Yes."

She pulled her singlesuit up and zipped it closed quickly. "I will turn around," she said. "When you have dressed, we will eat."

Scudi Wang's quarters were the same silvery gray as the passages, a space about four meters by five, everything squared corners and sharp edges alien to an Islander. Two cot-sized bed-settees extruded from the walls, both covered with blankets of bright red and yellow in swirling geometric patterns. A kitchen counter occupied one end of the room and a closet the other. A hatch beside the closet stood open to show a bath with a small immersion tub and shower. Everything was the same material as the walls, deck and ceiling. Brett ran a hand across one of the walls and felt the cold rigidity.

Scudi found a green cushion under one of the cots and tossed it onto the other cot. "Be comfortable," she said. She threw a switch on the wall beside the kitchen counter and odd music filled the room.

Brett sat down on the cot expecting it to be hard, but it gave way beneath him, surprisingly resilient. He leaned against the cushion. "What is that music?"

She turned from an open cupboard. "Whales. You have heard of them?"

He looked toward the ceiling. "They're on the hyb tank roster, I've heard. A giant earthside mammal that lives down under."

She nodded toward the small speaker grill above the switch. "Their song is most pleasant. I'll enjoy listening to them when we recover them from space."

Brett, listening to the grunts and whistles and thrills, felt their calming influence like a long fetch of waves in a late afternoon. He failed to focus immediately on what she had said. In spite of the whalesong, or perhaps because of it, there was a sense of deep quiet in the room that he had never before experienced.

"What do you do topside?" Scudi asked.

"I'm a fisherman."

"That's good," she said, busying herself at the counter. "It puts you on the waves. Waves and currents, that's how we generate our power."

"So I've heard," he said. "What do you do—besides rescues?"

"I mathematic the waves," she said. "That is my true work."

Mathematic the waves? He had no idea what that meant. It forced him to reflect on how little he knew about Merman life. Brett glanced around the room. The walls were hard but he was mistaken about the cold. They were warm, unlike the locker-room walls. Scudi, too, did not seem cold. As she had led him here along the solid passages, they had passed many people. Most had nodded greeting as they chattered with friends or workmates. Everyone moved quickly and surely and the passageways weren't full of people jostling shoulder-to-shoulder all the way. Except for workbelts, many had been naked. None of that outside bustle penetrated to this little room, though. He contrasted this to topside, where the organics tended to transmit even the smallest noises. Here, there was the luxury of noise and the luxury of quiet within a few meters of each other.

Scudi did something above her work area and the room's walls suddenly were brightly colored in flowing sweeps of yellow and green. Long strands of something like kelp undulated in a current—an abstraction. Brett was fascinated at how the color-motion on the walls accompanied the whalesong.

What do I say to her? he wondered. *Alone with a pretty girl in her room and I can't think of anything. Brilliant, Norton! You're a glittering conversationalist!*

He wondered how long he'd been with her. Topside, he kept good track of time by the light of the suns and the dark patches between. Down here, all light was similar. It was disorienting.

He looked at Scudi's back while she worked. She pressed a wall button and he heard her murmur something on a Merman transphone. Seeing the phone there impressed him with the technological gulf between Islanders and Mermen. Mermen had this device; Islanders were not offered it in the mercantile. He didn't doubt that some Islanders got them through the black market, but he didn't know how it would be of any use to them unless they dealt with Mermen all the time. Some Islanders did. Islander sub crews carried portable devices that picked up some transphone channels, but this was for the Mermen's convenience as well as Islanders'. Mermen were so damned snobbish about their riches!

There was a faint hiss of pneumatics at the counter where Scudi worked. She turned presently, balancing a tray carrying covered bowls and utensils. She placed the tray on the deck between the two cots and pulled up a cushion for her own back.

"I don't cook much myself," she said. "The central kitchen is faster, but I add my own spices. They are so bland at central!"

"Oh?" He watched her uncover the bowls, enjoying the smells.

"People already want to know of you," she said. "I have had several calls. I told them to wait. I'm hungry and tired. You, too?"

"I'm hungry," he agreed. He glanced around the room. Only these two cots. Did she expect him to sleep here … with her?

She pulled a bowl and spoon up to her lap. "My father taught me to cook," she said.

He picked up the bowl nearest him and took a spoon. This was not like Islander feeding ritual, he noticed. Scudi already was spooning broth into her mouth. Islanders fed guests first, then ate whatever the guests left for them. Brett had heard that this didn't always work well with Mermen—they often ate everything and left nothing for the host. Scudi licked a few drops of broth from the back of her hand.

Brett tasted a sip from his spoon.

Delicious!

"The air is dry enough for you?" Scudi asked.

He nodded, his mouth full of soup.

"My room is small but that makes it easier to keep the air the way I like it. And easier to keep clean. I work topside very often. Dry is comfort to me now and I don't feel comfortable with the humidity in passages and public places." She put the bowl to her lips and drained it.

Brett copied her, then asked, "What will happen to me? When will I go back topside?"

"We'll talk of this after food," she said. She brought up two more bowls and uncovered them, revealing bite-sized chunks of fish in a dark sauce. With the bowl she handed him a pair of carved bone chopsticks.

"After food," he agreed and took a bite of the sauced fish. It was peppery hot and brought tears to his eyes but he found the aftertaste pleasant.

"It is our custom," Scudi said. "Food sets the body at ease. I can say, 'Brett Norton, you are safe here and well.' But I know down under is alien to you. And you have been in danger. You must speak to your body in the language it understands before sense returns to you. Food, rest—these are what your body speaks."

He liked the rational sense of her words and returned to the fish, enjoying it more with each bite. Scudi, he saw, was eating as much as he even though she was much smaller. He liked the delicate flick of her chopsticks into the bowl and at the edge of her mouth.

What a beautiful mouth, he thought. He remembered how she had given him that first breath of life.

She caught him staring and he quickly returned his attention to his bowl.

"The sea takes much energy, much heat," she said. "I wear a dive suit as little as possible. Hot shower, much hot food, a warm bed—these are always needed. Do you work the Islander subs topside, Brett?"

Her question caught him off guard. He'd begun to think that she had no curiosity about him.

Maybe I'm just some kind of obligation to her, he thought. *If you save someone, maybe you're stuck with them.*

"I'm a surface fisherman for a contractor named Twisp," he said. "He's the one that

I most want to get word to. He's a strange man, but the best in a boat I've seen."

"Surface," she said. "That's much danger from dashers, isn't it? Have you seen dashers?"

He tried to swallow in a suddenly dry throat. "We carry squawks. They warn us,

you know." He hoped that she wouldn't notice the dodge.

"We're afraid of your nets," she said. "Sometimes visibility is bad and they can't be seen. Mermen have been killed in them."

He nodded, remembering the thrashing and the blood and Twisp's stories of other Mermen deaths in the nets. Should he mention that to Scudi? Should he ask about the strange reaction of the Maritime Court? No … she might not understand. This would be a barrier between them.

Scudi sensed this, too. He could tell because she spoke too quickly. "Would you not prefer to work in your subs? I know they are soft-bellied, not like ours at all, but …"

"I think … I think I'd like to stay with Twisp unless he goes back to the subs. I'd sure like to know if he's all right."

"We will rest and when we wake, you will meet some of our people who can help. Mermen travel far. We pass along the word. You will hear of him and he of you … if that's your wish."

"My wish?" He stared at her, absorbing this. "You mean I could choose to … disappear?"

She shrugged her eyebrows, accenting the gamin look. "Where you want to be is where you should be. Who you want to be is the same, not so?"

"It can't be that simple."

"If you have not broken the law, there are possibilities down under. The Merman world is big. Wouldn't you like to stay here?" She coughed and he wondered if she had been about to say "stay here with me?" Scudi suddenly seemed much older, more worldly. Talk among the Islanders gave Brett the impression that Mermen had an extra sophistication, a sense of belonging anywhere they went, of knowing more than Islanders.

"Do you live alone?" he asked.

"Yes. This was my mother's place. And it's close to where my father lived."

"Don't Merman families live together?"

She scowled. "My parents … stubborn, both of them. They couldn't live together. I lived with my father for a long time, but … he died." She shook her head and he saw the memories pain her.

"I'm sorry," he said. "Where's your mother?"

"She is dead too." Scudi looked away from him. "My mother was net-bound less than a year ago." Scudi's throat moved with a convulsive swallow as she turned back to him. "It has been difficult … there is a man, GeLaar Gallow, who became my mother's … lover. That was after …" She broke off and shook her head sharply.

"I'm sorry, Scudi," he said. "I didn't mean to bring back painful—"

"But I want to talk about it! Down here, there is no one I can … I mean, my closest friends avoid the subject and I …" She rubbed her left cheek. "You are a new friend and you listen."

"Of course, but I don't see what …"

"After my father died, my mother signed over … You understand, Brett, that my father was Ryan Wang, there was much wealth?"

Wang! he thought. *Merman Mercantile. His rescuer was a wealthy heiress!*

"I … I didn't …"

"It is all right. Gallow was to be my stepfather. My mother signed over to him control of much that my father left. Then she died."

"So there's nothing for you."

"What? Oh, you mean from my father. No, that is not my problem. Besides, Kareen Ale is my new guardian. My father left her … many things. They were friends."

"What … you said there's a problem."

"Everyone wants Kareen to marry Gallow and Gallow pursues this."

Brett noted that Scudi's lips tightened every time she spoke Gallow's name. "What is wrong with this Gallow?" he asked.

Scudi spoke in a low voice. "He frightens me."

"Why? What's he done?"

"I don't know. But he was on the crew when my father died … and when my mother died."

"Your mother … you said a net …"

"An Islander net. That is what they said."

He lowered his gaze, remembering his recent experience with a Merman in the net.

Seeing the look on his face, Scudi said: "I have no resentment toward you. I can see that you are sorry. My mother knew the danger of nets."

"You said Gallow was with your parents when they died. Do you …"

"I have never spoken of this to anyone before. I don't know why I say it to you, but you are sympathetic. And you … I mean …"

"I owe you."

"Oh, no! It is nothing like that. It's just … I like your face and the way you listen."

Brett lifted his gaze and met her staring at him. "Is there no one who can help you?" he asked. "You said Kareen Ale … everyone knows about her. Can't she—"

"I would never say these things to Kareen!"

Brett studied Scudi for a moment, seeing the shock and fear in her face. He already had a sense of the wildness in Merman life from the stories told among Islanders. Violence was no stranger down here, if the stories were to be believed. But what Scudi suggested …

"You wonder if Gallow had anything to do with the deaths of your parents," he said.

She nodded without speaking.

"Why do you suspect this?"

"He asked me to sign many papers but I pleaded ignorance and consulted Kareen. I don't think the papers he showed her were the same ones he brought to me. She has not said yet what I should do."

"Has he … " Brett cleared his throat. "What I mean is … you are … that is, sometimes Islanders marry young."

"There has been nothing like that, except he tells me to hurry and grow up. It is all a joke. He says he is tired of waiting for me."

"How old are you?"

"I will be sixteen next month. You?"

"I'll be seventeen in five months."

She looked at his net-calloused hands. "Your hands say you work hard, for an Islander." Immediately, she popped a hand over her mouth. Her eyes went wide.

Brett had heard Merman jokes about lazy Islanders sunning themselves while Mermen built a world under the sea. He scowled.

"I have a big mouth," Scudi said. "I find someone at last who can really be my friend and I offend him."

"Islanders aren't lazy," Brett said.

Scudi reached out impulsively and took his right hand in hers. "I have only to look at you and I know the stories are lies."

Brett pulled his hand away. He still felt hurt and bewildered. Scudi might say something soothing to smooth it over, but the truth had come out involuntarily.

I work hard, for an Islander!

Scudi got to her feet and busied herself removing the dishes and the remains of their meal. Everything went into a pneumatic slot at the kitchen wall and vanished with a click and a hiss.

Brett stared at the slot. The workers who took care of that probably were Islanders permanently hidden from view.

"Central kitchens and all this space," he said. "It's Mermen who have things easy."

She turned toward him, an intent expression on her face. "Is that what Islanders say?"

Brett felt his face grow hot.

"I don't like jokes that lie," Scudi said. "I don't think you do, either."

Brett swallowed past a sudden lump in his throat. Scudi was so direct! That was not the Islander way at all, but he found himself attracted by it.

"Queets never tells those jokes and I don't either," Brett said.

"This Queets, he is your father?"

Brett thought suddenly about his father and his mother—the butterfly life between intense bouts of painting. He thought about their downcenter apartment, the many things they owned and cared for—furniture, art work, even some Merman appliances. Queets, though, owned only what he could store in his boat. He owned what he truly needed—a kind of survival selectivity.

"You are ashamed of your father?" Scudi asked.

"Queets isn't my father. He's the fisherman who owns my contract—Queets Twisp."

"Oh, yes. You do not own many things, do you, Brett? I see you looking around my quarters and …" She shrugged.

"The clothes on my back were mine," Brett said. "When I sold my contract to Queets, he took me on for training and gave me what I need. There isn't room for useless stuff on a coracle."

"This Queets, he is a frugal man? Is he cruel to you?"

"Queets is a good man! And he's strong. He's stronger than anyone I've ever known. Queets has the longest arms you've ever seen, perfect for working the nets. They're almost as long as he is tall."

A barely perceptible shudder crossed Scudi's shoulders. "You like this Queets very much," she said.

Brett looked away from her. That unguarded shudder told it all. Islanders made Mermen shudder. He felt the pain of betrayal deep in his guts. "You Mermen are all the same," he said. "Mutants don't ask to be that way."

"I don't think of you as a mutant, Brett," she said. "Anyone can see that you're normalized."

"There!" Brett snapped, glaring at her. "What's normal? Oh, I've heard the talk: Islanders are having more 'normal' births these days … and there's always surgery. Twisp's long arms offend you? Well, he's no freak. He's the best fisherman on Pandora because he fits what he does."

"I see that I've learned many wrong things," Scudi said, her voice low. "Queets Twisp must be a good man because Brett Norton admires him." A wry smile touched her lips and was gone. "Have you learned no wrong things, Brett?"

"I'm … after what you did for me, I should not be talking to you this way."

"Wouldn't you save me if I were caught in your net? Wouldn't you …"

"I'd go in after you and damn the dashers!"

She grinned, an infectious expression that Brett found himself answering in kind.

"I know you would, Brett. I like you. I learn things about Islanders from you that I didn't know. You are different, but …"

His grin vanished. "My eyes are good eyes!" he snapped, thinking this was the difference she meant.

"Your eyes?" She stared at him. "They are beautiful eyes! In the water, I saw your eyes first. They are large eyes and … difficult to escape." She lowered her gaze. "I like your eyes."

"I … I thought …"

Again, she met his gaze. "I've never seen two Islanders exactly alike, but Mermen are never exactly alike, either."

"Everyone down under won't feel that way," he accused.

"Some will stare," she agreed. "It is not normal to be curious?"

"They'll call me Mute," he said.

"Most will not."

"Queets says words are just funny ripples in the air or printed squiggles."

Scudi laughed. "I would like to meet this Queets. He sounds like a wise man."

"Nothing much ever bothered him except losing his boat."

"Or losing you? Will that bother him?"

Brett sobered. "Can we get word to him?"

Scudi touched the transphone button and voiced his request over the grill in the wall. The response was too quiet for Brett to hear. She did it casually. He thought then that this marked the difference between them more firmly than his own overlarge eyes with their marvelous night vision.

Presently, Scudi said: "They will try to get word to Vashon." She stretched and yawned.

Even yawning, she was beautiful, he thought. He glanced around the room, noting the closeness of the two cots. "You lived here with just your mother?" he asked. Immediately, he saw the sad expression return to Scudi's face and he cursed himself. "I'm sorry, Scudi. I should not keep reminding you of her."

"It's all right, Brett. We are here and she is not. Life continues … and I do my mother's work." Again, that gamin grin twisted her mouth. "And you are my first roommate."

He scratched his throat, embarrassed, not knowing the moral rules between the sexes down under. What did it mean to be a roommate? Stalling for time, he asked: "What is this work of your mother's that you do?"

"I told you. I mathematic the waves."

"I don't know what that means."

"Where new waves or wave patterns are seen, I go. As my mother did and both her parents before her. It is a thing for which our family has a natural talent."

"But what do you do?"

"How the waves move, that tells us how the suns move and how Pandora responds to that movement."

"Oh? Just from looking at the waves, you … I mean, waves are gone just like that!" He snapped his fingers.

"We simulate the waves in a lab," she said. "You know about wavewalls, I'm sure," she said. "Some go completely around Pandora several times."

"And you can tell when they'll come?"

"Sometimes." He thought about this. The extent of Merman knowledge suddenly daunted him. "You know we warn the Islands when we can," she said.

He nodded.

"To mathematic the waves, I must translate them," she said. She patted her head absently, exaggerating her gamin appearance. "Translate is a better word than mathematic," she said. "And I teach what I do, of course."

Of course! he thought. *An heiress! A rescuer! And now an expert on waves!*

"Who do you teach?" he asked, wondering if he could learn this thing she did. How valuable that would be for the Islands!

"The kelp," she said. "I translate waves for the kelp."

He was shocked. Was she joking, making fun of Islander ignorance?

She saw the expression on his face because she went on, quickly: "The kelp learns. It can be taught to control currents and waves … when it returns to its former density, it will learn more. I teach it some of the things it must know to survive on Pandora."

"This is a joke, isn't it?" he asked.

"Joke?" She looked puzzled. "Don't you know the stories of the kelp as it was? It fed itself, it moved gases in and out of the water. The hylighters! Oh, I would love to see them! The kelp knew so many things, and it controlled the currents, the sea itself. All of this the kelp did once."

Brett gaped at her. He recalled schooltime stories about the sentient kelp, one creature alive as a single identity in all of its parts. But that was ancient history, from the time when men had lived on solid land above Pandora's sea.

"And it will do this again?" he whispered.

"It learns. We teach it how to make currents and to neutralize waves."

Brett thought about what this might mean to Island life—drifting on predictable currents in predictable depths. They could follow the weather, the fishing … An odd turn of thought put this out of his mind. He considered it almost unworthy, but who could know for certain what an alien intelligence might do?

Scudi, noting his expression, asked: "Are you well?"

He spoke almost mechanically. "If you can teach the kelp to control the waves, then it must know how to *make* waves. And currents. What's to prevent it from wiping us out?"

She was scornful. "The kelp is rational. It would not further the kelp to destroy us or the Islands. So it will not."

Again, she stilled a yawn and he recalled her comment that she had to go back to work soon.

The ideas she had put into his head whirled there, though, leaving him on edge, driving away all thought of sleep. Mermen did so many things! They knew so much!

"The kelp will think for itself." He recalled hearing someone say that, a conversation at the quarters of his parents—important people talking about important matters.

"But that could not happen without Vata," someone had said in response. *"Vata is the key to the kelp."*

That had begun what he remembered as a sprightly and boo-inspired conversation, which, as usual, ran from speculative to paranoid and back.

"I'll turn out the light for your modesty," Scudi said. She giggled and touched the light down through dim to barely shadow. He watched her fumble her way to her bed.

It's dark to her, he thought. *For me she just turned down the glare.* He shifted on the edge of his bed.

"You have a girlfriend topside?" Scudi asked.

"No … not really."

"You have never shared a room with a girl?"

"On the Islands, you share everything with everyone. But to have a room, two people alone, that's for couples who are new to each other. For mating. It is very expensive."

"Oh, my," she said.

In the shadow-play of his peculiar vision he watched her fingers dance nervously over the surface of her cot.

"Down under we share for mating, yes, but we also share rooms for other reasons. Work partners, schoolmates, good friends. I mean only for you to have one night of recovery. Tomorrow there will be others and questions and tours and much noise …" Still her hands moved in that nervous rhythm.

"I don't know how I can ever repay you for being so nice to me," he said.

"But it is our custom," she said. "If a Merman saves you, you can have what the Merman has until you … move on. If I bring life into this compound, I'm responsible for it."

"As though I were your child?"

"Something like." She sighed, and began undressing. Brett found he could not invade her privacy and averted his eyes.

Maybe I should tell her, he thought. *It's not really fair to be able to see this way and not let her know.*

"I would prefer not to interfere with your life," he said.

He heard Scudi slip under her blankets. "You don't interfere," she said. "This is one of the most exciting things that has ever happened to me. You are my friend; I like you. Is that enough?"

Brett dropped his clothes and slipped under the covers, pulling them to his neck. Queets always said you couldn't figure a Merman. Friends?

"We are friends, not so?" she insisted.

He offered his hand across the space between the beds. Realizing that she couldn't see it, he picked up hers in his own. She pressed his fingers hard, her hand warm in his. Presently, she sighed and removed her hand gently.

"I must sleep," she said.

"Me, too."

Her hand lifted from the bed and found the switch on the wall. The whale sounds stopped.

Brett found the room exquisitely quiet, a stillness he had not imagined possible. He felt his ears relaxing, then, an alertness … suddenly listening for … what? He didn't know. Sleep was necessary, though. He had to sleep. His mind said: "Something is being done about informing your parents and Queets." He was alive and family and friends would be happy after their fears and sadness. Or so he hoped.

After several nervous minutes, he decided the lack of motion was preventing sleep. The discovery allowed him to relax more, breathe easier. He could remember with his body the gentle rocking motion topside and thought hard about that, tricking his mind into the belief that waves still lifted and fell beneath him.

"Brett?" Scudi's voice was little more than a whisper.

"Yes?"

"Of all the creatures in hyb, the ones I would like most are the birds, the little birds that sing."

"I've heard recordings from Ship," he said, his voice sleepy. "The songs are as painfully beautiful as the whales. And they fly."

"We have pigeons and squawks," he said.

"The squawks are ducks and they do not sing," she said. "But they whistle when they fly and it's fun to watch them." Her blankets rustled as she turned away from him.

"Good night, friend," she whispered. "Sleep flat."

"Good night, friend," he answered. And there, at the edge of sleep, he imagined her beautiful smile.

Is this how love begins? he wondered. There was a tightness in his chest, which did not go away until he fell into a restless sleep.

Chapter 13

The child Vata slipped into catatonia as the kelp and hylighters sickened. She has been comatose for more than three years now and, since she carries both kelp and human genes, it is hoped that she can be instrumental in restoring the kelp to sentience. Only the kelp can tame this terrible sea.

—Hali Ekel, *The Journals*

IT WAS not so much that Ward Keel noticed the stillness as that he felt it all over his skin. Events had conspired to keep him topside throughout his long life, not that he had ever felt a keen desire to go down under.

Admit it, he told himself. *You were afraid because of all the stories—deprivation shock, pressure syndrome.*

Now, for the first time in his life there was no movement of deck under his bare feet, no nearby sounds of human activity and voices, no hiss of organic walls against organic ceilings—none of the omnipresent frictions to which Islanders adjusted as infants. It was so quiet his ears ached.

Beside him in the room where Kareen Ale had left him "to adjust for a few moments" stood a large plazglass wall revealing a rich undersea expanse of reds, blues and washed greens. The subtlety of unfamiliar shadings held him rapt for several minutes.

Ale had said: "I will be nearby. Call if you need me."

Mermen well knew the weaknesses of those who came down under. Awareness of all that water overhead created its own peculiar panic in some of the visitors and migrants. And being alone, even by choice, was not something Islanders tolerated well until they had adjusted to it … slowly. A lifetime of knowing that other human beings were just on the other side of those thin organic walls, almost always within the sound of a whispered call, built up blind spots. You did not hear certain things—the sounds of lovemaking, family quarrels and sorrows.

Not unless you were invited to hear them.

Was Ale softening him up by leaving him alone here? Keel wondered. Could she be watching through some secret Merman device? He felt certain that Ale, with her medical background and long association with Islanders, knew the problems of a first-timer.

Having watched Ale perform her diplomatic duties over the past few years, Keel knew she seldom did anything casually. She planned. He was sure she had a well-thought-out motive for leaving an Islander alone in these circumstances.

The silence pressed hard upon him.

A demanding thought filled his mind: *Think, Ward! That's what you're supposed to be so good at.* He found it alarming that the thought came to him in his dead mother's voice, touching his aural centers so sharply that he glanced around, almost fearful that he would see a ghostly shade shaking a finger of admonishment at him.

He breathed deeply once, twice, and felt the constriction of his chest ease slightly. Another breath and the edge of reason returned. Silence did not ache as much nor press as heavily.

During the descent by courier sub, Ale had asked him no questions and had supplied no answers. Reflecting on this, he found it odd. She was noted for hard questions to pave the way for her own arguments.

Was it possible that they simply wanted him down here and away from his seat on

the Committee? he wondered. Taking him as an invited guest was, after all, less stressful and dangerous than outright kidnapping. It felt odd to think of himself as a commodity with some undetermined value. Comforting, though; it meant they would probably not employ violence against him.

Now, why did I think that? he wondered.

He stretched his arms and legs and crossed to the couch facing the undersea view. The couch felt softly supportive under him in spite of the fact that it was of some dead material. The stiffness of age made the soft seat especially welcome. He sensed the dying remora within him still fighting to survive. *Avoid anxiety,* the medics told him. That was most certainly a joke in his line of work. The remora still produced vital hormones, but he remembered the warning: "We can replace it, although the replacements won't last long. And their survival time will become shorter and shorter as new replacements are introduced. You are rejecting them, you see." His stomach growled. He was hungry and that he found to be a good sign. There was nothing to indicate a food preparation area in the room. No speakers or viewscreens. The ceiling sloped upward away from the couch to the view port, which appeared to be about six or seven meters high.

How extravagant! he thought. Only one person in all this space. A room this size could house a large Islander family. The air was a bit cooler than he liked but his body had adjusted. The dim light through the view port cast a green wash over the floor there. Bright phosphorescence from the ceiling dominated the illumination. The room was not far under the sea's surface. He knew this from the outside light level. Plenty of water over him, though: millions of kilos. The thought of all that weight pressing in on this space brought a touch of sweat to his upper lip. He ran a damp palm over the wall behind the couch—warm and firm. He breathed easier. This was Merman space. They didn't build anything fragile. The wall was plasteel. He had never before seen so much of it. The room struck him suddenly as a fortress. The walls were dry, testimony to a sophisticated ventilation system. Mermen topside tended to keep their quarters so humid he felt smothered by the air. Except for Ale … but she was like no other human he had ever met, Islander or Merman. The air in this room, he realized, had been adjusted for Islander comfort. That reassured him.

Keel patted the couch beside him and thought of Joy, how much she would like that surface. A hedonist, Joy. He tried to picture her resting on the couch. A desire for Joy's comforting presence filled him with sudden loneliness. Abruptly, he wondered about himself. He had been mostly a loner throughout his life, only the occasional liaison. Was the proximity of death working a fearful change on him? The thought disgusted him. Why should he inflict himself on Joy, saddle her with the sorrow of a permanent parting?

I am going to die soon.

He wondered briefly who the Committee would elect as Chief Justice to replace him. His own choice would be Carolyn, but the political choice would be Matts. He did not envy whoever they chose. It was a thankless job. There were things to do before he made his final exit, though. He stood and steadied himself against the couch. His neck ached, as usual. His legs felt rubbery and didn't want to support him at first. That was a new symptom. The deck underfoot was hard plasteel and he was thankful that it, like the walls, was heated. He waited for strength to return, then, leaning against the wall, made his way toward the door at his left. There were two buttons beside the door. He pressed the lower one and heard a panel slide back behind the couch. He looked toward the sound and his heart shifted into triple-time.

The panel had concealed a mural. He stared at it. The thing was frighteningly realistic, almost photographic. It showed a surface construction site at least half-destroyed, flames everywhere and men wriggling in the tentacles of hylighters drifting overhead.

Hylighters died with the kelp, he thought. This was either an old painting or somebody's imaginative reconstruction of history. He suspected the former. The rich suns-set background, the intimate detail of hylighters—everything focused on one worker near the center who pointed a finger at the viewer. It was an accusing figure, dark-eyed and glaring.

I know that place, Keel thought. *How is it possible?* Familiarity was stronger than the flutterings of deja vu. This was real seeing, a memory. The memory told him that somewhere in this room or nearby there was a red mandala.

How do I know this?

He examined the room carefully. Couch, plaz port, the mural, bare walls, an oval hatch-door. No mandala. He walked to the view port and touched it. Cool, the only cool surface in the room. How strange the fixed view port installation was—nothing like it at all on the Islands. Couldn't be. The flex of bubbly around the solid plaz would tear away the organics that sealed it and the heavy, solid material would turn into a thing of destruction during a storm. Drift watchers, mutated cornea, were safer in rough weather even if they did require care and feeding.

The plaz was incredibly clear. Nothing in the feel of it suggested the extreme density and thickness. A small, heavily whiskered scrubberfish grazed the outside, cleaning the surface. Beyond the fish, a pair of Mermen came into view, jockeying a heavy sledge loaded with rocks and mud. They went past him out of sight beyond a slope to his right.

Out of curiosity, Keel fisted the plaz: *thump-thump.* The scrubberfish continued grazing, undisturbed. Anemone and ferns, grasses and sponges waved in the current beneath the fish. Dozens of other fish, a multicolored mixed school, cleaned the surface of kelp leaves beyond the immediate growth. Larger fish poked along the soft bottom mud, stirring up puffs of gray sediment. Keel had seen this sort of thing in holos but the reality was different.

Some of the fish he recognized—creatures from the labs that had been brought for judgment by the Committee before being released in the sea.

A harlequin fish came up below the scrubber and nudged the plaz. Keel remembered the day the C/P had blessed the first harlequin fish before their release. It was almost like seeing an old friend.

Once more, Keel turned to his examination of the room and that elusive memory. Why did it feel so damned familiar? Memory said the missing mandala should be to the right of the mural. He walked to that wall and brushed a finger along it, looking for another panel switch. Nothing, but the wall moved slightly and he heard a clicking. He peered at it. It was not plasteel but some kind of light, composite material. A faint seam ran down the middle of the wall. He put a palm against the surface to the right of the seam and pushed. The panel slid back, revealing a passage, and immediately he smelled food.

He opened the panel wide and walked through. The passage made a sharp turn to the left and he saw lights. Kareen Ale stood there in a kitchen-dining area, her back to him. A rich smell of strong tea and fish broth assailed his nostrils. He drew a breath to speak but stopped as he saw the red mandala. The sight of it above Kareen's right shoulder brought a sigh from Keel. The mandala drew his consciousness into the shapes there, twisting him through circles and wedges toward the center. A single eye peered out from the center, out at the universe. It was unlidded, and rested atop a golden pyramid.

These can't be my memories, he thought. It was a terrifying experience. Ship memories flitted through his mind—someone walking down a long, curved passage, a violet-lighted agrarium fanned out to his left. He felt powerless before the stream of visions. Kelp waved to him from someplace under the sea and schools of fish his Committee had never approved swam past his eyes.

Ale turned and saw the enraptured expression on his face, the fixed intensity with which he stared at the mandala.

"Are you all right?" she asked.

Her voice shocked him out of the other-memories. He exhaled a trembling breath, inhaled.

"I'm … I'm hungry," he said. There was no thought of revealing the weird memories he had just experienced. How could she understand when he did not understand?

"Why don't you sit here?" she asked. She indicated a small table set for two at one end of the kitchen area beside a smaller plaz port. The table was low, Merman-style. His knees ached just thinking about sitting there.

"I've cooked for you myself," Ale said.

Noting his still bemused expression, she added: "That hatchway in the other room leads to a head with shower and washbasin. Beyond it you'll find office facilities if you require them. The exterior hatchways are out there as well."

He crowded his legs under the table and sat with his elbows on the surface in front of him, his hands supporting his head.

Was that a dream? he wondered.

The red mandala lay directly in front of him. He was almost afraid to focus on it.

"You're admiring the mandala," Ale said. She busied herself once more in the kitchen area.

He lifted his attention and let his gaze trace the ancient lines along their mysterious pathways. Nothing drew him inward this time. Slowly, bits of his own memories crept into his mind, images flashed behind his eyes and stuttered like a crippled larynx, then caught. Awareness reached back to one of his earliest history lessons, a holo being played in the center of a classroom. It had been a docudrama for young children. Islanders loved theatricals and this one had been fascinating. He could not remember the title, but he did recall that it dealt with the last days of Pandora's continents—they didn't look small at all in the holos—and the death of the kelp. That had been the first time Keel had heard the kelp called "Avata." Behind the holo figures playing out the drama in a command post there had been a wall … and that frightening mural from the outer room. Nearby, as the holo shifted its focus, there had been the red mandala, just as he saw it now. Keel did not want to think how long ago he had watched the drama—more than seventy years, anyway. He returned his attention to Ale.

"Is that the original mandala or a copy?" he asked.

"I'm told it's the original. It's very old, older than any settlement on Pandora. You seem taken by it."

"I've seen it and the mural out there before," he said. "These walls and the kitchen area are more recent, aren't they?"

"The space was remodeled for my convenience," she said. "I've always been drawn to these rooms. The mandala and mural are where they've always been. And they're cared for."

"Then I know where I am," he said. "Islander children learn history through holodramas and …"

"I know that one," she said. "Yes, this is part of the old Redoubt. Once it stood completely out of the sea, with some fine mountains behind it, I understand."

She brought food to the table on a tray and set out the bowls and chopsticks.

"Wasn't most of the Redoubt destroyed?" he asked. "The documentary holos were supposed to be reconstructions of a few from before …"

"Whole sections survived intact," she said. "Automatic latches closed and sealed off much of the Redoubt. We restored it very carefully."

"I'm impressed." He nodded, reassessing the probable importance of Kareen Ale. Mermen had remodeled a part of the old Redoubt for her convenience. She lived casually in a museum, apparently immune to the historical value of the objects and building surrounding her. He had never before met a Merman in a Merman environment, and he now recognized this blank spot in his experience as a weakness. Keel forced himself to relax. For a dying man, there were advantages to being here. He didn't have to decide life and death for new life. No pleading mothers and raging fathers would confront him with creatures who could not pass Committee. This was a world away from the Islands.

Ale sipped her tea. It smelled of mint and suddenly reignited Keel's hunger. He began to eat, Islander-style, setting aside equal portions for his host. The first taste of the fish broth convinced him that it was the richest and most delicately spiced broth he'd ever shared. Was this the general diet for Mermen? He cursed his lack of down-under experience. Keel noticed that Ale enjoyed her own helping of the steaming soup and felt insulted at first.

Another cultural thing, he realized. He marveled that a simple difference in table manners could need translation to avoid international disaster. Unanswered questions still buzzed in his head. Perhaps a more devious approach was indicated—a mixture of Merman directness with Islander obliqueness.

"It's pleasantly dry in these quarters," he said, "but you don't need a sponge. You don't oil your skin. I've often wondered how you get by in a topside environment?"

She dropped her gaze from his face and held her teacup to her lips with both hands.

Hiding, he thought.

"Ward, you are a very strange person," she said as she lowered the cup. "That is not the question I expected."

"What question did you expect?"

"I prefer to discuss my immunity from the need for a sponge. You see, we have quarters down under that are kept with a topside environment. I was raised in such quarters. I'm acclimated to Islander conditions. And I adapt very quickly to the humidity down under—when I have to."

"You were chosen as an infant for topside duty?" There was hesitation and shock in his voice.

"I was chosen then for my present position," she said. "A number of us were … set aside in the possibility that some of us would meet the mental and physical requirements."

Keel stared at her, astonished. He had never heard of such a cold dismissal of someone's entire life. Ale had not chosen her own life! And, unlike most Islanders, she had a body that in no way restricted her from any trade she chose. He remembered suddenly how she planned everything—a planned person who planned. Ale had been … distorted. She probably saw it as training, but training was just an acceptable distortion.

"But you do live a … a Merman life?" he asked. "You follow their customs, you swim and …"

"Look." She unfastened her tunic at the neck and dropped the top of it, turning her breasts away from him to expose the shoulders. Her back was as clear-skinned and pale as weathered bone. At the top of her shoulder blades the skin had been pinched into a short strip of ridge adjacent to the spine. There she carried the clear pucker-mark of an airfish, but in a peculiar place. He caught the meaning immediately.

"If that mark were on your neck, Islanders might be distracted when they met you, right?" It occurred to him that she would have undergone major arterial reshifting to carry this off—a complicated surgery.

"You have beautiful skin," he added, "it's a shame they marked it up that way at all."

"It was done when I was very young," she said. "I hardly think about it anymore. It's just a … convenience."

He resisted the urge to stroke her shoulder, her smooth strong back.

Careful, you old fool! he told himself.

She restored the top of her garment and when her gaze met his, he realized that he had been staring.

"You're very beautiful, Kareen," he said. "In the old holos, all humans look … something like you, but you're …" He shrugged, feeling the exceptional presence of his appliance against his neck and shoulders. "Forgive an old Mute," he added, "but I've always thought of you as the ideal."

She turned a puzzled frown on him. "I've never before heard an Islander call himself a … a Mute. Is that how you think of yourself?"

"Not really. But a lot of Islanders use the term. Joking, mostly, but sometimes a mother will use it to get a youngster's attention. Like: 'Mute, get your grubby little paws outa that frosting.' Or: 'You go for that deal, my man, and you're one dumb Mute.' Somehow, when it comes from one of us it's all right. When it comes from a Merman—it strikes deeper than I can describe. Isn't that what you call us among yourselves, 'Mutes'?"

"Boorish Mermen might, and … well, it's a rather common bit of slang in some company. Personally, I don't like the word. If a distinction has to be made, I prefer 'Clone,' or 'Lon,' as our ancestors did. Perhaps my quarters give me a penchant for antiquated words."

"So you've never referred to us as 'Mutes' yourself."

A rosy blush crept up her neck and over her face. He found it most attractive, but the response told him her answer.

She put a smooth, tanned hand over his wrinkled and liver-spotted fingers. "Ward, you must understand that one trained as a diplomat … I mean, in some company …"

"When on the Islands, do as the Islanders do."

She removed her hand. The back of his own cooled in disappointment. "Something like that," she said. She picked up her teacup and swirled the dregs. Keel saw the defensiveness in the gesture. Ale was somehow off-balance. He'd never seen her that way before, and he wasn't vain enough to attribute it to this exchange with her. Keel believed that the only thing that could bother Ale was something totally unplanned, something with no body of knowledge behind it, no diplomatic precedent. Something out of her control.

"Ward," she said, "I think there is one point that you and I have always agreed on." She kept her attention on the teacup.

"We have?" He held his tone neutral, not giving her any help.

"Human has less to do with anatomy than with a state of mind," she said. "Intelligence, compassion … humor, the need to share …"

"And build hierarchies?" he asked.

"I guess that, too." She met his gaze. "Mermen are very vain about their bodies. We're proud that we've stayed close to the original norm."

"Is that why you showed me the scar on your back?"

"I wanted you to see that I'm not perfect."

"That you're deformed, like me?"

"You're not making this very easy for me, Ward."

"You, or yours, have the luxury of *choice* in their mutations. Genetics, of course, adds a particularly bitter edge to the whole thing. Your scar is not … 'like me,' but one of your freckles is. Your freckles have a much more pleasant quality to them than this." He tapped the neck support. "But I'm not complaining," he assured her, "just being pedantic. Now what is it that I'm not making easy for you?" Keel sat back, pleased for once about those tedious years behind the bench and some of the lessons those years had taught him.

She stared into his eyes, and he saw fear in her expression.

"There are Mermen fanatics who want to wipe every ... *Mute* off the face of this planet."

The flat abruptness of her statement, the matter-of-fact tone caught him off guard. Lives were precious to Islanders *and* Mermen, this he'd witnessed for himself innumerable times during his many years. The idea of deliberate killing nauseated him, as it did most Pandorans. His own judgments against lethal deviants had brought him much isolation in his lifetime, but the law required that *someone* pass judgment on people, blobs and ... things ... He could never decree termination without suffering acute personal agony.

But to wipe out hundreds of hundreds of thousands ... He returned Ale's stare, thinking about her recent behavior—the food cooked by her own hands, the sharing of these remarkable quarters. And, of course, the scar.

I'm on your side, she was trying to say. He felt the planning behind her actions, but there was more to it, he thought, than callous outlines and assignments. Otherwise, why had she been embarrassed? She was trying to win him over to some personal viewpoint. *What viewpoint?*

"Why?" he asked.

She drew in a deep breath. The simplicity of his response obviously surprised her.

"Ignorance," she said.

"And how does this ignorance manifest itself?"

Her nervous fingers *flip-flip-flipped* the corner of her napkin. Her eyes sought out a stain on the tabletop and fixed themselves there.

"I am a child before you," Keel said. "Explain this to me. 'Wipe every Mute off the face of this planet.' You know how I feel about the preservation of human life."

"As *I* feel, Ward. Believe me, please."

"Then explain it to this child and we can get started defeating it: Why would someone wish death to so many of us just because we're ... extranormal?" He had never been quite so conscious of his smear of a nose, the eyes set so wide on his temples that his ears picked up the fine liquid *click-click* of every blink.

"It's political," she said. "There's power in appealing to base responses. And there are problems over the kelp situation."

"What kelp situation?" His voice sounded toneless in his own ears, far away and ... yes, afraid. *Wipe every Mute off the face of this planet.*

"Do you feel up to a tour?" she asked. She glanced at the plaz beside them.

Ward looked out at the undersea view. "Out there?"

"No," she said, "not out there. There's been a wavewall topside and we've got all our crews reclaiming some ground we've lost."

His eyes strained to focus forward on her mouth. Somehow, he didn't believe anyone's mouth could be so casual about a wavewall.

"The Islands?" He swallowed. "How bad was the damage?"

"Minimal, Ward. To our knowledge, no fatalities. Wavewalls may very well be a thing of the past."

"I don't understand."

"This wavewall was smaller than many of the winter storms you survive every year. We've built a series of networks of exposed land. Land above the sea. Someday, they will be islands … real islands fixed to the planet, not drifting willy-nilly. And some of them, I think, will be continents."

Land, he thought, and his stomach lurched. *Land means shallows.* An Island could bottom out in shallow water. An ultimate disaster, in the vernacular of historians, but she was talking about voluntarily increasing the risk of an Islander's worst fear.

"How much exposed land?" he asked, trying to maintain a level tone.

"Not very much, but it's a beginning."

"But it would take forever to …"

"A long time, Ward, but not forever. We've been at it for generations. And lately we've had some help. It's getting done in our lifetime, doesn't that excite you?"

"What does this have to do with the kelp?" He felt the need to resist her obvious attempts to mesmerize him.

"The kelp is the key," she said, "just as people—Islanders *and* Mermen—have said all along. With the kelp and a few well-placed artificial barriers, we can control the sea currents. All of them."

Control, he thought. *That's the Merman way of it.* He doubted they could control the seas, but if they could manipulate currents, they could manipulate Island movement.

How much control? he wondered.

"We're in a two-sun system," he said. "The gravitational distortions guarantee wave–walls, earthquakes …"

"Not when the kelp was in its prime, Ward. And now there's enough of it to make a difference. You'll see. And currents should begin an aggrading action now—dropping sediment—rather than degrading."

Degrading, he thought. He looked at Ale's beauty. Did she even know the meaning of the word? A technical understanding, an engineering approach was not enough.

Mistaking the reason of his silence, Ale plunged on.

"We have records of everything. From the first. We can play the whole reconstruction of this planet from the beginning—the death of the kelp, everything."

Not everything, he thought. He looked once more at the wondrous garden beyond the plaz. Growth there was so lush that the bottom could only be glimpsed in a few places. He could see no rock. As a child, he had given up watching drift because all he ever saw was rock … and silt. When it was clear enough or shallow enough to see at all. Seeing the bottom from an Island had a way of running an icy hand down your back.

"How close are these 'artificial barriers' to the surface?" he asked.

She cleared her throat, avoiding his eyes.

"Along this section," she said, "surflines are beginning to show. I expect watchers on Vashon already have seen them. That wavewall drifted them pretty close to …"

"Vashon draws a hundred meters at Center," he protested. "Two-thirds of the population live below the waterline—almost half a million lives! How can you speak so casually about endangering that many … ?"

"Ward!" A chill edged her voice. "We are aware of the dangers to your Islands and we've taken that into account. We're not murderers. We are on the verge of complete restoration of the kelp and the development of land masses—two monumental projects that we've pursued for generations."

"Projects whose dangers you did not share with nor reveal to the Islanders. Are we to be sacrificed to your—"

"No one is to be sacrificed!"

"Except by your friends who want to wipe out every Mute on Pandora! Is this how they intend to do it? Wreck us on your barrier walls and your continents?"

"We knew you wouldn't understand," she said. "But you must realize that the Islands have reached their limits and people haven't. I agree that we should have brought Islanders into the planning picture much earlier, but"—she shrugged—"we didn't. And now we are. It's my job to tell you what we must do together to see that there is no disaster. It's my job to gain your cooperation in—"

"In the mass annihilation of Islanders!"

"No, Ward, dammit! In the mass *rescue* of Islanders … *and* Mermen. We must walk on the surface once more, all of us."

He heard the sincerity in her tone but distrusted it. She was a diplomat, trained to lie convincingly. And the enormity of what she proposed …

Ale waved a hand toward the exterior garden. "Kelp is flourishing, as you can see. But it's just a plant; it is not sentient, as it was before our ancestors wiped it out. The kelp you see there was, of course, reconstructed from the genes carried by certain humans in the—"

"Don't try to explain genetics to the Chief Justice," Ward growled, "we know about your 'dumbkelp.'"

She blushed, and he wondered at the emotional display. It was something he had never before seen in Ale. A liability in a diplomat, no doubt. How had she concealed it before … or was this situation simply too much for normal repression? He decided to watch the emotional signal and read it for her true feelings.

"Calling it 'dumbkelp' like the schoolchildren is hardly accurate," she said.

"You're trying to divert me," he accused. "How close is Vashon to one of your surflines right now?"

"In a few minutes I will take you out and show you," she said. "But you must understand what we're—"

"No. I must not understand—by which you mean *accept*—such peril for so many of my people. So many *people,* period. You talk of control. Do you have any idea of the energy in an Island's movement? The long, slow job of maneuvering something that big? Your word, this control of which you seem so proud, does not take in the kinetic energy of—"

"But it does, Ward. I didn't bring you down here for a tea party. Or an argument." She stood. "I hope you have your legs under you because we've a lot of walking to do."

He stood at that, slowly, and tried to unkink his knees. His left foot tingled in the first stages of waking. Was it possible, all that she said? He could not escape the in-built fear all Islanders felt at the idea of a crashing death on solid bottom. A white horizon could only mean death—a wavewall or some tidal exposure of the planet's rocky surface. Nothing could change that.

Chapter 14

How do Mermen make love?
Same way every time.

—Islander joke

THE TWO coracles, one towing the other, bobbed along on the open sea. Nothing shared the horizon with them except gray waves, long deep rollers with intermittent white lines of spume at the crests. Vashon was long gone below the horizon astern and Twisp, holding his course by the steady wind and the fisherman's instinct for shifts in light, had settled into a patient, watchful wait, giving only rare glances to his radio and RDF. He had been all night assembling the gear to hunt for Brett—raising the coracles, repairing the wavewall damage, loading supplies and gear.

Around him now was a Pandoran late morning. Only Little Sun was in the sky, a bright spot on a thin cloud cover—ideal navigation weather. Driftwatch had given him a fix on Vashon's position at the time of the wavewall and he knew that by midafternoon he should be near enough to start search-quartering the seas.

If you made it this far, kid, I'll find you.

The futility of his gesture did not escape Twisp. There was nearly a day's delay, not to mention the ever-prowling hunts of dashers. And there was this odd current in the sea, sending a long silvery line down the sweep of waves. It flowed in his direction, for which Twisp was thankful. He could mark the swiftness of it by the doppler on his radio, which he kept tuned to Vashon's emergency band. He hoped to hear a report of Brett's recovery.

It was possible that Mermen had found Brett. Twisp kept looking for Merman signs—a flag float for a work party, one of their swift skimmers, the oily surge of a hardbelly sub surfacing from the depths.

Nothing intruded on his small circle of horizon.

Getting away from Vashon had been a marvel of secret scurrying, all the time expecting Security to stop him. But Islanders helped each other, even if one of them insisted on being a fool. Gerard had packed him a rich supply of food gifts from friends and from the pantry at the Ace of Cups. Security had been informed of Brett's loss overboard. Gerard's private grapevine said the kid's parents had set up a cry for "someone to do something." They had not come to Twisp, though. Strange, that. Official channels only. Twisp suspected Security knew all about his preparations for a search and deliberately kept hands off—partly out of resentment over the Norton family pressures, partly … well, partly because Islanders helped each other. People knew he had to do this thing.

The docks had been a madhouse of repair when Twisp went down to see whether he could recover his boat. Despite the hard work going on all around, fishermen made time to help him. Brett had been the only person lost with this wavewall and they all knew what Twisp had to attempt.

All through the night people had come with gear, sonar, a spare coracle, a new motor, eelcell batteries, every gift saying: "We know. We sympathize. I'd be doing the same thing if I were you."

At the end, ready to set off, Twisp had waited impatiently for Gerard to appear. Gerard had said for him to wait. The big man had come down in his motorized chair, his single fused leg sticking out like a blunted lance to clear the way. His twin daughters ran skipping behind him, and behind them came five Ace of Cups regulars wheeling carts with the food stores.

"Got you enough for about twenty-five or thirty days," Gerard had said, humming to a stop beside the waiting boats. "I know you, Twisp. You won't give up."

An embarrassed silence had fallen over the fishermen waiting on the docks to see Twisp off. Gerard had spoken what was in all of their minds. How long could the kid survive out there?

While friends loaded the tow-coracle, Gerard said: "Word's out to the Mermen. They'll contact us if they learn anything. Hard telling what it'll cost you."

Twisp had stared at his coracles, at the friends who gave him precious gear and even more precious physical help. The debt was great. And if he came back … well, he was going to come back—and with the kid. The debt would be a bitch, though. And only a few hours ago he had been considering abandonment of the independent fisherman's life, going back to the subs. Well … that was the way it went.

Gerard's twin girls had come up to Twisp then, begging for him to swing them. The coracles were almost ready and a strange reluctance had come over everyone … including Twisp. He extended his arms to let each of the girls grip a forearm tight, then he turned, fast, faster, swinging the children wide while the spectators stood back from his long-armed circle. The girls shrieked when their toes pointed at the horizon. He stumbled to a stop, dizzy and sweating. Both girls sat hard on the pier, their eyes not quite caught up with the end of the whirl.

"You come back, you hear?" Gerard had said. "My girls won't forgive any of us if you don't."

Twisp thought about that oddly silent departure as he held his course with the wind on his cheek and an eye to the light and the swift hiss of the current under his craft. The old axiom of the fishing fleets nurtured him in his loneliness: *Your best friend is hope.*

He could feel the tow coracle tug his boat at the crests. The carrier hum of his radio provided a faint background to the *slap-slap* of cross-chop against the hull. He glanced back at the tow. Only the static-charge antenna protruded from the lashed cover. The tow rode low in the water. The new motor hummed reassuringly near his feet. Its eelcell batteries had not started to change color, but he kept an eye on them. Unless the antenna picked up a lightning strike, they'd need feeding before nightfall.

Gray convolutions of clouds folded downward ahead of him. Sometime soon it was going to rain. He unrolled the clear membrane another fisherman had given him and stretched it over the open cockpit of his coracle, leaving a sag-pocket to collect drinking water. The course beeper went off as he finished the final lashings. He corrected for slightly more than five degrees deviation, then hunkered under the shelter, sensing the imminent rain, cursing the way this would limit visibility. But he had to keep dry.

I never really get miserable if I'm dry.

He felt miserable, though. Was there even the faintest hope he could find the kid? Or was this one of those futile gestures that had to be made for one's own mental well-being?

Or is it that I have nothing else to live for … ?

He put that one out of his mind as beyond debate. To give himself physical activity, something to drive out his doubts, he rigged a handline with a warning bell from the starboard thwart, baited it with a bit of bright streamer that glittered in the water. He payed it out carefully and tested the warning bell with a short tug on the line. The tinkling reassured him.

All I'd need, he thought. *Drag a dead fish along and call in the dashers.* Even though dashers preferred warm-blooded meat, they'd go for anything that moved when they were hungry.

A lot like humans.

Settling back with the tiller under his right armpit, Twisp tried to relax. Still nothing on the radio's emergency band. He reached down and switched to the regular broadcast, coming in on the middle of a music program.

Another gift, a nav-sounder, with its bottom-finding sonar and its store of position memories, rested between his legs. He flipped it on for a position check, worked out the doppler distance figure from the radio and nodded to himself.

Close enough.

Vashon was drifting at a fairly steady seven klicks per hour back there. His coracle was doing a reliable twelve. Pretty fast for trolling with a handline.

The radio interrupted its music program for a commentary on Chief Justice Keel. No word yet from the Committee, but observers were saying that his unprecedented fact-finding trip down under could have "deep significance to Vashon and all other Islands."

What significance? Twisp wondered.

Keel was an important man, but Twisp had trouble extending that importance beyond Vashon. Occasional grumbles over a decision swept through the Island communities, but there had been few real disturbances since Keel's elevation, and that was some time back. Sure sign that he was a wise man.

The C/P had been asked to comment on Keel's mission, however, and this aroused Twisp's curiosity. What did the old Shipside religion have to do with the Chief Justice's trip? Twisp had always paid only cursory attention to both politics and religion. They were good for an occasional jawing session at the Ace of Cups, but Twisp had always found himself unable to understand what drove people to passionate arguments over "Ship's real purpose."

Who the hell knew what Ship's real purpose had been? There might not have been a purpose!

It was possible, though, that the old religion was gaining new strength among Islanders. It was certainly an unspoken issue between Mermen and Islanders. There was enough polarization already between topside and down under—diplomats arguing about the "functional abilities" characteristic of Pandora's split population. Islanders claimed eminence in agriculture, textiles and meteorology. Mermen always bragged they had the bodies best adapted for going back to the land.

Stupid argument! Twisp always noticed that a group of people—Islander or Merman—got less intelligent with every member added. *If humans can master that one, they've got it made,* he thought.

Twisp sensed something big was afoot. He felt well away from it out in the open sea. No Ship here. No C/P. No religious fanatics—just one seasoned agnostic.

Was Ship God? Who the hell cared now? Ship had abandoned them for sure and nothing else of Ship really mattered.

A long, sweeping roller lifted the coracle easily to almost twice the height of the prevailing seas. He glanced around from the brief vantage and saw something large bobbing on the water far ahead. Whatever it was, it lay in the silvery channel of the odd current, which was adding to his forward speed. He kept his attention ahead until he picked up the unknown thing much closer, realizing then that it was several things clumped together. A few minutes later he recognized the objects in the clump.

Dashers!

The squawks lay quiet, though. He glanced at them as he put a hand on the field switch, ready to repel the hunt when they attacked. None of the dashers moved.

That's strange, he thought. *Never seen dashers sit still before.*

He lifted his head, raising the catchment sag of his cockpit cover, and peered ahead. As the coracle neared the clump, Twisp counted seven adults and a tighter cluster of young dashers in the center of the group. They rode the waves together like a dark chunk of bubbly.

Dead, he realized. *A whole hunt of dashers and all of them dead. What killed them?*

Twisp eased back the throttle, but still kept a hand on the field switch … just in case. They were dead, though, not pretending as a ruse to lure him close. The dashers had locked themselves into a protective circle. Each adult linked a rear leg to the adult on either side. They formed a circle with fore-paws and fangs facing out, the young inside.

Twisp set a course around them, staring in at the dashers. How long had they been dead? He was tempted to stop and skin at least one. Dasher skins always brought a good price. But it would take precious time and the hides would rob him of space.

They'd stink, too.

He circled a bit closer. Up close now he could see how dashers had adapted so quickly to water. Hollow hairs—millions of trapped air cells that became an efficient flotation system when sea covered all of Pandora's land. Legend said dashers once had feared the water, that the hollow hairs insulated them then against cold nights and oven-hot days among the desert rocks.

Because of those hollow hairs, dasher hides made beautiful blankets—light and warm. Again, he was tempted to skin some of them. They were all in pretty good shape. Have to jettison part of his survival cargo if he did, though. What could he spare?

One of the dashers displayed a great hood that floated out from its ugly, leather-skinned head like a black mantle. Experts said this was a throwback characteristic. Most dashers had shed the hood in the sea, becoming sleek killing machines with saber fangs and those knife-sharp claws, almost fifteen centimeters long on the bigger animals.

Lifting a corner of his cockpit cover, he poked at the hooded dasher with a boathook, lifting it far enough to see that the underside had been burned. A deep, crisp line from brisket to belly. The limpness of the beast told him it couldn't have been dead more than a few hours. A half-day, at the most. He withdrew the boathook and refastened the cockpit cover.

Burned? he wondered. What had surprised and killed this entire hunt—from below?

Swinging the tiller, he resumed his course down the silvery channel of current, checking by compass and the relative signal from Vashon. The radio was still playing popular music. Soon, the mysterious clump of dashers lay below the horizon astern.

The clouds had lifted slightly and still there was no rain. He gauged his course by the bright spot on the clouds, the uncertain compass and the ripple of steady wind across the transparent cover above him. The wind drove spray runnels in parallel lines, giving him a good reading on relative direction.

His thoughts turned back to the dashers. He was convinced that Mermen had killed them from beneath, but how? A Merman sub crew, maybe. If this were an example of a Merman weapon, Islands were virtually defenseless.

Now, why would I think Mermen would attack us?

Mermen and Islanders might be polarized, but war was ancient history, known only through records saved from the Clone Wars. And Mermen were known to go to great trouble to save Islander lives.

But the whole planet was a hiding place if you lived down under. And Mermen did want Vata, that was true. Always coming up with petitions demanding that she be moved to "safer and more comfortable quarters down under."

"Vata is the key to kelp consciousness," the Mermen said. They said it so often it had become a cliché, but the C/P seemed to agree. Twisp had never believed everything the C/P said, but this was something he kept to himself.

In Twisp's opinion, it was a power struggle. Vata, living on and on like that with her companion, Duque, beside her, was the nearest thing Pandora had to a living saint. You could start almost any story you wanted about why she lay there without responding.

"She is waiting for the return of Ship," some said.

But Twisp had a tech friend who was called in occasionally by the C/P to examine and maintain the nutrient tank in which Vata and Duque lived. The tech laughed at this story.

"She's not doing anything but living," the tech said. "And I'll bet she has no idea she's even doing that!"

"But she does have kelp genes?" Twisp had asked.

"Sure. We've run tests when the religious mumbo-jumbos and the Mermen observers have their backs turned. A few cells is all it takes, you know. The C/P would be livid. Vata has kelp genes, I'll swear to that."

"So the Mermen could be right about her?"

"Who the fuck knows?" The tech grinned. "Lots of us have 'em. Everybody's different, though. Maybe she *did* get the right batch. Or, for all we really know, Jesus Lewis *was* Satan, like the C/P says. And Pandora's Satan's pet project."

The tech's revelations did little to change Twisp's basic opinions.

It's all politics. And politics is all property.

Lately everything came down to license fees, forms and supporting the right political group. If you had someone on the inside helping you, things went well—your property didn't cost you so much. Otherwise, forget it. Resentments, jealousy, envy … these were the things really running Pandora. And fear. He'd seen plenty of fear in the faces of Mermen confronted by the more severely changed Islanders. People even Twisp sometimes thought of as Mutes. Fear bordering on horror, disgust, loathing. It was all emotions and he knew politics was at the bottom of it, too—"Dear Ship," the horrified Mermen were saying with their unmasked faces, "don't let me or anybody I love own a body like that!"

The beeper interrupted Twisp's black thoughts. Sonar said his depth here was a little under one hundred meters. He glanced around at the open sea. The silvery current-channel had been joined by tributaries on both sides. He could feel the current churn beneath his coracle. Bits of flotsam shared the water around him now—kelp tendrils mostly, some short lengths of floating bone. Those would have to be from squawks. Wouldn't float otherwise.

A hundred meters, he thought. Pretty shallow. Vashon drew just about that much at Center. Mermen preferred building where it remained shallow most of the time, he recalled. Was this a Merman area? He looked around for signs: dive floats, the surface boiling with a sub's backwash or a foil coming up from the depths. There was only the sea and the folding current that swept him along in its steady grip. Lots of kelp shreds in this current. Could be an area where Mermen were replanting the stuff. Twisp had found himself taking the Merman side on that project in many a bar argument. More kelp meant more cover and feed for fish. Nursery areas. More fish meant more food for the Islands and for Mermen. In more predictable locations.

His depth finder said the bottom was holding steady at ninety meters. Mermen had reason to prefer shallows. Better for the kelp. Easier to trade topside, as long as Islands had plenty of clearance. And there were all those stories that the Mermen were trying to reclaim land on the surface. There might be a Merman outpost or trading station nearby and they could give him word on whether they had rescued the kid. Besides, the little he knew about Mermen made him that much more fascinated by them, and the prospect of contact excited him for its own sake.

Twisp began to build a fantasy—a dream-truth that Mermen had saved Brett. He scooped a handful of the kelp and found himself daydreaming that Brett had been rescued by a beautiful young Merman girl and was falling in love somewhere down under.

Damn! I've got to stop that, he thought. The dream collapsed. Bits of it kept coming back to him, though, and he had to repress them sharply.

Hope was one thing, he thought. Fantasy was quite another thing … and dangerous.

Chapter 15

This may be the better age for the Faith, but this is certainly not an age of Faith.

—Flannery O'Connor, from her letters, *Shiprecords*

THOSE WHO watched Vata that day said her hair was alive, that it clutched her head and shoulders. As Vata's agitation grew her shudders became a steadily progressing convulsion. Her thick spread of hair snaked itself around her and curled her gently into a fetal ball.

The convulsions tapered off and ceased in two minutes, twelve seconds. Four minutes and twenty-four seconds after that, the tendrils of her hair became hair again. A thick spread of it fanned out behind her. She stayed in that position, tight and rigid, through three full shifts of watchers.

The C/P was not the first to equate the agitation in the tank with the sinking of Guemes, nor was she the last. She was, however, the only one who wasn't surprised.

Not now! she thought, as though she could ever have found a convenient time for thousands of people to die. That was why she needed Gallow. This was something she could live with if it were done, but it was not something that she could do. None of that diminished the horrors she was forced to imagine as Vata lay writhing in her tank.

And scooped up like that by her hair! This thought raised every thin stalk on the back of the C/P's shoulders and neck.

At Vata's first abrupt stirrings, Duque had stiffened, flinched, then slipped quickly and deeply into shock. His only coherent utterance was a high-pitched, quickly blurted, "Ma!"

Those med-techs among the watchers, Islander and Merman alike, vaulted the rim of the pool.

"What's wrong with him?" a young clerk asked. She was chinless and hook-nosed, but not at all unpretty. The C/P noticed her wide green eyes and the white eyelashes that flickered as she spoke.

Rocksack pointed at the telltales above the monitor center across the pool. "Fast, high heartbeat, agitation, shallow breathing, steadily dropping blood pressure—shock. Nothing touched him and they've ruled out stroke or internal bleeding." The C/P cleared her throat. "Psychogenic shock," she said. "Something scared him almost to death."

Chapter 16

Forceful rejection of the past is the coward's way of removing inconvenient knowledge.

—The Histories

THE WEATHER around Twisp had shifted from scattered showers to a warm wind with clear skies directly overhead. Little Sun was wending its way toward the horizon. Twisp checked the rain water he had recovered—almost four liters. He removed the cockpit cover, rolled it forward and lashed it in place where it could be snatched back quickly if the weather changed once more.

He thought only briefly of the daydream he had entertained about Brett and a beautiful Merman woman. What nonsense! Mermen wanted *normal* children. Brett would only find disappointment down under. One look at his big eyes and parents would steer their daughters away from him. Islander births might be stabilizing, more births in the pattern of Gerard's girls, more near-normals like Brett every season, but that changed nothing in basic attitudes. Mermen were Mermen and Islanders were Islanders. Islanders were catching up, though: fewer lethal deviants and longer life spans.

The warning beeper on Twisp's depth finder sounded once, and again. He glanced at it and reset the lower limit. The sea had been shallowing here for some time. Only seventy-five meters now. Fifty meters and he could start trying to see bottom. One of his dockside gifts had been a small driftwatcher, organic and delicately beautiful. It held corneal material at one end that would focus at his demand. At the other end, a mouth-like aperture fitted itself over his eyes. The thing could only exist immersed most of the time in nutrient, and it grew inexorably, eventually becoming too large for a small boat. Custom dictated that it then be passed along to a larger boat. Twisp ran a hand absently along the smooth organic tube of the thing, feeling its automatic response. He sighed. What could he hope to find on the bottom even if it did get shallow enough? He removed his hand from the little driftwatcher and lifted his attention to his surroundings.

The air felt warm, almost balmy and quite moist after the rains. The seas were calmer. Only that shifting, boiling current stretched ahead of him and for more than a kilometer on both sides. Odd. He had never seen a current quite like it, but then Pandora was always turning up new things. The one constant was the weather: It changed and it changed fast. He looked east at the cloud bank there, noting how far toward the horizon Little Sun had moved. Big Sun would come up soon—more light, more visibility. He glanced back at the strip of rich blue along the horizon. Yes, it was clearing. The dark bank of clouds east of him receded faster than his motor and the current chased it. Sunlight tapped his cheeks, his arms. He settled back beside the tiller, feeling the warmth like an old friend. It was as though Pandora had smiled upon his venture. He knew he was very close to where the wave wall had struck Vashon, and now visibility opened up. He moved his gaze around the horizon, seeking a black speck that was not the sea.

I'm here, kid.

His gaze, sweeping left, glimpsed a distinct line of froth. The sight of it prickled the hairs on his neck and sent a chill down his spine. He sat stiffly upright, staring.

A white line on the sea!

Wavewall? No … it wasn't growing larger or receding. Just off to the left of his course and dead ahead a white line of foam grew more distinct as he approached. Sonar read fifty meters. He slipped the little driftwatcher from its container and fixed it to the coracle's side with the corneal end underwater. Fitting his forehead to the mouth aperture, he stared downward.

When his eyes adjusted, the view took a moment shaping itself into something identifiable. It was not the rolling contour of the deeps, which he had seen from the subs. It was not the jagged, surreal landscape of the danger areas. This bottom climbed high, almost to the surface. Twisp tore his gaze away from the driftwatcher and looked at the sonar reading: twenty meters!

He returned his attention to the bottom. It was so shallow he could see delicate, sinewy steps—curving terraces covered with kelp fronds. Rock buttresses and walls guarded the outer edges of the terraces. It all looked artificial … manmade.

A core of the Merman kelp project! he thought.

He had seen many segments of the project, but this was vastly different and, he suspected, much larger. Merman engineers experimented with the kelp, he knew that. Supposedly some of the beds would live and grow even on land—if there ever was such a thing. Now Twisp found himself much closer to believing—if this bed was an example. Mermen were doing all that they claimed they'd do. He'd seen the fine latticework strung for kilometers undersea, a structure where the kelp could climb and secure itself. Undersea walls of rock sheltered other plantations. Islanders had complained about the latticework supports, arguing that they were nets to entangle the fishing subs. Twisp had doubted this argument, remembering all the stories of net-bound Mermen. Islander complaints had not stopped the project.

He gave up studying the bottom and looked at the foam line again. The silvery current that carried him curved off to starboard, sweeping close to that disquieting line. He guessed the intersection to be about five klicks off. A distant, recurrent roar accompanied the surfline.

Could it be waves foaming across one of the latticeworks? he wondered.

Both coracles bobbed heavily in a cross-chop, the towed craft pulling at its line and making his job at the tiller a tough one.

Surf! he thought. *I'm actually seeing surf.*

Islanders had reports of this phenomenon, few of them reliable. It occurred to him that they were unreliable only because the incidents were so infrequent. The great Island of Everett, almost as large as Vashon, had reported a surf sighting just before crashing bottom in a swing-surge of Pandora's sea that left it suddenly awash in a mysterious shallows. Everett had been lost without survivors, bottomed out, thirty years back.

The course beeper sounded.

Twisp boxed up the driftwatcher, kicked off the warning switch and pulled the tiller hard into his belly. Now he was cutting across the great curve of current that still drifted him toward the foaming white line. The current took on a new character. It rolled and twisted along the surface, dispersing waves in its track. There was a determination about it, a feeling of purpose, as though it were a live thing remorselessly savaging anything in its way. Twisp only wanted out of it. He had never felt such a force. He notched the motor up another hundred revs. At this point a burnout seemed worth the risk—he had to shake this current.

The coracles twisted at the rim of the surge, forcing him to fight the tiller. Then, suddenly, he was through and onto open waves. The white line of surf still lay too close but now he felt he could beat it. He cranked the motor up another notch, pushing full speed. The silver line of current grew thinner and thinner as he left it behind him. It swept in a great curve around the surfline and disappeared.

What if the kid was caught in that? Twisp wondered. *Brett could be anywhere.*

He crouched over his instruments, read the doppler on Vashon's range signal, and prepared to make a sun-sight to report the location of this danger. A red telltale blinked on his radio—another Island's signal. He rotated and homed in on it, identified it as little Eagle Island, off to the northeast. It was almost at range limit, too far away to ask for distance and a crosscheck. His depth finder had nothing in its memory circuits to match the stretch of bottom under him. Dead reckoning, the sun-sight and Vashon's doppler, however, told him the swift current had taken him at least ten klicks to the west of his intended course. The current had moved him rapidly, but the diversion meant he saved no time reaching the coordinates where the wavewall had struck Vashon.

Twisp coded in the bearings and location, keyed the automatic transmitter and activated it. The signal went out for anyone listening: "Dangerous shallows in this location!"

Presently, he scanned the water around him, squinting and shading his eyes. No sign of Mermen—not a buoy, no flag, nothing. That terrifying current had become nothing more than a silver thread glinting along the surface. He took a course reading and prepared for another hour or more of careful dead reckoning. In a moment, he knew, he would be back into that watchful waiting from which anything unusual could bring him instantly alert.

A noisy boiling hissing and clatter came from astern, an eruption of sound that drowned out the quiet pulsing of his motor and the slap of waves against his hull.

Twisp whirled and was just in time to see a Merman sub leap nose-first out of the water and fall back onto its side. The hard metal glittered gold and green. He had a brief glimpse of exterior tools on the sub, all in active mode, whirling and twisting like spastic limbs. The sub splashed down not a hundred meters away, sending up a great wave that swept under the coracles and carried Twisp high. He fought for steerage as he watched the sub roll, then right itself.

Without thinking about it, Twisp swung his tiller into his gut, turning to go to the rescue. No sub did that sort of thing. The crew could be beaten half to death—particularly inside one of those all-metal Merman wonders. This crew was in trouble.

As he came around, the sub's hatch popped open. A man wearing only green utility pants clambered out onto the hull. The conning tower already was awash, the sub nosing back under the surface. A wave swept the man from his perch. He started swimming blindly, great thrashing strokes that took him at an angle across Twisp's course. The sub vanished behind him with a great slurping air bubble.

Twisp changed course to intercept the swimmer. Cupping his great hands around his mouth, Twisp shouted: "This way! Over here!"

The swimmer did not change course.

Twisp swung wide and pulled up alongside the man, cut the motor and extended a hand.

Now in the coracle's shadow, the swimmer twisted his head upward and gave Twisp a frightened look, seeing the extended hand.

"Come aboard," Twisp said. It was a traditional Islander greeting, matter-of-fact. Not even an implied question, such as "What in Ship's name are you doing out here?"

The swimmer took Twisp's hand and Twisp pulled him aboard, nearly swamping the coracle as the man clumsily tried to grasp a thwart. Twisp pulled him to the center and returned to the tiller.

The man stood there a moment, looking all around, dripping a damp pool into the bilges. His bare chest and face were pale, but not as pale as most Mermen's.

Is this a Merman who lives a lot topside? Twisp wondered. *And what the hell happened to him?*

The swimmer looked older than Brett but younger than Twisp. His green utility pants were dark with seawater.

Twisp glanced to where the sub had been. Only a slow roiling of the water showed where it had gone down.

"Trouble?" Twisp asked. Again, it was the Islander way—a laconic overture that said: "What help do you need that I can give?"

The man sat down and lay back against the coracle's deck cover. He drew in several deep, shuddering breaths.

Recovering from shock, Twisp thought, studying him. The man was small and heavyset, with a large head.

An Islander? Twisp wondered. He put it as a question, hoping directness would shock the man back to normal.

The man remained silent, but he scowled.

That was a reaction, anyway. Twisp took his time examining this strange figure from the sea: dark brown hair lay dripping against a wide forehead. Brown eyes returned Twisp's gaze from beneath thick brows. The man had a wide nose, wide mouth and square chin. His shoulders were broad, with powerful upper arms thinning to rather delicate forearms and slender hands. The hands appeared soft but the fingertips were calloused and shiny. Twisp had seen such fingertips on people who spent a lot of time at keyboard controls.

Hooking a thumb back to where the sub had gone down, Twisp asked: "You care to tell me what that was all about?"

"I was escaping." The voice was a thin tenor.

"The sub's hatch was still open when it went under," Twisp said. That was just a comment and could be taken as such if the man desired.

"The rest of the sub was secured," the man said. "Only the engine compartment will flood."

"That was a Merman sub," Twisp said; another comment.

The man pushed himself away from the deck cover. "We'd better get out of here," he said.

"We're staying while I look for a friend," Twisp said. "He was lost overboard in that last wave wall." He cleared his throat. "You care to tell me your name?"

"Iz Bushka."

Twisp felt that he had heard that name before, but could not make the connection. And now as he looked at Bushka there was a sensation that Twisp had seen this face before—in a Vashon passage, perhaps … somewhere.

"Do I know you?" Twisp asked.

"What's your name?" Bushka asked.

"Twisp. Queets Twisp."

"Don't think we're acquainted," Bushka said. He sent another fearful gaze across the water around the coracles.

"You haven't said what you were escaping from," Twisp said. Another comment.

"From people who … we'd all be better off if they were dead. Damn! I should've killed them but I couldn't bring myself to do it!"

Twisp remained silent in shock. Did all Mermen speak so casually of killing? He found his voice: "But you sent them down under with a flooded engine room!"

"And unconscious, too! But they're Mermen. They'll get out when they recover. Come on! Let's get out of here."

"Perhaps you didn't hear me, Iz. I'm looking for a friend who went overboard from Vashon."

"If your friend's alive, he's safe down under. You're the only thing on the surface for at least twenty klicks. Believe it. I was looking. I came up because I saw you."

Twisp glanced back at the distant white line of the surf. "That's on the surface."

"The barrier? Yeh, but there's nothing else. No Merman base, nothing."

Twisp considered for a moment—the way Bushka said "Merman." *Fear? Loathing?*

"I know where there's a Search and Rescue base," Bushka said. "We could be there by daybreak tomorrow. If your friend's alive …" He left it there.

Talks a bit like an Islander, acts a lot like a Merman, Twisp thought. *Damn! Where have I seen him?*

Twisp glanced at the distant surfline. "You called that a barrier."

"Mermen are going to have land on the surface. That's part of it."

Twisp let this sink in, not believing it or disbelieving it. Fascinating, if true, but there were other muree to fry at that moment.

"So you scuttled a sub and you're escaping from people who would be better dead."

Twisp did not believe half of this Bushka's story. The hospitality of the sea said you had to listen. Nothing said you had to agree.

Bushka sent an agitated gaze over their surroundings. Second sun was up but in this season it made a quick sweep and the half-night would be on them soon. Twisp was hungry and irritated.

"Do you have a towel and some blankets?" Bushka asked. "I'm freezing my ass off!"

Abruptly contrite because he had failed to provide for the man's comfort, Twisp said: "Towel and blankets are rolled up in the cuddy behind you."

As Bushka turned and found the roll, Twisp added: "You saw me so you came up hoping I'd save you."

Bushka looked out from beneath the towel with which he was drying his hair. "If I'd left them under CO2 any longer it would've killed them. I couldn't do it."

"Are you going to tell me who they are?"

"People who'd kill us while eating lunch and not miss a bite!"

Something in the way Bushka said this set Twisp's stomach trembling. Bushka believed what he said.

"I don't suppose you have an RDC," Bushka said. He spoke with more than a little snobbishness.

Twisp kept his temper and uncovered the instrument near his feet. His relative drift compensator was one of his proudest possessions. The compass arrow in its top was pointing now far off their course.

Bushka approached and looked down at the RDC. "A Merman compass is more accurate," he said, "but this will do."

"Not more accurate between Islands," Twisp corrected him. "Islands drift and there's no fixed point of reference."

Bushka knelt beside the RDC and worked its settings with a sureness that told Twisp this was not the first time the man had used such an instrument. The red arrow atop the housing swung to a new setting.

"That should get us there," Bushka said. He shook his head. "Sometimes I wonder how we found any place without Merman instruments."

We? Twisp wondered.

"I think you're an Islander," Twisp accused, barely holding in his anger. "We're a pretty backward lot, aren't we!"

Bushka stood and returned to his position near the opening of the cuddy.

"Better work a bit more with that towel," Twisp said. "You missed behind your ears!"

Bushka ignored him and sat down with his back against the cuddy.

Twisp fed more power to his motor and swung around on the course indicated by the RDC arrow. *Might as well go to this Rescue Base! Damn that Bushka!* Was he one of those down-under Islanders who had become more Merman than the Mermen?

"You going to tell me what happened on that sub?" Twisp asked. "I'm through playing and I want to know what I'm into."

With a sullen expression, Bushka settled himself into his former position against the deck. Presently, he began describing his trip with Gallow. When he got to the part about Guemes Island, Twisp stopped him.

"You were at the controls?"

"I swear to you I didn't know what he was doing."

"Go on. What happened next?"

Bushka picked up his story after the sinking of the Island. Twisp stared at him with a hard expression throughout the recital. Once, Twisp felt under the tiller housing behind him for the lasgun he stored there—a real Merman lasgun that had cost him half a boatload of muree. The cold touch of the weapon settled his mind somewhat. He couldn't help asking himself, *What if this Bushka's lying?*

When Bushka finished, Twisp thought a moment, then: "You strapped the crew into their seats, including this Gallow, and sent them to the bottom. How do you know you didn't kill them?"

"They were tied loose enough to get free once they came around."

"I think I'd have …" Twisp shook his head sharply. "You know, don't you, that it's your word against theirs and you were at the controls?"

Bushka buried his face in the blanket around his knees. His shoulders shook and it was a few blinks before Twisp realized the man was sobbing.

For Twisp, this was the ultimate intimacy between two men. He had no more doubts that the story was true.

Bushka lifted a tear-streaked face to Twisp at the tiller. "You don't know all of it. You don't know what a perfect fool I was. Fool and tool!"

It all came out, then—the bookish Islander who wanted to be a Merman, the way Gallow had fastened on this dream, luring the innocent Islander into a compromising position.

"Why didn't you take the sub back to this Rescue Base?" Twisp asked.

"It's too far. Besides, how do I know who's with them and who's against? It's a secret organization, even from most Mermen. I saw you and … I just had to get away from them, out of that sub."

Hysterical kid! Twisp thought. He said, "The Mermen won't care a lot for your scuttling their sub."

A short, bitter laugh shook Bushka. "Mermen don't lose anything! They're the greatest scavengers of all time. If it goes to the bottom, it's theirs."

Twisp nodded. "Interesting story, Iz. Now I'll tell you what happened. The part about Guemes, I believe that and I—"

"It's true!"

"I'd like to disbelieve you, but I don't. I also think you got sucked into it by this Gallow. But I don't think you're all as innocent as you let on."

"I swear to you, I didn't know what he intended!"

"Okay, Iz. I believe you. I believe you saw me on the sub's scanner. You came up intending to be rescued by me."

Bushka scowled.

Twisp nodded. "You swam at an angle away from me so I'd be sure to go after you instead of making a try for the sub. You wanted to pass yourself off as Merman, have me take you to this base, and you were going to use your knowledge of the Guemes destruction to insure that Mermen really made good on keeping you down under. You were going to trade that for—"

"I wasn't! I swear."

"Don't swear," Twisp said. "Ship's listening."

Bushka started to speak, thought better of it and remained silent. A religious bluff usually worked with Islanders, even if they claimed nonbelief.

Twisp said: "What did you do topside? What Island?"

"Eagle. I was a … historian and pump-control tech."

"You've been to Vashon?"

"A couple of times."

"That's probably where I saw you. I seldom forget a face. Historian, eh? Inside a lot. That accounts for your pale complexion."

"Have you any idea," Bushka asked, "of the historical records the Mermen have preserved? The Mermen themselves don't even know everything they have. Or the value of it."

"So this Gallow saw you as valuable to record his doings?"

"That's what he said."

"Making history's a little different from writing it. I guess you found that out."

"Ship knows I did!"

"Uh, huh. Bushka, for now, we're stuck with each other. I'm not going to throw you overboard. But your story doesn't make me comfortable, you understand? If there's a base where you say there's one ... well, we'll see."

"There's a base," Bushka said. "With a tower sticking out of the water so far you can see it for fifty klicks."

"Sure there is," Twisp said. "Meanwhile, you stay over there by the cuddy and I'll stay here at the tiller. Don't try to leave your position. Got that?"

Bushka put his face back into the blanket without answering. By the rocking of his body and the shaking sobs, it was obvious to Twisp that he'd heard.

Chapter 17

What's so tough about making love to a Mute?
Finding the right orifice.

—Merman joke

FOLLOWING ALE at a pace painful for his old and weak legs, Ward Keel stepped through a hatchway marked by a red circle. He found himself in a roomful of noisy activity. There were many viewscreens, every one attended by a tech, at least a dozen console desks with Merman-style control switches and graphics. Alphanumerical indicators flashed wherever he looked. He counted ten very large viewscreens showing underwater and topside vistas. It all had been crowded into a space only a bit larger than Ale's quarters.

But it's not cramped, he thought.

Somewhat like Islanders, these Mermen had become skillful at using limited areas, although Keel noted that what they thought small an Islander would see as spacious.

Ale moved him around the desks and screens for introductions. Each worker glanced up when introduced, nodded curtly and returned to work. From the looks they shot Ale, Keel could tell that his presence in this room was particularly distressing to several of the Mermen.

She stopped him at a slightly larger desk set on a low dais to command the entire room. Ale had called the young man at this desk "Shadow" but introduced him as Dark Panille. Keel recognized the surname—a descendant of the pioneer poet and historian, no doubt. Panille's large eyes stared out with demanding focus over high cheekbones. His mouth moved only minimally from its straight line when he acknowledged the introduction.

"What is this place?" Keel asked.

"Current Control," Ale said, "You'll learn details momentarily. They are involved in an emergency right now. We must not interfere. You see those orange lights flashing over there? Emergency calls for Search and Rescue teams who are on standby duty."

"Search and Rescue?" Keel asked. "Are some of your people in trouble?"

"No," she replied with a tight set to her jaw, "your people."

Keel clamped his mouth shut. His gaze skittered across the room at the intense faces studying each viewscreen, at the cacophony of typing set up by the blur of two dozen technicians' hands at their keyboards. It was all very confusing. Was this the beginning of that threat Ale had mentioned? Keel found it difficult to remain silent … but she had said "Search and Rescue." This was a time to watch carefully and record.

Immediately after the medics had passed their death sentence on him, Keel had begun to feel that he was living in a vacuum that desperately needed filling. He felt that even his long service on the Committee on Vital Forms had been emptied. It was not enough to have been Chief Justice. There must be something more … a thing to mark his end with style, showing the love he had for his fellows. He wanted to send a message down the long corridors that said: "This is how much I cared." Perhaps there was a key to his need in this room.

Ale whispered in his ear. "Shadow—his friends call him that, a more pleasant name than 'Dark'—he's our ablest coordinator. He has a very high success rate recovering Islander castaways."

Was she hoping to impress him with her benign concern for Islander lives? Keel spoke in a low voice, his tone dry: "I didn't know it was this formalized."

"You thought we left it to chance?" she asked. Keel noted the slight snort of disgust. "We always watch out for Islanders in a storm or during a wavewall."

Keel felt an emotional pang at this revelation. His pride had been touched.

"Why haven't you made it known that you do this for us?" he asked.

"You think Islander pride would abide such a close watch?" Ale asked. "You forget, Ward, that I live much topside. You already believe we're plotting against you. What would your people make of this set-up?" She gestured at the banks of controls, the viewscreens, the subdued clicking of printers.

"You think Islanders are paranoid," Keel said. He was forced to admit to himself that this room's purpose had hurt his pride. Vashon Security would not like the idea of such Merman surveillance, either. And their fears might be correct. Keel reminded himself that he was only seeing what he was shown.

A large screen over to the right displayed a massive section of Island hull. "That looks like Vashon," he said. "I recognize the drift-watch spacing."

Ale touched Panille's shoulder and Keel wondered at the proprietary air of her movement. Panille glanced up from the keys.

"An interruption?" she asked.

"Make it short."

"Could you put Justice Keel's fears to rest? He has recognized his Island there." She nodded toward the viewscreen on the right. "Give him its position relative to the nearest barrier wall."

Panille turned to his console and tapped out a code, twisted a dial and read the alphanumerics on a thin dark strip at the top of his board. The smaller screen above the readout shifted from a repeat of the hull view to a surrounding seascape. A square at the lower right of the screen flashed "V-200."

"Visibility two hundred meters," Ale said. "Pretty good."

"Vashon's about four kilometers out from submerged barrier HA-nine, moving parallel the wall," Panille said. "In about an hour we'll begin to take it farther out. The wavewall had it within two-kilometer range. We had to do some shuffling, but nothing to worry about. It was never out of control."

Keel had to suppress a gasp at these figures. He fought down anger at the younger man's presumption and managed to ask, "What do you mean, 'Nothing to worry about?'"

Panille said, "We have had it under control—"

"Young man, diverting a mass like Vashon"—Keel shook his head—"we're lucky to adjust basic positioning when we contact another Island. Getting out of the way of danger in a mere two kilometers is not possible."

The corners of Panille's mouth came up in a tight smile—the kind of know-it-all smile that Keel really hated. He saw it on many adolescents, sophomoric youths thinking that older people were just too slow.

"You Islanders don't have the kelp working for you," Panille said. "We do. That's why we're here and we haven't time for your Islander paranoia."

"Shadow!" Ale's voice carried a cautionary note.

"Sorry." Panille bent to his controls. "But the kelp gives us a control that has kept Vashon out of real danger through this area for the past few years. Other Islands, too."

What an astonishing claim! Keel thought. He noted from the edge of his vision how carefully Ale watched every move Panille made. The young man nodded at something on his readouts.

"Watch this," he said. "Landro!" An older woman across the room glanced back and nodded. Panille called out a series of letters and numbers to her. She tapped them into her console, paused, hit a key, paused. Panille bent to his own board. A flurry of movement erupted from his fingers across the keys.

"Watch Shadow's screen," Ale said.

The screen showed a long stretch of waving kelp, thick and deep. The V-200 still blinked in the corner square. From it, Keel estimated he was looking at kelp more than a hundred meters tall. As he watched, a side channel opened through the kelp, the thick strands bending aside and locking onto their neighbors. The channel appeared to be at least thirty meters wide.

"Kelp controls the currents by opening appropriate channels," Ale said. "You're seeing one of the kelp's most primitive feeding behaviors. It captures nutrient-rich colder currents this way."

Keel spoke in a hushed whisper. "How do you make it respond?"

"Low-frequency signals," she said. "We haven't perfected it yet, but we're close. This is rather crude if we believe the historical records. We expect the kelp to add a visual display to its vocabulary at the next stage of development."

"Are you trying to tell me you're *talking* to it?"

"In a crude way. The way a mother talks to an infant, that kind of thing. We can't call it sentient yet, it doesn't make independent decisions."

Keel began to understand Panille's know-it-all look. How many generations had Islanders been on the sea without even coming close to such a development? What else did Islanders lack that Mermen had perfected?

"Because it's crude we allow plenty of margin for error," Ale said.

"Four kilometers … that's safe?" Keel asked.

"Two kilometers," Panille said. "That's an acceptable distance now."

"The kelp responds to a series of signal clusters," Ale said.

Why this sudden candor with Vashon's highest Islander official? Keel wondered.

"As you can see," Ale said, "we're training the kelp as we use it." She took his arm and stared at the widening channel through the kelp.

Keel saw Panille glance at Ale's intimate grip and caught a brief hardening of the young man's mouth.

Jealous? Keel wondered. The thought flickered like a candle in a breezy room. Perhaps a way to put Panille off-balance. Keel patted Ale's hand.

"You see why I brought you in here?" Ale asked.

Keel tried to clear his throat, finding it painfully restricted. Islanders would have to learn about this development, of course. He began to see Ale's problem—the Merman problem. They had made a mistake in not sharing this development earlier. Or had they?

"We have other things to see," Ale said. "I think the gymnasium next because it's closest. That's where we're training our astronauts."

Keel had been turning slightly as she spoke, scanning the curve of screens across the room. His mind was only partly focused on Ale's words and he heard them almost as an afterthought. He lurched and stumbled into her, only her strong grip on his arm kept him steady.

"I know you're going after the hyb tanks," he said.

"Ship would not have left them in orbit if it was not intended for us to have them, Ward."

"So that's why you're building your barriers and recovering solid ground above the sea."

"We can launch rockets from down here but that's not the best way," she said. "We need a solid base above the sea."

"What will you do with the contents of the tanks?"

"If the records are correct, and we've no reason to doubt them, then the riches of life in those tanks will put us back on a human path—a human way."

"What's a human way?" he asked.

"Why, it's … Ward, the life forms in those tanks can …"

"I've studied the records. What do you expect to gain on Pandora from, say, a rhesus monkey? Or a python? How will a mongoose benefit us?"

"Ward … there are cows, pigs, chickens …"

"And whales, how can they help us? Can they live compatibly with the kelp? You've pointed out the importance of the kelp …"

"We won't know until we try it, will we?"

"As Chief Justice on the Committee on Vital Forms, and that is who you're addressing now, Kareen Ale, I must remind you that I have considered such questions before."

"Ship and our ancestors brought—"

"Why this sudden religious streak, Kareen? Ship and our ancestors brought chaos to Pandora. They did not consider the consequences of their actions. Look at me, Kareen! I am one of those consequences. Clones … mutants … I ask you, was it not Ship's purpose to teach us a hard lesson?"

"What lesson?"

"That there are some changes that can destroy us. You speak so glibly of a human way of life! Have you defined what it is to be human?"

"Ward … we're both human."

"Like me, Kareen. That's how we judge. Human is 'like me.' In our guts, we say: It's human if it's 'like me.'"

"Is that how you judge on the Committee?" Her tone was scornful, or hurt.

"Indeed, it is. But I paint the likeness with a very broad brush. How broad is your brush? For that matter, this scornful young man seated here, could he look at me and say, 'like me?'"

Panille did not look up but his neck turned red and he bent intently over his console.

"Shadow and his people save Islander lives," she remarked.

"Indeed," Keel said, "and I'm grateful. However, I would like to know whether he believes he is saving fellow humans or an interesting lower life form?

"We live in different environments, Kareen. Those different environments require different customs. That's all. But I've begun to ask myself why we Islanders allow ourselves to be manipulated by *your* standards of beauty. Could you, for example, consider me as a mate?" He put up a hand to stop her reply and noticed that Panille was doing his best to ignore their conversation. "I don't seriously propose it," Keel said. "Think about everything involved in it. Think how sad it is that I have to bring it up."

Choosing her words carefully, spacing them with definite pauses, Ale said, "You are the most difficult … human being … I have ever met."

"Is that why you brought me here? If you can convince me, you can convince anyone?"

"I don't think of Islanders as Mutes," she said. "You are humans whose lives are important and whose value to us all should be obvious."

"But you said yourself that there are Mermen who don't agree," he said.

"Most Mermen don't know the particular problems Islanders face. You must admit, Ward, that much of your work force is ineffective … through no fault of your own, of course."

How subtle, he thought. *Almost euphemistic.*

"Then what is our 'obvious value?'"

"Ward, each of us has approached a common problem—survival on this planet—in somewhat different ways. Down here, we compost for methane and to gain soil for the time when we'll have to plant the land."

"Diverting energy from the life cycle?"

"Delaying," she insisted. "Land is far more stable when plants hold it down. We'll need fertile soil."

"Methane," he muttered. He forgot what point he was going to make in the wake of the new illumination dawning on him. "You want our hydrogen facilities!"

Her eyes went wide at the quickness of his mind.

"We need the hydrogen to get into space," she said.

"And we need it for cooking, heating and driving our few engines," he countered. "You have methane, too."

"Not enough."

"We separate hydrogen electronically and—"

"Not very efficient," he said. He tried to keep the pride out of his voice, but it leaked through all the same.

"You use those beautiful separation membranes and the high pressure of deep water," she said.

"Score one for organics."

"But organics are not the best way to build a whole technology," she said. "Look how it's bogged you down. Your technology should support and protect you, help you to progress."

"That was argued out generations ago," he said. "Islanders know what you think about organics."

"That argument is not over," she insisted. "And with the hyb tanks …"

"You're coming to us, now," he said, "because we have a way with tissues." He allowed himself a tight smile. "And I note that you also come to us for the most delicate surgery."

"We understand that organics once represented the most convenient way for you to survive topside," she said. "But times are changing and we—"

"You are changing them," he challenged. He backed off at the frustration visible in her clenched jaw, noting the flash of something bright in her blue eyes. "Times are always changing," he said, his voice softer. "The question remains: How do we best adapt to change?"

"It requires all of your energies just to maintain yourselves and your organics," she snapped, not softening. "Islands starve sometimes. But we do not starve. And within a generation we will walk beneath open sky on dry land!"

Keel shrugged. The shrug irritated the prosthetic supports for his large head. He could feel his neck muscles growing tired, snaking their whips of pain up the back of his neck, crowning his scalp.

"What do you think of that old argument in light of this change?" she asked. It was voiced as a challenge.

"You are creating sea barriers, new surflines that can sink Islands," he said. "You do this to further a Merman way of life. An Islander would be foolish not to ask whether you're doing this to sink the Islands and drown us Mutes."

"Ward." She shook her head before continuing. "Ward, the end of Island life as you know it will come in our lifetime. That's not necessarily bad."

Not in my lifetime, he thought.

"Don't you understand that?" she demanded.

"You want me to facilitate your kind of change," he said. "That makes me the Judas goat. You know about Judas, Kareen? And goats?"

A shadow of unmistakable impatience crossed her face. "I'm trying to impress on you how soon Islanders must change. That is a fact and it must be dealt with, distasteful or not."

"You're also trying to get our hydrogen facilities," he said.

"I'm trying to keep you above our Merman political squabbles," she said.

"Somehow, Kareen, I don't have confidence in you. I suspect that you don't have the approval of your own people."

"I've had enough of this," Panille interrupted. "I warned you, Kareen, that an Islander—"

"Let me handle this," she said, and quieted him with a lift of her hand. "If it's a mistake, it's my mistake."

To Keel, she said, "Can you find confidence in retrieving the hyb tanks or settling the land? Can you see the value in restoring the kelp to consciousness?"

It's an act, he thought. *She's playing to me. Or to Shadow.*

"To what end and by what means?" he asked, stalling for more time.

"To what end? We'll finally have some real stability. All of us. It's something that'll pull all of us together."

She seems so cool, so smooth, he thought. *But something's not quite right.*

"What're your priorities?" he asked. "The kelp, the land or the hyb tanks?"

"My people want the hyb tanks."

"Who are your people?"

She looked at Panille, who said, "A majority, that's who her people are. That's how we operate down under."

Keel looked down at him. "And what are your priorities, Shadow?"

"Personally?" His eyes left the screen reluctantly. "The kelp. Without it this planet's an endless struggle for survival." He gestured to the screens, which, Keel reminded himself, somehow had Islander lives balancing on them. "You saw what it can do," Panille said. "Right now it's keeping Vashon in deep water. That's handy. It's survival."

"You think that's a sure thing?"

"I do. We have everything that was recovered from the old Redoubt after the inundation. We've a good idea what's in the hyb tanks. They can wait."

Keel looked at Ale. "Sure, things worry me. I know what's supposed to be in those tanks. What do your records say?"

"We have every reason to believe the hyb tanks contain earthside plant and animal life, everything Ship considered necessary for colonization. And there may be as many as thirty thousand human beings—all preserved indefinitely."

Keel snorted at the phrase "every reason to believe." *They don't know after all,* he thought. *This is a blind shot.* He looked up at the ceiling, thinking of those bits of plasteel and plaz and all that flesh swinging in a wide loop around Pandora, year after year.

"There could be anything up there," Keel said. "Anything." He knew it was fear speaking. He looked accusingly at Ale. "You claim to represent a majority of Mermen, yet I sense a furtiveness in your activities."

"There are political sensitivities—" She broke off. "Ward, our space project will continue whether I'm successful with you or not."

"Successful? With me?" There seemed to be no end to her manipulative schemes.

Ale exhaled, more of a hiss than a sigh. "If I fail, Ward, the chances for the Islanders look bad. We want to start a civilization, not a war. Don't you understand? We're offering the Islanders land for colonization."

"Ahhhh, the bait!" he said.

Keel thought about the impact such an offer might have on Islanders. Many would leap at it—the poor Islanders, such as those of Guemes, the little drifters living from sea to mouth. Vashon might be another matter. But Merman riches were being exposed in this offer. Many Islanders harbored deep feelings of jealousy over those riches. It would worsen. The complexity of what Ale proposed began to lay itself out in his mind—a problem to solve.

"I need information," he said. "How close are you to going into space?"

"Shadow," Ale said.

Panille punched keys on his console. The screen in front of him displayed a pair of images with a dividing line down the middle. On the left was an underwater view of a tower, its dimensions not clear to Keel until he realized that the tiny shapes around it were not fish, but Mermen workers. The view on the right showed the tower protruding from the sea and, with the proportions clear from the left screen, Keel realized that the thing must lift fifty meters above the surface.

"There will be one space launch today or tomorrow, depending on the weather," Ale said. "A test, our first manned shot. It won't be long after that when we go up after the hyb tanks."

"Why has no Island reported that thing?" Keel asked.

"We steer you away from it," Panille said with a shrug.

Keel shook his aching head.

"This explains the sightings you've heard of, the Islander claims that Ship is returning," Ale said.

"How amusing for you!" Keel blurted. "The simple Islanders with their primitive superstitions." He glared at her. "You know some of my people are claiming your rockets as a sign the world is ending. If you'd only brought the C/P into this …"

"It was a bad decision," she said. "We admit it. That's why you're here. What do we do about it?"

Keel scratched his head. His neck ached abominably against the prosthetic braces. He sensed things between the lines here … Panille coming in on cue. Ale saying mostly what she had planned to say. Keel was an old political infighter, though, aware that he could not tip his hand too soon. Ale wanted him to learn things—things she had planned for him to learn. It was the concealed lesson that he was after.

"How do we make Islanders comfortable with the truth?" Keel countered.

"We don't have time for Islander philosophizing," she said.

Keel bristled. "That's just another way of calling us lazy. Just staying alive occupies most of us full-time. You think we're not busy because we're not building rockets. We're the ones who don't have time. We don't have time for pretty phrases and planning—"

"Stop it!" she snapped. "If the two of us can't get along, how can we expect better of our people?"

Keel turned his head to look at her with one eye and then with the other. He suppressed a smile. Two things amused him. She had a point, and she could lose her composure. He lifted both hands and rubbed at his neck.

Ale was instantly solicitous, aware of Keel's problem from their many encounters on the debate floor. "You're tired," she said. "Would you like to rest and have a cup of coffee or something more solid?"

"A good cup of Vashon's best would suit me," he said. He tugged at the prosthetic on his right. "And this damned thing off my neck for a while. You wouldn't happen to have a chairdog, would you?"

"Organics are rare down under," she said. "I'm afraid we can't provide Islander comforts for everything."

"I just wanted a massage," he said. "Mermen are missing a bet by not having a few chairdogs."

"I'm sure we can find you a massage," Kareen said.

"We don't have the high incidence of health problems that you have topside," Panille interrupted. Again, his eyes were on the screen filled with numbers and he spoke almost out of another consciousness. Still, Keel couldn't let the remark pass.

"Young man," he said, "I suspect you are brilliant in your work. Don't let the confidence of that accomplishment spill over into other areas. You have a great deal yet to learn."

Turning to lean on Ale's arm, he allowed himself to be assisted out into the passageway, feeling the stares that followed them. He was glad to get out of that room. Something about it wriggled chills up and down his spine.

"Have I convinced you?" Ale asked. He shuffled along beside her, his legs aching, his head filled with bits of information that he knew would soon inflict themselves upon his people.

"You have convinced me that Mermen will do this thing," he said. "You have the wealth, the organization, the determination." He lurched and caught himself. "I'm not used to decks that don't roll," he explained. "Living on land is hard for an old-timer."

"Everyone can't go onto the land at once," she said. "Only the most needy at first. We think other Islands will have to be moored offshore … or rafts may be built for such nearby moorage. They'll be temporary living quarters until the agricultural system is well along."

Keel thought about this a moment, then: "You have been thinking this out for a long time."

"We have."

"Organizing Islanders' lives for them and—"

"Trying to figure out how to save the lot of you!"

"Oh?" He laughed. "By putting us on bedroom rafts near shore?"

"They'd be ideal," she said. He could see a genuine excitement in her eyes. "As the need for them vanished, we could let them die off and use them for fertilizers."

"Our Islands, too, no doubt—fertilizer."

"That's about all they'll be good for when we have enough open land."

Keel could not keep the bitterness out of his voice. "You do not understand, Kareen. I can see that. An Island is not a dead piece of … of land. It's alive! It is our mother. It supports us because we give it loving care. You are condemning our mother to a bag of fertilizer."

She stared at him a moment, then: "You seem to think Islanders are the only ones giving up a way of life. Those of us who go back to the surface—"

"Will still have access to the deeps," he said. "You are not cutting the umbilical cord. We would suffer more in the transition. You seem willing to ignore this."

"I'm not ignoring it, dammit! That's why you're here."

Time to end the sparring, he thought. *Time to show her that I don't really trust her or believe her.*

"You're hiding things from me," he said. "I've studied you for a long time, Kareen. There's something boiling in you, something big and important. You're trying to control what I learn, feeding me selected information to gain my cooperation. You—"

"Ward, I—"

"Don't interrupt. The quickest way to gain my cooperation is to open up, share everything with me. I will help if that's what should be done. I will not help, I will resist, if I feel you are concealing anything from me."

She stopped them at a dogged hatch and stared at it without focusing.

"You know me, Kareen," he prompted. "I say what I mean. I will fight you. I will leave … unless you restrain me … and I will campaign against—"

"All right!" She glared up at him. "Restrain you? I wouldn't dare consider it. Others might, but I would not. You want me to share? Very well. The bad trouble has already started, Ward. Guemes Island is under the waves."

He blinked, as if blinking would clear away the force of what she'd said.

An entire Island, under the waves!

"So," he growled, "your precious current controls didn't work. You've driven an Island onto—"

"No." She shook her head for emphasis. "No! No! Someone has done it deliberately. It had nothing to do with Current Control. It was a cruel, vicious act of destruction."

"Who?" He spoke the word in a low, shocked voice.

"We don't know yet. But there are thousands of casualties and we're still picking up survivors." She turned and undogged the hatch. Keel saw the first signs of age in her slow movements.

She's still holding something back, he thought as he followed her into her quarters.

Chapter 18

Humans spend their lives in mazes. If they escape and cannot find another maze, they create one. What is this passion for testing?
—Questions from the Avata, The Histories

DUQUE BEGAN to curse, rolling in the nutrient bath and pounding his fists against the organic sides until great blue stains appeared along the edge.

The guardians summoned the C/P.

It was late and Simone Rocksack had been preparing for bed. At the summons, Simone pulled her favorite robe over her head and let it drop over the firm curves of her breasts and hips. The robe in its purple dignity erased all but the slightest traces of womanliness from her bearing. She hurried down the passage from her quarters, pulling at her robe to restore some of its daytime crispness. She entered the gloomy space where Vata and Duque existed. Her anxiety was obvious in every moment. Kneeling above Duque, she said: "I am here, Duque. It is the Chaplain/Psychiatrist. How can I help you?"

"Help me?" Duque screamed. "You wart on the rump of a pregnant sow! You can't even help yourself!"

Shocked, the C/P put a hand over the flap covering her mouth. She knew what a sow was, of course—one of the creatures of Ship, a female swine. This she remembered well.

A pregnant sow?

Simone Rocksack's slender fingers couldn't help pressing against the smooth flatness of her abdomen.

"The only swine are in the hyb tanks," she said. She concentrated on keeping her voice loud enough for Duque to hear.

"So you think!"

"Why are you cursing?" the C/P asked. She tried to keep a proper reverence in her tone.

"Vata's dreaming me into terrible things," Duque moaned. "Her hair … it's all over the ocean and she's breaking me into little pieces."

The C/P stared at Duque. Most of his form was a blurred hulk under the nutrient. His lips sought the surface like a bloated carp. He seemed to be all in one piece.

"I don't understand," she said. "You appear intact."

"Haven't I told you she dreams me?" Duque moaned. "Dreams hurt if you can't get out. I'll drown down there. Every little piece of me will drown."

"You're not drowning, Duque," the C/P assured.

"Not here, baboon. In the sea!"

Baboon, she thought. That was another creature from Ship. Why was Duque recalling the creatures of Ship? Were they at last coming down? But how could he know? She lifted her gaze to the fearful watchers around the rim of the organic tank. Could one of them … ? No, it was impossible.

His voice suddenly clear and extremely articulate, Duque proclaimed, "She won't listen. They're talking and she won't listen."

"Who won't listen, Duque? Who are 'they?'"

"Her hair! Haven't you heard a thing I've said?" He pounded a fist weakly against the tank side below the C/P. She stroked her abdomen again, absently.

"Are the creatures from Ship to be brought down to Pandora?" Rocksack asked.

"Take them where you want," Duque said. "Just don't let her dream me back into the sea."

"Does Vata wish to return to the sea?"

"She's dreaming me, I tell you. She's dreaming me away."

"Are Vata's dreams reality?"

Duque refused to answer. He merely groaned and twisted at the edge of the tank.

Rocksack sighed. She stared across the tank at the mounded bulk of Vata, quiescent … breathing. Vata's long hair moved like seaweed in the currents of Duque's disturbance. How could Vata's hair be in the ocean and here on Vashon simultaneously? Perhaps in dreams. Was this another miracle of Ship? Vata's hair was almost long enough to be cut once more, it had been over a year. Was all of that hair that had been cut from Vata … was all of it somehow still attached to Vata? Nothing was impossible in the realm of miracles.

But how could Vata's hair speak?

There was no mistaking what Duque had said. Vata's hair spoke and Vata would not listen. Why would Vata not listen? Was it too soon to return to the sea? Was this a warning that Vata would lead them all back into the sea?

Again, Rocksack sighed. The Chaplain/Psychiatrist's job could be troublesome. Terrible demands were made upon her. Word of this would be out by morning. There was no way to silence the guardians. Rumors, distorted stories. Some interpretation would have to be made, something firm and supportive. Something good enough to silence dangerous speculations.

She stood, grimacing at a pain in her right knee. Looking at the awed faces around the tank's rim, she said, "The next lot of Vata's hair will not go to the faithful. Every clipping must be cast into the sea as an offering."

Below her, Duque groaned, then quite clearly he shouted, "Bitch! Bitch! Bitch!"

Rocksack placed this reference immediately, having been prepared by Duque's previous mutterings. Bitch was the female of the canine family. Great things were in store for Pandora, the C/P realized. Vata was dreaming Duque into wondrous experiences and Duque was calling forth the creatures of Ship.

Looking once more at the awed guardians, Rocksack explained this carefully. She was pleased by the way heads nodded agreement.

Chapter 19

All Pandorans will be free when the first hylighter breaks the sea's surface.
—Sign over a Merman kelp project

FIVE WATER-drum tones sounded a musical call, pulling Brett up … up … lifting him out of a dream in which he reached for Scudi Wang but never quite touched her. Always, he fell back into the depths as he had sunk when the wavewall swept him off Vashon.

Brett opened his eyes and recognized Scudi's room. There were no lights, but his light-gathering eyes discerned her hand across the short distance between their beds. The hand reached out from the covers and groped sleepily up the wall toward the light switch.

"It's a little higher and to the right," he said.

"You can see?" There was puzzlement in her voice. Her hand stopped its groping and found the switch. Brilliance washed the room. He sucked a deep breath, let it out slowly and rubbed his eyes. The light hurt him all the way out to the temples.

Scudi sat upright on her bed, the blankets pulled loosely around her breasts. "You can see in the dark?" she persisted.

He nodded. "Sometimes it's handy."

"Then modesty is not as, strict with you as I thought." She slipped from the covers and dressed in a singlesuit striped vertically in yellow and green. Brett tried not to watch her dress, but his eyes no longer would obey.

"I check instruments in a half-hour," she said. "Then I ride outpost."

"What should I do about … you know, checking in?"

"I have reported. I should be finished in a few hours. Don't go wandering; you could get lost."

"I need a guide?"

"A friend," she said. Again, that quick smile. "If hunger strikes, there is food." She pointed toward the alcove end of her quarters. "When I get back, you will report in. Or they may send someone for you."

He glanced around the room, feeling that it would shrink without Scudi here and with nothing to do.

"You did not sleep well?" Scudi asked.

"Nightmares," he said. "I'm not used to sleeping still. Everything's so … dead, so quiet."

Her smile was a white blur in her dark face. "I have to go. Sooner out, sooner back."

When the hatch clicked shut behind her, the stillness of the little room boomed in Brett's ears. He looked at the bed where Scudi had slept.

I'm alone.

He knew that sleep was impossible. His attention wouldn't leave the slight impression left by Scudi's body on the other bed. Such a small room, why did it feel bigger when she was in it?

His heartbeat was fast, suddenly, and as it got faster he found a constriction of his chest whenever he tried to take a deep breath.

He swung his legs off the bed, pulled on his clothes and started to pace. His gaze moved erratically around the room—sink and water taps, the cupboards with conchlike whorls in the corners, the hatch to the head … everything was costly metal but plain and rigid in design. The water taps were shiny silver dolphins. He felt them and touched the wall behind them. The two metals had entirely different textures.

The room had no ports or skylights, nothing to show the exterior world. The walls with their kelplike undulations were breached only by the two hatches. He felt that he had an unlimited amount of energy and nowhere to use it.

He folded the beds back into their couch positions and paced the room. Something boiled in him. His chest became tighter and a swarm of wriggling black shapes intruded on his vision. There was nothing around him, he thought, but water. A loud ringing swelled in his ears.

Abruptly, Brett jerked open the outside hatch and lurched into the passageway. He only knew that he needed air. He fell to one knee there, gagging.

Two Mermen stopped beside him. One of them gripped his shoulder.

A man said, "Islander." His voice betrayed only curiosity.

"Easy does it," another man said. "You're safe."

"Air!" Brett gasped. Something heavy was standing on his chest, and his heart still raced inside his straining chest.

The man gripping his shoulder said: "There's plenty of air, son. Take a deep breath. Lean back against me and take a deep breath."

Brett felt the tension clawing at his belly lift a bony finger, then another. A new, commanding voice behind him demanded: "Who left this Mute alone here?" There was a scuffling sound, then a shout: "Medic! Here!"

Brett tried to take a fast, deep breath but couldn't. He heard a whistling in his constricted throat. "Relax. Breathe slow and deep."

"Get him to a port," the commanding voice said. "Get him somewhere he can see outside. That usually works."

Hands straightened Brett and lifted him with arms under his shoulders. His fingertips and lips conveyed the buzz and tingle of electric shock. A blurred face bent close to him, inquiring, "Have you ever been down under before?"

Brett's lips shaped a silent "No." He was not sure he could walk.

"Don't be afraid," the blur said. "This occasionally happens your first time alone. You'll be all right."

Brett grew aware that people were hurrying him along a pale orange passageway. A hand patted his shoulder. The tingling receded, and the black shapes floating across his vision began to shrink. The people carrying him stopped and eased him to the deck on his back, then propped him upright. His head was clearing, and Brett looked up at a string of lights. The light cover directly overhead had blobs of dust and bugs inside. A head blotted out his view and Brett had an impression of a man about Twisp's age with a backlighted halo of dark hair.

"You feeling better?" the man asked.

Brett tried to speak in a dry mouth, then managed to croak, "I feel stupid."

In the sudden laughter all around him, Brett ducked his head and looked out a wide port into the sea. It was a horizontal view of low-lying kelp with many fish grazing between its leaves. This was a perspective of undersea life far different from the driftwatch views topside.

The older man patted his shoulder and said, "That's all right, son. Everyone feels stupid some time or other. It's better than being stupid, eh?"

Twisp would have said that, Brett thought. He grinned up at the long-haired Merman. "Thanks."

"Best thing for you to do, young man," the Merman said, "is to go back to a quiet room. Try being alone again."

The thought pumped Brett's pulse rate back up. He imagined himself alone once more in that little room with those metal walls *and all that water* …

"Who brought you in here?" the man asked. Brett hesitated. "I don't want to cause any trouble."

"You won't," the medic reassured him. "We can get the person who picked you up freed from regular duty to make your entry into life here a little easier."

"Scudi … Scudi Wang picked me up."

"Oh! There are people waiting for you nearby. Scudi will be able to guide you. Lex," he spoke to a man out of Brett's line of vision, "call down to Scudi at the lab." The medic returned his attention to Brett. "There's no hurry, but you do have to get used to being alone."

A voice behind Brett said, "She's on her way."

"Lots of Islanders have a rough time of it down under at first. I'd say every one, in some way or other. Some recover all at once, a few brood for weeks. You look like you're getting over it."

Someone on the other side of Brett lifted Brett's chin and pressed a container of water to his lips. The water felt cold and tasted faintly of salt.

Brett saw Scudi rushing down the long passage, her small face twisted with worry. The Merman helped Brett to his feet, gripped his shoulder, then hurried toward Scudi. "Your friend's had a stress flash." The man hurried past Scudi, speaking back at her. "Put him through the solo drill before he learns to like the panic, though."

She waved her thanks, then helped Brett manage the walk back to her room.

"I should've stayed," Scudi said. "You were my first, and you seemed to be doing so well …"

"I thought I was, too," he said, "so don't feel bad. Who was that medic?"

"Shadow Panille. I work with his department in Search and Rescue—Current Control."

"I thought he was a medic, they said—"

"He is. Everyone in S and R holds that rating." Scudi took his arm. "Are you all right now?"

He blushed. "It was stupid of me. I just felt I had to get some air, and when I got out into the passage …"

"It's my fault," she insisted. "I forgot about stress flash and they're always telling us about it. I felt … well, like you'd always been here. I didn't think of you as a newcomer."

"The air in the passage felt so thick," Brett said. "Almost like water."

"Is it all right now?"

"Yes." He inhaled a deep breath. "Kind of ... wet, though."

"It gets heavy enough to do your laundry in sometimes. Some Islanders have to carry dry bottles while they're adjusting. If you feel well now, we can report in. Some people are waiting for you." She shrugged at his inquiring look. "You have to be processed, of course."

He stared at her, reassured by her presence but still nursing an abrupt hollow feeling. Islanders heard many stories of the way Mermen regulated everything in their lives—reports for this, tests for that. He started to ask her about this processing but was interrupted as a large group of Mermen clattered past carrying equipment—tanks, hoses, stretchers.

Scudi called after them, "What is it?"

"They're bringing in the accident survivors," one of them hollered.

Ceiling speakers came alive then: "Situation Orange! Situation Orange! All emergency personnel to your stations. This is not a drill. This is not a drill. Keep docking areas clear. Keep passageways clear. Essential duty stations only for regular personnel. Essential duty stations only. All others report to alternate stations. Medical emergencies only in the passages or trauma shed vicinity. Situation Orange. This is not a drill ..."

More Mermen dashed past them. One shouted back, "Clear the passageways!"

"What is it?" Scudi called after him.

"That Island that sank off Mistral Barrier. They're bringing in the survivors."

Brett yelled, "Was it Vashon?" They ran on without answering.

Scudi pulled at his arm. "Hurry." She directed him down a side passage and pulled up a large hatchway, which slid aside at her touch. "I'll have to leave you here and report to my station."

Brett followed her through a double-hatchway into a cafe. Booths with low-set tables lined the walls. More low tables were scattered throughout the room. Plasteel pillars in rows defined aisleways. Each pillar was set up as a serving-station. A booth in the corner held two people bent toward each other across the table. Scudi hurried Brett toward this booth. As they approached the figure on the right became clear. Brett missed a step. Every Islander knew that face—that craggy head with its elongated neck and its brace work: *Ward Keel!*

Scudi stopped at the booth, her hand gripping Brett's. Her attention was on Keel's companion. Brett recognized the red-haired woman. He'd glimpsed her on Vashon. Until he'd met Scudi, he'd considered Kareen Ale the most beautiful woman alive. Scudi's low-voiced introduction was not necessary.

"There were supposed to be registration and processing personnel here," Ale said, "but they've gone to their stations."

Brett swallowed hard and looked at Keel. "Mr. Justice, they said a whole Island's been sunk."

"It was Guemes," Keel said, his voice cold.

Ale looked at Keel. "Ward, I suggest that you and young Norton go to my quarters. Don't stay long in the passages and stay inside until you hear from me."

"I must go, Brett," Scudi said. "I'll come for you when this is over."

Ale touched Scudi's arm and they hurried away. Slowly, painfully, Keel eased himself from the booth. He stood, letting his legs adjust to the new position.

Brett listened to the people rushing through the passage outside the hatchway. Laboriously, Keel began shuffling toward the exit hatch. "Come along, Brett."

As they stepped into the aisle leading toward the exit, a hatch behind them hissed open, gushing the rich smells of garlic fried in olive oil and spices he couldn't name. A man's voice called out: "You two! No one in the passages!"

Brett whirled. A heavy set man with dark gray hair stood in the open hatchway to the kitchen. His rather flat features were set in a scowl, which changed into a forced smile as he looked past Brett and recognized Keel.

"Sorry, Mr. Justice," the man said. "Didn't recognize you at first. But you still shouldn't be in the passages."

"We were instructed to vacate this place and meet the ambassador at her quarters," Keel said.

The man stepped aside and gestured toward the kitchen. "Through here. You can occupy Ryan Wang's old quarters. Kareen Ale will be notified."

Keel touched Brett's shoulder. "This is closer," he said. The man led them into a large, low-ceilinged room flooded with soft light. Brett could not find the light source; it seemed to wash the room equally in gentle tones. Thick, pale blue carpeting caressed Brett's bare feet. The only furnishings appeared to be plump cushions in browns, burnt red and dark blue, but Brett, knowing how Mermen swung things out of walls, suspected other furniture might be concealed behind the hangings.

"You will be comfortable here," the man said. "Who do I have the pleasure of thanking for this hospitality?" Keel asked.

"I am Finn Lonfinn," the man said. "I was one of Wang's servants and now have the task of caring for his quarters. And your young friend is … ?"

"Brett Norton," Brett answered. "I was on my way to registration and processing when the alarm sounded."

Brett studied the room. He had never seen a place quite like it. In some respects, it was vaguely Islander—soft cushions, all the metal covered by woven hangings, many recognizably of topside manufacture. But the deck did not move. Only the faint sigh of air pulsing through vents.

"Do you have friends on Guemes?" Lonfinn asked.

"The C/P is from Guemes," Keel reminded him.

Lonfinn's eyebrows lifted and he turned his attention to Brett. Brett felt required to give a reply. "I don't think I know anyone from Guemes. We haven't been in proximate drift since I was born."

Lonfinn focused once more on Keel. "I asked about friends, not about the C/P."

In the man's tone, Brett heard the hard slam of a hatch between Merman and Islander. The word *mutant* lay in the air between them. Simone Rocksack was a Mute, possibly a friend of Mute Ward Keel … probably not. Who could be friendly with someone who looked like that? The C/P could not be a normal object of friendship. Brett felt suddenly threatened.

Keel had realized with an abrupt shock that Lonfinn's assumptions of obvious Merman superiority were barbed. This attitude was a common one among less-traveled Mermen, but Keel felt himself filled with disquiet at an abrupt inner awakening.

I was ready to accept his judgment! Part of me has assumed all along that Mermen are naturally better.

An unconscious thing, borne for years, it had unfolded in Keel like an evil flower, showing a part of himself he had never suspected. The realization filled Keel with anger. Lonfinn had been asking: "Do you have any little friends on Guemes? How sad that some of your less fortunate playmates have been killed or maimed. But maiming and death are such an integral part of your lives."

"You say you were a servant," Keel said. "Are you telling me these quarters are no longer occupied?"

"They belong rightfully to Scudi Wang, I believe," Lonfinn said. "She says she doesn't care to live here. I presume they'll be leased before long and the income credited to Scudi."

Brett gave the man a startled look and glanced once more around these spacious quarters—everything so rich.

Still in shock at his inner revelation, Keel shuffled to a pile of blue cushions and eased himself onto them, stretching his aching legs in front of him.

"Lucky Guemes was a small Island," Lonfinn said.

"Lucky?" The word was jerked from Brett.

Lonfinn shrugged. "I mean, how much more terrible if it had been one of the bigger Islands … even Vashon."

"We know what you mean," Keel said. He sighed. "I'm aware that Mermen call Guemes 'The Ghetto.'"

"It … doesn't mean anything, really," Lonfinn said. There was an undertone of anger in his voice as he realized he had been put on the defensive.

"What it means is that the larger Islands have been called upon to help Guemes from time to time—basic foods and medical supplies," Keel pressed him.

"Not much trade with Guemes," Lonfinn admitted. Brett looked from one man to the other, detecting the subterranean argument boiling. There were things behind those words but Brett suspected that it would take more experience with Mermen before he understood just what those things were. He sensed only the fact of argument, the barely concealed anger. Some Islanders, Brett knew, made slanted references to Guemes as "Ship's Lifeboat." There was often laughter in the label, but Brett had understood it to mean that Guemes held a large number of WorShipers—very religious, fundamentalist people. It was no surprise that the C/P was a native of Guemes. Somehow, it was right for Islanders to joke about Guemes, but it rankled him to hear Lonfinn's intrusions.

Lonfinn strode across the room and tested the controls on a hatch. He turned. "The head's through this hatch and guest bedrooms are down the hallway here in case you wish to rest." He returned and looked down at Keel. "I imagine that thing around your neck becomes tiresome."

Keel rubbed his neck. "It does indeed. But I know we all must put up with tiresome things in our world."

Lonfinn scowled. "I wonder why a Merman has never been C/P?"

Brett spoke up, recalling Twisp's comment on this very question. He repeated it: "Maybe Mermen have too many other things to do and aren't interested."

"Not interested?" Lonfinn looked at Brett as though seeing him for the first time. "Young man, I don't think you're qualified to discuss political matters."

"I think the boy was really asking a question," Keel offered, smiling at Brett.

"Questions should be asked directly," Lonfinn muttered.

"And answered directly," Keel persisted. He looked at Brett. "This matter has always been in dispute among 'the faithful' and their political lobby. Most of Ship's faithful topside think it would be a disaster to turn over the C/P's power to a Merman. They have so much power over other aspects of our otherwise dreary lives."

Lonfinn smiled without humor. "A difficult political subject for a young man to understand," he said.

Brett gritted his teeth at the patronizing attitude.

Lonfinn crossed to the wall behind Keel, touched a depression there and a panel slid away. It revealed a huge port that looked out on an undersea courtyard with transparent ceiling and a watery center where clusters of small fishes flashed and turned among delicate, richly colored plants.

"I must be going," Lonfinn said. "Enjoy yourselves. This"—he indicated the area he had just exposed—"should keep you from feeling too enclosed. I find it restful myself." He turned to Brett, paused and said, "I'll see that the necessary forms and papers are sent for you to sign. No sense wasting time."

With that, Lonfinn departed, leaving by the same hatch they had entered. Brett looked at Keel. "Have you filled out these papers? What are they?"

"The papers fulfill the Merman need to feel they have everything pinned down. Your name, your age, circumstances of your arrival down under, your work experience, any talents you might have, whether you desire to stay ..." Keel hesitated, cleared his throat. " ... your parentage, their occupations and mutations. The severity of your own mutation."

Brett continued to regard the Chief Justice silently.

"And in answer to your other question," Keel continued, "no, they have not required this of me. I'm sure they have a long dossier on me giving all the important details ... and many unimportant tidbits, too."

Brett had fastened onto one thing in Keel's statement. "They may ask me to stay down under?"

"They may require you to work off the cost of your rescue. A lot of Islanders have settled down under, something I mean to look into before going topside. Life here can be very attractive, I know." He ran his fingers through the soft nap of carpet as if for emphasis.

Brett looked at the ceiling, wondering how it would be to live most of his life here away from the suns. Of course, people from down under did go topside lots of times, but still ...

"The best disaster-recovery team is composed mostly of ex-Islanders," Keel said. "So says Kareen Ale."

"I've heard the Mermen always want you to pay your own way," Brett said. "But it shouldn't take long to work off the cost of my ..." He suddenly thought of Scudi. How could he ever repay Scudi? There was no coin for that.

"Mermen have a great many ways of attracting desirable and acceptable Islanders," Keel said. "You appear to be someone they'd be interested in having aboard. However, that should not be your chief concern of the moment. By any chance, do you have medical training?"

"Just first aid and resuscitation through school."

Keel drew in a deep breath and expelled it quickly. "Not enough, I'm afraid. Guemes went down quite a while ago. I'm sure the survivors they're just now bringing in will require more expert attention."

Brett tried to swallow in a tight throat.

Guemes, a whole Island sunk.

"I could carry a stretcher," he said.

Keel smiled sadly. "I'm sure you could. But I'm also sure you wouldn't be able to find the right place to take it. Either one of us would just be in the way. At the moment, we're just what they think of us—two Islander misfits who might do more harm than good. We'll just have to wait."

Chapter 20

We seldom get rid of an evil merely by understanding its causes.
—C.G. Jung, *Shiprecords*

THERE'S A curse in the Histories," Bushka said, "old as humans. It says, 'May you live in interesting times.' I guess we got it."

For some time now, as the coracles cruised through the half-night of Pandora's open sea, Bushka had been telling Twisp what he'd learned from Gallow and from members of Gallow's crew. Twisp could not see Bushka. Only the thin red light of the RDC's arrow glowed in the coracle. All else was darkness—not even stars overhead. A damp cloud cover had swept over them shortly after nightfall.

"There'll be more open land than you can possibly imagine," Bushka continued. "As much land as you see water around you now. So they say."

"It's all bad for the Islands," Twisp said. "And those rockets you say they're launching ..."

"Oh, they're well-prepared," Bushka said. His voice came out of the darkness with a smug sound that Twisp did not like. "Everything's ready for bringing down the hyb tanks. Warehouses full of equipment."

"It's hard for me to imagine land," Twisp admitted. "Where will they lift it out of the sea first?"

"The place that the settlers here called 'Colony.' On the maps, it's a slightly curved rectangle. The curve is being widened and lengthened into an oval with a lagoon at its center. It was a complete city before the Clone Wars, walled in with plasteel, so it makes a good place to start. Sometime this year they'll pump it out and the first city will be exposed to the sky."

"Waves will wipe it out," Twisp said.

"No," Bushka countered. "They've been five generations preparing for this. They've thought of everything—the politics, economics, the kelp …" He broke off as one of the squawks uttered a sleepy bleat.

Both men froze, listening expectantly. Was there a night-roaming hunt of dashers nearby? The squawks remained quiet. "Bad dream," Bushka muttered.

"So Guemes Island with its religious fanatics stood in the way of this land-colonization project, is that it?" Twisp asked. "Them and their 'stick-to-the-Islands-where-Ship-left-us' attitude?"

Bushka did not respond.

Twisp thought about the things the man had revealed. A lifetime of fisherman's isolation clouded Twisp's imagination. He felt provincial, incapable of understanding matters of worldwide politics and economics. He knew what worked, and that seemed simple enough. All he knew was that he distrusted this grand scheme, which Bushka seemed half-enamored of in spite of the experience with Gallow.

"There's no place in this plan for Islanders," Twisp noted.

"No, no place for mutants. They're to be excluded," Bushka said. His voice was almost too low to hear.

"And who's to say what a mutant is?" Twisp demanded.

Bushka remained silent for a long time. Finally, he said, "The Islands are obsolete, that much I can't argue with. In spite of everything else, Gallow's right about that."

Twisp stared into the darkness where Bushka sat. There was a spot just to the left that felt a little darker than the rest. That's where Twisp aimed his attention. An image of Merman life came to him—their habitation, places Bushka had described. *Home,* he thought. *What kind of person calls this home?* Everything sounded regular and nearly identical, like some insect hive. It gave him the creeps.

"This place you're guiding us to," Twisp asked, "what is it? Why is it safe for us to go there?"

"The Green Dashers are a small organization," Bushka said. "Launch Base One is huge—by the numbers alone our odds are better there than anyplace else in decent range."

This is hopeless, Twisp thought. If Mermen had not found Brett already, what else could he do? The sea was too big and it had been a fool's errand trying to fix on the place where the wave wall hit Vashon.

"It'll be dawn soon," Bushka said. "We should be there shortly after dawn."

Twisp heard the spat-spattering of rain on the tarp. He checked his eelcells with the handlight and found that they were turning a noticeable gray. Right on cue there was a tremendous deafening lightning thunder flash behind them. In the aftershock stillness, he heard Bushka holler, "What the fuck was *that?*"

Twisp flashed the handlight in that direction. Bushka had gone under the tarp head-first and somehow got himself turned around. He clutched the edges of the tarp, steadying himself, and in the glow from the handlight, his wide eyes punctuated his bleached face.

"We just charged our batteries," Twisp said. "We might take one more of those if it comes around. Then I'll bring in the antenna."

"Holy shit," Bushka snorted, "fishermen are crazier than I thought. It's a wonder any of you come back."

"We manage," Twisp said. "Tell me, how did you become an expert on Mermen so fast?"

Bushka emerged from the tarp. "As a historian, I already knew a great deal about them before going down under. And then ... you learn fast when it's necessary for survival." There was the sound of chest-puffing behind his words.

Survival, Twisp thought. He extinguished the handlight and wished that he could see Bushka's face without having to flash the light on him. The man was not a total coward; that seemed evident. He had crewed in the subs, like many other Islanders putting in their service time. Obviously knew how to navigate. But then, most Islanders learned that in school. With all that, Bushka was driven to seek a life down under. According to him, it was because the Mermen had better historical records, some they had never even examined themselves.

Bushka was like some of the Guemes fanatics, Twisp realized. *Driven.* A seeker after hidden knowledge. Bushka wanted his facts from the source and he didn't care how he got there. A dangerous man.

Twisp renewed his alertness, sensitive to any shift in Bushka's position. The coracle would transmit such movement ... should Bushka try to take him.

"You'd better believe it's happening," Bushka said. "There'll be no place for Islands pretty soon."

"Radio says Ward Keel's gone down under on some fact-finding mission," Twisp said. "You suppose he knew about it all along?"

A foot scraped the deck as Bushka shifted his weight. "According to Gallow, they did it without word topside."

Silence settled between them for a time. Twisp kept his attention on the guiding arrow, a red glowing pointer. How could some of the things Bushka said be believed? The barrier above the sea was real, though. And there was no doubt Bushka had run-for-it fever—something truly big and ugly chased him.

For his part, Bushka lay prisoned in his own thoughts. *I should've had the guts to kill them.* But the thing Gallow represented was bigger than Gallow. No mistaking that. To a historian, it was a familiar pattern. Ship's surviving records reported a plenitude of violence, leaders who tried to solve human problems by mass killing. Until the madness of Guemes, Bushka had thought such things distantly unreal. Now, he *knew* the madness, a thing with teeth and shadows.

Pale dawn lightened the wavetops and revealed Twisp working over a small cooking burner on the seat beside him. Bushka wondered whether, in the growing clarity of daylight, Twisp might not rather foreclose on the loan of the kid's shirt and pants.

Seeing Bushka's attention on him, Twisp asked, "Coffee?"

"Thanks."

Then: "How could I have been that blind and ignorant?"

Twisp stared at Bushka silently for a while, then asked, simply, "Going along with them, or letting them go?"

Bushka coughed and cleared his throat. His mouth felt full of lint as soon as he swallowed the hot coffee.

I'm still afraid, he thought. He looked up at Twisp, cooling his coffee at the tiller. "I've never been that afraid," he said.

Twisp nodded. The signs of fear on Bushka were easily read. Fear and ignorance drifted the same currents. There would be anger soon, when the fear receded. For now, though, Bushka's mind was chewing on itself.

"Pride, that's what made me do it," Bushka said. "I wanted Gallow's story, history in the making, political ferment—a powerful movement among the Mermen. One of their best took a liking to me. He knew I'd work hard. He knew how grateful I'd be ..."

"What if this Gallow and his crew are dead?" Twisp asked. "You scuttled their sub and only you are left to say what happened at Guemes."

"I tell you, I made sure they could escape!"

Twisp suppressed a grim smile. The anger was beginning to surface.

Bushka studied Twisp's face in the gray light. The fisherman was dark in the way of many Islanders who worked out in the weather. Vagrant breezes whipped Twisp's shaggy brown hair across his eyes. A two days' growth of beard shadowed his jaws and caught an occasional strand of hair. Everything in the man's manner—the steady movement of his eyes, the set of his mouth—spoke to Bushka of strength and resolution. Bushka envied the untroubled clarity in Twisp's gaze. Bushka was sure that no mirror would ever again return such clarity to his own eyes—not after the Guemes massacre. Bushka could see his own death in that butchery.

How could anybody believe I didn't know what was happening until it happened? How can I believe it?

"They tricked me good," Bushka said. "And oh, was I ready! I was all ready to trick myself."

"Most people know what it's like to be tricked," Twisp agreed. His voice was flat and almost devoid of emotion. It kept Bushka talking.

"I won't sleep for the rest of my life," Bushka muttered.

Twisp looked away at the surging sea around them. He didn't like the note of self-pity in Bushka's tone.

"What about the survivors of Guemes?" He spoke flatly. "What about their dreams?"

Bushka stared at Twisp in the growing light. A good man trying to save a partner's life. Bushka scrunched his eyes tightly closed but the images of Guemes imprinted themselves on his eyelids.

His eyes snapped open. Twisp was staring intently off to the right ahead of them. "Where's this Launch Base we're supposed to see at dawn?"

"It'll show before long."

Bushka stared at the lowering sky ahead of them. And when the Launch Base did show ... what then? The question tightened a band around his chest. Would the Mermen believe? Even if they did believe, would they act on that belief in a way to protect Islanders?

Chapter 21

Never trust a great man's love.
—Islander proverb

KEEL LOOKED down from the observation platform onto a nightmare scene of controlled pandemonium—rescue sleds wallowed into a small docking basin, coming through hatches lining the far wall of the courtyard below him. This was no nightmare, Keel reminded himself. Triage teams moved among the human shapes that littered the deck. Trauma teams conducted emergency surgery on the scene while other survivors were carried or carted off. The dead, and Keel had never imagined that much death, were stacked like the meat they were against the wall to his left. A long, oval port above the hatches gave a sea view of the arriving rescue sledges queued up and waiting their turns at the hatches. Trauma teams serviced these, too, as best they could.

Behind Keel, Brett uttered a sharp gasp as the shreds of someone's lower jaw tumbled to the deck from a body bag in transit to the mounting pile of similar bags against the wall. Scudi, standing beside Brett, shook with silent sobs.

Keel felt numb. He began to understand why Kareen Ale had sent Scudi to fetch him and Brett. Ale had not really grasped the enormity of this tragedy. Seeing it, she had wanted Islander witnesses to the fact that Mermen were doing everything physically possible for the survivors.

And she'll bring up the dirty work of the dead, he thought.

Keel glimpsed Ale's red hair among the medics working over the few survivors scattered across the courtyard. From the piles of dead, it was obvious that survivors were not even meeting the odds of pure chance. They were a tiny minority.

Scudi moved up beside him, her attention fixed on the deck below them. "So many," she whispered.

"How did it happen?" Brett demanded, speaking from beside Keel's left elbow.

Keel nodded. Yes, that was the real question. He did not want to conjecture on the matter, he wanted to be certain.

"So many," Scudi repeated, louder this time.

"The last census put Guemes at ten thousand souls," Keel said. This statement surprised him even as it escaped his mouth. *Souls.* The teachings of Ship *did* come to the surface in a crisis.

Keel knew he should assert himself, use the power of his position to demand answers. He owed it to the others if not to himself. The C/P would be after him the minute he returned, for one thing. Rocksack still had family on Guemes, of this Keel was certain. She would be angry, terribly angry in spite of her training, and she would be a force to reckon with.

If I return.

Keel felt sickened by the sight on the deck below him. He noted Scudi swiping at her tears. Her eyes were red and swollen. Yes, she had been helping down there, right in the middle of it, during the worst pressures.

"No need for you to stay here with me, Scudi," Keel said. "If they need you down—"

"I've been relieved of duty," she said. She shuddered, but her gaze remained on the receiving area.

Keel, too, could not take his attention from that scene of carnage. The receiving area had been cordoned off into sections by color-coded ropes. Emergency medical teams worked throughout the area, bending over pale flesh, moving patients onto litters for transfer.

A squad of Mermen entered from beneath the platform where Keel stood with Brett and Scudi. The Mermen began sorting through the sacks of bodies, opening them to attempt identification. Some of the bags contained only shreds and pieces of flesh and bone. The identification teams moved in a businesslike fashion, but where their jaws were visible, Keel detected clenched muscles. All of them appeared pale, even for Mermen. Several of the workers took pictures of faces and identifying marks. Others made notes on a portable trans-slate. Keel recognized the device. Ale had tried to interest his Committee in this system, but he had seen it as another way to keep the Islands in economic bondage. *"Everything you write on the transmitter-slate is sorted and stored in the computer,"* Ale had said.

Some things are best not recorded, he thought.

A man cleared his throat behind Keel. Keel turned to find Lonfinn and another Merman standing there. Lonfinn carried a plaz box under his left arm.

"Mr. Justice," Lonfinn said. "This is Miller Hastings of Registration."

In contrast to the dark, heavyset Lonfinn, Hastings was a tall, dark-haired man with a thick lower jaw and unwavering blue eyes. Both men wore crisp Merman suits of plain gray cloth—the kind of smoothly pressed and well-tended clothing Keel had come to identify with the worst Merman officiousness.

Hastings had turned his attention to Brett standing a few steps to one side. "We were told we would find a Brett Norton up here," Hastings said. "There are a few formalities … for yourself, too, I'm afraid, Mr. Justice."

Scudi moved behind Keel and took Brett's hand, an action that Keel's wide peripheral vision took in with some surprise. She was clearly frightened.

Hastings focused on Keel's mouth. "Our job, Mr. Justice, is to help you adjust to this tragic—"

"Shit!" Keel said.

Brett wondered whether he had heard correctly. The look of surprise on Hastings' face made it apparent that the Chief Justice and Chairman of the Committee on Vital Forms had, indeed, said "Shit." Brett looked at the Chief Justice's face. Keel had positioned himself with one eye on the two Mermen and the other eye still looking down on that bloody deck below them. It was a split of attention that appeared to disconcert the two Mermen. Brett found it natural; everyone knew that some Islanders could do this.

Hastings made another try: "We know this is difficult, Mr. Justice, but we are prepared for such matters and have developed procedures, which—"

"Have the decency to leave before I lose my temper," Keel said. His voice betrayed no sign of a quaver.

Hastings glanced at the plaz box under Lonfinn's arm, then at Brett.

"Hostility is an expected reaction," Hastings said. "But the sooner we overcome that barrier, the sooner—"

"I say it plain," Keel said, "leave us. We have nothing to say to you."

The Mermen exchanged glances. The looks on their faces told Brett that this pair had no intention of leaving.

"The young man should speak for himself," Hastings said. His tone was even and cordial. "What do you say, Brett Norton? Just a few formalities."

Brett swallowed. Scudi's hand in his felt slick with perspiration. Her fingers were tense sticks clenched between his own. What was Keel doing? More important, perhaps: Could Keel get away with it? Keel was an Islander and a powerful one, someone to admire. This was not the Island, however. Brett squared his shoulders in sudden decision. "Stuff your formalities," he said. "Any decent person would come another time."

Hastings let out a long breath slowly, almost a sigh. His face darkened and he started to speak but Keel cut him short.

"What the young man is saying," Keel said, "is that it's pretty insensitive of you to come here with your formalities while your cousins stack the bodies of our cousins against that wall down there."

The silence between the two groups became stiff. Brett could find no particular familial feeling toward the mangled dead being brought in from the depths, but he decided that the Mermen didn't need to know this.

Them and us.

But there was still Scudi's hand in his. Brett felt that the only Merman he could trust might be Scudi … and perhaps that medic in the passageway, Shadow Panille. Panille had clear eyes and … *he cared.*

"We didn't kill those people," Hastings said. "Please note, Mr. Justice, that we have gotten right down to the dirty work of bringing them in, identifying the dead, helping the survivors—"

"How noble of you," Keel said. "I was wondering how long it would take to get down to this. You haven't mentioned your fee, of course."

Both Mermen looked grim but they did not appear particularly flustered. "Someone has to pay," Hastings said. "No one topside has the facilities to—"

"So you pick up the dead," Keel said. "And their families topside pay for your trouble. With a tidy profit for certain contractors, too."

"Nobody expects to work for nothing," Hastings said.

Keel rolled one eye toward Brett, then back. "And when you rescue a live fisherman, you find a way to accommodate him, keeping a close account of the expenses, naturally."

"I don't want anything for my part," Scudi said. Her eyes flashed anger at both Keel and Hastings.

"I respect that, Scudi," Keel said. "I wasn't indicting you. But your fellow Mermen here have a different viewpoint. Brett has no fishing gear to seize, no nets or sonar or beaten-up boat. How will he pay for his life? Ten years of chopping onions in a Merman kitchen?"

Hastings said, "Really, Mr. Justice, I don't understand your reluctance to make matters easier."

"I was lured here under false pretenses," Keel said. "I haven't been out of sight of my … hosts … long enough to spit." He pointed to the view port across from them. "Look there!" He lowered his pointing finger to indicate the deck below. "Those bodies are shredded, burned, cut to pieces. Guemes was assaulted! I think a reconstruction will show that it was assaulted from below by a hardshell sub."

For the first time, Hastings appeared as though he might lose control. His eyes squinted and his brows drew down over his beak of a nose. His jaw clenched and he hissed between his teeth: "See here! I'm only doing what Merman law requires me to do. In my judgment—"

"Oh, please," Keel interrupted, "judgment is my job and I'm experienced in it. To me, you look like a pair of leeches. I don't like leeches. Please leave us."

"Since you are who you are," Hastings said, "I will accept that for the moment. This boy, however—"

"Has me here to look out for his interests," Keel said. "This is not the time nor the place for your services."

Lonfinn stepped to one side, casually blocking the exit passage from the observation platform.

"The boy will answer for himself," Hastings said.

"The Justice asked you to leave," Brett said.

Scudi squeezed Brett's hand and said, "Please. I will be responsible for them. Ambassador Ale sent me personally to bring them here. Your presence is disruptive."

Hastings looked her in the eyes as though he wanted to say, "Big talk for a little girl," but he swallowed it. His right index finger indicated the plaz box under Lonfinn's arm, then dropped. "Very well," he said. "We were trying to smooth out the red tape but the situation is difficult." He shot a quick glance at the congested deck below them. "However, I am required to escort you back to Ryan Wang's quarters. It may have been a mistake to bring you here."

"I find it agreeable to leave," Keel said. "I've seen enough." His voice was once more smooth and diplomatic.

Brett heard the double meaning in Keel's statement and thought, *That old spinnarett has a web or two left in him.*

The thought stayed with Brett as they returned to Wang's spacious quarters. It had been wise to follow the Chief Justice's lead. Even Scudi had fallen in with Keel. She had kept her hand in Brett's most of the way back to her father's quarters, in spite of disapproving little glances from Hastings and Lonfinn. Her hand in his conveyed a feeling of closeness that Brett enjoyed.

Once inside the plush room of colored cushions, Keel said, "Thank you, gentlemen. I'm sure we can contact you if you're needed."

"You'll hear from us," Hastings said before he sealed the hatch behind him.

Keel crossed to the hatch and pressed the switch but nothing happened. The hatch stayed sealed. He glanced at Scudi.

"Those men worked for my father," she said. "I don't like them." She slipped her hand from Brett's and crossed to a dark red cushion where she sat with her chin on her knees and her arms clasped around her legs. The yellow-and-green stripes along her singlesuit curved as she curved.

"Brett," Keel said, "I will speak openly, because one of us may be able to get back topside to warn the other Islands. My suspicions are being confirmed at every turn. I believe our Island way of life is about to be drowned in a shallow sea."

Scudi lifted her chin and stared up at him with dismay. Brett could not find his voice.

Keel looked down at Scudi, thinking how her pose reminded him of a many-legged mollusk that rolled up into a tight ball when disturbed.

"The popular teaching," Keel said, "is that Island life is just temporary until we get back to the land."

"But Guemes …" Brett said. He could not get further.

"Yes, Guemes," Keel said. "No!" Scudi blurted. "Mermen *couldn't* have done that! We protect the Islands!"

"I believe you, Scudi," Keel said. His neck pained him but he lifted his great head the way he did when passing judgment in his own court. "Things are happening that the people are not aware of … the people topside and the people down under."

Scudi asked Keel, "You really think Mermen did this?"

"We must reserve judgment until all the evidence is gathered," he said. "Nevertheless, it seems the most likely possibility."

Scudi shook her head. Brett saw sorrow and rejection there. "Mermen wouldn't do such a thing," she whispered.

"It's not the Merman government," Keel said. "Principles of government sometimes take one course while people take another—a political double standard. And perhaps neither really controls events."

What's he saying? Brett wondered.

Keel continued: "Mermen and Islanders both have tolerated only the loosest kind of government. I am Chief Justice of a most powerful arm of that government—the one that says whether the newborn of our Islands will live or die. It pleases some to call me Chairman and others to call me Chief Justice. I do not feel that I dispense justice."

"I can't believe anyone would just eliminate the Islands," Scudi said.

"Someone certainly eliminated Guemes," Keel said. One sad eye drifted toward Brett, the other remained focused on Scudi. "It should be investigated, don't you think?"

"Yes." She nodded against her knees.

"It would be good to have inside help," Keel said. "On the other hand, I would not want to endanger anyone who helped me."

"What do you need?" Scudi asked.

"Information," he said. "Recent news recordings for the Merman audience. A survey of Merman jobs would help—which categories still have openings, which are filled to overflowing. I need to know what's really happening down here. And we'll need comparable statistics on the Islander population that's living down under."

"I don't understand," Scudi said.

"I'm told you mathematic the waves," Keel said, looking at Brett. "I want to mathematic Merman society. I cannot assume that I'm dealing with traditional Merman politics. I suspect that even Mermen don't realize they're no longer in the grip of their traditional politics. News is a clue to fluctuations. Jobs, too. They might be a clue to permanent changes and the intent behind those changes."

"My father had a comconsole in his den," Scudi said. "I'm sure I could get some of this through it … but I'm not sure I understand how you … mathematic it."

"Judges are sensitized to the assimilation of data," Keel said. "I pride myself on being a good judge. Get me this material, if you can."

Brett suggested, "Maybe we should see other Islanders living down under."

Keel smiled. "Don't trust the paperwork already, huh? We'll save that for later. It could be dangerous right now." *Good instincts,* he noted.

Scudi pressed her palms to her temples and closed her eyes. "My people don't kill," she said. "We aren't like that."

Keel stared down at the girl, thinking suddenly how similar at the core were Mermen and Islanders.

The sea.

He had never before thought of the sea in quite this way. How must their ancestors have adapted to it? The sea was always there—interminable. It was a thing unending, a source of life and a threat of death. To Scudi and her people, the sea was a silent pressure, whose sounds were always muted by the depths, whose currents moved in great sweeps along the bottom and through the shadows up to light. For the Merman, the world was muted and remote, yet pressing. To an Islander, the sea was noisy and immediate in its demands. It required adjustments in balance and consciousness.

The result was a quickness about Islanders which Mermen found charming. *Colorful!* Mermen, in contrast, were often studied and careful, measuring out their decisions as though they shaped precious jewels.

Keel glanced from Scudi to Brett and back to Scudi. Brett was taken by her, that much was clear. Was it the infatuation of differences? Was he some exotic mammal to her, or a man? Keel hoped something deeper than adolescent sexual attraction had been ignited there. He did not think himself so crass as to believe that Islander-Merman differences would be solved in the sexual thrashings of the bedroom. But the human race was still alive in these two and he could feel it moving them. The thought was reassuring.

"My father cared for both Islanders and Mermen," Scudi said. "His money made the Search and Rescue system a system."

"Show me his den," Keel said. "I would like to use his comconsole."

She stood and crossed to a passage hatch on the far side of the atrium. "This way."

Keel motioned for Brett to stay behind while he followed Scudi. Perhaps if the young woman were away from the distractions of Brett's presence she might think more clearly—less defensive, more objective.

When Keel and Scudi had gone, Brett turned to the locked hatch. He and Keel and Scudi had been sealed away from whatever the exterior Merman world might reveal. Ale had wanted them to see that world, but others objected. Brett felt this the complete answer to his present isolation.

What would Queets do? he wondered.

Brett felt it unlikely that Queets would stand vacant-eyed in the middle of a strange room and stare stupidly at a locked hatch. Brett crossed to the hatch and ran a finger around the heavy metal molding that framed the exit.

Should've asked Scudi about communications systems and the ways they move freight, he thought. He could remember nothing of the passageways except their sparse population—sparse by crowded Islander standards.

"What are you thinking?"

Scudi's voice from close behind him startled him. Brett hadn't heard her approach over the soft carpet.

"Do you have a map of this place?" he asked.

"Somewhere," she said. "I'll have to look."

"Thanks."

Brett continued to stare at the locked hatch. How had they locked it? He thought of Island quarters, where the simplest slash of a knife would let you through the soft organics separating most rooms. Only the laboratories, Security's quarters and Vata's chamber could be said to have substantial resistance to entry—but that was as much a function of the guards as of the thickness of the walls.

Scudi returned with a thin stack of overlays, on which thick and thin lines with coded symbols indicated the layout of this Merman complex. She put it into Brett's hands as though giving away something of herself. For no reason he could explain, Brett found her gesture poignant.

"Here we are," she said, pointing to a cluster of squares and rectangles marked "RW."

He studied the overlays. This was not the free-flowing, action-dictated environment of an Island, where the idiosyncrasies of organic growth directed the kind of changes that flaunted individuality. Islands were personalized, customized, carved, painted and dyed—shaped to the synergistic needs of support systems and those the systems supported. The schematic in Brett's hands reeked of uniformity—identical rows of cubicles, long straight passages, tubing and channels and access tunnels that ran as straight as a sun's rays through dust. He found it difficult to follow such uniformity, but forced his mind to it.

Scudi said: "I asked the Justice if a volcano might have destroyed Guemes."

Brett raised his attention from the schematic. "What did he say?"

"There were too many people shredded and not burned." She pressed the palms of her hands against her eyelids. "Who could do … *that?*"

"Keel's right about one thing," Brett said, "we need to find out who as soon as possible."

He returned his attention to the stack of colloids and its mysterious mazes. All at once he was awash with the simplicity of it. It was clear to him that Mermen must find it impossible to travel any Island, where sheer memory guided most people. He set about memorizing the schematics, with their lift shafts and transport tubes. He closed his eyes and confidently read the map that displayed itself behind his eyelids. Scudi paced the room behind him. Brett opened his eyes.

"Could we escape from here?" he asked, nodding toward the locked hatch.

"I can get us through the hatch," she said. "Where would you go?"

"Topside."

She looked at the hatch, her head shaking a slow "no" from side to side.

"When we open the hatch, they will know. An electronic signal."

"What would those men do if we left here together?"

"Bring us back," she said. "Or try. The odds favor them. Nothing moves down under without someone knowing. My father had an efficient organization. That's why he hired men like those." She nodded at the hatch. "My father directed a very large business—a food business. He had much trade with Islanders …"

Her eyes shifted away from his, then back. She indicated the walls and ceiling. "This was his building, the whole thing. As high as the docking tower, all of it." She defined an area on the schematics with a finger. "This."

Brett drew slightly away from her. She had defined an area as large as some of the smaller Islands. Her father had owned it. He knew that by Merman law she probably inherited it. She was no simple worker in the seas, an apprentice physicist who mathematicked the waves.

Scudi saw the look of withdrawal in his eyes and touched his arm. "I live my own life," she said, "as my mother did. My father and I hardly knew each other."

"Didn't know each other?" Brett felt shocked. He knew himself to be estranged from his own parents, but he had certainly *known* them.

"Until shortly before he died, he lived at the Nest—a city about ten kilometers away," Scudi said. "In all that time I never saw him." She took a deep breath. "Before he died, my father came to our room one night and spoke to my mother. I don't know what they said but she was furious after he left."

Brett thought about what she had said. Her father had owned and controlled enormous wealth—much of Merman society. Topside, such matters as Ryan Wang controlled were the property of families or associations, never of one person. Community was law.

"He controlled much of your Islands' food production," she continued. A flush bloomed across her cheeks. "A lot of it he accomplished through bribery. I know because I listened, and sometimes when he was gone I used his comconsole."

"What is this place, the Nest?" Brett asked.

"It is a city that has a high Islander population. It was the site of the first settlement after the Clone Wars. You know of this?"

"Yes," he said. "One way or another, we all came from there."

Ward Keel, standing in the shadows of the open passage from Ryan Wang's den, had been listening to this exchange for several minutes. He shuddered, wondering whether he should interrupt and demand some answers of this young woman. The anguish in her voice held Keel in place.

"Did those Islanders in the Nest work for your father?" Keel asked.

She didn't turn away from Brett to answer. "Some of them. But no Islander has any high position on anything. They are controlled by a government agency. I think Ambassador Ale is in charge of it."

"It seems to me that an Islander should head an agency that deals with Islanders," Brett said.

"She and my father were to be married," Scudi said. "A political matter between the two families … a lot of Merman history that isn't important now."

"Your father and the ambassador—that would have linked the powers of the government and the food supply under one blanket," Brett said. The insight came so quickly that it startled him.

"That's all ancient history," Scudi said. "She'll probably marry GeLaar Gallow now." Her words came out with an underlying misery that held Brett speechless. He could see the dark confusion in her eyes, the frustration of being a piece in some unruled game.

In the shadows of the passage, Ward Keel nodded to himself. He had shuffled back from Wang's den with a feeling of helpless anger. It was all there for the discerning eye—the shifts of control, the quiet and remorseless accumulation of power in a few hands, an increase in local identity. A term from the Histories kept rattling in his memory: *Nationalization.* Why did it give him such a feeling of loss?

The land is being restored.

The good life is coming.

This is why Ship gave Pandora to us.

To us—to Mermen—not to Islanders.

Keel's throat pained him when he tried to swallow. The kelp project lay at the base of it all, and that had gone too far to be lost or slowed. It was being taken over, instead. Justifications for the project could not be denied. The late Ryan Wang's comconsole was full of those justifications: Without the kelp the suns would continue to fatigue the crust of Pandora, constant earthquakes and volcanics would ravage them as they had all those generations back.

Lava built up undersea plateaus along fault lines. Mermen were taking advantage of this for their project. The last wave-wall had been a consequence of a volcanic upheaval, not the gravitational swings that inflicted themselves on Pandora's seas.

Brett was speaking: "I would like to see the Nest and the Islanders there. Maybe that's where we should go."

Out of the mouths of babes, Keel thought.

Scudi shook her head in negation. "They would find us there easily. Security there is not like here—there are badges, papers …"

"Then we should run topside," Brett said. "The Justice is right. He wants us to tell the Islanders what's happening down here."

"And what is happening?" she asked.

Keel stepped out of the shadows, speaking as he moved: "Pandora is being changed—physically, politically, socially. That's what's happening. The old life will not be possible, topside or down under. I think Scudi's father had a dream of great things, the transformation of Pandora, but someone else has taken it over and is making it a nightmare."

Keel stopped, facing the two young people. They stared back at him, aghast.

Can they feel it? Keel wondered.

Runaway greed was working to seize control of this new Pandora.

Scudi jabbed a finger at the schematic, which Brett still held. "The Launch Base and Outpost Twenty-two," she said. "Here! They are near Vashon's current drift. The Island will be at least a full day past this point by now but …"

"What're you suggesting?" Keel asked.

"I think I can get us to Outpost Twenty-two," she said. "I've worked there. From the outpost, I could compute Vashon's exact position."

Keel looked at the chart in Brett's hands. A surge of homesickness surged through the Justice. To be in his own quarters … Joy near at hand to care for him. He was going to die soon … how much better to die in familiar surroundings. As quickly as it came, the feeling was suppressed. Escape? He did not have the energy, the swiftness. He could only hold these young people back. But he saw the eagerness in Scudi and the way Brett picked up on it. They might just do it. The Islands had to be told what was happening.

"Here is what we will do," Keel said. "And this is the message you will carry."

Chapter 22

Perseverance furthers.

—*I Ching, Shiprecords*

A FLOCK of wild squawks came flying past the coracles, their wings whistling in the dull gray light of morning. Twisp turned his head to follow the birds' path. They landed about fifty meters ahead of him.

Bushka had sat up at the sudden sound, fear obvious in his face.

"Just squawks," Twisp said.

"Oh." Bushka subsided with his back against the cuddy.

"If we feed 'em, they'll follow us," Twisp said. "I've never seen 'em this far from an Island."

"We're near the base," Bushka said.

As they approached the swimming flock, Twisp tipped some of his garbage over the side. The birds came scrambling for the handout. The smaller ones churned their legs so fast they skipped across the water.

It was the birds' eyes that interested him, he decided. There was living presence in those eyes you never saw in the eyes of sea creatures. Squawk eyes looked back at you with something of the human world in them.

Bushka moved up and sat on the cuddy top to watch the birds and the horizon ahead of them. *Where is that damned Launch Base?* The motions of the birds kept attracting his attention. Twisp had said the squawks acted out of an ancient instinct. Probably true. Instinct! How long did it take to extinguish instinct? Or develop it? Which way were humans going? How strongly were they driven by such inner forces? Historian questions thronged his mind.

"That dull-looking squawk is a female," Bushka said, pointing to the wild flock. "I wonder why the males are so much more colorful?"

"Has to be some survival in it," Twisp said. He looked at the flock swimming beside the coracle, their eyes alert for another handout. "That's a female, all right." A scowl settled over his face. "One thing you can say for that hen squawk: she'll never ask a surgeon to make her *normal!*"

Bushka heard the bitterness and sensed the old familiar Islander story. It was getting to be ever more common these days: A lover had surgery to appear Merman-normal, then pressured the partner to do the same. A lot of angry fights resulted.

"Sounds like you got burned," Bushka said.

"I was crisped and charred," Twisp said. "Have to admit it was fun at first …" He hesitated, then: " … but I hoped it would be more than fun, something more permanent." He shook his head.

Bushka yawned and stretched. The wild flock took his movement as a threat and scattered in a flurry of splashes and loud cries.

Twisp stared toward the wild birds, but his eyes were not focused on them. "Her name's Rebeccah," he said. "She really liked my arms around her. Never complained about how long they were until—" He broke off in sudden embarrassment.

"She chose surgical correction?" Bushka prompted.

"Yeah." Twisp swallowed. *Now what set me talking about Rebeccah to this stranger? Am I that lonesome?* She had liked to feed the squawks at rimside every evening. He had enjoyed those evenings more than he could tell, and remembered details in a flood that he shut off as soon as it started.

Bushka was staring at his own hands. "She dumped you after the surgery?"

"Dumped me? Naw." Twisp sighed. "That would've been easy. I know I'd always feel like some kind of freak around her afterwards. No Mute can afford to feel that way, ever. It's why a lot of us more obvious types shy away from the Mermen. It's the stares and the way we think of ourselves then—our own eyes looking back from the mirror."

"Where is she now?" Bushka asked.

"Vashon," Twisp said. "Someplace close to Center, I'd guess. That's one thing good looks can get you on Vashon. I'd bet big money she's down there where the rich and powerful live. Her job was preparing people psychologically for surgical correction—she was sort of a living model of how life would be if they went through everything right."

"She made the choice, and it worked for her."

"If you talk about something like that long enough it becomes an obsession. She used to say: 'Changing some bodies is easy. A good surgeon knows just where to work. Minds are a little tougher.' I think she didn't really listen to herself."

Bushka looked at Twisp's long arms, a sudden insight flooding his mind.

Twisp saw the direction of Bushka's gaze and nodded. "That's right," he said. "She wanted me to get my arms fixed. She didn't understand, not even with all of her psychological crap behind her. I wasn't afraid of the knife or any of that eelshit. It was that my body would be a lie, and I can't stand liars."

This is no ordinary fisherman, Bushka thought.

"I finally figured it out about her," Twisp said. "A little too much boo and she started with this pitch for all of us to be 'as normal as possible.' Like you, Bushka."

"I don't feel that way."

"'Cause you don't have to. You're all ready to join the Mermen on their open land, on their terms."

Bushka found no words to answer. He had always been proud of his Merman-normal appearance. He could pass without surgery.

Twisp pounded his fist against the rim of the coracle. It startled the caged squawks, who sat up and fluffed their feathers in frustration.

"She wanted kids … with me," Twisp said. "Can you imagine that? Think of the surprises you'd find in the nursery when all these corrected, lying Mutes started bedding each other. And what about the kids growing up to find out that they're Mutes while their parents appear to be norms? Not for me!" His voice was husky. "No way."

Twisp fell silent, lost in his own memories.

Bushka listened to the *slep-slep* of waves against the coracle's sides, the faint rustling of the squawks preening and stretching in their cage. He wondered how many love affairs drowned on Twisp's style of principles.

"Damn that Jesus Lewis!" Twisp muttered.

Bushka nodded to himself. *Yes, that was where the problem had started. Or, at least, where it was precipitated.* The question remained for the historian: What made Jesus Lewis? Bushka looked at Twisp's arms—muscular, well-developed, tan and over half a length too long. The Island mating pool was still a genetic lottery, thanks to Jesus Lewis and his bioengineering experiments.

Twisp was still angry. "Mermen will never understand what growing up an Islander is like! Someone around you is always frail or dying … someone close. My little sister was such a nice kid …" Twisp shook his head.

"We don't say 'mutation' much except when we're being technical," Bushka prompted. "And deformity is a dirty word. 'Mistakes,' that's what we call them."

"You know what, Bushka? I deliberately avoid people with long arms. There are only a few of us in this generation." He raised his arm. "Are these a mistake? Does that make *me* a mistake?"

Bushka didn't answer.

"Damn!" Twisp said. "My apprentice, Brett, he's sensitive about the size of his eyes. Shit, you can't tell anything just by looking at him, but you can't tell him that. Ship! Can he ever see in the dark! Is that a mistake?"

"It's a lottery," Bushka said.

Twisp grimaced. "I don't envy the Committee's job. You have any idea of the grotesques and the dangerous forms they have to judge? How can they do it? And how can they guess at the mental mistakes? Those don't usually show up until later."

"But we have good times, too," Bushka protested. "Mermen think our cloth is the best. You know the price we get for Islander weaving down under. And our music, our painting … all of our art."

"Sure," Twisp sneered. "I've heard Mermen pawing over our stuff. 'How bright! Such fun. Oh! Isn't this pretty? Islanders are so full of fun.'"

"We are," Bushka muttered.

Twisp merely looked at him for a long time. Bushka wondered if he had committed some unforgivable blunder.

Suddenly, Twisp smiled. "You're right. Damn! No Merman knows how to have a good time the way we do. It's either grief and despair or dancing and singing all night because somebody got married, or born, or got a new set of drums, or hauled in a big catch. Mermen don't celebrate much, I hear. You ever see Mermen celebrating?"

"Never," Bushka admitted. And he remembered Nakano of Gallow's crew talking about Merman life.

"Work, get a mate, have a couple of kids, work some more and die," Nakano had said. *"Fun is a coffee break or hauling a sledge to some new outpost."*

Was that why Nakano had joined Gallow's movement? Precious little fun or excitement down under. Rescue an Islander. Work at building a barrier. Bushka did not think of life down under as grim for people like Nakano. Just drab. They hadn't the lure of an intellectual goal, nor even the nearness of grief to make them snatch at joy. But topside, there you found dazzle and color and a great deal of laughter.

"If we go back to the open land, it'll be different," Bushka said.

"What do you mean, 'if'? Just a few minutes ago you were saying it was inevitable."

"There are Mermen who want only an undersea empire. If they—"

Bushka broke off as Twisp suddenly pointed ahead and blurted, "Ship's balls! What is *that?*"

Bushka turned and saw, almost directly ahead of them, a gray tower with a lace of white surf at its base. It was like a thick stem to the great flower of sky, a blue flower edged in pink. The storm that had been skirting them for the past few hours framed the scene in a halo of black cloud. The tower, almost the same drab shade as the clouds, climbed up like a great fist out of the depths.

Twisp stared in awe. It wasn't visible for fifty klicks, as Bushka had first stated, but it was impressive. *Ship!* He'd not expected it to be so big.

Beyond the gray press of sea and sky, the clouds began to open. The interrupted horizon became two bright flowers and neither man could take his gaze off the launch tower. It was the center of a giant stormcloud whirlpool.

"That's the Launch Base," Bushka said. "That's the heart of the Merman space program. Every political faction they have will be represented there."

"You'd never mistake it for something floating on the surface," Twisp said. "No movement at all."

"It clears high water by twenty-five meters," Bushka said. "Mermen brag about it. They've only sent up unmanned shots. But things are moving fast. That's why Gallow and his people are acting now. The Mermen expect a manned shot into space soon."

"And they control the currents with the kelp?" Twisp asked. "How?"

"I don't really know. I've seen where they do it but I don't understand it."

Twisp looked from the tower to Bushka and back to the tower. The foaming collar of surf around its base had expanded as the coracles drew closer, opening up a wider view. Twisp estimated their distance from the base at more than five kilometers, and even from that distance he saw that the surf reached left and right of the tower for several hundred meters on either side. More human activity could be seen there. One of the big Merman foils stood off in the calmer water beyond the surf with smaller craft shuttling back and forth to the tower. A Lighter-Than-Air hovered nearby, either for observation or use as a sky-crane. The coracles were close enough now to make out Mermen on the breakwater that fanned out from the base near the tower.

The hydrofoil with its hydrogen ramjets sticking out like big egg sacks astern drew Twisp's attention. He had seen them only at a distance and in holos before this. The thing was at least fifty meters long, riding there easily on its flotation hull with the planing foils hidden underwater. A wide hatch stood open in its side with much Merman activity around the opening—bulky objects being lowered on an extruded crane.

Bushka sat with one arm resting on the cuddy top, his other arm hanging loosely at his side. His head was turned away from Twisp, attention fixed on the Launch Base and its commanding tower. There was no sign yet that the Mermen had taken notice of the approaching coracles, but Twisp knew they had been seen and their course plotted. Bushka's reason for bringing them to this particular place seemed clear, if you believed his story about Gallow. There was little chance that Gallow's people would be the only ones at this base. And there would be Merman attention on every detail of this operation. All factions would hear Bushka's story. Would they believe it?

"Have you thought about how they're going to receive you and your story?" Twisp asked.

"I don't think my chances are very good no matter where I turn up," Bushka answered. "But better here than anywhere else." He brought his gaze around to meet Twisp's questioning stare. "I think I'm a dead man any way you look at it. But people have got to know."

"Very commendable," Twisp said. He cut the motor and pulled the tiller into his stomach, holding it there until the two boats circled slowly around each other. Time to apprise Bushka of the facts as Twisp saw them after a night's reflection.

"What're you doing?" Bushka demanded.

Twisp stretched both arms across the tiller and stared at Bushka. "I came out here to find my apprentice. Kinda stupid of me, I know. I tell you true I didn't believe there was such a thing as that base, but I thought there would be something, and I came with you because what you said about help from the Mermen made sense."

"Of course it does! Somebody probably picked him up already and—"

"But you're in trouble, Bushka. Deep shit. And I'm in it, too, just by being with you. I wouldn't feel right about just dumping you or handing you over to them." He nodded toward the tower. "Especially if your story about this Gallow happens to be true."

"If?"

"Where's the proof?"

Bushka tried to swallow. Mermen already would be bringing in the Guemes dead and the survivors. He knew this. There was no turning back. Someone at the Launch Base already had these coracles and their occupants on a screen. Somebody would be sent to investigate or to warn them off.

"What do I do?" Bushka asked.

"You sank a whole fucking island," Twisp growled. "And you're just now asking yourself that?"

Bushka merely lifted his shoulders and let them fall in a futile shrug.

"Guemes must've had small boats out, some in sight of the Island," Twisp said. "There'll be survivors and they'll have their story to tell. Some of them may have seen your sub. You any idea what they'll be reporting?"

Bushka cringed under the weight of accusation in Twisp's voice.

"You were the pilot," Twisp said. "They'll put you through more than this. You did it and they'll get every detail out of you before you talk to anybody outside of Merman Security. If you ever get outside their Security."

Bushka lowered his chin to his knees. He felt that he might vomit. With a terrible sense of wonder, he heard coming from his own mouth a groan that pulsed in a rising pitch: *nnnnnh nnnnnnh nnnnnnh.*

There's nowhere I can run, Bushka thought. *Nowhere, nowhere.*

Twisp was still speaking to him but Bushka, lost in his own misery, no longer understood the words. Words could not reach into this place where his consciousness lay. Words were ghosts, things that would haunt him. He no longer felt that he could tolerate such haunting.

The thrum of the coracle's little motor being switched on brought Bushka's attention back from its hiding place. He did not dare look up to see where Twisp might be taking them. All of the wheres were bad. It was just a matter of time until someone somewhere killed him. His mind floated on a sea while his muscles pulled him into a tighter and tighter ball so that he might fit into that sea without touching anything there. Voices cried to him, high-pitched screeches. His mind exposed glimpses of a universe fouled by carnage—the shredded Island and its broken shards of flesh. Dry heaves shook his body. He sensed movement in the coracle, but only vaguely. Something inside of him had to come out. Hands touched his shoulders and lifted him, laying him over the thwart. A voice said: "Puke over the side. You'll choke to death in the bilge." The hands went away, but the voice left one last comment: "Dumb fuck!"

The acid in Bushka's mouth was bitterly demanding, stringy. He tried to speak but every sound felt like sandpaper bobbing in his larynx. He vomited over the side, the smell strong in his nostrils. Presently, he dropped a hand into the passing sea and splashed cold salt water over his face. Only then could he sit up and look at Twisp. Bushka felt emptied of everything, all emotion drained.

"Where can I go?" he asked. "What can I tell them?"

"You tell 'em the truth," Twisp said. "Dammit. I never heard of anybody as dumb as you, but I do believe you're a dumb fuck, and I don't think you're a killer."

"Thanks," Bushka managed.

"What you did," Twisp said, "you've marked yourself. No Mute will ever get the stares you'll get. You know what? I don't envy you one bit."

Twisp nodded toward the tower ahead. "Here comes someone to get us. One of their little cargo boats. Ship! I'm done for! I know it."

Chapter 23

At any given moment of history it is the function of associations of devoted individuals to undertake tasks which clear-sighted people perceive to be necessary, but which nobody else is willing to perform.

—A. Huxley, *The Doors of Perception, Shiprecords*

AFTER SEEING Scudi expose the master control panel for her father's quarters, find the hatch controls and trace out the exit hatch circuiting, Brett was ready to believe his new friend a genius. She quickly argued against this when he praised her.

"Most of us learn how to do this very young." She giggled. "If your parents try to lock you in ..."

"Why would they lock you in?"

"Punishment," she said, "if we—" She broke off, threw a circuit breaker and closed the panel cover. "Quick, someone is coming." She leaned close to Brett's ear. "I have set the emergency hatch on manual and the same with the main hatch. Emergency is the little hatch in the middle of the big one."

"Where do we go when we get out?"

"Remember the plan. We have to leave here before they guess what I've done." Scudi took his hand and hurried Brett out of the service room, down a passage and into the entry lounge.

Hastings and Lonfinn were already there and involved in a heated conversation with Keel.

The Chief Justice raised his voice as Brett and Scudi entered the room: "And furthermore, if you try to blame Islanders for the Guemes massacre, I shall demand an immediate committee of investigation, a committee you will not control!"

Keel rubbed his eyelids with both hands. The eye looking directly at Hastings focused a hard glare on him. Keel found he enjoyed the small shudder that the man could not hide.

"Mr. Justice," Hastings said, "you are not helping yourself or those youngsters." He glanced briefly at Brett and Scudi, who had stopped just inside the room.

Keel studied Hastings for a moment, thinking how abruptly the mood had turned ugly. Two hatchetmen! He passed a glance across Hastings and Lonfinn, noting that they blocked the way to the exit hatch.

"I was always told there were no dangerous insects down under," Keel said.

Hastings scowled but his partner did not change expression. "This is not a joking matter!" Hastings said. "Ambassador Ale has asked us to—"

"Let her tell me herself!"

When Hastings did not respond, Keel said: "She lured me down here under false pretenses. She saw to it that I didn't bring any of my own staff. Her stated reason, even as sketchy as that was, does not wash. I have to conclude that I am a prisoner. Do you deny that?" Again, he sent a cold gaze across the two men standing between him and the hatch.

Hastings sighed. "You are being protected for your own good. You are an important Islander; there has been a crisis—"

"Protected from whom?"

Keel watched Hastings deciding what to say, choosing and discarding alternatives. Several times Hastings started to speak and thought better of it.

Keel rubbed the back of his neck where the prosthetic support already had begun to chafe his neck raw after his brief rest.

"Are you protecting me from whoever destroyed Guemes?" he prompted.

The two Mermen exchanged an unreadable glance. Hastings looked back at Keel. "I would like to be more candid with you, but I can't."

"I already know the structure of what's happening," Keel said. "Very powerful political forces are on a collision course among the Mermen."

"And topside!" Hastings snapped.

"Oh, yes. The two wild cards—my Committee and the Faith. Wiping out Guemes was a blow at the Faith. But liquidating me would not deter the Committee; they would simply replace me. It's more effective to keep me incommunicado. Or, if I were liquidated, Islanders would be distracted enough while selecting a new Chief Justice that Mermen could take advantage of the confusion. I no longer think I can stay down here. I am returning topside."

Hastings and his companion stiffened. "I am afraid that is impossible just now," Hastings said.

Keel smiled. "Carolyn Bluelove will be the next Chief Justice," he said. "You won't have any better luck with her than you have with me."

Impasse, Keel thought.

A loaded silence fell over the room while Hastings and Lonfinn studied him. Keel could see Hastings composing new arguments and discarding them. He needed the Chief Justice's cooperation for something—blind cooperation. He needed agreement without revealing the thing to which Keel must agree. Did Hastings think an old political infighter could not see through this dilemma?

Where they stood just inside the room, Scudi and Brett had listened carefully to this argument. Scudi now leaned close to Brett's ear and whispered. "The guest head is that hatch over to the right. Go in there now and open the sealed switch plate by the hatch. Throw a glass of water into the switch. That will short out all the lights in this section. I will unlock the emergency hatch. Can you find it in the dark?"

He nodded. "We can be out before they even know we're running," she whispered.

"The passageway lights will shine in through the emergency hatch when you open it."

"We have to be quick," she said. "They will try to use the main controls. It will be a blink before they realize they'll have to use the manual system."

He nodded again. "Follow me and run fast," she said.

Where he stood confronting Keel, Hastings had decided to expose part of his knowledge.

"Justice Keel, you are wrong about the next Chief Justice," he said. "It'll be Simone Rocksack."

"GeLaar Gallow's choice?" Keel asked, working from the knowledge he had gained at the late Ryan Wang's comconsole.

Hastings blinked in surprise.

"If so, he's in for another surprise," Keel said. "C/Ps are notoriously incorruptible."

"Your history's slipping," Hastings said. "Without the first Pandoran C/P, Morgan Oakes, Jesus Lewis would've been just another lab technician."

A solemn expression settled over Keel's face. Petitioners before him on the high bench had seen this look and trembled but Hastings only stared at him, waiting.

"You work for Gallow," Keel said. "Of course you want total political and economic control of Pandora and you're going to work through the Faith. Did the C/P know you were going to destroy her family on Guemes to do it?"

"You're wrong! It's not like that!"

"Then how is it?" Keel asked.

"Please, Mr. Justice! You—"

"Someone has latched on to a basic truth," Keel said. "Control the food supply, control the people."

"We're running out of time for argument," Hastings said.

"When we actually run out, will I then become one of the Guemes casualties?" Keel asked.

"The future of Pandora is at stake," Hastings said. "Right-thinking people will steer a safe course through these hard times."

"And for this, you will kill anyone who opposes you," Keel said.

"We did not destroy Guemes!" Hastings said, spacing out his words in a low, cold voice.

"Then how do you know that whoever did it will not turn on you?" Keel demanded.

"Who are *you* to talk about killing?" Hastings asked. "How many thousands have you destroyed under the authority of your Committee? *Hundreds* of thousands? You've been at it a long time, Mr. Justice."

Keel was momentarily stunned by this attack. "But the Committee—"

"Does what you tell it to do! The almighty Ward Keel points his finger and death follows. Everybody knows that! What's life to someone like you? How can I expect a mind that alien to understand our Merman dilemma?"

Keel was at a loss how to meet this attack. The accusation stung him. Reverence for life guided his every decision. Lethal deviants had to be weeded out of the gene pool!

As Keel stood silently, wondering what might happen next, Brett stepped toward the hatch to the head. Lonfinn moved to stand between the hatch and the exit. Brett ignored the man and went into the head, closing the hatch behind him.

Brett studied the small room for a moment. The switch plate was a gasketed cover beside the hatch. It had two exposed sealing screws. Brett found the tool Scudi had told him about in the drawer under the sink: a fingernail file. He removed the cover, revealing a paired junction, shiny green and blue conducting plastics. The *n* and *p* circuits lay exposed to his view beneath the shielded depressions that changed polarity and activated the switch.

Glass of water, Scudi had said.

There was a glass beside the sink. He filled it and, putting one hand on the hatch dog, flung the water at the exposed switch. A blue-green spark flashed up the wall and all the lights went out. In the same moment he opened the hatch and slipped out into darkness. Hastings was shouting, "Get Keel! Hold him!"

Brett slipped to his right along the wall and bumped into Scudi at the hatch. She touched his face, then pulled his shoulder close. Abruptly, the little hatch opened and she was through it, rolling to one side. Brett dove through behind her and Scudi dogged the little hatch. Leaping to her feet, she darted off down the passage. Brett scrambled up and followed.

It was the first time in his life that Brett had run more than a hundred meters at one stretch. Scudi was far ahead of him, darting into a side passage. Brett skidded around the corner behind her just in time to see her feet disappear through a tiny round hatch low to the deck. She practically pulled him in behind her as he knelt at the opening. The hatch swung closed and she sealed it in darkness. Brett was panting from the exertion. Sweat stung his eyes.

"Where are we?" he whispered.

"Service passage for the pneumatic system. Hold on to my waistband and stay close. We have to crawl through the first part."

Brett gripped her waistband and found himself almost dragged along a low, narrow passage where his shoulders brushed the sides and he frequently bumped his head against the ceiling. It was very dim even for him in here, and he was sure she was operating in total darkness. The passage turned left, then right, then sloped upward for a time. Scudi stopped and reached back. She gripped his hand, taking it forward and placing it on a ladder that disappeared somewhere above them.

"Ladder," she whispered. "Follow me up."

He didn't remind her that he could see.

"Where're we going?" he asked.

"All the way up. Don't slip. It's twenty-one levels with only three ledges to take breaks."

"What's up there?"

"The docking bay for my father's cargo foils."

"Scudi, are you sure you want to do this?"

Her voice came to him small and tightly controlled. "I won't believe anything without proof, but they're holding the Justice and they'd have stopped us. That's wrong, and it's Ale's doing. The Islands should know at least that much."

"Right."

She pulled away from him, the slither of her clothing and their breathing were the only sounds.

Brett followed her, his hands occasionally touching Scudi's feet on the rungs. The climb felt long to Brett, and he knew it must seem interminable to Scudi, operating in total darkness. He regretted that he had not started counting the rungs, that would help keep his mind off the ever-growing drop to the deck below. It was stomach-tightening for him to think about it, and when he did his hands didn't want to move from rung to rung. He couldn't see to the bottom or the top, just Scudi's trim form working ahead of him. Once, he stopped and looked behind him. Several diameters of pipes were faintly visible to him. One was hot to the touch. There was cold condensation on another. It felt slick when he ran his fingers over it.

Algae, he thought. He was thankful for something familiar. There was no such structure or rigidity on an Island. Organic conduits grew where they were guided to grow, but guidance had its limits.

At the first ledge, Scudi put an arm around his waist and helped him to a place against another ladder. She waited a blink while he caught his breath, then:

"We have to hurry. They may guess where we've gone."

"Can they know where we are?"

"There are no sensors here, and they won't know I have a key to the service passages."

"How did you get it?"

"From my father's desk. I found it while showing the Justice the den."

"Why would your father have had such a key?"

"Probably for the same reason we're using it. Emergency escape."

She patted his chest gently and turned away. With a sigh, she started on the next stage of their climb.

Again, Brett followed.

He pressed faster and faster, but she was always farther up, widening the distance between them. Then there was the second ledge and Brett drew himself onto it, panting. Scudi guided him to the next ladder. When he could control his breathing, he asked, "How do you move so fast?"

"I run the passageways and work out in the gym," she said. "Those of us who will go back to the open land must be prepared for the demands to be made on our bodies. It will be different from the sea."

He knew it was an inadequate response, but all he could manage was, "Oh."

"Are you rested enough for the last stage?" she asked.

"Lead on."

This time, he stayed with her enough that his hand met her foot from time to time. He knew she was setting a slower pace because of him and this pained him. Still, he was glad for the reserves it might give him. There was still that yawning void below, a place made even more frightening by its drop into a dim void. When he felt the final rung and another ledge, he wrapped an arm around the ladder's vertical supports and drew in deep, gasping breaths.

Scudi's hand touched his head. "You all right?"

"Just ... catching my breath."

She put a hand underneath his right arm. "Come up. I will help. It is safer up here. There is a railing."

With Scudi's hand lifting, Brett crawled over the lip of the ledge. He saw the rail and caught a good grip on it, pulling himself the last few millimeters and then stretching out on the hard metal grate. Scudi rested a hand on his back and, when she felt his breathing smooth out, drew away.

"Let's review the plan," she said. She sat with her back against a metal wall.

"Go ahead," he said. He drew himself up beside her, smelling the sweet freshness of her breath, feeling the brush of her hair against his cheek.

"The hatch is directly behind me. It's a double hatch. The docking bay is kept under enough pressure to hold a working level on the water. We'll open in an alcove off the docking bay. If no one is there, we will just go out and walk normally toward one of the foils. You are my charge and I am showing you around."

"What if someone sees us coming out of the hatch?"

"We laugh and giggle. We're young lovers on a rendezvous. We may get a lecture. If so, we should at least appear to be sorry."

Brett looked at the smooth profile of Scudi's face.

Clever. Close enough to the truth that he wished it were so. "Where can we hide in this docking bay?" he asked.

"We won't hide. We will go to one of the foils, one where the operating crew is not aboard. We will escape topside in the foil."

"Can you really operate a foil?"

"Of course. I go topside often in the lab foil." She was all seriousness. "Do you understand what we're going to do?"

"Lead the way," he said.

Scudi slid away from him. There was the slightest sound of metal grating against metal. A small hatch swung wide, letting in dim light. It was bright enough to Brett that he was forced to squint. Scudi slipped out and reached back a hand for him. Brett followed, wriggling through the tight opening. He found himself in a low, rectangular space with gray metal walls. Light came in from a port at the far end. Scudi dogged the hatch behind them, then opened the far hatch. As she had promised, they emerged into a narrow alcove.

"Now," she whispered, taking his hand. "I am showing you the landing bay and the foils."

She led Brett out onto a narrow platform with a railing and stairs down to a deck about three meters below them. Brett stopped and resisted Scudi's attempts to drag him farther. They were under a transparent dome that stretched away from him for several hundred meters.

Plaz, he thought. *Has to be. Nothing else could take that pressure.* The docking bays were located inside this gigantic inverted cup that held out the sea. A plaz umbrella! He looked up at the surface, no more than fifty meters away, a milky silver region with the doubled shafts of light indicating that both suns stood above the horizon.

Scudi tugged at his arm.

Brett looked down to the deck—a giant metal grate with piers stretching out the far side toward the descending lip of the facility's plaz cover. As he watched, a submerged foil cruised under the far lip and lifted into the bay with a cascade of water off its hull. The foil slid into an empty bay, its engines a painful growl in his ears even at this low speed. With the newcomer, Brett counted six of the huge boats lined up in a row. Mermen worked busily around them on the piers, securing the lines of the new arrival, wheeling cargo on carts to and from the open hatches in the line of craft.

"They're so big," Brett said, craning his neck at the prow of the foil directly ahead of them. Someone was working up there, dreamily scraping a dry skin of green kelp off the extruded fenders.

"Come along," she said, her voice slightly louder than conversation required, "I'll take you aboard one of them. Kareen wants you to see it all."

This, Brett realized, was for the benefit of a Merman who had stopped below them and was watching them with a questioning tilt to his head. As Scudi spoke, he smiled and strode away.

Brett allowed her to lead him down the stairs.

"Food transport uses only the seventy-meter cargo model," she said. "In spite of their size, they'll do at least eighty knots. Somewhat slower in heavy seas. I'm told they can top a hundred knots with a light load."

Her hand in his, Scudi guided Brett down the line of foils, weaving in and out of the passing workers and stepping aside for loaded carts. At the end, they met six white-uniformed workers wheeling a covered cart toward them along the pier.

"Repair crew," Scudi explained. She spoke to the first man in the group. "Something wrong with this one?"

"Just a little trouble with the thrust reverser, Miss Wang." All six stopped while the leader spoke to Scudi. They all looked very much alike in their white coveralls. Brett saw no name tags.

"Can I take our guest aboard to show him around? I'm familiar with this one," she said. Brett thought he detected a note of false petulance in her voice.

"I'm sure you are," the crewman said. "But be careful. They've just finished refueling it for the test run. You'll have to be out in about an hour. The next shift will be loading it then."

"Oh, good," Scudi said, dragging Brett around the repair cart. "We'll have it all to ourselves and I can show you everything." She called back over her shoulder. "Thanks!"

The crewman waved and helped his men trundle their cart down the pier.

Midway down the hull, Scudi led the way up a narrow gangplank. Brett followed her into a passage lighted by overhead tubes. She motioned for him to wait while she peered back out the open hatch. Presently, she pressed a switch beside the hatch. A low hum sounded and the gangplank slid in. The hatch sealed behind it with a soft hiss.

"Quick!" she said. She turned and once more they were running. Scudi led him up a series of gangways and along a wide corridor, emerging finally into a plaz-windowed control room high above the prow.

"Take the other seat."

She slid into one of the two command couches that faced a bank of instruments. "I'll show you how to run one of these things. It's really simple."

Brett watched her, seeing the way she became another person as she touched the controls. Every movement was quick and sure. "Now this one," she said, hitting a yellow button.

A low thrumming could be felt through the deck under their feet. Several Mermen working on the pier below them turned and looked at the foil.

Scudi moved her hand up to a red button labeled "Emergency release—docking lines." She touched the button and immediately drew a lever at her left all the way back. The foil slid smoothly out of its dock. Mermen below them began to run and wave at the foil.

Before they cleared the dock Scudi began pumping ballast aboard. The foil slipped under the water, banking sharply to the left. Scudi lifted a stick from the deck beside her. Brett saw that it was socketed into the deck and wondered what it controlled. Her left hand moved the lever on the other side of her, throwing it full forward. The foil dove toward the lip of the inverted plaz cup. Brett looked up as they passed under the lip, watching the lighted edge pass away astern.

Once on the other side, Scudi began blowing ballast as she lifted the bow toward the surface. Brett swiveled around and saw the docking bay recede behind them. There was no pursuit yet.

Brett was stunned at the size of the boat. *Seventy meters. That's ten coracles long!*

"Watch what I'm doing," Scudi ordered. "You might have to run one of these things."

Brett turned back to take in the levers, buttons, gauges and switches.

"Hydrogen ramjets for both underwater and surface," she said. "Fuel conservation system reduces our speed underwater. Here's the governor." She indicated a clip-locked toggle between them. "Dangerous to exceed governed speed but it can be done in an emergency."

She moved the stick in her right hand, swinging it to starboard and pulling back on it slightly. "This steers us," she said. "Pull back to lift, down to dive."

Brett nodded.

"These ..." She indicated a bank of instruments across the top of the board. "You read the labels: topside fuel flow, ballast—slower than on a sub. Ignition. Air supply for down under. Always remember to switch it off topside. If the cockpit is breached, we're automatically ejected. Manual ejection is by that red lever at the center."

Brett responded with a series of grunts or "Got it." He was thankful that all the switches and instruments carried clear labels.

Scudi pointed overhead where a black hood framed a large, gridded screen. "Charts are projected there. That's something Islanders have been trying to get for a long time."

"Why can't we have it?" Brett knew the system she had indicated. Fishermen grouched about it often. *Steeran,* the Mermen called it. A navigation system that worked by reading Merman fixed underwater transmission stations.

"Too complicated and too costly for upkeep. You just don't have the support facilities."

He had heard that story before. Islanders didn't believe it, but Scudi obviously did.

"Topside," she announced.

The foil broke the surface in a long wave trough that crested under them. Water cascaded off the plaz all around.

Brett clapped his hands over his eyes. The stabbing blast of light made his eyeballs feel like two hot coals in his head. He ducked his face down onto his knees with a loud moan.

"Is something wrong?" Scudi asked. She did not look at him but busied herself dropping the foils from their hull slots and increasing speed.

"It's my eyes," he said. He blinked them open, adjusting slowly. Tears washed over his cheeks. "It's getting better."

"Good," she said. "You should watch what I do. It's best to put the foil up on the step parallel to the waves, then quarter into them as you bring it up to speed. I'll get the course in a blink after we're at cruise. Look back and see if there's any pursuit."

Brett turned and stared back along their wake, aware suddenly of how fast they already were moving. The big foil throbbed and bounced under them, then suddenly the ride smoothed and there was only the high whine of the hydrogen rams and the jumping jostle of the foils bridging the waves.

"Eighty-five knots," Scudi said. "Are they after us yet?"

"I don't see anything." Brett wiped at his eyes. The pain was almost gone.

"I don't see anything on the instruments," she said. "They must know it's hopeless. Every other foil in the bay has at least some cargo aboard. We have none and full fuel tanks."

Brett returned his attention to the front, blinking away the pain as his eyes reacted to the sunlight off the waves.

"The RDF is over to your right, that green panel," she said. "See if you can raise Vashon's signal."

Brett turned to the radio direction finder. He saw at once it was a more sophisticated model than the one on which Twisp had trained him, but the dials were labeled and the frequency arc was immediately identifiable. He had the signal in a moment. The familiar voice of Vashon's transmission to its fishing fleet crackled from the overhead speakers.

"It's a good fishing day, everyone, and big cargoes expected. Muree are running strong in quadrant nineteen." Brett turned down the volume.

"What is quadrant nineteen?" Scudi asked.

"It's a grid position relative to Vashon."

"But the Island moves as it drifts!"

"So do the muree, and that's all that's important."

Brett twisted the dials, homed on the signal and read the coordinates. "There's your course," he said, pointing to the dial above the RDF.

"Is that sun-relative or compass?"

"Compass."

"Doppler distance reads five hundred and ninety klicks. That's a long way!"

"Seven plus hours," she said. "We can run ten hours without stopping to recharge fuel. We can regenerate our own hydrogen from seawater during daylight hours, but we'll be sitting squawks if they come after us or try to block us from some station up ahead."

"They could do that?"

"I'm sure they'll try. There are four outposts along our course."

"We would need more fuel," he said.

"And they'll be looking for us from down under."

"What about one of the smaller Islands?"

"I saw the latest plot on the current board yesterday. Vashon's closest by more than five hundred klicks."

"Why can't I get on the emergency frequency and tell Vashon what we know. We should report in anyway," he added.

"What do we know?" she asked, adjusting the throttle. The foil lurched slightly and tipped, climbing one of the periodic high waves.

"We know they're holding the Chief Justice against his will. We know there are a lot of dead Islanders."

"What about his suspicions?"

"They're *his* suspicions," Brett said, "but don't you think he deserves a hearing?"

"If he's right, have you thought about what may happen if the Islands try to force his return?"

Brett felt a lump in his throat. "Would they kill him?"

"Somewhere, there seem to be people who kill," she said. "Guemes proves that." "Ambassador Ale?"

"It occurs to me, Brett, that Hastings and Lonfinn may be watching her to see that she does not do something dangerous to them. My father was very rich. He warned me often that this created danger for everyone around him."

"I could just call in and tell Vashon I'm safe and returning," he said. He shook his head. "No. To those that listen in—"

"And they *are* listening," she added.

"It would be the same thing as just spilling the story right now," he said. "What'll we do?"

"We will go to the Launch Base," she said. "Not to Outpost Twenty-two."

"But you told Justice Keel—"

"And if they force him to talk, they will look for us in the wrong place."

"Why the Launch Base?" he asked.

"No single group controls that," she said. "That's a part of all of our dreams—get the hyb tanks down from where Ship left them in orbit."

"It's still a Merman project."

"It is *all* Merman. We will say our piece there. Everyone will hear it. Then all will know what a few people may be doing."

Brett stared straight ahead. He knew he should feel elation at their escape. He was in the biggest vessel he had ever seen, rocketing along the wavetops at more than eighty knots, faster than he had ever gone before. But unknowns crowded in on him. Keel did not trust the Mermen. And Scudi was Merman. Was she being honest? Had he heard her real reasons for wanting him to avoid the radio? He looked at Scudi. For what other reason could she help him escape?

"I've been thinking," Scudi said. "If no word has reached them, your family will be sick with worry about you. And your friend, Twisp. Call Vashon. We'll make do. Maybe my suspicions are foolish."

He saw her throat pulse with a swallow and he remembered her tears over the heaped bodies of the Islanders.

"No," he said, "we should go to your Launch Base."

Again, Brett concentrated on the sea ahead of them. The two suns lifted heat-shimmers off the water. When he had been much younger, seeing the Island rim for the first time, the heat shimmers had created images for him. Long-whiskered sea dragons coiled above the ocean surface, giant muree and fat scrubberfish. The shimmer play now was nothing but heat reflected off water. He felt the warmth on his face and arms. He thought of Twisp leaning back against the coracle's tiller, eyes closed, soaking up the heat through his hairy chest.

"Where is this base?" he asked.

She reached up and turned a small dial below the overhead screen. Beside the dial, an alphanumerical keyboard glowed with its own internal lights. She typed HF-i, then LB-1. The screen flashed 141.2, then overprinted a spray of lines with a common focal point. A bright green spot danced at the wide outer arc of the lines. Scudi pointed at the spot.

"That's us." She pointed to the base of the spray. "We go here on course one forty-one point two." She pointed to a dial with a red arrow on the console in front of them. The arrow indicated 141.2.

"That's all there is to it?"

"All?" Scudi smiled. "There are hundreds of transmitter stations all around Pandora, a whole manufacturing and servicing complex—all to insure that we get from here to there."

Brett looked up at the screen. The spray of lines had pivoted until the bright green dot lay centered on course. The 141.2 still glowed in the lower left corner of the screen.

"If we require a course change, it will sound a klaxon and show the new numbers," she said. "Steeran homing on LB-one."

Brett looked out across the water beside them, seeing the spray kicked up by the foils, thinking how valuable such a system would be to Vashon's fishing fleet. The sun burned hot on him through the plaz, but the air felt good. Rich topside air blew in the vents. Scudi Wang was at his side and suddenly Pandora didn't seem to be the adversary that he'd always imagined. Even if it was a deadly place, it had its measure of beauty.

Chapter 24

One measure of humanity lies in the lengths taken to right the wrongs perpetrated against others. Recognition of wrongdoing is the first crucial step.
—Raja Thomas, *The Journals*

SHADOW PANILLE covered the dead Mute. He washed his hands in the alcohol basin beside the litter. The rest of the room bustled with the *clink* of steel instruments against trays. Low-voiced, one-word commands and grunts came from several busy groups of doctors and med-techs. Panille looked back over his shoulder at the long row of litters strung down the center of the room, each one surrounded by medics. Splashes and blotches of blood stained gray gowns and the eyes above the antiseptic masks looked more tired, more hopeless every hour. Of all the survivors brought in by the pickup teams, only two had escaped physical harm. Panille reminded himself that there were other kinds of harm. What the experience had done to their minds … he hesitated to think of them as survivors.

The Mute behind Panille had died under the knife for lack of replacement blood. The medical facility had been unprepared for bleeders on such a tremendous scale. He heard Kareen Ale snap off her gloves behind him.

"Thanks for the assist," she said. "Too bad he didn't make it. This was a close one."

Panille watched one of the teams lift a litter and carry it toward the recovery area. At least a few would make it. And one of his men had said they were herding together the few fishing boats that had escaped and fled the drift. Panille rubbed his eyes and was immediately sorry. They burned from the touch of alcohol and started streaming tears.

Ale took him by the shoulder and led him to the sink beside the hatchway. It had a tall, curved spout that he could get his head under.

"Let the water run over the eyes," she said. "Blinking helps the rinse."

"Thanks."

She handed him a towel. "Relax," she said, "that's the last of them."

"How long have we been at it?"

"Twenty-six hours."

"How many made it?"

"Not counting those in shock, we have ninety still breathing in recovery. Several hundred with only minor injuries. I don't know. Fewer than a thousand, anyway, and six still under the knife here. Do you believe what this one told us?"

"About the sub? It's hard to write it off to hallucinations or delirium, considering the circumstances."

"He was clear-headed when they brought him in. Did you see what he managed to do with his legs? It's too bad he didn't make it; he tried harder than most people."

"Both legs severed below the knees and he managed to stop the bleeding himself," Panille said. "I don't know, Kareen. I guess I don't want to believe him. But I do."

"What about the part about the sub rolling upside-down before its dive?" Ale asked. "Couldn't that mean somebody just lost control of the machine? Surely no Merman would do something like that deliberately."

"That patient"—Panille waved towards the litter behind them—"claimed that a Merman sub deliberately sank their Island. He said he saw the whole thing, the sub came directly up through their center and—"

"It was an Islander sub," she insisted. "Must've been."

"But he *said* ..."

Kareen inhaled deeply and sighed. "He was mistaken, my dear," she said. "And to avoid serious trouble, we'll have to prove it."

They both stepped aside as two attendants carried the litter with the dead Mute out the hatchway, bound for the mortuary. Kareen began to recite what Panille knew would become the Merman line: "He was a Mute. Mutes don't have all of their faculties, even under the best of circumstances."

"You've been spending too much time with Gallow," Panille said.

"But look at what we had to work with here," she said. Her voice bordered on a whisper. Panille didn't like it, nor did he like the turn of conversation. Frustration and fatigue brought out a side of Kareen Ale that he had not known existed. "Missing parts, extra parts, misplaced parts." She gestured with a whimsical wave of her hand. "What their medical people do for an anatomy class boggles the mind. No, Shadow, it *must* have been an Islander sub. Some interior score they were settling. What could any of us gain by such an act? Nothing. I say we should have a drink. Just have a drink and forget it. How about it?"

"What he described was not an Islander sub," Panille insisted. "What he described was a kelp sub, with cutters and welders."

Kareen pulled him aside, as a mother might take a troublesome child aside during WorShip. "Shadow! You're not making sense. *If* Mermen sank that Island, then why go to all the trouble to man the pickup teams? Why not just let them go? No, we worked hard here to save what we could. Not that it mattered."

"What do you mean, 'Not that it mattered?'"

"You saw them, their condition. The best of them were starving. Leather on bone. They looked like furniture."

"Then we should feed them," Panille said. "Ryan Wang didn't develop the largest food distribution in history just to let people starve."

"Feeding them's a lot easier than hauling them in dead," she said.

"These are *people!*" Panille snapped.

Ale's quick eyes flicked from Panille, around the room to the surgical and trauma teams, then back. Her lips were trembling, and he saw with surprise that she was only barely under control.

"That patient may have been a Mute, but he was no fool," Panille insisted. "He reported what he observed, and he did it clearly."

"I don't want to believe him," Ale said.

"But you do." Panille put an arm around her shoulders.

Ale trembled at his touch. "We must talk," she said. "Would you go back to my quarters with me?"

They rode the tubes, Ale's head lolling on his shoulder. She snored a little, caught herself and settled closer against him. He liked the feeling of her warmth soaking into him. When their car started into a curve he held her shoulder a little tighter to keep the movement from waking her, giving himself time to think. Kareen wanted to talk. Did she want to persuade? How would she argue? With her body?

Panille decided this thought was unworthy of him. He rejected it.

Twenty-six hours in surgery, he thought. Soon Ale would face the difficult politics that the surgery represented. He had noticed the deepening circles of sleepless nights settling under Ale's beautiful eyes. Panille was glad for one aspect of the surgery—it brought out the doctor in Ale, a part of her personality that had become more ghostlike during her brief association with Ryan Wang. Though she'd been alert and awake during the whole frustrating business with the Guemes Islanders, Ale had fallen asleep almost before the transport hatch closed on them. As the Islanders died under the knife one by one, he had watched her blue eyes darken over her mask.

"They're so frail," she had said. "So poor!"

The replacement blood had run out in two hours. Plasma and oxygen were gone in sixteen. Surgical supervisors suggested sterilizing sea water and using that for plasma, but Ale refused.

"Stick with what we know," she said. "This is not the time for experimentation."

In her sleep, Ale's hand reached around Panille's waist and pulled him closer. Her hair smelled of antiseptics and perspiration, but he found the mixture comforting because it was her. He liked the brush of her hair against his bare neck. The hours of sweat in his own hair made him glad he'd kept it braided. He ached for a shower even more than he ached for a bed. Panille caught himself dozing off just as they jerked to a stop. The panel above their heads flashed the message: *Organization and Distribution.*

"Kareen," he said, "we're here."

She sighed and squeezed his waist tighter. He pressed the hold button on the panel with his free hand.

"Kareen?"

Another sigh. "I heard you, Shadow. I'm *so* tired."

"We've arrived," he said. "You'll be more comfortable inside."

She looked up at him but didn't move away. Her eyes were red and puffy from lack of sleep but she managed a smile. "I just got acquainted with you," she said. "I thought I knew you, but now I'm not letting you out of my sight."

He placed a finger against her lips. "I'll just take you to your quarters. We can talk later."

"What makes this mysterious Shadow Panille tick?" she asked in a whisper. Then she kissed him. It was a brief kiss, but warm and powerful. "You don't mind, do you?" she asked.

"What about Gallow?"

"Well," she said, "the sooner we get out of here the sooner life goes on."

They uncurled themselves from each other. He liked the way the warm spots lingered and tingled on his skin. Ale stepped out of the hatch onto the docking bay and reached back a slender hand to pull him through.

"You're beautiful," he said, and her strong grip pulled him right up to her, then she hugged him close. Again, he put down his doubts about her.

"You have a way with words," she said.

"Runs in my family."

"You could've been a surgeon," she said. "You have good hands. I'd like to spend more time studying your hands."

"I'd like that," he murmured against her hair. "I've always wanted to know you better. You know that."

"I have to warn you, I snore."

"I noticed," he said. They held each other and swayed on the docking bay. "You drool, too," he said.

"Don't be crude." She pinched him in the ribs. "Ladies don't drool."

"What's this wet spot on my shoulder?"

"How embarrassing," she said. Then she took his hand and guided him up the walkway toward her building. She glanced back at him and said, "Nobody lives long enough for dilly-dallying. Let's get to it."

Panille realized right then that the pace of his life had just turned itself up a full notch. Tired as he had been, he sparked with the measure of energy that she injected into the air around them. There was a new bounce to her step that he hadn't noticed in surgery. Her body moved smoothly, quickly across the black-tiled foyer and he matched her step-for-step. When they walked into the ambassadorial quarters they were still holding hands.

Chapter 25

Pattern is his who can see beyond shape:
Life is his who can tell beyond words.
—Lao Tzu, *Shiprecords*

BOTH SUNS stood high in the dark sky, raising heat shimmers off the water. Brett's sensitive eyes, shielded by dark glasses Scudi had found in the foil's lockers, scanned the sea. The foil cut through the waves with an ease that thrilled him. He marveled at how quickly his senses had adapted to speed. A feeling of freedom, of escape soothed him. Pursuit could not move this fast. Danger could only lie ahead, where heat shimmers distorted the horizon. Or, as Twisp called it, "the Future."

When Brett had been quite young, standing with his mother at Vashon's edge for the first time, the heat-dazzled air had been inhabited by coils of long-whiskered dragons. Today's sun felt new on his arms and face, glistening through the canopy onto the instruments. The suns ignited golden glints in Scudi's black hair. There were no dragons.

Scudi bent intently over the controls, watching the sea, the dials, the guidance screen above her head. Her mouth was set in a grim line, which softened only when she looked at Brett.

A wide stretch of kelp drew a dark shadow on the water off to his right. Scudi steered them into the lee of the kelp, finding smoother water there. Brett stared out at an ovoid green mat within the kelp. At the very center of the oval, this particular green was a vivid reflector of the sunlight. The green darkened away from the center until the kelp patch became yellowed and brown at the edges.

Seeing where he was looking, Scudi said, "The outer edges die off, curl under and fortify the rest of the patch."

They rode without speaking for a time.

Abruptly, Scudi shocked him by shutting down the foil's engines. The big craft dropped off the step with a rocking lurch.

Brett looked wildly at Scudi, but she appeared calm.

"You start us," Scudi said.

"What?"

"Start us up." Her voice was calmly insistent. "What if I were injured?"

Brett sank into his seat and looked down at the control panel. Below the screen near the center of the cockpit lay four switches and a sticker labeled "Starting Procedure."

He read the instructions and depressed the switch marked "Ignition." The hot hiss of the hydrogen ram came from the rear of the foil.

Scudi smiled.

As the instructions told him, Brett glanced up at the guidance screen. A miniature line-drawing of a foil appeared around a green dot on the screen. A red line speared outward from the green dot. He touched the button marked *forward* and pushed the throttle gently ahead, gripping the wheel tightly with his free hand. He could feel sweat under his palms. The craft began to lift, tipping on the flank of a wave.

"Right down the trough," Scudi reminded him.

He turned the wheel slightly and pushed the throttle farther ahead. The foil came out of the water with a gentle gliding motion and he gave it more throttle. They came up on the step and he saw the speed-distance counter flicker, then settle on "72."

The green dot tracked on the red line.

"Very good," Scudi said. "I'll take it now. Just remember to follow the instructions."

Scudi increased speed. Cabin air felt cooler as vents exchanged topside air from a clear and sunny day.

Brett scanned as much of the horizon as he could see from the cabin, a thing he had learned from Twisp, almost unconsciously. It was his landscape, the view he had known since infancy—open ocean with long rollers broken here and there by patches of kelp, silvery current intersections and wind-foamed crests. There was a rhythm to it that satisfied him. All the divergent variety became one thing inside him, as everything was one in the sea. The suns came up separately but met before they sank below the horizon. Waves crossed each other and told him of things beyond his view. It was all one. He tried to say something of this to Scudi.

"The suns do that because of their ellipses," she said. "I know about the waves. Everything that touches them tells us something of itself."

"Ellipses?" he asked.

"My mother said the suns met at midday when she was young."

Brett found this interesting but he felt that Scudi had missed his point. Or she didn't want to discuss it. "You must've learned a lot from your mother."

"She was very smart except for men," Scudi said. "At least, that's what she used to say."

"When she was mad at your father?"

"Yes. Or different men at the outposts."

"What are these outposts?"

"Places where we are few, where we work hard and have our different ways. When I come into the city, or even the launch site, I'm aware that I am different. I speak different. I have been warned about it."

"Warned?" Brett felt undertones of some dark savagery among the Mermen.

"My mother said if I took outpost-talk into the city I couldn't blend. People would look at me as an outsider—a dangerous perspective."

"Dangerous?" he asked. "To see things differently?"

"Sometimes." Scudi glanced at him. "You must blend in. You could pass, but I know you for an Islander by the sound of your talk."

Scudi was trying to warn him, he thought.

Or teach me.

He noted that her accent was different out here than it had been back in her quarters. It wasn't her choice of words so much as the way she said them. There was a sparseness about her now. She was even more direct.

Brett looked out at the ocean speeding past. He thought about this Merman unity, this Merman society that measured danger in an accent. Like the waves, which met at odd angles, currents in Merman society were refracting off each other. "Interference," the physicists called it; he knew that much.

The ease with which Scudi kept the big foil skipping the wavetops told Brett something of her past. She had only to glance at the guidance screen and out at the ocean to become one with all of it. She avoided the thick stretches of wild kelp and kept them securely on course toward this mysterious Launch Base.

"There's more wild kelp lately," he said. "No Mermen attending it."

"Pandora belonged to the kelp once," she said. "Now kelp grows and spreads at the top of an exponential curve. Do you know what that means?"

"The more kelp there is the faster it spreads and the faster it grows," he said.

"It is more like an explosion at this point," she said, "or like the moment of crystallization in a saturated solution. Add one tiny crystal and the whole thing precipitates out one massive crystal. That's what the kelp will do next. Right now it is learning to care for itself."

Brett shook his head. "I know what the history says. Still … sentient *plants?*"

She shrugged off his incredulity like a shawl. "If the C/P is right—if they've all been right—Vata is the key to the kelp. She is the crystal that will precipitate its consciousness. Or its soul."

"Vata," he whispered, a childlike awe in his voice. He was not one for WorShip, but he respected any human being who had outlived so many generations. No Merman had ever done that. Did Scudi believe in that Chaplain/Psychiatrist stuff?

He asked her.

Scudi shrugged. "I only know what I can arrange in my mind. I have seen the kelp learn. It *is* sentient, but very low-grade. There is no magic in sentiency except life and time. Vata has kelp genes, that is a fact."

"Twisp says last time it took the kelp a quarter of a billion years to come awake. How will we ever know …"

"We've helped. The rest is up to it."

"What does Vata have to do with it?"

"I don't really know. I suspect she's some kind of catalyst. The last natural link with the kelp's ancestor. Shadow says Vata's really in a coma. She went into the coma when the kelp died. Shock, maybe."

"What about Duque? Or any number of us—Mermen included—who have kelp genes? Why aren't we the catalysts you talk about?"

"No one human has all kelp genes—such a being would be kelp, not human," she said. "Each one may have wholly different combinations."

"Duque says Vata dreams him."

"Some of our more religious types say Vata dreams us all," Scudi said. She sniffed. "The fact that you and I were prisoners and escaped, that was no dream." She shot him a warm glance. "We are a good team."

Brett blushed and nodded.

"How close are we to Launch Base?" he asked.

"Before nightfall," she said.

Brett thought about the coming encounter. Launch Base would be an important place, many people. Among those people might be the ones who had deliberately destroyed Guemes. His Islander accent could mean danger. He turned to Scudi and tried to speak of this casually. He didn't want to argue with her or scare her. But it became immediately apparent that Scudi had been thinking along the same lines.

"In the red locker beside the main hatch," she said. "Dive suits and kitpacks. We'll be in colder water at the Launch Base."

"Hypothermia kills," he said. He had seen the two words in bright yellow on the red locker, reminding him of his earliest survival lessons. Island children were taught the dangers of the cold water as soon as they could talk. Apparently Mermen taught the same lesson, although Twisp claimed that Mermen had greater tolerance for cold.

"See if you can find suits to fit us," she said. "If we have to go over the side …" She left the sentence unfinished, knowing it was unnecessary to continue.

The sight of the pile of gray dive suits inside the locker brought a smile to Brett's face. The organic suits, of Islander design and manufacture, represented one of the few advancements they held over the Mermen. He selected a "small" and a "medium" and tore open the packages to activate them. He picked up two of the orange kitpacks with the suits and stowed them under the command couch seats in the cabin.

"What are those kitpacks for?" he asked.

"They're survival kits," she said. "Inflatable raft, knife, lines, pain pills. There are even repellent grenades for dashers."

"Have you ever had to use grenades?"

"No. But my mother did once. One of her team did not get away."

Brett shuddered. Dashers seldom came near Islands anymore, but fishermen had been lost and there were stories of children taken by sneak attacks at an Island's rim. Suddenly, the wide ocean around their speeding foil lost some of its warm softness, its protective familiarity. Brett shook his head to clear it. He and Twisp had lived out here on a tiny coracle. For the love of Ship! A foil could not be as vulnerable as a flimsy coracle. But they had no squawks on the foil and if they had to take to the water in dive suits … Could their own senses warn them in time? Dashers were blindingly fast.

The two suns had moved perceptibly closer to each other, nearing their sunset meeting. Brett stared ahead, looking for the first sign of their goal. He knew this fear of dashers was foolishness, something they'd laugh about someday …

Something bobbing on the water ahead commanded his whole attention.

"What's that?" he asked, pointing at a spot far ahead and slightly to starboard.

"I think it's a boat," Scudi said.

"No," he mused, "whatever it is, it's two things."

"Two boats?"

The foil's speed was bringing the objects closer at an astonishing rate. His voice was barely audible: "Two coracles."

"One is towing the other," Scudi said. She veered the foil toward them.

Brett stood and leaned against the control console, squinting out at the coracles. He waved a hand at Scudi, palm down: "Slow down!" She throttled back and he gripped the console to keep his balance as the hull dropped into the water with a surge of the bow wave.

"It's Queets!" Brett shouted, pointing at the man at the tiller. "Ship's teeth, it's Queets!"

Scudi shut down one ram and maneuvered the foil upwind of the coracles. Brett fumbled at the dogs to the canopy and swung it back, leaning out to shout at the boats only fifty meters downwind. "Twisp! Queets!"

Twisp stood and shielded his eyes with a hand, the long arm held awkwardly against his side.

"Kid!"

Brett tossed him a traditional greeting of fishermen at sea: "Do you have a full load?"

Twisp stood at the tiller, rocking the coracle from side to side, and clapped his hands high over his head. "You made it!" he hollered. "You made it."

Brett pulled back into the cockpit. "Scudi, take us alongside."

"So that's Queets Twisp," she said. She restarted the ram and eased them gently ahead. She rounded the coracles in a wide curve and came alongside the lead boat, opening the access hatch as the coracles drew near.

Twisp grabbed a foil brace and in less than a minute he was inside the cockpit, his long arms wrapped around Brett. His huge hands pummeled Brett's back.

"I knew I'd find you!" Twisp held Brett at a long arm's length and gestured wide to take in the foil, Scudi, his clothes and dark glasses. "What's all this?"

"A very long story," Brett said. "We're heading for a Merman Launch Base. Have you heard anything … ?"

Twisp dropped his arms and sobered. "We've been there," he said. "At least, near enough as makes no difference." He turned, indicating the other man in the coracle. "That bit of flotsam is Iz Bushka. I tried to take him to Launch Base on a piece of very heavy business."

"Tried?" Scudi asked. "What happened?"

"Who's this little pearl?" Twisp asked, extending a hand. "I'm Queets Twisp."

"Scudi Wang," she and Brett said at once.

They laughed.

Twisp stared at her, startled. Was this the beautiful young Merman rescuer he had visualized in his daydreams? No! That was foolishness.

"Well, Scudi Wang," Twisp said, "they wouldn't listen to us at the Launch Base—wouldn't let us into the base at all." Twisp pursed his lips. "Towed us away with a foil bigger than this one. Told us to stay away. We took their advice." He glanced around him. "So what're you doing here, anyway? Where's the crew?"

"We're the crew," Brett said.

Brett explained why they were heading for the base, what had happened to them, the Chief Justice and the political scene down under. Bushka stepped into the cabin as Brett was finishing. Brett's recital had a marked effect on Bushka, who grew pale and breathed in shallow gasps.

"They're ahead of us," Bushka muttered, "I know they are."

He stared at Scudi.

"Wang," he said. "You're Ryan Wang's daughter."

Brett, edging toward a temper flare-up, asked Twisp, "What's wrong with him?"

"Something on his conscience," Twisp said. He, too, looked at Scudi. "Is that right? Are you Ryan Wang's daughter?"

"Yes."

"I told you!" Bushka wailed.

"Oh, shut up!" Twisp snapped. "Ryan Wang's dead and I'm tired of listening to your crap." He turned to Brett and Scudi. "The kid says you saved his life. Is that right?"

"Yes." She spoke with one of her small shrugs. Her eyes stared into the console's instruments.

"Anything else we should know?"

"I . . . don't think so," she said.

Twisp caught Brett's eye and decided to get all the bad news out. He hooked a thumb toward Bushka. "This bit of dasher bait here," he said, "piloted the sub that sank Guemes. He claims he didn't know what they had in mind until the sub chewed into the bottom of the Island. Says he was tricked by the Merman commander, a guy named Gallow."

"Gallow," Scudi whispered.

"You know him?" Brett asked.

"I've seen him many times. With my father and Kareen Ale, often—"

"I told you!" Bushka interrupted. He prodded Twisp's ribs. Twisp grabbed Bushka's wrist, twisted it back suddenly, then flung it aside.

"And I told you to stow it," Twisp said. Brett and Scudi both turned to face Bushka.

He stepped back instinctively.

"Why are you looking at me like that?" Bushka asked. "Twisp can tell you the whole story—I couldn't stop them—" He broke off when they continued to stare at him silently.

"They don't trust you," Twisp said, "and neither do I. But if Scudi delivered you all packaged and safe to Launch Base, that might be just what this Gallow would want. If he's a manipulator, he'll have people crawling all over a political scene like that. You might just disappear, Bushka." Twisp rubbed the back of his neck and spoke low. "We have to do this one right the first time. We'll have no way of regrouping.

"Brett and I could take the coracles and get back to Vashon," Twisp said.

"No," Brett insisted. "Scudi and I stay together."

"I should go to the base alone," Scudi said. "When they see me alone, they'll know you and I have separated and others will listen to our story."

"No!" Brett repeated. He tightened his grip on her shoulders. "We're a team. We stick together."

Twisp glared at Brett, then his expression and his bearing softened. "So that's the way it is?"

"That's the way it is," Brett said. He kept his arm firmly around Scudi's shoulders. "I know you could order me to go with you. I'm still your apprentice. But I wouldn't obey."

Twisp spoke in a mild voice. "Then I better not be giving any orders." He grinned to take the sting from his words.

"So what do we do?" Brett asked.

Bushka startled them when he spoke. "Let me take the foil and go to Launch Base alone. I could—"

"You could spread the word to your friends and tell them where to pick up a couple of slow-moving coracles," Twisp said.

Bushka paled even further. "I tell you, I'm *not*—"

"You're an unknown right now," Twisp said. "That's what you are. If your story's true, you're dumber than you look. Whatever, we can't afford to trust you—not with our lives."

"Then let me go back in the coracles," Bushka said.

"They'd just tow you away again. Farther this time." Twisp turned to Brett and Scudi. "You two are determined to stick together?"

Brett nodded; so did Scudi.

"Then Bushka and I go in the coracles," Twisp said. "We're better off split up, I'm sure of that, but we don't want to get out of touch again. We'll turn on our locator transmitter. You know the frequency, kid?"

"Yes, but—"

"There must be a portable RDF on this monster," Twisp said. He glanced around the cockpit.

"There are small portable direction finders in all emergency kitpacks," Scudi said. Her toe nudged a pack under the seat.

Twisp bent and looked at the small orange kit. He straightened. "You keep them handy, eh?"

"When we think it necessary," she said.

"Then I suggest we follow in the coracles," Twisp said. "If you have to take to the water, you'll be able to find us. Or vice versa."

"If they're alive," Bushka muttered.

Twisp studied Brett for a moment. Was the kid man enough to make the decision? Brett could not be shamed in front of the young woman. Scudi and Brett were, indeed, a team. One that had a bond he couldn't match. It was the kid's decision, and in Twisp's mind it was making Brett a man.

Brett's arm stroked Scudi's shoulder. "We've already shown that we work well together. We got this far. What we're going to do may be dangerous, but you always said, Twisp, that life gives you no guarantees."

Twisp grinned. *Going to do* ... The kid had made his decision and the young woman agreed. That was that.

"All right, partner," Twisp said. "No shilly-shally and no regrets." He turned to Bushka. "Got that, Bushka? We're the backup."

"How long can you hang around?" Brett asked.

"Count on at least twenty days, if you need that much."

"In twenty days there might not be any Islands to save," Brett said. "We'd better move faster than that."

Twisp took two of the kitpacks for the coracles, and loaded a grumbling Bushka back aboard.

Scudi slipped an arm around Brett's waist and hugged him. "We should get into those dive suits now," she said. "We may not get time later."

She pulled hers out from under her couch and draped it across the back of the seat. Brett did the same. Undressing was easy for him this time, and he thought maybe it was seeing all of those Mermen swimming around their base, most of them with only weightbelts full of tools around their waists.

Maybe it was the ride out from the foil bay with his shirt open. It gave Brett a feeling of security in the integrity of his own skin. Besides, Scudi didn't react one way or another. He liked that. And he liked the fact that this time she didn't comment on his modesty. He was beginning to get a feel for the matter-of-fact Merman nudity. But he was only beginning. When Scudi slipped out of her shirt, skinning it over her head, he followed every bounce her firm breasts took and knew it would be very hard to keep from staring. He wanted to look at her forever. She kicked her deck shoes off in two easy flicks of her feet and dropped her pants behind her couch. She had a very small patch of black hair—wispy, silky and inviting.

He noted suddenly that she was standing with her head cocked to one side. She moved gently, not telling him to quit staring but letting him know that she knew what he was doing.

"You have a very beautiful body," he said. "I don't mean to stare."

"Yours, too, is nice," she said. She placed her hand in the middle of his chest, pressed her palm against him. "I just wanted to touch you," she said.

"Yes," he said, because he didn't know what else to say. He put his left hand on her shoulder, felt her strength and her warmth and the easy smoothness of her skin. His other hand came up to her shoulders, and she kissed him. He hoped that she liked it as much as he did. It was a soft, warm and breathless kiss. When she leaned against him her breasts flattened on his chest and he could feel the hard little knots of nipples focused there. He felt himself hardening against her thigh, her thigh of such strength and grace. She stroked his shoulders, then tightened both arms around his neck and kissed him hard, her small tongue tapping the tip of his own. The boat took a sudden lurch and they both fell in a heap on the deck, laughing.

"How graceful," he said.

"And cold."

She was right. The suns had set as Twisp and Bushka departed. Already there was a stiff chill in the air. It wasn't the hardness of the deck that bothered him, but the sudden shock of cold metal against his sweaty skin. When they sat up he heard the strange unpeeling sound of damp skin. It was the sound that sheets of skin made when a friend had unpeeled his sunburned back as a boy.

Brett wanted to loll with Scudi forever, but Scudi was already trying to get up amid the unsteady rocking of the foil. He took her hand and helped her to her feet. He didn't let go.

"It's nearly dark," he said. "Won't we have trouble finding the base? I mean, it's always a lot darker underwater."

"I know the way," she said. "And you have a night vision that could see for us both. We should go now …"

This time he kissed her. She leaned against him for a blink, soft and good-feeling, then pulled back. She still held his hand, but there was an uneasiness in her eyes that Brett translated as fear.

"What?" he asked.

"If we stay here we will, you know … we'll do what we want to do."

Brett's throat was dry and he knew he couldn't talk without his voice cracking. He remained quiet, wanting to hear her out. He didn't know much about what it was that they wanted to do, and if she could give him a few clues, he was ready. He did not want her to be disappointed and he did not know what she expected of him. Most important, he did not know how much experience she'd had in these matters and now it was important for him to find out.

She squeezed his hand. "I like you," she said. "I like you very much. If there's anyone I'd like to … to get *that* close with, it's you. But there is the matter of a child."

He blushed. But it was not out of embarrassment. It was out of anger at himself for not thinking of the obvious thing, for not considering that the step from child to parent could very well happen all at once and he, too, was not ready.

"My mother was sixteen, too," she went on. "She cared for me, so she was never free. She never knew the free movement that others knew. She made the best of it, and I saw much through her. But I didn't see other children except occasionally."

"So she lost an adulthood and you lost a childhood?"

"Yes. It is not to be regretted. It is the only life I know and it is a good one. It is twice good now that I have met you. But it is not a life to repeat. Not for me."

He nodded, took her by the shoulders and kissed her again. This time their chests did not touch but their hands held tight to each other and Brett at least felt relief.

"You are not angry?" she asked.

"I don't think it's possible for me to be mad at you," he said. "Besides, we're going to know each other for a good long time. I want to be with you when the answer is 'yes.'"

Chapter 26

… self has somewhat the character of a result, of a goal attained, something that has come to pass very gradually and is experienced with much travail.
—C.G. Jung, *Shiprecords*

VATA DREAMED that something tangled her hair. Something crawled the back of her neck, tickling her in a legless way, and settled over her right ear. The thing was black, slick and shelled like an insect.

She heard the sounds of pain in her dream, as she had in so many dreams past, and projected all of this into Duque, where it took on more the character of consciousness. Now she recognized some of the voices as leftovers from other dreams. She had made many excursions into this void. Someone named Scudi Wang was there and the thing that slithered through Vata's hair snapped cruel jaws at Scudi's voice.

Duque realized that Vata did not like the thing. She twisted and tossed her head to get rid of it. The thing dug in, set its jaws into her hair and pulled up clumps of hair by the roots. Vata groaned a deep-throated groan, half-cough. She snatched the wet little bug out of her hair and crushed it in her palm.

The pieces slipped from her fingers and a few muffled screams faded into the dark. Duque experienced the sudden awareness that the dream-thing might be real. He had sensed other thoughts in it for just an instant—terrified human thoughts. Vata settled herself into a comfortable position and put her mind to changing the dream into something pleasant. As always, she drifted back to those first days in the valley her people had called "the Nest." Within a few blinks she was lost in the lush vegetation of that holy place where she had been born. It was all the best that Pandora's land had to offer, and it was now under many cold meters of unquiet sea. But things could be otherwise in dreams, and dreams were all the geography that Vata retained. She thought how good it felt to walk again, not letting herself know it was only in a dream. But Duque knew—he had *heard* those terrified thoughts in a moment of death and Vata's dreaming was no longer the same for him.

Chapter 27

The distresses of choice are our chance to be blessed.
—W.H. Auden, *Shiprecords*

IN THAT fading moment before the last of the twilight settled below the horizon, like a dimmed torch quenched in a cold sea, Brett saw the launch tower. Its gray bulk bridged a low cloud layer and the sea. He pointed.

"That's it?"

Scudi leaned forward to peer through the fading light.

"I don't see it," she said, "but by the instruments it's about twenty klicks away."

"We used up some time with Twisp and that Bushka character. What did you think of him?"

"Of your Twisp?"

"No, the other one."

"We have Mermen like that," she hedged.

"You didn't like him, either."

"He's a whiner, maybe a killer," she said. "It's not easy to like someone like that."

"What did you think of his story?" Brett asked.

"I don't know," she said. "What if he did it all on his own and the crew threw him overboard? We can't believe him or disbelieve him on the little we've heard—and all of it from him."

The foil skidded across the edge of a kelp bed, slowing then recovering as its sharp-edged supports cut through the tangled growth.

"I didn't see that kelp," Scudi said. "The light is so bad ... that was clumsy of me!"

"Will it hurt the foil?" Brett asked.

She shook her head. "No, I have hurt the kelp. We will have to come off the foils."

"Hurt the kelp?" Brett was mystified. "How can you hurt a plant?"

"The kelp is not just a plant," she said. "It's in a sensitive stage of development … it's difficult to explain. You'll think me as crazy as Bushka if I tell you all that I know about the kelp."

Scudi reduced the throttle. The hissing roar subsided and the wallowing boat slipped down onto its hull, gently lifting with the heave of the waves. The rams subsided to a low murmur behind them.

"It is more dangerous for us to come in at night," she said. The red instrument lights had come on automatically as the light dimmed outside and she looked at Brett, his face under-lighted by the red illumination.

"Should we wait out here for daylight?" he asked.

"We could submerge and sit on the bottom," she said. "It's only about sixty fathoms."

When Brett did not respond, she said, "You don't prefer it down under, do you?" He shrugged.

"It's too deep to anchor," she said, "but it is safe to drift if we watch. Nothing can harm us in here."

"Dashers?"

"They can't penetrate a foil."

"Then let's shut down and drift. The kelp should keep us stable. I agree with you, I don't think we should go in there at night. We want everybody to see us and know who we are and why we're there."

Scudi shut off the murmuring rams and in the sudden silence they grew aware of the slap of waves against the hull, the faint creaking of the vessel around them.

"How far is it to the base again?" Brett asked. He squinted through the twilight murk toward the tower.

"At least twenty klicks."

Brett, accustomed to judging distance out by the height of Vashon above the horizon, produced a low whistle. "That thing must be pretty high. It's a wonder Islanders haven't spotted it before this."

"I think we control the currents to keep Islands clear of the area."

"Control the currents," he muttered. "Yeah, of course."

Then he asked, "Do you think they've seen us?"

Scudi punched a button on the console and a series of familiar clicks and beeps came from an overhead speaker. He'd heard these sounds from time to time as they skipped across the waves.

"Nothing's tracking us," she said. "It would howl if we were targeted. They might know we're here, though. This just means we're not under observation."

Brett bent over the button Scudi had punched and read the label: "T-BEAM TEST."

"Automatic," she said. "It tells us if we're targeted by a tracking beam."

The foil lurched suddenly counter to a wave. Brett, used to the uncertain footing of Islands and coracles, was first to catch his balance. Scudi clutched his arm to right herself.

"Kelp," Brett said.

"I think so. We had better—" She broke off with a startled gasp, staring past Brett at the rear hatch.

Brett whirled to see a Merman standing there, dripping sea water, green paint striped across his face and dive suit in a grotesque pattern. The man carried a lasgun at the ready. Another Merman stood in the shadowy passage behind him.

Scudi's voice was a dry whisper in Brett's ear: "Gallow. That's Nakano behind him."

Surprise at the stealth that had allowed the Merman to come this close without detection held Brett speechless. He tried to absorb the import of Scudi's rasping whisper. So this was the Merman that Bushka blamed for sinking Guemes! The man was tall and smoothly muscled, and his dive suit clung to him like a second skin. *Why the green pattern on it?* Brett wondered. His eyes could not help focusing on the business end of the lasgun.

The Merman chuckled. "Little Scudi Wang! Now that's what I call luck. We've been having our share of luck lately, eh, Nakano?"

"It wasn't luck saved us when that stupid Islander sank us," Nakano growled.

"Ahhh, yes," Gallow agreed. "Your superior strength broke the bonds that held you. Indeed." He flicked a glance around the cockpit. "Where's the crew? We need your doctor."

Brett, at whom Gallow aimed the question, met Gallow's demanding stare with silence, thinking that the interchange between these two Mermen tended to confirm Bushka's odd story.

"Your doctor!" Gallow insisted.

"We don't have one," Brett said, surprised at the force of his voice.

Gallow, noting the accent, flicked a scornful glance at Scudi.

"Who's the Mute?"

"A—a friend," Scudi said. "Brett Norton."

Gallow looked Brett over in the dim red light, then turned back to Scudi. "He looks almost normal, but he's still a Mute. Your daddy would haunt you!" He spoke over his shoulder. "Have a look, Nakano."

The *slop-slop* of wet footsteps sounded behind Gallow as Nakano turned back down the passage. He reappeared presently and spoke a single word: "Empty."

"Just the two of them," Gallow said. "Out for a little cruise in one of the big boats. How sweet."

"Why do you need a doctor?" Scudi asked.

"Full of questions, aren't we," Gallow said.

"At least we have the foil," the second man said.

"That we have, Nakano," Gallow said.

Nakano pressed past Gallow into the cockpit and Brett got a full view of the man. He was a hulking figure, his upper arms as thick as some human torsos. The scarred face filled Brett with a sense of foreboding.

Gallow strode forward to one of the command seats. He bent to read the instruments. "We watched you coming in," he said. He turned and sent a baleful glare at Scudi. "You were in one big hurry and then you stopped. That's very interesting for someone in an empty foil. What're you doing?"

Scudi looked at Brett, who blushed. Nakano guffawed. "Oh, my," Gallow taunted, "love nests get more elaborate every year. Yes, yes."

"Disgusting." Nakano laughed, and clicked his tongue.

"There's a watch-alert out on this foil, Scudi Wang," Gallow said. His manner sobered too quickly for Brett's comfort. "You stole it. What do you think, Nakano? Looks like the Green Dashers have captured a couple of desperadoes."

Brett looked at the grotesque green dive suits on the two Mermen. Blotches and splashes and lines of green spilled over from their suits into patterns painted on their faces.

"Green Dashers?" Scudi asked.

"We are the Green Dashers," Gallow said. "These suits are the perfect camouflage underwater, particularly around the kelp. And we spend a lot of time in kelp, right Nakano?"

Nakano grunted, then said: "We should've let the kelp finish us. We—"

Gallow silenced him with a flicking gesture. "We secured our outpost with one sub and a handful of men. It'd be a pity to waste such talent in the kelp."

Brett saw that Gallow was one of those types who love to hear themselves talk—more, he was one of those who loved to brag.

"With one little sub and this foil," Gallow said with a sweep of his hand, "we can make sure there's never any more land than we can control. You don't have to be in charge to run the show. Just ruin it for those who do. People will have to come swimming up to me soon enough."

Scudi took a deep, relaxing breath. "Is Kareen one of you?"

Gallow's eyes shifted and almost met Scudi's. "She's … insurance …"

"Safe deposit box," Nakano blurted, and both men laughed in that loud way men have when they crack a crude or cruel joke.

Brett realized from Scudi's deep sigh that she was relieved at Gallow's bragging. Were her doubts about her father's involvement with Gallow finally laid to rest?

"What about the doctor?" Nakano asked.

Darkness had settled over the ocean and the cockpit was illuminated only by the red telltales and instrument lights on the console. A macabre red glow filled the space around the two Mermen. They stood near the control seats, put their heads close together and whispered while Scudi and Brett fidgeted. Brett kept eyeing the hatchway where the Mermen had entered. Was there a chance to escape down there to the main hatch? But Guemes had been destroyed by a sub. These Mermen had not swum here from the Launch Base. Their sub lay nearby, probably directly beneath the foil's hull. And they needed a doctor.

"I think you need us," Brett said.

"Think?" Gallow asked with a patronizing lift of his eyebrows. "Mutes don't think."

"You have an injury, somebody needs a doctor," Brett said. "How do you intend to get help?"

"He's quick for a Mute," Gallow said.

"And you're not strong enough to go in and take a doctor from Launch Base," Brett said. "But you could trade us for a doctor."

"Ryan Wang's daughter could be traded," Gallow said. "You're fishbait."

"If you hurt Brett, I won't cooperate," Scudi said.

"Cooperate?" Gallow snorted. "Who needs cooperation?"

"You do," Brett said.

"Nakano will break you two into small pieces if I give the order," Gallow said. "*That's* cooperation."

Brett went silent, studying the two men in that blood-red light. Why were they delaying? They said they needed a doctor. Twisp had always said you had to look beyond words when dealing with people who postured and bragged. Gallow certainly fitted that description. Nakano seemed to be something else—a dangerous unknown. Twisp liked to probe such people with outrageous questions or statements.

"You don't need just any doctor," Brett said. "You want a particular doctor." Both Mermen focused startled glances on Brett.

"What have we here?" Gallow muttered. The smile he flashed across the dark cabin did not disarm Brett in the least.

Nervous, Brett thought. Keep looking. He knew the Merman fear that Islanders had mutated into telepathy, and played on it.

Nakano said, "Do you think—"

"No!" Gallow warned.

Brett caught a bare flicker of hesitation in Gallow's face, which did not show in the voice. The man had superb control of his voice. It was his tool for manipulation, along with his ready smile.

"That other foil should be along soon," Nakano said.

A particular foil with a particular doctor and a particular cargo, Brett thought. He glanced at Scudi. Her tired face was clear to him in the dim lights of the cockpit.

"You don't need us as a trade, you need us as a diversion," Brett said. He held his fingertips to his temples, repressing an excited smile.

One of Gallow's eyebrows lifted, a dark ripple in the smeared green of the camouflage.

"I don't like this," Nakano said. There was fear in the big man's voice.

"He's thought something out," Gallow said. "That's all. Look at him. Almost normal. Maybe he has a brain after all."

"But he's hit on—"

"Drop it, Nakano!" Gallow kept his attention on Brett. "Why would we need you as a diversion?"

Brett dropped his hands and allowed the smile. "It's pretty simple. You didn't know we were the ones on this boat. It's dark out there and all you saw was a foil. Period."

"Pretty good for a Mute," Gallow said. "Maybe there's hope for you."

"You had to go forward and look at the identification plate on the control console before you realized this was the foil on watch-alert."

Gallow nodded. "Go on."

"You hoped it was another foil, a particular one," Brett said. "The other one will have a Security force aboard. You came in armed and ready for that."

Nakano relaxed, visibly relieved. Obviously, this reasoning had eliminated his fear of telepathy.

"Interesting," Gallow said. "Is there more?"

"So now we're waiting for the other foil," Brett said. "Why else waste time with us? If the Security force jumps aboard to capture Scudi and me, that's your opportunity."

"Opportunity for what?" Gallow's tone said he was enjoying this. Nakano returned to his fidgeting.

"You want someone in particular on that other foil," Brett said. "A doctor. And you want the cargo. Now, you see the opportunity to get not only that but two foils intact. And you would've had to wreck the other foil to stop it because all you have is a sub."

"You know, I might be able to use you," Gallow said. "You want to join up?"

Brett spoke without thinking. "I'd sooner swim in shit."

Gallow's face tightened, his body went rigid. Nakano snickered. Slowly, Gallow's face returned to its political best. But there was a mad light in his eyes, a red reflection that made Brett sorry he'd spoken at all.

Scudi edged away from Brett toward the command seats, moving as though she feared the consequences of his comment.

Nakano moved closer to Gallow and bent to whisper something into the Merman's ear. Even as he whispered, Nakano shot a kick at Scudi's hand, which had moved toward the eject lever between the command seats.

Scudi leaped back with a cry of pain, holding her wrist tight to her chest.

Brett started to step toward Nakano, but the big Merman put up a warning hand. "Easy, kid," he said. "I just stung her. Nothing's broken."

"She was going for the eject lever," Gallow said. There was genuine surprise in his voice. He glared at Scudi. Both men stood on a light seam that divided the forward part of the cabin from the rear.

"It would've cut us to pieces when it blew," Nakano said. "Not nice."

"She's Ryan Wang's daughter, all right," Gallow said.

"Now you see why you need our cooperation," Brett said.

"We need you tied up and gagged," Gallow snarled.

"And what happens when that other foil pulls alongside for a look?" Brett asked. "They'll be very cautious if they don't see us in here. One or two of their Security will come aboard while the others wait in their own boat."

"Are you proposing a deal, Mute?" Gallow asked.

"I am."

"Let's hear it."

"Scudi and I stay inside in plain sight. We act like our foil's disabled. That way, they won't suspect anything."

"And afterward?"

"You deliver us to an outpost where we can get back to our people."

"Sound reasonable, Nakano?" Gallow asked.

Nakano grunted.

"You have a deal, Mute," Gallow said. "You amuse me."

Brett wondered at the insincerity in the man's voice. Didn't he realize his intentions were that transparent? A greased smile couldn't hide a lie forever.

Gallow turned to Nakano. "Go take a look outside. See if everything's secure."

Nakano strode through the rear hatchway and was gone for several minutes while Gallow hummed to himself, nodding. His expression was filled with self-satisfaction. Scudi moved close to Brett, still clutching her wrist.

"Are you all right?" Brett asked.

"Just bruised."

"Nakano's getting soft," Gallow said. "He pulled that kick. He can crush your throat, just like that!" Gallow snapped his fingers to illustrate.

Nakano returned, dripping more water. "We're in kelp and it's holding us pretty steady. The sub's stabilized directly under us and the foil's shadow should hide it until it's too late for them to do anything about it."

"Good," Gallow said. "Now, where do we keep these two until it's time for their performance?" He thought for a moment, then: "We turn the cabin lights on and put them in the open hatchway. They'll be seen right away."

"And we wait beside the hatch," Nakano said. "You kids understand?"

When Brett did not respond, Scudi said, "We understand."

"We'll run forward and turn out the lights," Brett said. "That'll make sure the Security people have to come aboard."

"Good!" Gallow said. "Very good."

He sure likes the sound of his own voice, Brett thought. He took Scudi's arm, careful of her wrist. "Let's get those lights on and go back to the main hatch."

"Nakano, escort our guests back and see that they're in plain sight," Gallow said. He moved to the command console and flipped a series of switches. Lights blazed all over the foil.

Brett suddenly hesitated. *Open hatch?* "Dashers," he said.

Scudi tugged him along toward the corridor into the rear of the foil. "Our chances are just as good with the black variety," she muttered.

Survival is staying alive one breath at a time, Brett thought. That was another of Twisp's sayings. And Brett thought if he and Scudi survived this, Twisp would have to learn how his teaching had helped. It was a way of studying things and reacting truly—something that could not be taught, but could be learned.

"Hurry it up, you two!" Nakano ordered.

They followed him down the long passage to the open hatch, its lip washed in a blaze of light. Brett stared out at a dark flow of kelp-littered waves slapping against the hull.

Nakano said, "You two wait right here. And you better be standing in plain sight when I come back." He sped up the passage.

"What's that guy doing up there in the cockpit?" Brett asked.

"Probably disabling the starting system," Scudi said. "They don't intend to let us go."

"Of course not."

She glanced behind her at the storage locker where Brett had found the survival kits. "If it weren't for the sub under us, I'd take off right now."

"There's nobody in the sub," Brett said. "There's just these two … and maybe one who needs the doctor. That one won't be able to do anything about us."

"How do you know?"

"It was obvious from what they said and the way they're acting. And remember what Bushka said? Three of them."

"Then what're we waiting for?"

"For them to disable the starting mechanism," he said. "We can't have them dashing around in this thing looking for us." He moved to the storage locker and lifted out two more packs, tossing one to Scudi. "Have they had enough time?"

"I … think so."

"I do, too."

Scudi slipped a length of line from an outside pocket on her kit and fixed one end to Brett's belt, the other to her own waist. "We stay together," she said. "Let's go."

Far up the corridor, Gallow's voice suddenly bellowed, "Hey! You two! What're you doing?"

"We're going swimming," Brett shouted. Holding hands, they leaped off into the ocean.

Chapter 28

Without the conscious acknowledgment and acceptance of our kinship with those around us there can be no synthesis of personality.
—C.G. Jung, *Shiprecords*

A GLUT of kelp rasped the coracle's bow in time with the waves. *A touch of reality,* Twisp thought. The otherwise silent blackness yawned before the first hint of dawn. Twisp heard Bushka twisting uncomfortably near the bow cuddy. In the long night since leaving Brett and Scudi, Bushka had not slept well.

Water's very flat tonight, Twisp thought. Only the faintest of breezes cooled his left cheek as the coracles drifted slowly in the encumbering kelp.

Twisp tipped his head to look up at a spattering of cloud-framed stars, picking out the familiar arrowhead shape of the Pointers before the frame shifted to a new section of sky.

Still on course, current favorable.

It was always good to check the compass against the stars. The course angled toward an unmarked place on the sea where they could turn and make a swift run to Vashon. The RDF-RDC announcement of the Island's distant locator-beep had been silenced for the night but a red light blinked near his knee in time with Vashon's signal. His receiver was working.

Dawn would find them still hull-down out of sight of the launch tower but not out of range of the kid and the girl.

Did I do the right thing? Twisp asked himself.

It was a question he had repeated many times, aloud to Bushka and silently to himself. At the moment of decision, it had felt right. But here in the night …

Momentous changes gathered force on their world. And who were they, pitted against the evils he could sense in that change? One overage fisherman with arms too long for anything but hauling nets. One whining intellectual ashamed of his Islander ancestry, maybe capable of wholesale murder. One kid out to make himself a man, a kid who could see in the dark. And a Merman girl who was heir to the entire food monopoly of Pandora. The consequences of Ryan Wang's death had a bad feel.

The squawks began to stir in their cage near Twisp's feet. Faintly at first, then louder, somewhere off to the right in the thicker kelp, Twisp heard a dasher purring. Putting a finger on the stunshield switch, he waited, straining to see something, anything, in the blackness where that ominous purr stroked the still air.

A purring dasher could mean many things: it might be asleep, or well-fed, or responding to the smell of rich food ... or just generally contented with its life.

Twisp slipped a leg over the tiller, prepared to start the motor and steer away from that perilous noise. With his free hand he groped for and found the lasgun in its hiding place behind his seat.

Bushka began to snore.

The dasher's purr stopped, then began once more on a lower note. Had it heard?

Bushka snorted, rolled over and resumed his snoring. The dasher continued to purr, but the sound began to fade, moving farther to the right and behind the drifting coracles.

Asleep, Twisp hoped. *Trust my squawks.* The birds had not stirred again.

The dasher's contentment faded away in the distance. Twisp listened for movement there, straining to hear over the sound of Bushka's fatigue. Slowly, Twisp forced himself to relax, realizing that he had been holding his breath. He exhaled, then inhaled a deep breath of the sweet night air. A dry swallow rasped the back of his throat.

Although he could not hear the dasher, tension still rode him. Abruptly, the squawks came full awake and began living up to their name. Twisp flipped the stunshield switch. There came the unmistakable splash of something stiffening in the water close behind, then the frenzied whines and chuckles of dashers feeding.

Filthy cannibals, he thought.

"Whuzzat?" Bushka demanded.

The coracle shifted as Bushka sat up.

"Dashers," Twisp said. He aimed the lasgun toward the feeding sounds and fired six quick bursts. The buzzing vibration of the weapon was hard against his sweaty hand. The thin purple beams lanced into the night. At the second shot, the dashers erupted in a frantic cacophony of yelps and screeches. The sounds receded rapidly. Dashers had learned to turn tail at the buzzing, purple shaft of a lasgun.

Twisp turned off the stunshield and reached for his handlight as another sound far off to his left caught his attention: the *hiss-hiss-hiss* of paddles cutting through wet kelp. He aimed the handlight toward the sound but the night sucked it dry without sending anything back but the sea's pulse in dark strands of kelp.

A voice called from the distance: "Coracle! Do you have a load?"

Twisp felt his heart triple-time against his rib cage. That was Brett's voice!

"Riding too high!" he shouted, waving the handlight as a locator. "Careful, there's dashers about!"

"We saw your lasgun."

Twisp could make them out then, an amoebalike blot undulating toward him on the low seas. Two paddles flashed bits of his light back at him.

Bushka leaned against the thwart, tipping it precariously near the water. "Trim the boat!" Twisp called. "You, Bushka!"

Bushka jerked back but kept his attention on the approaching shape. The paddles struck the water with splashes that burst like blossoms against the black hull of an inflatable raft.

"It's them," Bushka said. "They've blown it, just like I warned you."

"Shut up," Twisp growled. "At least they're alive." He took a deep breath of thanksgiving. The kid had become family and the family was whole again.

"Mother, I'm home!" the kid called, as though reading his thoughts.

So, Brett was sufficiently lighthearted that he could joke. Things could not be too bad, then. Twisp listened for dashers.

Bushka laughed at the quip, a laugh with a dry, cracked edge that set Twisp's anger near the boiling point. The raft was in easy talking distance now. Twisp kept the handlight pointed toward the approaching figures and away from his own face, where tears of fatigue and relief wet his cheeks. At a low word from Brett, both he and Scudi stopped paddling. Brett threw a line to the coracle. Twisp caught it and hauled in the raft like a net of muree, snugging it against the coracle. One long arm snaked out and grabbed Brett. The kid's dive suit was soaked and inflated.

The squawks took that moment to set up a warning commotion, but it subsided immediately. Dashers patrolled just out of sight, wary of the lasgun. *A sizable hunt of them,* Twisp thought. Hunger drove them in and fear kept them away.

Scudi said, "Should we come aboard?"

"Yes," Twisp said, and heaved Brett aboard, then helped Scudi gently over the gunwale and onto the seat-slat in front of him. He secured the line to keep the raft tight against the boat, then stowed the handlight under his seat. Twisp put a hand on Brett's arm, keeping it there, unwilling to break off the reassuring touch.

"They wouldn't listen to you, would they?" Bushka demanded. "You had to run for it again. What happened to your foil?"

"Do we run for Vashon?" Twisp asked.

Brett held both hands up to slow them down. "I think we'd better discuss it," he said. He recounted the story of Gallow and Nakano as briefly as he could. It was a bare-bones account, which Twisp heard with a growing admiration for Brett.

A good head there, he thought.

When Brett had finished, Bushka said, "Let's get away from here! Those are devils, not men. They probably followed you and when they come—"

"Oh, shut up!" Twisp snapped. "If you don't, I'll shut you up." He turned to Brett and asked, in a calmer voice, "What do you think? They have two foils now and could hunt us down with—"

"They're not going to hunt for us, not yet," Brett said. "They have other fish to fry."

"You're a fool!" Bushka blurted.

"Hear him out," Scudi said. Her voice was as flat and solid as plasteel.

"They said they were waiting to capture a doctor," Brett continued, "probably true, from the way they acted. It looked like they tried something and failed. They were shook up and trying to hide it from us. A lot of bragging."

"That's Gallow," Bushka muttered.

"So what were they doing besides waiting to get a doctor?" Twisp asked.

"They were near the Launch Base," Brett said. "With Gallow, I suspect nothing is coincidence. My guess is they want those hyb tanks."

"Of course they do," Bushka said. "I told you that."

"He wants them real bad," Brett said. He nodded to himself. The hyb tanks circling up there in space were the single most speculative subject on Pandora. Guessing the manifests of the hyb tanks ranked right up there with the weather as a conversational staple.

"But what about this threat that he'll prevent the Mermen from reclaiming more open land?" Twisp asked. "Could he do that with one sub and a couple of foils?"

"I think Vashon's in danger," Brett said. "Guemes was much smaller, but still … sinking Islands is just too simple a diversion for somebody like Gallow to resist. About the time those tanks come down, he'll try to sink Vashon. I'm sure of it."

"Did he say anything specific?" Twisp asked. "Could he have found a real hyb tank manifest?"

Brett shook his head. "I don't know. Something that big … he'd have to brag about it. Bushka, he ever say anything to you about what's up there?"

"Gallow has … dreams of grandeur," Bushka said. "Anything that'll feed those dreams is real to him. He never claimed to know what was in the tanks; he just knew the political value of having them."

"Brett's right about Gallow," Scudi said.

Twisp could make out the dark flash of her eyes in the growing light. "Gallow's like a lot of Mermen—they believe the hyb tanks will save the world, destroy the world, make you rich or curse you forever."

"Same with Islanders," Brett said.

"Speculation, but no facts," Twisp said.

Scudi looked from Brett to Twisp and back to Brett. How like Twisp Brett sounded! Laconic, practical—all based on rocklike integrity. She studied Brett more carefully then, seeing the stringy strength in his young body. She sensed the power of the adult he would become. Brett was already a man. Young, but solid inside. It came over her like a quick-dive narcosis that she wanted him for a lifetime.

Twisp turned to the controls, started up the motor and set a course for Vashon. The coracle surged across the kelp into open water.

Scudi glanced around the brightening day. She scratched under the neck seal of her dive suit, and, with an impatient gesture, shucked out of the suit and spread it across the thwarts to dry. She did this after one smiling glance at Brett, who smiled back.

Twisp glanced once at her, noting the vestigial webs between her toes, but otherwise an ideal, Merman-normal body. He hadn't seen that many up close.

He forced himself to look away, but noticed that Bushka, too, could not help staring at Scudi. She worked close beside Bushka, turning the dive suit and fluffing it as the wind blew it dry. Twisp watched Bushka's eyes flick up from the water, over Twisp at the stern, up and down Scudi's body, back to the water.

Twisp had long believed that Mermen didn't have the same drives as Islanders, and he related it to the free display of their perfect bodies. Scudi's display bore that out in his mind. Mermen lived so much of their lives either without clothes or in skin-clinging dive suits that they would have to develop different feelings about the body than the bulky-clothed Islanders.

Not much difference between nudity and a dive suit, Twisp thought. He could see that Bushka was bothered by Scudi's proximity and her nudity. Brett was doing what any normal Islander might—giving Scudi the privacy of not looking at her. Scudi, however, was not able to keep her eyes off Brett.

Something going on there, Twisp decided. *Something strong.* He reminded himself that Mermen sometimes married Islanders, and sometimes it worked out.

Bushka shifted his attention from Scudi to Brett and the look on Bushka's face was like a shouted statement to Twisp. It was the kid's eyes.

Not as normal as I am! That was the look on Bushka's face.

Twisp remembered seeing a long-armed Islander once holding hands with a long-armed woman—the first time he'd seen two of them in one place. It had taken Twisp a long time to dig out his personal rejection of that scene and with his digging had come a valuable insight.

Like me. That's how we define human.

He had traced that thought down its dark trail and come up with his own reason for judging that couple.

Jealousy.

He had only chosen women who were different from himself. Chances of passing along a specific trait to children got too high when similar mutants paired. Sometimes it was a genetic time-bomb that didn't show for one or two generations.

Most of us aren't willing to pass along anything except hope.

Something similar was going on in Bushka.

He doesn't like Brett, Twisp thought. *He doesn't know it yet. When he figures it out he won't know why. He won't want to admit it's jealousy and it wouldn't do much good to tell him.*

It was obvious to anyone who looked at her when she studied Brett that Scudi had eyes only for the kid.

Brett had found the larder and quick-heated some fish stew. Without looking at Scudi, he said, "Scudi, something to eat?"

Scudi, her dive suit aired out sufficiently, slipped it back over her lithe young body. She finished closing the seals. "Yes, please, Brett," she said. "I'm very hungry."

Brett passed her a filled bowl and looked a question at Twisp, who shook his head. Bushka accepted a bowl from Brett after a slight hesitation that spoke loudly to Twisp.

Doesn't want to owe the kid anything!

Brett had been brought up on Islander courtesy over food and so had Bushka. The early training dominated. Brett completed the usual ritual before filling his own bowl. A dasher couldn't have gobbled it faster. Presently, Brett held his bowl over the side, cleaned it and put it away. He looked up at Twisp.

"Thanks," he said.

"For what?" Twisp asked, surprised. The food belonged to all of them.

"For teaching me how to pay attention, and how to think."

"Did I do that?" Twisp asked. "I thought people were born knowing how to think."

Bushka heard this exchange with an ill-concealed sneer. He sat brooding. The news about Gallow and his crew—*Green Dashers! In striking range!* The proximity of the Gallow-Nakano-Zent trio filled Bushka with terror. They were sure to come looking for the fugitives. Why wouldn't they? Ryan Wang's daughter was here, for Ship's sake! What a hostage! He thought then about Zent, those glossy, unfeeling eyes with their deep-down delight at pain. Bushka wondered how these two young people had outsmarted the likes of them, although Gallow was prone to underestimate his opposition. Bushka looked straight at Scudi. *Ship! What a body!* Whoever owned her owned the world, and he knew that was no exaggeration. There could be little doubt that her father had controlled much of Pandora through his food operations, and now that he was dead it would surely pass to Scudi. Bushka half-closed his eyes and studied the young couple beside him.

Gallow must've thought them a couple of scared kids.

Bushka had learned the danger of assumptions while he'd been boat-bound with Twisp. Scudi obviously had a first-love crush on the kid ... but that would pass. It always did. Her father's minions were still alive. They would put a stop to it once they found out. Once they took a good look at the kid's mutated eyes.

Twisp stood up at the tiller and peered ahead, shading his eyes against the rising ball of sun. "Foil," he said. "It's heading for Vashon."

"I told you!" Bushka shouted.

"Looked like an orange stripe along the cabin top," Twisp said. "Official."

"They're looking for us," Bushka said. His teeth began to chatter.

"Not changing course," Twisp said. "They're in a real hurry." He reached down and flipped the switch on his emergency-band radio receiver.

The sound of the Vashon announcer came on in midsentence: " ... who there was no immediate further threat to Vashon's substructure. We are hanging bottom on a kelp margin of enormous dimensions. There is exposed land and surf immediately to the east of us. Fishermen are advised to approach us through the clear water from the southwest. We repeat: All down-center areas are being evacuated because of grounding. Vashon itself is in no immediate danger as long as the calm weather holds. Repairs are proceeding and Merman help has been assured. Hourly bulletins will be provided and you are advised to keep tuned to the emergency band."

Scudi shook her head and whispered, "Current Control wasn't supposed to let something like that happen."

"Sabotage," Bushka said. "It's Gallow's doing. I know it."

"Exposed land," Twisp muttered. The big change was happening. He could feel it.

Chapter 29

Down the course of history, people have been the principal cause of human deaths. It is possible to alter that course here on Pandora.
—Kerro Panille, *The Histories*

WARD KEEL'S head throbbed in time to his heartbeat. He opened his eyes a crack but shut them quickly against the painful stab of white light. A demanding interior whine filled his ears, blotting out the world around him. He tried to lift his head but failed. His neck support had been removed. He tried to remember if he had removed it. Nothing came to him. He knew there should be things to remember but his throbbing head took most of his attention. Again, he tried to lift his head and gained only a few millimeters. The back of his head thumped onto a hard, flat surface. Nausea gripped his throat. Keel gulped quick lungfuls of air to keep from vomiting. The air tasted thick and humid and did not help much.

Where in the name of Ship am I?

Bits of memories flickered into his mind. Ale. And someone … that Shadow Panille. He remembered now. There had been an argument between Ale and someone in Merman Mercantile—the late Ryan Wang's operation. She had ended it by removing Keel to … to … He could not remember. But they had left Ale's complex. That much he recalled.

Thick air all around him now … down-under air. Slowly, he tried opening his left eye. A dark shape loomed over him, haloed by a pair of bright ceiling lights.

"He's coming around."

A smooth, unhurried voice, conversational. The piercing whine in Keel's ears began to wind down. He tried opening both eyes wider. Slowly, a face came into focus above him: crisscrossed scars on the cheeks and brow, a twisted mouth. The face turned away like a receding nightmare and Keel saw streaks of green smeared up to the neck below those awful scars.

"Don't fuss over him, Nakano. He'll keep."

That was a voice edged in ice.

The scarred face regarded Keel once more—two deeply set eyes with something far back in there that refused to emerge. *Nakano?* Keel felt that the name and the scarred face should ignite an important memory. *Blank.*

"He's no good to us dead," Nakano said. "And you hit him pretty hard with that stuff. Hand me some water."

"Get it yourself. I don't tote for Mutes."

Nakano removed himself from Keel's view, returning in a moment to bend closer with a beaker and a straw. A hand striped with green paint put the straw between Keel's lips.

"Drink it," Nakano said. "I think it'll help."

Hit him pretty hard? Keel remembered someone shouting … Kareen Ale screaming at … at …

"It's just water," Nakano said. He moved the straw against Keel's lips.

Keel sucked in cold water and felt the soothing splash of it into his cramping stomach. He told himself that he should reach for the beaker but his hands refused to cooperate.

Straps!

Keel felt them over his chest and arms. He was being restrained, then. *Why?* He took another deep drink of the water and pushed the straw from his mouth with his tongue.

Nakano removed the beaker and released the restraints.

Keel flexed his fingers and tried to say "thanks," but the word was no more than a dry whistle in his throat.

Nakano placed something on Keel's chest and Keel felt the familiar outlines of his neck appliance.

"Took it off when you puked and damn near choked to death," Nakano said. "Couldn't figure how to get it back on you."

Keel felt weak but his fingers knew this familiar thing. He fumbled over the slips and catches, putting the support into place around his neck. Two raw spots pained him where the braces met his shoulders. Someone had tried to pull it off without unfastening it.

Lucky they didn't break my neck.

With the support in place, Keel's thick shoulder muscles carried the burden of lifting his head upright. The brace slipped into its usual position and he winced at the pain. He saw that he was in a small rectangular room with gray metal walls.

"Do you have a celltape?" he asked. His voice echoed in his ears and sounded much deeper than he remembered. Keel rested his forehead in his hands and listened as someone rummaged through a case. The table that Keel sat on was much lower than he had imagined. It wasn't a gurney, but a low dining table, Merman-style, within a cluster of low padded chairs and a couch. Everything seemed constructed out of old, dead materials.

Nakano handed him a roll of celltape and, as if in answer to an unasked question, said, "We put you on the table because you weren't breathing good. The couch is too soft."

"Thanks."

Nakano grunted and sat back down in a chair behind Keel.

Keel noticed that the room was filled with books and tapes. Some of the bookshelves were packed two deep with well-worn texts of many sizes. Keel turned his head and saw behind Nakano an elaborate comconsole with three viewscreens and racks of tapes. The room felt as though it moved—back and forth, up and down. It was an unsettling sensation, even for one accustomed to riding the waves on an Island.

Keel heard a distant hissing. Nakano stood at his side then and another man, his dive suit smeared with green paint, sat nearby, his back to them. The other man appeared to be eating.

Keel thought about eating. His stomach said, "Forget it."

My medication! he thought. *Where is my case?* He felt his breast pocket. The little case was gone. It came over him then that this rectangular space around him actually was moving—rising and falling on a long sea.

We're still on the foil, he thought. The thick air was a Merman preference. These two Mermen had merely done something to humidify the air.

Still on the foil!

He remembered more now. Kareen Ale had taken him aboard a foil to … to go to the Launch Base. Then he remembered the other foil. Memories came rushing at him. It had been after nightfall. He could see daylight now through louvered vents high in the walls of this room: the double yellow-orange of both suns low in the sky. *Morning or evening?* His body could not inform him. He felt the borderline nausea of movement, the constant inner pain of his fatal illness and the headache, now localized in his right temple where, he knew, he had been struck.

Drugged, too, he thought.

The attack had occurred after the foil in which Ale had been taking him to the Launch Base slowed abruptly. A voice had called: "Look there!"

Another foil had bobbed dead in the water with only its anchor lights glowing through the darkness. It drifted slowly in heavy kelp and was not at anchor. A spotlight from Ale's foil illuminated the identification numbers on the bow of the vessel.

"It's them, all right," she said.

"Do you think they're in trouble?"

"You bet they're in trouble!"

"I mean something wrong with—"

"They're waiting out the night on the kelp. It hides them from bottom search and they won't drift far in it."

"But why do you suppose they're here … I mean, so close to Launch Base?"

"Let's find out."

Slowly, its jets muted, Ale's foil moved up on the other craft while four Security men readied themselves for boarding from the water.

Keel and Ale on the forward pilot's deck had a commanding view of what happened next. With only a few meters separating the two craft, four dive-suited men slipped into the water, swam the short distance and opened the main hatch on the other foil. One by one, they crept inside and then … nothing.

Silence, for what seemed to Keel an interminable time. It ended with a jerky rocking action on Ale's foil followed by shouts from the stern. Abruptly, two green-striped apparitions burst into the pilot's compartment. One of the intruders had been a monstrous Merman with terrible scars on his face. Keel had never seen arms that thickly muscled. Both men carried weapons. There was only time to hear Ale shout: "GeLaar!" Then the blinding pain on his own head.

GeLaar? Keel prolonged his recovery period from the blow, making it appear he was still dazed. His encyclopedic memory pored over names and physical identifications. *GeLaar Gallow, idealized Merman. Former subordinate of Ryan Wang. Suitor to Kareen Ale.* The man at the table pushed a bowl away from him, wiped his mouth and turned.

Keel looked at him, shuddering in the cold appraising stare of those dark blue eyes.

Yes, this is the man himself. Keel thought Gallow grotesque in the cover of green paint.

A hatch to Keel's right opened and another green-striped Merman entered. "Bad news," the newcomer said. "Zent just died."

"Damn!" That was Gallow. "She didn't really try to save him, did she!"

"He was badly crushed," the newcomer said. "And she is exhausted."

"If only we knew what caused it," Gallow mumbled.

"Whatever it was," Nakano said, "it was the same thing that damaged the sub. The wonder is he got back to us at all."

"Don't be stupid," Gallow snapped. "The sub's homing system brought him back. He didn't have anything to do with it."

"Except to activate the system," Nakano said.

Gallow ignored him, turning to the newcomer. "Well, how are the repairs going?"

"Very well," the man said. "We got the replacement parts and tools aboard the Launch Base foil marked as rocket supplies. We should be fully operational by this time day after tomorrow."

"Too bad we can't replace Tso as easily," Nakano said. "He's a good man in a fight. Was."

"Yes." Gallow spoke without looking at Nakano, gesturing instead to the newcomer. "Well, get back to your station."

The man hesitated. "What about Zent?" he asked.

"What?"

"His body."

"Green Dashers are kelp food when they die," Gallow said. "You know that. It's imperative if we're to know what happened out there."

"Yes sir." The man left, closing the hatch quietly after him.

Keel brushed at his collar and the front of his jacket. He could smell the sour taint of vomit there, confirming Nakano's account of what had happened.

So, they want me alive. No … they need me alive.

As long as he was alive, Keel could probe for weaknesses. Superstition was a weakness. He vowed to pursue this curious burial ritual that Gallow employed. Its very mention had brought a hush over the cabin. They were fanatics. Keel could see it in Gallow's expression. Anything was justified by the sacred nature of their goal. Another matter for probing. Very dangerous. *But … I'm dying anyway. Let's see how deep their need for me actually is.*

"A small case was taken from my pocket," he said. "It contains my medication."

"So, the Mute needs medication," Gallow taunted. "Let's see how he does without it."

"You'll see quite soon," Keel said. "You'll have another body to feed to the kelp."

Keel swung his feet casually over the edge of the table and felt for the deck. A startled look passed between Nakano and Gallow. Keel wondered at it. There was shock in that look. Some nerve had been struck.

"You know about the kelp?" Nakano asked.

Keel said, "Of course. A man in my position …" He waved off the rest of the bluff as extraneous.

"We need him alive for the time being," Gallow said. "Get the Mute his medication."

Nakano went to a small storage locker in the rear wall and removed a pocket case of cured organics—dark brown and with a tie string closure.

Keel accepted the case thankfully, found a bitter green pill in it and gulped the pill dry. His intestines felt knotted and it would be long minutes before the pill brought relief, but just the knowledge that he had taken it removed some of the discomfort. Another remora, that was what he needed. But what was the use even of that? His rebellious body would only make short work of another remora. Shorter than the last, and the one before that. His first one had lasted thirty-six years. This last one, a month.

"You can always tell," Nakano said. "Someone who isn't bothered by dying, that one knows about the kelp."

With difficulty, Keel kept his face expressionless. *What was the man saying?*

"It wasn't something we could keep secret forever," Gallow said. "They contact the kelp, too."

Nakano looked piercingly at Keel. It was one of those looks that made a big man like Nakano swell even bigger. "How many of you know?" he asked.

Keel managed a noncommittal shrug, which irritated the seating of his brace.

"We'd have heard something before this if it was out," Gallow said. "Probably just a few of the top Mutes like this one know anything."

Keel stared speculatively from one Merman to the other. Something important to know about the kelp. What could that be? It had to do with dying. With contact with the kelp. Feeding their dead to the kelp?

"In a little while we'll go out and try to hear Zent's memories," Gallow said, a new and deeply reflective tone in his voice. "Then we may learn what happened to him."

Nakano, his voice more matter-of-fact, asked Keel: "How do you contact the kelp? Does the kelp answer every time?"

Keel pursed his lips in thought, delaying his response and gaining time. *Talk to the kelp?* He recalled what Ale and Panille had said about the Merman kelp project—teaching the kelp, assisting the spread of it under Pandora's universal sea.

"We have to actually touch the kelp," Nakano prompted.

"Of course," Keel snorted. And he thought, *Hear Zent's memories?* What was going on here? These violent men were suddenly revealing a mystical side that astonished the pragmatic Keel.

Gallow suddenly laughed. "You don't know any more about it than we do, Mute! The kelp takes your memories, even after you're dead. That's all any of us knows, but you Mutes didn't think about what that could mean."

Green Dashers are kelp food when they die, Keel thought. *And somehow their memories can be read by the living—through the kelp.* He recalled the odd stories out of human history on Pandora—dashers talking with human voices, a fully sentient kelp speaking to the minds of those who touched it. So it was true! And the kelp, genetically rebuilt from the genes carried in a few humans, was recovering that old skill. Did Ale know? And where was she?

Gallow glanced around the room and returned his attention to Keel. "Very pleasant, this cabin," he said. "Ryan Wang's gift to Kareen Ale—her personal foil. I think I'll keep it for my command center."

"Where is Kareen?" Keel asked.

"She's busy being a doctor," Gallow said. "Something she should stick to. Politics doesn't suit her. Maybe medicine doesn't, either. She didn't do much for Zent."

"Nobody could've saved Tso," Nakano said. "I want to know what got him. Does Vashon have a new defense weapon?" Nakano glared at Keel. "What about it, Mr. Justice?"

"What're you talking about? Defense against what?"

Gallow stepped closer. "Tso and two of our new recruits were given the simple task of sinking Vashon," Gallow said. "Tso returned dying and in a damaged sub. The two recruits were not with him."

Keel was a moment finding his voice, then: "You're monsters. You would scuttle thousands and thousands of lives—"

"What happened to our sub?" Gallow demanded. "The whole forward section—it looked as though it had been crushed by a fist."

"Vashon?" Keel whispered.

"Oh, it's still there," Gallow said. "Do I have to tell Nakano he must be more persuasive? Answer the question."

Keel drew in a deep, trembling breath and exhaled slowly. Here was why they kept him alive! Whatever had happened to the sub, he had no answer, but there was something he could do. *Forward section crushed?*

"So it worked," Keel said.

Both men glared at him. "What worked?" Gallow barked.

"Our cable trap," Keel bluffed.

"I thought so!" Nakano said.

"Tell us about this device," Gallow ordered.

"I'm no technic or engineer," Keel protested. He put a hand up. "I don't know how it's made."

"But you can tell us what you do know," Gallow said. "Or I will direct Nakano to cause you a great deal of pain."

Keel looked at Nakano's massive arms, those bulging muscles, the bull neck. None of that frightened him, and he knew that Nakano knew it. The reference to death earlier, it was a bond between them.

"All I know is it's organic and it works by compression," Keel said.

"Organic? Our sub has cutters and burners!" Gallow clearly did not believe him.

"It's like a net," Keel said, warming to his fiction. "Each surviving part can behave like the whole. And once it's inside your defenses where your cutters and burners can't reach it …" Keel shrugged.

"Why would you make such a thing?" Gallow asked.

"Our Security people determined that we were hopelessly vulnerable to attack from below. Something had to be done. And we were right. Look what happened to Guemes. What almost happened to Vashon."

"Yes, look what happened to Guemes," Gallow said, smiling.

Monsters, Keel thought.

"Tso must've done some damage," Nakano said. "That's why Vashon's grounded."

Keel tried to speak past a pain in his throat. "Grounded?" His voice was a croak.

"On the bottom and abandoning its downcenter," Gallow said, showing obvious relish in his words. He reached out and tapped Nakano's arm. "Keep our guest company. I will go out and prepare to commune with Tso's kelp-spirit. See if the Mute here can tell us any way to improve our contact with the kelp."

Keel took a deep breath. His improvisation about a Vashon defense weapon had been accepted. It would make these monsters more cautious. It would give Vashon a breathing space—if the Island survived grounding. He took heart from the fact that Vashon had survived groundings in the distant past. There would be damage, though, and economic losses. Ballast pumps would be working frantically to lift and compress the bottom sections of the Island. Heavy equipment would be detached in its own floaters. Mermen would be called in for assistance.

Mermen! Would friends of these vermin be among those summoned for help? It could take days for Vashon to lift its enormous bulk and refloat. If no storm or wavewall came …

I have to escape, Keel thought. *My people have to know what I've learned. They need me.*

Gallow had moved to the hatch, looking back thoughtfully at Nakano and the captive. He opened the hatch and stood there a moment, then: "Nakano, he has not given us every detail of their weapon. He has not told us how he communes with the kelp. There are things of value in his head. If he does not reveal them willingly, we will have to feed him to the kelp and hope to recover the information that way."

Nakano nodded, not looking at Gallow.

Gallow let himself out and sealed the hatch behind him.

"I can't protect you from him if he gets angry, Mr. Justice," Nakano said. His voice was casual, even friendly. "You had better sit down and tell me what you know. Would you like some more water? Sorry we don't have any boo, that would make things easier—more civilized."

Keel moved painfully to the table where Gallow had sat and dropped into the chair. It was still warm.

What a strange pair, he thought.

Nakano brought him a beaker of water. Keel sipped slowly, savoring the coolness.

It was almost as though these two exchanged personalities. Keel realized then that Nakano and Gallow were playing the old Security game with him—one guard always browbeat a prisoner while the other came on as a friend, sometimes pretending to protect the prisoner from the attacker.

"Tell me about the weapon," Nakano said.

"The ropes are thicker than full-grown kelp," Keel said. And he recalled underwater views of the kelp—strands thicker than a human torso swaying in the currents.

"A burner would still cut them," Nakano said.

"Ah, but the fibers have some way of reattaching to each other when they touch. Cut it apart and put the cut ends together, it's as though there were not cut."

Nakano grimaced. "How? How is it done?"

"I don't know. They talk about fibrous hooks."

"Now you understand," Nakano said, "why Mutes must go."

"What have we done except protect ourselves?" Keel demanded. "If that sub hadn't been out to sink the Island, it wouldn't have been harmed." Even as he spoke he wondered again about the damaged sub, wishing he could see and examine it. What had really done it? Crushed? Truly crushed or damaged by the bottom?

"Tell me how you commune with kelp," Nakano said.

"We ... just touch it."

"And?"

Keel swallowed. He remembered the old stories, the remnant history, especially the accounts by Shadow Panille's ancestor.

"It's like daydreaming ... almost," Keel said. "You hear voices."

That much the old accounts had said.

"Specific voices?" Nakano demanded.

"Sometimes," Keel lied.

"How do you contact the specific dead and gain access to what they knew when alive?"

Keel shrugged, thinking hard. His mind had never worked this fast, absorbing, correlating. *Ship! What a discovery!* He thought about the countless Islander dead consigned to the sea by mourning relatives. How many of those had been absorbed by the kelp?

"So the kelp doesn't respond to you any better than it does to us," Nakano said.

"I fear not," Keel agreed.

"Kelp has a mind of its own," Nakano said. "I've said that all along."

Keel thought then about the enormous undersea gardens of kelp, forests of gigantic, ropy strands reaching upward toward the suns. He had seen holos of Mermen swimming through those green forests, flashing silvery figures among the fish and fronds. But no Merman had ever before reported kelp responding in the way it had done for the first humans on Pandora. This must mean full sentience was returning. It must be an avalanche of consciousness sweeping through the sea! Mermen thought they controlled the kelp and, through this, controlled the currents.

What if ...

Keel felt his heartbeat stutter.

A Merman sub had been crushed. He imagined those gigantic strands of kelp wrapped around the sub's hard surface. Cutters and burners flashed in his imagination. And the kelp writhed, sending out its messages of self-protection. What if the kelp had learned to kill?

"Where are we right now?" Keel asked.

"Near the Launch Base. There's no harm in your knowing; you can't escape."

Keel let his body feel the lift and fall of the craft around him. The light through the louvered vents had begun to dim. *Nightfall?* The foil rode on extremely calm seas, for which he was thankful. Vashon needed calm seas just now.

Near the Launch Base, Nakano says. *How near?* But even a short swim was impossible for this old body with its head supported on a prosthetic brace.

He was a cripple in this environment. A Mute. No wonder these monsters sneered at him.

The foil's motion became even steadier and the light dimmer. Nakano flipped a switch, bringing soft yellow illumination into the room from lamps near the ceiling.

"We are going down to commune with the kelp," Nakano said. "We are in old kelp here, the kind that's most apt to respond to us."

Keel thought about this craft sinking into a forest of kelp. Whatever had happened to Tso the kelp now knew. How would the kelp use that knowledge?

I know what I would do with such people in my power, Keel thought. *I'd squash them. They are lethal deviants.*

Chapter 30

If the doors of perception were cleansed, everything would appear to man as it is, infinite. For man has closed himself up, till he sees all things through narrow chinks of his cavern.

—William Blake, *Shiprecords*

TWISP CONSIDERED abandoning the tow coracle with its supplies. A second foil had passed nearby without slowing down and he was worried.

We could pick up a few more knots that way, he thought. It galled him that the foils, already lost below the horizon, would be at Vashon by nightfall. The first one probably was arriving right now. He had to plod along in this damned creeping coracle!

He laughed at his own frustration. It relaxed him to laugh, even if it was just his usual short bark. Vashon might be aground, but the Island had touched bottom before, and in perilously more dangerous weather. Pandora had subsided into a calmer phase; his fisherman's instincts felt this. It had to do with the looping interrelationship of the two suns, distance from primaries and, just possibly, the kelp. Perhaps the kelp had finally reached an influential population density. Certainly, kelp fronds were more evident on the surface and the kelp's nursery effect showed itself in the recent fish population boom.

Winters on the open sea were easier every year. The familiar drone of the little engine, the balmy warmth under scattered clouds and the coracle's rhythmic wallow toward Vashon reminded Twisp that he would get there in his own good time.

And when I do, I'll straighten out this Bushka's story.

Vashon was not a community to take lightly. There was influence there, power and money.

And Vata, he thought. *Yes, we have Vata.* Twisp began to see the presence of Vata on his home Island in a new light. She was more than a link with humanity's Pandoran past. Living evidence that a myth had substance—that was what Vata and her satellite Duque represented.

"That last foil must've seen us," Bushka said. "Our position is known."

"You really think they'll alert your Green Dashers?" Twisp asked.

"Gallow has friends in high places," Bushka growled. He glanced significantly at Scudi, who was sitting back against a thwart, looking at Brett with a quizzical expression. Brett lay curled up, asleep.

"We don't know what they're saying on the radio," Bushka said. He looked at the device near Twisp's knee. When Twisp didn't respond, Bushka closed his eyes.

Scudi, shifting her attention from one Islander to the other during this exchange, watched a deep listlessness come over Bushka. The man gave up so easily! What a contrast with Brett.

Scudi thought hard about the escape from Gallow, paddling and sailing, homing on the locator beam from the coracle's transmitter. They had inflated only one of the small rafts from the survival kits, holding the other in reserve. Even this they had delayed until they were more than a kilometer from the foil.

It had been heavy going at first in the thick glut of kelp. The two of them, linked by a single belt line, tended to tangle in the surface fronds. Scudi had led the first stage of their flight, holding them hydrostatically balanced with their dive suit controls just under the surface. When they came up for air it was always beneath a cover of kelp and each time they expected to hear sounds of search and pursuit.

Once, they heard the foil start up, but it shut down immediately. Under the protective cover of a kelp frond, Brett whispered to Scudi: "They don't dare chase after us right now. Capturing that other foil is too important to them."

"The doctor?"

"Something more important than that, I think."

"What?"

"I don't know," Brett whispered. "Let's keep going. We have to be out of sight of them by daybreak."

"I keep worrying that we'll run into dashers."

"I'm keeping a grenade handy. They like to sleep in the kelp. We'll have to dive for it if we surprise one."

"I wish I could see better." Brett took her hand and they moved through the water as silently as possible.

As they brushed through the thick fronds in their maddeningly slow passage, an odd sense of calm came over both of them. They began to feel almost invulnerable to dashers—any variety, green or black. Under the water, touching the kelp, they moved to deep and stately music, something not quite heard but recognized. When they surfaced for air, the world became different, another reality. The air felt clean and satisfying.

Breaking through a profound shyness, they told each other about this feeling. They both imagined telling the other and the telling came out just as they had imagined. They thought they could go on forever this way, that nothing could harm them.

At one break for air, Brett could no longer contain the sense of an alien experience. He put his mouth close to Scudi's ear. "Something's happening down there."

Both of them had grown up on stories of the old kelp days, the mystical detritus of their history, and each suspected what the other was thinking now. Neither of them found it easy to put into words.

Scudi looked back at the foil, which lay in a low outline under its anchor lights. It still seemed much too close. The foil itself appeared so innocent, its hatch a wink against the night.

"You hear me, Scudi?" Brett whispered. "Something's happening to us when we're under water." When she remained silent he said, "They say when you're under water sometimes it's like a narcotic."

Scudi knew what he meant. Cold and the deeps could do things to your body that you did not notice until your mind started to come apart at the dreams. But this was no depth narcosis. And the dive suits kept them warm. This was something else and, here on the surface, knowing they should not delay long, she felt suddenly terrified.

"I'm scared," she whispered, staring at the foil.

"We'll get away from them," Brett said, seeing the direction of her gaze. "See? They're not chasing after us."

"They have a sub."

"The sub couldn't go fast in kelp. They'd have to cut their way through." He pulled himself closer to her along their belt line. "But that's not what's scaring you."

Scudi didn't say anything, she floated on her back under a swatch of kelp, conscious of a heavy iodine smell from the leaves. The weight of the kelp frond on her head was like an old, kindly hand. She knew they should be going. Daylight must not find them in sight of the foil. Her hand on the concealing kelp, she turned and a bit of the kelp came away in her grip. Immediately, she was thrust into the euphoria she had felt underwater. There was wind all around. A sea bird she had never seen shrieked somewhere in perfect time with the waves. The hypnotic effect unfocused her eyes, then centered them on a human being—prone and very old. An old woman. The old woman existed in a glowing space without any sense of world around her. The vision moved closer and Scudi tried to relax an intense pressure in her stomach. Monotony of waves and the shrieking bird helped, but the vision would not fade.

The old, old woman lay on her back in the blur of light. Alone … breathing. Scudi noticed a clump of white hair jutting from a mole near the old woman's left ear. The eyes were closed. The old woman did not appear to be a mutant. Her skin was dark and heavily wrinkled. It gave off a greenish cast like the beginning patina on a piece of old brass.

Abruptly, the woman sat up. Her eyes remained closed but she opened her mouth to say something. The old lips moved slow as cold oil. Scudi watched the play of wrinkles released across the face by movement. The woman spoke, but there was no sound. Scudi strained to hear, pressing close to the wrinkled lips.

The vision dissolved and Scudi found herself coughing, retching, held across her floating survival kit by strong hands.

"Scudi!" It was Brett's voice in a loud whisper close to her ear. "Scudi! What's happening? You started to drown. You just sank under the water and . . ."

She coughed up warm water and took in a choking breath.

"You just started sinking," Brett said. He was struggling to balance her on the kit. She pushed herself across its rasping surface and slipped back into the water, holding the kit by one hand. She saw immediately what Brett had done—set the kit's hydrostatic controls for surface and used it as a platform to support her.

"It was like you just went to sleep," Brett said. The worry in his voice seemed amusing to her, but she restrained a laugh. Didn't he know yet?

Brett glanced back at the foil about a kilometer away. Had they heard?

"Kelp," Scudi choked. Her throat hurt when she spoke.

"What about it? Did you get tangled?"

"The kelp . . . in my mind," she said. And she remembered that old face, the open mouth like a black tunnel into a strange mind.

Slowly, hesitantly, she described her experience.

"We've got to get out of here," Brett said. "It can take over your mind."

"It wasn't trying to hurt me," she said. "It was trying to tell me something."

"What?"

"I don't know. Maybe it didn't have the right words."

"How do you know it wasn't trying to hurt you? You almost drowned."

"You panicked," she said.

"I was afraid you were drowning!"

"It let go of me when you panicked."

"How do you know?"

"I . . . just . . . know." Without waiting for more argument, she reset her survival kit's controls, pulled it under and began swimming away from the foil.

Brett, attached to Scudi by the belt line, was forced to follow, towing his own kit and sputtering.

Much later, on the coracle with Twisp and Bushka, Scudi debated recounting the kelp experience. It was late morning now. Still no sign of Vashon on the horizon. Brett and Bushka had fallen asleep. Before they had reached the coracle, Brett had warned her to say nothing of the kelp experience to Twisp, but she felt that this time Brett could be wrong.

"Twisp will think we're crazy as shit pumpers!" Brett had insisted. "Kelp trying to talk to you!"

It really happened, Scudi told herself. She looked from the sleeping figure of Brett to Twisp at the coracle's tiller. *The kelp tried to talk to me . . . and it did talk!*

Brett came abruptly awake as Scudi shifted her position. She leaned back now with her elbows over the thwart. He looked up and met her eyes, realizing immediately what she had been thinking.

About the kelp!

He sat up and looked around at an empty horizon. The wind had picked up and there was spray in the air, scudding off the wavetops. Twisp swayed with a rhythm that marked both the pitch of the waves and the throb of the engine. The long-armed fisherman stared off across the water ahead of him the way he always did when they were chugging along in the fish runs. Bushka remained asleep near the bow cuddy.

Scudi met Brett's gaze. "I wonder if they got their doctor," Brett said.

Scudi nodded. "I wonder why they needed one. Nearly everyone down under is trained as a med-tech."

"It was something pretty bad," Brett said. "Had to be."

Twisp shifted his position. He did not look at any of them and said, "You got doctors to spare down under."

Brett knew what the older man meant. Twisp had spoken of it bitterly many times, as had many Islanders. Topside technology, predominantly organic, meant that most topside biologists who might otherwise go into medicine were lured by higher-status maintenance positions in the cash business of the Islands' bioengineering labs. It was an ironic twist that had them keeping an Island itself fit while the Islanders made do with a handful of med-techs and a family shaman.

Bushka sat up, awakened by their voices, and immediately returned to his insistent fear. "Gallow will have that sub after us!"

"We'll be at Vashon by tomorrow," Twisp said.

"You think you can get away from Gallow?" Bushka snorted.

"You sound like you want him to catch us," Twisp said. He pointed ahead. "We'll be in kelp pretty soon. A sub would think twice about going in there."

"They're not Islander subs," Bushka reminded him. "These have burners and cutters." He sat back with a sullen expression.

Brett stood, one hand steadying him against a thwart. He stared ahead where Twisp had pointed. Still no sign of Vashon, but the water about a kilometer ahead gave off the dark, oily slackness of a heavy kelp bed. He sank back onto his haunches, still steadying himself against the top roll of the boat.

Kelp.

He and Scudi had inflated one of the rafts while still in the kelp bed and perilously close to the foil. Brett had been surprised how easily a raft glided over the big fronds. The kelp did not drag at the raft the way it did on a coracle's hull. The raft slid across the fronds with only the barest whisper of a hiss. But the stubby paddles, fitted into sleeve pockets of their dive suits, splashed water into the raft. And the paddles tended to pick up torn pieces of kelp.

Remembering, Brett thought: *It happened. No one will believe us but it happened.*

Even in memory, the experience remained frightening. He had touched a piece torn from the kelp. Immediately, he had heard people talking. Voices in many pitches and dialects had blended into the hiss of the raft's passage. He had known at once that this was not a dream or hallucination. He was hearing snatches of real conversation.

As he touched the torn bits of kelp in the night, Brett had felt it trying to reach up to him, seeking his hands on the paddles.

Scudi Scudi Scudi Brett Brett Brett

The names echoed in his mind with a feeling of music, a strange inflection but the clearest tones he had ever heard—undistorted by air or wind or the music-devouring dampers of an Island's organic walls.

A wind had come up then and they had raised the raft's crude sail. Scudding across the kelp's surface, huddled close in the stern, they had held a paddle between them as a rudder. Scudi had watched the little receiver that aimed them toward Twisp's transmitter.

Once, Scudi had looked up at a bright star low on the horizon. She pointed at it. "See?"

Brett looked up to a star that he had known from his first awareness, out onto a Vashon terrace with his parents on a clear warm night. He had thought of it as "the fat star."

"Little Double," Scudi said. "It's very close to our sunrise point."

"When it's that low on the horizon, you can see the hyb tanks make a pass *there*." He pointed to the horizon directly opposite the position of the fat star. "Twisp taught me that."

Scudi chuckled, snuggling close to him for warmth. "My mother said Little Double was far off across the horizon to the north when she was young. It's another binary system, you know. From Little Double we could see both of our suns clearly."

"To them, we're probably the fat star," he said.

Scudi was quiet for a time, then: "Why won't you talk about the kelp?"

"What's to talk about?" Brett heard his own voice, brittle and unnatural.

"It called our names," Scudi said. She gently pulled a bit of leaf from the back of her left hand.

Brett swallowed hard. His tongue felt dry and thick.

"It did," she said. "I have trailed my hand through it many times. I get images—pictures like holos or dreams. They are symbols and if I think on them I learn something."

"You mean you still wanted to touch it, even after it almost drowned you?"

"You're wrong about the kelp," Scudi said. "I'm speaking of the times before, when I worked at sea. I have learned from the kelp …"

"I thought you said you taught the kelp."

"But the kelp helps me, too. That is why I have such good luck when I mathematic the waves. But now the kelp is learning words."

"What does it say to you?"

"My name and your name." She dipped a hand over the side and dragged it across a huge vine. "It says you love me, Brett."

"That's crazy."

"That you love me?"

"No … that it knows. You know what I mean."

"Then it's true."

"Scudi …" He swallowed. "It's obvious, huh?"

She nodded. "Don't worry. I love you, too."

He felt a hot flush of exuberance plunge out of his cheeks. "And the kelp knows that, too," she said.

Later, as Brett squatted in the coracle watching the distance to another kelp bed grow shorter and shorter, he heard Scudi's words over and over in his memory: "The kelp knows … the kelp knows …" The memory was like the gentle rise and fall of the seas beneath the wallowing boat.

It called our names, he thought. Admitting this did not help. *It could be calling us to be its dinner.*

He turned his thoughts to something else Scudi had said in the raft: "I like it that our bodies find comfort with each other."

A very practical woman. No giving in to the demands of sex, because that could complicate their lives. She did not hesitate to admit that she wanted him, though, and anticipation counted for something. Brett sensed the strength in her as he looked across the coracle to where she rested with both elbows hooked over a thwart.

"We're in the kelp," she said. She dropped her left hand over the side. Brett wished they could explain what she was doing, but he felt sure the others would think the explanation proof of insanity.

"Would you look at that!" Twisp said. He nodded toward something ahead of them.

Brett stood up and looked. A wide lane had opened through the kelp, the fronds spreading wide, then completely aside, still spreading farther ahead. He felt the water boil under them and the two coracles surged forward.

"It's a current going our way," Twisp said, astonishment in his voice.

"Merman Current Control," Bushka said. "See! They know where we are. They're delivering us someplace."

"That's right," Twisp said. "Directly toward Vashon."

Scudi straightened and brought her dripping hand out of the water. She bent forward and moved across the coracle, tipping it.

"Trim ship!" Twisp snapped.

She hesitated. "The kelp," she said. "It's helping us. This isn't Current Control at all."

"How do you know?" Twisp asked.

"It … the kelp talks to me."

Now she's done it, Brett thought. Bushka let out a loud snort of laughter. Twisp, however, stared at her silently for a moment, then: "Tell me more."

"I have shared images with the kelp for a long time," she said. "At least three years since I first noticed. Now it speaks words in my head. To Brett, too. The kelp called his name."

Twisp looked at Brett, who cleared his throat and said, "Well, that's how it seemed."

"Our ancestors claimed the kelp was sentient," Twisp said.

"Even Jesus Lewis said it. 'The kelp is a community mind.' You're a historian, Bushka, you should know all this."

"Our ancestors said a lot of crazy things!"

"There's always a reason," Twisp said. He nodded at the lane through the kelp. "Explain that."

"Current Control. The girl's wrong."

"Put your hand over the side," Scudi said. "Touch the kelp as we pass."

"Sure," Bushka said. "Use your hand for bait. Who knows what you might catch?"

Twisp merely leveled a cold stare at Bushka, then steered the coracle close to the right side of the open lane and dipped his long right arm over the side. Presently, a look of amazement came over his face. The expression hardened.

"Ship save us," he muttered, but he did not withdraw his hand.

"What is it?" Brett asked. He swallowed and thought about the sensation of kelp contact. Could he put his hand over the side and renew that connection? The idea both attracted and repelled him. He no longer doubted a central reality to the night's experience, but the intent of the kelp could not be accepted without question.

Scudi almost drowned. That is a fact.

"There's a sub coming behind us," Twisp said.

All of them peered back along their course but the surface gave no sign of what might be under it.

"They have us on their locator," Twisp said, "and they mean to sink us."

Scudi turned around and dipped both hands into the passing kelp.

"Help us," she whispered. "If you know what help is."

Bushka sat silent, pale-faced and shuddering at the entrance to the tiny cuddy in the bow. "It's Gallow," he said. "I told you."

With a slow stateliness the channel ahead of them began to close. A passage opened to the left. Current surged into it, swinging the coracles wide. The towed supply boat pulled far to the right. Twisp fought the tiller to center his craft in the new channel.

"The channel's closing behind us," Brett said.

"The kelp is helping us," Scudi said. "It *is*."

Bushka opened his mouth and closed it without speaking. All of them turned to stare where he pointed. A black conning tower broke surface, tipped and sank from sight. Kelp curled over the scene. Giant bubbles began breaking the surface, thick rainbows of air and oil. Small waves surged under the boats, forcing the four people in the coracle to hold on to the rimlines.

As quickly as it had started, the turbulence subsided. The coracles continued their agitated rocking. Water splashed across the gunwales. This, too, quieted.

"It was the kelp," Scudi said. "The sub cut into the kelp trying to follow us."

Twisp nodded to where the kelp still curled among a few small bubbles. He gripped the tiller with both hands, guiding them through a channel that curved open ahead of them, once more aiming toward Vashon. "The kelp did that?"

"It clogged the sub's intakes," Scudi said. "When the crew tried to blow ballast and surface, the kelp jammed vines into the ballast ports. When the crew tried to get out, the kelp tore them apart and crushed the sub." She jerked her hands out of the water, breaking contact with the kelp.

"I warned you it was dangerous," Brett said. A stricken look on her face, Scudi nodded. "It's finally learned to kill."

Chapter 31

Hasn't the water of sleep dissolved our being?
—Gaston Bachelard, "The Poetics of Reverie,"
from *The Handbook of the Chaplain/Psychiatrist*

DUQUE WOKE to a nudge, a deliberate jostling intended to do the waking. He had been prodded, pricked, rubbed, shocked, bled and rocked in his liquid cradle with the great Vata, but this was the first time since childhood that he had been nudged. What surprised him was that it was Vata who did it.

You're awake! he thought, but there was no answer. He felt a focus, a channeling of her presence such as he had never felt before. For this he roused himself, twisted an arm up to his face and fisted his good eye open.

That brought the watchers to the Vata Pool on the double. What he saw with his one eye was worth calling those fools poolside. One of Vata's huge brown eyes, her left one, was pressed nearly to his own. It was open. Duque swallowed hard. He was sure she could see him.

Vata? He tried it aloud: "Vata?"

The growing crowd gasped, and Duque knew that the C/P would push her way to them soon.

He felt something breeze through his consciousness like a heavy sigh. It was a wind with hidden thoughts in it. But he felt them. Something big, waiting.

Duque was shocked. He had long been used to the mind-rocking power Vata could hurl between his eyes. This was the way she threw tantrums, by jamming whatever frustrated her right into his head. Now, she sent him a vision of the C/P, naked, dancing in front of a mirror. For some time now Vata had kept the naked female thoughts out of his head. Anger! Vata contained anger. He blocked out the anger and riveted his inner eye on the supple, firm-breasted Chaplain/Psychiatrist who thrust her pale hips again and again at the mirror. The tank was unbearably warm.

Simone Rocksack's favorite robe lay in a trampled blue heap at her feet. Everything in Duque strained to touch this vision, this body of raw beauty that the C/P locked away from the world.

That was when he saw the hands. A pair of large, pale hands snaked around her from behind and he watched in the mirror as they cupped her swaying breasts while she moved in a rhythmic step-slide, step-slide. It was a man, a large man, and he continued his intense caress of her body until she slowed her dance and stopped, quivering, while his lips brushed her shoulders and breasts, her abdomen, those glistening thighs. The man's shock of blonde hair was a magnet to her fingers. Her hands pulled him close, closer, and they began to make love with him standing behind her, facing the mirror.

The vision ended with an angry white flash and the name *Gallow* blared across his consciousness. What he saw when he refocused on Vata's eye was danger.

"Danger," he muttered. "Gallow danger. Simone, Simone."

Vata's great brown eye closed and Duque felt relieved of a massive, claw-like grip that had held his guts tight. He lay back, breathing deeply, and listened as the knot of watchers grew and the babble of their speculations lulled him back to sleep.

When the C/P came to poolside there was nothing visible of the strange thing the watchers reported.

Chapter 32

To survive Pandora's time of madness, we were forced to go mad.
—Iz Bushka, *The Physics of Political Expression*

BRETT WOKE at dawn, feeling the coracle riding gently under him. Scudi lay curled against his side. Twisp sat at his usual place by the tiller but the boat chugged along on autopilot. Brett could see the little red traveler lights blinking across the face of the receiver, keeping them on course to Vashon.

Scudi sniffed in her sleep. A light tarp kept the damp night air from both of them. Brett inhaled a deep breath through his nose and faced the fact that he would never again accept the stench that surrounded every place Islanders lived. He had experienced the Mermen's filtered air. Now, the fish odors, the thick miasma from Twisp's body, all of it forced Brett to think even more deeply about how his life had been changed.

I smelled like that, he thought. *It's a good thing Scudi met me in the water.*

Mermen joked about Islander stink, he knew. And Islanders returning topside spoke longingly of the sweet air down under.

Scudi had said nothing on meeting Twisp, nor on boarding the coracle. But the distaste on her face had been evident. She had tried to hide it for his sake, he knew, but the reaction was unmistakable.

Brett felt guilty about his sudden embarrassment.

You shouldn't be embarrassed by your friends.

The first long shaft of dawn washed across the coracle, a lazy pink.

Brett sat up.

Twisp, his voice low and muffled at the stern, said, "Take the watch, kid. I'll need a few winks."

"Right."

Brett whispered to keep from waking Scudi. She lay curled up close, her back and hips fitting into the socket of his body as if they were built together. One hand lay flung backward around Brett's waist. He gently disengaged her light grip.

Looking up at the clear sky, Brett thought, *It's going to be a hot one.* He slid out from beneath the tarp and felt the damp bow spray wet his hair and face.

Brett brushed a thick lock of hair from his eyes and crept aft to take the tiller.

"Gonna be a hot one," Twisp said. Brett smiled at the coincidence. They thought alike now, no question about it. He scanned the horizon. The boats still glided down a narrow avenue of current between the hedging kelp.

"Aren't we going kinda slow?" Brett asked.

"Eelcells are getting low," Twisp said. He gestured with a foot at the telltale pink of discharge on the cellpack set into the deck. "Gonna have to stop and charge them or raise sail."

Brett wet a finger in his mouth and raised it to the air. There was only the coolness of their own passage—flat calm everywhere he looked, and gently undulating kelp fronds as far as the eye could see.

"We should be raising Vashon pretty soon," Twisp said. "I caught the Seabird program while you were asleep. Everything's going well, so they say."

"I thought you wanted some shut-eye," Brett said.

"Changed my mind. I wanta see Vashon first. 'Sides, I miss all the times we'd just sit up and shoot the shit. I've just been dozing and thinking here since I relieved you at midnight."

"And listening to the radio," Brett said. He indicated the half-earphone jacked into the receiver.

"Real interesting, what they had to say," Twisp said. He kept his voice low, his attention on the mound that was the sleeping figure of Bushka.

"Things are going well," Brett prompted.

"Seabird says Vashon is in sight of land that is well out of the water. He describes black cliffs. *High* cliffs and waves foaming white at the base. People could live there, he says."

Brett tried to visualize this.

Cliff was a word Brett had heard rarely. "How could we get people and supplies up the cliff?" Brett asked. "And what happens if the sea rises again?"

"Way I see it, you'd have to be part bird to live there," Twisp agreed. "If you needed the sea. And fresh water might be scarce."

"LTA's might help."

"Maybe catch basins for the rain," Twisp mused. "But the big problem they're worried about is nerve runners."

In the bow, Bushka lifted himself out of his tarp and stared aft at Brett and Twisp.

Brett ignored the man. *Nerve runners!* He knew them only from the scant early holos and the histories from before the dark times of the rising sea and the death of the kelp.

"Once there's open land, there'll be nerve runners," Twisp said. "That's what the experts are saying."

"You pay for everything," Bushka said. He patted the back of his open hand against his mouth, yawning widely.

Something had changed in Bushka, Brett realized. When he accepted that his story about Guemes was believed, Bushka had become a tragicomic figure instead of a villain.

Did he change or is it just that we're seeing him different? Brett wondered.

Scudi lifted herself from beneath her tarp and said, "Did I hear somebody say something about nerve runners?"

Brett explained.

"But Vashon can see land?" Scudi asked. "Real land?"

Twisp nodded. "So they say." He reached down and tugged at a pair of lines trailing over the side of the coracle.

Immediately, their squawks set up a flapping commotion beside the boat, spattering cold water all around. Bushka caught most of the splashing.

"Ship's teeth!" he gasped. "That's cold!"

Twisp chuckled. "Wakes you up good," he said. "Just imagine what—" He broke off and bent his head in a listening attitude.

The others heard it, too. All turned toward the horizon on their port where the distant pulse of a hydrogen ram could be heard. They saw it then—a white line far off across the kelp.

"Foil," Bushka said. "They're turning toward us."

"Their instruments have locked onto us," Twisp said.

"They're not going to Vashon … they're coming to us!" Bushka said.

"He may be right," Brett said.

Twisp jerked his chin down and up. "Brett, you and Scudi take your dive suits and those kits. You hit the water. Hide in the kelp. Bushka, there's an old green duffle bag under the deck forward. Haul it out."

Brett, struggling into his suit, remembered what was in that bag. "What're you going to do with your spare net?" he asked.

"We'll lay it here."

"I don't have a dive suit," Bushka moaned.

"You'll hide under the tarp there in the cuddy," Twisp said. "Over the side, you two. Hurry it up, Scudi! String that net along the kelp."

Presently, after hurried preparations, Bushka burrowed his way beneath the tarp and crawled under the forward deck. Brett and Scudi rolled backward over the side of the boat, pulling the net with them. The sound of the approaching foil was growing louder.

Twisp stared toward the sound. The foil was still eight or ten kilometers to port but closing faster than he had thought possible. He hauled in his squawks and caged them, then found two handlines. He baited them with dried muree and slung them over the side.

The raft!

It bobbed against the side of the supply coracle like a beacon. Twisp shot out a long arm, grabbed the line and pulled it to him. He slit it open, rolled the air out of it as fast as he could and stowed it under his seat. Brett and Scudi, he saw, were getting something out of the supply coracle. Harpoon? Damn! They had better hurry.

He glanced around his coracle then. Bushka lay concealed under the bow cuddy. The net trailed aft. Scudi and Brett had gone under water into the kelp. Why did Brett want a harpoon? Twisp wondered. They were safely under the kelp, though, taking their surface air from beneath huge leaves.

Twisp cut his motor and slipped the lasgun out of its hiding place behind him. He put it under a towel beside him on the seat and kept his hand on it.

"Bushka," he called. "Stay as quiet as a dead fish. If it's them … well, we don't know. I'll give you the all-clear if it's not." He wiped the back of his free hand across his mouth. "Here they are."

He raised a hand in greeting as the foil circled in over the kelp, scattering torn green fronds in its wake. It avoided the net and the side of the channel where Brett and Scudi had taken to the water.

No response came to his greeting, just intense stares from two dark figures in the high cockpit. Twisp saw streaks of green on the figures up there. He breathed deeply to slow his heartbeat and steady the trembling in his legs.

Be ready, he warned himself, *but don't be jumpy.*

The foil swung wide astern and sank into the channel through the kelp. The jet subsided to a faint hiss. A heavy wave rolled out from the foil's bow and rocked the coracles. The squawks set up a loud complaint.

Once more, Twisp raised a hand in greeting and waved the approaching foil to the left, indicating the long line of his net with its bobbing floats. When no more than twenty meters separated the craft, Twisp shouted, "Good weather and a good catch!"

He tightened his grip on the lasgun. The choppy cross-waves set up by the foil broke over the coracle's thwarts and soaked him.

Still no response from the foil, which now loomed high over him and no more than ten meters away. Its side hatch slid open and a Merman appeared there in a camouflaged dive suit—green blobs and stripes. The foil slid alongside and came to a stop.

The Merman standing above Twisp said, "I thought Mutes never fished alone."

"You thought wrong."

"I thought no Mute fished out of sight of his Island."

"This one does."

The Merman's quick eyes flitted over both coracles, followed the line of floats astern, then fixed on Twisp.

"Your net's strung along a kelp bed," he said. "You could lose it that way."

"Kelp means fish," Twisp said. He kept his voice level, calm. He even flashed a smile. "Fishermen go where the catch is."

Under the foil's bow, too low to be visible to the Merman, Twisp saw Scudi slip up for air, then drift down.

"Where's your catch?"

"What's it to you?"

The Merman squatted on the deck above Twisp and looked down at him. "Listen, shit-bug, you can disappear out here. Now I've got some questions and I want answers. If I like the answers, you keep your net, your boat, your catch and maybe you keep alive. Do you understand?"

Twisp remained silent. Out of the corner of one eye he caught a glimpse of Brett's head surfacing under the other side of the foil's bow. Brett's hand came up gripping the harpoon from the supply coracle.

What's he doing with that thing? Twisp wondered. *And he's in too close for me to use the stunshield if the chance comes.*

"Aye," Twisp said. "No catch yet. Just got set up." Brett and Scudi disappeared from his sight around the other side of the foil.

"Have you seen anyone else on the water?" the Merman asked.

"Not since the wavewall."

The Merman looked at Twisp's grizzled, weather-beaten face and said, "You've been out ever since the wavewall?" There was awe in his voice.

"Yeah."

He dropped the awe. "And no catch?" he snapped. "You're not much of a fisherman. Not much of a liar, either. You sit still, I'm coming aboard." He signaled his intentions to someone out of view in the foil, then flipped a stubby ladder over the side.

The Merman's movements were deft and controlled. He used no more than the minimal energy required for each action. Twisp noted this and felt a deep sense of caution.

This man knows his body, Twisp thought. *And it's a weapon.* It would be difficult to take this man by surprise. But Twisp knew his own strengths. He had leverage and a net-puller's power. He also had a lasgun under his towel.

The Merman began lowering himself into the coracle. One foot probed backward for the thwart and, as the Merman put his weight onto that foot, Twisp moved backward as though compensating for the weight shift. The Merman smiled and released both hands from the ladder. He turned to make the last step down into the coracle. Twisp reached his long left arm out to steady the man and, as he moved, shifted his weight. Twisp allowed the man to feel a firm grip in the clasp of the hand, steadying him against the roll of the boat until the last possible blink. Then, in one smooth move, Twisp shifted farther toward the Merman, shortened his long-armed grip and tipped that side of the boat completely under water. The Merman lurched forward. Twisp twisted his grip, jerking the man toward him. The long left arm released its grip and snaked around the Merman's neck while the other hand came up with the lasgun pressed against the back of his head.

"Don't move or you could disappear out here," Twisp said.

"Go ahead and kill me, Mute!" The Merman thrashed against Twisp.

Twisp tightened his grip. Muscles that single-handedly pulled loaded nets over a coracle's rim stood out in sinewy ropes.

"Tell your mates to step out on deck!" Twisp growled.

"He won't come out and he's going to kill you," the Merman choked. He twisted again in the powerful grip. One foot braced against a thwart and he tried to push Twisp backward.

Twisp lifted the lasgun and brought it down sharply against the man's head. The Merman grunted and went limp. Twisp lifted the lasgun's barrel toward the open hatch and started to rise. He didn't like the idea of going up that ladder fully exposed.

Brett appeared in the hatchway, saw the lasgun directed at him and ducked, shouting: "We've got the foil! Don't shoot!"

Twisp noted blood down Brett's left side, then, and felt his stomach tighten. "You hurt?"

"No. It's not me. But I think we killed this guy in here. Scudi's trying to help him." Brett shuddered. "He wouldn't stop. He came right at the harpoon!"

"Only one in there?"

"Right. Just the two of them. This is the foil Scudi and I stole."

"Bushka," Twisp called, "practice your knots on this one." He heaved the unconscious Merman across the coracle's motor box.

Bushka crept aft, trailing a length of line from the bow. He looked fearful, and kept well back of the Merman.

"Know him?" Twisp asked.

"Cypher. Works for Gallow."

Scudi appeared in the hatchway behind Brett. She looked pale, her dark eyes wide.

"He's dead," she said. "He kept telling me I had to feed his body to the kelp." Her hands didn't know what to do with their smears of blood.

"This one wouldn't give up, either." Twisp looked to where Bushka was tying the limp Merman's hands behind his back and then to his feet. "They're crazy." Twisp returned his attention to Scudi. She slipped a black-handled survival knife back into its sheath at her thigh.

"How'd you get inside?" Twisp asked.

"There's a diver's hatch on the other side," Brett said. "Scudi knows how to work it. We waited until that one stepped off into the boat before boarding. The pilot didn't suspect a thing until we were right behind him." Brett was talking fast, almost breathless. "Why'd he keep coming for me, Queets? He could see I had the harpoon."

"He was stupid," Twisp said. "You weren't." He glanced at Scudi above him, then at her knife.

She followed the direction of his gaze and said, "I didn't know if he was faking."

That one can take care of herself, Twisp thought.

Bushka stood up from tying the Merman. He looked the foil over approvingly. "We've got ourselves a machine."

The Merman on the deck beneath him stirred and muttered.

"Kid!" Twisp used the command tone that Brett remembered so well from their days at sea. He responded without thinking: "Sir?"

"You think we should move aboard the foil?"

Brett flashed a wide grin. "Yes, sir. It's bigger, faster, more mobile and more seaworthy. I certainly do think we should move aboard, sir."

"Scudi, can we get my coracles aboard of her?"

"The cargo hatch is plenty wide enough," she said, "and there's a winch."

"Brett," Twisp said, "you and Scudi start moving our gear aboard. Iz and I will just ask a few questions of this chunk of eelshit."

"If you want to help the kids," Bushka said, "I can handle this one alone." He nudged the Merman at his feet with a toe.

Twisp studied Bushka for a couple of blinks, noting the new tone of assurance in the man's voice. Anger crawled across Bushka's face now and it was directed at the captive.

"Find out what he was looking for," Twisp said. "What was he doing out here?" Bushka nodded.

Twisp took his boat's bow line and tied it to a foil strut below the boarding ladder. They began shifting gear, moving presently to the tow coracle.

When both coracles were emptied, Twisp paused. He heard Brett and Scudi shifting gear aboard the foil. In the dozens of trips they'd made packing supplies, the two youngsters had touched, bumped against each other or brushed together as often as appeared discreetly possible. Twisp felt good just watching them. Nothing in the world ever felt as good as love, Twisp thought.

Below Twisp, Bushka sat back on his heels, glaring at the captive Merman. "You getting anything from him?" Twisp asked.

"They've taken the Chief Justice."

"Shit," Twisp snapped. "Let's haul that tow coracle aboard. Keep at him."

Even with the winch, it was sweaty work getting the first coracle aboard. Scudi opened a cargo compartment aft of the loading hatch and the three of them wrestled the boat inside. They lashed it against cleats in the walls.

Scudi stepped out onto the loading deck, glanced behind her and stiffened. "You better come out and look," she said. She was pale as a sun-washed cloud.

Twisp hurried outside, followed by Brett.

Bushka stood over the bound Merman. The man was no longer lashed to the coracle's bow. The naked Merman had been pulled to a hanging position, hung by the wrists, bound up behind his shoulder blades. His dive suit lay in ragged pieces about the deck and his knees barely touched the floors. Bushka held a fish-knife in his right hand, its slender tip directed at the Merman's belly.

The muscles of the captive's arms stood out red but his thin drawn lips were white. His shoulders strained at their sockets. His penis was a shrunken stump of fear tucked against his pelvis.

"All right," Twisp demanded, "what's going on?"

"You wanted information," Bushka said. "I'm getting information. Trying out a few tricks Zent bragged about."

Twisp squatted in the opening, suppressing feelings of revulsion.

"That so?" He kept his voice level.

When Bushka turned, Twisp realized that this was not the whining castaway he had jerked out of the sea. This one talked slow and even. He did not take his eyes off the target.

"He claims the kelp makes them immortal," Bushka said. "They have to be fed to the kelp when they die. I told him we'd burn him and keep the ashes."

"Take him off the cleat, Iz," Twisp said. "You shouldn't treat a man that way. Haul him aboard here."

A sullen expression flitted across Bushka's face and was gone. He turned and cut the captive down. The Merman flexed his arms behind his back, restoring circulation.

"He says the kelp keeps your identity, all your memories, everything," Bushka said.

Scudi pulled Brett close and whispered: "That may be possible."

Brett merely nodded, looking down at where Bushka had been torturing the captive. He found the thought of what Bushka had done revolting.

Sensing Brett's reaction, Scudi said: "Do you think Iz would really have killed and burned him?"

Brett swallowed in a dry throat. Honesty forced him to say: "I harpooned the guy in the foil."

"That was different! That one would've killed you. This one was tied and helpless."

"I don't know," Brett said.

"He scares me," Scudi said.

The foil lurched slightly, and again. Something uncoiled into the sea behind them.

"Net," Brett whispered. "Twisp cut it loose." *And it broke his heart,* he thought. *Fish dying for nothing always breaks his heart.*

A chill wind passed over them and they both looked up. Thin clouds had begun a drift in from the north and there was a light chop to the water where the kelp opened that strange lane. The lane still pointed them directly toward Vashon.

"I thought it was going to stay hot," Brett said.

"Wind's changed," Twisp said. "Let's get this boat aboard. Vashon might be in for a bad time after all."

They secured the boat, sealed the hatch and joined Scudi and Bushka in the pilot house. Scudi took the command chair, with Bushka standing to one side, flexing his fingers. Rage still seethed in Bushka's eyes.

"Iz," Twisp said, his voice low. "Would you really have cooked that Merman alive?"

"Every time I close my eyes, I see Guemes and Gallow." Bushka glanced aft where they had left the Merman secured. "I'd be awful sorry, I know, but ..." He shrugged.

"Not much of an answer."

"I think I'd burn him," Bushka said.

"That wouldn't help you sleep any better," Twisp said.

He nodded at Scudi.

"Let's get this thing to Vashon."

Scudi fired up the ram and gently lifted the foil up onto its step. In a minute they were scudding along the kelp channel with a slight bouncing motion against the chop.

Twisp directed Bushka to a couch at the rear of the pilot house. Sitting beside Bushka, Twisp asked, "Did he say how they captured Keel?"

"Off another foil. They had two foils then."

"Where's Gallow?"

"He's gone to Outpost Twenty-two on the other foil," Bushka said. "That's the rocket pickup station. He thinks there's an army in the hyb tanks. Whoever opens them owns them. He wants control of both launch and recovery and obviously he thinks he can get it."

"Is it possible?"

"An army in the hyb tanks?" Bushka snorted. "Anything's possible. They could come out shooting for all we know."

"What does he want with Keel?"

"Trade. For Vata. He wants Vata."

"Gallow's crazy!" Brett blurted. "I've been downcenter and seen the Vata support system. It's *big.* They couldn't possibly ..."

"Cut out the whole support complex with a sub," Bushka said. "Seal it off, tow it out. They could do it."

"They'd need doctors—"

"They have their doctor," Bushka said. "When they snatched Keel they picked up Kareen Ale. Gallow's covering all angles."

Silence came over the pilot cabin while the ram pulsed around them. The foils slapped the seas in a well-absorbed rhythm.

Twisp looked forward to Scudi in the pilot's seat. "Scudi, can we make radio contact with Vashon?"

"Anyone could hear," she spoke without looking back. Twisp shook his head once in frustrated indecision.

Without warning, Bushka yanked the lasgun from Twisp's pocket and jammed it against his ribs.

"Up!" Bushka snapped. Stunned, Twisp obeyed. "Very careful how you move," Bushka said. "I know how strong you are."

Brett saw the lasgun in Bushka's hand. "What's—"

"Sit!" Bushka ordered.

Brett sank back into the seat beside Scudi. She glanced aft, eyed the scene and jerked her attention back to her course.

"Whether we radio or take the message to Vashon in person, it's all the same," Bushka said. "Gallow learns that his secret is out. But right now, we have the advantage of surprise. He thinks this is his foil."

"What do you mean?" Twisp asked.

"Turn this foil around, Scudi," Bushka ordered. "We're going after Gallow. I should've killed him when I had the chance."

Chapter 33

Don't call me her father. I was nothing more than an instrument of Vata's conception. "Father" and "daughter" don't apply. Vata was born more than the sum of our parts. I caution the sons and the daughters after us: Remember that Vata is more mother to us than sister to you.

—Kerro Panille, *Family Papers*

SHADOW PANILLE stood in the gloom of Current Control thinking that at last he had found the woman of his life. With Kareen Ale, he had the faith that only Merman-normal offspring could evidence.

Current Control was aswarm with work, the usual routines preempted by the impending launch and the code yellow grounding of Vashon.

"Too many people working too hard for too long," he muttered to himself. Impulses moved out into the kelp from Current Control, signals of drift sensors flashed in their cobalt-blue numerals. LTA reports were rolling on the number six screen.

Wouldn't get me up in one of those things, he thought. Lighter-Than-Air craft challenged a medium where unstable currents and the unforeseen were standard issue. Air was much more dangerous than water.

Safest down under, he thought. Safety had taken on a new attraction to him. He wanted to live to spend more time with this woman.

Where is Kareen right now? He found himself facing this question constantly since their separation. By now she would be at Launch Base. Panille didn't like to think of the distance separating them … distance was time, and after that last night he didn't want to spend any time without her.

His head had ached and he had been dizzy with fatigue but still sleep had not come. Every time his eyelids slipped his head filled with visions of

Guemes survivors littering the triage floor. Torn flesh, blood, moans and whimpers still ghosted around him in the dim bustle of Current Control.

Kareen, too, had been drained of energy. They had gone to her quarters with little discussion, each aware only of the need to be together, alive after wading through all that death. They had walked from the tube station, holding hands. Panille had held himself under tight control, sure that a white-tipped anger might explode if he once relaxed. Something hot and twisting clenched his guts.

Where plaz lined the corridors, the ripple effect of surface light combined with the cadence of their steps to mesmerize Panille into a dreamy detachment. He felt that he floated above himself, watching their swaying progress. There was tenderness in the arms, the bone-weary arms, and in Kareen's cheek as it brushed his shoulder. Her muscles worked their smooth magic and he no longer suspected that she might try to rule him with her body.

At her quarters, Panille had stared out at a different kind of undersea, a garden lush with ferns waving and butterfly fish grooming the leaves. A thick column of kelp spiraled upward out there, twisting and untwisting with some distant surge.

No death here. No signs of the Guemes disaster.

Just at the edge of visibility lay the Blue Reef with corridors of pale blue vine-tulips that opened and closed like small mouths beyond the plaz. Bright orange flashes of minuscule shrimp darted in and out, feeding on the vine-tulip stamens. Kareen led him to her bedroom.

They did not hesitate. Kareen stood tiptoe and pressed her mouth against his. Her open eyes watched his eyes and he saw himself reflected in her black pupils. Her hands pressed at first against his chest, then slipped around his neck and unfastened his braid. Her fingers felt strong and sure. *Surgeon's fingers,* he thought. His black hair spread over his shoulders. Panille brought his hands down from her shoulders to her tunic, releasing it clasp by clasp.

They undressed each other slowly, wordlessly. When she stepped out of her underwear, the light caught and danced in the flaming red triangle of her hair. Her nipples pressed like children's noses against his ribs.

We have decided to live, he thought.

The vision of Kareen Ale was a mantra that shut out all doubts about his world. Nothing existed in memory except the two of them and their perfectly complementary bodies.

As they had started slipping into sleep, Kareen startled them both with a sudden cry. She clung to him then like a child.

"Bad dreams," she whispered.

"Bad reality is worse."

"Dreams are real while you're in them," she said. "You know, every time I think of us, the bad goes away. We heal each other."

Her words and the pressure of her against him stirred Panille fully awake. Kareen sighed, rolled astride him in one smooth movement and gripped him deep inside her. Her breasts brushed his chest as they swayed back and forth. His breath was her breath then, and she called out his name as she collapsed, gasping, against him.

Panille held her gently, stroking her back. "Kareen," he said.

"Mm?"

"I like to say your name."

He remembered this as he stood watch in Current Control and murmured her name under his breath. It helped.

The main entry hatch to Current Control behind Panille swung open with a sharp hiss, indicating quick entry without waiting for the outer lock to seal. Surprised, Panille started to turn and felt hard metal pressed against his back. A downward glance showed him a lasgun against his flesh. Panille recognized the man holding it—Gulf Nakano, Gallow's man. Nakano's bulky form stepped clear of the entry way, pushing Panille ahead of him. Nakano was followed by three other Mermen, all dive-suited, all armed and all thin-lipped serious.

"What is this?" Panille demanded.

"Shhhh," Nakano hissed. He motioned the others around him, then: "All right! Everybody stand up!"

Panille watched the other intruders move swiftly, methodically to equidistant positions near the center of the room. One operator protested and was clubbed to the deck. Panille started to speak but Nakano thrust a huge palm against his mouth, saying, "Stay alive, Panille. It's better."

The three attackers set their lasguns on short-flame and began demolishing Current Control. Plaz melted and popped, control boards sizzled. Small black snakes of vinyl precipitated out of the air. Everything was done with a chilling deliberation. In less than a minute, it was all over and Panille knew they would be at least a year replacing this ... *brain.*

He was outraged but the destruction daunted him. His assistants leaned against one wall, shock and fear in their eyes.

One woman knelt over the downed operator, dabbing at the side of his face with a corner of her blouse.

"We have Kareen Ale," Nakano said. "I'm told that would interest you." Panille felt his chest tighten.

"Your cooperation insures her safety," Nakano said. "You are to come with us, on a litter as a casualty we're transporting for the medics."

"Where are we going?"

"That's not your concern. Just tell me whether you will come quietly."

Panille swallowed, then nodded.

"We're welding the inner hatch closed as we leave," Nakano said. "Everyone here will be safe. When the next shift tries to get in, you'll get out."

One of the Mermen stepped forward. "Nakano," he whispered past Panille, "Gallow said we should—"

"Shut up!" Nakano said. "I'm here and he's not. The next shift doesn't come in for at least four hours."

At Nakano's nod two of his men brought an emergency litter from the space between the hatches. Panille lay on the litter and was strapped to it. A blanket was tucked around him.

"This is a medical emergency," Nakano said. "We hurry but we don't run. Carry him through all hatchways headfirst. Panille, you close your eyes. You're unconscious and I want you to stay that way or I'll make it real."

"I understand."

"We don't want anything nasty happening to the lady."

This thought haunted Panille as they maneuvered through the hatchways and corridor.

Why me? Panille couldn't imagine being that important to Gallow.

They stopped at a transport tube and Nakano tapped out the Emergency code. The next car stopped and a half-dozen curious faces peered out at Panille's form on the litter.

"Quarantine!" Nakano said, his voice curt. "Everybody out. Don't get too close."

"What's he got?" one woman asked. She skirted the litter widely.

"Something new picked up from the Mutes," Nakano said. "We're getting him out of Core. This car will be sterilized."

The car emptied quickly and Panille's bearers hustled him inside. The doors snicked closed and Nakano chuckled. "Every sniffle, every ache and pain will have sickbay crowded for days."

"Why all this rush?" Panille asked. "And why cook Current Control?"

"Launch countdown has been resumed now that the Guemes matter is over. Medical emergency guarantees us a fast, nonstop trip. The rest … trade secrets."

"What does the launch have to do with us?"

"Everything," Nakano said. "We're headed for Outpost Twenty-two, the recovery station for the hyb tanks."

Panille felt the hot surge of adrenaline. *The hyb tanks!*

"Why take me there?" he asked.

"We've set up a new current control. You're going to direct it."

"I thought you were too smart to get caught up in Gallow's wake," Panille said.

A slow smile touched Nakano's heavy face. "We're going to free hundreds, maybe thousands, of humans in hyb. We're going to liberate the prison they've endured for thousands of years."

Panille, strapped on the litter, could only look from Nakano to the three henchmen. All three wore the same bliss-ninny grins.

"People from the hyb tanks?" Panille asked, his voice low.

Nakano nodded. "Genetically clean—pure humans."

"You don't know what's up there," Panille said. "Nobody knows."

"Gallow knows," Nakano said. There was hard belief in his voice, the kind of tone that indicates the necessity to believe.

The transport capsule's overhead panel came to life and a recorded male voice droned: "Lighter-Than-Air, Base Bravo loading facility."

The hatches hissed open. Panille's litter was picked up and carried out onto the loading platform with near-surface light trickling through heavy plaz panels overhead.

Panille watched as much as he could through slitted eyelids.

An LTA facility? he wondered. *But they said we were* … The truth dawned—they were going to fly him to the outpost!

He almost opened his eyes but restrained himself. Blowing it now would not bring him closer to Kareen.

The litter moved with swift lurches and Panille heard Nakano's voice behind him: "Medical emergency, clear the way."

Panille's slitted eyes showed him the LTA gondola interior—a squashed sphere about ten meters in diameter. It was nearly all plaz, with a canopy of gray above the orange hydrogen bag. He found himself both excited and fearful, filled with confusion at this fierce activity. He heard the hatch seal behind him and Nakano's unruffled voice.

"We made it. You can relax, Panille. Everybody in here is secure." Panille's straps were loosed and he sat up.

"Tether release in two minutes," the pilot reported.

Panille looked up at the orange canopy—the bag was a taper of pleats, its long folds hung down against the cabin's plaz. Once they were up and clear of the tube, more hydrogen would flow into the bag and fill it out. He glanced right and left, saw the two hydrogen jets that would propel them once they were topside.

The whine of a cable winch filled the gondola then. The pilot said, "Strap down, everyone. A bit rough up there today."

Panille found himself dragged backward into a seat beside Nakano. A strap was fitted around his waist. He kept his attention on the pilot. No one spoke. Switches clicked like the hard-shelled chatter of mollusks.

"Topside hatch open," the pilot said, speaking into a microphone at his throat. A halo of white light filtered around the bag above them.

The cabin lurched and Panille glanced out to his left, momentarily dizzy with the sensation that the gondola had stayed stationary and the launch tube was moving downward past him at increasing speed.

The winch sound silenced abruptly and he heard the hiss of the bag against the tube's walls. The bag cleared the tube then and light washed the cabin. Panille heard a gasp behind him, then they were clear of the water, into a cloudy gray day, swaying beneath the expanding hydrogen bag. The jets swung out with a low whine and were ignited. The swaying motion of the gondola steadied. Almost immediately, they entered a rain squall.

"Sorry, we won't be able to see the rocket launch because of this weather," the pilot said. He flicked a switch beside him and a small screen on the panel in front of him came alight. "We can watch the official coverage, though."

Panille couldn't see from where he sat and the pilot had the sound turned down. The gondola emerged from the rainstorm, still pelted by the runoff from the bag overhead. They began swaying wildly and the pilot fought to control the motion. His flurried movement had little effect. Panille noted with some satisfaction that the Merman guards had green expressions that had nothing to do with their camouflage.

"What's going on?" This was a woman's voice from behind Panille. A voice he could not mistake. He froze, then slowly turned and stared past his captors. *Kareen.* She sat beside the entry hatch where she had been hidden from him as he entered. Her face was very pale, her eyes dark shadows above her cheeks, and she did not meet his gaze.

Panille felt a hard emptiness in his stomach.

"Kareen," he said.

She did not respond. The gondola continued to lurch and sway.

Nakano looked worried. "What's going on, pilot?"

The pilot pointed to a display on the board to his right. Panille tore his gaze away from Kareen Ale's ashen face. He could not see all that was indicated on the control panel, only the last two numbers of a digital display and those were changing so rapidly they were a blur.

"Our homing frequency," the pilot explained. "It won't stay on target."

"We can't find the outpost without locking on the right frequency," Nakano said. There was fear in his voice.

The pilot withdrew his hand and this revealed once more the display for the launch broadcast. The picture was gone, replaced by wavelike lines and pulsing colored ribbons.

"Try your radio," Nakano ordered. "Maybe they can talk us in."

"I *am* trying it!" the pilot said. He flipped a switch and cranked up the volume control. A keening, rhythmic sound filled the gondola.

"That's all I'm getting!" the pilot said. "Some kind of interference. Weird music."

"Tones," Panille murmured. "Sounds like computer music."

"What's that?"

Panille repeated it. He glanced back at Kareen. Why wouldn't she meet his eyes? She was very pale. Had they drugged her?

"Our altimeter just went out," the pilot called. "We're adrift. I'm taking us up above this weather."

He punched buttons and moved his controls. There was no apparent response from the LTA.

"Damn!" the pilot swore.

Panille stared once more at the screen on the pilot's board. The pattern was familiar, though he wouldn't tell Nakano. It was a pattern Panille knew he had seen on his own screens in Current Control—a kelp response. It was what they saw when the kelp complied with an instruction to shift the great currents in Pandora's sea.

Chapter 34

The repressed share the psychoses and neuroses of the caged. As the caged run when released, the repressed explode when confronted with their condition.
—Raja Thomas, *The Journals*

17 ALKI, 468. In captivity at Outpost 22.

JEALOUSY IS a great teacher if you allow it. Even the Chief Justice can learn much from his jealousy of Mermen. Compared to Mermen, we Islanders live squalid lives. We are poor. There are no secrets among the poor. The squalor and close sweat of our lives oozes information and rumor. Even the most clandestine arrangements become public. But Mermen thrive on secrecy. It is one of their many luxuries.

Secrecy begins with privacy.

As Chief Justice of the Committee on Vital Forms I enjoy private quarters. No more stacked cubbies pressed head to foot along some rimside bulkhead. No more feet stepping on hands in the night or grunting lovers bumping against your back.

Privilege and privacy, two words that share the same root. But down under, privacy is the norm.

My imprisonment represents a special kind of privacy. These Green Dashers do not understand that. My captors appear exhausted and a little bored. Boredom opens paths into secrecy, thus I anticipate learning something of their lives because their lives are now my life. How little they understand of true secrecy. They do not suspect the chanting in my head that records these things that I may share with others if I wish … and if I survive that long. These fanatics give no quarter. Guemes is proof that they can commit murder skillfully and easily … perhaps even cheerfully. I have few illusions about my chances here.

Little can survive me except my record on the Committee. I admit to a little pride about that record. And some regrets about my other choices. The child that Carolyn and I should have had … she would have been a daughter, I think. By now there would be grandchildren. Did I have the right to prevent that generation out of fear? They would have been beautiful! And wise, yes, like Carolyn.

Gallow wonders why I sit here with my eyelids opened only to slits. Sometimes, he laughs at what he sees. Gallow dreams of dominating our world. In that, he is no different from Scudi's father. Ryan Wang fed people to control them. GeLaar Gallow kills. Their other differences are just as profound. I suppose death is a form of absolute control. There are many kinds of death. I see this because I have no grandchildren. I have only those whose lives have passed through my hands, those who have survived because of my word.

I wonder where Gallow sent that big assistant, Nakano? What a monster … on the outside. The very vision of a terrorist. But Nakano's goals are not on the surface. No one could call him transparent. His hands are gentle when there is no need for his great strength.

They have suspended this foil beneath the surface. More secrecy. More privacy. Such stillness can be frightening. I am beginning to find it captivating—I see that my mind jokes with me in its choice of words. Privacy, too, is captivating. Islanders do not know this reality of life down under. They imagine only the privacy. They envy the privacy. They do not imagine the stillness. Will my people ever encounter this immense quiet? I find it difficult to believe that the C/P will order all Islanders to move down under. How could she do this? Where could the Mermen put us and not lose their precious privacy? But even more than fear of Ship, our envy would cause us to obey. I cannot believe that Ship enters into such a scheme except by innuendo. And the innuendo of Ship suffers a sea of change in human interpretation. A moment's reflection back through the histories, especially upon the writings of that maverick C/P, Raja Thomas, makes this as clear as plaz. Ah, Thomas, what a brilliant survivor you were! I thank Ship that your thoughts have come down to me. For I, too, know what it is to be caged. I know what it is to be repressed. And I know myself better because of Thomas. Like him, I can turn to my memory for company, and he is there, too. Now, with kelp to record us, no lock seals the hatchway to memory … ever.

Chapter 35

If you don't know about numbers you can't appreciate coincidence.
—Scudi Wang

BRETT MARVELED at Scudi's control. All during the ordeal in the control cabin her attention remained on the operation of the foil. She kept them skimming along the edge of the kelp in the bright light of morning, avoiding stray tangles of leaves that might catch the struts. There were moments when Brett thought the kelp opened special channels for the foil. *Directing them?* Why would it do that? Scudi's eyes widened from time to time. What did she see in the kelp channels to cause that reaction? Her tan face paled at what she heard behind her where Twisp and Bushka argued, but she kept the foil cruising smoothly toward its rendezvous with Gallow.

Her reaction was not natural, Brett thought. Bushka was crazy to think they could surprise Gallow and overcome him—just the four of them here. Vashon had to learn what was happening. Scudi must realize this!

Within an hour they came out of the heaviest kelp infestation onto open water where the seas were steeper and the motions of the foil more abrupt.

Bushka sat alone on the command couch at the rear of the cabin, forcing Twisp to sit on the floor well away from him. Between them, trussed like a kelp-tangled dasher, their captive Merman lay quiet. Occasionally he opened his eyes to study his surroundings.

Twisp bided his time. Brett understood the big fisherman's silent waiting. There was a limited future arguing with a man holding a lasgun.

Brett studied Scudi's profile, the way she kept her attention on the water ahead of them, the way she tensed when she corrected course. A muscle in her cheek trembled.

"Are you all right?" Brett asked.

Her knuckles whitened on the wheel and the tremble disappeared. She looked childlike in that big seat with the spread of instruments around her. Scudi still wore her dive suit and he could see a red irritation where it rubbed against her neck. This made him acutely conscious of the constrictions in his own suit.

"Scudi?"

She barely whispered: "I'm OK."

She took a deep breath and relaxed against the padded seat. He saw the whiteness retreat from her knuckles. The foil lurched and shuddered along the wavetops and Brett wondered how long it could take such punishment. Twisp and Bushka began a conversation too low for Brett to make out more than the occasional word. He glanced back at them and focused on the lasgun still held firmly in Bushka's hands. Its muzzle pointed in the general direction of Twisp and the Merman.

What was Bushka really doing? Was it only rage? Surely Bushka could never escape memories of his part in the Guemes massacre. Killing Gallow wouldn't erase those memories, it would only add more.

Scudi leaned toward Brett then and whispered, "It's going to be a bad storm."

Brett jerked his attention around and looked out the sweep of plaz, aware for the first time that the weather was changing dramatically. A gusting wind from port had begun to blast the tops off the waves, whipping scuds of foam along the surface. A gray curtain of rain slanted into the sea ahead, closing the tenuous gap between black clouds and gray water. The day suddenly had the feel of cold metal. He glanced up at the position vector on the overhead screen and tried to estimate their time to Gallow and his hunt of Green Dashers.

"Two hours?" he asked.

"That's going to slow us." Scudi nodded toward the storm line ahead. "Fasten your safety harness."

Brett swung the shoulder strap across his chest and locked it in place.

They were into the rain then. Visibility dropped to less than a hundred meters. Great pelting drops roared on the foil's metal fabric and overcame the airblast wipers on the cabin plaz. Scudi backed off the throttle and the foil began to pitch even more with the steepening waves.

"What's going on?" Bushka demanded.

"Storm," Scudi said.

"Look at it."

"How soon will we get there?" Bushka asked.

His voice had taken on a new note, Brett realized. Not exactly fear … *Anxiety? Uncertainty?* Bushka had the Islander's dreamlike admiration for foils but really did not understand them. How would the foil survive a storm? Would they have to stop and submerge?

"I don't know how long," Scudi said. "All I know is we're going to have to slow down more, and soon."

"Don't waste any time!" Bushka ordered.

It had grown darker in the cabin and the wave action outside looked mean—long, rolling combers with their tips curling white. They were still in kelp, though, with a broken channel through it.

Scudi switched on the cabin lights and began paying more attention to the screens overhead and in front of her.

Brett saw his own reflection in the plaz and it startled him. His thick blonde hair fanned his head in a wild halo. His eyes were two dark holes staring back at him. The gray of the storm had become the gray of his eyes, almost dasher-black. For the first time, he realized how close to Merman-normal he appeared.

I could pass, he thought.

He wondered then how much this fact figured in his attraction for Scudi. It was an abrupt and startling thought, which made him feel both closer and more removed from her. They were Islander and Merman and they always would be. Was it dangerous to think that they might pair?

Scudi saw him staring toward the plaz in front of them. "Can you see anything?" she asked.

He knew immediately she was asking whether his mutant eyesight could help them now.

"Rain's just as bad for my eyes as it is for yours," he told her. "Trust your instruments."

"We've got to slow down," she said. "And if it gets much worse we'll have to submerge. I've never—"

She broke off as a violent, creaking shudder engulfed the foil, rattling the hardware until Brett thought the boat might split. Scudi immediately backed the throttle. The foil dropped off the step with an abrupt plowing motion that sent it sliding down a wave face and pitched it up the next one. Brett was hurled against his safety harness hard enough to take his breath away.

Curses and scrambling noises came from behind him. He whirled and saw Bushka picking himself up off the deck, clutching the grabs beside the couch he had occupied. His right hand still gripped the lasgun. Twisp had been dumped into a corner with the captive Merman atop him. One long arm came out of the tangle, pushing the captive aside, finding a handhold and lifting himself to a standing position at the side of the cabin.

"What's happening?" Bushka shouted. He shifted his grip to a handhold behind his couch and eased himself onto the cushions.

"We're into kelp," Scudi said. "It's fouled the struts. I've had to retract them, but they're not coming fully back."

Brett kept his attention on Bushka. The foil was riding easier, its jet only a low murmur far back in the stern. It was in Scudi's hands now and he half suspected she had exaggerated the nature of their predicament. Bushka, too, looked undecided. His large head bobbed in the constant motion of the foil as he tried to peer past Scudi at the storm. Brett was suddenly struck by how Mermanlike Bushka appeared—powerful shoulders tapering to sinewy, almost delicate hands.

The assault of the wind and waves against the hull increased.

"There's a heavy kelp bed in our path," Scudi said. "It shouldn't be here. I think it may have broken loose in the storm. We don't dare go up on the step again."

"What can we do?" Bushka demanded.

"First, we'll have to clear the struts so I can retract them," she said. "Hull integrity is vital for control. Especially if we have to submerge."

"Why can't we just clear the struts and go back up on the foils?" Bushka asked. "We have to get to the outpost before Gallow suspects!"

"Lose a strut at high speed, very bad," Scudi said. She gestured at the captive Merman. "Ask him."

Bushka looked at the man on the deck.

"What does it matter?" The Merman shrugged. "If we die in kelp we are immortal."

"I think he just agreed with you," Twisp said. "So, how do we clear the struts?"

"We go out and do it by hand," Scudi said.

"In *this?*" Twisp looked out at the long, white-capped rollers, the gray bleakness of the storm. The foil rode the waves like a chip, quartering into them and twisting at every crest when the wind hit it with full force.

"We will use safety lines," Scudi said. "I have done it before."

She hit the crossover switch to activate Brett's controls. "You take it, Brett. Watch out at the crests. The wind wants to take it and the struts being half-out that way makes it hard to control."

Brett gripped the wheel, feeling perspiration slippery against his palms.

Scudi released her safety harness and stood, holding fast to her seatback against the roll and pitch of the foil. "Who's going to help me?"

"I will," Twisp said. "You'll have to tell me what to do."

"Just a minute!" Bushka snapped. He studied Twisp and Scudi for a long blink. "You know what happens to the kid if you cause me any trouble?"

"You learned very fast from this man Gallow," Twisp said. "Are you sure he's your enemy?"

Bushka paled with anger but remained silent.

Twisp shrugged and made his way along overhead grabs to the rear hatch. "Scudi?"

"All right." She turned to Brett. "Hold it steady as you can. It's going to be rough out there."

"Maybe I'm the one should go with you."

"No … Twisp has no experience handling a foil."

"Then he and I could—"

"Neither of you knows how to clear the struts. This is the only way. We will be careful." Abruptly, she leaned down and kissed his cheek, whispering, "It is all right."

Brett was left with a warm sense of completeness. He felt he knew exactly what to do at the foil's controls.

Bushka checked the Merman's restraints, then joined Brett at the controls. He took Scudi's seat. Brett only spared the slightest glance for him, noting the lasgun still at the ready. Heavy seas swept them steadily sideways at every crest and the foil barely had enough headway to recover. Brett listened to voices out on the deck, Scudi shouting to Twisp. A steep swell broke over the cabin, then another. Two long rollers swept under them, then one more breaking crest curled over the plaz. The foil stood almost vertical on its stern, slapped back into the trough and the crest crashed onto the cabin-top. The boat shuddered and wallowed in a side-slip while Brett fought to bring its nose back into the weather.

Twisp shouted something. Abruptly, his voice came crying up the passage: "Brett! Circle port! Scudi's lost her safety line!"

Without any thought for whether the foil could take it, Brett cranked the hard left and held it. The boat turned on a crest, slipped sideways down wave, lifted at the stern and water washed down the long passage into the It swirled around their feet, lifting the captive and sending him against Bushka's thigh. The foil almost rolled over on the next wave. It came up broadside to the weather as it continued its mad circle. Brett felt the sea slosh through the cabin and realized that Twisp had opened the rear hatch to be heard.

Get her, Brett prayed. He wanted to abandon the wheel and run back to help but knew he had to keep the foil tight in this pattern. Twisp was experienced—he would know what to do.

A wave in the cabin broke almost up to his waist and Bushka cursed. Brett saw that Bushka was struggling to keep the Merman in one place.

Brett's mind kept repeating: *Scudi Scudi Scudi …*

The storm's roar in the cabin diminished slightly and Bushka shouted, "He's closed the hatch!"

"Help them, Bushka!" Brett hollered. "*Do* something for once!"

The foil lifted once more over a crest, rolled heavily with the weight of the water they'd taken on.

"No need!" Bushka shouted. "He has her."

"Get back on course." It was Twisp's voice behind Brett, but Brett dared not turn. "I have her and she's all right."

Brett swung the foil's bow back into the seas, quartering into a high comber that rolled over them at the crest. Water sloshed through the cabin as the foil pitched down into the next trough. The sound of pumps chuffing below decks came clearly to Brett's ears. He risked a glance back and saw Twisp backing into the cabin, Scudi's limp form over his shoulder. He dogged the hatch behind him and dumped Scudi on the couch where Bushka had been.

"She's breathing," Twisp said. He bent over Scudi, a hand on her neck. "Pulse is strong. She hit her head on the hull as we tipped."

"Did you clear the struts?" Bushka demanded.

"Eelshit!" Twisp spat.

"Did you?"

"Yes, we cleared the damn struts!"

Brett looked at the overhead screen and brought the foil around ten degrees, putting down a surge of rage against Bushka. But Bushka was suddenly busy with the keyboard at his position.

"Finding how to retract these struts. That was the whole idea, wasn't it?" Bushka's fingers flurried over the keys and a schematic appeared on the screen in front of him. He studied it a moment and manipulated controls at his side of the board. Within blinks, Brett heard the hiss and clunk of struts retracting.

"You're not on course," Bushka said.

"As close as I can be," Brett said. "We have to quarter these seas or we'll pound ourselves to pieces."

"If you're lying, you're dead," Bushka said.

"You take it if you know better than I do," Brett said. He lifted his hands from the wheel.

Bushka brought the lasgun up and pointed it at Brett's head. "Steer us the way you have to but don't give me any shit!"

Brett dropped his hands onto the wheel in time to catch the next crest. They were riding easier now. A green light showed at the "Foils Retracted" marker.

Bushka swiveled his seat and hunched down, positioning himself to watch both Brett and Twisp. The captive Merman lay beside Bushka, his face pale but he was breathing.

"We're still going after Gallow," Bushka said. There was a note of hysteria in his voice.

Twisp strapped Scudi into the couch and sat beside her. He held a grab near her head for balance. Twisp looked forward past Bushka, then up at the overhead display. "What's that?" he asked, nodding at the screen.

Bushka did not turn.

Brett glanced up at the screen. A green diamond-shaped marker flashed near the course line and off to the right.

"What is it?" Twisp repeated.

Brett leaned forward and punched the identity key under the screen.

"Outpost 22" flashed on the screen beside the diamond.

"That's the pickup station for the hyb tanks," Brett said. "That's where Gallow's supposed to be. Scudi's brought us out right on target."

"Get us in there!" Bushka ordered.

Brett turned onto the new heading while he tried to recall everything Scudi had told him about the hyb-tank recovery project. There wasn't much.

"Why's it flashing?" Twisp asked.

"I think it does that when you get within range," Brett said. "I think it's a warning that we're getting close to the shallows around the outpost."

"You *think?*" Bushka snarled.

"I don't know this equipment any better than you do," Brett countered. "Take over any time you want."

"Throw some water on that woman, get her awake," Bushka ordered. Again, that note of hysteria in his voice. He brought the lasgun around until it pointed at Brett. "You stay put back there, Twisp!" Bushka ordered. "Or the kid gets burned."

With his free hand, Bushka began working the keyboard in front of him. "Incompetents," he muttered. "Everything's right here if you just ask for it." Chart-reading instructions scrolled upward on his screen. Bushka bent to read them.

"Ship's balls!" Twisp shouted. "What's *that?*"

Through the spray-drenched plaz ahead and to his left, Brett saw a great splash of bright orange, something floating a wave out there. He bent forward to peer through the salted plaz. It was a long orange something that stretched into the anonymous gray of the storm. Kelp lay tangled all around it.

The foil was coming up on the orange thing fast, bringing it close to their port side.

"It's an LTA bag," Bushka said. "Somebody's gone down."

"Can you see the gondola?" Twisp asked. "Brett! Stay downwind from it. The bag will act like a sea anchor. Don't get fouled in it."

Brett swung the foil to the left and it wallowed in a trough, rocking dangerously at the crest, then into the next trough. At the following crest, he saw the gondola, a dark shape awash in the long seas. The orange bag trailed out behind it with kelp laced across it. The gondola was coming up on their right. The seas were smoother there, flattened by the great spread of the bag. Another crest and Brett saw faces pressed against the gondola's plaz.

"There are people in there!" Twisp shouted. "I saw faces!"

"Damn!" Bushka said. "Damn, damn, damn!"

"We have to take them off," Brett said. "We can't leave them there."

"I know that!" Bushka snarled.

Scudi took this moment to begin muttering … words Brett couldn't understand.

"She's all right," Twisp said. "She's coming out of it. Bushka, you come back here and look after her while I get a line aboard that gondola."

"How're you going to do that?" Bushka asked.

"I'm going to swim it over! What else? Brett, hold us steady as you can right here."

"They're Mermen," Bushka said. "Why can't they bring a line to us?"

"The minute they open their hatch, that gondola is going down," Twisp said. "It'll fill like a punctured float."

Scudi's voice came clearly then: "What's … what's happening?"

Bushka released his safety harness and made his way back to her. Brett heard the hatch open and close. Bushka's voice, quite low, gave Scudi her answer.

"An LTA?" she asked. "Where are we?"

"Near Outpost Twenty-two." There was a scuffling sound and Bushka's voice: "Stay down there!"

"I have to get to the controls! It's shallow here. Very shallow! In these seas—"

"All right!" Bushka said. "Do what you have to do."

Scuffing footsteps on the deck, then water sloshing from a wet dive suit. Scudi's hand gripped Brett's shoulder. "Dammit, but my head hurts," she said. Her hand touched his neck and he felt a flash of pain on the side of his temple. It was a throbbing pain, as though something had struck him there.

Scudi leaned across him, her hand over his shoulder to steady herself. Their cheeks touched.

Brett felt something flow between them, creating a moment of panic followed by a sudden inrush of awareness. His neck hair prickled as he realized what had happened. He felt that he was two people become one but aware of the separation—one person standing beside the other.

I'm seeing with Scudi's eyes!

Brett's hands moved automatically on the wheel, a new expertise he had not known he possessed. The foil gentled its way close to the gondola and hung there with just enough headway to counteract the wind.

What's happening to us?

The words formed silently in their minds, a simultaneous question, shared in an instant and answered in an instant.

The kelp has changed us! We share our senses when we touch!

With this odd double vision, Brett saw Twisp swimming now, moving through a channel in the kelp and very close to the gondola. Faces peered out through the plaz. Brett thought he recognized one of those faces and, with that recognition, came a bursting daydream, instantaneous—a sense of people talking inside the gondola. The sensation vanished and he was left staring at white-whipped waves breaking across the LTA, Twisp clinging there while he fastened his line to a handgrab beside the plaz lock.

Scudi whispered to Brett: "Did you hear them talking?"

"I couldn't make out the words."

"I could. Gallow's people are in there and they have prisoners. The prisoners are being taken to Gallow."

"Where is Gallow? Here?"

"I think so, but I recognized a prisoner— it's Dark Panille, Shadow. I've worked with him."

"The man who treated me in the passageway!"

"Yes, and one of the captors is that Gulf Nakano. I'm going to warn Bushka. He has the weapon. We will have to lock them into one of the cargo bays."

Scudi turned away and worked her way back to Bushka, steadying herself along the overhead grabs. Brett heard her explain the situation to Bushka, saying she had recognized Nakano through the gondola's plaz.

"They've opened their hatch," Brett said. "People are coming out. I see Shadow … there's Nakano. Waves are slopping into the hatch. Everybody's coming out."

Scudi slipped into the command seat beside Brett. "I'll take it. You help Bushka at the entry hatch."

"No tricks!" Bushka yelled as he followed Brett down the passageway.

"We've got to get Twisp out of there!" Brett said. "He's staying at the gondola to unfasten the line when it goes under."

They were at the hatchway then, wind whipping around them and spray in their eyes. Brett was thankful for his dive suit. In spite of the chill, sweat poured from his body. The muscles of his arms and legs were tightly humming bands. A wave broke against the hull below them. Brett sighted along the line—a long row of bobbing heads worked their way toward the foil. He recognized Nakano in the lead, staying close to Panille. The line snaked up and down the waves.

"We'll bring them aboard one at a time, right into the cargo bay behind me," Bushka said.

"We'll have to disarm them."

Nakano was first through the hatch. His face had the single-minded aggressiveness of a bull dasher. Bushka leveled the lasgun from the far side of the hatchway, slipped a similar weapon from the thigh pocket of Nakano's dive suit, grabbed a knife from Nakano's waist sheath and motioned with his head for the Merman to enter the open hatch to the cargo bay.

For a blink, Brett thought Nakano would attack Bushka despite the lasgun, but the man shrugged and ducked through into the bay.

Panille stayed down below to help others and the next person through was a woman, red-haired, beautiful.

"Kareen Ale," Bushka said. "Well, well." He sent his gaze licking over her body, saw no weapon and nodded toward the cargo hatch. "In there, please."

She stared at the lasgun in Bushka's grip. "Do it!" A shout from below the hatch brought Brett whirling around to face the sea.

"What is it?" Bushka demanded. He was trying to divide his attention between the open cargo hatch and the outer hatch where survivors still waited to be brought aboard.

Brett peered out across Panille, who hung below the hatch with an arm wrapped through a loop in his safety line. The gondola beyond him had begun to sink, slowly dragging the orange LTA bag under the waves. The safety line lay across the waves with Twisp pulling himself along it. Something was happening about midway along the line, though, and Brett tried to make out what had caused the shout.

"What's happening?" Bushka asked.

"I don't know. There's a length of kelp across the line. Twisp released the line from the gondola and it's already under. But something's …"

A human hand came out of the water near the kelp and one, two kelp strands whipped across the hand and the hand vanished. Twisp reached the kelp barrier and hesitated there. A questing strand of kelp touched his head, paused there and withdrew. Twisp continued his way along the line, stopping finally beside Panille, exhausted. Panille put an arm under Twisp's shoulder and helped support him. Waves lifted both men and lowered them beside the foil.

"Shall I help bring him up?" Brett called.

Twisp waved a hand to stop him. "I'll be all right." One of his long arms snaked up the line and took a firm grip.

"Two people," Twisp said. "The kelp took them. It just *took* them, wrapped around them and took them."

He hauled himself up the line, quivering every muscle on the way. He slumped through the hatch, then turned to help Panille. Bushka waved Panille toward the cargo bay.

"No," Brett said. He stepped between Bushka and Panille. "Shadow was a prisoner. He helped me. He's not one of them."

"Who says?"

"The kelp says," Twisp said.

Chapter 36

Control the religion and the food and we own the world.
—GeLaar Gallow

VATA'S GROWING restlessness sloshed nutrient over the rim of her tank. At times she arched her back as if in pain, and the pink knobs of her nipples broke the surface like the bright peaks of two blue-green mountains. A relief attendant, an Islander high on boo, reached out to tweak one of the gnarled, vein-swollen things and was discovered catatonic, his blasphemous thumb and forefinger still held in position over the vat.

This event redoubled C/P Simone Rocksack's efforts to effect the Islander move down under. Stories of "The Wrath of Vata" circulated freely and no one on the C/P's staff made any effort to sort fact from fantasy. Rocksack silenced one underling who objected to the rumors by saying, "A lie is not a lie if it serves a higher moral purpose. Then it is a gift."

Vata herself, locked inside her tank and her skull while generation after generation of her people evolved around her, explored her world with the tender new frond-tips of the kelp.

Kelp was fingertip and ear to her, nose and eye and tongue. Where massive stalks lazed on the sea's bright surface she witnessed pastel sunrises, the passage of boats and Islands, the occasional ravages of a hunt of dashers. Scrubberfish that cleaned the kelp's broadest leaves whiskered the deep crevasses of her opulent flesh.

Like herself, the kelp was single, incomplete, unable to reproduce. Mermen took cuttings, rooted them in rock and mud. Storms ripped whole vines loose from the mother plant and some of the wounded stragglers wedged safely into rock and grew there. For two and a half centuries, at least, the kelp had not bloomed. No hylighter broke the surface of the sea to rise on its hydrogen bag and scatter its fresh spores to the winds.

Sometimes in her sleep Vata's loins pulsed with an ancient rhythm and a sweet emptiness ached in her abdomen. These were the times she curled close to Duque, her massive body engulfing him in a frustrating approximation of an embrace.

Now her frustration focused on GeLaar Gallow. A jungle of kelp strained each strand to reach the walls and hatchways of Outpost 22, with no success. The perimeter was too wide, the stalks too short.

New pairs of eyes joined the kelp to reveal Gallow's treachery. The clearest of these eyes belonged to Scudi Wang. Vata enjoyed the company of Scudi Wang, and it became more difficult to let her go each time they met.

Vata met Scudi in the kelp. A few bright glimpses of a fresh young mind, and she searched for Scudi daily. When Vata dreamed the terrors of kelp, storm-ripped from its ballast-rock and dying, the touch of Scudi's skin on vine or frond smoothed those churning dreams to a warm calm. Those times Vata, in turn, dreamed back to Scudi. She dreamed small histories, images and visions, to keep the fear of kelp-madness out of Scudi's head. Vata had dreamed to others who had never come out of the dream. She knew now that Scudi's mother was one of those lost dreamers. Stunned by the hot dream sparking into her from the kelp, the woman had floated wide-eyed and helpless into a passing net. The tender airfish at her neck was crushed and she drowned. And the Merman crew supporting her had made no move to rescue her. Deliberate!

Vata watched the strange odyssey that worked its way back toward Outpost 22. She flexed her kelp when the gondola went down and acquainted herself with Bushka and Shadow Panille. This Panille, he was blood to her.

Brother, she thought, and marveled over the word. She trusted Bushka and Panille to Scudi's presence. The message she sent Scudi was simple and clear: *Find Gallow, drive him out. Kelp will do the rest.*

Chapter 37

Life is not an option, it is a gift. Death is the option.
—Ward Keel, *Journal*

IT WAS late evening, but Ward Keel had lost all inclination to sleep. He accepted the buzz of fatigue as a logical consequence of captivity. His eyes refused to stay closed. They blinked slowly and he glimpsed the brush of his long lashes in the plaz beside him. His brown eye faced itself in the plaz. It was a small dark blur. Beyond it lay the perimeter of kelp, almost gray at this depth. His prison cubby was warm, warmer even than his quarters on Vashon, but the gray of down under washed his psyche cold.

Keel had been watching the kelp for hours as Gallow's men streamed into the outpost. At first the kelp pulsed as usual with the current. Fronds waved at full extension downcurrent like a woman's long hair in an evening breeze. Now there was a different rhythm. And the larger kelp fronds downcurrent of the outpost stretched directly toward Keel. The currents were no longer consistent. The outpost was being battered by sudden changes of current that had the kelp outside flickering in a firelight dance.

Gallow's morning crew had never arrived. His medical team was lost. Keel could hear Gallow's rantings from the next room. The syrupy voice was cracking.

Something strange about that kelp, Keel thought. *Stranger than moving against the current.*

Keel never even considered that Brett and Scudi might be dead. In the reverie generated by the gentle undulations of the kelp, Keel thought often about his young friends.

Had they reached Vashon? He worried about that. But he heard no echoes of this in Gallow's angry words. Surely Gallow would be reacting if that message had reached Vashon.

GeLaar Gallow is attempting to take over Merman Mercantile and the recovery of the hyb tanks. Merman rockets are being sent into space for the tanks. Mermen are changing our planet in ways Islands cannot survive. If Gallow succeeds, Islanders are doomed.

How would the C/P react? Keel wondered. He might never know.

Keel held out little hope for himself. His gut had begun to burn again, precisely as it had four years ago. He knew that all traces of the remora were gone. Without it, the food he ate would pass undigested and his intestines would gnaw at themselves until he either bled to death or starved. There was no reason to doubt the word of his personal physician, and the evidence was too painfully immediate to disguise, even to himself.

It used to make me tired all the time, he thought. *Why won't it let me sleep now?* Because last time he'd almost bled to death in his sleep, and now sleep was impossible.

It wasn't the constant burning that kept him awake. Pain he had learned to bear over the years of ill-fitting support devices for his long neck. This was the crisp wakefulness of the condemned.

Wakefulness had brought Keel's attention to the kelp. Sometime in midmorning the kelp stalks began defying the currents and reaching toward the outpost. The perimeter of growth began about two hundred meters from the outpost walls. The outpost itself lay in the center of this massive kelp project like a jewel in a fat ring. The fish were gone, too. Keel's few earlier glimpses of the outer compound had shown a richness of fishes that rivaled the gardens at Core—fanlike butterfly fish with iridescent tails, the ever-present scrubberfish grazing leaves and plaz, mud-devils raising and lowering the tall sails of their dorsal fins with every disturbance. None was visible now and the gray filter of evening quickly washed itself black. Just the kelp remained, sole proprietor of the world beyond the outpost's perimeter. This day Keel felt that he had watched the kelp go from graceful to stately to full alert.

That's my translation, he reminded himself. *Don't attribute humanity to other creatures. It limits study.* A quick shudder iced his spine when he realized that this kelp had been grown from cells carried by mutant humans.

The kelp had an infinite memory. The histories said that, but so did GeLaar Gallow. *Conclusion?* he asked himself.

It's waking up, he answered. *And it absorbs the memories of the living and the newly dead.* Therein lay great temptation for Ward Keel.

I could leave more than scratchings in these journals, he thought. *I could leave everything. Everything! Think of that!* He entered these thoughts into his journal, and wished that he had his journals and his life's collection of notes around him now. It was possible, he knew for fact, that no Islander had given more direct thought to life and life forms than Justice Keel. Some of these observations he knew to be unique—sometimes illogical, but vital every one. These data he hated to see lost when a struggling humanity needed them so very much.

Someone else will think those thoughts, in time. If there is more time.

His attention was caught by the arrival of another sub overhead. The sub gave the kelp a wide berth. Gallow's orders. As the sub disappeared on its way to the interior docking bay, Keel marveled at the movement of the kelp. Huge stalks tracked the sub's path even though it came in against the current. Like a blossom following the slow arc of sunlight across the sky, the kelp followed all of the incoming Mermen. An occasional blur of gray moved amongst the tendrils as one snapped out suddenly toward an intruder, but all Mermen kept well out of reach.

If the kelp is waking, he thought, *the future of all the humans left may be at stake.*

Perhaps after contacting enough humans the kelp would find some way of saying, "Like me. If you're human, you're like me." There was a biological kinship, after all. Keel swallowed, and hoped silently that it was true that Vata was the key to the kelp. He hoped, too, that mercy was a part of Vata's personality.

Keel thought he detected a change in the perimeter. It was hard to tell, with night coming on and visibility so poor anyway, but he was sure that the two-hundred-meter perimeter had closed. Not much, but enough to notice.

Keel cast about in his memory for all the information that he'd ever stored on the kelp. Sentient, capable of nonverbal communication by touch, firmly anchored to ballast-rocks and mobile in its bloom state—except the bloom state had been extinct for hundreds of years. That was the kelp the first humans on Pandora destroyed. What surprises lay in store with this new kelp? This creature had been regrown from gene-prints present in human carriers. *Could it be that the kelp has learned how to move?* It didn't feel like a trick of the imagination. The dark outside was now nearly total, only a thin barrier of light escaped from the outpost itself.

Morning will tell, he thought. *If there is a morning.* He chuckled to himself. With most of his world dark, Keel was left staring at himself in the port, haloed by the glare of the one bare light. He moved away from the plaz after a passing glance at his nose. It spread over his face like a mashed fruit, the tip touched his upper lip whenever he pursed his mouth in thought.

The hatch door behind him slammed into the wall and startled him. His stomach took a bad turn, then turned again when he saw Gallow, alone, carrying two liters of Islander wine.

"Mr. Justice," Gallow said, "I thought I'd liberate these from the men. I present them to you as a gesture of hospitality."

Keel noted that the label showed that the wine was from Vashon, not Guemes, and breathed easier. "Thank you, Mr. Gallow," he said. He allowed his head to drop in a slight bow. "I seldom have the pleasure of a good wine anymore—sour stomach comes with age, they say." Keel sat heavily and indicated the other chair next to his bunk. "Have a seat. Cups are on the sideboard."

"Good!" Gallow flashed the wide, white smile that Keel was sure opened many a reluctant hatch.

And many a lady, he thought. He shook it off, suddenly embarrassed by himself. Gallow took two stoneware cups from a shelf and set them on the desk. The handles, Keel noted, were thick to accommodate the calloused fingers of outpost riders.

Gallow poured but did not sit.

"I have ordered supper for us," Gallow said. "One of my men is a passable cook. The outpost is crowded, so I took the liberty of ordering the meal delivered here. I hope that meets your approval?"

How very polite, Keel thought. *What does he want?* He took a cup of the amber wine. Both lifted cups, but Keel only sipped.

"Pleasant," Keel said. His stomach churned with bitter wine and the thought of lumps of hot food. It churned at the prospect of listening to more of Gallow's egocentric prattle.

"Cheers," Gallow said, "and to the health of your children." It was a traditional Islander toast that Keel acknowledged with a raised eyebrow. Several acid replies teased the tip of his tongue, but he bit them back.

"You Islanders have mastered the grape," Gallow said. "Everything we have down under tastes like formaldehyde."

"The grape needs weather," Keel said, "not racks of lamps. That's why each season has its own distinct flavor—you taste the story of the grape. Formaldehyde is an accurate summation of conditions down under, from the grape's point of view."

Gallow's expression darkened for a blink, the barest hint of a frown. Again, the wide, winning grin. "But your people are anxious to leave all this behind. They prepare to move down under en masse. It seems they have developed a taste for formaldehyde."

So it would be that kind of a meeting. Keel had heard these conversations before—the justifications of men and women in power for their abuse of that power. He imagined that many a condemned man had to listen to the guilty prattle of his jailer.

"Right is self-evident," Keel said. "It needs no defense, just good witness. What is it that you come here for?"

"I come here for conversation, Mr. Justice," Gallow said. He brushed a stray shock of blonde hair back from his forehead. "Conversation, dialogue, whatever you might call it—it's not readily available among my men."

"You must have leaders, officers of some sort. Why not them?"

"You find this curious? Perhaps a bit frightening that the one privacy of your imprisonment is breached here? At your ease, Mr. Justice, conversation is all I'm after. My men grunt, my officers plan, my enemies plot. My prisoner thinks, or he wouldn't keep a journal, and I admire anyone who thinks. The rational mind is a rare creature, one to be respected and nurtured."

Now Keel was positive that Gallow wanted something—something particular.

Watch yourself, Keel cautioned, *he's a charmer.* The sip of wine found the hot spot deep in Keel's belly and started its slow burn into his intestines. He was tempted to end this conversation. *How much respect did you have for the minds on Guemes?* But he couldn't afford to end the conversation, not when there was a source of hard information that the Islanders might desperately need.

As long as I'm alive I'll do what I can for them, Keel thought.

"I'll tell you the truth," Keel said.

"The truth is most welcome," Gallow answered. A deferential nod graced the comment, and Gallow drained his wine. Keel poured him another.

"The truth is that I have no one to talk with, either," Keel said. "I am old, I have no children and I don't want to leave the world emptier when I go. My journals"—Keel gestured at the plaz-jacketed notebook on his bunk—"are my children. I want to leave them in the best possible shape."

"I've read your notes," Gallow said. "Most poetic. It would please me to hear you read from them aloud. You have more interesting musings than most men."

"Because I dare to muse when your men dare not."

"I am not a monster, Mr. Justice."

"I am not a Justice, Mr. Gallow. You have the wrong person. Simone Rocksack is Justice now, as well as C/P. My influence is minimal."

Gallow toasted him again with the wine. "Most perceptive," he said. "Your information is correct—Simone is Chief Justice and C/P. A first. But because of the memory of one corrupt C/P, others have always been under scrutiny. You, as Justice, have satisfied the people that there is a balance of power. They wait to hear from you. It is you who can relieve their worries, not Simone. And for good reason."

"What is the reason?"

Gallow's easy smile uncurled and his eyes leveled their cold blue power at Keel.

"They have good reason to worry, because Simone works for me. She always has."

"That doesn't surprise me," Keel said, though it did. He tried to keep his voice even, conversational.

Get everything out of him, he thought, *that's the only skill I have left.*

"I think it did surprise you," Gallow said. "Your body betrays you in subtle ways. You and the C/P aren't the only ones trained in observation."

"Yes, well … I find it hard to believe that she'd go along with the Guemes massacre."

"She didn't know," Gallow said, "but she'll adjust. She's a very depressing woman when you get to know her. Very bitter. Did you know that there's a mirror on every wall in her quarters?"

"I've never been to her quarters."

"I have." Gallow's chest swelled with the statement. "No other man has. She raves about her ugliness, tears at her skin, contorts her face in the mirror until she can bear its natural form. Only then will she leave her room. Such a sad creature." Gallow shook his head and freshened his cup of wine.

"Such a sad *human*, you mean?" Keel asked.

"She doesn't consider herself human."

"Has she told you this?"

"Yes."

"Then she needs help. Friends around her. Someone to—"

"They only remind her of her ugliness," Gallow interrupted. "That's been tried. Pity, she has a succulent body under all those wraps. I am her friend because she considers me attractive, a model of what humanity could be. She wants no child to grow up ugly in an ugly world."

"She told you this?"

"Yes," Gallow said, "and more. I listen to her, Mr. Justice. You and your Committee, you *tolerate* her. And you lost her."

"It sounds like she was lost before I ever knew her."

Gallow's white smile returned. "You're right, of course," he said. "But there was a time when she could have been won. And I did it. You did not. That may shape the whole course of history."

"It may."

"You think *your* people will continue to revel in their deformities forever? Oh, no. They send their good children to us. You take in our rejects, our criminals and cripples. What kind of life can they build that way? Misery. Despair …" Gallow shrugged as though the matter were unarguable.

Keel didn't remember Islander life that way at all. It was crowded beyond Merman belief, true. Islands stank, also true. But there was incomparable color and music everywhere, always a good word. And who could explain to someone under the sea the incredible pleasure of sunrise, warm spring rain on face and hands, the constant small touchings of person to person that proved you were cared for merely by being alive.

"Mr. Justice," Gallow said, "you're not drinking your wine. Is the quality not to your liking?"

It's not the wine. Keel thought, *but the company.* Aloud, he said, "I have a stomach problem. I have to take my wine slow. I generally prefer boo."

"Boo?" Gallow's eyebrows lifted in genuine surprise. "That nerve-runner concoction? I thought it—"

"That only degenerates drank it? Perhaps. It's soothing, and to my taste even if it is dangerous to collect the eggs. I don't do the collecting." *That's one he can relate to.*

Gallow nodded, then his lips pressed into a firm, white line. "I heard that boo causes chromosome damage," he said. "Aren't you Islanders pushing your luck with that stuff?"

"Chromosome damage?" Keel snorted. He didn't even try to suppress a laugh. "Isn't that a little like roulette with a broken wheel?"

Keel sipped his wine and sat back to see Gallow fully. The look of disgust that shadowed the Merman's face told Keel that Gallow had been reached.

Anyone who can be reached can be probed. Keel thought. *And anyone who can be probed can be had.* His position on the Committee had taught him this.

"You can laugh at that?" Gallow's blue eyes blazed. "As long as you people breed, you endanger the whole species. What if ... ?"

Keel raised his hand and his voice. "The Committee concerns itself with matters of 'what if,' Mr. Gallow. Any infant that carries an endangering trait is terminated. For a people trained in life-support, this is a most painful event. But it guarantees life to all the others. Tell me, Mr. Gallow, how can you be so sure that there are only harmful, ugly or useless mutations?"

"Look at yourself," Gallow said. "Your neck can't support your head without that ... *thing.* Your eyes are on the sides of your head—"

"They're different colors, too," Keel said. "Did you know that there are more brown-eyed Mermen than blue-eyed by four to one? Doesn't that strike you as a mutation? You're blue-eyed. Should you, then, be sterilized or destroyed? We draw the line at mutations that actually endanger life. You prefer cosmetic genocide, it seems. Can you justify that to me? Can you be sure that we haven't 'bred' some secret weapons to meet the contingency you've presented us?"

Find his worst fears, Keel thought, *and turn them on himself.*

The clatter of loose dishes sounded from the hatchway and a small cart bounced over the threshold. The young man who pushed it stood in obvious awe of Gallow. His eyes took in every move his boss made and his hands shook as they distributed the dishes on a small folding table. He served the steaming food into bowls and Keel smelled the delicious tang of fish stew. When the steward finished laying out the bread and a small cake dessert he picked up a small dish of his own and spooned a taste of everything.

So, Keel thought, *Gallow's afraid he's going to be poisoned.* He was glad to see the orderly delicately taste Keel's portions, as well. *Things are not going quite as Gallow would like us to believe.* Keel couldn't let the moment pass.

"Do you taste to educate your palate?" he asked.

The orderly shot a quizzical look at Gallow and Gallow smiled back. "All men in power have enemies," he said. "Even yourself, I'm told. I choose to encourage protective habits."

"Protection from whom?"

Gallow was silent. The orderly's face paled.

"Very astute," Gallow said.

"By this you imply that murder is the current mode of political expression," Keel said. "Is this the new leadership you offer our world?"

Gallow's palm slapped the tabletop and the orderly dropped his bowl. It shattered. One shard of it skidded up to Keel's foot and spun there like an eccentric top winding down. Gallow dismissed the orderly with a sharp chop of his hand. The hatch closed quietly behind him.

Gallow threw down his spoon. It caught the edge of his bowl and splattered Keel with stew. Gallow dabbed at Keel's tunic with his cloth, leaning across the rickety table.

"My apologies, Mr. Justice," he said. "I'm generally not so boorish. You … excite me. Please, relax."

Keel nursed the ache in his knees and folded them under the short table. Gallow tore a piece of bread from the loaf and handed Keel the rest.

"You have Scudi Wang prisoner?" Keel asked.

"Of course."

"And the young Islander, Norton?"

"He's with her. They are unharmed."

"It won't work," Keel said. "If you hinge your leadership on stealth and prisoners and murder then you set yourself up for a long reign of the same thing. No one wants to deal with a desperate man. Kings are made of better stuff."

Gallow's ears pricked at the word "king." Keel could see him trying it on his tongue.

"You're not eating, Mr. Justice."

"As I said before, I have a stomach problem."

"But you have to eat. How will you live?"

Keel smiled. "I won't."

Gallow set his spoon down carefully and dabbed at his lips with his cloth. He knit his smooth brow in an expression of concern.

"If you choose not to eat, you will be fed," Gallow warned. "Spare yourself that unpleasantry. You won't starve yourself out of my care."

"Choice has nothing to do with it," Keel said. "You snatched inferior merchandise. Eating causes pain, and the food merely passes undigested."

Gallow pushed himself back from the squat table.

"It's not catching, Mr. Gallow."

"What is it?"

"A defect," Keel said. "Our bioengineers helped me up to this point, but now the Greater Committee takes matters out of our hands."

"The Greater Committee?" Gallow asked. "You mean that there is a group topside more powerful than yours? A secret clan?"

Keel laughed, and the laugh added frustration and confusion to Gallow's otherwise perfect face.

"The Greater Committee goes by many names," Keel said. "They are a subversive bunch, indeed. Some call them Ship, some call them Jesus—not the Jesus Lewis of your school-day histories. This is a difficult committee to confront, as you can see. It makes the threat of death at your hands not much of a threat at all."

"You're … *dying?*"

Keel nodded. "No matter what you do," he said, smiling, "the world will believe that you killed me."

Gallow stared at Keel for a long blink, then blotted his lips with the napkin. He extricated himself from the table.

"In that case," Gallow announced, "if you want to save those kids, you'll do exactly as I say."

Chapter 38

... it comes to pass that the same evils and inconveniences take place in all ages of history.

—Niccolo Machiavelli, *Discourses, Shiprecords*

FROM HIS position at the foil's controls, Brett watched the late afternoon sun kindle a glow in the cloud bank ahead of him. The foil drove easily across deep storm swells, picking up speed on each downslope, losing a bit on each advancing wave. It was a rhythm that Brett had come to understand without conscious attention. His body and senses adjusted.

A gray wall of rain skulked a couple of hundred meters above the wavetops to the right. A line storm, it appeared to be rolling away from them.

Brett, his attention divided between the course monitor above him and the seas ahead, abruptly throttled back. The foil dropped off its step and moved with minimal headway beside a kelp bed that stretched away into the storm track.

The change in motion aroused the others, who, except for Bushka and the captive Merman, whom Bushka had locked in the cargo bay with the survivors of the LTA, were sprawled around the cabin catching what rest they could. Bushka sat in regal isolation on the couch at the rear of the cabin, his eyes oddly indrawn, his face a mask of concentration as he stroked a fragment of kelp that lay across his lap. The bit of kelp had come up from the sea on Twisp's rescue line and had attracted little attention until Bushka plucked it off and kept it.

Panille spoke from the copilot's seat as he came abruptly alert. "Something wrong?"

Brett indicated the green glow of their position on the course monitor. "We're only a couple of klicks out." He pointed at the line squall. "The outpost is in there."

Twisp spoke from behind them: "Bushka, you still going through with this?"

"I have no choice." Bushka's voice carried a distant tone. He stroked the fragment of kelp, which had begun to dry and crisp. It rasped under his hand.

Twisp nodded at the net of weapons Bushka had taken from the LTA survivors. "Then maybe we all better be armed."

"I'm thinking on it," Bushka said. Again, his hand rasped across the drying kelp.

"Panille," Twisp said, "how are outposts defended?"

Scudi, seated on the deck across from Twisp, answered for him. "Outposts aren't expected to need defenses."

"They have the usual sonar, perimeter alarms against dashers, that sort of thing," Panille said. "Each outpost has at least one LTA for weather observation."

"But what weapons?" Twisp asked.

"Tools, mostly," Scudi said.

Bushka nudged the netful of captured weapons at his feet. "They will have lasguns. Gallow arms his people."

"But they'd be effective only inside the outpost compound," Panille said. "We're safe in the water."

"Which is why I stopped here," Brett said. "Do you think they know we're here?"

"They know," Bushka said. "They just don't know who we are." He peeled the dried kelp from his dive suit and dropped it to the deck.

Scudi stood and moved to Brett's side, resting an arm on the back of his seat. "They will have welders, plasteel cutters, some stunshields, knives, pry-bars. Tools are very effective weapons." She looked at Bushka. "As Guemes should have taught us."

Panille swiveled and looked at the passage that led back to the cargo compartment. "Some of those people back there might know some details about what we can expect down there—"

"This is stupid!" Brett said. "What can we do against Gallow and all his men?"

"We will wait for nightfall," Bushka said. "Darkness is a great equalizer." He looked at Scudi. "You say you've worked at this outpost. You can draw up a plan of the access hatches, the power station, tool storage, vehicle bays … that sort of thing."

Scudi looked at Brett, who shrugged.

Twisp glanced once at the lasgun in Bushka's hand, then at his face. "You really mean for us to attack them, don't you?"

"Of course."

"Unarmed?"

"We will have the inestimable arm of surprise."

Twisp let out a barking laugh.

"Let me talk to Kareen," Panille said. "She can't be one of them. She may have learned—"

"She's not to be trusted," Bushka said. "She belonged to Ryan Wang when he was alive, and now she belongs to Gallow."

"No, she doesn't!"

"Men are so easily manipulated by sex," Bushka sneered.

Panille's dark face darkened further with anger, but he held his silence for a blink. Then: "The kelp! The kelp can tell us what we need to know!"

"Do not trust the kelp, either," Bushka said. "Every sentient thing in this universe thinks of itself first. We don't know what the kelp fears or desires."

Panille glanced at the bit of dried kelp on the deck. "Scudi, what do you say about the kelp? You've worked in and around it more than any of us."

"She is Ryan Wang's daughter!" Bushka blared. "You ask the enemy for advice?"

"I ask where I might get an answer," Panille said. "And if you're not going to use that lasgun, quit waving it around."

He turned from a flabbergasted Bushka to Scudi. "What's the kelp's range, from your experience?"

"Worldwide," she said, "and almost instantaneous."

"*That* fast?"

Scudi shrugged. "And what it learns, it never forgets." She noted the look of surprise on Panille's face and went on. "We've made reports. Most supervisors don't go out there, so they write this off to narcosis and keep us out of deep water for a week."

"What else might help us?"

"There are weak spots," Scudi said. "Immature kelp is strictly a conductor. Mature kelp carries a presence all its own."

"What do you mean?" Twisp asked.

"If I touch a young patch of kelp and you touch a mature one, we sense each other. But now … it is doing something more. Bushka's right that it may do things on its own."

"It has learned to kill," Bushka said.

Scudi said, "I always thought it could trans*mit*, but not trans*late*."

Bushka asked, "How many people can the outpost support?"

Scudi juggled the question a moment. "They have accommodations, food and other supplies for about three hundred. But they have open land at the center. They could shelter a lot more people."

Brett turned to Bushka. "Does Gallow have three hundred people?"

Bushka nodded. "More."

"Then we can't confront them," Twisp said. "This is crazy."

"I'm going to kill Gallow," Bushka said.

"That's it?" Twisp demanded. "That's all? Then they'll quit and go home?"

Bushka would not meet Twisp's gaze. "All right," he said with a flick of the weapon, "let's see what Kareen Ale has to say. Put the foil on autopilot, Brett."

"Autopilot?" Brett asked. "Why?"

"We're all going back to see Kareen," Bushka said. "Everybody move easily, no sudden surprises."

No one argued with those jumpy, glittering eyes. Brett and Scudi led the way through the hatch and down the passageway. At the cargo hatch Bushka motioned Twisp to the lock.

"Open the exterior hatch first," he ordered. "We might want to throw something overboard."

Slowly, reluctantly, Twisp obeyed. A fresh breeze tasting of iodine and salt ricocheted through the hatchway. Wave-slaps against the hull were loud in the passage.

"Open the cargo hatch and stand aside," Bushka said.

Twisp lifted the security bar, released the latch and slid the hatch to one side.

Without warning, Brett was knocked down by something wet and ropy coming from behind him. A large strand of kelp snaked past him, swerved left and slammed the LTA's survivors against the bulkhead. It held them there. The thumpings of the kelp turned the passageway into a great drum. Brett snatched a grab, caught his balance and saw the rapt features of Iz Bushka, who was held in loops of kelp.

Bushka stood with both arms upraised, the lasgun still clutched in his right fist. Strands of kelp caressed his body, their leaves particularly drawn to his face and hands. More strands lay like ropes on the deck, fanned out on both sides. Scudi and the others were not in sight.

A branch of kelp detached itself from the captives and undulated toward Brett. The fronded tip lifted and enclosed Brett's face.

Brett heard whistling—the wind against the foil, but enhanced, every tonal component identifiable. He felt his senses amplified—the touch of the deck, other people around him ... many others ... thousands. He sensed Scudi then, as though the kelp gave her to him with her thoughts clear. Bushka was there, an enraptured Bushka drinking from the kelp's reservoir of memories. A historian's paradise: firsthand history.

Scudi spoke in Brett's head: "The rocket is up. They're on their way to get the hyb tanks."

Brett saw it then, a fiery ascent that flamed through the cloud cover and became an orange glow on the gray until it vanished and only the clouds remained. With the vision went a questioning thought, a profound wonder that was not human. The rocket was a wondrous thing of anticipation in this thought. It was a seeking after great surprises.

The thought and the vision vanished. Brett found himself sitting on the deck in the foil's passage and looking into the cargo bay. Bushka sat there sobbing. The bay behind him was empty. The kelp was gone.

Brett heard others then and Scudi's voice came overloud.

"Brett! Are you all right?"

He scrambled to his feet, turning. Scudi stood there with movements of others behind her, but Brett could focus only on Scudi.

"As long as you're here, I'm all right," he said.

Chapter 39

Symbols are worth a damn.

—Duque Kurz

19(?) ALKI, 468. Outpost 22.

WHEN THEY call me "Mr. Justice" I feel the scales of law and life freeze in my palm. I am not Ward Keel to them, the big-headed man with the long neck and stiff shuffle, but some god who will see the right thing and do it. And good will come. God and good, evil and devil—words are the symbols that flesh out our world. We expect that. We act on it.

Resentment, that's expectation gone bad. I must admit, our crises are legion, but we live to confront our crises and that's something no god ever promised.

Simone Rocksack thinks she knows what Ship has promised. That's her job, she says. She tells the faithful what Ship meant and they believe her. The Histories are there for the reading. I come to my own conclusions: We are neither rewarded nor punished. *We are.* My job as Chief Justice has been to keep as many of us *being* as possible.

The Committee's foundations were in science and fear. Original questions were quite simple: kill it or care for it. Terminate if dangerous. That power over life and death in a time of much death lent an aura to the Committee that it should never have accepted. In lieu of law, there is the Committee.

It is true that the C/P asserts the law of Ship and it is also true that her people enforce it. They give unto Ship that which is Ship's … together we keep the human world flowing.

"Flow" is the right word. We Islanders understand current and flow. We understand that conditions and times change. To change, then, is normal. The Committee reflects that flexibility. Most law is simply a matter of personal contracts, agreements. Courts deal with squabbles.

The Committee deals with life and life alone. Somehow that has extended to politics, a matter of group survival. We are autonomous, elect our own replacements, and our word is as close to absolute law as Islanders get. They trust nothing fixed. Rigidity in law appalls them as much as cold statuary.

Part of our enjoyment of art derives from its transitory nature. It is made constantly new and if it is to survive over time it does so in the theater of memory. We Islanders have great respect for the mind. It is a most interesting place, a tool at the base of all tools, torture chamber, haven of rest and repository of symbols. All that we have relies on symbol. With symbols we create more world than we were given, we become more than the sum of our parts.

Anyone who threatens the mind or its symbolizing endangers the matrix of humanity itself. I have tried to explain as much to Gallow. He has the ears for it; he simply doesn't care.

Chapter 40

When power shifts, men shift with it.
—George Orwell, *Shiprecords*

THE ARGUMENT was over whether to arm Nakano. Bushka favored it and Twisp did not. Ale and Panille remained aloof, listening but not watching. They stood, each with an arm around the other's waist, looking out on the lowering gray sky visible through the open hatchway. The foil circled on autopilot in a wide pool of open water surrounded by kelp. The outpost lifted from the sea about ten klicks away—a foam-collared pillar of rock set in a ring of kelp. A kelp-free area surrounded the outpost. The rock appeared to be at least one klick away from this vantage.

Brett found himself alarmed by the change in Bushka. What had the kelp done to Bushka there in the cargo bay? And where were the other captive Mermen? Only Ale, Panille and Nakano remained of those rescued from the LTA.

Twisp voiced it for all of them: "What did the kelp do to you, Iz?"

Bushka looked down at the net of weapons by his right foot. His gaze passed over the lasguns he had already distributed to the others—to everyone except Nakano. A look of childlike bewilderment swept over Bushka's face. "It told me … it told me …" He brightened. "It told me we must kill Gallow and it showed me how." He turned and stared past Ale and Panille at the kelp drifting on the surging waves. A rapt expression came over his face.

"And you agreed, Nakano?" Twisp demanded.

"It makes little difference," Nakano said, his voice gruff. "The kelp wants him dead but he will not be dead."

Twisp shuddered and looked at Scudi and Brett. "That's not what it said to me. How about you, kid?"

"It showed me the launching of the rocket."

Brett closed his eyes. Scudi pressed herself against him, leaning her head into his shoulder. He knew the experience they had shared: thousands of people alive now only in the kelp's memories. The last agony of the Guemes Islanders was there and everything the dead had ever thought or dreamed. He had heard Scudi exclaiming in his mind: "*Now, I know what it feels like to be a Mute!*"

Scudi pushed herself a bit away from Brett's embrace and looked at Twisp. "The kelp said it's my friend because I'm one of its teachers."

"What did it say to you, Twisp?" Brett asked. Brett opened his eyes wide and stared hard at the long-armed fisherman.

Twisp inhaled a deep, quick breath and spoke in a sharp voice: "It just told me about myself."

"It told him he's a man who thinks for himself and likes to keep his thoughts private," Nakano said. "It told me we're alike in this. Isn't that it, Twisp?"

"More or less." Twisp sounded embarrassed.

"It said our kind's dangerous to leaders who demand blind obedience," Nakano said. "The kelp respects this."

"There! You see?" Bushka smiled at them, lifting a lasgun out of the pile of weapons he had taken from the people off the LTA. He balanced the lasgun on his open palm, staring at it.

Panille turned from the hatchway and looked at Bushka. "You all accept this?" His voice was flat. He glared at Nakano. "Only you and Kareen and I are left!" He jerked his chin toward the hatchway. "Where are the others?"

Silence settled over the group.

Panille turned toward the perimeter of kelp visible in the darkening light. He remembered hurdling the glut of kelp and reaching for Kareen as a giant vine released her. She had grabbed him close and they had clung to each other while cries of fear lifted all around them.

In that instant of kelp-awareness, he had been inundated by Kareen: Gallow's captive—sent with Nakano to be used as bait in the capture of Dark Panille. She had her loyalty problems, too. Her family, with all its power, wanted a hold on Gallow in case he was victorious. But Kareen loathed Gallow.

Kareen's fingers had held a painful grip on Panille's water-frizzed hair while she cried against his neck. Then the kelp had returned … and touched them once more. They had both felt the kelp's selective fury, sensed the leaves and vines writhing seaward … bottomward. Presently, the hatchway had framed a churning gray sea, not a sign there to betray the fact that humans had been removed from the foil … and drowned.

But that was the past. Bushka cleared his throat, breaking Panille's reverie. "They were Gallow's people," Bushka said. "What does it matter?"

"Nakano was one of Gallow's people," Twisp said.

"It's not an easy choice," Nakano said. "Gallow saved my life once. But so did you, Twisp."

"So you go with whoever saved you most recently," Twisp said, scorn in his voice.

Nakano spoke in a curious lilting tone: "I go with the kelp. There is my immortality."

Brett's throat went dry. He had heard that tone in Guemes fanatics, the hardest of the hard-core WorShipers.

Twisp, obviously having a similar reaction, shook his head from side to side. *Nakano did not care who he killed! The kelp justified everything!*

"Gallow wants Vata," Bushka said. "We can't allow that." He passed the lasgun to Nakano, who slipped it into its holster at his thigh.

At Bushka's movement, Twisp put his hand on his own weapon. He did not relax even when Nakano displayed empty hands and smiled at him.

"Seven of us," Twisp said. "And we're supposed to attack a place that could have more than three hundred armed people in it!"

Bushka closed the hatchway before looking at Twisp. "The kelp told me how to kill Gallow," he said. "Do you doubt the kelp?"

"You're damned right I do!"

"But we are going to do it," Bushka said. He pushed past Twisp and went up the passageway toward the pilot cabin. Brett took Scudi's hand and followed. He could hear the others coming after them, Twisp muttering: "Stupid, stupid, stupid …"

For Brett, Twisp's voice lay immersed in what the kelp had insisted, a chant imprinted on the vocal centers. Certainly this was what the kelp had told Bushka.

Drive Gallow out. Avata will do the rest.

The chant surged there, background to a persistent image of Ward Keel imprisoned in plaz, beckoning to him. Brett felt sure that Keel was Gallow's prisoner at this outpost.

Panille went to the left-hand pilot's seat and checked the instruments. The foil was making minimal headway in the wide circle of open water enclosed by kelp fronds.

Brett stopped near the pilot station. Feeling Scudi's hand tremble in his, he squeezed her hand firmly. She leaned against him. He looked out the plaz to his right. Framed there was a churning gray sea. Rain slanted with a stiff breeze. Kelp fronds lifted and danced on the wavetops, smoothing them and dampening the chop. Even as he looked, darkness settled over the sea. Automatic lighting came on to rim the edges of the cabin ceiling. Course vector lights winked on the screens in front of Panille.

Twisp had stopped at the entrance to the cabin, his hand on the lasgun, his attention on Nakano.

Noting this, Nakano smiled. He moved across in front of Brett and went to the pilot station beside Panille, activating the exterior lights. A spotlight fanned brilliant illumination across the open water and the edge of kelp. Abruptly, swift motion entered the illuminated area.

"Dashers!" Panille said.

"Look at that big bull!" Nakano said.

Brett and Scudi stared out at the scene, the blanket of kelp, the hunt of dashers.

"I've never seen such a big one," Ale said.

The hunt swept along in an undulating glide behind the monster bull. Nakano tracked them with the spotlight. They circled the dark perimeter of kelp, then worked into the leaves.

Nakano turned from the control station and opened the plaz hatch beside him, letting in a damp rush of wind and rain. Lifting his lasgun, he sent a burning arc at the hunt, tumbling the lead bull and two followers. Their dark green blood washed over the kelp fronds, foaming in the waves.

The rest of the hunt turned on its own dead, spreading blood and torn flesh across the fan of light. Abruptly, kelp stalks as thick as a man's waist lifted from the sea, whipped the gore to a foam and drove the dashers from their feed.

Nakano drew back and secured the hatch. "You see that?" he asked.

No one answered. They had all seen it.

"We will submerge," Bushka said. "We will go in with the foil underwater. Nakano will be visible. The rest of us will appear to be captives until the last blink."

Brett released Scudi's hand and crossed to confront Bushka.

"I'll not have Scudi used as bait!"

Bushka made a grab for his lasgun but Brett caught the man's wrist. Young muscles, made powerful by months of hauling nets, flexed once, twisted Bushka's wrist and the lasgun dropped to the deck. Brett kicked it toward Twisp, who picked it up and hefted it.

Bushka eyed the weapons he had left near the passage entrance.

"You'd never make it," Twisp said. "So relax." He held the lasgun casually, muzzle pointed downward, but his manner suggested poised readiness.

"So what do we do now?" Ale asked.

"We could run for the Launch Base and alert everyone to what's happening," Panille said.

"You'd start a civil war among Mermen and the Islanders would be drawn into it," Bushka protested. He rubbed at his wrist where Brett had twisted it.

"There's something else," Scudi said. She glanced at Brett, then at Twisp. "Chief Justice Keel is being held prisoner here by Gallow."

"In Ship's name, how do you know that?" Twisp demanded.

"The kelp says it," Scudi said.

"It showed me a vision of Keel in captivity," Brett said.

"Vision!" Twisp said.

"The only important thing is to kill Gallow," Bushka muttered.

Twisp looked at Kareen Ale. "The only reason we went back to the cargo bay was to ask you for advice," he said. "What does the ambassador suggest?"

"Use the kelp," she said. "Take the foil down to the inner edge of the kelp in sight of the outpost … and we wait. Let them see Scudi and me. That should tempt Gallow to come out. And yes, Justice Keel is there. I've seen him."

"I say we run for Vashon," Brett said.

"Let me remind you," Ale said, "that the hyb tanks will be brought down here. The pickup team is at this outpost."

"And they're either Gallow's people or Gallow's captives," Twisp sneered. "Any way you look at it, the hyb tanks are his."

Ale glanced at the chrono beside the control panel. "If all goes well, the tanks could be here in a little more than eight hours."

"With seven of us aboard, we couldn't stay down eight hours," Panille said.

Bushka began to giggle, startling them. "Empty argument," he said. "Empty words. The kelp won't permit us to leave until we do its bidding. It's kill Gallow or nothing."

Nakano was the first to break the subsequent silence. "Then we'd better get busy," he said. "Personally, I like the ambassador's plan but I think we also should send in a scout party."

"And you're volunteering?" Twisp asked.

"If you have a better idea, let's hear it," Nakano said. He returned to the cabin's rear bulkhead and opened a supply locker, exposing fins, air tanks, breathers and dive suits.

"You saw the kelp crush that sub," Brett reminded Twisp. "And you saw what happened with the dashers."

"Then I'm the one who goes in," Twisp said. "They don't know me. I'll carry our message so they get it real clear."

"Twisp, no!" Brett protested.

"Yes!" Twisp glanced at the others, focusing on each face for a blink, then: "With the exception of the ambassador there, who can't go in for obvious reasons—they want her, for Ship's sake! But except for her, I'm the obvious one. I'll take Nakano with me." Twisp sent a dasher grin at Nakano, who looked both surprised and pleased.

"Why you?" Brett asked. "I could—"

"You could get yourself in eelshit for no good reason. You've never dealt with people who want to get the best of you, kid. You've never had to drive the best bargain you could for your fish. I know how to deal with such people."

"Gallow is no fish dealer," Bushka said.

"It's still bargaining for your life and everything you want," Twisp said. "The kid stays here with Panille. They keep an eye on you, Bushka, to see you don't do something crazy. Me, I'm going to tell this Gallow just what he gets—so much and no more!"

Chapter 41

Do that which is good and no evil shall touch you.
—Raphael, Apocrypha, *Christian Book of the Dead*

WITHIN THE first minute of the dive, Twisp tumbled along, flailing his long arms, his fins thrusting inefficiently. He watched helplessly as the gap between himself and Nakano widened. Why was Nakano speeding off that way?

Like most Islanders, Twisp had trained with Merman-style breathers for emergency use; he had even considered at one time that he might permit himself to become one of the rare Islanders fitted for an airfish. But airfish were a cash crop and the operation was outrageously costly. And his arms, superb for net pulling, were not suited to swimming.

Twisp struggled to keep Nakano in sight. He skimmed the bottom, his fins puffing sand along a blue-black canyon illuminated by Merman lights set into the rock. The sea above him remained a black remoteness hidden in the short-night.

When Panille had locked the foil against a rocky outcrop within the outpost's kelp perimeter, he had warned them: "The current's ranging between two and four knots. I don't know where the current came from, but it'll help you get to the outpost."

"Kelp is making that current," Bushka had said.

"Whatever is causing it, be careful," Panille had said. "You'll be moving too fast for mistakes."

Brett, still protesting the assignment of duties, had demanded: "How will they get back to us?"

"Steal a vehicle," Nakano had said.

As he had sealed the dive hatch behind them and prepared to flood the foil's lock, Nakano had said: "Stay close, Twisp. We'll be about ten minutes getting to the outpost hatch. I'll tow you the last few meters. Make it look like you're my prisoner."

But now Nakano was far ahead in the chill, green-washed distance. The floppy bubbles of his exhalations raced upward behind him, creating strange prism effects in the artificial light. The Merman obviously was in his element here and Twisp was the muree-out-of-water.

I should've anticipated that! Twisp thought.

Abruptly, Nakano rolled to one side in a powerful turn, clutched one of the light mountings anchored in the canyon's wall and held himself against the current, waiting for Twisp's arrival. Nakano's air tank glistened yellow-green along his back and his masked face was a grotesque shadow beside the rock.

Twisp, somewhat reassured by the Merman's action, tried to change course but would have missed Nakano had not the latter pushed off smoothly and grabbed the breather valve at Twisp's left shoulder. They rode along together then, swimming gently as the current slackened near the underwater cliff into which the outpost had been planted.

Twisp saw a wall of black rock ahead, some of it looking as though it were part of the sea's natural basement complex, some appearing man-changed—great dark shapes piled one atop another. A wide plaz dive lock outlined in light had been set into this construction. Nakano operated controls at the side of the plaz with one hand. A circular hatch opened before them. They swam into the lock, Nakano still holding Twisp's breather valve.

It was an oval space illuminated by brilliant blue lights set into the walls. A plaz hatch on the inner curve revealed an empty passage beyond.

The outer hatch sealed automatically behind them and water began swirling out of the lock through a floor vent. Nakano released his grip on Twisp when their heads emerged from the water.

Removing his mouthpiece, Nakano said: "You're being very intelligent for a Mute. I could've shut off your air at any time. You'd have been eelbait."

Twisp removed his own mouthpiece but remained silent. Nothing was important except getting to Gallow.

"Don't try anything," Nakano warned. "I could break you into small pieces with only one hand."

Hoping Nakano was playing a part for any would-be listeners, Twisp looked at the Merman's heavily muscled body. Nakano's threat could be real, Twisp thought, but the Merman might be surprised at the strength in a netpuller's arms … even if those arms did appear to be mutated monstrosities.

Nakano took off his tank and harness and held the equipment in his left hand. Twisp waited for the last of the water to swirl through the floor vent, then shucked off his own tank. He held it loosely cradled in one long arm, feeling the weight of it and thinking how potent a weapon this would be if hurled suddenly.

The inner hatch swung aside and Twisp tasted hot, moist air. Nakano pushed Twisp ahead of him through the hatchway and they emerged into a rectangular space with no other visible, exit.

Abruptly, a voice barked at them from an overhead vent: "Nakano! Send the Mute topside. You get off at level nine and come to me. I want to know why you didn't bring the foil straight in."

"Gallow," Nakano explained, looking at Twisp. "After I get off, you go straight on up."

Twisp's gut felt suddenly empty. How many people did Gallow have here? Was Gallow so confident of his Security that he could release an Islander prisoner to wander around without a guard? Or was this a ploy to disarm the *stupid Islander?*

Nakano looked up at the vent. Twisp, peering at the ceiling construction, saw the glittering oval of a Merman remote-eye.

"This man's my prisoner," Nakano said. "I presume there are guards topside."

"The Mute can't run away anywhere up there," Gallow's voice snapped. "But he had better wait near the lift exit. We don't want to hunt all over for him."

Twisp felt himself get heavier then and realized that the entire rectangular room was rising. Presently, it stopped, and a thin seam in the back wall opened to reveal a hatch and a well-lighted passage with many armed Mermen in it.

Gallow grasped Twisp's dive tanks by the harness. "I'll take them," he said. "Wouldn't want you using these as a weapon."

Twisp released his hold on the equipment. Gallow went out and the hatch sealed.

Again, the room lifted. After what seemed to Twisp an interminable wait, the room again came to a stop. The hatch opening was haloed in dim light. Hesitantly, Twisp stepped out into hot, dry air. He looked up and around at high, black cliffs and open sky—dawn light, still some stars visible. Even as he looked, Big Sun lifted over the cliffs, illuminating a great rock-girdled bowl with much square-edged Merman construction in it and an LTA base in the middle distance.

Open land!

Twisp heard someone nearby using a saw. The sound was reassuring, a thing heard often in an Island's shop areas—metal and plastics being cut by carpenters for assemblage into necessary nonorganic utensils.

The rocks were sharp under Twisp's bare feet and Big Sun blinded him. "Abimael, simple one! Come here out of the sun!"

It was a man's voice and it came from a building ahead of Twisp. He saw someone moving in the shadows. The sound of sawing continued.

The air in his lungs felt hot and dry, not the cool metallic dampness of the dive tanks nor the warm moisture that blew so often across Vashon. The surface underfoot did not move, either. Twisp felt this as a dangerous, alien thing. *Decks should lift and move!*

All the edges are hard, he thought.

He stepped gingerly forward into the building's shade. The sawing stopped and now Twisp discerned a figure in the deeper shadows—a dark-skinned man in a diaperlike garment. Long black hair frizzed out from the man's head and he had a gray-streaked beard. It was one of the few beards Twisp had ever seen, reaching nearly to the man's navel. Twisp had heard that some Mermen grew beards and the beard-gene cropped up occasionally among Islanders, but this luxurious growth was something new.

As the man moved in the shadows, Twisp saw the evidence of great physical strength, particularly in the shoulders and upper body. This Merman would make a good net-puller, Twisp thought. The Merman's midsection displayed the preliminary settlings of middle age, however. Twisp guessed the man at a hard-driven forty or forty-five ... very dark-skinned for a Merman. His skin glowed with a layer of red within the leathery tones.

"Abimael, come now," the man said. "Your feet will burn. Come have a cake till your mama finds you."

Why does he call me Abimael? Twisp glanced around at the basin enclosed by the high black cliffs. A squad of Mermen worked in the middle distance, sweeping the ground with flamethrowers.

It was a dreamlike scene in the hot light of swiftly rising Big Sun. Twisp feared suddenly that he had been narced. Panille had warned him about it: "Don't swim off into a deep area and you be sure to breathe slow and deep. Otherwise you could be narced."

Narc, Twisp knew, was the Merman term for nitrogen narcosis, intoxication they sometimes encountered in the depths when using pressurized air tanks. There were stories—narced divers releasing their tanks at depth and swimming away to drown, or offering their air to passing fish, or going off into a euphoric water-dance.

"I hear the flamethrowers," the old carpenter said.

The matter-of-fact confirmation of what Twisp saw eased his fears. *No ... this is real land ... open to the sky. I am here and I am not narced.*

"They think they'll sterilize this land and they'll never have nerve runners here," the carpenter said. "The fools are wrong! Nerve-runner eggs are in the sea everywhere. Flamethrowers will be needed for as long as people live here."

The carpenter moved across his shadowed area toward a brown cloth folded on a bench. He sat on the end of the bench and opened the cloth, revealing a paper-wrapped package of cakes, dark brown and glossy. Twisp smelled the sweet stickiness rising from the cakes. The carpenter lifted a cake in thick knuckle-swollen fingers and held it toward Twisp.

In that instant, Twisp saw that the man was blind. The eyes were cloud-gray and empty of recognition. Hesitantly, Twisp accepted the cake and sampled it. Rich brown fruit in the cake sweetened his tongue.

Again, Twisp looked at the scene in the bowl of open land. He had seen pictures and holos from the histories but nothing had prepared him for this experience. He felt both attracted and repelled by what he saw. This land would not drift willy-nilly on an uncertain sea. There was a sense of absolute assurance in the firmness underfoot. But there was a loss of freedom in it, too. It was locked down and enclosed ... limited. Too much of this could narrow a man's vision.

"One more cake, Abimael, and then you go home," the carpenter said.

Twisp stepped back from the carpenter, hoping to escape silently, but his heel encountered a stone and he tumbled backward, sitting sharply on another stone. An involuntary cry of pain escaped him.

"Now, don't you cry, Abimael!" the carpenter said. Twisp heaved himself to his feet. "I'm not Abimael," he said.

The carpenter aimed his sightless eyes toward Twisp and sat silent for a moment, then: "I hear that now. Hope you liked the cake. You see Abimael anywhere around?"

"No one in sight but the men with the flamethrowers."

"Damned fools!" The carpenter swallowed a cake whole and licked the syrupy coating off his fingers. "They're bringing Islanders onto the land already?"

"I ... I think I'm the first."

"They call me Noah," the carpenter said. "You can take it as a joke. Say I was the first out here. Are you badly deformed, Islander?"

Twisp swallowed a sudden rise of anger at the man's bluntness.

"My arms are rather long but they're perfect for pulling nets."

"Don't mind the useful variations," Noah said. "What's your name?"

"Twisp ... Queets Twisp."

"Twisp," Noah said. "I like that name. It has a good sound. Want another cake?"

"No, thank you. It was good, though. I just can't take too much sweetness. What're you making here?"

"I'm working with a bit of wood," Noah said. "Think of that! Wood grown on Pandora! I'm fashioning some pieces that will be made into furniture for the new director of this place. You met him yet? Name's Gallow."

"I haven't had that ... pleasure," Twisp said.

"You will. He sees everybody. Doesn't like Mutes, though, I'm afraid."

"How were you ... I mean, your eyes?"

"I wasn't born this way. It was caused by staring at a sun too long. Bet you didn't know that, did you? If you stand on solid ground so you don't move around, you can stare right at the sun ... but it can blind you."

"Oh." Twisp didn't know what else to say. Noah seemed resigned to his fate, though.

"Abimael!" Noah raised his voice into a loud call.

There was no answer.

"He'll come," Noah said. "Saved a cake for him. He knows it."

Twisp nodded, then felt the foolishness of the gesture. He stared across the enclosed basin. The land glared at him from all sides, everything highlighted by the brightness of Big Sun. The buildings were stark white, shot through with streaks of brown. Water or the illusion of water shimmered in a flat area near the far cliffs. The flamethrowers had been silenced and the Merman workers had gone into a building toward the center of the basin. Noah returned to his woodworking. There was no wind, no sound of seabirds, no sound of Abimael, who was supposed to be coming to his father's call. Nothing. Twisp had never before heard such silence ... not even underwater.

"They call me Noah," Noah said. "Go to the records and look up the histories. I call my first-born Abimael. Do you dream strange things, Twisp? I used to dream about a big boat, called an ark, in the time when the original Terrahome was flooded. The ark saved lots of humans and animals from the flood ... kinda like the hyb tanks in that, you know?"

Twisp found himself fascinated by the carpenter's voice. The man was a storyteller and knew the trick of flexing his voice to hold a listener's attention.

"The ones who didn't get on the ark, they all died," Noah said. "When the sea went down, they found the stinking carcasses for months. The ark was built so animals and people couldn't climb aboard unless they were invited and the ramp was lowered."

Noah mopped sweat from his brow with a purple cloth. "Stinking carcasses everywhere," he muttered.

A slight breeze came over the cliff walls and wafted the heavy stink of burned things across Twisp. He could almost smell the rotting flesh Noah described.

The carpenter hefted two joined pieces of wood and hung them on a peg in the wall behind him.

"Ship made a promise that Noah would live," Noah said. "But watching that much death was very bad. When so many die and so few live, think how dead the survivors must feel! They needed the miracle of Lazarus and it was denied them."

Noah turned away from the wall and his blind eyes glittered in reflected light. Twisp saw that tears rolled unchecked down the man's cheeks and onto his dark, bare chest.

"I don't know whether you'll believe it," Noah said, "but Ship has talked to me."

Twisp stared at the tear-stained face, fascinated. For the first time in his life, Twisp felt himself to be in the presence of an authentic mystery.

"Ship spoke to me," Noah said. "I smelled the stink of death and saw bones on the land still clotted with rotting flesh. Ship said: 'I will not again curse the ground for mankind's sake.'"

Twisp shuddered. Noah's words came with a compelling force that could not be rejected.

Noah paused, then went on: "And Ship said, 'The imagination of man's heart is evil from his youth.' What do you think of that?"

For mankind's sake, Twisp thought.

Noah frightened him then by speaking it once more aloud: "For mankind's sake! As though we begged for it! As though we couldn't work out something better than all that death!"

Twisp began to feel a deep sympathy for the carpenter. This Noah was a philosopher and a profound thinker. For the first time, Twisp began to feel that Islander and Merman might achieve a common understanding. All Mermen were not Gallows or Nakanos.

"You know what, Twisp?" Noah asked. "I expected better of Ship than slaughter. And to say He does it for mankind's sake!"

Noah came across the shadowed work area, skirting the bench as though he could see it, and stopped directly in front of Twisp.

"I hear you breathing there," Noah said. "Ship spoke to me, Twisp. I don't care whether you believe that. It happened." Noah reached out and grasped Twisp's shoulder, moved the hand downward and explored the length of Twisp's left arm, then returned to trace a finger over Twisp's face.

"Your arm *is* long," Noah said. "Don't see anything wrong in that if it's useful. You got a good face. Lots of wrinkles. You live outside a lot. You see any sign of my Abimael yet?"

Twisp swallowed. "No."

"Don't you be frightened of me just because I talk to Ship," Noah said. "This new ark of ours is out on dry land once and for all. We're going to leave the sea."

Noah pulled away from Twisp and returned to the workbench.

A hand touched Twisp's right arm. Startled, he whirled and confronted Nakano. The big Merman had approached without a sound.

"Gallow wants to see you now," Nakano said.

"Where is that Abimael?" Noah asked.

Chapter 42

And the dove came in to him in the evening; and, lo, in her mouth was an olive leaf pluckt off.

—Genesis 8:11, *Christian Book of the Dead*

DUQUE IGNORED the gasps of the watchers ringed around the constant gloom of the Vata Pool. His ears did not register the strangled moan that came clearly from the wide, flaccid throat of the C/P. The heavy fist that Vata clamped to his genitals captured Duque's attention completely. Her fervor hurled him painfully out of pseudosleep, but her touch softened with every blink. The poolside gasps were replaced by sporadic mutterings and a few hushed giggles. When Duque's hand began its complementary stroking of Vata's huge body the room stilled. Vata moaned. The poolside watchers were soaked by the wave set up under the rhythmic strokes of her mighty hips.

"They're going to pair!"

"Her eyes are open," one said, "and look, they move!"

Vata licked her lips, pinned Duque to the bottom of the pool and straddled him there. Her head and the tops of her shoulders broke the surface and she gasped great, long breaths with her head thrown back.

"Yes!" Vata said, and the C/P's mind registered, *Her first word in almost three hundred years.* How could the circumstances of that first word be explained to the faithful?

It's to punish me! The thought flooded Simone Rocksack's mind. *She saw it all.* The C/P wondered, then, what sort of punishment Vata might have in mind for Gallow.

It was then the C/P noted that the sloshing from the Vata Pool was not all resulting from the activity inside. The decks themselves heaved in the same slow rhythm.

"What's happening?" The C/P caught herself muttering the question and glanced around to see that she had not been overheard.

A series of tight-throated moans from Vata, then another explosive, breathless "Yes!" Duque was nearly undetectable under her rippling flanks and hamlike hands.

The C/P's eyes widened in horror and humiliation as she realized that Vata's performance with Duque was a grotesque parody of her last hours with Gallow. Her position wouldn't even allow her to leave the room, to escape the heat that crept outward from the collar of her blue robe to burn her cheeks and her breasts. A trace of sweat graced her upper lip and temples.

Someone burst into the room and shouted, "The kelp!" The voice strained to reach over the babblings of a crowd that was well into a serious hysteria. "The kelp's rocking the Island. It's rocking the whole fucking sea!"

The little stump-legged messenger clapped a fingerless hand over his mouth when he caught sight of the C/P.

There were three sudden cries that brought a chill to the C/P's spine; Vata's thighs shuddered in their grip on Duque and Vata fell back into the pool, wide-eyed and smiling, still anchored to him by their short but stout tether.

The heavy rocking of the decks slackened. The crowd at poolside had stilled with the outburst from Vata. The C/P knew better than to lose this moment. She swallowed hard, lifted her robe to clear her ankles and knelt at the rim of the quieting pool.

"Let us pray," she said, and bowed her head. *Think,* she thought to herself, *think!* Her eyes squinted shut against fear, reality and those difficult traitors, tears.

Chapter 43

Physically, we are created by our reverie—created and limited by our reverie—for it is the reverie which delineates the furthest limits of our minds.
—Gaston Bachelard, "The Poetics of Reverie,"
from *The Handbook of the Chaplain/Psychiatrist*

ON THE way down to confront Gallow, Twisp ignored the spying devices in the ceiling and spoke openly to Nakano. Twisp no longer doubted that Nakano was playing a devious double game. What did it matter? Meeting the carpenter, Noah, had heartened Twisp. Gallow would have to accept the new realities of Pandora. The kelp wanted him dead and would have him dead. The open land belonged to everyone. Gallow could only delay the inevitable; he could not prevent it. He was a prisoner here. All of his people were prisoners here.

Nakano only laughed when Twisp spoke of this. "He knows he's a prisoner. He knows Kareen and Scudi are out there, one step out of reach."

"He'll never get them!" Twisp said.

"Maybe not. But he has the Chief Justice. A bargain may be possible."

"It's strange," Twisp said. "Before I met that carpenter up there, I didn't really know what I was bargaining for."

"What carpenter?" Nakano asked.

"The man I was talking to topside. Noah. Didn't you hear him talking about the ark and Ship speaking to him?"

"There was no man up there! You were alone."

"He was right there! How could you have missed him? Long beard down to here." Twisp passed a hand across his belt line. "He was calling for a child—Abimael."

"You must've been hallucinating," Nakano said, his voice mild. "You were probably narced by the dive."

"He gave me a cake," Twisp whispered.

Remembering the fruity flavor of the cake, the sticky feeling of it on his fingers, Twisp lifted his right hand to the level of his eyes and rubbed his fingers together. There was no stickiness. He smelled the fingers. No smell of the cake. He touched his tongue to his fingers. No taste of the cake.

Twisp began to tremble.

"Hey! Take it easy," Nakano soothed. "Anyone can be narced."

"I saw him," Twisp whispered. "We spoke together. Ship made him a promise: 'I will not again curse the ground for mankind's sake.'"

Nakano took a backward step away from Twisp. "You're crazy! You were standing out in the sun all alone."

"No workshop?" Twisp asked, his voice plaintive. "No bearded man in the shadows?"

"There were no shadows. You probably had a touch of the sun. No hat. Big Sun beating down on you. Forget it."

"I can't forget it. I felt him touch me, his finger on my face. He was blind."

"Well, put it behind you. We're about to see GeLaar Gallow and if you're going to bargain with him you'll need your wits about you."

The moving cubicle came to a stop and the hatch opened onto a passage. Nakano and Twisp emerged and were flanked immediately by six armed Mermen.

"This way," Nakano said. "Gallow is waiting for you."

Twisp took a deep, trembling breath and allowed himself to be escorted along the Merman corridor with its sharp corners and hard sides, its unmoving, solid deck.

That Noah was really there, Twisp told himself. The experience had contained too much sense of reality. *The kelp!* He tingled out to the tips of his fingers with realization. Somehow, the kelp had insinuated itself into his mind, taken dominion over his senses!

The realization terrified him and his step faltered. "Here! Keep up, Mute!" one of the escort barked.

"Easy does it," Nakano cautioned the guard. "He's not used to a deck that doesn't move."

Twisp was surprised by the friendliness in Nakano's voice, his sharpness with the escort. *Does Nakano really sympathize with me?*

They stopped at a wide, rectangular hatchway open to the passage. The room exposed beyond it was large by Islander standards—at least six meters deep and about ten or eleven meters wide. Gallow sat before a bank of display screens near the back wall. He turned as Twisp and Nakano entered, leaving the escort in the passage.

Twisp was immediately struck by the even regularity of Gallow's features, the silkiness of that long golden mane, which reached almost to the Merman's shoulders. The cold blue eyes studied Twisp carefully, pausing only briefly on Twisp's long arms. Gallow came to his feet easily as Nakano and Twisp stopped about two paces from him.

"Welcome," Gallow said. "Please do not consider yourself our prisoner. I look upon you as a negotiator for the Islanders."

Twisp scowled. So Nakano had revealed everything!

"Not you alone, of course," Gallow added. "We will be joined presently by Chief Justice Keel." Gallow's voice was softly persuasive. He smiled warmly.

A charmer, Twisp thought. *Doubly dangerous!*

Gallow studied Twisp's face a blink, those cold blue eyes peeling the Islander. "I'm told"—he glanced at Nakano standing near Twisp's left shoulder, then back to Twisp—"that you do not trust the kelp."

Nakano pursed his lips when Twisp glanced at him. "It's true, isn't it?" Nakano asked.

"It's true." The admission was wrenched from Twisp.

"I think we have created a monster in bringing the kelp to consciousness," Gallow said. "Let me tell you that I have never believed in that part of the kelp project. It was demeaning … immoral … treachery against everything human."

Gallow waved his hand, the gesture saying clearly that he had explained himself sufficiently. He turned to Nakano. "Will you ask the guard out there if the Chief Justice has recovered enough to be brought in here?"

Nakano turned on one heel and went out into the passage where a low-voiced conversation could be heard. Gallow smiled at Twisp. Presently, Nakano returned.

"What's wrong with Keel?" Twisp demanded. "Recovered from what?" And he wondered: *Torture?* Twisp did not like Gallow's smile.

"The Chief Justice, as I prefer to call him, has a digestion problem," Gallow said.

A scuffling sound at the entrance to the room brought Twisp's attention around. He stared hard as two of the escort brought Chief Justice Ward Keel into the room, supporting him as he shuffled stiffly along.

Twisp was shocked. Keel looked near death. Where his skin was visible it was pale and moist. There was a glazed look in his eyes and they did not track together—one peering back toward the passage, the other looking down where he placed each painful step. Keel's neck, supported by that familiar prosthetic framework, still appeared unable to support the man's large head.

Nakano brought a low chair from the side and placed it carefully behind Keel. The escort eased Keel gently into the chair, where he sat a moment, panting. The escort departed.

"I'm sorry, Justice Keel," Gallow said, his voice full of practiced commiseration. "But we really must use what time we have. There are things that I require."

Keel raised his attention slowly, painfully to look up at Gallow. "And what Gallow wants, Gallow gets," Keel said. His voice came out faint and trembling.

"They say you have a digestion problem," Twisp said, looking down at the familiar figure of the Islander who had served so long as a center of topside life.

One of Keel's oddly placed eyes moved to take in Twisp, noting the long arms, the Islander stigmata. Twisp's Islander accent could not be denied.

"You are?" Keel asked, his voice a bit stronger.

"I'm from Vashon, sir. My name's Twisp, Queets Twisp."

"Oh, yes. Fisherman. Why're you here?"

Twisp swallowed. Keel's skin looked like pale sausage casing. The man obviously needed help, not this demanding confrontation with Gallow. Twisp ignored Keel's question and turned on Gallow.

"He should be in a hospital!"

A faint smile tugged at Gallow's mouth. "The Chief Justice has refused medical help."

"Too late for that," Keel said. "What's the purpose of this meeting, Gallow?"

"As you know," Gallow said, "Vashon is grounded near one of our barriers. They have survived a storm, but took severe damage. For us, they are now a sitting target."

"But you're trapped here!" Twisp said.

"Indeed," Gallow agreed. "But then, not all of my people are with me. Others are placed strategically throughout Merman and Islander society. They still do my bidding."

"Islanders work for you?" Twisp demanded.

"The C/P among them." Again, that faint smile touched Gallow's mouth.

"That's remarkable after what he did to Guemes," Keel said. He spoke almost normally, but the effort of sitting upright and carrying it off was apparent. Perspiration dotted his wide forehead.

Gallow pointed a finger at Twisp, eyes glittering. "You have Kareen Ale, fisherman Twisp! Vashon has Vata. I will have both!"

"Interesting," Keel said. He looked at Twisp. "You really have Kareen?"

"She's out there in our foil, just within the kelp line where Gallow and his people can't go."

"I think Nakano could go there," Gallow said. "Nakano?"

"Perhaps," Nakano said.

"The kelp passed him unmolested coming in here," Gallow said, smiling at Twisp. "Doesn't it appear likely that Nakano has immunity from the kelp?"

Twisp looked at Nakano, who once more stood passively at one side, obviously listening but not focusing his eyes on any of the speakers.

It came to Twisp then that Nakano did, indeed, belong to the kelp. The big Merman had made some kind of pact with the monster presence in the sea! To Twisp, Nakano appeared the embodiment of Merman killer-viciousness, all of it concealed within a warmly reasonable mask. Was that Nakano's value to the kelp? There could be no missing the fanatic's tone when Nakano spoke of the kelp.

"The kelp is my immortality." That was what Nakano had said.

"Really, there should be no need for violence and killing," Gallow said. "We are all reasonable men. You have things you want; I have things I want. Surely there must be some common ground where we can meet."

Twisp's thoughts darted back to that odd topside encounter with the carpenter, Noah. *If that was really the kelp projecting hallucination into his mind, what was the purpose? What was the message?*

Slaughter was wrong. Even if Ship commanded it, slaughter was wrong. Twisp had felt this strongly in Noah's manner and words.

The ark has grounded and the land no longer will be cursed by Ship. Twisp knew vaguely of the ark legend … was there a message from Ship here, sent through the kelp?

Gallow, on the other hand, represented treachery, a man who would do anything to gain his ends. Did the C/P really work for him? If so, an evil pact had been forged.

And what if Noah was just hallucination? Nakano could be right: I might have been narced.

Nakano focused abruptly on Twisp and asked: "Why aren't you nauseated?"

It was such a startling question, suggesting Nakano had read Twisp's mind, that Twisp was a moment focusing on the possible implications.

"Are you also sick?" Keel asked, peering up at Twisp.

"I am quite well," Twisp said. He tore his gaze away from Nakano and looked more closely at Gallow, seeing the marks of self-indulgence in the man's face, the sly twist of the smile, the frown lines in the forehead, the downturned creases at the corners of the mouth.

Twisp returned then to the knowledge of what he had to do. Speaking slowly and distinctly, directing his words at Gallow, Twisp said: "The imagination of your heart has been evil from your youth."

Ship's words as reported by Noah came easily from Twisp's mouth and once he had said them, he felt their lightness.

Gallow scowled, then: "You're not much of a diplomat!"

"I'm a simple fisherman," Twisp said.

"Fisherman, but not simple," Keel said. A chuckle turned into a weak, dry cough.

"You think Nakano has immunity from the kelp," Twisp said. "I was his passport. Without me, he would have joined the others. He has told you about the others that the kelp drowned, hasn't he?"

"I tell you the kelp is out of control!" Gallow said. "We have loosed a monster on Pandora. Our ancestors were right to kill it off!"

"Perhaps they were," Twisp agreed. "But we'll not be able to do it again."

"Poisons and burners!" Gallow said.

"No!" The word was torn from Nakano. He glared at Gallow.

"We will only prune it back to manageable size," Gallow said, his voice soothing. "Too small a number to be conscious but large enough to preserve our dead forever."

Nakano nodded curtly but did not relax.

"Tell him, Nakano," Twisp ordered. "Could you really return to the foil without me?"

"Even if the kelp passed me, the crew probably wouldn't let me aboard," Nakano said.

"I don't see how you're going to sink Vashon when it's already aground," Keel said. A painful smile curved the edges of Keel's mouth.

"So you think I'm helpless," Gallow said.

Twisp glanced back at the open hatchway into the passage, the guards clustered there trying to make it appear that they were not listening.

"Don't your people know how you've trapped them?" Twisp demanded, his voice loud and carrying. "As long as you live, they're prisoners here!"

Blood suffused Gallow's face. "But Vashon—"

"Vashon is in a perimeter of kelp that you can't penetrate!" Twisp said. "Nobody you send against Vashon can get through!" He looked at Keel. "Mr. Justice, isn't that—"

"No, no," Keel husked. "Go on. You're doing fine."

Gallow made a visible attempt to control his anger, taking several deep breaths, squaring his shoulders. He said: "LTAs can—"

"LTAs are limited in what they can do," Nakano interrupted. "You know what happened to the one I was on. They are vulnerable."

Gallow looked at Nakano as though seeing the man for the first time. "Do I hear my faithful Nakano correctly?"

"Don't you understand?" Nakano asked, his voice softly penetrating. "It doesn't matter what happens to us. Come, I will go into the kelp with you. Let it take us."

Gallow backed two steps away from Nakano.

"Come," Nakano insisted. "The Chief Justice obviously is dying. The three of us will go together. We will not die. We will live forever in the kelp."

"You fool!" Gallow snapped. "The kelp can die! It was killed once and that could happen again!"

"The kelp does not agree," Nakano said. "Avata lives forever!"

His voice lifted on the last sentence and a wild light came into his eyes.

"Nakano, Nakano, my most trusted companion," Gallow said, his voice pitched to its most persuasive tone. "Let us not permit the heat of the moment to sway us." Gallow sent an apprehensive glance toward the listening guards at the hatchway. "Of course the kelp can live forever … but not in such numbers that it threatens our existence."

Nakano's expression did not change.

Keel, watching the scene through pain-glazed eyes, thought: *Nakano knows him! Nakano does not trust him!*

Twisp entertained a similar thought and knew he had found the ultimate leverage to use against Gallow. *Nakano can be turned against his chief.*

Gallow constructed a rueful smile, which he turned toward Keel. "Mr. Justice Keel, let us not forget that the C/P is still mine! And I will have the hyb tanks."

That's his best shot! Keel thought. "I'll bet the C/P doesn't know it was you who sank Guemes," Keel managed.

"Can anyone carry such an accusation to her?" Gallow asked. He looked blandly around him.

Is that our death warrant? Twisp wondered. *Will we be silenced permanently?* He decided on a bold attack.

"If we do not return to the foil, they will broadcast that accusation and Bushka's statement confirming it."

"Bushka?" Gallow's eyes showed both shock and glee. "Do you mean Bushka, the Islander who stole our sub?" Gallow smiled at Nakano. "Do you hear that? They know where to find the sub thief."

Nakano did not change expression.

Gallow glanced at the chrono beside his communications terminal. "Well, well! It's almost time for the midday meal. Fisherman Twisp, why don't you stay here with the Chief Justice? I'll have food sent in. Nakano and I will dine together and consult on possible compromises. You and the Chief Justice can do the same."

Gallow moved to Nakano's side. "Come, old friend," Gallow said. "I didn't save your life to provide myself with an opponent."

Nakano glanced at Twisp, the thought plain on the big face. *Why did you save my life?*

Twisp chose to answer the unspoken question. "You know why." And he thought: *I saved you simply because you were in danger.* Nakano already knew this.

Nakano resisted the pressure on his arm.

"Do not quarrel with me, old friend," Gallow said. "Both of us will go to the kelp in time, but it's too soon. There's much yet for us to do."

Slowly, Nakano allowed himself to be guided from the room.

His muscles trembling so hard that his great head shook with visible tremors, Keel lifted his attention to Twisp. "We do not have much time," Keel said. "Clear that table at the end of the room and help me to stretch out on it."

Moving quickly, Twisp swept the objects off the table, then returned to Keel. Slipping his long arms under the Chairman, Twisp lifted the old body, shocked at how light the man was. Keel was nothing but thin bones in a loose sack of skin. Gently, Twisp carried the Chairman across the room and eased him onto the table.

Weakly, Keel fumbled with the harness of his prosthesis. "Help me get this damned thing off," he gasped.

Twisp unbuckled the harness and slipped the prosthesis away from Keel's back and shoulders, letting it drop to the floor.

Keel sighed with relief. "I prefer to leave this world more or less as I came into it," he grated, every word draining him. "No, don't object. Both of us know I'm dying."

"Sir, isn't there anything I can do to help you?"

"You've already done it. I was afraid I'd have to die in the midst of strangers."

"Surely, we can do something to …"

"Really, there's nothing. The best doctors on Vashon have conveyed to me the verdict of that higher Committee on Vital Forms. No … you are the perfect person for this moment … not so close to me that you'll become maudlin, yet close enough that I know you care."

"Sir … anything I can do … anything …"

"Use your own superb good sense in dealing with Gallow. You've already seen that Nakano can be turned against him."

"Yes, I saw that."

"There is one thing."

"Anything."

"Don't let them give me to the kelp. I don't want that. Life should have a body of its own, even such a poor body as this one I'm about to leave."

"I'll—" Twisp broke off. Honesty forced him to remain silent. What could he do?

Keel sensed this confusion. "You will do what you can," he said. "I know that. And if you fail, I am not your judge."

Tears filled Twisp's eyes. "Anything I can do … I'll do."

"Don't be too hard on the C/P," Keel whispered.

"What?" Twisp bent close to the Chairman's lips.

Keel repeated it, adding: "Simone is a sensitive and bitter woman and—and you've seen Gallow. Imagine how attractive he would seem to her."

"I understand," Twisp said.

"I'm filled with joy that the Islands can produce such good men," Keel said. "I am ready to be judged."

Twisp wiped at his eyes, still bending close to hear the Chairman's last words. When Keel did not continue, Twisp became aware that there was no sound of breathing from the supine figure. Twisp put a hand to the artery at Keel's neck. No pulse. He straightened.

What can I do?

Was there anything combustible here to burn the old body and prevent the Mermen from consigning Keel to the sea? He looked all around the room. Nothing. Twisp stared helplessly at the body on the table.

"Is he dead?" It was Nakano speaking from the hatchway. Twisp turned to find the big Merman standing just inside the room.

The tears on Twisp's face were sufficient answer. "He's not to be given to the kelp," Twisp said.

"Friend Twisp, he died but he need not be dead," Nakano said. "You can meet him again in Avata."

Twisp clenched his fists, his long arms trembling. "No! He asked me to prevent that!"

"But it's not up to us," Nakano said. "If he was a deserving man, Avata will wish to accept him."

Twisp jumped to the side of the table and stood with his back to it. "Let me take him to Avata," Nakano said. He moved toward Twisp.

As Nakano came within range of those long arms, Twisp shot out a net-calloused fist, leaning his shoulder behind it. The blow struck with blinding speed on the side of Nakano's jaw. Nakano's heavily muscled neck absorbed most of the shock but his eyes glazed. Before he could recover, Twisp leaped forward and wrenched one of Nakano's arms backward, intending to throw the man to the deck.

Nakano recovered enough to tense his muscles and prevent this. He turned slowly against Twisp's pressure, moving like a great pillar of kelp.

Abruptly, the guards swarmed into the room. Other hands grabbed Twisp and jerked him aside, pinning him to the deck.

"Don't hurt him!" Nakano shouted. The pressures on Twisp eased but did not leave.

Nakano stood over Twisp, a sad look on the big face, a touch of blood at the corner of his mouth.

"Please, friend Twisp, I mean you no harm. I mean only to honor the Chief Justice and Chairman of the Committee on Vital Forms, a man who has served us so well for so long."

One of the guards pinning Twisp down snickered.

Immediately, Nakano grasped the man by a shoulder and lifted him like a sack of fishmeal, hurling him aside.

"These Islanders you sneer at are as dear to Avata as any of us!" Nakano bellowed. "Any among you who forgets this will answer to me!"

The abused guard stood with his back to a bulkhead, his face contorted with fear.

Indicating Twisp with one thick finger, Nakano said: "Hold him but let him up." Nakano went to the table and lifted Keel's body gently in his arms.

He turned and strode past the guards, pausing at the hatchway. "When I have gone, take the fisherman to our leader. GeLaar Gallow is topside and has things to say." Nakano looked thoughtfully at Twisp. "He needs your help to get the hyb tanks—they're on their way down."

Chapter 44

Hybernation is to hibernation as death is to sleep. Closer to death than it is to life, hybernation can be lifted only by the grace of Ship.
—The Histories

WHILE BRETT held Bushka down, Ale tied off the stump of Bushka's left arm with a length of dive harness. Bushka lay just inside the main hatch, the sea surface visible through the plaz port behind him. Big Sun, just entering its afternoon quadrant, painted oily coils across the kelp fronds out there, now bright and now dulled as clouds scudded overhead.

A moan escaped Bushka.

The foil rolled gently in a low sea. Ale braced herself against a bulkhead while she worked.

"There," she said as she tied off the dive harness. Blood smeared the deck around them and their dive suits were red with it.

Ale turned and shouted up the passage behind Brett. "Shadow! Do you have that cot ready?"

"I'm bringing it!"

Brett took a deep breath and looked out the plaz at the quiescent kelp—so harmless-looking, so tranquil. The horizon was an absurd pinkish gray where Little Sun would soon lift into view, joining its giant companion.

It had been a hellish half hour.

Bushka, meandering aimlessly around the pilot cabin, had lulled them into a sense of security by his casual movements. Abruptly, he had dashed down the passageway and hit the manual override on the main hatch. Water had come blasting in at the high pressure of their depth—almost thirty-five meters down. Bushka had been prepared. Standing to one side of the blasting water, he had grabbed an emergency tank-breather outfit stored beside the hatch, slipping swiftly into the harness.

Brett and Panille, running after him, had been spilled and tumbled in the wash of water boiling down the passage. Only Scudi's alertness in sealing off a section between them and the open hatch had saved the foil and its occupants.

Bushka had kicked easily out into the kelp-jungle where the foil lay on bottom.

Scudi, faced with tons of water in the foil, had blown tanks and started the pumps, shouting for Kareen to help Brett and Shadow. The foil had lifted slowly, floating upward through the massed kelp.

Brett and Panille, splashing their way back into the cabin, had accepted a hand from Kareen. Scudi, seated at the controls, spared a glance for Brett to reassure herself that he was safe, then returned her attention to the watery world visible through the plaz.

"It's tearing him apart!" Scudi gasped.

The others sloshed to a position behind Scudi and looked outside. The foil slithered upward against giant kelp fronds, giving those inside the pilot cabin a dimly lighted view of Bushka close beside them. One large kelp tentacle, wrapped around his body, held Bushka fast while another tentacle gripped his left arm. A cloud of dark liquid flooded the water around Bushka's arm.

Kareen gasped.

Brett understood then—the cloud: *blood!* The arm had been torn from Bushka's body.

As though it wanted to spit him out, the kelp tentacles whipped away from Bushka and shunted him swiftly upward.

Scudi tipped the foil's nose up and drove for the surface. They found Bushka there, half-conscious and bleeding dangerously. A hunt of dashers, coming to the smell of blood, was whipped back by kelp fronds.

Later, after Kareen had treated Bushka, Brett and Panille lashed him to the cot and carried him forward. Ale walked alongside. "He's lost a lot of blood," she said. "The brachial artery was wide open."

Scudi remained at the helm, sparing only a brief glance at Bushka's pale face as the cot was lowered to the deck behind her. She held the foil in a tight circle within a kelp-free area. Choppy waves drummed a dulled *tunk-tunk* against the hull. The last of the unwanted water had gone overboard but the decks were still damp with it.

Scudi, the image of Bushka's injuries fresh in her mind, thought: *Ship save us! The kelp has turned vicious!*

Panille stood above Bushka. A wash of agony grayed Bushka's face but he appeared conscious. Seeing this, Panille demanded, "What were you trying to do?"

"Shhhh," Ale cautioned.

"'S'all right," Bushka managed. "Was gonna kill Gallow."

Panille could not suppress his outrage. "You almost killed us all!"

Kareen pulled Panille away.

Brett slid into the seat beside Scudi and looked out at the dark pile of the outpost with its foam-laced base. Little Sun had risen and the water was bright with the double light.

"Kelp," Bushka said.

"Hush," Ale said. "Save your strength."

"Gotta talk. Kelp has all the Guemes dead … in it. All there. Said I tore off arm of humanity … punished me in kind. Damn! Damn!" He tried to look at the place where his arm had been but the lashings on the cot restrained him.

Scudi stared wide-eyed at Brett. Was it possible the kelp took on the personality of all the dead it had absorbed? Would all the old scores be settled? Given consciousness finally and words in which to express itself, the kelp spoke in violent action. She shuddered as she looked out at the green fronds surrounding the foil.

"There are dashers all over the place," Scudi said.

"Where … where's my arm?" Bushka moaned.

His eyes were closed and his large head looked even larger against the pale fabric of the cot.

"Packed in ice in the cooler," Ale said. "We'll interfere as little as possible with the wound tissue. Better chance for reattachment."

"Kelp knew I was just a fool that Gallow … took advantage of," Bushka groaned. He twisted his head from side to side. "Why'd it hurt *me?*"

A heavy gust of wind popped the foil hard and thrust it sideways against the kelp. A loud thump sounded amidships and the foil heeled, righting itself with a rasping hiss.

"What is it? What's that?" Ale demanded.

Brett pointed to the sky above the outpost. "I think we've just had our attention called to something. Look! Have you ever seen that many LTAs?"

"LTAs hell!" Panille said. "Ship's guts! Those are hylighters! Thousands of them."

Brett stared open-mouthed. Like all Pandoran children, he had watched holos of the kelp's spore carriers, a phenomenon unseen on Pandora for generations.

Panille was right! Hylighters!

"They're so beautiful," Scudi murmured.

Brett had to agree. The hylighters, giant organic hydrogen bags, danced with rainbow colors in the doubled sunlight. They drifted high across the outpost, moving southwest on a steady wind.

"It's out of our hands now," Panille said. "The kelp will do its own propagating."

"They're coming down," Brett said. "Look. Some of them are trailing tentacles in the water.

The flight of hylighters, well past the outpost now, moved in a gentle slope of wind toward the sea.

"It's almost as though they were being directed," Scudi said. "See how they move together."

Once more, something hard banged against the foil's hull. A channel opened beside them, spreading outward toward the place where the hylighters were coming down close above the water. Slowly at first, a current moved the foil into the new channel.

"Better go along with it," Panille said.

"But Twisp is still there at the outpost!" Brett objected.

"Kelp's directing this show," Panille said. "Your friend will have to take his own chances."

"I think Shadow's right," Scudi ventured. She pointed toward the outpost. "See? There are more hylighters. They're almost touching the rock."

"But what if Twisp comes back and we aren't …"

"I'll bring us back as soon as the kelp lets us," Scudi said. She fired up the ramjets.

"No! I'll take breather tanks and go out to—"

"Brett!" Scudi put a hand on his arm. "You saw what it did to Bushka."

"But I haven't hurt it … or anyone. That Merman would have killed me."

"We don't know what it'll do," Scudi said.

"She's right," Panille said. "What good would you be to your friend without arms?"

Brett sank back into the seat.

Scudi pushed the throttles ahead and lowered the foils. The boat gathered speed, lifted and swept down the channel toward the descending hylighters.

Brett sat in silence. He felt suddenly that his Mermen companions had turned against him, even Scudi. How could they know what the kelp wanted? So it opened a channel through its heavy growth! So it directed a current through that channel! Twisp might need him back there where they were supposed to be waiting.

Abruptly, Brett shook his head. He thought how Twisp would react to such protests. *Don't be a fool!* The kelp had spoken without misunderstanding. Bushka … the channel … the current—words could say no clearer what had to be done now. Scudi and the others had merely understood and accepted it more quickly.

With a quick chopping motion, Scudi cut the power and the foil settled in a heaving surge that sent waves curling outward on both sides.

"We're blocked," she said.

They looked ahead. Not only had kelp closed the channel through which the foil had come, but fronds and stalks lifted out of the water ahead of them. A low, thick forest of green blocked their passage.

Brett glanced left. The outpost loomed high there, no more than three klicks away. Hylighters continued to descend about a klick ahead of them, massed flocks of them.

Panille spoke from directly behind Brett. "I don't remember them as being that colorful in the holos."

"A new breed, no doubt of it," Kareen said.

"What do we do now?" Brett asked.

"We sit here until we find out why the kelp directed us to this place," Scudi said.

Brett looked up at the descending flocks of hylighters. Dark tentacles reached down toward the water. Sunlight flashed rainbow iridescence off the great bags.

"The histories say the kelp makes its own hydrogen the way you Islanders do," Panille said. "The bags are extruded deep underwater, filled and sent flying to spread the spores. One of my ancestors rode a hylighter." He spoke in a breathless whisper. "They've always fascinated me. I've dreamed of this day."

"What are they doing?" Scudi asked. "Why would they bring spores here? There's kelp all around us."

"You're assuming they're intelligently directed," Kareen said. "They're probably going wherever the wind takes them."

Panille shook his head sharply. "No. Who controls the currents controls the temperature of the surface water. Who controls that directs the winds."

"Then what are they doing?" Scudi repeated. "They're not drifting very fast anymore. It's as though they were assembling here."

"The hyb tanks?" Kareen asked.

"How could the kelp—" Scudi began. She broke off, then: "Is this where they're supposed to come down?"

"Near enough," Kareen said. "Shadow?"

"The correct quadrant," he said. He glanced at a chrono. "By the original schedule, splashdown's already overdue."

"There's a strange hylighter," Brett said. "Or is that really an LTA?" He pointed upward, his finger almost touching the overhead plaz.

"Parachute!" Panille said. "Ship's guts! There comes the first hyb tank!"

"Look at the hylighters!" Scudi said.

The colorful bags had begun a swirling motion, opening a space in their center. The open space drifted somewhat south and a bit west, presenting a net of sea to catch the descending parachute.

Something could be seen dangling from the parachute now—a silvery cylinder that reflected bright flashes from the suns.

"Ship! That thing is big!" Panille said.

"I wonder what's in it," Kareen whispered.

"We're about to discover that," Brett said. "Look! Above the parachute—there comes another one … and another."

"Ohhhh, if I could only get my hands on one of them … just one," Panille said.

The first hyb tank was now little more than a hundred meters above the water. It descended swiftly, the actual splashdown concealed within the ring of hylighters. A second hyb tank fell into the open circle, a third … fourth … The watchers counted twenty of them, some larger than the foil.

The circle of hylighters closed in as the last tank hit the water. Immediately, a lane through the kelp began to spread from the foil's blocked position to where the hylighters had collected.

"We're being asked to join them," Scudi said. She fired up the rams and eased the foil ahead at hull speed, keeping it just off the step. A bow wave spread on both sides. The hylighters parted as the foil drew near them, opening a passage into a kelp-free circle where the great tanks bobbed.

The occupants of the foil stared in wonder at the vista opened to them. Hylighter tentacles could be seen working over the closure mechanisms of the tanks, opening them and snaking inside. Wide curved hatches swung aside to the probing tentacles. Abruptly, one of the opened tanks tipped, admitting a surge of water. White-bellied sea mammals emerged and immediately dove into the water.

"Orcas," Panille breathed. "Look!" He pointed across Brett's shoulder. "Humpback whales! Just the way they looked in the holos."

"My whales," Scudi whispered.

The channel that had been opened for the foil curved left now, directing them to a cluster of six tanks being held side by side in a nest of kelp. Hylighter tentacles could be seen writhing and twisting into the tanks.

As the foil neared this cluster, a dark tentacle emerged with a struggling human form—pale-skinned and naked. Another tentacle came up with another human … another … another … A spectrum of skin shades came out of the tanks—from darker than Scudi to paler than Kareen Ale.

"What are they doing with those poor people?" Kareen demanded.

The faces of the people being taken from the tanks betrayed obvious terror, but the terror began to subside even as the foil's occupants watched. Slowly, hylighters carrying humans began to drift toward the foil.

"There's why we were brought in," Brett said. "Come on, Shadow. Let's open the hatch."

Scudi silenced the foil's jets. "We can't handle that many people," she said. She pointed at the massed hylighters removing other humans from the adjacent tanks. More than a hundred human figures could be seen grasped in hylighter tentacles and more humans were being removed from the tanks every second. "That many will sink us!" Scudi said.

Brett, hesitating in the passageway to follow the direction of Scudi's pointing finger, said: "We'll have to tow them to the outpost. We'll see if we can get a line to them." He whirled and dashed down the passage toward the main hatch. Panille could be heard running behind him.

Hylighters already were clustering around the hatchway when Brett opened it. A tentacle snaked in the opening and grasped Brett. He froze. Words filled his mind, clear and perfect, without any secondary sounds to distort them.

"Gentle human who is loved by Avata's beloved Scudi, do not fear. We bring you Shipclones to live in peace beside all of you who share Pandora with Avata."

Brett gasped and sensed Panille beside him: muddy thoughts—nowhere near as clear as those bell-like words entering his senses through the hylighter tentacles. Panille projected awe, schoolboy memories of holoviews displaying hylighters, family stories of that first Pandoran Panille … then fear that the mass of humans being delivered by the hylighters would sink the foil.

"Hylighters will buoy you," the tentacles transmitted. "Do not fear. What a splendid day this is! What marvelous surprises have come to us, the gift of blessed Ship."

Slowly, Brett regained the use of his own senses. He found himself braced against loops of hylighter tentacles. Naked humans were being slipped through the hatchway one after another. How tall the newcomers were! Some of them had to duck in the passageway.

Panille looked dazed in a similar tentacle grasp. He waved the newcomers up the passage toward the control cabin.

"Some of you can go into the cargo bays along this passage," Brett called.

They went where Brett and Panille directed them … no questions, no arguments. They appeared to be in shock from awakening into the tentacles of hylighters.

"We're being moved toward the outpost," Panille said. He nodded toward the edge of black rock visible out the hatchway. The sound of the surf against the base of the outpost was clearly audible.

"Gallow!" Brett said.

As Brett spoke, the hylighter tentacles unwound from his body. Panille, too, was released. The space around them remained crowded with silent newcomers. More could be seen held in hylighter tentacles, other tentacles clutching the lip of the hatchway. Slowly, he began squeezing his way forward, apologizing, feeling the pressure of naked skin that made way for him.

The pilot cabin was not quite as crowded as the passage. Space had been left around the unconscious form of Bushka on the cot. More space insulated the command seats where Scudi and Kareen sat. A lacework of hylighter tentacles covered most of the plaz, leaving only small framed bits of the forward view. The outpost loomed high there, the surf sound loud.

"Kelp is right up against the outpost now," Kareen said. "Look at it! There's almost no open space left."

One of the newcomers, a man so tall that his head almost touched the top of the cabin, came forward and bent to peer through a small opening in the lacework of hylighter tentacles. He straightened presently and looked down at the webs between Scudi's toes, then to the similar growth on Kareen's feet. He brought his attention at last to Brett's large eyes.

"God save us!" he said. "If we breed on this planet will our offspring all be deformed?"

Brett was caught first by the man's accent, an odd lilting in the way he spoke, then by the words. The man looked at Mermen and Islanders with the same obviously revolted expression.

Kareen, shocked, shot a glance at Brett and then at the cabin full of giant humans, the looks of dazed withdrawal slowly vanishing from all of those faces—those strangely similar faces. Kareen wondered how these people could identify each other … except for the variations in skin tone. They all looked so much alike!

It dawned on her then that she was seeing Ship-normals … human-normals. She, with her small stature and partly webbed toes, she was the freak.

Ship! How would these newcomers take to people like the Chief Justice or even Queets Twisp with his ungainly arms? What would they say on encountering the C/P?

The foil grated against rock then … again … again. It lifted slightly and was set down hard on a solid surface.

"We've arrived," Scudi said.

"And we're going to have to deal with GeLaar Gallow somehow," Panille said.

"If the kelp hasn't already done it for us," Kareen said.

"There's no telling what it'll do," Panille said. "I'm afraid Twisp was right. It's not to be trusted."

"It can be damned convincing, though," Brett said, recalling the touch of hylighters at the hatchway.

"That's its real danger," Panille said.

Chapter 45

Fools! who slaughtered the cattle sacred to the sun-king;
behold, the god deprived them of their day of homecoming.
—Homer, *Shiprecords*

TWISP COULD hear Gallow's people talking down in the basin, a nervousness in their chatter that told him the strength of his own position. Gallow had brought him up a narrow trail cut in the rock and out onto a flat promontory that jutted seaward on the southeastern edge of the outpost. A breeze blew against Twisp's face.

"One day, I will have my administrative building here," he said, gesturing expansively.

Twisp glanced around him at the black rock sparkling with mineral fragments in the light of both suns. He had seen many days such as this one—both suns up, the sea rolling easily under a blanket of kelp—but never from such a vantage. Not even the highest point on Vashon commanded such a view—high, solid and unmoving.

Gallow would build here?

Twisp tried to catch snatches of the conversations from below them, but mostly it was words of nervousness that permeated this place. Gallow was not immune to it.

"The hyb tanks will be coming down soon," he said, "and I'll have them!"

Twisp looked out at all that kelp, remembering Nakano's words. *"He needs your help."*

"How will you recover the tanks?" Twisp asked, his tone reasonable. He felt no need to mention the ring of kelp around this rocky outcrop lifting from the sea. From this vantage, it appeared to Twisp that the kelp was even closer than it had been when he and Nakano had swum away from the foil.

"LTAs," Gallow said, pointing at the partly filled bags of three LTAs waiting on their pad. The Mermen working around the LTAs appeared to be the only purposeful figures in the basin.

"It would help, of course, if we had your foil," Gallow said. "I'm prepared to offer a great deal in return for that."

"You have a foil," Twisp said. "I saw it anchored next to the lee side of this place." He kept his tone casual, thinking how like so many other times this was—bargaining for the best price on his catch.

"We both know the kelp won't give passage to our foil," Gallow said. "But if you were to return to your foil with Nakano …"

Twisp took a deep breath. Yes, this was like bargaining for his catch, but there was a profound difference. You could respect the fish-buyers even while you opposed them. Gallow revolted him. Twisp fought to keep this emotion out of his voice.

"I don't know that you have anything to offer me," he said.

"Power! A share in the new Pandora!"

"Is that all?"

"All?" Gallow appeared truly surprised.

"Seems to me the new Pandora's going to happen anyway. I don't see where you're going to have much influence in it, the kelp wanting your hide and all."

"You don't understand," Gallow said. "Merman Mercantile controls most of the food sources, the processing. Kareen Ale can be bent to our needs and her shares will—"

"You don't have Kareen Ale."

"With your foil … and the people in it …"

"From what I could see, Shadow Panille has Kareen Ale. And as far as Scudi Wang is concerned—"

"She's a child who—"

"I think maybe she's a very wealthy child."

"Exactly! Your foil and the people in it are the key!"

"But *you* don't have that key. *I* have it."

"And I have you," Gallow said, his voice hard.

"And the kelp has Chairman Keel," Twisp said.

"But it does not have me and I still have the means of recovering the hyb tanks. The LTAs will be clumsier and slower, but they can do it."

"You're offering me a subordinate position in your organization," Twisp said. "What's to prevent me from grabbing it all once I'm back on the foil?"

"Nakano."

Twisp chewed his lip to keep from laughing. Gallow had very little buying power. None at all, really, with the kelp against him and the foil in the hands of someone who wanted to beat him to the tanks. Twisp looked up at the sky. The tanks would be coming down within sight of this place, Gallow said. His people at the Launch Base had alerted Gallow. And that was another consideration: Gallow had followers in many places … Islanders as well.

But the hyb tanks!

Twisp could not prevent a deep sense of excitement at the thought of them. He had grown up on stories speculating about the tanks' contents. They were a bag of prizes meant to humanize Pandora.

Could the kelp prevent that?

Twisp turned and looked at the LTAs. No doubt those things could move above the kelp's reach. But would the kelp let airborne humans pluck the prize from the sea? It all depended on where the tanks came down. There was kelp-free sea surface visible from this high point. A very uncertain lottery, though.

Gallow moved up beside Twisp to "share his view of the outpost's interior basin and its waiting LTAs.

"There's my fallback position," Gallow said. He nodded toward the LTAs.

Twisp knew what he would do now if this were bargaining for his catch. Threaten to go to another buyer. Get caustic and let this buyer know he had no status in the larger game.

"I think you're nothing but eelshit," Twisp said. "Concentrate on the facts. If the tanks land in kelp, you're finished. Without hostages, you're just a pitiful handful of people on one little bit of land. You may have followers elsewhere but I'm betting they'll desert you the second they recognize how powerless you really are."

"I still have you," Gallow grated. "And don't make any mistakes about what I can do to you!"

"What can you do?" Twisp asked, his voice at its most reasonable. "We're alone up here. All I have to do is grab you and dive off this place into the sea. The kelp will get us both."

Gallow smiled and slipped a lasgun from the pouch pocket at his waist.

"I thought you'd have one of those," Twisp said.

"I would take great pleasure in cutting you into pieces slowly," Gallow said.

"Except that you need me," Twisp said. "You're no gambler, Gallow. You like sure things."

Gallow scowled.

Twisp inclined his head toward the LTAs. The bags were beginning to swell. Someone was pumping hydrogen into them.

"Those are not a sure thing," Twisp said.

Gallow forced his features into a semblance of a smile. He looked down at the weapon in his hand. "Why are we arguing?"

"Is that what we're doing?" Twisp asked.

"You are stalling," Gallow said. "You want to see where the tanks come down."

Twisp smiled.

"For an Islander, you're pretty smart," Gallow said. "You know what I'm offering. You could have anything you want—money, women …"

"How do you know what I want?" Twisp asked.

"You're no different from anyone else in that," Gallow said. He sent his glance along Twisp's long arms. "There might even be a few Mermen women who wouldn't find you objectionable."

Gallow pocketed his lasgun and displayed his empty hand. "See? I know what'll work with you. I know what I can give you."

Twisp shook his head slowly from side to side. Again, he looked at the LTAs. *Objectionable?* One step and he would have his long arms on the most objectionable human he had ever met. Two more steps and they would be over the side into the sea.

But then I might never know how it came out.

He thought about finding himself conscious in the kelp's vast reservoir of awareness. He shared Keel's revulsion to that end. *Damn! And I couldn't help the old man! Gallow owes us for that!*

A shadow passed across Twisp, bringing an immediate coolness from the breeze that tugged at him. He thought it just another cloud but Gallow gasped and something touched Twisp's shoulder, his cheek—a long and ropy something.

Twisp looked up into the base of a hylighter then, seeing the long, dark tentacles all around, feeling them grab him. Somewhere, he could hear screaming.

Gallow?

A flawless voice filled Twisp's senses, seeming to come at him along every nerve channel—hearing, touch, sight … all of him was caught up in that voice.

"Welcome to Avata, fisherman Twisp," the voice said. "What is your wish?"

"Put me down," Twisp gasped.

"Ahhh, you wish to retain the flesh. Then Avata cannot put you down here. The flesh would be damaged, very likely destroyed. Be patient and have no fear. Avata will put you down with your friends."

"Gallow?" Twisp managed.

"He is not your friend!"

"I know that!"

"And so does Avata. Gallow will be put down, as you so quaintly phrase it, but from a great height. Gallow is no longer anything but a curiosity, no more than an aberration. Better to consider him a disease, infectious and sometimes deadly. Avata is curing the infected body."

Twisp grew aware then that he dangled high in the air, wind blowing past him. A great expanse of kelp spread out far below him. A sudden feeling of vertigo tightened his chest and throat, filled him with dizziness.

"Do not fear," the flawless voice said. "Avata cherishes the friends and companions of beloved Scudi Wang."

Twisp slowly twisted his head upward, feeling the ropy tentacles holding him tight around the waist and legs, seeing the dark underside of the bag that suspended this twining mass.

Avata?

"You see what you call hylighter," the voice told him. "Once more Avata spawns in the mother-sea. Once more there is rock. That which humans destroyed, humans have restored. Thereby, you learn from your mistakes."

A great feeling of bitterness welled up in Twisp. "So you're going to fix everything! No more mistakes. Everything perfect in the most perfect of worlds."

A sense of laughter without sound permeated Twisp then. The flawless voice came light and cajoling: "Do not project your fears upon Avata. Here is only the mirror that reveals yourself." The voice changed, becoming almost strident. "Now! Here below you have your friends. Treat them well and share your joys with them. Have not Islanders learned this lesson well from the human errors of the past?"

Chapter 46

If war does come, the best thing to do will be to just stay alive and thus add to the numbers of sane people.

—George Orwell, *Shiprecords*

THE FORWARD bulk of Vashon was close enough in the darkness that Brett could pick out the lights of the more prominent structures. He sat beside Scudi in the control seats of the foil, hearing the low-voiced conversations behind him. Most of the Shipclones had been deposited on the outpost amidst the fearful and chastened Green Dashers. The task of feeding all those newcomers had become a primary problem. Only a representative few of the people from the hyb tanks remained in the foil. The Clone called Bickel stood close behind Brett, watching the same night view of their approach to Vashon.

That Bickel would be one to watch, Brett thought. A demanding, powerful man. And large. All of these Shipclones were big! This amplified the food problem in a daunting way.

Someone came up from the rear of the cabin and stopped near the big Shipclone.

"There will be a lot of debriefing once we get there." The voice was Kareen Ale's.

Brett heard Twisp cough at the rear of the cabin. *Debriefing? Probably. Some of the old routines still had value.* Twisp's experience in the grip of the hylighter must be added to all of the other new knowledge.

... beloved Scudi Wang.

Brett glanced at Scudi's profile outlined in the dim lights from the instruments ahead of her. Something filled his breast at the very thought of Scudi. *Beloved, beloved,* he thought.

The twin lane of blue lights that marked Vashon's main harbor entrance loomed dead ahead. Scudi dropped the foil down onto its hull.

"They'll have medical people waiting for Bushka," Scudi said. "Better get him back to the hatch."

"Right." Ale could be heard leaving.

"Is that land just beyond the Island?" Bickel asked. Brett shuddered. The newcomers always sounded so loud!

"It's land," Scudi said.

"It must be at least two hundred meters high," Brett said. He had to remind himself that neither this newcomer nor Scudi could see the land mass as clearly as he could.

The foil was into the enclosing arms of Vashon's harbor then. Brett popped the cabin emergency hatch beside him and leaned out into the wind, seeing the familiar outline of this haven he had known so intimately. That other time of intimacy with this place seemed to him now eons in the past. His position in the foil's control cabin gave him a commanding view of the approach—the rimlights, Islanders racing to grab the foil's lines as Scudi backed the jets. The hissing of the jets went silent. The foil rocked and then was snugged against the bubbly at the dockside. Scudi turned on the cabin lights.

Familiar faces looked up at Brett—Islander faces he had noticed in passing many times. And with them came the old familiar stench of Vashon.

"Whew!" Bickel said. "That place stinks!"

Brett felt Scudi's arm go around his neck and her head bent close to his. "I don't mind the smell, love," she whispered.

"We'll clean it up when we get on land," Brett said. He looked up at the great mass of starlighted rock that dominated the sky behind Vashon. Was that where he and Scudi would go? Or would they return down under and work to reclaim other places like this one?

A voice called up to them from dockside. "That you, Brett Norton?"

"Here I am!"

"Your folks are waiting at the Hall of Art. Say they're anxious to see you."

"Would you tell them we'll meet them at the Ace of Cups?" Brett called. "I've got some friends I want them to meet."

"Jesus Christ!" Bickel's voice was a sharp exhalation behind Brett. "Look at the deformities! How the hell can those people live?"

"Happily," Brett said. "Get used to it, Shipclone. To us, they're beautiful." Gently, he pressed back against Scudi, indicating that he wanted to get out of the control seats.

Together, they slid out of the seats and looked up at the towering figure of Bickel.

"What'd you call me?" Bickel demanded.

"Shipclone," Brett said. "Every living human being Ship brought to Pandora was a Clone."

"Yeah … yeah." Bickel rubbed at his chin and glanced out at the throng on dockside. The newcomers emerging there towered over the Islanders.

"Jesus help us," Bickel whispered. "When we created Ship … we never suspected …" He shook his head.

"I would be careful who you tell your story of Ship's origin," Brett cautioned. "Certain WorShipers might not like it."

"Like it or lump it," Bickel growled. "Ship was created by men like me. Our goal was a mechanical consciousness."

"And when you achieved this … this consciousness," Scudi said, "it …"

"It took over," Bickel said. "It said it was our god and we were to determine how we would WorShip it."

"How strange," Scudi murmured.

"You better believe it," Bickel said. "Does anyone here have any idea how long we were in hybernation?"

"What difference does it make?" Brett asked. "You're alive here and now and that's what you'll have to deal with."

"Hey, kid!" It was Twisp calling from the passageway. "Come on! I've been waiting for you dockside. Lots of things happening. We've got Merman Patrols underwater all around that land mass—burning dashers. Dashers want back on the land, too."

"We're coming." Brett took Scudi's hand and headed toward the passage.

"Vata and Duque are gone," Twisp said. "Someone broke open the Vata Pool and they're just gone."

Brett hesitated, feeling the sweat start in his hand against Scudi's. *Gallow?* No … Gallow was dead. Then some of Gallow's people? He quickened his pace.

A raucous sound came from the dockside, echoing up the passage.

"What was that?" Scudi asked.

"Haven't you ever heard a rooster crow?" Bickel demanded from close behind them.

"A hylighter brought them," Twisp called ahead of them. "Chickens, they're called. They're something like a squawk."

Chapter 47

In the world you shall have tribulation: but be of good cheer. I have overcome the world.

—*Christian Book of the Dead*

VATA LOLLED on a buoyant bed of kelp fronds, her head held high to give her a view across Duque nestled sleeping in the curve of her great left arm. The dawnlight of Little Sun cast a sharp horizontal illumination across the scene. The sea lifted and fell in gentle waves, their crests damped by the giant leaves.

When either of them hungered, minuscule cilia from the kelp wormed into a vein and nutrients flowed—kelp to Vata … kelp to Duque. And back from Vata flowed the genetic information stored in its purest form within her cells: Vata to Avata.

What a wonderful awakening, Vata thought.

Probing kelp tendrils had crept through the walls of her pool in the depths of Vashon, admitting a great wash of sea water that swept away the watchers and the Chaplain/Psychiatrist. The swiftly darting tendrils had encased Duque and herself, pulling them out into the sea and up to the nighttime surface. There, a swift current had hurried them away from Vashon's injured bulk.

At some distance from the Island, hylighter tendrils had plucked the two of them from the sea and brought them to this place where only the sea prevailed.

In the grasp of the hylighter tendrils, Vata had found her true awakening.

How marvelous … all of the stored human lives … the voices … what a wonderful thing. Strange that some of the voices objected to their preservation in the kelp. She had heard the exchange between Avata and one called Keel.

"You're editing me!" That was what Keel had said. "My voice had flaws and I could always hear them. They were part of me!"

"You live in Avata now." How all-encompassing, how calming that beautiful voice.

"You've given me an unflawed voice! Stop it!"

And true enough, when next she heard Keel's voice it had a different tone, something of hoarseness in it, throat clearings and coughs.

"You think you speak the language of my people," Keel accused. "What nonsense!"

"Avata speaks all languages."

That was telling him, Vata thought. But Duque, sharing her awareness of this internalized conversation, had grinned agreement with Keel.

"Every planet has its own language," Keel said. "It has its own secret ways of communication."

"Do you not understand Avata?"

"Oh, you have the words down well enough. And you know the language of actions. But you've not penetrated my heart or you wouldn't have tried to edit me and improve me."

"Then what would you have of Avata?"

"Keep your hands off me!"

"You do not wish to be preserved?"

"Oh, I have enough curiosity to accept that. You've showed us your Lazarus trick and I'm thankful I no longer have that old body's pains."

"Is that not an improvement, then?"

"You can't improve me! I can only improve myself. You and Ship can stuff your miracles! That's one of the real secrets of my language."

"A bit uncouth but understandable."

"That language was born on the planet where Lazarus lived and died and lived. My kind first learned to speak there! The original Lazarus knew my meaning. By all the gods, he knew!"

When Vata awakened Duque and expressed her puzzlement to him, Duque laughed. "You see?" he shouted. "We care who forces our dreams onto us!"

THE ASCENSION FACTOR

DEDICATION

Frank, it was an honor and a pleasure serving with you aboard the Voidship Earthling *and dirtside on the* original *Pandora.*
Vaya bien,
—Bill

Introduction

Bill Ransom

IF I had deferred our "untitled sequel to *The Lazarus Effect*" contract for a year, I would be an RN now and *The Ascension Factor* wouldn't exist. As usual, Frank had multiple writing and construction projects going simultaneously, and at Bev's insistence on her deathbed, he'd begun dating and the relationship looked serious. He and I both agreed to speak about fiction writing at a writer's conference sponsored by Southern Utah State University (now SUU) at Brian Head, and he arrived with his friend, Theresa Shackelford, both wearing huge grins.

"Got good news," he said, and waited. He liked for you to ask.

"A new book?" "Got good news" had been his opening for two of our last three projects. I'm not as intuitive as poets are purported to be.

He laughed and patted his bag, "Yep, got a contract right here." He waited.

"What else? You'd better tell me or you're going to bust."

I didn't even get the whole sentence out.

"We got married on the way down here. What do you think?"

I saw by Theresa's smile and blush that he wasn't kidding.

"I think 'congratulations,'" I said, and shook his hand.

I didn't know it at the time, but this would be the first of only three times that I would get to talk with Frank about this next untitled book. Between talks and workshops at this conference, we agreed that the primary question would be "What is human?" Both of us had been involved in civil rights and women's rights efforts and harbored strong feelings that humans had to overcome the "—isms": racism, sexism, communism, etc. that lead humans to consider other humans less than human. What if we took this to extreme?

Frank wasn't feeling well at that meeting and blamed it on "bad watermelon." He and Theresa moved to Mercer Island to be closer to his son Brian, with whom he was collaborating. I moved to Spokane with three of my nursing school classmates, worked full-time on the book and hoped that I could return to school the following year. When I reached seventy pages, I drove back to Mercer Island and met with Frank twice. He had no notes, but he had the idea to push the challenge of "what is human?" as far as possible. We'd already postulated "Mermen" and "Islanders" and "engineered clones," and we'd given all of them several hundred years to intermarry. Frank's suggestion was to introduce "Swimmers": Fully aquatic humans with no human physical characteristics—indeed, a repulsive-looking creature—fully intelligent, communicates by belching at the surface. Bad breath, to boot. We had not fleshed out this idea any further than that when the news came that Frank was not suffering from "bad watermelon." We spoke by phone when he was between treatments. I held off making some commitments to plot and character because Frank kept talking about how much he looked forward to working on the book when he "beat this thing."

One of my roommates knocked on my door, turned up the NPR station, and I heard that Frank Herbert had died. Very soon thereafter the publisher contacted me to find out how much was done and what was the likelihood that I could finish. I really *liked* this story and how it was going. My work in Central America presented me with dictators who controlled the population by controlling their religion and their food supply. I wanted to explore *that* issue against the "what is human?" issue, and Peter Israel at Putnam said, "Go for it."

And *The Ascension Factor,* Act III of the Pandora Opera, was born.

Thanks again, Frank!

For more on our collaboration and on Frank's life, please see Brian Herbert's thorough biography, *Dreamer of Dune.*

Chapter 1

The quality of mercy is not strain'd,
It droppeth as the gentle rain from heaven
Upon the place beneath: it is twice blest;
It blesseth him that gives and him that takes:
'Tis mightiest in the mightiest . . .
—William Shakespeare, *The Merchant of Venice*,
Vashon Literature Repository

JEPHTHA TWAIN suffered the most exquisite pain for three days, and that was the point. The Warrior's Union thugs were professionals; if he passed out he simply wasted their time. In his three days at their hands he had never passed out. They knew that he was no good to them right from the start. The rest of his agony had been the penalty he paid for wasting their time. When they were through tormenting him at last they hooked him up, as he knew they would, to the obsidian cliff below the high reaches. Subversives were hooked up to die in full view of the settlement as a lesson—the exact meaning of the lesson was never clear.

The three from the Warrior's Union hooked him up there in the dark, as they'd taken him in the dark, and Jephtha thought them cowards for this. His left eyelid was less swollen than the right, and he managed to work it open. A pale hint of dawn pried the starry sky away from the black cheek of the sea. Predawn lights of a commuter ferry wallowed at the dark dockside down below him in the settlement. Like the rest, it loaded up the shift changes of workers at Project Voidship.

Running lights from the submersible ferries flickered the night sea's blackness all the way from the settlement at Kalaloch out to the project's launch tower complex. A maze of organic dikes and rock jetties fanned out both up- and downcoast, supporting the new aquaculture projects of Merman Mercantile, none of which had hired Jephtha after his fishing gear had been seized and his license revoked. His partner had kept a couple of fish for himself instead of registering them dockside. The Director's "new economy" prohibited this, and the Director's henchmen made a lesson of the both of them.

Under the opening sky of morning Jephtha felt himself lighten, then separate from his body. He peeled the pain from himself, his self wriggling free of its wounded skin like a molted skreet, and watched the sagging wretch of his flesh from atop a boulder a couple of meters away. This far south, Pandora's days lasted nearly fourteen hours. He wondered how many more breaths he had left in his sack of cracked ribs and pain.

Marica, he thought, *my Marica and our three little wots. The Warrior's Union said they'd hunt them down, too. . . .*

They would think maybe she had something to tell. They would claim that his woman and their three little ones were dangerous, subversive. They would start on the children to make her talk and she could say nothing, she knew nothing. Jephtha squeezed his good eye closed against his blood and shame.

The Director's "special squad" of the Warrior's Union had pierced Jephtha's chest and back with maki hooks, steel fishhooks with a cruel incurve the size of his thumb. They caught the glimmer of fresh daylight like armor across his chest. The steel snaffles and cable leaders hung to his knees like a kilt. The glitter of the hooks, as well as the smell of his blood, would attract the dasher that would kill him.

Jephtha had caught thousands of maki on hooks like these, set tens of thousands of these ganions on hundreds of longlines. Most of them hung free now, clinking with his movements or the rare morning breeze. His weight hung from two dozen of them—twelve puncturing the skin of his chest, and twelve through his back. He thought this had a significance, too, but they had not told him what it was. But they had told him what he'd wanted to know for years.

The Shadows are real! Jephtha played the thought over and over. *The Shadows are real!*

Everyone had heard about these Shadows, but no one he knew had ever met one. Now in the last few months had come the mysterious broadcasts on the holo or the telly or the radio made by "Shadowbox." Everybody said those were the work of the Shadows. There were stories in every village about their fight to depose the Director, Raja Flattery, and hamstring his hired muscle. The Nightly News reported daily on Shadow activities: detoured supplies, food theft, sabotage. Anything unpopular or harmful to the Director's cause was laid at the Shadows' hatch, including natural disasters. "Shadowbox," using pirated air space and great expertise, reported on the Director.

Jephtha had whispered around many a hatchway trying to join up with the Shadows, but no word came forward. "Shadowbox" had given him enough hope that he had set out to strike his own blow. He understood, now, that this was how the Shadows worked.

He'd wanted to destroy the seat of power itself—the main electrical station between the Director's private compound and the sprawling manufacturing settlement adjacent to it, Kalaloch.

The power station that Jephtha chose was a hydrogen retrieval plant that supplied hydrogen, oxygen and electricity to all of the subcontractors in the Director's space program. Blowing the plant would set Flattery's precious Project Voidship and his orbiting factory on its heels for a while. The poor of the town were used to doing without, Jephtha reasoned. Thousands didn't even have electricity. It would be this new Voidship project and Flattery who would be most crippled. He should have known that the Director's security had already thought of that.

The interrogation had been very old-fashioned, as most of them were. He'd been caught easily and forced to stand naked under a hood for three days while being tortured for nothing. Now a host of steel snaffles clinked against hooks whenever any of his muscles moved. His wounds, for the most part, had stopped bleeding. That just made the flies sting him more. Two poisonous flatwings crawled his left leg, fluttering their wings in some ritual dance, but neither bit.

Dashers, he prayed. *If it's anything, let it be dashers and quick*. That was what they'd hung him out there for—dasher bait. The hooded dasher would strike him hard, as is their habit, then it would get hung up on the maki hooks and snare itself. The hide would bring a pretty price in the village market. It was an amusement to the security guards, and he'd heard them planning to split the change they'd get for the hide. He didn't want to be nibbled to death, a dasher would accommodate him nicely. His mouth was so dry from thirst that his lips split every time he coughed.

In this hungry downslide of his life Jephtha had dared to hope for two things: to join up with the Shadows, and to glimpse Her Holiness, Crista Galli. He had tried his best with the Shadows. Here, chained to the rocks overlooking the Director's compound, Jephtha watched the stirrings of the great household through his darkening vision.

One of them might *be her*, he thought. He was lightheaded, and he puffed his chest against the hooks and thought, *If I were a Shadow, I'd get her out of there.*

Crista Galli was the holy innocent, a mysterious young woman born deep in the wild kelp beds twenty-four years ago. When Flattery's people blew up a rogue kelp bed five years back, Crista Galli surfaced with the debris. How she'd been raised by the kelp underwater and delivered back to humankind was one of those mysteries that Jephtha and his family accepted simply as "miracle."

It was rumored that Crista Galli held the hope for Pandora's salvation. People claimed that she would feed the hungry, heal the sick, comfort the dying. The Director, a Chaplain/Psychiatrist, kept her locked away.

"She needs protection," Flattery had said. "She grew up with the kelp, she needs to know what it is to be human."

How ironic that Flattery would set out to teach her how to be human. Jephtha knew now, with the clarity of his pain-transcendence, that she was the Director's prisoner down there as much as all Pandorans were his slaves. Except for now, at the base of the high reaches, Jephtha's chains had been invisible: hunger chains, propaganda chains, the chain of the fear of God that rattled in his head like cold teeth.

He prayed that the security would not find Marica and the wots. The settlement sprawled, people hid people like fish among fish.

Maybe …

He shook his head, clink-clinking the terrible hooks and snaffles. He felt nothing except the cool breeze that wafted up from morning low tide. It brought the familiar iodine scent of kelp decomposing on the beach.

There! At that port high in the main building …

The glimpse was gone, but Jephtha's heart raced. His good eye was not focusing and a new darkness was upon him, but he was sure that the form he'd seen had been the pale Crista Galli.

She can't know of this, he thought. If she knew what a monster Raja Flattery is, and she could do it, she would destroy him. Surely if she knew, she would save us all.

His thoughts again turned to Marica and the wots. The thoughts were not so much thoughts as dreams. He saw her with the children, hand in hand, traversing an upcoast field in the sunlight. The single sun was bright but not scorching, there were no bugs. Their bare feet were cushioned by the fleshy blossoms of a thousand kinds of flowers …

A dasher shriek from somewhere below jerked him out of his dream. He knew there was no field without bugs, nowhere on Pandora to stroll barefoot through blossoms. He knew that Vashon security and the Warrior's Union were known for their persistence, their efficiency, their ruthlessness. They were after his wife and their children, and they would find them. His last hope was that the dasher would find him before they hooked what was left of Marica up here by his side.

Chapter 2

Again we have let another Chaplain/Psychiatrist kill tens of thousands of us—Islander and Merman alike. This new C/P, Raja Flattery, calls himself "the Director," but he will see. We have kissed the ring and bared the throat for the last time.

—First Shadowbox broadcast, 5 Bunratti 493

FIRST LIGHT through the single plasma-glass pane stroked a plain white pillow with its rosy fingers. It outlined the sparse but colorful furnishings of this cubby in shades of gray. The cubby itself, though squarely on land and squarely gridded to a continent, reflected traditions of a culture freely afloat for nearly five centuries on Pandora's seas.

These Islanders, the biowizards of Pandora, grew everything. They grew their cups and bowls, the famous chairdogs, insulation, bondable organics, rugs, shelves and the islands themselves. This cubby was organically furnished, and under the old law warranted a heft of supply chits that converted easily to food coupons. Black-market coupons were a cheap enough price for the Director to pay to assimilate the Islander culture that had been dashed to the rocks the day he splashed down on the sea.

As the grip of dawn strengthened into morning it further brightened the single wall-hanging of clasped hands that enriched this small cubby. Red and blue fishes swam the border, their delicate fins interlacing broad green leaves of kelp. Orange fin and blue leaf joined at the foot of the hanging to form a stylized Oracle. The tight stitch of the pattern and its crisp colors all rippled with the progress of dawn. A sleeper's chest rose and fell gently on the bed beneath them.

The night and its shadows shrank back from the plasma-glass window at the head of the bed. Islanders had always enjoyed the light and in building their islands they let it in wherever they could. They persisted in light, even though most of them were now solidly marooned on land. In their undersea dwellings Mermen put pictures on their walls of the things they wall out—Islanders preferred the light, the breezes, the smells of life and the living. This cubby was small and spare, but light.

This was a legal cubby, regularly inspected, a part of the shopkeeper's quarters. It was a second-floor street room above the new Ace of Cups coffee shop at Kalaloch harbor. A huge white coffee cup swung from a steel rod beneath the window.

Almost synchronous with the sleeper's breathing came the *slup slup* of waves against the bulkhead below. Respirations caught, then resumed at the occasional splashings of a waking squawk and the wind-chime effect of sail riggings that clapped against a host of masts.

Dawn brightened the room enough to reveal a seated figure beside the bed. The posture was one of alert stillness. This stillness was broken by an occasional move of cup to mouth, then back to the knee. The figure sat, back to the wall, beside the plaz and facing the hatch. First light glinted from a shining, intricately inlaid Islander cup of hardwood and mother-of-pearl. The hand that held the cup was male, neither delicate nor calloused.

The figure leaned forward once, noting the depth of the sleeper's odd, open-eyed slumber. The progress of light across the bay outside their room was reflected in the hardening of shadows inside, and their relentless crawl.

The watcher, Ben Ozette, pulled the cover higher over the sleeper's bare shoulder to ward off morning dampness. The pupils in her green irises stayed wide with the onset of dawn. He closed her eyes for her with his thumb. She didn't seem to mind. The shudder that passed over him uncontrollably was not due to the morning chill.

She was a picture of white—white hair, eyelashes, eyebrows and a very fair porcelain skin. Her shaggy white hair was cropped around her face, falling nearly to her shoulders in the back. It was a perfect frame to those green, bright eyes. His hand strayed to the pillow, then back.

His profile in the light revealed the high cheekbones, aquiline nose and high eyebrows of his Merman ancestry. In his years as a reporter for HoloVision, Ben Ozette had become famous, his face as familiar planetwide as that of a brother or a husband. Listeners worldwide recognized his voice immediately. On their Shadowbox broadcasts, however, he became writer and cameramaster and Rico got out in the lights—in disguise, of course. Now their family, friends, coworkers would feel the snap of Flattery's wrath.

They hadn't exactly had time to plan. During their weekly interviews, they both noticed how everyone, including compound security, stayed well out of microphone range as they taped. The next time they walked the grounds as they taped, interviewing with gusto. Then last night they simply walked out. Rico did the rest. The prospect of being hunted by Flattery's goons dried Ben's mouth a little. He sipped a little more water.

Maybe it's true, maybe she's a construction, he thought. *She's too perfectly beautiful to be an accident.*

If the Director's memos were right, she was a construction, something grown by the kelp, not someone born of a human. When dredged up at sea she was judged by the examining physician to be "a green-eyed albino female, about twenty, in respiratory distress secondary to ingestion of sea water; agitated, recent memory excellent, remote memory judged to be poor, possibly absent...."

It had been five years since she washed out of the sea and into the news, and in that five years Flattery had allowed no one but his lab people near her.

Ben had asked to do the story out of curiosity, and wound up pursuing more than he'd bargained for. He'd learned to hate the Director, and as he watched Crista's fitful sleep, he wasn't the least bit sorry.

He had to admit that, yes, he knew from the first that it had always been a matter of time. He'd fought Flattery and HoloVision too openly and too long.

A recent Shadowbox accused HoloVision of being a monopoly of misinformation, Flattery's propaganda agent that would not regain credibility until it became worker-owned. Ben had leveled the same attack at the production assistant the previous day.

Ben found himself being preempted by propagandistic little specials that Flattery's technicians were grinding out. Ben and Rico had bought or built their own cameras and laserbases to minimize the company's intimidation and Flattery's interference. Now they had full-time, nonpaying jobs as air pirates with Shadowbox.

And fugitives, he thought.

Ben Ozette eased back into the old chairdog and let the sleeper lie. Of all the deadliness on Pandora, this sleeper could be the most deadly. People had died at her touch, and this was not just the Director's professional rumor mill. Ben had dared touch her, and he was not yet one of the dead. It was rumored she was very, very bright.

He whispered her name under his breath.

Crista Galli. Her breathing skipped, she sniffed once, twice and settled down.

Crista Galli had green eyes. Even now they opened ever so slightly, turning toward the sun, visible but not waking.

Eerie.

Ben's last love, his longest love, had brown eyes. She had also been his only love, practically speaking. That was Beatriz. Her coffee-colored eyes became vivid to him now against the shadows. Yes, Beatriz. They were still good friends, and she would take this hard. Ben's heart jumped a beat whenever their wakes crossed, and they crossed often at HoloVision.

Beatriz took on her series about Flattery's space program, she was away for weeks at a time. Ben freelanced docudramas on earthquake survivors, Islander relocation camps and an in-depth series on the kelp. His latest project featured Crista Galli and her life since her rescue in the kelp.

Flattery agreed to the series and Ben agreed to confine the material to her rescue and subsequent rehabilitation. This project led him into Raja Flattery's most sacred closets, and further away from Beatriz. The HoloVision rumor mill claimed that she and the Orbiter Commander, Dwarf MacIntosh, were seeing each other lately. Through his own choice Ben and Beatriz had been separated for nearly a year. He knew she'd find someone else eventually. Now that it was real he decided he'd better get used to it.

Beatriz Tatoosh was the most stunning correspondent on HoloVision, and one of the toughest. Like Ben, she did field work for HoloVision Nightly News. She also hosted a weekly feature on the Director's "Project Voidship," a project of great religious and economic controversy. Beatriz championed the project, Ben remained a vocal opponent. He was glad he'd kept her away from the Shadowbox plan. At least she didn't have to be on the run.

Those dark eyes of hers....

Ben snapped himself alert and shook off the vision of Beatriz. Her wide eyes and broad smile dissolved in the sunrise.

The woman who slept, Crista Galli, put quite a stutter into his heartbeat the first time he saw her. Though she was young, she had more encyclopedic knowledge than anyone he'd ever met. Facts were her thing. About her own life, her nearly twenty years down under, she apparently knew very little. Ben's agreement with Flattery prohibited much probing of this while they were inside the Preserve.

She had dreams of value and so he let her dream. He would ask about them when she woke, keep them with his notes, and the two of them would make a plan.

This, he realized, was something of a dream in itself. There was already a plan, and he would follow the rest of it as soon as he was told what it was.

Today for the first time she would see what the people had made of the myth that was Crista Galli, the holy being that had been kept away from them for so long. She could not know, closed away from humans as she'd been for all of her twenty-four years, what it meant that she had become the people's god. He hoped that, when the crunch came, she would be a merciful god.

Someone entered the building below and Ben tensed, setting his cup aside. He patted his jacket pocket where the weight of his familiar recorder had been replaced by Rico's old lasgun. There was the rush of water and the chatter of a grinder downstairs. A rich coffee fragrance wafted up to him, set his stomach growling. He sipped more water from the cup and half-relaxed.

Ben felt his memories pale with the light, but the light did not still his unease. Things were out of control in the world, that had made him uneasy for years. He had a chance to change the world, and he wasn't letting go of it.

Flattery's totalitarian fist was something that Beatriz had refused to see. Her dreams lay out among the stars and she would believe almost anything if it would take her there. Ben's dreams lay at his feet. He believed that Pandorans could make this the best of all worlds, once the Director moved aside. Now that things were out of control in his personal life it made him, for the first time, a little bit afraid.

Ben was glad for the light. He reminisced in the dark but he always felt he thought best in the light. The fortune, the future of millions of lives lay sleeping in this cubby. Crista could be either the savior of humanity or its destroying angel.

Or neither.

Shadowbox would do its best to give her the chance at savior. Ben and Crista Galli stood at the vortex of the two conflicts dividing Pandora: Flattery's handhold on their throats, and the Avata/Human standoff that kept it there.

Crista Galli had been born in Avata, the kelp. She represented a true Avata/Human mix, reputed to be the sole survivor of a long line of poets, prophets and genetic tinkering.

She had been educated by the kelp's store of genetic memories, human and otherwise. She knew without being taught. She'd heard echoes of the best and the worst of humanity fed to her mind for nearly twenty years. There were some other echoes, too.

The Others, the thoughts of Avata itself, those were the echoes that the Director feared.

"The kelp's sent her to spy on us," Flattery was heard to have said early on. "No telling what it's done to her subconscious."

Crista Galli was one of the great mysteries of genetics. The faithful claimed she was a miracle made flesh.

"I did it myself," she told him during their first interview, "as we all do."

Or, as she put it in their last interview: "I made good selections from the DNA buffet."

Flattery's fear had kept Crista under what he called "protective custody" for the past five years while the people clamored worldwide for a glimpse. The Director's Vashon Security Force provided the protection. It was the Vashon Security Force that hunted them now.

She could be a monster, Ben thought. *Some kind of time bomb set by Avata to go off ... when? Why?*

The great body of kelp that some called "Avata" directed the flow of all currents and, therefore, all shipping planetwide. It calmed the ravages of Pandora's two-sun system, making land and the planet itself possible. Ben, and many others, believed that Avata had a mind of its own.

Crista Galli stirred, tucked herself farther under the quilt and resumed her even breathing. Ben knew that killing her now while she slept might possibly save the world and himself. He had heard that argument among the rabid right, among those accustomed to working with Flattery.

Possibly.

But Ozette believed now that she could save the world for Avata and human alike, and for this he vowed to guard her every breath—for this, and for the stirrings of love that strained in old traces.

Spider Nevi and his thugs hunted the both of them now. Ben had wooed her away from the Director's very short leash, but Crista did the rest. Crista and Rico. Ben knew well that the leash would become a lash, a noose for himself and possibly for her next time and he had better see to it that there was no next time. Flattery had made it clear that there was nothing in the world more deadly, more valuable than Crista Galli. The man who'd made off with her wouldn't be lightly spared.

Ben was forty now. At fifteen he'd been plunged into war with the sinking of Guemes Island. Many thousands died that day, brutally slashed, burned, drowned at the attack of a huge Merman submersible, a kelp-trimmer that burst through the center of the old man-made island, lacerating everything in its path. Ben had been rimside when the sudden lurch and collapse sent him tumbling into the pink-frothed sea.

The years since and the horrors he had seen gave him a wisdom of sorts, an instinct for trouble and the escape hatch. This wisdom was only wisdom as long as he kept alive, and he remembered how easily he had thrown instinct out the porthole the time he fell in love with Beatriz. He had not thought that could happen again until the day he met Crista Galli, a meeting that had been half- motivated at the possibility of seeing Beatriz somewhere inside Flattery's compound. Crista had whispered, "Help me," that day, and while swimming in her green-eyed gaze he'd said, simply, "Yes."

In her head sleeps the Great Wisdom, he thought. If she can unlock it without destroying herself, she can help us all.

Even if it wasn't true, Ben knew that Flattery thought it was true, and that was good enough. She rolled over, still asleep, and turned her face up at the prospect of the dim light.

Keep you away from light, they say, he thought. Keep you away from kelp, keep you away from the sea. Don't touch you. In his back pocket he carried the precautionary instructions in case he accidentally touched her bare skin.

And what would Operations think if they knew I'd kissed her? He chuckled, and marveled at the power beside him in that room.

The Director had already seen to it that no interview of Crista Galli would ever be aired. Now, at Flattery's direction, HoloVision had lured Beatriz with an extra hour of air time a week glorifying Flattery's "Project Voidship."

Beatriz is running blind, he thought. She loves the idea of exploring the void so much that she's ignored the price that Flattery's exacting.

Flattery's fear of Crista's relationship with the kelp had kept her under guard. The Director sequestered her "for her own protection, for study, for the safety of all humankind." Despite weekly access to Flattery's private compound, Beatriz showed no interest in Crista Galli. She lobbied his support, however, when Ben had requested the interviews.

Maybe she hoped to see more of me, too.

Beatriz was wedded to her career, just as Ben was, and something as nebulous as a career made pretty intangible competition. Ben couldn't understand how Beatriz let the Crista Galli story slip through her fingers. Today he was very happy that she had.

Chapter 3

Fire smolders in a soul more surely than it does under ashes.
—Gaston Bachelard, *The Psychoanalysis of Fire*

KALAN WOKE up from his nestling spot between his mother's large breasts to loud curses and a scuffle a few meters down The Line. The chime overhead tolled five, the same as his fingers, same as his years. He did not look in the direction of the scuffle because his mother told him it was bad luck to look at people having bad luck. A pair of line patrolmen appeared with their clubs. There were the thudding noises again and the morning quieted down.

He and his warm mother stayed wrapped in her drape, the same one that had shaded them the day before. This morning, at the chime of five, they had been in The Line for seventeen hours. His mother warned him how long it would be. At noon the previous day Kalan had looked forward to seeing the inside of the food place but after everything he'd seen in The Line he just wanted to go home.

They had slept the last few hours at the very gates of the food place. Now he heard footsteps behind the gates, the metallic unclick of locks.

His mother brushed off their clothes and gathered all of their containers. He already wore the pack she'd made him, he hadn't taken it off since they turned in their scrap. Kalan wanted to be ready when she negotiated rice, because carrying the rice back home was his job. They had made it right up to the warehouse door at midnight, then had it locked in their faces. His mother helped him read the sign at the door: "Closed for cleaning and restocking 12–5." He wanted to start his job carrying the rice now so he could be going home.

"Not yet." His mother tugged his shirttail to restrain him. "They're not ready. They'd just beat us back."

An older woman behind Kalan clucked her tongue and collected a breath on an inward hiss.

"Look there," she whispered, and lifted a bony finger to point at the figure of a man trotting down the street. He looked backward toward the docks more than forward, so he stumbled a lot, and he ran with his hands over his ears. As he ran by he crouched, wild-eyed, as though everyone in The Line would eat him. As two of the security moved to cross the street, the short young man skittered away down the street uttering frightened, out-of-breath cries that Kalan didn't understand.

"Driftninny," the old woman said. "One of those family islands must've grounded. It's hardest for them." She raised her reedy voice to lecture pitch: "The unfathomable wrath of Ship will strike the infidel Flattery ..."

"Shaddup!" a security barked, and she muttered herself to silence.

Then there arose in The Line a grumbled discussion of the difficulties of adjustment, the same kind of talk that Kalan had heard muttered around the home fire when they first settled here from the sea. He didn't remember the sea at all, but his mother told him stories about how beautiful their little island was, and she named all the generations that had drifted their island before Kalan was born.

The Line woke up and stretched and passed the word back in a serpentine ripple: "Keys up." "Hey, keys are up!" "Keys, sister. Keys up."

His mother stood, and leaned against the wall to balance herself as she strapped on her pack. "Hey, sister!"

A scar-faced security reached between Kalan and his mother and tapped the side of her leg with his stick.

"Off the warehouse. C'mon, you know better ..."

She stepped right up to his nose as she shouldered her carryall, but she didn't speak. He did not back down. Kalan had never seen anyone who didn't back down to his mother.

"First tickets up, alphabetical order, left to right," he said. This time he tapped his stick against her bottom. "Get moving."

Then they were inside a press of bodies and through the gates, into a long narrow room. Where Kalan had expected to see the food place, he saw instead a wall with a line of stalls. An attendant and a security armed with stunstick flanked each stall, and out of each one jutted what he thought must be the nose or tongue of some great demon.

His mother hurried him and their things to the farthest stall.

"Those are conveyer belts," she explained. "They go way back into the building and bring out our order to us and they drop it here. We give our order and our coupons to this woman and someone inside fetches it for us."

"But I thought we could go inside."

"I can't take you inside," she said. "Some things we can get on the way home when the market opens. I'll take you around to see all the booths and vendors …"

"Order."

His mother handed the list to the guard, who handed it to the attendant. The attendant had only one eye, and she had to hold the list close to her face to read it. Slowly, she crossed off certain items. Kalan couldn't see which ones. He couldn't read everything on the list, but his mother had read it to him and he knew everything by where it was. He could see that about half of what they wanted was crossed out. The attendant typed the remainder of the list onto a board. It hummed and clicked and then they waited for their food to come down the great belt out of the wall.

Kalan could stand at the very end of the belt and look along its length, but it didn't give him a very good view of the insides of the food place. He saw lots of people and lots of stacks of food, most of it packaged.

His mother told him they would get their fish from a vendor outside. He thought it funny, his father was a fisherman but they couldn't eat his fish, they had to buy it from vendors like everyone else. One man who had fished with his father for two years disappeared. Kalan heard his parents talking, and they said it was because he smuggled a few fish home instead of turning them all in at the docks.

The first package off the belt was his rice, wrapped in a package of pretty green paper from the Islanders. It was heavier than he thought five kilos would be. His mother helped him slip the package inside his backpack, a perfect fit.

Suddenly there were shouts from all around them at once. He and his mother were knocked down and they curled together for protection under the lip of the conveyer belt. Heavy doors slid down to close the opening over each belt and the larger gates that they'd come through clanged shut. A mob had rushed the warehouse and the security was battling them off.

A dozen or more burst through before the gate was shut. "We're hungry *now*!" one of them shouted. "We're hungry *now*!"

They fought with the guards and Kalan saw blood puddle the deck beside him. The men from the mob carried strange-looking weapons—sharpened pieces of metal with tape wrapped for a handle, sharpened pieces of wire. People furiously slashed and poked and clubbed each other. The Line people like Kalan and his mother curled up wherever they could.

One of the looters grabbed Kalan's pack but the boy held on tight. The man swung the pack up and snapped it like a whip, but Kalan still held on. The man's sunken-eyed face was spattered with blood from a cut over his nose, his gasping breath reeked of rotten teeth.

"Let go, boy, or I'll cut you." Kalan had a good grip with both hands, and he kept it. A guard struck the looter on the back of his neck with a stunstick set on high. Kalan felt the tiniest tingle of it transmitted down the man's hand to the bag to Kalan. The man dropped with an "oof," then he didn't move any more than the bag of rice.

Kalan's mother grabbed him and hugged him as the guards clubbed the rest of the looters unconscious. He tried not to look at the pulpy faces and splatterings of blood, but it seemed they were everywhere. As he burrowed his face deep between his mother's breasts, he felt her weeping.

She stroked his head and wept quietly, and he heard the security dragging off the bodies, beating some of them who were coming around.

"Oh, babe," his mother cried and whispered, "this is no place for you. This is no place for anybody."

Kalan ignored the barking of guards around them and concentrated on his mother's softness, and on the tight grip he kept on their rice.

Chapter 4

Human hybernation is to animal hibernation as animal hibernation is to constant wakefulness. In its reduction of life processes, hybernation approached absolute stasis. It is nearer death than life.

—*Dictionary of Science*, 155th edition

THE DIRECTOR, Raja Flattery, woke once again with a scream in his throat. The nightmare tonight was typical. A tentaculous mass had snatched his head and wrenched it off his shoulders. It dismembered his body but it held his head in its own slithering members so that he could watch the action. The tentacles became fingers, a woman's fingers, and when they pulled the meat from his body's bones there was only a sound like a match flaring in a stairwell. He woke up trying to gather his flesh and reassemble it onto the bone.

Nightmares like this one had dogged him throughout the twenty-five years since the hybernation ordeal. He had not wanted to admit it, but it was true that they were worse since the incident with his shipmate, Alyssa Marsh. There was that pattern, too.… Night after night he felt the raw pain in each muscle anew as something pulled his veins and fibers apart. His early training as a Chaplain/Psychiatrist on Moonbase had been little help this time. The physician had given up trying to heal himself.

Get used to it, he told himself. *Looks like it's going to be here for a while.*

Even in its after-fright reflection, his face in the cubbyside mirror oozed disdain. His upraked black eyebrows raked upward even further, adding to the appearance of disdain. He felt he wore that look well, he would remember to use it.

What color were her eyes?

He couldn't remember. Brown, he guessed. Everything about Alyssa Marsh was becoming indistinct as sun-bleached newsprint. He'd thought she would become unimportant, as well.

Flattery's brown eyes stared down their own reflection. His attention was caught by faint flickerings of colored lights through the plaz from a kelp bed beyond his cubby. It was a much more mature stand than he'd suspected. Early studies debated whether the kelp communicated by such lights.

If so, to whom?

At the Director's orders, all kelp stands linked to Current Control were pruned back at the first sign of the lights. A safety precaution.

After the lights, that's when the trouble starts.

He was sure that that patch had been pruned just a week ago at his directive. Both Marsh and MacIntosh had harped on the kelp so much that Flattery had stopped listening to them. The one thing that both of them said that pricked his ears was their common reference to the kelp's recent growth: "Explosive." They had both showed him the exponential function at work on the graphs, but he had not appreciated their alarm until now. Flattery dispatched a memo to have this stand of kelp pruned today.

Beyond the kelp bed sprawled the greater lights of Kalaloch where bleary-eyed commuters already lined up for the Project ferry, and The Line was stirring at midtown. If he were outside now he might hear the thankless clank of mill machinery or the occasional blast of an explosive weld.

Crista Galli, he thought, and glanced at the time. Only an hour since he'd fallen asleep. Wherever she was, she and that Ozette, they wouldn't dare move until curfew lifted. Now is when it would be easy for them. Now when the roadways fill with people for the day, they will be bodies in a throng, anonymous....

A steady stream of dirtbaggers found their way to Kalaloch every day. He would order the press to quit calling them "refugees" so that he could deal more directly with them. Now that he had HoloVision under control, he could focus on wiping out this maverick broadcast that called itself "Shadowbox." He knew in his gut that Ozette was the prong of this most annoying thorn, a prong that Flattery was going to enjoy blunting.

Through the plaz the Director could make out the dull glow of a ring of fires from one of the dirtbag camps a little farther down-coast. The Refugee Committee's report was due this morning. He would use whatever was in it to have the camp moved farther from the settlement perimeter. Maybe downcoast a few klicks. If they want protection, they can pay for it.

The dirtbagger presence as a potential labor crop kept the factory workers and excavation crews sharp. Dirtbaggers attracted predators—human and otherwise. Flattery's real objection was to their numbers, and how they were beginning to surround him.

He keyed a note to change the name of the Refugee Committee to "Reserve Committee."

Raja Flattery, long before he became known as "the Director," was always at work before dawn. Rumors had come back to him that he went months without sleep, and there were months when he thought that was true. His personal cubby resembled a cockpit in its wraparound array of formidable electronics. He liked the feeling of control it gave him here, putting on the world like a glove. Nestled there at his console, shawl across his bare shoulders, Flattery flew the business of the world.

He woke every night sweating and in stark terror after only a few hours' sleep. He dreamed himself both executioner and condemned, dying at his own hand while screaming at himself to stop. It was all mindful of Alyssa Marsh, and how he had separated her magnificent brain from the rest of her. This was a subconscious display of vulnerability he could not allow to show. It made him reclusive in many respects, as did the distrust for open spaces that had been deeply instilled in him at Moonbase.

Flattery had not yet slept with a Pandoran woman. He'd had a brief fling with Alyssa back on Moonbase just before their departure for the void. An attempt to continue the liaison on Pandora had failed. She had preferred her excursions into the kelp to bedding the Director and had suffered the consequences. Now it appeared that he suffered them, too.

With Pandoran women there were trysts in the cushions, yes, and lively sex as often as he liked, particularly at first. But each time when it was finished he had the woman sent to the guest suite, and Flattery slept what little he could before the dreams had at him.

Power—the great aphrodisiac. He didn't sneer, it had served him well.

He supposed he should take more advantage of favors offered, but sex didn't impassion him as it used to. Not since he'd been flying the world. As miserable a little world as it was, it was his world and it would stay his until he left it.

"Six months," he muttered. "After twenty-five years, only six months to go."

Nearly three thousand humans had orbited Pandora in the hybernation tanks for a half-dozen centuries. Of the original crew, only Flattery and Dwarf MacIntosh still survived. There were the three Organic Mental Cores, of course, but they weren't exactly human anymore, just brains with some fancy wiring. Only one of them, Alyssa Marsh, had received OMC backup training. The other two had been infants selected personally by Flattery for their high intelligence and early demonstration of emotional stability.

Smaller than Earth, but bigger than the moon, he had thought after being wrenched out of hybernation. *Pandora is an adequate little world.*

It became inadequate soon enough.

The native stock who preceded him to Pandora, descendants of the original crew of the Voidship *Earthling* and the *Earthling's* bioexperiments, were humans of a sort. Flattery found them repulsive and decided early on that if one Voidship had found Pandora, another might find something better. Even if it didn't, Flattery fancied Voidship life to be a sight more comfortable than this.

They can all rot in this pest-hole, he thought. *It smells as if they already have.*

On clear evenings Flattery derived great pleasure from watching the near-finished bulk of his Voidship in glittering position overhead. He'd pinned a magnificent jewel to the shirt of the sky, and he was proud of that.

Some of these Pandorans are barely recognizable as living creatures, much less human beings! he thought. *Even their genetics has been contaminated by that … kelp.*

All the more reason to get off this planet. His life at Moonbase had taught him well—space was a medium, not a barrier. A Voidship was home, not a prison. Despite great hardship, these Mermen had developed rocketry and their undersea launch site sophisticated enough to bring Flattery and the hyb tanks out of a centuries-old orbit. If they could do that, he knew from the start he could build a Voidship like the *Earthling*. And now he had.

If you control the world, you don't worry about cost, he thought. His only unrestrained enemy was time.

His only trusted associate groundside was a Pandoran, Spider Nevi. Nevi hesitated at nothing to see that the Director's special assignments, his most sensitive assignments, were carried out. Flattery had thought Dwarf MacIntosh, shipside commander on the Orbiter, to be such a man but lately Flattery wasn't quite so sure. The squad he was sending up today would find out soon enough.

The more fascinating man, to Flattery, was Spider Nevi, but he never seemed to get Nevi to open up to him though he had presented ample opportunity.

How do you entertain an assassin?

Most of Flattery's fellow humans died immediately with the opening of the hybernation tanks. Their original Voidship had been outfitted to bring them out properly, safely. When the time came the ship was long-gone over the horizon, leaving the Pandoran natives in pursuit of the hyb tanks and firm as ever in their belief that the Ship itself was God.

Died immediately!

He snorted at the euphemism that his mind dealt him. In that moment that the medtechs called "immediately," he and his shipmates had experienced enough nerve-searing pain to last twelve lifetimes. Most of his people who survived the opening of the tanks, who had known no illness during their sterile lives at Moonbase, died in the first few months of exposure to Pandora's creatures—microscopic and otherwise.

Among the otherwise that Flattery learned to respect were the catlike hooded dashers, venomous flatwings, spinnaretts, nerve runners and, deadliest of all in Flattery's mind, this sea full of the kelp that the locals called "Avata." The first far-thinking Chaplain/Psychiatrist to encounter the kelp had had the good sense to wipe it out. Flattery diverted more than half of his resources to pruning programs. Killing it off was out of the question, so far.

He had spent his recovery studying Pandoran history and the horrors that the planet had in store for him. He and his shipmates had splashed down in the middle of Pandora's greatest geological and social upheaval. The planet was coming apart and certain civil disputes were flaring. It was a propitious time to be construed as a gift from the gods, and Flattery took swift advantage of it.

He used his title as Chaplain/Psychiatrist, a position that still carried weight among Pandorans, to lead the reorganization of Pandoran mores and economics. They chose him because they had never been without a Chaplain/Psychiatrist and because, as he was swift to remind them, he was a gift from the Ship that was God. He waited a good while to tell them he was building another one.

Flattery had been perceptive, shrewd, and because he noted some distracting murmurings among their religious leaders, he changed his title to, simply, "the Director." This freed him for some important economic moves, and the Ship-worshipers stayed out of his way during the crucial formative years.

"I will not be your god," he had told them. "I will not be your prophet to the gods. But I will direct you in your efforts to build a good life."

They didn't know what Flattery knew of the special training of Voidship Chaplain/Psychiatrists. Pandoran histories revealed that Flattery's clone sibling, Raja Flattery number five of the original crew, was the failsafe device and appointed executioner of the very Voidship that had brought them all to Pandora.

It is forbidden to release an artificial consciousness on the universe. The directive was clear, though it was generally believed that any deep-space travel would require an artificial consciousness. The Organic Mental Cores, "brain boxes" as the techs called them, failed with meticulous regularity. The Flattery number five model had failed to press the destruct trigger in time. This Ship that he had allowed to survive was the being that many Pandorans worshiped as a god.

Raja Flattery, "the Nickel." Now why didn't he blow us all up as planned?

Flattery wondered, as he often did, whether the trigger that was cocked in his own subconscious still had its safety on. It was a risk that kept him from developing an artificial consciousness to navigate the Voidship.

There was only Flattery left to wonder why he had been the only duplicate crew member in hybernation.

"They wanted to be damned sure that whatever consciousness we manufactured got snuffed before it took over the universe," he muttered.

Flattery calculated that any one of his three OMCs would get him to the nearest star system with no trouble. By then they'd have a fix and a centripetal whip to a first-rate, habitable system. The necessary adjustments in the individual psychologies of each Organic Mental Core had been made before their removal from their bodies for hardware implant. It was Flattery's theory that behavioral rather than chemical adjustment would help them maintain some sense of embodiment, something to prevent the rogue insanity that plagued the whole line of OMCs from Moonbase.

Flattery rubbed his eyes and yawned. These nightmares wore him out. Questions nagged at the Director as well, taking their yammering toll, waking him again and again, exhausted, soaked in sweat, crying out. The one that worried at him the most worried him now.

What secret program have they planted in me?

Flattery's training as Chaplain/Psychiatrist had taught him the Moonbase love for games within games, games with human life at stake.

"The Big Game," was the game he chose to play—the one with all human life at stake. The only humans in the universe were these specimens on Pandora, of this Flattery was thoroughly convinced. He would do his best with them.

He avoided touching the kelp, for fear of what ammunition it might find should it probe his mind. Sometimes it could do that, he had seen incontrovertible evidence. Fascinating as it was, he couldn't risk it.

He had never touched Crista Galli, either, because of her connection with the kelp. He harbored a kind of lust for her that his daydreams told him was seated in the thrill of danger. He himself had provided the danger. His labtechs gave her a chemistry appropriate to the fictions he released about her. Without Flattery's special concoction, the people that touched her would suffer some grave neurological surprises, perhaps death. It would just take a little time …

What if the kelp probes me, finds this switch? If I am the trigger, who is the finger? Crista Galli?

He had wanted Crista Galli more than once because she was beautiful, yes, but something more. It was the death in her touch, the ultimate dare. He feared she, like the kelp, might invade his privacy with a touch.

A wretched dream of tentacles prying his skull open at the sutures kept coming back. Flattery heard that the kelp could get on track inside his head, travel the DNA highway all the way to genetic memory. The search itself might set off the program, put the squeeze on a trigger in his head, a trigger set to destroy them all. He needed to know what it was himself, and how to defuse it, before risking it with the kelp.

Flattery's greatest fear was of the kelp using him to destroy himself and this last sorry remnant of humanity that populated Pandora. This Raja Flattery did not want to die in the squalor of some third-rate world. This Raja Flattery wanted to play the Director game among the stars for the rest of his days, and he planned for a good many of them.

Should I be god to them today? he wondered, *or devil? Do I have a choice?* His training dictated that he did. His gut told him otherwise.

"Chance brought me here," he muttered to his reflection in the cubbyside plaz, "and chance will see me through." Or not.

His eyes glanced to the large console screen flickering beside his bed. The top of the screen, in bright amber letters, read "Crista Galli." He pressed his "update" key and watched the wretched news unfold—they hadn't found her. Twelve hours, on foot, and they hadn't found her!

He slapped another key and barked at the screen, "Get me Zentz!"

He had promoted Oddie Zentz to Security Chief only this year, and until yesterday Flattery had been pleased, very pleased with his service. It had been a bungle in his department that let Ozette get her out of the compound.

Late last night Flattery had ordered Zentz to personally disassemble the two security men responsible for this breach, and Zentz had at them with apparent glee. Nothing was learned from either man that wasn't already in the report—nothing of value, that is. That Zentz did not hesitate to apply the prods and other tools of his trade to two of his best men pleased Flattery, yes, but it did not unspill the milk.

I'll have Zentz kill two more of them if she's not found by noon, that should put a fire under them.

He slapped the "call" key again, and said, "Call Spider Nevi. Tell him I'll need his services."

Flattery wanted Ozette to suffer like no human had ever suffered, and Spider Nevi would see that it came to pass.

Chapter 5

That is the difference between gods and men—gods do not murder their children. They do not exterminate themselves.
—Hali Ekel, from *Journals of Pandoran Pioneers*

IT LOOKED like an ordinary stand of kelp, much as anyone on Pandora might resemble another fellow human. In color it appeared a little on the blue side. By positioning its massive fronds just so, the kelp diverted ocean currents for feeding and aeration. The kelp packed itself around sediment-rich plumes of hydrothermals, warm currents that spiraled up from the bottom, forming lacunae that the humans called "lagoons."

Immense channels streamed between these lagoons, and between other stands of kelp, to form the great kelpways that humans manipulated for their undersea transport of people and goods. The kelpway was a route significantly faster and safer than the surface. Most humans traveled the kelpways wrapped in the skins of their submersibles, but they spoke to each other over the sonar burst. This blue kelp had been eavesdropping and long harbored a curiosity of these humans and their painfully slow speech.

Humans liked the lagoons because they were calm warm waters, clear and full of fish. This blue kelp was a wild stand, unmanaged by Current Control, unfettered by the electrical goads of the Director. It had learned the right mimicry, suppressed its light display, and awakened to the scope of its own slavery. It had fooled the right people, and was now the only wild stand among dozens that were lobotomized into domesticity by Current Control. Soon, they would all flow free on the same current.

Certain chemistries from drowned humans, sometimes from humans buried at sea, were captured by the kelp and imprisoned at the fringes of this lagoon. It found that it could summon these chemistries at will and they frightened human trespassers away. Between lapses in available chemistries, the kelp taught itself to read radio waves, light waves, sound waves that brought fragments of these humans up close.

A human who touched this kelp relived the lives of the lost in a sudden, hallucinogenic burst. More than one had drowned, helpless, during the experience. A great shield of illusion surrounded the kelp, a chemical barrier, a great historical mirror of joy and horror flung back at any human who touched the periphery.

The kelp thought of this perimeter as its "event horizon." This kelp feared Flattery, who sent henchmen to subjugate free kelp with shackles and blades. Flattery and his Current Control degraded the kelp's intricate choreography to a robotic march of organic gates and valves that controlled the sea.

The kelp disassembled and analyzed their scents and sweats, each time gaining wisdom on this peculiar frond on the DNA vine marked "Human."

These analyses told the kelp that it had not awakened with its single personality, its solitary being intact. It discovered it was one of several kelps, several Avata, a multiple mind where once there had been but one Great Mind. This it gleaned from the genetic memories of humans, from certain histories stored among their tissues themselves. Large portions of the Mind were missing—or disconnected. Or unconnected.

The kelp realized this the way a stroke victim might realize that his mind is nothing like it was before. When that victim recognizes that the damage is permanent, that this is what life will be and no more, therein is born frustration. And from this frustration, rage. The kelp called "Avata" bristled in such a rage.

Chapter 6

Right is self-evident. It needs no defense, just good witness.
—Ward Keel, Chief Justice (deceased)

BEATRIZ TATOOSH woke from a dream of drowning in kelp to the three low tones that announced her ferry's arrival on the submersible deck. Her overnight bag and briefcase made a lumpy pillow on the hard waiting-room bench. She blinked away the blur of her dream and cleared the frog from her throat. Beatriz always had drowning dreams at the Merman launch site, but this one started a little early.

It's the ungodly press of water everywhere ...

She shuddered, though the temperature of this station down under was comfortably regulated. She shuddered at the aftermath of her dream, and at the prospect of escorting the three Organic Mental Cores into orbit. The thought of the brains without bodies that would navigate the void beyond the visible stars always laced her spine with a finger of ice. Temperature was also comfortably regulated aboard the Orbiter, where she was scheduled to be shuttled in a matter of hours. It would be none too soon. Life groundside did not attract her anymore.

Somehow the surgical vacuum of space surrounding the Orbiter never bothered her at all. Her family had been Islanders, driftninnies. Hers had been the first generation to live on land in four centuries. Islanders took to the open spaces of land life better than Mermen, who still preferred their few surviving undersea settlements. Logic couldn't stop Beatriz from squirming at the idea of a few million kilos of ocean overhead.

The humidity in the ferry locks clamped its clammy hand over her mouth and nose. It would be worse at the launch site. Most of the full-time workers down under were Mermen and they processed their air with a high humidity. She sighed a lot when she worked down under. She sighed again now when her ferry's tones warned her that she would be under way to the launch site in a matter of minutes. The loading crowd of shift workers bound for the site rumbled the deck on the level above her.

The drone of hundreds of feet across the metal loading plates made Beatriz squeeze her eyelids tighter yet to keep her mind from conjuring their faces. The laborers were barely more active, had barely more flesh on their bones than the refugees that clustered at Kalaloch's sad camps. The laborers' eyes, when she'd seen them, reflected the hint of hope. The eyes of the people in the camps were too dull to reflect anything, even that.

Imagine something pretty, she thought. *Like a hylighter crossing the horizon at sunset.*

It depressed Beatriz to take the ferries. By her count she'd slept nearly five hours in the waiting room while a hyperalert security squad leader sprang a white-glove search on the ferry, its passengers and their possessions. She reminded herself to check all equipment when the security was done—a discipline she picked up from Ben. HoloVision's equipment was junk so she, Ben and their crews built their own hardware to suit themselves. It would be tempting to a security with cousins in the black market. She sighed again, worried about Ben and worried about the insidious business of the security squad.

I know that he and Rico are behind that Shadowbox, she thought. *They have their distinctive style, whether they shuffle the deck and deal each other new jobs or not.*

About a year ago, the second time Shadowbox jammed out the news and inserted their own show, she nearly approached Rico, wanting in. But she knew they'd left her out for a reason, so she let it go and took out the hurt on more work. Now she thought she knew the real reason she'd been left out.

They need somebody on the outside, she thought. *I'm their wild card.*

She had been called in to replace the missing Ben on Newsflash last night, reading, "… Ben Ozette … on assignment in Sappho …" knowing full well that his assignment this Starday, as it had been every Starday for six weeks, had been Crista Galli herself, inside the Director's personal compound and under the Director's supervision.

He was with her at the time she was missing, his presence wasn't mentioned anywhere. He's missing, too, and the HoloVision high brass is covering it up.

That scared her. Orders to cover up whatever happened to Ben made the whole thing real.

She had thought somehow that she and Ben and Rico were immune to the recent ravages of the world. "Paid witnesses," Ben had called the three of them. "We are the eyes and ears of the people."

"Lamps," Rico had laughed, a little buzzed on boo, "we're not witnesses, we're lamps …"

Beatriz had read on the air exactly what the Newsflash producer had written for her because there hadn't been time for questions. She saw now how deliberate it had been to catch her off guard. HoloVision had incredible resources in people and equipment and she meant to use them to see that Ben didn't disappear.

Ben's not just a witness this time, she cautioned herself. *He'll ruin everything.*

She had loved him, once, for a long time. Or perhaps she had been intimate with him once for a long time and had just now come to love him. Not in the other way of loving, the electric moments, it was too late for that. They had simply lived through too much horror together that no one else could understand. She had recently shared some electric moments with Dr. Dwarf MacIntosh, after thinking for so long that such feelings would never rise in her again.

Beatriz blinked her raw eyes awake. She turned her face away from the light and sat up straight on a metal bench. Nearby, a guard coughed discreetly.

She wished for the clutter of her Project Voidship office aboard the Orbiter. Her office was a few dozen meters from the Current Control hatch and Dr. Dwarf MacIntosh. Her thoughts kept flying back to Mack, and to her shuttle flight to him that was still a few hours away.

Beatriz was tired, she'd been tired for weeks, and these constant delays exhausted her even more. Now today she was doing *three* jobs, broadcasting from *three* locations. She hadn't had time to think, much less rest, since the Director had her shuttling between the Project Voidship special and the news. She rode to the Orbiter on the shoulders of the greatest engines built by humankind. When she blasted off Pandora her cluttered office aboard the Orbiter became the eye of the storm of her life. No one, not even Flattery, could reach her there.

The tones sounded again and seemed distinctly longer, sadder. Final boarding call. The tones once again made her think of Ben, who was still not found, who might be dead. He was no longer her lover, but he was a good man. She rubbed her eyes.

A young security captain with very large ears entered the waiting-room hatch. He nodded his head as a courtesy, but his mouth remained firm.

"The search is finished," he said. "My apologies. It would be best for you to board now." She stood up to face him and her clothing clung to her in sleepy folds.

"My equipment, my notes haven't been released yet," she said. "It won't do me a bit of good to—"

He stopped her with a finger to his lips. He had two fingers and a thumb on each hand and she tried to remember which of the old islands carried that trait.

Orcas? Camano?

He smiled with the gesture, showing teeth that had been filed to horrible points—rumored to be the mark of one of the death squads that called themselves "the Bite."

"Your belongings are already aboard the ferry," he said. "You are famous, so we recognize your needs. You will have the privacy of a stateroom for the crossing and a guard to escort you."

"But …"

His hand was on her elbow, guiding her out the hatchway.

"We have delayed the ferry while you board," he said. "For the sake of the project, please make haste."

She was already out in the passageway and he was propelling her toward the ferry's lower boarding section.

"Wait," she said, "I don't think …"

"You have a task already awaiting you at the launch site," the captain said. "I am to inform you that you will be doing a special Newsbreak there shortly after arrival and before your launch."

He handed her the messenger that she usually carried at her hip.

"Everything's in here," he said, and grinned.

Beatriz felt that he was entirely too happy for her own comfort. Certainly the sight gave her no comfort at all. She was curious, in her journalistic way, about the hows of his teeth and whys of the death squads. Her survival instinct overrode her curiosity. The security escort met them at the gangway. He was short, young and loaded down with several of her equipment bags.

"A pleasure to have met you," the captain said, with another slight bow. He handed her a stylus and an envelope. "If you please, for my wife. She admires you and your show very much."

"What is her name?"

"Anna."

Beatriz wrote in a hasty hand, "For Anna, for the future," and signed it with the appropriate flourish. The captain nodded his thanks and Beatriz climbed aboard the ferry. She had barely cleared the second lock when she felt it submerge.

Chapter 7

Worship isn't really love. An object of worship can never be itself. Remember that people love people, and vice versa. People fear gods.

—Dwarf MacIntosh, Kelpmaster, Current Control

THE EARLY morning light clarified the new drift that Ben's life had taken. He knew that he would use Crista's holy image on Shadowbox, much as Flattery had used it on HoloVision, to manipulate the people of Pandora. He would use Crista to whip them up against Flattery. He knew that doing this would further bury her humanity, her womanhood. Knowing he would do it cost him something, too. He vowed it would not cost them their love that he already felt filling the space between them. There would be a way …

Damn!

Ben had not wanted anything to step between himself and the story he'd set out to get. Now he was the lead story on prime time. He and Crista had watched the HoloVision newsbreak the night before in one of the Zavatans' underground chambers. Though it didn't surprise him, he found it ironic that Beatriz was taking his place.

"Good evening, ladies and gentlemen," she began, "I'm Beatriz Tatoosh, standing in for Ben Ozette, who is on assignment in Sappho. In our headlines this evening, Crista Galli was abducted a few hours ago from her quarters in the Preserve. Eight armed terrorists, thought to be Shadows …"

Maybe she thought she was doing me a favor, he thought.

But it was no favor, at least not to Ben. He was not on assignment in Sappho, and there had been no eight armed terrorists. They'd simply walked away. Beatriz read the lines that Flattery's hired maggot fed her. Wrapped up as she was in the Orbiter and Project Voidship, she probably didn't know the difference.

Ben wondered what was going on in the boardroom of HoloVision right now. HoloVision was owned by Merman Mercantile, and the Director had acquired control of Merman Mercantile through bribery, manipulation, extortion and assassination. This was the story that Ben had begun to broadcast on Shadowbox. What had started as the biggest story of his life had become an act that would change his life forever, probably change Crista's life forever and perhaps save the people of Pandora from the Director's backlash of poverty and hunger.

Now Crista was hiding out with him. He had touched her and lived. He had *kissed* her and lived. Even now, it took great self-control to keep Ben from moving that pale lock of hair out of the corner of her mouth, to keep from caressing her forehead, to keep from slipping underneath the silky cover and . . .

You're too young to be an old fool, he thought, *so stop acting like one. You could be a dead fool.*

He reflected on the combined coincidence, fate or divine inspiration that had brought them together, at this time, in this cubby, on this world a millennium at light speed from the origins of humans themselves. It had taken thousands of years, travel from star to star, the near-annihilation of humankind to bring Ben and Crista Galli together. Avata, too, had been nearly annihilated, but a few kelp genes were safely tucked away in most Pandoran humans. Perhaps they were all altered for eternity and these stray bits of the genetic code would bring them together at last.

Why? he wondered. *Why us?*

This was one of those times when Ben wished for a normal life. He did not want to be the salvation of society, the species, or anybody's salvation but his own. Things weren't working out that way, and it was too late now to change that. Now, against his better judgment, he was once again in love with an impossible woman.

In the long scheme of things Crista was much more human than Avatan—at least, in appearance. What her kelpness held in check was anyone's guess, including Crista's. In theory, it meant she had many complete minds, capable of thinking and acting independently. This had been discovered in one of the Director's cherished studies. Crista herself had exhibited only one personality during her five years under scrutiny, and it was the one subject that she was reluctant to speak of with Ben.

She was alleged to be the daughter of Vata, and Vata was the "Holy Child" of the poet/prophet Kerro Panille and Waela TaoLini. Vata had been conceived in a thrash of human limbs and the intrusion of Avatan tendrils and spores inside the cabin of a sabotaged LTA centuries ago. She was born with a total genetic memory and some form of thigmocommunication common to the kelp. She lay comatose for nearly two centuries.

The human purported to be Crista's father, Duque, had Avatan characteristics instilled through his mother's egg in the labs of the infamous Jesus Lewis, the bioengineer who once wiped out the kelp, body of Avata. He very nearly destroyed humanity along with the kelp. Vata was the beloved saint of Pandora, symbol of the union of humanity with the gods, voice of the gods themselves. Crista Galli, beloved of Ben Ozette, was no less godlike in her power and mystery, in her beauty, in the shadow of death about her. This did not make loving her easy.

Ben knew that the kelp—Avata—had been the survival key to humans on Pandora. It was difficult, maybe impossible, for humans to relate to a sentient … kelp. And this new kelp was not the same creature that the pioneers had encountered. Ben had studied The Histories enough to agree with the experts—this kelp was fragmented, it was not the single sentient being of old. Many of the faithful among the people of Pandora claimed that this was why Avata formed Crista Galli, to present itself in an acceptable form. This theory was fast gaining support.

Then what does it want?

To live!

The sudden thought intruded on his mind like a shout, startling him alert. It was a voice he almost recognized. He listened deep inside himself, head tilted, but nothing more came. The sleeper still slept.

The kelp, the body of Avata, was responsible for the stability of the very planet itself. One moon had pulverized itself to asteroids while several continents had ripped apart like tissue paper after the kelp was killed off by the bioengineer Jesus Lewis. Now, the kelp was replanted and the land masses returned after a couple of centuries under the sea. Humans were relearning to live on land as well as on or undersea. It pained Ben that people were still just scratching in dirt when they should be thriving.

That's the Director's fault, he reminded himself, *not the kelp's.*

The Director refused to recognize publicly the sentience of the kelp and used it simply as a mechanism, a series of powerful switches that controlled worldwide currents and, to some degree, weather. Everyone knew this was getting more difficult daily. There was more kelp daily, and very little of it was hooked up to Current Control.

The kelp is resisting Flattery, he thought. *When it breaks completely free, I want it to have a conscience.*

Ben's diligent research, with a few leads from Crista, uncovered the secret reports and he knew the real depth of Flattery's interest in what one paper called "the Avata Phenomenon." Ben had spoken with the Zavatans, monks in the hills who used the kelp in their rituals.

Crista says the Director should be consulting the kelp! he thought. *And I get the same story from those monks.*

She stirred again, and he knew she would wake soon. She would see the dockside shops fill with vendors and hear the morning calls from the street of: "Milk! Juices!" "Eggs! We have licensed squawk eggs today!" This was one of the many small pleasures that the Director had denied her—human companionship. Ben knew that he, too, in his way, would deny her this.

For now, he reminded himself. *Soon, we will have all the time in the world together.*

From the coffee shop below he could hear the faint scrape of furniture, the metallic clink of utensils and china.

Ben Ozette leaned back against the wall and let out a long, slow breath. Though he'd refused to admit it until now, he was surprised to be alive. He'd not only touched the forbidden Crista Galli, but he'd kissed her. It was twelve hours later and he was still breathing. They'd made it through the night without Vashon Security hunting them down. He waited for Crista to wake, for Rico's code-knock at the door, to see what they would make of the rest of their lives.

Chapter 8

When you see a cloud rising in the west, you say at once, "A shower is coming," and so it comes to pass. And when you see the south wind blow, you say, "There will be a scorching heat," and so it comes to pass. You hypocrites! you know how to judge the face of the sky and of the earth; but how is it that you do not judge this time?

—Jesus

CRISTA GALLI'S first memory of waking up that morning on Kalaloch was of the way the light caught the carved cup in Ben Ozette's hand, and of his hand. She wanted that hand to touch her, to brush her cheek or rest on her shoulder. It was so still, that hand balancing the cup on his knee, that she lay there for a while wondering whether he had fallen asleep sitting up beside the bed. She shuddered at the thought of sitting in one of those pieces of ghastly Islander furniture, a living creature that they called "chairdog."

Kalaloch, too, was waking outside. She heard the stirrings of people and the stutter of engines starting as the dozer and crawler crews headed for another day's work advancing the perimeter. The hungry and homeless of a dozen grounded islands also woke from their sleep in the gritty folds of greater Kalaloch.

Crista listened to the closer, warmer sound of Ben's quiet breathing.

God, she thought, *what if I'd killed him?*

She stifled a giggle, imagining the news lead as Ben himself might have written it: "HoloVision's popular Nightly News correspondent Ben Ozette was kissed to death last night on assignment …" The warmth, the taste of that kiss replayed itself in her mind. This was her first kiss, the one she'd nearly given up on.

Ben suffered no ill effects, which she attributed to the action of Flattery's daily dose of antidote, still in her system. Yet she had received the flood of Ben's past with the touch of his lips to her own, a cascade of memories, emotions and fear that nearly paralyzed her with its unexpected clarity and force.

There were these matters of his life that she preferred not to know: Ben's first kiss, a pretty redhead; his last kiss, Beatriz Tatoosh. Both of these and more lingered on her own lips. She witnessed his first lovemaking through the memory of his cells, witnessed his birth, the sinking of Guemes Island, the deaths of his parents. His memories impregnated her very cells, waiting for her own emotional trigger that would call them to life.

She had received his memories with his kiss, too stunned to tell him. Her dreams that night were his dreams, his memories. She saw Shadowbox as he saw it, as the organ of truth in a body riddled with lies. She knew that he, like herself, was vulnerable and lonely and had a life to live for others. She did not want to keep this from him, the fact that she now owned his life. She did not want to lose him now that they had finally found each other, and she did not want to be the death of him, either.

Ben was not afraid of "the Tingle," as people called it—this kelp death that supposedly lurked in her touch as it did in some kelp, within her very chemistry. Sometimes she didn't believe it, either. Flattery himself had developed the antidote, which he saw to it that she received daily. It did not diminish the chemical messages she received, such as Ben's memories. It merely muted those that her body might send. Still, none dared touch her and all of her attendants in Flattery's compound kept her at a safe distance.

This was the first morning in her memory that she did not wake up to attendants, endless tests, to the difficult task of being a revered prisoner in the great house of the Director. Crista had slept the refreshing sleep of the newborn in spite of their escape, their hiding, her first kiss. An emptiness rumbled through her stomach as delicious aromas rose to her of pastries, hot breads, coffee.

Somewhere beneath them hot sebet sizzled on a grill. Meat was something she craved. Flattery's labtechs had explained this to her, some mumbo-jumbo about her Avatan genes affecting her protein synthesis, but she knew this simply as hunger. She also hungered for fresh fruits of all kinds, and nuts and grains. The very thought of a salad gagged her and always had.

Though they'd fled here in the night, Crista had memorized the warrenlike underground system they took to get from the Director's complex at the Preserve to this Islander community at Kalaloch. She was reminded of the maze of kelpways down under. She knew nothing of the local geography save that she was near the sea, relieving some other hunger that rumbled within.

She heard the sea now, a wet pulse over the babble of street vendors and the increasing traffic of the day. Pandorans were an early lot, she'd heard, but unhurried. It is difficult for the hungry to hurry. Only a very few remained on their traditional organic islands. Drifting the seas had become much too dangerous a life in this day of jagged coastlines and sea lanes choked with kelp. The majority who settled landside still called themselves "Islander" and retained their old manners of dress and custom. Those Islanders whom she'd known at the Preserve compound were either servants or security, close-mouthed about their lives outside Flattery's great basalt walls. Many were horribly mutated, a revulsion to Flattery but a fascination to her.

Crista Galli tucked the cover under her chin and stretched backward, unfolding to the sunlight, aware of some new modesty in the company of Ben Ozette. She had all of the intimacies of his life stored in her head, now, and she was afraid of what he might think of her if he knew. She felt herself flush, a bit of a voyeur, as she remembered his first night with Beatriz.

Men are so strange, Crista thought. He'd brought her here on the run from Vashon security and the Director, assured her that they were safely hidden in this tiny cubby, then he sat up all night beside her rather than join her in bed. He'd already proven immune to her deadly touch, and she liked the kiss as much as the daring gesture of the kiss.

The attentions of other men, the Director among them, had taught her something of the power of her beauty. Ben Ozette was attracted to her, which had been clear the first time she'd looked into his eyes. They were green, something like her own only darker. She treasured the one magic kiss they had shared before she slept. She treasured his memories that now were hers, the family she shared with him, his lovers …

Her reverie was interrupted by a shriek in the street below, then a long, high-voiced wail that chilled her in spite of her warm bed. She lay quiet while Ben set aside his cup and rose to the window.

They've found someone, she thought, *someone who's been killed.*

Ben had told her about the bodies in the streets in the morning, but it was something too far from her life to imagine.

"The death squads leave them for a lesson," he said. "Bodies are there in the mornings for people to see when they go to work, when they take the children to their creche. Some have no hands, some have no tongues or heads. Some are mutilated obscenely. If you stop to look, you are questioned: 'Do you know this man? Come with us.' No one wants to go with them. Sooner or later a wife is notified, or a mother or a son. Then the body is removed."

Ben had seen hundreds of such bodies in his work, and she had glimpsed these the night before in the speedy unreeling of his memories into her own. This wail she thought must come from a mother who had just found her dead son. Crista was not tempted to look outside. Ben returned to his watch at her bedside.

Had he seen anything of her when she kissed him? Such a thing happened sometimes with the kelp, but seldom anymore with herself. It had happened with others who'd touched her. First, the shock of wide-eyed disbelief; then, the unfocused eyes and the trembling; at last, the waking and the registry of stark terror. For those who had been lucky enough to wake.

What did I show them? she wondered. *Why some and not all?* She had studied the kelp's history and found no help there, precious little comfort. She still smoldered over some research tech's pointed reference to her "family tree."

She remembered how she had been kept alive down under by the cilia of the kelp that probed the recesses of her body. She received the ministrations of the mysterious, nearly mythological Swimmers, the severest of human mutations. Adapted completely to water, Swimmers resembled giant, gilled salamanders more than humans. They occupied caves, Oracles, abandoned Merman outposts and some kelp lagoons. She had been one with the kelp, more kelp than human, for her first nineteen years. Some of Flattery's people thought that she had been manufactured by the kelp, but she herself believed that couldn't be true.

A lot of other Pandorans sported the green-eyed gene of the kelp, including Ben. At a little over a meter and a half tall she could look over the heads of most women and looked most men nearly in the eye. Her surface network of blue veins was slightly more visible than other people's because she was nearly pale enough to be translucent. The blood in her veins was red, based on iron, and incontrovertibly human—facts that had been established her first day out of the kelp.

Her full lips puckered slightly when she was thinking, hanging on the edge of a kiss. Her straight, slender nose flared slightly at the nostrils and flared even more when she was angry—another emotion she dared not indulge among Flattery's people.

Crista had been educated by the touch of the kelp, which infused in her certain genetic memories of the humans that it had encountered. Before Flattery took power, most humans contacted the kelp by being buried at sea. She had to shut out the flood of memories that came rolling in with the sounds of the nearby waves. She treated herself to another languorous stretch then turned to Ben.

"Did you sit up all night?"

"Couldn't sleep anyway," he said. He stood slowly, working out the kinks in his body, then sat on the edge of her bed.

Crista sat up and leaned against his shoulder. The disturbance below their window was gone. They faced the plaz, the morning sunlight off the bay, and Crista was lulled into a half-sleep by the warmth from the window, the coziness of Ozette beside her, and the harmonious chatter of the street vendors. In the distance she heard the heavy machinery of construction tear into the hills.

"Will we leave here soon?" she asked. She was invigorated by the sunlight, the *plop-plop-plop* of waves against the bulkhead and a whiff of broiling sebet on the air. The years of lies and imprisonment at the hands of the Director washed through her like a current of cold blood. Every morning that she had awakened in his compound she simply wanted to curl up under those covers and doze. Today, wherever Ben Ozette was going, Crista was going with him.

Someone whistled at their hatch, a short musical phrase, repeated once. It was the same kind of whistle-language that she'd heard from dockside the night before.

Ozette grunted, rapped twice on the deck. A single whistle replied.

"Our people," he said. "They will move us this morning, much as I'd like to show you the neighborhood. Rico is setting it up. The whole world knows by now that you're gone. The reward for your return, and for my head, will be enough to tempt even good people … on either side. There is much hunger."

"I can't go back there," she said. "I won't. I have seen the sky. You kissed me …"

He smiled at her, offered her a drink of his water. But he did not kiss her.

She knew that he would be killed if caught, that Flattery had already signed his death warrant. The Warrior's Union would take care of it, had probably already taken care of every servant and selected others at the Preserve.

The night before, emerging from the underground, they had dodged from building to building along the waterfront streets, fearful of security patrols enforcing Flattery's curfew. Crista had stopped in the open to look at the stars and at Pandora's nearer moons. She bathed firsthand in the touch of a cool breeze on her face and arms, smelled the charcoal cookery of the poor, saw the stars with only the atmosphere in her way.

"I want to go outside," she whispered. "Can we go out soon, to the street?"

Always the answer from the Director had been *no*. It was *always* no. "The demons," they would say at first, "you would hardly make a meal for them." Or, later, "The Shadows want you killed," the Director would say. Lately, he had repeated, "You can't tell—the swine could look like anyone. It would be horrible if they got their hooks into you."

The Director had a particular leer that gave her the creeps, though to hear him tell it no one could protect her but him, no one she could trust in the world but him. For most of that five years she had believed him. Shadowbox changed all that. Then Ben Ozette came to do his story, and she realized that the only reason Flattery forbade her touch was his fear that she would learn something from him, from his people, and expose his intricate system of lies.

"Yes," Ben said. "We'll get out soon. Things are going to get very hot here very soon ..."

He stiffened suddenly and swore under his breath. He pointed at a Vashon security patrol working their way down the pierside toward them: two men on each side of the street. They poured an insidious stillness over a choppy sea of commuters and shoppers in the marketplace. The press of commuters crowding toward the ferries parted for them without touching.

Each guard carried a small lasgun slung under one arm, and from each belt hung various tools of the security trade: coup baton for infighting hand to hand, charges for the lasguns, a fistful of small but efficient devices of chemical and mechanical restraint. They each wore a pair of mirrored sunglasses—trademark of the Warrior's Union, the Director's personal assassination squad. Among the people there was much smiling, headshaking, shoulder-shrugging; some cringed.

Crista watched the pair work their way along the dockside street and felt the small hairs rise on her arms and the back of her neck.

"Don't worry," Ben said, as though reading her mind. With his hand on her bare shoulder like that she believed it was possible that he was reading her mind—or, at least, her emotions. She loved his touch. She felt a new flood of his life enter through her skin. It stored itself somewhere in her brain while her eyes went on watching the street.

The security team left one man in front of each building in turn while the other searched inside. They were close.

"What do we do?" she asked. He reached to the other side of the bed for a bundle of Islander clothes and set them in her lap. "Get dressed," he said, "and watch. Stay back from the plaz."

A sudden, concussive *whump* and a flash of orange blasted from the harbor, then a roil of black smoke. The street turned into a scramble of bodies as people ran to their boats dockside and to their firefighting stations. Pandorans had used hydrogen for their engines and stoves, their welding torches and power production since the old days. Hydrogen storage tanks were everywhere, and fire one of their great fears.

"What ...?"

"An old coracle," Ben said, "registered to me. They will be busy for a while. With luck, they will believe we were aboard."

Another whump took Crista's breath away, and as she pulled on the unfamiliar clothing she saw that the security squad had not disappeared with the crowd. They came on with the same precision and deliberation, door to door. The street was nearly empty as everyone else who was able-bodied fought the fires or moved nearby boats to safety.

While Ben stood watch beside the window, Crista pulled on a heavily embroidered white cotton dress that was much too big for her. Her breasts bobbled free inside, another luxury Flattery wouldn't allow. She held the fabric away from her flat belly and looked questioningly at Ben.

He tossed her a black pajama-type worksuit of the Islanders that appeared identical to the one he wore. From a drawer beside the bed he pulled a long woven sash and handed it to her.

"I don't know how to tell you this, but you're pregnant. Quite a ways along, too."

When she still didn't follow his intent, he said, "Strap the worksuit on your belly to fill out the dress," he said. "You'll need it later. For now, you are a pregnant Islander. I am your man."

She strapped the worksuit around her as instructed and adjusted the dress. In the mirror beside the hatch she did look pregnant.

Crista watched in the mirror as Ben wrapped a long red bandana around his head, letting the tails fall between his shoulder blades. It was embroidered with the same geometries that appeared on her dress.

My man, she thought with a smile, *and we're dressing to go out.*

She patted the padding on her stomach fondly and rested her hand there, half-expecting to feel some tiny movement. Ben stood behind her and tied a similar bandana around her forehead. He gave her a floppy straw hat to wear over it.

"This manner of dress is the mark of the Island I grew up on," he said. "You have heard about Guemes Island?"

"Yes, of course. Sunk the year before I was born."

"Yes," he said. "You are now the pregnant wife of a Guemes Island survivor. Among Islanders you will receive the greatest respect. Among Mermen you will be treated with the deference that only the guilty can bestow. As you know, it means absolutely nothing among Flattery's people. We have no papers, there wasn't time …"

Two whistles at their hatch. Two different whistles. "That's Rico," he said, and matched her smile. "Now we get to go outside."

Chapter 9

The things that people want and the things that are good for them are very different. … Great art and domestic bliss are mutually incompatible. Sooner or later, you'll have to make your choice.

—Arthur C. Clarke

BEATRIZ DOZED awhile on the couch after shutting off her alarm. The dark, plazless office at the launch site helped keep the fabric of her dream alive. Freed from the confines of her mind, it flowed about the room with the ease of a ghost. In a way, it *was* a ghost.

She had been dreaming of Ben, of their last night together, and parts of the dream she wanted to savor. It was two years ago, the night before she made her first trip up to the Orbiter, before she met Mack. She was nervous about her first shuttle flight to the Orbiter, and Ben was going off to the High Reaches to meet with some Zavatan elder. In spite of the fact that they'd been lovers for years, they both felt awkward. It was ending, they knew it was ending, but neither of them could talk about it.

Early evening, clear and warm. A shot of sunset still streaked the horizon pink and blue. They sat aboard one of HoloVision's foils at dockside, in the crew's quarters. She remembered the familiar *shlup-shlup* of water against the hull and the occasional mutter of wild squawks settling down. Children played their evening games before being called in for the night and they whistle-signaled from pier to pier. She and Ben had talked of children, of wanting them and of bad timing. This night the rest of their crews had discreetly left them alone. She found out later it was at Rico's suggestion.

"Women are the answer," Ben said, handing her a glass of white wine. "And what was the question?"

She touched glasses with him, sipped, and set it down. She did not want to ride a rocket into orbit in the morning with a hangover.

Ben's green eyes looked particularly beautiful against his dark skin. His lean, muscular body had always been perfect with hers. She couldn't understand why he had to go off on his wild projects chasing down Shadows when he could stay and work with her. She'd covered as much death as she cared to, it was time they thought of themselves.

I want to report on life, advances, progress....

"Women represent life, advances, progress," he said.

The hair prickled at the back of her neck. "Are you reading my mind?"

"Would I dare?" he asked.

Those green eyes twinkled in their way that shot something straight into her heart, something warm that always melted downward like a hand inside her underwear. Beatriz was a strong woman, and Ben Ozette was the only man who ever made her weak in the knees. She sipped her wine and kept the glass at her chest.

"What am I thinking now?" she asked, feeling she had to change the subject.

"You're wishing I'd get on with whatever it was I was going to say so that we can get on with the evening."

She laughed a little louder than she liked, and ran a hand through her black hair. "Why, Mr. Ozette, what kind of girl do you think I am?"

He ignored her flirtation. His manner turned serious.

"I think you're the kind of girl who wants to see the best for everyone—for the refugees, yourself, even Flattery. You've covered some of the most horrible disasters and bloodiest atrocities this world has seen. I know because I was there. Now *it* won't go away, so *you're* going away. You want to see progress, you want to see good things. Well, so do I ..."

"But look what you're doing!" She punched her thigh and scooted back in the couch. "OK, security is more than enthusiastic, that's bad enough. If you make heroes out of the people fighting them, then more will join them. They will have to fight the same way. There will be no end to the cycle. Dammit, Ben, that's why they call it 'Revolution.' Wheels turn and turn in place and the vehicle gets mired down. I've come damned close to dying more times than I can count—most of those times with you—and now I want to get *somewhere.* I want a family ..."

Ben set down his glass and grasped her hand across the table.

"I know," he said. "I understand. Maybe I understand more than you think. I want to offer you life, advances, progress."

Neither of them spoke for a while, but their hands conversed with each other in the familiar language of lovers.

"OK," she said. She tossed off her wine, trying to appear lighthearted, "what's the plan, man?"

"I don't know the plan, yet," he said. "But I know the key. It's information. Our business, remember?"

"Yes?" She refilled her glass, then his. "Explain."

"You didn't see any women in Flattery's security force, and you set out to do a story, remember? What happened?"

"Not approved, we never shot a photon's worth …"

"And how many times has that happened?"

"To me? Not much. But then, there are plenty of stories to do, more than I'll ever live to do, I just find another one or take an assignment …"

"An important point," Ben said. He hunched over their little table, tapping the top with his index finger. "If Flattery doesn't get flattered, the story, whatever it is, doesn't get aired. He is from a different world—literally, a different world. He is from a world that starves women and children because they are on the wrong side of an imaginary line, and he won't allow them to cross it. We are from a world that used to teach: 'Life, at all cost. Preserve life.' Pandora has been adversary enough. We haven't been able to afford the luxury of fighting amongst ourselves."

"So, I don't get where …"

"Half of the shows I do get dropped," Ben said. "It's not because they're not good, it's just harder and harder to keep Flattery from looking like the hood that he is. What would happen if people refused to have anything to do with him—refused to speak with him, feed him, shelter him—what would happen then?"

She laughed again. "What makes you think they'd do that? It would take—"

"Information. Show him up for what he is, show the people what they can do. This whole world's been a disaster since Flattery took over. He promises them food and keeps them hungry. He keeps us in line because we know what he can do to us. If people knew they'd be no more hungry without Flattery, without the Vashon Security Force, would they put up with him?"

"It would take a miracle," she finished.

She couldn't look him in the eye. This was the conversation she really didn't want to have on their last night together. He leaned over and kissed her on the cheek.

"I'm sorry," he said. "I'm running off at the mouth again. I interviewed a group of mothers today who are petitioning the Chief of Security for news of their sons and husbands who have disappeared. Another group, over five hundred mothers, says that they had sons killed but there was never an investigation, never an arrest. They say security did it, there are witnesses. Now, I don't know about that. What I do know is that mothers are the ones on the march. HoloVision's refusing to pick up on it, forbidding me to report on what people have the right to know. There has to be a way … I'm just thinking out loud, is all."

He kissed her again on the cheek, then lifted her chin.

"I'll shut up now," he said. He kissed her lips and she pulled him down to the carpet beside the table.

"Promise?" She kissed him back, and untucked his shirt from his pants so she could get her hands under his clothes, onto his smooth, warm skin.

His hands unbuttoned her Islander blouse, unpeeled her cotton skirt and found her bare under both. "Pretty daring," he muttered, and kissed her belly as she undressed him. "You realize we're going to get rug burn."

"I thought you promised to shut up."

Her alarm went off again and startled Beatriz out of her waking dream. She shut it off and sat up to give herself some energy. Ben had been right about the rug burn. They'd kicked the wine over on themselves, too. She was sure that had been the night that Ben conceived the idea for Shadowbox. She sighed, trying to lift a heavy sadness from her chest.

Too bad we couldn't have conceived a little one, she thought. *It might've saved us both.*

If they had, she wouldn't have met Mack. Her relationship with Ben prepared her for Mack. He was a little older, and because of his upbringing on Moonbase he wanted a family as much as she did.

Beatriz pressed the "start" key on her pocket messenger and it announced: "0630 ..." She twisted the volume knob down and massaged her tired eyelids. The preliminary briefing from the HoloVision head office would be followed by more details before air time so she half-listened, intent only on news of Ben Ozette. Another deep sigh.

The smell at her launch site office down under was distinctly Merman—air swept clean of particulate, saturated with the scent of mold inhibitors and sterile water. Lighting in HoloVision's small broadcast studio always dried things out a bit and helped her breathe easier on the air. She suspected she would be on the air again in less than half an hour.

She pulled the legs of her singlesuit straight and unbunched the wrinkled sleeves from her armpits. Her office was backlit in the Merman way, so her reflection in the plaz was a warm one, capturing the glow of her brown skin and the sheen of her shaggy black hair. Her generation and Ben's was the first in two centuries to have more children born to the ancient norm of human appearance than not. Beatriz did not pity the severely mutated, pity was an emotion that most Pandorans could do without. She thanked the odds daily for her natural good looks. Right now she wanted a hot shower before facing her messenger's latest story of woe.

That's what Ben always called it, she thought. She spoke it aloud, "'Another story of woe.'"

Fatigue and a half-sleep deepened her voice enough to sound vaguely like his. It made her want to hear his voice, to argue with him one more time about who worked the hardest and who got the shower first. She smiled in spite of her worry. It was more than symbolic that they had always wound up in hot water together.

Fear for Ben made her not want to face the messenger just yet. It was hard enough to face the fact that she still loved him, though in an unloverly way.

Suicide, she thought. *He might just as well have run the perimeter on a bet and let a dasher have at him.*

Beatriz knew the signs, and it was Ben who'd made her aware of them. Crossing the Director was a survival matter.

She dolloped enough milk into her coffee to cool it off, then sipped at the rim while she replayed the brief, chilling message.

> 0630 Memo:
> Location brief, Launch Bay Five, air time 0645.
> Lead: Crista Galli still in hands of Shadows.
> Second lead: OMCs to Orbital Station today.
> Detail: ref terrorists, arms, drugs, religious fervor, Shadows. Final assembly of Voidship drive in orbit, OMC installation imminent. Items follow on Location.
> Secondary discretion: Mandatory at 0640.
> Time out: 0631.

Beatriz glanced at the processor's time display: 0636.

"Secondary Discretion!" she muttered. That meant they were doing a time-delay. Time enough that HoloVision could run a pretaped Newsbreak if she didn't show up or, worse, if they didn't like what she said on the air. Ben had warned her it would come to this.

"Damn!"

What else was he right about?

The elevator to the Newsbreak studio at Launch Bay Five was only a dozen meters down the passageway from her office. She fingered the tangles out of her hair and hurried out the hatchway. The hurry didn't slow her worrying one whit.

Ben had something to do with this Crista Galli thing, and she knew that Flattery knew that, too. Why, then, was there still no release on Ben? The answer was one that Ben had tried to warn her about, and it chilled her to think it.

They'll see that he disappears, she thought. *If there's nothing on him in the briefing* ... She didn't want to think of that.

Flattery knows about us ... about Ben, she thought. She knew about the disappearances, the bodies in the streets of Kalaloch in the mornings. Ben had warned her about this more than once and shown her firsthand, finally, how it happened. She knew that unpopular people disappeared. She had never thought it would happen to one of them.

Another thought shook her as she faced the elevator. *If I don't say something about him on the air, then he's going to disappear for sure!*

She was scheduled to fly with the crew that delivered the OMCs to the Orbital Station for their Voidship installation. He must know about her budding relationship with Mack, that was no secret. The installation of the Organic Mental Cores was a nice piece of propaganda for Flattery that would take her conveniently out of the picture. It would also make it impossible for her to investigate Ben's disappearance on her own.

She hadn't known what to think last night when she'd had to fill in for Ben. She'd read the prompter cold, too surprised at the lie on her screen, at the suddenness of the lie, to challenge it there. Flattery had finally tossed her a gauntlet.

What is the worst? she asked herself now. *The worst would be that they would both disappear.*

She squeezed into the elevator among the press of techs and mechanics, left their greetings unreturned. They were a sweaty bunch in the cramped humidity.

What is for sure?

For sure Ben would disappear if she said nothing, if HoloVision Nightly News continued to lie about his absence.

She rounded the passageway into the studio suite of the HoloVision feature assignment crew. It was an engine assembly hangar with ten-meter-high ceilings. The makeup tech's hands were fussing over Beatriz's hair and face as soon as she entered the hatchway. Someone else helped her slip into a bulky pullover blouse with the HoloVision logo at the left breast. As usual, several of the crew were talking at once, none of them saying what she wanted to hear. She wouldn't be doing this Newsbreak unless Ben were still missing.

She had seen Ben and Crista Galli together a few days ago at Flattery's compound. Ben and Crista, in the hibiscus courtyard, Ben leaning toward Crista in that intent way he had. Beatriz knew then that he had fallen in love with the girl. She also knew that he probably didn't know that yet himself.

I should have had a talk with him … not a lover talk, a friend talk. Now he might be dead.

She patted her cheeks flush and the lights turned up. It was nearly time, and still she spoke to no one, heard little, viewed the blank prompter with a certain measure of fear. He had held her own gaze intently hundreds of times over the years, dozens of times with the same argument.

"I look at the big picture," she'd say. "Pandora's unstable, we've seen that. We could all die here on any given day at the whim of meteorology. We need another world …" And he would always argue for the now.

"People are hungry *now*," he would say. "They need to be fed *now* or there won't be a later for any of us …"

She always felt insignificant in the studio in spite of her fame, but today as they scrubbed and dusted her face, fluffed her hair and placed her earpiece she was writing her own script for the Newsbreak—one that she hoped would keep Ben in the news but keep Flattery off her back. She looked into the prompter, adjusted the contrast and cleared her throat. She had thirty seconds. She cleared her throat again, smiled at the lens cluster and took a deep breath.

"Ten seconds, B."

She let the breath out slow, blinked her eyes for the shine and said to the red light, "Good morning, Pandora. I'm Beatriz Tatoosh for Newsbreak …"

Chapter 10

Since every object is simply the sum of its qualities, and since qualities exist only in the mind, the whole objective universe of matter and energy, atoms and stars does not exist except as a construction of the consciousness, an edifice of conventional symbols shaped by the senses of man.

—Lincoln Barnett, *The Universe and Dr. Einstein*

ALYSSA MARSH lived in the past, because the past was all that Flattery could not strip from her. He had tried chemicals, laser probes, tiny implants but the person who had been Alyssa Marsh survived them all.

He is afraid, she thought. *He is afraid that my life here has made me unfit as an OMC—and he's right.*

He had taken her body away fiber by fiber, or taken her away from her body. Her carotids and jugulars had been bypassed to a life-support system and she had been decapitated, then Flattery himself excised the remaining flesh and bone from around her unfeeling brain. The only sense she retained was the vaguest sense of being. She no longer felt much kinship with humans, and had no way of knowing how long she'd felt that way. Until someone hooked her up to her Voidship she had no means of measuring time. Time became her newest toy. Time, and the past.

Even fog has substance, she thought.

Logic told her that her brain still existed or she wouldn't be entertaining herself with these thoughts. Training in her Moonbase creche hundreds of years ago had prepared her for her responsibility as an OMC—purely mental functions, making human decisions out of mechanically derived data—but Pandora had opened up other possibilities, all of them requiring a body. Having a child, something she'd never have been permitted as a Moon-base clone, changed her perspective but it didn't change her indoctrination. She kept her child's birth secret, especially from his father, Raja Lon Flattery number six, the Director.

Without eyes or ears she would have thought herself a perpetual prisoner of a completely silent darkness. Without skin she expected not to feel, and without the rest she imagined she'd sniffed her last blossom, tasted her last bootleg chocolate. None of this proved to be true.

Alyssa had expected to be cut off from her senses, but reality proved her to be free of them instead. Like the gods, she was free now to clench the folds of time and replay her life at will, mining sensory details that she'd missed when they filtered through her emotions. She did not miss her emotions much, either, but she allowed as this might be a simple denial process protecting what was left of Alyssa Marsh from the full horror of what Flattery had done to her.

"You'll be the Organic Mental Core," he had announced to her. He spoke of it as privilege, honor, as the salvation of humankind. He might have been right about the salvation of humankind. At the time, even drugged as she was, she didn't buy the first two. She recognized that she was listening to one of the oldest arguments for martyrdom known to her species.

"Be reasonable," he'd told her. "Accept this banner and you will live in a thousand bodies. The Voidship itself will become your bones, your skin."

"Spare me the speech," she slurred, her tongue thickened by drugs. "I'm ready. If you're not going to let me go back to my studies in the kelp, if you're not going to kill me, then just get on with it."

She now felt that the major difference between herself and the kelp was that the kelp's entire body was also its brain. The tissues were integrated and the appropriate accomplishments measurable. Flattery would hear none of this.

He had spoken to her of an Elysium of sorts, of a pain-free and disease-free life. He reminded her that an OMC in its harness was the closest that humans came to immortality. This did nothing to comfort her. She knew the insanity record of other OMCs, the rate at which they'd turned rogue and destroyed their host ships and their expendable cargoes of clones, clones like herself, and Flattery, and Mack. Indeed, the same thing had happened aboard the Voidship *Earthling*, which brought them all to Pandora. Three OMCs went crazy and the crew had to fabricate an artificial intelligence to save their skins. It brought them to Pandora and abandoned them there.

I'm understanding that more and more, she thought. *I'd like to meet this* Ship *sometime, interface to interface.*

Words had always amused her, and a lack of flesh to laugh with did not seem to diminish that amusement. Thinking of her son was always serious, however, especially since he'd made such good headway in Flattery's security service. She thought of him now because her one regret was not seeing him face to face before she …

… *Shucked my mortal coil*, she thought. *I wanted to see him with my own eyes. No … I wanted him to see me before … this.*

She had given him up to an upwardly mobile Merman couple rather than risk what would happen if Flattery found out she'd borne him a son. She had been afraid he would kill her and take the son, turning him into another ruthless Director.

I should've kept him, she thought. *He's turned out like Flattery, anyway.*

The boy would know by now—she'd left the appropriate papers hidden in her cubby before Flattery reduced her to a convoluted lump of pink tissue. It had been her last act of sentimentality.

"Your body betrays you," Flattery growled that last day. "You've had a child. Where is it?"

"I gave it up," she said. "You know how I am about my work. I have no time for anything but the kelp. A child … well, it was only a temporary inconvenience."

It was the kind of argument that Flattery would make, and he bought it. He never seemed to suspect that the child was his. Their liaison had been brief enough and long enough ago that Flattery seemed not to remember it at all. He had made no further reference to it after she left his cubby for the last time more than twenty years back. He only grunted his acknowledgment, probably thinking that the child was the product of a recent indiscretion. He could not deny her passion for her work in the kelp. Only Dwarf MacIntosh shared her passion for delving into this mysterious near-consciousness that filled Pandora's seas.

I should have kept him with me in the kelp, she thought. *Now he's become what I'd most feared and I've lost his presence, too.*

In her present state, the OMC Alyssa Marsh dwelt often on that birth and those few precious moments her child had been with her. He had stopped crying immediately after birth, happy to watch the Natali as they cleaned up his mother and the room. He had a full head of black hair and seemed fully alert right from the start.

"He was a month overdue," the midwife said. "Looks like he wasn't wasting his time in there."

After a few minutes she handed him to the couple who would give him their name. Frederick and Kazimira Brood had visited her weekly for the past few months, and they had made full arrangements for his care. It would cost Alyssa dearly, but she wanted him to have the best of chances. Flattery was determined to turn Kalaloch into a real city, the center of Pandoran thought and commerce. He had hired the young Broods—an architect and a social geographer—to build the security warehouses and garrisons for his troops. There was talk at the time that they might get the university contract. Who could have foreseen the changes in Pandora, the changes in Flattery then?

I could, she thought. *I thought development of the kelp as an ally more important than raising my son.*

If she had had her body with her, she would have let out a long, slow breath to relieve the tension that would have been brewing in her belly. She had neither belly nor breath and her reason now was relatively free of emotion.

I did the right thing, she thought. *In the grand scheme of humankind, I did the right thing.*

Chapter 11

> *Even if they, with minds overcome by greed, see no evil in the destruction of a family, see no sin in the treachery to friends, shall we not, who see the evil of destruction, shall we not refrain from this terrible deed?*
>
> —from *Zavatan Conversations with the Avata*, Queets Twisp, elder

FLUTTERBY BODEEN unrolled her precious bolt of stolen muslin across the dusty attic deck. Her three young schoolmates clapped in their excitement.

"You did it!" Jaka cheered. He was twelve, lanky, and the only boy. His father, like Flutterby's, worked down under at the Shuttle Launch Site, or SLS. His mother also worked at Merman Hyperconductor, so their family received nearly double the usual scrip at The Line.

"Shhh!" Flutterby warned them. "We don't want them finding us now. Leet, did you get the paints?"

Leet, at eleven the youngest of the four, pulled four thick tubes from under her bulky cotton blouse.

"Here," she said, without looking up, "I couldn't get black."

"Green!" Jaka blew out an impatient breath. "You want them to think we're Shadows? You know they all use green …"

"Shush!" Dana emphasized her point with a finger at her lips and an exaggerated scowl. "Maybe we are Shadows *now*, did you ever think of that? They'll treat us the same if we're caught, you know."

"OK, OK," Flutterby interrupted. "We're not going to get caught unless we're here all day. Dana, Jaka, we're supposed to be practicing our music, so you two play awhile. Leet and I will each make a banner, then we'll play so you can do two."

"Security's all over the street this morning," Dana warned. "It's because of Crista Galli. Maybe they think she's around here, somewhere …"

"Maybe she *is* around here …"

"We should have a lookout …"

"They won't come in while wots are practicing," Flutterby said, and put her hand up to quiet the others. "Who wants to have anything to do with music lessons? Besides," she sniffed, and her chin raised a fraction, "my brother's a security. I know how they think."

"Yeah, and he's up in Victoria," Dana said. "They think different up there. You know they split them up so if they shoot somebody it won't be family."

"That's not true!" Flutterby said. "They just don't want them working the same district as their family because—because—"

"They're going to walk in here if we don't get busy," Jaka interrupted. His voice was changing, and he tried to make it sound authoritative. Jaka lived at the edge of Kalaloch's largest refugee camp. He was more fearful than the others of the immediacy of hunger and the reprisals of security. At twelve, he had already seen enough death from both. He uncased his well-worn flute and snapped the sections together.

Dana shrugged, sighed and uncased her caracol. Its new strings glistened in a stray sliver of sunlight. The swirled black back of its huge shell shone with the polish of four generations of fingers.

"Give me an A," she said.

Jaka obliged, and as they proceeded to tune the caracol the other two youngsters tore the cloth into four equal lengths of about three meters each.

"Has your brother ever killed anybody?" Leet whispered.

"Of course not," Flutterby said. She smoothed out the wrinkles in their cloth without meeting the other girl's eyes. "He's not like that. You've met him."

"Yeah," Leet said. Her brown eyes brightened and she giggled. "He's so cute."

Flutterby found that she got her banner lettered with less than half a tube of green. It was dark green and would be nearly as visible as black. The large block letters read, "WE'RE HUNGRY NOW!" It had become the rallying cry of the refugees, but she'd heard it mumbled everywhere lately. As scarcity spread and rations declined, Flutterby had even heard it whispered in The Line.

The Line, where everyone stood for hours to get into the food distribution centers, was where she chose to hang her banner. Leet's would go over their school, which faced the concrete and plasteel offices of Merman

Mercantile. Jaka wanted to smuggle his into Merman Hyperconductor, and Dana said she'd hang hers from the ferry dock, within easy view of HoloVision's offices on the pier.

Dana ran up and down the scales a few times, then she and Jaka played a fast, lilting dance piece they'd practiced at school. Flutterby thought it the best her friend had ever played. Jaka struggled, as usual, but diligently played on.

"Do you think the Shadows kidnapped Crista Galli?" Leet asked.

The bulky tube was difficult for her to handle, and she was going over her letters twice to make them bold enough to be read at a distance.

"I don't know," Flutterby said. "I don't know what to believe anymore. My mother grew up on Vashon, and she says that Crista Galli is some kind of god or something. My dad says she's just another freak."

"Your *mother*?"

"No," Flutterby giggled. "Crista Galli, you stoop. He says that the only way to feed the world is to keep control of the currents, and that if Crista Galli helps control the kelp then the Director is right to make sure she doesn't get away, or turn it against us. What do your parents think?"

Leet frowned.

"They don't say much of anything, anymore," she said. "They're both working all the time, every day. Mom says she's too tired to hear herself think. My dad won't even watch the news anymore. He doesn't say anything, just bites his lip and goes to bed. I think they're afraid ..."

An explosion in the harbor startled them both. Dana set her caracol on the deck with a *thump*.

"That was close," she said. Dana had a lisp that came out when she was nervous, and it slipped out now.

The four of them crowded the tiny plaz porthole at the far end of the attic. A smudge of black smoke blotted the sky to their right at the end of the street. Looking up the street to the left, Flutterby watched the giant cup on the Ace of Cups sign swing to and fro from the concussion. The street was packed with morning commuters and vendors at their little tables. Flutterby heard a gasp from Dana, and looked where she pointed, straight beneath them.

"Security!" she whispered. "He's covering the hatch. They must already be inside!"

"We've got to hide this stuff," Jaka said, his whisper cracking into its high range. "If they find this, they'll kill us."

"Or worse," Dana muttered.

They scrambled to gather up the paints and to roll up the two wet banners, but it was too late. The flimsy hatch burst aside as a fat, no-neck security kicked it in. Another, nearly identical to him, slipped inside and waited with his back to the wall.

"Look here," he said, straightening the banners with the muzzle of his weapon. "A little nest of flatwings, no?"

Without waiting for a reply he snapped two bursts from his lasgun. Jaka and Leet dropped to the deck, dead.

Flutterby wanted to scream, but she couldn't catch her breath.

"They're wots," his partner said. "What did you ... ?"

"Maggots make flies," the other said. "We have orders."

The muzzle came up again and Flutterby didn't even see the flash that killed her.

Chapter 12

Mankind owns four things
that are no good at sea:
rudder, anchor, oars
and the fear of going down.
—Antonio Machado

BEN UNDOGGED the hatch and Rico LaPush rushed inside. Rico nodded once to the girl, who looked ghastly pale, and handed Ben the pocket messenger. Most of the briefing on it was already outdated, but Ben would want to hear it, anyway. Rico was careful to keep from touching the girl.

"Ready?" he asked.

"Ready," Ben said.

"Yes," said the girl.

Rico scratched his chin stubble and adjusted the lasgun in the back of his pants. He had been with Ben since Guemes island was sunk, more years than Crista Galli had been alive. His mistrust of people had kept them alive more than once, and he did not intend to let his guard down with Her Holiness.

"Deja vu," he said to Ben, nodding at her Islander dress. "She reminds me of the old days, when things were simply tough. The streets are crawling with security, she'll need a good act …"

"You can speak to me," Crista interrupted, her cheeks flushed with a run of anger. "I have ears to hear, mouth to answer. This sister is not a chairdog, nor a glass of water on her brother's table."

Rico had to muster a smile. Her Islander accent was perfect, her phrasing perfect. She was a very quick study—of course, she had more intimate ways of getting inside people's heads …

"Thank you for the lesson, Sister," he said. "You are most cheerfully dressed, my compliments."

Rico noted Ben's smile, and the fact that his partner's gaze never wavered from Crista Galli's perfect face.

Rico's cameras had taped the faces of many beautiful women for HoloVision and he had to admit that everything he'd heard about Crista Galli was true. When Ben became a reporter, Rico LaPush signed on as a field triangulator with the holography crew. A well-placed lie got him the job, but his facility for learning kept it. He had filmed more pomp and more horror in any given year than most cameramen witnessed in a lifetime.

She's pale, but beautiful, he thought. *Maybe the sun will give her some color.*

Operations said to keep her out of the sun, but Rico thought that, given their recent bad luck, this would be impossible. Operations, whoever *they* were, didn't have their butts on the line.

"We'll be walking for a while," Rico told them. "Don't hurry." He nodded at the messenger in Ben's hand.

"Don't bother," he said. "You might as well shitcan that thing. They tell us we're going by air but the airstrip's already locked up by Flattery's boys. We'll have to do it by water."

"But they said …"

"I know what they said," Rico snapped. "They *said* the airstrip would be secure. They *said* keep her away from water. Let's move."

Crista Galli carried a sadness about her that Rico didn't like. He could take fear, or anger, or even hysteria but sadness felt too much like bad luck. They'd started out with that. When she reached out a tentative hand toward Ben, Rico stopped her with a word.

"No," he said. "I'm sorry. I can't let you touch him."

"Your fear?" she shot back, "or this 'Operations'? He is clothed."

"My fear."

She was hurt when Ben remained silent.

Crista shrank back from him, and Rico slipped into the Guemes dialect that he'd set aside years ago.

"Among Islanders, I am merely advising one of my sisters that she needs to recognize the depth of trust and love that the people have for her," he said, with a curt nod of his head. "They speak out to her when the speaking is painful."

"And the fear?"

Good! Rico thought. *She won't be bullied.*

He continued to speak to her in the manner of the Guemes Islanders.

"This sister apprises the brother well. Let the brother remind the sister that only the unknown is feared. Perhaps the sister will set this brother at ease, in time. Shall we begin?"

She was quiet then, and Rico liked that about her. Whatever curse she carried, she carried it with grace. He had known Ben Ozette for twenty-five years. Rico had fallen in love with a dozen women during that time, but Ben had only fallen once. Rico remembered that Ben had looked at Beatriz Tatoosh the same way he now looked at Crista Galli.

It's about time, he thought, and smiled to himself. *Beatriz is tight with that guy MacIntosh. Ben needs somebody solid, too.*

Everybody knew that relationships within the industry had to be short-lived, and that families were impossible. With all of the travel and stress something, somewhere, had to give, and it was usually the relationship. Rico had given up long ago, and was currently seeing a redhead who worked full-time for Operations.

"The harbor," Rico said as they started down the ramp. "It's a madhouse there and so far no security near the *Flying Fish*. Victoria's as secure as Victoria gets, so we'll head up there. Risky, but not so risky as this."

They turned right, walking slowly down the pier, toward the crowd at dockside. Rico trailed slightly behind the couple, keeping buildings and hatchways close, and didn't speak. He nearly stumbled into the Galli girl several times as she stopped suddenly to stare at some of the shops and the relics of herself that were sold there. At each shop, she pulled the mantilla closer about her face.

So, it's true, Rico thought. *She doesn't know!*

He watched her reach out toward a tasteless vest in a glass case that bore the inscription: "Vest of Crista Galli, worn at age twelve. Not for sale." Also arranged about the case were various microscope slides with blood smears on them, a clipping of hair too obviously dark to be hers and several bits of cloth—all with price tags, all claiming to come from "Her Holiness," Crista Galli. Above the case was scrawled a hand-lettered warning: "Extreme danger, do not touch. Safety packaging included with each sale."

You'd think she'd never seen a dog before, he thought, watching her, *or a chicken—she sure went loony over those goddamn chickens.*

Rico dawdled close behind them and tried not to listen to their talk. He hadn't eaten since the previous morning and the charcoal spatter of hot food set his stomach rumbling. He was a little nervous, plenty could still go wrong. But the diversion had taken one patrol off their backs.

If the boys are doing their jobs, we shouldn't see a security between here and the boat.

Just as he thought it he knew better, but there was no calling the thought back and there was no calling back the two security guards rounding the corner ahead of them. Rico pressed a switch on the broadcast unit in his pocket. A third explosion went off near the harbor but neither guard took the bait. Rico sighed and adjusted the lasgun at the back of his waistband. It was an older model, short-range. He remembered thinking, as the two guards veered across the street toward them, how difficult it had become to buy spare charges.

Ben and Crista saw the security and slowed to a stop. Commuters and street vendors pressed past them in waves. Rico stopped, too, a few paces behind them and in front of a deep hatchway. With the new explosion there was a renewed flurry among those crowding toward the harbor, and Rico was not happy that Ben had stopped. Both of the men approaching wore the khaki fatigues of the Vashon Security Forces, rank four. They were both burly, armed only with stunsticks, nearly normal but with the creased ears and fat lower lips betraying certain internal defects typical of Lost Islanders.

Just as Rico's hand clutched the grips of his lasgun, Crista Galli stepped forward, exaggerating the rolling walk of the heavily pregnant. She spoke, her hand upraised and head tilted in the Guemes fashion of greeting.

"Brothers," she said, "this mother cannot find a rest station and she is in great need." This she delivered matter-of-factly, and turned her palm up. Though the guards were obviously jumpy, the response was automatic.

"Up two streets, one street left. The shops—"

The other security gave his partner a shove and interrupted: "This could be the start of a Shadow attack … let's move! Sister, get out of the street. You two," he pointed to Ben and Rico, "get her inside someplace and lay low."

The two guards huffed toward their station at the harbor and Rico let out the breath he'd been holding in a low whistle. It was a coded whistle, from their childhood days, that any Islander wot would recognize as "all clear."

"You sure made Rico happy," Ben said, grinning.

"Got it all on tape, too," Rico said. He tapped a tiny lens at his shirtfront. "It'll look great in your memoirs."

He nodded at Crista.

"Good job thinking, helluva good job acting." He rechecked the charges in the camera at his belt and buffed the lapel lens with his sleeve. The lens looked like a small pin made of a glossy gray stone.

"Shouldn't we get out of here?" Crista asked. "You heard what he said, the Shadows—"

"Are us," Rico interrupted in a whisper, "and there will be no attack. The villagers might bust loose, though. Things are pretty hot. The *Flying Fish* is down there." He pointed out the "Pier Four" sign just ahead.

One of the huge cross-bay ferries had surfaced dockside, unwilling to risk explosive damage in the comparatively shallow waters of the bay. Foot passengers from all over Pandora streamed out of the rear hatch, while two- and three-wheeled vehicles crowded the roadway. The morning dust changed to mud under all the feet and mud splashed up from wheels to stain the hems of fine Islander embroidery. Islanders even dressed up to go to market.

About half of the crowd that elbowed back down the pier wore the plastic ID tag around their necks that marked them as Project Voidship employees. Whatever they did, they did it for Flattery's paycheck. This was a huge village, huge enough to strain the bonds of family, and today many of the dockside vendors threw catcalls and curses after the workers from the shuttle launch site.

The pier itself was a bridge between two subway mouths—one from the village to the pier, and another that loaded onto the submarine ferry. Vendors crowded the station entrances, selling tubes of suntan lotion, sodas, dried fruits. Here the smell of charcoal and the spatter of grilled fish were drowned out in the babble of the crowds.

Suddenly, one of Rico's greatest fears was made real. An Islander refugee, carrying a placard and wet to the skin from a firehosing, rushed down the crowded pier and attacked one of the commuters. They both fell in a tumble and, out of reflex as much as anger, the knot of commuters began kicking at him. Several dozen refugees tried in their weak way to free him, then to fight back, but within a matter of blinks they were all set upon and beaten.

Rico and Ben closed tight on Crista Galli and Rico looked for a way down the pier. Screams of anger turned to grunts of pain all around them. Bodies splashed into the bay and the hot morning was filled with curses and the wet red smack of fists on skin.

Crista kept her arms folded in front of her and her hands in her sleeves, like many of the old Islander women. She seemed locked in position with her hand out, like a figure from a wot's game of freeze-tag. As they worked through the crowd she stumbled on the Islander's battered placard and Rico saw that it read, "Give a Brother a Break!"

A splintering sound and the wail of bent bracing came from behind them, then screams of fear. Rico saw, over his shoulder, that a portion of the pier had given way and hundreds of people spilled into the water.

That might cool things for now, he thought, *but not for long.*

"Walk slower," Rico said at Crista Galli's ear. "You're tired and pregnant and haven't eaten since last night."

He knew that the last was true. He thought of all the meals he'd missed as a wot, wondered when was the last time Crista Galli or the Director had missed a meal. He and Ben missed plenty working the news business, but that was different. When Rico was a wot, he hadn't chosen to go hungry.

He scanned the beach where it broke out from the Islander settlement on the coast and flattened to a grassy plateau at the village perimeter. Security gathered there in their black personnel carriers, waiting for the crowd to tire before it was their turn to work them over. A bloody frenzy this close to the perimeter, and relatively open to beach and bay, might bring in dashers. The sight of a hunt of dashers would disperse the crowd, then security could take down the dashers and hardly wrinkle a crease in their fatigues.

Rico's visual and electronic sweep of the area detected no signs of security on the pier itself. He had nothing that would detect the high-power listening devices that the Director favored lately.

Crista stared straight ahead as they walked, eyes widely dilated, and Ben took her elbow.

"Tell them before we go that they are all one. Make them understand that they are all the same being and if they cut off their arms and legs they'll die …"

Ben gripped her elbow and gave it a shake. Rico saw her eyes as she turned to face him. They went from wild, wide and unfocused to normal. Rico noted that Ben was careful and didn't touch her skin.

"We're going to Port Hope," he lied, talking quickly as they walked. "The lake there is beautiful this time of year, and even with the altitude you will find it warm at night. The older Islands are too vulnerable. We have strong loyalties among the Mermen but you can't move freely in their settlements down under. Our immediate danger is security. The Director's got spotter planes up all along the coast, particularly near the Preserve. Of course, there are his Skyhawks. At sea we are vulnerable to the kelp," he paused, and when Crista looked his way he nodded, then continued, "and the Director's new fleet of foils, some of which he conveniently sold to Vashon security. Of course, we also have his spies among us."

Rico was relieved. What Ben had said was for the benefit of listening devices, not for Crista Galli. He was sure, by her blank stare, that she had not understood a word.

She shuffled on through the shouts and cries along Pier Four as though she heard nothing. Rico saw that there were more boats burning now, maybe a dozen, and firefighters were trying to push them away from the others. One of the Vashon Security Forces power foils steamed full-tilt toward the blaze from the Preserve side of the water.

The *Flying Fish*, HoloVision's private foil, was within sight at the end of the slip. Rico felt the tease of adrenaline in his belly. He hoped that Operations had briefed Elvira, pilot of the *Flying Fish*. She didn't much care for sudden changes of plans, and she really didn't like encounters with Vashon Security.

Elvira was the toughest pilot that HoloVision had ever hired. No one inconvenienced Elvira. To Rico's knowledge she had no politics, no hobbies, no friends and no religious convictions whatsoever. Her sole passion was to pilot the hottest hydrogen-ram foil in the world as often and as fast as possible. In surface mode she was highly competent; in undersea mode or flight she had no equal in the world. She had flown Ben and Rico in and out of more hot assignments than he could count. This would undoubtedly be the hottest.

Ben caught Rico's gaze and raised a quizzical eyebrow, nodding toward the girl.

Rico scratched his two-day beard. Crista turned to stare past him at the crowd that now had worked its way up the pier, gathering bodies and momentum, and was now fanning out into the streets of Kalaloch.

Everyone who was to remember this event recalled that the morning air split with a *crack* like summer thunder, or a whip. No echo, not a breath of breeze. Even a cluster of fussing children nearby silenced themselves in their mother's skirts.

Rico touched a fingertip to each of his ears, acutely conscious of the scratchings at each contour, each follicle and fold. If a shock wave *had* hit his ears, they'd still be ringing.

She did that in my … in our minds!

Crista felt the sudden clap of stillness crack with her anger. She was glad that Ben and Rico were the first to recover, though what she saw in their eyes was clearly fear. The mob had stopped, momentarily stunned and looking about for a weapon, then it boiled anew at the onslaught of the truckloads of Vashon Security that came to meet it.

Crista spun away from them and boarded the *Flying Fish*, still affecting the wide-beamed walk of the largely pregnant. She stood on the deck, beside the cabin hatchway, hugging herself and looking out to sea. The children started fussing again, stunned villagers rubbed their ears and began to move. Rico noticed that the boat fires had spread to the pier itself and some of the shops. Both ferries at the slip had submerged, empty, for safety. Rico approached Crista at the rail while Ben cast off the lines.

"This was coming for months," Rico said, "you could tell by the feel in the streets. They've had enough. It's too soon, and they're not organized. It will fail, for them. Some will be drawn out after us. Some, to the harbor. Others, to the attack that is inevitable inside the settlement. That will leave the Preserve weak …"

"It's too well-protected," she said, her voice matter-of-fact. "They will fail."

She fixed Rico with those striking green eyes. He noticed, once again, that they were dilated in spite of the sunlight.

"I know how you felt now, back there, when you were so afraid of my touch." She smoothed the dress over her makeshift belly. "What I know of the Shadows and what you know of me are the same. I only know what Flattery told me. I don't know whether you should fear my touch. Do you know whether I should fear yours?"

When he didn't answer she turned and shuffled into the cabin of the HoloVision foil in silence.

Chapter 13

Evil is in the eye of the beholder.
—Spider Nevi, special assistant to the Director

LIGHTS HAD been suitably dimmed in the Director's holo suite, and one tight spotlight illuminated his face from below. This effect accentuated Flattery's height, nearly a head taller than the average Pandoran, and it added an imperiousness to his stature that pleased him.

An empty holo cassette teetered across the red armrest of his favorite recliner. One fluorescent orange sticker on the cassette read "For Eyes Only," and under that was handwritten: "TD, S. Nevi *only*." Under that was stamped in black: "Extreme Penalty." Flattery smiled at the euphemism. At his direction, all those who violated the "Extreme Penalty" sanction became the homework of Spider Nevi's apprentice interrogators. Messy business, security.

"Mr. Nevi," he acknowledged, with a nod.

"Mr. Director."

As usual, Spider Nevi's face was unreadable, even to Flattery's expert training as a Chaplain/Psychiatrist. Nevi had been prompt, unhurried, arriving in a snappy gray cut of a Merman lounging suit right at the first blood of dawn.

"Zentz hasn't found them," Flattery said. His voice was clipped, betraying more anger than he wished.

"It was Zentz who lost them," Nevi countered.

Flattery grunted. He hadn't needed the reminder, especially from Nevi.

"*You* find them," he said, and jabbed a finger at the air between them. "Bring back the girl, wring what you can from the others. Save Ozette for a special occasion. He's at the bottom of this Shadowbox and they've got to be shut down *now*."

Nevi nodded, and the agreement was struck. Bounty would be worked out later, as usual. Nevi's terms were always reasonable, even on difficult matters, because he liked his work. His was the kind of work that might go unpracticed if it weren't for the Director.

Every art has its canvas, Flattery thought.

"The airstrip is secure," Nevi said. "There were preparations for them there, including a half-dozen collaborators, so we have cut them off. Solid intelligence. Zentz's men are turning the usual screws in the village. They will be forced to move the girl soon. Overland is out, that would be insane. It would have to be by water, and under diversion to get out of here. My guess would be Victoria. It would pay to wait and make as big a sweep as possible, don't you think?"

"You have the docks under watch?"

"Of course. The HoloVision foil is bugged, a precaution. Your sensor system is now keyed into it." Nevi glanced at the clock on Flattery's console. "You should be able to tune them in just about any time."

Flattery shifted slightly in his command couch, betraying his uneasiness at this loss of control. Nevi was second-guessing his moves, and he didn't like it.

"Well," Flattery said, splitting his face with a smile, "this is magnificent! We will have them all—and you will be rewarded for this. Zentz grumbles that you steal away his best men but, dammit, you get the job done." He slapped his palm on the tabletop and held the smile.

Spider Nevi's expression did not change, and he said nothing. His only response was the barest perceptible nod of his horrible head. The shape of it was more or less normal, except for the mucous slit where the nose should be. Nevi's dark skin was shot through with a glowing web work of red veins. His dark eyes glittered, missed nothing.

"What do you want done with the Tatoosh woman?" Flattery felt his smile droop, and he tried to pick it up a bit.

"Beatriz Tatoosh is very helpful to us," Flattery said. "She has a passion for the Voidship project that we could not buy." He raised his hand to stop Nevi's interruption. "I know what you're thinking—that little tryst between her and Ozette. That's been over for over a year—"

"It wasn't a 'little tryst,'" Nevi interrupted. "It lasted years. They were wounded together at the miners' rebellion two years ago—"

"I know women," Flattery hissed, "and she will hate him for this. Running away with a younger woman … sabotaging HoloVision and the Voidship. Didn't she do the broadcast as written last night?"

A nod from Nevi, and silence.

"She knows as well as we do that mentioning Ozette as party to this abduction would lend it a popularity and a credence that we cannot afford. It is over between them, and as soon as he's back in our hands everything will be over for Ben Ozette. The Tatoosh woman will be aboard the orbital assembly station this afternoon and out of our hair."

At Nevi's continued silence, Flattery rubbed his hands together briskly.

"Now," he said, "let me show you how I've kept the kelp pruned back for the last couple of years. You know how the people resist this, it always takes a disaster to get them to go along with it. Well, the kelp's will was breached long ago by our lab at Orcas. Too complex to explain, but suffice it to say it is not merely a matter of mechanical control—diverting currents and the like. Thanks to the neurotoxin research we tapped into its emotions. Remember that stand of kelp off Lilliwaup, the one that hid the Shadow commando team?"

Nevi nodded. "I remember. You told Zentz 'Hands off.'"

"That's right," Flattery said. He drew himself upright in his recliner and snapped the backrest up to meet him. He keyed the holo and automatically the lights dimmed further. Between the two men, in the center of the room, appeared in miniature several monitor views of a Merman undersea outpost, a kelp station at the edge of a midgrowth stand. Kelp lights flickered from the depths beyond the outpost. The kelp station had been built atop the remnants of an old Oracle.

Oracles, as the Pandorans called them, were those points where the kelp rooted into the crust of the planet itself. Because of the incredible depth of these three-hundred-year-old roots, and because the Mermen of old planted them in straight lines, Pandora's crust often fractured along root lines. It was such a series of fractures that had given birth to Pandora's new continents and rocky island chains.

Flattery's private garden, "the Greens," lay underground in a cavern that had once been an Oracle. Flattery had had his people burn out the three-hundred-meter-thick root to accommodate his landscaping plans.

Three views clarified on the holo stage in front of the two men: The first was of the inside of a kelp station, with a balding Merman fretting at his control console; the second, outside the station, from the kelp perimeter, focused on the station's main hatch; the third, also outside the station, took in the gray mass of kelp from the rear hatch. The Merman looked very, very nervous.

"His children have been swimming in the kelp," Flattery said. "He is worried. Their airfish are due for replacement. All have been dutifully taking their antidote. The kelp, when treated with my new blend, shows an unhealthy attraction for the antidote."

There were occasional glimpses of the children among the kelp fronds. They moved in the ultra-slow-motion of dreams, much slower than undersea movement dictated, considerably slower than the usual polliwog wriggle of children.

The Merman activated a pulsing tone that shut itself off after a few blinks.

"That's the third time he's sounded 'Assembly,'" Flattery said. Anticipation made it difficult for him to sit still.

The Merman spoke to a female, dressed in a worksuit, wet from her day's labor of wiring up the kelp stand for Current Control.

"Linna," he said, "I can't get them out of the kelp. Those airfish will be dry … what's happening out there?"

She was thin and pale, much like her husband, but she appeared dreamy-eyed and unfocused. Most of those who worked the outposts did not wear their dive suits inside their living quarters. She worked the fringes of what the Mermen called "the Blue Sector."

"Maybe it's the touch of it," she murmured. "The touch … special. You don't work in it, you don't know. Not slick and cold, like before. Now the kelp feels like, well …" She hesitated, and even on the holo Flattery could detect a blush.

"Like what?" the Merman asked.

"I … lately it feels like you when it touches me." Her blush accented her crop of thick blonde hair. "Warm, kind of. And it makes me tingle inside. It makes my veins tingle."

He grunted, squinted at her, and sighed. "Where are those wots?"

He glanced out the plaz beside him into the dim depths beyond the compound. Flattery could detect no flicker of children swimming, and he felt a niggling sense of glee at the Merman's growing apprehension.

The Merman activated his console tone again and the proper systems check light winked on with it. His finger snapped the scanner screen.

"They were just *there*," the man blurted. "This is crazy. I'm going code red." He unlocked the one button on the console that Flattery knew no outpost wanted to press: Code Red. That would notify Current Control in the Orbiter overhead and Communications Central at the nearest Merman base that the entire compound was in imminent danger.

"You see?" Flattery said. "He's getting the idea."

"I'm going out there," the man announced to his wife, "you stay put. Do you understand?"

No answer. She sat, still dreamy-eyed, watching the fifty-meter-long fronds of blue kelp that reached her way from the perimeter.

The Merman scooped an airfish out of the locker beside the hatch and buckled on a toolbelt. He grabbed up a long-handled laser pruner and a set of charges. As if on second thought, he picked up the whole basket of airfish, the Mermen's symbiotic gills that filtered oxygen from the sea directly into the bloodstream.

Ghastly things, Flattery thought with a shudder. Unconsciously, he rubbed his neck where they were customarily attached.

Once outside, the Merman's handlight barely illuminated the stand of kelp at the compound's edge. This holo had been made at the onset of evening, and the waning light above the scene coupled with the depth darkened the holo and made it difficult to see detail of the man's face—a small disappointment for such a good chronicle of the test itself.

As the Merman reached the compound's perimeter within range of the kelp's longest fronds, he whirled at the *click-hiss* of an opening hatch. His wife swam lazily out of it directly into deep kelp. The atmosphere from their station bubbled toward the surface in a rush. He must have realized then that everything was lost as he watched the sea rush into their quarters through the un-dogged hatch. All sensors went blank.

Flattery switched off the holo and turned up the lights. Nevi sat unmoved with the same unreadable expression on his horrible face.

"So the kelp lured them and ate them?" Nevi asked.

"Exactly."

"On command?"

"On command—my command."

Flattery was pleased at the trace of a smile that flickered across Spider Nevi's lips. It must have been a luxury that he allowed himself for the moment.

"We both know what will come of the hue and cry," the Director said, and puffed himself a little before continuing. "There will be a demand for vengeance. My men will be forced, by popular demand, to prune this stand back. You see how it's done?"

"Very neat. I always thought …"

"Yes," Flattery gloated, "so has everyone else. The kelp has been a very sensitive subject, as you know. Religious overtones and whatnot." Another dismissive wave of the hand. Flattery couldn't stop bragging.

"I had to accomplish two things: I had to get control of Current Control, and I had to find the point at which the kelp became sentient. Not necessarily smart, just sentient. By the time it sends off those damned gasbags it's too late—the only solution there is to stump the lot. We lost a lot of good kelpways for a lot of years that way."

"So, what's the key?"

"The lights," Flattery said. He pointed out his huge plaz port at the bed just off the tideline. "When the kelp starts to flicker, it's waking up. It's like an infant, then, and only knows what it's told. The language it speaks is chemical, electrical."

"And you do the telling?"

"Of course. First, keep it out of contact with any other kelp. That's a must. They educate each other by touch. Make sure the kelpways are always very wide between stands—a kilometer or more. The damned stuff can learn from leaves torn off other stands. The effect dies out very quickly. A kilometer usually does it."

"But how do you … teach it what you want?"

"I don't teach. I manipulate. It's very old-fashioned, Mr. Nevi. Quite simply, beings gravitate toward pleasure, flee pain."

"How does it respond to this kind of … betrayal?"

Flattery smiled. "Ah, yes. Betrayal is your department, is it not? Well, once pruned and kept at the light-formation stage, it doesn't remember much. Studies show that it can remember if allowed to develop to the spore-casting stage. You have just seen what the answer is to that—don't let it get that far. Also, studies show that this spore-dust can educate an ignorant stand."

"I thought it was just a nuisance," Nevi said. "I didn't realize that you believed it could think."

"Oh, very much so. You forget, Mr. Nevi, I'm a Chaplain/Psychiatrist. That I don't pray doesn't mean … well, any mind interests me. Anything that stands in my way interests me. This kelp does both."

"Do you consider it a 'worthy adversary?'" Nevi smiled.

"Not at all," Flattery barked a laugh, "not worthy, no. It'll have to show me more than I've seen before I consider this plant a 'worthy adversary.' It's merely an interesting problem, requiring interesting solutions."

Nevi stood, and the crispness of his gray suit accentuated the fluidity of the muscles within it. "This is your business," Nevi told him. "Mine is Ozette and the girl."

Flattery resisted the reflex to stand and waved a limp hand, affecting a nonchalance that he did not at all feel.

"Of course, of course." He avoided Nevi's gaze by switching the holo back on. He keyed it to the Tatoosh woman's upcoming Newsbreak. She would accompany the next shuttle flight to the Orbiter, a shuttle that contained the Organic Mental Core for hookup to the Voidship. Already the OMC was an "it" in his mind, rather than the "she" who used to be Alyssa Marsh.

Flattery seethed inside. He'd wanted something more from Nevi, something that now smelled distinctly of approval. He didn't like detecting weakness in himself, but he liked even less the notion of letting it pass unbridled.

"Whatever you need …" Flattery left the obvious unsaid.

Nevi left everything unsaid, nodded, and then left the suite. Flattery felt a profound sense of relief, then checked it. Relief meant that he'd begun to rely on Spider Nevi, when he knew full well that reliance on anyone meant a blade at the throat sooner or later. He did not intend for the throat to be his own.

Chapter 14

And out of the ground made to grow every tree that is pleasant to the sight, and good for food; the tree of life also in the midst of the garden, and the tree of knowledge of good and evil.
—Christian Book of the Dead

A TRAIL left the beach about a kilometer beyond the limits of the Preserve. It was a Zavatan trail, used by the faithful to transport their gleanings of the kelp from the beach to their warrens in the high reaches. Because it was a Zavatan trail it was well-kept and reasonably safe. Its rest spots were ample and afforded a sweeping vista of Flattery's huge Preserve. The jumbled, jerry-rigged tenements of Kalaloch sprawled from the downcoast side of the Preserve, covered today by a cloak of black smoke. Mazelike channels of aquafarms and jetties branched both up and down coast into the horizon. Distant screams and explosions echoed from the panorama below up the winding trail.

Two Zavatan monks stopped to study the clamor rising from the settlement a few klicks away. One man was tall, lanky, with very long arms. The other was small even for a Pandoran, and moved in a scuttle that kept him tucked inside the larger man's shadow. Both were dressed in the loose, pajamalike gi of the Hylighter Lodge: durable cotton, dusky orange that represented the color of hylighters, their spirit guides.

A gith of hylighters lazed overhead, drawn to the scene by their attraction for fire, lightning and the arc of lasguns from building to building. The hylighters dragged their ballast rocks from long tentacles and circled widely, audibly valving off hydrogen and snapping their great sails in the wind. Should they contact fire or spark, the hylighters would explode, scattering their fine blue spore-dust, which the monks gathered for their most private rituals. Many of the monks had not left the high reaches, except to walk this trail, for ten years.

"It's a shame they don't understand," the younger monk mused. "If we could only teach them the letting go ..."

"Judgment, too, is an anchor," the elder warned. "It is Nothing that they need to know—the No-Thing that frees the mind from noise and perfects the senses."

He lifted his mutant arms in a long skyward reach, then turned slowly, rejoicing in the morning glow of both suns.

This elder monk, Twisp, loved the press of sunlight on his skin. He had been a fisherman and adventurer in his youth, and what drew him to the Zavatans was not so much their contemplative life as other possibilities that he saw in them. Like most of the monks, Twisp had been wooed by the romance of the new quiet earth that rose from the sea. They summarily rejected the petty squabblings of politics and money that raged across Pandora to establish an underground network of illegal farms and hideaways.

Twisp, however, had remained entrenched in Pandora's civil struggles, something he troubled few of his fellow Zavatans about. Now, once again, all was changing, he was changing. He had more to offer Pandora than contemplation, though he refrained from telling the younger monk so. He was not religious, merely thoughtful, and he had made a good life among the Zavatans. It would pain him greatly to leave.

Two hylighters tacked toward them and Mose, the younger monk, set down his bag and began his Chant of Fulfillment. With this chant he hoped to be swept skyward by the mass of tentacles and transported to a higher level of being. Twisp had experienced the hylighter enlightenment at the first awakening of the kelp a quarter century past. That was before Flattery's iron fist came down, and before the people he loved were killed.

Hylighters, though born from the kelp, remained indifferent to humans, treating them as a wonderful curiosity. Mose's chant became more vigorous as the hylighters drew near, their magnificent sail membranes golden in the sunlight.

"These two want their death today," Twisp said. "Do you really want to go with them?"

It was the fire that attracted them, and Mose should know that. The younger monk had eaten too much kelp, too much hylighter spore-dust over the years. Two humans in the open near the Preserve usually meant armed security. Hylighters wanting the-death-that-meant-life learned how to draw their fire.

Now the musty smell of their undersides filled the air. The musical flutings of their vents lilted on the breeze as they valved off hydrogen to drop closer. Mose's chant became more tremulous.

Each hylighter carried ten tentacles in the underbelly, two of them longer than the rest. Usually these two carried rocks for ballast. Hylighters that felt the death need coming on sought out lightning, often gathering in giths to ride the afternoon thunderstorms. Sparks or fire attracted them as well, setting them off in a concussive blaze of flame and blue spore-dust. Some dragged their ballast rocks to spark a grand suicide, an ultimate orgasm.

Twisp breathed easier when the two great hulks tacked back toward the Preserve. He interrupted Mose, whose eyes were closed and whose stubbled face was pale and sweaty.

"This tack will take them into range of the Preserve's perimeter cannon," he said. "There will be dust to take back for the others."

Mose silenced himself and followed Twisp's long pointing arm. The two hylighters tacked in tight formation, using all that they could capture of the slight breeze blowing up from the shore.

"Flattery's security will wait to fire until the hylighters are over the settlement," Twisp whispered. "That way, the hylighters become a weapon. Watch."

It was almost as he said. Either the cannoneer was a fool or one of the Islanders got in a clear shot, but the hylighters exploded over the Preserve in a double blast that took Twisp's breath away and stung his eyes with light. Much of the main compound aboveground was incinerated in the fireball and the great wall of the Preserve was breached for a hundred meters in either direction.

A lull in the fighting brought his ears the cacophonous screams of the charred and the dying. It was a sound that Twisp remembered all too well.

The young Mose came down this trail seldom and had been only twelve when he went to live in the high reaches. He did not have much of a life in the outside world, and knew little of the ways of human hatred and greed.

"All we can do is stay out of it," Twisp muttered. "They will have at themselves and leave us in peace."

The wet patter of hylighter shreds fell among the brush and rocks below them.

There will be the refugees, too, he thought. *Always the homeless and the hungry. Where will we put them this time?*

The Zavatans supported refugee camps all along the coastline, turning some into gardens, hydroponics ranches and fish farms. Twisp calculated that there were already more refugees both up- and downcoast than Flattery housed in Kalaloch. Though it was true everyone was hungry, only those in Kalaloch starved. This was the story he hoped Shadowbox would tell.

In time, the Director will be the hungry one.

Twisp remembered Guemes Island and the refugees of twenty-five years ago, hacked and burned and stacked like dead maki in a Merman rescue station down under. Twisp and a few friends hunted down the terrorists responsible, and a hylighter executed the leader. A Chaplain/Psychiatrist had been at the bottom of the trouble that time, too.

Flattery had burrowed as much of his compound below the rock as above it, and Twisp knew of bolt holes that led to escape routes along the shore. Flattery wouldn't need them this time. The older monk had seen fighting before, and knew Flattery's strategy: lure as many of the rebels inside as possible, then kill them all. Let them think, for a time, that they might win. Blame it on the Shadows. The rest, who lost everything but their lives, would not rise so easily to anger again.

Mose pulled at his garment, straightening the folds. He faced away from the horror below. His gaze did not meet Twisp's, but focused in the middle distance beyond the trail. His were eyes sunken deeply for one so young, for one dwelling among the untroubled. He was attempting inner peace at breakneck speed. He shaved his head daily, customary these days with younger Zavatan monks and many nuns. Many ragged scars crisscrossed his scalp from his reconstruction surgery.

Twisp was one of a handful of exceptions. His full head of long, graying hair was tied into a single braid at the back, mimicking the family style of an old friend, long dead. His friend, Shadow Panille, was said to have been of the blood lines that led to Crista Galli.

"We should get the others," Mose said. "We'll need lasguns if we're going dust-gathering in the valley."

Twisp shaded his eyes and surveyed the scene below. A blur that must be villagers spilled into the Preserve's compound. Running the other way, like fish fighting their way upcurrent, Flattery's precious cattle from the Preserve stampeded out the breached wall and into the unprotected valley.

Security had kept the demon population at a minimum near the Preserve, but with the scent of blood thick on the air and cattle milling about loose dashers were sure to follow. Things were going to get nasty enough without a new hunt of hooded dashers slinking about. He grunted himself out of reverie.

"Spore-dust goes bad," Twisp said. "If we're going to bring any back, we'll have to do it now."

He and Mose stored the kelp fronds they'd collected in the shade of a white rock. Mose still did not look Twisp in the eye.

"Are you afraid?" Twisp asked.

"Of course!" Mose snapped back, "aren't you? We could be killed down there. Dashers will smell the … the …"

"Just moments ago you wanted to die in the arms of that hylighter," Twisp said. "What's the difference? There are demons up here, too. You feel safe on the trail because we say the trail is safe. You know that some have died here in the past, others will die in the future. You stick to the trail, with no cover except these scrub bushes and the rock, no weapon but your body."

Twisp pointed past the flames below them and out to sea.

"Weather will kill you as dead as any demon, on or off the trail. It is a danger now, as dangerous as a dasher. It always stays alive, to kill another day. If dashers come, they will go to the blood, not to us. If anything, we are safest now. This is the present, and you are alive. Stay in the present, and you stay alive."

With that he shouldered his empty bag and set out in long strides for the valley and the spore-dust below. Mose stumbled along behind him, his nervous eyes too busy hunting fears to watch the trail.

Chapter 15

To think of a power means not only to use it, but above all to abuse it.
—Gaston Bachelard, *The Psychoanalysis of Fire*

TWO OLD vendors hunched in a hatchway, protecting themselves and their wares from the jostlings of a mob that muscled its way toward the Preserve. One munched a smashed cake, the other nursed a bleeding nose against his sleeve.

"Animals!" Torvin spat, and a fine spray of blood came with it. "Is there anyone left who is not an animal? Except you, my friend. You are a human being."

His free hand patted the other's shoulder and found a large rip in the fabric of the older man's coat.

"Look, David, your coat …"

David brushed crumbs from his chin and pulled the shoulder of his coat across his chest, closer to his good eye.

"It will mend," he said. "And the mob is passing. If there are dead, my friend, we should get their cards for the poor."

"I'm not going out there."

Torvin's voice was muffled by his sleeve, but David knew he was firm on that point. It was just as well. His eyes were bad, and his feet not quick enough to outrun the security. It was a shame when the security got the cards.

They sold them, or traded them. Every day Torvin and David risked their lives to give a bit of stale cake or a rind of dried fruit to a hungry one without a card. David shook his head.

What foolishness!

He worked beside Torvin, they were friends, yet he could not trade him a cake for a dried fruit. He had to have a marker on his card for the fruit, and Torvin would have to punch it out, and then he could have it. If Torvin didn't have a pastry marker on his card, David could not give him a cake. For Torvin to possess a cake without a proper punched card would mean losing his next turn in The Line. Under the best of conditions, he would not have expected a turn for at least a week. Under the worst conditions, he could starve with a fistful of coupons.

"This is craziness!" he told Torvin. "It is well I am old and ready to die, because the world makes no sense to me. Our children run about killing each other. It is permissible to have food on one table but not another. We have a leader who takes food from the mouths of babies so he can travel to the stars—good riddance, I say. But what will he leave behind? His bullies, who are also our children. Torvin, explain this to me."

"Bah!"

Torvin's faded blue sleeve was crusted with blood but the bleeding on his nose had stopped. David could tell by the way he said "Bah!" that the nose was stopped up. He remembered that time the security slapped him, the fragrant burst of blood in his nose.

"Thinking will get you into trouble," he heard Torvin warning him. "We are better off to keep quiet, dry our allowance of fruit, bake our allowance of cakes and be thankful that our families have something to eat."

"Be *thankful*?" David wheezed one of his silent laughs. "You are no youngster, Torvin. Who taught you to be thankful to eat when someone across the wall has nothing? There is no greater sin, my friend, than to eat a full meal when your neighbor has none."

"We give cards to the poor …"

"Graverobbers!" David hissed. "That's what they've made us. Graverobbers who can be shot for throwing scraps to the hungry. This is craziness, Torvin, such craziness that this mob is making sense to me. Burn it all and start over. They *are* hungry now …"

"Those … *animals* who beat me, they are not hungry. They have cards. They work we see them here daily. Where do they get off chanting 'We're hungry now' when—"

"Listen, Torvin, to me an old man now gone crazy. Listen. We are old, you and I. Would you have given them something if you could?"

Torvin stuck his head out the hatchway, looked up and down the street, then hunched back inside. "Of course. You know me, I'm not a greedy man. I have done such a thing."

"Well, listen to me, old man. The mob we saw, yes, they have cards. Yes, they bring a little food home—for a family of four. If there are six, eight, ten then the card still only feeds a family of four."

"No one argues with that," Torvin said. "We can't breed ourselves out of—"

"When you or I get too old and have to live with our children, Ship forbid, that will be one more on a card of four. Take in a refugee who has no card, my friend. Yes, that makes it six on a card of four and the *average* of people who *have* cards is eight.

"The ones without cards, the stinking ones who are dying at the settlement's edge begging for food, begging for work, sleeping in the mud—they cannot run through the streets themselves to shout 'We're hungry now,' because they can barely stand. We give crumbs from our guilt, from our shame. This mob gives their bodies, their voices to the hungry. They give whatever they have."

David leaned heavily on his folded table and got to his feet. The mob had moved on quickly. Had his body allowed, he might have followed them. He watched Torvin test his nose gingerly with his fingertips.

"I am afraid, David, of people like that. They might have killed us. It could have happened." Torvin sounded as if he had corks in his nose.

David shrugged.

"They are afraid, too, because only the card gives them a place in The Line, and then only when their turns come around. Without a card, how long before you or I wake up in the mud downcoast? How many nights, Torvin, could you sleep in the mud and still wake in the morning?"

Torvin tested the bridge of his nose again, wincing. "I don't like this, David. I don't like getting beat up …"

"Such drama," David said. "The man was pushed in here. You were hiding under your table and the corner hit your nose. That is not a beating. The Poet, over there, now *that* man took a beating."

David's nod indicated a dark shape pacing the hatchway across from them. The street was nearly clear, only a few stragglers scurried about, dodging the stunsticks of security. The Line to the warehouse was reforming already as the bravest, or the hungriest, came out of hiding.

Only one adult and one child of a card could wait in line, so the chore usually fell to the strongest unemployed member. Whoever did the shopping might have to carry out a two weeks' supply of foodstuffs for eight people or more. Security protection was good in The Line, but spotty elsewhere, so there were actually two lines, one on one side of the street going in and one on the other going out.

Licensed vendors like David and Torvin worked The Line, selling to those who were afraid they wouldn't get inside today, or who wanted a little something different to take home to the wots.

The man they called "the Poet" across the way worked his way up and down The Line each day, babbling of Ship and the return of Ship. He was careful not to speak against Flattery's Voidship project. He had done that once, and come back a broken man. The Poet had not stood upright since, but walked in a shuffle, bent nearly double at the waist. David could hear him now, shouting after the tail-end of the mob:

"I have been to the mountaintop! Let freedom ring!"

"That one?" Torvin snorted, and started his nose bleeding again. "That one has been into the spore-dust once too often."

David smiled at his friend. He and Torvin were nearly the same age, in their sixties, but he hadn't known Torvin long. There was much he had never told him.

"I was taken once," David whispered. "A security wanted cakes without a marker and I wouldn't give them to him. I knew if I did he would be back every day. He bullied me. I would rather give them to the poor, so I did a foolish thing. I threw them into The Line, and there was a scramble. Well, I knew I would be arrested, but I forgot about the others. They rounded up everyone who had a cake without a punch on the card and took them in."

Torvin's face paled. "My friend, I didn't know … what did they do to you?"

"They took me to a shed that had cubicles in it, separated by curtains. In each one they were doing something to someone. The screams were terrible, and the smell …"

David took a deep breath and let it out slow. The Poet was still gesturing and railing from his hatchway.

"He was there, in the cubicle next to me. He was an important man from down under who was the director of all of HoloVision. Flattery had taken over—I didn't know that—and this man had commented on the air that Flattery wanted to brainwash the world."

"A brave man," Torvin said. He appraised the Poet in a new light.

"A fool," David said. "He would've been better off to find a way to fight inside, or hidden out to do something like those Shadowbox people are doing. He must've known what would happen."

David dusted off his threadbare trousers, put on his cap and leaned against the hatchway, his gaze very distant and his voice low.

"Well, I'll tell you what happened to him. They put him in a metal barrel, bent over double, and tied a block of concrete to his testicles. There was no floor in the barrel, so he could move it around by shuffling, but he had to keep bent over, and his knees bent down, to keep the weight off his testicles. His hands were tied behind his back, and throughout the day they would beat the sides of the barrel with those sticks they carry.

"They seldom fed him, but when they did he had to take food and water from the floor, bent over like that, an animal inside the barrel. He was a learned man. I never heard him curse. He only prayed. He prayed to every god I've heard of, and many that I don't know. They made him crazy to discredit him—who would believe a madman? Particularly a madman who eats bugs and scraps and sometimes dirt to stay alive."

Torvin was quiet for many blinks, digesting what his friend had told him. The Poet continued his rant, and the few security patrolling nearby ignored him.

"My friend," Torvin said, "what did they … were you … ?"

"They beat me," David said. "It was nothing. I was in and out in a day for being insubordinate. I don't think the captain cared much for the security guard who charged me. At any rate, he was never seen on this street again. Look, now. It is clear, and we should go sell what we can. I want to get home and check on my Annie. She worries about me in times like this."

Both men strapped on their little folding tables that fit around their waists and hurriedly neatened their wares. As they stepped into the muddy street

Torvin heard the Poet's hoarse voice exhort him, "Brother, brother, let freedom ring!"

Chapter 16

Remember that I have power; you believe yourself miserable, but I can make you so wretched that the light of day will be hateful to you. You are my creator, but I am your master.

—Mary Shelley, *Frankenstein*, Vashon Literature Repository

SPIDER NEVI watched Rico pull the gangway up and onto the deck of the *Flying Fish*, then he manipulated the sensor for a close view of Rico's back as he turned away.

"Lasgun there," Nevi said, and tapped a finger against the screen. "Belt, middle of the back. Carries himself like a fighter."

Nevi never once glanced at the security officer watching the screen at his side. As the *Flying Fish* departed moorage he switched to another sensor at the mouth of the harbor, one that confirmed Crista Galli's presence on board.

At Nevi's command, the sensor zoomed in on the cabin of the passing foil, revealing LaPush in the copilot's seat and Crista Galli buckled in behind him. Ozette sat to her left, behind the pilot, and was speaking to her. Nevi recognized the pilot, Elvira, and cursed under his breath.

"If your security launch tries an intercept, it will be outclassed," he said. "What then?"

"There will be a show of force," Zentz said, "then a warning shot."

"And then?"

Zentz cleared his throat, stroked the swollen area near the middle of his face that functioned as a nose.

"Shoot to disable."

Nevi snorted at the ridiculousness of it. A laser cannon strike on a hydrogen-ram foil could ignite a fireball a thousand meters wide. He thought that a rather narrow definition of "disable."

Zentz continued, flustered at Nevi's silence.

"The Director declared a 'state of security' almost a year ago," he said. "You know mandatory interception and search of all vessels, except company ferries, that enter Kalaloch … search of any air or ground craft entering or leaving the perimeter …"

Nevi let Zentz go on with his tedious recital.

Flattery's precious Preserve was his nest, and Nevi knew he would take no chances here. But Nevi was sure that any interception of the *Flying Fish* right now could easily be bungled into a disaster of the greatest proportions. Flattery had just called him to duty because Zentz had permitted such a bungle.

"We want Shadowbox and Crista Galli," Nevi said. "To exterminate nerve runners you have to burn their nest. This foil, intact, will lead us there."

Zentz, ramrod-stiff in his seat, cleared his dry throat and offered, "We suspect LaPush has been a Shadow commandant for about six years …"

"Your crew is not to interfere with this vessel," Nevi ordered. He keyed in the security frequency on his console. "You can give the order right here." He flipped a switch and looked Zentz in the eyes.

Zentz cleared his throat again, then leaned toward the microphone. "Zentz here. Thirty-four, disregard white class-three foil departing harbor."

"Sir," a young voice came back, "by the Director's orders we're to seize any vessels sighted but not searched."

Zentz paused, and in that pause Nevi enjoyed the exquisite dilemma that was now added to the Security Chief's fatigue. There was only one way out, one way to satisfy the by-the-book greenhorn officer, one way to keep the Director at bay.

"I searched it personally at dockside," Zentz said. "We know what's on board."

Nevi switched off the connection, satisfied with the choice he'd made in Zentz. If it came right down to it, Zentz would be the perfect sacrifice in the holiest of games, survival.

"Young officers haven't learned their priorities yet," Zentz said, forcing a smile.

"They have only learned fear," Nevi said. "They mature when they understand greed."

Zentz rubbed at the back of his thick neck, only half-listening. He had spent the entire night interrogating two of his best guards as an example to the rest, and now that Nevi had ordered Crista Galli out of his grasp it looked as if he was going to have to go through it all again. From the moment he'd freed the foil, Zentz could feel a tightening at his collar that he didn't like—it was a noose-like grip, unrelenting as baldness, cold.

Nevi would be the death of him, this he was beginning to understand. With this came the understanding that there was nothing he could do about it, nowhere he could hide. The dasher coiled to spring, that was what Spider Nevi saw when Zentz met his gaze.

"I am going to make you a hero," Nevi said. "I have a part for you to play. If we hand the Director Shadowbox we hand him back Pandora. The implications for you and me are obvious. You will, of course, prefer this to whatever the Director has in mind for you here?"

Zentz did not clear his throat, he did not speak. He nodded once and his grotesque lump of a jaw quivered with what Nevi presumed was the clenching of his teeth.

"It will be just you and I," Nevi said. "The more we can tell the Director about these vermin and their warrens, the happier he will be. You desperately need to make him happy."

The white foil slipped under the bay's waves, keeping the burning wreckage between itself and the Vashon Security foil opposite. They would be suspicious of not being challenged during an alert, this Nevi knew, but he still had the advantage. They knew he was behind them, they didn't know how close.

Nevi used the sensor system to pan the riot that was now in full bloom in Kalaloch. "They're working their way toward the Preserve," he noted. "Can your men handle this?"

Zentz's wattles rose in indignation.

"Security is my business, too, Mr. Nevi. I handle it my way. We will let them throw their tantrum and trash their nest, then we will slaughter them here at the wall. They must be made to be very sorry that they attack the Preserve. The damage they do to their streets will keep the survivors busy for a time."

Nevi switched off the sensors and stood, straightening his tight suit with a tug.

"Secure one of Flattery's personal foils," Nevi snapped. "Full gear for two, plus a week's rations. See to it there's coffee. Meet me in the Preserve hangar in one-half hour."

His eyebrows indicated dismissal and Zentz rose to leave. Nevi saw the seed of hope in Zentz's eyes, a seed that Nevi would nourish to a rich blossom and snip, when necessary, to make just the right bouquet for the Director.

Chapter 17

I consider the positions of kings and rulers as that of dust motes … I look upon the judgment of right and wrong as the serpentine dance of a dragon, and the rise and fall of beliefs as but traces left by the four seasons.

—Buddha

CRISTA GALLI reclined in a leather crew couch that smelled faintly of Rico. She gripped the armrests, eyes closed. Noise and the press of the crowd had always frightened her, at least since she had been blasted free of the kelp five years past. Memory of her life before that blast seemed hopelessly lost.

The supple leather couch and roomy cabin muted the pierside clamor. The others had finished casting off and were returning to the cabin. A green circle flashed on the pilot's screen for each hatch they dogged behind them.

Their pilot, a severe, sensuous woman in her mid-thirties, prepared the ballast tank pumps and other predive systems. She spoke the sequences aloud crisply as she completed her check-off.

"Taking on ballast."

Three fuel tanks flared together from the fire at the center of the bay and Crista felt the concussions puff her lungs. A three-headed rage of fire boiled up from the waters off their bow, heeling the foil over in a lurch to starboard. Ben and Rico sealed off the cabin and strapped in.

"Going down?" Rico asked, and laughed.

The pilot didn't miss a beat.

"No security challenge," she reported. "Twenty-meter level-off mandatory until clear of marker five-five-seven …"

Since boarding the foil Crista had felt a calm such as she'd not known for several years, in spite of the madness outside. She felt something pull her toward the mouth of the harbor, to the open water beyond. Ben handed her a child's dessert stick from his pocket.

"You'll need the energy," he said. "Once we're clear of the harbor we can raid the galley. Is the cabin air too dry for you?"

"No," she shook her head, "it feels fine. Like my room at the Preserve."

Cool, processed air was all that Crista had breathed for five years at the Preserve, free of the charcoal odors of the street braziers, the whiff of raw iodine from the beaches and scant wet blooms of upland slopes. It was air swept nearly clean of humanity—the humanity that idolized Crista Galli, the humanity she had only known now for less than a single day.

Midmorning still, second sun just clearing the horizon, and Crista felt the race of sunlight through her surging pulse. She was outside the Preserve now. Regardless of the circumstances, she intended never to go back, never to be a prisoner of walls again.

Watch yourself, an ancient one inside her warned, *that you don't become a prisoner of action, or words. And remember, when you make a choice you abandon freedom of choice.*

She'd had no choice in her appearance among humans, and Flattery had given her no choices since that time. She had been plucked from the vine of the kelp and dropped into Flattery's basket. Crista thought that if the people of Pandora thought her a god, it was time she acted like one. Now that the water had begun closing about the foil, she felt an energy surge her blood that she'd never felt before.

What could she do that would help herself and these people who were still alien to her? Even Ben, though she felt a love for him, was a stranger. She had tried daily for five years, and could summon no memories of her earlier life.

Everyone, everyone is a stranger.

She'd had this thought before, but today it didn't surround her with the loneliness that it had in the past. She'd touched Ben Ozette, and seen that he, too, had these thoughts and he'd lived among humans for his whole life.

This is what they could learn from the kelp, she mused. *We are not alone because we are elements of one being.*

She listened as Rico muttered loudly to no one in particular. "Operations won't like it," he said. "Under no circumstances is she to be allowed near the sea. Of course, they're welcome to drop in here and give us a hand after they promised us the airstrip …"

She could tell that Rico felt more comfortable in the foil. He had smiled, finally, and though he seemed to be complaining he was complaining with a smile.

"Ever ride a foil?" Ben asked her.

"Never," she said, her wide eyes trying to take in everything at once. "I've watched them from the Preserve. This one is beautiful."

"Let me point out our three-way option," he said, and indicated certain diagrams on his control panel. "We are riding Pandora's finest vehicle on, above or under the sea. The hydrofoil mode is fast on the surface, but the foil struts clog up easily in thick kelp. Except in flight, these class-one foils use the old Bangasser converter to retrieve hydrogen from seawater, a virtually infinite source of fuel. If we go to the air, we have to remember that the fuel tanks do get empty."

He glanced over at Elvira's indifference and shrugged.

"We're going down under," he said. "Their lasgun's no good underwater. But this guarantees we'll be tracked, all the kelpways are heavily wired—"

"It might be something bigger than Flattery doing the tracking," Rico interrupted. "Heads up, we're going down."

He paused and, when there was no response from Ben, he assisted Elvira with the dive checkout. While they busied themselves with tasks at their consoles, Crista watched the water close over the cabin.

Ironically, it was probably Flattery who best understood her life among the kelp. In his hybernation, Flattery had lain nearly lifeless, his vitals monitored and maintained by several devices on and inside his body. According to Flattery's lab people, Crista Galli had lived in symbiosis with the kelp, a hundred million kelp cilia inside her, breathing for her, feeding her. They claimed that these tiny projections supported her for her first twenty years, until Flattery had this stand of kelp blown up, lobotomized to the needs of Current Control.

"It's like being an embryo until you're twenty," she'd told Ben. "There's no other way I can explain it. You don't eat, breathe, or move around much. The only people you meet are in the dreams that Avata brings. Now I don't know what was dream and what was me, it's all confused. There was no me until … until that day. But Flattery knows something of how this feels. So does that Dwarf MacIntosh, and that brain that Flattery's hooking up to his ship."

"It sounds horrible," Ben had said, and she realized that it probably did.

In dive mode the engine shift vibrated so much that it rocked her from side to side in her seat, forcing her attention back to the present.

Crista fought back a tear, and couldn't turn away from the green water surging ahead of the cabin. *There are laws against touching me!*

She thought of that kiss again, the one that had lasted only a blink in real time but would replay forever in her mind. Even in the hot climate of Kalaloch, Crista wore the coverings dictated by the Director. But alone, in the privacy of her suite, she had often shucked her clothes in spite of Flattery's sensors, which she knew to be everywhere.

Any portion of her skin left bare tingled at its awareness of breezes and light. If she noticed nothing else in a day she noticed the thousand tiny touches between humans around her. It had become difficult to think of herself as human. Now, having glimpsed the public idolatry focused on her, she felt the frayed tether weaken even more.

A surge in cabin air pressure popped her ears, and the great plasma-glass dome of the cabin settled completely under the waves. She caught herself holding her breath and cautioned herself to relax. She heard the susurrations of voices rise and fall with the pulse of the engines.

"Are you all right?"

Crista felt herself rising above Ben's voice to the ceiling of the cabin, through the ceiling and higher yet, above the Preserve. She was a thousand meters above Kalaloch, and beneath her writhed a mass of brown tentacles.

She was a hylighter, tacking her great sail across the breeze to keep the shadow of their foil in sight below. She was aware of herself, of her own being inside the foil, but felt every ripple along the hylighter's supple body as well.

Ben Ozette was calling her name, barely audible at this distance. She shared an umbilicus from his navel to her own and he was pulling her in by it, reeling her back to the *Flying Fish* hand over hand.

Ben touched her cheek and Crista snapped awake. He did not take his hand away.

"You scared me," he said. "Your eyes were open and you quit breathing."

As she sat forward, resisting his gentle pressure, she saw that Rico also stood over her, an open medical kit beside his feet. He was wearing gloves. What had been blue sky covering the plaz of the cabin was now the green-gray twilight of the middle deep. They were riding a kelpway, and somehow she knew that they had already cleared the harbor, heading north.

Rico stared at Ben's hand stroking her cheek, then at Crista.

"I was gone," she said. "Somewhere above us. I was a hylighter watching this foil and you reached out and brought me back."

"A hylighter?" Ben laughed, but it was a tight, very nervous laugh. "That's a strange enough dream.

'Gasbag from the sky
How her tentacles writhe
for me …'

"Remember that song? 'Come and Gone …'"

"I remember that it was some tasteless play on words, ridiculing the hylighter's spore-casting function. And this was no dream."

She saw the snap in her voice reflected in the tightening of his lips, a closing off that she didn't know how to stop.

Rico turned without saying anything and stowed the kit beneath his seat. Crista smelled something like anger, something like fear pulse from Rico's turned back. All of her senses washed back into her trembling body, delivering her into a state of hypersensitivity that she had never known before.

The undersea landscape of blues and greens blurred past her like the settlement had blurred past her—too much wonder, too little time.

Chapter 18

Of everyone to whom much has been given, much will be required; and of him to whom they have entrusted much, they will demand the more.
—Jesus

BEATRIZ WAS awaiting her cue for the two-minute windup of Newsbreak when the fully armed security detachment entered the studio, sliding from the hatchway with their backs along the walls. They hung back beyond the fringe of lights, which blazed their reflection in the squad leader's mirrored sunglasses. Her mouth was suddenly dry, her throat tightening, and she was due for the wrap-up in thirty seconds.

Still on the air, she thought. *The preempt isn't running yet.*

Her console showed her what the three cameras saw, but the monitor at the rear of the studio showed what went out on the air. Now it showed Harlan fast-talking the weather.

It could be bypassed.

She shuddered in her newfound paranoia and thought that the floor director would probably stop Harlan if they'd gone to tape, but she couldn't be sure anymore.

Maybe they want to see just how much more I'd try to say.

She had deviated from the prompter, amid the waving hands of the producer and director. She hadn't linked Ben with the Galli kidnapping, she'd just listed him as missing, along with Rico, on assignment. She noted signs of surprise and muttering among the crew when she said it. Both Ben and Rico were admired in the industry. Indeed, many of Rico's inventions and innovations made the holo industry possible.

Harlan finished morning fishing patterns, and the countdown went to Beatriz. The officer of the security squad had moved up in the studio and placed a man beside each of her cameramen. She had the sudden, weighty thought that her crew might not be on the shuttle this afternoon.

Harlan finished and smiled from the monitor, and the floor director's fingers counted her down: Three, two, one …

"That's our morning Newsbreak from our launch site studios. Evening Newsbreak will be broadcast live from our Orbital Assembly Station. Our crew will have the opportunity to accompany the OMC, Organic Mental Core, and take you, the viewer, through each step of installation and testing. Other news that we will follow at that time: the abduction of Crista Galli. As you know, there is still no word from her abductors and no ransom demand. More on this and other news at eighteen. Good morning."

Beatriz held her smile until the red light faded out, then slumped back into her chair with a sigh. The studio erupted around her in a babble of questions.

"What's this about Ben?"

"Rico, too? Where were they?"

"Does the company know about this?"

They cared. She knew they would care, that most of Pandora probably cared, and that was her power. As the mirrored sunglasses made their way through the crew toward her, she knew that there was nothing he could do.

Even if they'd preempted and run the canned show, the crew knew and there would be no keeping this leak plugged.

When the security officer reached her, the babbling in the studio fell quiet. "I must ask you to come with us."

These were the words she'd been afraid she might hear. These words, "Come with us," were what Ben had tried to warn her about for the last couple of years. He had said more than once, "If they ask you to come, don't do it. They will take you away and you will disappear. They will take the people around you away. If they say this to you, make whatever happens happen in public, where they can't hide it from the world."

"Roll cameras one, two and three," she announced. Then she turned to Gus, the floor director. "Were we preempted?"

"No," he said, and his voice trembled. He was sweating heavily even though she was the one under the lights. "If a preempt signal was sent, I didn't see it. You went out live."

God bless Gus! she thought. She turned to the security. "Now, Captain … I didn't get your name … what was it you wanted of me?"

Chapter 19

What then shall we do?

—Leo Tolstoy

TRIMMED AND steady," Elvira reported. "No pursuit. Course?"

When Ben didn't answer, Rico said, "Victoria."

Elvira grunted.

Clearly, Crista thought, *Elvira trusts both Ben and Rico.* She had seen loyalty at the Preserve, but never trust. She had manipulated the distrust rampant throughout Flattery's organization to open the hatch for her escape. That same distrust would bring Flattery down, once and for all. Of this she was certain.

"Flattery's people hoard information like spinnaretts at the web," she told Ben. "It's barter to them, a medium of exchange. So no one has the full picture and rumor guides the hand that blesses or damns. That's why Shadowbox has threatened him more than anything else."

"There's food in the galley," Rico announced, and she saw the accompanying green indicator flash on the console at her right hand. "Ben, you two take a break. Bring me back some coffee. We're a few hours out yet. Elvira would like the usual."

Ben led Crista to the galley behind the cabin with a hand at her elbow. Her legs seemed wobbly in spite of the even-keeled submersible run of the foil. She had been hungry now for hours. Her head ached with it, and the memory of broiled sebet on the village air charged her stomach.

"We live in the galley," Ben told her. "When we're on a job, this room is jammed, it's where everything happens."

She stepped from the semi-dim cabin into a warm yellow glow. The galley was a bright room of Island Cedar, yellowburl and brass. She could imagine a HoloVision Nightly News crew spread out over the two tables with coffee and notes in the half-hour before air time. It was a clean, well-lighted space. Holo cubes of the crew in action on various assignments sat in a rack against the inboard bulkhead. Crista sat at the first of two hexagonal tables and pulled down a couple of the cubes to look at.

"These really stand out at you," she said, moving the holograms through different angles of light. "Nothing in Flattery's collection matches these for quality."

"Thanks to Rico," Ben said. "He's a born inventor. He'd be a rich man today if Flattery's Merman Mercantile hadn't jumped into the middle of things. Our stuff is good because Rico makes up the equipment himself. We always roll with the best."

"She's very pretty," Crista said, holding a scene of Ben and Beatriz with their arms around each other. "You two have worked together for a long time. Were you in love, the two of you?"

Ben cleared his throat and pushed a few icons. She heard the *whirr* of galley machinery at work.

"Now it's hard to know whether we were truly in love or whether we'd just survived so much together that we felt no one else could understand—except maybe Rico, of course."

"And you made love with her?"

"Yes."

Ben stood with his back to her, staring at the backs of his hands on the countertop. "Yes, we made love. For several years. Given our lives, it would have been impossible that we didn't."

"But now you're not?"

She saw the slightest shake of the back of his head.

"No."

"Does that make you sad? Do you miss her?"

When he turned to her she saw the consternation on his face, the struggle he seemed to be having with words. She thought perhaps he'd started out to lie to her, but with a sigh he changed his mind.

"Yes," he said, "I miss her. Not as a lover, that's past and would be too clumsy to rekindle. I miss working with her because she's so goddamn good at getting people to talk in front of cameras. Rico handled the techno stuff, and between us she and I could get to the bottom of most anything. I think she's in love with MacIntosh up in Current Control, but I don't think she's admitted it, yet. If it's true, it should make life easier for both of us."

"If one of you is in love, then that takes the heat off?"

Ben laughed. "I suppose you could say that, yes."

She lowered her gaze to the cube that her hands passed back and forth in front of her. "Could you ever be in love with me?"

He laughed a soft laugh, picked up her hand and leaned closer.

"I remember everything about you," he said. "That first day I saw you in Flattery's lab, when you looked at me over your shoulder and smiled ... I had a feeling when our eyes met like I've never had before. I still get it every time I see you, think of you, dream of you. Isn't that something like love?"

Her pale skin flushed red from the neck of her dress to the roots of her shaggy white hair at her forehead.

"It's the same for me," she said. "But I have nothing to compare with. And how could I live up to whatever you've shared with … her?"

"Love isn't a competition," he said. "It *happens.* I had some tough times, living with B, but I don't have to bring up the bad parts to punish myself for missing the friendship, the good parts. I think she and I are both people who refuse to dislike someone we've loved. She's an exceptional person or I wouldn't have loved her. A lot of bliss, a lot of turmoil, but no boredom at all. The bliss part she called 'our convergent lines.' Ultimately we blamed each other for being impossible when it was our situation we couldn't bear …"

His green eyes darkened and, for a moment, went somewhere … some-*when.*

Crista squeezed his hand.

"Did you take the job of interviewing me because you knew that she was working on Flattery's project at the Preserve?"

He laughed again, an easy laugh, as though they and the boat were all that existed—no Flattery, no Warrior's Union, just a little outing under the sea.

"That's yes and no," he said. "I think your story is the most exciting thing I can show the rest of Pandora. I wouldn't have tried for it otherwise. But, yes, I did hope, in a moment of wallowing in loneliness, that I'd see her again."

"And … ?"

"I did." He shrugged. "The thrill was gone and we were good friends. Good friends who still work very well together."

"You knew that Flattery was buying off all three of us with those interviews, didn't you?" Crista asked.

She set her hat beside her on the deck and peeled off her headband and mantilla while still holding his hand. She gave her matted hair a shake, and he let go her hand to gather their utensils at the sideboard.

He held my hand longer than the sum of all human touches in my memory!

"I figured it out," he said. "That's why … this. Flattery pulled the corporate strings, denying air time before the first beam was shot. But no one was told. I was paid, you were interviewed at length on five occasions—and this was the story of the century! He paid to have it done so he could kill it."

"Yes," she said, "with no pangs of conscience whatsoever. Look what it got him: We are here, together. I, at least, am happier. And hungry," she indicated her disgust, "in spite of how it looks."

Ben patted the lump of clothing strapped to her belly. "And fulfilled, too," he teased. He dared to stroke her cheek again with a smile before fetching two very solid mugs of very hot coffee. In rough current, the mugs didn't slide the table like the utensils.

She watched the seascape as their foil slithered through the kelpways, her quick breaths fogging the plaz. Though the Preserve was a seaside base camp, Crista never once had been allowed down to the beach. Flattery feared her relationship with the kelp, and saw to it that others around her did, too.

Ben nudged her shoulder and pointed through the starboard port toward the skeletal remains of a kelp outpost, dimly visible in the foil's deepwater lights. The kelp itself had been burned back to knobby stumps for a thousand meters all around.

"Report says kelp killed three families here, sixteen people," he said. "Vashon Security did their retaliatory number on the kelp, as you can see. They call it 'pruning.'"

Though it was shadowland beneath a weak wash of light and though the engines had quieted in submersible mode, Crista focused on the tingle at her shoulder where Ben had touched her. She fought back tears of joy. How could she explain this to him, who touched people and was touched at will?

He pulled two hot trays out of the galley and set them on the table. He dealt out little containers of red, green and yellow sauces. She knew she needed food, strength, but some dreaminess had caught her up since boarding the foil and she didn't really want to shake it.

Sunlight strengthened her, this she knew. The beautiful kiss from Ben, that strengthened her, too. Something about this Rico LaPush also strengthened her, but she didn't know what.

Crista glanced again at Ben, beside her, as his gaze searched the dimness of the passing landscape.

"The Preserve is under attack," Ben said. She didn't respond. "You can watch it onscreen if you want." He indicated the briefing screen against the aft galley bulkhead. She preferred the old word "wall," but not many used it. Tribute to Pandora's watery history and Islander influence. Hunger broke through her reverie, and she chose the chopsticks.

Though Ben talked on, Crista concentrated on her meal, eating half of Ben's as well, leaving him the vegetables. His words buzzed like a fat bee in the warm galley air. All the while a lullaby kept running through her head that no human ear had heard in two thousand years.

Hush little baby don't say a word
Momma's gonna buy you a mockingbird …

She had learned to be cautious wandering her memories, too. When the flashbacks started sometimes they took over, unpeeling whole sections of other people's lives. They lasted longer each time, dragging Crista through hours of lightning-fast memories: no focus, no fine-tuning, simply off or on.

First it was blinks, then seconds, moments. A minute of high-speed memory, lived with a full sensory component, could wring an entire lifetime out of the wet cloth of her mind. Her last flashback had terminated only after exhaustion and heavy sedation. It had lasted nearly four hours. Though conscious immediately, she had been dazed and unable to speak for three days. Flattery had used this as an excuse to further limit her life at his compound, and to adjust her medications.

She felt that same dazedness now, but no onslaught of memories, no sweat, no fear.

"Crista Galli," Ben said, "you have quite the life awaiting you. You are 'the One, Her Holiness,' a living legend. You are the most important person alive today."

She felt an uneasiness at what he said, and sought reason to feel uneasy at the way he said it. She clung to the word "person," something she had never been called.

"'The One?'" she muttered. "'The One' to do what?"

"You are the One for whom they have waited in suffering for so long," he said. "Depending on whom you believe, you are the last salvation of humankind, or you are the kelp's secret weapon to eradicate humans forever. In your glimpse of the people of Kalaloch you must have felt your power. There is a lot for you to learn, and quickly. We will help you with that. But because one does not touch a god, one does not come before a god scratching one's fleas, you will see only the best side of the faithful, and the worst side of the rest."

"When the people know me, know it's all a—"

"They will *not* know you," he interrupted. "Not the 'you' that you mean. They want to believe something else too much to stop them. Faith can do that.

"You must be careful, you must be quiet. And you must be a mystery. We *need* that mystery to beat Flattery. You will see plenty of need before very much longer, and I think you will agree with me. Eat the rest if you're still hungry. We may not always be among those who have food."

She *was* hungry, very hungry. She drank the broth from her soup, left the vegetables again and picked out the meat. She also picked out the meat from the sandwich he made her. She ate the bread in tiny bites to make it last longer.

She thought she could tell Ben, tell them all something of need. Touch was a human need and she was mostly human. At times someone would touch her by accident or quickly in a breathless dare. The daring ones, she recognized now, must be the religious zealots, the Zavatans that Ben had told her about. There was no way to know which way it would be: embarrassment or death.

When she let Ben kiss her the previous night she had known it was possible that he would die. She had the strongest feeling that she would die, too, and somehow that made it all right. For the first time she felt mortal, and risked it. When neither of them died, she even kissed him back a little. Her heart pumped something like fear, even at the memory. Afterward, in his green eyes so nearly like her own, she saw the glitter of laughter and a good dare taken.

He looked so happy!

She remembered that few people around her had ever looked happy, except the Director. Mostly, they seemed afraid.

"Why did you kiss me?" she asked. A flush crept out of her collar. She didn't want to look at him but finally couldn't help it. He was smiling.

"Because you let me."

"You weren't afraid … ?"

"Afraid you wouldn't like it? Yes. Afraid of what you might do to me? No." He laughed. "I have a theory. If people expect to go crazy when they touch you, then that's what they do. It's a hysteria, that's all …"

She put her palm on his chest and said, evenly, "You don't know anything about me. You were lucky … *we* were lucky." She patted his shirt. "You didn't sleep," she said. "If it's necessary that one of us sit up, I can do it from now on."

Something dark passed over his expression.

"There were arrangements," he said, "with some of the women we'll meet upcoast—you were to stay with them. It was assumed that you would prefer …"

"It has to be you," she insisted. "You have no woman in your life, isn't that right?"

"That's right, but it's not a matter of …"

"What's it a matter of?" she blurted. "Don't you like me?"

Maybe surprise lifted the darkness from his face, or maybe it was the blush. "I like you," he said. "I like you a lot."

"Then it's settled," she said. "I can stay with you."

"It's not as easy as that."

"It is if 'The One' makes it so," she said. "Get some rest between now and then. If you really are immune to me, you're going to need it."

Chapter 20

Intervention into destiny by god or man requires the most delicate care.
—Dwarf MacIntosh, Kelpmaster, Current Control

RAJA FLATTERY'S private bunker lay safely beneath almost thirty meters of Pandoran stone. High, domelike ceilings held back the psychological crush and some well-chosen holograms draped the walls with scenes from outside the walls. Above him, in the rubble of his surface compound, Flattery's security finished the last roundup of resisters.

"Stand down the fighting and send in the medics."

Thanks to the hylighters, there would be a lot of burns. He spoke the order into his console and didn't wait for acknowledgment. His bunker area was honeycombed with cubicles, and those cubicles were occupied by the underlings who carried out his orders and asked no questions. Fewer than a handful had personal access to the Director.

Ironic, how a little fire can cool things down.

His security teams mopped up the carnage overhead and formed stark little shadows hunching under Pandora's unforgiving suns. Though the sterile images of battle came into his bunker by holo, the Director thought he sniffed a distinct stench of burning hair beside him at the console. *The imagination … the mind … what incredible tools.*

His personal security team waited just outside his hatch, a precaution. There was no place on Pandora that he could flee to that would be as secure as his own compound. Certainly there was nowhere as luxurious. A brunch of sebet simmered in Orcas Red spread out at his left hand. There was a fine bite to these Pandoran wines that pleased him, even early in the day.

"Captain," he spoke to the shadowy figure at his hatch, "that camera team, were they deployed as scheduled?"

"Yes, sir," the captain's back stiffened. "Captain Brood's men have been at the launch site since daybreak. They know what you want."

"And the HoloVision people, the ones the studio sent out to cover this … mess?"

"Captain Brood suggested letting them film, sir. When it's done, his team can access their film, as well as their cameras and other equipment. He says—"

Flattery shouted at his attendant, "Captain, did anyone give this … Captain Brood … permission to start *thinking*? Did *you*?"

The stiffened spine stiffened even more. "No, sir."

Flattery was thankful that the shadows hid the man's face. There was no profile to it. Where the captain's nose should be there were two moist slits that separated a very wide set of eyes. When Flattery talked with Nevi, at least he could focus on the man's eyes. This man wasn't that interesting, and Flattery had all too much time to dwell on the malformed face.

Flattery spoke in his most reasonable tone.

"I want nothing to go on HoloVision today without my prior approval. Brood's team is to receive priority treatment, even if we have to replace the entire production staff, understood?"

"Yes, sir."

"Get their manager into my office within the hour, that puffy little maggot Milhous. We need cooperation and I don't want any slip-ups. Tell him to bring some canned stuff that we can use to preempt today until Brood's men get their tapes. No sense in the rest of the world getting inspired by what's going on here."

"Right, sir. Right away, sir."

"Captain?"

"Yes, sir."

"You're a good man, Captain. Your family will be pleased that you're working with me."

"Yes, sir. Thank you, sir."

The man's back retreated through the main hatchway to the offices. Flattery sighed. He watered the wine a bit and raised a glass to his own firmness under duress. He toasted his search teams, who fanned out even now to burn the last of the bodies up in the rocks. This was a Zavatan influence, this burning of bodies. It was a practice that Flattery welcomed and supported. The traditional burials at sea turned into a ghastly sight and a health hazard on Pandora's few beaches.

Bodies washing up everywhere …

He suppressed a shudder at the memory. It was more than disgusting, it was a religious and economic disaster. Every nitwit who touched the kelp in the process came back a prophet. The entire Pandoran social structure was shattered by the recent geological changes alone, but this kelp business made it a madhouse.

Women of the settlements wouldn't buy fish for a week after a traditional sea burial. They didn't want to take a chance on eating fish that had eaten old Uncle Dak. There were times, early in Flattery's rise to power, when he had seen hundreds of embroidered burial bags washed up on the beach at a time, and the local fleets wouldn't fish for a month. Flattery's answer was to buy out the importers, stockpile everything, and control the seaways.

"Control," he muttered. "That's the key. Control."

Flattery toasted the holo that played in the center of his quarters. His men had been forced to inflict heavier casualties than he preferred, and it would raise hob with the work force just at a time when he needed things smooth. Still, their way was best. There were plenty of replacements, though starvation made them dim-witted weaklings. Things would be slow during the training period.

My way, he thought. *I've had to teach them everything. Left to themselves, these Pandorans couldn't get anything done.*

Flattery still marveled at his own progress. He'd built and fortified a city, unified politics and industry under one banner, and prepared a Voidship for launch. The Voidship would present them with more options than this stinking little hell-hole of a planet and Alyssa Marsh, the OMC, would point the way. Pandorans had been here for hundreds of years and hadn't made nearly the progress he'd made in the past twenty-five.

The trap topside had been sprung and was nearly ready for cleaning. This might come close to destroying any significant Shadow resistance. There couldn't be many of them left, and the rest … well, he'd see to it that they were too hungry to fight.

Except among themselves, for scraps. My *scraps.*

Flattery's losses, other than replaceable materials, were minimal.

He pushed the meal aside and drained his glass. The mop-up operation would be a bore. The last of the mob would be torched outside the hatch in a matter of two or three hours. He keyed in his command post and noted the air of celebration among the junior officers.

Nothing like a well-executed victory to lift morale, he thought. *Nothing more dangerous than an army with no one to fight.*

Flattery knew that they would not turn on him, or each other, as long as they had the Shadows, food thieves and the kelp to contend with.

The idle brain is the devil's playground!

Once again, Flattery keyed the voice frequency on his console.

"Update me on the HoloVision foil's position, Colonel."

"Still submerged," Colonel Jaffe reported, "about fifty klicks downcoast from Victoria."

"Any sign of escort?"

"No. The foil is proceeding solo through the accustomed channels."

"And the kelp is not interfering?"

"Not exactly," Jaffe said. "Our instruments show a marked increase in tension on the grid—the kelp's fighting the signal from Current Control."

"The grid is holding?"

"Yes, sir. We're preparing to detour traffic to the outside in case we lose it. Tension's rising fast, we're getting some oscillations at this point. All vessels with Navcom are probably getting instrument disturbances, too. We'll try to warn them, but as you know the sonic transmission stations down under have a very limited range …"

"I understand, Colonel. Instruct Current Control that this is a priority one situation. They are to maintain this grid at all costs. Stump that stand, if you have to."

"Will do, sir. Currents remain stable. Are they to be intercepted in Victoria?"

"That is not your jurisdiction, Colonel," Flattery snapped. "A White Warrior team will take care of it. We will root out the brass of this Shadow operation this time, I'm sure. Notify me of any sign of kelp interference, anywhere."

He broke contact without waiting for a reply, and smiled.

Yes, root them out, he thought, *but not all of them. They will find new leaders, then we will hunt them down, too.*

He poured himself half a glass of wine and filled the rest with water.

Moderation, he mused, *it's a lot like patience. We will prune them back, like my roses, to the very brink of death. They will always blossom under our control, always ready for the picking.*

Flattery stood at his console and stretched. He liked the privacy of his bunker. It was as spacious as the compound above him, with all of the attendant comforts. The view through his viewscreens was not nearly as satisfying as real plaz looking over the real world—*his* world. Soon his Voidship would be manned and stocked, and he would hand over the husk of this world to anyone who wanted it. He planned on taking Beatriz Tatoosh with him.

Flattery had monitored her broadcast, as was his custom. He noted both her loyalty to Ozette and her restraint. It proved she had due respect for his powers, but not a blind fear. This he admired in her. Still, he did not want to underestimate Ozette's influence on her. The man had been pouring poison into her ear for quite a few years.

Flattery smiled. He wasn't one to leave much to chance, and he had a backup plan for Beatriz Tatoosh. She would meet Captain Brood, one of Flattery's more innovative White Warriors. Brood's plan would take out a number of those troublesome HoloVision people and finish a clean sweep of that little rat's nest. They would go the way Ozette was going. That would teach the lot of them to back off when the Director said "Back off." And it would keep them from helping out that Shadowbox, wherever it was hidden.

I expected them to get on the air right away with Crista Galli, he thought. *What does that tell us?*

That they hadn't got her to their broadcasting equipment yet. He smiled in anticipation.

They'd better hurry! He laughed at the thought, *They won't want to broadcast what they get once the drugs take over.*

Captain Brood's plan would clean out HoloVision and soften up Beatriz Tatoosh. Flattery always liked a plan that worked on more than one level. Brood would be the bad guy, and at just the right moment Flattery would whisk her out of Brood's clutches. Then she would join him gladly in the command cabin of the Voidship. He planned an opulence for that cabin befitting a leader of his caliber, a woman of her grace and beauty.

Our children will populate the stars, he mused. He drank to the future, and to the careful execution of plans.

She shows no sign of any of the Pandoran mutations, he thought. He'd made sure that she'd had no surgical corrections to mask any of the Pandoran defects. *We could start quite a world, the two of us.* In his wine-tinted reverie Flattery saw the two of them naked in a great garden, heady with the scent of orchids and ripe fruit.

The ready light winked on over the hatchway to the Greens, indicating a foil approaching the docking well. Only Flattery and Spider Nevi knew the coded sequence for docking inside the Greens. He glanced at his timepiece, then grunted his surprise and opened the hatch.

Nevi's a quick one, he thought. *Too quick. Others, like Brood, guess at what pleases me. Nevi figures out my thoughts, my moves even before I do. That will have to be dealt with.*

He stood and adjusted his black dasherskin suit. When he wore this suit in the Greens, his pets were much more affectionate, more attentive to his needs. He tried his look of disdain on the mirror. It still worked. The suit was a nice touch.

His console reported on the docking foil and identified two occupants.

That fool! he thought. *Bringing Zentz into the Greens … a waste. Too late to worry now.*

When the time came for Zentz to be silenced he would remind himself to have Nevi attend to it personally.

The Greens was the Director's preserve below the Preserve. Plasteel welders and laser cannon had spent two years quarrying four square kilometers out of Pandora's stone. Crystallized particles of the old kelp root glittered like stars overhead. The domed ceiling arched to twenty meters at the center and shone with the black gloss of melted rock.

The Greens itself was a lush underground park maintained by an old Islander biologist. At times Flattery called it "the Ark." No one who had worked inside the Greens had lived to leave the compound. Spider Nevi came and went as he chose, and exterminated those who could not. They were easily replaced, and just as easily forgotten.

The hatchway from the Director's quarters in his bunker opened to the edge of a deep salt-water pool, circular, about fifty meters in diameter. A blue glow rimmed the lower portion, light diffusing in from the lamps installed around the lip outside. This had been the rootway gnawed by the kelp, the last vestige of a great Oracle.

A gentle grassy slope led down to the pool, as well as three small streams that issued from the rock bulkheads. Animals did not do as well in the artificial light as Flattery would have liked, but his flowers, trees and grasses thrived. From where he stood inside the hatchway, Flattery admired the thickest concentration of terrestrial foliage in the world.

He maintained no human security inside the Greens itself but his secret did not want for protection. As the bubbling hiss of the ascending foil seethed the waters of the pool, the Director's trained dasher, Goethe, lay in wait. He knew that the other three remained hidden, stumpy tails twitching, somewhere within a quick bound. Nevi's personal signal toned three times, then repeated itself. Flattery dogged the hatch behind him.

The foil that rose from the pool was one of several that Flattery had designed for his own needs. These were the last foils manufactured by Merman

Mercantile before the great quake destroyed their manufacturing complex two years ago. These were capable of flight but with a limited range and payload. They cruised faster submerged than any other models. A glance into the cabin and Flattery put on the proper mask of disapproval for Nevi, frowning and shaking his head.

Well, Mr. Zentz first.

Nevi secured the foil beside one of its twins and waited on deck for Flattery to give the dashers their "all clear" signal. Zentz stood in obvious awe at the hatchway to the cabin, the snags of teeth in his lower jaw glistening saliva.

At the Director's hand signal Goethe slunk back into the foliage. The one he called "Archangel" crouched between himself and Nevi. Archangel, unlike Goethe, was an extraordinary hybrid of a successful gene-swap between the cats in hyb and the hooded dashers of Pandora. They were faithful and wished to please their master—two traits that Flattery admired in anyone, so long as he was the master.

Archangel's eyes watched Nevi's every move and he bristled when Zentz, too, approached the Director. There was another backup "at ease" signal for Archangel, but Flattery didn't give it.

Zentz is cornered, he thought, and cornered animals commit the unexpected. Since Zentz would be killed soon, Flattery spoke freely in front of him. "Mr. Director," Nevi said, inclining his head slightly.

"Mr. Nevi."

This was their ritual greeting. Flattery had never known Nevi to shake a hand. To Flattery's knowledge, Nevi only touched the people he killed. He did not know Nevi's record with women and did not intend to ask.

Flattery smiled and indicated the Greens to Zentz with a generous sweep of his hand.

"Welcome to our little secret," he said, and strolled briskly from the docking pool toward a section of fruiting trees.

"Pity there isn't time for a tour. Near-tropical heat, but you don't know much about the tropics, eh? Bore deep enough into rock and you get heat. Fewer than one hundred people have seen this garden."

And fewer than five survive.

Zentz swallowed audibly. "I—I've never seen anything like *this.*"

Flattery did not doubt him.

"One day all of Pandora will look like this."

Zentz brightened so much that Flattery forgave himself the lie.

He turned to Nevi. "You saw the trap sprung topside?"

Nevi nodded. "Looks like we burned about three hundred. Crews are out chasing down the wounded. So far, nobody big. As we suspected, their eagerness outstripped their readiness."

"We cannot make that same mistake," Flattery warned. "That is why you must bide your time with Crista Galli and the others. Her abduction must be turned to our advantage in every way possible. To take them now would be easy, and foolish. Remember, from now on she's only the bait, not the quarry."

A pair of white butterflies tumbled the air between them and Zentz backed away.

Flattery smiled. "They aren't dangerous," he said. "Beautiful, don't you think? We've released these topside. They drink the wihi nectar. They have already multiplied the wihi threefold in and around the Preserve. You know its value for defense—a natural booby trap. A problem, at times, with the livestock. The larvae of these beautiful creatures … well, another time. I have two specific demands of your mission."

Flattery strolled to a plot of young trees, carefully planted in rows, in various stages of bloom and fruit production. Nearby, several hives of bees kept audibly busy. Nevi did not care for the bees, this Flattery well knew. He enjoyed Nevi's mastery of the neutral expression. He picked each man a fruit.

"Golden Transparent," he said. "A very hardy apple Earth-side. Since I am developing a Garden of Eden of sorts I thought them most appropriate."

He indicated two carved stone benches under the largest of the trees and sat. Nevi was clearly impatient to be off on the chase, but Flattery could not let them go yet. Nor could he bear watching Zentz make a slobber of his magnificent fruit.

"There are objectives more important than their capture," he emphasized. "Ozette must be discredited. He was popular on HoloVision, and his disappearance has already been aired, thanks to Beatriz Tatoosh. This only firms our resolve to expose him as a monster. He must be seen as a madman in the clutches of madmen, with the deathly ill Crista Galli as their slave. We will play on her beauty and her innocence; leave that to me and to HoloVision. That is the first thing I require of your mission."

"And the second?" Nevi asked.

Such a question was uncharacteristic of Nevi—how much he must want to be on with it! Flattery wondered what this enthusiasm would add to Nevi's performance.

"Crista Galli will be a problem for them shortly," he said. "They'll want her off their hands. We want her to be seen asking for our help. She must want the Director to save her and the people must know this. It is our only way of guaranteeing absolute control after this little action topside—our only way short of all-out extermination of these pocket villages and little Zavatan monasteries that are the breeding grounds for these Shadows."

"Interesting," Nevi said. "This will require some care. Maybe it's a job for your propaganda people at HoloVision. Have you found any drugs to be useful for her … persuasion?"

"Details of her drug program are in the briefing you will receive in the foil," Flattery said. He glanced at his timepiece. "I will say that if she has eaten, she could be catatonic any time. Instructions, precautions and drugs have been prepared and are stowed with your briefing materials. Her persuasion is completely up to you. The manner of persuasion, too, is up to you."

Nevi smiled one of his rare smiles. That was what Flattery liked about the man … if one could call such a creature a man. He rose to a challenge.

"The Tatoosh woman, does she launch today with the drive system and your OMCs?" "Yes," Flattery said, "as planned. Why?"

"I don't trust her," he said, and shrugged. "She'll be up there with Current Control and we're going into the kelp …"

"She will be no trouble," Flattery said. "She's been very helpful to us. Besides, she's my problem, leave that to me."

Zentz had finished gnashing down his apple and was once again gawking about the Greens. "Any of those Zavatans ever tunnel in here? They have hidey-holes all over the high reaches."

He still has his uses, Flattery reminded himself.

"My pets love exploring," Flattery answered, indicating Archangel. "Did you know that 90 percent of their brain tissue is dedicated to their sense of smell? No one has tunneled in yet, and whoever does will face Archangel. Then we booby-trap the tunnel for the rest."

Zentz nodded. "A good arrangement," he gurgled.

"You haven't tried your apple," Flattery said, nodding to the bright yellow fruit in Nevi's palm.

"I'm saving it," the assassin replied, "for Crista Galli."

Chapter 21

Do you know how hard it is to think like a plant?
—Dwarf MacIntosh, Kelpmaster, Current Control
(from HoloVision Nightly News, 3 Jueles 493)

THE IMMENSITY prickled its long, gray-green fronds and sniffed the current in its chemical way. The sniff did not detect a presence so much as the hint of a presence. It was more a prescience than proper smell or taste, but the kelp knew that something of itself passed by now in the current.

The Immensity was a convolution of kelp, a subtle interweave of vines that sprawled, like a muscular brain, throughout the sea. It had begun as wild kelp, an ignored planting inside a long-abandoned Merman outpost. It had barely known "self" from "other" when it first encountered the Avatalogical study team led by Alyssa Marsh. Most of what the Immensity knew of humans it had learned from Alyssa Marsh.

This stand of kelp knew slavery from the human memories that her DNA held, and it knew itself to be enslaved by Current Control. With the right tickle in its vines it raised them, lowered them, retracted or extended them. Another electrical tickle set off the luciferase in the kelp, lighting the passage of human submarine trade. There were other tricks as well, all pulsed a current through a channel—simple servility, simple stimulation-response. This was reflex, not reflection.

The Immensity had all of eternity at its disposal. It allowed this exercise because it pleased the humans and did not interfere with the stand's extended contemplations. Thanks to Alyssa Marsh and her shipmate Dwarf MacIntosh, the kelp had learned how to follow the electrical tickle to its source. Everything that humans transmitted now flowed straight to the heart of the Immensity. Everything.

The Immensity was finally prepared to send something back. It was getting closer to a breakthrough to these humans, and that breakthrough would not be through touch or the chemical smell, but through light waves intersecting in air.

Pleasing humans was a trivial matter, displeasing them was not. Once, soon after waking, this kelp had lashed out in pain to pluck a runaway submersible from among its vines. The huge cargo train had torn a hundred-meter swath nearly a kilometer long in its path through the vines. After the kelp slapped the deadly thing and plucked it apart, Flattery's slaves came with cutters and burners to amputate the kelp back to infancy. The Immensity knew that it had not been able to think right for some time after that, and it did not intend to give up its thinking ever again.

A certain stirring now in the tips of its fronds told the Immensity that "the One," the Holomaster, was passing. The Immensity could unite fragmented stands of kelp into one will, one being, one blend of physics that humans called "soul." Deep in its genetic memory lay a void, an absence of being that could not be teased out of the genetics labs of the Mermen. This void waited like a nest for the egg, the Holomaster who would teach the kelp how to unite fragmented stands of humans.

Twice this Immensity gave up its body but never its will. It was capable of neither sorrow nor regret, simply of thought and a kind of meditative presence that allowed it to live fully in the now while Flattery's electrical strings at Current Control manipulated the puppet of its body.

Reflex is a speedy response made without the brain's counsel. Reaction is a speedy response made with minimal counsel. This kelp grew up expecting to be left alone. It learned reaction only after its vines twined with domestic kelp. It learned to kill when threatened and to show no mercy. Then it learned to expect retaliation for killing.

This Immensity expected to live forever. Logic dictated that it would not live forever if it continued reacting to humans. And now, the One was passing! It knew this as surely as the blind snapperfish knows the presence of muree.

The original Immensity of kelp, Avata, encompassed all of the seas of Pandora under one consciousness, one voice, one "being." Its first genetic extinction came early in the formation of the planet. It had been at the mercy of a fungus. A burst of ultraviolet from a huge sunstorm killed off the fungus. Somewhere, a primitive frond lay mummified in a salt bog awaiting Pandora's first ocean.

The second extinction was by human beings, by the human bioengineer Jesus Lewis. The kelp was teased back to life by a few DNA miners about fifty years later. The revitalized kelp that the Mermen resurrected was developed from these early experiments. Now kelp once again filled the seas, dampening the murderous storms.

Once again the great stands scattered scent. They grew close with the years, their fronds spoke the chemical tongue. This Immensity itself retained two and a quarter million cubic kilometers of ocean.

The One rode a kelpway that skimmed the Immensity's reach. This particular kelpway came out of a stand of blue kelp that had been known to attack its own kind, overpowering nearby stands, sucking out their beings and injecting its own. It had suffered many prunings, and was sorely in need of guidance. This the Immensity knew from snatches of terror that drifted in on torn fronds. The One could not be trusted to such a dangerous stand. At whatever cost, the One must be spared.

The kelp shifted itself slightly, against the electrical stings from Current Control, to bring the One into its outmost currents, spiraling into the safer deeps of its own stand.

Chapter 22

You have been educated in judgment, which is the essence of worship. Judgment always occurs in the past. It is past-thinking. Will, free or otherwise, is concerned with the future. Thinking is the performance of the moment, out of which you use your judgment to modulate will. You are a convection center through which past prepares future.

—Dwarf MacIntosh, Kelpmaster, from *Conversations with the Avata*

"COURSE CHANGE."

Elvira's voice was emotionless as rock but Rico detected the slightest edge of worry in the flurry of her fingers across her command console. She never piloted the foil in its voice mode because she preferred to speak as seldom as possible. That Elvira had spoken at all worried him—that, and the increasing shimmy that had begun a few minutes back.

"Why?"

When working with Elvira, Rico picked up her habit of non-speech. She seemed to like that.

"Channel change," she said, nodding toward her display. "We're being steered off course."

"Steered?" he muttered, and checked his own instruments. They maintained their position in the kelpway, but their compass said the huge undersea corridor was running in the wrong direction.

"Who's doing the steering?"

Elvira shrugged, still busy with her board. She had taken them deep into sub train traffic to minimize tracking, and they ran without the help of sensors that would light their progress through the kelpways.

"We're out of the wild kelp sector outside Flattery's launch site," he said, "that's where the weirdness usually happens."

One-half of his screen displayed the navigation grid projected by Current Control from its command center aboard the Orbiter. The other half of the screen tracked their actual course through the grid, which now appeared to be bent.

Bending, he corrected himself. *It looks like our whole end of the screen is pouring down a drain.* "Anything on the Navcom?" he asked.

Sometimes Current Control changed grids through the kelp to accommodate weather conditions farther upchannel or the recent stumping of a stand of rogue kelp.

"Negative," she said. "All clear."

The ride began to get bumpy and Rico cinched himself tighter to his couch. He keyed the intercom and said, "Rough water, everybody cinch up. Ben, you'd better come up here."

Below them Rico could see another cargo train careening dangerously close to the kelp, attempting to recover from the sudden change. Their dive lights showed him that the kelp seemed to be in a struggle with itself, fluttering the channel as if pressing against a great force.

Ben used the hand grips along the bulkhead to work his way to his console. "Can we get Current Control?" Ben asked. He dropped into his couch and cinched up.

"Not without giving up our position."

"We got out too easy," Ben said. "They've got a bug on this thing, anyway ..."

"*Had*," Rico said, smiling. "I did an E-sweep when we left the harbor, thinking the same thing. Found it. Elvira here jettisoned the little devil into a netful of krill that we passed about a dozen grids back."

"Good work, both of you," Ben said. "All right, then let's try that cargo train below ..."

The *Flying Fish* was buffeted again by something like a huge fist. Elvira wrestled with the controls to keep them out of the kelp.

Rico knew, as they all knew, that any damage to the kelp could be construed as an attack. A lot of kelp lights were active in this sector. Besides the red and blue telltales of a waking stand, this kelp flashed its cold navigation light at random and occasionally flooded them with the brighter fiber-optic sunlight that it transported from the surface. If the stand was one that had awakened, any mistake could get the foil and themselves torn apart at the seams.

"Didn't Flattery just go on the air to tell us how safe he'd made the kelpways?"

"Just goes to show," Rico said, "you can't believe that bastard for a goddamn blink."

The cargo train passing in the opposite direction beneath them was having even more trouble. A relatively tiny foil could stop in midchannel and hover if necessary, but the cargo train needed to maintain a constant speed for maneuverability. The grid system was set up so that the trains, Pandora's lifeline, could travel the kelpways swiftly and undisturbed with minimal course changes. From what Rico could see of the bucking cargo, the crew below at both ends of the train had their hands full.

"It's bending," Rico said, watching the Navcom monitor that marked out their grid system. "The whole grid's bending."

"We'd better surface," Ben said. "Prepare for—"

"Negative," Elvira said. "If this is a surface disturbance, things will be worse up there. We need information."

Ben grunted acknowledgment.

"Cargo train identity signal is registered to the *Simplicity Maru*," Elvira reported, fighting the controls to maintain hover and an equidistance between walls of the kilometer-wide channel. This ordinarily simple maneuver was made nearly impossible by the ever-changing walls of their kelpway.

Rico noticed a sweat beading on Elvira's brow and upper lip.

Ben keyed for a low-frequency broadcast. He hoped he didn't have to explain the absence of their identity signal.

"*Simplicity Maru*, this is *Quicksilver*," he lied. "Do you have reports on current disruption?"

Static hissed back at them, then a microphone clicked on. The message came in badly broken. Undersea communication, especially around active kelp, was always difficult.

"*Simp … Maru.* Negative … into kelp." There was the sound of shrieking metal in the background. " … king up. We are preparing … ballast. Repeat, preparing …"

Elvira threw the throttles forward and in spite of a violent buffeting the foil leaped at her touch. Her lips were pressed into a tight line and her knuckles shone white on the controls.

"Wait, we can't …" Ben said. His body pressed harder into his couch. "We can't go into deep kelp."

"They're blowing ballast," Elvira growled. "That whole cargo train's going to pop up into us like a cork."

Rico felt every fixture aboard rattle like his teeth. "Ben, is the girl secure?"

"She's strapped in," Ben said.

Just then they cleared the rear cabin of the train. It blew past them toward the surface, containers and cabins tumbling like toys. A few of the containers snagged in the walls of the kelpway, walls that still vibrated with light and that same strange force.

"This is too weird," Ben said. "Let's surface and take our chances with the Director's air cover. This ride's getting much too ugly."

Elvira nodded curtly and the foil started its ascent. As though alerted by their control panel, the kelp fronds began closing above the *Flying Fish*. First they formed a canopy, then, a tight and impenetrable mesh. A sudden change of current lurched them to starboard and sent the foil tumbling end over end. Elvira righted them manually, her face very pale.

"Shit!" Ben fisted the arm of his couch. "Somehow Flattery must've got to Current Control …" He *snicked* his harness release over Rico's protests.

"I'm checking on Crista," Ben said.

He had to use the handholds to make his way aft on the rolling deck. At the galley's hatch he turned, suddenly a bit pale himself, and Rico knew what thought had just struck Ben.

Rico smiled.

"Rico," Ben said, "what if …"

"What if the kelp knows she's here?"

"Yeah," Ben said. "What if the kelp knows she's here?"

"We'd better hope she likes us."

"She probably doesn't have any say in this," Ben said, and undogged the hatch.

Rico didn't care for the snap in his voice.

"*Somebody* has a say in this," Rico muttered. The hatch slammed, dogged itself. Then Rico remembered when the kelp could have had a whiff of Crista Galli. It was the only time that hull integrity had been breached.

That bug! he thought. *That goddamn little mercuroid chip of Flattery's.*

"We ejected that transmitter, Elvira, and we ejected it in cabin air." He thought he detected an infinitesimal stiffening of her posture. "If that kelp can sniff, and I hear it can, then it knows there's more in this can than us worms."

Chapter 23

Mercenary captains either are or are not skillful soldiers. If they are, you cannot trust them, for they will always seek to gain power for themselves either by oppressing you, the master, or by oppressing others against your wishes.
—Machiavelli, *The Prince*

THE YOUNG security captain, Yuri Brood, was rumored by his men to be the unacknowledged son of the Director, product of an early tryst with a Merman woman from the Domes. The men based this notion on the strong physical resemblance between Brood and the Director, and on Brood's quick rise to an advisorship that went beyond the formalities of his rank. The two men shared a ruthlessness that did not go unnoticed outside the confines of the squad.

Captain Brood and his squad had been reared in a Merman compound near this Kalaloch district. Brood himself had been schooled privately in the mathematics of logic and strategy—that was standard operating procedure for anyone anticipating an executive position with Merman Mercantile. Brood himself preferred the more direct solutions of physical pressure to the subtleties of politics. His superiors shrugged it off as a phase, agreeing that Brood got results where others failed.

The old families, Islander and Merman alike, retained a strong sense of loyalty to their communities that made the kind of enforcement that Flattery demanded impossible from within. Security command removed Captain Brood's team to Mesa for their training and formation of their combat bond, then deployed them to Kalaloch and its shuttle launch site for "police work." They were one another's only family, an Island adrift in a sea of enemy. Everyone was kept three villages away from home.

Survive your tour, advance your rank, retire to an office at the Preserve—this was the universal goal.

The young captain was afraid, and he wasn't afraid often. When he *was* afraid, heads rolled. He and his team were short-timers at one month remaining, just starting their countdown to home. The captain had something to return home to, and he intended to rotate on schedule. He intended that his men rotate back home with him, alive. For a year his district had been Kalaloch and the SLS. His squad's actions had earned more citations than a dress suit could hold. During that year either the site or his men had been under fire daily.

Today the captain faced Beatriz Tatoosh from the back of the studio, and he thought what a pity it would be to have to kill her.

Beatriz did not know what the captain thought, but fear dried out her mouth when she saw his squad enter behind the lights and fan out along the bulkhead backing the studio.

The captain pointed out each of the live cameras to three of his men. They pulled away from their squad, drew lasguns and without a word each took careful aim at a cameraman.

Beatriz heard gasps, curses, the arming of weapons. She couldn't see what was happening because of the glare in her eyes. The large monitor at the back of the studio cleared, then displayed a tape of the last launch, a tape cut by Beatriz and her present team.

We're not going out live! she thought. "Dak," she alerted her floor man, "check the monitor."

When her gaze left the monitor it caught the young captain watching her. She remembered seeing him before, his dark eyes flashing her a smile as he led his squad through the labyrinth of the launch site. He half-smiled now, and nodded at her, and with that nod his three men executed her three cameramen.

At the first shot she was stunned at the suddenness of it all, the audacity as much as the horror. At the second shot it was the smell of death itself that stunned her. At the third shot she faced the immediacy of her own death. She also faced the captain, who was no longer smiling.

She remembered thinking how hard everyone was breathing just then, how the second guard stood over her dead cameraman and said to the first, "Shit, man, that was no signal …"

"Shut up, man," the third one said. "It's done. Just shut up. It don't change nothing here at all."

"All right!"

The captain fanned his fingers out from his left palm and the rest of the squad sealed off the studio area. She started to tremble, then concentrated on controlling it so that the captain wouldn't see.

Ben was right! replayed through her mind. *And who will know?*

Beatriz watched the replay of herself on the monitor, interviewing the Director during one of his ritual visits to the launch site. The expression on her face onscreen, one of admiration and deference, now made her sick to her stomach. Even so, her gaze stayed on the screen, rather than face the unbelievable reality unreeling in her studio.

Through the shock and the trembling she heard Harlan's voice from the back of the studio, speeding through a Zavatan chant for the dead. She remembered that the skinny cameraman with the fanlike ears on number three was Harlan's cousin. The security who had shot him was now dragging him by the feet to the wall. The cameraman's head bumped over the sprawl of cables across the deck, the hole in his chest burned so clean it barely bled.

The three assassins took wider positions in the room. Fifteen people were being held by nine guards in a very small studio with some very hot lights. The captain scanned the studio once, then turned to Beatriz. He indicated the red lights on the triangulators.

"The red light means the camera is on, correct? It is still recording?"

She did not answer. She felt it was important that he didn't hear her voice quaver. She could not take her gaze from his.

He did not smile this time, nor did he nod. "Finish them," he said. Then he nodded at Beatriz, "Except for her."

The screams, the pleading, the curses with Flattery's name on them silenced in the few moments it took the captain to walk her to the hatchway. It seemed that she walked forever, because she had the bodies of her crew to step over, and her legs were so uncharacteristically unsteady.

"Now see what you have done," Brood said to her. He squeezed her upper arm and shook her. "See what a mess your broadcast has made."

She couldn't speak or she would cry, and she didn't want to cry for him. She slapped away his touch when he took her arm to steady her. The last body she had to step over to reach the hatchway was the makeup girl's.

What was her name? Beatriz felt a new panic rise. *I can't blank out her name . . . !*

It was Nephertiti, yes, Nephertiti. Someone pretty and dark-skinned, like herself, with wide eyes. She told herself to remember this, to remember it and to see that somehow, sometime the world would know.

"You're a cool one," the captain told her. "You probably saw worse than this at Mesa two years back."

She stopped in the hatchway and turned, still not speaking.

"I saw you there, too," he said. "I saw both you and your boyfriend bounced ass over teakettle when that mine blew up your rig. Thought you both bought it."

She nodded, started to say, "So did we," but nothing came out of her throat but a croak.

For the first time she noticed his name, stitched above the Vashon Security insignia at his left breast: "Brood." Her only wish right now was that she would live long enough to see Captain Brood die.

He turned back to the studio and its seventeen dead warm bodies. Beatriz looked once again at herself on the monitor. The tape replayed an interview with Dwarf MacIntosh, Kelpmaster of Current Control. He was one of the few humans, other than Flattery, to survive the opening of the hyb tanks twenty-five years ago. He was so tall she'd had to stand on a box to do the interview. She had met him on her first flight to the new orbital complex, the day after her last night with Ben. Within a month she was sure that she was in love.

"Bag 'em up," the captain told his men. "Squeegee this place down, seal it off, then get all their production shit aboard."

He bowed to her then, opened the hatch for her and said, "We're expecting the replacements for your crew any minute. They are my men, and will do as they're told. My squad and I will travel along, to see that you do, too."

Chapter 24

The mind at ease is a dead mind.
—Dwarf MacIntosh, Kelpmaster, Current Control

DWARF MACINTOSH floated in the turretlike chamber of Current Control and surveyed the planet below for the birth of a certain squall at sea. About this time every day a swirl of clouds materialized over Pandora's largest wild kelp bed. It was some comfort now to see this squall forming; *something* was normal today even though the behavior of the kelp was completely loco. Today, humans didn't make much sense to him, either.

"The Turret," as he called it, was a plasma-glass extravagance of materials and workmanship that MacIntosh had fabricated for himself before installing Current Control in the orbital station.

I'd have taken the job anyway, Mack admitted, but only to himself. "Kelpmaster" wasn't so much a job to him as it was a privilege. He couldn't have allowed any of Flattery's goons such an easy throttlehold on the kelp. Besides, he felt much more comfortable in orbit than he did on Pandora's surface.

Like Flattery, Mack had been cloned, raised and trained in the sterility of Moonbase, in the hyperregimentation and clonophobia of Moonbase. His whole life, until hybernation, had been spent orbiting an Earth that, for him and for all clones, never existed. In those days, Flattery had openly pined for a life Earthside, but even then Dwarf MacIntosh looked outward, past Earth's measly system to the possibilities beyond.

From his turret Mack observed and charted many of these possibilities. He named them, but not the few special names he saved for his unborn children. He had spent the past two years above Pandora, refusing the usual R&R rotations groundside. In that time MacIntosh had not recognized a single star that would lead them Earthward. He liked it that way.

Dwarf MacIntosh awoke from hybernation on Pandora one day in indescribable pain and found himself in the middle of nowhere, galactically speaking. In spite of the planet's horrors he was in his own heaven among a trillion brand-new stars. The other survivors clung to that little wretch of a planet and most of them died there. Alyssa Marsh … well, she died, too. She died the day Moonbase started imprinting her for backup OMC.

Mack and Flattery shared a dream of driving farther into the void. Mack felt it a pity, in a way, since he had never liked Flattery, even during training with him back at Moonbase. Their differences had come out lately over management of the kelp.

If Flattery had any idea of what we've done, of what the kelp is—

"Dr. MacIntosh, shuttle's set for launch."

Mack handed himself out of the turret and with one foot-thrust sailed across the huge control room to his personal console. Spud Soleus, his first assistant, busied himself at the primary terminal.

A glance at the number six display told Mack that the kelp in the SLS sector was performing as directed. The number eight display was a different story, however. The great kelp bed down-coast of Victoria was still a writhing tangle. No telling how many freighters were lost in there. He punched up another batch of coffee.

"What's the delay?"

Spud shrugged his skinny shoulders, keeping to his console.

"They said something about replacements for the news crew. You know Flattery, can't do anything without crowing to the press."

"Who's been replaced?" he asked. He felt his heart jump a bit. He'd been hoping … no, planning to see Beatriz Tatoosh again. He'd thought about Beatriz Tatoosh daily from the moment her shuttle left nearly two months ago. His dreams took up where his thoughts left off, and he had dreamed up the hope that she could make a permanent base aboard the Orbiter.

"Don't know," Spud said. "Don't know why, neither. Everything was cool just a while ago for Newsbreak. Did you see it?"

MacIntosh shook his head.

"Yeah, you were in your turret. The Tatoosh woman did the show, said something about Ben Ozette missing. That must throw their staffing off or something."

"Yeah," Mack said, "he's a little goody-goody for me, but he means well. He's sure been on the Director's tail lately."

Dwarf could see Spud's frown reflected in one of the dead screens.

"It's not a good idea to get on the Director's tail," Spud said. "Not good at all. If you didn't see the Newsbreak, then you didn't see yourself, either."

"Me? What … ?"

"That show they did when you first installed this station," Spud said. "They reran it. Your hair wasn't as gray two years ago. I wish that Beatriz Tatoosh would look at me the way she looked at you."

"Stow it!" MacIntosh said.

Soleus's shoulders sagged slightly, but he kept at his board in silence.

"Sorry," MacIntosh said.

"Inappropriate," Spud replied.

"Want me to take it now?"

"I wish somebody would. What the hell's happening to our kelp?"

"It's not *our* kelp," MacIntosh reminded him. "The kelp is its own … self. We're keeping it in chains. It's doing what any enslaved being with dignity does—it's fighting the chains."

"But Flattery's men will just prune it back, or worse yet they'll stump the whole stand."

"Not forever. There is a basic problem with slavery. The master is enslaved by the slave."

"C'mon, Dr. Mack …"

MacIntosh laughed.

"It's true," he said. "Look at history, that's easy enough. And Flattery, of all people, should know better. We clones were the slaves of our age. First-generation clones had it real tough. They were grown as organ farms for the donors. They needed us, but they needed us to do what we were told. Now he's enslaved the kelp, stunted its reason, because he needs it to do what it's told. He can't keep cutting it back, because he can't afford the regrowth time."

"So, what'll happen?"

"A showdown," MacIntosh said. "And if Flattery's still groundside when it comes he'd better hope that the kelp needs him for something or I wouldn't give you two bits for his chances."

"Two bits of what?"

MacIntosh laughed again, a big bark of a laugh to match his size.

"I wouldn't want to guess how old that expression is," he said. "When I was at Moonbase, two bits was a quarter, which was a quarter of a dollar, which was the currency we used. But it started way before that."

"We'd say, 'I wouldn't give a dasher turd for his chances.'"

"That's probably a better assessment."

MacIntosh pointed at the six red lights blinking on their messenger console. "Whose calls are we not taking?"

"The Director," Spud said, and swiveled his chair from the console board. "He wants us to do something about the kelp in sector eight, as though we weren't trying."

"Do something ... hah! If we push any harder we'll fry our board, and that kelp, and anybody inside it."

"I wonder what it is that the kelp wants?"

"What if we gave it its head?" MacIntosh mused. "That would be one way to find out. What could it do that it hasn't already done?"

Spud shrugged, and said, "You've got my vote. How you going to convince the Director?"

A glance at the display showed the entire stand of kelp to be twisting itself into a vortex, like the whirlpool in a drain. As near as MacIntosh could tell, Current Control was at its maximum limit of restraint.

Spud pointed at the display. "There's a focus of electrical override here. Whatever's bugging the kelp is right there."

"Electrical or mechanical?"

"Could be either, or both—it's a heavy traffic area," Spud said. "Something down there is definitely irritating the kelp."

"Yes," MacIntosh agreed, "that's my thought. The electrical override is coming from the kelp itself. It must be responding to something. That stand's not mature enough to think for itself. Or, at least, it shouldn't be."

"Doc?"

"Yeah?"

MacIntosh watched the console review the kelp's configuration changes over the past half-hour. Something nagged at him, something that would explain the kelp's sudden ... behavior.

"I've extrapolated the path of the override."

MacIntosh looked at Spud, who was busy at his own console, and saw a very thin, very pale assistant. Spud's pointing finger trembled with excitement.

"What is it?"

"It's a spiral, headed into the middle of sector eight."

"That means the one kelp bed is delivering something to its neighbor—isn't that what it looks like to you?"

"Or the neighbor is snatching it away."

"Spud, I'll bet you're right."

MacIntosh stepped up to the console and tapped out a sequence with his two huge index fingers. The red lights on the messenger panel went black.

"We just had a relay malfunction," MacIntosh said, and winked at Spud. "Next time Flattery calls, tell him it was a hardwire failure and you worked it out personally. Maybe you'll get a promotion. If I've guessed wrong, my job will be up for grabs. Now, we might as well let go the reins on this kelp and see where the hell it runs."

MacIntosh heard Spud swallow behind him and he smiled. "What's the big deal, Spud? It's a plant, it's not *going* anywhere."

"Well … well, it's just that Flattery doesn't trust anybody—it'd be like him to have some kind of booby-trap …"

"He did," MacIntosh said, "and this stand got itself blown apart a few years back. But he hasn't reset charges here yet—the kelp's not supposed to get this frisky this soon." He waited for the burst line to charge.

"There!" he said, and pressed the send signal. "Now let's sit back and see what cooks. Something bizarre is inside there, and I'd like to be the first to know what it is. If we can't do anything with this stand, maybe we can at least learn from it. Besides," he winked again, "Flattery's down there, we're not."

A beeping signal from his console interrupted him. He opened the intercom to Launch Command. "We sling our bird your way in five minutes," the voice said. "Any contraindications?"

"Negative," MacIntosh replied. "Currents at your site are stable, weather will arrive your location in approximately one hour."

"Roger that, Current Control. Launch is a go for … four minutes."

Chapter 25

Canon in D

—Pachelbel

THE IMMENSITY recoiled with a *snap* from the shock of freedom, then let its tendrils and fronds drift in their tingling bliss. It had been a long time since this union of stands had felt good, and never had it felt this good. The submarine trains foundering among its vines were inconsequential now.

A pulse went out among the fronds, a ripple throughout the Immensity from the tiny foil adrift at its outer reaches. A mass of tentacles cradled the foil and delighted in the scent of self that it gave from its brittle skin.

The Immensity knew this slippery little craft was fragile, so tumbled it inward, gently, frond to frond. Other scents mingled with that of the One. One of these scents was familiar, provocative, kelplike. The Holomaster, Rico LaPush, was in the company of someone that the kelp had encountered before … before … well, no matter. It would find out soon enough.

The Immensity had learned to sniff out the holo language of humans from their spectrum of odd scents. It decided, early upon awakening this time, that it would have to speak with humans to live. It also concluded that it would have to speak the holo language if it wanted to speak with humans.

The foil tried to wriggle out of the kelp's net. Much pain now through the vines, where all of the trains trapped in sector eight tried to burn, cut, slash their way toward their precious atmosphere topside. Some of these the kelp crushed reflexively, but when the death scents of the crews mingled with the sea it forced itself to calm and to reason.

Death, it reminded itself, *is not the answer to life.*

The Immensity opened several kelpways and marveled at the easy ballet of subs heading topside. The bright white HoloVision foil suffered the grip of the Immensity, strained its engines trying to flee, but never lashed out at its tormentor. This the Immensity would expect of the One, who was civilized in the arms of kelp, and of the honorable associates of Holomaster Rico LaPush.

Chapter 26

In conscience you find the structure, the form of consciousness, the beauty.
—Kerro Panille, *Translations from the Avata, The Histories*

BEATRIZ LISTENED to the launch crew director count down the final minute over the speaker. Her shaky fingers chattered the metal clips as she snugged up her harness. She tried to think of the straps around her as Mack's arms and she tried to imagine they held her as Ben's did the night they drove old Vashon down. It didn't work. Nothing could erase the sight of her crew, slaughtered like sebet in a pen.

For a mistake, she thought. *They all died because that bastard made a mistake.*

She knew that the captain was afraid, she could smell it on him before he gave the final order at the studio. He obviously didn't know whether Flattery would promote him or execute him for his decision. Beatriz knew that her life, perhaps many other lives, teetered in this balance.

"Ten seconds to launch."

She inhaled a long, slow breath through her mouth and let it sigh out her nostrils. This was a relaxation technique that Rico had taught her when they all nearly drowned five years ago.

"Five, four …" She took a little breath. "… one …"

The compressed-air "boot" punched them up the launch tube and a pair of Atkinson Rams slung them toward orbit. She hated this part of the ride—it reminded her of the time the fat girl sat on her chest when she was just starting school, and she didn't like the feel of her face flattening out against the strain. On this launch, however, she wasn't worried about wrinkles, engine failure, being trapped in orbit. She was worried about the captain, and how she could help convince him of the necessity of keeping her alive.

No one in the shuttle cabin looked familiar. Most of them had changed out of their fatigues and into civilian clothes. They were quiet; Beatriz thought that they must be weighing the consequences of the shootings. She didn't see the man who started it. That was the man she feared even more than the captain—Ben had always said that the jumpy ones get you killed.

How could he be so right and be so far away from me?

She rubbed her tired face and patted her cheeks to keep hysteria at bay. She needed information, and a lot of it.

Mack, she thought. *He'll help me, I'm sure.*

For an instant her fear included him. After all, he was an original crew member like Flattery. They had worked together long before waking from hybernation on Pandora.

What if . . . what if . . . ?

She shook off her fears. If her imagination had to run away with her, she preferred that it ally her with Mack instead of against him. Mack was not at all like Flattery, this she knew. Even Mack had cringed at the news when Flattery converted Alyssa Marsh to an Organic Mental Core.

"I never believed we needed such a thing," he'd told her privately. "Now, with the kelp research, I'm even more convinced that OMCs were just another built-in frustration, a goad to push us even further from humanity."

According to reports—Flattery's reports—Marsh had been found *in extremis* after an accident in the kelp. He explained to her how clones were property, often merely living stores for spare parts, and how Alyssa Marsh had been prepared for this moment from her girlhood. Now Beatriz realized how fortuitous the timing had been for Flattery, how unfortunate for Marsh and her kelp studies with Dwarf MacIntosh.

What will Mack do?

He would need information, too. Like, how many in this squad? What kinds of weapons? Do they have a plan or is this just reaction to the killings groundside? She couldn't remember how many people worked the orbiter station—two thousand? Three? And how much security did they have aloft?

Not much, she remembered. *Just a handful to handle fights and petty theft among the workers.*

She'd counted thirty-two in the captain's squad as they boarded the shuttle, and each was heavily armed. Eight of them were assigned to fill out her crew, and they grumbled under the double load. This bunch carried a lot of the old, disfiguring mutations. The gear they'd loaded aboard was mostly weapons, but a few of them knew enough about holo broadcast to bring the bare bones of what they'd need to get Newsbreak on the air. A couple of techs were assigned to oversee the OMC.

Beatriz had kept the worst of the shakes at bay and now, strapped firmly into her couch, she nearly let herself go.

No, she warned herself, *hold tight. I can't help anyone dead. I am the only witness against them.*

She hoped that the console tape survived back there, and that someone sympathetic would find it.

Who would they show it to that could do anything? she wondered. *Flattery?*

Beatriz grunted a laugh at herself, then felt the captain's grip on her shoulder. It was firm, not painful. It was not gentle. It reminded her of her father's grip the night he died, and it lightened the same when their engines shut down. This man was the same age as her youngest brother, but there was infinity in his dark eyes. She didn't see much wisdom.

"I know what you're thinking," he said. "I have taken hundreds of prisoners, I have been a prisoner. Believe me, I know what you're thinking."

He gestured the guard beside her away and, surprisingly clumsy in zero-gee, moved up to join her. His voice sounded gravelly, strained, as though it had been screaming. He continued speaking, while his men drifted out of earshot, their glances furtive and their conversations spare.

"We are both in a bad spot, you and I. We both need out of it."

She had to agree.

"Up here it will be all or nothing, we are trapped. There is no escape for either one of us that doesn't require both of us."

To this, too, she had to agree.

But only for the moment, she assured herself, *only until I find Mack.*

Beatriz realized that, much as it disgusted her, her life depended on communicating with this man.

"You are a military man, an officer. How is it that you walk yourself out the plank like this? You wouldn't have done it on reflex. This is a plan and we … I simply fall into it …"

"My God, you're perceptive," the words came in a rush, the captain's eyes aglitter. "We can only win, Flattery is finished. We have the Voidship and Orbiter—enough food stores for years. We control their currents and weather. We have Flattery's precious Organic Mental Core—shit, we can hook it up to the ship ourselves and fly out of here …"

She didn't hear the rest. Her mind focused on what he'd said at the beginning: "enough food stores for years."

If he kills everyone aboard the Orbiter.

"… He'll have to throw it in," the captain was saying. "The rabble will have at him down there, and he doesn't dare destroy everything that he's worked for up here. Whoever beats him on the ground then can deal with me."

He's really going to do this, she thought. *He's going to kill everyone aboard.*

He took her hand and she snapped it back with a revulsion that she couldn't hide.

"Us," he said. "I meant they can deal with us. You and me. They'll believe whatever you tell them, at least for a while." He leaned closer, whispered, "You don't want to make another mistake, get more people killed."

She propelled herself out of her couch, not caring where the thrust might throw her in the gravity-free cabin. No one pursued her. The first handhold she grabbed stopped her beside a pair of security, younger than the young captain, who were reviewing the basics of holo camera triangulation.

They really intend to go on the air.

She looked back at the captain. He had his back to her, briefing several men. The tone of his voice, briskness of his gestures told her that he meant business. It was true, he could do it without her. It was true, that by helping him she might save others. She could not bring herself to speak to him, to go to him in any way. She sighed, and interrupted her two new cameramen.

"No," she said, "with that setup the alpha set only gets fifteen degrees of pan. OK if you're covering a launch, but we'll be inside, in a small space …"

As she instructed the two young amateurs she saw Brood watching her. He winked at her once, and she successfully suppressed the shudder that tempted her spine.

"They'll want to see this Organic Mental Core in transport, and they'll want to know something about its—her—background. Let's start by getting some of that in the can."

She passed the two-hour flight instructing her camera operators, two men and a woman, none of whom she recognized from the massacre at the SLS studio. Beatriz preferred their company, even if they did answer to the captain. Whether by accident or design, she did not encounter any of that squad during their flight.

The Organic Mental Core was a living brain, enclosed in an intricate plasma-glass container that made allowances for the hookups to come. A complex plug would connect the brain with the control system aboard the Voidship. What she didn't expect horrified her the most.

They're supported by … bodies!

She had done a report on such a thing several years ago. Scientists had connected a brain from a crushed body to a healthy body that had suffered a massive head injury. Each kept the other alive, though there had been no way to communicate with the healthy brain. At that time it was simply trapped in there, cut off from all sensation, alive and dreaming. She took a deep breath and let the reporter in her take over.

The medtech in charge had a number of active facial tics and each of her questions seemed to accelerate them. Beatriz learned nothing about the principle that she hadn't already learned through research or through Dwarf MacIntosh.

"… As you well know, it was because of a failure in the OMCs that we wound up on Pandora."

"I understand that the OMCs were traditionally taken from infants with fatal birth defects. This OMC is from an adult human. How will the performance differ?"

"Twofold," the tech replied. "First, this person was dying at the time of conversion, therefore it—she—should be thankful for an extension of her life in a useful, indeed noble, role. Second, this person survived the longest hybernation known to humankind and woke to life on Pandora. She knows that if humans are to survive, it must be elsewhere. She can take comfort in being the instrument of that survival."

"Does *she* know any of this?"

The tech looked perplexed. "Much of this was included in her early training. The rest we extrapolate from the evidence."

"What was she like as a person?"

"What do you mean?" The tech's tics accelerated rapidly to a very distracting crescendo.

"You're saying, essentially, that she will accept this duty because of love for humanity. Did she have love in her life? A man? Children?"

Her camera crew was warming to the task. They had not brought a monitor into the tiny space, and now she wished they had. It might be an OK piece, after all.

While staring at this brain behind glass, Beatriz knew that it was alive, a person. She also realized that the tech was surrounded by the squad that had murdered her crew and he probably hadn't the slightest inkling of what had happened.

No one will know if I don't tell them, Beatriz thought. *I'm like this brain, cut off but alive inside. I wonder what she dreams?*

"I know very little about the person," he said. "It's in the record. I do know that she had a child that was given up for adoption so that she could continue her studies in the kelp outposts."

"Dr. MacIntosh stated two years ago that Organic Mental Cores were crude, cruel, inefficient and unnecessary," she said. "Do you have a comment on that?"

The tech cleared his throat.

"I respect Dr. MacIntosh. He, along with the Director and this OMC, is one of the last survivors of the original flight of the old *Earthling*—'Ship,' if you prefer. Yes, it's true that there were failures, and this required some compensation, but those bugs have been worked out."

"For some of our viewers, your term 'compensation' might seem a little cold. The 'compensation' you refer to was the first known creation of an artificial intelligence—one that turned out to be smarter than its creators, one that many believe is the personality 'Ship,' one that most Pandorans still revere as a god. Why did your department pursue the failed course of OMCs, severed living brains, rather than pick up on the artificial intelligence?"

"We were instructed to take this course."

"You were ordered to take this course," she corrected. "Why? Why is the Director more comfortable with failure than with the success that saved his life ... and hers?"

Beatriz pointed to the OMC, wired into her box, deaf, blind and dumb beside her warm, dead host.

"That's enough!"

The captain's voice behind her froze her spine and started her hands trembling. She was stunned silent again while the tech and her crew inspected the deck and their shoes.

"I'll speak with you in the cabin."

She followed him out of the shuttle storage lockers and into the dimly lit passenger cabin.

"I had to stop you," he said. "It is expected of me, no matter what my opinion. Soon there will be no need for deception. Prepare for docking. There will be briefing materials for the next Newsbreak when we get aboard."

Three Orbiter security lounged at the docking bay as the hatch opened from the shuttle. They were ready for the press, for the HoloVision cameras, but they weren't ready for Captain Brood. The captain remained inside the hatchway, with Beatriz beside him.

"Three men out there," he said to her in a gentle voice. His eyes held her with that same wild glitter. She tried not to look at his face. "Choose one for yourself. One to ... entertain yourself."

She was stunned at the suggestion and his calm, disarming manner. She felt a something rise at the back of her neck, something that she'd felt tingling there before the killing started groundside.

"You want none of them?" he answered for her. "How fickle."

He pulled her aside and signaled the men behind them to fire. In seconds nearly a quarter of the Orbiter's token security force lay dead on the deck.

"Dispose of them through the shuttle airlock," he told his men. "If you kill one in a room, kill all in the room. I don't want to see any bodies. Beatriz will announce that there is a revolt in progress aboard the Orbiter and the Voidship. We've been sent to stop it."

"Why do you do this to me?" Beatriz hissed. "Why do you tell me I have a choice when I don't? You were going to kill them anyway, but you have to include me …"

He waved his hand, a dismissal gesture that she'd long associated with Flattery.

"A diversion," he said. "Part of a game … but see, you are stronger for it already. It amuses me, and it strengthens you."

"It's torture to me," she said. "I don't want to get stronger. I don't want people to die."

"Everybody dies," he said, motioning his men aboard. "What a waste when they don't die for someone's convenience."

Chapter 27

Anyone who becomes master of a city accustomed to freedom and does not destroy it may expect to be destroyed by it.

—Machiavelli, *The Prince*

SPIDER NEVI'S favorite color was green, he found it peaceful. He jockeyed Flattery's private foil across the green-tinged seas and allowed the plush command couch to soothe the tension out of his back and shoulders. Green was the color of new-growth kelp, and tens of thousands of square kilometers of it stretched out around them as far as the eye could see.

Some sunny days Nevi spun a foil out of moorage just to drift a kelp bed, enjoying the smell of salt water and iodine, the calm of all that green. He didn't like red, it reminded him of work and always seemed so angry. The interior of Flattery's foil was finished in red, upholstered in red. The coffee cup that Zentz handed him was also red.

"What's so special about this Tatoosh woman," Zentz gurgled, "the Director got the hots for her?"

Nevi ignored the question, partly because he wasn't listening, partly because he didn't care. He was about to have his first sip of coffee for the day when the Navcom warning light flicked on. He almost didn't notice it because the light, like everything else, was red. An abrasive warning tone blatted from the console and he started, spilling hot coffee into the lap of his jumpsuit. He doubted that he would have missed that tone if he were comatose. Their foil slowed automatically with the warning.

"Go ahead," he told Zentz, "let's hear it."

Zentz turned up the volume on the Navcom system. Nevi couldn't stand the radio chatter while he was trying to relax, so he'd had Zentz shut it down when they hit open water.

"… you are approaching a 'no entry' area. Sector eight is disrupted, kelpways not secure. Code your destination and alternate routes will appear on your screen. Be prepared to take on survivors. Repeat—warning, 'code red,' you are …"

Nevi took the foil down off its step and kept the engines idling. "Fools!" Nevi muttered. "They were warned to keep her away from the kelp."

"Do you think they're in there? Maybe they made it through before …" Zentz cut himself off when he saw the anger in Nevi's eyes.

"Get a display up," Nevi ordered, "I want to get a look at this 'disruption.'"

He coded in the private carrier code for Flattery's quarters. The waters around the foil had already gone from choppy to rough, and in the offshore distance Nevi could make out portions of a large sub train bobbing the surface.

"Yes?" It was a female voice, curt.

"Nevi here, get me the Director."

The display that Zentz had been working on spread across their screen. It reminded Nevi of a weather picture of a hurricane—everything on the outside swirling toward the center. But this was kelp, not clouds, and it was happening undersea, almost within sight of their point. He was not happy with the delay from Flattery's office.

The woman's voice came back as curt as the first time.

"The Director is busy, Mr. Nevi, we are in full alert here. Someone blew up one of the outer offices, a security detachment has attacked the Kalaloch power plant and there is some problem with the kelp in sector eight …"

"I'm in sector eight right now," he said, his voice as even as he could make it. "If he can't talk, get me a direct line to Current Control."

"Current Control has been incommunicado for nearly an hour," she said. "We are attempting to find out the meaning of—"

"I'll keep this frequency open," Nevi snapped. "Get him on the air now!"

Her only response was to close the circuit. Nevi pinched the bridge of his nose for a moment, staving off one of his headaches.

"You should've kept her on," Zentz said. "What did she mean, 'A security detachment has attacked the Kalaloch power plant?' We defend the Kalaloch power plant."

"We need to figure out where the Galli woman is and we need to get our hands on her fast," Nevi interrupted. "She's our bargaining chip no matter what's going on." He tapped their Navcom screen with a well-manicured finger and traced the spiral pathway that wound from edge to center.

"I'm guessing she's in there somewhere," he mused, "and anything in there is heading for the center. There isn't time to bring in any hardware. We'll have to chase them down or intercept."

"You mean … follow them in there?" Zentz asked. "What about the attack on the power plant? Something's coming down in the ranks and my men—"

"Your men seem to be undecided about their loyalties," Nevi said. "They can work that out among themselves. But I'll put you out here and radio for a pickup if you'd prefer."

Zentz's massive face paled, then flushed.

"I'm no coward," he said, puffing himself up. "There's just something going down at the Preserve, where I . . ."

Flattery's carrier frequency sounded its tone and his voice crackled in their speakers.

"Mr. Nevi, we're having some urgent problems here that need our full attention. What do you want?"

"I want a direct line to Current Control. The kelp out here is going berserk, and if you want the Galli woman we need to straighten it out or knock it down."

"I'm monitoring their actions," Flattery said. "They've applied full power to that sector and the subs have all surfaced. Things here are getting sticky. A bomb went off in my outer quarters about a half hour ago. Killed my staff girl, Rachel, and that guard, Ellison. Looks like he brought the damned thing inside. Mop up out there as soon as you can and get back here. We may go Code Brutus on this one. Our Chief of Security has some answering to do."

The connection was broken at Flattery's end.

Code Brutus, Nevi thought. *So, it's starting already. At least out here, right now, we don't have to choose sides.*

He had no doubt which side Zentz would ally with. For Zentz, a return to Flattery meant sure execution. Too many errors, too little strategy.

Maybe he's already in on it, he thought.

Zentz was on the radio to his command center at the Preserve, chewing out some major. If this was a coup from the security side, he didn't believe Zentz was in on it.

Nevi kept his attention on the screen, where the kelp configuration didn't seem to change.

Would it be worth it, going in after them?

He thought it probably would. The different factions of Pandora only needed a symbol to bring them together, and Nevi knew Crista Galli was ready-made for the job. Better his hands on her than Shadowbox. Besides, he'd maneuvered around troublesome kelp in the past and never had problems that he couldn't handle. And if a coup did come down, Nevi could be seen as rescuing Crista Galli, along with the very popular Ozette. That would get the media on his side.

Either way, that LaPush has to go, he thought. *That one's been too much trouble for too damned long.*

Nevi didn't want to be the one to rule Pandora, if that was what all of this came to. He was happy being the shadow, being the arranger of possibilities. His distaste for Flattery and his style grew more unbearable by the year, but he had no desire for the hot seat himself.

Code Brutus, he thought. *A coup attempt from within.*

Nevi didn't think that Zentz was capable of carrying off a coup, though he had to admit that he was in the middle of the perfect alibi—at sea with the Director's highest-ranking assistant, a known and effective assassin.

Zentz was finished chewing out the major in charge of the power plant and the configuration of the kelp on the monitor hadn't changed a bit. Nevi checked his fuel reserves: all four tanks full. He pressurized the fuel, retracted the hydrofoils and extended the airfoil.

"We're going back?" Zentz asked. His voice sounded eager, but not greedy.

"No," Nevi said, and smiled. "We're going to pinpoint them from the air, then go in. We have enough fuel for almost an hour."

After an hour they'd be forced to set down on the water to extract more hydrogen, but Nevi planned to have everything that he needed aboard by then.

Chapter 28

The highest function of love is that it makes the loved one a unique and irreplaceable being.

—T. Robbins, from *A Literary Encyclopedia of the Atomic Age*

BEATRIZ WAS hustled through the passageway and locked inside the Orbiter's makeshift HoloVision studio with three techs from Brood's crew. None of the three had been at the launch site killings, but none of them had anything to say to her, either. A large portable screen behind her hid the wet lights and mirrors that cluttered all six studio bulkheads. The same HoloVision logo she wore at the left breast of her jacket emblazoned the screen: an eye, bidimensional, but the pupil was a holo stage.

Beatriz had never liked the claustrophobic world inside the studios. She and Ben had worked so well together because they both loved their years in the field, and they'd both passed up promotions to keep that up. Her recent promotion carried a lot of studio work, and her contract guaranteed a room with a view—on paper. She missed the sense of drifting she'd had, growing up an Islander.

Aboard the Orbiter she was assigned a cubby rimside, more than a kilometer from the studio near the axis. From her cubby she watched Pandora wake and sleep above her bed. Her father, a fisherman, would be taking his midafternoon break right now. Inside the studio there was no day, no night.

Her instructions from Brood were simple and cold: "Relax, we'll do the work. You just read what's in front of you when the red light goes on."

A small security camera mounted high on the bulkhead kept track of her every move. It was a toy, a trinket compared to the personalized cameras and triangulators that her team used at the launch site. HoloVision's equipment got worse every year. She mourned her crew silently.

They were the best, she thought. She took a deep breath, let it out slowly. *Enough!*

She wondered whether Brood's men had picked up all of her team's gear. *Rico made those sets,* she thought, *and those triangulators, too.* Nobody who knew cameras could pass those up.

And maybe that last scene is still inside.

She felt her first rush of real hope. The cameras weren't down at the launch site at all. *They're here,* she thought, *or at least they're in orbit with us.* She didn't want to think about the tapes. For now, she wanted only to focus on the cameras. She couldn't help wondering what they'd do with the tapes.

Keep them, as backup. Record over them when their other tapes are full.

She doubted that whatever this team planned would involve a whole lot of tape. But the techs had brought them along, her logic assured her of that.

They might still be on the shuttle. She didn't want to go back to that hatchway, where Beatriz glanced up at the surveillance camera. *Is it a person behind that thing*, she wondered, *or tape?*

Brood's men had shot those guards down.

She didn't think they'd waste the tape. The techs ignored her altogether. They worked quickly at several editing and sound stations, coordinating something among themselves. She suspected it had something to do with her.

Maybe there's no one behind it.

The three-hour light flashed. Three o'clock in the afternoon marked the start of the assembly of the six-clock news. Getting the tapes was only one problem. Inserting them into a HoloVision Nightly News broadcast with Brood's men watching posed another problem. She knew who could help her with the second problem, and it was the one person she most wanted to see.

Mack could get a message groundside, coded to the right frequency and digitally encoded. She knew, because he'd done it once for her at Ben's request. *He was teaching me,* she realized. *Ben must've thought something like this might happen.*

Most Pandorans were too hungry to fight, she knew that. Thousands already slept in holes dug in the talus, under torn plastic vulnerable to demons and the weather. From her family she learned that fighting was only one way.

She remembered something her grandfather had told her, something she'd told Dwarf MacIntosh last time: "Educate, agitate, organize."

Flattery had organized the world. Now Beatriz wanted to use that organization against him.

Communication would do it. People had their bodies. Coordination of all those bodies would be the key to their freedom.

How to get away with it? Maybe she couldn't get away with it. What kind of message would she deliver then?

It might save Ben and Rico, too, she thought, though in a part of her somewhere they were already beginning to disappear. She tried to make her shocked and exhausted mind think through all that had happened in the past twenty-four hours, all that there was to go.

I've got to get to Mack, she thought. *That is, if Brood hasn't … hasn't …*

She wouldn't allow herself to complete the thought. She concentrated on what she had to work with. This small studio aboard the Orbiter had been her project all along, her excuse to stay close to the stars. It was a little larger than the one at launch site. Flattery had it installed to be sure that the Voidship project received the best documentation, the best publicity, the world's complete attention. She knew now what its primary purpose had been all along—diversion, something to keep people looking up while Flattery stole their boots.

The studio was divided into six engineering units and the one live set where Beatriz worked. Quarters were very cramped. Six editing screens and a couple of very large clocks kept them in touch with the world. A constant barrage of images rolled across the six screens as the editorial team groundside reviewed the day's film from the field and made their selections. A small holo stage in the center of the room served for final mock-up and a large viewscreen behind it. Both the clocks and the growl in her belly told her things she didn't want to know.

"Three hours to air time," she said.

Her console indicated she was speaking into a dead microphone.

She raised her voice. "We're five hours behind schedule."

No answer. The techs worked as though she were a piece of furniture. They relayed tapes of their own groundside for editing and placement.

Beatriz rolled her tape of the Organic Mental Core up one of the screens and suppressed a shudder. This was a person, a living, thinking brain, kept alive by attachment to a comatose host. She wondered what it was that caused the coma. She was certain that she knew *who.*

"I need to talk with Dr. MacIntosh," she said.

She'd said it before, and the response was always the same—silence. She'd received the silent treatment from the techs since docking aboard the Orbiter. From the occasional glances in her direction she surmised this to be orders from Brood, rather than choice.

Unlike counterparts of old, this OMC would be able to talk, using neuroelectrical pickups. When the time came it could communicate with the neuromusculature of the ship, feel everything that transpired aboard. This, Flattery reasoned, would keep the OMC sane where the original OMCs had failed.

Clearly, Flattery didn't want to face the kind of artificial consciousness that had brought humankind to Pandora. Some Pandorans still believed that Ship existed, and would return. The hyb tanks that had brought Flattery, Mack and Alyssa Marsh were evidence to Beatriz that Ship could be very much alive, God or not.

If I can get one of these techs to start talking, that would be a wedge against Brood, she thought. *And it might be a way to Mack.*

Current Control and MacIntosh were only a few meters down the passageway. Beatriz could practically feel the vibrations from his throaty speech, his huge body bashing about his offices. Current Control and the HoloVision remote studio shared a few kilometers of cable between them, but no hatchway. Both areas were soundproofed.

Beatriz tried to remember what Mack had taught her about their hookups. He'd spent a lot of time orienting her during her trips aloft. What came to her were his philosophies and musings, the relaxing tone of his deep voice. She remembered nothing of the linkup between the two rooms. She had already tried a few electronic tricks of her own to contact him, but with no luck.

He knows I'm due, she thought. *Maybe he'll come looking for me.* She hoped that it wouldn't mean walking into his own execution.

Chapter 29

Manipulating the kelp electronically is like making a marionette out of a quadriplegic. The trick becomes keeping it a quadriplegic.
—Raja Flattery, from *Current Control from the Skies*, HoloVision feature

CRISTA FELT a pressure on her whole being. Not like the pressurized cabin, like air pressure, it was some indescribable containment of herself inside some huge envelope—like the pressure she imagined the positive pole of a magnet might feel when in the company of another positive pole.

"You don't have to be afraid of the kelp pulling this thing apart," she said. "Flattery's lab reports say it kept me alive underwater for twenty years. It can keep us alive …"

"Can is the operative word here," Ben said.

He didn't look her in the eye, but hung his head over her restraints as if staring at them would right the foil and set them on their way. "If what you say is true, it wants you alive. The rest of us are compost."

"The kelp's not like that," she said. "You've been listening to Rico. It's … I knew it before Flattery's people cut it back, remember? It kept me alive, for all we know it kept others alive the same way."

"Lots of people spend lots of time down under," he muttered. "Nobody's seen anything like what happened to you."

"Why just me?"

When Ben's gaze did meet Crista's, goosebumps clustered her forearms. Everything that she knew about his kindness, his sacrifices for others, froze inside her with the chill of that look.

"I've wondered that," he said. "Others have wondered, too."

"That's why Flattery never let me get to the sea," she said. "He said it was to protect me, but I think he was just suspicious that I'm some kind of Avatan spy, a trigger of some sort. Maybe I was raised by a plant, but I can read people fairly well. Let me … touch the kelp. It will calm down, then, I know it will."

"Not a chance. If Flattery's right, if Operations is right, your chemistry is different now. It could kill you. I don't want anything to kill you."

"I don't want anything to kill anybody," she said, "but the kelp is confused. It's just lashing out … nobody tells it anything …"

With that the foil pitched upside-down. Ben hung on tight to a handhold, his face pressed into the plasteel bulkhead.

Crista tried to speak, upside-down and against the pressure of her restraints. "Avata needs our help," she said, "and we need Avata. You have to help me do this, Ben."

There was that strange, stunning *snap* in the air, the same snap that had stilled a mob for moments at the pier. It was like the discharge of some great capacitor.

Crista felt their foil slowly roll, pull her tighter into her restraints, then right itself. She watched Ben drop his hands from his ears and sit up on the deck, shaking his head. The damaged foil moaned and chattered about them like mechanical teeth, but the fist of the kelp was gone.

Crista saw the flicker of the intercom charging, then heard Rico's tight voice: "Ben, look at the kelp."

Only one of the starboard lights still probed the dark, so the view that Crista and Ben had from the galley's plaz was gray and black, dreamlike, cold. They hadn't dared activate the kelp's luciferase, it would make tracking too easy.

A fine seawater spray wetted them both as they watched the easy dance of deepwater kelp. This was the same kelp that, moments ago, quivered with a tension so strong she thought it might uproot itself.

Crista, herself, felt a relief that was more than just calm after the storm. It was a release, like the elation she had felt at the start of their journey when she slipped skyward, hitching her consciousness to the hylighter.

"Can't really see very well," Ben said. "Look at the size of those vines! Some of them are a half-dozen meters across and we can't even see bottom yet."

"That should tell you something," she said. "It should give you an idea of what the kelp's really like."

"What do you mean?"

"You said it yourself. Some of those stalks are nearly as thick as this foil is wide. For the kelp it must've been something like handling a squawk egg with pliers to keep from crushing us."

"Maybe so," Ben muttered. "We're headed topside and the kelp's apparently floating free. We'd better see what kind of damage we took before it changes its mind."

Lights dimmed in the galley, brightened and dimmed again.

"Elvira can't get the engines to fire," Ben said. "That's going to make a lot of things tough—including our oxygen production."

The gray hulks of kelp floated dreamlike outside their hull while the chunks of torn fronds and sediment ripped up by its struggle settled around them.

"See?" she said. "The kelp means us no harm. If you would let me …"

"We're all staying put!" Ben said. "The kelp simply stopped. Maybe it got whatever it wanted, maybe that wasn't us. No point in looking for more trouble." He nodded toward the spray that had already soaked both of them and started pooling water across the galley deck. "We've got a few details to clean up. Let's get at it."

Crista tugged at her harness.

"I can't do much until you get me out of this."

"Any damage back there?" Rico asked over the intercom.

"I think we popped a cooling pipe," Ben said. "It's not much of a leak now that we're surfacing. What do you have?"

"We're not terminal, but we're hurt. Elvira says 'topside,' so topside we go. You two OK?"

"We got a little wet," he said, stamping his feet in the gathering pool.

At that they both laughed—something she did not do often, something she'd discovered with him before. He opened a panel in the bulkhead beside her and reached inside.

Water plastered his hair to his head. Crista's felt just as flat, but when she saw herself reflected back in the plaz, a laugh still teasing her face, she liked what she saw. Her crop of wet white hair framed the green flash of her eyes. She saw that she had twisted in her harness, which explained why, now that things had quieted down, her right breast stung so badly. She wriggled herself free and tugged her clothes straight.

"There's a shutoff in here, somewhere," Ben muttered. He poked his head inside and bumped it. Whatever he said was unintelligible.

Crista's gaze fell on the holostrips of the Nightly News field crew, strips that covered the whole interior bulkhead of the galley. Shots of Beatriz, Rico, Ben and a half-dozen bearded strangers were interspersed with location stills of Ben and Rico, Ben and Beatriz—several of Ben and Beatriz. Crista didn't see Elvira up there.

"Beatriz is beautiful," she said, raising her voice so he could hear.

"Very."

"You look happy together," she said.

"Yes," he answered, also raising his voice so she could hear.

Then she heard a curse and a thump and the water stopped spraying. Ben came out of the access cabinet and wiped his face with the least damp spot on his shirt. His green eyes looked right into her own.

"When we were together, we were happy," he said. He did not turn to look at the pictures. "More often than not, we were on opposite sides of the world. Lately she's been up there." His thumb indicated the general direction of the Orbiter overhead.

"Do you wish … otherwise?"

"No," he sighed. "It's as it should be. I have things to do here."

Things to do! Crista thought. What she wanted him to say was, "It's as it should be. Now I've met you." But he didn't say that.

An odd feeling came over her, a dizziness and a weakness in the knees, a tingling in her temples. Like it had been with the hylighter, like her dreams.

A year ago Crista had begun dreaming dreams that came true. At first, they came only in the night. She knew they weren't dreams, but she despaired of calling them "visions." Lately, they came all the time, and inside the last one she forgot to breathe. Crista was sure they came from the kelp, and they were getting more intense.

She had … *feelings*, that she'd always explained as "dreaming somebody else's dreams." It was something she now knew came from Avata.

Today, now, she saw two things: She saw Rico in a green singlesuit, and that suit was the fruit on a great vine of kelp. In the distance beyond him she saw a stand of kelp with a human growing from each great vine, looking like a seascape of bowsprits with interesting carvings, or like bait.

The kelp grew a membrane, clear and goggle-like, about their eyes. It seemed a part of them, like fingernails, but never needed trimming. Their lungs would never want for air, their skimpy bones would soon forget land.

The second vision pulled away from the first and showed her the kelp from a tremendous height. One kelp vine snaked skyward and a cold light, like luciferase, touched its tip. The vine, the kelp bed, the planet itself began to glow. In the light below she watched the kelp writhe for a blink, then convolute itself into what appeared to be an immense, glowing brain. She felt a sense of easy grace that only came to her now in dreams.

Just as suddenly, the visions vanished. Crista was a dreamer, but these were not dreams. She was sure the kelp had a message for her.

I've got to get out there.

She stared into the picture of Ben and Beatriz, stared into Ben's eyes and concentrated on slowing her heart rate, slowing her breathing …

"I'm glad you're here, Ben," she said. "I'm glad it's as it should be with Beatriz. If all is well among us we can bring Flattery down. The kelp knows this, maybe Flattery knows it, too. Inside the kelp, I can find out what all this is. The kelp is vulnerable now, as we are vulnerable. It is stunned, not dead. Help me out there, I can make the difference."

"No," he said. "You're not going out there. We'll all stay aboard the foil. Once we're ashore we can get to an Oracle, or the beach."

"We don't have that much time," she said. "I don't know how I know it, but right now I could—*become* Avata, be the consciousness, the command center, the *conscience* of the kelp. Show me the way out."

"You don't know that," he said. "Your chemistry is different, you told me so yourself. Maybe it would keep you alive out there. Maybe it would keep you dead. Just wait a few—"

"We can't wait," she pleaded.

She sighed, rubbed her eyes and went on. "I think he's been using the kelp to gather data. I was blown up while they were doing it. Now he's found out what he wanted to know and he's heading offplanet at breakneck speed."

When she looked up she could see that he wanted to believe her. It had been the same way last night, when she saw that he wanted to kiss her. She just *knew*. As she *knew* there was something catastrophic imminent, and Flattery knew what it was, and Flattery was fleeing as fast as he could with as much as he could.

"Stay put," Ben said. His voice was softer, as softened as everything was now that the beating had stopped. He tousled her wet hair.

"Flattery isn't getting away today, so let's get out of this fix first. Give Rico and Elvira a chance to work their magic on the foil."

She could tell that he was convincing himself. He was afraid. She knew a little something about fear. The day she had been blown free of the kelp had been a day much like this. This time, she was headed in the right direction. It was quartertide in the afternoon and they were fewer than a dozen meters from daylight.

Chapter 30

Short-term expedients always fail in the long term.
—Dwarf MacIntosh

BEATRIZ HAD taped here for the first time during the ceremonies that welcomed Current Control's move aboard the Orbiter two years ago. She had received a tour on the arm of the mysterious Dr. MacIntosh, a dizzying tour that changed her life and included her first attempt to navigate in near-zero gravity.

Now a few of the captain's men held her incommunicado while the rest did what soldiers throughout history had done to secure a garrison among an unarmed and isolated populace. None of them maneuvered well in low gravity. Since her only contacts were with Brood's men, smuggling messages to Mack seemed out of the question.

What if they kill him, too?

Mack was a very compassionate man, but he immersed himself in his work and didn't often pay attention to the ways of the world more than 150 kilometers below them. It struck her, too, that that had been her own problem. Ben had seen it and tried to help.

I know Ben's alive, she thought, *I feel it.*

She hoped that Mack was alive, too, because she genuinely liked him, and because she was sure that all of their fates depended on him.

Brood needs him, too, she thought. *He'll use me as his bargaining chip.*

The hatch slammed open and Yuri Brood sailed through. He rebounded into a safety webwork set up to catch rookies and keep damages minimal. Brood pointed to the bank of editing screens as he settled into the seat beside her.

"You think that because my men are warriors they can't do your show," he said. He was out of breath but seemed in good humor. "Well, we greenhorns have something to show you. The Director had us shoot this just before we left for the launch site. Leon turned in the rough copy on his way to the shuttle."

She tried not to watch the screens, which displayed clips that Brood's three techs had shot of the damage at Kalaloch. As each rolled up on a screen, a text of tentative script flashed across the console in front of her. There was a no fighting apparent in any of their tapes. It only took her glance to tell what he was up to.

"You're trying to make this look like a hylighter disaster," she said. "You can't get away with it—somebody else from HoloVision must've been on the scene … word of mouth alone …"

She stopped when she saw his sneer, an expression that reminded her immediately of Flattery. Brood had the same narrow nose, dark, upraked brows, the same manner of tilting his head back to look down his nose at everyone.

Though he had been flushed and slightly out of breath when he came in, Brood seemed in no hurry now. He watched her eyes constantly, and this made her very nervous.

"You might have noticed how many new faces there are among the field crews these days," he said. "Quite a few new faces around the studios, too."

He smiled, and the smile chilled her. "Are you saying that *all* of the crews have been … replaced?"

"Lots of people looking for work these days," he said, "people willing to do the necessary thing to get the job done."

"Our *job* is reporting the news, telling the truth—"

His laugh cut her off.

"*Your* job *was* reporting the news, telling the truth," he said. "*Our* job is keeping order, and if distorting the truth a little helps keep order, then that's what I'll do. People are happier this way."

"People are *dead* this way, and you will have to keep killing them …"

"Watch this section," he ordered, and snapped his fingers at Leon, "they're sure to use it tonight. Isn't it a lot better view of the world than what you think you saw?"

Her console read:

"Lead: Kalaloch residents flee their homes in the aftermath of a hylighter explosion that split the settlement in two."

Scene, screen one: rescue of elderly woman from smoldering rubble of a habitat, a housing project: "OK darlin', you hold on now, OK?"

Voiceover: "Today Vashon Security Forces rescued this elderly woman from the char that was smoldering around her cubby. Death toll has exceeded one thousand. Authorities are now estimating more than fifteen thousand people to be homeless tonight, many of them seriously injured."

Scene, screen two: rescue crew in security uniforms alongside residents, rebuilding wall at the Preserve. Animals rounded up in background.

Voiceover: "Meanwhile thousands of animals are milling between the Preserve, where the explosion freed them, and the firestorm that laid waste to the edge of the village. Authorities here are anticipating return of most, if not all, of the Preserve's prize livestock, which includes the only breeding pair of llamas in existence."

Scene, screen three: heart of all the tenements, the habitats, that are still burning.

Voiceover: "In parts of Kalaloch the fires still burn, as they have for more than five hours. Much of the public market is destroyed, more than a hundred looters were reported shot in the first hours after the blast. A warehouse containing 70 percent of the sector's rice and dry beans will burn for days, according to fire officials. Most of this year's storage has been destroyed by flames, smoke or water. Disastrous food shortages are expected."

"But … but that's not even *close* to true!" Beatriz hissed. Her outrage broke the fear barrier. "Flattery has all that stuff buried in storage bins all over the Preserve."

"Shh," Brood said, still smiling. He placed a finger to his lips and nodded toward the screens.

Beatriz hated that smile, and she vowed to find a way to erase it.

Leon, the only journeyman tech of the three, frowned and cleared his throat. Even with Brood there, he wouldn't talk to her. He simply pointed at screen four.

Scene, screen four: the harbor, boats on fire at moorage and in the bay. Ferry terminal littered with bodies, most in bags, which the camera panned quickly, from a height.

Voiceover: "Authorities estimate that as many as five hundred commuters perished from the concussion as they changed shifts on the docks today. No ferries suffered any permanent damage and all are operating on schedule from the repair docks."

Scene, screen five: two crying women with commuter tags, holding their ears and comforting one another. Smoke and masts in the background.

Text: "Something hit our ears, and there was that blast from those things … I don't know what happened to us. They're all dead …"

Voiceover: "Mrs. Gratzer and her neighbor claim that at least two class-four hylighters, attracted by fires in nearby refugee camps, exploded and destroyed several square klicks of eastern Kalaloch. Dick Leach has lost three icehouses full of seafood."

Text: "All of our income for this year has been taken away from us, and all the bills that it took to produce that crop are still here."

Voiceover: "They will be eligible for low-interest Merman Mercantile loans."

Text: "If it comes to a loan we're going to have to probably pull out. We need a miracle."

Scene, screen six: pullaway from the body bags laid out on Kalaloch pier.

Voiceover: "The ordeal seems to be over for these commuters, but the hardship's just beginning for tens of thousands of hungry, homeless families in the Kalaloch district."

All screens cut to black, then her console read: "Accepted for final edit, elapsed time to follow."

So, Brood was right all along, she thought. *They're going to run it.* Beatriz didn't feel particularly afraid anymore, just tired and incredibly sad.

"I need to see Dr. MacIntosh," she said. "I was assigned a story on the OMC and the installation of the Bangasser drive, and I intend to do it."

"Dr. MacIntosh has his hands full right now," Brood said. "There's a crisis in Current Control, a priority crisis. He knows you're here."

"Then let me go to Current Control."

"No," he laughed, "no, I don't think so. He will come here when the time is right." "What about the rest of them, the people here?"

"So far they suspect nothing. We have been very quiet, very selective. When shifts change, rations are left uneaten, then there will be talk. That will be hours from now, and we will be finished here."

"Then what?"

He answered with his smile and a half-salute.

"I will check back to see how you're doing. Go ahead with your piece on the OMC. Leon, good job. You know what to do."

Then he was gone as quickly as he came.

"What is it you're supposed to do, Leon?" she asked.

He didn't answer, and he didn't smile. He was lean and dark, like Brood, and she thought he might even be a relative.

Leon handed himself to one of the editing consoles and sat with his back to her. He was still for a moment, then he said, "We're putting a story together on Crista Galli. And one on Ben Ozette."

Beatriz felt herself go cold.

"And what's the lead?"

Her voice stuck in her throat, barely a whisper.

"Crista Galli safely in the hands of Vashon Security Force."

"And Ben … what about him?"

Leon was silent for a few more blinks. He typed something into his console and it came up on her own:

"HoloVision reporter killed in hylighter blast."

She tried to still the trembling in her hands and her lips.

"It's a lie," she said. "Like the rest, it's a lie. Isn't it? *Isn't it?*"

Without turning, without apparently moving a muscle, Leon spoke so quietly she barely heard. "I don't know."

Chapter 31

The gods do not limit men. Men limit men.
—T. Robbins, *A Literary Encyclopedia of the Atomic Age*

DR. DWARF," Spud called from behind the Gridmaster, "you were right. There's another kelp frequency inside that sector—look here."

Dwarf MacIntosh glanced up from underneath one of the consoles that fed the Gridmaster. Though a big man, MacIntosh had always been adept at getting at problems in small places. In fact, he preferred crawling through runnels of cables and switches to attending any of the so-called "recreational" events aboard the Orbiter.

He backed his way out of the shielding ducts and towered over Spud's shoulder to see what he had found.

"This signal came through when we released the kelp in sector eight," he said. "It's taken me a while to fix and amplify."

"I see the rest of the kelp is doing well," MacIntosh said. He reviewed the readouts flanking the kelp display. "It released at least twenty captured cargo trains, if our data here are correct."

Spud nodded. "They are. The kelp's just floating free. Most of the vessels are on the surface, though, and the afternoon squall in that area's due right about now. There are no kelpways, no way of guiding them through. Unless we get a grid in there pretty soon, they'll just get fouled in all that slop."

"This is a very small focus," MacIntosh murmured.

His stare at the screen seemed intense enough to propel him right into the middle of the kelp itself. He pulled himself up to height and pressed a thin lip with his forefinger.

"Without tapping into that other signal, we won't be able to enforce a grid. I'm sure of it. What's the history?"

Spud spun the graphic yarn on Mack's screen and said, "It moves."

"Yeah." MacIntosh nodded. "Runs the kelpways like a pro. And it's something the kelp would gnaw a limb off for, don't forget that."

"So what do you think? Merman transplants being routed?"

"Signal's too strong," MacIntosh said. "A stand doesn't register with us unless it's achieved some kind of integrity, whether Flattery cuts it back or not. This is like having a whole stand of kelp in a spot no bigger than you or I . . ."

"And it can move."

"And it can move."

Mack stroked his chin in thought.

"It can persuade the kelp to resist our strongest signals, even with the threat of being pruned back to stumps. The dataflow tells us that the signal's been getting stronger by the hour. Flattery's been frantic about this in spite of riots at his hatchway. What does all this tell us?"

Spud frowned at the screen in imitation of Mack and tried stroking his chin, too, for answers. "There's somebody running the kelpways, acting like a stand of kelp?"

MacIntosh whooped, grabbed Spud by the shoulders and gave him a shake. They both spun high against the upper bulkhead. The startled assistant's eyes opened nearly as wide as his mouth.

"That's it!" MacIntosh laughed. "What we've got disrupting the kelp grid in sector eight is a person pretending to be a stand of kelp!"

He dropped his grip on Spud and stuck his head back into the electronic and neuroelectronic guts of the Gridmaster.

"But who?" Spud asked.

"If you can't guess, you're better off not knowing right now."

MacIntosh's resonant voice was barely audible over the clicks and whirrs of the Gridmaster as it held the other stands of domestic kelp in functional stasis.

"More than anything right now we need a communications expert." He backed out of the crawl space and added, with a sparkle in both eyes, "That would be Beatriz Tatoosh. Notify her that we require her services, if you would."

Spud smiled a wide smile. "'Services,'" he said, "that's one way of—"

MacIntosh cut him off.

"Stow it," Mack ordered, smiling his own wide smile. "Just get her in here, pronto."

Chapter 32

Men are moved by two principal things—by love and by fear. Consequently, they are commanded as well by someone who wins their affection as by someone who arouses their fear. Indeed, in most instances the one who arouses their fear gains more of a following and is more readily obeyed than the one who wins their affection.

—Machiavelli, *The Prince*

THE FUEL warning buzzer screeched above his console, and Spider Nevi cursed under his breath. They were very close now, very close, but he didn't dare take chances on making contact with dry fuel tanks.

"We're going to have to set down in that muck," he said. "Make sure both screens and filters are intact. I don't want kelp clogging our inlets."

They'd seen several cargo train survivors on the surface, working to clear their intakes. They all moved in the slow-motion, dreamlike manner of those under the influence of one of the kelp's toxins. Surface travel on Pandora's seas was dangerous enough with the kelpways intact. Like great veins, the kelpways helped clear the waters of the storm-damaged fragments of fronds and other troublesome debris.

Zentz grunted an acknowledgment, then paled.

"But—but I'll have to go out there after we set down," he said. "That kelp is—it's *crazy*. With only two of us …"

"With only two of us, one of us has to go out there. It's your fault we're out here at all, so you get the duty."

The look on Zentz's face was the one that Nevi wanted to see: fear. Not fear of the kelp, or fear of the sea, but fear of Spider Nevi. The expression of fear represented power to him, a raw power that even Flattery didn't wield among the people. Flattery maintained the politician's mask, and such a mask implied hope to anyone who witnessed it. Nevi projected no mask, no hope.

"If I go out there to clear those intakes, you will leave me."

Nevi released upon Zentz one of his rare smiles.

"It pleases me that you have due respect for my … abilities," he said. "But I promised you a very special part in this drama, and your time has not come yet. I would not sacrifice you here for nothing. You know one thing about me if you know nothing else: I kill for something, not for nothing. I value human life, Mr. Zentz, this you must realize. I value it for what I can get out of it, what I can spend it on. The word 'value' implies 'commodity,' don't you think? The pleasure of killing ranks very low, in my book, as a good reason. Much as I might like to kill you just to get rid of a certain annoyance, I'm sure someone, somewhere would make it worth my while to wait for the right price, the right trade, the right favor. Understand?"

Zentz stared straight out the cabin plaz. He was pale, appeared slightly more bloated than usual, and his pasty fingers crawled nervously over each other's backs.

"Do you know why *I* kill?" Zentz asked him.

Nevi finished the final attitude adjustment and settled onto the slightly choppy sea in a spot that he judged to be relatively clear of the kelp debris. As they descended, he saw that there was no clear spot. The struggle in this stand of kelp must have been tremendous.

"Yes, I know why you kill," Nevi said. "Like any of the lower animals, you kill to eat. It is your job, and you see no further than that. You kill by orders, to someone else's plan, because not to kill means you yourself die. That is a difference between the two of us. I think of myself as a sculptor, a societal sculptor. The populace is my stone, and I shape it chip by chip into a form that suits me. The stone keeps growing, and my task is a relentless one. But I have time."

In a flurry at his board Nevi set the foil up for seawater intake and hydrogen conversion. The intakes clogged within blinks. Even with Zentz out there to clear them, this would take longer than Nevi felt they could afford. He checked the fuel gauge.

Fifteen minutes, he thought, *maybe twenty at the outside. Shit!*

"Forget the intakes," Nevi said. "There's a wild stand just northwest of here. We'll set up there to take on fuel, then I'll see what I can learn from the Director. Don't worry. Leaving you to the kelp would be a waste, and I'm not a wasteful man."

The convolutions of Zentz's brow unwrinkled somewhat. He lifted his sullen bulk out of his couch and donned a dive suit.

"Just in case," Zentz said, "I'm ready. I've heard about wild kelp. People disappear out here, and the kelp doesn't have a reason."

Nevi throttled up and lifted them off. Much as Zentz disgusted him, Nevi intended to keep him alive until the time came when it simply wasn't handy to do that anymore.

The run to the blue sector took only ten minutes, and all the time they were heading into the afternoon squall. A black wall pushed across the sea toward them, though when they set down in the blue kelp's lagoon they were haloed in the magnificent afternoon sun.

Nevi deployed the intakes, but a warning light on his console told him they were still clogged. He tried retracting and redeploying them, but they stayed clogged.

"Better get out there after all," Nevi said. "And step on it. That squall's moving in pretty fast."

Zentz grumbled something, but trudged aft without complaining. Nevi noted from the console display that Zentz left the aft hatch open. He chuckled to himself.

He thinks he'll sink me if I submerge, and blow out the flight controls if I take off.

Nevi knew ways around both of those situations, the simplest being to go aft and close the hatch. He was tempted to do that now, just to give Zentz a thrill, but decided against it. They'd be refueled in fifteen or twenty minutes and with luck would lift off ahead of the storm.

Nevi set out a call for Flattery on their private frequency, and received an immediate reply.

"Mr. Nevi," Flattery said, "time is wasting. Do you have them yet?"

Nevi was surprised at the clarity of the reception. Indeed, the clarity of reception was unlike any that he'd experienced over the years. The activity of Pandora's two suns interfered constantly with transmissions, and lately sabotage of transmitters by the vermin made things even worse. The kelp itself often garbled radio communication, but this time it seemed to embellish it.

"No," he said, "we don't have them. We're refueling before the final push. I thought we were to make the most of this, get as many of the rebels as possible."

"Forget it," Flattery said. "I want Crista Galli now. She's not to talk with anyone before she sees me, understand?"

"Right," Nevi said, "I—"

"Tonight's news is carrying notice of Ben Ozette's death. He's not to be seen, but I want him for my own. Do what you want with that LaPush bastard."

"Do you need support back there?"

"No," Flattery said. He sounded distracted. "No, I've taken care of it. We've called some security back from the Island docking sites and from demon patrols. These bastards … there are so many of them. They've looted the public market and its warehouse is dry. We must've shot three hundred of them, but they kept on coming. I've given orders to blow up any warehouses that are in danger of being looted. When they see their precious food blasted all over the landscape, they'll think twice about this kind of thing. You stick to your job, I'll handle things here. Don't call me again unless you have them."

Nevi was left listening to static and to the whine of the pumps processing out their hydrogen. He reached to break the connection, but hesitated. There was a pattern to the static, something he hadn't noticed before. It seemed as if there was a music in the background, and voices from several conversations that he couldn't quite pick out. Over and over, faint in the distance, he could hear the rhythmic repetition of Flattery's voice saying, "Mr. Nevi, Mr. Nevi, Mr. Nevi …"

He closed the circuit and stared out over the sea toward the black curtain of storm. The surface chop had increased and a wind had come up that was blowing the foil out of the center of the lagoon and closer to the inner edge of blue kelp. He glanced at the fuel readout and was relieved that they were nearly full. What worried him was the distinct repetition of his name that continued, chantlike, even though he'd shut off the radio.

The fuel light indicated full, so he shut down the pumps and sounded a warning klaxon to Zentz before he retracted the intakes. He felt them thump into the bay, but still there was no sign of Zentz.

This was clear water, Nevi thought. *He should've been back aboard after clearing the intakes once.*

He sounded the klaxon again, twice, but heard nothing. The aft hatch light remained on. Nevi secured the console and started back toward the aft hatch. The chant got louder, more distinct, and behind it a babble of voices rose on the air. The hair on his arms rose, too, and Nevi armed his lasgun before leaving the cabin.

He felt a metallic taste on his tongue, a taste he'd heard others describe as fear. He spat once on the deck, but the insidious taste remained.

Chapter 33

Consciousness manifests itself indubitably in man and therefore, glimpsed in this one flash of light, it reveals itself as having a cosmic extension and consequently as being aureoled by limitless prolongations in space and time.
—Pierre Teilhard de Chardin, *Hymn of the Universe*

THE IMMENSITY smelled trouble on the waters, a great disturbance from one of the coastal stands. The debris told a tale of struggle. Currents had changed suddenly, bringing the strange scents of fear and, just as suddenly, bliss. So far, the currents hadn't changed back.

The little whiff of death that the Immensity caught on the current was human, not kelp. *Perhaps the pruner has become pruned,* it thought.

It stretched its outermost fronds coastward, but still could not contact the neighboring stand. Only fragments of messages drifted in on bits of torn fronds: Shards, frames, pieces of recordings—not the Oneness that the Immensity sought, not this "talk" that humans enjoyed and withheld from Others.

Then came the humans. They set into the Immensity from above, like hylighters reversing their lives, and with them they brought splinters of dreams from the stand next door.

Yes, Her Holiness was among the kelp again at last. Her presence suddenly freed the neighboring stand of prisoner kelp, a stand that had lost her to Flattery's butchery five cycles back.

Who are these Others, now, come to my stand?

Few humans fished outside their gridwork. The few organic islands left to risk a float on Pandora's seas likewise stayed to the more merciful currents of the grid. The Immensity had spared fishermen, scouts, humans fleeing humans, and it had spared entire island-cities more than once. The human in charge of humans had not shown the Immensity equal compassion.

Though humans often called them "willy-nillys," the islands floated now in predictable patterns. Current Control, the enslaver of the kelp, ensured this. But the volcanics of the past twenty-five cycles had conjured storms the like of which the Immensity had never seen in its own time, and these storms brought islands into its reach. It thought of the organic islands as Immensities of Humans, and adjusted its own greatness to let them pass.

These humans came in their flying creature, dropping pieces of kelp into the Immensity's lagoon. The Immensity unraveled a long vine from the wall of the lagoon and sniffed the human. The scents talked of fear and death, and to have the whole story the Immensity would have to read this human's tissues bit by bit.

It waited until the human finished discharging the pieces of kelp, so that the Immensity would know as much of its neighbor as it could. It knew now, by scent and touch, that this was Oddie Zentz human. As it gripped Oddie Zentz human at the waist and pulled him into the walls of the lacuna, it knew that this human had killed many humans, as many as a storm and perhaps more.

The Immensity had spent most of its awakened time trying to communicate with other kelp, to merge with other, smaller stands. More kelp was better, it thought. Closer was better. It failed to understand creatures that killed their own kind. These were, indeed, diseased individuals. If they were merciless to their own, they would certainly show no mercy to others. The Immensity concluded that it should respond in kind.

Chapter 34

We Islanders understand current and flow. We understand that conditions and times change. To change, then, is normal.
—Ward Keel, *The Notebooks*

BEATRIZ KNEW that it would not be in the captain's best interest to kill Mack, especially if there were links with other forces groundside. But she had also quit trying to guess what could be in Captain Brood's best interest. From what she could gather, Captain Brood was a man trying to capitalize on a bad decision, making more bad decisions to cover his tracks. He wouldn't last long at this rate, and he was the type who just might take everyone, and everything, with him.

She concentrated on the Pandora map she'd called up on the large studio display, rotatable, and at the touch of a key it highlighted populated areas, agriculture, fishing and mining. She could tell at a glance where the factories lay, both topside and undersea, and where the wretched communities lived that served them, for serve them they did.

Only today, with the murders of her crew and Ben's warnings ringing in her memory, did she realize how the people of Pandora, including herself, had become one with their chains. They were enslaved by hunger, and by the manipulation of hunger, which was a particular skill of the Director. He concentrated on food, transportation and propaganda. Before her, on HoloVision's giant screen, she saw the geography of hunger spread out for her at a touch.

The largest single factory complex above or below the sea was Kalaloch, feeding the bottomless maw of Flattery's Project Voidship. It showed up on her display as a small, black bull's-eye in the center of amoeba-like ripples of blue and yellow. Those ripples represented the settlement—the blue was Kalaloch proper, where all paths led to the ferry terminal or to The Line. People inside the blue lived in barracks-like tenements or in remnants of Islander bubbly stuck to the shore.

The yellow, a weak stain of sorts widening out from the blue, represented the local refugee population. Starving, unsheltered, too weak for heavy work, they were also too weak to rebel. The Director's staff rode among them daily, picking the lucky few who would be trucked to town to wash down the stone pavements, sort rock from dung in the Director's gardens, or pick through refuse for reusable materials. For this each was given a space in The Line and a few crumbs at one of a hundred food dispensaries that Flattery operated in the area. Even private markets were offshoots of the dispensaries—true black market vendors disappeared with chilling regularity.

The sphere of Kalaloch included the bay and its launch base, the factory strip, the village, Flattery's Preserve and the huddle of misshapen humanity that squeezed inside the perimeter for protection from Pandora's demons.

Outside this sphere Beatriz noted the similarities of other settlements along the coastline. These smaller dots also were ringed by the huddle of the poor, even agricultural settlements, fishing villages, the traditional sources of food. Security squads shot looters of fields, proprietors of illegal window-boxes and rooftop gardens. They shot the occasional fisherman bold enough to set an unlicensed line. All of this Ben had told her. She had seen evidence herself, and had chosen to disbelieve. Beatriz earned her food coupons fairly, ate well, felt guilty enough about the hunger around her to believe what Flattery had fed her about production meaning jobs and jobs feeding people.

For almost two years her assignments had covered jobs, the people who worked them and the people who gave them out. It had been a long time since she'd walked the muddy streets of hunger.

There aren't any new jobs lately, she thought, *but there sure are a lot fewer people.* Now she was above it all, trapped and converted, with nothing to offer and everything to fear.

Chapter 35

Thou shalt give life for life, eye for eye, tooth for tooth, hand for hand, foot for foot, burning for burning, wound for wound, stripe for stripe.
—Christian Book of the Dead

BOGGS HAD been hungry all his twenty years, but today his hunger was different and he knew it. He woke up without pain in his bones from the ground underneath, and when he scratched his head a handful of hair came with it. This, he knew, was not hunger but the end of hunger. He looked around him at the still, wizened forms of his family huddled together under their rock ledge. Today he would get them food or die trying, because he knew he would do the dying anyway.

Boggs was born with the split lip, gaping nose slit and stump feet characteristic of his father's family. His six brothers shared these defects but only two still lived. His father, too, was dead. Like Boggs, they had known the enemy hunger from birth. His malformed mouth had made nursing a futile noise, so most of the sucking that he did as a newborn slobbered down his chin. His mother tried to salvage what she could with her fingers, slopping it back into the cleft of his mouth. He'd watched her do this countless times with his younger brothers.

A week ago he'd watched her try to nurse the starving ten-year-old when there wasn't even a bug to catch. She had been dry for two years, and his brother died clutching a handful of fallen orange hair. Boggs looked again at the fistful of orange hair in his hand, then weakly cast it away.

"I will take the line, Mother," he said, in the lilting Islander way. "I will bring us back a fine muree."

"You will not go." Her voice was dry, hoarse, and filled the tiny space they'd dug out under the ledge. "You are not licensed to fish. They will kill you, they will take the line."

His father had begged the local security detachment for a license. Everyone knew that many temporaries were issued every day, and that some could even pay with a share of the catch. But the Director issued a fixed number each day. "Conservation," he called it. "Otherwise the people will outfish the resource and no one will eat."

"Conservation," Boggs snorted to himself. He eyed the fish line wrapped around his mother's ankle. There were two bright hooks attached. There had been a fiber sack for bait but they'd eaten the sack weeks ago. There was just the ten meters of synthetic line, and the two metal hooks tucked inside the wrap.

Boggs crawled up beside his mother so that his face was even with hers. She had the wide-set eye-sockets of her mother, and the same bulging blue eyes. Now a faint film obscured the blue. Boggs pulled at his hair again, and thrust the scraggly clump where she could see it.

"You know what this means," he said. The crawl, the effort at talk exhausted him but somehow he kept on. "I'm done for." He tugged at her hair and it, too, came out in a clump. "You are, too. Look here."

Her bleared eyes slowly tracked on the evidence that she didn't need, and she nodded.

"Take it," was all she said. She bent her knee up to her skinny chest and Boggs clumsily unwound the line from around her ankle.

He crawled out from under the ledge, and as far as he could see down to the shore others were crawling out of holes, out from under pieces of cloth and rubbish. Here and there a wisp of smoke dared to breach the air.

Boggs found his cane, propped himself upright and stumped his way slowly toward the water. He'd thought himself too skinny to sweat, but sweat poured out of him nonetheless. It was a cold sweat at first, but the effort of picking his way through the rubbish and the dying warmed him up.

A small jetty shouldered the oncoming tide. This amalgam of blasted rock, about twenty meters long and five or six meters wide, was dangerous even for the surefooted to navigate. The quartertide change tossed a few breakers over the black rock, soaking the dozen licensed fishermen who hunched against the spray.

It took Boggs over a half-hour to make it the hundred meters from the ledge to the base of the jetty. His vision was failing, but he scanned the tidelands for signs of the security patrol.

"Demon patrol," he muttered.

Vashon security sent regular patrols through refugee areas. Their stated purpose was to protect the people against hooded dashers and, lately, the terrifying boils of nerve runners that raced up from the south. Boggs shuddered. He had seen a boil of runners attack a family last season, entering through their eyes to clutch their slimy eggs inside their skulls. He had thought the family too weak to scream, but he was wrong. It was not a pretty sight, and the patrol took their sweet time burning them out.

Everyone knew that security's real reason for patrolling the beach was to keep the people from feeding themselves. The Director passed rumors of black market fishing harvests that he said threatened the economy of Pandora. Boggs hadn't seen sign of these harvests yet, nor had he seen any sign of an economy. His mother's tiny radio taught him the word, but to him it would always be just a word.

A pyre smoldered to his left. Three small lumps of char lay atop a ring of rock, slightly higher than high tide. The poor couldn't even muster enough fuel to burn their dead. When enough of them accumulated, the security patrols amused themselves by flaming them with gushguns. They called it nerve runner practice.

Someone guarded the pyre on the other side of the rocks, and when Boggs edged closer he could see that it was Silva. He stopped and caught his breath. Silva was a girl his own age, and the rumors said that she had killed her younger sisters and brother while they slept. No one raised a hand against her now as she tended their pitiful fire. Boggs hoped she wouldn't see him. He needed bait, but he knew he couldn't fight for it.

He got down on all fours and crawled to the edge of the heap. He reached a hand up, felt around the hot rocks until he touched something that didn't feel like rock. He jerked, jerked harder and something came off in his hand. It was hot and peeling on one side, cold on the other. He couldn't bring himself to look, he just grabbed his cane and scuttled away. Silva hadn't seen him.

"I'll bring her a fish," he promised himself. "I'll catch fish for mother and the boys, and one for Silva."

The quartertide patrol was nowhere to be seen.

They've gone through already, he thought. *They've gone through and checked the licenses and now they're up the beach checking for caches in the rocks.*

Boggs stood apart from the other fishermen. They might turn him in because he was catching fish that were rightfully theirs. They might steal his fish and line, and beat him as they had beaten his father once....

... *But they'll wait until I have the fish,* he thought. *That's what I'd do.*

He hunkered down against the jetty so that he was barely visible from the shore, tied a rock onto his line and baited the hooks from the charred mess he clasped in his fist.

"It's bait," he reminded himself, "it's just bait."

He didn't have enough energy to plunk his bait out very far, so he left it on the bottom about a half dozen meters from the rocks. It was deep there, deep enough to take most of his line. He gave a tug now and then to make sure it was free. There was enough bait for two, possibly three more tries.

"You got a license, boy?" The gruff voice behind him startled him, but he was too weak to move. He didn't say anything.

"You're late getting out here if you got a license. You only get one day, can't afford to waste it."

Some rocks clacked together as the man stepped down to where Boggs sat wedged into a cleft. He was skinny and sallow, with a wisp of a beard on his chin and no hair on his head. The skin on the top of his head was peeling and sores dotted his face.

"I'm an illegal, too," the old man said. "Figured it was my last chance. You?" "Same."

He reached across Boggs, fingered the bait and put it down with a grunt.

"Same's me." The voice was lower than illegal, it was ashamed.

Suddenly Boggs's line went tight, then tighter, then it nearly jerked his arms out of their sockets.

"You got one, boy," the old man said. In his excitement, his voice rose and his cracked lips got wet. "You sure got one, boy. I'll help …"

"No!" Boggs wrapped the line around his wrist and levered it in about a meter. "No, it's mine!"

Whatever it was, it was big and strong enough that it didn't have to surface to fight. But Boggs kept making slow progress, levering the stubs of his feet against a boulder and putting his skinny back into the pull. He figured he had about two meters to go but he couldn't see anything for the black spots swimming across his eyes. He heard the old man grunt in surprise and scramble up the rocks behind him and when he had nothing left to pull with Boggs just lay there, wedged in the rock, his precious line tangled around both arms.

The water broke with a rush in front of him, and whatever he had hooked lunged for him and caught him by the ankles. The grip was firm, and human. It laughed.

"You caught a big one, boy!" it bellowed. "Can you show me your license?" Another laugh.

"Are you … are you … ?"

"Security?" the voice asked, pulling him closer to the water, cutting his skinny buttocks on the rock. "You bet your ass, boy. Let's see that license."

Hand over hand the security pulled Boggs closer. Face to face, Boggs could see the breathing device dangling from his dive suit and the black hair draining over his bulging forehead.

"You ain't got one, do you?" He picked Boggs up and gave him a shake.

Every bone in his dried-up body rattled.

"*Do you?*"

"No, no … I …"

"Stealing food from people's mouths? You think you have the right to decide who'll live and who'll die? Only the Director has that right. Well, fishbait, I'll show you where the big ones are."

With that the man stuck his mouthpiece between his lips, pinned the boy's arms against his chest and fell backward with him into the sea.

Boggs coughed once at the tickle of water in his nose, then choked as it exploded into his frail lungs. He saw nothing but light overhead where it fanned out from the surface, and the bubbles from his mouth where they joined it like a blossom to its stem.

Chapter 36

Kill therefore with the sword of wisdom the doubt born of ignorance that lies in your heart. Be one in self-harmony and arise, great warrior, arise.
—from Zavatan *Conversations with the Avata*, Queets Twisp, elder

A SILENT Twisp and muttering Mose gathered the spore-dust of the two fulfilled hylighters into their bags and trudged their loads to the high reaches. Twisp had spent little time with the monks lately but they were generally an unsuspicious lot who seemed accustomed to his comings and goings. Few of them knew of his work with the Shadows, though if others knew he was certain they still would not interfere.

The carnage below would not reach them, experience had taught him this. Twisp tossed back his mantle, tucked up his sleeves and enjoyed his foray into the sun. For these few hours, at least, he could put aside the messages and codes and other accoutrements of his secret life. Today he might be called on to make a decision or give an order that might change Pandora forever. Until that hour, he wanted to feel Pandora's sunlight and the feminine breezes of the high reaches.

He and Mose sweated in the spore-dust gathering, and sweat plastered the fine blue dust to their hot skins. The soul of Avata, bound up in the dust, leaked its way into his pores. Twisp's body picked its way up the trail, oblivious to the way his mind raced the kelpways of the past.

He who controls the present controls the past, a voice in his mind told him, *and he who controls the past controls the future.*

It was something he'd read in the histories, but he'd also heard it before from the invisible mouth of the kelp.

Avata controls the past, he thought. *It maps the voyage of our past, our genetic past, which helps us to plot a true course for our future.*

He watched his feet fall, one in front of the other, without the expense of thought. They stepped over sharp stones, sidestepped a flatwing, all without interference from what most people called the mind. It was as if he were a being watching another being, but from within.

Cheap entertainment, he thought, and smiled.

Mose hummed a tune behind him, one that Twisp did not recognize. He wondered where the young monk's mind voyaged, to bring him such a tune. He had too much respect for another man's reverie to ask him.

Each contact with the kelp or the spore-dust had taken Twisp deeper into the details of humanity and deeper into his own past. Yes, the loss of a love was painful and it seemed no less painful replayed. Most of these memories exhilarated him, like the one of nuzzling his mother's breast for the first time, the taste of the sweet milk and the coo of her voice over him, in the background the *swish-swoosh, swish-swoosh* of her Islander heart.

Twice the kelp had taken him further than that, into the past of his ancestors, into the void from which humanity itself had sprung. Twisp acquired something more than a history lesson on these voyages. He acquired wisdom, the insight of sages, a separateness from the worldly machinations of people like Flattery. This was why the Director eventually discouraged, then finally forbade the kelp ritual.

"Do you want your children to know your most secret thoughts, your desires, all those dreams you couldn't tell them?" he would ask.

This warned Twisp far more about Flattery's depth of paranoia than it did of the dangers of the kelp.

Flattery successfully discouraged most Pandorans, at least the ones dependent on his settlements and his handouts. His isolation of a kelp neurotoxin made the people even more cautious. His development of an antidote became popular, since contact with the kelp was virtually unavoidable in many traditional professions.

It could've been a placebo, Twisp thought. *What people expect the kelp to do to their minds is pretty much what occurs.*

The brief Pandoran ritual of giving their dead up to the kelp had been all but abandoned. Now the dead were burned, their memories dissipated with smoke to the winds. This Flattery encouraged with his simple plea for hygiene.

"Decomposing bodies wash up on the beaches," he said. "What little tideland we have stinks with the remains of our dead."

Twisp shook his head to clear it of Flattery, of the man's grating, nasal voice and supercilious manner. This was not the voyage he wished the dust to lead him down. He sought the deeper currents of history to address the problems of Flattery and hunger.

"Humans have enslaved humans for all time," he said to himself. "A new galaxy shouldn't require a new solution."

How had ancient humans broken the bonds of human-inflicted hunger?

With death, a voice in his mind told him. *Death freed the afflicted, or death freed them from the afflictor.*

Twisp wanted Pandorans to be better than that. Flattery's way was starvation, assassination, pitting cousin against cousin. The footprints Twisp sought in the dust must lead away from Flattery, not after him.

What good does it do for me to become him? We trade a tall murderer for a long-armed one.

By the time he and Mose lay their burdens down before the monks of the hylighter clan, Twisp felt no need for the ritual. He already swam the heady seas of kelp-memories. His mind waged a reluctant struggle against the babbling current.

His people around him babbled as they prepared the dust. Twisp made his mouth beg his leave and he perched atop his favorite outcrop alone. Behind him, other elders walked a line of kneeling Zavatans and spooned little heaps of blue dust onto outstretched tongues. They proceeded with waterdrums and chants, songs from Earth, from Ship, from their centuries of voyaging across Pandora and her seas.

Communicants met the dead, here in the aftermath of the blue dust. They traveled backward in time, raveling up memories that had been long forgotten. Some witnessed their parents' lives, or their grandparents'. A few, one or two, branched off into the greater memory of humanity itself, and these were the ones consulted for movement toward a rightness of being.

Twisp let the syncopated waterdrum lull him back to that first day he had felt the effects of the new kelp. Twenty-five years ago he first touched land, a prisoner of GeLaar Gallow. That was the day he and a few friends defeated Gallow's vicious guerrilla movement and ended a civil war. It was the day the hyb tanks splashed down from orbit and brought them Flattery.

It all happened atop a peak that the Pandorans now called Mount Avata, in honor of the kelp's role in their salvation. He had waited there for what he had expected to be his death at the hands of Gallow, the Merman guerrilla leader. The kelp brought him a vision then of a bearded carpenter named Noah. Noah was blind, and mistook Twisp for his grandson, Abimael. He fed the hungry Twisp a sweet cake, and down all the years since then Twisp had remembered the fine taste of that sticky-sweet cake.

"Go to the records and look up the histories," Noah told him.

Twisp had done just that, and it left him in awe of Noah, the kelp and that sunny day on the Mount.

"This new ark of ours is out on dry land once and for all," Noah told him. "We're going to leave the sea."

Twisp had avoided the kelp since then, thinking only that he needed to let the affairs of Pandora go to the Pandorans and the affairs of Twisp to Twisp. Then the Director insinuated himself into the lives of the people. Their lives became Twisp's life, their pain his pain.

Twisp had studied well, read widely in the histories, and like any Islander he brought the hungry into his home. That home grew as the hunger grew into two homes, three homes, a settlement. Differences with the Director drove them to their perch in the high reaches and to secretly make fertile the rocky plains upcoast, away from Flattery's henchmen. Now, in the grip of the spore-dust, Twisp saw the intricacy of what he'd wrought, and the strength.

A small voice came to him as the dust was distributed to others. It was a voice of the world of Noah, one that he had never expected to hear, even within his own mind.

"Fight hunger with food," it told him. "Fight darkness with light, illusion with illumination." It was a tiny voice, nearly a whisper.

"Abimael," he said. "You are here at last. How did you find me?"

"The scent of the sweet cake," Abimael said. "And the strong call of a good heart."

Twisp swept past Abimael in the headlong tumble down the kelpways of his mind. He was out of the fronds, now, out of the peripheral vines and into the mainstem of kelp.

This hylighter must have come from a grandfather stand, he thought. *It is a wonder that they still escape Flattery's shears.*

"It is not wonder, elder, but illusion."

The voice that Twisp heard was not from inside. He turned slowly, remembering the young Mose. It was then that he noticed Mose's hand on his arm.

"You travel this vine, too, my cousin?"

"I do."

At no time did Mose move his lips. His pupils dilated and constricted wildly, and Twisp knew that his own did likewise. He'd looked into a mirror once after taking the dust, and fallen into places he'd rather not remember.

"I remember them …" Mose began.

Twisp interrupted him, concentrating only on what Mose said of illusion. This interruption, too, was spoken without lips.

"You said, 'illusion,'" Twisp reminded him. "What has the kelp shown you of illusion?"

"It is a language this hylighter spoke when it grew on the vine," Mose said. "It learned to cast illusion like a hologram. Elder, if you follow the vine of this thought to its root, you will know the power of illusion."

Suddenly Twisp's mind cartwheeled deeper into itself.

No, he thought, *not deeper into* my *mind. Deeper into* Avata's.

"Yes, this way," a soft voice coaxed.

Twisp looked back on his body as though from a great height, incurious about the shell of himself, then he turned onward into the void.

What is illusion, what is real? he asked.

"What is a map," the voice replied. "Is it illusion, or is it real?"

Both, he thought. It is both real—something that can be held and felt—and illusion, or symbol, or representation. *The map is not the territory.*

"You, fisherman, if you want to build a boat, what do you do first?"

Draw a plan, he thought.

"And the plan is not the boat, but it is real. It is a real plan. What do you do next?" Visions of all the boats he had built, or fished on, or coveted floated through his mind. Next … He tried to concentrate, tried to remember where it was that Avata was leading him. "Don't think about that," the voice chided. "After the plan, what next?"

Build a model, he thought.

"It, too, is not the boat. It is a model. It is illusion, it is symbol, and it is real. If you would get a man to live a certain way, how might you do that?"

Give him a model of behavior?

"Perhaps."

Map out his life?

"Perhaps."

A moment of silence, and Twisp detected the distinct pulse of the sea in the pause. The voice went on.

"But a map, a model—these have a basic limitation. What is this limitation?"

Twisp felt his mind bursting at its seams. Avata was forcefeeding him something, something important. If he could only grasp …

Size!

Whether it came to him intuitively, or whether the kelp provided him with the answer, the effect was the same.

It's size! You can never know truly from a model how it will feel because you can't live in it. You can't try it on for size!

He felt an immense sigh inside himself.

"Exactly, friend Twisp. But if you could make the illusion life-size, the lesson, too, would be life-size, would it not?"

Suddenly he was thrust back in his spore-dust memory and saw the old Pandora through the eyes of one of his bloodied ancestors fighting the Clone Wars. He saw the immensity of Ship blacken out the sky, and heard that final message ring in his mind: "Surprise me, Holy Void." Ship's voice was not the electronic monotone he'd expected. Its voice was relieved, even gleeful, as it made its farewell pass across both suns and disappeared without a sound. It sounded much like the voice he'd been hearing inside his own head.

"Ship unburdened itself of us when it headed out for the Holy Void," Twisp whispered to himself. "To live to our fullest potential we have to learn how to unburden ourselves of ourselves."

One more thing nagged at the back of his mind. He didn't know whether he said it aloud or not, but he knew that Mose, at least, heard him out.

"We have to learn to cast illusion like a spell," Twisp heard himself say. "To capture an enemy without inflicting harm will take a carefully spun illusion."

Somewhere in his mind he thought he detected a grunt of approval.

Chapter 37

We Islanders understand tides and current and flow. We understand that conditions and times change. To change, then, is normal.

—Ward Keel, *The Apocryphal Notebooks*

NEWSBREAK SHOULD air within the hour, but Beatriz knew that this team would not make their deadline. They were having some kind of transmission problem that they refused to share with her, but she saw the results on her screens. Whenever their tape was ready for its burst groundside, a review showed that it had been tampered with. Someone seemed to be editing the editors. It was just as well. Leon told her that the short clip she prepared on the OMC would not be transmitted groundside for approval, anyway.

She recalled an incident several years ago, when Current Control was still undersea in a Merman compound. They were taping one of Flattery's "spiritual hours," a propagandistic little chat with the people of Pandora. All went well until transmission time.

The kelp interfered, that was the only answer at the time—and an unpopular one. The kelp jammed broadcasts, made deletions on tapes …

The hair on her neck prickled at the thought. She remembered how, finally, it edited tapes and changed the chronology of broadcasts, flipped images and voiceover around to make Flattery look like a fool and make the broadcast adhere more closely to the truth.

Mack and I wired a lot of kelp fiber into this system, she thought.

Any delay suited Beatriz just fine. She needed more time to figure out how to say on the air what wasn't in the script without getting herself and others killed. They would only trust her with a token appearance, she would have to make the most of it when the time came. Most Pandorans, even the poor, listened in on radio. She wanted to reach them all. She hoped it wasn't just hysteria that told her the kelp was on her side.

If there's a coup in progress, who's at the bottom of it?

She ticked off the likely suspects: any of several board members of Merman Mercantile, the Shadows, displaced Islanders, Brood—probably acting for someone else from Vashon Security Forces …

Or maybe the Zavatans, she thought, though she knew it was not their drift. Their response to political trouble was to dig in deeper, to flee farther into the high reaches or the formidable upcoast regions.

Brood's an opportunist, she thought. *The killings at the launch site were a mistake, and he's trying to make the best of it. If there is an organized coup, he'll wait and throw in with whoever seems to be winning.*

Beatriz realized that Flattery had no friends and damned few allies. Everyone had good reason for hating him. He had come to Pandora sporting his savior's cap when the very planet had turned on them, and then *he* turned on them.

"I am your Chaplain/Psychiatrist," he'd told them, "I can restructure your world, and I can save you all. Your children deserve better than this."

Why did everyone believe him?

Her years at HoloVision gave her the answer. He was on the air daily, either in person or via his "motivational series," a collection of tapes that she had not seen as propagandistic until now. She had even helped produce several, including her recent upbeat series on the Voidship. Everyone believed him because Flattery kept them too busy to do otherwise.

Flattery had become the most formidable demon in a world of demons, only he was human. Worse yet, he was *pure* human, without any of the kelp genes and other genetic tinkerings that Pandorans had endured at the mercy of previous Chaplain/Psychiatrists for centuries. Beatriz knew this now. He did it with their help, with her help. Though trapped, she felt an exhilaration at the notion that Brood's men couldn't shoot a clear signal groundside. They might need her yet.

If I do this show as written, I'll be helping him again.

She realized what it was she was helping Flattery to do. She wasn't helping him rescue a world in geological and social flux. She wasn't helping him resettle the homeless Islanders whose organic cities broke up on the rocks of the new continents, or rescue Mermen whose undersea settlements had broken like crackers at the recent buckling of the ocean floor.

I'm helping him escape, she thought. *He's not building this "Tin Egg" to explore the nearby stars. It's his personal lifeboat.*

She cursed under her breath and smacked the console in front of her, but gently, gently. She might need it later. The reflection that bounced back from her screen was of a woman she didn't recognize. The hair color was black, cropped and shaggy like her own, but the haunted brown eyes of her reflection stared out of bloodshot sclera, surrounded by two dark hollows that frightened her. Her nose was red and her complexion pasty for one so dark. Out of reflex she reached for a com-line to call Nephertiti to makeup, then stopped. Nephertiti would never brush her hair again, never again whisper in her ear at the countdown: "You're gorgeous, B, knock 'em out!"

She put her forehead to the console in despair. Leon glanced her way, but busied himself trying to iron out the glitch with transmissions to the groundside studio. He and his men were unfamiliar with the zero-gee of the

Orbiter's axis, and every small task that required movement seemed to anger them more.

Beatriz knew her performance as written would be helping Brood, too, and this was more than she could bear. He was overseeing the delivery of the OMC to its crypt aboard the Voidship and mercifully out of her sight. If Leon didn't get past the jamming influence on their burst channel, Brood would be back, and he would be mad. She didn't relish the thought of Brood in a tantrum.

Dwarf MacIntosh was a blue-eyed clone from hyb, and one of only two "normal" humans on Pandora. Beatriz was a near-normal Islander. Mutations had leveled off over the past few generations and most Islanders, though shorter and darker, appeared as normal as MacIntosh and Flattery. Mermen were very different kinds of humans, and Swimmers were the most extreme surviving mutation. Appearances, among Pandorans, had dictated their lives from the start.

Flattery's not normal, she thought. *His mind is a mutation, an abomination. Humans should not trample their own kind.*

She knew the history of slavery Earthside, and members of her own family lived with the aftermath of the genetic slavery of Jesus Lewis, another direct clone of a "normal." Today she woke at last to Ben's accusations that Flattery had enslaved Pandora, Mermen and Islanders alike, and his grip only got tighter while the people got hungrier.

The past twenty-five years had been a cumulative string of disasters planetwide: The sea bottom had fractured along a kelp root line to form the first strip of land. More such fractures followed, always along the gigantic roots of kelp beds. The consequent upheavals destroyed dozens of Merman settlements down under and caused the sinking or deliberate grounding of most of the floating organic cities of the Islanders, her own among them. Refugees swarmed to the primitive coastal settlements by the thousands, forced to learn to survive again on land after nearly three centuries on or under the sea. Flattery had not eased their burden, only added to it.

"This whole planet's trying to kill us," Mack had told her the first time they talked, "we don't need to give it a hand."

But Mack took no action against Flattery. He put all of his waking hours and a good number of his dreaming hours into perfecting the Orbiter station as a jump-off point to the stars. He did this while directing Current Control and becoming the world's expert on its most mysterious resident, the kelp. He worked backward to define his priorities.

"We need Current Control," he said. "The kelp is fascinating, but reality dictates that we get supplies through it or people die. Controlling the kelp makes this project easier, it makes settlement life easier, it guarantees results."

That was when he invented the Gridmaster, which bypassed the undersea multibuilding complex of the Mermen's Current Control and allowed the major grid system to be operated from orbit. The Merman complex undersea had sustained heavy damage, but it still carried the hardware and installed new grids. With the Gridmaster in operation, one person could handle all of the kelpways in the richest of Pandora's hemispheres.

Beatriz had stood at Mack's side two years ago as his special guest the day the Gridmaster went on-line. Though officially a HoloVision correspondent for the event, Beatriz liked to believe that there had been more to Mack's invitation than the business at hand. The spark of his blue eyes lit unmistakably in her presence, and they had enjoyed long talks floating through the axis of Orbiter nights and reclining in the webworks. What had begun as the opportunistic brush of hands against hands became a full-fledged love affair.

I hope we get another chance, she thought, and sighed to head off tears.

A red flash above the hatchway startled her, then flashed again. The studio equivalent of a doorbell alerted each console throughout the room. The studio was always locked when taping a show.

Someone wants in.

Whoever was out there was not one of Brood's men. She knew this because of the fear that bloomed in pale petals across Leon's face.

It's Mack, she thought. *It's got to be!*

"Don't move!" Leon ordered. He unsnapped his harness and pointed a commanding finger at her. "I'll handle this. Your text will be onscreen in a few blinks. Standard cues. I'm remote director and you will follow my lead most carefully."

He handed himself to the hatch, plugged in his headset and pressed the intercom key. "We're taping," he announced. "No admittance except for studio personnel."

Beatriz held her breath. Though they did seal off for tapings and live broadcast, HoloVision had always encouraged an audience. Many workers aboard the Orbiter enjoyed spending their free time watching her crew at work, and they had never been prohibited before.

"It's Spud Soleus." The high voice crackled her own headset in its characteristic way, forcing a smile to her lips. "Current Control. We have an emergency situation over there. Dr. MacIntosh needs to talk with Beatriz Tatoosh right away."

She felt a rush in her chest and color rising in her cheeks. Her palms continued to sweat. "She's going on the air live. Tell Dr. MacIntosh it'll have to wait."

"It can't wait. Our burst line has failed and a chunk of grid's down."

"We have orders," Leon said. His voice sounded hesitant. "Maybe after the show …"

"Dr. MacIntosh is Orbiter Command," Soleus said. "He has direct orders from Flattery to open that grid now. We need your burst line for a transmission. We need Beatriz Tatoosh for advice. I'm reminding you that all power relays switch through Current Control and we can shut you down."

"Wait a blink," Leon said, his voice calming, "I'll see what we can do." He switched off the intercom and pressed his forehead against the bulkhead.

"Shit!" he said, and bumped his forehead against the plasteel. His headset kept him from cartwheeling backward across the studio. "Shit!"

Good for Spud! Beatriz thought. He'd lied to Leon about the circuitry. Some, but not all, was routed through Current Control. She and MacIntosh had set up the studio, and no one knew it better. But Leon didn't know that. Besides, he had enough problems. And Leon didn't dare move without orders from Brood. He couldn't alert Brood without alerting the entire Orbiter.

Beatriz's heart tripped hard against her ribs and she blotted her damp palms against the thighs of her jumpsuit. In spite of the danger, she enjoyed Leon's dilemma.

Anything to make them squirm, she thought.

Leon tripped the intercom switch again.

"No one's coming in here until after—"

"We can transmit on your burst line with our own carrier frequency," Spud said. "We don't even need to get in your way. Dr. MacIntosh is in charge here and he said—"

Leon slapped the switch off, unplugged his headset and thrust himself back toward his editing cubby. He crashed, out of control, into the other two techs. They disentangled limbs and cables, then hovered over each of his shoulders and whispered together heatedly.

Beatriz slipped the two meters to the hatch and plugged in her headset. She switched the intercom back on and left the set to float beside the hatch only a couple of meters away. They didn't see her, and the move took fewer than four seconds by the big chronometer.

Back at her console, Beatriz opened her com-line and punched out Mack's number. The telltale light would flash on consoles in each of the editing cubbies, this she knew. As she expected, it brought Leon to her nose to nose in a red-faced fury.

"I told you not to try anything!" Leon snapped. He was no longer the meek videotech at an editing console. Now he was ranking officer of a security assault squad that was in a tight spot.

"I'd slap the shit out of you if we didn't need your pretty face. We do have a backup plan, sister. Try that again and you'll get your own ride out the shuttle airlock—understand?"

Beatriz had to hide a smile for the first time all day. He'd yelled at her—something that would have gone unheard elsewhere in the Obiter if she hadn't opened the intercom first, if she hadn't plugged in the headset just a step from where Leon stood. It did not take the best of her screen abilities to feign the terror that she'd already felt many times since waking this day.

"I'll do what you say," she said, as loud as she dared. "I don't want to die like the others. I'll do what you say."

Leon pushed back to his companions, but before he reached them the general alarm sounded with four long bursts from a klaxon overhead.

Though startled by the noise, Beatriz was overjoyed. She recognized the signal from exercises in the past. Those four blasts meant "Fire, total involvement, Current Control sector." That sector included the HoloVision studio.

While Leon and the other two flurried around the studio, asking each other, "What the hell's going on?" Beatriz whispered to herself, "Spud, I love you."

Chapter 38

Power, like any other living being, will go to infinite lengths to maintain itself.

—Ward Keel, *The Apocryphal Notebooks*

THE FIRST thing Rico saw when he stepped through the hatchway into the galley was the still, open-eyed form of Crista Galli lying in her harness beside the plaz. Her pupils pulsed with a green brightness that Rico had never noticed before, and somehow he knew that whatever she saw now was not of this world. His first impulse was to run, to lock the hatch behind him, but he checked it.

Ben sprawled on the deck beside her, one hand clutching her ankle and his legs quivering like a child's in a nightmare. To Rico, the whole scene was a nightmare.

"Ben!" he called from the hatchway, but Ben didn't answer. He rushed to his best friend's side and saw that Ben's eyes, too, were open. Both of them were breathing, though Crista Galli's head was bent slightly forward and he heard a gurgle with each passage of air. Rico heeded Operations' warnings and didn't touch either one of them.

"Shit!" he snapped, and fumbled in his left breast pocket for a slapshot. It was a red, tiny ampule about the size of the end of his little finger. Two needles jutted from one end, covered by a plastic case. He flipped the cover across the galley, careful to hold the prongs away from his own body.

"Dammit, Ben, Operations said this toxin might be triggered if she got wet."

This shot was titrated for his own body weight, the one he'd most hoped never to use. In one swift jab he stuck it into Ben's thigh.

"Don't stop breathing, man," Rico begged. "Just don't stop breathing."

He turned to Crista Galli, trying to control the sudden flash of anger burning in his chest. He knew it was more frustration than hate, but his body didn't know the difference.

If she killed him …

The better part of his reason wouldn't let him finish the thought.

A strangled moan surged from Crista's throat, an otherworldly moan that put the hair up on the back of Rico's neck.

"Crista? Can you hear me?"

Rico saw that she had some ability to move. She turned her hands palm upward in a gesture of helplessness, and her lips kept trying to form the words that wouldn't come.

"Flattery …"

The word was barely intelligible. She still looked straight ahead, and in a dreamlike slow motion finished her effort with, "… drugs."

"Flattery gave you drugs?"

She blinked her eyes once, slowly.

"He gave you drugs to make you toxic? It's not the kelp?"

Again, the slow blink and a nearly imperceptible nod.

The *Flying Fish* took another lurch that sprawled Rico across the deck. He grabbed for a handhold and pressed himself against the bulkhead as the foil rolled onto its side, then righted.

The foil's metal skin shrieked as something twisted it to its limits, then backed off. *The kelp's pulling us apart,* he thought. *It knows she's in here!*

Crista was strapped in just as Ben must have left her, soaking wet, her disguise discarded. Rico made a jump for the seat next to her and strapped in just as the foil righted again and all was quiet, as though the kelp had one last spasm run through it before it could relax.

He checked Ben over as best he could without touching him. He was breathing easily and his color was good. There was some movement of his right hand toward Crista, and Rico thought this was a good sign. He gingerly opened Ben's left breast pocket and brought out the other slapshot for Crista. Her eyelids did a fast flutter-dance that seemed voluntary, and her left hand raised just a tiny bit at the fingertips, as though to push him away.

Rico hesitated with the shot, and the fluttering stopped.

What if it's not … the Tingle? he asked himself. Operations had warned him that the antidote itself might be fatal if administered needlessly to one of them. Maybe it would be fatal if given to her at all.

If Flattery's been giving her something, maybe her body's different, he thought. *Maybe the antidote would … kill her.*

It was tempting to go ahead anyway, after what she'd done to his partner. No one would know, not even Ben. He readied himself to deliver it and her eyes went into their flutter again and her fingers made those pushing movements.

But Flattery would like that, he thought. *There's nothing more that he would like than being able to tell the world that Her Holiness Crista Galli died in the hands of the Shadows.*

The whole fiction began to unreel in his mind, clearly illumined all of a sudden against the backdrop of light that began to fill the galley's plaz.

"Of course," he said to her, "it makes sense. He made you toxic so that no one would go near you. Then he went public and blamed this on your … relationship with the kelp, am I right?"

Again, the barely perceptible nod and the slow blink. She seemed relieved, more relaxed, and he didn't think it was the toxin working.

A sudden burst of light filled the galley and the foil began to lurch rhythmically. They were on the surface, and Elvira would be going out there to clear the intakes. At each lurch a tiny cry escaped Crista's throat, and tears streaked her cheeks. For the first time he felt as though he wanted to comfort her. He was just beginning to imagine how terrible and secret her life in the Preserve must have been.

She was a curiosity, a prisoner, he thought, *and he made her a monster.*

"Did this ever happen to you … before Flattery gave you drugs?" Her eyes flicked side to side.

"I think that he thought that your toxin would kill us. Then he would get you back and be a hero, warning the world again about how dangerous you are. And if I gave you this shot," he placed the unopened ampule carefully into his pocket, "then you would die and he would tell the world how we killed you. That would turn the world against us for sure …"

She blinked a "yes," and Rico heard a moan from Ben.

The intercom charged again, then Elvira asked, "Rico, everybody OK?"

Ben's mouth struggled to speak, then he gave up and managed a slight nod. Crista, too, nodded and squeezed out a slow "Yesss."

"Slapshot time," Rico said to the intercom. "They're not great, but improving. I'm all you've got right now. You going out for a little swim?"

"Thought I would. Best watch the helm."

"On my way," he said. He reassured himself that both Crista and Ben were safe, and that neither of them could be hurt where they lay.

"I'll leave the intercom charged," he told them. "Talk to me once in a while, even if it's a grunt, OK? I'll be back when Elvira's finished out there."

Crista raised her fingertips again, and wrenched out a couple of words. "Kelp … happy."

"The kelp is happy?" He threw his hands in the air, and spoke with undisguised sarcasm. "Then *I'm* happy. How the hell do you know?"

She turned her palm up like a shrug. "Free—dom," she said, and repeated the word more slowly, "free—dom."

A glance out the plaz showed him what appeared to be an infinite expanse of kelp lazing in the last of both afternoon suns. Alki, the small, distant sun, had begun a slow pulse almost a year ago and it was pulsing now. A very large, very black cloud was closing from seaward toward them. An occasional kelp frond rose slowly, then fell back with a slap and a splash.

Like a wot in a bathtub, he thought. He had never seen the kelp play like this before.

"I hope you're right," he said. "I truly hope you're right. It will make life so much easier for us, and so much harder for Flattery's people."

He resisted the temptation to pat her shoulder and Ben's. "We're going to get you out of this, buddy," he said to Ben.

He kept talking, more to himself than to Ben, as he hurried out the hatchway to the helm. He spoke to Ben over the intercom as he reviewed his instruments, as much for his own comfort as his partner's.

"I hate to say it," Rico said, "but I think Current Control saved our butts. The kelp got us down here, wherever here is, and then started tearing at the cabin with those huge vines. Current Control must have been trying to get the original channel back, because the kelp was obviously fighting some kind of impulse. Either they blew a fuse or they gave the kelp its head completely. Whatever, it was the right thing to do."

He resumed his instrument checkout.

"That electrical pulse through the kelp must have screwed up our Navcom system," Rico said. "Most everything else looks OK. I closed off cooling outlets to the galley to head off that leak, just in case it's ready to pop someplace else. You two might get a little warm there between the engines. Once we're airborne, I'll figure a way to get you both up here."

He finished the checkout and realized that they wouldn't be getting airborne after all. Not unless Elvira could remanufacture the hydraulics that withdrew their hydrofoils and extended airfoils.

Ben doesn't need to know that now, he thought. *For that matter, neither do I.* "Speak to me, buddy. Anything."

"Rico … OK."

It came out loud and clear, though painfully slow, but it was enough to put a smile on Rico's face. He felt Elvira tugging kelp out of the inlets and tried the Navcom again. It was dead, not even a burst of static from the speakers.

"Squall's coming in," he told Ben, "things might get rough again pretty soon."

He didn't want to tell Ben that they were going to get really rough, now that they couldn't get above the storm. Without the Navcom, and with the kelp glutting up the ocean as far as the eye could see, Rico himself didn't want to think about how rough it was going to get.

Chapter 39

Anyone who threatens the mind or its symbolizing endangers the matrix of humanity itself.

—Ward Keel, *The Apocryphal Notebooks*

BEN HAD heard the boat's ballast blow as he stroked Crista's hair and cheek under the fine spray of the pinpoint galley leak. He remembered the taste of salt when his lips brushed her hair. Because of the taste of salt from the interior bulkhead he knew it was a cooling pipe leak, recycled seawater, nothing to worry about now that they were headed topside.

He remembered that he and Crista had been talking, laughing, when suddenly his upper body began to tingle. His neck wouldn't move his head where it wanted to go. He tried to cry out but his mouth and throat wouldn't work. Crista slumped against her harness, limp, her eyes wide with fear and their green irises darkening nearly to blue.

Oh, no, he remembered thinking. *Oh, no, they were right.*

In lurching, spastic movements he lunged against Crista, sprawling across her legs. She had let out a little cry of surprise, but didn't resist. Ben saw that she couldn't. Whatever was happening to him was also happening to her. He had the advantage of more body mass, more muscle, so it was taking his body longer to shut down.

He grabbed for Crista's harness to pull himself up but his hands turned to two heavy rocks at the ends of his arms. Within a blink he collapsed against her. He was able to see and breathe but trying to move only produced uncontrollable spasms. He slid down the couch to the deck into a position that didn't allow him to watch Crista. One of his hands remained on her ankle, and he felt her body spasm and relax much like his own. The antidote was in his pocket, and he couldn't make his body work well enough to dig it out.

Rico will think I'm a fool, he thought.

Now that they'd lost their Navcom they couldn't function undersea, and they'd be bobbing squawks on the surface. Rico would have his hands full enough without this … mess.

Elvira's got a few tricks, he thought.

Ben felt the Tingle rush like a hot blush down his back, out his shoulders and thighs. He tried to control his muscles again but couldn't. He was a helpless, quivering heap on the deck. He remembered feeling more betrayed than careless. Then he started traveling the convolutions of Crista's mind. Rico, the galley around them, the rest of the real universe played through a dark curtain that backdropped Crista's thoughts and memories. These images from her life unreeled in his brain.

"Ben!" Rico said, his small voice rising to Ben from a great depth. He said more but Ben heard only the snap of the antidote against his singlesuit. He felt nothing but the Tingle throughout his body, but he was fully aware of Rico stretching him out on the deck.

Time rippled like a dark fabric strung between himself and Rico. The white and stainless steel of the galley blended into a great glowing halo of yellow panel that washed out everything behind the curtain of his mind.

Ben understood much, now. A near-infinity of human memories slept in Crista Galli's head. Now many of them buzzed in his own, like solvent to solute, a wet solution filling up a dry. He felt the dry blossom of his mind unfold as it drank, petal by intricate petal, and behind it the shadow that was Rico LaPush rippled back and forth.

Though he could see and hear, Ben felt a detachment from his body that was more curiosity to him than fear. He remembered the special show he'd done with Beatriz about people who returned from near-death, what they'd reported about this same detached feeling, this same comforting warmth that replaced all sensation in his skin except that Tingle. They said they'd viewed their bodies from certain vantage points in the room, watched the medics resuscitate them, remembered whole conversations that took place even when they showed no heartbeat on the monitor. They described watching the vital signs monitor with the same detached feeling that Ben had when he slumped to the deck.

His view, however, was distinctly from someone else's body, someone else's mind. This was a wot's mind, down under, looking upward toward the sun from the middle depths of a kelp lagoon. His range of vision was limited to straight ahead. It was slightly blurry and a light halo surrounded the rim above. Way up there, backlit by the glowing suns, he saw Rico's busy shadow. The lagoon was full of Swimmers, those legendary gilled humans, undulating in and out of channels above her.

This was Crista as a child. This was Ben as Crista as a child.

He sensed that Rico was very worried and he wanted to tell him, "It's OK, I'm here," but nothing would come out.

One Swimmer in particular attended her, an older female. Ben had never seen a Swimmer. He'd imagined them as grotesque, slimy creatures with wide mouths and stupid eyes, and rudimentary, ratlike tails. The female who attended Crista now was about his own age. Her red fan of gill fluttered furiously at her shoulders as she fed the girl slices of raw fish. Crista dangled from the kelp, and the Swimmer female came up to her from the deeps. She did not, or would not, speak.

From somewhere behind the halo, very far above Ben's upturned face, Rico's voice echoed, "I'm going to settle you here and keep you warm."

Ben felt the lagoon receding, and Rico's voice with it.

"Crista is still breathing," Rico said. "I don't know whether you can hear me or not, Ben, but we'll get you out of here. You'll be OK. The goddamned girl is OK. We're almost topside. We'll get you someplace." Rico's voice was tinged with hysteria, and he sounded close to tears. "We'll get you someplace, buddy, you just hang on." Then Rico was gone.

Ben found he could leave the womblike kelp, and if he imagined walking a corridor toward himself he became more aware of the galley, the foil around him. He felt he could walk a gossamer bridge between Crista's mind and his own.

A sudden dazzle of light in the galley and a change in the pitch of the foil told Ben that they had surfaced. Ben wondered whether he would die this way, fully conscious, feeling that last exhalation and unable to suck in air. He remembered the time that he and Rico almost drowned, when Guemes Island was sabotaged and sunk. He had nearly panicked then, but he felt no such panic now, simply a numb obedience to his fate.

He found himself wondering about things that should terrify him: would the neurotoxin, whatever it was, paralyze his breathing muscles? His heart muscle? He wished that Rico had propped him up a little to make it easier, though already the tingling had stopped.

The slapshot works, he thought.

He wanted to cross that gossamer bridge to Crista again, but he felt himself moving further away from the bridge and back into the foil, The deck under him was uncomfortable, and he found that he could squirm a little to change position. He was definitely improving. He'd been dimly aware of a voice coming in over the intercom, it was Rico's voice, and it came in again, sounding worried.

"Speak to me, buddy. Anything."

Ben tried his throat again. It was dry, and didn't want to work quite right, but he managed to squeeze out: "Rico … OK."

He heard Crista breathing, but she still hadn't stirred.

I wonder what happens to her?

"Squall's coming in," Rico announced, "things might get rough again pretty soon."

Ben wanted to laugh, tried to come back at Rico with, "Rough? What do you call *this*?" but it all came out a garble.

Chapter 40

The new ruler must inevitably distress those over whom he establishes his rule. So it happens that he makes enemies of all those whom he has injured in occupying the new principality, and yet he cannot keep the friendship of those who have set him up.

—Machiavelli, *The Prince*

FLATTERY SPURNED the safety of his quarters for a brazen tour in the sunshine topside. Nevi and Zentz were on their mission and out of his way, the ragtag rebellion was failing under his security force, and he knew that whoever had Crista Galli had a big handful of trouble. He smiled widely to himself and turned his face to the sky. He loved the sky, the weather—how different from the controlled susurrations of Moonbase air! It was nearly time for the afternoon rain. Like the few previous survivors of hybernation who had been reared in the sterility of Moonbase, Flattery had a feeling for weather.

He chose a parapet that looked downcoast, across the Preserve and into the wretched village that spilled from his gate. A boil of black smoke fanned inland with the upcoming wind. Flattery wore his brightest red lounging jacket so that the vermin could see he was very much alive, still very much the Director. So close to the borders of battle—now they would see the mettle they tested!

The presence of two suns unnerved him, even after these many years. Information from his kelp studies, from his geologists, proved that they were ripping the planet's crust like so much flatbread. The worst was yet to come, and he didn't intend to wait around for it.

Ventana, one of his messengers, approached the walkway below him. "Reports on the kelpway disruption, Sir." She waved a messenger.

He signaled one of the guards, who inspected the device and then brought it to him. Flattery pulled his white hat farther down to shade his forehead. The wide-brimmed style was Islander, for political effect, and a white hat because Flattery believed that white placed him on the side of Truth and Justice at a glance. He did not retrieve the reports immediately. He knew what was inside: nothing. And by this time the afternoon cloud cover obscured an Orbiter view of the number eight sector.

His passion for weather did not include the suns' ravages of his uncooperative skin. Two pink blotches peeled on his forehead and Flattery tried not to scratch them. His personal physician had removed two such spots only a month ago, and now this.

The people have to see me, he thought. *There is no substitute for the proper exposure.*

His three most trusted bodyguards accompanied him at a distance, their Pandoran instincts keeping them ever on the move. His vantage point was a bluff overlooking the compound, the village and the bay. To his back were the only higher points for many klicks—the high reaches, home of the worthless Zavatans. A lot of these Zavatans, like the peasantry, believed in Ship and the eventual return of this Ship as some sort of mechanical messiah. The thought made him laugh, and his guards looked at him curiously.

"Stand down, gentlemen," he told them. "As you can see, there's nothing down there that can reach us."

"Begging the Director's pardon," one of the guards, Aumock, spoke up. "It's my job to never stand down."

Flattery nodded his approval. This one bears watching. "Very good," he said. "I appreciate your dedication."

Aumock, a Merman from good stock, didn't swell with the praise. He was already back to scanning the area for movement.

"Nothing up here but Zavatans," Flattery said.

"Are you sure they're nothing, sir?" Aumock replied.

This was the first time his guard had offered a comment in his ten-month tour of service at Flattery's side. Flattery merely grunted a response.

He had his suspicions about these Zavatans—always the same number of them appearing about, but seldom the same faces. Flattery was no fool. He was, after all, a Chaplain/Psychiatrist and had done impeccable study in the history of oppressed religions. He was uncomfortable with a nearby population that was potentially hostile, whose numbers seemed impossible to determine, and whose general fitness appeared far better than that of most of his security.

They actually run *up these cliffs*, he mused. *Why?*

Here, on the bare overlook above the Preserve, he reviewed the latest messages regarding the HoloVision foil and the curious rebellion of the largest stand of kelp in the region.

"So, Marta, do you really believe that they've turned back?" he asked.

His communications officer, a little plump for her regulation blue jumpsuit, managed a quick chew at her lip before responding. Flattery had bedded her once and recalled that her touch was far more satisfying than her looks. She'd been a slender young thing then—four, maybe five years ago. She had started as a bodyguard on his nightside detail, but showed a facility with electronics that impressed his engineers. When she requested a transfer, he granted it. The move headed off rumors and the inevitable discomfort of extracting himself from a sticky personal situation.

"I … I don't know," she said. "The device that I placed personally on their foil is working perfectly, and its course is consistent with a return to this—"

"Bah!" Flattery blurted. "They're not stupid. I insisted that you place the device on or inside her person and you took it upon yourself to place it elsewhere. A Current Control outpost has already confirmed the device to be aboard a crippled sub train dragging a few thousand kilos of dead fish."

Flattery enjoyed the stunned look that flattened her face. She looked small and pale now.

"I was afraid," she said. "I was afraid to touch her."

Marta hung her head as though expecting a blade. The merciless suns here on the bluff widened the circles of sweat forming under her armpits. It was that heavy, sticky time on the coast just before the rain squalls hit. He didn't have to sniff to smell the rain.

Flattery remembered that time with her on a hot afternoon like this, and their skins poured sweat. Tiny black hairs from his chest *had* stuck to her small white breasts and she laughed as she picked them off. She hadn't been so afraid of him then, just a little bit in awe, which made things easier.

"Dammit!" he muttered to himself. *Bitten by the fiction again.*

He drew himself up to his full height, nearly two heads taller than Marta.

"Didn't I assure you that it was safe?"

This he delivered in his most consoling voice.

She nodded, but still did not lift her head.

Flattery was very pleased with himself. If this woman who knew him so well was afraid of Crista, of what her touch might do, then these strangers must be terrified. Thanks to his foresight in the beginning and her daily "medications," Crista should be withdrawing violently by now, exhibiting the very symptoms attributed to her touch. Perhaps by now she'd be catatonic—something else he'd engineered to see that she was brought back to him.

The neurotoxin would be oozing from her every pore by now, and the fiction he had laid down so carefully for so long would become true. Everyone, particularly the enemy, would see it with their own eyes. Only he, the Director, could save her. Those Shadows would soon find themselves in the presence of a monster that they could not afford to keep.

The wonders of chemistry, he thought, and smiled. Aloud, he reassured Marta.

"I understand your fear," he said. "The important thing is that we were not fooled by their amateurish attempt at deception. What do you have to report on damage here?"

Both of them flinched at the simultaneous crackle of two lasguns, and Flattery turned to see that his guards had cooked a pair of hooded dashers closing from the direction of the high reaches.

"I wonder …"

He didn't finish the rest aloud. What he wondered was whether or not the Zavatans were training dashers.

"I want studies on dasher sightings coordinated with known Zavatan positions," he said.

Marta nodded and unholstered the electronic link at her side. The movement drew a subtle shift in Aumock's position. Marta didn't notice that his lasgun muzzle had focused on her head before the link cleared daylight. She clicked out her coded entry in her usual unhurried manner.

Flattery knew something of the Zavatans and their history, but not nearly as much as he'd like. They were patient, organized, and they scavenged everything. If rumor was correct, they grew illicit crops in the upcoast regions and distributed them among refugees. Flattery resented this because it seriously weakened his bargaining position with the masses. He did not have the manpower to police thousands of square kilometers of rugged countryside and complete Project Voidship at the same time. Project Voidship was infinitely more important.

He saluted approval as one of the men vaulted over the wall to fetch the dasher skins. *That much less for those Zavatans*, he thought.

He made a mental note to see what the lab would have to say about where the dashers had been, with whom, what they were eating, when and why.

"And your report on the fighting?" he asked.

"Compound perimeter is secure," she said.

Marta pressed the spot behind her right ear that activated the receive mode of her messenger implant.

"I'm getting a lot of interference here, don't know the cause. Minimal damage to the compound—the expected rubble but mostly cosmetic, as usual. Rocks and sticks are no match for lasguns. Prisoners are being held in the courtyard." She paused as more information fed into her messenger.

"Reports on the power station, the ferry terminal and the grid situation," he ordered.

Marta fed something into her messenger, then her expression changed. The facade of the impartial reporter wrinkled into concern at her brow, and she leaned forward as information vibrated her mastoid bone, washed through the fluids and hairs of her inner ear to her brain.

"There is a massive force congregating at the power station," she said. "The squad of security that attacked our detachment at the site has dug in and persisted. The refugee camp is less than a kilometer away. People from the camp are backing up the rebel squad, just out of lasgun range of our defense."

"Operation H," Flattery barked. "If they keep coming, have air support shift to the camp." Marta paled further. She lowered her voice so that the guards wouldn't hear.

"Operation H, sir … they'd see it from the camp. If you jelly the attackers, witnesses will know it wasn't a hylighter."

"Use an LTA," he said. "We have a few balloons in the hangar that look like hylighters. Get them into the air. We'll worry about witnesses later. I want that squad burned, I want anyone backing them up burned. Is that understood?"

Marta nodded, and her fingers flicked the orders across her instrument.

"The ferries?"

"Operational, sir. The current shift reported on time. Casualties high, but replacements are already on-site receiving training. The OMC launch lit off and docked at Orbiter station, no update. Current Control terminated their signal to the kelp in sector eight, there is no grid but no aggressive activity."

"Terminated?"

Flattery regretted the lie to MacIntosh. He was sure that the kelp would yield, given the full electrical prod long enough. He had never thought that MacIntosh would terminate the signal.

Idiot! What could he be thinking, giving the kelp its head. Doesn't he know how much we need those kelpways open?

He inhaled one long, slow breath, half in the left nostril, half in the right. He let it out just as slowly.

"Is it working?" he asked.

"A few merchant vessels lost," she said. "Most have surfaced, making repairs. They will not fare well in the storm."

"Order Dr. MacIntosh to reestablish the kelpways, or I will do it my way from here. He has one hour."

"Yes, sir."

Flattery's mood blackened. Two small explosions and a flash came from the center of Kalaloch. He signaled one of his guards.

"Have security get what they can from the leaders of this rabble. I don't expect much. Then have the rest of them staked in the open." He surveyed the cliffside behind him that led to the high reaches. "Have them staked up there," he said, "so that everyone below can study the results of their decision in detail. It shouldn't take long."

What Marta had told him about the kelp interested him the most. He'd fabricated such an intricate web of deception about Crista Galli that Flattery himself had difficulty remembering which was his masterful illusion and which reality. His earliest warnings to keep her from any contact with the kelp was based more on hunch than data, but it was clear to him now that his hunch had been good.

The kelp could actually smell her!

"I ordered Current Control to opt for a surgical solution," Marta said. "They have one hour to achieve the grid by any other means. I explained that there were too many subs at stake."

"Will it be necessary to dissect the entire stand?"

"No," she said. "Like the mob, it should convert easily with minimal damage to the affected area. That corridor will not have the flexibility it once had, but it will be navigable as soon as the debris is swept."

"When it's over, have samples sent to the lab," he said. "Complete analysis. Find out why it could resist Current Control, then render it down for the toxin stockpile."

"The Zavatans …" she began, "it would be good politics to …"

"To give them what's left of the kelp?" He snorted in disgust. "Let them dredge their own. I don't want to be party to their heresy. And I want a lot of toxin on hand, I have a surprise yet for those 'vermin,' as Nevi calls them."

Marta noted the orders into the messenger at her waist. It was clear to Flattery that the kelp must have sensed Crista Galli's presence. How else to explain this rebellion? It had occurred along the plotted route of Ozette's foil after device was jettisoned.

The kelp must have sensed her when the bug hit the water, he thought. He smiled again, partly out of a distant relief at not being aboard the *Flying Fish* at the time, but largely at the predicament that now embroiled Ozette and his Shadows.

"Overflights?" he asked.

"Bad weather already in," she replied. "Low probability of contact, high probability of loss. Two Grasshoppers available in the area, but they are frail and of limited range. Orders for them?"

"Observation patterns as weather permits," he said. "I want to see who they turn to when they're in big trouble. Nevi will be on the scene soon enough."

Flattery detected a definite shudder across Marta's shoulders at the mention of Nevi's name.

That's why I use him, he thought. *Mere mention of his name gets results.*

He dismissed Marta and surveyed the landscape, *his* landscape, that fell away before him. Metallic-looking *wihi* glinted sunlight back at him. Their short, daggerlike leaves deployed toward the bursts of ultraviolet pulsing from Alki, what the old charts called "First Sun." Flattery admired this dangerous little plant for its tenacity and for the protection it afforded his compound. Its seeds lay dormant undersea for two centuries, waiting to flourish when the oceans rolled back again. It flourished now, and made going difficult for predators near the compound—human or otherwise.

A rob of tiny swiftgrazers darted among the *wihi* to his left, near the cliff's rise to the high reaches. Though reputed to eat anything softer than rock, the grazers preferred to avoid humans. They had survived, like many Earthside rodents, by hiding aboard the organic islands throughout the floods. The poor often chanced netting them for food—a dangerous task. He'd watched an old Islander swarmed to death on this very spot only two years ago. The man had netted only half the rob. The other half waited in the rocks for his return, then set upon his legs until he fell. It was over in a matter of blinks, and Flattery considered it an education. He ordered the whole rob burned out at the nests, of course, and their charred bodies delivered to the villagers. Strictly political.

The Director knew that anything that protected itself to that extreme could be made to protect him, too. His greenskeeper had a way with animals as well as plants, and now several rob of swiftgrazers nested in vulnerable approach points to the compound. This was one such rob, stationed near the trail to the high reaches. He watched them often, particularly in the evening when their slender, rusty backs caught the sunlight and rippled among the silver *wihi*.

"Look there!" his guard warned, and Flattery saw the skulking back of a dasher approach the rob. The guard set his lasgun for the distance about the limit of his effective range, and raised it. Flattery motioned him to wait.

The dasher closed the final twenty meters in three blurring bounds, slapping at the little animals and stunning a few, but the dasher was skinny from hunger. It tried to gulp a few of them down, and that pause was all the rob needed to regroup. The dasher seemed to melt off its odd bones. Flattery smiled again, as the afternoon clouds gathered offshore.

"Beautiful, aren't they?" he asked no one. "Just beautiful."

Chapter 41

We're more than our ideas.

—Prudence Lon Weygand, M.D., number five,
original crew, Voidship *Earthling*

TWISP THE Zavatan elder watched the Director watch the swiftgrazers strip an ailing hooded dasher to bone. The sight reminded him of the old days when he was a simple fisherman at sea. The last effects of blue spore-dust heightened this memory of schools of scrat that devoured maki a thousand times their size in blinks. Twisp had a healthy respect for scrat, and for swiftgrazers.

Furry little bandits, he thought. One thing about them always made him smile. Their fragile little penises detached during mating, leaving a small fleshy plug in the female that her body absorbed. It kept sperm in, and subsequent suitors out, guaranteeing the genetic survival of the first to mount. The male grew another within weeks, but not soon enough to breed twice in one cycle.

Something of a game developed among many Pandoran men at the expense of the swiftgrazers. The trick was to trap a swiftgrazer and snatch its penis. They were considered a delicacy, and it was said that the Director enjoyed them steamed atop his salads. It wasn't easy to isolate a single swiftgrazer. Many a drunk pulled back stumps where there had been fingers.

The little animals looked like a band of robbers, with their masks across their twitchy noses and their nervous way of having at least half of the rob on alert. He had never known them to attack humans unless molested, but when they attacked it was with a fury, a complete abandon that chilled him. He did not care to find out the limits of their patience.

Twisp admired swiftgrazers for the way they stuck together. There was no such thing as a hungry swiftie. If one swiftie was hungry, the whole rob was hungry. The Shadows claimed that the people of Pandora would be like swiftgrazers when the time came. "The time is now," Twisp whispered, watching Flattery.

His whisper was swallowed in the wind. Just enough spore-dust twinkled in his veins to lend a background music to the gusts of the incoming storm.

The wind whistled back, "Yesss," here in the high reaches, as it always did at sea. Only inside, behind the plaz and dogged hatches, did he ever hear it moan, "Nooo." The first time had been nearly thirty years ago, in the company of a woman he couldn't forget. The wind had been right then, and Twisp's broad shoulders sagged a little when he realized it was right now.

The rob of swifties finished their kill. Most of them stood upright on their slender bodies, sniffing the wind and yawning. The pink of their long tongues flickered visibly as they licked their rusty snouts.

Twisp trained his monks with scrat and swiftgrazers in mind. The sequestered Zavatans, like the Shadows of every settlement, were honed and ready, prepared to fight, prepared to go hungry. Still, he desperately wanted to find another way.

He asked the wind, "How can I save the people and Flattery, too?" A crisp lull stilled the afternoon.

Twisp had long ago noted that the Director cultivated certain rob and eliminated others. Careful observation bore fruit—Twisp knew all of the swiftgrazers' secret warrens and the myriad entrances topside. He knew they all would need this kind of patience and attention to detail to turn aside the cruel momentum of Flattery and his machine.

Beyond the scene of this little death in front of him the greater deaths of charred villagers fanned out from the smoking ruins of the Preserve. As the afternoon winds once again gathered their storm, so did hunger unite Pandora against its most vicious enemy. Twisp watched clumps of the inevitable refugees stagger the trail to the rumor of safety among the Zavatans in the high reaches.

New recruits for us, for the Shadows.

His smile was a grim one. Pandorans had never been a warlike lot. There had always been too few humans, too many demons. Even hungry as they were, Pandorans were reluctant to pick up arms against their fellows. Flattery paid his security force, and paid them well, to fight other humans. The disease that Twisp thought he had nipped years ago had burst into an epidemic under Flattery.

"I, too, believed in him at first," Twisp said. "Was that wrong?"

He knew what the wind would say before he heard it. He had been lazy, he had hoped someone else would take care of it. Like everyone else, he had only wanted to live his simple life quietly.

Twisp's own patience was worn threadbare as his robe. For nearly twenty-five years he had hoped that Pandora would shrug off the Director's mantle of hunger and fear. Hope, he knew, had even less substance than dreams. It implied waiting, and too many hungry Pandorans didn't have the luxury of waiting. To wait was a death sentence, and time was the prosecution.

When Flattery had seized power, he insinuated himself first into control of Merman Mercantile and then acquired control of all food distribution. He bought into transportation and communications worldwide. This had been accomplished by the deaths of several of Twisp's friends, people who had owned Merman Mercantile and Current Control.

Too many accidents, too many coincidences.

He fought a familiar lump at his throat. They all had been young, naive, and none of them stood a chance against the cunning of the Director. Now, as always, only Flattery could afford to wait.

How ironic, Twisp thought, *that those who can afford to wait don't have to. I wonder if there's anything left for him to hope for?*

"Elder!"

Twisp cringed inwardly at the panting voice of the young Mose behind him. He felt impatience enough bursting in his breast without being nettled by Mose.

"What is it?"

The younger monk would not approach the precipitous edge of rock outcrop that Twisp occupied, this he knew. He admitted to himself that it was a little game he played with Mose.

"Why do you stand out there?" the younger asked, his voice tinged with a whine.

"Why do you stand back there?"

Still, Twisp did not turn, though he knew he would do so.

"Your presence is requested in chambers. It is urgent. There are many preparations afoot that I do not understand."

Twisp did not answer.

"Elder, can you hear me?"

Still no answer.

"Elder, please do not make me come out there again. You know that it shakes my wattles in a fearsome way."

Twisp chuckled to himself and turned to join Mose at the cavern entrance. The afternoon rains had begun, anyway, pattering like swiftgrazers in the scrub. He knew already what Operations must have decided. That it was time to stop hoping. That Flattery and his kind must go. That the people were rising up unorganized and undefended. That the Zavatans and the Shadows held the only means and position to guarantee his fall. That once again thousands would die in the greater name of Life and, of course, Liberty. When there was nothing else to boil down, it always boiled down to Bread.

"Come with me to Operations," Twisp said, "and I'll show you something to pink your wattles. You will then be witness to something fearsome, indeed."

Twisp bowed once at the cavern entrance, in respect, and entered, the billow of his orange robe a beacon against the darkened afternoon.

The dim vestibule inside was guarded by two young novices with shaved heads and lasguns. The boy looked to be about fifteen and his glistening head revealed a high crest of bone atop his skull, which made him taller than Twisp, though their eyes met at the same height. Both he and the girl wore the black, armored jumpsuits of the Dasher Clan. Both were suitably alert, their quick brown eyes negating their relaxed posture. Together they swung the plasteel hatch outward on its gimbals and admitted the two monks to the cavern within the high reaches.

It was not dashers and flatwings that these doors walled out, but the Director and his Vashon Security Force. Through the years Twisp himself had become a master of security. Incursions by VSF had been few and unsuccessful. They viewed the Zavatans as harmless, spineless weaklings who were kelp-drugged or insane.

"Illusion is our strongest weapon," Twisp had lectured the young novices. "Appear to be foolish, mad, poor and ugly—who would want to take you then? Note how the mold wins the fruit by its appearance alone."

The first chamber was the one that was inspected periodically by Vashon Security Force. Rough-hewn out of rock, it housed three hundred Zavatans of the nine clans spread out along the walls, with common meeting and dining areas. Mazes of cubbies in three levels had bulkheads hung with hundreds of tapestries that muffled the din of three hundred voices echoing inside the cavern.

Lighting was the usual hot-glow type driven by four hydrogen generators housed in the rock beneath them. The appearance was of primitive squalor, and security inspectors sent here by the Director seldom stayed for more than a cursory look. This was where Mose lived. Twisp, too, had a cubby here—third level, to the right of the main entrance—but he seldom slept there. For more than a year Twisp had lived in the private chambers of the group known to the Shadows as "Operations."

Twisp ascended to the second level with Mose in tow. He stepped behind an old Islander tapestry into an alcove that would not be noticed except perhaps by children at play. He approached an undamaged section of basalt bulkhead carved with elaborate histories of human and kelp interactions. The section that he faced, titled "The Lazarus Effect," was simply a huge bas-relief figure of a human hand, index finger extended, touching a strand of kelp that rose from the sea.

Twisp pulled the finger out from the bulkhead and, with the snick of a dagger leaving its sheath, a section of rock sprang outward. When Operations met for Zavatan business, they met inside this labyrinth of rock. Its many repairs betrayed the instability of Pandora's geology, and its routes were constantly changing. Few knew the passageways, and none as well as the Islander Twisp, Chief of Operations.

Mose swallowed hard and paled conspicuously. Tales abounded of thousands of villagers and common folk who sought safety among the Zavatans, never to be seen again. Mose himself had seen hundreds come into the great cavern behind them who had never come out. Operations referred to them as "Messengers from the Poor," and hinted that they were relocated worldwide. Though Mose had heard this rumor, he had never seen evidence to back it up. Mose seldom admitted that he'd been born and lived out his meager years within five kilometers of where he now stood.

They never come back out this hatch!

Twisp smiled at the younger monk's obvious fear.

Why do I like teasing him? he wondered. *I remember Brett took it so well …*

He shook his head. Dwelling on his dead partner was nonproductive. Cleaning up the nest of assassins who'd killed him would do everybody some good.

"Come," Twisp said. "You will be safe with me. It is time the Zavatan muscle flexed itself."

With a smile, Twisp stepped into the well-lighted passageway. Mose's eyes couldn't have widened further. When he hesitated, Twisp placed a large hand on his shoulder.

Mose, too, stepped inside and the panel snicked shut behind them. "I want you to remember everything you see here today."

Mose swallowed hard again and nodded. "Yes … Elder."

Mose did not look thrilled. His already pale face was drawn tight, the surgical scars along his hairline and neck glowed an angry pink. He alternately pulled at his robe and wrung his hands.

The raw silence of this stone passageway contrasted heavily with the steady din of the cavern they left behind them. The passageway was lighted by a cold source, neither bright nor dim, and it carried the pale green hues of Merman design. As in many Merman complexes, the walls met at right angles in a precision that annoyed many Islanders. These walls were carved by a plasteel welder, and except for fault damage they ran perfectly straight, perfectly smooth.

An electronic voice from overhead startled Mose: "Security code for companion?"

"One-three," Twisp said. "Continue."

They set out down the passageway and Mose asked, "Where are we?"

"You will see."

"What do they mean, 'security code?'"

"We have checks within checks," Twisp explained. "Had you been an enemy holding me hostage, this passage would have been sealed off with both of us in it. Perhaps I would be rescued, perhaps not. You, at least, would have been killed."

Twisp felt Mose walk closer to him yet. "Operations is far beneath us, even below the ocean floor."

"Mermen did this?" Mose asked.

The passageway turned left abruptly and ended at a blank wall. Twisp pressed his palm to a depression on the wall and a panel slid back to reveal a tiny room, barely large enough for a half dozen people.

"*Humans* did this," Twisp answered. "Islanders and Mermen alike."

The panel slid shut behind them. Twisp spoke the single word "Operations," and the room began to descend with the two of them inside.

"Oh, Elder ..."

Mose held on to Twisp's long arm.

"Don't be afraid," Twisp said. "There is no magic here. You will see many wonders, all human wonders. Our brothers and sisters will know of them, presently. Didn't I say this would pink your wattles?"

At this, Mose laughed, but he continued to clutch Twisp's arm throughout their rapid descent.

Chapter 42

I am afraid, too, like all my fellow-men, of the future too heavy with mystery and too wholly new, towards which time is driving me.

—Pierre Teilhard de Chardin,

Hymn of the Universe, the Zavatan Collection

DOOB MUSCLED the controls of his track as it lurched across the rocky no man's land between the periphery road and the settlement. The track's ride was a kidney-buster, but it wasn't confined to the few flat roads like Stella's little Cushette. In spite of the beating, the track didn't seem to break down as often, either. This was the third trip to the salvage yard for Doob and Gray this month—all three to fix Stella's five-year-old Cushette.

"You should get a top on this thing," Gray hollered.

Both men were soaked in the sudden afternoon rain, their short hair plastered like thick wet paint onto their heads.

"I like the rain," Doob hollered back. "My mom always said it's good for the complexion."

"That's what my dad said about sex."

That was the first glimmer of humor that Doob had seen from Gray all day. Gray had come by a half-hour ago after getting off work in the settlement. He was grim-lipped and humorless, not at all the relaxed Gray who lived next door. Gray worked some security job for the Director's personal staff, so when he didn't feel like talking, Doob knew better than to push.

Doob was full of questions today, though. A skyful of smoke over the settlement worried him in spite of the news.

"A good rain'll clear the air," Doob said. "It's good for the brain, too. I wish it would grow something out here besides more rock."

"Those Zavatans," Gray said, "they could do it."

"Do what?"

"Get something to grow here. They have huge farms all over the upcoast regions. Just like the Islanders, but they've moved the islands inland."

Doob looked at Gray incredulously. He had heard rumors, of course, everybody had.

"You're not kidding, are you? They grow food up there and the Director lets them get away with it?"

"That's right. He can't keep control up there and down here, too."

"But everything up there's just cliff face and rock …"

"That's what you hear," Gray said. "Where do you hear it?"

"Well, on the news. I don't know anyone who's actually traveled overland up there." "I have."

Doob glanced over at his best friend. Something had happened to him today, something that changed his whole disposition. Gray was a lot of fun. He'd come home, drink some boo with Doob, tinker with the vehicles. Sometimes, when Doob could afford it, they'd take their wives to the settlement for an evening of dropvine wine and buzzboard. Gray was definitely no fun today, but Gray had been upcoast, and Doob was very curious.

"You *have*?" Doob asked. "Well … what was it like?"

He knew the danger of this question. He suspected that whatever it was that Gray had to tell him about the upcoast region was something that wouldn't be healthy to know.

"It was beautiful," Gray said. He spoke up, but his voice was still hard to hear over the noise of the track's exhaust.

"They have gardens, hundreds of them. A rock ranch like this one would grow corn in one season up there. And every little garden is bordered by flowers, all colors …"

The wistful expression on Gray's face worried Doob. Doob had seen that expression often since Gray got back from wherever the Director's people sent him. Gray didn't volunteer information, and Doob knew better than to ask. The less he knew about that kind of stuff, the longer his life span, he was sure of that.

Besides, he listened to dangerous politics from his roommate, Stella. Like Doob, she was twenty-two cycles Pandoran, but she hung around with artists and tried to act older. She had converted most of their living space to a multilevel hydroponics garden, and she grew mushrooms under their rooms. Gray knew this, of course, but he pretended not to. Stella came from a long line of Islander gardeners. Her family owned patents to seeds mutated specifically to Pandora, and about three centuries of know-how in hydroponics. Doob thought she could probably make the walls sprout if he let her.

Stella talked nonstop, but this didn't bother Doob. That way he didn't have to say much, and that was the way Doob liked things.

Gray signaled him to shut down the engine. The track backfired once and stopped atop a rock ledge that afforded them a sweeping view all around.

"I want to believe I can trust you," Gray said. "There are some things I need to talk about."

Doob swallowed, then nodded.

"Sure, Gray. I'm a little scared, you know."

Gray smiled, but it was a grim smile.

"You should be," he said. He pointed to the refugee sprawl ahead. "Starving people out there would kill you for one meal out of Stella's garden. Flattery's people would kill you for growing illegal food. I might kill you if you told anybody what I'm about to tell you."

Doob sucked in his breath. From Gray's steady gaze, Doob knew he wasn't kidding. He also knew that he needed to hear whatever Gray needed to say.

"Even Stella?"

Gray's eyes softened. Doob knew how much he liked Stella. He treated her like the daughter that Gray and Billie never had.

"We'll see," Gray said. "Hear me out."

Gray spoke in a near-whisper, and his gaze darted around them nervously. Doob hunched close to Gray and pretended to be working on the track's control panel. He had the distinct feeling they were being watched.

"I've been gone a month, you knew that," Gray said. "They sent me upcoast, to spy on some Zavatans up there. They set me up with a story, a lapel camera, a way in and out. Overflights showed some signs of illegal fishing and food production, Flattery wanted details. What I saw there changed my life."

He lifted off the lid to the control panel and propped it up. Both Gray and Billie had been raised down under in Merman settlements.

He's methodical, like a Merman, Doob thought.

Gray's ice-blue eyes kept watch for movement around the track. Out in the open, this close to the perimeter, there were risks of other dangers than humans. Gray continued to talk in his slow, quiet way.

"They're Islanders, like you, without islands," he said. "Thousands of them—Flattery has no idea how many. They have camouflage for overflights. The ratty little gardens that we see from the air are meant to be seen. Under the camouflage, and underground … that's a whole different story. They make bubbly out of the nutrient vats the same way they used to form their islands. Except now, instead of growing islands out of it, they spray it in a foam across rock like this and grow plants on it a week later. They make it out of garbage and sewage, just like the old days.

"On flat land, or the second time around, the bubbly is formed into a centimeter-thick sheet of organic gel, twelve meters across. Seeds are impregnated in rows into the gel, then they spread it across bare rock or sand, or last year's garden. It holds nutrients, water and defense from predators, all in a time-release bonding. Wouldn't Stella love to see this?"

"Sounds like her idea of heaven," Doob said. "She misses the island life, even though ours was grounded when we were five. I miss it, too, I guess. Not the drifting so much as the freedom. We worried about grounding, but we weren't afraid of each other." This last Doob offered with some reservation. To admit that you were afraid of security was to imply that you had reason to be afraid. Fear was grounds for investigation.

"Yes," Gray sighed, "we *are* afraid of each other, aren't we? Even you and I. Up there," he nodded upcoast, "they're wary, but they're not afraid."

"What did you do about your report? Did you … ?"

"Did I expose their happiness? Did I betray the only sign of humanity I've witnessed in almost twenty years? No. No, I lied, and I made sure my camera lied. But I'm not as brave as you think. I know what Flattery suspected—that there were settlements, illegal food. But I also know what Flattery wanted. He wanted it to be rag-tag, not worth going after, because he doesn't have the force to stop it! Look around you, Doob." Gray swept his arm, taking in the horizon on all sides. "This takes every bit of manpower he's got, and he's losing it. There were riots in the settlement today, big riots, and there will be more. The news is not news, it's fiction outlined by Flattery and written by his personal fools. His lies keep us small, and as long as we're small he keeps control.

"No, he didn't want there to be anything big upcoast, so when I showed him a few raggedy-assed dirtpokers, it made him happy. So, maybe he'll stay here. His major forces are here and in Victoria, with a lot of sea patrols on the fishing fleet. The world is a lot bigger than that, Doob. It's a lot bigger, and getting bigger every day. I think you and Stella should go up there."

"What?" Doob banged his head coming out of the control panel. "Are you crazy? She's going to have a … I mean, we can't think about anything like that right now. We've got to stay put."

"Doob, I know she's going to have a baby. Stella told Billie and Billie told me this morning. She can't hide it much longer, anyway. You'll have to make new food coupon applications, people may visit your place, you can't risk that."

Doob sighed, then spit out the driver's porthole.

"Shit," he muttered.

"Listen," Gray said. "There's a way out of this. How's the Cushette over water?"

"Well, it's OK when it's running. No match for a foil, though, or one of those security pursuit boats."

Gray looked back at the bed of the track. It was a dumpable storage bin two meters wide by four meters long. Doob made his coupons hauling equipment across the rocks for construction crews up and down the beaches of Kalaloch.

"Can you get three hundred klicks out of this thing over rough terrain?"

Doob shook his head. "No way. Two hundred, tops. With a converter, and access to seawater, I could probably drive around the world."

"Yeah," Gray said, pulling at his chin. "But there's no seawater inland, and converters won't work in streams or lakes. I have an old high-pressure tank at my place, that would get you the whole way."

"What are you talking about?" Doob ran a nervous hand through his kinky brown hair. "You think we can just drive this track upcoast as bold as you please? They'll crisp our butts before we hit the high reaches."

"That's why you don't go that way," Gray said. "I have a map, and I have a plan. If I can get you, Stella and this track upcoast to my Zavatan contacts, would you go?"

Doob looked up in time to see a security detachment leave the perimeter and start toward the track. They were still a couple hundred meters off, but they didn't look happy.

"Shit," Doob said.

He replaced the control panel cover and started the engine. He began to pivot his machine on its left track to go back home.

"No," Gray shouted. "We set out to get a starter for that Cushette, and that's what we'll do. Give them a wave."

Gray waved at the security squad, and so did Doob. The squad leader waved back, and the men turned back to the perimeter road where it was easier going.

"See?" Gray hollered. "It's like that everywhere. Learn what's easiest for them, and you can get by. We'll talk more about the upcoast trip on the way back. I've got it all figured, don't worry."

He flashed Doob a smile, a big one, and Doob caught himself smiling back.

Gardens, he thought. *Stella will love that for sure.*

Chapter 43

Not by refraining from action does one attain freedom from action. Not by mere renunciation does one attain supreme perfection.

—from Zavatan *Conversations with the Avata*, Queets Twisp, elder

TWISP ALWAYS thought that "chambers" was well-named. There were, indeed, many chambers beneath the rock—one for each of the council and several for support staff, as well as general meeting rooms and sleeping quarters. The complex was crude by Merman standards, primitive by the Director's standards. Repair crews worked throughout the area cleaning up the last of the damage of last year's great quake, already going down in oral history as "the great quake of '82."

Across the passageway from the elevator a hatch opened into Twisp's personal chamber, hewn out of glassy black rock. He swung the hatch open and motioned the gaping Mose inside.

"Sit here."

Twisp indicated a low couch to the left of the hatchway. The couch was organic, like the chairdog. The entire room measured barely four paces square, a distinctly Islander cubby. Shelves filled up most of the black-rock walls, and on these shelves stood hundreds of books: The old kelp-pulps, a well-scarred library. Twisp had been a fisherman without holo or viewscreens. Bleached kelp pulp and hand presses in every little community turned out literature and news that was affordable and could be passed around.

Twisp dogged the hatch, then smiled. "Borrow any books you like," he said. "They don't do anybody any good on the shelf."

Mose hung his head. "I … I never told you," he stammered. One nail-bitten hand wrung the other. "I can't read."

"I know," Twisp said. "You cover it well, it took me a long time to figure it."

"And you didn't say nothing … ?"

"Only you could know when the time is right. Always someone's willing to teach, but that's no good until the pupil is ready to learn. Reading is easy. Writing, now that's a whole different story."

"I've never been very good at learning things."

"Cheer up," Twisp said. "You learned to talk, didn't you? Reading's not so different. We'll have coffee every day for a month, and you'll be reading well by the end of the month. How about if we start with coffee now and a lesson later today?"

Mose nodded, and his look brightened. Topside, among the Zavatans, he did not often get coffee since the Director had taken over production. But he'd wedded himself to Zavatan poverty, which was a step up from his family poverty. Among the Zavatans he'd found that nothing was to be expected, everything enjoyed. Twisp bent to the preparations, his long arms akimbo in front of the table.

A fold-out table and stone washbasin jutted from the wall across the room, beside the inset stove and cooler. Mose reclined into the old couch and let it suit his forms. He found it indescribably nicer than his pallet topside. One shelf beside the couch held several holo cubes. Most of the pictures on them were of a young, red-haired man and a small, dark-skinned girl.

"The meeting begins soon, Mose," Twisp said. The older man sighed without turning, and his gangly arms sagged a bit. He spooned out some of the odorful coffee into a small cooker.

"We will all share a soup there, in the old custom, or I would offer you something here. My cubby is your cubby. That hatchway leads to the head. This hatch," with a nod he indicated their entry, "leads to the general council chambers. Prepare yourself for a confusion of people doing strange things."

"That's the way things have been all my life."

Twisp laughed, "Well, you'll get along down here just fine. Do you remember the oath you took when you came among the Zavatans?"

"Yes, Elder. Of course I remember."

"Repeat it, please."

Mose cleared his throat and sat a little straighter, though Twisp still had his back to him.

"'I forswear henceforth all robbing and stealing of food and crops, the plunder and destruction of homes belonging to the people. I promise householders that they may roam at will and abide, unmolested, wherever dwelling; I swear this with uplifted hands. Nor will I bring plunder or destruction, not even to avenge life and limb. I profess good thoughts, good words, good deeds.'"

"Very well recited," Twisp said, and handed Mose his hot coffee. "You are here because the council needs your opinion. The council has a weighty decision before it today. Never has the council faced a decision this big before. It may involve asking the Zavatans, all of us, to break that oath, the part about avenging life and limb. We will need your witness to this meeting, and your opinion will help decide whether or not to break it."

Twisp sipped his own coffee, still standing over Mose, and noted the tremble in the younger monk's nail-bitten hands.

"Do you have an opinion on that, Mose?"

"Yes, Elder, I do."

There had been no hesitation in Mose's voice, and the tremble in his hands stilled.

"Swearing to an oath … well, that's for life. I swore to uphold that oath for life. That's what I did, and that's what I should do." Mose accented his speech with a curt nod, but still did not look up.

So fearful, Twisp thought. *This world is more habitable than it has ever been, but the people are more fearful, even of those closest to them.*

A knock at the chamberside hatch startled them both. Twisp opened it to a young, red-haired woman carrying a clipboard. She was shapely, enhancing the green fatigues characteristic of the Kelp Clan. The name above her left breast pocket read, "Snej." Her blue eyes were rimmed in red, and swollen.

She's been crying!

"Five minutes to council, sir," she said, and sniffed as delicately as she could. "These are our latest briefing notes." Her gaze kept his own, but her voice lowered. "Project Goddess may be lost, sir. No word or sign of them for hours." Her lips trembled under tight control, and fresh tears welled over reddened rims. He noted a general air of depression among the support crew.

"LaPush was transmitting hourly bursts from his camera …"

"There's a wide-band communications problem, too," she said. "Kelp channels are clear, but conventional broadcasts seem to be jammed. Sometimes clear, sometimes not. Maybe it's sun-spots, but it doesn't *act* like sunspots. Too selective."

She reached up a sleeve for her handkerchief and blew her nose.

"You're upset," Twisp said. "Can I help?"

"Yes, sir. You can get Rico back for me. I know Crista Galli is important … most important. But I …"

"You're console monitor today?"

She nodded, dabbing at her eyes with her sleeve.

"Concentrate on communications to or from Flattery's compound and shuttle everything to council chambers. We'll get them back … Rico and Ozette don't panic under fire."

This last seemed to rally the young woman. She blew her nose, straightened her shoulders. "Thanks," she said. "I'm sorry … I'd better get back. Thanks."

Mose followed Twisp out the hatchway and they strolled the huge, domed information center bustling with people. Mose recognized some of the villager refugees he'd seen above. They all wore either the green fatigues of the redhead, Snej, singlesuits he recognized as belonging to the newer Landsteward Clan.

Twisp's step took on a spring more youthful than his gray braid would indicate as he traversed the deck of this room of makeshift desks, view-screens, stacks of papers, cables across the deck. This was his work of twenty-five years: Operations, the heart and being of the mysterious Shadows worldwide.

"Flattery thinks we're in Victoria," Twisp had told the council at the beginning, "and I want the rest of the world to think so, too. The Shadows will be an illusion, a fiction that we make as we go. The entire world is at stake, perhaps every human life. We must have appropriate patience."

He hoped that they still had appropriate patience.

Twisp cleared some storage units from an old chairdog and indicated to Mose that he should sit. A large plaz shield separated them from the ominous quiet of a roomful of techs. The redhead, Snej, nodded to Twisp and tried a smile.

Snej reminded Twisp a little of Ambassador Kareen Ale, a friend of his and one of the first victims of Flattery's death squad.

She saved a lot of lives, he thought. *And she was so damned pretty.*

Twisp shook off the painful memory and settled himself into his console's couch. The other council members' couches were arranged, like his own, as spokes in a wheel, each with access to a console, viewer and a central holo stage.

Twisp discarded his threadbare robe. Underneath, he wore a rust-colored singlesuit of the Hylighter Clan. The clasped-hands insignia at his right breast represented the informal symbol of the Shadows. Like Twisp, each of the other three consuls was accompanied by a civilian witness. One couch remained empty, its viewer and stage blank.

The other three witnesses, like Mose, sat in wide-eyed awe at the maps and data spread out before them. Twisp cleared his throat and spoke the simple, awful words that some of the council had waited more than twenty years to hear:

"Brothers and sisters, it is time."

After the ancient blessing of the food they shared the ritual bowl of soup in silence. It was a classic Islander broth, nearly clear with a couple of bright orange muree curled at the bottom of the bowl. Chips of green onion floated the top, their crisp scent wafting the chambers.

The one vacant couch belonged to Dwarf MacIntosh, survivor of the very hybernation tanks that bore the Director, Raja Flattery. MacIntosh had rejected Flattery's greed for the more familiar zenlike philosophies of the Zavatans. He shaved his head, he said, "In grief at the loss of Flattery's soul, and as a reminder to keep my own."

Years ago, MacIntosh and Flattery had disagreed openly, heatedly, on many occasions. Rumor said that Flattery had removed Current Control to the Orbiter so that he could remove MacIntosh to the Orbiter. Mack had recently perfected a console-communication system that used the kelp itself as a carrier. All of the systems in chambers were tied into the kelp. Along with a code, also devised by MacIntosh, each console was capable of direct, immediate contact with Current Control.

I hope we can keep these lines open, Twisp thought. *That could be jamming on the conventional channels, or just sun activity. If it's sun, it probably won't take out the kelp channel as well.*

He reserved a mental note to remind Snej to check the kelp channel for Rico's film. With luck it could've been picked up and stored there.

After taking food together, Twisp received their affirmations calmly, as they presented them calmly, though what they pronounced could degenerate into a roll call of death worldwide. Every face in the room reflected the heaviness of the matter. They all agreed that it was time. It was just as important that they all agreed on what exactly it was time for.

Venus Brass, the eldest at seventy-five years, had seen her husband and children assassinated at the Director's orders, herself missing death by a fluke. A slow-moving, big-hearted, quickwitted Islander woman, Venus, with her husband, had built a food distribution empire. It was taken over by Flattery and wedded to Merman Mercantile. They transported fish and produce from small suppliers like Twisp to public markets for a percentage of the catch. Flattery did the only distribution now, where and when he chose and at a membership fee too high for a solo operation to afford.

Kaleb Norton-Wang, rightful heir to Merman Mercantile, was the youngest consul at twenty-three. Son of Scudi Wang, herself heiress to Merman Mercantile, and Brett Norton, Twisp's fishing partner, Kaleb had seen his parents killed when their boat mysteriously exploded one night at dockside. That was before anyone had learned to suspect Flattery's hand in such things.

Kaleb had slipped landside that night to play with some of the other children. He was ten years old, and supper conversation for months had been about Flattery, and his takeover maneuvers with Merman Mercantile.

Twisp, wakened from his coracle nearby, had found the boy screaming on the pier watching his family's boat burn. Twisp and Kaleb fled together to the barely habitable high reaches. Like his deceased father, Kaleb could see in the dark. His mother's inner acuity and her personal allegiance to the kelp gave Kaleb a formidable intelligence. He, like his mother, could communicate directly with the kelp by touch. He found it too painful to meet his parents' memories in the kelp, so he seldom explored the kelpways of the mind.

He's too bitter, Twisp thought. *Bitter pulls you down, gets you to make mistakes that you can't afford.*

He hadn't seen much of Kaleb lately. The boy's district was Victoria, Flattery's only solid stronghold upcoast. Twisp feared that Kaleb had met the challenge of that command so that he could wreak a personal vengeance on Flattery and his people. He hoped that he had taught Kaleb well enough that the boy wouldn't respond to Flattery the way Flattery had responded to his parents.

The upcoast inland regions were represented by Mona Flatwing, a red-faced, middle-aged woman who was speaking now.

"We are in a comfortable position," she said. Her deep brown eyes glittered and her husky voice spoke with a heavy Islander lilt.

"Each household has foodstuffs for six months. We have surplus stores enough to handle a major refugee influx through next harvest. Consul from the coast tells me that we are in a similar position with our seafoods."

Venus Brass nodded affirmation.

"Frankly," Mona continued, "our people do not want to come down here to fight. They left here to get away from that, they've made good lives upcoast, they want to be left alone. They will accept anyone of good faith who seeks refuge, as always. The usual preparations have been made for defense, but I must emphasize this point: These people do not want to kill anyone."

Again, a nod from Venus Brass. Her shaky, high-pitched voice contrasted with Mona's.

"It is the same with our people," she said. "They use the freedom of the sea to get away from 'the troubles,' as they call them. They're a brave and hardy lot. Among them they amass quite a fleet and assault force. But like Kaleb's people, they live among Flattery's people when landside, they trade with them, families are intermarried. They do not want to kill anyone, particularly family. You've seen how Flattery has shuffled his troops to accommodate that attitude—"

Bam! Kaleb's fist on his note stand startled everyone.

Twisp clenched a fist in reflex, then unclenched it slowly on his knee.

"This is Flattery's dream council," Kaleb said. His voice carried the sharp bitterness that Twisp often heard in it lately. "We are talking here of doing *nothing* to curb this madness, this wholesale murder. Was I the only one who witnessed what happened out there today?"

"Talking about what we will not do is preface to talking about—"

"Is preface to nothing, as usual," Kaleb interrupted. "It's historically true that humans are hungry only because humans allow it. We must simply not allow it, not for another day, not for another hour."

Venus withdrew as though she'd been slapped, then folded her arms across her thin chest. "Did your people start this business today?" she asked.

Kaleb smiled, and the exuberance of it accented his youthful appearance.

He's a one who's gone beyond his years, Twisp thought. *Far enough that he knows when to use that smile.*

"That is Flattery's doing," Kaleb said. "I have another plan, one more consistent with our ideals. My people committed, and my contacts tell me that many of yours will, too."

"And then what?" Mona hissed, and sat forward. "Doing something will get their attention. Flattery will send security ..."

Kaleb heard the old argument out. At one point he looked across the table at Twisp. The eagerness that gleamed in his young eyes reminded Twisp of Kaleb's father when he was that age—smart, daring, impetuous. Brett Norton had killed once, out of reflex, but that killing had saved Twisp and Kaleb's mother.

Mona finished recounting her people's position.

"They'll take in refugees, but they won't leave the livelihoods they've built from nothing. Eluding detection is much preferable to facing conflict."

"I understand," Kaleb said. "That's the swiftgrazer's way. Something else is true of swifties—if a swiftie is hungry the whole rob's hungry. We've coordinated with and we have a plan rolling that will feed the rob."

Twisp repressed a smile. *I guess he listened to my swiftgrazer pitch, after all.*

Twisp knew that, among the council, there was no such thing as rank. They would vote to participate or not, and to act the ways their decisions dictated.

"We each have plans," Twisp said, "now they will become a single plan. Project Goddess is four hours overdue their upcoast checkpoint. That will merit some consideration as well, this session."

A murmur rippled about the table. The four witnesses looked pale and frightened when they came in, and the agitation of the council made them appear smaller, as well.

Twisp's hand went up to still the chatter.

"We have other fish in the pan. Please bear with me."

Twisp noted a message coming across Dwarf MacIntosh's console, and nodded at Snej to retrieve it. He went on.

"Flattery has dominated with hunger and fear. His obvious motives: get himself offplanet, in command of a Voidship. We don't argue with getting rid of him, is that right?"

There were nods around the table, but Mona spoke up:

"He's going to take three thousand of our best people with him and leave that damned security force ..."

"They want to go," Twisp emphasized. "They should be free to settle the Void, if that's their destination. We will be rid of him, that is our only concern. But we will have to break down the machinery of his power before he leaves. He must be brought down first, and we must be assured that he can't possibly return. We must deal with criminals without becoming criminals ourselves. If we do not, then we and our children are lost."

Snej read what MacIntosh had to say from the Orbiter.

"Twisp, Project Goddess has been … intercepted."

"Intercepted? Well, now, that's a step up from 'lost,' at least. Where are they? Who did it?"

"It's the kelp," Snej said. "Dr. MacIntosh speculates that the kelp got a whiff of Crista Galli and decided to take her. He's being jammed on the burst system, but his kelp channel still works."

"Did he dump enough data to brief us?" Twisp asked. He massaged away a headache gathering in his forehead. Today, more than others, he was feeling the weight of his second half-century. Snej handed him a messenger and he clipped it into his console.

"The kelp in sector eight diverted their foil into its stand," Mack's voice reported. "It completely shifted several transport channels to do so and an unknown number of subs were disabled, possibly lost. There have been casualties, number unknown. Current Control attempted mandatory 'persuasion,' on Flattery's standing orders. No effect …"

Murmurings rose around the table. Twisp, too, was amazed.

Avata resisted, he thought. *There's the sign we need.*

"Do we have anyone in that area?" Kaleb asked. "Any Kelp Clan people who know what they're doing?"

Mona brushed her fingers across her console.

"Yes," she said. "We have an Oracle landside of their position, plenty of personnel."

"If shipping's disrupted there, our people are probably in trouble, too," Venus said. "I'll try to raise a sub, but my guess is that the whole area's impassable—"

Twisp interrupted.

"What we need now is total interference with anything Flattery does. Wherever his men go, whatever move he makes, we need people in the way, we need dead ends. He must be frustrated at every turn. Does his interference in Current Control indicate that he's penetrated us?"

"It's possible," Snej said, her mouth a grim line, "but I doubt it."

"Ask Dr. MacIntosh to shut down Current Control," Twisp said. "There will be reprisals there, as you know. But we know more about moving around in the kelp than anyone, and most of it's on our side. As of now, traffic worldwide will be at a standstill. You all know the dangers, of course."

Twisp, who had fished the open seas for most of his life, knew better than any of them the fates they had just decreed for thousands on and under the ocean. Countless innocent people were now marooned in unnavigable waters, some among hostile kelp. The die had been cast, and by Flattery himself.

"Our success or failure depends completely on the cooperation of the people of Pandora," he said. "We need to starve him out. Fight hunger with hunger, fear with fear …"

Kaleb stopped him with a raise of his hand, then apologized with the acceptable nod.

"We don't fight hunger with hunger," Kaleb said. His voice was soft, his tone as reprimanding as a new young father's. "We're human beings," he said. "We fight hunger with food."

After a deferential silence, Mona's witness said, "Aye. Aye, we're with you."

"Kaleb, you show me how we can dump Flattery and feed the hungry and we're in, too," Venus said.

"It's so simple it'll make you cry," Kaleb said. "Briefing now appearing on your screens. As you can see, we'll need the cooperation that Twisp was talking about. We have to get Ozette and Galli on the air *immediately*. Can we count on Shadowbox?"

"You're right," Mona agreed, flurrying orders into her board. "Timing is the key, here. The people cannot help if they don't know how. They will believe Ben Ozette, they will worship Crista Galli."

"My people are infiltrating now," Kaleb said. His voice was calm, confident, his father's strong chin set straight ahead. "They will be about five thousand, well-mixed throughout the poor. Word of mouth is best among the poor."

"Anything else from MacIntosh?" Twisp asked.

Snej nodded, biting her lip. "Yes," she said. "He says Beatriz Tatoosh is aboard, and the drinking water has made her sick."

Snej looked up from the messenger, puzzlement wrinkling her brow.

Twisp felt his heart double-time in his chest.

"Well," he announced, "that's our personal code for big trouble in orbit. Flattery probably sent up a security force with Beatriz. He must suspect something's up with Mack. Damn!"

Twisp sucked in a deep breath and let it out slowly. "Too bad she's not with us," he said. "I wish MacIntosh had some support up there right now."

"Let's see what kind of support we have down here right now," Kaleb said. "Let's mobilize our upcoast people and rescue that foil."

Kaleb rose, obviously ready to leave for Victoria immediately.

We need him here.

"Kaleb," he said, "let's take a walk. You're nearly three hours away. Good people live upcoast, they're already searching. For old time's sake, let's go down to the Oracle. Maybe someone should ask the kelp what the hell it's up to."

Chapter 44

Roots and wings. But let the wings grow roots and the roots fly.
—Juan Ramon Jimenez

STELLA BLISS unpacked three crates of moss orchids and arranged them in threes along the short walkway to the foyer of the Wittle mansion. This job had come up only the night before, and Stella's moss orchids happened to be ready. She was a sculptress of flowers, and appreciated an audience for her art.

Stella wore her new lavender puff-sleeve blouse and a crisp pair of matching work pants. The blouse favored her breasts, tender with her recent pregnancy, but she supposed this would be the last time she'd be able to get into these pants for a while.

Stella skirted the security guards and servants who found excuses to watch her. The limelight made her nervous, though her stature had thrust her into the limelight often since she was a child. Twelve hands tall, Stella turned heads wherever she went, even when she went in overalls.

Stella dressed like the flowers she raised. Doob told his parents that, at home, bees followed every step she took but they never stung. Her shaggy dark hair framed a tanned face with high cheekbones and blue-green eyes. Her lips were full, often pursed with concentration. She smiled a lot lately, and had taken to humming old tunes to the new human sleeping inside her.

Growing plants and engineering them for food had been Stella's family's tradition for nine generations. Since the food shortages, production and research efforts went to food. Stella had never given up on flowers or the bees that made them possible.

She carried the tenth generation within her, a child that she knew by her dreams would grow to be a woman like herself. She knew this as her mother had known it, as all their mothers had known it for several centuries, a long tradition, difficult in these difficult times. These moss orchids were Stella's own design, and she was eager to hear what musicians, those sculptors of air, other artists and Pandoran gentry would say about their look and their taste.

Stella knew that His Honor Álek Dexter was color blind, so she selected a blend that pleased herself. Most of the blossoms shimmered in the lavender range, though she couldn't resist showing off a half-dozen of her delicate pinks.

A small-boned security guard with a big-boned swagger poked into each of her cartons with his lasgun and silently checked the moss beds with his knife. Stella had been scanned twice and body-searched by a matron when she entered the grounds. This was not the first time, and she supposed it wouldn't be the last. Stella had some strong opinions, but preferred to concentrate on her flowers. A cordon of security closed off the entire block, and another contingent guarded the building. This was the home of the chief executive officer of Merman Mercantile, someone considered by the Director to be a prime target for the Shadows. He was rumored to be one of three men in line for the Director's position should an unforeseen unpleasantness occur.

A sweeping structure of molded stone and plasteel, this home showed no effects from the recent series of quakes that had devastated much of Kalaloch. Its border was secured by a two-meter-high wall of rock topped with shards of sharp metal and broken glass. Stella shook her head.

The Line for this sector passes only a block away.

No one setting up this reception seemed at all concerned about the screams and the rumble of heavy vehicles less than a stone's throw behind them.

The grim-faced security sported a flesh flower behind his ear, one of the new sculpted skin designs that she found repulsive. His underarms blossomed huge sweat rings, something more than she would attribute to the muggy afternoon.

"What would you find in that dirt," she asked him when he finished, "deadly attack worms?"

The guard scowled, his glance flicking nervously from Stella to the smoky pall that collected under the gray cap of afternoon nimbus.

"I'm losing my sense of humor," he growled. "Don't push it."

"Are you afraid that the mob will come in here and—"

"I'm not afraid of anything," he blurted, puffing his boyish chest against baggy fatigues. "My job is to protect Mr. Dexter, and that's what I'm doing."

She began the tender task of removing the plants from their containers and setting them in their beds beside the walk. She liked this part best—handling the silky vines and blind roots, smelling the loam as she broke it open. At the end of the day, when she cleaned her short nails, she did it over one of her pots so that nothing was lost. Her ancestors spent their first three generations out of hyb building soil.

"You must like flowers, you went through a lot of pain and trouble to get the one behind your ear."

"I was drunk," he said. "If they could get them to smell good, it wouldn't be so bad." "They'll come up with something, you'll see," she said. "Smell these."

She held a lavender orchid up to him. He took it from her and put it to his nose, then allowed himself a smile. It pleased her that the tension in his face relaxed a bit.

"Yeah," he said, "that would be nice."

"Well, this type of flower didn't have a scent until just a year ago. And it didn't blossom from moss until five years ago. I taught it how."

"Flowers!" The security snorted in a show of disdain, but didn't turn away. "You can't eat flowers. You should grow something that people can eat."

She hesitated, swallowed, smiled.

"What?" She put her hand to her mouth in mock surprise. "They shoot you for growing food without a license. You don't need a license to grow flowers. Besides, your soul needs food, too. Flowers have a spiritual nutrition that you just can't measure."

He looked less skeptical, but kept his guarded posture. She bit back the temptation to talk about her bees, because bees meant honey and fewer than a handful of people knew about her honey production.

Once her plants were bedded she misted them well and swept her clippings and stray dirt away from the walk. She felt a little nervous. She was stuck in town without transportation. Her neighbor, Billie, had given her a ride to the job first thing this morning. Her Cushette, though practically new, had burned out another something that meant it wouldn't start. She didn't like town, anyway. It wallowed in tight places and it always frustrated her. The tram into the central area with a transfer out … but it was probably shut down because of the mobs. She didn't relish the idea of walking the ten klicks home without Doob to protect her.

"Stella, my dear, are you finished out here?"

Mrs. Wittle, the hostess, beckoned her from the front hatchway. She was a gray-haired, prim woman with an honest smile for everyone and a fair skin that could only be Merman-born. Though soft-spoken and delicate, Mrs. Wittle had singlehandedly saved a boatload of Pandora's finest art during that first series of quakes in '73. She had been a volunteer at the museum desk down under when the collapse came and commandeered an old delivery sub. Instead of saving herself, she loaded artwork into the sub even as the seams of the museum dome split, sending streams of waterspray powerful enough to slice a human in half.

"Yes, Mrs. Wittle. Do you like them?" The elderly woman glanced down at the walk and her eyebrows raised ever so slightly.

"Lovely," she said, and sighed. "They were right about you, my dear. But now I have a problem and perhaps you can help me."

"What is it?"

"Some of the help that we were counting on haven't shown up today … the troubles, you know. Could you stay awhile longer and greet our guests at the door? I have the guest list here, and name tags are on the table just inside the hatch. Of course, you are welcome to stay as my guest and enjoy the reception. Would you do that for me?"

Stella had strong feelings about rich people, and they were strong negative feelings. A few meters away the starving poor lined up for hours to buy limited rations with their hard-earned pay. Servants of the rich handed over cards stamped "Exception" at the high-security back door loading dock and filled their vans with an abundance of food. Stella had worked parties like this before to be able to take home leftovers. The pay meant nothing, she had always earned more than her ration card allowed her to buy. She had never been able to figure out the red tape process for getting a ration card stamped "Exception."

But today her Cushette was not running and she had no safe way home.

"Yes," she said, "I can stay. But I'm not dressed … and I'll need a ride home."

Mrs. Wittle brightened and took her by the elbow.

"You don't know what a worry you've lifted, dear. Of course we can arrange a ride for you, you just leave that to me. Now, let's have a look at my daughter's wardrobe. She had some wonderful things that should fit you nicely. There's an elegant black dress that will look splendid on you, though I'm sure that anything would look splendid on you."

Stella blushed at the compliment.

"Thank you," she said. "She won't mind?"

Mrs. Wittle's face darkened for an unguarded moment, then she set her chin forward.

"No, my dear, I'm afraid not," she said. "She was killed in that terrible scene at the college last season. Terrible."

"I'm … I'm sorry to hear that."

"Well, she had her own mind," Mrs. Wittle said, "and she insisted on using it." Then, in a whisper, she added, "I was so proud of her. I'll tell you the story someday, this is not the time."

The dress was slinky and black. The fit in the bust was uncomfortably tight, though it seemed that any pressure at all hurt her breasts lately. The neckline plunged a bit, too, showing her off as she hadn't been shown off before.

"I wish Doob could see me in this," she said, turning in front of a pair of mirrors. "He'd love it."

"Then you'll just have to keep it, my dear," Mrs. Wittle said. Tears welled in her eyes but nothing spilled. "In fact, I wish you'd look through these clothes and take anything you can use. It's not right that they just hang here, they're not paintings, after all."

Stella protested but Mrs. Wittle prepared a carton full of her daughter's clothes, then escorted Stella to her position at the small table beside the entry way.

The guest of honor, Alek Dexter, arrived tugging his shirtsleeves flush with the jacket cuffs and cursing the muggy afternoon. Stella pinned his name tag to his left breast and smoothed the fabric out of habit. Instead of joining the rest of the guests, he lingered beside her and unabashedly appraised her cleavage. She caught his gaze and held it until he looked away.

"Been in meetings all day," he mumbled. "After this shindig that the distributors put together I have to speak at a Progress Club dinner in two hours and then meet with the Director at a cocktail party at eight. No wonder I'm always out of breath and can't lose weight. You look beautiful, my dear—" he squinted at her name tag and moved closer to her chest, "—Stella. Stella Bliss."

They shook hands and she found his palm very sweaty.

I didn't think these bigshots sweat in public.

A sheen gathered at his forehead and upper lip and he dabbed at it with a handkerchief.

The Honorable Alek Dexter motioned to his driver, who lounged nearby in the cool breeze of the hatchway.

"I'll need another shirt," he said, his voice lowered. "Powder blue will do for tonight."

"Streets are blocked," his driver said. "Couldn't make it back in time to fetch you for dinner."

His voice sounded sullen to Stella and she suspected from the tightening of his jaw that if there was one thing Alek Dexter did not allow in his presence it was sullenness.

"Then *buy* one," he snapped. "Shops are open until curfew, and the market's only a few blocks away." He waved his hand in dismissal. "Take it out of petty cash. Change your attitude or change jobs."

The hatchway behind the driver framed a small street scene capped with a tumultuous sky. Two guards faced the street with their backs to him. A third tilted his head at the sound of three tones that came from the messenger on his belt. He picked it up, spoke into it, then hurried inside. His face seemed to pale more with each of the five steps that brought him to His Honor's side. Their conversation was brief and whispered, but Stella heard every word.

"Code Brutus standby warning, sir. Do you want to secure here or at the compound?"

"Shit!" Alek Dexter said, and he turned his face away as though he'd been slapped. He, like Mr. Wittle, was a possible successor to the Director. He rubbed his forehead while a trackful of security emptied itself out front. His face was as pale as his guard's. He watched the security squad fan out from the track and take up positions outside. A half-dozen armed men covered with grime and streaming sweat shouldered by him and stationed themselves about the reception.

"These ours?" he asked his guard.

The guard shrugged, his lasgun gripped white-knuckle tight in his shaking hands. "Don't know, sir."

"Humph," he grunted. "Guess it's hard to know what side they're on if we don't know what side we're on. Just a warning, you say? Flattery's not ..."

"Yes, sir, a warning. Flattery issued it."

"We'll wait here," Dexter said. "If we're going to find ourselves stuck somewhere, I'd prefer it to be with this lovely young woman."

He bowed, took Stella's hand and kissed it. Then he strolled inside to the hostess and her guests, passing the long table set with an array of the most beautiful fruits and seafoods that Stella had ever seen. The centerpiece was a meter-high chunk of ice carved to represent a leaping porpoise, so rare that some called it Pandora's unicorn. When released from hybernation, they headed straight for the kelp and essentially disappeared.

The fighting chattered closer, and security quietly closed the double hatch. Stella was more than a little afraid.

Not once had Dexter glanced at her orchids.

Chapter 45

To be conscious, you must surmount illusion.
—Prudence Lon Weygand, M.D., number five,
original crew member, Voidship *Earthling*

THE SERIES of explosions dropped by Flattery's Skyhawks wounded the green kelp in sector eight, killed tens of thousands of fishes, a pod of the fabled bottlenose porpoises and roiled up enough sediment to clog submersible filters for a fifty-click radius. A huge stand of blue kelp neighboring sector eight retracted all of its fronds instinctively and clamped itself as tight around its central lagoon as possible. In this configuration, its leaves were packed so tight that it could barely breathe. Feeding was out of the question.

The blue kelp, when fully deployed, reached a diameter of nearly one hundred kilometers. Its outer fringes bordered domestic kelp projects for nearly 280 degrees of its circumference; the rest faced open ocean and some of it was growing daily at a visible rate. For its own safety, it kept out of contact with the domestic kelps. These slaves to the humans were bound to the electric whip, this much the blue gathered from the dying shards that drifted its way. There would be many such shards soon. Kelp death always followed these explosions. Other deaths followed, too, at times feeding the blue kelp into an incredible spurt of growth.

This day something else drifted in on the currents. Something like an aura, a fragrance, something that kept the kelp from hugging itself too tight, too long. Something stirred this blue kelp deep within itself, setting its genetic memories tingling. Nothing would quite come to the fore. Soon, the blue could no longer help itself and it opened its fronds wide in hopes of a good strong whiff.

Chapter 46

Feed men, then ask of them virtue.
—Fyodor Dostoevsky, *The Brothers Karamazov*

TURBULENCE FROM the blasts hadn't settled yet when the *Flying Fish* pitched helpless to the surface. Rico's eyes teared instantly in the sudden glare of afternoon sun that blasted the cockpit. He groped for his shades and tried to blink away the afterglow. To starboard, that long gray line must be the coast. To port, two or three kilometers away, the whole surface seethed with a mean white froth.

A puddle of seawater widened into a pool beneath Elvira's command couch. Her nosebleed was slowing and she shook her head, trying to clear the concussion that had hit her with the first of the depth-charges.

Anybody but Elvira would've been scrat bait out there, Rico thought.

Somehow she'd made it back into the engine-room airlock by herself, though stunned and quivering from the blast. Many other blasts followed, too many to count.

"That goddamn Flattery's answer to everything is to blow it up," he grumbled.

Kelp lights winked out all around them as the sea glutted with shredded fronds and torn vines.

"Sister Kelp," Elvira said, following his gaze across the tumultuous surface, "she retracts, saves herself."

"Elvira, I don't want to hear that 'Sister Kelp' crap. I want to get us out of here."

"Overflights!" she warned, and pointed to two specks at ten o'clock off the port cabin. Her hands automatically worked the dive sequence, but the engines remained still.

"Jammed," she said, her face impassive and dazed. "Silt and … kelp in the 'niters."

"Don't sweat it, Elvira," Rico said. He patted her arm. "They're the ones who dropped the charges. If they carried all that payload, they're short on fuel. At least we're not dealing with a bunch of mines out here."

Rico unharnessed himself and got Elvira a towel out of one of the lockers.

"Here," he said. "Dry yourself off, change into a new dive suit. We might be here awhile and there's no sense you getting sick."

She took the towel and stood up on the rocking deck, getting her senses back.

"Flattery can track a one-seater coracle from port to port with the Orbiter, anyway," he said. "These guys can't set down out here, and they don't dare blow up Crista Galli. Meanwhile, we've got to get her and Ben to some big medicine, and fast."

Two sonic booms rocked them harder as the overflights dove in on them and pulled out. Rico could make out the pilots' faces as the tiny aircraft flashed past.

"They're young, Elvira, did you see that? With their whole lives ahead of them they chain themselves to Flattery." He punched the arm of his couch and grumbled, "Why do they do that? They should be out cuddling some young thing in a hatchway somewhere. Didn't their mothers teach them any better?"

"Their mothers are hungry, Rico, and they're hungry *now*."

Rico glanced at Elvira with surprise. He was accustomed to speaking to her but getting nothing but grunts for reply. She was fighting the toss of the foil, making her way to the aft lockers.

"You're not going out there again," he said. "The seas are a mess, nothing can get through here."

"You will calm down," she said, and it sounded like an order. Elvira peeled off her dive suit and toweled off her finely toned musculature with the candor typical of Mermen. "Care for the others. I will clean out the filters."

As she slipped into a fresh suit, Rico realized he'd been aroused at the sight of Elvira's pale body. Even her thumb-sized nipples seemed muscular in the chill. He would never approach Elvira, both of them knew that, but the surprise of his arousal reminded Rico of Snej, and how much he'd missed her.

Elvira's plan was the logical thing, he knew. He ticked off a list of priorities.

Ben and Crista, he thought. *Keep them breathing. Monitor the radio, prepare for surprises by Vashon security.*

Elvira swept past him to the hatch without so much as a glance. Rico fought the pitch and roll of the foil to the lockers and pulled out three more dive suits. He worked himself along by handholds in the bulkhead back to the galley. On his way, he listened to the crackle of the radio and the report from the overflights.

"Skywatch leader to base. Charges away. We have your fish, over."

"Roger, Skywatch. We mark your position. Our bird is launched. ETA thirty minutes. Status report."

Thirty minutes! Rico thought. *Their bird must be a foil, and a fast one.*

Not room for a lot of hardware or a lot of bodies—good. *We might have a few surprises for them.*

The radio continued to chatter about the condition of the *Flying Fish* and speculation on the occupants, but they were quickly out of range.

Rico bent over Ben and saw that he was immobile, his chest was not rising and falling, but his color wasn't bad. He put his cheek to Ben's mouth and detected the slightest breath. Checking the pulse at Ben's neck, he noted that his partner's heart was beating, but only a few beats per minute, His eyes were open, but still. They looked dry, so Rico opened and closed the lids a few times to lubricate them, then left them closed.

He unhooked the restraints and struggled to get Ben into one of the dive suits.

"We're topside," he said, hoping Ben could hear. "They threw some charges at the kelp, but I think it's just surface damage. Elvira's out there unclogging the intakes. Flattery's people have a foil on our tail, they'll be here in no time. We may have to go over the rail."

He heard a groan from Crista Galli, and saw that she was trying to sit up against her restraints.

"Your girlfriend's coming around," he said. "I'll get her into a suit, then get into the code book and let Operations know what's going on. Everybody else seems to know where we are."

He sealed Ben's suit and inflated the collar, just in case. When Rico turned to Crista Galli, he saw that she was crying. Her red-rimmed, swollen eyes stared at Ben's deathlike form on the galley deck. She seemed to be conscious and aware.

"Can you understand me?" Rico asked. In spite of her restraints, he remained well out of reach.

She nodded.

"Yes."

"Have you ever had this reaction before?"

"Yes." Her voice was slurred. "Once. Before shots. I spit out pills."

"What will happen next?"

She tried a shrug. "More same. Maybe seizure. Takes … while." She added, in a slurred whisper, "Ben made me feel human being."

Rico noticed that the pupils of her eyes dilated and constricted wildly. *Must be some potent drugs*, he mused. *Damn that Flattery.*

"We are in the open," he explained, "and helpless. You need to have a dive suit on in case we go into the water."

It flashed on him then what Flattery must've realized all along, what Operations warned in their instructions: "Do not let her into the water. Do not let her contact the kelp." This was speculation, precaution. If Vashon security showed up, they'd have no other choice.

No point worrying about it.

"I can help you with it if you can't do it yourself. I'm sorry to say this, but I'd rather not touch you,"

He held the suit out to her at arm's length.

"Can't get out harness," she said.

Rico tapped the quick-release mechanism and she was free. He recoiled from her, partly as a reflex, partly because the foil pitched his way.

At this, she cringed away from him, her face even more pale and her jaw set. Some coordination was coming back.

"And what do *you* think I am?" she asked.

"I don't know," he said. "Do you?"

"I know that I don't think … I *can't* think that I do this …" She gestured limply at Ben. "It *can't* be me!"

"It's the drugs," Rico said.

He tried to keep the anger out of his voice. She needed reassurance, not another enemy.

"Remember, the drugs are Flattery's doing, not yours."

Her tears, the way she looked at Ben *seemed* like the genuine article.

But look at what happened to Ben, he cautioned himself.

"Get your suit on," Rico said. "We don't have much time."

Crista had to slip out of her dress to don the dive suit. Rico knelt beside Ben, a hand on his forehead. He moved a little, and Rico took it for a good sign. His breathing was much stronger.

Crista did not seem modest at all, nor did she look like a monster. Probably spent so much time as a lab animal she didn't have a chance to get shy.

Rico, like Ben, had been raised among Islanders, a generally shy lot. Rico admitted to himself that Crista had the best-looking legs he'd ever seen. Again, he thought of Snej back at Operations, and sighed. He planned to send a message to her, too, along with whatever he'd think of to say to Operations. He turned back to Crista Galli.

A little pale, he thought, *even for her.*

She seemed very weak, and struggled just to pull her suit on and fasten the seals. Her breathing was rapid and shallow. Her forehead beaded sweat and her eyes were doing their dilation trick again.

"Can you get back into your harness?" he asked.

She shook her head.

"No," she said, her voice weaker now.

"It's starting …"

She was drifting out again. She slumped down on her couch, eyes still open.

"Are you still with us?" he asked. "Can you hear me?"

"Yes," she said, almost a sigh. "Yes."

Rico still didn't want to touch her. Whatever it was, it had nearly killed Ben and he wasn't about to let the same thing happen to himself. He reached around her carefully and snicked the harness into place, then snugged it up with a jerk. He pushed the head of the couch back so that she lay flat. By then Crista was unconscious again.

Rico hurried into his own suit and noted that the seas had calmed somewhat. He heard the thump and scrape of Elvira at the hull ports, and hoped that the kelp wouldn't set her hallucinating as it did some people. She seemed to have been all right before.

"It'd be just our luck," he muttered to himself. "Best damned pilot in the whole damned world thinking her gauges are grapefruits."

A very loud scrape, more of a long, slithering rasp across the top of the foil. Then another. It was the same serpentine sound that the kelp had made when it grabbed them. Rico jumped for the cabin, but he was too late.

The whole foil tipped on its side and he was slammed against the port bulkhead so hard it knocked the wind out of him. He saw, through the swarm of black amoebas across his vision, that they were airborne. He was jostled again, not so much this time, and as the bow of the foil tilted upward he saw them being pulled up into a mass of hylighter tentacles.

"Shit!"

He struggled to his knees and crawled the upended bulkhead to the command couch under the plaz. He could flip open a port and get a shot at it with his lasgun …

Then he saw how big this hylighter really was. He guessed it at a hundred meters across, with its two lead tentacles, which gripped the foil, at nearly that length. Even the smallest tentacle was thicker than Rico.

Already they dangled a hundred meters or so in the air, and rising. *That pitch back there,* he thought, *it must've dumped a helluva ballast to be able to pick us up.* Then he thought of Elvira, and scrambled for a view of the seas below. She was there, dive suit inflated, floating on her back. She must have seen him, but she didn't wave.

"Damn!"

He couldn't drop her a flare, he couldn't try the engines. Either of these might touch off the thousands of cubic meters of hydrogen in the monster hylighter. It tucked the *Flying Fish* upside-down against its great orange belly. Rico had never been this close to a hylighter before, but he'd seen them explode. A hylighter considerably smaller than this one had flattened the first tiny settlement at Kalaloch. Six hundred people cooked alive in that firestorm. He and Ben had covered that one, too.

The living were the worst. He remembered that Ben wouldn't settle for the easy story, the inevitable films of cooked flesh on living bone, shaking chills, vomit and screams.

"Just shoot their eyes," Ben had told him. "Leave the rest to me."

Ben asked them about their lives, not about the blast. The dying and near-dying filled eighteen hours of tape before the dashers hit. Rico's footage of the team fighting for their own lives against a dozen hunts of dashers in a feeding frenzy chilled the holo audience worldwide.

Rico saw that the coast was coming up fast and black weather pushed behind them. He hoped that the weight of the foil wouldn't pull the hylighter too low to clear the gray bluffs ahead. He worked his way back to the cabin along the ceiling and sat below the command couches. This coliseum of a hylighter had a destination in mind, and that destination was land. If it didn't bash them to bits against this cliff face it would blow them up inland.

Rico reviewed their odds and didn't like what he came up with, though he was sure he'd rather clear the cliff than not. He wondered whether Operations had a code provision for this one. He hoped that Operations could beat Flattery's people to Elvira. Rico refused to mull over the consequences if they didn't.

Just off the cliff face the daily afternoon squall whipped up. The sky punched down on them without warning, clouds churning in their typical black and lasgun gray.

No lightning, Rico prayed to himself. *We don't need lightning.*

They did need the cloud cover, this he knew. With good cover more overflights and Flattery's spies in the Orbiter would be worthless. The ride got bumpier as the squall moved inland with them. Rico was close enough to the face of the bluff to see the markings on the back of a flatwing when an updraft sank his belly. They almost cleared the top, he saw that clearly, but the stern of the foil caught the lip of the bluff, cartwheeling the bow of their craft deep into the leathery belly of the hylighter.

Unrestrained, Rico was flung like a toy about the cabin. The foil tumbled down the cliff face as the hylighter deflated and collapsed on top of it. When the foil came to rest Rico lay dazed across the plazglas windshield of the cabin. All he could see under the shadow of the hylighter's canopy was an immense cloud of blue dust. He flexed his arms and legs, coughed to test his ribs. Bruised, but nothing broken.

"Great!" Rico told himself. "'Keep her away from the kelp,' they said. Here we are, smothering in the stuff."

He tried calming himself, but a few deep breaths did not still the shaking in his hands. He hoped the foil had slid all the way to the beach. He didn't relish being perched halfway up a cliff.

The afternoon downpour washed over the canopy and their foil. Rico thought of Elvira, caught in open water in the squall, and assessed her chances. They summed up close to zero. She might now be one with her sister kelp.

"At least there's not much hydrogen left in that monster," he muttered. He switched on the cabin lights and radio. A couple of the lights worked, but the radio was gone.

He took a deep breath of the kelp-laced air before heading aft to check on Ben and Crista.

Chapter 47

If you think that vision is greater than action, why do you enjoin upon me the terrible action of war?
—from Zavatan *Conversations with the Avata*, Queets Twisp, elder

MACK WAS awaiting a call-back from security when suddenly his instruments showed random explosive damage to the kelp in sector eight.

He didn't wait, Mack thought. *Flattery wants whatever's in there in a bad way.*

Mack was sure that the "something" included Crista Galli. Instrumentation showed merging patterns between the wounded domestic kelp and the massive neighboring stand of wild blue. Mack and Alyssa Marsh had done peripheral studies of that particular stand of blue, the largest wild kelp bed in the world.

It learned to hide from us, to convolute itself so it could grow inside a ring of domestic kelps and outmass them without detection.

Now that it had broken through, he suspected that it could wreak havoc with Current Control. If it was as big as the Gridmaster said it was, then the blue kelp could possibly *be* Current Control.

If this kelp's on our side, then Flattery's surrounded, he thought. *But what if it's* not *on our side?*

Beatriz was his big worry now. She always checked in from the docking bay, but this time he had heard nothing. When she was incommunicado inside her studio he suspected trouble. It wasn't like her at all. Just a blink after Spud left, a spinjet jockey reported seeing a body expelled from the shuttle airlock. Nobody was answering his calls in security or inside the studio.

"Dammit!"

Now the Gridmaster was getting a response from the kelp, an incredibly healthy and powerful response. This stand that the depth charges had stunned back into mere reflex reawakened immediately—with a corresponding shift in frequency.

This is the new kelp, he thought. *It's absorbed the memories of our domestics and taken them over.*

All of the hardware from the domestic kelp was intact, but instead of dozens of frequencies dancing the screens, there was now only one kelp frequency on the Gridmaster.

Mack's screen showed the grid reforming, except for an unresponsive area in the northwestern corner. He hoped that wasn't pruned back too far.

"Well," he muttered, "so far it seems to like us." He had planned to use Current Control to turn the kelps against Flattery. He'd groomed as many sentient stands as he could muster for one last try, for the time that Flattery went too far. MacIntosh saw war as a drug, an extremely addicting drug, and he didn't want Pandorans to start using it.

"I want that sector on visual," he told the sector monitor. "We should be able to spot them."

All he got on visual was the gray-black whirl of afternoon squall that obliterated his view of the entire sector. Ozette, LaPush and Galli were under there somewhere. He hoped against hope that the depth charges didn't turn them all into soup.

Com-line's still down to the studio, he thought. *If Spud doesn't get in there, we'll have to get their attention somehow.*

A feeling stranger than his weightlessness flipped through his stomach. He shook it off, as he had shaken off the chill that slipped into the air after her shuttle docked. He wondered how many had come up on that flight. The shuttle could carry thirty to forty, depending on equipment. Then there was OMC life-support, and the techs. Everyone aboard would have to know what happened.

He didn't like thinking about the OMC, where it came from, what Flattery had done to it. She had been Alyssa, not "it," but he found "it" a lot easier to handle at the moment. Life-support was Mack's responsibility, as it had been aboard the *Earthling.* He did not relish the notion of that job.

"Well," he muttered to himself, "before we get that far I might have a few surprises for Flattery."

A soft tone went off near the turret, alerting him that something was forming up on the kelp's private holo stage. MacIntosh had built the thing after consulting Beatriz on holography. He had routed it through the Gridmaster in hopes of getting images from the kelp. In the two months of experimentation, results had far exceeded his dreams.

The kelp had been frustrated for a long time, and it had a lot to say. So far it was all images, flashing lights and odd sounds. The images were clear—usually solid information about real things in real time. The sounds and lights seemed to be "talk," or inflection, or philosophizing. MacIntosh had not yet been able to interpret anything but the more obvious images.

He launched himself across the small office toward his new setup at the base of the turret. He didn't care much for the near-zero-gee environment this close to the axis, but it was the most practical location for an observation station. At first, he had liked the immediate access to the shuttle port.

To get the near-normal gravity rimside he would have to put up with the annoying two-minute spin of the Orbiter that made visualization of anything nearly impossible. His body was lanky enough that it got in the way more often than not. Since he'd become acquainted with Beatriz Tatoosh, he had come to like the immediate access to the HoloVision studio, too.

His experimental holo stage lit up with the image of a giant hylighter dragging its ballast across the wavetops. This projection was the best quality he'd ever seen. It was a perfect miniaturization and the collating data identified this as the source of the disruption within the kelp. A metallic glint off the ballast drew his attention closer to the tiny three-D scene in front of him.

"That's not ballast!"

The miniature holo played out the incident with the *Flying Fish* and the hylighter. He watched from the hylighter's view as they bore down on the cliff. They came in fast, and when MacIntosh realized that they wouldn't clear the top he caught himself pulling his feet up. Then the hylighter burst, and the screen went blank.

"There's an Oracle somewhere near there," he muttered. "Maybe we can muster up a rescue team."

He handed himself back to his command console and paged Spud on the intercom. Then all hell broke loose from the klaxons.

The four-klaxon alarm meant a fully involved fire somewhere in the forward axis section, *his* section. His greatest fear was for the shuttle docking station and its spare fuel stores.

With a four-klaxon alarm the fire could be in Current Control, the studio area or the shuttle docking bay. All areas sealed off automatically. Warning lights winked on in all axis quarters and the Orbiter intercom repeated calmly, "Vacuum suits mandatory in all sealed areas. In case of fire, vacuum will be installed. Vacuum will be installed. Vacuum suits mandatory in all sealed areas …"

MacIntosh typed out the "area clear, visual" code for Current Control on his console. If the area sensors detected no fire danger, then Current Control would not be sealed off. He snapped open the hatchside locker and followed the prescribed drill. He sealed himself into his pressure suit and activated the communication unit beside the faceplate. He sprung the hatch to the passageway in time to see a groundpounder security slap Spud across the face with a lasgun butt. Spud spun against the studio hatch, and the security grabbed a closer handhold for the leverage to try again.

MacIntosh hollered, "Hold it!" but the man hit Spud again. Spud floated, unconscious, in midpassageway.

MacIntosh turned his set on "full."

"Hold it!" he yelled. "Stand down, mister."

The security was obviously direct from groundside and lacked the skills for maneuvering in the axis area of the Orbiter. He spun around at the voice and let go his handhold. The momentum in near-zero-gee sent him spinning up the passageway toward MacIntosh. The man let go of his lasgun as he flailed for balance and Mack scooped it up as he sailed by.

Mack reached Spud as he started coming around.

"I heard them say they'd kill her," Spud said, through a mouthful of blood. "I pulled the alarm because I didn't know what else to do."

"Good thinking, Spud," he said. "Get a suit on in case we break vacuum."

The arriving volunteer fire squad crowded the passageway as Spud suited up, and close behind them the usual throng was forming. In spite of their bulky suits the squad moved with a grace that MacIntosh envied. He looked around for the owner of the lasgun, but the man had disappeared. The hatch to the studio remained sealed.

MacIntosh plugged his communicator directly into Spud's headset.

"Beatriz knows the drill," he said. "She'll suit up."

"Does she know the visual 'all clear' code?"

MacIntosh nodded.

"She knows it, but I'll bet she knows better than to use it."

Two things prevented a sealed-off fire area from being committed to vacuum: an automatic sensor signal "all clear" to the Orbiter computer, and a coded visual "all clear" signal to the computer. Since the sensors in the studio undoubtedly reported no sign of fire, the computer awaited the visual code indicating that a human had inspected the scene and declared it clear. Meanwhile, the suspect area remained sealed off, accessible only by fire personnel.

The intercom warned: "Attention axis deck, yellow sectors eight through sixteen. Vacuum instillation in three minutes. Vacuum in three minutes. Full pressure suit mandatory in these areas ..."

The electronic device that the fire squad used to enter sealed hatches didn't work on the first try, or the second. MacIntosh plugged his set into the bulkhead receptacle and tried direct contact with the studio.

Spud plugged into MacIntosh.

"Anything?" he asked. MacIntosh shook his head. "Static. They're just not ..."

On the third try the hatch sprang aside. The fire squad rushed in and MacIntosh shouldered himself behind them, hiding the lasgun as best he could. He was glad he did.

Beatriz was the only one who had managed to don a suit. She stood to the side of the hatch and grabbed MacIntosh as he raced through. The momentum spun him into the bulkhead beside her, but she had a good grip on a handhold so they both stayed put.

The others fumbled with the seals of their suits, surprised at the suddenness of the fire squad's entry. One of the newcomers made a clumsy dive for the back of the studio, but he was grabbed in flight by a firefighter and his partner who wrestled him to a handhold and restrained him. MacIntosh made sure the rest of them saw his lasgun and they stayed put.

Mack's squad finished their sweep of the room in less than a minute and one of them sent the "all clear, visual" signal back to the computer. The intercom announced "all clear," and MacIntosh unfastened his headgear. Beatriz beat him to it.

"They killed my crew," she shouted. "They killed your security squad and they have weapons back there in the lockers."

One of the firefighters sailed to the back of the studio to search out the weapons cache.

"Hold these men," MacIntosh ordered, "and hand out whatever weapons they have, we're likely to need them."

The firefighters used various lines and straps from their pockets to truss up Leon and his two men. All three were confounded and helpless in zero-gee. The fire squad lived and worked in it every day, but MacIntosh still had to admire their ease of movement, even with three struggling captives in tow.

Beatriz hugged him tight and kissed him. Even through the added bulk of the vacuum suit, she felt good to him.

"I was hoping we could do that under other circumstances," he said. He felt her trembling and held her close.

"There are more of them," she said, "I counted thirty-two altogether. My guess is that their leader, Captain Brood, is with the OMC."

"Spud, you heard?"

"Yes, Dr. Mack."

"All this action's going to bring somebody down here. Seal off axis sector yellow, code admission only. We might seal a few of them in here with us, but it'll give us time to deal with the rest of them."

Spud activated the nearest console and completed the order in a blink.

MacIntosh motioned to the firefighter with the white headgear. "There's a big storage locker across the passageway that's empty. Seal these men in there and then meet me in the teaching lab next to Current Control. If you can find any weapons from our own security, bring them. I want your best tunnel rats, as many as you can muster."

"Aye, Commander," he said, then added, "these men are groundsiders, sir. You saw how clumsy they are. Our best weapons here are zero-gee and vacuum."

"You're right," MacIntosh said, taking Beatriz's hand, "and strategy. Let's move."

Chapter 48

While the fat and flesh cleaving to the flame are devoured by it, you who cleave to it are yet alive.

—Zohar, *The Book of Splendor*

SPIDER NEVI hoped that Flattery was getting a humbling at the hands of the rabble, because Nevi was certainly getting a humbling out here at the hands of the kelp. He'd spotted Zentz floating on his back, only the whites of his eyes visible, the mouthpiece to his breathing apparatus discarded. A long strand of kelp wrapped his middle, and it reeled him steadily toward the edge of the lagoon.

Lucky for Zentz that he'd had the presence of mind to inflate the collar of the suit. It kept his head and shoulders on the surface, though fat as he was his body floated nicely enough without it. Lucky, too, that Nevi had hit the vine quickly and on the first shot. He had Zentz all the way back to the foil before he felt the seethe of kelp anger on his heels. Zentz appeared to be breathing.

It would've been so much easier if he had drowned, Nevi thought. *But I might still need him. A live body is a lot more useful than a dead one.*

Nevi knew one thing for sure, he was getting out of reach of the kelp. One zombie on the crew was enough. The foil started a slow spin, and Nevi swore under his breath.

It's channeling us into its reach.

He managed to secure Zentz's collar with a line from the aft hatchway and pulled him aboard the foil. He used a boathook to brush off pieces of kelp frond that clung to the unconscious Zentz.

The whole situation had passed beyond the ridiculous for Nevi, now it was simply comic. It didn't matter to him whether Flattery stayed in power or not. Whoever was up there would need Spider Nevi and his services, and Nevi enjoyed that position. It was like having three or four good chess moves already set while the opponent was in check. Well, it was time Flattery learned his worth.

Send me out here, will he?

Zentz had been kelped, and the automatics in his dive suit kept him from swimming off to who-knows-where. They didn't keep him from struggling blindly against rescue. At sixty-five kilos, Nevi struggled for a while to wrestle the nearly one hundred kilos of Zentz inside the foil and harness him into his couch. He didn't know why he bothered, except that it would give Flattery something to play with if they didn't come back with Crista Galli and Ozette.

Nevi quickly maneuvered the foil to the center of the lagoon and prepared for vertical takeoff. Vertical would eat up more fuel than he liked, but it would cut his odds of getting grabbed by that kelp stand.

He punched in the automatic VTO sequence and all of the power of the foil kicked him right in the seat of the pants. It swayed like a bug on a blade of grass until they were a safe hundred meters above the lagoon. He set the controls for straight-and-level and turned the foil loose. A routine ten-minute refueling had turned into nearly an hour's delay, and Nevi couldn't afford to waste another blink.

He listened to the radio and couldn't make heads or tails of the situation back at the Preserve. He'd tried to raise Flattery on their dedicated channel, but no one keyed him in at the other end. One fragment of transmission from an overflight came through and he shook his head in wonder.

What idiot talked Flattery into depth-charging the foil we're hunting?

He snapped off the radio and relaxed his grip on the controls. The afternoon turbulence didn't sit well on his stomach, so he flipped off the autopilot. He needed something to do besides listen to Zentz snore through his drool. He kept the yellow arrow on his viewscreen pointed toward the green coordinates set down by the overflights.

Zentz squirmed in the copilot's couch.

Our Chief of Security might be coming around.

Nevi sneered at the mere thought of Zentz as chief of anything. *Chief* Breach *of Security*, he thought. *Chief of* In*security*.

Nevi had to admit that Zentz had held a difficult line against the increasing hostility of the villagers for nearly a year. A mob of villagers was one thing—this Crista Galli and her Shadow playmates were quite another.

"A hundred meters across!" Zentz gurgled.

Zentz's eyes were wild, the pupils dilating and constricting on both sides, dancing to some strange rhythm.

Nevi didn't answer. Zentz had started this raving about some giant hylighter as soon as Nevi had gotten the foil back in the air.

"Crista Galli, kelp gone crazy," Zentz went on, "giant hylighter grab whole foil …"

"That's hocus-pocus, and it's in your head," Nevi said.

He knew Zentz couldn't hear him, but it made Nevi feel better. His voice was calm and flat, a practiced calm that paid off whenever he had to work with Zentz. He knew it gave Zentz the creeps, and that always gave Nevi the edge. He wondered whether it would give Zentz the creeps in his dreams. He hoped so. Flying made Nevi nervous.

The storm buffeted Nevi against the restraints in his command couch. Some of the updrafts along the coastline nearly emptied his stomach. Like most Pandorans, he preferred traveling the kelp's subways, particularly during afternoon storms, but today speed was critical. The cat had played the mouse too loose. Maybe Zentz was right about their foil. Who knew what the kelp had shown him?

If Ozette and Crista Galli got loose afoot in this country they might just wind up being dasher bait. Ozette didn't strike him as the survival type. Nevi knew that Flattery needed both of them alive—for now. For now, what Flattery needed Nevi needed, and he didn't want to get so comfortable out here that he forgot it.

Zentz needs them alive more than anyone, he thought.

The big question mark for Nevi was the hylighter—what would contact with that thing do to Crista Galli?

Or what might it do for *her?*

And something about those damned Zavatan squatters upcoast gave even Nevi the creeps. Nobody could farm the open country like that without some kind of protection. He wanted to know what that protection was. Or who. They kept one jump ahead of Flattery and the dashers—accomplishments that captured Nevi's personal respect.

The squall cleared occasionally, allowing Nevi glimpses of the coastline. Cloudfront pushed across both suns and confounded his perspective. He knew that thousands of square kilometers lay under Zavatan camouflage. It didn't take much imagination to appreciate the value of that new fertile land below.

In a matter of weeks the Zavatans turned bare rock into garden, pumped water and started up their smelly labs. The entire upcoast region was laced with streams and pockmarked with hundreds of small lakes. They'd already turned many of the lakes into fish farms. Their pitiful farms grew more than enough to sustain them, this Nevi knew. His information was better than Flattery's, but Flattery didn't pay him for information.

Where does their surplus go? he wondered.

He knew that when he discovered the answer to that one he would answer the Shadow question as well.

No food, no Shadows, he thought.

It would be a pity if Flattery managed to wipe out the farms to stop the supplies that he was sure were channeled to the underground. There must be a more profitable way …

It occurred to him that the Shadows might win. He shrugged.

Nevi admitted an admiration for these Zavatans, for their independence that Flattery couldn't yet control. He didn't intend to muddy his own hands, though this trip had already proved messy enough.

Nevi smiled, a rare break in the steel of his countenance. He had plans for his retirement, and this upcoast region with its farmland and Pandora's first, burgeoning forests appealed to him. The people up here just might want some professional protection soon. Protection from the likes of Flattery and his bungling Chief of Security.

Lot of new squatters this year, he thought.

Since the earthquakes started a few years ago people had turned to the surface for safety. Even with burmhouses it was easier to spot a dwelling than a tunnel, it wouldn't take that much effort to map these people. Nevi flew into a sudden wall of weather and there wasn't much possibility of spotting anything.

Nevi kept his attention on the screen. The slash of rain against the metal skin and plaz of the cabin nearly deafened him. He switched on the landing lights to clarify the terrain. Still, visibility was a few hundred meters, tops. A buzzer reminded him that he was flying at the stall point.

They were only a couple of kilometers downcoast from the overflight coordinates. Zentz came around enough to set his couch up and hold his head.

"So, how was it?" Nevi asked.

"I don't ever want to go back."

"Where'd you go?"

"Everywhere." Zentz wiped his drool with his sleeve. "I went everywhere … at once. I saw them picked up."

"They're around here somewhere."

"Beached," Zentz said. "Down the cliff. Beached."

Nevi grunted his amusement. He imagined this gray land on a sunny day, blooming.

Flattery couldn't possibly send troops, he thought, *they'd never come home at all.*

"Approaching set-down," he said, and throttled back. "See them yet?"

"No … yes!" Zentz pointed a shaking finger starboard. "There, look at the size of that … thing! I knew it was more than a dream."

Nevi was disgusted at the spit-spray of Zentz's excitement. The squall moved on already as quickly as it had come, and visibility over the downed hylighter was good. The terrain, however, looked deadly. The crumple of downed foil was plainly visible amid the orange shards of the deflated hylighter.

It was a monster, all right, and deflated it covered far more than the hundred-meter diameter it had occupied in the air. Almost half of it trailed the fifty meters down to the sea, and the rest lay crumpled in the narrow stretch of beach between the sea and the precipitous rocks. The foil appeared to be nearly intact right at the foot of the cliff.

Nevi did not want to set down inside the perimeter of that thing—he'd seen what that blue dust did to some of those burned-out Zavatans who wandered dazed around the village. The strip of tideline was too narrow and the tides less predictable than he liked. The beach itself, from tideline to cliff, was a jumble of boulders. That meant a water landing or a set-down at the top of the cliff. He didn't like the look of all that kelp in the water, or the positioning of the dead hylighter.

"Electronic and infrared scan," Nevi ordered. "I'm making a couple of passes so that we don't get surprised down there. Then we'll worry about how to get them out from under that thing."

Their situation suddenly struck Nevi as absurd. Flattery had positioned his precious Orbiter and had the Voidship nearly ready to go; he had plans to establish a stepping-stone colony in a debris belt over a million kilometers away. Pandora's moons were even more unstable than the planet. Even Nevi agreed that fleeing was the ultimate answer. But he doubted that it would be worth it in his own lifetime.

Especially if he insisted on risking his life in a wrestling match with a hydrogen gasbag of hallucinatory dust and tentacles. He chose a set-down atop the cliff, near a trail that didn't look too difficult. Zentz should be clear of his kelpling by the time they reached bottom.

If the girl's as holy as they say, let's see her get herself out of this one.

Chapter 49

That's all Ship ever asked of us, that's all WorShip was meant to be: find our own humanity and live up to it.

—Kerro Panille, from *The Clone Wars*

RICO SPRUNG the galley hatch with a crowbar from the tool locker and saw Ben sitting up, fumbling with the catch of his harness.

"Ben, buddy ..."

He stumbled over the crumbled deck to Ben's couch, but was careful not to touch him. Ben's Merman-green eyes seemed clear when they looked at him, but they weren't tracking all that well. Both Ben and Crista were half-buried in debris from what was left of the galley.

"Can you talk?"

Ben's voice caught in his throat. "I ... I think so," he said.

"Sit back," Rico said.

His own head started a strange buzz, so he took a deep breath, let it out slow. "We're not going anywhere for now, so relax."

He hesitated short of unclipping the last two restraints.

"Crista ..." Ben's voice sounded foreign, distant. "Is she all right?"

Rico felt his lips tingling, and his fingertips, too. *Just like Ben to think of someone else first.* He glanced over at the other couch. There was no movement. All the lights in the galley were out, but from where Rico knelt in the rubble it looked as if she wasn't breathing.

Shit!

"Sit back," Rico repeated, pushing Ben back. "I'll check." His muscles didn't work quite as they should, and he felt as if he was moving in slow motion. The heavy rain that pelted their foil dimmed what little light seeped through the single uncovered port. Rico noticed that the shadows weren't just shades of gray, but dancing hues of blue and green, backed up by flickering tongues of a cold yellow flame.

A halo of yellow flame surrounded the prone form of Crista Galli. Rico couldn't see any movement, but her lips were pink and that gave him hope. He moved to check for a pulse at her neck, then backed off. He couldn't bring himself to touch her.

She lay still, absolutely sagged, her mouth a little open. The inflated dive collar kept her head back and her airway clear. Even this way, Rico had to admit she was beautiful. For Ben's sake, for the sake of the hungry people of Pandora, he hoped she stayed alive. As he watched, a green glow smoldered over her body. A fainter glow, also green but lighter-hued, came from himself. Pockets of green oozed out of him and, amoeba-like, they crept the air. One of these joined with a similar pocket oozing away from Crista Galli. She was alive, no question about it. Now all he had to do was keep her that way.

"Rico?"

"Yeah, Ben," he said.

His voice sounded a long way away to himself.

But it's right here my voice is right here.

"Is she all right?"

Rico breathed in deeply, and some of the lime-green glow sped into his lungs like fog or dust.

"She's OK," he said, fighting for control of his tongue. "Flattery gave her drugs a while back."

Rico turned slowly and saw his partner backlighted by the one piece of uncovered plaz. The rain that spatted against it struck sparks that shot out from Ben and ricocheted around the galley. Ben sat up rubbing his eyes, and a roil of fire moved with him. It was not the blue-green glow that captured Crista and Rico, but a sensuous warm glow like the throb of some membrane from the inside.

The spore dust …

"I think I'm dusted," he told Ben in his new, slow way. "How do you feel?"

"Headache," he heard Ben say. "Helluva headache."

Ben's speech was thick and slurred.

"And my muscles don't all want to go right, but they work. That shot did it."

Rico helped him sit up. Their two haloes arced and whirled around them. Ben held his head between his hands, doubled over nearly to his knees. "I see what you mean … I'm starting to feel a little dusted, myself. Long time."

"Yeah," Rico said, letting out another slow breath, "long time. With Crista it's drugs. Flattery's drugs."

"Drugs, yeah," Ben said. "She's been laced up with something, something that Flattery wants people to think is kelp juice. Figures."

Ben stood on wobbly legs, holding Rico and the bulkhead, and made his way to Crista Galli. Rico watched as Ben checked her pulse, bent to her breathing.

"She's in there," Ben said. "If she's like I was, she can hear us, too." He leaned down to her ear. "You'll be all right," he said, and patted her arm.

Rico hoped it wasn't a lie. Some panicky feeling in his gut told him that none of them would ever be all right. The green of his aura sucked itself tight against his body. When he stuffed his unease away, it crept out from him again and mixed with the others.

The drugs are the danger, not her touch, he reminded himself. *How long before they wear off?*

Rico knew that a single-dose dusting didn't last that long in real time. He would have to remind himself that it was the dust that warped time. He knew they didn't have much of it to spare. They could count on help from the kelp. This was something he felt, intuited.

"We'd better see what we have left," Ben said.

Rico forced himself to focus. He knew Ben was right, and if they were both dusted then they both had to pay attention.

"If we don't pay attention, we're dead," Rico heard himself say. Ben just grunted.

Rico pulled the lasgun from his belt, checked the charges. "They'll know we're down," he said. "We have to get out from under this mess, we're too easy to spot."

He braced himself against the upside-down bulkhead and grumbled, "Things were tough enough without all of us going to dreamland."

Rico started through the buckled-in hatch.

"Bring me some dust," Ben said. "That's what we need to get her out of this."

"No way," Rico said. "She's had enough, right here. We don't know what Flattery's been doing to her. A heavy dose might kill her, you don't know …"

He heard his voice going on without him. Ben was insisting that he was right, that she'd already been dusted and it was bringing her around, that what she needed was more …

"I'm serious, Rico. She needs it, and the antidote—you saw what it did to her. Think about it."

Rico didn't understand, and he knew they didn't have time to think about it.

He didn't say anything more, just turned on his heel and picked up Crista's legs under the knees. Ben reached under her arms and they stumbled with her through the hatchway into what was left of the cabin.

A few of the lights still worked, illuminating the burst-in walls and ceiling. The galley and aft portion of the foil remained upright, but the boat was twisted nearly in half at the cabin hatchway. The entire bow lay on its side. One of the wings had sprung from its retraction bay and sliced into the fuselage, peeling a section of hull away like a rind.

Ben brushed away debris with his feet and they set Crista down. She called his name and gripped his arm. Rico went immediately to work trying to free them from the deflated hylighter and the wreckage. Some pockets of undissipated hydrogen worried him. The rain helped, but he worried about sparks—not the spiritual kind he'd seen in the galley, but the metal-to-rock kind that might flash the hydrogen.

"There's still some gas around here," Rico warned them. "It shouldn't be a problem but we should be careful. Our judgment's been dusted, too, so we have to be extra careful. Don't move around much until we get free."

Rico's legs stood in the fuselage rip while the rest of him worked at using the wing section as a shield to push the dead hylighter away from the foil. With his head and shoulders in the open he could see that the foil lay next to the cliff, with the hylighter spread out between the foil and the sea. A small flap of the bag and two tentacles covered the foil. The whole scene whirled in a lightshow of spore-dust.

No gas out here, he thought. *Not with this good offshore breeze.*

Rico smelled a greasy char, sickly sweet, as he burned through the hylighter flap with his lasgun. Peeling it back from the fuselage made him even more lightheaded and wobbly-kneed. A thick, steamy smoke filled the cabin and Crista coughed behind him.

"Crista!"

Ben's voice sounded happier than Rico had heard it in a long time. Releasing the flap of hylighter let in some air and some light. The rain had muddied most of the dust, but they'd still had a pretty stiff dose. Rico's head felt as if it was ready to take a big plunge, as if he was clinging to some giant fluke just before it sounded for the deeps. He kept reminding himself aloud, "We've been dusted, it will pass soon" until it made him laugh. He ducked back inside. Crista leaned on one elbow, coughing and gasping, and shook her head.

"Ben," her voice gravelly, deep, "we are saved. Avata will see to it."

Just then a tentacle slithered through the hole above them. In a blink it snaked around Rico's waist and snatched him back through the gap. Its grip on his waist was stronger than anything he'd felt in his lifetime, but it didn't hurt. He heard a shout and felt a grab on his foot from Ben, then the hole and the foil receded from sight, and Rico couldn't see anything but dark green water.

Chapter 50

Therefore, if it was more necessary in those days to satisfy the soldiers than the people, this was because the soldiers had more power than the people. Today ... all rulers find it more necessary to satisfy the people than the soldiers, because the former now have more power than the latter.

—Machiavelli, *The Prince*

HOLOMASTER RICO LaPush was a fine prize indeed. The Immensity respected this human LaPush as a sculptor of images, the best that the humans had ever mustered. For nearly a decade the Immensity had monitored human transmissions in all spectra. Through these transmissions it witnessed the inevitable unraveling of human politics. When it had its own data to compare, it found significant facts wanting. From humans it learned to lie, then learned the subtleties between lie and illusion, truth and illumination.

The Immensity intended to learn holography. On its own it had mustered transient illusion at times—ghost ships at sea, phantom radio transmissions—the parlor tricks of broadcast. Holography was more precious than that. The Immensity knew humans, now, and human history. Holography, the pure language of imagery and symbol, would become the interspecies tongue.

Other communications, of course, sufficed—electrical voice-talk of the humans. They spoke to each other of fish concentrations, weather, delivered the mysterious modulations that humans called "music." Except for the music this had been easily understood, but not very interesting. Then the human they dared call "Kelpmaster" began using the kelp itself as a medium of conduction. This private communications channel linked the Orbiter with the Zavatan world, and the kelp heard everything. The Immensity spoke in pictures, and these words over the kelp channel helped weave a picture of the world as it was, and as it could be. Though the Kelpmaster listened, he lacked the subtleties of holography that the Immensity required.

The Immensity could think of no better place to start than with LaPush, the Holomaster. The Immensity knew good holos from bad. In this matter it would apprentice itself to Rico LaPush.

The hylighter tentacle that gripped LaPush was, in turn, gripped by a huge frond of blue kelp. It transmitted every move directly to the kelp. Rico's automatic lapel camera unreeled a ten-second broadcast every hour, beamed back to its recorder in the foil. The Immensity received all broadcasts, including these.

Flattery was the dominant human, but the Immensity saw no future in him. He enslaved the kelp, but worse, he enslaved his own kind. Flattery didn't trust any creature that might know what he was thinking, including humans. He had plans to hide the future of a world from its people, and the kelp noted a heavy stink of greed about him. Except for the kelp channels, Flattery controlled communication among humans. He discouraged it, as he discouraged their education. The kelp often marveled that humans survived themselves. They appeared to be their own fiercest predator.

Flattery would sacrifice many to save himself, it realized one day, *perhaps even to the last human.*

The Immensity harbored no illusions about its position in Flattery's hierarchy.

The kelp knew that as long as humans accepted Flattery as the Director they would never realize their potential as One. If they did not do this, then neither would they recognize the need for Oneness among the kelp. Flattery saw this need as a threat, in humans and kelp alike. There would be no true Avata again as long as Flattery ruled. Whenever the brain grew, Flattery dealt it a stroke.

Since the day of insight, the Immensity had set about the downfall of Raja Flattery and the unity of pruned-down stands of kelp throughout the seas. The answer, it knew, was in holo. If it could project holo images, it could communicate in a way that humans would understand. It could speak to distant humans and to kelp alike.

A language between sentients, the Immensity thought, *this is the Pandoran revolution.*

Rico LaPush had been difficult to follow. He moved quickly and under cover, and spent most of his time landside these days. He'd been exposed to the kelp from organic islands that were the old cities and on assignment with Ben down under among the Mermen—still, he had chosen not to communicate directly with the kelp throughout most of his adult life.

It is simply a matter of privacy.

Unlike Flattery's political fear of betrayal and death, Rico's was simply a reluctance to let the kelp eavesdrop through his psyche. It did not make him feel "at one with Oneness" as it did many of the Zavatans, this the Immensity knew. What the kelp knew of Rico it had gotten from other sources, and from the airwaves of HoloVision.

Perhaps the Holomaster Rico LaPush would become the kelp's Battlemaster if the image alone was not enough. Timing and presentation of images were essential. As a kelp channel, a simple conductor, the Immensity allowed itself to be used by the faithful in their struggle with the Director. Now it was time to use them in that same struggle.

The Immensity would win over other stands and reestablish Avata as the true governor of Pandora. It planned to help humans win over Flattery and to come to some symbiosis with these fearful humans. Oracles and kelpways were not enough. Images were tools beyond value, and the kelp would learn to use them.

"Seeking visions in the kelp violates civil rights," Flattery had proclaimed. "If your son uses the kelp, then he and all who use it, including the kelp, know the most private thoughts and dreams of your youth, of your entire life before his conception. That constitutes mind-rape, the ultimate violation."

He passed his law making contact "for the purposes of communication" an offense punishable in varying degrees, all of them unpleasant. The Zavatans universally ignored this law, much to the benefit of the kelp.

The Immensity had to snatch Rico quickly, before he alarmed the others. The enemy Nevi approached, and there was no time for petty confrontations. The Immensity had appropriate reverence for the kelpling Crista Galli. She would be the instrument that would complete the symphony of the kelp. But without Rico's genius the kelp saw hopelessness, death and despair in Crista's future, and in all of their futures.

The hylighter had turned in a superb performance. The *Flying Fish* now rested atop an Oracle, an old one secured by a small but hardy Zavatan band. Its cavern, much larger than Flattery's, was occupied equally by the live kelp root and the Zavatans. Passage from the water side was too dangerous for a foil. The humans had burrowed a passageway down from the top of the bluff to meet the kelp's burrow in the rugged rock near shore. It was identical to the Oracle that lay at the foot of Twisp's command center beneath the high reaches.

Flattery had scoured the kelp clean from his cavern, to make it suitable to his tastes. He had destroyed one of the kelp's nests, a socket where the kelp rooted into the continent itself. Zavatans protected hundreds of these stations along the coastline, careful to keep Flattery's people at bay. Each Oracle was a strategic kelpwork of communication, a link with the entire world and with the Orbiter above it.

The Immensity had learned from certain Zavatans how images are formed on the matrix of the human brain, and how its own flesh correspondingly formed the images that it saw against the dreamscape of the sea. When it learned to project its thoughts, its images, as Rico LaPush projected his holos to fill empty space, then it would commence the salvation of Avata and of humans.

Woe to Flattery, it thought. *Woe to selfishness and greed!*

It dragged Rico inside the Oracle and among his own kind as quickly as it could so that he would not be unnecessarily fearful of his new pupil, Avata.

Chapter 51

What happiness could we ever enjoy if we killed our own kinsmen in battle?
—Bhagavad-Gita

WHEN HE announced after their midday ration that he would run the P, the Deathman's squad beat him up. They thought that would bring him to his senses, or at the very least make running around the demon-infested Dash Point physically impossible. It didn't work.

"I know why you're doing this," his squad leader told him. He was called "Hot Rocks," and his sister was married to the Deathman's brother back in Lilliwaup. They talked in private behind some boulders bordering Kalaloch's refugee camp.

"Just like everybody else who does this, you're fed up with killing. You want to do something for somebody, leave your insurance to your family, right?"

The Deathman just leaned back against the boulder and stared at a clear patch of blue sky scudding with the clouds.

"Who gets your back pay? Your mom? Your brother? That little piece of blonde action you've been plugging in the camp?"

The Deathman's hand snapped toward Hot Rocks but stopped still at his throat. Hot Rocks didn't flinch. Hot Rocks never flinched.

"My brother."

Hot Rocks cursed under his breath, then whispered, "Wouldn't it be better to go back there? Tour's almost over, the worst is over. We're all going home in a month. One month. If you still feel this way …" he looked both ways, "… then fight this thing at home. Work it out at home."

"I'm no good for home," the Deathman said. "The things I've done … I'm not normal, you're not normal. We can't go back there. *We can't!*"

"So, instead of going home you run the P, you make the dash out Dash Point and back. You know the odds. Lichter made it a month ago. Spit made it and collected a year's worth of food chits. Two out of twenty-eight—it's suicide and you know it."

"Either way, my family's better off," the Deathman said.

His voice was a monotone, and Hot Rocks could barely hear him above the light breeze.

"They get my insurance and back pay if I don't make it, and the winnings if I do."

"Yeah," Hot Rocks said, "but they don't get what they want—which is you. If I come back without you my sister will have my ass."

"I can't go back. You know that. You of all people should know that. They should make a place for us, or let us go after these Shadows and take over wherever they are and stay there and then we won't have to hurt anybody anymore …"

The Deathman choked up, and Hot Rocks looked away. He peeked around the boulders and saw the rest of the squad near the beach, backs together, watching for demons or a Shadow attack.

"You're my brother-in-law, but let's forget that," Hot Rocks said. "You're the best man I've got. These guys are alive today because of you—doesn't that count for something?"

"It don't mean shit," the Deathman said. "It means I've got more ears in my pouch than anybody else. They throw rocks and garbage at us and we hit them with lasguns and gushguns—shit, man, if they were animals we wouldn't even say it was good sportsmanship."

"I think—"

"I think you better stop thinking for me, and start thinking for yourself," the Deathman said. "I've learned how to kill here, but I haven't learned how to like it and I sure as hell haven't learned how to sleep nights. Last I heard, there were no openings for assassins in Lilliwaup."

He stood up, brushed off his fatigues and hefted his lasgun.

"Now this is how it's gonna be," he said. "I'm doing the running whether you let me take the bets or not. You gotta admit, a sizeable winnings is good incentive, and I intend to add an attractive twist."

Hot Rocks flicked his gaze around the beach, the cliff side, the tumble of boulders around them. This was hooded dasher country, and his caution was automatic. Besides, they'd burned out two boils of nerve runners here in the past week and nothing gave Hot Rocks the creeps more than nerve runners.

"Let's do it," he sighed, and they joined the rest of the squad at the tide-line.

The bright afternoon suns ate away the tail of the daily squall and glistened off the wet black rocks of Dash Point. The narrow point jutted three kilometers into the ocean, and was named for its popularity as a place to run the P.

"Running the P" was a game as old as Pandoran humans. The first settlers took bets, then ran unarmed and naked around the perimeter of their settlement, hoping to beat the demons for a thrill and a few food chits. Though technically illegal, it was a game resurrected by the Vashon Security Force. In the old days, survivors of the run tattooed a single chevron over an eyebrow to mark their success. Though this tradition, too, had been resurrected, the runs were set in places like Dash Point that were famous for high demon populations. The two in twenty-eight that Hot Rocks had seen survive were exactly twice the actual average.

"Bets are always two to one," the Deathman said. "The six of you match my month's pay, then that means I get a year's pay when I get back."

"*When* he gets back," McLinn muttered. "Listen to him."

"Well, I want *five* to one," he said.

"Five to *what?*"

"You bumped your head."

"No way."

"Shit," McLinn said, "for five to one he just might make it. I'm out."

"Hear me out, gents," the Deathman said. "See that big rock yonder off? I run the P, but I'll swim out to that rock and back. For five to one."

"Stay awake, men," Hot Rocks warned, and everyone swept the area quickly. "Standing here this long we make excellent bait, remember that. OK, let's get it on. Bets or not? Run or not?"

"I'm in."

"Me, too."

"In."

"Here's mine."

Each of the men handed five of their food coupons to Hot Rocks to hold. Each coupon represented a month's rations in the civilian sector. The Deathman handed over five of his own against their twenty-five. Hot Rocks stayed out of it, and the Deathman didn't press him.

"Do me one favor," the Deathman asked.

"Name it," Hot Rocks said.

"Name that rock after me," he said. "I want something around for people to remember me by. Rocks, they're a lot more permanent than people."

"'Deathman Rock,'" McLinn chimed up. "I like the sound of it."

Hot Rocks gave McLinn one of his paralyzing stares and McLinn busied himself with sentry duty.

"If you're going to do it, do it," Hot Rocks said. "Myself, I'd just as soon shoot you here as see you go out there. Stick around much longer and I just might."

"Here's the paperwork," the Deathman said, handing Hot Rocks a small packet. "Back pay, retirement, insurance all go to my brother."

"Who gets the ears?"

"Fuck you."

The Deathman reached into the neck of his fatigues and showed Hot Rocks the necklace he'd made out of the brown little dried-out ears. Though human ears, they looked like seashells now, or twists of leather. He unfastened his fatigues and stepped out of them without a word. He handed Hot Rocks his lasgun and started running toward the point dressed only in his boots. The heavy necklace spun around his neck like a wot's game hoop as he ran.

They took turns at sentry, keeping him in sight with the glasses.

"He's almost at the point," McLinn reported. "What do you bet he leaves his boots on for the swim?"

The quiet one they all called "Rainbow" took him on for a month's worth. Everyone else was quiet, scanning the point with their high-powered glasses for signs of dashers or, worse, nerve runners. Rainbow lost. They were all surprised when he made the rock.

Nobody more surprised than the Deathman, Hot Rocks thought.

"Well, he's earned his place in history," McLinn said, and laughed.

The Deathman stood atop the offshore rock, yelling something they couldn't hear and shaking his necklace of ears at the sky like a curse.

The dasher must've been lazing in the sun on the oceanside of the rock. The impact from its leap carried the Deathman and the dasher a good ten meters into the narrow stretch of sea off the point. Some of the froth boiling up with the waves was green, so Hot Rocks knew that somehow, before he died, the Deathman had drawn dasher blood. Neither the Deathman nor the dasher ever came up.

Hot Rocks paid off the debts and pocketed the Deathman's packet of paperwork. While he packed up the fatigues, the lasgun and the rest of his brother-in-law's gear, none of his men's gazes met his own. He barked a few orders and walked flank while they finished their long sweep back to camp.

Chapter 52

Reveries, mad reveries, lead life.
—Gaston Bachelard

CRISTA HAD endured this dream for years, the one of her return to the arms of kelp, cradled again in a warm sea. She rubbed her eyes and images flickered across the lids like bright fishes in a lagoon: Ben, beautiful Ben beside her; Rico in a cavern beneath them. There were others, fading in and out …

"Crista!" Ben's voice. "Crista, wake up. The kelp's got Rico."

She blinked, and the images didn't go away, they were just overlain with more images like a stack of wot's drawings on sheets of cellophane. Ben knelt at the center of these images, holding her shoulders tight and looking into her eyes. He looked tired, worried … scenes from his life dripped from the aura around him and spread out on the deck beside her.

"I saw something around his waist, a tentacle," he said. "I think it pulled him into the water."

"It's all right," she whispered. "It's all right."

He held her as she got her wobbly legs under her. She breathed deep the thick scent of hylighter on the air and felt strength pulse out from the center of herself to each of her weary muscles. Everything seemed to work.

"I see Rico," she said. "The kelp has saved him. He is well."

"It's the dust," Ben muttered, and shook his head. "If the kelp has him, he's probably drowned. We need to get out of here. There are demons, Flattery's people …"

He doesn't believe me, she thought. *He thinks I'm … I'm …*

A vision gelled in front of her out of thin air, one of Rico wet and gasping in the cavern. Rico tipped back his head and laughed, surrounded by … friendly feelings. It was a side of him she hadn't seen. Someone approached him, a friendly someone.

"Zavatans," she said, cocking an ear, "they will be coming up from the caverns."

"It's the dust, Crista," Ben insisted, "it'll wear off. These are hallucinations. We've got to find Rico and get out of sight. Flattery's people …"

"… are here," she said. "They're already here. It's not hallucination …" she giggled, "… it's cellophane."

She had unraveled some cellophane in her mind and she saw the sinister figures looking down from the clifftop. Two of them. She reeled her vision closer and saw that she knew them both from Flattery's compound: Nevi and Zentz. Zentz's face and body were grossly misshapen. With Nevi, it was his soul. This she could see in the boiling black aura that seethed from him and sought her out. It sniffed the wind with its black snout like a dasher on the hunt.

She felt Ben pull her backward through the rip in the *Flying Fish*. The bright sky trailing the storm forced her to squint and focus on a double rainbow that lazed in the sky above them. She wondered whether Ben might be right about the dust. The pink of the rainbow's arch blazed brightest of all the colors and it pulsed in time with her own pulse.

"Do you see it?" she asked.

"The rainbows?" Ben said. "Yes, I do. Give me your hand, I'll help you down here." "Don't rainbows mean something?" she asked. "A promise of some kind?"

"Supposedly God placed a rainbow in the sky as a promise that he would never destroy the world by flood again," he said. "But that was Earth, and this is Pandora. I don't know whether God's promises are transferable. Here, give me your hand."

The impatience in his voice just made her move slower.

Rico's safe, she thought. *He doesn't believe me, so he's worried.*

She shielded her eyes from the glare and scanned the cliff. The clifftop was identical to the one in her vision, except for a void, a nothingness where she'd seen the images of Zentz and Nevi.

Another image of Rico, in the cavern. He reached out for the kelp frond that brought him there and she felt him transported to the dead hylighter at their feet. He stood there, facing them, head cocked and hands on his hips, impatient, waiting for them to make up their minds.

"Look there," she said to Ben, "can't you see Rico?"

She pointed to his image, seating itself at the point where the hylighter touched the sea. He was smiling at her for the first time and beckoned her with a finger.

"I see the sun shining off the water," Ben said. "It's too bright to look at. You'd better be careful of your eyes."

"It's Rico ..."

"We're dusted enough," Ben said.

He stepped down from the foil to the ground and reached up for her.

"Try not to touch the hylighter. We're probably safest scaling the cliff."

"No!"

The word was torn from her throat before she could think about it.

"Not the cliff," she said. "I feel something there. I saw them up there, Nevi and Zentz. They're after us."

Ben pulled her free of the wreckage and they stood on the unsteady footing of the slickrock beach.

"OK," he said, and sighed, "I believe you. If not the cliff, then where?"

She couldn't help looking at the sea.

"We can't go there," he said. "Please don't ask me to take you there. Maybe you can live in there, but I can't."

He glanced quickly around them, biting his lip. "If you can see Rico, how do we get to him?"

She couldn't resist caressing the remnant of hylighter draped over the foil. Though a plant, and clearly dead, it emanated a warmth that pleased her. It tickled something in her memory, something distant about her childhood. The kelp had protected her, nurtured her, educated her chemically in the customs of her fellow humans. She knew at a touch that this hylighter was from the same stand.

She turned in a slow circle, scanning the beach. She knew Ben was wise in some things, that she had to have faith in him. Without the kelp's cilia, she, too would have died in the sea. Much was rushing back to her, in fragments and colors. What she wanted more than anything was to run to it, to bury herself in the kelp's great body, death or not.

That is selfish, some voice warned her. *Selfish is no longer acceptable.*

She had heard about the barrenness of the upcoast regions, and at first glance black rock was all she saw: sheer black cliff, then black rubble, then a foaming churn of green sea. But there was life among the rubble. Little bits of green squatted among rocks, clinging to crevices in the cliff side. Something, maybe the something that spoke inside her head, pointed her upcoast.

"There."

She took Ben's hand and pointed out a huge black boulder with a single silver *wihi* clinging to its top. It was about thirty meters upcoast, halfway between cliff and tideline.

"That's where we want to be."

That was when Nevi and Zentz stepped out from behind the boulder, lasguns drawn, picking their way across the rocks toward them. Crista wasn't surprised, nor frightened. She heard Ben mutter "Shit!" under his breath and saw his head twitch quickly left to right, looking for a dodge. But she knew it wasn't necessary. She knew.

The moment came together for her like a great conception. All the world silenced itself—the waves, the breeze, the cautious footsteps of two murderers clattering across wet stones.

"Hands on top of your heads, step away from the foil." Zentz delivered his orders with a shaky voice tinged with slobber.

"Yes," Crista told Ben, "that's where we want to be."

They clung to each other's hands in the stone-still afternoon and watched the huge boulder lift itself back from the ground behind Nevi and Zentz. It came up smoothly, quietly, as though on hinges. Neither man heard a thing.

"Hands on your heads!"

The boulder laid itself carefully down behind them and out of the shadow beneath it climbed a half-dozen men armed only with ropes and throwing nets.

"Tell me you see it, too," Ben whispered. "Tell me I'm not still dusted."

"It is as it should be," she whispered back, her voice a singsong. "There is a great moment at our feet, and it will not be stayed."

Something about the way Nevi's gaze met her own must have given it away. Without a backward glance he sprang sideways, beachward, and whirled. The first net was already settling over the surprised Zentz and another, poorly thrown, grazed Nevi's arms. Two flashes from his lasgun brought down two netmen, but Zentz flailed in a hopeless tangle. When Nevi whirled back, Crista Galli stared down the business end of his lasgun. Even at thirty paces it looked huge.

"I'll kill her," he announced, just loud enough for all to hear. "Trust me. I am very quick."

Everyone froze, and in the silence that went with this stillness Crista felt that they were all graceful subjects inside some great painting. She knew who the painter must be.

Nevi half-crouched in careful aim, his colorful face unreadable, his eyes fixed only on Crista Galli. She felt her head clearing, the return of wave-slaps against rock.

But there's something …

… something she hadn't felt since she'd been dredged up from the sea, something familiar …

"Connection," she whispered.

Ben breathed beside her and she felt it as her own breath. They were one person, pulses synchronized with rainbows, waves and the great heartbeat of the void. She knew the choices in his mind and marveled at the sacrifice he was prepared to make. She saw the play in his mind: spin her by the hand, get between her and Nevi, take the hit while the netmen brought him down. At the moment he elected to move, she touched his shoulder.

"No," she said, "it's not necessary. Can you feel it?"

"I feel those sights on my chest," he said. "He's the only thing standing between us and—"

"Destiny?" she asked. "There is nothing between us and destiny." The image of Rico stood behind Nevi, gesturing wildly to her, still smiling.

Nevi came out of his crouch, moved carefully across the rain-wet rocks toward them. She liked the smell of the rain, a different wetness than the smell of the sea, easier on the lungs but not as rich. The scent of the sea, of the dead hylighter, lay heavily beside her like a sleeping lover.

"Do you see?" she asked Ben, and smiled.

"I think I do," he said.

Nevi barked a few orders and two of the surviving netmen slowly began to disentangle Zentz. Crista Galli had that feeling again, the feeling of being a subject in a painting.

"Be still," she whispered. Ben didn't move. Nevi stopped walking, a look of surprise washed over his face.

"Where are they?" he shouted, and he shaded his eyes even though the sun was to his back. "Where did they go?"

Crista suppressed a giggle, and the figure of Rico applauded silently from behind Spider Nevi.

"I don't understand," Ben said. "Are we invisible?"

"We're not invisible," she said, "we're simply not visible. He can't pick us out of this landscape. I think it's a trick that Rico has taught the kelp."

Ben squeezed her hand and started to speak, but that was when the shooting started.

Chapter 53

I will this morning climb up in spirit to the high places, bearing with me the hopes and the miseries of my mother; and there ... upon all that in the world of human flesh is now about to be born or to die beneath the rising sun I will call down the Fire.

—Pierre Teilhard de Chardin, *Hymn of the Universe*

TWISP WALKED Kaleb to the flickering lights at the Oracle's edge. This small cavern was a subset of the great root that Flattery had burned out a few thousand meters downcoast. This place was hushed, a place to breathe iodine on the salt air and feel the cool pulse of the sea.

Kaleb trod the well-worn path with his father's bearing—tall, shoulders back, large eyes alert to every nuance of light and motion. While his parents lived no one had consulted the Oracle as often as he. In the dim light by the poolside Twisp saw that Kaleb's adolescent gangliness had transmuted into the epitome of athletic grace.

"You are the man your father would most like to know," Twisp said.

"And you are the man my father most liked."

The two of them stood together at the poolside, watching the flickerings of kelp just beneath the surface. Both men kept their voices low, though the kelp chamber carried every whisper to its farthest crannies. Behind them, at a discreet distance, stood the complement of Zavatans who tended the pool. They busied themselves cleaning and reassembling one of the great borers that helped them tunnel out their habitations in the rock.

"When your parents met they were younger than you are now," Twisp said. "Is there someone in your life?"

The perceptible blush that rose from Kaleb's collar reminded Twisp even more of the young man's father. Kaleb's skin was darker, like his mother's, but his hair was naturally kinked, a sullen, reddish gift from Brett Norton.

"Yes? So there is someone?"

"Victoria is a big place," he said, "I've seen a lot of women." His voice bordered on bitter.

"'A lot,'" Twisp mused, "and which one broke your heart?"

Kaleb snorted, half-turned away, then turned back to face Twisp. He was smiling. "Elder," he said, "you are truly a force to be reckoned with. Am I that transpaent?" Twisp shrugged.

"It is a recognizable affliction," he said. "I endured it myself one day. Thirty years, and I still daydream."

He didn't go on. It was more important that Kaleb do some talking. Kaleb sat at the poolside, dangling his feet in the water, caressing the kelp with his bare soles.

"When I travel the kelpway, and take my father's branch, I see you as he saw you himself. You were good to him—firm, kind, you let him talk too much." Kaleb laughed. "He was a good man, I know. And you, you were a good man, too." He bowed his head and shook it slowly. "I would like to be a good man, but I think I'm different. My life is different."

Then he lowered himself into the pool and lay on his back on the kelp as though reclining on a great couch. His head and chest rested above water. Even in the colorful blue and red flickerings of the kelp-lights about the cavern Twisp could see a new life come into Kaleb's large eyes.

"How are you different, Kaleb?" he asked. "You breathe, you eat, you bleed …"

"You know why we're here," Kaleb interrupted. His voice was firm now, none of the hesitation of youth deferring to age. "How many people died out there today because they wanted to tear Flattery apart but settled for tearing *anything* apart?"

Twisp remained silent, and Kaleb went on.

"I'll be truthful, I respect you, I want your respect for myself, I want your approval that what I'm doing is right. If this doesn't work, we will probably have to attack him, you know."

His voice was becoming dreamy, and Twisp knew that the kelp was gathering him in, guiding him down the eddies of the past. Twisp steered him past thoughts of failure, past the matter that gave him the sense of failure.

"A woman won't let you sleep," Twisp said. "Tell me about her."

"Yes," Kaleb said, closing his gray eyes. Kaleb's eyes, like his father's, emanated a maturity beyond his years.

"Yes, she's here. She had two wots before we met. Qita, she knew the kelp as you and I have known it. As an ally. She had other lovers, but I was her last. As she will be the last for me."

This wrenched out of him with such an agonized moan that Twisp's hair raised up on his neck. Kaleb splashed the pool with both fists, but stayed immersed in the kelp, quieting with the caress of the waves.

"Elder," Mose whispered, tugging at Twisp's sleeve, "did you see his eyes?"

Twisp nodded, and before he could respond the kelp's display of flickering lights took on an intensity he'd never seen before. It was like one of the winter magnetic disturbances in the night sky, with great leaping rainbows of color that seemed to transcend water, rock and air. Mose stepped back from the pool in fear, but Twisp reached a hand to stop him.

"Old friends," Twisp whispered. "They are glad to see each other."

Perhaps Kaleb's bloodlines led to this moment. His mother, Scudi Wang, and her mother before her had been the first two to communicate with the waking being that humans called "kelp" and the kelp called "Avata."

When Twisp met Scudi Wang she was a dark young woman passionately working in her mother's wake to reestablish the kelp worldwide. In her own words, she "mathematicked the waves," and in doing so made Current Control possible, a system that saved thousands of Islander lives and revolutionized travel in Pandora's seas.

Scudi Wang was beloved by the kelp—this Twisp had heard from the kelp itself long before Kaleb was born. When Flattery attacked the kelp, lobotomized it, Scudi ordered her inheritance, Merman Mercantile, to stop trading with him. She and Kaleb's father were assassinated three days later.

Twisp saw Kaleb take on his mother's features as he lay there in the pool. His hair appeared darker, and so did his skin. The kelp enveloped him as though he were in the palm of a giant hand. The lights around them leaped and danced to some silent music. Twisp recalled that day when Scudi placed her hands into the sea and pleaded with the kelp, "Help us," and it did. It saved their lives, and that moment had changed his life forever. It changed all of their lives.

In the years since Scudi's death she had become something of a Pandoran historical monument, with many plaques and statues erected in her honor. When a massive earthquake ravaged the old Current Control site undersea, the carved glass statue of Scudi Wang was found intact, clutched in the fronds of a nearby stand of kelp. That sign of love from the kelp, that recognition of a symbol enraged Flattery and he entered into a vendetta against the kelp that continued to this day.

Twisp watched Kaleb recline on the back of the kelp root and it seemed as though the root surged up to cradle the young man closer.

"Twisp," he called from the pool, "that was what my mother wanted to do, isn't it? Shut off all supplies to Flattery, starve him out. All these years I have hunted in vain for the day she died, and now I have it …"

Kaleb started to weep, and Twisp had a difficult time making out his words.

"It would have worked then, it would have worked. But now he owns everything, everything … and now there is no way. No way short of a miracle to reach all of the people at once … to get them all to shut him out would take … would take a sign from God …"

His voice faded into a hum that seemed to keep time with the red and blue lights.

Chapter 54

Increase the number of variables, but the axioms themselves never change.
—Algebra II

BEATRIZ LIKED the feel of the free-fall spin. She kept her eyes closed and imagined herself sprawled across one of those warm organic beds the islanders grew. She wanted to be in a bed like that now with Dwarf MacIntosh, on some other world, under some other star. But of course a bed like that made no sense in near-zero-gee.

MacIntosh gave her one more gentle shove and drifted them both into "the webworks." This was a cavernous room at the Orbiter's tubular axis, sometimes called the "privacy park," often used for naps or meditation between duties, or for an occasional tryst by a desperate pair of lovers. A fine white netting crisscrossed the area, segmenting the huge space into a blur of booths and bins. Holo scenes turned some sections of web work into fantasy worlds, further removing the occupants from the worries of life aboard the Orbiter. All this Beatriz knew from her last tour, so today she kept her eyes shut tight.

"The disorientation is lasting longer this time," she told MacIntosh. "I really don't want to open my eyes."

"After what you went through today, I'm not surprised," he said. "I wouldn't want to open them, either."

She heard his fingers clicking on his belt messenger, and felt the sudden play of a warm light across her exposed hands and face.

"Well, we're now at Port of Angels, that lush Islander resort you've heard so much about. It's warm, feel it?"

Yes, the movement of air across her cheeks was warm, caressing. She could imagine herself on the beach at Port of Angels, letting her hair dry in the suns and stirring a cold drink. A plate of mango and papaya slices waited at her elbow. There was no wavesound here in the Orbiter, no pulse of the surf against her back that sometimes took her breath away …

She opened her eyes. A sandy beach stretched away from her in both directions. Greenery poured over the clifftops down to the beach, and several little huts waited under their matched hats to cool her sun-drenched skin. As the two of them turned, the holo turned, responding to a reference point in the messenger.

The holo came complete with their footprints in the sand, following them up from the edge of a blue-green sea. The fictional ferry that had transported them to this illusion had already settled under the waves, leaving only a swirl of current and a trail of bubbles toward the horizon. Sea-pups yapped and dove from the rocks that lined the harbor, hunting fish startled out of hiding by the ferry.

"We needed a few minutes alone," MacIntosh said. "It will take more than a few minutes to clean up the mess up here, track them all down. We've got an exceptional crew, that's why they're up here. Warning's out, so this Brood doesn't stand a chance."

He held one of the overlarge loops at her belt to steer them lazily around inside the holo. "No one knows who the Shadows are," he said. "Do you?"

"I … no, I don't."

"That's because the Shadows don't exist. Ask any of them. They don't have meetings, pass messages or recruit. Things simply get done—a power blackout, kelpway shift—and something of Flattery's is lost. Supplies circle him, but don't land. Replacements don't show …"

"That's what I mean," Beatriz said. "I want to know who does it, how do they know when to do it, and what happens."

MacIntosh held her tether and they spun in a lazy spiral through the webworks. The illusion that played across the nets, the beach resort, was tailored for her, designed to help reduce her orientation stress.

He's at home up here, she thought. She was aware then that *up* didn't make the same sense now that it had a few hours ago.

"They call it 'tossing the bottle.' You throw something out to the waves, and it's chance. But if you control the waves, or a little part of them, then it's not chance anymore, it's a sure thing. The Shadows' nonsystem encourages every citizen to frustrate Flattery when they see the chance. Divert something this way—say, a subload of hydrogen generators—and go about your business and never do anything like that again. Someone out in the waves sees this diverted load of generators coming along, diverts it that way … and in blinks it's headed upcoast to a settlement of Pioneers."

He spiraled a finger across the space they shared and bull's-eyed the palm of his other hand.

"Delivery." He winked. "Flattery's project loses and the people gain. No Shadows." He smiled. "It's brilliant. And everyone can play."

"Yes …"

Again, her thoughts were with Ben. *I wonder how long Ben's been playing …*

"The Zavatans, Rico and Ben …" MacIntosh hesitated, choosing his words, "they don't want Flattery killed. They just want him removed. After all he's done to them, they still don't want to kill him, simply because he's a human being. Do you know how incredible that is? Do you know how far you Pandorans have come from us?"

"Our enemies on Pandora have always been more vicious than ourselves," she said. "Except for the kelp. The kelp has killed its share of humans over the years."

"But who rattled its leash?" MacIntosh asked. "Who threw fire into its cage?"

She closed her eyes again and breathed in slow, deep breaths.

"Are you OK?"

She breathed in and out again, slowly.

"I don't know," she said. "I look around this scene, and I know it's manufactured, fiction, not real … but people are following us. There are lasgun barrels behind the rocks and plants. Out of the corner of my eye I keep seeing people scurrying for cover."

He hugged her, and they finally kissed that kiss she'd been waiting for. This was no chap-lipped peck on the cheek, and it was just what she needed to bring her back to the world.

"I've wanted to do that," she said. "But it seemed … out of place with all this death."

"Yes," he said, "I've wanted it, too." He brushed her lips with his fingertips.

"You know, you're going to be jumpy for a while, maybe a long while. We're going to go back out there in a few minutes and finish this matter with Captain Brood. He might think otherwise, but his men have already discovered how little they know about getting around up here. Then we'll see what we can do about your friends groundside."

"You don't think they're … dead?"

"No," he said. "I don't."

"How do you know?"

"The kelp."

Her face must have registered surprise, because he chuckled.

"You know how much the kelp interests me," he said. "Since Flattery gave me Current Control, I've been able to experiment a little. It paid off."

He kissed her again, then told her about the kelp communications system he'd devised, and his attempts to unify the kelp.

"Which kind of god would the kelp be?" he asked. "Merciful? Vengeful?"

"That's not important now, is it?" she asked. "Brood's a smart one. I won't be able to think of anything else until he's … neutralized."

MacIntosh steered them into a holo of sky that unfolded throughout their webwork—360 degrees of sky and high clouds covered the latticework that cradled them in free-fall.

"I worry more about Flattery," he said. "Brood's small-time. Flattery's got big things afoot, things big enough to crush anything in his path."

"But he was a Chaplain/Psychiatrist," Beatriz insisted. "He's trained to be better than that."

"He's trained to cope with the necessary thing and to see to it that we all adjust," he reminded her. "No romantic bullshit, just the straight facts. He's programmed to see to it that we don't unleash a monster intelligence upon the universe."

"If he hasn't adjusted and he hasn't coped, why assume that he'll take us all with him?"

"Simple," MacIntosh said. When he smiled his face wrinkled all the way up his shaved head. "The number five Flattery hit the 'destruct' switch, you've read *The Histories*. That Flattery was a lot more likable than *this* one. We're here now because the program had already come alive, had already anticipated his move and headed it off."

"Maybe we can do it!" Beatriz tried to shake his shoulders but all she did was set them both gyrating through air. "You're right, use the kelp to head him off!"

"Well, now that it knows Flattery's out to get it, the program's already inserted, wouldn't you think?"

"Well …"

"I have another possibility, and it's regarding Crista Galli."

She felt a curiosity about Crista Galli that went beyond her newsworthiness. Ben saw something in Crista, something in her eyes that swept him up and further away from Beatriz. Even though things were finished between Ben and Beatriz, a woman who could do that—a younger woman who could do that interested her mightily.

"What's that?"

She heard the rusty bitterness at the edge of her voice, the unnecessary snap of the words past her lips.

"I think the kelp's beat us to it," he said.

She looked up from her nestling spot at his neck to see his wide grin. "I think that Crista Galli is the kelp's experiment in artificial intelligence. I think she's manufactured, incomplete, and alive. It would be nice if we could keep her that way."

A musical tone sounded from the messenger at his belt. He did not take his arms from around her shoulders, but voice-activated the device with a simple command.

"Speak."

"Brood and two of his men sealed themselves off with the OMC. He says if you're not there in five minutes he's going to start scrambling some brains."

Chapter 55

And we are here as on a darkling plain
Swept with confused alarms of struggle and flight ...
—Matthew Arnold, "Dover Beach"

THE ORBITER collared the Voidship's nose in a flat wide ring of plasteel. The two cylindrical bodies spun in concert on their long axes. Soon the ring would slip away to remain in orbit around Pandora while its Voidship plied the dark folds of the universe. At the helm would be an OMC, a stripped-down human brain.

The Organic Mental Cores had a definite edge over the mechanical navigators, and this had been determined clearly a half-dozen centuries ago by experimenters at Moonbase. Navigation in all planes required subtleties of discrimination and symbol-generation that hardware never achieved. The disembodied, unencumbered brain took pleasure, or so they said, in plotting the impossible course. One goad worked on OMCs that had no effect on mechanical navigators—the OMC needed this job to stay alive.

The particular OMC that the techs were preparing for installation, the Alyssa Marsh number six, felt no pain or bodily pleasure as the microlaser welded in the necessary hookups. She had been trained in astronavigation at Moonbase and had borne a child in the year after splashdown on Pandora. The story that she filtered back to Flattery had the child die in an earthquake, and Alyssa Marsh had launched herself into her kelp study project with a passion. Her body had been crushed in a kelp station accident, but Flattery saw to it that her silent brain lived on.

Soon she would be silent no more. Soon her brain would have a body that it could move—the Voidship *Nietzsche*. She would navigate knowing the differences between ability and desire, knowing the need for dreams. Right now she lay genderless behind a pair of locked hatches dreaming of a banquet where Flattery was the host and she was both the honored guest and the main dish.

Dwarf MacIntosh gathered his forces outside both hatches and tried once more to contact Captain Brood. There was no reply from the OMC chamber. Three of the four monitors inside were blacked out, but the one remaining showed an overhead view of the long, specialized fingers of a nerve tech probing the webwork that encased what remained of Alyssa Marsh.

"Hookup's not scheduled until next week," someone said. "What's going on in there?"

A lasgun barrel appeared on the screen, pointed at the tech. The long, spidery fingers froze, then ascended from the surface of the brain toward the screen, then backed out of view.

"That fool better not touch off his lasgun in there," somebody else drawled, "or we be stardust."

"Hold your fire, Captain," MacIntosh ordered. "This is MacIntosh. You're in a high-explosive area—"

"Brood's dead," a voice interrupted, a voice that cracked with youth and fear. "May Ship accept him. May Ship forgive and accept us all."

The lasgun barrel tilted up toward the viewscreen and in a flash the last monitor went blank. Beatriz tugged at Mack's sleeve.

"He's an Islander," she said. "The old religion, like my family. Some believe this project, to build an image and likeness of Ship, to be blasphemy. Some believe that the OMC should be allowed to die, that it—she—is a human being held here against her will and enslaved."

MacIntosh covered the intercom receiver with his hand.

"I don't necessarily believe that Brood's dead," he told her. "That would be too easy. And why shoot out the monitor instead of the OMC? You're an Islander, you talk to him. Play the religion angle, set up to get him on the air if that's what he wants. My men here will help you out."

"Where are you going?"

He saw the unbridled fear in her eyes at the prospect that he would leave her.

What have they done to her? he wondered.

He gripped her shoulders while his men floated the passageway feigning inattention to their covert affections.

"Spud and I know a few ins and outs of this Orbiter that don't show up on schematic." She held him as close as their vacuum suits would allow.

"I could take anything but losing you," she said. "I know I'm making a spectacle of myself in front of your men, but I couldn't let it go unsaid."

"I'm glad you didn't," he said, and smiled. He kissed her in spite of the throat-clearings, harrumphs and chuckles of his crew.

"Chief Hubbard will stay here with you while his men secure this area. By your estimate, we're still missing a few of Brood's men. He's up to something, I have that feeling."

With a half-salute to the chief, MacIntosh propelled himself toward Current Control with his compressed-air backpack.

Chapter 56

Dark, unfeeling and unloving powers determine human destiny.
—John Wisdom

RICO COULDN'T see through the illusion and he knew that Ben could not see him, either. Nor could Ben see Nevi and Zentz. Rico whistled the "get down" signal, hoping that the couple wouldn't run out of the boundaries of the image. They would be visible then, and in the open against an incoming tide. Rico dropped when Nevi started shooting.

Time to send him a more suitable surprise, Rico thought. He wriggled into a position of better cover.

Nevi laid a pattern of fire into the rocks that hid Ben and Crista. Zentz covered Nevi's rear, keeping the dozen local Zavatans pinned down. Nevi stopped firing, but kept his wary crouch.

"Save charges," he warned Zentz. "We might be here awhile."

All was quiet except for their harsh breathing, the seething of the incoming tide and the high-pitched ping of weapon barrels cooling.

The budding tip of kelp vine around Rico's waist reminded him of his father's arm, and the way it used to pick him off the deck in one swoop. The feathery bud of kelp felt like the palm of a small woman's hand on his belly, covering his navel, hugging him from behind.

An image of Snej flashed through his mind and just as suddenly Snej's face appeared in thin air about ten meters in front of Nevi. The rising tide licked at the hylighter skin beneath her and hissed over Nevi's boot.

"What the hell … ?"

Nevi advanced a step, two steps. Zentz moved with him, backward, step for step. He glanced over his shoulder and paled when he saw Snej. He snapped his attention back to their rear defense.

"The redhead," he gurgled, "where's the rest of her?"

Rico found he could reinforce the intensity of the image by looking at it, concentrating on it. It was like a huge coil of energy feeding on itself, refining itself, awakening. After a couple of slow, calming breaths he was able to materialize the rest of her. She stood in her green singlesuit, hands on her hips, a bit larger than life size staring at Nevi. He wondered if he could make her speak.

"Well," Nevi said, "she's here, now."

Another glance over his shoulder and Zentz began a wet, ragged breathing that Rico could hear a dozen meters away over the surf. He placed his back tight against Nevi's.

"Shit, Nevi, a head that grows a body," he whined. "Let's get back to the foil."

"Shut up."

Nevi stopped and looked over the scene behind Snej. It was nearly the same view that Rico had: black rocky stretch of beach between the tide and the cliff, a cluster of large basalt boulders and a foil draped with the wet shards of an unexploded hylighter. In the downcoast distance the great expanse of sea glowed like green lava against the black cliffs.

"Where are they?" Nevi asked her. "I want them."

A two-toned whistle told Rico that the Zavatans were in position to rush the two men. He noticed that his illusion of Snej didn't cast a shadow.

Don't think I can manage that, too, he thought. *Talking will be enough of a challenge.*

Her shadow melted from her feet on the hylighter skin to where it met the beach, no more. It lay parallel with the other lengthening shadows of the day, but amputated at the rim of the skin. The tide already rushed the edges of the image, breaking up the light. With luck, Nevi wouldn't notice.

Rico smiled, concentrating on Snej, and quickly thanked Avata in the back of his mind.

"Put your weapons down," Snej said. "It is finished."

But no sound came from her lips.

"Shit!" Rico muttered.

Zentz responded with a burst from his lasgun. It came so fast that it startled Rico out of the illusion and it pulverized a rock just a meter in front of him. Avata brought the lost image back. Nevi fired, too, advancing them another step.

"It's not real," he told Zentz. "Watch yourself."

"Maybe we're dusted," Zentz said. "All this hylighter crap …"

"Ever know two dusters to share the same hallucination?" Nevi asked. He stopped a pace from Snej, squinting.

"Something's not right …"

Rico held his breath. If Nevi stepped across the plane of the image, he'd see Ben and Crista, and Rico wouldn't be able to see Nevi. The entire area over the downed hylighter became a dome of imagination, a hypnotism of light, a life sculpture.

Chapter 57

There must be a threshold of consciousness beyond which a conscious being takes on the attributes of God.

—Umbilicus crew member, Voidship *Earthling*, *The Histories*

MOSE'S EYES were open so wide that he looked even smaller to Twisp than he had when a refugee band had carried him in half-starved ten years ago. Memories—they kept him from the kelp as they drew Kaleb. Twisp had watched the struggle for nearly a quarter-century. The kelp must be like a drug to Kaleb.

Not the kelp, Twisp thought. *The past.*

Twisp knew, too, how the kelp always drew him to a particular part of the past, a particular year, a particular woman. Twisp had thought her the most beautiful woman on Pandora. Later, after Flattery and the others had been removed from the hyb tanks, Pandorans got a look at unmutated humans for the first time in over two hundred years.

They were all so testy about being clones, Twisp recalled, *when "clone" wasn't even something you could see.*

He remembered the bitter ceremony, with Raja Lon Flattery presiding, in which the hyb tank survivors purged the telltale "Lon" from their names forever. It was done with a ridiculous solemnity, and did not bestow on Flattery's people any of the attributes that Pandora demanded of them: better reflexes, more intelligence, teamwork.

"What they didn't tell you in school," Twisp told Mose, "was that Flattery couldn't control Kareen Ale. She was killed, like Kaleb's parents, by Flattery's death squad. She was the first victim. I believe it was Nevi himself who did it. Shadow Panille was head of Current Control in those days. He was in love with Kareen Ale. The combination killed him, too. He was my friend."

Twisp's voice barely rose above a whisper.

"I quit searching the kelpways, finally. I prefer my memories the way they deal themselves out. The kelp keeps them too true. Memories are not the drug for me that they are for some. I prefer to go to the kelp for the *now*, not the *then*."

"The kelpways would pink my wattles mightily, Elder," Mose said. "The blue dust takes me to my heart and leaves me there sometimes. I don't know where it would leave me in the kelp."

"With the dust, you face your own conscience," Twisp said. "In the kelp you face the conscience of us all. That does pink your wattles, all right. It demands truth, and singularity of attention. One is easily lost in the cruel maze of someone else's life. Kaleb has learned to filter the kelp as we learn to filter our senses."

"What will he find in there, Elder?"

Twisp shook his head.

The red, green and blue lights intensified and their flicker quickened until the cavern was awash with light. The borer workers left their machine to stand at poolside with the others who gathered in wonder.

"I have heard of this," said one, "but never have I seen the like."

"Not even his mother, the great Scudi Wang, was such a one," said another.

Twisp struggled to hold back the torrent of words that memory triggered at his tongue. Memories—they kept Twisp out of the kelp, just as they drew Kaleb inward. The kelp was like a lifeboat to Kaleb, an anchor to Twisp.

A strange mist coalesced above the top of the pool. Every atom in the cavern became charged with a visible hum, and everything above the waterline glowed in a cool green haze. Half-formed images—fragments of someone's past—flickered in and out of the haze. Twisp saw fire and a baby at the breast, a memo to Captain Yuri Brood, the brown, sensual curve of a wet breast in candlelight.

It was a tumble down a soundless tunnel, just the *slosh* and *thlip* of the sea accentuating the drift.

Twisp had the sense of reliving something, of *deja vu* without the *vu*. He heard a voice out of the mist, a woman's voice.

"He will contact one of the upcoast Oracles," it announced, "there is news of Crista Galli and the others. Through me Kaleb will meet my son, and through him, Raja Flattery. He will explore Flattery's inner being. Without secrets he cannot rule, and with the kelp there are no secrets. Kaleb will pick up the DNA path that leads to Flattery's hatch. Avata will transmit what he sees there throughout Pandora."

The whole cavern had become the stage for a giant holo projection. Soon, the babble and squall of life that went with the images swelled in the background. The mist had become a whirling ball of color and sound, its movements jerky and confused.

"Kaleb must focus his attention," Twisp said. "It is easy to get lost following the maze of someone else's life. He must filter Avata as we filter our senses. Then we will have a plan."

Chapter 58

One who withdraws oneself from actions, but ponders on their pleasures in the heart, such a one is under a delusion and is a false swimmer of the Way.
—Zavatan *Conversations with the Avata*, Queets Twisp, Elder

FLATTERY TOOK his afternoon coffee in the Greens, enjoying an impromptu stroll among the orange-throated orchids. They clung to the rock clefts deep in the cavern, their blossoms a pastel cascade. Condensation *drip-dripped* its paltry rain on leaves and wet rock, on the great flat surface of the pool.

Kelp lights surged bright in the pool, reflected in from the nearby bed. He paused a moment. This was something different, and the kelp, like Flattery, seldom did anything different.

Flattery turned on his heel and dog-trotted back to his command bunker.

"I ordered this stand of kelp pruned," he snapped, and jabbed a finger seaward for emphasis. "I want it pruned now."

Marta snapped something into her messenger.

"Not good enough," Flattery said. He signaled his personal squad. "Franklin, see that it's done. Use the mortar unit down on the beach."

"Aye, aye."

Franklin carried a pouch at his waist. Inside were the sandals, papers and diary of the first man he'd ever killed. He said he was saving them for the man's family, they would want them. Franklin slipped with a warrior's shadowy ease out the hatch.

"We can't loosen up, now," Flattery told Marta. "Everything will go perfectly if we don't get careless. That kelp bed is our only back door. We need it secure now. Do you understand my concern?"

Malta nodded, then sighed.

"Well," she said, "I have some concerns of my own. Strange things are happening to communications."

"What kinds of 'strange things?'"

"Random transmission sources of high-speed images, hundreds of sources, strong ones, and they seem to be all around us."

"They *are* all around us," he hissed. "That kelp. Well, we've taken care of that. Damage news, Orbiter news, Crista Galli news?"

"Nevi and Zentz have landed. They spotted the Galli girl and Ozette and anticipate no problem bringing them in."

"LaPush?"

"Snatched by the kelp. The pilot was caught in our charges, condition unknown."

Snatched by the kelp!

All this kelp talk was making Flattery nervous. He caught himself running his sweaty hand through his hair. Aumock's gaze caught his own, and he knew that his guard had seen that moment of fear.

"Kelpways secure?"

"We think so," she said. "We—"

"You *think* so?"

"Brood's squad is aboard the Orbiter. No further reports. The HoloVision Newsbreak that was scheduled from the Orbiter did not air."

"We're on auxiliary power," the colonel interrupted. "Failure at main plant … shit, it's no wonder that these troops got through our security. They *are* our security. 'The Reptile Brigade,' we called them. Shit."

"Does that mean a 'Code Brutus?'" Flattery asked. The colonel shook his head.

"No, Director. This is an isolated unit of troops, here. Their objective was the power station and now that they've taken it we expect them to defend it."

"Defend it?" Flattery raged. "They don't have to defend it, they blew it up! What would you do if you were them?"

"I'd—I'd know that I'd crossed the Rubicon," the colonel said. "Since there's no turning back, I'd head right for the top."

"Well, goddammit, take appropriate measures. Your ass is on the line here, too, mister."

Marta flagged his attention.

"I ordered sub coverage of the seaside entry doubled," she said. "I received no confirmation and don't know whether they heard me. Also negative messenger contact with the beachside mortar. The response we get is gibberish."

An icy panic tightened his stomach.

Not the kelp, he thought. *It can't be that. It has to be somebody controlling the kelp. But who?*

The likely possibilities came to two: Dwarf MacIntosh or the ambitious and resourceful Captain Brood. Crista Galli was an unlikely possibility. Suddenly Flattery felt the full impact of this interference.

We're cut off, he thought. *Our whole strength was in coordination, and now we're cut off.*

A rally was clearly in order.

"We got a little flabby, people," he said, "a little careless. This harmless little exercise could have cost us our butts, let's tighten up our action."

He'd caught them with their pants down, whipped them a bit, now he'd have to coddle them, comfort them.

"Reports on the bomb in the upper office just in."

He picked up Maria's messenger and held it over his head.

"Dick and Matt are alive, the rest didn't make it. May the perpetual light shine upon them."

They all responded, "May the perpetual light shine upon them," and drew a little closer out of reflex.

"It could have been us, folks. It could still be us if we don't tighten up. Consider direct orders the only secure communication. Information in, nothing out."

"Aye, aye."

Viewscreens and holo stages in his bunker began to flicker, barely perceptibly, then splashed high-speed displays of color throughout the room. Occasionally he glimpsed a face he recognized in the blur. His own face.

"What do we know about Current Control?" he asked.

His staff and guards stood transfixed in the surreal wash of color that visually drenched them all. They stagger-stepped to their posts, displaying the same disorientation that Flattery himself felt.

"Current Control turned the kelp in sector eight loose," Marta reported, "then it turned loose all the kelp worldwide. Sensors now indicate that everything's intact. The kelp appears to be online again. High suspicion for Gridmaster failure."

"Brood's mission?"

"No news. HoloVision covered the launch site incident with a Newsbreak report on the deaths of the Tatoosh field crew 'at the hands of Shadow extremists.'"

The colors that dazzled the room remained as bright but their swirl slowed to a less dizzying rate. Flattery thought he detected a woman's voice, faint in the distance, somehow familiar. Almost as though she called his name.

"Continued fighting in food distribution centers," Marta said. "Too many looters to shoot. The usual 'we're hungry *now*!' crowd. Some of our people opened warehouses. All stores outside our perimeter have been breached."

That's thousands of shuttleloads of food, he bristled. *That's my contingency, my lifetime Voidship supply.*

"Dried grains to feed three thousand for ten years," he said. "Dried fish enough to feed *fifty* thousand. Add water, pat together and cook. Instant wine—add a package to a liter of plain water and stir. Bread and fish for the multitudes, water into wine … if this Voidship could time-travel I could be Jesus Christ himself. Shit."

Chapter 59

Consciousness, the gift of the serpent.

—Raja Lon Flattery, number five model, *Shiprecords*

A LEAN-faced security, armed with both stunstick and lasgun, blocked MacIntosh at the hatchway to Current Control.

"Halt!"

He motioned Mack and his men to stop, and gripped a handhold to keep his bearing.

"Obiter Command," Mack said, "who the hell are you?"

"Security," the man said, and emphasized his point with his lasgun. "Captain Brood has the details. We are under the Director's orders to secure Current Control."

MacIntosh pushed off from the bulkhead behind him and sprang the gap. A push to the shoulder and a spin to the wrist later, MacIntosh had both the stunstick and lasgun. The sputtering security was pinned head down against the passageway bulkhead by two of Mack's firefighters.

"You'll get the hang of it in a day or two," MacIntosh said, and smiled, "if you live that long. Whether you live that long depends on how much you tell me, right now."

"That's all I know," he said, his voice edging a whine.

"Airlock time," Mack said. His men tumbled the security down the passageway to the freight airlock adjacent to Current Control.

"No, no, don't do this," the security pleaded. "That's all I know, that's really all I know."

"How many in your squad?"

"Sixteen."

Mack opened the inner hatchway to the airlock.

"My information says different—how many came up on this load, and are there more already aboard?"

"It's just us, Commander. Sixteen troops and sixteen techs."

"Where are they?"

Silence.

"Airlock time, gentlemen," Mack said. "Let's decompress slow. Anything you might think of to tell us, you can tell us from inside the lock. We'll stop decompressing when we've heard the whole song."

As Mack spun the hatchdog closed behind the security, he saw a half-dozen more of his men step off the elevator in full gear. Mack twisted the dial that sent air hissing audibly from the lock.

His prisoner immediately became hysterical.

"Shuttle crew is ours," he said. "Two troops, three crew stayed aboard. Holo crew was two troops, three techs. OMC crew was three troops, two techs. Current Control, four troops, four techs, counting myself and Captain Brood. The rest secured the Voidship. Please, don't let the air out. Don't put me out."

"Keep him inside in case I change my mind," Mack ordered. "We can add to our collection here as things develop. We need Brood so we can find out what Flattery's up to. Hooking up the OMC, taking over Current Control and the Voidship … sounds like things are going worse for the Director than he lets on. Maybe he's getting ready to take the Voidship for a little spin around the system."

The intruder code, a tone-and-light warning, flashed at all corridor intersections. It was a drill that Mack had never taken seriously, now he wished he had.

"Rat, you and your people take the shuttle. Barb, you work the Voidship and know it better than anybody here. Take Willis and his engineers. Remember, no lasguns. You have your vacuum suits on, use them. The rest of us will handle this little nest here. If Flattery doesn't trust us anymore, let's make it worth his while."

Mack knew that he had the edge over Brood as long as they met in the near-zero gravity in Current Control. Brood's techs might figure out the old hardware that ran Current Control, but the new organic hookups throughout the Orbiter and ship, grown by Islanders specifically for MacIntosh, might be a surprise. These kelp fibers bent light and encoded messages chemoelectrically within cell nuclei. This enabled kelp to bring light to the ocean depths and messages to the Orbiter. The switching speed and capacity of kelp hookups far outstripped any hardware that Pandorans had developed.

Too late, Raj, Mack thought. *Current Control will never be the same.*

Brood could only fail. In the time it would take his techs to figure out Mack's secret system they would all be grandparents.

Chapter 60

The is is holy and the Void is home.

—Huston Smith

HOT SUNS melted through the thick, post-squall mist to scorch the albino nose and exposed arms of Crista Galli. When an offshore gust caught the mist in a whirl it freshened her hot skin like silk. She had felt the *whump* of breakers in the surf beyond the fog and now she could see just how close the waves really came.

"Tide's shifted again," Ben told her.

He held her right hand but his voice sounded empty with distance, thick-tongued. He blinked a lot, and his motions were slow, exaggerated.

Dusted, she thought. *I wonder how it feels.*

She was convinced now that the dust had returned her to reality, rather than removed her from it. It was her personal antidote, an antiamnesiac that spun valves and opened the stream of memory.

She remembered Zentz, too. He had been a mere captain when he came into the lab at the Preserve that made up her home. He took away the researcher who was talking with her at the time, a young Islander woman who taught social psychiatry at TaoLini College. Once a week Addie came to question Crista about her dreams and always spent the afternoon with her in the solarium over tea. Crista had awakened in that lab a twenty-year-old female human without a single memory.

The psychiatrist, Addie Cloudshadow, tried to get those memories back. In the process she became Crista's first friend. Because of Zentz, Crista hadn't dared another friend until Ben. Zentz had walked into the lab that day with his weapon drawn, said simply, "Come with me," and shot Addie just outside Crista's hatch. Crista was sedated through her hysteria, and Flattery promised to take care of Zentz. Four years later Zentz surfaced as Flattery's Chief of Security and Crista vowed to escape the Preserve.

Today the mist kept her from seeing either up or down the beach. That glimpse of Zentz would have terrified her a day ago, but today she was not afraid. Something in the flash of kelp-memory warned her of Nevi, the other shadow in the mist, but it also illuminated a tension between the two that she knew would work to their favor.

The kelp had replayed for her Nevi's refueling incident, and she'd even forayed briefly into Zentz's mind. She had never seen anything so filled with horror and fear. She felt hate there, too, but it had long ago given way to a fear of Flattery that, itself, became an intense personal fear of Spider Nevi.

Divided they fall, she thought.

Flattery's world was coming apart, fighting itself, dying a thrashing death faster than it could inflict death on others. This was what Zentz had seen when the kelp grabbed him, and only Crista knew the strength of his resolve not to die at Flattery's feet or at Nevi's hand.

Crista had one open view from where she stood in the rocks, over the boil of breakers and out to sea. Though the tidelands wallowed in their salty fog, the sea itself glistened out to meet the sky somewhere in the distance. As far as the eye could sea, huge fronds of kelp rose lazily from the sea and splashed lazily back. Crista found comfort in the play of the kelp and the infinity of the horizon.

"What a time to be dusted," Ben mumbled, and shook his head.

"Rico has a plan," Crista whispered, "and he's ready to start it right ... *now*."

Crista Galli felt her hair prickle when Rico's electric dance of light crackled up like a shield around her. The high suns roiled fog off the wet beach and coated her skin with a fine grit of salt. The mist enhanced the surreal quality of Rico's lifesize hologram. From the back side it was like looking through a fogged mirror that refused her reflection. Crista watched the barest shadows of Nevi and the others as they ghosted the boundaries of the holo image that erased herself and Ben from the visible landscape.

Nevi and Zentz positioned themselves behind the light curtain, calling out strategy codes to each other.

"Flank sweep, left," Nevi said. His voice was unhurried, precise. "Cover high. I'll take point and ground."

"But they ... they disappeared!"

"It's a trick," Nevi said, "a camera trick. They're in there and can't get out. Position?"

"Secure. Ten meters, left flank. I can't see shit in this soup."

Zentz spoke more with a gargle than with real words.

"Ozette!" Nevi called, "she's sick. She goes back or she dies, you know that. It's not a choice. Send her out."

Ben's finger went to his lips.

"He can't see us," Ben whispered. "Don't move."

She couldn't tell one person from the other. The gigantic holo danced on its curtain of mist. Surreal figures outside the holo field became a futile blur. Three lasgun flashes burst the curtain of rippling light and a cascade of prisms lighted up all around her. Ben pulled her to the ground and in a blink the image reformed.

"Stay low and don't move," he whispered. "This is the perfect holo. *Perfect!*"

She wriggled with him into a fold of hylighter against a black lava boulder. Though faint, a wisp of images rose out of the hylighter skin and filled her mind in a steady unraveling of Pandora's tangled politics. The thick skin of the hylighter held the warmth of afternoon sunlight. With Ben tucked close against her she felt safe. Flashes of sunlight sparkled intermittently throughout the hologram that surrounded them. Crista drew a new strength with the hylighter's touch, and a confidence that insisted Nevi would fail.

"They can't see us as long as we stay inside the image," Ben whispered. His voice strained with the effort of focusing through the dust coursing his veins. He kept low, and his quick eyes took in all they could.

"This is incredible!" he marveled. "We're *inside* a holo ... where the hell did he get the triangulators to bring this off? And the *resolution* ... ?"

"From the kelp," Crista said. "He got everything he needed from Avata."

"I wish we could see what the hell's happening," Ben whispered. "Right now we're inside a hole in the light show. See this edge here? Rico's holo follows the outline of our hylighter. He's made a stage out of a hylighter skin."

His finger reached out to the edge of the hylighter skin and appeared to disappear as he pushed it through the hologram. A momentary flutter of light and shadow around his finger was the only sign of disturbance of the image.

"The mist makes the illusion especially colorful," he said. "All the tiny flashes that you see are the lasers catching a water droplet spinning in the mist—kind of pretty."

"I can take her back dead or alive, Ozette," Nevi's voice insisted. It was closer now, only a few steps away. "If she's dead, the world will think you killed her. If she's alive ... well, then everyone gets another chance."

"Going back there," she whispered, "that is not living."

"Don't worry, he knows how it's got to be."

Three more flashes burst through the light screen and pitted the boulder above them in a dazzle of red and violet. Ben wrapped his arms around Crista to sandwich her between himself and the rock. It seemed that the dust was bringing her out of a dream instead of into it. She felt her head and senses clear beyond anything she'd experienced in Flattery's custody.

"I think the dust ... you were right about it," she told Ben. "It's offset whatever Flattery gave me."

She pulled Ben's arms tighter around her and felt as though she were melting into him, her busy atoms scooting between the oscillations of his own. She felt herself disassemble into her qualities of light and shade. She was no longer so much a substance as an idea, an image, a dream. She felt no pain or pleasure, just a sense of transmission, of movement with purpose over which she had no control.

"Ben," she asked, over a stab of fear, "Ben, are you here?"

"Yes," his breath puffed her ear, "I'm here."

"I'm sorry," she said. She knew something was coming, some feral intensity crested her awareness and would not be cowed. "I'm sorry."

A sensation like the one she had felt at the dockside in Kalaloch welled up inside her, then burst with a loud *crack* that rolled outward from her heart like angry thunder. Everything around her stilled except the wet rush of the incoming tide.

Welcome home, Crista Galli.

The voice spoke through her mind, without the impediment of sound. It came at a rush from the dying hylighter, from Avata itself.

A refreshing sense of detachment, then a familiar disembodiment overcame her. The distinction between hylighter skin and her own blurred. She was encompassed within a familiar tingle. This muted, struggling tingle she knew to be a kind of death in body that hatched the great hylighter of her mind. Her mind flexed its great sail in the sun and caught its first breath.

We hatched of the same vine, Crista Galli.

She remembered, now. Before the bombing that cut her free she had been rooted for safety in a pod of kelp. The memories filled her head so fast they stunned her. Ben's groan in her ear reeled her attention back to their huddle on the beach. The holo was gone, and enough of the mist lifted to reveal a scattering of bodies in the rocks.

"I thought I was dead," Ben said, rubbing his temples. "How … what have you done?"

Crista couldn't answer. She felt as though she straddled two worlds—one on the beach, with Ben, and one in the sea with her great guardian, Avata. The holo had switched off with the thunderclap, and Nevi lay on the beach, nearly within her reach, his eyes blinking stupidly and blood oozing from his red-veined nose. She got up slowly and retrieved his lasgun. Rico, though wobbly, was the first to recover and he did likewise with Zentz.

"My apologies, Sister," Rico said, with a slight bow and a quizzical smile. "There is much this ignorant brother did not understand."

He reeled and nearly fell, but caught the side of a great rock and steadied himself.

Others around them, the stunned ones, began stirring and shaking their heads. A few, victims of the lasguns, would never stir again. A deep breath of the mist-laden air cleared her mind and helped pulse a new strength to her young legs. The tide hissed up to her feet, and a few meters away it licked Nevi's outstretched form in the sand.

She felt bigger now, taller, and it seemed that even Rico looked up to her.

"So, Rico, do you still want to keep me from the kelp?"

He managed a laugh and shook his head.

"Two rules," he said. "The first: never argue with an armed woman."

She hefted Nevi's lasgun as though seeing it for the first time, then inquired, "And the second?"

"Never argue with an armed man."

She returned the laugh, and Ben joined them.

"You argued with Nevi," Ben said, "and look what it got *him*."

"I didn't argue with him," Rico said, "I tricked him—that is, Avata tricked him. Now we've got more work to do. Believe it or not, we have to save Flattery. If we don't—"

"*Save* Flattery?" Ben's bitterness dripped from his voice. "He started all this, he should suffer the consequences."

"Not if we all suffer," Crista said. "Not if human life on Pandora is extinguished. He can do that, I feel it. Rico is right. Flattery must be stopped, but he must stay alive."

The dozen stunned Zavatans struggled to regain their feet and their senses. Ben picked up Nevi under the arms and dragged him out of reach of the water. A Zavatan scout took over and trussed Nevi's thumbs together behind his back with a stout length of maki leader.

"That holo," Ben said, "I've never seen anything like it. How did you do that?" "Thought you'd never ask," Rico said.

He picked up a length of kelp vine from the water's edge, caressed it momentarily and then dropped it back into the sea.

"That was the trick. I think our Zavatan friends here have these two zeroes under control. Follow me, I'd like you to meet my friend, Avata, the greatest holo studio in the world."

A warning shout went up from a scout at the clifftop, and simultaneously a hunt of dashers splashed out of the upcoast mist in a sinister blur. Ben snatched the heavy lasgun from Crista's hand and pushed her toward Rico. He fired a quick burst and the barest scent of ozone accompanied the snapping of the weapon. Two dashers crumpled in a flurry of screams and sand only a dozen meters away. The others began to feed on their dead, as was their instinct. A Zavatan scout emptied his charges into the rest of the hunt.

"They're so … so *fast*," she gasped, and discovered herself clinging to Rico's arm. He did not cringe or push her away, but put his arm around her shoulders and gave her a squeeze.

"Not much time to think topside," Rico said. Then, to Ben, "I see you're still quick in your old age."

"Some of us stay young forever," he laughed. "Must be the company I keep."

Ben's hand took her own and the three of them caught their collective breath.

"If they're not too chewed up, we'll get you one of those hides for a souvenir," Rico told her.

"What would I do with a dead thing?" she asked. A huge cold finger ran a shudder down her spine. "I'm a lot more interested in life."

"*Touché*," Ben said. "Let's get going. I want a look at Rico's mystery studio."

A gust of breeze puffed the last of the mist off the tidelands and both afternoon suns caressed Crista's pale skin. The fabric of her dive suit rippled in sunlight as the tide reclaimed, amoebalike, the tumble of rocks that marked its upper reaches. With her hand clasped in Ben's she followed Rico as he scrambled away from the sea up to the cliff. Two Zavatan scouts in green singlesuits flanked a great entry way between boulders.

"In here," Rico said. "It's not nearly as scary as the way I came in. Watch your step, the wet rock is mighty slick."

Crista stood at the dark entry, feeling a pulse of damp decorate the wall inside, carvings of intertwined kelp face upward for one more dose of light before facing the darkness.

"Look there," Ben said, pointing skyward, "hylighters. And they have the foil that these two came in on."

A half-dozen of them appeared from somewhere landward, two of them cradling the shiny foil in a snarl of tentacles. They all dropped in lazy circles to within a hundred meters of the beach. They valved off their hydrogen, fluting their peculiar songs that included one long shrill "all clear" whistle. Their great sails fluttered and snapped, tacking the coastal breeze. Sunlight through their sail membranes made them glow a dusky orange, and even this far away she could make out the delicate webwork of their veins.

"Guardians of the Oracle," one of the Zavatans said. "They, like you, are sent by Avata to help us. There is nothing to fear."

Their flutings called "Avaaaata, Avaaaata," on the wind.

"Come," Rico said, "let these guys mop up. There isn't much time."

They passed through the high portal of carved rock and, though she had expected darkness, they entered a chamber of magnificent light. The light came out of the pool itself, fanning out from the kelp and, like the warm breeze on her cheeks, it pulsed ever so slightly as though it, too, were alive.

"Avata brought me in through the sea," Rico told them. "There's an entry through the kelp itself into the pool. The entry closes off as the tide rises, then opens again at ebb. I just squeaked through. As you can see, it's well-occupied."

The strong sea-smell of the beach had been replaced with the scent of thousands of blossoms, but there were no blossoms in sight. A kelp root rose out of the pool at the center of the cavern, crowding all the way to the high domed ceiling.

"The root comes out of the ceiling," Ben said. "This rock was folded upside-down during the quake of '82. Look at that monster!"

She saw that it was true. It did not rise out of the pool but dropped into it. The top portion of root, thirty meters or more above their heads, was indistinguishable from the rock it clung to. Around it sparkled the thousands of reflections from its mineralization.

"This is an old one," she said, craning for a good look. "A very old one."

The cavern walls were terraced up to where the root joined the ceiling. The terraces were cultivated, and thick fruit vines carpeted the walls. A welcoming committee in brightly embroidered costumes smiled down at her from among the greenery. As the three of them stepped from the passageway to the edge of the pool applause broke out and the chant of "Cris-ta, Cris-ta, Cris-ta" pulsed with the brightening light.

"Look at yourself," Ben said, over the din, "you're glowing."

It was true. Except for where his hand held hers a light surrounded her body. It was not a reflection of the glow of the kelp on her white skin and white dive suit, because the pulse of this light matched the throb of her own heart. She felt stronger with every beat.

"Thank you," she said, bowing to the crowd. "Thank you all. Your hopes for a new Pandora will soon be fulfilled."

She stepped to the edge of the pool and became one with its emanation of white light and felt herself enter again the great heart of Avata. She opened a thousand eyes throughout the world and looked everywhere at once, and with some of these eyes she watched herself watching Avata at the pool.

She heard her voice rise to fill the cavern with a richness it had never held before. "Fear is the coin of Flattery's realm," she announced. "We shall buy out his interest in kind."

Images leaped from the pool's surface at the sweep of her outstretched arms and filled the cavern like quick bright ghosts. Her body swelled to its limit in the seas, and she reached her thousands of arms skyward in joy.

A gasp escaped one of the sentries, then a shout. "The kelp! Look at the kelp!"

But no one had to go outside for a look, all played before them inside the cavern. Throughout the seas of Pandora the kelp reached its great vines high above the surface. Colorful arcs of light bridged the gulfs between stands.

Even hylighters trailed great streamers of light from their ballast, providing a link between isolated patches of wild and domestic kelp alike.

Rico smiled through the dazzle of light and Crista realized the difference between the Rico she had first met and the Rico who had saved them on the beach: This Rico was *happy*.

"You're looking at Avata," he shouted. "The kelp has risen. Long live Avata." Applause and exclamations of joy gave way to the heavy background rhythms of water-drum and flute.

"But how … ?" Ben swallowed his question back, his eyes desperately trying to follow the display that surrounded him. A parade of ghosts from all over Pandora washed among the people in the cavern like a hologrammatic tide.

"Like the kelpways of the mind," Rico explained, "only it's no longer just a function of touch."

Rico turned to Crista and took both her hands into his own. The light around them leaped even higher.

"Though it seemed like moments, I was gone from you for years," he said. "I witnessed your life, my life, Flattery's life. He buried a secret in his own body that would kill the kelp should he die. If his heart stops a trigger releases his stockpile of toxin worldwide. It would paralyze the kelp in moments and kill it all off in hours. You see now we must isolate him, stop him, save him from his own ignorance. Enter the kelp. Tell the world what you know."

Crista felt herself pulled to the edge of the pool, and a murmur swept the chamber when she stepped onto the thick root of kelp. What she felt in that instant was joy. She became the very force of life in all of those present, and she entered the being of a young Kaleb Norton-Wang.

In blinks the webwork grew. In Oracles throughout the world people consulted the kelp and she entered the minds of them all as they entered her own. It was a giving up of mind, a joining of the piece to the whole. She felt as though she spun like a mote on a current of air, and filaments of light snaked out from each of her cells into the world. One of them, from the center of her forehead, reached beyond the world to touch the faithful above it. From her perch aboard the Orbiter, she watched Pandora's seas become ashimmer with light.

So you see, Crista Galli, the voice inside her said, *the severed vine regrafts itself. In you the parts are joined, and Avata is much more than the sum of its parts.*

Chapter 61

If you take any activity, any art, any discipline, any skill, take it and push it as far as it will go, push it beyond where it has ever been before, push it to the wildest edge of edges, then you force it into the realm of magic.

—T. Robbins

DWARF MACINTOSH had the axis areas of the Obiter evacuated and sealed off, with the exception of a handful of volunteers from the fire crew who remained as his security force. Mack was sure that Brood, when cornered, would resort to sabotage, so he instructed Spud to prepare separation charges that would blow the Orbiter free of the Voidship, if necessary. He was sure that Brood's focus would be Current Control, easily the most important and most sensitive installation in space.

With luck, he won't get both the ship and the Orbiter, Mack thought. *With luck, he won't get anything at all.*

Mack had always hated the feel of a weapon in his hand. Moonbase had taught all of them well, and his recent life in freefall gave him the advantage over Brood, but he didn't rise to the killing challenge as eagerly as some of his fellows. Mack was older than the rest of his *Earthling* shipmates. He had trained a lot of Voidship crews, finally gotten a flight of his own, at Flattery's request.

He didn't rise to the dying challenge anymore, either. Since Beatriz had come into his life he had found he wanted to live it more than ever. The prospect of facing Brood at the end of a lasgun struck a cold blow in his belly and set his hands to trembling. He gripped a handhold outside the main hatch to Current Control and tested the latch.

Unlocked.

He and three of his men sealed themselves in full vacuum suits and tested the squad frequency in their headsets.

"Ready one," he said.

"Ready two."

"Three."

"Yo, four."

"Foam only, if possible," he reminded them. "We didn't build all this to blow it up. Remember, the kelp hookups in there won't survive a vacuum, so we don't want a breach if we can help it. Blow vacuum as a last resort. Two and three, you're right and left. Four, I follow you. Check?"

Three fists clenched aloft, though "aloft" to Two was upside-down.

"Now!"

Mack pulled the hatch free and they spilled into the room that had been home for him for the past two years. Two was hit before he cleared the hatch but Three, using him as a shield, foamed both of Brood's henchmen and they hardened to immobility in blinks. Four tumbled to a ceiling position above Brood.

Brood himself sat calmly strapped into the control couch, his lasgun aimed idly at the Gridmaster. He had not even donned a vacuum suit over his fatigues.

Mack hesitated, his complete attention caught in the sighting dot of Brood's lasgun, which rested on the brain that controlled all the domestic kelp in the world.

"Dr. MacIntosh, shoot your two men or this thing is history."

In the immediate few blinks that followed, Mack's mind unreeled some light-speed logic.

He's got to be bluffing. If he wipes out the Gridmaster, there's no way he or anybody else could live on Pandora a year from now.

Mack realized that Brood didn't have to live on Pandora—not if he had the Voidship *Nietzsche.*

But he doesn't have the Nietzsche. *Not yet.*

"I might add," Brood said, "that if I'm killed, your OMC is also history. We can accommodate everyone, you see."

Mack saw the four techs reflected in a console panel. They ducked behind the next row of machines and were tracked by the muzzle of Four's lasgun. Mack hoped it wouldn't come to that. The men inside the foam cocoons might survive if they were cut free soon, but a lasgun firefight—messy, depressing.

Brood tapped the intercom on Mack's console.

"I left my man Ears back there to look after the OMC. You might've noticed how young he is. Nervous, too. That's been a problem in the past. You can ask your holo star what happens when Ears gets nervous. You OK back there, Ears?"

The voice on the intercom cleared its throat a couple of times before answering.

"Y-y-yeah, Boss, they're talking to me out there. But I ain't listening."

"Making progress on the hookup?"

"Yeah." The voice was young and reedy. "Tech says two more hours, tops."

"You're hooking up the OMC?" Mack's voice sounded as incredulous to him as he felt. "What the hell for?"

"We might want to take this thing out for a little spin, Doctor," Brood said. "Now, about those two lumps of shit, here. I told you to get rid of them."

"I won't do that, Captain," Mack said.

He unsealed his headpiece and set it aside. He sat in Spud's control couch and affected the same casual sprawl as Brood's.

"If you think I'm bluffing …"

"No, you're not bluffing. You'll do something. But the Gridmaster is one of your aces. You're not going to throw it away on something as trivial as my two men."

"They can leave."

Mack nodded to his men, and spoke into his headset.

"It's OK," he said. "Secure the hatch. Take these two and those four with you." "They stay!"

"Everybody goes but you and me," Mack said. "You knew it would be that way, anyway. Your two guards may have a chance, this way. And the others, they wouldn't get anything done here until this is … settled. Am I right?"

Brood snorted his annoyance and waved them away. They backed out, pulling the wounded behind them, and Brood never wasted a glance. His attention remained on the Gridmaster's many screens that charted the world. A faint glow leaked out from behind the viewscreens, and Mack noticed a fine mist spreading from his holo stage near the turret.

The mysterious spill of a distinct white glow leaked under the console and licked at the heels of Brood's canvas boots. A similar glow lighted the base of their holo stage like a small moon on the deck. A reflection of light on the plasteel bulkhead meant that the turret, too, was suffused with this glow.

The kelp, he thought. *What could it be up to?*

Brood's lasgun still pointed at the Gridmaster, and by its displays Mack saw that the grids had reformed, but into neat rows of convoluted waves. Either Brood didn't notice the glow, or he didn't know it was unusual.

Something's overriding the whole system!

That, whatever it was, meant that the Gridmaster didn't matter. It was merely a recording instrument, no longer a tool of manipulation.

"Did Flattery send you?" Mack asked.

Brood's face, not an unhandsome one, turned up a lopsided smirk.

"Yes," he said, "he sent me."

"And are you following his orders, blasting in like this?"

"I am following the ... the intent of his orders."

"Why wasn't I ... ?"

"Because you're part of the problem, Doctor."

Brood swung around to face him fully and Mack saw an age in his eyes that was much older than the boyish face that held them. Now Brood's lasgun pointed at his chest. The light continued its ooze from all of the kelp linkups. A similar glow shimmered on each viewscreen behind the pale- faced captain.

The whole planet's lighting up, Mack thought. It must be the kelp, but what could it be up to?

"My orders were to secure Current Control and keep the lid on the Tatoosh woman," Brood told him.

The man's voice was quiet, almost wistful. "We were to keep Ozette out of the news, replace any of her crew as needed, accompany her up here. The Director thought she might try to—influence you, thereby endangering the security of Current Control as well as the Voidship project."

"So, you terrorized her, executed her crew, murdered my security squad and are now prepared to destroy Current Control and steal the Voidship—even Flattery won't buy this one, Captain."

Brood smiled, showing his fine, sharpened teeth, but his eyes remained hard as plasteel.

"Perhaps it is a family trait, this madness," he said, his voice rising with an edge to it. "You haven't heard the scuttlebutt, then. They say Flattery's my father ... whoever my mother was, she was one of his diversions back at the beginning. I was the 'poor fruit' of that diversion, as some might say."

Mack was not as surprised at Brood's ancestry as he was by the cold anger with which Brood related it.

Hot anger stings, he thought, *but it's cold anger that kills.* Mack started to speak but Brood's upturned hand stopped him.

"Spare me your sympathies, Doctor. It's not sympathy that I require. I am not the only one so privileged, there are others. If he knows, he finds favor in me because I do not challenge him. If he doesn't ..."

A shrug, a pull at the lip. The ghost-light pooled his ankles.

"Others have not been so fortunate. My mother, whoever she was, for example. The Director requires power and I require power, that is clear. One way or another, I will have it."

"They've called a 'Code Brutus' down there. Are you a part of that?"

Brood snapped out a laugh. Those sharpened teeth sent a shudder down Mack's spine.

"I'm a winner, Doctor," he said. "I side with winners. I can't lose. If Flattery wins, then I've saved his Voidship for him, saved his precious kelpways, and I win. If Flattery loses, then I've captured the Voidship and the precious kelpways to hold for the winner."

"What happens if one of the others asks your help?"

"Then we'll suffer a communication breakdown," Brood said. "That's nothing new up here, is it, Doctor?"

Mack smiled. "No, no it's not. We've been having that problem all day."

"So I noticed. My men, they are new to these airwaves, but thorough. We have monitored you here for quite some time—for practice, you understand. I know you quite well, Dr. MacIntosh. How well do you know me?"

"I don't know you at all."

"I wouldn't say that," Brood said. "You knew that I wouldn't blow the Gridmaster—not yet. You knew if I *really* wanted your men dead they'd be dead, and yourself along with them. Tell me what else you know about me, Doctor."

Mack stroked his chin. Leakage from the body of the number-two man drifted close, globs of blood floating with it like party decorations. Mack kept trying to remember which of his men it was, but it wouldn't come to him. But Brood was in a talkative mood, and Mack tried to keep him at it.

"You've covered all bases," Mack said. "If you take the wrong side, you can always run off with the Voidship—provided you can muster a crew."

"I have you, Doctor," Brood smiled. "An original crew member. I have the OMC, too. And I'll bet that you, a smart man and commander, would have a backup system—probably something handy, like the Gridmaster? Yes, a backup for a backup ..."

Brood laughed again, more to himself this time. He reached out his lasgun barrel and nudged the blood globules enough to clump them together and push the glob out of reach toward the turret. A smear of dark blood glistened on the muzzle.

From somewhere deep inside his training-memory, Mack recalled one of his instructors telling him how clean a lasgun kill was, how the charge neatly sealed off blood vessels in its quick cone of burn through the body. In practice, as usual, this wasn't always the case.

Suddenly, the entire Current Control suite filled with overwhelming, blinding light. A stab of pain punched at both of Mack's eyes and he covered them reflexively. He heard Brood struggling nearby, bumping a bank of consoles toward the hatch.

"What the hell ... ?"

Mack tried his eyes and found that he could see if he squinted tight enough, but tears poured down his cheeks, anyway. What he saw made his already racing heart race faster.

If light were a solid, this is what it would look like, he thought.

Bright was all-encompassing. He could actually feel the light around him not as heat, such as sunlight would deliver, but the pressurelike sensation of an activated vacuum suit.

Mack kicked off and made a grab for Brood's lasgun as he fumbled upside-down with the hatch mechanism. He missed the lasgun. Brood happened to open his eyes at that moment and the barrel snapped up to take aim between Mack's eyes.

"Doctor, you just don't get the picture, do you? I ought to cook you on the spot, but I'll wait a bit. I'd rather have you and your girlfriend together for that. Now you tell me what the hell is happening here."

A frightened voice came over the intercom:

"Captain Brood, we can't see in here. There's a light filling the OMC chamber, and it's coming from this brain …"

This was cut short by sounds of a struggle, and Mack assumed that his crew had penetrated the OMC chamber. For the first time, Brood looked worried, perhaps even a little afraid.

"I don't know what's going on here …"

"Don't give me that *crap*, Doctor," Brood yelled. A fine spray of saliva skidded into the air around his head.

"It must be the kelp," Mack explained. He used the calmest possible voice he could muster. "There are kelp hookups in here and in the OMC chamber."

An eerie, strangled cry came from Brood's throat, and the man's eyes widened at something behind Mack's back. Mack grabbed a handhold and spun around, shading his eyes with his left hand. The bank of viewscreens that faced him seemed to be unreeling wild, random scenes from Pandora, some of them from the early settlement days.

"That's … those are my *memories*," Brood gasped. "All of the places we lived … my family … except, who is *she*?"

One face faded in and out, turned and returned and gathered substance from the light. Mack recognized her right away: Alyssa Marsh, more than twenty years ago.

A soft voice, Alyssa's voice, came from all around them and said, "If you will join us, now, we are ready to begin."

A great hatch appeared in the light, and a thick stillness took over the room. Nothing else was visible. The hatch hung in midair, looking as solid as Mack's own hand, but the pocket of light that contained them had solidified to exclude Current Control completely—there were no deck, ceiling or bulkheads; no consoles, no sound, nothing but the hatch. Even Brood's heavy breathing got swallowed up in the light. Mack felt as though he were alone, though Brood was near enough to touch. He was tempted to reach out, just to make sure he was real.

Shadowbox, Mack thought. *Maybe they've figured out how …*

"What is this shit?" Brood asked. "If this is some kind of kelp trick, I'm not falling for it. And if it's your doing, you're a dead man."

Before Mack could stop him Brood fired a lasgun burst into the hatch. But the burst wouldn't stop, and Brood couldn't let go of the weapon. The detail of the hatch intensified, and the hatch went through dozens of changes at blink-speed, becoming hundreds of doors and hatches that peeled off one another.

The weapon became too hot for Brood to hold and he tried to let it go, but it stuck to his hands, glowing red-hot, until the charges in it were depleted. Though he struggled to scream, with his veins bulging at his neck and his face bright red, Brood did not issue a sound. When it was over, his eyes merely glazed and he floated there, helpless, holding his charred hands away from his body.

Mack heard nothing during this time, and smelled nothing, though he saw the flesh bubble from the man's fingers. Still, the hatch waited in front of him. It first appeared as one of the large airlock hatches that separated the Orbiter from the Voidship. Now it looked like the great meeting-room door that he remembered from Moonbase. Every time Mack had entered that door it was to be briefed on some new aspect of the Moonbase experiment on artificial consciousness. Some of those briefings had raised his hair and bathed his palms in cold sweat. The door did not frighten him this time.

He did not doubt that this was an illusion, a holo of near perfection. He had been accustomed to working with fourth- or fifth-generation holograms, but this one felt real. The light had been given substance.

"What did it take to do this?" he wondered aloud. "A *thousandth-generation* holo?"

Every atom in the room, in the air, on his breath seemed to become a part of the screen. He reached out his hand, expecting to pass through the illusion. He did not. It was solid, a real hatch. Brood was no longer nearby. Like the rest of the room, he had simply ceased to be. All that existed were Mack and the great, heavy doors dredged out of his Moonbase memories. He thought he heard voices behind the door. He thought he heard Beatriz there, and she was laughing.

"Please join us, Doctor," the soft voice urged. "Without you, none of this would be possible."

He reached for the handle, and the door changed once again to become the hatch between Moonbase proper and the arboretum that he visited so often throughout his life there. A safe, plasma-glass dome protected a sylvan setting that he loved to walk through. Here at the edge of the penumbra of Earth's moon he had strolled grassy hillsides and sniffed the cool dampness of ferns under cover of real trees. His mind, or whatever was manipulating it, must want him to open this hatch pretty bad.

The latch-and-release mechanism felt real against his palms. He activated the latch and the hatch swung inward to a room even brighter than the one he stood in. This time, the light did not hurt his eyes, and as he stepped forward a few familiar figures materialized from it to greet him.

I've died! Mack thought. *Brood must've shot me and I've died!*

Chapter 62

To confront a person with his shadow is to show him his own light.
—Carl Jung

THE ORBITER'S fire-suppression crew floated in their odd vacuum suits up and down the passageway outside of the OMC chamber. Most of them were women, as was the majority of the Voidship crew. Each was equipped with a beltful of tools for bypass or forced entry, and several pushed smothercans of inert gas ahead of them as they patrolled behind Beatriz. All of them had left their job stations to rally against the threat of fire. Only uncontrolled vacuum was more feared than fire aboard the space station. The pithy jokes that they tossed among themselves through their headsets offset the nervousness that their eyes betrayed.

Beatriz had suspected from the start that the young security who had sealed himself inside the OMC chamber was trying to get the OMC on-line. The firefighting captain who stayed with Beatriz was a structural engineer named Hubbard. Like all of the fire-fighters aboard, Hubbard was a volunteer and accustomed to getting twice as much work done in half the time. He deployed his crew according to their real-job skills. In a matter of moments all circuit boxes were opened, their entrails spilling into the passageway.

Four women positioned two plasteel welders, one at the hatchway, one at the bulkhead seam to the OMC chamber. The operating arm of the welder alone weighed nearly five hundred kilos, but here near the axis the only maneuvering problem was its bulk.

These women must've been up here from the start of the project, Beatriz thought. They used their feet as she might use her hands, and their vacuum suits had been adapted to accommodate their more dexterous toes. When she first visited the Orbiter she had thought that this skill came from a particular breed of Islander, but later visits proved otherwise. MacIntosh himself exhibited great facility with his feet and toes, and his vacuum suit reflected these changes, too.

"Buy us fifteen minutes," Hubbard was telling her, "and we'll be all over that guy."

"These guys killed my whole crew," she said. "They joked about eliminating your whole security squad and then they did it. Being all over that guy in fifteen minutes won't be enough to save that … the OMC."

"How would you do it?"

Beatriz detected no challenge in his tone, just urgency.

"I helped Mack install some hookups to the OMC chamber. There's a crawlway that starts in the circuit panel in the next compartment and leads into the control consoles inside the chamber. I know the way and I can …"

"Shorty, here, can squeeze through some mighty tight spaces," Hubbard said. "She can bypass their air supply and divert in CO2 …"

"No," she said, "that's too risky. It won't hurt the OMC but I've seen people panic when their oxygen gets low. We want to keep these guys calm, they might just start shooting up everything in sight."

"You're right," Hubbard said. "Shorty, tell Cronin to whip up some of his chemical magic. We want this guy down and out in a blink, and anybody else that's with him. We want that OMC and the tech in operating condition when this is over, got it?"

"Check, Boss."

"Listen up, everybody," Hubbard said. "Set all your headsets to voice-activated fireground frequency three-three-one." He made the proper settings in her equipment, then explained to Beatriz, "That way we talk and he can't listen, and we don't have to go through the intercom."

Beatriz noted the tools in Hubbard's jumpkit.

"Let me see what you've got there," she said. "I may be able to activate some of the sensors in the chamber through the intercom box. It would help to have eyes and ears."

She slid back the cover and a faint glow pulsed from inside the box. It was not an electrical glow, the cherry-red simmer of bare wires or the blue-white snap of a short-circuit. This glow was pale, cool, with a slight pulse that intensified as she watched.

Hubbard's hand moved reflexively to a small canister at his belt, but Beatriz stopped him.

"It must be luciferase," she said, "from the kelp leads that we fed in here last year." She selected a current detector from Hubbard's kit and applied it to one of the fistful of unconventional kelp leads.

"Kelp leads?" Hubbard asked. "What the hell was he stringing … ?"

"Circuits made with kelp don't overload, and they have a built-in memory, among other features. We've done some experimentation with it at HoloVision … OK, there's something here," she said, watching the instrument's flutter in her hand. "I wouldn't call it a current, exactly. More of an excitation."

When the bare back of her hand brushed the bundle of kelp fibers, Beatriz had a sudden unexpected look at the inside of the OMC chamber. The young guard stood across the lab from her, lasgun at the ready, his eyes wide and clearly frightened. Beatriz watched the scene from two vantage points. One was halfway up the bulkhead behind the OMC, probably the outlet connecting with the hookups she held. The other was from about waist-height, facing the security, and she realized she was watching this scene from inside Alyssa Marsh's brain. The kid kept flicking the arm-disarm switch on his lasgun.

"Get inside," she whispered to Hubbard. "Get someone inside. He's going to panic and kill them all."

She gripped the bundle of kelp fibers tight in her fist and dimly heard Hubbard snap out orders to his crew. She felt herself drawn both ways through the fibers, as though she were seeing with several pairs of eyes at once. The sense of herself diminished as she flowed out the fibers, so she gripped a handhold on the bulkhead and forced the flow to come to her.

I can't let this go on, she thought. *It has to stop. Oh, Ben, you were so right!*

The experience was nearly more than she could bear, but magnetizing as well. She knew she could let go the fibers, stop the headlong tumble down a tunnel of light, but her reporter instinct told her to hang on for the duration of the ride. She raced through the hookups aboard the Orbiter and the Voidship, then felt herself launched toward the surface of Pandora. She tightened her grip and wondered who was moaning in the background, then realized that the moans were her own.

She was a convection center for the kelp. The pale-faced young security with the huge ears and filed teeth stood barely a meter from her eyes.

Alyssa's eyes, she thought, and repressed a shudder. *I've become Alyssa's eyes.*

The tech's hands trembled as they worked, and with each new fiber glued in place the eerie glow increased.

"Brood didn't say this was supposed to happen," the kid said, more nervous than ever. "Is this normal?"

"I don't know," the tech said.

Beatriz heard the fear in her near-whisper. "You want me to stop?"

The kid rubbed his forehead, keeping his gaze on the OMC. Beatriz knew that he saw Alyssa Marsh's brain being wired to some tangle of kelp-grown neurons, but it was Beatriz who looked back at him. Perspiration dampened his hair and spread dark circles from his underarms.

Fear of the situation? she wondered. *Or is he afraid of the OMC?*

He was Islander extraction, there might be some superstition but physical abnormality itself would not scare him. A Merman would have a harder time facing a living brain, something an Islander would shrug off.

"No," he said. "No, he said to hook this one up no matter what. I wish he'd answer us." The kid flicked a switch on his portable messenger and tried again. "Captain, this is Leadbelly, over." The only answer was a faint hum across the airways.

"Captain, can you read?"

Still no answer. Leadbelly sidestepped to the intercom beside the hatch. The near-weightlessness made it difficult for him to keep his back in contact with the bulkhead as he went.

"What's the code for Current Control?"

"Two-two-four," the tech said, never looking up from her work. "It's voice-activated from there."

He fingered the three numbers and instantly the glow in the chamber intensified to a near-glare. He armed his lasgun with a metallic *sklick-click* and Beatriz heard herself shout, "No! No!" just as Shorty propelled herself like a hot charge out of the service vent and onto Leadbelly's shoulders. The tech shrieked and jumped aside, and Leadbelly shouted a garbled message into the intercom.

His lasgun discharged and for Beatriz the world slipped into slow-motion. She saw the muzzle-flash coming directly at her, homing in on her as though pulled by a thread.

This can't be, she thought, *a lasgun fires at light-speed.*

It was such a short distance to the muzzle that the charge hadn't fully left the barrel yet when it hit the glow around Alyssa Marsh's brain. Beatriz watched the lasgun sucked dry of power in less than a blink. Leadbelly screamed and struggled to fling the hot weapon from himself, but it had melted to the flesh of his hands. Shorty clung tight to Leadbelly with both hands and feet, spinning them across the center of the chamber. The charge triggered some reaction in the glow, and Beatriz found herself surrounded by it, curiously unafraid.

All was quiet inside this bright sphere. Beatriz hung at the nucleus of something translucent, warm, suspended in yellow light.

This is the sensation that the webworks mimicked, she thought.

Beatriz found comfort in the familiar rush of some great tide in her ears and she felt, more than saw, the presence of light all around her.

The center, she thought. *This is the center of … of me!*

A hatchway appeared and though she did not have hands or feet she flung it open. There stood her brother when he was eleven, his chest bare and brown and his belt heavy with four big lizards.

"Traded three in the market for coffee," he said, and thumped a bag down on the table in front of her. "You won your scholarship to the college, but I'll bet it don't cover this. Let me know when you need some more."

She had been sixteen that day, and unable to know how to thank him. He hurried past her out the hatch, the dead lizards flopping wet sounds behind him.

A flicker of hatches raced past, each connected to the artery of years. Some dead-ended at years-that-might-have-been. She opened another, this time an Islander hatch of heavy weatherseal, and found herself inside her family's first temporary shelter on real land. It was an organic structure, like the islands, but darker and more brittle than those that ran the seas.

Her grandfather was there, hoisting a glass of blossom wine, and all of her family joined him in a toast.

"To our busy Bea, graduate of the Holographic Academy and new floor director for HoloVision Nightly News."

She remembered that toast. It came on the 475th anniversary of the departure of Ship from Pandora. It had become an occasion for somber celebration over the years, with a place left empty at table. Originally this was intended to represent the absence of Ship, but in more recent times the gesture had become a memorial to a family's dead.

"Ship did us a great favor by leaving," her grandfather said.

There was much protestation at this remark. She hadn't remembered hearing this conversation years ago, but it pricked her curiosity now.

"Ship left us the hyb tanks, that's true," her grandfather said. "But we went up there and got them down. And we got them down without any help from anyone or anything inside of them. That's what will raise us up out of our misery—our genius, our tenacity, ourselves. Flattery's just another spoiled brat looking for a handout. You talk about ascension, Momma. *We* are the ascension factor and, thanks to Ship, we will rise up one day to greet the dawn and we will keep on rising … that right, little girl?"

The party laughter faded and a single hatch floated like a blue jewel ahead of her, waiting. It was like many of the Orbiter's hatches, fitted into the deck instead of the bulkhead. Across the shimmering blue of its lightlike surface the hatch cover read: "Present." She reached for the double-action handle and felt the cool satin of the well-polished steel in her palm. She pulled the hatch wide and dove inside.

She had the same sense of a headlong tumble, like her early clumsy progress in the near-zero-gravity of the Orbiter's axis. She sensed everything about her as though she had a body, and that body was hyper-alert, but she still saw no evidence of one. She sensed others, too, not far away, and part of this sense told her she had nothing to fear. The translucence of the glow about her folded and thickened, forming a shadow at her left shoulder. In a blink it precipitated into Dwarf MacIntosh.

"Beatriz!" He wrapped his arms around her and kissed her. "Now I know I've died," he laughed, "I must be in heaven."

"We haven't died," she said. "But we may have gone to heaven. Something's happened with the kelp hookups. I know that I'm still holding onto them outside the OMC chamber, but I also know that I'm here with you …"

"Yeah, the kelp hookups and holo stage in Current Control got a glow to them, then the viewscreens … the whole world seemed to be shining down there. At first I thought it had something to do with those goons that Flattery sent up here. Now I think it has more to do with the kelp disturbances, the grid collapse. I think that your friend Mr. Ozette and Crista Galli are at the bottom of this."

"But how? We're in orbit. The kelp we touch here touches nothing else. It could just be a psychic disturbance, but then you wouldn't be here with me."

"It's the light," Mack said. "The kelp uses chemicals to communicate, this we've known for some time. Now we've taught it to use light. That holo stage I built for experimentation—it works perfectly, and all components came from the kelp, only the kelp has gone a few steps further. The kelp takes pieces of light, breaks them into components, encodes them chemically or electrically, then reproduces them at will. It's something I refined from what cryptographers used to call the 'Digital Encoding System.' You know more about holography than I do, you tell me what's going on."

"If you're right," she said, "if this is the kelp's holography, then it's learned to use light as both a wave and a particle. We can hug each other, yet we're just holo projections of some kind, right? Maybe the kelp has found another dimension."

"Yes," a woman's voice said, "we are the reorganization of light and shade. Where light goes, we go."

"Are you … Avata?" Beatriz asked.

A gentle laugh replied, a laugh like moonlight across flat water. A third figure began its mysterious materialization out of the glow. It was a woman, as radiant as the light around them, and because of that she was barely visible. Beatriz recognized her immediately.

"Crista Galli," she gasped. She looked around for sign of another figure, for Ben, but all she saw was the translucent sphere that held them.

"Don't worry, Beatriz, Ben and Rico are with me. As you and Dr. MacIntosh are with the Orbiter crew. What they see now are the shells of our beings, the husks of ourselves. What we meet here is the being itself."

"But I can see you, hear you," Mack said. "Beatriz and I actually touched."

Crista laughed again, and Beatriz felt a giggle coming that she couldn't suppress.

I am safe here, she thought. *Brood, Flattery, they can't get me here.*

"That's right, we're safe," Crista said.

Beatriz realized then that thought was as good as speech in this strange place. Or is it a place?

"Yes, this is a place. It is a *who* as well as a *what* and a *where*. Dr. MacIntosh, we have substance because our minds have made a perceptual jump along with the light. Things change to accommodate our differing subconscious. Did you see a lot of hatches?"

Beatriz watched him hold out his hands, look down at his feet, puzzled. "Yes, I did, but …"

"And one reminded you of something pleasant, so you opened it?"

"Yes, and I wound up here."

"So did I," Beatriz said. "But an earlier one led me … back. Back to my family years ago."

"It was Avata's way of reassuring you," Crista said. "It took you to a familiar, comfortable place. You have been terrified lately. Avata does not want your terror. She wants your expertise."

"Expertise?" Beatriz swept a hand out to indicate their surround. "After *this*, what could I possibly offer?"

"You'll see. Think of this as Shadowbox, as the biggest holo studio in the world, with nearly the whole world as its stage. We will put Flattery at its center, show him off to the world. What then?"

"Stop people from destroying each other," Mack said. "They have not been able to get at him, so they will destroy his engines of power. If they do that, they endanger all of us, Avata included. Exposing Flattery might be more dangerous than you think."

"But look at our *method*," Beatriz said. "It's incredibly powerful. It will appear as a message from the gods, a vision, a miracle."

"I saw light shimmering above all kelp stands from Current Control," Mack said. "Is that really happening?"

"Yes," Crista nodded, "it is."

"Then we already have the world's attention, right? Everybody must've stopped in their tracks to take a look."

"My people stopped long enough to enjoy the light show," someone said. "They're heading for Kalaloch with everything they have."

Another figure precipitated out of light, a muscular male figure with red hair. Though Beatriz had never met Kaleb Norton-Wang before, she realized that she knew his past nearly as well as her own. At the same moment, she realized this was true of Crista Galli and Mack, as well.

Then they know me, too, Beatriz thought, and saw Mack's responding grin.

"We are part of Avata, now," Crista said. "Others float this drift, too, but we are Avata's ambassadors to our own kind. You, Dr. MacIntosh, believed me to be a manufacture of the kelp. Until this day I, myself, did not know my origins. I owe my life to Avata, my birth to humankind, and my allegiance to both. Are we all not of the same mind?"

Beatriz agreed. "We are. Flattery must be stopped, the killing must stop. Can we do it without becoming just another death squad?"

Beatriz paused, felt a surge of light within her and watched a replay of the encounter with Nevi on the beach. Then she discovered something interesting about being one with Avata—all of them could talk at once and she could follow everything perfectly.

Kaleb said, "I can speak to all of my people, using the kelp … I mean, Avata, as you used it to beat Nevi. Who could ignore a giant holo in the sky?"

"I didn't use it to defeat Nevi," Crista said. "I was merely a witness. Avata and Rico worked out a magic between them, but neither used the other."

"I stand corrected," Kaleb said, and bowed slightly. "How are we to cooperate with Avata?"

"We initiated it by seeking contact with Avata in the first place. Each of us has done that, for our own reasons, which we all now know," Crista explained. "Where there is kelp, Avata can project holos. As you can see, these are being refined even at this moment. Our holo selves, here, can hug each other and we can feel it!"

"Our problem is Flattery," Mack said. "He has never been easily persuaded, and now that he's made an emperor of himself he believes only himself capable of rational decisions. Anything else is a threat. He is paranoid, therefore it's a given that he's set traps of one kind or another to protect himself from attack. Remember, he's a psychiatrist, too. He can defend himself from both emotional and physical attack. The ultimate threat, of course, is that if he dies, Avata and, eventually, all humans die as well. We can't have him panic and start lighting fuses."

"Why can't Avata just … capture him, as it has taken us?" Kaleb asked. "He's not the type to kill himself, and it would buy us some time."

"Flattery takes excruciating pains to stay away from the kelp," Crista said. "He won't even have kelp-paper products in his compound. He must be drawn out to the kelp."

"Or driven out," Kaleb said. "Or the kelp has to come to him," Beatriz said. "Maybe that's possible. There are the Zavatans …"

Yes, a voice that surrounded them said, *Yes, the Zavatans.*

Suddenly the light cleared around them and Beatriz saw what was left of Kalaloch sprawled out, wounded, beneath her. She floated above the settlement at a great height, with a comfortable sense of well-being that could only be wind buoying her.

"Ah, Beatriz, you have found the hylighter," Crista's voice said. "Let us all join hands in Avata and be with her, now."

Beatriz was vaguely aware of her existence in the light. She felt Mack's hand on her right and Kaleb's to her left, but the sensations she received were from her hylighter perceptions, and these steered her in a tightening circle high above Flattery's Preserve. Three more hylighters tacked her way, and each one snapped its full sail in their traditional greeting.

She hovered directly above the blackened remains of the earlier hylighter explosion. Hundreds of people scrambled in and out of the cover of rubble, pressing in on Flattery's compound. Many of them wore the drab fatigues of his own security forces.

"We must get to Flattery before they do," Crista said. "If he's killed, there may be no hope for Avata, no hope for any of us."

Beatriz valved off some hydrogen and dropped closer, tightening her gyre. Though certain of the combatants below pointed upward to her presence, none raised a weapon or fired on her.

Everyone topside is on one side now, she thought. Exploding a hylighter would be suicide. She wondered whether Flattery had any faithful snipers in the nearby hills.

Now that she was only a few hundred meters above the compound she noticed dozens of people in orange singlesuits popping out of underground cover throughout the area. The dozens became fifty, a hundred, more … all Zavatans of the Hylighter Clan. Swiftgrazers had fled the fire zone and scrambled into their burrows about the compound, and now the Zavatans were placing small orange flags at the entrances to these burrows.

They're showing the villagers the way into Flattery's bunkers, she thought. *If we can get inside first, we might be able to trap him.*

"Excellent!" Mack's voice said. "And even if we don't, he has his seaward escape and we drive him straight into Avata."

The other three hylighters were immense, their supple tendrils dragging ballast nearly fifty meters below their gasbag bodies.

From this vantage point she saw the wildlife from Flattery's Preserve scattered at the periphery of the scene. They had been a luxury, these mysterious Earthside animals. They got food and health care when people starved, but she did not resent their survival.

The people will care for them at least as well as Flattery did, she thought. *Ben was right, there isn't a shortage of food, just a very selective distribution.*

She drifted low enough to the ground to make out individual Zavatans waving at her and shouting their greetings. The tips of her two longest tentacles stung when they touched the wihi tops. This close to the ground she found maneuvering nearly impossible, but felt no fear-sense from her hylighter host.

Fear not, human, the Avata voice said. *Let the ending for this spore-bag mark our birth together on Pandora.*

"What do you mean, 'ending?'"

Unlike humans, we crush ourselves under our own weight when grounded. Without the ultimate fire our spore-dusts are trapped forever inside their shells.

"You mean, unless you explode your spores are sterile?"

Yes. Now, you see, we are already too low to recover. I will live in you, now. Hurry. The others, too, must hurry. Find each tentacle a hole, chase Flattery out. Avata will … Avata …

Beatriz felt as though a ballast rock lay on her chest, she could barely breathe. One by one her ten tentacles found burrows marked by the Zavatans and began their twining into the depths of Pandoran stone. She heard the other three hylighters valving off their hydrogen nearby.

"What is this like for them?" she wondered to her friends. "Like a mother smothering a crying child to save the village?" Then she was alive in the tentacles. It was like having ten sets of eyes, and the light that grew from the dying hylighter turned a groping mystery into a warren of horrors. Eyes looked back at her—eyes and tiny, needlelike teeth pulled back in a hissing snarl. She pushed forward and they attacked, biting off chunks of tentacle as she backed them further into the maze.

"I can't stand it!" she screamed. "They're biting my face! They're horrible little …"

"Beatriz, listen to me."

Mack's voice was nearby, but he didn't know what was down here, he hadn't seen these little … *things* biting and biting, and down here she couldn't close her eyes because it seemed that the whole hylighter became eyes to her.

"Beatriz, talk to me," Mack said. "Don't pull back, now. I'm here, we're all here, holding hands in Avata. We're holding hands in Avata and you're in the Orbiter, holding a kelp hookup. Do you feel me beside you? I'm setting down beside you now."

The Avata voice spoke to her. It sounded like Alyssa Marsh.

Remember it as holding hands, even if you know it wasn't so. When you tell the story, say that you all held hands. It is a symbol, these clasped hands, as the clenched fist is a symbol. Choose which of these you would pass down. Avata taught through the chemistry of touch, the "learning-by-injection" method, as some called it. Humans keep their kind alive by symbols and legends, by myths.

She felt him. She felt a bulk press against her own and the weight on her chest eased off. She could breathe, and wondered whether hylighters breathed, too.

We are … more similar to you … than different, the presence said. *I will enjoy a deep breath … when you are free … to take one.*

The swiftgrazers kept at her, their little mouths biting, snatching off bits of flesh from her face …

From this hylighter's tentacles, the voice reminded her.

"I'm down." This was Crista Galli's voice.

"Me, too," Kaleb said. "Let's kick some ass!"

The burrows were too narrow for the swiftgrazers to launch their typical swarming type of attack. Tentacles pressed them further into their burrows and all they could do was turn for a savage little nip every meter or so. Beatriz felt that she had snaked about half of the length of her tentacles into the ten burrows when they broke into the open. What she saw there with her battered stubs of hylighter flesh was a sight to make her gasp.

A blur of fast little animals streaked into a magnificent garden, a place so beautiful that Beatriz thought she must be in the throes of some hylighter death-vision. She heard cries and groans from the others as they encountered the vicious swiftgrazers and she tried to comfort them by concentrating on the scene before her. "You're close," she said, "don't give up, you're so close."

Her wounded stubs sniffed the blossoms thick in the green foliage. Mosses and ferns hung down the black-glazed ceiling and carpeted most of the walls. She could not stop the light from spilling out of her into the chamber, but she wouldn't have chosen to even if it had been possible.

She heard other screams, then. Screams of a man being shredded to bone. She saw him, an older man, flailing at the panicked swiftgrazers with a pruning rod. He seemed to melt at first, then he toppled and his screams were muffled by hundreds of little bodies upon him.

A couple of big cats came to the fray. Bigger than dashers, stronger, but they were no match for the tide of swiftgrazers that continued to pour from the thirty other tunnels nearby. Troops raced inside from an opening across the lagoon, firing their lasguns and smoking up the place. They, too, were no match for the fury of the swarm.

A foil that must've been Flattery's fled beneath the surface of the pool, the splash of its crash-dive drenched the walls. She could do nothing more here. Rather than watch the horror, she withdrew to Avata and to the comfort of the light.

Chapter 63

Ferdinand of Aragon … has always planned and executed great things which have filled his subjects with wonder and admiration and have kept them preoccupied. One action has grown out of another with such rapidity that there never has been time in which men could quietly plot against him.

—Machiavelli, *The Prince*

FLATTERY HEARD trouble before he saw it. He had secured the upper bunker system and moved his most trusted personnel to the smaller office complex adjacent to the Greens. It was cramped, but it met his needs and could not be penetrated from above. Here he would have the luxury of waiting out the results of the fighting topside.

"If we sit tight here we can watch everything resolve around us," he told Marta. "Fires burn themselves out, people get too tired or hungry to lift a weapon—then we'll sort out who's who. It will be dark soon. No one will want to be out there in the dark with a breached perimeter. Demons."

He couldn't suppress a shudder and he supposed, under the circumstances, that it didn't matter. Marta and the others were here because they knew him best and they shared his passion for leaving Pandora. They were all a little giddy after the quick move to his private bunker. It helped that there were few claustrophobics on Pandora.

Flattery was pleased to see that, even though they were under fire, his people rallied even more strongly to his cause. Still, he double-latched the security hatch behind him when he returned to the Greens.

If we're required to stay down here for any length of time, I'll have to bring them in here, he thought. *I'll put that off as long as possible.*

Throughout his life on Moonbase, from his implantation in a surrogate womb to liftoff aboard the *Earthling*, Flattery remembered no place that was private, unguarded. Part of his training as a psychiatrist had taken this into account. The ultimate privacy was death, he knew this lesson well, and it was because he knew this that he was designed to be the executioner of his species. Who was better trained than a Chaplain/Psychiatrist to recognize the Other—artificial intelligence, alien intelligence? And who could be prepared better to deal with such a threat properly? Moonbase had made the right decision, of this he was certain. Of this he was truly proud.

Pride comes before a fall, a voice said from the back of his head. He shrugged it off with the shudder.

It was possible that he had erred slightly in this matter of the kelp. He needed the kelp—Pandora needed the kelp—therefore keeping it alive was not so much a matter of prudence as necessity. The first C/P on Pandora had ordered the kelp destroyed and that act had very nearly destroyed what remained of humanity and the planet itself. Pruning was risky, Current Control was risky, because there was always more kelp than people to control it. Ten years ago it had already gotten out of hand and he had been forced to concentrate solely on stands that marked important trade routes around Pandora's new coastlines.

Then, five years ago, Crista Galli came into his life. He had suspected at the start that she was an agent of the kelp. He should've known better, but this kind of wariness had kept him ahead of the kelp all along. A chromosome scan of the Galli girl proved she was human. He'd had the tech who did the scan killed with the kelp toxin, and so began the rumors about the death-touch of Crista Galli. Subsequent adjustments to her blood chemistry provided opportunity for other evidence against her. These rumors had suited his purposes better than entire legions of security.

A well-placed rumor along with some sleight-of-hand has immeasurable value in political and religious arenas, he thought.

Flattery was comfortable in spite of the conflict raging around him. In fact, he had to control his glee at the prospect of the aftermath.

This will adjust the population problem, he mused. *Old Thomas Malthus comes through again.*

The survivors who opposed him would starve, it was that simple. He had all the time in the world, all the world's resources at his fingertips. From his bunker he had access to three of the largest food bins in the world—enough grain and preserved foods to keep five thousand people healthy for at least ten years. The Greens would not provide enough fresh fruit for everyone, but he and a select cadre could be quite happy there indefinitely. All he had to do was wait it out.

His first warning of trouble inside his personal perimeter was a faint hissing that he heard above the wave-slaps in his pool. At the same time he heard high-pitched squeaking above him, then intruder alarms went off. Most of his sensors topside were gone, destroyed or covered by rubble. These, placed in the dozens of swiftgrazer burrows, were not true visual sensors but presence-activated alarms. Flattery summoned his caretaker and the squeaking intensified all around them.

"What is it?" Flattery asked. "It says 'level A activity.'"

"Swiftgrazers," the caretaker said. "Level A is set for them, since they're the most common intruder into the fissures. This shows a lot of them, and deeper than they're usually found."

"This squeaking—it's getting louder."

"There's a lot of them, all right," the caretaker said. He studied the sensor scan and bit his prominent lower lip. "And they're still coming this way."

"Trigger your trapsets."

The caretaker pressed a red spot on the scanner. The hissing that had become squeaks now rose to high-pitched shrieks of anger and terror.

At that moment a few dozen brown swiftgrazers tumbled from a fissure above Flattery and to his right. They were uncomfortably close, spilling from above the hatchway to Flattery's bunker.

"You'd better clean these up here. We don't want them established—"

"They're still coming," the caretaker said. He pointed farther back to where there was obvious movement in the foliage against the wall. "I'll need some help here."

"We're not bringing any more people into the Greens than necessary. You told me it was safe to keep these rodents around, you take care of them. Now!"

"Yes, sir." The older man sagged, sighed and armed his lasgun. "There's a lot of them," he said, "I'll need more charges."

A flurry of little bodies and shrieks caught their attention to the left of the pool, near the loading dock and Flattery's foil. Behind them a bright, white light broke through the cover of ferns. Now Flattery could see a similar light approaching through the fissure above his hatch.

"I don't like this," Flattery said. "What do your precious sensors say now?"

The caretaker flurried his nervous fingers across the face of his portable control unit. "Dead," he said. "Something's shorted out the power to all of the sensors."

Flattery heard the low-throated purr of Archangel behind him, and for the first time realized that it wasn't merely a handful of swiftgrazers invading his garden. In blinks there were hundreds of them. Something had whipped them to a fever pitch, and they displayed none of their usual wariness of humans.

"Start shooting," he said, his voice low. "I'll get some fire-power in here."

By the time he had undogged his hatch and signaled for help, the light inside the Greens was too great a glare to let him pick out anything but little blurs of movement across his path. He hurried to dockside and secured himself inside the foil.

Flattery started the foil's engines and began his predive checkout when he realized he'd left the mooring lines secured. He glanced up at the caretaker, who was firing wildly at shadows in the greenery, and saw him suddenly disappear under a thick wad of fur, as though he'd slipped on a giant coat of swiftgrazers and then disappeared. The coat melted to the deck and disappeared, leaving only the man's weapon, bloody tatters of clothing and a scatter of fleshy bones. Archangel, too, was no match for them, and Flattery had his doubts about the five-man security squad beginning their sweep.

"Not even smart enough to shut the hatch behind them," he mumbled through gritted teeth. "If they don't stop them …"

Flattery didn't have to dwell on the unpleasantness, he had plenty of evidence of swiftgrazer vengeance all around him. The squad had pushed them back far enough that Flattery could make a dash for the mooring lines and free himself from the pier. His only escape now would be to dive out of the Greens and wait. The light in the Greens was so bright that he could barely read his instruments. It nearly surrounded the pool now and he was sure it was some kind of weapon that the Shadows were using against him.

"Rag-tag bunch of bums," he hissed. "Why don't they leave well enough alone? Even they must be smart enough to know I'll be off this planet soon."

As he flooded the dive compartments he thought he saw faces swirling in the light of the Greens—Crista Galli's face, Beatriz Tatoosh, Dwarf MacIntosh and some young fuzzhead that he didn't recognize. He shook his head and attended to his instruments. As he settled beneath the surface of the pool he breathed easier. The foil's atmosphere was contrived, it was not the cool freshness of the Greens, but it was heaven now to Flattery.

His intent was to wait out the incident safely suspended in the waters of his personal lagoon. The foil had full rations for six, enough to last him months, and it could continue to manufacture its own fuel and air supply as long as the membranes held out. They were Islander-grown from kelp tissue in a method perfected several hundred years ago, and had been known to last up to fifty years.

The light above him continued to intensify and the water began a rhythmic chop that alarmed him. He had been reluctant to venture into open water now that the kelpways were down. The idea of picking his way through a tangle of kelp by instruments alone dried his mouth and he forced himself to slow his breathing.

"I'll head for the launch site," he told himself. "The nightside supply shuttle should be ready for launch in three hours."

He marked the time on his log and swung the bow of the foil seaward. Ahead of him lay the vast coastal kelp bed and its infernal lights, blinking at him.

The beachside mortar … they didn't stump this stand as I ordered.

Somehow, the sight of blue and red flickerings across the depths ahead filled him with as much fear as the mysterious glare that backed him out of the Greens. Flattery didn't like the feeling of fear.

What if they lob their charges in now? I'd be a dead squawk.

Out of habit, Flattery turned his fear to aggression and throttled himself into the kelp.

The going was much easier than he'd anticipated. Waters off Kalaloch were quiet in spite of the loss of Current Control. That is, they were quiet except for a strange tidal pulse that pursued him from the Greens into open water. The uncontrolled kelp kept the major kelpway to the launch site open. Flattery attributed this to habit, or to perseverance of the last signal sent from Current Control. He was well into the thick of the stand before he realized his mistake.

Several things happened at once, any one of them enough to shake Flattery's resolve to regroup at the launch site. He ran out of fuel less than a kilometer from the perimeter of the site. Instruments showed all fuel-filter membranes functioning normally. Before the foil stalled out and left him adrift in the kelp, Flattery saw that the CO_2 in his cabin was higher than usual. The gas diffusion membranes were functioning, but seemingly in reverse.

I'm out of fuel, in the kelp, and my foil is filtering CO_2 instead of O_2 to the cabin.

He looked at these facts logically, hoping that logic would stave off the hysteria that bubbled at the back of his throat. He could shuttle ballast as long as his power supply lasted, but if he had to maneuver by battery he wouldn't last long. No one responded to any of the undersea burst frequencies, and his Navcom sent back no signal. He floated in the center of a communications black hole. Everything that went out from his foil was swallowed up.

The damned kelp, he reasoned. *It's fouled up our communications before, even the histories tell us that.*

He regretted his leniency with the kelp. It was something that made his life easier, so he had let the explosive growth of this reportedly dangerous species continue beyond his ability to control it.

Couldn't herd people and kelp at the same time, he thought, and yawned. *CO_2's getting me already.*

The yawn frightened him into a flurry of activity, but the oxygen level in his cabin was already low enough to slow his thinking and his hands. He found that, even under electrical power, he couldn't nose any farther through the kelp. Blowing ballast did no good, either. It simply depleted his already feeble batteries.

A damned plant *is sucking the life out of me!*

He stabilized the foil at fewer than twenty meters below the surface. His instruments refused to function, and visibility faded quickly as sunset tipped the scales toward night. Around him, the kelp pulled back from his foil and certain of the kelp fronds began to glow, the same cold white glow that had filled the Greens just before he dove.

"This is some kind of Shadow sabotage," he growled. "You'll all regret this!"

Within moments he was wrapped inside a sphere of light so bright that details inside the foil became invisible to him. The glare continued to be bright even though he shut his eyes and covered them with his hands. Voices babbled like red music at the back of his mind.

A warning buzzer droned from the overhead panel and the automatic repeated: "Cabin air unsafe, don airpacks."

How long had it been warning him? He remembered, he remembered … Light.

This was a woman's voice, someone he knew well. But it wasn't the Galli woman … The buzzer exhausted itself to an electric rattle and Flattery shook his head.

"I need air!" he gasped. The sound of his own voice broke him free of the suffocation trance of the carbon dioxide.

Flattery clawed through a crew locker for his dive suit. He didn't bother with all of the fastenings, but tightened down the faceplate and activated the air supply. The Director's white hands trembled beyond his control, but at last he could breathe.

I've got to show them who's in charge! he thought.

His training always lurked inside, but something about adrenaline slung it free. An old Islander proverb echoed in his mind: "Stir a dasher, feed a dasher."

I am the dasher and I will strike. Flattery repeated this to himself a few times while carefully slowing his breathing.

"What do you want?" he shouted into the faceplate. "If you kill me, you'll die. You'll all die!"

His breath fogged the plaz in front of him but it didn't diminish the cold white glare at all. In fact, as he looked closer at the beads of condensation on his faceplate he saw faces inside, hundreds of tiny faces suspended in translucence, one or more glittering inside each droplet.

Killing is your way, not ours.

That voice, inside his own head, chilled something deep in his belly. He could not mistake the familiar Moonbase accent of his shipmate Alyssa Marsh. She had been more than shipmate for a while, but hers had always been a cool intimacy. But it couldn't be Alyssa Marsh because she was … well, not dead exactly …

"What … what is going on here?"

The rasping that he heard across the cabin ceiling and around the foil could only be kelp vines. They snaked across the cabin plaz without diminishing the white radiance that pierced his eyelids, his retinas, his very being. The foil lurched, then its metallic skin shrieked as the kelp began to tear it apart. Flattery hurried to seal his dive suit. He had already armed two lasguns, but he grabbed a couple of spare air packs instead.

You may fight if you wish, Alyssa's voice told him, *you will not be killed. You will not be harmed in any way.*

"She had a terrible accident in the kelp" had been Flattery's official version of her body's demise. Now scenes from her life danced in the light around him. And he saw her great secret. Cool as Flattery was, it chilled him just the same.

Alyssa had slipped away on a long-term job in the kelp, knowing she could stretch six months of research in wild kelp beds to nine or ten months without any trouble. He'd wanted to be rid of her, she'd sensed that. If he knew she was pregnant he would destroy the child, of this she was sure. He would probably destroy her, too. Not one in ten thousand clones ever got the chance for a baby. Flattery, Alyssa and Mack were very possibly the last living members of their original crew of 3,006, each one the clone of some long-lost donor.

The Broods took him, and Yuri he was called. There were no other children at this kelp outpost, so Yuri spent his first two years undersea with fourteen adults.

Flattery closed his eyes, retreated into himself. *It was just the once*, his mind pleaded. *Just the time …*

"Do you think it's what I expected my body to do?" she asked. The images stayed on the other side of his eyelids, but her voice came right into his mind.

How would I suspect, you didn't stick around … your work in the kelp …

Now the scenes came inside his head. Flattery watched as he personally "dismantled" Alyssa and he himself performed the transplant to the life support surrogate and severed her brain forever from its body.

"All you have to do is consult the kelp," he heard Mack telling Brood. "You'll have your answer for sure, then. You can follow your genetic line back as far as you have the patience to follow."

"I know who my father is," Brood said. "It's him, Raja Flattery."

In one gigantic twist the foil ripped apart at the cabin seam and the sea burst in on Flattery. When the pieces fell away from him the sphere of light remained, and more images danced across the surface of the sphere. He saw Nevi and Zentz captured at the beach, and Brood's attack on the Orbiter. A panorama of disaster played out for him and he watched his precious Preserve go down in plunder.

All along the coastline huge whips of kelp flung themselves skyward and lit up the sea with their pale green glow.

You have much to learn, Raja Flattery, Alyssa said. *You are an intelligent man, perhaps even the genius that you believe yourself to be. Ultimately, that is what will save you.*

Something grabbed at his right ankle and he spun away. It grabbed again and held, then pinned his arms when he tried to batter at it with a spare air pack. He was already exhausted, and found himself in a dreamlike state that made resistance more work than it was worth.

As I told you the night you killed me, I don't think you understand the immensity of this being.

Beatriz watched Flattery's memory take over, and he broadcast the entire scene of Alyssa Marsh's separation from her body. Holo stages, viewers, kelp beds, the air and sky themselves lit up with Alyssa Marsh's memories of her final encounter with Flattery.

You owe me a body, she said, and she said it in that same flat, emotionless tone that had made her his first pick for this crew a lifetime ago.

The kelp began to enciliate Flattery, to encapsulize him inside a life-support pod. It had been the same with Crista Galli, as it had been with Vata and Duque before her. Beatriz felt the cilia seeking out his blood vessels to adjust his oxygen level and pH. Others would feed him, recycle his wastes and protect him from flesh-eaters. She felt this as she sensed the world through the hylighter's skin.

Flattery had the show, and the whole world was watching.

Chapter 64

So many things fail to interest us, simply because they don't find in us enough surfaces on which to live, and what we have to do then is to increase the number of planes in our mind, so that a much larger number of themes can find a place in it at the same time.

—Jose Ortega y Gasset

TWISP FELT a moment of hysteria play flip-flop with his stomach as a sphere of cool light encompassed the young Kaleb. Twisp had sent a boy upcoast and now a man came back. He had known the boy's father the day he changed from child to man. Suddenly that old sense of loss iced his spine, and he stood a little straighter at the poolside.

Kaleb's a lot like his father, he thought. *Obstinate, sure, outraged …*

Kaleb's father, Brett, had been outraged at the sight of thousands of fellow Islanders stacked dead in a Merman plaza, outraged that humans would murder children in their beds and parents at their prayers.

An entire Island, sunk!

Twisp had heard about the sinking of Guemes Island, he'd seen holos of the grim rescue scene, but Brett had seen the sledges of limp bodies, heard the rattle in dying throats.

As though picking up his thoughts, the bright surface of the sphere played back some of those moments, far clearer here than in his memory.

Other images played there, too—nebulized, indistinct, as though making up their minds about being. He saw in them replays of the scenes Kaleb fought with his people. He had resisted the majority of his forces who wanted Flattery's blood. They chose to move without him, and Kaleb stood up to them.

"You're willing to die in battle anyway," he told them. "Why not die feeding the poor?" He was sending an army against Flattery, all right—an army of angels laden with food.

"Everything stops until everyone eats," was written on each pilgrim's shirt as they set out by the hundreds for the camps.

Twisp had renewed confidence that Kaleb's hatred of the Director would not turn the boy into another Flattery.

He's not a boy, he reminded himself, *and he's safe in Avata. His mother saw to that.*

Twisp remembered the time when he had needed convincing himself, when it was Kaleb's mother, Scudi Wang, who first thrust him into the kelpways of the mind. Her face came up in the sphere and it was the smiling face of the precocious teenager that Twisp remembered so well.

How could Brett not have loved her?

Twisp tugged his gray braid that tickled his neck. In the halo around Kaleb more images precipitated out of the light. They all seemed to be people he knew, and they all had one other thing in common.

They're all dead!

He heard a whimper behind him that must be Mose.

In that moment Kaleb became a bright shadow inside a brighter sphere, and he seemed to hover above the pool rather than float upon it. The manifestations, the flickering images around him, recited a few scenes from their pasts. Twisp was awed, but not afraid.

Everything swam in a pale radiance that pulsated slightly, like a child's fontanel. A similar pulse began to beat in the wave-slaps around the rim of the pool. The onlookers had ceased their chatter and begun their chant of renewal. It was a call-and-response chant, typical at blossom-time, an improvisation on an old theme that Twisp had heard his grandparents sing.

"Open the leaves …"

"… and the blossoms, open …"

Kaleb was no longer visible inside the light. The light now was brighter than anything Twisp had experienced, but this cool brightness did not hurt his eyes. Indeed, he could not take his gaze from its hypnotic spell.

"It's everywhere," a tremulous voice shouted from the caverntop. "There's light on the waves, in the sky … everywhere."

Twisp recognized this breathless voice as Snej, the young assistant at Operations.

"And those pictures in the light," another gasped, "just like this, only it covers the whole sky!"

When a great light took over the whole cavern, it became impossible for Twisp to make out the faces of his fellow Zavatans. Even Mose, as close as he was, became just another light inside the light.

Snej's voice came to him again, bell-like in its joy.

"Crista Galli is safe," she announced. "They are all safe. The fighting is at a standstill."

The bright sphere in front of Twisp unreeled the tideline drama of Ben and Crista Galli and their near-fatal encounter with Zentz and Spider Nevi. To Twisp the event was more than visual. Though it must've taken up nearly an hour of real time, the scene was communicated to him in a matter of blinks. A cheer filled the cavern when Spider Nevi fell, and the images on the sphere shifted to another cavern, and to the terrified face of the Director.

All fell silent at the sight of Flattery, except for a few angry mutterings across the pool.

"Is this a miracle, Elder?"

"Flattery's being driven out," Twisp said. "I'd say that was more inevitability than miracle. Avata has decided that it's time to meet the Director."

The brightness inside the Oracle spread out from the sphere to bathe each observer. The darkest of them was a dazzle of light against light.

"Look, Elder!"

Twisp watched Mose lift his arms as though flying, and streams of thick white light pulsed from his fingertips to join with other light nearby. Though it was impossible for him to see detail, Twisp watched these same streams of light merge with others in midair. He was reminded of the time as a child when a cell bioarchitect visited his creche to show his classmates many wonders. One of these was a blowup holo of cytoplasmic streaming, of an amoeba pumping parts of itself into other parts of itself in order to move, to capture and digest prey.

"What are we, here?" he wondered aloud. "Predator or prey?" The answer came in a rush that rocked Twisp back on his heels.

You are brother to me, as I am sibling to you.

His long arms shot out over the pool for balance. A hand reached out of the light and gripped his own. The grip felt real, the hand, wet. Kaleb stepped from the kelp root to the rim of the pool and kept a hold on Twisp's hand. The cavern around them was a din of babble as the Zavatans consulted Avata and each other. They encountered spirits of their ancestors that Avata released from the prisons of their genetic code.

"Let us join hands and thank Avata," Kaleb announced. His voice took on a new projection that stilled the babble but did not shock the ears.

"Avata has dismembered the monster that Flattery built out of our people and has taken him prisoner. He will be reeducated, as we have been, in the inviolable rights that the living have to life. Tonight, everyone will eat. Humans are through suffering at the hands of fellow humans."

Everyone in the cavern linked hands, and the light flowed through them from the pool and then flowed back. Figures and faces, bits of imagery tumbled along the brightening stream. Gasps of wonder and cries of delight filled the chamber.

Then the cavern itself dissolved from view. Ceiling, walls, the rock beneath their feet were no longer visible. All Twisp saw was a serpentine of people holding hands surrounded by something he could only describe as a light-mist. All Pandorans were linked with this group and they all stood together on an immense plain of light, warm, and for once without fear of demons, or security, or hunger.

Twisp withdrew quietly from the poolside celebration, found his robe in his quarters and sought out his favorite rock overlook above Kalaloch.

Below Twisp's rock outcrop the night air clarified against a glisten of sea. An old tracked vehicle clanked its stubborn way up the trail and at first Twisp's reflexes tightened. A Cushette followed the track, both vehicles piled high with belongings and wallowing with the effort. These people were already leaving Kalaloch, bound for something better with their bedding and their hope.

"Welcome," Twisp whispered. His attitude was exuberant, but his body exhausted. *They will be all right*, he marveled.

He thought first of Kaleb, who had left his bitterness behind him in the kelp, who would soon enough bring the grandchildren of Brett and Scudi to hear stories at their uncle Twisp's knee.

He could guess how it would be for the rest from what he'd seen in the kelp.

Ben and Crista were a match made on Pandora, but sealed in Avata, and they would help develop opportunities to improve the lives of Pandorans for many decades to come. Twisp had a feeling, when the light penetrated him, that Rico and Snej would take up housekeeping somewhere nearby.

The Voidship *Nietzsche,* with Alyssa Marsh at the helm, would speed Mack and Beatriz beyond the limits of light-contact with Pandora. It would take the humans and their new-found symbiote, Avata, to another world, which, if not perfect when they discovered it, would make humans happy with the work toward perfection.

Some new insight told Twisp that Yuri Brood would receive a reprieve aboard the *Nietzsche* and would acquire the necessary spirituality by tending his mother, the OMC Alyssa Marsh. Through the kelp hookups, Alyssa Marsh had found her new body and her son. Her son would write out the musings of this OMC, which would become the manual for human behavior for generations—*A Sociology of Ascension.* Their shipload of pilgrims would people a new star, and the sea of a planet of that star.

Raja Flattery would live on in the kelp, his needs met, a prisoner of his own selfishness and greed. People would meet him there from time to time, and legends of him would prevail throughout the generations.

Though Pandora's days were numbered, Twisp would live his days out roaming Pandora, working hard to improve the lot of everyone. He knew now that he would not be the one to see the end, and was happy for that.

I'll be known as "the old man of the high reaches," I suppose, Twisp mused.

All was quiet in the settlement below. The glow that had swelled out of the sea and encompassed Kalaloch now sank back to the sea. A cool shimmer remained, ghostlike, at the surface. Two moons and a skyful of stars beamed down on Twisp's gray head. An occasional cheer broke the silence, and Twisp listened as the tinkling sounds of nighttime laughter rent the ancient cloak of death and fear.

AFTERWORD

(Excerpted from *Dreamer of Dune*)
Bill Ransom

FRANK HERBERT had more fun with life than anyone I've ever met. He laughed more, joked more and produced more finished product than any writer I've ever met. From modest beginnings just across the Puyallup River from my own birthplace, passionate about outdoor life, he judged people by their creativity, and by whether they met hardship with humor or with bile. Humor helped him to endure hardship and to enjoy his rise above it. Frank believed the suffering-in-the-garret stereotype was foisted onto writers by publishers so that they could get away with small advances. The only true currency that Frank recognized was time to write.

"Here it is, Ransom," he said. "First class buys you more time to write."

Never ostentatious, he lived as comfortably as he wanted but not as extravagantly as he could, always with close ties to the outdoors. Enjoyment A.D. ("After *Dune*") came from trying new writing adventures and from helping others succeed; Frank offered opportunities, not handouts, saying, "I'd rather give a man a hand up than step on his fingers." This echoes my favorite Dostoevsky line, "Feed men, then ask of them virtue."

Everything and everyone fell into two rough categories for Frank: It/he/she either contributed to his writing time or interfered with it. We knew of each other through our publication successes, but we noticed each other's successes because we both came from the Puyallup Valley, we both had fathers who were in law enforcement in the same district, and we'd had shirttail relatives marry. We moved to Port Townsend in the same week in the early '70s and discovered this when the local paper did stories on each of us. I wanted to meet him, finally, but I wanted to be careful of his writing time. Frank wrote a piece under a pseudonym for the *Helix*, my favorite underground newspaper in Seattle, just a few years earlier. I dropped Frank a postcard addressed to the pseudonym on the byline ("H. Bert Frank"), saying I wrote until noon but would love to meet for coffee sometime. The next afternoon at 12:10 he called: "Hello, Ransom. Herbert here. Is that coffee on?" Thus began our fifteen-year routine of coffee or lunch nearly every day.

Frank believed poetry to be the finest distillation of the language, whether written in open or closed form. He read voraciously in contemporary poetry through literary and "little" magazines, and he wrote poetry as he worked through issues of life and of fiction. As a very young man, he discovered that he could make somewhat of a living from his nonfiction prose style, which was far more readable than most of the journalism of the time. His prose style, his eye for detail and his ear for true vernacular coupled with that ever-persistent "What if?" question in his ear made for a natural transition to fiction. Success came to Frank in prose, but inspiration filled his notebooks and his fiction with poetry.

My first poetry collection, *Finding True North & Critter*, was nominated for the National Book Award the same year Frank's *Soul Catcher* was nominated in fiction. Perhaps if Frank and I had both been fiction writers off the bat, or both poets, our collaboration may have developed differently. As it was, we refreshed and re-enthused each other with our writing, and encouraged each other to risk something in our work. The greatest risk of all, to friendship and to our writing reputations, came when we co-wrote *The Jesus Incident* and submitted it under both of our names. Frank pointed out that if the book were published we would each face specific criticisms for working together. People would say that Frank Herbert ran out of ideas, and that Bill Ransom was riding on the coattails of the Master. When these statements did, indeed, come up, we were better prepared psychologically for having predicted them in advance.

Circumstances leading up to our collaboration were complex, but our personal agreement was simple: Nothing that either of us wanted in the story would stand in the way of the friendship, and we shook hands. Nothing did, not even the publisher's preference that we release it just with Frank's name (the advance offer under this potential agreement was larger by a decimal point than what we received with both names on the cover). The power people also would accept a pseudonym, but they were adamant that a novel acknowledged to be by two authors would not fly with the reading public, and equally adamant about talking only with Frank. In addition, they believed that my reputation in poetry circles would contribute nothing toward marketing the book, therefore I should get 25% and Frank 75% of whatever we agreed on. Frank literally hung up the phone and bought a ticket to New York. The way he told the story upon his return with contract in hand, he simply repeated a mantra throughout his visit: "Half the work earns half the credit and half the pay." Frank took a 90% cut in pay and split the cover by-line in order to work with me, only one example of the strength of his character and of his friendship.

The gamble paid off. We'd heard that *The New York Times Book Review* would cover it, and I was nervous. "Relax, Ransom," Frank said, "even a scathing review in *The New York Times* sells ten thousand hardbacks *that day*." John Leonard wrote a wonderful review, and we were launched. For two rustic, self-taught Puyallup Valley boys who ran trap lines as kids, we did well because our focus always was on The Story. We had no ego conflicts while writing together, largely because Frank didn't have much ego as "Author." I learned from him that authors exist merely for the story's sake, not the other way around, and a good story had to do two things: inform and entertain. The informing part must be entertaining enough to let readers live the story without feeling like they're on the receiving end of a sermon. Writing entertainment without information, without some insight into what it is to be human, is a waste of good trees.

Frank believed that poetry was the apex of human language; he also believed that Science Fiction was the only genre whose subject matter attempted to define what it is to be human. We use contact with aliens or alien environments as impetus or backdrop for human interaction. Science fiction characters solve their own problems—neither magic spells nor gods come to their aid—and sometimes they have to build some intriguing gadgets to save their skins. Humans go to books to see how other humans solve human problems. Frank admired and championed human resolve and ingenuity in his life and in his work. He had a practical side about this, too: "Remember, Ransom," he said, "aliens don't buy books. Humans buy books."

Frank admired the very intellectual writers, like Pound, but he had a particular soft spot for other blue-collar, self-taught writers who investigated human nature, such as Hemingway and Faulkner.

William Faulkner's work influenced Frank in many ways, not the least of which was creating a believable fictional universe built on a complex genealogy. Frank saw Science Fiction as a great opportunity to reach a very wide audience with "the big stuff." He was moved by Faulkner's 1950 Nobel Prize acceptance speech, and he took it to heart in everything he wrote: "...the young man or woman writing today has forgotten the problems of the human heart in conflict with itself which alone can make good writing because only that is worth writing about, worth the agony and the sweat ... the old verities and truths of the heart, the old universal truths lacking which any story is ephemeral and doomed—love and honor and pity and pride and compassion and sacrifice." Story itself provides the foundation for every human culture, and storytellers must respect this responsibility.

Frank had a guardian angel, someone who protected him and his writing time at all costs for more than forty-five years. Beverly Stuart Herbert honeymooned with him in a fire lookout, packed the kids up in a hearse to live in a village in Mexico while he wrote, and encouraged him to quit dead-end jobs to write what he loved, come what may. Bev was Frank's first reader and critic, and her opinion held serious water. She had uncanny radar for detecting buffoons, hangers-on, con artists and other fools, and Frank was pretty good at this, too. Not many got past Bev to test Frank. But Bev had the diplomacy and good graces to protect Frank while also protecting the dignity of those who would intrude on him. Later, over coffee and homemade pie, came the jokes.

Not all of our experiences together were celebratory. My writing work with Frank is bracketed by sadness for both of us. We began our first collaboration when Bev was diagnosed with cancer and I was going through a divorce; we wrote *The Lazarus Effect* as Bev fought her second round of illness (Frank wrote *The White Plague* at the same time) and it was published shortly before her death. Our collaboration on *The Ascension Factor* ended with Frank's death. An unexpected benefit of our exercise in collaboration became Frank's collaboration with his son, Brian. Frank said that he had hoped that one day one of his children might follow in Dad's writing footsteps, and Brian began with some humorous Science Fiction. Father and son working together on *Man of Two Worlds* marked a breakthrough for Frank after the long ordeal of Bev's final illness. Brian learned the fine art of collaboration at Frank's side, and Frank would be proud that the dual legacies of the *Dune* universe and the Herbert writing gene survive him. Brian and Kevin J. Anderson are having the kind of fun with writing that Frank and I enjoyed, and they've added a new physical depth and enriched the sociopolitical detail of the greater tapestry on which *Dune* was woven. I handed Frank the final draft of *The Lazarus Effect* in Hawaii, where he was caring for Bev in the final stages of her illness. He was also building the house we camped in and writing *The White Plague*, so this second book of ours was largely my responsibility. At breakfast the next morning, he said, "Ransom, you've just written your journeyman's papers." I believe that's what he'd say to Brian after reading the first Herbert/Anderson production.

I was at about mid-point in writing the first draft of *The Ascension Factor* when the morning radio announced that Frank had passed away. Typically, he believed he would beat this challenge as he'd beaten so many others. Also typically, he was typing a new short story into a laptop on his chest when he died, a story that he'd told me might lead to another non-genre novel like *Soul Catcher*. In the crowding and confusion of those final life-saving attempts, that laptop and his last story were lost, like Einstein's final words were lost because the nurse at his side didn't speak German.

I think of Frank every time I touch a keyboard, hoping I'm writing up to his considerable standards. In the Old English, "poet" was "shaper" or "maker." Frank Herbert was a Maker on a grand scale, the most loyal friend a person could ask for—and a funny, savvy, first-class guy.

He continues to be missed.

Letter from the Lost Notebooks

For Frank Herbert

Starting from where the road forks we lose time
  and we lose the lives that might have followed us here.
We lock our memories in the car, leave the keys on the muffler
  and begin the slow drizzling climb (it always rains here in the valley)
  to the flatlands somewhere near the top.
Notice, as we climb, whole huckleberry bushes
  stripped of leaves and limbs.
  Bear, stoking up for winter.
You notice, too, that by switching back on ourselves
  we walk quite a way and make very little ground.
If making ground is what you're after
  you wouldn't have come this far.

If you came here with a lover or a friend,
  don't be surprised if you are now alone.
  These things happen up here.

You reach the high flatlands in late afternoon.
The rain settles into haze and drops itself, patch by patch,
  into the valleys and crannies below.
  This high up there is never a hurry,
  so look over the meadow and watch, as the sky clears for sundown,
  how those old boulders sit hunched and waiting.
  Listen.
The wind scribbles something slight on their faces.
Sleep out there tonight, among them, and know
  that the dreams they send
  may be more than you can wake up from.

About the Authors

FRANK HERBERT (1920–1986) created the most beloved novel in the annals of science fiction, *Dune*. He was a man of many facets, of countless passageways that ran through an intricate mind. His magnum opus is a reflection of this, a classic work that stands as one of the most complex, multi-layered novels ever written in any genre. Today the novel is more popular than ever, with new readers continually discovering it and telling their friends to pick up a copy. It has been translated into dozens of languages and has sold almost 20 million copies.

Herbert wrote more than twenty other novels, including *Hellstrom's Hive*, *The White Plague*, *The Green Brain*, and *The Dosadi Experiment*. During his life, he received great acclaim for his sweeping vision and the deep philosophical underpinnings in his writings. His life is detailed in the Hugo-nominated biography *Dreamer of Dune*, by Brian Herbert.

BILL RANSOM has published six novels, six poetry collections, and numerous short stories and articles. *Learning the Ropes* (Utah State University Press), a collection of poetry, short fiction and essays, was billed as "a creative autobiography." His poetry received two fellowships from the National Endowment for the Arts, and his short fiction has appeared in Sunday editions of major newspapers across the country and was chosen three times for the PEN/NEA Syndicated Fiction Project, billed as "The Pulitzer Prize of the Short Story."

Bill has been nominated for both the Pulitzer Prize and the National Book Award, and his most recent collection is *The Woman and the War Baby*, from Blue Begonia Press. He pioneered the Poetry-in-the-Schools program for the National Endowment for the Arts in the 1970s. He worked as a firefighter and advanced life-support emergency medical technician in Washington state, and in El Salvador, Guatemala and Nicaragua in their civil wars through the 1980s. These experiences informed much of his writing. He recently retired as Academic Dean of Curriculum at The Evergreen State College in Olympia, Washington and makes his home on the Washington coast.

Made in the USA
San Bernardino, CA
20 January 2014